From the Library of
Sherrill Hieber

Foundations
of Fear

Foundations of Fear

Edited by
DAVID G. HARTWELL

A TOM DOHERTY ASSOCIATES BOOK
NEW YORK

FOUNDATIONS OF FEAR

Copyright © 1992 by David G. Hartwell

All rights reserved, including the right to reproduce
this book, or portions thereof, in any form.

A Tor Book
Published by Tom Doherty Associates, Inc.
175 Fifth Avenue
New York, N.Y. 10010

TOR® is a registered trademark of Tom Doherty Associates, Inc.

ISBN 0-312-85074-3

First edition: September 1992

Printed in the United States of America

0 9 8 7 6 5 4 3 2 1

To the editors and anthologists who first gave the genre a canon in the 1920s–1940s;

To the publishers who stuck with it and gave the genre an identity for better or worse;

To the writers who often ignored them all and just wrote powerfully and well;

And finally, to my children, Alison and Geoffrey, without whom I couldn't have completed the book during difficult times.

Acknowledgments

This book continues the revaluation of horror literature I began in *The Dark Descent*, and so to the same people and books given credit there I continue my indebtedness. Discussions with Alfred Bendixen (and of course his books) have proven helpful, and with Robert Hadji, whose wide reading in and out of the genre and considered critical judgement have influenced several of my choices for inclusion herein. The support of those who were enthusiastic enough about *The Dark Descent* to demand that I continue working in this area—particularly Joanna Russ—carried me through a number of rough spots. Certainly the most important acknowledgement is to Kathryn Cramer, not only for discussion, critical commentary, and moral support, but for sharing with me her unfinished writings and researches on horror publishing and the distinctions between category and genre, and on Henry James, as well as her published work surveying influences among horror writers today. At every point her creative insights have been provocative and useful. The critical reconsideration of the evolution of horror in literature begun by Kathryn Cramer, Peter D. Pautz, and myself five years ago has borne a variety of fruits, including all our various anthologies. This is only the most recent.

No acknowledgement would be complete without proper recognition of the support of my publisher, Tor Books, who took a chance. To Tom Doherty, publisher, and Melissa Singer, editor, for patient enthusiasm, my sincere gratitude.

Contents

Introduction

I High and Low

There is no delight the equal of dread.
                    —Clive Barker, "Dread"

. . . if not the highest, certainly the most exacting form of literary art.
                    —L. P. Hartley on the ghost story

Taken as a whole, the output . . . stands in need of critical study, not to erect theories upon subterranean surmises, but by using direct observation and following educated taste . . . to enlarge for all readers the repertory of the well-wrought and the enjoyable.
                    —Jacques Barzun, Introduction to
                    The Penguin Encyclopedia of Horror and the Supernatural

We dislike to predict the future of the horror story. We believe its powers are not yet exhausted. The advance of science proves this. It will lead us into unexplored labyrinths of terror and the human desire to experience new emotions will always be with us. . . . Some of the stories now being published in *Weird Tales* will live forever.
                    —editorial, *Weird Tales* (vol. 4, no. 2; 1924)

This anthology of horror literature is a companion volume to *The Dark Descent*, continuing a panorama of examples and an examination of the evolution of horror as a mode of literary expression from its roots in stories in the early Romantic period to the rich varieties of contemporary fiction. In *The Dark Descent*, it was observed that the short story has, until the 1970s, been the dominant literary genre of horror throughout its evolution (horror was in at the origination of the short story and has evolved with and through it); and that it is now evident that the horror novel is in a period of rapid development and proliferation, for the first time achieving dominance over the shorter forms. So it is a particularly appropriate historical moment for us to look back over the growth and spread of horror stories.

Furthermore, a general consideration of literary examples yields several conclusions about the nature of horror. First, that horror is not in the end either a marketing category or a genre, but a literary mode that has been used in every genre and category, the creation of an atmosphere and emotional environment that sparks a transaction between the reader and the text which yields the horrific response. Horrific poems and plays and novels predate the inception of the short story. There can and have been western horror stories, war horror stories, ghost stories, adventure stories, mystery stories, romances—the potential exists in every category.

But by the early twentieth century, horror began to spread and separate in two directions, in literary fiction and in popular literature, mirroring the Modernist distinction between high art and low, a distinction that is rapidly disintegrating today in the post–Modern period, but remains the foundation of marketing all literature in the twentieth century. For most of the century, horror has been considered narrowly as a marketing category or a popular genre, and dismissed by most serious readers and critics. In many ways, horror is associated with ghosts and the supernatural, which in a way stand for superstition and religion—and one of the great intellectual, cultural and spiritual battles of the past 150 years has been on the part of intellectuals, to rid western civilization of the burdens of Medieval religion and superstition, especially in the wake of the great battles over Darwin and Evolution. The Modernist era, which began in the late nineteenth century, is an era of science.

The death of horror was widely announced by Modernist critics (particularly Edmund Wilson, who devoted two essays to demolishing it), the specialists such as Lovecraft and Blackwood denounced, and the psychological investigations of Henry James, Franz Kafka, Joseph Conrad and D. H. Lawrence enshrined as the next stage in literary evolution, replacing superstition and the supernatural as the electric light had replaced the flame.

Yet it was precisely at that moment, in the 1920s and 1930s, that the first magazines devoted to horror began to appear, that the first major collections and anthologies of horror fiction from the previous hundred years were done, and the horror film came into prominence. Significantly, Lovecraft, in his classic study, *Supernatural Horror in Literature* (1936, revised), in examining the whole history of western literature concluded that over centuries and in a large preponderance of texts, the true sensations of horror occur rarely, and momentarily—in parts of works, not usually whole works. He wrote this during the generation when horror was actually becoming a genre, with an audience and a body of classic texts. A threshold had been reached after a century of literary evolution, in which a parallel evolution of the ghost story and the horror story had created a rich and varied body of tropes, conventions, texts, and passed, and the horror genre was established as a vigorous variety of popular literature, in rich interaction with the main body of the literature of this century ever since. One can speculate that, since the religious and superstitious beliefs had passed from overt currency in the reading public, their transformation into the subtext of horror fiction fulfilled certain desires, if not needs, in the audience and writers. As was noted in *The Dark Descent*, the most popular current of horror fiction for decades has been moral allegories of the power of evil.

The giant of the magazines of horror was *Weird Tales*, founded in 1923 and published until the 1950s (and recently revived). It was there that H. P. Lovecraft, Frank Belknap Long, Robert E. Howard, Clark Ashton Smith, and many others flourished. Davis Grubb, Tennessee Williams, Ray Bradbury, and many other literary writers also published early work in *Weird Tales*, which was hospitable to all forms of the weird and horrific and supernatural in literature. "Up to the day the first issue of *Weird Tales* was placed on the stands, stories of the sort you read between these covers each month were taboo in the publishing world. . . . Edgar Allan Poe . . . would have searched in vain for a publisher before the advent of this magazine," said the editorial of the first anniversary issue in 1924.

One of the conditions that favors genrification is an accessible category market, and *Weird Tales* provided this, along with a letter column in which the names and addresses of correspondents were published. This allowed readers and writers to get in touch with each other, and they did. The Lovecraft circle was composed of writers, poets and readers, and generated thousands of letters among them over several decades, forming connections that lasted years after Lovecraft's death in 1937, some at least until the death of August Derleth in the 1960s. Some of the early correspondents were involved, as Lovecraft was, in the amateur journalism movement of the teens and twenties, and they generated amateur magazines and small press publications, which flourished from the 1930s to the 1960s—their descendents exist today. The World Fantasy Awards has a separate category award for excellence in fan publishing each year, and there are many nominees. So *Weird Tales* was seminal not only in creating a genre, but also in creating a field, a subculture of devotees.

In the 1940s and 1950s, the development of the popular form continued and, through a series of historical accidents, came under the protective umbrella of the science fiction field, as did the preponderance of fantasy literature. H. P. Lovecraft and many of his circle published in the science fiction magazines of the 1930s. And the letter-writing subcultures generated by the science fiction magazines interpenetrated with the horror field, creating one body, so that by the late 1930s the active fans commonly identified themselves as fans of the fantasy fiction field.

In 1939, the great science fiction editor, John W. Campbell, Jr., whose magazine, *Astounding Stories*, dominated science fiction, founded a companion magazine, *Unknown*, devoted to fantasy and horror, and to modernizing the style and atmosphere of the fiction. Campbell, who had written an influential science fiction horror story in 1938, encouraged his major science fiction writers to work for his new magazine, and in the five years of its existence, *Unknown* confirmed a bond between horror and science fiction that has not been broken, a bonding that yielded the flowering of SF horror movies in the fifties and encouraged a majority of the important horror writers for the next fifty years. Shirley Jackson once told me in conversation that she had a complete run of *Unknown*. "It's the best," she said. Several of Jackson's stories first appeared in the 1950s in *The Magazine of Fantasy and Science Fiction* (as did, for instance, one of the earliest translations of Jorge Luis Borges). Since the 1930s, a majority of the horror stories in the English language have first appeared in genre magazines.

> In times when censorship or conventions operated to deter authors from dealing specifically with certain human situations, the occult provided a reservoir of images which could be used to convey symbolically what could not be presented literally.
> Glen St John Barclay, *Anatomy of Horror*

Meanwhile, from the 1890s onward, to a large extent under the influence of Henry James, writers such as Walter de la Mare, Edith Wharton, and others devoted significant portions of their careers to the literary ghost story. "In a certain sense, all of his stories are ghost stories—evocations of a tenuous past; and his most distinguished minor work is quite baldly cast in this rather vulgar, popular form. 'The "ghost story," ' he wrote in one of his prefaces, 'as we for convenience call it, has ever been for me the most possible form of the fairy tale.' But at a deeper level than he consciously sought in doing his intended stories of terror (he called, we remember, even 'The Turn of the Screw' a 'potboiler'), James was forever closing in on the real subject that haunted him always: the necrophilia that has always so oddly been an essential part of American romance," says critic Leslie Fiedler.

At the time of his death, Henry James was writing *The Sense of the Past*, a supernatural novel in which a character named Ralph becomes obsessed with a portrait and is translated into the past as a ghost from the future. The supernatural and ghosts were major strains in the work of this great and influential writer throughout his career and, under the pressure of his Modernist admirers, have often been ignored or banished from consideration by being considered only as psychological metaphors during most of the twentieth century. Virginia Woolf, for example, in defending the ghost stories, says the ghosts "have their origin within us. They are present whenever the significant overflows our powers of expressing it; whenever the ordinary appears ringed by the strange. . . . Can it be that we are afraid? . . . We are afraid of something unnamed, of something, perhaps, in ourselves." True, of course, but a defense of the metaphorical level of the text at the expense of the literal surface—which is often intentionally difficult to figure out.

Since the Modernists considered the supernatural a regressive and outmoded element in fiction, the contemporaries and followers of James who were strongly influenced by the literal level of his supernaturalism have been to a large extent banished from the literary canon. Most of them are women writers. A few, such as Edith Wharton, still have critical support, but not on the whole for their supernatural works. Those whose best work was largely in the supernatural, such as Violet Hunt and Gertrude Atherton, Harriet Prescott Spofford and Mary Wilkins Freeman, have been consigned to literary history and biographical criticism, marginalized. In the recent volume, *Horror: 100 Best Books* (1988—covering literature from Shakespeare to Ramsey Campbell), five women writers were chosen for the list, omitting novelists such as Anne Radcliffe, Emily Brontë, and Ann Rice, and every short story collection by a woman—except Marjorie Bowen's and Lisa Tuttle's.

Horror, often cast as ghost story, was an especially useful mode for many woman writers, allowing them a freedom to explore the concerns of feminism symbolically and nonrhetorically with powerful effect. Alfred Bendixen, in the introduction to his excellent anthology, *Haunted Women* (1985), says: "Supernatural fiction opened doors for American women writers, allowing them to move into otherwise forbidden regions. It permitted them to acknowledge the needs and fears of women, enabling them to examine such 'unladylike' subjects as sexuality, bad marriages, and repression." He goes on to identify stories rescued from virtual oblivion and observe that "most of the stories . . . come from the 1890s and early 1900s—a period when the feminist ghostly tale attracted the talents of the finest women writers in America and resulted in some of their most powerful and intriguing work." Alan Ryan, in his excellent anthology, *Haunting Women* (1988), adds the work of Ellen Glasgow, May Sinclair, Jean Rhys, and Isak Dinesen, extending the list into the present with works by Hortense Calisher, Muriel Spark, Ruth Rendell and others. "One recurring theme," say Ryan, ". . . is a female character's fear of a domineering man, who may be father, husband, or lover."

Richard Dalby, in the preface to his *Victorian Ghost Stories by Eminent Women Writers* (1988—from Charlotte Brontë to Willa Cather), claims that "over the past 150 years Britain has led the world in the art of the classic ghost story, and it is no exaggeration to state that at least fifty percent of quality examples in the genre were by women writers." And in the introduction to that same volume, Jennifer Uglow observes, "although—perhaps because—they were written as unpretentious entertainments, ghost stories seemed to give their writers a license to experiment, to push the boundaries of fiction a little further. . . . Again and again we find that the machinery of this most conventional genre frees, rather than restricts, the women who use it."

An investigation of the horror fiction of the nineteenth and early twentieth centuries reveals that a preponderance of the supernatural fiction was written by women and that, buried in the works of a number of women writers whose fiction has been ignored or excluded from the literary canon, there exist significant landmarks in the evolution of horror. Harriet Prescott Spofford, for instance, is emerging as one of the major links between Poe and the later body of American women writers. Gertrude Atherton's "The Bell in the Fog" is both an homage to and critique of Henry James—and perhaps an influence on *The Sense of the Past*. It is provocative to wonder, since women were marginalized in English and American society, and since popular women writers were the most common producers of supernatural fiction, ghostly or horrific, whether supernatural fiction was not in part made marginal because of its association with women and feminine concerns. Just as James (except for "The Turn of the Screw") was forgotten as a writer of supernatural fiction for most of the Modernist era (although it was an important strain throughout his career), so were most of the women who wrote in that mode in the age of electricity. But the flame still burns, can illuminate, can heat the emotions.

In the contemporary period, much of the most popular horror is read by women (more than sixty percent of the adult audience is women in their thirties and forties, according to the most recent Gallup Poll surveys of reading). Best-selling horror most often addresses the traditional concerns of women (children, houses, the supernatural), as well as portraying vividly the place of women and their treatment in society.

Intriguingly, the same Gallup Poll indicates that in the teenage readership, an insignificant percentage ("0%") of girls read horror. The teenage audience is almost exclusively male. Perhaps this is because a very large amount of genre horror fiction (that is published in much smaller numbers of copies than best-selling horrific fiction) is extremely graphic and characteristically features extensive violence, often sexual abuse, torture, or mutilation of women alive, who then return for supernatural vengeance and hurt men. One wonders if this is characteristic of boys' concerns.

L. P. Hartley, in the introduction to Cynthia Asquith's anthology, *The Third Ghost Book* (1955), remarked, "Even the most impassioned devotee of the ghost story would admit that the taste for it is slightly abnormal, a survival, perhaps, from adolescence, a disease of deficiency suffered by those whose lives and imaginations do not react satisfactorily to normal experience and require an extra thrill." And a more recent comment: "Our fiction is not merely in flight from the physical data of the actual world . . . it is, bewilderingly and embarrassingly, a gothic fiction, nonrealistic and negative, sadist and melodramatic—a literature of darkness and the grotesque in a land of light and affirmation. . . . our classic [American] literature is a literature of horror for boys." So says Leslie Fiedler in his classic study, *Love and Death in the American Novel*. Still, one suspects that the subject of who reads horror, and why, and at what age, has been muddied by the establishment of genre and category marketing, and is more complex than has been illuminated by market research and interpretation to date.

II   The Sublime Transaction

The sublime provided a theory of terror in literature and the other arts.
—Carl Woodring, *The Penguin Encyclopedia of Horror and the Supernatural*

. . . confident skepticism is required by the genre that exploits the supernatural. To feel the unease aimed at in the ghost story, one must start by being certain that there is no such thing as a ghost.
—Jacques Barzun,
Introduction to *The Penguin Encyclopedia of Horror and the Supernatural*

Supernatural horror, in all its bizarre constructions, enables a reader to taste a selection of treats at odds with his well-being. Admittedly, this is not an indulgence likely to find universal favor. True macabrists are as rare as poets and form a secret society unto themselves, if only because their memberships elsewhere were cancelled, some of them from the moment of birth. But those who have sampled these joys marginal to stable existence, once they have gotten a good whiff of other worlds, will not be able to stay away for long. They will loiter in moonlight, eyeing the entranceways to cemeteries, waiting for some terribly propitious moment to crash the gates.

> —Thomas Ligotti,
> "Professor Nobody's Little Lectures on Supernatural Horror"

The transaction between reader and text that creates the horrific is complex and to a certain extent subjective. Although the horrifying event may be quite overt, a death, a ghost, a monster, it is not the event itself but the style and atmosphere surrounding it that create horror, an atmosphere that suggests a greater awe and fear, wider and deeper than the event itself. "Because these ideas find proper expression in heightened language, the practiced reader of tales in our genre comes to feel not merely the shiver of fear, but the shiver of aesthetic seizure. In a superior story, there is a sentence, a word, a thing described, which is the high point of the preparation of the resolution. Here disquiet and vision unite to strike a powerful blow," said Jacques Barzun. M. R. James said that the core of the ghost story is "those things that can hardly be put into words and that sound rather foolish if they are not properly expressed." It is useful to examine literary history and criticism to illuminate some of the sources of horror's power.

We do know, from our study of history, that there was a time in our culture when the sublime was the goal of art, the Romantic era. Poetry, drama, prose fiction, painting strove to embody it. Horror was one of its components. Carl Woodring, summarizing the subject in *The Penguin Encyclopedia of Horror and the Supernatural*, says: "As did the scholars of tragedy, [Edmund] Burke and others who analyzed the sublime asked why such awesomeness gave pleasure when it might be expected to evoke only fear or abhorrence. Immanuel Kant, in his *Critique of Judgment* (1790), explained: "Whereas the beautiful is limited, the sublime is limitless, so that the mind in the presence of the sublime, attempting to imagine what it cannot, has pain in the failure but pleasure in contemplating the immensity of the attempt." Kant noted that the sublime could be mathematical—"whereby the mind imagines a magnitude by comparison with which everything in experience is small—or it could be dynamic—whereby power or might, as in hurricanes or volcanoes, can be pleasurable rather than frightening if we are safe from the threat of destruction."

One response to this aesthetic was the rise of Gothic fiction in England and America, and in Germany, "the fantastic." Jacques Barzun gives an eloquent summary of this period in his essay, "Romanticism," in the aforementioned Penguin *Encyclopedia*. "What is not in doubt is the influence of this literature. It established a taste for the uncanny that has survived all the temporary realisms and naturalisms and is once again in high favor, not simply in the form of tales of horror and fantasy, but also as an ingredient of the 'straight' novel." He goes on to discuss at length the fantastic, the Symbolist aspect of Romanticism, tracing its crucial import in the works of major literary figures in England, France and America. Here, if anywhere, is the genesis of horror fiction.

If the short story of the supernatural is often considered as an "inferior" literary genre, this is to a great extent due to the works of those authors to whom preternatural was synonymous with horror of the worst kind. To many writers the supernatural was merely a pretext for describing such things as they would never have dared to mention in terms of reality. To others the short story of the supernatural was but an outlet for unpleasant neurotic tendencies, and they chose unconsciously the most hideous symbols. . . . It is indeed a difficult task to rehabilitate the pure tale of horror and even harder, perhaps, for a lover of weird fiction, for pure horror has done much to discredit it.

—Peter Penzoldt, *The Supernatural in Fiction*

Now that we have an historical and aesthetic background for the origins of horror literature, let us return to the nature of its power. Horror comes from material on the edge of repression, according to the French critic, Julia Kristeva, material we cannot confront directly because it is so threatening to our minds and emotional balances, material to which we can gain access only through literary indirection, through metaphor and symbol. Horror conjoins the cosmic or transcendental and the deeply personal. Individual reactions to horror fiction vary widely, since in some readers' minds the material is entirely repressed and therefore the emotional response entirely inaccessible.

But as Freud remarked in his essay on the uncanny, horror shares with humor the aspect of recognition—even if an individual does not respond with the intended emotional response, he or she recognizes that that material is supposed to be humorous or horrific. Indeed, one common response to horror that does not horrify is laughter. Note again the M. R. James comment above.

The experience of seeing an audience of teenage boys at the movies laugh uproariously at a brutal and grotesque horror film is not uncommon. I have taught horror literature to young students who confess some emotional disturbance late in the course as the authentic reaction of fear and awe begins to replace the dark humor that was previously their reaction to most horror.

Boris Karloff remarked, in discussing his preferred term for the genre, "horror carries with it a connotation of revulsion which has nothing to do with clean terror." Material on the edge of repression is often dismissed as dirty, pornographic. It is not unusual to see condemnations of genre horror on cultural or moral grounds. One need only look at the recent fuss over Brett Easton Ellis' novel, *American Psycho* (1990) to see these issues in the foreground in the mainstream. Certain horror material is banned in Britain.

And I have spoken to writers, such as David Morrell, who confess to laughing aloud during the process of composition when writing a particularly horrific scene—which I interpret as an essential psychological distancing device for individuals aware of confronting dangerous material. L. P. Hartley, in the introduction to his first collection, *Night Fears* (1924) said: "To put these down on paper gives relief. . . . It is a kind of insurance against the future. When we have imagined the worst that can happen, and embodied it in a story, we feel we have stolen a march on fate, inoculated ourselves, as it were, against disaster." Peter Penzoldt, in his book, *The Supernatural in Fiction*, concurs: ". . . the weird tale is primarily a means of overcoming certain fears in the most agreeable fashion. These fears are represented by the skillful author as pure fantasy, though in fact they are only too firmly founded in some repression. . . . Thus a healthy-minded even if very imaginative person will benefit more from the reading of weird fiction than a neurotic, to whom it will only be able to give a momentary relief."

There is a fine border between the horrific and the absurdly fantastic that generates much fruitful tension in the literature, and indeed deflates the effect when handled indelicately. Those who never read horror for pleasure, but feel the need to condemn those who do, like to point to the worst examples as representative of the genre. Others laugh. But the stories that have gained reputations for quality in the literature have for most readers generated that aesthetic seizure which is the hallmark of sublime horror.

III   Category, Genre, Mode

The modern imagination has indeed been well trained by psychiatry and avant-garde novels to accept the weird and horrible. Often, these works are themselves beyond rational comprehension. But stories of the supernatural—even the subtlest—are accessible to the common reader; they make fewer demands on the intellect than on the sensibility.
—*Jacques Barzun,*
Introduction to The Penguin Encyclopedia of Horror and the Supernatural

Genres are essentially literary institutions, or social contracts between a writer and a specific public, whose function is to specify the proper use of a particular cultural artifact.
—Frederic Jameson, *Magical Narratives*

A category is a contract between a publisher and a distribution system.
—Kathryn Cramer, unpublished dissertation

. . . one thing we know is real: horror. It is so real, in fact, that we cannot quite be sure that it couldn't exist without us. Yes, it needs our imaginations and our awareness, but it does not ask or require our consent to use them. Indeed, both at the individual and collective levels, horror operates with an eerie autonomy.
—Thomas Ligotti,
"Professor Nobody's Little Lectures on Supernatural Horror"

S ir Walter Scott, to whom some attribute the creation of the first supernatural story in English, said, "The supernatural . . . is peculiarly subject to be exhausted by coarse handling and repeated pressure. It is also of a character which is extremely difficult to sustain and of which a very small proportion may be said to be better than the whole." This observation, while true, has certainly created an enduring environment in which critics can, if they choose, judge the literature by its worst examples. The most recent announcement of the death of horror literature occurs in Walter Kendrick's *The Thrill of Fear* (1991), which demise Kendrick attributes to the genrification of the literature as exemplified by the founding of *Weird Tales*: "*Weird Tales* helped to create the notion of an entertainment cult by publishing stories that only a few readers would like, hoping they would like them fiercely. There was nothing new to cultism, but it came fresh to horror. Now initiates learned to adore a sensation, not a person or a creed, and the ephemeral embarked on its strange journey from worthlessness to great price. . . . By about 1930, scary entertainment had amassed its full inventory of effects. It had recognized its history, begun to establish a canon, and even started rebelling against the stultification canons bring. Horrid stories would continue to flourish; they would spawn a score of sub-types, including science-fiction and fantasy tales. . . ." But three lines later he ends his discussion of literature, and his chapter, by declaring that by 1940, films had taken over from literature the job of scary entertainment. Thus evolution marches on and literature is no longer the fittest. It seems to me very like saying that lyric poetry is alive and well in pop music.

That an intelligent critic could find nothing worthwhile to say about horror in literature beyond the creation of the genre is astonishing in one sense (it betrays a certain ignorance), but in other ways not surprising. Once horror became a genre (as, under the influence of Dickens in the mid-nineteenth century, had the ghost story told at Christmas), it became in the hands of many writers a commercial exercise first and foremost. One might, upon superficial examination, not perceive the serious aesthetic debates raging among many of the better writers, from those of the Lovecraft circle, to Campbell's new vision in *Unknown*, to today's discussions among Stephen King, Peter Straub, Ramsey Campbell, David Morrell, Karl Edward Wagner, and others on such topics as violence, formal innovation, appropriate style (regardless of current literary fashion), and many others. That money and popularity was a serious consideration for Poe and Dickens, as well as King and Straub, does not devalue them aesthetically. Never mind that Henry James was distraught that he was not more popular and commercial, and expressed outrage at "those damned scribbling women" who outsold him—even his so-called "pot-boilers."

The curious lie concealed in James' last phrase (which he used to describe "The Turn of the Screw"), and in the public protestations of many writers before and since, up to Stephen King, today, is illuminated by Julia Briggs. In her *Night Visitors*, she states her opinion, based upon wide reading and study, that the supernatural horror story "appealed to serious writers largely because it invited a concern with the profoundest issues: the relationship between life and death, the body and the soul, man and his universe and the philosophical conditions of that universe, the nature of evil. . . . it could be made to embody symbolically hopes and fears too deep and too important to be expressed more directly." She then goes on to say, "The fact that authors often disclaimed any serious intention . . . may paradoxically support this view. The revealing nature of fantastic and imaginative writing has encouraged its exponents to cover their tracks, either by self-deprecation or other forms of retraction. The assertion of the author's detachment from his work may reasonably arouse the suspicion that he is less detached than he supposes."

To further complicate the matter, the marketing of literature in the twentieth century has become a matter of categories established by publishers upon analogy with the genre magazines. Whereas a piece of genre horror implies a contract between the writer and the audience, the marketing category of horror implies that the publisher will provide to the distribution system a certain quantity of product to fill certain display slots. Such material may or may not fulfill the genre contract. If it does not, it will be packaged to invoke its similarity to genre material and will be indistinguishable to the distribution system from material that does. As we discussed above, horror itself may exist in any genre as a literary mode, and, as a mode, is in the end an enemy of categorization and genrification. It is in part the purpose of this anthology to bring together works of fiction from within the horror genre together with works ordinarily labelled otherwise in contemporary publishing, from science fiction to thriller to "literature" (which is itself today a marketing category).

I have previously discussed, in the introduction to *The Dark Descent*, my observations that horror literature occurs in three main currents: the moral allegory, which deals with manifest evil; the investigation of abnormal psychology through metaphor and symbol;

the fantastic, which creates a world of radical doubt and dread. Whether one or another of those currents is dominant in an individual work does not exclude the presence or intermingling of the others. Rather than taking the myopic stance that horror means what the marketing system says it does today, I have applied my perceptions of horror to the literature of the past two centuries to find accomplished and significant works that manifest the delights of horror and which mark signposts in the development of horror. Horror literature operates with an "eerie autonomy" not only without regard to the reader, but without regard to the marketing system. Critic Gary Wolfe's observation that "horror is the only genre named for its effect on the reader" should suggest that the normal usage of genre is somewhat suspect here.

IV   Short Forms

Why an ever-widening circle of connoisseurs and innocents seek out and read with delight stories about ghosts and other horrors has been accounted for on divers grounds, most of them presupposing complex motives in our hidden selves. That is what one might expect in a age of reckless psychologizing. It is surely simpler and sounder to adduce historical facts and literary traditions. . . .
    —Jacques Barzun,
        Introduction to The Penguin Encyclopedia of Horror and the Supernatural

It is all the more astonishing to find English weird fiction the property of the drama in Elizabethan days, and later see it confined to the Gothic novel. On first reflection this development seems strange because the supernatural appears to flow more easily into the short tale in verse or prose. The human mind cannot leave the solid basis of reality for long, and he who contemplates occult phenomena must sooner or later return to logical thinking in terms of reality lest his reason be endangered. . . .
    —Peter Penzoldt, The Supernatural in Fiction

A horror that is effective for thirty pages can seldom be sustained for three hundred, and there is no danger of confusing the bare scaffolding of the ghost story with the rambling mansion of the Gothic novel.
    —Julia Briggs, Night Visitors

C ommentators on horror agree that the short story has always been the form of the horror story: "Thus if it is to be successful the tale of the supernatural must be short, and it matters little whether we accept it as an account of facts or as a fascinating work of art," says Peter Penzoldt. At the same time, most of them have observed that some of the very best fiction in the history of horror writing occurs at the novella length. Julia Briggs, for instance, after having given the usual set of observations on the dominance of the short form, states: "There are, however, a number of full-length ghost stories of great importance. Most of these, written in the last century, are short in comparison to the standard Victorian three-volume novel, though their length would be quite appropriate for a modern novel. More accurately described as long–short stories, or novellas, they include [Robert Louis Stevenson, Vernon Lee, Oscar Wilde, Arthur

Machen, Henry James]. They are quite distinct from the broad-canvas full-length novel of the period not only in being shorter, but also in using what is essentially a short-story structure, introducing only a few main characters within a strictly limited series of events. The greater length and complexity is often the result of a sophistocated narrative device or viewpoint. In each of these the angle or angles from which the story is told is of crucial importance to the total effect, while the action itself remains comparatively simple."

Only in a collection of this size could one gather a significant selection of novellas, and I have included a number of them to emphasize the importance of that length. I have excluded familiar masterpieces such as Robert Louis Stevenson's "Dr. Jekyll and Mr. Hyde," Henry James' "The Turn of the Screw," and Conrad's "The Heart of Darkness" in favor of significant works such as Daphne Du Maurier's "Don't Look Now" and H. P. Lovecraft's sequel to Poe's *Narrative of Arthur Gordon Pym*, "At the Mountains of Madness," John W. Campbell, Jr.'s "Who Goes There?" (from which the classic horror film, *The Thing*, was made), Gerald Durrell's "The Entrance," and others.

I have included several examples of horror from the science fiction movement by writers such as Robert A. Heinlein, Frederik Pohl and Philip K. Dick, Octavia Butler and George R. R. Martin, wherein horror is the dominant emotional force for the fiction, and a sampling of horror stories by women often excluded from notice in the history and development of horror, such as Gertrude Atherton, Violet Hunt, Harriet Prescott Spofford, and Mary Wilkins Freeman. Contemporary masters and classic names in horror are the backbone of the book, Peter Straub and Arthur Machen, Clive Barker and E. T. A. Hoffmann, and many others, but for most readers there will be a few literary surprises. Horror literature is a literature of fear and wonder. Here, then, the *Foundations of Fear*.

Daphne Du Maurier (1907–1989)

Don't Look Now

Daphne Du Maurier was the granddaughter of George Du Maurier, who invented the infamous Svengali in his popular Victorian novel, *Trilby*. One of the most popular novelists of the last fifty years, she almost single-handedly kept alive the Gothic romance tradition in the mid-twentieth century, in such novels of mystery and suspense as *Rebecca* (1938) and *My Cousin Rachel* (1952). Her stories are collected in the volumes *The Apple Tree* (1952), *The Breaking Point* (1959) and *Echoes from the Macabre* (1976); *Classics of the Macabre* (1987) reprints the best stories from the others. Her story "The Birds" was the basis of the famous Alfred Hitchcock movie. Nicholas Roeg filmed "Don't Look Now" superbly. "I have always enjoyed," she says, "the challenge and discipline of constructing a short story generally based on some personal experience . . . I saw two old women, the twins, who in the story are like a sinister Greek chorus, sitting at a table in St. Mark's Square. On the way back to my hotel after dark, a child, as I thought, was jumping from a cellar into a narrow boat. These two quite different incidents and the atmosphere of Venice, especially the eeriness of the back streets at night, set me thinking, and ideas began to develop into a story." And the result is one of the finest supernatural horror novellas of the century, slick, colloquial, yet attaining high intensity and tragic force. It makes an interesting comparison to Gertrude Atherton's "The Bell in the Fog". Rarely do stories of the occult generate such conviction (usually they have the same defect as religious fiction—requiring an a priori belief—in order to attain convincing horripilation). "Don't Look Now" also mixes a good bit of humor into the early scenes, only to emphasize the darkness underneath later. This novella is a triumph.

D on't look now," John said to his wife, "but there are a couple of old girls two tables away who are trying to hypnotise me."

Laura, quick on cue, made an elaborate pretence of yawning, then tilted her head as though searching the skies for a non-existent aeroplane.

"Right behind you," he added. "That's why you can't turn round at once—it would be much too obvious."

Laura played the oldest trick in the world and dropped her napkin, then bent to scrabble for it under her feet, sending a shooting glance over her left shoulder as she straightened once again. She sucked in her cheeks, the first telltale sign of suppressed hysteria, and lowered her head.

"They're not old girls at all," she said. "They're male twins in drag."

Her voice broke ominously, the prelude to uncontrolled laughter, and John quickly poured some more chianti into her glass.

"Pretend to choke," he said, "then they won't notice. You know what it is—they're criminals doing the sights of Europe, changing sex at each stop. Twin sisters here on Torcello. Twin brothers tomorrow in Venice, or even tonight, parading arm-in-arm across the Piazza San Marco. Just a matter of switching clothes and wigs."

"Jewel thieves or murderers?" asked Laura.

"Oh, murderers, definitely. But why, I ask myself, have they picked on me?"

The waiter made a diversion by bringing coffee and bearing away the fruit, which gave Laura time to banish hysteria and regain control.

"I can't think," she said, "why we didn't notice them when we arrived. They stand out to high heaven. One couldn't fail."

"That gang of Americans masked them," said John, "and the bearded man with a monocle who looked like a spy. It wasn't until they all went just now that I saw the twins. Oh God, the one with the shock of white hair has got her eye on me again."

Laura took the powder compact from her bag and held it in front of her face, the mirror acting as a reflector.

"I think it's me they're looking at, not you," she said. "Thank heaven I left my pearls with the manager at the hotel." She paused, dabbing the sides of her nose with powder. "The thing is," she said after a moment, "we've got them wrong. They're neither murderers nor thieves. They're a couple of pathetic old retired schoolmistresses on holiday, who've saved up all their lives to visit Venice. They come from some place with a name like Walabanga in Australia. And they're called Tilly and Tiny."

Her voice, for the first time since they had come away, took on the old bubbling quality he loved, and the worried frown between her brows had vanished. At last, he thought, at last she's beginning to get over it. If I can keep this going, if we can pick up the familiar routine of jokes shared on holiday and at home, the ridiculous fantasies about people at other tables, or staying in the hotel, or wandering in art galleries and churches, then everything will fall into place, life will become as it was before, the wound will heal, she will forget.

"You know," said Laura, "that really was a very good lunch. I did enjoy it."

Thank God, he thought, thank God. . . . Then he leant forward, speaking low in a conspirator's whisper. "One of them is going to the loo," he said. "Do you suppose he, or she, is going to change her wig?"

"Don't say anything," Laura murmured. "I'll follow her and find out. She may have a suitcase tucked away there, and she's going to switch clothes."

She began to hum under her breath, the signal, to her husband, of content. The ghost was temporarily laid, and all because of the familiar holiday game, abandoned too long, and now, through mere chance, blissfully recaptured.

"Is she on her way?" asked Laura.

"About to pass our table now," he told her.

Seen on her own, the woman was not so remarkable. Tall, angular, aquiline features, with the close-cropped hair which was fashionably called an Eton crop, he seemed to remember, in his mother's day, and about her person the stamp of that particular generation. She would be in her middle sixties, he supposed, the masculine shirt with collar and tie, sports jacket, grey tweed skirt coming to mid-calf. Grey stockings and laced black shoes. He had seen the type on golf-courses and at dog shows—invariably showing not sporting breeds but pugs—and if you came across them at a party in somebody's house they were quicker on the draw with a cigarette-lighter than he was himself, a mere male, with pocket-matches. The general belief that they kept house with a more feminine, fluffy companion was not always true. Frequently they boasted, and adored, a golfing husband. No, the striking point about this particular individual was that there were two of them. Identical twins cast in the same mould. The only difference was that the other one had whiter hair.

"Supposing," murmured Laura, "when I find myself in the *toilette* beside her she starts to strip?"

"Depends on what is revealed," John answered. "If she's hermaphrodite, make a bolt for it. She might have a hypodermic syringe concealed and want to knock you out before you reached the door."

Laura sucked in her cheeks once more and began to shake. Then, squaring her shoulders, she rose to her feet. "I simply must not laugh," she said, "and whatever you do, don't look at me when I come back, especially if we come out together." She picked up her bag and strolled self-consciously away from the table in pursuit of her prey.

John poured the dregs of the chianti into his glass and lit a cigarette. The sun blazed down upon the little garden of the restaurant. The Americans had left, and the monocled man, and the family party at the far end. All was peace. The identical twin was sitting back in her chair with her eyes closed. Thank heaven, he thought, for this moment at any rate, when relaxation was possible, and Laura had been launched upon her foolish, harmless game. The holiday could yet turn into the cure she needed, blotting out, if only temporarily, the numb despair that had seized her since the child died.

"She'll get over it," the doctor said. "They all get over it, in time. And you have the boy."

"I know," John had said, "but the girl meant everything. She always did, right from the start, I don't know why. I suppose it was the difference in age. A boy of school age, and a tough one at that, is someone in his own right. Not a baby of five. Laura literally adored her. Johnnie and I were nowhere."

"Give her time," repeated the doctor, "give her time. And anyway, you're both young still. There'll be others. Another daughter."

So easy to talk. . . . How replace the life of a loved lost child with a dream? He knew Laura too well. Another child, another girl, would have her own qualities, a separate identity, she might even induce hostility because of this very fact. A usurper in the cradle, in the cot, that had been Christine's. A chubby, flaxen replica of Johnnie, not the little waxen dark-haired sprite that had gone.

He looked up, over his glass of wine, and the woman was staring at him again. It was not the casual, idle glance of someone at a nearby table, waiting for her companion to return, but something deeper, more intent, the prominent, light blue eyes oddly penetrating, giving him a sudden feeling of discomfort. Damn the woman! All right, bloody stare, if you must. Two can play at that game. He blew a cloud of cigarette smoke into the air and smiled at her, he hoped offensively. She did not register. The blue eyes continued to hold his, so that he was obliged to look away himself, extinguish his cigarette, glance over his shoulder for the waiter and call for the bill. Settling for this, and fumbling with the change, with a few casual remarks about the excellence of the meal, brought composure, but a prickly feeling on his scalp remained, and an odd sensation of unease. Then it went, as abruptly as it had started, and stealing a furtive glance at the other table he saw that her eyes were closed again, and she was sleeping, or dozing, as she had done before. The waiter disappeared. All was still.

Laura, he thought, glancing at his watch, is being a hell of a time. Ten minutes at least. Something to tease her about, anyway. He began to plan the form the joke would take. How the old dolly had stripped to her smalls, suggesting that Laura should do likewise.

And then the manager had burst in upon them both, exclaiming in horror, the reputation of the restaurant damaged, the hint that unpleasant consequences might follow unless . . . The whole exercise turning out to be a plant, an exercise in blackmail. He and Laura and the twins taken in a police launch back to Venice for questioning. Quarter of an hour. . . . Oh, come on, come on. . . .

There was a crunch of feet on the gravel. Laura's twin walked slowly past, alone. She crossed over to her table and stood there a moment, her tall, angular figure interposing itself between John and her sister. She was saying something, but he couldn't catch the words. What was the accent, though—Scottish? Then she bent, offering an arm to the seated twin, and they moved away together across the garden to the break in the little hedge beyond, the twin who had stared at John leaning on her sister's arm. Here was the difference again. She was not quite so tall, and she stooped more—perhaps she was arthritic. They disappeared out of sight, and John, becoming impatient, got up and was about to walk back into the hotel when Laura emerged.

"Well, I must say, you took your time," he began, and then stopped, because of the expression on her face.

"What's the matter, what's happened?" he asked.

He could tell at once there was something wrong. Almost as if she were in a state of shock. She blundered towards the table he had just vacated and sat down. He drew up a chair beside her, taking her hand.

"Darling, what is it? Tell me—are you ill?"

She shook her head, and then turned and looked at him. The dazed expression he had noticed at first had given way to one of dawning confidence, almost of exaltation.

"It's quite wonderful," she said slowly, "the most wonderful thing that could possibly be. You see, she isn't dead, she's still with us. That's why they kept staring at us, those two sisters. They could see Christine."

Oh God, he thought. It's what I've been dreading. She's going off her head. What do I do? How do I cope?

"Laura, sweet," he began, forcing a smile, "look, shall we go? I've paid the bill, we can go and look at the cathedral and stroll around, and then it will be time to take off in that launch again for Venice."

She wasn't listening, or at any rate the words didn't penetrate.

"John, love," she said, "I've got to tell you what happened. I followed her, as we planned, into the *toilette* place. She was combing her hair and I went into the loo, and then came out and washed my hands in the basin. She was washing hers in the next basin. Suddenly she turned and said to me, in a strong Scots accent, 'Don't be unhappy any more. My sister has seen your little girl. She was sitting between you and your husband, laughing.' Darling, I thought I was going to faint. I nearly did. Luckily, there was a chair, and I sat down, and the woman bent over me and patted my head. I'm not sure of her exact words, but she said something about the moment of truth and joy being as sharp as a sword, but not to be afraid, all was well, but the sister's vision had been so strong they knew I had to be told, and that Christine wanted it. Oh John, don't look like that. I swear I'm not making it up, this is what she told me, it's all true."

The desperate urgency in her voice made his heart sicken. He had to play along with her, agree, soothe, do anything to bring back some sense of calm.

"Laura, darling, of course I believe you," he said, "only it's a sort of shock, and I'm upset because you're upset. . . ."

"But I'm not upset," she interrupted. "I'm happy, so happy that I can't put the feeling into words. You know what it's been like all these weeks, at home and everywhere we've been on holiday, though I tried to hide it from you. Now it's lifted, because I know, I just know, that the woman was right. Oh Lord, how awful of me, but I've forgotten their name—she did tell me. You see, the thing is that she's a retired doctor, they come from Edinburgh, and the one who saw Christine went blind a few years ago. Although she's studied the occult all her life and been very psychic, it's only since going blind that she has really seen things, like a medium. They've had the most wonderful experiences. But to describe Christine as the blind one did to her sister, even down to the little blue-and-white dress with the puff sleeves that she wore at her birthday party, and to say she was smiling happily. . . . Oh darling, it's made me so happy I think I'm going to cry."

No hysteria. Nothing wild. She took a tissue from her bag and blew her nose, smiling at him. "I'm all right, you see, you don't have to worry. Neither of us need worry about anything any more. Give me a cigarette."

He took one from his packet and lighted it for her. She sounded normal, herself again. She wasn't trembling. And if this sudden belief was going to keep her happy he couldn't possibly begrudge it. But . . . but . . . he wished, all the same, it hadn't happened. There was something uncanny about thoughtreading, about telepathy. Scientists couldn't account for it, nobody could, and this is what must have happened just now between Laura and the sisters. So the one who had been staring at him was blind. That accounted for the fixed gaze. Which somehow was unpleasant in itself, creepy. Oh hell, he thought, I wish we hadn't come here for lunch. Just chance, a flick of a coin between this, Torcello, and driving to Padua, and we had to choose Torcello.

"You didn't arrange to meet them again or anything, did you?" he asked, trying to sound casual.

"No, darling, why should I?" Laura answered. "I mean, there was nothing more they could tell me. The sister had had her wonderful vision, and that was that. Anyway, they're moving on. Funnily enough, it's rather like our original game. They *are* going round the world before returning to Scotland. Only I said Australia, didn't I? The old dears. . . . Anything less like murderers and jewel thieves."

She had quite recovered. She stood up and looked about her. "Come on," she said. "Having come to Torcello we must see the cathedral."

They made their way from the restaurant across the open piazza, where the stalls had been set up with scarves and trinkets and postcards, and so along the path to the cathedral. One of the ferryboats had just decanted a crowd of sightseers, many of whom had already found their way into Santa Maria Assunta. Laura, undaunted, asked her husband for the guidebook, and, as had always been her custom in happier days, started to walk slowly through the cathedral, studying mosaics, columns, panels from left to right, while John, less interested, because of his concern at what had just happened, followed close behind, keeping a weather eye alert for the twin sisters. There was no sign of them. Perhaps they had gone into the church of Santa Fosca close by. A sudden encounter would be embarrassing, quite apart from the effect it might have upon Laura. But the anonymous, shuffling tourists, intent upon culture, could not harm her, although from his own point of view they made artistic appreciation impossible. He could not concentrate, the cold clear beauty of what he saw left him untouched, and when Laura touched his sleeve, pointing to the mosaic of the Virgin and Child standing above the frieze of the Apostles, he nodded in sympathy yet saw nothing, the long, sad face of the Virgin infinitely remote, and turning on sudden impulse stared back over the heads of the tourists towards the door, where frescoes of the blessed and the damned gave themselves to judgement.

The twins were standing there, the blind one still holding on to her sister's arm, her sightless eyes fixed firmly upon him. He felt himself held, unable to move, and an impending sense of doom, of tragedy, came upon him. His whole being sagged, as it were, in apathy, and he thought, "This is the end, there is no escape, no future." Then both sisters turned and went out of the cathedral and the sensation vanished, leaving indignation in its wake, and rising anger. How dare those two old fools practise their mediumistic tricks on him? It was fraudulent, unhealthy; this was probably the way they lived, touring the world making everyone they met uncomfortable. Give them half a chance and they would have got money out of Laura—anything.

He felt her tugging at his sleeve again. "Isn't she beautiful? So happy, so serene."

"Who? What?" he asked.

"The Madonna," she answered. "She has a magic quality. It goes right through to one. Don't you feel it too?"

"I suppose so. I don't know. There are too many people around."

She looked up at him, astonished. "What's that got to do with it? How funny you are. Well, all right, let's get away from them. I want to buy some postcards anyway."

Disappointed, she sensed his lack of interest, and began to thread her way through the crowd of tourists to the door.

"Come on," he said abruptly, once they were outside, "there's plenty of time for postcards, let's explore a bit," and he struck off from the path, which would have taken them back to the centre where the little houses were, and the stalls, and the drifting crowd of people, to a narrow way amongst uncultivated ground, beyond which he could see a sort of cutting, or canal. The sight of water, limpid, pale, was a soothing contrast to the fierce sun above their heads.

"I don't think this leads anywhere much," said Laura. "It's a bit muddy, too, one can't sit. Besides, there are more things the guidebook says we ought to see."

"Oh, forget the book," he said impatiently, and, pulling her down beside him on the bank above the cutting, put his arms round her.

"It's the wrong time of day for sightseeing. Look, there's a rat swimming there the other side."

He picked up a stone and threw it in the water, and the animal sank, or somehow disappeared, and nothing was left but bubbles.

"Don't," said Laura. "It's cruel, poor thing," and then suddenly, putting her hand on his knee, "Do you think Christine is sitting here beside us?"

He did not answer at once. What was there to say? Would it be like this forever?

"I expect so," he said slowly, "if you feel she is."

The point was, remembering Christine before the onset of the fatal meningitis, she would have been running along the bank excitedly, throwing off her shoes, wanting to paddle, giving Laura a fit of apprehension. "Sweetheart, take care, come back . . ."

"The woman said she was looking so happy, sitting beside us, smiling," said Laura. She got up, brushing her dress, her mood changed to restlessness. "Come on, let's go back," she said.

He followed her with a sinking heart. He knew she did not really want to buy postcards or see what remained to be seen; she wanted to go in search of the women again, not necessarily to talk, just to be near them. When they came to the open place by the stalls he noticed that the crowd of tourists had thinned, there were only a few stragglers left, and the sisters were not amongst them. They must have joined the main body who had come to Torcello by the ferry service. A wave of relief seized him.

"Look, there's a mass of postcards at the second stall," he said quickly, "and some eye-catching head scarves. Let me buy you a head scarf."

"Darling, I've so many!" she protested. "Don't waste your lire."

"It isn't a waste. I'm in a buying mood. What about a basket? You know we never have enough baskets. Or some lace. How about lace?"

She allowed herself, laughing, to be dragged to the stall. While he rumpled through the goods spread out before them, and chatted up the smiling woman who was selling her wares, his ferociously bad Italian making her smile the more, he knew it would give the body of tourists more time to walk to the landing stage and catch the ferry service, and the twin sisters would be out of sight and out of their life.

"Never," said Laura, some twenty minutes later, "has so much junk been piled into so small a basket," her bubbling laugh reassuring him that all was well, he needn't worry any more, the evil hour had passed. The launch from the Cipriani that had brought them from Venice was waiting by the landing stage. The passengers who had arrived with them, the Americans, the man with the monocle, were already assembled. Earlier, before setting out, he had thought the price for lunch and transport, there and back, decidedly steep. Now he grudged none of it, except that the outing to Torcello itself had been one of the major errors of this particular holiday in Venice. They stepped down into the launch, finding a place in the open, and the boat chugged away down the canal and into the lagoon. The ordinary ferry had gone before, steaming towards Murano, while their own craft headed past San Francesco del Deserto and so back direct to Venice.

He put his arm around her once more, holding her close, and this time she responded, smiling up at him, her head on his shoulder.

"It's been a lovely day," she said. "I shall never forget it, never. You know, darling, now at last I can begin to enjoy our holiday."

He wanted to shout with relief. It's going to be all right, he decided, let her believe what she likes, it doesn't matter, it makes her happy. The beauty of Venice rose before them, sharply outlined against the glowing sky, and there was still so much to see, wandering there together, that might now be perfect because of her change of mood, the shadow having lifted, and aloud he began to discuss the evening to come, where they would dine—not the restaurant they usually went to, near the Fenice theatre, but somewhere different, somewhere new.

"Yes, but it must be cheap," she said, falling in with his mood, "because we've already spent so much today."

Their hotel by the Grand Canal had a welcoming, comforting air. The clerk smiled as he handed over their key. The bedroom was familiar, like home, with Laura's things arranged neatly on the dressing-table, but with it the little festive atmosphere of strangeness, of excitement, that only a holiday bedroom brings. This is ours for the moment, but no more. While we are in it we bring it life. When we have gone it no longer exists, it fades into anonymity. He turned on both taps in the bathroom, the water gushing into the bath, the steam rising. "Now," he thought afterwards, "now at last is the moment to make love," and he went back into the bedroom, and she understood, and opened her arms and smiled. Such blessed relief after all those weeks of restraint.

"The thing is," she said later, fixing her ear-rings before the looking-glass, "I'm not really terribly hungry. Shall we just be dull and eat in the dining-room here?"

"God, no!" he exclaimed. "With all those rather dreary couples at the other tables? I'm ravenous. I'm also gay. I want to get rather sloshed."

"Not bright lights and music, surely?"

"No, no . . . some small, dark, intimate cave, rather sinister, full of lovers with other people's wives."

"H'm," sniffed Laura, "we all know what *that* means. You'll spot some Italian lovely of sixteen and smirk at her through dinner, while I'm stuck high and dry with a beastly man's broad back."

They went out laughing into the warm soft night, and the magic was about them everywhere. "Let's walk," he said, "let's walk and work up an appetite for our gigantic meal," and inevitably they found themselves by the Molo and the lapping gondolas dancing upon the water, the lights everywhere blending with the darkness. There were other couples strolling for the same sake of aimless enjoyment, backwards, forwards, purposeless, and the inevitable sailors in groups, noisy, gesticulating, and dark-eyed girls whispering, clicking on high heels.

"The trouble is," said Laura, "walking in Venice becomes compulsive once you start. Just over the next bridge, you say, and then the next one beckons. I'm sure there are no restaurants down here, we're almost at those public gardens where they hold the Biennale. Let's turn back. I know there's a restaurant somewhere near the church of San Zaccaria, there's a little alleyway leading to it."

"Tell you what," said John, "if we go down here by the Arsenal, and cross that bridge at the end and head left, we'll come upon San Zaccaria from the other side. We did it the other morning."

"Yes, but it was daylight then. We may lose our way, it's not very well lit."

"Don't fuss. I have an instinct for these things."

They turned down the Fondamenta dell'Arsenale and crossed the little bridge short of the Arsenal itself, and so on past the church of San Martino. There were two canals ahead, one bearing right, the other left, with narrow streets beside them. John hesitated. Which one was it they had walked beside the day before?

"You see," protested Laura, "we shall be lost, just as I said."

"Nonsense," replied John firmly. "It's the left-hand one, I remember the little bridge."

The canal was narrow, the houses on either side seemed to close in upon it, and in the daytime, with the sun's reflection on the water and the windows of the houses open, bedding upon the balconies, a canary singing in a cage, there had been an impression of warmth, of secluded shelter. Now, ill-lit, almost in darkness, the windows of the houses shuttered, the water dank, the scene appeared altogether different, neglected, poor, and the long narrow boats moored to the slippery steps of cellar entrances looked like coffins.

"I swear I don't remember this bridge," said Laura, pausing, and holding on to the rail, "and I don't like the look of that alleyway beyond."

"There's a lamp halfway up," John told her. "I know exactly where we are, not far from the Greek quarter."

They crossed the bridge, and were about to plunge into the alleyway when they heard the cry. It came, surely, from one of the houses on the opposite side, but which one it was impossible to say. With the shutters closed each one of them seemed dead. They turned, and stared in the direction from which the sound had come.

"What was it?" whispered Laura.

"Some drunk or other," said John briefly. "Come on."

Less like a drunk than someone being strangled, and the choking cry suppressed as the grip held firm.

"We ought to call the police," said Laura.

"Oh, for heaven's sake," said John. Where did she think she was—Piccadilly?

"Well, I'm off, it's sinister," she replied, and began to hurry away up the twisting alleyway. John hesitated, his eye caught by a small figure which suddenly crept from a cellar entrance below one of the opposite houses, and then jumped into a narrow boat below. It was a child, a little girl—she couldn't have been more than five or six—wearing a short coat over her minute skirt, a pixie hood covering her head. There were four boats moored, line upon line, and she proceeded to jump from one to the other with surprising agility, intent, it would seem, upon escape. Once her foot slipped and he caught his breath, for she was within a few feet of the water, losing balance; then she recovered, and hopped on to the furthest boat. Bending, she tugged at the rope, which had the effect of swinging the boat's after-end across the canal, almost touching the opposite side and another cellar entrance, about thirty feet from the spot where John stood watching her. Then the child jumped again, landing upon the cellar steps, and vanished into the house, the boat swinging back into midcanal behind her. The whole episode could not have taken more than four minutes. Then he heard the quick patter of feet. Laura had returned. She had seen none of it, for which he felt unspeakably thankful. The sight of a child, a little girl, in what must have been near danger, her fear that the scene he had just witnessed was in some way a sequel to the alarming cry, might have had a disastrous effect on her overwrought nerves.

"What are you doing?" she called. "I daren't go on without you. The wretched alley branches in two directions."

"Sorry," he told her. "I'm coming."

He took her arm and they walked briskly along the alley, John with an apparent confidence he did not possess.

"There were no more cries, were there?" she asked.

"No," he said, "no, nothing. I tell you, it was some drunk."

The alley led to a deserted *campo* behind a church, not a church he knew, and he led the way across, along another street and over a further bridge.

"Wait a minute," he said. "I think we take this right-hand turning. It will lead us into the Greek quarter—the church of San Georgio is somewhere over there."

She did not answer. She was beginning to lose faith. The place was like a maze. They might circle round and round forever, and then find themselves back again, near the bridge where they had heard the cry. Doggedly he led her on, and then surprisingly, with relief, he saw people walking in the lighted street ahead, there was a spire of a church, the surroundings became familiar.

"There, I told you," he said. "That's San Zaccaria, we've found it all right. Your restaurant can't be far away."

And anyway, there would be other restaurants, somewhere to eat, at least here was the cheering glitter of lights, of movement, canals beside which people walked, the atmosphere of tourism. The letters "Ristorante", in blue lights, shone like a beacon down a left-hand alley.

"Is this your place?" he asked.

"God knows," she said. "Who cares? Let's feed there anyway."

And so into the sudden blast of heated air and hum of voices, the smell of pasta, wine, waiters, jostling customers, laughter. "For two? This way, please." Why, he thought, was one's British nationality always so obvious? A cramped little table and an enormous menu scribbled in an indecipherable mauve biro, with the waiter hovering, expecting the order forthwith.

"Two very large camparis, with soda," John said. "*Then* we'll study the menu."

He was not going to be rushed. He handed the bill of fare to Laura and looked about him. Mostly Italians—that meant the food would be good. Then he saw them. At the opposite side of the room. The twin sisters. They must have come into the restaurant hard upon Laura's and his own arrival, for they were only now sitting down, shedding their coats, the waiter hovering beside the table. John was seized with the irrational thought that this was no coincidence. The sisters had noticed them both, in the street outside, and had followed them in. Why, in the name of hell, should they have picked on this particular spot, in the whole of Venice, unless . . . unless Laura herself, at Torcello, had suggested a further encounter, or the sister had suggested it to her? A small restaurant near the church of San Zaccaria, we go there sometimes for dinner. It was Laura, before the walk, who had mentioned San Zaccaria. . . .

She was still intent upon the menu, she had not seen the sisters, but any moment now she would have chosen what she wanted to eat, and then she would raise her head and look across the room. If only the drinks would come. If only the waiter would bring the drinks, it would give Laura something to do.

"You know, I was thinking," he said quickly, "we really ought to go to the garage tomorrow and get the car, and do that drive to Padua. We could lunch in Padua, see the cathedral and touch St. Antony's tomb and look at the Giotto frescoes, and come back by way of those various villas along the Brenta that the guidebook cracks up."

It was no use, though. She was looking up, across the restaurant, and she gave a little gasp of surprise. It was genuine. He could swear it was genuine.

"Look," she said, "how extraordinary! How really amazing!"

"What?" he said sharply.

"Why, there they are. My wonderful old twins. They've seen us, what's more. They're staring this way." She waved her hand, radiant, delighted. The sister she had spoken to at Torcello bowed and smiled. False old bitch, he thought. I know they followed us.

"Oh, darling, I must go and speak to them," she said impulsively, "just to tell them how happy I've been all day, thanks to them."

"Oh, for heaven's sake!" he said. "Look, here are the drinks. And we haven't ordered yet. Surely you can wait until later, until we've eaten?"

"I won't be a moment," she said, "and anyway I want scampi, nothing first. I told you I wasn't hungry."

She got up, and, brushing past the waiter with the drinks, crossed the room. She might have been greeting the loved friends of years. He watched her bend over the table and shake them both by the hand, and because there was a vacant chair at their table she drew it up and sat down, talking, smiling. Nor did the sisters seem surprised, at least not the one she knew, who nodded and talked back, while the blind sister remained impassive.

"All right," thought John savagely, "then I *will* get sloshed," and he proceeded to down his campari and soda and order another, while he pointed out something quite unintelligible on the menu as his own choice, but remembered scampi for Laura. "And a bottle of Soave," he added, "with ice."

The evening was ruined anyway. What was to have been an intimate, happy celebration would now be heavy-laden with spiritualistic visions, poor little dead Christine sharing the table with them, which was so damned stupid when in earthly life she would have been tucked up hours ago in bed. The bitter taste of the campari suited his mood of sudden self-pity, and all the while he watched the group at the table in the opposite corner, Laura apparently listening while the more active sister held forth and the blind one sat silent, her formidable sightless eyes turned in his direction.

"She's phoney," he thought, "she's not blind at all. They're both of them frauds, and they could be males in drag after all, just as we pretended at Torcello, and they're after Laura."

He began on his second campari and soda. The two drinks, taken on an empty stomach, had an instant effect. Vision became blurred. And still Laura went on sitting at the other table, putting in a question now and again, while the active sister talked. The waiter appeared with the scampi, and a companion beside him to serve John's own order, which was totally unrecognisable, heaped with a livid sauce.

"The signora does not come?" enquired the first waiter, and John shook his head grimly, pointing an unsteady finger across the room.

"Tell the signora," he said carefully, "her scampi will get cold."

He stared down at the offering placed before him, and prodded it delicately with a fork. The pallid sauce dissolved, revealing two enormous slices, rounds, of what appeared to be boiled pork, bedecked with garlic. He forked a portion to his mouth and chewed, and yes, it was pork, steamy, rich, the spicy sauce having turned it curiously sweet. He laid down his fork, pushing the plate away, and became aware of Laura, returning across the room and sitting beside him. She did not say anything, which was just as well, he thought, because he was too near nausea to answer. It wasn't just the drink, but reaction from the whole nightmare day. She began to eat her scampi, still not uttering. She did not seem to notice he was not eating. The waiter, hovering at his elbow, anxious, seemed aware that John's choice was somehow an error, and discreetly removed the plate. "Bring me a green salad," murmured John, and even then Laura did not register surprise, or, as she might have done in more normal circumstances, accuse him of having had too much to drink. Finally, when she had finished her scampi and was sipping her wine, which John had waved away, to nibble at his salad in small mouthfuls like a sick rabbit, she began to speak.

"Darling," she said, "I know you won't believe it, and it's rather frightening in a way, but after they left the restaurant in Torcello the sisters went to the cathedral, as we did, although we didn't see them in that crowd, and the blind one had another vision. She said Christine was trying to tell her something about us, that we should be in danger if we stayed in Venice. Christine wanted us to go away as soon as possible."

So that's it, he thought. They think they can run our lives for us. This is to be our problem from henceforth. Do we eat? Do we get up? Do we go to bed? We must get in touch with the twin sisters. They will direct us.

"Well?" she said. "Why don't you say something?"

"Because," he answered, "you are perfectly right, I don't believe it. Quite frankly, I judge your old sisters as being a couple of freaks, if nothing else. They're obviously unbalanced, and I'm sorry if this hurts you, but the fact is they've found a sucker in you."

"You're being unfair," said Laura. "They are genuine, I know it. I just know it. They were completely sincere in what they said."

"All right. Granted. They're sincere. But that doesn't make them well-balanced. Honestly, darling, you meet that old girl for ten minutes in a loo, she tells you she sees Christine sitting beside us—well, anyone with a gift for telepathy could read your unconscious mind in an instant—and then, pleased with her success, as any old psychic expert would be, she flings a further mood of ecstasy and wants to boot us out of Venice. Well, I'm sorry, but to hell with it."

The room was no longer reeling. Anger had sobered him. If it would not put Laura to shame he would get up and cross to their table, and tell the old fools where they got off.

"I knew you would take it like this," said Laura unhappily. "I told them you would. They said not to worry. As long as we left Venice tomorrow everything would come all right."

"Oh, for God's sake," said John. He changed his mind, and poured himself a glass of wine.

"After all," Laura went on, "we have really seen the cream of Venice. I don't mind going on somewhere else. And if we stayed—I know it sounds silly, but I should have a nasty nagging sort of feeling inside me, and I should keep thinking of darling Christine being unhappy and trying to tell us to go."

"Right," said John with ominous calm, "that settles it. Go we will. I suggest we clear off to the hotel straight away and warn the reception we're leaving in the morning. Have you had enough to eat?"

"Oh, dear," sighed Laura, "don't take it like that. Look, why not come over and meet them, and then they can explain about the vision to you? Perhaps you would take it seriously then. Especially as you are the one it most concerns. Christine is more worried over you than me. And the extraordinary thing is that the blind sister says you're psychic and don't know it. You are somehow *en rapport* with the unknown, and I'm not."

"Well, that's final," said John. "I'm psychic, am I? Fine. My psychic intuition tells me to get out of this restaurant now, at once, and we can decide what we do about leaving Venice when we are back at the hotel."

He signalled to the waiter for the bill and they waited for it, not speaking to each other, Laura unhappy, fiddling with her bag, while John, glancing furtively at the twins' table, noticed that they were tucking into plates piled high with spaghetti, in very un-psychic fashion. The bill disposed of, John pushed back his chair.

"Right. Are you ready?" he asked.

"I'm going to say goodbye to them first," said Laura, her mouth set sulkily, reminding him instantly, with a pang, of their poor lost child.

"Just as you like," he replied, and walked ahead of her out of the restaurant, without a backward glance.

The soft humidity of the evening, so pleasant to walk about in earlier, had turned to rain. The strolling tourists had melted away. One or two people hurried by under umbrellas. This is what the inhabitants who live here see, he thought. This is the true life. Empty streets by night, and the dank stillness of a stagnant canal beneath shuttered houses. The rest is a bright façade put on for show, glittering by sunlight.

Laura joined him and they walked away together in silence, and emerging presently behind the ducal palace came out into the Piazza San Marco. The rain was heavy now, and they sought shelter with the few remaining stragglers under the colonnades. The orchestras had packed up for the evening. The tables were bare. Chairs had been turned upside down.

The experts are right, he thought. Venice is sinking. The whole city is slowly dying. One day the tourists will travel here by boat to peer down into the waters, and they will see pillars and columns and marble far, far beneath them, slime and mud uncovering for brief moments a lost underworld of stone. Their heels made a ringing sound on the pavement and the rain splashed from the gutterings above. A fine ending to an evening that had started with brave hope, with innocence.

When they came to their hotel Laura made straight for the lift, and John turned to the desk to ask the night porter for the key. The man handed him a telegram at the same time. John stared at it a moment. Laura was already in the lift. Then he opened the envelope and read the message. It was from the headmaster of Johnnie's preparatory school.

> Johnnie under observation suspected
> appendicitis in city hospital here.
> No cause for alarm but surgeon thought wise
> advise you.
> Charles Hill

He read the message twice, then walked slowly towards the lift where Laura was waiting for him. He gave her the telegram. "This came when we were out," he said. "Not awfully good news." He pressed the lift button as she read the telegram. The lift stopped at the second floor, and they got out.

"Well, this decides it, doesn't it?" she said. "Here is the proof. We have to leave Venice because we're going home. It's Johnnie who's in danger, not us. This is what Christine was trying to tell the twins."

The first thing John did the following morning was to put a call through to the headmaster at the preparatory school. Then he gave notice of their departure to the reception manager, and they packed while they waited for the call. Neither of them referred to the events of the preceding day, it was not necessary. John knew the arrival of the telegram and the foreboding of danger from the sisters was coincidence, nothing more, but it was pointless to start an argument about it. Laura was convinced otherwise, but intuitively she knew it was best to keep her feelings to herself. During breakfast they discussed ways and means of getting home. It should be possible to get themselves, and the car, on to the special car train that ran from Milan through to Calais, since it was early in the season. In any event, the headmaster had said there was no urgency.

The call from England came while John was in the bathroom. Laura answered it. He came into the bedroom a few minutes later. She was still speaking, but he could tell from the expression in her eyes that she was anxious.

"It's Mrs. Hill," she said. "Mr. Hill is in class. She says they reported from the hospital that Johnnie had a restless night and the surgeon may have to operate, but he doesn't want to unless it's absolutely necessary. They've taken X rays and the appendix is in a tricky position, it's not awfully straightforward."

"Here, give it to me," he said.

The soothing but slightly guarded voice of the headmaster's wife came down the receiver. "I'm so sorry this may spoil your plans," she said, "but both Charles and I felt you ought to be told, and that you might feel rather easier if you were on the spot. Johnnie is very plucky, but of course he has some fever. That isn't unusual, the surgeon says, in the circumstances. Sometimes an appendix can get displaced, it appears, and this makes it more complicated. He's going to decide about operating this evening."

"Yes, of course, we quite understand," said John.

"Please do tell your wife not to worry too much," she went on. "The hospital is excellent, a very nice staff, and we have every confidence in the surgeon."

"Yes," said John, "yes," and then broke off because Laura was making gestures beside him.

"If we can't get the car on the train, I can fly," she said. "They're sure to be able to find me a seat on a 'plane. Then at least one of us would be there this evening."

He nodded agreement. "Thank you so much, Mrs. Hill," he said, "we'll manage to get back all right. Yes, I'm sure Johnnie is in good hands. Thank your husband for us. Goodbye."

He replaced the receiver and looked round him at the tumbled beds, suitcases on the floor, tissue paper strewn. Baskets, maps, books, coats, everything they had brought with them in the car. "Oh God," he said, "what a bloody mess. All this junk." The telephone rang again. It was the hall porter to say he had succeeded in booking a sleeper for them both, and a place for the car, on the following night.

"Look," said Laura, who had seized the telephone, "could you book one seat on the midday 'plane from Venice to London today, for me? It's imperative one of us gets home this evening. My husband could follow with the car tomorrow."

"Here, hang on," interrupted John. "No need for panic stations. Surely twenty-four hours wouldn't make all that difference?"

Anxiety had drained the colour from her face. She turned to him, distraught.

"It mightn't to you, but it does to me," she said. "I've lost one child, I'm not going to lose another."

"All right, darling, all right . . ." He put his hand out to her but she brushed it off, impatiently, and continued giving directions to the porter. He turned back to his packing. No use saying anything. Better for it to be as she wished. They could, of course, both go by air, and then when all was well, and Johnnie better, he could come back and fetch the car, driving home through France as they had come. Rather a sweat, though, and the hell of an expense. Bad enough Laura going by air and himself with the car on the train from Milan.

"We could, if you like, both fly," he began tentatively, explaining the sudden idea, but she would have none of it. "That really *would* be absurd," she said impatiently. "As long as I'm there this evening, and you follow by train, it's all that matters. Besides, we shall need the car, going backwards and forwards to the hospital. And our luggage. We couldn't go off and just leave all this here."

No, he saw her point. A silly idea. It was only—well, he was as worried about Johnnie as she was, though he wasn't going to say so.

"I'm going downstairs to stand over the porter," said Laura. "They always make more effort if one is actually on the spot. Everything I want tonight is packed. I shall only need my overnight case. You can bring everything else in the car." She hadn't been out of the bedroom five minutes before the telephone rang. It was Laura. "Darling," she said, "it couldn't have worked out better. The porter has got me on a charter flight that leaves Venice in less than an hour. A special motor launch takes the party direct from San Marco in about ten minutes. Some passenger on the charter flight cancelled. I shall be at Gatwick in less than four hours."

"I'll be down right away," he told her.

He joined her by the reception desk. She no longer looked anxious and drawn, but full of purpose. She was on her way. He kept wishing they were going together. He couldn't bear to stay on in Venice after she had gone, but the thought of driving to Milan, spending a dreary night in a hotel there alone, the endless dragging day which would follow, and the long hours in the train the next night, filled him with intolerable depression, quite apart from the anxiety about Johnnie. They walked along to the San Marco landing stage, the Molo bright and glittering after the rain, a little breeze blowing, the postcards and scarves and tourist souvenirs fluttering on the stalls, the tourists themselves out in force, strolling, contented, the happy day before them.

"I'll ring you tonight from Milan," he told her. "The Hills will give you a bed, I suppose. And if you're at the hospital they'll let me have the latest news. That must be your charter party. You're welcome to them!"

The passengers descending from the landing stage down into the waiting launch were carrying hand-luggage with Union Jack tags upon them. They were mostly middle-aged, with what appeared to be two Methodist ministers in charge. One of them advanced towards Laura, holding out his hand, showing a gleaming row of dentures when he smiled. "You must be the lady joining us for the homeward flight," he said. "Welcome aboard, and to the Union of Fellowship. We are all delighted to make your acquaintance. Sorry we hadn't a seat for hubby too."

Laura turned swiftly and kissed John, a tremor at the corner of her mouth betraying inward laughter. "Do you think they'll break into hymns?" she whispered. "Take care of yourself, hubby. Call me tonight."

The pilot sounded a curious little toot upon his horn, and in a moment Laura had climbed down the steps into the launch and was standing amongst the crowd of passengers, waving her hand, her scarlet coat a gay patch of colour amongst the more sober suiting of her companions. The launch tooted again and moved away from the landing stage, and he stood there watching it, a sense of immense loss filling his heart. Then he turned and walked away, back to the hotel, the bright day all about him desolate, unseen.

There was nothing, he thought, as he looked about him presently in the hotel bedroom, so melancholy as a vacated room, especially when the recent signs of occupation were still visible about him. Laura's suitcases on the bed, a second coat she had left behind. Traces of powder on the dressing table. A tissue, with a lipstick smear, thrown in the wastepaper basket. Even an old toothpaste tube squeezed dry, lying on the glass shelf above the washbasin. Sounds of the heedless traffic on the Grand Canal came as always from the open window, but Laura wasn't there any more to listen to it, or to watch from the small balcony. The pleasure had gone. Feeling had gone.

John finished packing, and leaving all the baggage ready to be collected he went downstairs to pay the bill. The reception clerk was welcoming new arrivals. People were sitting on the terrace overlooking the Grand Canal reading newspapers, the pleasant day waiting to be planned.

John decided to have an early lunch, here on the hotel terrace, on familiar ground, and then have the porter carry the baggage to one of the ferries that steamed direct between San Marco and the Porta Roma, where the car was garaged. The fiasco meal of the night before had left him empty, and he was ready for the trolley of hors d'œuvres when they brought it to him, around midday. Even here, though, there was change. The headwaiter, their especial friend, was off-duty, and the table where they usually sat was occupied by new arrivals, a honeymoon couple, he told himself sourly, observing the gaiety, the smiles, while he had been shown to a small single table behind a tub of flowers.

"She's airborne now," John thought, "she's on her way," and he tried to picture Laura seated between the Methodist ministers, telling them, no doubt, about Johnnie ill in hospital, and heaven knows what else besides. Well, the twin sisters anyway could rest in psychic peace. Their wishes would have been fulfilled.

Lunch over, there was no point in lingering with a cup of coffee on the terrace. His desire was to get away as soon as possible, fetch the car, and be en route for Milan. He made his farewells at the reception desk, and, escorted by a porter who had piled his baggage on to a wheeled trolley, made his way once more to the landing stage of San Marco. As he stepped on to the steam ferry, his luggage heaped beside him, a crowd of jostling people all about him, he had one momentary pang to be leaving Venice. When, if ever, he wondered, would they come again? Next year . . . in three years. . . . Glimpsed first on honeymoon, nearly ten years ago, and then a second visit, *en passant*, before a cruise, and now this last abortive ten days that had ended so abruptly.

The water glittered in the sunshine, buildings shone, tourists in dark glasses paraded up and down the rapidly receding Molo, already the terrace of their hotel was out of sight as the ferry churned its way up the Grand Canal. So many impressions to seize and hold, familiar loved façades, balconies, windows, water lapping the cellar steps of decaying palaces, the little red house where d'Annunzio lived, with its garden—our house, Laura called it, pretending it was theirs—and too soon the ferry would be turning left on the direct route to the Piazzale Roma, so missing the best of the Canal, the Rialto, the further palaces.

Another ferry was heading downstream to pass them, filled with passengers, and for a brief foolish moment he wished he could change places, be amongst the happy tourists bound for Venice and all he had left behind him. Then he saw her. Laura, in her scarlet coat, the twin sisters by her side, the active sister with her hand on Laura's arm, talking earnestly, and Laura herself, her hair blowing in the wind, gesticulating, on her face a look of distress. He stared, astounded, too astonished to shout, to wave, and anyway they would never have heard or seen him, for his own ferry had already passed and was heading in the opposite direction.

What the hell had happened? There must have been a hold-up with the charter flight and it had never taken off, but in that case why had Laura not telephoned him at the hotel? And what were those damned sisters doing? Had she run into them at the airport? Was it coincidence? And why did she look so anxious? He could think of no explanation. Perhaps the flight had been cancelled. Laura, of course, would go straight to the hotel, expecting to find him there, intending, doubtless, to drive with him after all to Milan and take the train the following night. What a blasted mix-up. The only thing to do was to telephone the hotel immediately his ferry reached the Piazzale Roma and tell her to wait—he would return and fetch her. As for the damned interfering sisters, they could get stuffed.

The usual stampede ensued when the ferry arrived at the landing stage. He had to find a porter to collect his baggage, and then wait while he discovered a telephone. The fiddling with change, the hunt for the number, delayed him still more. He succeeded at last in getting through, and luckily the reception clerk he knew was still at the desk.

"Look, there's been some frightful muddle," he began, and explained how Laura was even now on her way back to the hotel—he had seen her with two friends on one of the ferry services. Would the reception clerk explain and tell her to wait? He would be back by the next available service to collect her. "In any event, detain her," he said. "I'll be as quick as I can." The reception clerk understood perfectly, and John rang off.

Thank heaven Laura hadn't turned up before he had put through his call, or they would have told her he was on his way to Milan. The porter was still waiting with the baggage, and it seemed simplest to walk with him to the garage, hand everything over to the chap in charge of the office there and ask him to keep it for an hour, when he would be returning with his wife to pick up the car. Then he went back to the landing station to await the next ferry to Venice. The minutes dragged, and he kept wondering all the time what had gone wrong at the airport and why in heaven's name Laura hadn't telephoned. No use conjecturing. She would tell him the whole story at the hotel. One thing was certain: he would not allow Laura and himself to be saddled with the sisters and become involved with their affairs. He could imagine Laura saying that they also had missed a flight, and could they have a lift to Milan?

Finally the ferry chugged alongside the landing stage and he stepped aboard. What an anticlimax, thrashing back past the familiar sights to which he had bidden a nostalgic farewell such a short while ago! He didn't even look about him this time, he was so intent on reaching his destination. In San Marco there were more people than ever, the afternoon crowds walking shoulder to shoulder, every one of them on pleasure bent.

He came to the hotel and pushed his way through the swing door, expecting to see Laura, and possibly the sisters, waiting in the lounge to the left of the entrance. She was not there. He went to the desk. The reception clerk he had spoken to on the telephone was standing there, talking to the manager.

"Has my wife arrived?" John asked.

"No, sir, not yet."

"What an extraordinary thing. Are you sure?"

"Absolutely certain, sir. I have been here ever since you telephoned me at a quarter to two. I have not left the desk."

"I just don't understand it. She was on one of the vaporettos passing by the Accademia. She would have landed at San Marco about five minutes later and come on here."

The clerk seemed nonplussed. "I don't know what to say. The signora was with friends, did you say?"

"Yes. Well, acquaintances. Two ladies we had met at Torcello yesterday. I was astonished to see her with them on the vaporetto, and of course I assumed that the flight had been cancelled, and she had somehow met up with them at the airport and decided to return here with them, to catch me before I left."

Oh hell, what was Laura doing? It was after three. A matter of moments from San Marco landing stage to the hotel.

"Perhaps the signora went with her friends to their hotel instead. Do you know where they are staying?"

"No," said John, "I haven't the slightest idea. What's more, I don't even know the names of the two ladies. They were sisters, twins, in fact—looked exactly alike. But anyway, why go to their hotel and not here?"

The swing-door opened but it wasn't Laura. Two people staying in the hotel.

The manager broke into the conversation. "I tell you what I will do," he said. "I will telephone the airport and check about the flight. Then at least we will get somewhere." He smiled apologetically. It was not usual for arrangements to go wrong.

"Yes, do that," said John. "We may as well know what happened there."

He lit a cigarette and began to pace up and down the entrance hall. What a bloody mix-up. And how unlike Laura, who knew he would be setting off for Milan directly after lunch—indeed, for all she knew he might have gone before. But surely, in that case, she would have telephoned at once, on arrival at the airport, had the flight been cancelled? The manager was ages telephoning, he had to be put through on some other line, and his Italian was too rapid for John to follow the conversation. Finally he replaced the receiver.

"It is more mysterious than ever, sir," he said. "The charter flight was not delayed, it took off on schedule with a full complement of passengers. As far as they could tell me, there was no hitch. The signora must simply have changed her mind." His smile was more apologetic than ever.

"Changed her mind," John repeated. "But why on earth should she do that? She was so anxious to be home tonight."

The manager shrugged. "You know how ladies can be, sir," he said. "Your wife may have thought that after all she would prefer to take the train to Milan with you. I do assure you, though, that the charter party was most respectable, and it was a Caravelle aircraft, perfectly safe."

"Yes, yes," said John impatiently, "I don't blame your arrangements in the slightest. I just can't understand what induced her to change her mind, unless it was meeting with these two ladies."

The manager was silent. He could not think of anything to say. The reception clerk was equally concerned. "Is it possible," he ventured, "that you made a mistake, and it was not the signora that you saw on the vaporetto?"

"Oh no," replied John, "it was my wife, I assure you. She was wearing her red coat, she was hatless, just as she left here. I saw her as plainly as I can see you. I would swear to it in a court of law."

"It is unfortunate," said the manager, "that we do not know the name of the two ladies, or the hotel where they were staying. You say you met these ladies at Torcello yesterday?"

"Yes . . . but only briefly. They weren't staying there. At least, I am certain they were not. We saw them at dinner in Venice later, as it happens."

"Excuse me. . . ." Guests were arriving with luggage to check in, the clerk was obliged to attend to them. John turned in desperation to the manager. "Do you think it would be any good telephoning the hotel in Torcello in case the people there knew the name of the ladies, or where they were staying in Venice?"

"We can try," replied the manager. "It is a small hope, but we can try."

John resumed his anxious pacing, all the while watching the swing-door, hoping, praying, that he would catch sight of the red coat and Laura would enter. Once again there followed what seemed an interminable telephone conversation between the manager and someone at the hotel in Torcello.

"Tell them two sisters," said John, "two elderly ladies dressed in grey, both exactly alike. One lady was blind," he added. The manager nodded. He was obviously giving a detailed description. Yet when he hung up he shook his head. "The manager at Torcello says he remembers the two ladies well," he told John, "but they were only there for lunch. He never learnt their names."

"Well, that's that. There's nothing to do now but wait."

John lit his third cigarette and went out on to the terrace, to resume his pacing there. He stared out across the canal, searching the heads of the people on passing steamers, motorboats, even drifting gondolas. The minutes ticked by on his watch, and there was no sign of Laura. A terrible foreboding nagged at him that somehow this was prearranged, that Laura had never intended to catch the aircraft, that last night in the restaurant she had made an assignation with the sisters. Oh God, he thought, that's impossible, I'm going paranoiac. . . . Yet why, why? No, more likely the encounter at the airport was fortuitous, and for some incredible reason they had persuaded Laura not to board the aircraft, even prevented her from doing so, trotting out one of their psychic visions, that the aircraft would crash, that she must return with them to Venice. And Laura, in her sensitive state, felt they must be right, swallowed it all without question.

But granted all these possibilities, why had she not come to the hotel? What was she doing? Four o'clock, half-past four, the sun no longer dappling the water. He went back to the reception desk.

"I just can't hang around," he said. "Even if she does turn up, we shall never make Milan this evening. I might see her walking with these ladies, in the Piazza San Marco, anywhere. If she arrives while I'm out, will you explain?"

The clerk was full of concern. "Indeed, yes," he said. "It is very worrying for you, sir. Would it perhaps be prudent if we booked you in here tonight?"

John gestured, helplessly. "Perhaps, yes, I don't know. Maybe . . ."

He went out of the swing-door and began to walk towards the Piazza San Marco. He looked into every shop up and down the colonnades, crossed the piazza a dozen times, threaded his way between the tables in front of Florian's, in front of Quadri's, knowing that Laura's red coat and the distinctive appearance of the twin sisters could easily be spotted, even amongst this milling crowd, but there was no sign of them. He joined the crowd of shoppers in the Merceria, shoulder to shoulder with idlers, thrusters, window-gazers, knowing instinctively that it was useless, they wouldn't be here. Why should Laura have deliberately missed her flight to return to Venice for such a purpose? And even if she had done so, for some reason beyond his imagining, she would surely have come first to the hotel to find him.

The only thing left to him was to try to track down the sisters. Their hotel could be anywhere amongst the hundreds of hotels and pensions scattered through Venice, or even across the other side at the Zattere, or further again on the Giudecca. These last possibilities seemed remote. More likely they were staying in a small hotel or pension somewhere near San Zaccaria handy to the restaurant where they had dined last night. The blind one would surely not go far afield in the evening. He had been a fool not to have thought of this before, and he turned back and walked quickly away from the brightly lighted shopping district towards the narrower, more cramped quarter where they had dined last evening. He found the restaurant without difficulty, but they were not yet open for dinner, and the waiter preparing tables was not the one who had served them. John asked to see the *padrone*, and the waiter disappeared to the back regions, returning after a moment or two with the somewhat dishevelled-looking proprietor in shirtsleeves, caught in a slack moment, not in full tenue.

"I had dinner here last night," John explained. "There were two ladies sitting at that table there in the corner." He pointed to it.

"You wish to book that table for this evening?" asked the proprietor.

"No," said John. "No, there were two ladies there last night, two sisters, due sorelle, twins, gemelle"—what was the right word for twins?—"Do you remember? Two ladies, sorelle vecchie . . ."

"Ah," said the man, "si, si, signore, la povera signorina." He put his hands to his eyes to feign blindness. "Yes, I remember."

"Do you know their names?" asked John. "Where they were staying? I am very anxious to trace them."

The proprietor spread out his hands in a gesture of regret. "I am ver' sorry, signore, I do not know the names of the signorine, they have been here once, twice, perhaps for dinner, they do not say where they were staying. Perhaps if you come again tonight they might be here? Would you like to book a table?"

He pointed around him, suggesting a whole choice of tables that might appeal to a prospective diner, but John shook his head.

"Thank you, no. I may be dining elsewhere. I am sorry to have troubled you. If the signorine should come . . ." he paused, "possibly I may return later," he added. "I am not sure."

The proprietor bowed, and walked with him to the entrance. "In Venice the whole world meets," he said smiling. "It is possible the signore will find his friends tonight. Arrivederci, signore."

Friends? John walked out into the street. More likely kidnappers. . . . Anxiety had turned to fear, to panic. Something had gone terribly wrong. Those women had got hold of Laura, played upon her suggestibility, induced her to go with them, either to their hotel or elsewhere. Should he find the Consulate? Where was it? What would he say when he got there? He began walking without purpose, finding himself, as they had done the night before, in streets he did not know, and suddenly came upon a tall building with the word "Questura" above it. This is it, he thought. I don't care, something has happened, I'm going inside. There were a number of police in uniform coming and going, the place at any rate was active, and, addressing himself to one of them behind a glass partition, he asked if there was anyone who spoke English. The man pointed to a flight of stairs and John went up, entering a door on the right where he saw that another couple were sitting, waiting, and with relief he recognised them as fellow-countrymen, tourists, obviously a man and his wife, in some sort of predicament.

"Come and sit down," said the man. "We've waited half an hour but they can't be much longer. What a country! They wouldn't leave us like this at home."

John took the proffered cigarette and found a chair beside them.

"What's your trouble?" he asked.

"My wife had her handbag pinched in one of those shops in the Merceria," said the man. "She simply put it down one moment to look at something, and you'd hardly credit it, the next moment it had gone. I say it was a sneak thief, she insists it was the girl behind the counter. But who's to say? These Ities are all alike. Anyway, I'm certain we shan't get it back. What have you lost?"

"Suitcase stolen," John lied rapidly. "Had some important papers in it."

How could he say he had lost his wife? He couldn't even begin . . .

The man nodded in sympathy. "As I said, these Ities are all alike. Old Musso knew how to deal with them. Too many Communists around these days. The trouble is, they're not going to bother with our troubles much, not with this murderer at large. They're all out looking for him."

"Murderer? What murderer?" asked John.

"Don't tell me you've not heard about it?" The man stared at him in surprise. "Venice has talked of nothing else. It's been in all the papers, on the radio, and even in the English papers. A grizzly business. One woman found with her throat slit last week—a tourist too—and some old chap discovered with the same sort of knife wound this morning. They seem to think it must be a maniac, because there doesn't seem to be any motive. Nasty thing to happen in Venice in the tourist season."

"My wife and I never bother with the newspapers when we're on holiday," said John. "And we're neither of us much given to gossip in the hotel."

"Very wise of you," laughed the man. "It might have spoilt your holiday, especially if your wife is nervous. Oh well, we're off tomorrow anyway. Can't say we mind, do we, dear?" He turned to his wife. "Venice has gone downhill since we were here last. And now this loss of the handbag really is the limit."

The door of the inner room opened, and a senior police officer asked John's companion and his wife to pass through.

"I bet we don't get any satisfaction," murmured the tourist, winking at John, and he and his wife went into the inner room. The door closed behind them. John stubbed out his cigarette and lighted another. A strange feeling of unreality possessed him. He asked himself what he was doing here, what was the use of it? Laura was no longer in Venice but had disappeared, perhaps forever, with those diabolical sisters. She would never be traced. And just as the two of them had made up a fantastic story about the twins, when they first spotted them in Torcello, so, with nightmare logic, the fiction would have basis in fact; the women were in reality disguised crooks, men with criminal intent who lured unsuspecting persons to some appalling fate. They might even be the murderers for whom the police sought. Who would ever suspect two elderly women of respectable appearance, living quietly in some second-rate pension or hotel? He stubbed out his cigarette, unfinished.

"This," he thought, "is really the start of paranoia. This is the way people go off their heads." He glanced at his watch. It was half-past six. Better pack this in, this futile quest here in police headquarters, and keep to the single link of sanity remaining. Return to the hotel, put a call through to the prep school in England, and ask about the latest news of Johnnie. He had not thought about poor Johnnie since sighting Laura on the vaporetto.

Too late, though. The inner door opened, the couple were ushered out.

"Usual claptrap," said the husband sotto voce to John. "They'll do what they can. Not much hope. So many foreigners in Venice, all of 'em thieves! The locals all above reproach. Wouldn't pay 'em to steal from customers. Well, I wish you better luck."

He nodded, his wife smiled and bowed, and they had gone. John followed the police officer into the inner room.

Formalities began. Name, address, passport. Length of stay in Venice, etc., etc. Then the questions, and John, the sweat beginning to appear on his forehead, launched into his interminable story. The first encounter with the sisters, the meeting at the restaurant, Laura's state of suggestibility because of the death of their child, the telegram about Johnnie, the decision to take the chartered flight, her departure, and her sudden inexplicable return. When he had finished he felt as exhausted as if he had driven three hundred miles nonstop after a severe bout of 'flu. His interrogator spoke excellent English with a strong Italian accent.

"You say," he began, "that your wife was suffering the after-effects of shock. This had been noticeable during your stay here in Venice?"

"Well, yes," John replied, "she had really been quite ill. The holiday didn't seem to be doing her much good. It was only when she met these two women at Torcello yesterday that her mood changed. The strain seemed to have gone. She was ready, I suppose, to snatch at every straw, and this belief that our little girl was watching over her had somehow restored her to what appeared normality."

"It would be natural," said the police officer, "in the circumstances. But no doubt the telegram last night was a further shock to you both?"

"Indeed, yes. That was the reason we decided to return home."

"No argument between you? No difference of opinion?"

"None. We were in complete agreement. My one regret was that I could not go with my wife on this charter flight."

The police officer nodded. "It could well be that your wife had a sudden attack of amnesia, and meeting the two ladies served as a link, she clung to them for support. You have described them with great accuracy, and I think they should not be too difficult to trace. Meanwhile, I suggest you should return to your hotel, and we will get in touch with you as soon as we have news."

At least, John thought, they believed his story. They did not consider him a crank who had made the whole thing up and was merely wasting their time.

"You appreciate," he said, "I am extremely anxious. These women may have some criminal design upon my wife. One has heard of such things. . . ."

The police officer smiled for the first time. "Please don't concern yourself," he said. "I am sure there will be some satisfactory explanation."

All very well, thought John, but in heaven's name, what?

"I'm sorry," he said, "to have taken up so much of your time. Especially as I gather the police have their hands full hunting down a murderer who is still at large."

He spoke deliberately. No harm in letting the fellow know that for all any of them could tell there might be some connection between Laura's disappearance and this other hideous affair.

"Ah, that," said the police officer, rising to his feet. "We hope to have the murderer under lock and key very soon."

His tone of confidence was reassuring. Murderers, missing wives, lost handbags were all under control. They shook hands, and John was ushered out of the door and so downstairs. Perhaps, he thought, as he walked slowly back to the hotel, the fellow was right. Laura had suffered a sudden attack of amnesia, and the sisters happened to be at the airport and had brought her back to Venice, to their own hotel, because Laura couldn't remember where she and John had been staying. Perhaps they were even now trying to track down his hotel. Anyway, he could do nothing more. The police had everything in hand, and, please God, would come up with the solution. All he wanted to do right now was to collapse upon a bed with a stiff whisky, and then put through a call to Johnnie's school.

The page took him up in the lift to a modest room on the fourth floor at the rear of the hotel. Bare, impersonal, the shutters closed, with a smell of cooking wafting up from a courtyard down below.

"Ask them to send me up a double whisky, will you?" he said to the boy. "And a ginger ale," and when he was alone he plunged his face under the cold tap in the wash-basin, relieved to find that the minute portion of visitor's soap afforded some measure of comfort. He flung off his shoes, hung his coat over the back of a chair and threw himself down on the bed. Somebody's radio was blasting forth an old popular song, now several seasons out-of-date, that had been one of Laura's favourites a couple of years ago. "I love you, Baby . . ." He reached for the telephone, and asked the exchange to put through the call to England. Then he closed his eyes, and all the while the insistent voice persisted, "I love you, Baby . . . I can't get you out of my mind."

Presently there was a tap at the door. It was the waiter with his drink. Too little ice, such meagre comfort, but what desperate need. He gulped it down without the ginger ale, and in a few moments the ever-nagging pain was eased, numbed, bringing, if only momentarily, a sense of calm. The telephone rang, and now, he thought, bracing himself for ultimate disaster, the final shock, Johnnie probably dying, or already dead. In which case nothing remained. Let Venice be engulfed. . . .

The exchange told him that the connection had been made, and in a moment he heard the voice of Mrs. Hill at the other end of the line. They must have warned her that the call came from Venice, for she knew instantly who was speaking.

"Hullo?" she said. "Oh, I am so glad you rang. All is well. Johnnie has had his operation, the surgeon decided to do it at midday rather than wait, and it was completely successful. Johnnie is going to be all right. So you don't have to worry any more, and will have a peaceful night."

"Thank God," he answered.

"I know," she said, "we are all so relieved. Now I'll get off the line and you can speak to your wife."

John sat up on the bed, stunned. What the hell did she mean? Then he heard Laura's voice, cool and clear.

"Darling? Darling, are you there?"

He could not answer. He felt the hand holding the receiver go clammy cold with sweat. "I'm here," he whispered.

"It's not a very good line," she said, "but never mind. As Mrs. Hill told you, all is well. Such a nice surgeon, and a very sweet Sister on Johnnie's floor, and I really am happy about the way it's turned out. I came straight down here after landing at Gatwick—the flight OK, by the way, but such a funny crowd, it'll make you hysterical when I tell you about them—and I went to the hospital, and Johnnie was coming round. Very dopey, of course, but so pleased to see me. And the Hills are being wonderful, I've got their spare room, and it's only a short taxi-drive into the town and the hospital. I shall go to bed as soon as we've had dinner, because I'm a bit fagged, what with the flight and the anxiety. How was the drive to Milan? And where are you staying?"

John did not recognise the voice that answered as his own. It was the automatic response of some computer.

"I'm not in Milan," he said. "I'm still in Venice."

"Still in Venice? What on earth for? Wouldn't the car start?"

"I can't explain," he said. "There was a stupid sort of mix-up . . ."

He felt suddenly so exhausted that he nearly dropped the receiver, and, shame upon shame, he could feel tears pricking behind his eyes.

"What sort of mix-up?" Her voice was suspicious, almost hostile. "You weren't in a crash?"

"No . . . no . . . nothing like that."

A moment's silence, and then she said, "Your voice sounds very slurred. Don't tell me you went and got pissed."

Oh Christ . . . If she only knew! He was probably going to pass out any moment, but not from the whisky.

"I thought," he said slowly, "I thought I saw you, in a vaporetto, with those two sisters."

What was the point of going on? It was hopeless trying to explain.

"How could you have seen me with the sisters?" she said. "You knew I'd gone to the airport. Really, darling, you are an idiot. You seem to have got those two poor old dears on the brain. I hope you didn't say anything to Mrs. Hill just now."

"No."

"Well, what are you going to do? You'll catch the train at Milan tomorrow, won't you?"

"Yes, of course," he told her.

"I still don't understand what kept you in Venice," she said. "It all sounds a bit odd to me. However . . . thank God Johnnie is going to be all right and I'm here."

"Yes," he said, "yes."

He could hear the distant boom-boom sound of a gong from the headmaster's hall.

"You had better go," he said. "My regards to the Hills, and my love to Johnnie."

"Well, take care of yourself, darling, and for goodness' sake don't miss the train tomorrow, and drive carefully."

The telephone clicked and she had gone. He poured the remaining drop of whisky into his empty glass, and sousing it with gingerale drank it down at a gulp. He got up, and crossing the room threw open the shutters and leant out of the window. He felt light-headed. His sense of relief, enormous, overwhelming, was somehow tempered with a curious feeling of unreality, almost as though the voice speaking from England had not been Laura's after all but a fake, and she was still in Venice, hidden in some furtive pension with the two sisters.

The point was, he *had* seen all three of them on the vaporetto. It was not another woman in a red coat. The women *had* been there, with Laura. So what was the explanation? That he was going off his head? Or something more sinister? The sisters, possessing psychic powers of formidable strength, had seen him as their two ferries had passed, and in some inexplicable fashion had made him believe Laura was with them. But why, and to what end? No, it didn't make sense. The only explanation was that he had been mistaken, the whole episode an hallucination. In which case he needed psychoanalysis, just as Johnnie had needed a surgeon.

And what did he do now? Go downstairs and tell the management he had been at fault and had just spoken to his wife, who had arrived in England safe and sound from her charter flight? He put on his shoes and ran his fingers through his hair. He glanced at his watch. It was ten minutes to eight. If he nipped into the bar and had a quick drink it would be easier to face the manager and admit what had happened. Then, perhaps, they would get in touch with the police. Profuse apologies all round for putting everyone to enormous trouble.

He made his way to the ground floor and went straight to the bar, feeling self-conscious, a marked man, half-imagining everyone would look at him, thinking, "There's the fellow with the missing wife." Luckily the bar was full and there wasn't a face he knew. Even the chap behind the bar was an underling who hadn't served him before. He downed his whisky and glanced over his shoulder to the reception hall. The desk was momentarily empty. He could see the manager's back framed in the doorway of an inner room, talking to someone within. On impulse, cowardlike, he crossed the hall and passed through the swing-door to the street outside.

"I'll have some dinner," he decided, "and then go back and face them. I'll feel more like it once I've some food inside me."

He went to the restaurant nearby where he and Laura had dined once or twice. Nothing mattered any more, because she was safe. The nightmare lay behind him. He could enjoy his dinner, despite her absence, and think of her sitting down with the Hills to a dull, quiet evening, early to bed, and on the following morning going to the hospital to sit with Johnnie. Johnnie was safe, too. No more worries, only the awkward explanations and apologies to the manager at the hotel.

There was a pleasant anonymity sitting down at a corner table alone in the little restaurant, ordering vitello alla Marsala and half a bottle of Merlot. He took his time, enjoying his food but eating in a kind of haze, a sense of unreality still with him, while the conversation of his nearest neighbours had the same soothing effect as background music.

When they rose and left, he saw by the clock on the wall that it was nearly half-past nine. No use delaying matters any further. He drank his coffee, lighted a cigarette and paid his bill. After all, he thought, as he walked back to the hotel, the manager would be greatly relieved to know that all was well.

When he pushed through the swing-door, the first thing he noticed was a man in police uniform, standing talking to the manager at the desk. The reception clerk was there too. They turned as John approached, and the manager's face lighted up with relief.

"Eccolo!" he exclaimed. "I was certain the signore would not be far away. Things are moving, signore. The two ladies have been traced, and they very kindly agreed to accompany the police to the Questura. If you will go there at once, this agente di polizia will escort you."

John flushed. "I have given everyone a lot of trouble," he said. "I meant to tell you before going out to dinner, but you were not at the desk. The fact is that I have contacted my wife. She did make the flight to London after all, and I spoke to her on the telephone. It was all a great mistake."

The manager looked bewildered. "The signora is in London?" he repeated. He broke off, and exchanged a rapid conversation in Italian with the policeman. "It seems that the ladies maintain they did not go out for the day, except for a little shopping in the morning," he said, turning back to John. "Then who was it the signore saw on the vaporetto?"

John shook his head. "A very extraordinary mistake on my part which I still don't understand," he said. "Obviously, I did not see either my wife or the two ladies. I really am extremely sorry."

More rapid conversation in Italian. John noticed the clerk watching him with a curious expression in his eyes. The manager was obviously apologizing on John's behalf to the policeman, who looked annoyed and gave tongue to this effect, his voice increasing in volume, to the manager's concern. The whole business had undoubtedly given enormous trouble to a great many people, not least the two unfortunate sisters.

"Look," said John, interrupting the flow, "will you tell the agente I will go with him to headquarters and apologise in person both to the police officer and to the ladies?"

The manager looked relieved. "If the signore would take the trouble," he said. "Naturally, the ladies were much distressed when a policeman interrogated them at their hotel, and they offered to accompany him to the Questura only because they were so distressed about the signora."

John felt more and more uncomfortable. Laura must never learn any of this. She would be outraged. He wondered if there were some penalty for giving the police misleading information involving a third party. His error began, in retrospect, to take on criminal proportions.

He crossed the Piazza San Marco, now thronged with after-dinner strollers and spectators at the cafés, all three orchestras going full blast in harmonious rivalry, while his companion kept a discreet two paces to his left and never uttered a word.

They arrived at the police station and mounted the stairs to the same inner room where he had been before. He saw immediately that it was not the officer he knew but another who sat behind the desk, a sallow-faced individual with a sour expression, while the two sisters, obviously upset—the active one in particular—were seated on chairs nearby, some underling in uniform standing behind them. John's escort went at once to the police officer, speaking in rapid Italian, while John himself, after a moment's hesitation, advanced towards the sisters.

"There has been a terrible mistake," he said. "I don't know how to apologise to you both. It's all my fault, mine entirely, the police are not to blame."

The active sister made as though to rise, her mouth twitching nervously, but he restrained her.

"We don't understand," she said, the Scots inflection strong. "We said goodnight to your wife last night at dinner, and we have not seen her since. The police came to our pension more than an hour ago and told us your wife was missing and you had filed a complaint against us. My sister is not very strong. She was considerably disturbed."

"A mistake. A frightful mistake," he repeated.

He turned towards the desk. The police officer was addressing him, his English very inferior to that of the previous interrogator. He had John's earlier statement on the desk in front of him, and tapped it with a pencil.

"So?" he queried. "This document all lies? You not speaka the truth?"

"I believed it to be true at the time," said John. "I could have sworn in a court of law that I saw my wife with these two ladies on a vaporetto in the Grand Canal this afternoon. Now I realise I was mistaken."

"We have not been near the Grand Canal all day," protested the sister, "not even on foot. We made a few purchases in the Merceria this morning, and remained indoors all afternoon. My sister was a little unwell. I have told the police officer this a dozen times, and the people at the pension would corroborate our story. He refused to listen."

"And the signora?" rapped the police officer angrily. "What happen to the signora?"

"The signora, my wife, is safe in England," explained John patiently. "I talked to her on the telephone just after seven. She did join the charter flight from the airport, and is now staying with friends."

"Then who you see on the vaporetto in the red coat?" asked the furious police officer. "And if not these signorine here, then what signorine?"

"My eyes deceived me," said John, aware that his English was likewise becoming strained. "I think I see my wife and these ladies but no, it was not so. My wife in aircraft, these ladies in pension all the time."

It was like talking stage Chinese. In a moment he would be bowing and putting his hands in his sleeves.

The police officer raised his eyes to heaven and thumped the table. "So all this work for nothing," he said. "Hotels and pensiones searched for the signorine and a missing signora inglese, when here we have plenty, plenty other things to do. You maka a mistake. You have perhaps too much vino at mezzo giorno and you see hundred signore in red coats in hundred vaporetti." He stood up, rumpling the papers on his desk. "And you, signorine," he said, "you wish to make complaint against this person?" He was addressing the active sister.

"Oh no," she said, "no, indeed. I quite see it was all a mistake. Our only wish is to return at once to our pension."

The police officer grunted. Then he pointed at John. "You very lucky man," he said. "These signorine could file complaint against you—very serious matter."

"I'm sure," began John, "I'll do anything in my power . . ."

"Please don't think of it," exclaimed the sister, horrified. "We would not hear of such a thing." It was her turn to apologise to the police officer. "I hope we need not take up any more of your valuable time," she said.

He waved a hand of dismissal and spoke in Italian to the underling. "This man walk with you to the pension," he said. "Buona sera, signorine," and, ignoring John, he sat down again at his desk.

"I'll come with you," said John. "I want to explain exactly what happened."

They trooped down the stairs and out of the building, the blind sister leaning on her twin's arm, and once outside she turned her sightles eyes to John.

"You saw us," she said, "and your wife too. But not today. You saw us in the future."

Her voice was softer than her sister's, slower, she seemed to have some slight impediment in her speech.

"I don't follow," replied John, bewildered.

He turned to the active sister and she shook her head at him, frowning, and put her finger on her lips.

"Come along, dear," she said to her twin. "You know you're very tired, and I want to get you home." Then, sotto voce to John, "She's psychic. Your wife told you, I believe, but I don't want her to go into trance here in the street."

God forbid, thought John, and the little procession began to move slowly along the street, away from police headquarters, a canal to the left of them. Progress was slow, because of the blind sister, and there were two bridges. John was completely lost after the first turning, but it couldn't have mattered less. Their police escort was with them, and anyway, the sisters knew where they were going.

"I must explain," said John softly. "My wife would never forgive me if I didn't," and as they walked he went over the whole inexplicable story once again, beginning with the telegram received the night before and the conversation with Mrs. Hill, the decision to return to England the following day, Laura by air, and John himself by car and train. It no longer sounded as dramatic as it had done when he had made his statement to the police officer, when, possibly because of his conviction of something uncanny, the description of the two vaporettos passing one another in the middle of the Grand Canal had held a sinister quality, suggesting abduction on the part of the sisters, the pair of them holding a bewildered Laura captive. Now that neither of the women had any further menace for him he spoke more naturally, yet with great sincerity, feeling for the first time that they were somehow both in sympathy with him and would understand.

"You see," he explained, in a final endeavour to make amends for having gone to the police in the first place, "I truly believed I had seen you with Laura, and I thought . . ." he hesitated, because this had been the police officer's suggestion and not his, "I thought that perhaps Laura had some sudden loss of memory, had met you at the airport, and you had brought her back to Venice to wherever you were staying."

They had crossed a large square and were approaching a house at one end of it, with a sign PENSIONE above the door. Their escort paused at the entrance.

"Is this it?" asked John.

"Yes," said the sister. "I know it is nothing much from the outside, but it is clean and comfortable, and was recommended by friends." She turned to the escort. "Grazie," she said to him, "grazie tanto."

The man nodded briefly, wished them "Buona notte," and disappeared across the campo.

"Will you come in?" asked the sister. "I am sure we can find you some coffee, or perhaps you prefer tea?"

"No, really," John thanked her, "I must get back to the hotel. I'm making an early start in the morning. I just want to make quite sure you do understand what happened, and that you forgive me."

"There is nothing to forgive," she replied. "It is one of the many examples of second sight that my sister and I have experienced time and time again, and I should very much like to record it for our files, if you will permit it."

"Well, as to that, of course," he told her, "but I myself find it hard to understand. It has never happened to me before."

"Not consciously, perhaps," she said, "but so many things happen to us of which we are not aware. My sister felt you had psychic understanding. She told your wife. She also told your wife, last night in the restaurant, that you were to experience trouble, danger, that you should leave Venice. Well, don't you believe now that the telegram was proof of this? Your son was ill, possibly dangerously ill, and so it was necessary for you to return home immediately. Heaven be praised your wife flew home to be by his side."

"Yes, indeed," said John, "but why should I see her on the vaporetto with you and your sister when she was actually on her way to England?"

"Thought transference, perhaps," she answered. "Your wife may have been thinking about us. We gave her our address, should you wish to get in touch with us. We shall be here another ten days. And she knows that we would pass on any message that my sister might have from your little one in the spirit world."

"Yes," said John awkwardly, "yes, I see. It's very good of you." He had a sudden rather unkind picture of the two sisters putting on headphones in their bedroom, listening for a coded message from poor Christine. "Look, this is our address in London," he said. "I know Laura will be pleased to hear from you."

He scribbled their address on a sheet torn from his pocket-diary, even, as a bonus thrown in, the telephone number, and handed it to her. He could imagine the outcome. Laura springing it on him one evening that the "old dears" were passing through London on their way to Scotland, and the least they could do was to offer them hospitality, even the spare room for the night. Then a seance in the living room, tambourines appearing out of thin air.

"Well, I must be off," he said. "Goodnight, and apologies, once again, for all that has happened this evening." He shook hands with the first sister, then turned to her blind twin. "I hope," he said, "that you are not too tired."

The sightless eyes were disconcerting. She held his hand fast and would not let it go. "The child," she said, speaking in an odd staccato voice, "the child . . . I can see the child . . ." and then, to his dismay, a bead of froth appeared at the corner of her mouth, her head jerked back, and she half-collapsed in her sister's arms.

"We must get her inside," said the sister hurriedly. "It's all right, she's not ill, it's the beginning of a trance state."

Between them they helped the twin, who had gone rigid, into the house, and sat her down on the nearest chair, the sister supporting her. A woman came running from some inner room. There was a strong smell of spaghetti from the back regions. "Don't worry," said the sister, "the signorina and I can manage. I think you had better go. Sometimes she is sick after these turns."

"I'm most frightfully sorry . . ." John began, but the sister had already turned her back, and with the signorina was bending over her twin, from whom peculiar choking sounds were proceeding. He was obviously in the way, and after a final gesture of courtesy, "Is there anything I can do?", which received no reply, he turned on his heel and began walking across the square. He looked back once, and saw they had closed the door.

What a finale to the evening! And all his fault. Poor old girls, first dragged to police headquarters and put through an interrogation, and then a psychic fit on top of it all. More likely epilepsy. Not much of a life for the other sister, but she seemed to take it in her stride. An additional hazard, though, if it happened in a restaurant or in the street. And not particularly welcome under his and Laura's roof should the sisters ever find themselves beneath it, which he prayed would never happen.

Meanwhile, where the devil was he? The square, with the inevitable church at one end, was quite deserted. He could not remember which way they had come from police headquarters, there had seemed to be so many turnings.

Wait a minute, the church itself had a familiar appearance. He drew nearer to it, looking for the name which was sometimes on notices at the entrance. San Giovanni in Bragora, that rang a bell. He and Laura had gone inside one morning to look at a painting by Cima da Conegliano. Surely it was only a stone's throw from the Riva degli Schiavoni and the open wide waters of the San Marco lagoon, with all the bright lights of civilisation and the strolling tourists? He remembered taking a small turning from the Schiavoni and they had arrived at the church. Wasn't that the alleyway ahead? He plunged along it, but halfway down he hesitated. It didn't seem right, although it was familiar for some unknown reason.

Then he realised that it was not the alley they had taken the morning they visited the church, but the one they had walked along the previous evening, only he was approaching it from the opposite direction. Yes, that was it, in which case it would be quicker to go on and cross the little bridge over the narrow canal, and he would find the Arsenal on his left and the street leading down to the Riva degli Schiavoni to his right. Simpler than retracing his steps and getting lost once more in the maze of back streets.

He had almost reached the end of the alley, and the bridge was in sight, when he saw the child. It was the same little girl with the pixie hood who had leapt between the tethered boats the preceding night and vanished up the cellar steps of one of the houses. This time she was running from the direction of the church the other side, making for the bridge. She was running as if her life depended on it, and in a moment he saw why. A man was in pursuit, who, when she glanced backwards for a moment, still running, flattened himself against a wall, believing himself unobserved. The child came on, scampering across the bridge, and John, fearful of alarming her further, backed into an open doorway that led into a small court.

He remembered the drunken yell of the night before which had come from one of the houses near where the man was hiding now. This is it, he thought, the fellow's after her again, and with a flash of intuition he connected the two events, the child's terror then and now, and the murders reported in the newspapers, supposedly the work of some madman. It could be coincidence, a child running from a drunken relative, and yet, and yet . . . His heart began thumping in his chest, instinct warning him to run himself, now, at once, back along the alley the way he had come—but what about the child? What was going to happen to the child?

Then he heard her running steps. She hurtled through the open doorway into the court in which he stood, not seeing him, making for the rear of the house that flanked it, where steps led presumably to a back entrance. She was sobbing as she ran, not the ordinary cry of a frightened child, but the panic-stricken intake of breath of a helpless being in despair. Were there parents in the house who would protect her, whom he could warn? He hesitated a moment, then followed her down the steps and through the door at the bottom, which had burst open at the touch of her hands as she hurled herself against it.

"It's all right," he called. "I won't let him hurt you, it's all right," cursing his lack of Italian, but possibly an English voice might reassure her. But it was no use—she ran sobbing up another flight of stairs, which were spiral, twisting, leading to the floor above, and already it was too late for him to retreat. He could hear sounds of the pursuer in the courtyard behind, someone shouting in Italian, a dog barking. This is it, he thought, we're in it together, the child and I. Unless we can bolt some inner door above he'll get us both.

He ran up the stairs after the child, who had darted into a room leading off a small landing, and followed her inside and slammed the door, and, merciful heaven, there was a bolt which he rammed into its socket. The child was crouching by the open window. If he shouted for help someone would surely hear, someone would surely come before the man in pursuit threw himself against the door and it gave, because there was no one but themselves, no parents, the room was bare except for a mattress on an old bed, and a heap of rags in one corner.

"It's all right," he panted, "it's all right," and held out his hand, trying to smile.

The child struggled to her feet and stood before him, the pixie hood falling from her head on to the floor. He stared at her, incredulity turning to horror, to fear. It was not a child at all but a little thickset woman dwarf, about three feet high, with a great square adult head too big for her body, grey locks hanging shoulder-length, and she wasn't sobbing anymore, she was grinning at him, nodding her head up and down.

Then he heard the footsteps on the landing outside and the hammering on the door, and a barking dog, and not one voice but several voices, shouting, "Open up! Police!" The creature fumbled in her sleeve, drawing a knife, and as she threw it at him with hideous strength, piercing his throat, he stumbled and fell, the sticky mess covering his protecting hands.

And he saw the vaporetto with Laura and the two sisters steaming down the Grand Canal, not today, not tomorrow, but the day after that, and he knew why they were together and for what sad purpose they had come. The creature was gibbering in its corner. The hammering and the voices and the barking dog grew fainter, and, "Oh, God," he thought, "what a bloody silly way to die . . ."

Robert A. Heinlein (1907–1988)

They

Robert A. Heinlein was the greatest science fiction writer of the mid-twentieth century, author of the classic *Stranger in a Strange Land* and many other novels. A certain small but significant and influential portion of his work was done in fantasy and horror, particularly for John W. Campbell's *Unknown*. The single story that had the most impact, however, is "They," first published in *Unknown* in 1941. Along with L. Ron Hubbard's "Fear," Fritz Lieber's "Smoke Ghost," and Heinlein's own "The Unpleasant Profession of Jonathan Hoag," it became for many writers one of the paradigms of the "new style" of horror and supernatural fiction in the 1940s and 1950s, which rejected the traditional supernatural trappings of good and evil, and the traditional settings (old houses, antiquarian discoveries), along with the florid styles of earlier writers, especially the Lovecraftians, in favor of unornamented prose, contemporary urban settings, and an almost Existential approach to the psychology of horror, through which the nature of reality was brought into question, Existential doubts raised with horrifying potential. Fritz Leiber says, if you are looking for significant stories that underpin contemporary horror, look to Fitz-James O'Brien's "What Was It?" and Robert A. Heinlein's "They."

They would not let him alone.

They would never let him alone. He realized that that was part of the plot against him—never to leave him in peace, never to give him a chance to mull over the lies they had told him, time enough to pick out the flaws, and to figure out the truth for himself.

That damned attendant this morning! He had come busting in with his breakfast tray, waking him, and causing him to forget his dream. If only he could remember that dream—

Someone was unlocking the door. He ignored it.

"Howdy, old boy. They tell me you refused your breakfast?" Dr. Hayward's professionally kindly mask hung over his bed.

"I wasn't hungry."

"But we can't have that. You'll get weak, and then I won't be able to get you well completely. Now get up and get your clothes on and I'll order an eggnog for you. Come on, that's a good fellow!"

Unwilling, but still less willing at that moment to enter into any conflict of wills, he got out of bed and slipped on his bathrobe. "That's better," Hayward approved. "Have a cigarette?"

"No, thank you."

The doctor shook his head in a puzzled fashion. "Darned if I can figure you out. Loss of interest in physical pleasures does not fit your type of case."

"What is my type of case?" he inquired in flat tones.

"Tut! Tut!" Hayward tried to appear roguish. "If medicos told their professional secrets, they might have to work for a living."

"What is my type of case?"

"Well—the label doesn't matter, does it? Suppose you tell me. I really know nothing about your case as yet. Don't you think it is about time you talked?"

"I'll play chess with you."

"All right, all right." Hayward made a gesture of impatient concession. "We've played chess every day for a week. If you will talk, I'll play chess."

What could it matter? If he was right, they already understood perfectly that he had discovered their plot; there was nothing to be gained by concealing the obvious. Let them try to argue him out of it. Let the tail go with the hide! To hell with it!

He got out the chessmen and commenced setting them up. "What do you know of my case so far?"

"Very little. Physical examination, negative. Past history, negative. High intelligence, as shown by your record in school and your success in your profession. Occasional fits of moodiness, but nothing exceptional. The only positive information was the incident that caused you to come here for treatment."

"To be brought here, you mean. Why should it cause comment?"

"Well, good gracious, man—if you barricade yourself in your room and insist that your wife is plotting against you, don't you expect people to notice?"

"But she was plotting against me—and so are you. White, or black?"

"Black—it's your turn to attack. Why do you think we are plotting against you?"

"It's an involved story, and goes way back into my early childhood. There was an immediate incident, however—" He opened by advancing the white king's knight to KB3. Hayward's eyebrows raised.

"You make a piano attack?"

"Why not? You know that it is not safe for me to risk a gambit with you."

The doctor shrugged his shoulders and answered the opening. "Suppose we start with your early childhood. It may shed more light than more recent incidents. Did you feel that you were being persecuted as a child?"

"No!" He half rose from his chair. "When I was a child I was sure of myself. I knew then, I tell you; I knew! Life was worthwhile, and I knew it. I was at peace with myself and my surroundings. Life was good and I assumed that the creatures around me were like myself."

"And weren't they?"

"Not at all! Particularly the children. I didn't know what viciousness was until I was turned loose with other children. The little devils! And I was expected to be like them and play with them."

The doctor nodded. "I know. The herd compulsion. Children can be pretty savage at times."

"You've missed the point. This wasn't any healthy roughness; these creatures were different—not like myself at all. They looked like me, but they were not like me. If I tried to say anything to one of them about anything that mattered to me, all I could get was a stare and a scornful laugh. Then they would find some way to punish me for having said it."

Hayward nodded. "I see what you mean. How about grown-ups?"

"That is somewhat different. Adults don't matter to children at first—or, rather they did not matter to me. They were too big, and they did not bother me, and they were busy with things that did not enter into my considerations. It was only when I noticed that my presence affected them that I began to wonder about them."

"How do you mean?"

"Well, they never did the things when I was around that they did when I was not around."

Hayward looked at him carefully. "Won't that statement take quite a lot of justifying? How do you know what they did when you weren't around?"

He acknowledged the point. "But I used to catch them just stopping. If I came into a room, the conversation would stop suddenly, and then it would pick up about the weather or something equally inane. Then I took to hiding and listening and looking. Adults did not behave the same way in my presence as out of it."

"Your move, I believe. But see here, old man—that was when you were a child. Every child passes through that phase. Now that you are a man, you must see the adult point of view. Children are strange creatures and have to be protected—at least, we do protect them—from many adult interests. There is a whole code of conventions in the matter that—"

"Yes, yes," he interrupted impatiently, "I know all that. Nevertheless, I noticed enough and remembered enough that was never clear to me later. And it put me on my guard to notice the next thing."

"Which was?" He noticed that the doctor's eyes were averted as he adjusted a castle's position.

"The things I saw people doing and heard them talking about were never of any importance. They must be doing something else."

"I don't follow you."

"You don't choose to follow me. I'm telling this to you in exchange for a game of chess."

"Why do you like to play chess so well?"

"Because it is the only thing in the world where I can see all the factors and understand all the rules. Never mind—I saw all around me this enormous plant, cities, farms, factories, churches, schools, homes, railroads, luggage, roller coasters, trees, saxophones, libraries, people and animals. People that looked like me and who should have felt very much like me, if what I was told was the truth. But what did they appear to be doing? They went to work to earn the money to buy the food to get the strength to go to work to earn the money to buy the food to get the strength to go to work to get the strength to buy the food to earn the money to go to—' until they fell over dead. Any slight variation in the basic pattern did not matter, for they always fell over dead. And everybody tried to tell me that I should be doing the same thing. I knew better!"

The doctor gave him a look apparently intended to denote helpless surrender and laughed. "I can't argue with you. Life does look like that, and maybe it is just that futile. But it is the only life we have. Why not make up your mind to enjoy it as much as possible?"

"Oh, no!" He looked both sulky and stubborn. "You can't peddle nonsense to me by claiming to be fresh out of sense. How do I know? Because all this complex stage setting, all these swarms of actors, could not have been put here just to make idiot noises at each other. Some other explanation, but not that one. An insanity as enormous, as complex, as the one around me had to be planned. I've found the plan!"

"Which is?"

He noticed that the doctor's eyes were again averted.

"It is a play intended to divert me, to occupy my mind and confuse me, to keep me so busy with details that I will not have time to think about the meaning. You are all in it, every one of you." He shook his finger in the doctor's face. "Most of them may be helpless automatons, but you're not. You are one of the conspirators. You've been sent in as a troubleshooter to try to force me to go back to playing the role assigned to me!"

He saw that the doctor was waiting for him to quiet down.

"Take it easy," Hayward finally managed to say, "Maybe it is all a conspiracy, but why do you think that you have been singled out for special attention? Maybe it is a joke on all of us. Why couldn't I be one of the victims as well as yourself?"

"Got you!" He pointed a long finger at Hayward. "That is the essence of the plot. All of these creatures have been set up to look like me in order to prevent me from realizing that I was the center of the arrangements. But I have noticed the key fact, the mathematically inescapable fact, that I am unique. Here am I, sitting on the inside. The world extends outward from me. I am the center—"

"Easy, man, easy! Don't you realize that the world looks that way to me, too. We are each the center of the universe—"

"Not so! That is what you have tried to make me believe, that I am just one of millions more just like me. Wrong! If they were like me, then I could get into communication with them. I can't. I have tried and tried and I can't. I've sent out my inner thoughts, seeking some one other being who has them, too. What have I gotten back? Wrong answers, jarring incongruities, meaningless obscenity. I've tried. I tell you. God!—how I've tried! But there is nothing out there to speak to me—nothing but emptiness and otherness!"

"Wait a minute. Do you mean to say that you think there is nobody home at my end of the line? Don't you believe that I am alive and conscious?"

He regarded the doctor soberly. "Yes, I think you are probably alive, but you are one of the others—my antagonists. But you have set thousands of others around me whose faces are blank, not lived in, and whose speech is a meaningless reflex of noise."

"Well, then, if you concede that I am an ego, why do you insist that I am so very different from yourself?"

"Why? Wait!" He pushed back from the chess table and strode over to the wardrobe, from which he took out a violin case.

While he was playing, the lines of suffering smoothed out of his face and his expression took a relaxed beatitude. For a while he recaptured the emotions, but not the knowledge, which he had possessed in dreams. The melody proceeded easily from proposition to proposition with inescapable, unforced logic. He finished with a triumphant statement of the essential thesis and turned to the doctor. "Well?"

"Hm-m-m." He seemed to detect an even greater degree of caution in the doctor's manner. "It's an odd bit, but remarkable. 'S pity you didn't take up the violin seriously. You could have made quite a reputation. You could even now. Why don't you do it? You could afford to, I believe."

He stood and stared at the doctor for a long moment, then shook his head as if trying to clear it. "It's no use," he said slowly, "no use at all. There is no possibility of communication. I am alone." He replaced the instrument in its case and returned to the chess table. "My move, I believe?"

"Yes. Guard your queen."

He studied the board. "Not necessary. I no longer need my queen. Check."

The doctor interposed a pawn to parry the attack.

He nodded. "You use your pawns well, but I have learned to anticipate your play. Check again—and mate, I think."

The doctor examined the new situation. "No," he decided, "no—not quite." He retreated from the square under attack. "Not checkmate—stalemate at the worst. Yes, another stalemate."

He was upset by the doctor's visit. He couldn't be wrong, basically, yet the doctor had certainly pointed out logical holes in his position. From a logical standpoint the whole world might be a fraud perpetrated on everybody. But logic meant nothing—logic itself was a fraud, starting with unproved assumptions and capable of proving anything. The world is what it is!—and carries its own evidence of trickery.

But does it? What did he have to go on? Could he lay down a line between known facts and everything else and then make a reasonable interpretation of the world, based on facts alone—an interpretation free from complexities of logic and no hidden assumptions of points not certain. Very well—

First fact, himself. He knew himself directly. He existed.

Second facts, the evidence of his "five senses," everything that he himself saw and heard and smelled and tasted with his physical senses. Subject to their limitations, he must believe his senses. Without them he was entirely solitary, shut up in a locker of bone, blind, deaf, cut off, the only being in the world.

And that was not the case. He knew that he did not invent the information brought to him by his senses. There had to be something else out there, some otherness that produced the things his senses recorded. All philosophies that claimed that the physical world around him did not exist except in his imagination were sheer nonsense.

But beyond that, what? Were there any third facts on which he could rely? No, not at this point. He could not afford to believe anything that he was told, or that he read, or that was implicitly assumed to be true about the world around him. No, he could not believe any of it, for the sum total of what he had been told and read and been taught in school was so contradictory, so senseless, so wildly insane that none of it could be believed unless he personally confirmed it.

Wait a minute— The very telling of these lies, these senseless contradictions, was a fact in itself, known to him directly. To that extent they were data, probably very important data.

The world as it had been shown to him was a piece of unreason, an idiot's dream. Yet it was on too mammoth a scale to be without some reason. He came wearily back to his original point: Since the world could not be as crazy as it appeared to be, it must necessarily have been arranged to appear crazy in order to deceive him as to the truth.

Why had they done it to him? And what was the truth behind the sham? There must be some clue in the deception itself. What thread ran through it all? Well, in the first place he had been given a superabundance of explanations of the world around him, philosophies, religions, "common sense" explanations. Most of them were so clumsy, so obviously inadequate, or meaningless, that they could hardly have expected him to take them seriously. They must have intended them simply as misdirection.

But there were certain basic assumptions running through all the hundreds of explanations of the craziness around him. It must be these basic assumptions that he was expected to believe. For example, there was the deepseated assumption that he was a "human being," essentially like millions of others around him and billions more in the past and the future.

That was nonsense! He had never once managed to get into real communication with all those things that looked so much like him but were so different. In the agony of his loneliness, he had deceived himself that Alice understood him and was a being like him. He knew now that he had suppressed and refused to examine thousands of little discrepancies because he could not bear the thought of returning to complete loneliness.

He had needed to believe that his wife was a living, breathing being of his own kind who understood his inner thoughts. He had refused to consider the possibility that she was simply, a mirror, an echo—or something unthinkably worse.

He had found a mate, and the world was tolerable, even though dull, stupid, and full of petty annoyance. He was moderately happy and had put away his suspicions. He had accepted, quite docilely, the treadmill he was expected to use, until a slight mischance had momentarily cut through the fraud—then his suspicions had returned with impounded force; the bitter knowledge of his childhood had been confirmed.

He supposed that he had been a fool to make a fuss about it. If he had kept his mouth shut they would not have locked him up. He should have been as subtle and as shrewd as they, kept his eyes and ears open and learned the details of and the reasons for the plot against him. He might have learned how to circumvent it.

But what if they had locked him up—the whole world was an asylum and all of them his keepers.

A key scraped in the lock, and he looked up to see an attendant entering with a tray. "Here's your dinner, sir."

"Thanks, Joe," he said gently. "Just put it down."

"Movies tonight, sir," the attendant went on. "Wouldn't you like to go? Dr. Hayward said you could—"

"No, thank you. I prefer not to."

"I wish you would, sir." He noticed with amusement the persuasive intentness of the attendant's manner. "I think the doctor wants you to. It's a good movie. There's a Mickey Mouse cartoon—"

"You almost persuade me, Joe," he answered with passive agreeableness. "Mickey's trouble is the same as mine, essentially. However, I'm not going. They need not bother to hold movies tonight."

"Oh, there will be movies in any case, sir. Lots of our other guests will attend."

"Really? Is that an example of thoroughness, or are you simply keeping up the pretense in talking to me? It isn't necessary, Joe, if it's any strain on you. I know the game. If I don't attend, there is no point in holding movies."

He liked the grin with which the attendant answered this thrust. Was it possible that this being was created just as he appeared to be—big muscles, phlegmatic disposition, tolerant, doglike? Or was there nothing going on behind those kind eyes, nothing but robot reflex? No, it was more likely that he was one of them, since he was so closely in attendance on him.

The attendant left and he busied himself at his supper tray, scooping up the already-cut bites of meat with a spoon, the only implement provided. He smiled again at their caution and thoroughness. No danger of that—he would not destroy this body as long as it served him in investigating the truth of the matter. There were still many different avenues of research available before taking that possibily irrevocable step.

After supper he decided to put his thoughts in better order by writing them; he obtained paper. He should start with a general statement of some underlying postulate of the credos that had been drummed into him all his "life." Life? Yes, that was a good one. He wrote:

"I am told that I was born a certain number of years ago and that I will die a similar number of years hence. Various clumsy stories have been offered me to explain to me where I was before birth and what becomes of me after death, but they are rough lies, not intended to deceive, except as misdirection. In every other possible way the world around me assures me that I am mortal, here but a few years, and a few years hence gone completely—nonexistent.

"WRONG—I am immortal. I transcend this little time axis; a seventy-year span on it is but a casual phase in my experience. Second only to the prime datum of my own existence is the emotionally convincing certainty of my own continuity. I may be a closed curve, but, closed or open, I neither have a beginning nor an end. Self-awareness is not relational; it is absolute, and cannot be reached to be destroyed, or created. Memory, however, being a relational aspect of consciousness, may be tampered with and possibly destroyed.

"It is true that most religions which have been offered me teach immortality, but note the fashion in which they teach it. The surest way to lie convincingly is to tell the truth unconvincingly. They did not wish me to believe.

"Caution: Why have they tried so hard to convince me that I am going to die in a few years? There must be a very important reason. I infer that they are preparing me for some sort of a major change. It may be crucially important for me to figure out their intentions about this—probably I have several years in which to reach a decision. Note: Avoid using the types of reasoning they have taught me."

The attendant was back. "Your wife is here, sir."

"Tell her to go away."

"Please, sir—Dr. Hayward is most anxious that you should see her."

"Tell Dr. Hayward that I said that he is an excellent chess player."

"Yes, sir." The attendant waited for a moment. "Then you won't see her, sir?"

"No, I won't see her."

He wandered around the room for some minutes after the attendant had left, too distrait to return to his recapitulation. By and large they had played very decently with him since they had brought him here. He was glad that they had allowed him to have a room alone, and he certainly had more time free for contemplation than had ever been possible on the outside. To be sure, continuous effort to keep him busy and to distract him was made, but, by being stubborn, he was able to circumvent the rules and gain some hours each day for introspection.

But, damnation!—he did wish they would not persist in using Alice in their attempts to divert his thoughts. Although the intense terror and revulsion which she had inspired in him when he had first rediscovered the truth had now aged into a simple feeling of repugnance and distaste for her company, nevertheless it was emotionally upsetting to be reminded of her, to be forced into making decisions about her.

After all, she had been his wife for many years. Wife? What was a wife? Another soul like one's own, a complement, the other necessary pole to the couple, a sanctuary of understanding and sympathy in the boundless depths of aloneness. That was what he had thought, what he had needed to believe and had believed fiercely for years. The yearning need for companionship of his own kind had caused him to see himself reflected in those beautiful eyes and had made him quite uncritical of occasional incongruities in her responses.

He sighed. He felt that he had sloughed off most of the typed emotional reactions which they had taught him by precept and example, but Alice had gotten under his skin, 'way under, and it still hurt. He had been happy—what if it had been a dope dream? They had given him an excellent, a beautiful mirror to play with—the more fool he to have looked behind it!

Wearily he turned back to his summing up:

"The world is explained in either one of two ways; the common-sense way which says that the world is pretty much as it appears to be and that ordinary human conduct and motivations are reasonable, and the religio-mystic solution which states that the world is dream stuff, unreal, insubstantial, with reality somewhere beyond.

"WRONG—both of them. The common-sense scheme has no sense to it of any sort. Life is short and full of trouble. Man born of woman is born to trouble as the sparks fly upward. His days are few and they are numbered. All is vanity and vexation. Those quotations may be jumbled and incorrect, but that is a fair statement of the common-sense world is-as-it-seems in its only possible evaluation. In such a world, human striving is about as rational as the blind darting of a moth against a light bulb. The common-sense world is a blind insanity, out of nowhere, going nowhere, to no purpose.

"As for the other solution, it appears more rational on the surface, in that it rejects the utterly irrational world of common sense. But it is not a rational solution, it is simply a flight from reality of any sort, for it refuses to believe the results of the only available direct communication between the ego and the Outside. Certainly the 'five senses' are poor enough channels of communication, but they are the only channels."

He crumpled up the paper and flung himself from the chair. Order and logic were no good—his answer was right because it smelled right. But he still did not know all the answer. Why the grand scale to the deception, countless creatures, whole continents, an enormously involved and minutely detailed matrix of insane history, insane tradition, insane culture? Why bother with more than a cell and a strait jacket?

It must be, it had to be, because it was supremely important to deceive him completely, because a lesser deception would not do. Could it be that they dare not let him suspect his real identity no matter how difficult and involved the fraud?

He had to know. In some fashion he must get behind the deception and see what went on when he was not looking. He had had one glimpse; this time he must see the actual workings, catch the puppet masters in their manipulations.

Obviously the first step must be to escape from this asylum, but to do it so craftily that they would never see him, never catch up with him, not have a chance to set the stage before him. That would be hard to do. He must excel them in shrewdness and subtlety.

Once decided, he spent the rest of the evening in considering the means by which he might accomplish his purpose. It seemed almost impossible—he must get away without once being seen and remain in strict hiding. They must lose track of him completely in order that they would not know where to center their deceptions. That would mean going without food for several days. Very well—he could do it. He must not give them any warning by unusual action or manner.

The lights blinked twice. Docilely he got up and commenced preparations for bed. When the attendant looked through the peephole he was already in bed, with his face turned to the wall.

Gladness! Gladness everywhere! It was good to be with his own kind, to hear the music swelling out of every living thing, as it always had and always would—good to know that everything was living and aware of him, participating in him, as he participated in them. It was good to be, good to know the unity of many and the diversity of one. There had been one bad thought—the details escaped him—but it was gone—it had never been; there was no place for it.

The early-morning sounds from the adjacent ward penetrated the sleepladen body which served him here and gradually recalled him to awareness of the hospital room. The transition was so gentle that he carried over full recollection of what he had been doing and why. He lay still, a gentle smile on his face, and savored the uncouth, but not unpleasant, languor of the body he wore. Strange that he had ever forgotten despite their tricks and stratagems. Well, now that he had recalled the key, he would quickly set things right in this odd place. He would call them in at once and announce the new order. It would be amusing to see old Glaroon's expression when he realized that the cycle had ended—

The click of the peephole and the rasp of the door being unlocked guillotined his line of thought. The morning attendant pushed briskly in with the breakfast tray and placed it on the tip table. "Morning, sir. Nice, bright day—want it in bed, or will you get up?"

Don't answer! Don't listen! Suppress this distraction! This is part of their plan—But it was too late, too late. He felt himself slipping, falling, wrenched from reality back into the fraud world in which they had kept him. It was gone, gone completely, with no single association around him to which to anchor memory. There was nothing left but the sense of heartbreaking loss and the acute ache of unsatisfied catharsis.

"Leave it where it is. I'll take care of it."

"Okey-doke." The attendant bustled out, slamming the door, and noisily locked it.

He lay quite still for a long time, every nerve end in his body screaming for relief.

At last he got out of bed, still miserably unhappy, and attempted to concentrate on his plans for escape. But the psychic wrench he had received in being recalled so suddenly from his plane of reality had left him bruised and emotionally disturbed. His mind insisted on rechewing its doubts, rather than engage in constructive thought. Was it possible that the doctor was right, that he was not alone in his miserable dilemma? Was he really simply suffering from paranoia, delusions of self-importance?

Could it be that each unit in this yeasty swarm around him was the prison of another lonely ego—helpless, blind, and speechless, condemned to an eternity of miserable loneliness? Was the look of suffering which he had brought to Alice's face a true reflection of inner torment and not simply a piece of play-acting intended to maneuver him into compliance with their plans?

A knock sounded at the door. He said "Come in," without looking up. Their comings and goings did not matter to him.

"Dearest—" A well-known voice spoke slowly and hesitantly.

"Alice!" He was on his feet at once, and facing her. "Who let you in here?"

"Please, dear, please—I had to see you."

"It isn't fair. It isn't fair." He spoke more to himself than to her. Then: "Why did you come?"

She stood up to him with a dignity he had hardly expected. The beauty of her childlike face had been marred by line and shadow, but it shone with an unexpected courage. "I love you," she answered quietly. "You can tell me to go away, but you can't make me stop loving you and trying to help you."

He turned away from her in an agony of indecision. Could it be possible that he had misjudged her? Was there, behind that barrier of flesh and sound symbols, a spirit that truly yearned toward his? Lovers whispering in the dark—"*You do understand, don't you?*"

"*Yes, dear heart, I understand.*"

"*Then nothing that happens to us can matter, as long as we are together and understand*—" Words, words, rebounding hollowly from an unbroken wall—

No, he couldn't be wrong! Test her again— "Why did you keep me on that job in Omaha?"

"But I didn't make you keep that job. I simply pointed out that we should think twice before—"

"Never mind. Never mind." Soft hands and a sweet face preventing him with mild stubbornness from ever doing the thing that his heart told him to do. Always with the best of intentions, the best of intentions, but always so that he had never quite managed to do the silly, unreasonable things that he knew were worthwhile. Hurry, hurry, hurry, and strive, with an angelfaced jockey to see that you don't stop long enough to think for youself—

"Why did you try to stop me from going back upstairs that day?"

She managed to smile, although her eyes were already spilling over with tears. "I didn't know it really mattered to you. I didn't want us to miss the train."

It had been a small thing, an unimportant thing. For some reason not clear to him he had insisted on going back upstairs to his study when they were about to leave the house for a short vacation. It was raining, and she had pointed out that there was barely enough time to get to the station. He had surprised himself and her, too, by insisting on his own way in circumstances in which he had never been known to be stubborn.

He had actually pushed her to one side and forced his way up the stairs. Even then nothing might have come of it had he not—quite unnecessarily—raised the shade of the window that faced toward the rear of the house.

It was a very small matter. It had been raining, hard, out in front. From this window the weather was clear and sunny, with no sign of rain.

He had stood there quite a long while, gazing out at the impossible sunshine and rearranging his cosmos in his mind. He reexamined long-suppressed doubts in the light of this one small but totally unexplainable discrepancy. Then he had turned and had found that she was standing behind him.

He had been trying ever since to forget the expression that he had surprised on her face.

"What about the rain?"

"The rain?" she repeated in a small, puzzled voice. "Why, it was raining, of course. What about it?"

"But it was not raining out my study window."

"What? But of course it was. I did notice the sun break through the clouds for a moment, but that was all."

"Nonsense!"

"But darling, what has the weather to do with you and me? What difference does it make whether it rains or not—to us?" She approached him timidly and slid a small hand between his arm and side. "Am I responsible for the weather?"

"I think you are. Now please go."

She withdrew from him, brushed blindly at her eyes, gulped once, then said in a voice held steady: "All right. I'll go. But remember—you can come home if you want to. And I'll be there, if you want me." She waited a moment, then added hesitantly: "Would you . . . would you kiss me good-bye?"

He made no answer of any sort, neither with voice nor eyes. She looked at him, then turned, fumbled blindly for the door, and rushed through it.

The creature he knew as Alice went to the place of assembly without stopping to change form. "It is necessary to adjourn this sequence. I am no longer able to influence his decisions."

They had expected it, nevertheless they stirred with dismay.

The Glaroon addressed the First for Manipulation. "Prepare to graft the selected memory track at once."

Then, turning to the First for Operations, the Glaroon said: "The extrapolation shows that he will tend to escape within two of his days. This sequence degenerated primarily through your failure to extend that rainfall all around him. Be advised."

"It would be simpler if we understood his motives."

"In my capacity as Dr. Hayward, I have often thought so," commented the Glaroon acidly, "but if we understood his motives, we would be part of him. Bear in mind the Treaty! He almost remembered."

The creature known as Alice spoke up. "Could he not have the Taj Mahal next sequence? For some reason he values it."

"You are becoming assimilated!"

"Perhaps. I am not in fear. Will he receive it?"

"It will be considered."

The Glaroon continued with orders: "Leave structures standing until adjournment. New York City and Harvard University are now dismantled. Divert him from those sectors.

"Move!"

H. P. Lovecraft (1890–1937)

At the Mountains of Madness

Howard Phillips Lovecraft is the most important American horror writer since Poe. Like Poe, he was a theoretician, poet and writer. His essay, *Supernatural Horror in Literature,* is, despite its gorgeous prose excesses, the best piece of criticism and history of the genre. Arkham House, the most distinguished publisher of horror fiction of this century, was founded after his death in 1937 by August Derleth and Donald Wandrei, two writers of his circle, specifically to publish Lovecraft's collected works. His influence has been enormous since the initial appearances of his works in *Weird Tales* in the 1920s and 1930s, not only on the circle that gathered around him in his lifetime, including Clark Ashton Smith, Robert E. Howard, Derleth, Wandrei, Robert Bloch, Fritz Leiber and others, but on much of the literature in the English language (and to a certain extent in Europe and elsewhere—in a same manner as Poe, Lovecraft was noticed early in France, where his reputation is perhaps higher than here. Even Jorge Luis Borges wrote a consciously Lovecraftian story or two). It is particularly interesting that he chose, in this novella, the longest work he wrote published during his lifetime, to create what is essentially a sequel to Poe's "unfinished" *Narrative of Arthur Gordon Pym.* This piece was first published in *Astounding,* shortly before the Campbell era, one of the few Lovecraft stories to appear in a magazine other than *Weird Tales* (of which he was a mainstay). It is also one of the crucial links between science fiction and horror, a work that helped to forge the bond between the two categories that has lasted until the present.

I

I am forced into speech because men of science have refused to follow my advice without knowing why. It is altogether against my will that I tell my reasons for opposing this contemplated invasion of the antarctic—with its vast fossil-hunt and its wholesale boring and melting of the ancient ice-cap—and I am the more reluctant because my warning may be in vain. Doubt of the real facts, as I must reveal them, is inevitable; yet if I suppressed what will seem extravagant and incredible there would be nothing left. The hitherto withheld photographs, both ordinary and aërial, will count in my favour; for they are damnably vivid and graphic. Still, they will be doubted because of the great lengths to which clever fakery can be carried. The ink drawings, of course, will be jeered at as obvious impostures; notwithstanding a strangeness of technique which art experts ought to remark and puzzle over.

In the end I must rely on the judgment and standing of the few scientific leaders who have, on the one hand, sufficient independence of thought to weigh my data on its own hideously convincing merits or in the light of certain primordial and highly baffling mythcycles; and on the other hand, sufficient influence to deter the exploring world in general from any rash and overambitious programme in the region of those mountains of madness. It is an unfortunate fact that relatively obscure men like myself and my associates, connected only with a small university, have little chance of making an impression where matters of a wildly bizarre or highly controversial nature are concerned.

It is further against us that we are not, in the strictest sense, specialists in the fields which came primarily to be concerned. As a geologist my object in leading the Miskatonic University Expedition was wholly that of securing deep-level specimens of rock and soil from various parts of the antarctic continent, aided by the remarkable drill devised by Prof. Frank H. Pabodie of our engineering department. I had no wish to be a pioneer in any other field than this; but I did hope that the use of this new mechanical appliance at different points along previously explored paths would bring to light materials of a sort hitherto unreached by the ordinary methods of collection. Pabodie's drilling apparatus, as the public already knows from our reports, was unique and radical in its lightness, portability, and capacity to combine the ordinary artesian drill principle with the principle of the small circular rock drill in such a way as to cope quickly with strata of varying hardness. Steel head, jointed rods, gasoline motor, collapsible wooden derrick, dynamiting paraphernalia, cording, rubbish-removal auger, and sectional piping for bores five inches wide and up to 1000 feet deep all formed, with needed accessories, no greater load than three seven-dog sledges could carry; this being made possible by the clever aluminum alloy of which most of the metal objects were fashioned. Four large Dornier aëroplanes, designed especially for the tremendous altitude flying necessary on the antarctic plateau and with added fuel-warming and quick-starting devices worked out by Pabodie, could transport our entire expedition from a base at the edge of the great ice barrier to various suitable inland points, and from these points a sufficient quota of dogs would serve us.

We planned to cover as great an area as one antarctic season—or longer, if absolutely necessary—would permit, operating mostly in the mountain-ranges and on the plateau south of Ross Sea; regions explored in varying degree by Shackleton, Amundsen, Scott, and Byrd. With frequent changes of camp, made by aëroplane and involving distances great enough to be of geological significance, we expected to unearth a quite unprecedented amount of material; especially in the pre-Cambrian strata of which so narrow a range of antarctic specimens had previously been secured. We wished also to obtain as great as possible a variety of the upper fossiliferous rocks, since the primal life-history of this bleak realm of ice and death is of the highest importance to our knowledge of the earth's past. That the antarctic continent was once temperate and even tropical, with a teeming vegetable and animal life of which the lichens, marine fauna, arachnida, and penguins of the northern edge are the only survivals, is a matter of common information; and we hoped to expand that information in variety, accuracy, and detail. When a simple boring revealed fossiliferous signs, we would enlarge the aperture by blasting in order to get specimens of suitable size and condition.

Our borings, of varying depth according to the promise held out by the upper soil or rock, were to be confined to exposed or nearly exposed land surfaces—these inevitably being slopes and ridges because of the mile or two-mile thickness of solid ice overlying the lower levels. We could not afford to waste drilling depth on any considerable amount of mere glaciation, though Pabodie had worked out a plan for sinking copper electrodes in thick clusters of borings and melting off limited areas of ice with current from a gasoline-driven dynamo. It is this plan—which we could not put into effect except experimentally on an expedition such as ours—that the coming Starkweather-Moore Expedition proposes to follow despite the warnings I have issued since our return from the antarctic.

The public knows of the Miskatonic Expedition through our frequent wireless reports to the *Arkham Advertiser* and Associated Press, and through the later articles of Pabodie and myself. We consisted of four men from the University—Pabodie, Lake of the biology department, Atwood of the physics department (also a meterologist), and I representing geology and having nominal command—besides sixteen assistants; seven graduate students from Miskatonic and nine skilled mechanics. Of these sixteen, twelve were qualified aëroplane pilots, all but two of whom were competent wireless operators. Eight of them understood navigation with compass and sextant, as did Pabodie, Atwood, and I. In addition, of course, our two ships—wooden ex-whalers, reinforced for ice conditions and having auxiliary steam—were fully manned. The Nathaniel Derby Pickman Foundation, aided by a few special contributions, financed the expedition; hence our preparations were extremely thorough despite the absence of great publicity. The dogs, sledges, machines, camp materials, and unassembled parts of our five planes were delivered in Boston, and there our ships were loaded. We were marvellously well-equipped for our specific purposes, and in all matters pertaining to supplies, regimen, transportation, and camp construction we profited by the excellent example of our many recent and exceptionally brilliant predecessors. It was the unusual number and fame of these predecessors which made our own expedition—ample though it was—so little noticed by the world at large.

As the newspapers told, we sailed from Boston Harbour on September 2, 1930; taking a leisurely course down the coast and through the Panama Canal, and stopping at Samoa and Hobart, Tasmania, at which latter place we took on final supplies. None of our exploring party had ever been in the polar regions before, hence we all relied greatly on our ship captains—J. B. Douglas, commanding the brig *Arkham*, and serving as commander of the sea party, and Georg Thorfinnssen, commanding the barque *Miskatonic*—both veteran whalers in antarctic waters. As we left the inhabited world behind the sun sank lower and lower in the north, and stayed longer and longer above the horizon each day. At about 62° South Latitude we sighted our first icebergs—table-like objects with vertical sides—and just before reaching the Antarctic Circle, which we crossed on October 20 with appropriately quaint ceremonies, we were considerably troubled with field ice. The falling temperature bothered me considerably after our long voyage through the tropics, but I tried to brace up for the worse rigours to come. On many occasions the curious atmospheric effects enchanted me vastly; these including a strikingly vivid mirage—the first I had ever seen—in which distant bergs became the battlements of unimaginable cosmic castles.

Pushing through the ice, which was fortunately neither extensive nor thickly packed, we regained open water at South Latitude 67°, East Longitude 175°. On the morning of October 26 a strong "land blink" appeared on the south, and before noon we all felt a thrill of excitement at beholding a vast, lofty, and snow-clad mountain chain which opened out and covered the whole vista ahead. At last we had encountered an outpost of the great unknown continent and its cryptic world of frozen death. These peaks were obviously the Admiralty Range discovered by Ross, and it would now be our task to round Cape Adare and sail down the east coast of Victoria Land to our contemplated base on the shore of McMurdo Sound at the foot of the volcano Erebus in South Latitude 77° 9'.

The last lap of the voyage was vivid and fancy-stirring, great barren peaks of mystery looming up constantly against the west as the low northern sun of noon or the still lower horizon-grazing southern sun of midnight poured its hazy reddish rays over the white snow, bluish ice and water lanes, and black bits of exposed granite slope. Through the desolate summits swept raging intermittent gusts of the terrible antarctic wind; whose cadences sometimes held vague suggestions of a wild and half-sentient musical piping, with notes extending over a wide range, and which for some subconscious mnemonic reason seemed to me disquieting and even dimly terrible. Something about the scene reminded me of the strange and disturbing Asian paintings of Nicholas Roerich, and of the still stranger and more disturbing descriptions of the evilly fabled plateau of Leng which occur in the dreaded *Necronomicon* of the mad Arab Abdul Alhazred. I was rather sorry, later on, that I had ever looked into that monstrous book at the college library.

On the seventh of November, sight of the westward range having been temporarily lost, we passed Franklin Island; and the next day descried the cones of Mts. Erebus and Terror on Ross Island ahead, with the long line of the Parry Mountains beyond. There now stretched off to the east the low, white line of the great ice barrier; rising perpendicularly to a height of 200 feet like the rocky cliffs of Quebec, and marking the end of southward navigation. In the afternoon we entered McMurdo Sound and stood off the coast in the lee of smoking Mt. Erebus. The scoriac peak towered up some 12,700 feet against the eastern sky, like a Japanese print of the sacred Fujiyama; while beyond it rose the white, ghost-like height of Mt. Terror, 10,900 feet in altitude, and now extinct as a volcano. Puffs of smoke from Erebus came intermittently, and one of the graduate assistants—a brilliant young fellow named Danforth—pointed out what looked like lava on the snowy slope; remarking that this mountain, discovered in 1840, had undoubtedly been the source of Poe's image when he wrote seven years later of

> "—the lavas that restlessly roll
> Their sulphurous currents down Yaanek
> In the ultimate climes of the pole—
> That groan as they roll down Mount Yaanek
> In the realms of the boreal pole."

Danforth was a great reader of bizarre material, and had talked a good deal of Poe. I was interested myself because of the antarctic scene of Poe's only long story—the disturbing and enigmatical *Arthur Gordon Pym*. On the barren shore, and on the lofty ice barrier in the background, myriads of grotesque penguins squawked and flapped their fins; while many fat seals were visible on the water, swimming or sprawling across large cakes of slowly drifting ice.

Using small boats, we effected a difficult landing on Ross Island shortly after midnight on the morning of the 9th, carrying a line of cable from each of the ships and preparing to unload supplies by means of a breeches-buoy arrangement. Our sensations on first treading antarctic soil were poignant and complex, even though at this particular point the Scott and Shackleton expeditions had preceded us. Our camp on the frozen shore below the volcano's slope was only a provisional one; headquarters being kept aboard the *Arkham*. We landed all our drilling apparatus, dogs, sledges, tents, provisions, gasoline tanks, experimental ice-melting outfit, cameras both ordinary and aërial, aëroplane parts, and other accessories, including three small portable wireless outfits (besides those in the planes) capable of communicating with the *Arkham*'s large outfit from any part of the antarctic continent that we would be likely to visit. The ship's outfit, communicating with the outside world, was to convey press reports to the *Arkham Advertiser*'s powerful wireless station on Kingsport Head, Mass. We hoped to complete our work during a single antarctic summer; but if this proved impossible we would winter on the *Arkham*, sending the *Miskatonic* north before the freezing of the ice for another summer's supplies.

I need not repeat what the newspapers have already published about our early work: of our ascent of Mt. Erebus; our successful mineral borings at several points on Ross Island and the singular speed with which Pabodie's apparatus accomplished them, even through solid rock layers; our provisional test of the small ice-melting equipment; our perilous ascent of the great barrier with sledges and supplies; and our final assembling of five huge aëroplanes at the camp atop the barrier. The health of our land party—twenty men and 55 Alaskan sledge dogs—was remarkable, though of course we had so far encountered no really destructive temperatures or windstorms. For the most part, the thermometer varied between zero and 20° or 25° above, and our experience with New England winters had accustomed us to rigours of this sort. The barrier camp was semi-permanent, and destined to be a storage cache for gasoline, provisions, dynamite, and other supplies. Only four of our planes were needed to carry the actual exploring material, the fifth being left with a pilot and two men from the ships at the storage cache to form a means of reaching us from the *Arkham* in case all our exploring planes were lost. Later, when not using all the other planes for moving apparatus, we would employ one or two in a shuttle transportation service between this cache and another permanent base on the great plateau from 600 to 700 miles southward, beyond Beardmore Glacier. Despite the almost unanimous accounts of appalling winds and tempests that pour down from the plateau, we determined to dispense with intermediate bases; taking our chances in the interest of economy and probable efficiency.

Wireless reports have spoken of the breath-taking four-hour nonstop flight of our squadron on November 21 over the lofty shelf ice, with vast peaks rising on the west, and the unfathomed silences echoing to the sound of our engines. Wind troubled us only moderately, and our radio compasses helped us through the one opaque fog we encountered. When the vast rise loomed ahead, between Latitudes 83° and 84°, we knew we had reached Beardmore Glacier, the largest valley glacier in the world, and that the frozen sea was now giving place to a frowning and mountainous coastline. At last we were truly entering the white, aeon-dead world of the ultimate south, and even as we realised it we saw the peak of Mt. Nansen in the eastern distance, towering up to its height of almost 15,000 feet.

The successful establishment of the southern base above the glacier in Latitude 86° 7', East Longitude 174° 23', and the phenomenally rapid and effective borings and blastings made at various points reached by our sledge trips and short aëroplane flights, are matters of history; as is the arduous and triumphant ascent of Mt. Nansen by Pabodie and two of the graduate students—Gedney and Carroll—on December 13–15. We were some 8500 feet above sea-level, and when experimental drillings revealed solid ground only twelve feet down through the snow and ice at certain points, we made considerable use of the small melting apparatus and sunk bores and performed dynamiting at many places where no previous explorer had ever thought of securing mineral specimens. The pre-Cambrian granites and beacon sandstones thus obtained confirmed our belief that this plateau was homogeneous with the great bulk of the continent to the west, but somewhat different from the parts lying eastward below South America—which we then thought to form a separate and smaller continent divided from the larger one by a frozen junction of Ross and Weddell Seas, though Byrd has since disproved the hypothesis.

In certain of the sandstones, dynamited and chiselled after boring revealed their nature, we found some highly interesting fossil markings and fragments—notably ferns, seaweeds, trilobites, crinoids, and such molluscs as lingulellae and gasteropods—all of which seemed of real significance in connexion with the region's primordial history. There was also a queer triangular, striated marking about a foot in greatest diameter which Lake pieced together from three fragments of slate brought up from a deep-blasted aperture. These fragments came from a point to the westward, near the Queen Alexandra Range; and Lake, as a biologist, seemed to find their curious marking unusually puzzling and provocative, though to my geological eye it looked not unlike some of the ripple effects reasonably common in the sedimentary rocks. Since slate is no more than a metamorphic formation into which a sedimentary stratum is pressed, and since the pressure itself produces odd distorting effects on any markings which may exist, I saw no reason for extreme wonder over the striated depression.

On January 6, 1931, Lake, Pabodie, Daniels, all six of the students, four mechanics, and I flew directly over the south pole in two of the great planes, being forced down once by a sudden high wind which fortunately did not develop into a typical storm. This was, as the papers have stated, one of several observation flights; during others of which we tried to discern new topographical features in areas unreached by previous explorers. Our early flights were disappointing in this latter respect; though they afforded us some magnificent examples of the richly fantastic and deceptive mirages of the polar regions, of which our sea voyage had given us some brief foretastes. Distant mountains floated in the sky as enchanted cities, and often the whole white world would dissolve into a gold, silver, and scarlet land of Dunsanian dreams and adventurous expectancy under the magic of the low midnight sun. On cloudy days we had considerable trouble in flying, owing to the tendency of snowy earth and sky to merge into one mystical opalescent void with no visible horizon to mark the junction of the two.

At length we resolved to carry out our original plan of flying 500 miles eastward with all four exploring planes and establishing a fresh sub-base at a point which would probably be on the smaller continental division, as we mistakenly conceived it. Geological specimens obtained there would be desirable for purposes of comparison. Our health so far had remained excellent; lime-juice well offsetting the steady diet of tinned and salted food, and temperatures generally above zero enabling us to do without our thickest furs. It was now midsummer, and with haste and care we might be able to conclude work by March and avoid a tedious wintering through the long antarctic night. Several savage windstorms had burst upon us from the west, but we had escaped damage through the skill of Atwood in devising rudimentary aëroplane shelters and windbreaks of heavy snow blocks, and reinforcing the principal camp buildings with snow. Our good luck and efficiency had indeed been almost uncanny.

The outside world knew, of course, of our programme, and was told also of Lake's strange and dogged insistence on a westward—or rather, northwestward—prospecting trip before our radical shift to the new base. It seems he had pondered a great deal, and with alarmingly radical daring, over that triangular striated marking in the slate; reading into it certain contradictions in Nature and geological period which whetted his curiosity to the utmost, and made him avid to sink more borings and blastings in the west-stretching formation to which the exhumed fragments evidently belonged. He was strangely convinced that the marking was the print of some bulky, unknown, and radically unclassifiable organism of considerably advanced evolution, notwithstanding that the rock which bore it was of so vastly ancient a date—Cambrian if not actually pre-Cambrian—as to preclude the probable existence not only of all highly evolved life, but of any life at all above the unicellular or at most the trilobite stage. These fragments, with their odd marking, must have been 500 million to a thousand million years old.

II

Popular imagination, I judge, responded actively to our wireless bulletins of Lake's start northwestward into regions never trodden by human foot or penetrated by human imagination; though we did not mention his wild hopes of revolutionising the entire sciences of biology and geology. His preliminary sledging and boring journey of January 11–18 with Pabodie and five others—marred by the loss of two dogs in an upset when crossing one of the great pressure-ridges in the ice—had brought up more and more of the Archaean slate; and even I was interested by the singular profusion of evident fossil markings in that unbelievably ancient stratum. These markings, however, were of very primitive life-forms involving no great paradox except that any life-forms should occur in rock as definitely pre-Cambrian as this seemed to be; hence I still failed to see the good sense of Lake's demand for an interlude in our time-saving programme—an interlude requiring the use of all four planes, many men, and the whole of the expedition's mechanical apparatus. I did not, in the end, veto the plan; though I decided not to accompany the northwestward party despite Lake's plea for my geological advice. While they were gone, I would remain at the base with Pabodie and five men and work out final plans for the eastward shift. In preparation for this transfer one of the planes had begun to move up a good gasoline supply from McMurdo Sound; but this could wait temporarily. I kept with me one sledge and nine dogs, since it is unwise to be at any time without possible transportation in an utterly tenantless world of aeon-long death.

Lake's sub-expedition into the unknown, as everyone will recall, sent out its own reports from the short-wave transmitters on the planes; these being simultaneously picked up by our apparatus at the southern base and by the *Arkham* at McMurdo Sound, whence they were relayed to the outside world on wave-lengths up to fifty metres. The start was made January 22 at 4 AM; and the first wireless message we received came only two hours later, when Lake spoke of descending and starting a small-scale ice-melting and bore at a point some 300 miles away from us. Six hours after that a second and very excited message told of the frantic, beaver-like work whereby a shallow shaft had been sunk and blasted; culminating in the discovery of slate fragments with several markings approximately like the one which had caused the original puzzlement.

Three hours later a brief bulletin announced the resumption of the flight in the teeth of a raw and piercing gale; and when I despatched a message of protest against further hazards, Lake replied curtly that his new specimens made any hazard worth taking. I saw that his excitement had reached the point of mutiny, and that I could do nothing to check this headlong risk of the whole expedition's success; but it was appalling to think of his plunging deeper and deeper into that treacherous and sinister white immensity of tempests and unfathomed mysteries which stretched off for some 1500 miles to the half-known, half-suspected coast-line of Queen Mary and Knox Lands.

Then, in about an hour and a half more, came that doubly excited message from Lake's moving plane which almost reversed my sentiments and made me wish I had accompanied the party.

"10:05 PM On the wing. After snowstorm, have spied mountainrange ahead higher than any hitherto seen. May equal Himalayas allowing for height of plateau. Probable Latitude 76° 15′, Longitude 113° 10′ E. Reaches far as can see to right and left. Suspicion of two smoking cones. All peaks black and bare of snow. Gale blowing off them impedes navigation."

After that Pabodie, the men, and I hung breathlessly over the receiver. Thought of this titanic mountain rampart 700 miles away inflamed our deepest sense of adventure; and we rejoiced that our expedition, if not ourselves personally, had been its discoverers. In half an hour Lake called us again.

"Moulton's plane forced down on plateau in foothills, but nobody hurt and perhaps can repair. Shall transfer essentials to other three for return or further moves if necessary, but no more heavy plane travel needed just now. Mountains surpass anything in imagination. Am going up scouting in Carroll's plane, with all weight out. You can't imagine anything like this. Highest peaks must go over 35,000 feet. Everest out of the running. Atwood to work out height with theodolite while Carroll and I go up. Probably wrong about cones, for formations look stratified. Possibly pre-Cambrian slate with other strata mixed in. Queer skyline effects—regular sections of cubes clinging to highest peaks. Whole thing marvellous in red-gold light of low sun. Like land of mystery in a dream or gateway to forbidden world of untrodden wonder. Wish you were here to study."

Though it was technically sleeping-time, not one of us listeners thought for a moment of retiring. It must have been a good deal the same at McMurdo Sound, where the supply cache and the *Arkham* were also getting the messages; for Capt. Douglas gave out a call congratulating everybody on the important find, and Sherman, the cache operator, seconded his sentiments. We were sorry, of course, about the damaged aëroplane; but hoped it could be easily mended. Then, at 11 PM, came another call from Lake.

"Up with Carroll over highest foothills. Don't dare try really tall peaks in present weather, but shall later. Frightful work climbing, and hard going at this altitude, but worth it. Great range fairly solid, hence can't get any glimpses beyond. Main summits exceed Himalayas, and very queer. Range looks like pre-Cambrian slate, with plain signs of many other upheaved strata. Was wrong about volcanism. Goes farther in either direction than we can see. Swept clear of snow above about 21,000 feet. Odd formations on slopes of highest mountains. Great low square blocks with exactly vertical sides, and rectangular lines of low vertical ramparts, like the old Asian castles clinging to steep mountains in Roerich's paintings. Impressive from distance. Flew close to some, and Carroll thought they were formed of smaller separate pieces, but that is probably weathering. Most edges crumbled and rounded off as if exposed to storms and climate changes for millions of years. Parts, especially upper parts, seem to be of lighter-coloured rock than any visible strata on slopes proper, hence an evidently crystalline origin. Close flying shews many cave-mouths, some unusually regular in outline, square or semicircular. You must come and investigate. Think I saw rampart squarely on top of one peak. Height seems about 30,000 to 35,000 feet. Am up 21,500 myself, in devilish gnawing cold. Wind whistles and pipes through passes and in and out of caves, but no flying danger so far."

From then on for another half-hour Lake kept up a running fire of comment, and expressed his intention of climbing some of the peaks on foot. I replied that I would join him as soon as he could send a plane, and that Pabodie and I would work out the best gasoline plan—just where and how to concentrate our supply in view of the expedition's altered character. Obviously, Lake's boring operations, as well as his aëroplane activities, would need a great deal delivered for the new base which he was to establish at the foot of the mountains; and it was possible that the eastward flight might not be made after all this season. In connexion with this business I called Capt. Douglas and asked him to get as much as possible out of the ships and up the barrier with the single dog-team we had left there. A direct route across the unknown region between Lake and McMurdo Sound was what we really ought to establish.

Lake called me later to say that he had decided to let the camp stay where Moulton's plane had been forced down, and where repairs had already progressed somewhat. The ice-sheet was very thin, with dark ground here and there visible, and he would sink some borings and blasts at that very point before making any sledge trips or climbing expeditions. He spoke of the ineffable majesty of the whole scene, and the queer state of his sensations at being in the lee of vast silent pinnacles whose ranks shot up like a wall reaching the sky at the world's rim. Atwood's theodolite observations had placed the height of the five tallest peaks at from 30,000 to 34,000 feet. The windswept nature of the terrain clearly disturbed Lake, for it argued the occasional existence of prodigious gales violent beyond anything we had so far encountered. His camp lay a little more than five miles from where the higher foothills abruptly rose. I could almost trace a note of subconscious alarm in his words—flashed across a glacial void of 700 miles—as he urged that we all hasten with the matter and get the strange new region disposed of as soon as possible. He was about to rest now, after a continuous day's work of almost unparalleled speed, strenuousness, and results.

In the morning I had a three-cornered wireless talk with Lake and Capt. Douglas at their widely separated bases; and it was agreed that one of Lake's planes would come to my base for Pabodie, the five men, and myself, as well as for all the fuel it could carry. The rest of the fuel question, depending on our decision about an easterly trip, could wait for a few days; since Lake had enough for immediate camp heat and borings. Eventually the old southern base ought to be restocked; but if we postponed the easterly trip we would not use it till the next summer, and meanwhile Lake must send a plane to explore a direct route between his new mountains and McMurdo Sound.

Pabodie and I prepared to close our base for a short or long period, as the case might be. If we wintered in the antarctic we would probably fly straight from Lake's base to the *Arkham* without returning to this spot. Some of our conical tents had already been reinforced by blocks of hard snow, and now we decided to complete the job of making a permanent Esquimau village. Owing to a very liberal tent supply, Lake had with him all that his base would need even after our arrival. I wirelessed that Pabodie and I would be ready for the northwestward move after one day's work and one night's rest.

Our labours, however, were not very steady after 4 PM; for about that time Lake began sending in the most extraordinary and excited messages. His working day had started unpropitiously; since an aëroplane survey of the nearly exposed rock surfaces shewed an entire absence of those Archaean and primordial strata for which he was looking, and which formed so great a part of the colossal peaks that loomed up at a tantalising distance from the camp. Most of the rocks glimpsed were apparently Jurassic and Comanchian sandstones and Permian and Triassic schists, with now and then a glossy black outcropping suggesting a hard and slaty coal. This rather discouraged Lake, whose plans all hinged on unearthing specimens more than 500 million years older. It was clear to him that in order to recover the Archaean slate vein in which he had found the odd markings, he would have to make a long sledge trip from these foothills to the steep slopes of the gigantic mountains themselves.

He had resolved, nevertheless, to do some local boring as part of the expedition's general programme; hence set up the drill and put five men to work with it while the rest finished settling the camp and repairing the damaged aëroplane. The softest visible rock—a sandstone about a quarter of a mile from the camp—had been chosen for the first sampling; and the drill made excellent progress without much supplementary blasting. It was about three hours afterward, following the first really heavy blast of the operation, that the shouting of the drill crew was heard; and that young Gedney—the acting foreman—rushed into the camp with the startling news.

They had struck a cave. Early in the boring the sandstone had given place to a vein of Comanchian limestone full of minute fossil cephalopods, corals, echini, and spirifera, and with occasional suggestions of siliceous sponges and marine vertebrate bones—the latter probably of teliosts, sharks, and ganoids. This in itself was important enough, as affording the first vertebrate fossils the expedition had yet secured; but when shortly afterward the drill-head dropped through the stratum into apparent vacancy, a wholly new and doubly intense wave of excitement spread among the excavators. A good-sized blast had laid open the subterrene secret; and now, through a jagged aperture perhaps five feet across and three feet thick, there yawned before the avid searchers a section of shallow limestone hollowing worn more than fifty million years ago by the trickling ground waters of a bygone tropic world.

The hollowed layer was not more than seven or eight feet deep, but extended off indefinitely in all directions and had a fresh, slightly moving air which suggested its membership in an extensive subterranean system. Its roof and floor were abundantly equipped with large stalactites and stalagmites, some of which met in columnar form; but important above all else was the vast deposit of shells and bones which in places nearly choked the passage. Washed down from unknown jungles of Mesozoic tree-ferns and fungi, and forests of Tertiary cycads, fan-palms, and primitive angiosperms, this osseous medley contained representatives of more Cretaceous, Eocene, and other animal species than the greatest palaeontologist could have counted or classified in a year. Molluscs, crustacean armour, fishes, amphibians, reptiles, birds, and early mammals—great and small, known and unknown. No wonder Gedney ran back to the camp shouting, and no wonder everyone else dropped work and rushed headlong through the biting cold to where the tall derrick marked a new-found gateway to secrets of inner earth and vanished aeons.

When Lake had satisfied the first keen edge of his curiosity he scribbled a message in his notebook and had young Moulton run back to the camp to despatch it by wireless. This was my first word of the discovery, and it told of the identification of early shells, bones of ganoids and placoderms, remnants of labyrinthodonts and thecodonts, great mososaur skull fragments, dinosaur vertebrae and armour-plates, pterodactyl teeth and wing-bones, archaeopteryx debris, Miocene sharks' teeth, primitive bird-skulls, and skulls, vertebrae, and other bones of archaic mammals such as palaeotheres, xiphodons, dinocerases, eohippi, oreodons, and titanotheres. There was nothing as recent as a mastodon, elephant, true camel, deer, or bovine animal; hence Lake concluded that the last deposits had occurred during the Oligocene age, and that the hollowed stratum had lain in its present dried, dead, and inaccessible state for at least thirty million years.

On the other hand, the prevalence of very early life-forms was singular in the highest degree. Though the limestone formation was, on the evidence of such typical imbedded fossils as ventriculites, positively and unmistakably Comanchian and not a particle earlier;

the free fragments in the hollow space included a surprising proportion from organisms hitherto considered as peculiar to far older periods—even rudimentary fishes, molluscs, and corals as remote as the Silurian or Ordovician. The inevitable inference was that in this part of the world there had been a remarkable and unique degree of continuity between the life of over 300 million years ago and that of only thirty million years ago. How far this continuity had extended beyond the Oligocene age when the cavern was closed, was of course past all speculation. In any event, the coming of the frightful ice in the Pleistocene some 500,000 years ago—a mere yesterday as compared with the age of this cavity—must have put an end to any of the primal forms which had locally managed to outlive their common terms.

Lake was not content to let his first message stand, but had another bulletin written and despatched across the snow to the camp before Moulton could get back. After that Moulton stayed at the wireless in one of the planes; transmitting to me—and to the *Arkham* for relaying to the outside world—the frequent postscripts which Lake sent him by a succession of messengers. Those who followed the newspapers will remember the excitement created among men of science by that afternoon's reports—reports which have finally led, after all these years, to the organisation of that very Starkweather-Moore Expedition which I am so anxious to dissuade from its purposes. I had better give the messages literally as Lake sent them, and as our base operator McTighe translated them from his pencil shorthand.

"Fowler makes discovery of highest importance in sandstone and limestone fragments from blasts. Several distinct triangular striated prints like those in Archaean slate, proving that source survived from over 600 million years ago to Comanchian times without more than moderate morphological changes and decrease in average size. Comanchian prints apparently more primitive or decadent, if anything, than older ones. Emphasise importance of discovery in press. Will mean to biology what Einstein has meant to mathematics and physics. Joins up with my previous work and amplifies conclusions. Appears to indicate, as I suspected, that earth has seen whole cycle or cycles of organic life before known one that begins with Archaeozoic cells. Was evolved and specialised not later than thousand million years ago, when planet was young and recently uninhabitable for any life-forms or normal protoplasmic structure. Question arises when, where, and how development took place."

"Later. Examining certain skeletal fragments of large land and marine saurians and primitive mammals, find singular local wounds or injuries to bony structure not attributable to any known predatory or carnivorous animal of any period. Of two sorts—straight, penetrant bores, and apparently hacking incisions. One or two cases of cleanly severed bone. Not many specimens affected. Am sending to camp for electric torches. Will extend search area underground by hacking away stalactites."

"Still later. Have found peculiar soapstone fragment about six inches across and an inch and a half thick, wholly unlike any visible local formation. Greenish, but no evidences to place its period. Has curious smoothness and regularity. Shaped like five-pointed star with tips broken off, and signs of other cleavage at inward angles and in centre of surface. Small, smooth depression in centre of unbroken surface. Arouses much curiosity as to source and weathering. Probably some freak of water action. Carroll, with magnifier, thinks he can make out additional markings of geologic significance. Groups of tiny dots in regular patterns. Dogs growing uneasy as we work, and seem to hate this soapstone. Must see if it has any peculiar odour. Will report again when Mills gets back with light and we start on underground area."

"10:15 PM Important discovery. Orrendorf and Watkins, working underground at 9:45 with light, found monstrous barrel-shaped fossil of wholly unknown nature; probably vegetable unless overgrown specimen of unknown marine radiata. Tissue evidently preserved by mineral salts. Tough as leather, but astonishing flexibility retained in places. Marks of broken-off parts at ends and around sides. Six feet end to end, 3.5 feet central diameter, tapering to 1 foot at each end. Like a barrel with five bulging ridges in place of staves. Lateral breakages, as of thinnish stalks, are at equator in middle of these ridges. In furrows between ridges are curious growths. Combs or wings that fold up and spread out like fans. All greatly damaged but one, which gives almost seven-foot wing spread. Arrangement reminds one of certain monsters of primal myth, especially fabled Elder Things in *Necronomicon*. These wings seem to be membraneous, stretched on framework of glandular tubing. Apparent minute orifices in frame tubing at wing tips. Ends of body shrivelled, giving no clue to interior or to what has been broken off there. Must dissect when we get back to camp. Can't decide whether vegetable or animal. Many features obviously of almost incredible primitiveness. Have set all hands cutting stalactites and looking for further specimens. Additional scarred bones found, but these must wait. Having trouble with dogs. They can't endure the new specimen, and would probably tear it to pieces if we didn't keep it at a distance from them."

"11:30 PM Attention, Dyer, Pabodie, Douglas. Matter of highest—I might say transcendent—importance. *Arkham* must relay to Kingsport Head Station at once. Strange barrel growth is the Archaean thing that left prints in rocks. Mills, Boudreau, and Fowler discover cluster of thirteen more at underground point forty feet from aperture. Mixed with curiously rounded and configured soapstone fragments smaller than one previously found—star-shaped but no marks of breakage except at some of the points. Of organic specimens, eight apparently perfect, with all appendages. Have brought all to surface, leading off dogs to distance. They cannot stand the things. Give close attention to description and repeat back for accuracy. Papers must get this right.

"Objects are eight feet long all over. Six-foot five-ridged barrel torso 3.5 feet central diameter, 1 foot end diameters. Dark grey, flexible, and infinitely tough. Seven-foot membraneous wings of same colour, found folded, spread out of furrows between ridges. Wing framework tubular or glandular, of lighter grey, with orifices at wing tips. Spread wings have serrated edge. Around equator, one at central apex of each of the five vertical, stave-like ridges, are five systems of light grey flexible arms or tentacles found tightly folded to torso but expansible to maximum length of over 3 feet. Like arms of primitive crinoid. Single stalks 3 inches diameter branch after 6 inches into five sub-stalks, each of which branches after 8 inches into five small, tapering tentacles or tendrils, giving each stalk a total of 25 tentacles.

"At top of torso blunt bulbous neck of lighter grey with gill-like suggestions holds yellowish five-pointed starfish-shaped apparent head covered with three-inch wiry cilia of various prismatic colours. Head thick and puffy, about 2 feet point to point, with three-inch flexible yellowish tubes projecting from each point. Slit in exact centre of top probably breathing aperture. At end of each tube is spherical expansion where yellowish membrane rolls back on handling to reveal glassy, red-irised globe, evidently an eye. Five slightly longer reddish tubes start from inner angles of starfish-shaped head and end in sac-like swellings of same colour which upon pressure open to bell-shaped orifices 2 inches maximum diameter and lined with sharp white tooth-like projections. Probable mouths. All these tubes, cilia, and points of starfish-head found folded tightly down; tubes and points clinging to bulbous neck and torso. Flexibility surprising despite vast toughness.

"At bottom of torso rough but dissimilarly functioning counterparts of head arrangements exist. Bulbous light-grey pseudo-neck, without gill suggestions, holds greenish five-pointed starfish-arrangement. Tough, muscular arms 4 feet long and tapering from 7 inches diameter at base to about 2.5 at point. To each point is attached small end of a greenish five-veined membraneous triangle 8 inches long and 6 wide at farther end. This is the paddle, fin, or pseudo-foot which has made prints in rocks from a thousand million to fifty or sixty million years old. From inner angles of starfish-arrangement project two-foot reddish tubes tapering from 3 inches diameter at base to 1 at tip. Orifices at tips. All these parts infinitely tough and leathery, but extremely flexible. Four-foot arms with paddles undoubtedly used for locomotion of some sort, marine or otherwise. When moved, display suggestions of exaggerated muscularity. As found, all these projections tightly folded over pseudo-neck and end of torso, corresponding to projections at other end.

"Cannot yet assign positively to animal or vegetable kingdom, but odds now favour animal. Probably represents incredibly advanced evolution of radiata without loss of certain primitive features. Echinoderm resemblances unmistakable despite local contradictory evidences. Wing structure puzzles in view of probable marine habitat, but may have use in water navigation. Symmetry is curiously vegetable-like, suggesting vegetable's essentially up-and-down structure rather than animal's fore-and-aft structure. Fabulously early date of evolution, preceding even simplest Archaean protozoa hitherto known, baffles all conjecture as to origin.

"Complete specimens have such uncanny resemblance to certain creatures of primal myth that suggestion of ancient existence outside antarctic becomes inevitable. Dyer and Pabodie have read *Necronomicon* and seen Clark Ashton Smith's nightmare paintings based on text, and will understand when I speak of Elder Things supposed to have created all earth-life as jest or mistake. Students have always thought conception formed from morbid imaginative treatment of very ancient tropical radiata. Also like prehistoric folklore things Wilmarth has spoken of—Cthulhu cult appendages, etc.

"Vast field of study opened. Deposits probably of late Cretaceous or early Eocene period, judging from associated specimens. Massive stalagmites deposited above them. Hard work hewing out, but toughness prevented damage. State of preservation miraculous, evidently owing to limestone action. No more found so far, but will resume search later. Job now to get fourteen huge specimens to camp without dogs, which bark furiously and can't be trusted near them. With nine men—three left to guard the dogs—we ought to manage the three sledges fairly well, though wind is bad. Must establish plane communication with McMurdo Sound and begin shipping material. But I've got to dissect one of these things before we take any rest. Wish I had a real laboratory here. Dyer better kick himself for having tried to stop my westward trip. First the world's greatest mountains, and then this. If this last isn't the high spot of the expedition, I don't know what is. We're made scientifically. Congrats, Pabodie, on the drill that opened up the cave. Now will *Arkham* please repeat description?"

The sensations of Pabodie and myself at receipt of this report were almost beyond description, nor were our companions much behind us in enthusiasm. McTighe, who had hastily translated a few high spots as they came from the droning receiving set, wrote out the entire message from his shorthand version as soon as Lake's operator signed off. All appreciated the epoch-making significance of the discovery, and I sent Lake congratulations as soon as the *Arkham*'s operator had repeated back the descriptive parts as requested; and my example was followed by Sherman from his station at the McMurdo Sound supply cache, as well as by Capt. Douglas of the *Arkham*. Later, as head of the expedition, I added some remarks to be relayed through the *Arkham* to the outside world. Of course, rest was an absurd thought amidst this excitement; and my only wish was to get to Lake's camp as quickly as I could. It disappointed me when he sent word that a rising mountain gale made early aërial travel impossible.

But within an hour and a half interest again rose to banish disappointment. Lake was sending more messages, and told of the completely successful transportation of the fourteen great specimens to the camp. It had been a hard pull, for the things were surprisingly heavy; but nine men had accomplished it very neatly. Now some of the party were hurriedly building a snow corral at a safe distance from the camp, to which the dogs could be brought for greater convenience in feeding. The specimens were laid out on the hard snow near the camp, save for one on which Lake was making crude attempts at dissection.

This dissection seemed to be a greater task than had been expected; for despite the heat of a gasoline stove in the newly raised laboratory tent, the deceptively flexible tissues of the chosen specimen—a powerful and intact one—lost nothing of their more than leathery toughness. Lake was puzzled as to how he might make the requisite incisions without violence destructive enough to upset all the structural niceties he was looking for. He had, it is true, seven more perfect specimens; but these were too few to use up recklessly unless the cave might later yield an unlimited supply. Accordingly he removed the specimen and dragged in one which, though having remnants of the starfish-arrangements at both ends, was badly crushed and partly disrupted along one of the great torso furrows.

Results, quickly reported over the wireless, were baffling and provocative indeed. Nothing like delicacy or accuracy was possible with instruments hardly able to cut the anomalous tissue, but the little that was achieved left us all awed and bewildered. Existing biology would have to be wholly revised, for this thing was no product of any cell-growth science knows about. There had been scarcely any mineral replacement, and despite an age of perhaps forty million years the internal organs were wholly intact. The leathery, undeteriorative, and almost indestructible quality was an inherent attribute of the thing's form of organisation; and pertained to some palaeogean cycle of invertebrate evolution utterly beyond our powers of speculation. At first all that Lake found was dry, but as the heated tent produced its thawing effect, organic moisture of pungent and offensive odour was encountered toward the thing's uninjured side. It was not blood, but a thick, dark-green fluid apparently answering the same purpose. By the time Lake reached this stage all 37 dogs had been brought to the still uncompleted corral near the camp; and even at that distance set up a savage barking and show of restlessness at the acrid, diffusive smell.

Far from helping to place the strange entity, this provisional dissection merely deepened its mystery. All guesses about its external members had been correct, and on the evidence of these one could hardly hesitate to call the thing animal; but internal inspection brought up so many vegetable evidences that Lake was left hopelessly at sea. It had digestion and circulation, and eliminated waste matter through the reddish tubes of its starfish-shaped base. Cursorily, one would say that its respiratory apparatus handled oxygen rather than carbon dioxide; and there were odd evidences of air-storage chambers and methods of shifting respiration from the external orifice to at least two other fully developed breathing-systems—gills and pores. Clearly, it was amphibian and probably adapted to long airless hibernation-periods as well. Vocal organs seemed present in connexion with the main respiratory system, but they presented anomalies beyond immediate solution. Articulate speech, in the sense of syllable-utterance, seemed barely conceivable; but musical piping notes covering a wide range were highly probable. The muscular system was almost preternaturally developed.

The nervous system was so complex and highly developed as to leave Lake aghast. Though excessively primitive and archaic in some respects, the thing had a set of ganglial centres and connectives arguing the very extremes of specialised development. Its five-lobed brain was surprisingly advanced; and there were signs of a sensory equipment, served in part through the wiry cilia of the head, involving factors alien to any other terrestrial organism. Probably it had more than five senses, so that its habits could not be predicted from any existing analogy. It must, Lake thought, have been a creature of keen sensitiveness and delicately differentiated functions in its primal world; much like the ants and bees of today. It reproduced like the vegetable cryptogams, especially the pteridophytes; having spore-cases at the tips of the wings and evidently developing from a thallus or prothallus.

But to give it a name at this stage was mere folly. It looked like a radiate, but was clearly something more. It was partly vegetable, but had three-fourths of the essentials of animal structure. That it was marine in origin, its symmetrical contour and certain other attributes clearly indicated; yet one could not be exact as to the limit of its later adaptations. The wings, after all, held a persistent suggestion of the aërial. How it could have undergone its tremendously complex evolution on a new-born earth in time to leave prints in Archaean rocks was so far beyond conception as to make Lake whimsically recall the primal myths about Great Old Ones who filtered down from the stars and concocted earth-life as a joke or mistake; and the wild tales of cosmic hill things from Outside told by a folklorist colleague in Miskatonic's English department.

Naturally, he considered the possibility of the pre-Cambrian prints' having been made by a less evolved ancestor of the present specimens; but quickly rejected this too facile theory upon considering the advanced structural qualities of the older fossils. If anything, the later contours shewed decadence rather than higher evolution. The size of the pseudo-feet had decreased, and the whole morphology seemed coarsened and simplified. Moreover, the nerves and organs just examined held singular suggestions of retrogression from forms still more complex. Atrophied and vestigial parts were surprisingly prevalent.

Altogether, little could be said to have been solved; and Lake fell back on mythology for a provisional name—jocosely dubbing his finds "The Elder Ones."

At about 2:30 AM, having decided to postpone further work and get a little rest, he covered the dissected organism with a tarpaulin, emerged from the laboratory tent, and studied the intact specimens with renewed interest. The ceaseless antarctic sun had begun to limber up their tissues a trifle, so that the head-points and tubes of two or three shewed signs of unfolding; but Lake did not believe there was any danger of immediate decomposition in the almost sub-zero air. He did, however, move all the undissected specimens closer together and throw a spare tent over them in order to keep off the direct solar rays. That would also help to keep their possible scent away from the dogs, whose hostile unrest was really becoming a problem even at their substantial distance and behind the higher and higher snow walls which an increased quota of the men were hastening to raise around their quarters. He had to weight down the corners of the tent-cloth with heavy blocks of snow to hold it in place amidst the rising gale, for the titan mountains seemed about to deliver some gravely severe blasts. Early apprehensions about sudden antarctic winds were revived, and under Atwood's supervision precautions were taken to bank the tents, new dog-corral, and crude aëroplane shelters with snow on the mountainward side. These latter shelters, begun with hard snow blocks during odd moments, were by no means as high as they should have been; and Lake finally detached all hands from other tasks to work on them.

It was after four when Lake at last prepared to sign off and advised us all to share the rest period his outfit would take when the shelter walls were a little higher. He held some friendly chat with Pabodie over the ether, and repeated his praise of the really marvelous drills that had helped him make his discovery. Atwood also sent greetings and praises. I gave Lake a warm word of congratulation, owning up that he was right about the western trip; and we all agreed to get in touch by wireless at ten in the morning. If the gale was then over, Lake would send a plane for the party at my base. Just before retiring I despatched a final message to the *Arkham* with instructions about toning down the day's news for the outside world, since the full details seemed radical enough to rouse a wave of incredulity until further substantiated.

III

None of us, I imagine, slept very heavily or continuously that morning; for both the excitement of Lake's discovery and the mounting fury of the wind were against such a thing. So savage was the blast, even where we were, that we could not help wondering how much worse it was at Lake's camp, directly under the vast unknown peaks that bred and delivered it. McTighe was awake at ten o'clock and tried to get Lake on the wireless, as agreed, but some electrical condition in the disturbed air to the westward seemed to prevent communication. We did, however, get the *Arkham*, and Douglas told me that he had likewise been vainly trying to reach Lake. He had not known about the wind, for very little was blowing at McMurdo Sound despite its persistent rage where we were.

Throughout the day we all listened anxiously and tried to get Lake at intervals, but invariably without results. About noon a positive frenzy of wind stampeded out of the west, causing us to fear for the safety of our camp; but it eventually died down, with only a moderate relapse at 2 PM. After three o'clock it was very quiet, and we redoubled our efforts to get Lake. Reflecting that he had four planes, each provided with an excellent short-wave outfit, we could not imagine any ordinary accident capable of crippling all his wireless equipment at once. Nevertheless the stony silence continued; and when we thought of the delirious force the wind must have had in his locality we could not help making the most direful conjectures.

By six o'clock our fears had become intense and definite, and after a wireless consultation with Douglas and Thorfinnssen I resolved to take steps toward investigation. The fifth aëroplane, which we had left at the McMurdo Sound supply cache with Sherman and two sailors, was in good shape and ready for instant use; and it seemed that the very emergency for which it had been saved was now upon us. I got Sherman by wireless and ordered him to join me with the plane and the two sailors at the southern base as quickly as possible; the air conditions being apparently highly favourable. We then talked over the personnel of the coming investigation party; and decided that we would include all hands, together with the sledge and dogs which I had kept with me. Even so great a load would not be too much for one of the huge planes built to our especial orders for heavy machinery transportation. At intervals I still tried to reach Lake with the wireless, but all to no purpose.

Sherman, with the sailors Gunnarsson and Larsen, took off at 7:30; and reported a quiet flight from several points on the wing. They arrived at our base at midnight, and all hands at once discussed the next move. It was risky business sailing over the antarctic in a single aëroplane without any line of bases, but no one drew back from what seemed like the plainest necessity. We turned in at two o'clock for a brief rest after some preliminary loading of the plane, but were up again in four hours to finish the loading and packing.

At 7:15 AM, January 25th, we started flying northwestward under McTighe's pilotage with ten men, seven dogs, a sledge, a fuel and food supply, and other items including the plane's wireless outfit. The atmosphere was clear, fairly quiet, and relatively mild in temperature; and we anticipated very little trouble in reaching the latitude and longitude designated by Lake as the site of his camp. Our apprehensions were over what we might find, or fail to find, at the end of our journey; for silence continued to answer all calls despatched to the camp.

Every incident of that four-and-a-half-hour flight is burned into my recollection because of its crucial position in my life. It marked my loss, at the age of fifty-four, of all that peace and balance which the normal mind possesses through its accustomed conception of external Nature and Nature's laws. Thence forward the ten of us—but the student Danforth and myself above all others—were to face a hideously amplified world of lurking horrors which nothing can erase from our emotions, and which we would refrain from sharing with mankind in general if we could. The newspapers have printed the bulletins we sent from the moving plane; telling of our nonstop course, our two battles with treacherous upper-air gales, our glimpse of the broken surface where Lake had sunk his mid-journey shaft three days before, and our sight of a group of those strange fluffy snow-cylinders noted by Amundsen and Byrd as rolling in the wind across the endless leagues of frozen plateau. There came a point, though, when our sensations could not be conveyed in any words the press would understand; and a later point when we had to adopt an actual rule of strict censorship.

The sailor Larsen was first to spy the jagged line of witch-like cones and pinnacles ahead, and his shouts sent everyone to the windows of the great cabined plane. Despite our speed, they were very slow in gaining prominence; hence we knew that they must be infinitely far off, and visible only because of their abnormal height. Little by little, however, they rose grimly into the western sky; allowing us to distinguish various bare, bleak, blackish summits, and to catch the curious sense of phantasy which they inspired as seen in the reddish antarctic light against the provocative background of iridescent ice-dust clouds. In the whole spectacle there was a persistent, pervasive hint of stupendous secrecy and potential revelation; as if these stark, nightmare spires marked the pylons of a frightful gateway into forbidden spheres of dream, and complex gulfs of remote time, space, and ultra-dimensionality. I could not help feeling that they were evil things—mountains of madness whose farther slopes looked out over some accursed ultimate abyss. That seething, half-luminous cloud-background held ineffable suggestions of a vague, ethereal *beyondness* far more than terrestrially spatial; and gave appalling reminders of the utter remoteness, separateness, desolation, and aeon-long death of this untrodden and unfathomed austral world.

It was young Danforth who drew our notice to the curious regularities of the higher mountain skyline—regularities like clinging fragments of perfect cubes, which Lake had mentioned in his messages, and which indeed justified his comparison with the dream-like suggestions of primordial temple-ruins on cloudy Asian mountain-tops so subtly and strangely painted by Roerich. There was indeed something hauntingly Roerich-like about this whole unearthly continent of mountainous mystery. I had felt it in October when we first caught sight of Victoria Land, and I felt it afresh now. I felt, too, another wave of uneasy consciousness of Archaean mythical resemblances; of how disturbingly this lethal realm corresponded to the evilly famed plateau of Leng in the primal writings. Mythologists have placed Leng in Central Asia; but the racial memory of man—or of his predecessors—is long, and it may well be that certain tales have come down from lands and mountains and temples of horror earlier than Asia and earlier than any human world we know. A few daring mystics have hinted at a pre-Pleistocene origin for the fragmentary Pnakotic Manuscripts, and have suggested that the devotees of Tsathoggua were as alien to mankind as Tsathoggua itself. Leng, wherever in space or time it might brood, was not a region I would care to be in or near; nor did I relish the proximity of a world that had ever bred such ambiguous and Archaean monstrosities as those Lake had just mentioned. At the moment I felt sorry that I had ever read the abhorred *Necronomicon*, or talked so much with that unpleasantly erudite folklorist Wilmarth at the university.

This mood undoubtedly served to aggravate my reaction to the bizarre mirage which burst upon us from the increasingly opalescent zenith as we drew near the mountains and began to make out the cumulative undulations of the foothills. I had seen dozens of polar mirages during the preceding weeks, some of them quite as uncanny and fantastically vivid as the present sample; but this one had a wholly novel and obscure quality of menacing symbolism, and I shuddered as the seething labyrinth of fabulous walls and towers and minarets loomed out of the troubled ice-vapours above our heads.

The effect was that of a Cyclopean city of no architecture known to man or to human imagination, with vast aggregations of night-black masonry embodying monstrous perversions of geometrical laws and attaining the most grotesque extremes of sinister bizarrerie. There were truncated cones, sometimes terraced or fluted, surmounted by tall cylindrical shafts here and there bulbously enlarged and often capped with tiers of thinnish scalloped discs; and strange, beetling, table-like constructions suggesting piles of multitudinous rectangular slabs or circular plates or five-pointed stars with each one overlapping the one beneath. There were composite cones and pyramids either alone or surmounting cylinders or cubes or flatter truncated cones and pyramids, and occasional needle-like spires in curious clusters of five. All of these febrile structures seemed knit together by tubular bridges crossing from one to the other at various dizzy heights, and the implied scale of the whole as terrifying and oppressive in its sheer giganticism. The general type of mirage was not unlike some of the wilder forms observed and drawn by the Arctic whaler Scoresby in 1820; but at this time and place, with those dark, unknown mountain peaks soaring stupendously ahead, that anomalous elder-world discovery in our minds, and the pall of probable disaster enveloping the greater part of our expedition, we all seemed to find in it a taint of latent malignity and infinitely evil portent.

I was glad when the mirage began to break up, though in the process the various nightmare turrets and cones assumed distorted temporary forms of even vaster hideousness. As the whole illusion dissolved to churning opalescence we began to look earthward again, and saw that our journey's end was not far off. The unknown mountains ahead rose dizzingly up like a fearsome rampart of giants, their curious regularities shewing with startling clearness even without a field-glass. We were over the lowest foothills now, and could see amidst the snow, ice, and bare patches of their main plateau a couple of darkish spots which we took to be Lake's camp and boring. The higher foothills shot up between five and six miles away, forming a range almost distinct from the terrifying line of more than Himalayan peaks beyond them. At length Ropes—the student who had relieved McTighe at the controls—began to head downward toward the left-hand dark spot whose size marked it as the camp. As he did so, McTighe sent out the last uncensored wireless message the world was to receive from our expedition.

Everyone, of course, has read the brief and unsatisfying bulletins of the rest of our antarctic sojourn. Some hours after our landing we sent a guarded report of the tragedy we found, and reluctantly announced the wiping out of the whole Lake party by the frightful wind of the preceding day, or of the night before that. Eleven known dead, young Gedney missing. People pardoned our hazy lack of details through realisation of the shock the sad event must have caused us, and believed us when we explained that the mangling action of the wind had rendered all eleven bodies unsuitable for transportation outside. Indeed, I flatter myself that even in the midst of our distress, utter bewilderment, and soul-clutching horror, we scarcely went beyond the truth in any specific instance. The tremendous significance lies in what we dared not tell—what I would not tell now but for the need of warning others off from nameless terrors.

It is a fact that the wind had wrought dreadful havoc. Whether all could have lived through it, even without the other thing, is gravely open to doubt. The storm, with its fury of madly driven ice-particles, must have been beyond anything our expedition had encountered before. One aëroplane shelter—all, it seems, had been left in a far too flimsy and inadequate state—was nearly pulverised; and the derrick at the distant boring was entirely shaken to pieces. The exposed metal of the grounded planes and drilling machinery was bruised into a high polish, and two of the small tents were flattened despite their snow banking. Wooden surfaces left out in the blast were pitted and denuded of paint, and all signs of tracks in the snow were completely obliterated. It is also true that we found none of the Archaean biological objects in a condition to take outside as a whole. We did gather some minerals from a vast tumbled pile, including several of the greenish soapstone fragments whose odd five-pointed rounding and faint patterns of grouped dots caused so many doubtful comparisons; and some fossil bones, among which were the most typical of the curiously injured specimens.

None of the dogs survived, their hurriedly built snow enclosure near the camp being almost wholly destroyed. The wind may have done that, though the greater breakage on the side next the camp, which was not the windward one, suggests an outward leap or break of the frantic beasts themselves. All three sledges were gone, and we have tried to explain that the wind may have blown them off into the unknown. The drill and ice-melting machinery at the boring were too badly damaged to warrant salvage, so we used them to choke up that subtly disturbing gateway to the past which Lake had blasted. We likewise left at the camp the two most shaken-up of the planes; since our surviving party had only four real pilots—Sherman, Danforth, McTighe, and Ropes—in all, with Danforth in a poor nervous shape to navigate. We brought back all the books, scientific equipment, and other incidentals we could find, though much was rather unaccountably blown away. Spare tents and furs were either missing or badly out of condition.

It was approximately 4 PM, after wide plane cruising had forced us to give Gedney up for lost, that we sent our guarded message to the *Arkham* for relaying; and I think we did well to keep it as calm and non-committal as we succeeded in doing. The most we said about agitation concerned our dogs, whose frantic uneasiness near the biological specimens was to be expected from poor Lake's accounts. We did not mention, I think, their display of the same uneasiness when sniffing around the queer greenish soapstones and certain other objects in the disordered region; objects including scientific instruments, aëroplanes, and machinery both at the camp and at the boring, whose parts had been loosened, moved, or otherwise tampered with by winds that must have harboured singular curiosity and investigativeness.

About the fourteen biological specimens we were pardonably indefinite. We said that the only ones we discovered were damaged, but that enough was left of them to prove Lake's description wholly and impressively accurate. It was hard work keeping our personal emotions out of this matter—and we did not mention numbers or say exactly how we had found those which we did find. We had by that time agreed not to transmit anything suggesting madness on the part of Lake's men, and it surely looked like madness to find six imperfect monstrosities carefully buried upright in nine-foot snow graves under five-pointed mounds punched over with groups of dots in patterns exactly like those on the queer greenish soapstones dug up from Mesozoic or Tertiary times. The eight perfect specimens mentioned by Lake seemed to have been completely blown away.

We were careful, too, about the public's general peace of mind; hence Danforth and I said little about that frightful trip over the mountains the next day. It was the fact that only a radically lightened plane could possibly cross a range of such height which mercifully limited that scouting tour to the two of us. On our return at 1 AM Danforth was close to hysterics, but kept an admirably stiff upper lip. It took no persuasion to make him promise not to shew our sketches and the other things we brought away in our pockets, not to say anything more to the others than what we had agreed to relay outside, and to hide our camera films for private development later on; so that part of my present story will be as new to Pabodie, McTighe, Ropes, Sherman, and the rest as it will be to the world in general. Indeed—Danforth is closer mouthed than I; for he saw—or thinks he saw—one thing he will not tell even me.

As all know, our report included a tale of a hard ascent; a confirmation of Lake's opinion that the great peaks are of Archaean slate and other very primal crumpled strata unchanged since at least middle Comanchian times; a conventional comment on the regularity of the clinging cube and rampart formations; a decision that the cave-mouths indicate dissolved calcareous veins; a conjecture that certain slopes and passes would permit of the scaling and crossing of the entire range by seasoned mountaineers; and a remark that the mysterious other side holds a lofty and immense super-plateau as ancient and unchanging as the mountains themselves—20,000 feet in elevation, with grotesque rock formations protruding through a thin glacial layer and with low gradual foothills between the general plateau surface and the sheer precipices of the highest peaks.

This body of data is in every respect true so far as it goes, and it completely satisfied the men at the camp. We laid our absence of sixteen hours—a longer time than our announced flying, landing, reconnoitring, and rock-collecting programme called for—to a long mythical spell of adverse wind conditions; and told truly of our landing on the farther foothills. Fortunately our tale sounded realistic and prosaic enough not to tempt any of the others into emulating our flight. Had any tried to do that, I would have used every ounce of my persuasion to stop them—and I do not know what Danforth would have done. While we were gone, Pabodie, Sherman, Ropes, McTighe, and Williamson had worked like beavers over Lake's two best planes; fitting them again for use despite the altogether unaccountable juggling of their operative mechanism.

We decided to load all the planes the next morning and start back for our old base as soon as possible. Even though indirect, that was the safest way to work toward McMurdo Sound; for a straight-line flight across the most utterly unknown stretches of the aeon-dead continent would involve many additional hazards. Further exploration was hardly feasible in view of our tragic decimation and the ruin of our drilling machinery; and the doubts and horrors around us—which we did not reveal—made us wish only to escape from this austral world of desolation and brooding madness as swiftly as we could.

As the public knows, our return to the world was accomplished without further disasters. All planes reached the old base on the evening of the next day—January 27th—after a swift nonstop flight; and on the 28th we made McMurdo Sound in two laps, the one pause being very brief, and occasioned by a faulty rudder in the furious wind over the ice-shelf after we had cleared the great plateau. In five days more the *Arkham* and *Miskatonic*, with all hands and equipment on board, were shaking clear of the thickening field ice and working up Ross Sea with the mocking mountains of Victoria Land looming westward against a troubled antarctic sky and twisting the wind's wails into a wide-ranged musical piping which chilled my soul to the quick. Less than a fortnight later we left the last hint of polar land behind us, and thanked heaven that we were clear of a haunted, accursed realm where life and death, space and time, have made black and blasphemous alliances in the unknown epochs since matter first writhed and swam on the planet's scarce-cooled crust.

Since our return we have all constantly worked to discourage antarctic exploration, and have kept certain doubts and guesses to ourselves with splendid unity and faithfulness. Even young Danforth, with his nervous breakdown, has not flinched or babbled to his doctors—indeed, as I have said, there is one thing he thinks he alone saw which he will not tell even me, though I think it would help his psychological state if he would consent to do so. It might explain and relieve much, though perhaps the thing was no more than the delusive aftermath of an earlier shock. That is the impression I gather after those rare irresponsible moments when he whispers disjointed things to me—things which he repudiates vehemently as soon as he gets a grip on himself again.

It will be hard work deterring others from the great white south, and some of our efforts may directly harm our cause by drawing inquiring notice. We might have known from the first that human curiosity is undying, and that the results we announced would be enough to spur others ahead on the same age-long pursuit of the unknown. Lake's reports of those biological monstrosities had aroused naturalists and palaeontologists to the highest pitch; though we were sensible enough not to shew the detached parts we had taken from the actual buried specimens, or our photographs of those specimens as they were found. We also refrained from shewing the more puzzling of the scarred bones and greenish soapstones; while Danforth and I have closely guarded the pictures we took or drew on the super-plateau across the range, and the crumpled things we smoothed, studied in terror, and brought away in our pockets. But now that Starkweather-Moore party is organising, and with a thoroughness far beyond anything our outfit attempted. If not dissuaded, they will get to the innermost nucleus of the antarctic and melt and bore till they bring up that which may end the world we know. So I must break through all reticences at last—even about that ultimate nameless thing beyond the mountains of madness.

IV

It is only with vast hesitancy and repugnance that I let my mind go back to Lake's camp and what we really found there—and to that other thing beyond the frightened mountain wall. I am constantly tempted to shirk the details, and to let hints stand for actual facts and ineluctable deductions. I hope I have said enough already to let me glide briefly over the rest; the rest, that is, of the horror at the camp. I have told of the wind-ravaged terrain, the damaged shelters, the disarranged machinery, the varied uneasiness of our dogs, the missing sledges and other items, the deaths of men and dogs, the absence of Gedney, and the six insanely buried biological specimens, strangely sound in texture for all their structural injuries, from a world forty million years dead. I do not recall whether I mentioned that upon checking up the canine bodies we found one dog missing. We did not think much about that till later—indeed, only Danforth and I have thought of it at all.

The principal things I have been keeping back relate to the bodies, and to certain subtle points which may or may not lend a hideous and incredible kind of rationale to the apparent chaos. At the time I tried to keep the men's minds off those points; for it was so much simpler—so much more normal—to lay everything to an outbreak of madness on the part of some of Lake's party. From the look of things, that daemon mountain wind must have been enough to drive any man mad in the midst of this centre of all earthly mystery and desolation.

The crowning abnormality, of course, was the condition of the bodies—men and dogs alike. They had all been in some terrible kind of conflict, and were torn and mangled in fiendish and altogether inexplicable ways. Death, so far as we could judge, had in each case come from strangulation or laceration. The dogs had evidently started the trouble, for the state of their ill-built corral bore witness to its forcible breakage from within. It had been set some distance from the camp because of the hatred of the animals for those hellish Archaean organisms, but the precaution seemed to have been taken in vain. When left alone in that monstrous wind behind flimsy walls of insufficient height they must have stampeded—whether from the wind itself, or from some subtle, increasing odour emitted by the nightmare specimens, one could not say. Those specimens, of course, had been covered with a tent-cloth; yet the low antarctic sun had beat steadily upon that cloth, and Lake had mentioned that solar heat tended to make the strangely sound and tough tissues of the things relax and expand. Perhaps the wind had whipped the cloth from over them, and jostled them about in such a way that their more pungent olfactory qualities became manifest despite their unbelievable antiquity.

But whatever had happened, it was hideous and revolting enough. Perhaps I had better put squeamishness aside and tell the worst at last—though with a categorical statement of opinion, based on the first-hand observations and most rigid deductions of both Danforth and myself, that the then missing Gedney was in no way responsible for the loathsome horrors we found. I have said that the bodies were frightfully mangled. Now I must add that some were incised and subtracted from in the most curious, cold-blooded, and inhuman fashion. It was the same with dogs and men. All the healthier, fatter bodies, quadrupedal or bipedal, had had their most solid masses of tissue cut out and removed, as by a careful butcher; and around them was a strange sprinkling of salt—taken from the ravaged provision-chests on the planes—which conjured up the most horrible associations. The thing had occurred in one of the crude aëroplane shelters from which the plane had been dragged out, and subsequent winds had effaced all tracks which could have supplied any plausible theory. Scattered bits of clothing, roughly slashed from the human incision-subjects, hinted no clues. It is useless to bring up the half-impression of certain faint snow-prints in one shielded corner of the ruined enclosure—because that impression did not concern human prints at all, but was clearly mixed up with all the talk of fossil prints which poor Lake had been giving throughout the preceding weeks. One had to be careful of one's imagination in the lee of those overshadowing mountains of madness.

As I have indicated, Gedney and one dog turned out to be missing in the end. When we came on that terrible shelter we had missed two dogs and two men; but the fairly unharmed dissecting tent, which we entered after investigating the monstrous graves, had something to reveal. It was not as Lake had left it, for the covered parts of the primal monstrosity had been removed from the improvised table. Indeed, we had already realised that one of the six imperfect and insanely buried things we had found—the one with the trace of a peculiarly hateful odour—must represent the collected sections of the entity which Lake had tried to analyse. On and around that laboratory table were strown other things, and it did not take long for us to guess that those things were the carefully though oddly and inexpertly dissected parts of one man and one dog. I shall spare the feelings of survivors by omitting mention of the man's identity. Lake's anatomical instruments were missing, but there were evidences of their careful cleansing. The gasoline stove was also gone, though around it we found a curious litter of matches. We buried the human parts beside the other ten men, and the canine parts with the other 35 dogs. Concerning the bizarre smudges on the laboratory table, and on the jumble of roughly handled illustrated books scattered near it, we were much too bewildered to speculate.

This formed the worst of the camp horror, but other things were equally perplexing. The disappearance of Gedney, the one dog, the eight uninjured biological specimens, the three sledges, and certain instruments, illustrated technical and scientific books, writing materials, electric torches and batteries, food and fuel, heating apparatus, spare tents, fur suits, and the like, was utterly beyond sane conjecture; as were likewise the spatter-fringed ink-blots on certain pieces of paper, and the evidences of curious alien fumbling and experimentation around the planes and all other mechanical devices both at the camp and at the boring. The dogs seemed to abhor this oddly disordered machinery. Then, too, there was the upsetting of the larder, the disappearance of certain staples, and the jarringly comical heap of tin cans pried open in the most unlikely ways and at the most unlikely places. The profusion of scattered matches, intact, broken, or spent, formed another minor enigma; as did the two or three tent-cloths and fur suits which we found lying about with peculiar and unorthodox slashings conceivably due to clumsy efforts at unimaginable adaptations. The maltreatment of the human and canine bodies, and the crazy burial of the damaged Archaean specimens, were all of a piece with this apparent disintegrative madness. In view of just such an eventuality as the present one, we carefully photographed all the main evidences of insane disorder at the camp; and shall use the prints to buttress our pleas against the departure of the proposed Starkweather-Moore Expedition.

Our first act after finding the bodies in the shelter was to photograph and open the row of insane graves with the five-pointed snow mounds. We could not help noticing the resemblance of these monstrous mounds, with their clusters of grouped dots, to poor Lake's descriptions of the strange greenish soapstones; and when we came on some of the soapstones themselves in the great mineral pile we found the likeness very close indeed. The whole general formation, it must be made clear, seemed abominably suggestive of the starfish-head of the Archaean entities; and we agreed that the suggestion must have worked potently upon the sensitised minds of Lake's overwrought party. Our own first sight of the actual buried entities formed a horrible moment, and sent the imaginations of Pabodie and myself back to some of the shocking primal myths we had read and heard. We all agreed that the mere sight and continued presence of the things must have coöperated with the oppressive polar solitude and daemon mountain wind in driving Lake's party mad.

For madness—centring in Gedney as the only possible surviving agent—was the explanation spontaneously adopted by everybody so far as spoken utterance was concerned; though I will not be so naive as to deny that each of us may have harboured wild guesses which sanity forbade him to formulate completely. Sherman, Pabodie, and McTighe made an exhaustive aëroplane cruise over all the surrounding territory in the afternoon, sweeping the horizon with field-glasses in quest of Gedney and of the various missing things; but nothing came to light. The party reported that the titan barrier range extended endlessly to right and left alike, without any diminution in height or essential structure. On some of the peaks, though, the regular cube and rampart formations were bolder and plainer; having doubly fantastic similitudes to Roerich-painted Asian hill ruins. The distribution of cryptical cave-mouths on the black snow-denuded summits seemed roughly even as far as the range could be traced.

In spite of all the prevailing horrors we were left with enough sheer scientific zeal and adventurousness to wonder about the unknown realm beyond those mysterious mountains. As our guarded messages stated, we rested at midnight after our day of terror and bafflement; but not without a tentative plan for one or more range-crossing altitude flights in a lightened plane with aërial camera and geologist's outfit, beginning the following morning. It was decided that Danforth and I try it first, and we awaked at 7 AM intending an early trip; though heavy winds—mentioned in our brief bulletin to the outside world—delayed our start till nearly nine o'clock.

I have already repeated the non-committal story we told the men at camp—and relayed outside—after our return sixteen hours later. It is now my terrible duty to amplify this account by filling in the merciful blanks with hints of what we really saw in the hidden trans-montane world—hints of the revelations which have finally driven Danforth to a nervous collapse. I wish he would add a really frank word about the thing which he thinks he alone saw—even though it was probably a nervous delusion—and which was perhaps the last straw that put him where he is; but he is firm against that. All I can do is to repeat his later disjointed whispers about what set him shrieking as the plane soared back through the wind-tortured mountain pass after that real and tangible shock which I shared. This will form my last word. If the plain signs of surviving elder horrors in what I disclose be not enough to keep others from meddling with the inner antarctic—or at least from prying too deeply beneath the surface of that ultimate waste of forbidden secrets and unhuman, aeon-cursed desolation—the responsibility for unnamable and perhaps immensurable evils will not be mine.

Danforth and I, studying the notes made by Pabodie in his afternoon flight and checking up with a sextant, had calculated that the lowest available pass in the range lay somewhat to the right of us, within sight of camp, and about 23,000 or 24,000 feet above sea-level. For this point, then, we first headed in the lightened plane as we embarked on our flight of discovery. The camp itself, on foothills which sprang from a high continental plateau, was some 12,000 feet in altitude; hence the actual height increase necessary was not so vast as it might seem. Nevertheless we were acutely conscious of the rarefied air and intense cold as we rose; for on account of visibility conditions we had to leave the cabin windows open. We were dressed, of course, in our heaviest furs.

As we drew near the forbidding peaks, dark and sinister above the line of crevasse-riven snow and interstitial glaciers, we noticed more and more the curiously regular formations clinging to the slopes; and thought again of the strange Asian paintings of Nicholas Roerich. The ancient and wind-weathered rock strata fully verified all of Lake's bulletins, and proved that these hoary pinnacles had been towering up in exactly the same way since a surprisingly early time in earth's history—perhaps over fifty million years. How much higher they had once been, it was futile to guess; but everything about this strange region pointed to obscure atmospheric influences unfavourable to change, and calculated to retard the usual climatic processes of rock disintegration.

But it was the mountainside tangle of regular cubes, ramparts, and cave-mouths which fascinated and disturbed us most. I studied them with a field-glass and took aërial photographs whilst Danforth drove; and at times relieved him at the controls—though my aviation knowledge was purely an amateur's—in order to let him use the binoculars. We could easily see that much of the material of the things was a lightish Archaean quartzite, unlike any formation visible over broad areas of the general surface; and that their regularity was extreme and uncanny to an extent which poor Lake had scarcely hinted.

As he had said, their edges were crumbled and rounded from untold aeons of savage weathering; but their preternatural solidity and tough material had saved them from obliteration. Many parts, especially those closest to the slopes, seemed identical in substance with the surrounding rock surface. The whole arrangement looked like the ruins of Machu Picchu in the Andes, or the primal foundation-walls of Kish as dug up by the Oxford–Field Museum Expedition in 1929; and both Danforth and I obtained that occasional impression of *separate Cyclopean blocks* which Lake had attributed to his flight-companion Carroll. How to account for such things in this place was frankly beyond me, and I felt queerly humbled as a geologist. Igneous formations often have strange regularities—like the famous Giants' Causeway in Ireland—but this stupendous range, despite Lake's original suspicion of smoking cones, was above all else non-volcanic in evident structure.

The curious cave-mouths, near which the odd formations seemed most abundant, presented another albeit a lesser puzzle because of their regularity of outline. They were, as Lake's bulletin had said, often approximately square or semicircular; as if the natural orifices had been shaped to greater symmetry by some magic hand. Their numerousness and wide distribution were remarkable, and suggested that the whole region was honeycombed with tunnels dissolved out of limestone strata. Such glimpses as we secured did not extend far within the caverns, but we saw that they were apparently clear of stalactites and stalagmites. Outside, those parts of the mountain slopes adjoining the apertures seemed invariably smooth and regular; and Danforth thought that the slight cracks and pittings of the weathering tended toward unusual patterns. Filled as he was with the horrors and strangenesses discovered at the camp, he hinted that the pittings vaguely resembled those baffling groups of dots sprinkled over the primeval greenish soapstones, so hideously duplicated on the madly conceived snow mounds above those six buried monstrosities.

We had risen gradually in flying over the higher foothills and along toward the relatively low pass we had selected. As we advanced we occasionally looked down at the snow and ice of the land route, wondering whether we could have attempted the trip with the simpler equipment of earlier days. Somewhat to our surprise we saw that the terrain was far from difficult as such things go; and that despite the crevasses and other bad spots it would not have been likely to deter the sledges of a Scott, a Shackleton, or an Amundsen. Some of the glaciers appeared to lead up to wind-bared passes with unusual continuity, and upon reaching our chosen pass we found that its case formed no exception.

Our sensations of tense expectancy as we prepared to round the crest and peer out over an untrodden world can hardly be described on paper; even though we had no cause to think the regions beyond the range essentially different from those already seen and traversed. The tough of evil mystery in these barrier mountains, and in the beckoning sea of opalescent sky glimpsed betwixt their summits, was a highly subtle and attenuated matter not to be explained in literal words. Rather was it an affair of vague psychological symbolism and aesthetic association—a thing mixed up with exotic poetry and paintings, and with archaic myths lurking in shunned and forbidden volumes. Even the wind's burden held a peculiar strain of conscious malignity; and for a second it seemed that the composite sound included a bizarre musical whistling or piping over a wide range as the blast swept in and out of the omnipresent and resonant cave-mouths. There was a cloudy note of reminiscent repulsion in this sound, as complex and unplaceable as any of the other dark impressions.

We were now, after a slow ascent, at a height of 23,570 feet according to the aneroid; and had left the region of clinging snow definitely below us. Up here were only dark, bare rock slopes and the start of rough-ribbed glaciers—but with those provocative cubes, ramparts, and echoing cave-mouths to add a portent of the unnatural, the fantastic, and the dream-like. Looking along the line of high peaks, I thought I could see the one mentioned by poor Lake, with a rampart exactly on top. It seemed to be half-lost in a queer antarctic haze; such a haze, perhaps, as had been responsible for Lake's early notion of volcanism. The pass loomed directly before us, smooth and windswept between its jagged and malignly frowning pylons. Beyond it was a sky fretted with swirling vapours and lighted by the low polar sun—the sky of that mysterious farther realm upon which we felt no human eye had ever gazed.

A few more feet of altitude and we would behold that realm. Danforth and I, unable to speak except in shouts amidst the howling, piping wind that raced through the pass and added to the noise of the unmuffled engines, exchanged eloquent glances. And then, having gained those last few feet, we did indeed stare across the momentous divide and over the unsampled secrets of an elder and utterly alien earth.

V

I think that both of us simultaneously cried out in mixed awe, wonder, terror, and disbelief in our own senses as we finally cleared the pass and saw what lay beyond. Of course we must have had some natural theory in the back of our heads to steady our faculties for the moment. Probably we thought of such things as the grotesquely weathered stones of the Garden of the Gods in Colorado, or the fantastically symmetrical wind-carved rocks of the Arizona desert. Perhaps we even half thought the sight a mirage like that we had seen the morning before on first approaching those mountains of madness. We must have had some such normal notions to fall back upon as our eyes swept that limitless, tempest-scarred plateau and grasped the almost endless labyrinth of colossal, regular, and geometrically eurhythmic stone masses which reared their crumbled and pitted crests above a glacial sheet not more than forty or fifty feet deep at its thickest, and in places obviously thinner.

The effect of the monstrous sight was indescribable, for some fiendish violation of known natural law seemed certain at the outset. Here, on a hellishly ancient table-land fully 20,000 feet high, and in a climate deadly to habitation since a pre-human age not less than 500,000 years ago, there stretched nearly to the vision's limit a tangle of orderly stone which only the desperation of mental self-defence could possibly attribute to any but a conscious and artificial cause. We had previously dismissed, so far as serious thought was concerned, any theory that the cubes and ramparts of the mountainsides were other than natural in origin. How could they be otherwise, when man himself could scarcely have been differentiated from the great apes at the time when this region succumbed to the present unbroken reign of glacial death?

Yet now the sway of reason seemed irrefutably shaken, for this Cyclopean maze of squared, curved, and angled blocks had features which cut off all comfortable refuge. It was, very clearly, the blasphemous city of the mirage in stark, objective, and ineluctable reality. That damnable portent had had a material basis after all—there had been some horizontal stratum of ice-dust in the upper air, and this shocking stone survival had projected its image across the mountains according to the simple laws of reflection. Of course the phantom had been twisted and exaggerated, and had contained things which the real source did not contain; yet now, as we saw that real source, we thought it even more hideous and menacing than its distant image.

Only the incredible, unhuman massiveness of these vast stone towers and ramparts had saved the frightful thing from utter annihilation in the hundreds of thousands—perhaps millions—of years it had brooded there amidst the blasts of a bleak upland. "Corona Mundi . . . Roof of the World . . ." All sorts of fantastic phrases sprang to our lips as we looked dizzily down at the unbelievable spectacle. I thought again of the eldritch primal myths that had so persistently haunted me since my first sight of this dead antarctic world—of the daemoniac plateau of Leng, of the Mi-Go, or Abominable Snow-Men of the Himalayas, of the Pnakotic Manuscripts with their pre-human implications, of the Cthulhu cult, of the *Necronomicon*, and of the Hyperborean legends of formless Tsathoggua and the worse than formless star-spawn associated with that semi-entity.

For boundless miles in every direction the thing stretched off with very little thinning; indeed, as our eyes followed it to the right and left along the base of the low, gradual foothills which separated it from the actual mountain rim, we decided that we could see no thinning at all except for an interruption at the left of the pass through which we had come. We had merely struck, at random, a limited part of something of incalculable extent. The foothills were more sparsely sprinkled with grotesque stone structures, linking the terrible city to the already familiar cubes and ramparts which evidently formed its mountain outposts. These latter, as well as the queer cave-mouths, were as thick on the inner as on the outer sides of the mountains.

The nameless stone labyrinth consisted, for the most part, of walls from 10 to 150 feet in ice-clear height, and of a thickness varying from five to ten feet. It was composed mostly of prodigious blocks of dark primordial slate, schist, and sandstone—blocks in many cases as large as $4 \times 6 \times 8$ feet—though in several places it seemed to be carved out of a solid, uneven bed-rock of pre-Cambrian slate. The buildings were far from equal in size; there being innumerable honeycomb-arrangements of enormous extent as well as smaller separate structures. The general shape of these things tended to be conical, pyramidal, or terraced; though there were many perfect cylinders, perfect cubes, clusters of cubes, and other rectangular forms, and a peculiar sprinkling of angled edifices whose five-pointed ground plan roughly suggested modern fortifications. The builders had made constant and expert use of the principle of the arch, and domes had probably existed in the city's heyday.

The whole tangle was monstrously weathered, and the glacial surface from which the towers projected was strown with fallen blocks and immemorial debris. Where the glaciation was transparent we could see the lower parts of the gigantic piles, and noticed the ice-preserved stone bridges which connected the different towers at varying distances above the ground. On the exposed walls we could detect the scarred places where other and higher bridges of the same sort had existed. Closer inspection revealed countless largish windows; some of which were closed with shutters of a petrified material originally wood, though most gaped open in a sinister and menacing fashion. Many of the ruins, of course, were roofless, and with uneven though wind-rounded upper edges; whilst others, of a more sharply conical or pyramidal model or else protected by higher surrounding structures, preserved intact outlines despite the omnipresent crumbling and pitting. With the field-glass we could barely make out what seemed to be sculptural decorations in horizontal bands—decorations including those curious groups of dots whose presence on the ancient soapstones now assumed a vastly larger significance.

In many places the buildings were totally ruined and the ice-sheet deeply riven from various geologic causes. In other places the stonework was worn down to the very level of the glaciation. One broad swath, extending from the plateau's interior to a cleft in the foothills about a mile to the left of the pass we had traversed, was wholly free from buildings; and probably represented, we concluded, the course of some great river which in Tertiary times—millions of years ago—had poured through the city and into some prodigious subterranean abyss of the great barrier range. Certainly, this was above all a region of caves, gulfs, and underground secrets beyond human penetration.

Looking back to our sensations, and recalling our dazedness at viewing this monstrous survival from aeons we had thought pre-human, I can only wonder that we preserved the semblance of equilibrium which we did. Of course we knew that something— chronology, scientific theory, or our own consciousness—was woefully awry; yet we kept enough poise to guide the plane, observe many things quite minutely, and take a careful series of photographs which may yet serve both us and the world in good stead. In my case, ingrained scientific habit may have helped; for above all my bewilderment and sense of menace there burned a dominant curiosity to fathom more of this age-old secret—to know what sort of beings had built and lived in this incalculably gigantic place, and what relation to the general world of its time or of other times so unique a concentration of life could have had.

For this place could be no ordinary city. It must have formed the primary nucleus and centre of some archaic and unbelievable chapter of earth's history whose outward ramifications, recalled only dimly in the most obscure and distorted myths, had vanished utterly amidst the chaos of terrene convulsions long before any human race we know had shambled out of apedom. Here sprawled a palaeogean megalopolis compared with which the fabled Atlantis and Lemuria, Commoriom and Uzuldaroum, and Olathoë in the land of Lomar are recent things of today—not even of yesterday; a megalopolis ranking with such whispered pre-human blasphemies as Valusia, R'lyeh, Ib in the land of Mnar, and the Nameless City of Arabia Deserta. As we flew above that tangle of stark titan towers my imagination sometimes escaped all bounds and roved aimlessly in realms of fantastic associations—even weaving links betwixt this lost world and some of my own wildest dreams concerning the mad horror at the camp.

The plane's fuel-tank, in the interest of greater lightness, had been only partly filled; hence we now had to exert caution in our explorations. Even so, however, we covered an enormous extent of ground—or rather, air—after swooping down to a level where the wind became virtually negligible. There seemed to be no limit to the mountain-range, or to the length of the frightful stone city which bordered its inner foothills. Fifty miles of flight in each direction shewed no major change in the labyrinth of rock and masonry that clawed up corpse-like through the eternal ice. There were, though, some highly absorbing diversifications; such as the carvings on the canyon where that broad river had once pierced the foothills and approached its sinking-place in the great range. The headlands at the stream's entrance had been boldly carved into Cyclopean pylons; and something about the ridgy, barrel-shaped designs stirred up oddly vague, hateful, and confusing semi-remembrances in both Danforth and me.

We also came upon several star-shaped open spaces, evidently public squares; and noted various undulations in the terrain. Where a sharp hill rose, it was generally hollowed out into some sort of rambling stone edifice; but there were at least two exceptions. Of these latter, one was too badly weathered to disclose what had been on the jutting eminence, while the other still bore a fantastic conical monument carved out of the solid rock and roughly resembling such things as the well-known Snake Tomb in the ancient valley of Petra.

Flying inland from the mountains, we discovered that the city was not of infinite width, even though its length along the foothills seemed endless. After about thirty miles the grotesque stone buildings began to thin out, and in ten more miles we came to an unbroken waste virtually without signs of sentient artifice. The course of the river beyond the city seemed marked by a broad depressed line; while the land assumed a somewhat greater ruggedness, seeming to slope slightly upward as it receded in the mist-hazed west.

So far we had made no landing, yet to leave the plateau without an attempt at entering some of the monstrous structures would have been inconceivable. Accordingly we decided to find a smooth place on the foothills near our navigable pass, there grounding the plane and preparing to do some exploration on foot. Though these gradual slopes were partly covered with a scattering of ruins, low flying soon disclosed an ample number of possible landing-places. Selecting that nearest to the pass, since our next flight would be across the great range and back to camp, we succeeded about 12:30 PM in coming down on a smooth, hard snowfield wholly devoid of obstacles and well adapted to a swift and favourable takeoff later on.

It did not seem necessary to protect the plane with a snow banking for so brief a time and in so comfortable an absence of high winds at this level; hence we merely saw that the landing skis were safely lodged, and that the vital parts of the mechanism were guarded against the cold. For our foot journey we discarded the heaviest of our flying furs, and took with us a small outfit consisting of pocket compass, hand camera, light provisions, voluminous notebooks and paper, geologist's hammer and chisel, specimen-bags, coil of climbing rope, and powerful electric torches with extra batteries; this equipment having been carried in the plane on the chance that we might be able to effect a landing, take ground pictures, make drawings and topographical sketches, and obtain rock specimens from some bare slope, outcropping, or mountain cave. Fortunately we had a supply of extra paper to tear up, place in a spare specimen-bag, and use on the ancient principle of hare-and-hounds for marking our course in any interior mazes we might be able to penetrate. This had been brought in case we found some cave system with air quiet enough to allow such a rapid and easy method in place of the usual rock-chipping method of trail-blazing.

Walking cautiously downhill over the crusted snow toward the stupendous stone labyrinth that loomed against the opalescent west, we felt almost as keen a sense of imminent marvels as we had felt on approaching the unfathomed mountain pass four hours previously. True, we had become visually familiar with the incredible secret concealed by the barrier peaks; yet the prospect of actually entering primordial walls reared by conscious beings perhaps millions of years ago—before any known race of men could have existed—was none the less awesome and potentially terrible in its implications of cosmic abnormality. Though the thinness of the air at this prodigious altitude made exertion somewhat more difficult than usual; both Danforth and I found ourselves bearing up very well, and felt equal to almost any task which might fall to our lot. It took only a few steps to bring us to a shapeless ruin worn level with the snow, while ten or fifteen rods farther on there was a huge roofless rampart still complete in its gigantic five-pointed outline and rising to an irregular height of ten or eleven feet. For this latter we headed; and when at last we were able actually to touch its weathered Cyclopean blocks, we felt that we had established an unprecedented and almost blasphemous link with forgotten aeons normally closed to our species.

This rampart, shaped like a star and perhaps 300 feet from point to point, was built of Jurassic sandstone blocks of irregular size, averaging 6 × 8 feet in surface. There was a row of arched loopholes or windows about four feet wide and five feet high; spaced quite symmetrically along the points of the star and at its inner angles, and with the bottoms about four feet from the glaciated surface. Looking through these, we could see that the masonry was fully five feet thick, that there were no partitions remaining within, and that there were traces of banded carvings or bas-reliefs on the interior walls; facts we had indeed guessed before, when flying low over this rampart and others like it. Though lower parts must have originally existed, all traces of such things were now wholly obscured by the deep layer of ice and snow at this point.

We crawled through one of the windows and vainly tried to decipher the nearly effaced mural designs, but did not attempt to disturb the glaciated floor. Our orientation flights had indicated that many buildings in the city proper were less ice-choked, and that we might perhaps find wholly clear interiors leading down to the true ground level if we entered those structures still roofed at the top. Before we left the rampart we photographed it carefully, and studied its mortarless Cyclopean masonry with complete bewilderment. We wished that Pabodie were present, for his engineering knowledge might have helped us guess how such titanic blocks could have been handled in that unbelievably remote age when the city and its outskirts were built up.

The half-mile walk downhill to the actual city, with the upper wind shrieking vainly and savagely through the skyward peaks in the background, was something whose smallest details will always remain engraved on my mind. Only in fantastic nightmares could any human beings but Danforth and me conceive such optical effects. Between us and the churning vapours of the west lay that monstrous tangle of dark stone towers; its outré and incredible forms impressing us afresh at every new angle of vision. It was a mirage in solid stone, and were it not for the photographs I would still doubt that such a thing could be. The general type of masonry was identical with that of the rampart we had examined; but the extravagant shapes which this masonry took in its urban manifestations were past all description.

Even the pictures illustrate only one or two phases of its infinite bizarrerie, endless variety, preternatural massiveness, and utterly alien exoticism. There were geometrical forms for which an Euclid could scarcely find a name—cones of all degrees of irregularity and truncation; terraces of every sort of provocative disproportion; shafts with odd bulbous enlargements; broken columns in curious groups; and five-pointed or five-ridged arrangements of mad grotesqueness. As we drew nearer we could see beneath certain transparent parts of the ice-sheet, and detect some of the tubular stone bridges that connected the crazily sprinkled structures at various heights. Of orderly streets there seemed to be none, the only broad open swath being a mile to the left, where the ancient river had doubtless flowed through the town into the mountains.

Our field-glasses shewed the external horizontal bands of nearly effaced sculptures and dot-groups to be very prevalent, and we could half imagine what the city must once have looked like—even though most of the roofs and tower-tops had necessarily perished. As a whole, it had been a complex tangle of twisted lanes and alleys; all of them deep canyons, and some little better than tunnels because of the overhanging masonry or overarching bridges. Now, outspread below us, it loomed like a dream-phantasy against a westward mist through whose northern end the low, reddish antarctic sun of early afternoon was struggling to shine; and when for a moment that sun encountered a denser obstruction and plunged the scene into temporary shadow, the effect was subtly menacing in a way I can never hope to depict. Even the faint howling and piping of the unfelt wind in the great mountain passes behind us took on a wilder note of purposeful malignity. The last stage of our descent to the town was unusually steep and abrupt, and a rock outcropping at the edge where the grade changed led us to think that an artificial terrace had once existed there. Under the glaciation, we believed, there must be a flight of steps or its equivalent.

When at last we plunged into the labyrinthine town itself, clambering over fallen masonry and shrinking from the oppressive nearness and dwarfing height of omnipresent crumbling and pitted walls, our sensations again became such that I marvel at the amount of self-control we retained. Danforth was frankly jumpy, and began making some offensively irrelevant speculations about the horror at the camp—which I resented all the more because I could not help sharing certain conclusions forced upon us by many features of this morbid survival from nightmare antiquity. The speculations worked on his imagination, too; for in one place—where a debris-littered alley turned a sharp corner—he insisted that he saw faint traces of ground markings which he did not like; whilst elsewhere he stopped to listen to a subtle imaginary sound from some undefined point—a muffled musical piping, he said, not unlike that of the wind in the mountain caves yet somehow disturbingly different. The ceaseless *five-pointedness* of the surrounding architecture and of the few distinguishable mural arabesques had a dimly sinister suggestiveness we could not escape; and gave us a touch of terrible subconscious certainty concerning the primal entities which had reared and dwelt in this unhallowed place.

Nevertheless our scientific and adventurous souls were not wholly dead; and we mechanically carried out our programme of chipping specimens from all the different rock types represented in the masonry. We wished a rather full set in order to draw better conclusions regarding the age of the place. Nothing in the great outer walls seemed to date from later than the Jurassic and Comanchian periods, nor was any piece of stone in the entire place of a greater recency than the Pliocene age. In stark certainty, we were wandering amidst a death which had reigned at least 500,000 years, and in all probability even longer.

As we proceeded through this maze of stone-shadowed twilight we stopped at all available apertures to study interiors and investigate entrance possibilities. Some were above our reach, whilst others led only into ice-choked ruins as unroofed and barren as the rampart on the hill. One, though spacious and inviting, opened on a seemingly bottomless abyss without visible means of descent. Now and then we had a chance to study the petrified wood of a surviving shutter, and were impressed by the fabulous antiquity implied in the still discernible grain. These things had come from Mesozoic gymnosperms and conifers—especially Cretaceous cycads—and from fan-palms and early angiosperms of plainly Tertiary date. Nothing definitely later than the Pliocene could be discovered. In the placing of these shutters—whose edges shewed the former presence of queer and long-vanished hinges—usage seemed to be varied; some being on the outer and some on the inner side of the deep embrasures. They seemed to have become wedged in place, thus surviving the rusting of their former and probably metallic fixtures and fastenings.

After a time we came across a row of windows—in the bulges of a colossal five-ridged cone of undamaged apex—which led into a vast, well-preserved room with stone flooring; but these were too high in the room to permit of descent without a rope. We had a rope with us, but did not wish to bother with this twenty-foot drop unless obliged to—especially in this thin plateau air where great demands were made upon the heart action. This enormous room was probably a hall or concourse of some sort, and our electric torches shewed bold, distinct, and potentially startling sculptures arranged round the walls in broad, horizontal bands separated by equally broad strips of conventional arabesques. We took careful note of this spot, planning to enter here unless a more easily gained interior were encountered.

Finally, though, we did encounter exactly the opening we wished; an archway about six feet wide and ten feet high, marking the former end of an aërial bridge which had spanned an alley about five feet above the present level of glaciation. These archways, of course, were flush with upper-story floors; and in this case one of the floors still existed. The building thus accessible was a series of rectangular terraces on our left facing westward. That across the alley, where the other archway yawned, was a decrepit cylinder with no windows and with a curious bulge about ten feet above the aperture. It was totally dark inside, and the archway seemed to open on a well of illimitable emptiness.

Heaped debris made the entrance to the vast left-hand building doubly easy, yet for a moment we hesitated before taking advantage of the long-wished chance. For though we had penetrated into this tangle of archaic mystery, it required fresh resolution to carry us actually inside a complete and surviving building of a fabulous elder world whose nature was becoming more and more hideously plain to us. In the end, however, we made the plunge; and scrambled up over the rubble into the gaping embrasure. The floor beyond was of great slate slabs, and seemed to form the outlet of a long, high corridor with sculptured walls.

Observing the many inner archways which led off from it, and realising the probable complexity of the nest of apartments within, we decided that we must begin our system of hare-and-hound trail-blazing. Hitherto our compasses, together with frequent glimpses of the vast mountain-range between the towers in our rear, had been enough to prevent our losing our way; but from now on, the artificial substitute would be necessary. Accordingly we reduced our extra paper to shreds of suitable size, placed these in a bag to be carried by Danforth, and prepared to use them as economically as safety would allow. This method would probably gain us immunity from straying, since there did not appear to be any strong air-currents inside the primordial masonry. If such should develop, or if our paper supply should give out, we could of course fall back on the more secure though more tedious and retarding method of rock-chipping.

Just how extensive a territory we had opened up, it was impossible to guess without a trial. The close and frequent connexion of the different buildings made it likely that we might cross from one to another on bridges underneath the ice except where impeded by local collapses and geologic rifts, for very little glaciation seemed to have entered the massive constructions. Almost all the areas of transparent ice had revealed the submerged windows as tightly shuttered, as if the town had been left in that uniform state until the glacial sheet came to crystallise the lower part for all succeeding time. Indeed, one gained a curious impression that this place had been deliberately closed and deserted in some dim, bygone aeon, rather than overwhelmed by any sudden calamity or even gradual decay. Had the coming of the ice been foreseen, and had a nameless population left en masse to seek a less doomed abode? The precise physiographic conditions attending the formation of the ice-sheet at this point would have to wait for later solution. It had not, very plainly, been a grinding drive. Perhaps the pressure of accumulated snows had been responsible; and perhaps some flood from the river, or from the bursting of some ancient glacial dam in the great range, had helped to create the special state now observable. Imagination could conceive almost anything in connexion with this place.

VI

It would be cumbrous to give a detailed, consecutive account of our wanderings inside that cavernous, aeon-dead honeycomb of primal masonry; that monstrous lair of elder secrets which now echoed for the first time, after uncounted epochs, to the tread of human feet. This is especially true because so much of the horrible drama and revelation came from a mere study of the omnipresent mural carvings. Our flashlight photographs of those carvings will do much toward proving the truth of what we are now disclosing, and it is lamentable that we had not a larger film supply with us. As it was, we made crude notebook sketches of certain salient features after all our films were used up.

The building which we had entered was one of great size and elaborateness, and gave us an impressive notion of the architecture of that nameless geologic past. The inner partitions were less massive than the outer walls, but on the lower levels were excellently preserved. Labyrinthine complexity, involving curiously irregular differences in floor levels, characterised the entire arrangement; and we should certainly have been lost at the very outset but for the trail of torn paper left behind us. We decided to explore the more decrepit upper parts first of all, hence climbed aloft in the maze for a distance of some 100 feet, to where the topmost tier of chambers yawned snowily and ruinously open to the polar sky. Ascent was effected over the steep, transversely ribbed stone ramps or inclined planes which everywhere served in lieu of stairs. The rooms we encountered were of all imaginable shapes and proportions, ranging from five-pointed stars to triangles and perfect cubes. It might be safe to say that their general average was about 30 × 30 feet in floor area, and 20 feet in height; though many larger apartments existed. After thoroughly examining the upper regions and the glacial level we descended story by story into the submerged part, where indeed we soon saw we were in a continues maze of connected chambers and passages probably leading over unlimited areas outside this particular building. The Cyclopen massiveness and giganticism of everything about us became curiously oppressive; and there was something vaguely but deeply unhuman in all the contours, dimensions, proportions, decorations, and constructional nuances of the blasphemously archive stonework. We soon realised from what the carvings revealed that this monstrous city was many million years old.

We cannot yet explain the engineering principles used in the anomalous balancing and adjustment of the vast rock masses though the function of the arch was clearly much relied on. The rooms we visited were wholly bare of all portable contents, a circumstance which sustained our belief in the city's deliberate desertion. The prime decorative feature was the almost universal system of mural sculpture; which tended to run in continuous horizontal bands three feet wide and arranged from floor to ceiling in alternation with bands of equal width given over to geometrical arabesques. There were exceptions to this rule of arrangement, but its preponderance was overwhelming. Often, however, a series of smooth cartouches containing oddly patterned groups of dots would be sunk along one of the arabesque bands.

The technique, we soon saw, was mature, accomplished, and aesthetically evolved to the highest degree of civilised mastery though utterly alien in every detail to any known art tradition of the human race. In delicacy of execution no sculpture I have ever seen could approach it. The minutest details of elaborate vegetation, or of animal life, were rendered with astonishing vividness despite the bold scale of the carvings; whilst the conventional designs were marvels of skilful intricacy. The arabesques displayed a profound use of mathematical principles, and were made up of obscurely symmetrical curves and angles based on the quantity of five. The pictorial bands followed a highly formalised tradition, and involved a peculiar treatment of perspective; but had an artistic force that moved us profoundly notwithstanding the intervening gulf of vast geologic periods. Their method of design hinged on a singular juxtaposition of the cross-section with the two-dimensional silhouette, and embodied an analytical psychology beyond that of any known race of antiquity. It is useless to try to compare this art with any represented in our museums. Those who see our photographs will probably find its closest analogue in certain grotesque conceptions of the most daring futurists.

The arabesque tracery consisted altogether of depressed lines whose depth on unweathered walls varied from one to two inches. When cartouches with dot-groups appeared—evidently as inscriptions in some unknown and primordial language and alphabet—the depression of the smooth surface was perhaps an inch and a half, and of the dots perhaps a half-inch more. The pictorial bands were in counter-sunk low relief, their background being depressed about two inches from the original wall surface. In some specimens marks of former colouration could be detected, though for the most part untold aeons had disintegrated and banished any pigments which may have been applied. The more one studied the marvellous technique the more one admired the things. Beneath their strict conventionalisation one could grasp the minute and accurate observation and graphic skill of the artists; and indeed, the very conventions themselves served to symbolise and accentuate the real essence of vital differentiation of every object delineated. We felt, too, that besides these recognisable excellences there were others lurking beyond the reach of our perceptions. Certain touches here and there gave vague hints of latent symbols and stimuli which another mental and emotional background, and a fuller or different sensory equipment, might have made of profound and poignant significance to us.

The subject-matter of the sculptures obviously came from the life of the vanished epoch of their creation, and contained a large proportion of evident history. It is this abnormal historic-mindedness of the primal race—a chance circumstance operating, through coincidence, miraculously in our favour—which made the carvings so awesomely informative to us, and which caused us to place their photography and transcription above all other considerations. In certain rooms the dominant arrangement was varied by the presence of maps, astronomical charts, and other scientific designs on an enlarged scale—these things giving a naive and terrible corroboration to what we gathered from the pictorial friezes and dadoes. In hinting at what the whole revealed, I can only hope that my account will not arouse a curiosity greater than sane caution on the part of those who believe me at all. It would be tragic if any were to be allured to that realm of death and horror by the very warning meant to discourage them.

Interrupting these sculptured walls were high windows and massive twelve-foot doorways; both now and then retaining the petrified wooden planks—elaborately carved and polished—of the actual shutters and doors. All metal fixtures had long ago vanished, but some of the doors remained in place and had to be forced aside as we progressed from room to room. Window-frames with odd transparent panes—mostly elliptical—survived here and there, though in no considerable quantity. There were also frequent niches of great magnitude, generally empty, but once in a while containing some bizarre object carved from green soapstone which was either broken or perhaps held too inferior to warrant removal. Other apertures were undoubtedly connected with bygone mechanical facilities—heating, lighting, and the like—of a sort suggested in many of the carvings. Ceilings tended to be plain, but had sometimes been inlaid with green soapstone or other tiles, mostly fallen now. Floors were also paved with such tiles, though plain stonework predominated.

As I have said, all furniture and other moveables were absent; but the sculptures gave a clear idea of the strange devices which had once filled these tomb-like, echoing rooms. Above the glacial sheet the floors were generally thick with detritus, litter, and debris; but farther down this condition decreased. In some of the lower chambers and corridors there was little more than gritty dust or ancient incrustations, while occasional areas had an uncanny air of newly swept immaculateness. Of course, where rifts or collapses had occurred, the lower levels were as littered as the upper ones. A central court—as in other structures we had seen from the air—saved the inner regions from total darkness; so that we seldom had to use our electric torches in the upper rooms except when studying sculptured details. Below the ice-cap, however, the twilight deepened; and in many parts of the tangled ground level there was an approach to absolute blackness.

To form even a rudimentary idea of our thoughts and feelings as we penetrated this aeon-silent maze of unhuman masonry one must correlate a hopelessly bewildering chaos of fugitive moods, memories, and impressions. The sheer appalling antiquity and lethal desolation of the place were enough to overwhelm almost any sensitive person, but added to these elements were the recent unexplained horror at the camp, and the revelations all too soon effected by the terrible mural sculptures around us. The moment we came upon a perfect section of carving, where no ambiguity of interpretation could exist, it took only a brief study to give us the hideous truth—a truth which it would be naive to claim Danforth and I had not independently suspected before, though we had carefully refrained from even hinting it to each other. There could now be no further merciful doubt about the nature of the beings which had built and inhabited this monstrous dead city millions of years ago, when man's ancestors were primitive archaic mammals, and vast dinosaurs roamed the tropical steppes of Europe and Asia.

We had previously clung to a desperate alternative and insisted—each to himself—that the omnipresence of the five-pointed motif meant only some cultural or religious exaltation of the Archaean natural object which had so patently embodied the quality of five-pointedness; as the decorative motifs of Minoan Crete exalted the sacred bull, those of Egypt the scarabaeus, those of Rome the wolf and the eagle, and those of various savage tribes some chosen totem-animal. But this lone refuge was now stripped from us, and we were forced to face definitely the reason-shaking realisation which the reader of these pages has doubtless long ago anticipated. I can scarcely bear to write it down in black and white even now, but perhaps that will not be necessary.

The things once rearing and dwelling in this frightful masonry in the age of dinosaurs were not indeed dinosaurs, but far worse. Mere dinosaurs were new and almost brainless objects—but the builders of the city were wise and old, and had left certain traces in rocks even then laid down well-nigh a thousand million years . . . rocks laid down before the true life of earth had advanced beyond plastic groups of cells . . . rocks laid down before the true life of earth had existed at all. They were the makers and enslavers of that life, and above all doubt the originals of the fiendish elder myths which things like the Pnakotic Manuscripts and the *Necronomicon* affrightedly hint about. They were the Great Old Ones that had filtered down from the stars when earth was young—the beings whose substance an alien evolution had shaped, and whose powers were such as this planet had never bred. And to think that only the day before Danforth and I had actually looked upon fragments of their millennially fossilised substance . . . and that poor Lake and his party had seen their complete outlines. . . .

It is of course impossible for me to relate in proper order the stages by which we picked up what we know of that monstrous chapter of pre-human life. After the first shock of the certain revelation we had to pause a while to recuperate, and it was fully three o'clock before we got started on our actual tour of systematic research. The sculptures in the building we entered were of relatively late date—perhaps two million years ago—as checked up by geological, biological, and astronomical features; and embodied an art which would be called decadent in comparison with that of specimens we found in older buildings after crossing bridges under the glacial sheet. One edifice hewn from the solid rock seemed to go back forty or possibly even fifty million years—to the lower Eocene or upper Cretaceous—and contained bas-reliefs of an artistry surpassing anything else, with one tremendous exception, that we encountered. That was, we have since agreed, the oldest domestic structure we traversed.

Were it not for the support of those snapshots soon to be made public, I would refrain from telling what I found and inferred, lest I be confined as a madman. Of course, the infinitely early parts of the patchwork tale—representing the pre-terrestrial life of the star-headed beings on other planets, in other galaxies, and in other universes—can readily be interpreted as the fantastic mythology of those beings themselves; yet such parts sometimes involved designs and diagrams so uncannily close to the latest findings of mathematics and astrophysics that I scarcely know what to think. Let others judge when they see the photographs I shall publish.

Naturally, no one set of carvings which we encountered told more than a fraction of any connected story; nor did we even begin to come upon the various stages of that story in their proper order. Some of the vast rooms were independent units so far as their designs were concerned, whilst in other cases a continuous chronicle would be carried through a series of rooms and corridors. The best of the maps and diagrams were on the walls of a frightful abyss below even the ancient ground level—a cavern perhaps 200 feet square and sixty feet high, which had almost undoubtedly been an educational centre of some sort. There were many provoking repetitions of the same material in different rooms and buildings; since certain chapters of experience, and certain summaries or phases of racial history, had evidently been favourites with different decorators or dwellers. Sometimes, though, variant versions of the same theme proved useful in settling debatable points and filling in gaps.

I still wonder that we deduced so much in the short time at our disposal. Of course, we even now have only the barest outline; and much of that was obtained later on from a study of the photographs and sketches we made. It may be the effect of this later study—the revived memories and vague impressions acting in conjunction with his general sensitiveness and with that final supposed horror-glimpse whose essence he will not reveal even to me—which has been the immediate source of Danforth's present breakdown. But it had to be; for we could not issue our warning intelligently without the fullest possible information, and the issuance of that warning is a prime necessity. Certain lingering influences in that unknown antarctic world of disordered time and alien natural law make it imperative that further exploration be discouraged.

VII

The full story, so far as deciphered, will shortly appear in an official bulletin of Miskatonic University. Here I shall sketch only the salient high lights in a formless, rambling way. Myth or otherwise, the sculptures told of the coming of those star-headed things to the nascent, lifeless earth out of cosmic space—their coming, and the coming of many other alien entities such as at certain times embark upon spatial pioneering. They seemed able to traverse the interstellar ether on their vast membraneous wings—thus oddly confirming some curious hill folklore long ago told me by an antiquarian colleague. They had lived under the sea a good deal, building fantastic cities and fighting terrific battles with nameless adversaries by means of intricate devices employing unknown principles of energy. Evidently their scientific and mechanical knowledge far surpassed man's today, though they made use of its more widespread and elaborate forms only when obliged to. Some of the sculptures suggested that they had passed through a stage of mechanised life on other planets, but had receded upon finding its effects emotionally unsatisfying. Their preternatural toughness of organisation and simplicity of natural wants made them peculiarly able to live on a high plane without the more specialised fruits of artificial manufacture, and even without garments except for occasional protection against the elements.

It was under the sea, at first for food and later for other purposes, that they first created earth-life—using available substances according to long-known methods. The more elaborate experiments came after the annihilation of various cosmic enemies. They had done the same thing on other planets; having manufactured not only necessary foods, but certain multicellular protoplasmic masses capable of moulding their tissues into all sorts of temporary organs under hypnotic influence and thereby forming ideal slaves to perform the heavy work of the community. These viscous masses were without doubt what Abdul Alhazred whispered about as the "shoggoths" in his frightful *Necronomicon*, though even that mad Arab had not hinted that any existed on earth except in the dreams of those who had chewed a certain alkaloidal herb. When the star-headed Old Ones on this planet had synthesised their simple food forms and bred a good supply of shoggoths, they allowed other cell-groups to develop into other forms of animal and vegetable life for sundry purposes; extirpating any whose presence became troublesome.

With the aid of the shoggoths, whose expansions could be made to lift prodigious weights, the small, low cities under the sea grew to vast and imposing labyrinths of stone not unlike those which later rose on land. Indeed, the highly adaptable Old Ones had lived much on land in other parts of the universe, and probably retained many traditions of land construction. As we studied the architecture of all these sculptured palaeogean cities, including that whose aeon-dead corridors we were even then traversing, we were impressed by a curious coincidence which we have not yet tried to explain, even to ourselves. The tops of the buildings, which in the actual city around us had of course been weathered into shapeless ruins ages ago, were clearly displayed in the bas-reliefs; and shewed vast clusters of needle-like spires, delicate finials on certain cone and pyramid apexes, and tiers of thin, horizontal scalloped discs capping cylindrical shafts. This was exactly what we had seen in that monstrous and portentous mirage, cast by a dead city whence such skyline features had been absent for thousands and tens of thousands of years, which loomed on our ignorant eyes across the unfathomed mountains of madness as we first approached poor Lake's ill-fated camp.

Of the life of the Old Ones, both under the sea and after part of them migrated to land, volumes could be written. Those in shallow water had continued the fullest use of the eyes at the ends of their five main head tentacles, and had practiced the arts of sculpture and of writing in quite the usual way—the writing accomplished with a stylus on waterproof waxen surfaces. Those lower down in the ocean depths, though they used a curious phosphorescent organism to furnish light, pieced out their vision with obscure special senses operating through the prismatic cilia on their heads—senses which rendered all the Old Ones partly independent of light in emergencies. Their forms of sculpture and writing had changed curiously during the descent, embodying certain apparently chemical coating processes—probably to secure phosphorescence—which the bas-reliefs could not make clear to us. The beings moved in the sea partly by swimming—using the lateral crinoid arms—and partly by wriggling with the lower tier of tentacles containing the pseudo-feet. Occasionally they accomplished long swoops with the auxiliary use of two or more sets of their fan-like folding wings. On land they locally used the pseudo-feet, but now and then flew to great heights or over long distances with their wings. The many slender tentacles into which the crinoid arms branched were infinitely delicate, flexible, strong, and accurate in muscular-nervous coördination; ensuring the utmost skill and dexterity in all artistic and other manual operations.

The toughness of the things was almost incredible. Even the terrific pressures of the deepest sea-bottoms appeared powerless to harm them. Very few seemed to die at all except by violence, and their burial-places were very limited. The fact that they covered their vertically inhumed dead with five-pointed inscribed mounds set up thoughts in Danforth and me which made a fresh pause and recuperation necessary after the sculptures revealed it. The beings multiplied by means of spores—like vegetable pteridophytes as Lake had suspected—but owing to their prodigious toughness and longevity, and consequent lack of replacement needs, they did not encourage the large-scale development of new prothalli except when they had new regions to colonise. The young matured swiftly, and received an education evidently beyond any standard we can imagine. The prevailing intellectual and aesthetic life was highly evolved, and produced a tenaciously enduring set of customs and institutions which I shall describe more fully in my coming monograph. These varied slightly according to sea or land residence, but had the same foundations and essentials.

Though able, like vegetables, to derive nourishment from inorganic substances; they vastly preferred organic and especially animal food. They ate uncooked marine life under the sea, but cooked their viands on land. They hunted game and raised meat herds—slaughtering with sharp weapons whose odd marks on certain fossil bones our expedition had noted. They resisted all ordinary temperatures marvellously; and in their natural state could live in water down to freezing. When the great chill of the Pleistocene drew on, however—nearly a million years ago—the land dwellers had to resort to special measures including artificial heating; until at last the deadly cold appears to have driven them back into the sea. For their prehistoric flights through cosmic space, legend said, they had absorbed certain chemicals and became almost independent of eating, breathing, or heat conditions; but by the time of the great cold they had lost track of the method. In any case they could not have prolonged the artificial state indefinitely without harm.

Being non-pairing and semi-vegetable in structure, the Old Ones had no biological basis for the family phase of mammal life; but seemed to organise large households on the principles of comfortable space-utility and—as we deduced from the pictured occupations and diversions of co-dwellers—congenial mental association. In furnishing their homes they kept everything in the centre of the huge rooms, leaving all the wall spaces free for decorative treatment. Lighting, in the case of the land inhabitants, was accomplished by a device probably electro-chemical in nature. Both on land and under water they used curious tables, chairs, and couches like cylindrical frames—for they rested and slept upright with folded-down tentacles—and racks for the hinged sets of dotted surfaces forming their books.

Government was evidently complex and probably socialistic, though no certainties in this regard could be deduced from the sculptures we saw. There was extensive commerce, both local and between different cities; certain small, flat counters, five-pointed and inscribed, serving as money. Probably the smaller of the various greenish soapstones found by our expedition were pieces of such currency. Though the culture was mainly urban, some agriculture and much stock-raising existed. Mining and a limited amount of manufacturing were also practiced. Travel was very frequent, but permanent migration seemed relatively rare except for the vast colonising movements by which the race expanded. For personal locomotion no external aid was used; since in land, air, and water movement alike the Old Ones seemed to possess excessively vast capacities for speed. Loads, however, were drawn by beasts of burden—shoggoths under the sea, and a curious variety of primitive vertebrates in the later years of land existence.

These vertebrates, as well as an infinity of other life-forms—animal and vegetable, marine, terrestrial, and aërial—were the products of unguided evolution acting on life-cells made by the Old Ones but escaping beyond their radius of attention. They had been suffered to develop unchecked because they had not come in conflict with the dominant beings. Bothersome forms, of course, were mechanically exterminated. It interested us to see in some of the very last and most decadent sculptures a shambling primitive mammal, used sometimes for food and sometimes as an amusing buffoon by the land dwellers, whose vaguely simian and human foreshadowings were unmistakable. In the building of land cities the huge stone blocks of the high towers were generally lifted by vastwinged pterodactyls of a species heretofore unknown to palaeontology.

The persistence with which the Old Ones survived various geologic changes and convulsions of the earth's crust was little short of miraculous. Though few or none of their first cities seem to have remained beyond the Archaean age, there was no interruption in their civilisation or in the transmission of their records. Their original place of advent to the planet was the Antarctic Ocean, and it is likely that they came not long after the matter forming the moon was wrenched from the neighbouring South Pacific. According to one of the sculptured maps, the whole globe was then under water, with stone cities scattered farther and farther from the antarctic as aeons passed. Another map shews a vast bulk of dry land around the south pole, where it is evident that some of the beings made experimental settlements though their main centres were transferred to the nearest sea-bottom. Later maps, which display this land mass as cracking and drifting, and sending certain detached parts northward, uphold in a striking way the theories of continental drift lately advanced by Taylor, Wegener, and Joly.

With the upheaval of new land in the South Pacific tremendous events began. Some of the marine cities were hopelessly shattered, yet that was not the worst misfortune. Another race—a land race of beings shaped like octopi and probably corresponding to the fabulous pre-human spawn of Cthulhu—soon began filtering down from cosmic infinity and precipitated a monstrous war which for a time drove the Old Ones wholly back to the sea—a colossal blow in view of the increasing land settlements. Later peace was made, and the new lands were given to the Cthulhu spawn whilst the Old Ones held the sea and the older lands. New land cities were founded—the greatest of them in the antarctic, for this region of first arrival was sacred. From then on, as before, the antarctic remained the centre of the Old Ones' civilisation, and all the discoverable cities built there by the Cthulhu spawn were blotted out. Then suddenly the lands of the Pacific sank again, taking with them the frightful stone city of R'lyeh and all the cosmic octopi, so that the Old Ones were again supreme on the planet except for one shadowy fear about which they did not like to speak. At a rather later age their cities dotted all the land and water areas of the globe—hence the recommendation in my coming monograph that some archaeologist make systematic borings with Pabodie's type of apparatus in certain widely separated regions.

The steady trend down the ages was from water to land; a movement encouraged by the rise of new land masses, though the ocean was never wholly deserted. Another cause of the landward movement was the new difficulty in breeding and managing the shoggoths upon which successful sea-life depended. With the march of time, as the sculptures sadly confessed, the art of creating new life from inorganic matter had been lost; so that the Old Ones had to depend on the moulding of forms already in existence. On land the great reptiles proved highly tractable; but the shoggoths of the sea, reproducing by fission and acquiring a dangerous degree of accidental intelligence, presented for a time a formidable problem.

They had always been controlled through the hypnotic suggestion of the Old Ones, and had modelled their tough plasticity into various useful temporary limbs and organs; but now their self-modelling powers were sometimes exercised independently, and in various imitative forms implanted by past suggestion. They had, it seems, developed a semi-stable brain whose separate and occasionally stubborn volition echoed the will of the Old Ones without always obeying it. Sculptured images of these shoggoths filled Danforth and me with horror and loathing. They were normally shapeless entities composed of a viscous jelly which looked like an agglutination of bubbles; and each averaged about fifteen feet in diameter when a sphere. They had, however, a constantly shifting shape and volume; throwing out temporary developments or forming apparent organs of sight, hearing, and speech in imitation of their masters, either spontaneously or according to suggestion.

They seem to have become peculiarly intractable toward the middle of the Permian age, perhaps 150 million years ago, when a veritable war of re-subjugation was waged upon them by the marine Old Ones. Pictures of this war, and of the headless, slime-coated fashion in which the shoggoths typically left their slain victims, held a marvellously fearsome quality despite the intervening abyss of untold ages. The Old Ones had used curious weapons of molecular disturbance against the rebel entities, and in the end had achieved a complete victory. Thereafter the sculptures shewed a period in which shoggoths were tamed and broken by armed Old Ones as the wild horses of the American west were tamed by cowboys. Though during the rebellion the shoggoths had shewn an ability to live out of water, this transition was not encouraged; since their usefulness on land would hardly have been commensurate with the trouble of their management.

During the Jurassic age the Old Ones met fresh adversity in the form of a new invasion from outer space—this time by half-fungous, half-crustacean creatures from a planet identifiable as the remote and recently discovered Pluto; creatures undoubtedly the same as those figuring in certain whispered hill legends of the north, and remembered in the Himalayas as the Mi-Go, or Abominable Snow-Men. To fight these beings the Old Ones attempted, for the first time since their terrene advent, to sally forth again into the planetary ether; but despite all traditional preparations found it no longer possible to leave the earth's atmosphere. Whatever the old secret of interstellar travel had been, it was now definitely lost to the race. In the end the Mi-Go drove the Old Ones out of all the northern lands, though they were powerless to disturb those in the sea. Little by little the slow retreat of the elder race to their original antarctic habitat was beginning.

It was curious to note from the pictured battles that both the Cthulhu spawn and the Mi-Go seem to have been composed of matter more widely different from that which we know than was the substance of the Old Ones. They were able to undergo transformations and reintegrations impossible for their adversaries, and seem therefore to have originally come from even remoter gulfs of cosmic space. The Old Ones, but for their abnormal toughness and peculiar vital properties, were strictly material, and must have had their absolute origin within the known space-time continuum; whereas the first sources of the other beings can only be guessed at with bated breath. All this, of course, assuming that the non-terrestrial linkages and the anomalies ascribed to the invading foes are not pure mythology. Conceivably, the Old Ones might have invented a cosmic framework to account for their occasional defeats; since historical interest and pride obviously formed their chief psychological element. It is significant that their annals failed to mention many advanced and potent races of beings whose mighty cultures and towering cities figure persistently in certain obscure legends.

The changing state of the world through long geologic ages appeared with startling vividness in many of the sculptured maps and scenes. In certain cases existing science will require revision, while in other cases its bold deductions are magnificently confirmed. As I have said, the hypothesis of Taylor, Wegener, and Joly that all the continents are fragments of an original antarctic land mass which cracked from centrifugal force and drifted apart over a technically viscous lower surface—an hypothesis suggested by such things as the complementary outlines of Africa and South America, and the way the great mountain chains are rolled and shoved up—receives striking support from this uncanny source.

Maps evidently shewing the Carboniferous world of an hundred million or more years ago displayed significant rifts and chasms destined later to separate Africa from the once continuous realms of Europe (then the Valusia of hellish primal legend), Asia, the Americas, and the antarctic continent. Other charts—and most significantly one in connexion with the founding fifty million years ago of the vast dead city around us—shewed all the present continents well differentiated. And in the latest discoverable specimen—dating perhaps from the Pliocene age—the approximate world of today appeared quite clearly despite the linkage of Alaska with Siberia, of North America with Europe through Greenland, and of South America with the antarctic continent through Graham Land. In the Carboniferous map the whole globe—ocean floor and rifted land mass alike—bore symbols of the Old Ones' vast stone cities, but in the later charts the gradual recession toward the antarctic became very plain. The final Pliocene specimen shewed no land cities except on the antarctic continent and the tip of South America, nor any ocean cities north of the fiftieth parallel of South Latitude. Knowledge and interest in the northern world, save for a study of coast-lines probably made during long exploration flights on those fan-like membraneous wings, had evidently declined to zero among the Old Ones.

Destruction of cities through the upthrust of mountains, the centrifugal rending of continents, the seismic convulsions of land or sea-bottom, and other natural causes was a matter of common record; and it was curious to observe how fewer and fewer replacements were made as the ages wore on. The vast dead megalopolis that yawned around us seemed to be the last general centre of the race; built early in the Cretaceous age after a titanic earth-buckling had obliterated a still vaster predecessor not far distant. It appeared that this general region was the most sacred spot of all, where reputedly the first Old Ones had settled on a primal sea-bottom. In the new city—many of whose features we could recognise in the sculptures, but which stretched fully an hundred miles along the mountain-range in each direction beyond the farthest limits of our aërial survey—there were reputed to be preserved certain sacred stones forming part of the first sea-bottom city, which were thrust up to light after long epochs in the course of the general crumpling of strata.

VIII

Naturally, Danforth and I studied with especial interest and a peculiarly personal sense of awe everything pertaining to the immediate district in which we were. Of this local material there was naturally a vast abundance; and on the tangled ground level of the city we were lucky enough to find a house of very late date whose walls, though somewhat damaged by a neighbouring rift, contained sculptures of decadent workmanship carrying the story of the region much beyond the period of the Pliocene map whence we derived our last general glimpse of the pre-human world. This was the last place we examined in detail, since what we found there gave us a fresh immediate objective.

Certainly, we were in one of the strangest, weirdest, and most terrible of all the corners of earth's globe. Of all existing lands it was infinitely the most ancient; and the conviction grew upon us that this hideous upland must indeed be the fabled nightmare plateau of Leng which even the mad author of the *Necronomicon* was reluctant to discuss. The great mountain chain was tremendously long—starting as a low range at Luitpold Land on the coast of Weddell Sea and virtually crossing the entire continent. The really high part stretched in a mighty arc from about Latitude 82°, E. Longitude 60° to Latitude 70°, E. Longitude 115°, with its concave side toward our camp and its seaward end in the region of that long, ice-locked coast whose hills were glimpsed by Wilkes and Mawson at the Antarctic Circle.

Yet even more monstrous exaggerations of Nature seemed disturbingly close at hand. I have said that these peaks are higher than the Himalayas, but the sculptures forbid me to say that they are earth's highest. That grim honour is beyond doubt reserved for something which half the sculptures hesitated to record at all, whilst others approached it with obvious repugnance and trepidation. It seems that there was one part of the ancient land—the first part that ever rose from the waters after the earth had flung off the moon and the Old Ones had seeped down from the stars—which had come to be shunned as vaguely and namelessly evil. Cities built there had crumbled before their time, and had been found suddenly deserted. Then when the first great earth-buckling had convulsed the region in the Comanchian age, a frightful line of peaks had shot suddenly up amidst the most appalling din and chaos—and earth had received her loftiest and most terrible mountains.

If the scale of the carvings was correct, these abhorred things must have been much over 40,000 feet high—radically vaster than even the shocking mountains of madness we had crossed. They extended, it appeared, from about Latitude 77°, E. Longitude 70° to Latitude 70°, E. Longitude 100°—less than 300 miles away from the dead city, so that we would have spied their dreaded summits in the dim western distance had it not been for that vague opalescent haze. Their northern end must likewise be visible from the long Antarctic Circle coast-line at Queen Mary Land.

Some of the Old Ones, in the decadent days, had made strange prayers to those mountains; but none ever went near them or dared to guess what lay beyond. No human eye had ever seen them, and as I studied the emotions conveyed in the carvings I prayed that none ever might. There are protecting hills along the coast beyond them—Queen Mary and Kaiser Wilhelm Lands—and I thank heaven no one has been able to land and climb those hills. I am not as sceptical about old tales and fears as I used to be, and I do not laugh now at the pre-human sculptor's notion that lightning paused meaningfully now and then at each of the brooding crests, and that an unexplained glow shone from one of those terrible pinnacles all through the long polar night. There may be a very real and very monstrous meaning in the old Pnakotic whispers about Kadath in the Cold Waste.

But the terrain close at hand was hardly less strange, even if less namelessly accursed. Soon after the founding of the city the great mountain-range became the seat of the principal temples, and many carvings shewed what grotesque and fantastic towers had pierced the sky where now we saw only the curiously clinging cubes and ramparts. In the course of ages the caves had appeared, and had been shaped into adjuncts of the temples. With the advance of still later epochs all the limestone veins of the region were hollowed out by ground waters, so that the mountains, the foothills, and the plains below them were a veritable network of connected caverns and galleries. Many graphic sculptures told of explorations deep underground, and of the final discovery of the Stygian sunless sea that lurked at earth's bowels.

This vast nighted gulf had undoubtedly been worn by the great river which flowed down from the nameless and horrible westward mountains, and which had formerly turned at the base of the Old Ones' range and flowed beside that chain into the Indian Ocean between Budd and Totten Lands on Wilkes's coast-line. Little by little it had eaten away the limestone hill base at its turning, till at last its sapping currents reached the caverns of the ground waters and joined with them in digging a deeper abyss. Finally its whole bulk emptied into the hollow hills and left the old bed toward the ocean dry. Much of the later city as we now found it had been built over that former bed. The Old Ones, understanding what had happened, and exercising their always keen artistic sense, had carved into ornate pylons those headlands of the foothills where the great stream began its descent into eternal darkness.

This river, once crossed by scores of noble stone bridges, was plainly the one whose extinct course we had seen in our aëroplane survey. Its position in different carvings of the city helped us to orient ourselves to the scene as it had been at various stages of the region's age-long, aeon-dead history; so that we were able to sketch a hasty but careful map of the salient features—squares, important buildings, and the like—for guidance in further explorations. We could soon reconstruct in fancy the whole stupendous thing as it was a million or ten million or fifty million years ago, for the sculptures told us exactly what the buildings and mountains and squares and suburbs and landscape setting and luxuriant Tertiary vegetation had looked like. It must have had a marvellous and mystic beauty, and as I thought of it I almost forgot the clammy sense of sinister oppression with which the city's inhuman age and massiveness and deadness and remoteness and glacial twilight had choked and weighed on my spirit. Yet according to certain carvings the denizens of that city had themselves known the clutch of oppressive terror; for there was a sombre and recurrent type of scene in which the Old Ones were shewn in the act of recoiling affrightedly from some object—never allowed to appear in the design—found in the great river and indicated as having been washed down through waving, vine-draped cycad-forests from those horrible westward mountains.

It was only in the one late-built house with the decadent carvings that we obtained any foreshadowing of the final calamity leading to the city's desertion. Undoubtedly there must have been many sculptures of the same age elsewhere, even allowing for the slackened energies and aspirations of a stressful and uncertain period; indeed, very certain evidence of the existence of others came to us shortly afterward. But this was the first and only set we directly encountered. We meant to look farther later on; but as I have said, immediate conditions dictated another present objective. There would, though, have been a limit—for after all hope of a long future occupancy of the place had perished among the Old Ones, there could not but have been a complete cessation of mural decoration. The ultimate blow, of course, was the coming of the great cold which once held most of the earth in thrall, and which has never departed from the ill-fated poles—the great cold that, at the world's other extremity, put an end to the fabled lands of Lomar and Hyperborea.

Just when this tendency began in the antarctic it would be hard to say in terms of exact years. Nowadays we set the beginning of the general glacial periods at a distance of about 500,000 years from the present, but at the poles the terrible scourge must have commenced much earlier. All quantitative estimates are partly guesswork; but it is quite likely that the decadent sculptures were made considerably less than a million years ago, and that the actual desertion of the city was complete long before the conventional opening of the Pleistocene—500,000 years ago—as reckoned in terms of the earth's whole surface.

In the decadent sculptures there were signs of thinner vegetation everywhere, and of a decreased country life on the part of the Old Ones. Heating devices were shewn in the houses, and winter travellers were represented as muffled in protective fabrics. Then we saw a series of cartouches (the continuous band arrangement being frequently interrupted in these late carvings) depicting a constantly growing migration to the nearest refuges of greater warmth—some fleeing to cities under the sea off the far-away coast, and some clambering down through networks of limestone caverns in the hollow hills to the neighbouring black abyss of subterrene waters.

In the end it seems to have been the neighbouring abyss which received the greatest colonisation. This was partly due, no doubt, to the traditional sacredness of this especial region; but may have been more conclusively determined by the opportunities it gave for continuing the use of the great temples on the honeycombed mountains, and for retaining the vast land city as a place of summer residence and base of communication with various mines. The linkage of old and new abodes was made more effective by means of several gradings and improvements along the connecting routes, including the chiselling of numerous direct tunnels from the ancient metropolis to the black abyss—sharply down-pointing tunnels whose mouths we carefully drew, according to our most thoughtful estimates, on the guide map we were compiling. It was obvious that at least two of these tunnels lay within a reasonable exploring distance of where we were; both being on the mountainward edge of the city, one less than a quarter-mile toward the ancient river-course, and the other perhaps twice that distance in the opposite direction.

The abyss, it seems, had shelving shores of dry land at certain places; but the Old Ones built their new city under water—no doubt because of its greater certainty of uniform warmth. The depth of the hidden sea appears to have been very great, so that the earth's internal heat could ensure its habitability for an indefinite period. The beings seem to have had no trouble in adapting themselves to part-time—and eventually, of course, whole-time—residence under water; since they had never allowed their gill systems to atrophy. There were many sculptures which shewed how they had always frequently visited their submarine kinsfolk elsewhere, and how they had habitually bathed on the deep bottom of their great river. The darkness of inner earth could likewise have been no deterrent to a race accustomed to long antarctic nights.

Decadent though their style undoubtedly was, these latest carvings had a truly epic quality where they told of the building of the new city in the cavern sea. The Old Ones had gone about it scientifically; quarrying insoluble rocks from the heart of the honeycombed mountains, and employing expert workers from the nearest submarine city to perform the construction according to the best methods. These workers brought with them all that was necessary to establish the new venture—shoggoth-tissue from which to breed stone-lifters and subsequent beasts of burden for the cavern city, and other protoplasmic matter to mould into phosphorescent organisms for lighting purposes.

At last a mighty metropolis rose on the bottom of that Stygian sea; its architecture much like that of the city above, and its workmanship displaying relatively little decadence because of the precise mathematical element inherent in building operations. The newly bred shoggoths grew to enormous size and singular intelligence, and were represented as taking and executing orders with marvellous quickness. They seemed to converse with the Old Ones by mimicking their voices—a sort of musical piping over a wide range, if poor Lake's dissection had indicated aright—and to work more from spoken commands than from hypnotic suggestions as in earlier times. They were, however, kept in admirable control. The phosphorescent organisms supplied light with vast effectiveness, and doubtless atoned for the loss of the familiar polar auroras of the outer-world night.

Art and decoration were pursued, though of course with a certain decadence. The Old Ones seemed to realise this falling off themselves; and in many cases anticipated the policy of Constantine the Great by transplanting especially fine blocks of ancient carving from their land city, just as the emperor, in a similar age of decline, stripped Greece and Asia of their finest art to give his new Byzantine capital greater splendours than its own people could create. That the transfer of sculptured blocks had not been more extensive, was doubtless owing to the fact that the land city was not at first wholly abandoned. By the time total abandonment did occur—and it surely must have occurred before the polar Pleistocene was far advanced—the Old Ones had perhaps become satisfied with their decadent art—or had ceased to recognise the superior merit of the older carvings. At any rate, the aeon-silent ruins around us had certainly undergone no wholesale sculptural denudation; though all the best separate statues, like other moveables, had been taken away.

The decadent cartouches and dadoes telling this story were, as I have said, the latest we could find in our limited search. They left us with a picture of the Old Ones shuttling back and forth betwixt the land city in summer and the sea-cavern city in winter, and sometimes trading with the sea-bottom cities off the antarctic coast. By this time the ultimate doom of the land city must have been recognised, for the sculptures shewed many signs of the cold's malign encroachments. Vegetation was declining, and the terrible snows of the winter no longer melted completely even in midsummer. The saurian livestock were nearly all dead, and the mammals were standing it none too well. To keep on with the work of the upper world it had become necessary to adapt some of the amorphous and curiously cold-resistant shoggoths to land life; a thing the Old Ones had formerly been reluctant to do. The great river was now lifeless, and the upper sea had lost most of its denizens except the seals and whales. All the birds had flown away, save only the great, grotesque penguins.

What had happened afterward we could only guess. How long had the new sea-cavern city survived? Was it still down there, a stony corpse in eternal blackness? Had the subterranean waters frozen at last? To what fate had the ocean-bottom cities of the outer world been delivered? Had any of the Old Ones shifted north ahead of the creeping ice-cap? Existing geology shews no trace of their presence. Had the frightful Mi-Go been still a menace in the outer land world of the north? Could one be sure of what might or might not linger even to this day in the lightless and unplumbed abysses of earth's deepest waters? Those things had seemingly been able to withstand any amount of pressure—and men of the sea have fished up curious objects at times. And has the killer-whale theory really explained the savage and mysterious scars on antarctic seals noticed a generation ago by Borchgrevingk?

The specimens found by poor Lake did not enter into these guesses, for their geologic setting proved them to have lived at what must have been a very early date in the land city's history. They were, according to their location, certainly not less than thirty million years old; and we reflected that in their day the sea-cavern city, and indeed the cavern itself, had had no existence. They would have remembered an older scene, with lush Tertiary vegetation everywhere, a younger land city of flourishing arts around them, and a great river sweeping northward along the base of the mighty mountains toward a far-away tropic ocean.

And yet we could not help thinking about these specimens—especially about the eight perfect ones that were missing from Lake's hideously ravaged camp. There was something abnormal about that whole business—the strange things we had tried so hard to lay to somebody's madness—those frightful graves—the amount *and nature* of the missing material—Gedney—the unearthly toughness of those archaic monstrosities, and the queer vital freaks the sculptures now shewed the race to have. . . . Danforth and I had seen a good deal in the last few hours, and were prepared to believe and keep silent about many appalling and incredible secrets of primal Nature.

IX

I have said that our study of the decadent sculptures brought about a change in our immediate objective. This of course had to do with the chiselled avenues to the black inner world, of whose existence we had not known before, but which we were now eager to find and traverse. From the evident scale of the carvings we deduced that a steeply descending walk of about a mile through either of the neighbouring tunnels would bring us to the brink of the dizzy sunless cliffs above the great abyss; down whose side adequate paths, improved by the Old Ones, led to the rocky shore of the hidden and nighted ocean. To behold this fabulous gulf in stark reality was a lure which seemed impossible of resistance once we knew of the thing—yet we realised we must begin the quest at once if we expected to include it on our present flight.

It was now 8 PM, and we had not enough battery replacements to let our torches burn on forever. We had done so much of our studying and copying below the glacial level that our battery supply had had at least five hours of nearly continuous use; and despite the special dry cell formula would obviously be good for only about four more—though by keeping one torch unused, except for especially interesting or difficult places, we might manage to eke out a safe margin beyond that. It would not do to be without a light in these Cyclopean catacombs, hence in order to make the abyss trip we must give up all further mural deciphering. Of course we intended to revisit the place for days and perhaps weeks of intensive study and photography—curiosity having long ago got the better of horror—but just now we must hasten. Our supply of trail-blazing paper was far from unlimited, and we were reluctant to sacrifice spare notebooks or sketching paper to augment it; but we did let one large notebook go. If worst came to worst, we could resort to rock-chipping—and of course it would be possible, even in case of really lost direction, to work up to full daylight by one channel or another if granted sufficient time for plentiful trial and error. So at last we set off eagerly in the indicated direction of the nearest tunnel.

According to the carvings from which we had made our map, the desired tunnel-mouth could not be much more than a quarter-mile from where we stood; the intervening space shewing solid-looking buildings quite likely to be penetrable still at a sub-glacial level. The opening itself would be in the basement—on the angle nearest the foothills—of a vast five-pointed structure of evidently public and perhaps ceremonial nature, which we tried to identify from our aërial survey of the ruins. No such structure came to our minds as we recalled our flight, hence we concluded that its upper parts had been greatly damaged, or that it had been totally shattered in an ice-rift we had noticed. In the latter case the tunnel would probably turn out to be choked, so that we would have to try the next nearest one—the one less than a mile to the north. The intervening river-course prevented our trying any of the more southerly tunnels on this trip; and indeed, if both of the neighbouring ones were choked it was doubtful whether our batteries would warrant an attempt on the next northerly one—about a mile beyond our second choice.

As we threaded our dim way through the labyrinth with the aid of map and compass—traversing rooms and corridors in every stage of ruin or preservation, clambering up ramps, crossing upper floors and bridges and clambering down again, encountering choked doorways and piles of debris, hastening now and then along finely preserved and uncannily immaculate stretches, taking false leads and retracing our way (in such cases removing the blind paper trail we had left), and once in a while striking the bottom of an open shaft through which daylight poured or trickled down—we were repeatedly tantalised by the sculptured walls along our route. Many must have told tales of immense historical importance, and only the prospect of later visits reconciled us to the need of passing them by. As it was, we slowed down once in a while and turned on our second torch. If we had had more films we would certainly have paused briefly to photograph certain bas-reliefs, but time-consuming hand copying was clearly out of the question.

I come now once more to a place where the temptation to hesitate, or to hint rather than state, is very strong. It is necessary, however, to reveal the rest in order to justify my course in discouraging further exploration. We had wormed our way very close to the computed site of the tunnel's mouth—having crossed a second-story bridge to what seemed plainly the tip of a pointed wall, and descended to a ruinous corridor especially rich in decadently elaborate and apparently ritualistic sculptures of late workmanship— when, about 8:30 PM, Danforth's keen young nostrils gave us the first hint of something unusual. If we had had a dog with us, I suppose I would have been warned before. At first we could not precisely say what was wrong with the formerly crystal-pure air, but after a few seconds our memories reacted only too definitely. Let me try to state the thing without flinching. There was an odour—and that odour was vaguely, subtly, and unmistakably akin to what had nauseated us upon opening the insane grave of the horror poor Lake had dissected.

Of course the revelation was not as clearly cut at the time as it sounds now. There were several conceivable explanations, and we did a good deal of indecisive whispering. Most important of all, we did not retreat without further investigation; for having come this far, we were loath to be balked by anything short of certain disaster. Anyway, what we must have suspected was altogether too wild to believe. Such things did not happen in any normal world. It was probably sheer irrational instinct which made us dim our single torch—tempted no longer by the decadent and sinister sculptures that leered menacingly from the oppressive walls—and which softened our progress to a cautious tiptoeing and crawling over the increasingly littered floor and heaps of debris.

Danforth's eyes as well as nose proved better than mine, for it was likewise he who first noticed the queer aspect of the debris after we had passed many half-choked arches leading to chambers and corridors on the ground level. It did not look quite as it ought after countless thousands of years of desertion, and when we cautiously turned on more light we saw that a kind of swath seemed to have been lately tracked through it. The irregular nature of the litter precluded any definite marks, but in the smoother places there were suggestions of the dragging of heavy objects. Once we thought there was a hint of parallel tracks, as if of runners. This was what made us pause again.

It was during that pause that we caught—simultaneously this time—the other odour ahead. Paradoxically, it was both a less frightful and a more frightful odour—less frightful intrinsically, but infinitely appalling in this place under the known circumstances . . . unless, of course, Gedney. . . . For the odour was the plain and familiar one of common petrol—every-day gasoline.

Our motivation after that is something I will leave to psychologists. We knew now that some terrible extension of the camp horrors must have crawled into this nighted burial-place of the aeons, hence could not doubt any longer the existence of nameless conditions—present or at least recent—just ahead. Yet in the end we did let sheer burning curiosity—or anxiety—or auto-hypnotism—or vague thoughts of responsibility toward Gedney—or what not—drive us on. Danforth whispered again of the print he thought he had seen at the alley-turning in the ruins above; and of the faint musical piping—potentially of tremendous significance in the light of Lake's dissection report despite its close resemblance to the cave-mouth echoes of the windy peaks—which he thought he had shortly afterward half heard from unknown depths below. I, in my turn, whispered of how the camp was left—of what had disappeared, and of how the madness of a lone survivor might have conceived the inconceivable—a wild trip across the monstrous mountains and a descent into the unknown primal masonry—

But we could not convince each other, or even ourselves, of anything definite. We had turned off all light as we stood still, and vaguely noticed that a trace of deeply filtered upper day kept the blackness from being absolute. Having automatically begun to move ahead, we guided ourselves by occasional flashes from our torch. The disturbed debris formed an impression we could not shake off, and the smell of gasoline grew stronger. More and more ruin met our eyes and hampered our feet, until very soon we saw that the forward way was about to cease. We had been all too correct in our pessimistic guess about that rift glimpsed from the air. Our tunnel quest was a blind one, and we were not even going to be able to reach the basement out of which the abyssward aperture opened.

The torch, flashing over the grotesquely carven walls of the blocked corridor in which we stood, shewed several doorways in various states of obstruction; and from one of them the gasoline odour—quite submerging that other hint of odour—came with especial distinctness. As we looked more steadily, we saw that beyond a doubt there had been a slight and recent clearing away of debris from that particular opening. Whatever the lurking horror might be, we believed the direct avenue toward it was now plainly manifest. I do not think anyone will wonder that we waited an appreciable time before making any further motion.

And yet, when we did venture inside that black arch, our first impression was one of anticlimax. For amidst the littered expanse of that sculptured crypt—a perfect cube with sides of about twenty feet—there remained no recent object of instantly discernible size;

so that we looked instinctively, though in vain, for a farther doorway. In another moment, however, Danforth's sharp vision had descried a place where the floor debris had been disturbed; and we turned on both torches full strength. Though what we saw in that light was actually simple and trifling, I am none the less reluctant to tell of it because of what it implied. It was a rough levelling of the debris, upon which several small objects lay carelessly scattered, and at one corner of which a considerable amount of gasoline must have been spilled lately enough to leave a strong odour even at this extreme super-plateau altitude. In other words, it could not be other than a sort of camp—a camp made by questing beings who like us had been turned back by the unexpectedly choked way to the abyss.

Let me be plain. The scattered objects were, so far as substance was concerned, all from Lake's camp; and consisted of tin cans as queerly opened as those we had seen at that ravaged place, many spent matches, three illustrated books more or less curiously smudged, an empty ink bottle with its pictorial and instructional carton, a broken fountain pen, some oddly snipped fragments of fur and tent-cloth, a used electric battery with circular of directions, a folder that came with our type of tent heater, and a sprinkling of crumpled papers. It was all bad enough, but when we smoothed out the papers and looked at what was on them we felt we had come to the worst. We had found certain inexplicably blotted papers at the camp which might have prepared us, yet the effect of the sight down there in the pre-human vaults of a nightmare city was almost too much to bear.

A mad Gedney might have made the groups of dots in imitation of those found on the greenish soapstones, just as the dots on those insane five-pointed grave-mounds might have been made; and he might conceivably have prepared rough, hasty sketches— varying in their accuracy or lack of it—which outlined the neighbouring parts of the city and traced the way from a circularly represented place outside our previous route—a place we identified as a great cylindrical tower in the carvings and as a vast circular gulf glimpsed in our aërial survey—to the present five-pointed structure and the tunnel- mouth therein. He might, I repeat, have prepared such sketches; for those before us were quite obviously compiled as our own had been from late sculptures somewhere in the glacial labyrinth, though not from the ones which we had seen and used. But what this art-blind bungler could never have done was to execute those sketches in a strange and assured technique perhaps superior, despite haste and carelessness, to any of the decadent carvings from which they were taken—the characteristic and unmistakable technique of the Old Ones themselves in the dead city's heyday.

There are those who will say Danforth and I were utterly mad not to flee for our lives after that; since our conclusions were now—notwithstanding their wildness— completely fixed, and of a nature I need not even mention to those who have read my account as far as this. Perhaps we were mad—for have I not said those horrible peaks were mountains of madness? But I think I can detect something of the same spirit—albeit in a less extreme form—in the men who stalk deadly beasts through African jungles to photograph them or study their habits. Half-paralysed with terror though we were, there was nevertheless fanned within us a blazing flame of awe and curiosity which triumphed in the end.

Of course we did not mean to face that—or those—which we knew had been there, but we felt that they must be gone by now. They would by this time have found the other neighbouring entrance to the abyss, and have passed within to whatever night-black fragments of the past might await them in the ultimate gulf—the ultimate gulf they had never seen. Or if that entrance, too, was blocked, they would have gone on to the north seeking another. They were, we remembered, partly independent of light.

Looking back to that moment, I can scarcely recall just what precise form our new emotions took—just what change of immediate objective it was that so sharpened our sense of expectancy. We certainly did not mean to face what we feared—yet I will not deny that we may have had a lurking, unconscious wish to spy certain things from some hidden vantage-point. Probably we had not given up our zeal to glimpse the abyss itself, though there was interposed a new goal in the form of that great circular place shewn on the crumpled sketches we had found. We had at once recognised it as a monstrous cylindrical tower figuring in the very earliest carvings, but appearing only as a prodigious round aperture from above. Something about the impressiveness of its rendering, even in these hasty diagrams, made us think that its sub-glacial levels must still form a feature of peculiar importance. Perhaps it embodied architectural marvels as yet unencountered by us. It was certainly of incredible age according to the sculptures in which it figured—being indeed among the first things built in the city. Its carvings, if preserved, could not but be highly significant. Moreover, it might form a good present link with the upper world—a shorter route than the one we were so carefully blazing, and probably that by which those others had descended.

At any rate, the thing we did was to study the terrible sketches—which quite perfectly confirmed our own—and start back over the indicated course to the circular place; the course which our nameless predecessors must have traversed twice before us. The other neighbouring gate to the abyss would lie beyond that. I need not speak of our journey—during which we continued to leave an economical trail of paper—for it was precisely the same in kind as that by which we had reached the cul de sac; except that it tended to adhere more closely to the ground level and even descend to basement corridors. Every now and then we could trace certain disturbing marks in the debris or litter under foot; and after we had passed outside the radius of the gasoline scent we were again faintly conscious—spasmodically—of that more hideous and more persistent scent. After the way had branched from our former course we sometimes gave the rays of our single torch a furtive sweep along the walls; noting in almost every case the well-nigh omnipresent sculptures, which indeed seem to have formed a main aesthetic outlet for the Old Ones.

About 9:30 PM, while traversing a vaulted corridor whose increasingly glaciated floor seemed somewhat below the ground level and whose roof grew lower as we advanced, we began to see strong daylight ahead and were able to turn off our torch. It appeared that we were coming to the vast circular place, and that our distance from the upper air could not be very great. The corridor ended in an arch surprisingly low for these megalithic ruins, but we could see much through it even before we emerged. Beyond there stretched a prodigious round space—fully 200 feet in diameter—strown with debris and containing many choked archways corresponding to the one we were about to cross. The walls were—in available spaces—boldly sculptured into a spiral band of heroic proportions; and displayed, despite the destructive weathering caused by the openness of the spot, an artistic splendour far beyond anything we had encountered before. The littered floor was quite heavily glaciated, and we fancied that the true bottom lay at a considerably lower depth.

But the salient object of the place was the titanic stone ramp which, eluding the archways by a sharp turn outward into the open floor, wound spirally up the stupendous cylindrical wall like an inside counterpart of those once climbing outside the monstrous towers or ziggurats of antique Babylon. Only the rapidity of our flight, and the perspective which confounded the descent with the tower's inner wall, had prevented our noticing this feature from the air, and thus caused us to seek another avenue to the sub-glacial level. Pabodie might have been able to tell what sort of engineering held it in place, but Danforth and I could merely admire and marvel. We could see mighty stone corbels and pillars here and there, but what we saw seemed inadequate to the function performed. The thing was excellently preserved up to the present top of the tower—a highly remarkable circumstance in view of its exposure—and its shelter had done much to protect the bizarre and disturbing cosmic sculptures on the walls.

As we stepped out into the awesome half-daylight of this monstrous cylinder-bottom—fifty million years old, and without doubt the most primally ancient structure ever to meet our eyes—we saw that the ramp-traversed sides stretched dizzily up to a height of fully sixty feet. This, we recalled from our aërial survey, meant an outside glaciation of some forty feet; since the yawning gulf we had seen from the plane had been at the top of an approximately twenty-foot mound of crumbled masonry, somewhat sheltered for three-fourths of its circumference by the massive curving walls of a line of higher ruins. According to the sculptures the original tower had stood in the centre of an immense circular plaza; and had been perhaps 500 or 600 feet high, with tiers of horizontal discs near the top, and a row of needle-like spires along the upper rim. Most of the masonry had obviously toppled outward rather than inward—a fortunate happening, since otherwise the ramp might have been shattered and the whole interior choked. As it was, the ramp shewed sad battering; whilst the choking was such that all the archways at the bottom seemed to have been recently half-cleared.

It took us only a moment to conclude that this was indeed the route by which those others had descended, and that this would be the logical route for our own ascent despite the long trail of paper we had left elsewhere. The tower's mouth was no farther from the foothills and our waiting plane than was the great terraced building we had entered, and any further sub-glacial exploration we might make on this trip would lie in this general region. Oddly, we were still thinking about possible later trips—even after all we had seen and guessed. Then as we picked our way cautiously over the debris of the great floor, there came a sight which for the time excluded all other matters.

It was the neatly huddled array of three sledges in that farther angle of the ramp's lower and outward-projecting course which had hitherto been screened from our view. There they were—the three sledges missing from Lake's camp—shaken by a hard usage which must have included forcible dragging along great reaches of snowless masonry and debris, as well as much hand portage over utterly unnavigable places. They were carefully and intelligently packed and strapped, and contained things memorably familiar enough—the gasoline stove, fuel cans, instrument cases, provision tins, tarpaulins obviously bulging with books, and some bulging with less obvious contents—everything derived from Lake's equipment. After what we had found in that other room, we were in a measure prepared for this encounter. The really great shock came when we stepped over and undid one tarpaulin whose outlines had peculiarly disquieted us. It seems that others as well as Lake had been interested in collecting typical specimens; for there were two here, both stiffly frozen, perfectly preserved, patched with adhesive plaster where some wounds around the neck had occurred, and wrapped with patent care to prevent further damage. They were the bodies of young Gedney and the missing dog.

X

Many people will probably judge us callous as well as mad for thinking about the northward tunnel and the abyss so soon after our sombre discovery, and I am not prepared to say that we would have immediately revived such thoughts but for a specific circumstance which broke in upon us and set up a whole new train of speculations. We had replaced the tarpaulin over poor Gedney and were standing in a kind of mute bewilderment when the sounds finally reached our consciousness—the first sounds we had heard since descending out of the open where the mountain wind whined faintly from its unearthly heights. Well known and mundane though they were, their presence in this remote world of death was more unexpected and unnerving than any grotesque or fabulous tones could possibly have been—since they gave a fresh upsetting to all our notions of cosmic harmony.

Had it been some trace of that bizarre musical piping over a wide range which Lake's dissection report had led us to expect in those others—and which, indeed, our overwrought fancies had been reading into every wind-howl we had heard since coming on the camp horror—it would have had a kind of hellish congruity with the aeon-dead region around us. A voice from other epochs belongs in a graveyard of other epochs. As it was, however, the noise shattered all our profoundly seated adjustments—all our tacit acceptance of the inner antarctic as a waste as utterly and irrevocably void of every vestige of normal life as the sterile disc of the moon. What we heard was not the fabulous note of any buried blasphemy of elder earth from whose supernal toughness an age-denied polar sun had evoked a monstrous response. Instead, it was a thing so mockingly normal and so unerringly familiarised by our sea days off Victoria Land and our camp days at McMurdo Sound that we shuddered to think of it here, where such things ought not to be. To be brief—it was simply the raucous squawking of a penguin.

The muffled sound floated from sub-glacial recesses nearly opposite to the corridor whence we had come—regions manifestly in the direction of that other tunnel to the vast abyss. The presence of a living water-bird in such a direction—in a world whose surface was one of age-long and uniform lifelessness—could lead to only one conclusion; hence our first thought was to verify the objective reality of the sound. It was, indeed, repeated; and seemed at times to come from more than one throat. Seeking its source, we entered an archway from which much debris had been cleared; resuming our trail-blazing—with an added paper-supply taken with curious repugnance from one of the tarpaulin bundles on the sledges—when we left daylight behind.

As the glaciated floor gave place to a litter of detritus, we plainly discerned some curious dragging tracks; and once Danforth found a distinct print of a sort whose description would be only too superfluous. The course indicated by the penguin cries was precisely what our map and compass prescribed as an approach to the more northerly tunnel-mouth, and we were glad to find that a bridgeless thoroughfare on the ground and basement levels seemed open. The tunnel, according to the chart, ought to start from the basement of a large pyramidal structure which we seemed vaguely to recall from our aërial survey as remarkably well preserved. Along our path the single torch shewed a customary profusion of carvings, but we did not pause to examine any of these.

Suddenly a bulky white shape loomed up ahead of us, and we flashed on the second torch. It is odd how wholly this new quest had turned our minds from earlier fears of what might lurk near. Those other ones, having left their supplies in the great circular place, must have planned to return after their scouting trip toward or into the abyss; yet we had now discarded all caution concerning them as completely as if they had never existed. This white, waddling thing was fully six feet high, yet we seemed to realise at once that it was not one of those others. They were larger and dark, and according to the sculptures their motion over land surfaces was a swift, assured matter despite the queerness of their sea-born tentacle equipment. But to say that the white thing did not profoundly frighten us would be vain. We were indeed clutched for an instant by a primitive dread almost sharper than the worst of our reasoned fears regarding those others. Then came a flash of anticlimax as the white shape sidled into a lateral archway to our left to join two others of its kind which had summoned it in raucous tones. For it was only a penguin—albeit of a huge, unknown species larger than the greatest of the known king penguins, and monstrous in its combined albinism and virtual eyelessness.

When we had followed the thing into the archway and turned both our torches on the indifferent and unheeding group of three we saw that they were all eyeless albinos of the same unknown and gigantic species. Their size reminded us of some of the archaic penguins depicted in the Old Ones' sculptures, and it did not take us long to conclude that they were descended from the same stock—undoubtedly surviving through a retreat to some warmer inner region whose perpetual blackness had destroyed their pigmentation and atrophied their eyes to mere useless slits. That their present habitat was the vast abyss we sought, was not for a moment to be doubted; and this evidence of the gulf's continued warmth and habitability filled us with the most curious and subtly perturbing fancies.

We wondered, too, what had caused these three birds to venture out of their usual domain. The state and silence of the great dead city made it clear that it had at no time been an habitual seasonal rookery, whilst the manifest indifference of the trio to our presence made it seem odd that any passing party of those others should have startled them. Was it possible that those others had taken some aggressive action or tried to increase their meat supply? We doubted whether that pungent odour which the dogs had hated could cause an equal antipathy in these penguins; since their ancestors had obviously lived on excellent terms with the Old Ones—an amicable relationship which must have survived in the abyss below as long as any of the Old Ones remained. Regretting—in a flareup of the old spirit of pure science—that we could not photograph these anomalous creatures, we shortly left them to their squawking and pushed on toward the abyss whose openness was now so positively proved to us, and whose exact direction occasional penguin tracks made clear.

Not long afterward a steep descent in a long, low, doorless, and peculiarly sculptureless corridor led us to believe that we were approaching the tunnel-mouth at last. We had passed two more penguins, and heard others immediately ahead. Then the corridor ended in a prodigious open space which made us gasp involuntarily—a perfect inverted hemisphere, obviously deep underground; fully an hundred feet in diameter and fifty feet high, with low archways opening around all parts of the circumference but one, and that one yawning cavernously with a black arched aperture which broke the symmetry of the vault to a height of nearly fifteen feet. It was the entrance to the great abyss.

In this vast hemisphere, whose concave roof was impressively though decadently carved to a likeness of the primordial celestial dome, a few albino penguins waddled—aliens there, but indifferent and unseeing. The black tunnel yawned indefinitely off at a steep descending grade, its aperture adorned with grotesquely chiselled jambs and lintel. From that cryptical mouth we fancied a current of slightly warmer air and perhaps even a suspicion of vapour proceeded; and we wondered what living entities other than penguins the limitless void below, and the contiguous honeycombings of the land and the titan mountains, might conceal. We wondered, too, whether the trace of mountain-top smoke at first suspected by poor Lake, as well as the odd haze we had ourselves perceived around the rampart-crowned peak, might not be caused by the tortuous-channelled rising of some such vapour from the unfathomed regions of earth's core.

Entering the tunnel, we saw that its outline was—at least at the start—about fifteen feet each way; sides, floor, and arched roof composed of the usual megalithic masonry.

The sides were sparsely decorated with cartouches of conventional designs in a late, decadent style; and all the construction and carving were marvellously well preserved. The floor was quite clear, except for a slight detritus bearing outgoing penguin tracks and the inward tracks of those others. The farther one advanced, the warmer it became; so that we were soon unbuttoning our heavy garments. We wondered whether there were any actually igneous manifestations below, and whether the waters of that sunless sea were hot. After a short distance the masonry gave place to solid rock, though the tunnel kept the same proportions and presented the same aspect of carved regularity. Occasionally its varying grade became so steep that grooves were cut in the floor. Several times we noted the mouths of small lateral galleries not recorded in our diagrams; none of them such as to complicate the problem of our return, and all of them welcome as possible refuges in case we met unwelcome entities on their way back from the abyss. The nameless scent of such things was very distinct. Doubtless it was suicidally foolish to venture into that tunnel under the known conditions, but the lure of the unplumbed is stronger in certain persons than most suspect—indeed, it was just such a lure which had brought us to this unearthly polar waste in the first place. We saw several penguins as we passed along, and speculated on the distance we would have to traverse. The carvings had led us to expect a steep downhill walk of about a mile to the abyss, but our previous wanderings had shewn us that matters of scale were not wholly to be depended on.

After about a quarter of a mile that nameless scent became greatly accentuated, and we kept very careful track of the various lateral openings we passed. There was no visible vapour as at the mouth, but this was doubtless due to the lack of contrasting cooler air. The temperature was rapidly ascending, and we were not surprised to come upon a careless heap of material shudderingly familiar to us. It was composed of furs and tent-cloth taken from Lake's camp, and we did not pause to study the bizarre forms into which the fabrics had been slashed. Slightly beyond this point we noticed a decided increase in the size and number of the side-galleries, and concluded that the densely honeycombed region beneath the higher foothills must now have been reached. The nameless scent was now curiously mixed with another and scarcely less offensive odour—of what nature we could not guess, though we thought of decaying organisms and perhaps unknown subterrene fungi. Then came a startling expansion of the tunnel for which the carvings had not prepared us—a broadening and rising into a lofty, natural-looking elliptical cavern with a level floor; some 75 feet long and 50 broad, and with many immense side-passages leading away into cryptical darkness.

Though this cavern was natural in appearance, an inspection with both torches suggested that it had been formed by the artificial destruction of several walls between adjacent honeycombings. The walls were rough, and the high vaulted roof was thick with stalactites; but the solid rock floor had been smoothed off, and was free from all debris, detritus, or even dust to a positively abnormal extent. Except for the avenue through which we had come, this was true of the floors of all the great galleries opening off from it; and the singularity of the condition was such as to set us vainly puzzling. The curious new foetor which had supplemented the nameless scent was excessively pungent here; so much so that it destroyed all trace of the other. Something about this whole place, with its polished and almost glistening floor, struck us as more vaguely baffling and horrible than any of the monstrous things we had previously encountered.

The regularity of the passage immediately ahead, as well as the larger proportion of penguin-droppings there, prevented all confusion as to the right course amidst this plethora of equally great cave-mouths. Nevertheless we resolved to resume our paper trail-blazing if any further complexity should develop; for dust tracks, of course, could no longer be expected. Upon resuming our direct progress we cast a beam of torchlight over the tunnel walls—and stopped short in amazement at the supremely radical change which had come over the carvings in this part of the passage. We realised, of course, the great decadence of the Old Ones' sculpture at the time of the tunnelling; and had indeed noticed the inferior workmanship of the arabesques in the stretches behind us. But now, in this deeper section beyond the cavern, there was a sudden difference wholly transcending explanation—a difference in basic nature as well as in mere quality, and involving so profound and calamitous a degradation of skill that nothing in the hitherto observed rate of decline could have led one to expect it.

This new and degenerate work was coarse, bold, and wholly lacking in delicacy of detail. It was counter-sunk with exaggerated depth in bands following the same general line as the sparse cartouches of the earlier sections, but the height of the reliefs did not reach the level of the general surface. Danforth had the idea that it was a second carving—a sort of palimpsest formed after the obliteration of a previous design. In nature it was wholly decorative and conventional; and consisted of crude spirals and angles roughly following the quintile mathematical tradition of the Old Ones, yet seeming more like a parody than a perpetuation of that tradition. We could not get it out of our minds that some subtly but profoundly alien element had been added to the aesthetic feeling behind the technique—an alien element, Danforth guessed, that was responsible for the manifestly laborious substitution. It was like, yet disturbingly unlike, what we had come to recognise as the Old Ones' art; and I was persistently reminded of such hybrid things as the ungainly Palmyrene sculptures fashioned in the Roman manner. That others had recently noticed this belt of carving was hinted by the presence of a used torch battery on the floor in front of one of the most characteristic designs.

Since we could not afford to spend any considerable time in study, we resumed our advance after a cursory look; though frequently casting beams over the walls to see if any further decorative changes developed. Nothing of the sort was perceived, though the carvings were in places rather sparse because of the numerous mouths of smooth-floored lateral tunnels. We saw and heard fewer penguins, but thought we caught a vague suspicion of an infinitely distant chorus of them somewhere deep within the earth. The new and inexplicable odour was abominably strong, and we could detect scarcely a sign of that other nameless scent. Puffs of visible vapour ahead bespoke increasing contrasts in temperature, and the relative nearness of the sunless sea-cliffs of the great abyss. Then, quite unexpectedly, we saw certain obstructions on the polished floor ahead— obstructions which were quite definitely not penguins—and turned on our second torch after making sure that the objects were quite stationary.

XI

Still another time have I come to a place where it is very difficult to proceed. I ought to be hardened by this stage; but there are some experiences and intimations which scar too deeply to permit of healing, and leave only such an added sensitiveness that memory re-inspires all the original horror. We saw, as I have said, certain obstructions on the polished floor ahead; and I may add that our nostrils were assailed almost simultaneously by a very curious intensification of the strange prevailing foetor, now quite plainly mixed with the nameless stench of those others which had gone before us. The light of the second torch left no doubt of what the obstructions were, and we dared approach them only because we could see, even from a distance, that they were quite as past all harming power as had been the six similar specimens unearthed from the monstrous star-mounded graves at poor Lake's camp.

They were, indeed, as lacking in completeness as most of those we had unearthed—though it grew plain from the thick, dark-green pool gathering around them that their incompleteness was of infinitely greater recency. There seemed to be only four of them, whereas Lake's bulletins would have suggested no less than eight as forming the group which had preceded us. To find them in this state was wholly unexpected, and we wondered what sort of monstrous struggle had occurred down here in the dark.

Penguins, attacked in a body, retaliate savagely with their beaks; and our ears now made certain the existence of a rookery far beyond. Had those others disturbed such a place and aroused murderous pursuit? The obstructions did not suggest it, for penguin beaks against the tough tissues Lake had dissected could hardly account for the terrible damage our approaching glance was beginning to make out. Besides, the huge blind birds we had seen appeared to be singularly peaceful.

Had there, then, been a struggle among those others, and were the absent four responsible? If so, where were they? Were they close at hand and likely to form an immediate menace to us? We glanced anxiously at some of the smooth-floored lateral passages as we continued our slow and frankly reluctant approach. Whatever the conflict was, it had clearly been that which had frightened the penguins into their unaccustomed wandering. It must, then, have arisen near that faintly heard rookery in the incalculable gulf beyond, since there were no signs that any birds had normally dwelt here. Perhaps, we reflected, there had been a hideous running fight, with the weaker party seeking to get back to the cached sledges when their pursuers finished them. One could picture the daemoniac fray between namelessly monstrous entities as it surged out of the black abyss with great clouds of frantic penguins squawking and scurrying ahead.

I say that we approached those sprawling and incomplete obstructions slowly and reluctantly. Would to heaven we had never approached them at all, but had run back at top speed out of that blasphemous tunnel with the greasily smooth floors and the degenerate murals aping and mocking the things they had superseded—run back, before we had seen what we did see, and before our minds were burned with something which will never let us breathe easily again!

Both of our torches were turned on the prostrate objects, so that we soon realised the dominant factor in their incompleteness. Mauled, compressed, twisted, and ruptured as they were, their chief common injury was total decapitation. From each one the tentacled starfish-head had been removed; and as we drew near we saw that the manner of removal looked more like some hellish tearing or suction than like any ordinary form of cleavage. Their noisome dark-green ichor formed a large, spreading pool; but its stench was half overshadowed by that newer and stranger stench, here more pungent than at any other point along our route. Only when we had come very close to the sprawling obstructions could we trace that second, unexplainable foetor to any immediate source—and the instant we did so Danforth, remembering certain very vivid sculptures of the Old Ones' history in the Permian age 150 million years ago, gave vent to a nerve-tortured cry which echoed hysterically through that vaulted and archaic passage with the evil palimpsest carvings.

I came only just short of echoing his cry myself; for I had seen those primal sculptures, too, and had shudderingly admired the way the nameless artist had suggested that hideous slime-coating found on certain incomplete and prostrate Old Ones—those whom the frightful shoggoths had characteristically slain and sucked to a ghastly headlessness in the great war of re-subjugation. They were infamous, nightmare sculptures even when telling of age-old, bygone things; for shoggoths and their work ought not to be seen by human beings or portrayed by any beings. The mad author of the *Necronomicon* had nervously tried to swear that none had been bred on this planet, and that only drugged dreamers had ever conceived them. Formless protoplasm able to mock and reflect all forms and organs and processes—viscous agglutinations of bubbling cells—rubbery fifteen-foot spheroids infinitely plastic and ductile—slaves of suggestion, builders of cities—more and more sullen, more and more intelligent, more and more amphibious, more and more imitative—Great God! What madness made even those blasphemous Old Ones willing to use and to carve such things?

And now, when Danforth and I saw the freshly glistening and reflectively iridescent black slime which clung thickly to those headless bodies and stank obscenely with that new unknown odour whose cause only a diseased fancy could envisage—clung to those bodies and sparkled less voluminously on a smooth part of the accursedly re-sculptured wall *in a series of grouped dots*--we understood the quality of cosmic fear to its uttermost depths. It was not fear of those four missing others—for all too well did we suspect they would do no harm again. Poor devils! After all, they were not evil things of their kind. They were the men of another age and another order of being. Nature had played a hellish jest on them—as it will on any others that human madness, callousness, or cruelty may hereafter drag up in that hideously dead or sleeping polar waste—and this was their tragic homecoming.

They had not been even savages—for what indeed had they done? That awful awakening in the cold of an unknown epoch—perhaps an attack by the furry, frantically barking quadrupeds, and a dazed defence against them and the equally frantic white simians with the queer wrappings and paraphernalia . . . poor Lake, poor Gedney . . . and poor Old Ones! Scientists to the last—what had they done that we would not have done in their place? God, what intelligence and persistence! What a facing of the incredible, just as those carven kinsmen and forbears had faced things only a little less incredible! Radiates, vegetables, monstrosities, star-spawn—whatever they had been, they were men!

They had crossed the icy peaks on whose templed slopes they had once worshipped and roamed among the tree-ferns. They had found their dead city brooding under its curse, and had read its carven latter days as we had done. They had tried to reach their living fellows in fabled depths of blackness they had never seen—and what had they found? All this flashed in unison through the thoughts of Danforth and me as we looked from those headless, slime-coated shapes to the loathsome palimpsest sculptures and the diabolical dot-groups of fresh slime on the wall beside them—looked and understood what must have triumphed and survived down there in the Cyclopean water-city of that nighted, penguin-fringed abyss, whence even now a sinister curling mist had begun to belch pallidly as if in answer to Danforth's hysterical scream.

The shock of recognising that monstrous slime and headlessness had frozen us into mute, motionless statues, and it is only through later conversations that we have learned of the complete identity of our thoughts at that moment. It seemed aeons that we stood there, but actually it could not have been more than ten or fifteen seconds. That hateful, pallid mist curled forward as if veritably driven by some remoter advancing bulk—and then came a sound which upset much of what we had just decided, and in so doing broke the spell and enabled us to run like mad past squawking, confused penguins over our former trail back to the city, along ice-sunken megalithic corridors to the great open circle, and up that archaic spiral ramp in a frenzied automatic plunge for the sane outer air and light of day.

The new sound, as I have intimated, upset much that we had decided; because it was what poor Lake's dissection had led us to attribute to those we had just judged dead. It was, Danforth later told me, precisely what he had caught in infinitely muffled form when at that spot beyond the alley-corner above the glacial level; and it certainly had a shocking resemblance to the wind-pipings we had both heard around the lofty mountain caves. At the risk of seeming puerile I will add another thing, too; if only because of the surprising way Danforth's impression chimed with mine. Of course common reading is what prepared us both to make the interpretation, though Danforth has hinted at queer notions about unsuspected and forbidden sources to which Poe may have had access when writing his *Arthur Gordon Pym* a century ago. It will be remembered that in that fantastic tale there is a word of unknown but terrible and prodigious significance connected with the antarctic and screamed eternally by the gigantic, spectrally snowy birds of that malign region's core. *"Tekeli-li! Tekeli-li!"* That, I may admit, is exactly what we thought we heard conveyed by that sudden sound behind the advancing white mist—that insidious musical piping over a singularly wide range.

We were in full flight before three notes or syllables had been uttered, though we knew that the swiftness of the Old Ones would enable any scream-roused and pursuing survivor of the slaughter to overtake us in a moment if it really wished to do so. We had a vague hope, however, that non-aggressive conduct and a display of kindred reason might cause such a being to spare us in case of capture; if only from scientific curiosity. After all, if such an one had nothing to fear for itself it would have no motive in harming us. Concealment being futile at this juncture, we used our torch for a running glance behind, and perceived that the mist was thinning. Would we see, at last, a complete and living specimen of those others? Again came that insidious musical piping—*"Tekeli-li! Tekeli-li!"*

Then, noting that we were actually gaining on our pursuer, it occurred to us that the entity might be wounded. We could take no chances, however, since it was very obviously approaching in answer to Danforth's scream rather than in flight from any other entity. The timing was too close to admit of doubt. Of the whereabouts of that less conceivable and less mentionable nightmare—that foetid, unglimpsed mountain of slime-spewing protoplasm whose race had conquered the abyss and sent land pioneers to recarve and squirm through the burrows of the hills—we could form no guess; and it cost us a genuine pang to leave this probably crippled Old One—perhaps a lone survivor—to the peril of recapture and a nameless fate.

Thank heaven we did not slacken our run. The curling mist had thickened again, and was driving ahead with increased speed; whilst the straying penguins in our rear were squawking and screaming and displaying signs of a panic really surprising in view of their relatively minor confusion when we had passed them. Once more came that sinister, wide-ranged piping—*"Tekeli-li! Tekeli-li!"* We had been wrong. The thing was not wounded, but had merely paused on encountering the bodies of its fallen kindred and the hellish slime inscription above them. We could never know what that daemon message was—but those burials at Lake's camp had shewn how much importance the beings attached to their dead. Our recklessly used torch now revealed ahead of us the large open cavern where various ways converged, and we were glad to be leaving those morbid palimpsest sculptures—almost felt even when scarcely seen—behind.

Another thought which the advent of the cave inspired was the possibility of losing our pursuer at this bewildering focus of large galleries. There were several of the blind albino penguins in the open space, and it seemed clear that their fear of the oncoming entity was extreme to the point of unaccountability. If at that point we dimmed our torch to the very lowest limit of travelling need, keeping it strictly in front of us, the frightened squawking motions of the huge birds in the mist might muffle our footfalls, screen our true course, and somehow set up a false lead. Amidst the churning, spiralling fog the littered and unglistening floor of the main tunnel beyond this point, as differing from the other morbidly polished burrows, could hardly form a highly distinguishing feature; even, so far as we could conjecture, for those indicated special senses which made the Old Ones partly though imperfectly independent of light in emergencies. In fact, we were somewhat apprehensive lest we go astray ourselves in our haste. For we had, of course, decided to keep straight on toward the dead city; since the consequences of loss in those unknown foothill honeycombings would be unthinkable.

The fact that we survived and emerged is sufficient proof that the thing did take a wrong gallery whilst we providentially hit on the right one. The penguins alone could not have saved us, but in conjunction with the mist they seem to have done so. Only a benign fate kept the curling vapours thick enough at the right moment, for they were constantly shifting and threatening to vanish. Indeed, they did lift for a second just before we emerged from the nauseously re-sculptured tunnel into the cave; so that we actually caught one first and only half-glimpse of the oncoming entity as we cast a final, desperately fearful glance backward before dimming the torch and mixing with the penguins in the hope of dodging pursuit. If the fate which screened us was benign, that which gave us the half-glimpse was infinitely the opposite; for to that flash of semi-vision can be traced a full half of the horror which has ever since haunted us.

Our exact motive in looking back again was perhaps no more than the immemorial instinct of the pursued to gauge the nature and course of its pursuer; or perhaps it was an automatic attempt to answer a subconscious question raised by one of our senses. In the midst of our flight, with all our faculties centred on the problem of escape, we were in no condition to observe and analyse details; yet even so our latent brain-cells must have wondered at the message brought them by our nostrils. Afterward we realised what it was—that our retreat from the foetid slime-coating on those headless obstructions, and the coincident approach of the pursuing entity, had not brought us the exchange of stenches which logic called for. In the neighbourhood of the prostrate things that new and lately unexplainable foetor had been wholly dominant; but by this time it ought to have largely given place to the nameless stench associated with those others. This it had not done—for instead, the newer and less bearable smell was now virtually undiluted, and growing more and more poisonously insistent each second.

So we glanced back—simultaneously, it would appear; though no doubt the incipient motion of one prompted the imitation of the other. As we did so we flashed both torches full strength at the momentarily thinned mist; either from sheer primitive anxiety to see all we could, or in a less primitive but equally unconscious effort to dazzle the entity before we dimmed our light and dodged among the penguins of the labyrinth-centre ahead. Unhappy act! Not Orpheus himself, or Lot's wife, paid much more dearly for a backward glance. And again came that shocking, wide-ranged piping—"Tekeli-li! Tekeli-li!"

I might as well be frank—even if I cannot bear to be quite direct—in stating what we saw; though at the time we felt that it was not to be admitted even to each other. The words reaching the reader can never even suggest the awfulness of the sight itself. It crippled our consciousness so completely that I wonder we had the residual sense to dim our torches as planned, and to strike the right tunnel toward the dead city. Instinct alone must have carried us through—perhaps better than reason could have done; though if that was what saved us, we paid a high price. Of reason we certainly had little enough left. Danforth was totally unstrung, and the first thing I remember of the rest of the journey was hearing him light-headedly chant an hysterical formula in which I alone of mankind could have found anything but insane irrelevance. It reverberated in falsetto echoes among the squawks of the penguins; reverberated through the vaultings ahead, and—thank God—through the now empty vaultings behind. He could not have begun it at once—else we would not have been alive and blindly racing. I shudder to think of what a shade of difference in his nervous reactions might have brought.

"South Station Under—Washington Under—Park Street Under—Kendall—Central—Harvard. . . ." The poor fellow was chanting the familiar stations of the Boston–Cambridge tunnel that burrowed through our peaceful native soil thousands of miles away in New England, yet to me the ritual had neither irrelevance nor home-feeling. It had only horror, because I knew unerringly the monstrous, nefandous analogy that had suggested it. We had expected, upon looking back, to see a terrible and incredibly moving entity if the mists were thin enough; but of that entity we had formed a clear idea. What we did see—for the mists were indeed all too malignly thinned—was something altogether different, and immeasurably more hideous and detestable. It was the utter, objective embodiment of the fantastic novelist's 'thing that should not be'; and its nearest comprehensible analogue is a vast, onrushing subway train as one sees it from a station platform—the great black front looming colossally out of infinite subterraneous distance, constellated with strangely coloured lights and filling the prodigious burrow as a piston fills a cylinder.

But we were not on a station platform. We were on the track ahead as the nightmare plastic column of foetid black iridescence oozed tightly onward through its fifteen-foot sinus; gathering unholy speed and driving before it a spiral, re-thickening cloud of the pallid abyss-vapour. It was a terrible, indescribable thing vaster than any subway train—a shapeless congeries of protoplasmic bubbles, faintly self-luminous, and with myriads of temporary eyes forming and unforming as pustules of greenish light all over the tunnel-filling front that bore down upon us, crushing the frantic penguins and slithering over the glistening floor that it and its kind had swept so evilly free of all litter. Still came that eldritch, mocking cry—*"Tekeli-li! Tekeli-li!"* And at last we remembered that the daemoniac shoggoths—given life, thought, and plastic organ patterns solely by the Old Ones, and having no language save that which the dot-groups expressed—*had likewise no voice save the imitated accents of their bygone masters.*

XII

Danforth and I have recollections of emerging into the great sculptured hemisphere and of threading our back trail through the Cyclopean rooms and corridors of the dead city; yet these are purely dream-fragments involving no memory of volition, details, or physical exertion. It was as if we floated in a nebulous world or dimension without time, causation, or orientation. The grey half-daylight of the vast circular space sobered us somewhat; but we did not go near those cached sledges or look again at poor Gedney and the dog. They have a strange and titanic mausoleum, and I hope the end of this planet will find them still undisturbed.

It was while struggling up the colossal spiral incline that we first felt the terrible fatigue and short breath which our race through the thin plateau air had produced; but not even the fear of collapse could make us pause before reaching the normal outer realm of sun and sky. There was something vaguely appropriate about our departure from those buried epochs; for as we wound our panting way up the sixty-foot cylinder of primal masonry we glimpsed beside us a continuous procession of heroic sculptures in the dead race's early and undecayed technique—a farewell from the Old Ones, written fifty million years ago.

Finally scrambling out at the top, we found ourselves on a great mound of tumbled blocks; with the curved walls of higher stonework rising westward, and the brooding peaks of the great mountains shewing beyond the more crumbled structures toward the east. The low antarctic sun of midnight peered redly from the southern horizon through rifts in the jagged ruins, and the terrible age and deadness of the nightmare city seemed all the starker by contrast with such relatively known and accustomed things as the features of the polar landscape. The sky above was a churning and opalescent mass of tenuous ice-vapours, and the cold clutched at our vitals. Wearily resting the outfit-bags to which we had instinctively clung throughout our desperate flight, we rebuttoned our heavy garments for the stumbling climb down the mound and the walk through the aeon-old stone maze to the foothills where our aëroplane waited. Of what had set us fleeing from the darkness of earth's secret and archaic gulfs we said nothing at all.

In less than a quarter of an hour we had found the steep grade to the foothills—the probable ancient terrace—by which we had descended, and could see the dark bulk of our great plane amidst the sparse ruins on the rising slope ahead. Half way uphill toward our goal we paused for a momentary breathing-spell, and turned to look again at the fantastic palaeogean tangle of incredible stone shapes below us—once more outlined mystically against an unknown west. As we did so we saw that the sky beyond had lost its morning haziness; the restless ice-vapours having moved up to the zenith, where their mocking outlines seemed on the point of settling into some bizarre pattern which they feared to make quite definite or conclusive.

There now lay revealed on the ultimate white horizon behind the grotesque city a dim, elfin line of pinnacled violet whose needle-pointed heights loomed dream-like against the beckoning rose-colour of the western sky. Up toward this shimmering rim sloped the ancient table-land, the depressed course of the bygone river traversing it as an irregular ribbon of shadow. For a second we gasped in admiration of the scene's unearthly cosmic beauty, and then vague horror began to creep into our souls. For this far violet line could be nothing else than the terrible mountains of the forbidden land—highest of earth's peaks and focus of earth's evil; harbourers of nameless horrors and Archaean secrets; shunned and prayed to by those who feared to carve their meaning; untrodden by any living thing of earth, but visited by the sinister lightnings and sending strange beams across the plains in the polar night—beyond doubt the unknown archetype of that dreaded Kadath in the Cold Waste beyond abhorrent Leng, whereof unholy primal legends hint evasively. We were the first human beings ever to see them—and I hope to God we may be the last.

If the sculptured maps and pictures in that pre-human city had told truly, these cryptic violet mountains could not be much less than 300 miles away; yet none the less sharply did their dim elfin essence jut above that remote and snowy rim, like the serrated edge of a monstrous alien planet about to rise into unaccustomed heavens. Their height, then, must have been tremendous beyond all known comparison—carrying them up into tenuous atmospheric strata peopled by such gaseous wraiths as rash flyers have barely lived to whisper of after unexplainable falls. Looking at them, I thought nervously of certain sculptured hints of what the great bygone river had washed down into the city from their accursed slopes—and wondered how much sense and how much folly had lain in the fears of those Old Ones who carved them so reticently. I recalled how their northerly end must come near the coast at Queen Mary Land, where even at that moment Sir Douglas Mawson's expedition was doubtless working less than a thousand miles away; and hoped that no evil fate would give Sir Douglas and his men a glimpse of what might lie beyond the protecting coastal range. Such thoughts formed a measure of my overwrought condition at the time—and Danforth seemed to be even worse.

Yet long before we had passed the great star-shaped ruin and reached our plane our fears had become transferred to the lesser but vast enough range whose re-crossing lay ahead of us. From these foothills the black, ruin-crusted slopes reared up starkly and hideously against the east, again reminding us of those strange Asian paintings of Nicholas Roerich; and when we thought of the damnable honeycombs inside them, and of the frightful amorphous entities that might have pushed their foetidly squirming way even to the topmost hollow pinnacles, we could not face without panic the prospect of again sailing by those suggestive skyward cave-mouths where the wind made sounds like an evil musical piping over a wide range. To make matters worse, we saw distinct traces of local mist around several of the summits—as poor Lake must have done when he made that early mistake about volcanism—and thought shiveringly of that kindred mist from which we had just escaped; of that, and of the blasphemous, horror-fostering abyss whence all such vapours came.

All was well with the plane, and we clumsily hauled on our heavy flying furs. Danforth got the engine started without trouble, and we made a very smooth takeoff over the nightmare city. Below us the primal Cyclopean masonry spread out as it had done when first we saw it—so short, yet infinitely long, a time ago—and we began rising and turning to test the wind for our crossing through the pass. At a very high level there must have been great disturbance, since the ice-dust clouds of the zenith were doing all sorts of fantastic things; but at 24,000 feet, the height we needed for the pass, we found navigation quite practicable. As we drew close to the jutting peaks the wind's strange piping again became manifest, and I could see Danforth's hands trembling at the controls. Rank amateur though I was, I thought at that moment that I might be a better navigator than he in effecting the dangerous crossing between pinnacles; and when I made motions to change seats and take over his duties he did not protest. I tried to keep all my skill and self-possession about me, and stared at the sector of reddish farther sky betwixt the walls of the pass—resolutely refusing to pay attention to the puffs of mountain-top vapour, and wishing that I had wax-stopped ears like Ulysses' men off the Sirens' coast to keep that disturbing wind-piping from my consciousness.

But Danforth, released from his piloting and keyed up to a dangerous nervous pitch, could not keep quiet. I felt him turning and wriggling about as he looked back at the terrible receding city, ahead at the cave-riddled, cube-barnacled peaks, sidewise at the bleak sea of snowy, rampart-strown foothills, and upward at the seething, grotesquely clouded sky. It was then, just as I was trying to steer safely through the pass, that his mad shrieking brought us so close to disaster by shattering my tight hold on myself and causing me to fumble helplessly with the controls for a moment. A second afterward my resolution triumphed and we made the crossing safely—yet I am afraid that Danforth will never be the same again.

I have said that Danforth refused to tell me what final horror made him scream out so insanely—a horror which, I feel sadly sure, is mainly responsible for his present breakdown. We had snatches of shouted conversation above the wind's piping and the engine's buzzing as we reached the safe side of the range and swooped slowly down toward the camp, but that had mostly to do with the pledges of secrecy we had made as we prepared to leave the nightmare city. Certain things, we had agreed, were not for people to know and discuss lightly—and I would not speak of them now but for the need of heading off that Starkweather-Moore Expedition, and others, at any cost. It is absolutely necessary, for the peace and safety of mankind, that some of earth's dark, dead corners and unplumbed depths be let alone; lest sleeping abnormalities wake to resurgent life, and blasphemously surviving nightmares squirm and splash out of their black lairs to newer and wider conquests.

All that Danforth has ever hinted is that the final horror was a mirage. It was not, he declares, anything connected with the cubes and caves of echoing, vaporous, wormily honeycombed mountains of madness which we crossed; but a single fantastic, daemoniac glimpse, among the churning zenith-clouds, of what lay back of those other violet westward mountains which the Old Ones had shunned and feared. It is very probable that the thing was a sheer delusion born of the previous stresses we had passed through, and of the actual though unrecognised mirage of the dead transmontane city experienced near Lake's camp the day before; but it was so real to Danforth that he suffers from it still.

He has on rare occasions whispered disjointed and irresponsible things about "the black pit", "the carven rim", "the proto-shoggoths", "the windowless solids with five dimensions", "the nameless cylinder", "the elder pharos", "Yog-Sothoth", "the primal white jelly", "the colour out of space", "the wings", "the eyes in darkness", "the moon-ladder", "the original, the eternal, the undying", and other bizarre conceptions; but when he is fully himself he repudiates all this and attributes it to his curious and macabre reading of earlier years. Danforth, indeed, is known to be among the few who have ever dared go completely through that worm-riddled copy of the *Necronomicon* kept under lock and key in the college library.

The higher sky, as we crossed the range, was surely vaporous and disturbed enough; and although I did not see the zenith I can well imagine that its swirls of ice-dust may have taken strange forms. Imagination, knowing how vividly distant scenes can sometimes be reflected, refracted, and magnified by such layers of restless cloud, might easily have supplied the rest—and of course Danforth did not hint any of those specific horrors till after his memory had had a chance to draw on his bygone reading. He could never have seen so much in one instantaneous glance.

At the time his shrieks were confined to the repetition of a single mad word of all too obvious source:

"Tekeli-li! Tekeli-li!"

Madeline Yale Wynne (1847–1918)

The Little Room

Madeline Yale Wynne was an American artist, poet, and short story writer, the daughter of the inventor of the Yale lock. She is remembered for her early contributions to the arts-and-crafts movement, especially in jewelry and enamelling long before the crafts became fashionable. The *Encyclopedia of Arts and Crafts* says, "she learned about metal in the workshops of her father. . . . The ideas for her jewels grew out of the metal itself, from what happened when she hit a coil of silver with a hammer or drove a blunt punch into sheet copper—a similar approach to that of Alexander Calder half a century later," and praises her work as "witty and intuitive." Alfred Bendixen reports that she was known for her attempts to interest other women in this art form. Her writing, however, has been substantially forgotten. Although apparently "The Little Room" received much praise and attention upon its original appearance in *Harper's Magazine,* no mention of it or her appears in most standard reference books. Her collection, *The Little Room and Other Stories* (1895), is a little known book. But in fact "The Little Room" is a minor masterpiece, on a par with Charlotte Perkins Gilman's "The Yellow Wall-Paper," which it predates. It is not only a subtle feminist work but also a mysterious meditation upon the nature of reality, the more powerful for its ambiguity. A unique haunted house story, it achieves considerable psychological depth through attention to nuance and detail, and careful use of allusion to events outside the story In the past. One wonders how many other stories of this quality have been forgotten.

H ow would it do for a smoking-room?"

"Just the very place! Only, you know, Roger, you must not think of smoking in the house. I am almost afraid that having just a plain, common man around, let alone a smoking man, will upset Aunt Hannah. She is New England—Vermont, New England—boiled down."

"You leave Aunt Hannah to me; I'll find her tender side. I'm going to ask her about the old sea-captain and the yellow calico."

"Not yellow calico—blue chintz."

"Well, yellow *shell* then."

"No, no! don't mix it up so; you won't know yourself what to expect, and that's half the fun."

"Now you tell me again exactly what to expect; to tell the truth, I didn't half hear about it the other day; I was wool-gathering. It was something queer that happened when you were a child, wasn't it?"

"Something that began to happen long before that, and kept happening, and may happen again—but I hope not."

"What was it?"

"I wonder if the other people in the car can hear us?"

"I fancy not; we don't hear them—not consecutively, at least."

"Well, mother was born in Vermont, you know; she was the only child by a second marriage. Aunt Hannah and Aunt Maria are only half-aunts to me, you know."

"I hope they are half as nice as you are."

"Roger, be still—they certainly will hear us."

"Well, don't you want them to know we are married?"

"Yes, but not just married. There's all the difference in the world."

"You are afraid we look too happy!"

"No, only I want my happiness all to myself."

"Well, the little room?"

"My aunts brought mother up; they were nearly twenty years older than she. I might say Hiram and they brought her up. You see, Hiram was bound out to my grandfather when he was a boy, and when grandfather died Hiram said he 's'posed he went with the farm, 'long o' the critters,' and he has been there ever since. He was my mother's only refuge from the decorum of my aunts. They are simply workers. They make me think of the Maine woman who wanted her epitaph to be: 'She was a *hard*-working woman.' "

"They must be almost beyond their working-days. How old are they?"

"Seventy, or thereabouts; but they will die standing; or, at least, on a Saturday night, after all the housework is done up. They were rather strict with mother, and I think she had a lonely childhood. The house is almost a mile away from any neighbours, and off on top of what they call Stony Hill. It is bleak enough up there, even in summer.

"When mamma was about ten years old they sent her to cousins in Brooklyn, who had children of their own, and knew more about bringing them up. She stayed there till she was married; she didn't go to Vermont in all that time, and of course hadn't seen her sisters, for they never would leave home for a day. They couldn't even be induced to go to Brooklyn for her wedding, so she and father took their wedding trip up there."

"And that's why we are going up there on our own?"

"Don't, Roger; you have no idea how loud you speak."

"You never say so except when I am going to say that one little word."

"Well, don't say it, then, or say it very, very quietly."

"Well, what was the queer thing?"

"When they got to the house, mother wanted to take father right off into the little room; she had been telling him about it, just as I am going to tell you, and she had said that of all the rooms, that one was the only one that seemed pleasant to her. She described the furniture and the books and paper and everything, and said it was on the north side, between the front and back rooms. Well, when they went to look for it, there was no little room there; there was only a shallow china-closet. She asked her sisters when the house had been altered and a closet made of the room that used to be there. They both said the house was exactly as it had been built—that they had never made any changes, except to tear down the old wood-shed and build a smaller one.

"Father and mother laughed a good deal over it, and when anything was lost they would always say it must be in the little room, and any exaggerated statement was called 'little-roomy.' When I was a child I thought that was a regular English phrase, I heard it so often.

"Well, they talked it over, and finally they concluded that my mother had been a very imaginative sort of a child, and had read in some book about such a little room, or perhaps even dreamed it, and then had 'made believe,' as children do, till she herself had really thought the room was there."

"Why, of course, that might easily happen."

"Yes, but you haven't heard the queer part yet; you wait and see if you can explain the rest as easily.

"They stayed at the farm two weeks, and then went to New York to live. When I was eight years old my father was killed in the war, and mother was broken-hearted. She never was quite strong afterwards, and that summer we decided to go up to the farm for three months.

"I was a restless sort of a child, and the journey seemed very long to me; and finally, to pass the time, mamma told me the story of the little room, and how it was all in her own imagination, and how there really was only a china-closet there.

"She told it with all the particulars; and even to me, who knew beforehand that the room wasn't there, it seemed just as real as could be. She said it was on the north side, between the front and back rooms; that it was very small, and they sometimes called it an entry. There was a door also that opened out-of-doors, and that one was painted green, and was cut in the middle like the old Dutch doors, so that it could be used for a window by opening the top part only. Directly opposite the door was a lounge or couch; it was covered with blue chintz—India chintz—some that had been brought over by an old Salem sea-captain as a 'venture.' He had given it to Hannah when she was a young girl. She was sent to Salem for two years to school. Grandfather originally came from Salem."

"I thought there wasn't any room or chintz."

"*That is just it.* They had decided that mother had imagined it all, and yet you see how exactly everything was painted in her mind, for she had even remembered that Hiram had told her that Hannah could have married the sea-captain if she had wanted to!

"The India cotton was the regular blue stamped chintz, with the peacock figure on it. The head and body of the bird were in profile, while the tail was full front view behind it. It had seemed to take mamma's fancy, and she drew it for me on a piece of paper as she talked. Doesn't it seem strange to you that she could have made all that up, or even dreamed it?

"At the foot of the lounge were some hanging shelves with some old books on them. All the books were leather-coloured except one; that was bright red, and was called the *Ladies' Album*. It made a bright break between the other thicker books.

"On the lower shelf was a beautiful pink sea-shell, lying on a mat made of balls of red shaded worsted. This shell was greatly coveted by mother, but she was only allowed to play with it when she had been particularly good. Hiram had shown her how to hold it close to her ear and hear the roar of the sea in it.

"I know you will like Hiram, Roger; he is quite a character in his way.

"Mamma said she remembered, or *thought* she remembered, having been sick once, and she had to lie quietly for some days on the lounge; then was the time she had become so familiar with everything in the room, and she had been allowed to have the shell to play with all the time. She had had her toast brought to her in there, with make-believe tea. It was one of her pleasant memories of her childhood; it was the first time she had been of any importance to anybody, even herself.

"Right at the head of the lounge was a light-stand, as they called it, and on it was a very brightly-polished brass candlestick and a brass tray with snuffers. That is all I remember of her describing, except that there was a braided rag rug on the floor, and on the wall was a beautiful flowered paper—roses and morning-glories in a wreath on a light blue ground. The same paper was in the front room."

"And all this never existed except in her imagination?"

"She said that when she and father went up there, there wasn't any little room at all like it anywhere in the house; there was a china-closet where she had believed the room to be."

"And your aunts said there had never been any such room?"

"That is what they said."

"Wasn't there any blue chintz in the house with a peacock figure?"

"Not a scrap, and Aunt Hannah said there had never been any that she could remember; and Aunt Maria just echoed her—she always does that. You see, Aunt Hannah is an up-and-down New England woman. She looks just like herself; I mean, just like her character. Her joints move up and down or backward and forward in a plain square fashion. I don't believe she ever leaned on anything in her life or sat in an easy chair. But Maria is different; she is rounder and softer—she hasn't any ideas of her own, she never had any. I don't believe she would think it right or becoming to have one that differed from Aunt Hannah's, so what would be the use of having any? She is an echo, that's all.

"When mamma and I got there, of course I was all excitement to see the china-closet, and I had a sort of feeling that it would be the little room after all. So I ran ahead and threw open the door, crying, 'Come and see the little room.'

"And, Roger," said Mrs. Grant, laying her hand in his, "there really was a little room there, exactly as mother had remembered it. There was the lounge, the peacock chintz, the green door, the shell, the morning-glory, and the rose paper, *everything exactly as she had described it to me.*"

"What in the world did the sisters say about it?"

"Wait a minute and I will tell you. My mother was in the front hall still talking with Aunt Hannah. She didn't hear me at first, but I ran out there and dragged her through the front room, saying, 'The room *is* here—it's all right.'

"It seemed for a minute as if my mother would faint. She clung to me in terror. I can remember now how strained her eyes looked and how pale she was.

"I called out to Aunt Hannah and asked her when they had had the closet taken away and the little room built; for in my excitement I thought that was what had been done.

" 'That little room has always been there,' said Aunt Hannah, 'ever since the house was built.'

" 'But mamma said there wasn't any little room here, only a china-closet, when she was here with papa,' said I.

" 'No, there has never been any china-closet there; it has always been just as it is now,' said Aunt Hannah.

"Then mother spoke; her voice sounded weak and far off. She said, slowly and with an effort, 'Maria, don't you remember that you told me that there had *never been any little room here,* and Hannah said so too, and then I said I must have dreamed it?'

" 'No, I don't remember anything of the kind,' said Maria, without the slightest emotion. 'I don't remember you ever said anything about any china-closet. The house has never been altered; you used to play in this room when you were a child, don't you remember?'

" 'I know it,' said mother, in that queer slow voice that made me feel frightened. 'Hannah, don't you remember my finding the china-closet here, with the gilt-edged china on the shelves, and then you said the *china-closet* had always been here?'

" 'No,' said Hannah, pleasantly but unemotionally, 'no, I don't think you ever asked me about any china-closet, and we haven't any gilt-edged china that I know of.'

"And that was the strangest thing about it. We never could make them remember that there had ever been any question about it. You would think they could remember how surprised mother had been before, unless she had imagined the whole thing. Oh, it was so queer! They were always pleasant about it, but they didn't seem to feel any interest or curiosity. It was always this answer: 'The house is just as it was built; there have never been any changes, so far as we know.'

"And my mother was in an agony of perplexity. How cold their grey eyes looked to me! There was no reading anything in them. It just seemed to break my mother down, this queer thing. Many times that summer, in the middle of the night, I have seen her get up and take a candle and creep softly downstairs. I could hear the steps creak under her weight. Then she would go through the front room and peer into the darkness, holding her thin hand between the candle and her eyes. She seemed to think the little room might vanish. Then she would come back to bed and toss about all night, or lie still and shiver; it used to frighten me.

"She grew pale and thin, and she had a little cough; then she did not like to be left alone. Sometimes she would make errands in order to send me to the little room for something—a book, or her fan, or her handkerchief; but she would never sit there or let me stay in there long, and sometimes she wouldn't let me go in there for days together. Oh, it was pitiful!"

"Well, don't talk any more about it, Margaret, if it makes you feel so," said Mr. Grant.

"Oh yes, I want you to know all about it, and there isn't much more—no more about the room.

"Mother never got well, and she died that autumn. She used often to sigh, and say, with a wan little laugh, 'There is one thing I am glad of, Margaret; your father knows now all about the little room.' I think she was afraid I distrusted her. Of course, in a child's way, I thought there was something queer about it, but I did not brood over it. I was too young then, and took it as a part of her illness. But, Roger, do you know, it really did affect me. I almost hate to go there after talking about it; I somehow feel as if it might, you know, be a china-closet again."

"That's an absurd idea."

"I know it; of course it can't be. I saw the room, and there isn't any china-closet there, and no gilt-edged china in the house, either."

And then she whispered; "But, Roger, you may hold my hand as you do now, if you will, when we go to look for the little room."

"And you won't mind Aunt Hannah's grey eyes?"

"I won't mind *anything*."

It was dusk when Mr. and Mrs. Grant went into the gate under the two old Lombardy poplars and walked up the narrow path to the door, where they were met by the two aunts.

Hannah gave Mrs. Grant a frigid but not unfriendly kiss; and Maria seemed for a moment to tremble on the verge of an emotion, but she glanced at Hannah, and then gave her greeting in exactly the same repressed and non-committal way.

Supper was waiting for them. On the table was the *gilt-edged* china. Mrs. Grant didn't notice it immediately, till she saw her husband smiling at her over his teacup; then she felt fidgety, and couldn't eat. She was nervous, and kept wondering what was behind her, whether it would be a little room or a closet.

After supper she offered to help about the dishes, but, mercy! she might as well have offered to help bring the seasons round; Maria and Hannah couldn't be helped.

So she and her husband went to find the little room, or closet, or whatever was to be there.

Aunt Maria followed them, carrying the lamp, which she set down, and then went back to the dish-washing.

Margaret looked at her husband. He kissed her, for she seemed troubled; and then, hand in hand, they opened the door. It opened into a *china-closet*. The shelves were neatly draped with scalloped paper; on them was the gilt-edged china, with the dishes missing that had been used at the supper, and which at that moment were being carefully washed and wiped by the two aunts.

Margaret's husband dropped her hand and looked at her. She was trembling a little, and turned to him for help, for some explanation, but in an instant she knew that something was wrong. A cloud had come between them; he was hurt, he was antagonised.

He paused for an appreciable instant, and then said, kindly enough, but in a voice that cut her deeply:

"I am glad this ridiculous thing is ended; don't let us speak of it again."

"Ended!" said she. "How ended?" And somehow her voice sounded to her as her mother's voice had when she stood there and questioned her sisters about the little room. She seemed to have to drag her words out. She spoke slowly: "It seems to me to have only begun in my case. It was just so with mother when she—"

"I really wish, Margaret, you would let it drop. I don't like to hear you speak of your mother in connection with it. It—" He hesitated, for was not this their wedding-day? "It doesn't seem quite the thing, quite delicate, you know, to use her name in the matter."

She saw it all now; *he didn't believe her*. She felt a chill sense of withering under his glance.

"Come," he added, "let us go out, or into the dining-room, somewhere, anywhere, only drop this nonsense."

He went out; he did not take her hand now—he was vexed, baffled, hurt. Had he not given her his sympathy, his attention, his belief—and his hand?—and she was fooling him. What did it mean? She so truthful, so free from morbidness—a thing he hated. He walked up and down under the poplars, trying to get into the mood to go and join her in the house.

Margaret heard him go out; then she turned and shook the shelves; she reached her hand behind them and tried to push the boards away; she ran out of the house on to the north side and tried to find in the darkness, with her hands, a door, or some steps leading to one. She tore her dress on the old rose-trees, she fell and rose and stumbled, then she sat down on the ground and tried to think. What could she think—was she dreaming?

She went into the house and out into the kitchen, and begged Aunt Maria to tell her about the little room—what had become of it, when they had built the closet, when they had bought the gilt-edged china?

They went on washing dishes and drying them on the spotless towels with methodical exactness; and as they worked they said that there had never been any little room, so far as they knew; the china-closet had always been there, and the gilt-edged china had belonged to their mother, it had always been in the house.

"No, I don't remember that your mother ever asked about any little room," said Hannah. "She didn't seem very well that summer, but she never asked about any changes in the house; there hadn't ever been any changes."

There it was again: not a sign of interest, curiosity, or annoyance, not a spark of memory.

She went out to Hiram. He was telling Mr. Grant about the farm. She had meant to ask him about the room, but her lips were sealed before her husband.

Months afterwards, when time had lessened the sharpness of their feelings, they learned to speculate reasonably about the phenomenon, which Mr. Grant had accepted as something not to be scoffed away, not to be treated as a poor joke, but to be put aside as something inexplicable on any ordinary theory.

Margaret alone in her heart knew that her mother's words carried a deeper significance than she had dreamed of at that time. "One thing I am glad of, your father knows now," and she wondered if Roger or she would ever know.

Five years later they were going to Europe. The packing was done; the children were lying asleep, with their travelling things ready to be shipped on for an early start.

Roger had a foreign appointment. They were not to be back in America for some years. She had meant to go up to say good-bye to her aunts; but a mother of three children intends to do a great many things that never get done. One thing she had done that very day, and as she paused for a moment between the writing of two notes that must be posted before she went to bed, she said:

"Roger, you remember Rita Lash? Well, she and Cousin Nan go up to the Adirondacks every autumn. They are clever girls, and I have entrusted to them something I want done very much."

"They are the girls to do it, then, every inch of them."

"I know it, and they are going to."

"Well?"

"Why, you see, Roger, that little room—"

"Oh—"

"Yes, I was a coward not to go myself, but I didn't find time, because I hadn't the courage."

"Oh! *that* was it, was it?"

"Yes, just that. They are going, and they will write us about it."

"Want to get—?"

"No; I only want to know."

Rita Lash and Cousin Nan planned to go to Vermont on their way to the Adirondacks. They found they would have three hours between trains, which would give them time to drive up to the Keys farm, and they could still get to the camp that night. But, at the last minute, Rita was prevented from going. Nan had to go to meet the Adirondack party, and she promised to telegraph Rita when she arrived at the camp. Imagine Rita's amusement when she received this message: "Safely arrived; went to Keys farm; it is a little room."

Rita was amused, because she did not in the least think Nan had been there. She thought it was a hoax; but it put it into her mind to carry the joke further by really stopping herself when she went up, as she meant to do the next week. She did stop over. She introduced herself to the two maiden ladies, who seemed familiar, as they had been described by Mrs. Grant.

They were, if not cordial, at least not disconcerted at her visit, and willingly showed her over the house. As they did not speak of any other stranger's having been to see them lately, she became confirmed in her belief that Nan had not been there.

In the north room she saw the roses and morning-glory paper on the wall, and also the door that should open into—what?

She asked if she might open it.

"Certainly," said Hannah; and Maria echoed, "Certainly."

She opened it, and found the china-closet. She experienced a certain relief; she at least was not under any spell. Mrs. Grant left it a china-closet; she found it the same. Good.

But she tried to induce the old sisters to remember that there had at various times been certain questions relating to a confusion as to whether the closet had always been a closet. It was no use: their stony eyes gave no sign.

Then she thought of the story of the sea-captain, and said, "Miss Keys, did you ever have a lounge covered with India chintz, with a figure of a peacock on it, given to you in Salem by a sea-captain, who brought it from India?"

"I dunno as I ever did," said Hannah. That was all. She thought Maria's cheeks were a little flushed, but her eyes were like a stone wall.

She went on that night to the Adirondacks. When Nan and she were alone in their room, she said: "By the way, Nan, what did you see at the farmhouse, and how did you like Maria and Hannah?"

Nan didn't mistrust that Rita had been there, and she began excitedly to tell her all about her visit. Rita could almost have believed Nan had been there if she hadn't known it was not so. She let her go on for some time, enjoying her enthusiasm, and the impressive way in which she described her opening the door and finding the "little room." Then Rita said: "Now, Nan, that is enough fibbing. I went to the farm myself on my way up yesterday, and there is *no* little room, and there *never* has been any; it is a china-closet, just as Mrs. Grant saw it last."

She was pretending to be busy unpacking her trunk, and did not look up for a moment; but as Nan did not say anything, she glanced at her over her shoulder. Nan was actually pale, and it was hard to say whether she was more angry or frightened. There was something of both in her look. And then Rita began to explain how her telegram had put her in the spirit of going up there alone. She hadn't meant to cut Nan out. She only thought—Then Nan broke in: "It isn't that; I am sure you can't think it is that. But I went myself, and you did not go; you can't have been there, for *it is a little room.*"

Oh, what a night they had! They couldn't sleep. They talked and argued, and then kept still for a while, only to break out again, it was so absurd. They both maintained that they had been there, but both sure the other one was either crazy or obstinate beyond reason. They were wretched; it was perfectly ridiculous, two friends at odds over such a thing; but there it was—"little room," "china-closet," "china-closet," "little room."

The next morning Nan was tacking up some tarlatan at a window to keep the midges out. Rita offered to help her, as she had done for the past ten years. Nan's "No, thanks," cut her to the heart.

"Nan," said she, "come right down from that stepladder and pack your satchel. The stage leaves in just twenty minutes. We can catch the afternoon express train, and we will go together to the farm. I am either going there or going home. You had better go with me."

Nan didn't say a word. She gathered up the hammer and tacks, and was ready to start when the stage came round.

It meant for them thirty miles of staging and six hours of train, besides crossing the lake; but what of that, compared to having a lie lying round loose between them! Europe would have seemed easy to accomplish, if it would settle the question.

At the little junction in Vermont they found a farmer with a wagon full of meal-bags. They asked him if he could not take them up to the old Keys farm and bring them back in time for the return train, due in two hours.

They had planned to call it a sketching trip, so they said: "We have been there before, we are artists, and we might find some views worth taking; and we want also to make a short call upon the Misses Keys."

"Did ye calculate to paint the old *house* in the picture?"

They said it was possible they might do so. They wanted to see it, anyway.

"Waal, I guess you are too late. The *house* burnt down last night, and everything in it."

Jean Ray (1887–1964)

The Shadowy Street

Raymundus Joannes Maria De Kremer (1887–1984), who wrote under the pseudonym "Jean Ray," was a Belgian journalist and European pulp writer sometimes called "The Belgian Poe." Significantly, at least four of his stories were translated and published in the 1930s in *Weird Tales*. It was not until 1965, however, that a collection of his work appeared in English, in a garish paperback original entitled *Ghouls in my Grave*, at the dying end of the mass market horror boomlet of the early 1960s. It contains several of his better stories, including "The Shadowy Street," which is perhaps his masterpiece. The influence of Lovecraft and Poe is clear, particularly in the pseudoscientific mentions of Einstein and the Lorenz-Fitzgerald contraction. But one must also look back to the earlier Hoffmanesque tales of the Romantic period for characters fascinated by golden riches, which suggest a folktale morality at work. Still, this tale is firmly in the horror genre and deserves a wider audience.

O n a Rotterdam dock, winches were fishing bales of old paper from the hold of a freighter. The wind was fluttering the multicolored streamers that hung from the bales when one of them burst open like a cask in a roaring fire. The longshoremen hastily scooped up some of the rustling mass, but a large part of it was abandoned to the joy of the little children who gleaned in the eternal autumn of the waterfront.

There were beautiful Pearsons engravings, cut in half by order of Customs; green and pink bundles of stocks and bonds, the last echoes of resounding bankruptcies; pitiful books whose pages were still joined like desperate hands. My cane explored that vast residue of thought, in which neither shame nor hope was now alive.

Amid all that English and German prose I found a few pages of France: copies of *Le Magasin Pittoresque*, solidly bound and somewhat scorched by fire.

It was in looking through those magazines, so adorably illustrated and so dismally written, that I found the two manuscripts, one in German, the other in French. Their authors had apparently been unaware of each other, and yet the French manuscript seemed to cast a little light on the black anguish that rose from the German one like a noxious vapor—insofar as any light can be shed on that story which appears to be haunted by such sinister and hostile forces!

The cover bore the name Alphonse Archipetre, followed by the word *Lehrer*. I shall translate the German pages:

124

The German Manuscript

I am writing this for Hermann, when he comes back from sea.

If he does not find me here, if I, along with my poor friends, have been swallowed up by the savage mystery that surrounds us, I want him to know our days of horror through this little notebook. It will be the best proof of my affection that I can give him, because it takes real courage for a woman to keep a journal in such hours of madness. I am also writing so that he will pray for me, if he believes my soul to be in peril. . . .

After the death of my Aunt Hedwige, I did not want to go on living in our sad Holzdamm house. The Rückhardt sisters offered to let me stay with them. They lived in a big apartment on the Deichstrasse, in the spacious house of Councillor Hühnebein, an old bachelor who never left the first floor, which was littered with books, paintings, and engravings.

Lotte, Eleonore, and Meta Rückhardt were adorable old maids who used all their ingenuity in trying to make life pleasant for me. Frida, our maid, came with me; she found favor in the eyes of the ancient Frau Pilz, the Rückhardts' inspired cook, who was said to have turned down ducal offers in order to remain in the humble service of her mistresses.

That evening. . . .

On that evening, which was to bring unspeakable terror into our calm lives, we had decided against going to a celebration in Tempelhof, because it was raining in torrents. Frau Pilz, who liked to have us stay home, had made us an outstanding supper: grilled trout and a guinea-hen pie. Lotte had searched the cellar and come up with a bottle of Cape brandy that had been aging there for over twenty years. When the table had been cleared, the beautiful dark liquor was poured into glasses of Bohemian crystal. Eleonore served the Lapsang Souchong tea that an old Bremen sailor brought back to us from his voyages.

Through the sound of the rain we heard the clock of Saint Peter's strike eight. Frida was sitting beside the fire. Her head drooped over her illustrated Bible; she was unable to read it, but she liked to look at the pictures. She asked for permission to go to bed. The four of us who remained went on sorting colored silks for Meta's embroidery.

Downstairs, the councillor noisily locked his bedroom door. Frau Pilz went up to her room, bade us good night through the door, and added that the bad weather would no doubt prevent us from having fresh fish for dinner the next day. A small cascade was splattering loudly on the pavement from a broken rain gutter on the house next door. A strong wind came thundering down the street; the cascade was dispersed into a silvery mist, and a window slammed shut on one of the upper stories.

"That's the attic window," said Lotte. "It won't stay closed." She raised the garnet-red curtain and looked down at the street. "I've never seen it so dark before. I'm not sleepy, and I certainly have no desire to go to bed. I feel as though the darkness of the street would follow me, along with the wind and the rain."

"You're talking like a fool," said Eleonore, who was not very gentle. "Well, since no one is going to bed, let's do as men do and fill our glasses again."

She went off to get three of those beautiful Sieme candles that burn with a pink flame and give off a delightful smell of flowers and incense.

I felt that we all wanted to give a festive tone to that bleak evening, and that for some reason we were unsuccessful. I saw Eleonore's energetic face darkened by a sudden shadow of ill-humor. Lotte seemed to be having difficulty in breathing. Only Meta was leaning placidly over her embroidery, and yet I sensed that she was attentive, as though she were trying to detect a sound in the depths of the silence.

Just then the door opened and Frida came in. She staggered over to the armchair beside the fire and sank into it, staring wild-eyed at each of us in turn.

"Frida!" I cried. "What's the matter?"

She sighed deeply, then murmured a few indistinct words.

"She's still asleep," said Eleonore.

Frida shook her head forcefully and made violent efforts to speak. I handed her my glass of brandy and she emptied it in one gulp, like a coachman or a porter. Under other circumstances we would have been offended by this vulgarity, but she seemed so unhappy, and the atmosphere in the room had been so depressing for the past few minutes, that it passed unnoticed.

"Fräulein," said Frida, "there's. . . ." Her eyes, which softened for a moment, resumed their wild expression. "I don't know. . . ."

Eleonore uttered an impatient exclamation.

"What have you seen or heard? What's wrong with you, Frida?"

"Fräulein, there's . . ." Frida seemed to reflect deeply. "I don't know how to say it. . . . There's a great fear in my room."

"Oh!" said all three of us, reassured and apprehensive at the same time.

"You've had a nightmare," said Meta. "I know how it is: you hide your head under the covers when you wake up."

"No, that's not it," said Frida. "I hadn't been dreaming. I just woke up, that's all, and then . . . How can I make you understand? There's a great fear in my room. . . ."

"Good heavens, that doesn't explain anything!" I said.

Frida shook her head in despair:

"I'd rather sit outside in the rain all night than go back to that room. No, I won't go back!"

"I'm going to see what's happening up there, you fool!" said Eleonore, throwing a shawl over her shoulders.

She hesitated for a moment before her father's old rapier, hanging among some university insignia. Then she shrugged, picked up the candlestick with its pink candles, and walked out, leaving a perfumed wake behind her.

"Oh, don't let her go there alone!" cried Frida, alarmed.

We slowly went to the staircase. The flickering glow of Eleonore's candlestick was already vanishing on the attic landing.

We stood in the semidarkness at the foot of the stairs. We heard Eleonore open a door. There was a minute of oppressive silence. I felt Frida's hand tighten on my waist.

"Don't leave her alone," she moaned.

Just then there was a loud laugh, so horrible that I would rather die than hear it again. Almost at the same time, Meta raised her hand and cried out, "There! . . . There! . . . A face. . . . There. . . ."

The house became filled with sounds. The councillor and Frau Pilz appeared in the yellow haloes of the candles they were holding.

"Fräulein Eleonore!" sobbed Frida. "Dear God, how are we going to find her?"

It was a frightening question, and I can now answer it: *We never found her.*

Frida's room was empty. The candlestick was standing on the floor and its candles were still burning peacefully, with their delicate pink flames.

We searched the whole house and even went out on the roof. We never saw Eleonore again.

We could not count on the help of the police, as will soon be seen. When we went to the police station, we found that it had been invaded by a frenzied crowd; some of the furniture had been overturned, the windows were covered with dust, and the clerks were being pushed around like puppets. Eighty people had vanished that night, some from their homes, others while they were on their way home!

The world of ordinary conjectures was closed to us; only supernatural apprehensions remained.

Several days went by. We led a bleak life of tears and terror.

Councillor Hühnebein had the attic sealed off from the rest of the house by a thick oak partition.

One day I went in search of Meta. We were beginning to fear another tragedy when we found her squatting in front of the partition with her eyes dry and an expression of anger on her usually gentle face. She was holding her father's rapier in her hand, and seemed annoyed at having been disturbed.

We tried to question her about the face she had glimpsed, but she looked at us as though she did not understand. She remained completely silent. She did not answer us, and even seemed unaware of our presence.

All sorts of wild stories were being repeated in the town. There was talk of a secret criminal league; the police were accused of negligence, and worse; public officials had been dismissed. All this, of course, was useless.

Strange crimes had been committed: savagely mutilated corpses were found at dawn. Wild animals could not have shown more ardent lust for carnage than the mysterious attackers. Some of the victims had been robbed, but most of them had not, and this surprised everyone.

But I do not want to dwell on what was happening in the town; it will be easy to find enough people to tell about it. I will limit myself to the framework of our house and our life, which, though narrow, still enclosed enough fear and despair.

The days passed and April came, colder and windier than the worst month of winter. We remained huddled beside the fire. Sometimes Councillor Hühnebein came to keep us company and give us what he called courage. This consisted in trembling in all his limbs, holding his hands out toward the fire, drinking big mugs of punch, starting at every sound, and crying out five or six times an hour, "Did you hear that? Did you hear? . . ."

Frida tore some of the pages out of her Bible, and we found them pinned or pasted on every door and curtain, in every nook and cranny. She hoped that this would ward off the spirits of evil. We did not interfere, and since we spent several days in peace we were far from thinking it a bad idea.

We soon saw how terribly mistaken we were. The day had been so dark, and the clouds so low, that evening had come early. I was walking out of the living room to put a lamp on the broad landing—for ever since the terrifying night we had placed lights all over the house, and even the halls and stairs remained lighted till dawn—when I heard voices murmuring on the top floor.

It was not yet completely dark. I bravely climbed the stairs and found myself before the frightened faces of Frida and Frau Pilz, who motioned me to be silent and pointed to the newly-built partition.

I stood beside them, adopting their silence and attention. It was then that I heard an indefinable sound from behind the wooden wall, something like the faint roar of giant conch shells, or the tumult of a faraway crowd.

"Fräulein Eleonore, . . ." moaned Frida.

The answer came immediately and hurled us screaming down the stairs: a long shriek of terror rang out, not from the partition above us, but from downstairs, from the councillor's apartment. Then he called for help at the top of his lungs. Lotte and Meta had hurried out onto the landing.

"We must go there," I said courageously.

We had not taken three steps when there was another cry of distress, this time from above us.

"Help! Help!"

We recognized Frau Pilz's voice. We heard her call again, feebly.

Meta picked up the lamp I had placed on the landing. Halfway up the stairs we found Frida alone. Frau Pilz had disappeared.

At this point I must express my admiration of Meta Rückhardt's calm courage.

"There's nothing more we can do here," she said, breaking the silence she had stubbornly maintained for several days. "Let's go downstairs. . . ."

She was holding her father's rapier, and she did not look at all ridiculous, for we sensed that she would use it as effectively as a man.

We followed her, subjugated by her cold strength.

The councillor's study was as brightly lighted as a traveling carnival. The poor man had given the darkness no chance to get in. Two enormous lamps with white porcelain globes stood at either end of the mantelpiece, looking like two placid moons. A small Louis XV chandelier hung from the ceiling, its prisms flashing like handfuls of precious stones. Copper and stone candlesticks stood on the floor in every corner of the room. On the table, a row of tall candles seemed to be illuminating an invisible catafalque.

We stopped, dazzled, and looked around for the councillor.

"Oh!" Frida exclaimed suddenly. "Look, there he is! He's hiding behind the window curtain."

Lotte abruptly pulled back the heavy curtain. Herr Hühnebein was there, leaning out the open window, motionless.

Lotte went over to him, then leapt back with a cry of horror.

"Don't look! For the love of heaven, don't look! He . . . he . . . his head is gone!"

I saw Frida stagger, ready to faint. Meta's voice called us back to reason:

"Be careful! There's danger here!"

We pressed up close to her, feeling protected by her presence of mind. Suddenly something blinked on the ceiling, and we saw with alarm that darkness had invaded two opposite corners of the room, where the lights had just been extinguished.

"Hurry, protect the lights!" panted Meta. "Oh! . . . There! . . . There he is!"

At that moment the white moons on the mantelpiece burst, spat out streaks of smoky flame, and vanished.

Meta stood motionless, but she looked all around the room with a cold rage that I had never seen in her before.

The candles on the table were blown out. Only the little chandelier continued to shed its calm light. I saw that Meta was keeping her eyes on it. Suddenly her rapier flashed and she lunged forward into empty space.

"Protect the light!" she cried. "I see him! I've got him! . . . Ah! . . ."

We saw the rapier make strange, violent movements in her hand, as though an invisible force were trying to take it away from her.

It was Frida who had the odd but fortunate inspiration that saved us that evening. She uttered a fierce cry, picked up one of the heavy copper candlesticks, leapt to Meta's side, and began striking the air with her gleaming club. The rapier stopped moving;

something very light seemed to brush against the floor, then the door opened by itself, and a heartrending clamor arose.

"That takes care of one of them," said Meta.

One might wonder why we stubbornly went on living in that murderously haunted house.

At least a hundred other houses were in the same situation. People had stopped counting the murders and disappearances, and had become almost indifferent to them. The town was gloomy. There were dozens of suicides, for some people preferred to die by their own hands rather than be killed by the phantom executioners. And then, too, Meta wanted to take vengeance. She was now waiting for the invisible beings to return.

She had relapsed into her grim silence; she spoke to us only to order us to lock the doors and shutters at nightfall. As soon as darkness fell, the four of us went into the living room, which was now a dormitory and dining room as well. We did not leave it until morning.

I questioned Frida about her strange armed intervention. She was able to give me only a confused answer.

"I don't know," she said. "It seemed to me I saw something. . . . A face. . . . I don't know how to say what it was. . . . Yes, it was the great fear that was in my room the first night."

That was all I could get out of her.

One evening toward the middle of April, Lotte and Frida were lingering in the kitchen. Meta opened the living-room door and told them to hurry. I saw that the shadows of night had already invaded the landings and the hall.

"We're coming," they replied in unison.

Meta came back into the living room and closed the door. She was horribly pale. No sound came from downstairs. I waited vainly to hear the footsteps of the two women. The silence was like a threatening flood rising on the other side of the wall.

Meta locked the door.

"What are you doing?" I asked. "What about Lotte and Frida?"

"It's no use," she said dully.

Her eyes, motionless and terrible, stared at the rapier. The sinister darkness arrived. It was thus that Lotte and Frida vanished into mystery.

Dear God, what was it? There was a presence in the house, a suffering, wounded presence that was seeking help. I did not know whether Meta was aware of it or not. She was more taciturn than ever, but she barricaded the doors and windows in a way that seemed designed more to prevent an escape than an intrusion. My life had become a fearful solitude. Meta herself was like a sneering specter.

During the day, I sometimes came upon her unexpectedly in one of the halls; in one hand she held the rapier, and in the other she held a powerful lantern with a reflector and a lens that she shone into all the dark corners.

During one of these encounters, she told me rather impolitely that I had better go back to the living room, and when I obeyed her too slowly she shouted furiously at me that I must never interfere with her plans.

Her face no longer had the placid look it had worn as she leaned over her embroidery only a few days before. It was now a savage face, and she sometimes glared at me with a flame of hatred in her eyes. For I had a secret. . . .

Was it curiosity, perversity, or pity that made me act as I did? I pray to God that I was moved by nothing more than pity and kindness.

I had just drawn some fresh water from the fountain in the wash-house when I heard a muffled moan: "Moh. . . . Moh. . . ."

I thought of our vanished friends and looked around me. I saw a well-concealed door that led into a storeroom in which poor Hühnebein had kept stacks of books and paintings, amid dust and cobwebs.

"Moh. . . . Moh. . . ."

It was coming from inside the storeroom. I opened the door and looked into the gray semidarkness. Everything seemed normal. The lamentation had stopped. I stepped inside. Suddenly I felt something seize my dress. I cried out. I immediately heard the moaning very close to me, plaintive, supplicating, and something tapped on my pitcher.

I put it down. There was a slight splashing sound, like that of a dog lapping, and the level of the water in my pitcher began to sink. The thing, the being, was drinking!

"Moh! . . . Moh! . . ."

Something caressed my hair more softly than a breath.

"Moh. . . . Moh. . . ."

Then the moaning changed to a sound of human weeping, almost like the sobbing of a child, and I felt pity for the suffering invisible monster. But there were footsteps in the hall; I put my hands over my lips and the being fell silent.

Without a sound, I closed the door of the secret storeroom. Meta was coming toward me in the hall.

"Did I hear your voice just now?" she asked.

"Yes. My foot slipped and I was startled. . . ."

I was an accomplice of the phantoms.

I brought milk, wine, and apples. Nothing manifested itself. When I returned, the milk had been drunk to the last drop, but the wine and the apples were intact. Then a kind of breeze surrounded me and passed over my hair for a long time. . . .

I went back, bringing more fresh milk. The soft voice was no longer weeping, but the caress of the breeze was longer and seemed to be more ardent.

Meta began looking at me suspiciously and prowling around the storeroom.

I found a safer refuge for my mysterious protégé. I explained it to him by signs. How strange it was to make gestures to empty space! But he understood me. He was following me along the hall like a breath of air when I suddenly had to hide in a corner.

A pale light slid across the floor. I saw Meta coming down the spiral staircase at the end of the hall. She was walking quietly, partially hiding the glow of her lantern. The rapier glittered. I sensed that the being beside me was afraid. The breeze stirred around me, feverishly, abruptly, and I heard that plaintive "Moh! . . . Moh! . . ."

Meta's footsteps faded away in the distance. I made a reassuring gesture and went to the new refuge: a large closet that was never opened.

The breeze touched my lips and remained there a moment. I felt a strange shame.

May came.

The twenty square feet of the miniature garden, which poor, dear Hühnebein had spattered with his blood, were dotted with little white flowers.

Under a magnificent blue sky, the town was almost silent. The cries of the swallows were answered only by the peevish sounds of closing doors, sliding bolts, and turning keys.

The being had become imprudent. He sought me out. All at once I would feel him around me. I cannot describe the feeling; it was like a great tenderness surrounding me. I would make him understand that I was afraid of Meta, and then I would feel him vanish like a dying wind.

I could not bear the look in Meta's fiery eyes.

On May 4, the end came abruptly.

We were in the living room, with all the lamps lighted. I was closing the shutters. Suddenly I sensed his presence. I made a desperate gesture, turned around, and met Meta's terrible gaze in a mirror.

"Traitress!" she cried.

She quickly closed the door. He was imprisoned with us.

"I knew it!" she said vehemently. "I've seen you carrying pitchers of milk, daughter of the devil! You gave him strength when he was dying from the wound I gave him on the night of Hühnebein's death. Yes, your phantom is vulnerable! He's going to die now, and I think that dying is much more horrible for him than it is for us. Then your turn will come, you wretch! Do you hear me?"

She had shrieked this in short phrases. She uncovered her lantern. A beam of white light shot across the room, and I saw it strike something like thin, gray smoke. She plunged her rapier into it.

"Moh! . . . Moh! . . ." cried the heartrending voice, and then suddenly, awkwardly, but in a loving tone, my name was spoken. I leapt forward and knocked over the lantern with my fist. It went out.

"Meta, listen to me," I begged, "have pity. . . ."

Her face was contorted into a mask of demoniac fury.

"Traitress!" she screamed.

The rapier flashed before my eyes. It struck me below the left breast and I fell to my knees.

Someone was weeping violently beside me, strangely beseeching Meta. She raised her rapier again. I tried to find the words of supreme contrition that reconcile us with God forever, but then I saw Meta's face freeze and the sword fell from her hand.

Something murmured near us. I saw a thin flame stretch out like a ribbon and greedily attack the curtains.

"We're burning!" cried Meta. "All of us together!"

At that moment, when everything was about to sink into death, the door opened. An immensely tall old woman came in. I saw only her terrible green eyes glowing in her unimaginable face.

A flame licked my left hand. I stepped back as much as my strength allowed. I saw Meta still standing motionless with a strange grimace on her face, and I realized that her soul, too, had flown away. Then the monstrous old woman's eyes, without pupils, slowly looked around the flame-filled room and came to rest on me.

I am writing this in a strange little house. Where am I? Alone. And yet all this is full of tumult, an invisible but unrestrained presence is everywhere. He has come back. I have again heard my name spoken in that awkward, gentle way. . . .

*   *   *   *   *   *

Here ends the German manuscript, as though cut off with a knife.

*   *   *   *   *   *

The French Manuscript

The town's oldest coachman was pointed out to me in the smoky inn where he was drinking heady, fragrant October beer.

I bought him a drink and gave him some tobacco. He swore I was a prince. I pointed to his droshky outside the inn and said, "And now, take me to Saint Beregonne's Lane."

He gave me a bewildered look, then laughed.

"Ah, you're very clever!"

"Why?"

"You're testing me. I know every street in this town—I can almost say I know every paving-stone! There's no Saint Bere. . . . What did you say?"

"Beregonne. Are you sure? Isn't it near the Mohlenstrasse?"

"No," he said decisely. "There's no such street here, no more than Mount Vesuvius is in Saint Petersburg."

No one knew the town, in all its twisting byways, better than that splendid beer-drinker.

A student sitting at a nearby table looked up from the love letter he had been writing and said to me, "There's no saint by that name, either."

And the innkeeper's wife added, with a touch of anger, "You can't manufacture saints like sausages!"

I calmed everyone with wine and beer. There was great joy in my heart.

The policeman who paced up and down the Mohlenstrasse from dawn till dark had a face like a bulldog, but he was obviously a man who knew his job.

"No," he said slowly, coming back from a long journey among his thoughts and memories, "there's no such street here or anywhere else in town."

Over his shoulder I saw the beginning of Saint Beregonne's Lane, between the Klingbom distillery and the shop of an anonymous seed merchant.

I had to turn away with impolite abruptness in order not to show my elation. Saint Beregonne's Lane did not exist for the coachman, the student, the policeman, or anyone else: it existed only for me!

How did I make that amazing discovery? By an almost scientific observation, as some of my pompous fellow-teachers would have said. My colleague Seifert, who taught natural science by bursting balloons filled with strange gases in his pupils' faces, would not have been able to find any fault with my procedure.

When I walked along the Mohlenstrasse, it took me two or three seconds to cover the distance between the distillery and the seed merchant's shop. I noticed, however, that when other people passed by the same place they went immediately from the distillery to the shop, without visibly crossing the entrance of Saint Beregonne's Lane.

By adroitly questioning various people, and by consulting the town's cadastral map, I learned that only a wall separated the distillery from the shop.

I concluded that, for everyone in the world except myself, that street existed outside of time and space.

I knew that mysterious street for several years without ever venturing into it, and I think that even a more courageous man would have hesitated. What laws governed that unknown space? Once it had drawn me into its mystery, would it ever return me to my own world?

I finally invented various reasons to convince myself that that world was inhospitable to human beings, and my curiosity surrendered to my fear. And yet what I could see of that opening into the incomprehensible was so ordinary, so commonplace! I must admit, however, that the view was cut off after ten paces by a sharp bend in the street. All I could see was two high, badly whitewashed walls with the name of the street painted on one of them in black letters, and a stretch of worn, greenish pavement with a gap in which a viburnum bush was growing. That sickly bush seemed to live in accordance with our seasons, for I sometimes saw a little tender green and a few lumps of snow among its twigs.

I might have made some curious observations concerning the insertion of that slice of an alien cosmos into ours, but to do so I would have had to spend a considerable amount of time standing on the Mohlenstrasse; and Klingbom, who often saw me staring at some of his windows, became suspicious of his wife and gave me hostile looks.

I wondered why, of all the people in the world, I was the only one to whom that strange privilege had been given. This led me to think of my maternal grandmother. She was a tall, somber woman, and her big green eyes seemed to be following the happenings of another life on the wall in front of her.

Her background was obscure. My grandfather, a sailor, was supposed to have rescued her from some Algerian pirates. She sometimes stroked my hair with her long, white hands and murmured, "Maybe he . . . Why not? After all . . ." She repeated it on the night of her death, and while the pale fire of her gaze wandered among the shadows she added, "Maybe he'll go where I wasn't able to return. . . ."

A black storm was blowing that night. Just after my grandmother died, while the candles were being lit, a big stormy petrel shattered the window and lay dying, bloody and threatening, on her bed.

That was the only odd thing I remembered in my life; but did it have any connection with Saint Beregonne's Lane?

It was a sprig of the viburnum bush that set off the adventure.

But am I sincere in looking there for the initial tap that set events in motion? Perhaps I should speak of Anita.

Several years ago, in the Hanseatic ports one could see the arrival of little lateen-rigged ships creeping out of the mist like crestfallen animals.

Colossal laughter would immediately shake the port, down to the deepest beer cellars.

"Aha! Here come the dream ships!"

I always felt heartbroken at the sight of those heroic dreams dying in formidable Germanic laughter.

It was said that the sad crews of those ships lived on the golden shores of the Adriatic and the Tyrrhenian Sea in a mad dream, for they believed in a fantastic land of plenty, related to the Thule of the ancients, lying somewhere in our cruel North. Not having much more knowledge than their forefathers of a thousand years ago, they had carefully nurtured a heritage of legends about islands of diamonds and emeralds, legends that had been born when their forefathers encountered the glittering vanguard of an ice floe.

The compass was one of the few items of progress that their minds had seized upon in the course of the centuries. Its enigmatic needle, always pointing in the same direction, was for them a final proof of the mysteries of the North.

One day when a dream was walking like a new Messiah on the choppy waters of the Mediterranean, when the nets had brought up only fish poisoned by the coral on the bottom, and when Lombardy had sent neither grain nor flour to the poverty-stricken lands of the South, they had hoisted their sails in the offshore wind.

Their flotilla had dotted the sea with its hard wings; then, one by one, their ships had melted into the storms of the Atlantic. The Bay of Biscay had nibbled the flotilla and passed the remainder on to the granite teeth of Brittany. Some of the hulls were sold to firewood merchants in Germany and Denmark; one of the ships died in its dream, killed by an iceberg blazing in the sun off the Lofoten Islands.

But the North adorned the grave of that flotilla with a sweet name: "the dream ships." Although it made coarse sailors laugh, I was deeply moved by it, and I might well have been willing to set sail with those dreamers.

Anita was their daughter.

She came from the Mediterranean when she was still a baby in her mother's arms, aboard a tartan. The ship was sold. Her mother died, and so did her little sisters. Her father set out for America on a sailing ship that never returned. Anita was left all alone, but the dream that had brought the tartan to those moldering wooden docks never left her: she still believed in the fortune of the North, and she wanted it fiercely, almost with hatred.

In Tempelhof, with its clusters of white lights, she sang, danced, and threw red flowers that either fell on her like a rain of blood or were burned in the short flames of the Argand lamps. She would then pass among the crowd, holding out a pink conch shell. Silver was dropped into it, or sometimes gold, and only then did her eyes smile as they rested for a second, like a caress, on the generous man.

I gave gold—I, a humble teacher of French grammar in the Gymnasium, gave gold for one look from Anita.

Brief notes:

I sold my Voltaire. I had sometimes read my pupils extracts from his correspondence with the King of Prussia; it pleased the principal.

I owed two months' room and board to Frau Holz, my landlady. She told me she was poor. . . .

I asked the bursar of the school for another advance on my salary. He told me with embarrassment that it was difficult, that it was against regulations. . . . I did not listen any longer. My colleague Seifert curtly refused to lend me a few thalers.

I dropped a heavy gold coin into the conch shell. Anita's eyes burned my soul. Then I heard someone laughing in the laurel thickets of Tempelhof. I recognized two servants of the Gymnasium. They ran away into the darkness.

It was my last gold coin. I had no more money, none at all. . . .

As I was walking past the distillery on the Mohlenstrasse, I was nearly run over by a carriage. I made a frightened leap into Saint Beregonne's Lane. My hand clutched the viburnum bush and broke off a sprig of it.

I took the sprig home with me and laid it on my table. It had opened up an immense new world to me, like a magician's wand.

Let us reason, as my stingy colleague Seifert would say.

First of all, my leap into Saint Beregonne's Lane and my subsequent return to the Mohlenstrasse had shown that the mysterious street was as easy to enter and leave as any ordinary thoroughfare.

But the viburnum sprig had enormous philosophical significance. It was "in excess" in our world. If I had taken a branch from any forest in America and brought it here, I would not have changed the number of branches on earth. But in bringing that sprig of viburnum from Saint Beregonne's Lane I had made an intrinsic addition that could not have been made by all the tropical growths in the world, because I had taken it from a plane of existence that was real only for me.

I was therefore able to take an object from that plane and bring it into the world of men, where no one could contest my ownership of it. Ownership could never be more absolute, in fact, because the object would owe nothing to any industry, and it would augment the normally immutable patrimony of the earth. . . .

My reasoning flowed on, wide as a river, carrying fleets of words, encircling islands of appeals to philosophy; it was swollen by a vast system of logical tributaries until it reached a conclusive demonstration that a theft committed in Saint Beregonne's Lane was not a theft in the Mohlenstrasse.

Fortified by this nonsense, I judged that the matter was settled. My only concern would be to avoid the reprisals of the mysterious inhabitants of the street, or of the world to which it led.

When the Spanish conquistadores spent the gold they had brought back from the new India, I think they cared very little about the anger of the faraway peoples they had despoiled.

I decided to enter the unknown the following day.

Klingbom made me waste some time. I think he had been waiting for me in the little square vestibule that opened into his shop on one side and his office on the other. As I walked past, clenching my teeth, ready to plunge into my adventure, he grabbed me by my coat.

"Ah, professor," he said, "how I misjudged you! It wasn't you! I must have been blind to suspect you! She's left me, professor, but not with you. Oh, no, you're a man of honor! She's gone off with a postmaster, a man who's half coachman and half scribe. What a disgrace for the House of Klingbom!"

He had dragged me into the shadowy back room of his shop. He poured me a glass of orange-flavored brandy.

"And to think that I mistrusted you, professor! I always saw you looking at my wife's windows, but I know now that it was the seed merchant's wife you had your eye on."

I masked my embarrassment by raising my glass.

"To tell you the truth," said Klingbom, pouring me out some more of the reddish liquid, "I'd be glad to see you put one over on that malicious seed merchant: he's delighted by my misfortune."

He added, with a smile, "I'll do you a favor: the lady of your dreams is in her garden right now. Why don't you go and see her?"

He led me up a spiral staircase to a window. I saw the poisonous sheds of the Klingbom distillery smoking among a tangled array of little courtyards, miniature gardens, and muddy streams narrow enough to step across. It was through that landscape that the secret street ought to run, but I saw nothing except the smoky activity of the Klingbom buildings and the seed merchant's nearby garden, where a thin form was leaning over some arid flower beds.

One last swallow of brandy gave me a great deal of courage. After leaving Klingbom, I walked straight into Saint Beregonne's Lane.

Three little yellow doors in the white wall . . .

Beyond the bend in the street, the viburnum bushes continued to place spots of green and black among the paving stones; then the three little doors appeared, almost touching each other. They gave the aspect of a Flemish Beguine convent to what should have been singular and terrible.

My footsteps resounded clearly in the silence.

I knocked on the first of the doors. Only the futile life of an echo was stirred behind it. Fifty paces away, the street made another bend.

I was discovering the unknown parsimoniously. So far I had found only two thinly whitewashed walls and those three doors. But is not any closed door a powerful mystery in itself?

I knocked on all three doors, more violently this time. The echoes departed loudly and shattered the silence lurking in the depths of prodigious corridors. Sometimes their dying murmurs seemed to imitate the sound of light footsteps, but that was the only reply from the enclosed world.

The doors had locks on them, the same as all the other doors I was used to seeing. Two nights before, I had spent an hour picking the lock on my bedroom door with a piece of bent wire, and it had been as easy as a game.

There was a little sweat on my temples, a little shame in my heart. I took the same piece of wire from my pocket and slipped it into the lock of the first little door. And very simply, just like my bedroom door, it opened.

Later, when I was back in my bedroom among my books, in front of the table on which lay a red ribbon that had fallen from Anita's dress, I sat clutching three silver thalers in my hand.

Three thalers!

I had destroyed my finest destiny with my own hand. That new world had opened for me alone. What had it expected of me, that universe more mysterious than those that gravitate toward the bottom of Infinity? Mystery had made advances to me, had smiled at me like a pretty girl, and I had entered it as a thief. I had been petty, vile, absurd.

Three thalers!

My adventure should have been so prodigious, and it had become so paltry!

Three thalers reluctantly given to me by Gockel, the antique dealer, for that engraved metal dish. Three thalers. . . . But they would buy one of Anita's smiles.

I abruptly threw them into a drawer: someone was knocking on my door.

It was Gockel. It was difficult for me to believe that this was the same malevolent man who had contemptuously put down the metal dish on his counter cluttered with barbarous and shabby trinkets. He was smiling now, and he constantly mingled my name—which he mispronounced—with the title of "Herr Doktor" or "Herr Lehrer."

"I think I did you a great injustice, Herr Doktor," he said. "That dish is certainly worth more."

He took out a leather purse and I saw the bright yellow smile of gold.

"It may be," he went on, "that you have other objects from the same source . . . or rather, of the same kind."

The distinction did not escape me. Beneath the urbanity of the antique dealer was the spirit of a receiver of stolen goods.

"The fact is," I said, "that a friend of mine, an erudite collector, is in a difficult situation and needs to pay off certain debts, so he wants to sell part of his collection. He prefers to remain unknown: he's a shy scholar. He's already unhappy enough over having to part with some of the treasures in his showcases. I want to spare him any further sadness, so I'm helping him to sell them."

Gockel nodded enthusiastically. He seemed overwhelmed with admiration for me.

"That's my idea of true friendship!" he said. "Ach, Herr Doktor, I'll reread Cicero's

De Amicitia this evening with renewed pleasure. How I wish that I had a friend like your unfortunate scholar has found in you! But I'll contribute a little to your good deed by buying everything your friend is willing to part with, and by paying very good prices. . . ."

I had a slight stirring of curiosity:

"I didn't look at the dish very closely," I said loftily. "It didn't concern me, and besides, I don't know anything about such things. What kind of work is it? Byzantine?"

Gockel scratched his chin in embarrassment.

"Uh . . . I couldn't say for sure. Byzantine, yes, maybe. . . . I'll have to study it more carefully. . . . But," he went on, suddenly recovering his serenity, "in any case it's sure to find a buyer." Then, in a tone that cut short all further discussion: "That's the most important thing to us . . . and to your friend, too, of course."

Late that night I accompanied Anita in the moonlight to the street where her house stood half-hidden in a clump of tall lilacs.

But I must go back in my story to the tray I sold for thalers and gold, which gave me for one evening the friendship of the most beautiful girl in the world.

The door opened onto a long hall with a blue stone floor. A frosted window pane cast light into it and broke up the shadows. My first impression of being in a Flemish Beguine convent became stronger, especially when an open door at the end of the hall led me into a broad kitchen with a vaulted ceiling and rustic furniture, gleaming with wax and polish.

This innocuous scene was so reassuring that I called aloud:

"Hello! Is there anyone upstairs?"

A powerful resonance rumbled, but no presence cared to manifest itself.

I must admit that at no time did the silence and absence of life surprise me; it was as though I had expected it. In fact, from the time when I first perceived the existence of the enigmatic street, I had not thought for one moment of any possible inhabitants. And yet I had just entered it like a nocturnal thief.

I took no precautions when I ransacked the drawers containing silverware and table linen. My footsteps clattered freely in the adjoining rooms furnished like convent visiting-rooms, and on a magnificent oak staircase that. . . . Ah, there *was* something surprising in my visit! That staircase led nowhere! It ran into the drab wall as though it continued on the other side of it.

All this was bathed in the whitish glow of the frosted glass that formed the ceiling. I saw, or thought I saw, a vaguely hideous shape on the rough plaster wall, but when I looked at it attentively I realized that it was composed of thin cracks and was of the same order as those monsters that we distinguish in clouds and the lace of curtains. Furthermore, it did not trouble me, because when I looked a second time I no longer saw it in the network of cracks in the plaster.

I went back to the kitchen. Through a barred window, I saw a shadowy little courtyard that was like a pit surrounded by four big, mossy walls.

On a sideboard there was a heavy tray that looked as though it ought to have some value. I slipped it under my coat. I was deeply disappointed: I felt as though I had just stolen a few coins from a child's piggy bank, or from an old-maid aunt's shabby woolen stocking.

I went to Gockel, the antique dealer.

The three little houses were identical. In all of them, I found the same clean, tidy kitchen, the same sparse, gleaming furniture, the same dim, unreal light, the same serene quietness, the same senseless wall that ended the staircase. And in all three houses, I found identical candlesticks and the same heavy tray.

I took them away, and . . . and the next day I always found them in their places again. I took them to Gockel, who smiled broadly as he paid me for them.

It was enough to drive me mad; I felt my soul becoming monotonous, like that of a whirling dervish. Over and over again, I stole the same objects from the same house, under the same circumstances. I wondered whether this might not be the first vengeance of that unknown without mystery. Might not damnation be the unvarying repetition of sin for all eternity?

One day I did not go. I had resolved to space out my wretched incursions. I had a reserve of gold; Anita was happy and was showing wonderful tenderness toward me.

That same evening, Gockel came to see me, asked me if I had anything to sell, and, to my surprise, offered to pay me even more than he had been paying. He scowled when I told him of my decision.

"You've found a regular buyer, haven't you?" I said to him as he was leaving.

He slowly turned around and looked me straight in the eyes.

"Yes, Herr Doktor. I won't tell you anything about him, just as you never speak to me of . . . your friend, the seller." His voice became lower: "Bring me objects every day; tell me how much gold you want for them, and I'll give it to you, without bargaining. We're both tied to the same wheel, Herr Doktor. Perhaps we'll have to pay later. In the meantime, let's live the kind of life we like: you with a pretty girl, I with a fortune."

We never broached the subject again. But Anita suddenly became very demanding, and Gockel's gold slipped between her little fingers like water.

Then the atmosphere of the street changed, if I may express it that way. I heard melodies. At least it seemed to me that it was marvelous, faraway music. Summoning up my courage again, I decided to explore the street beyond the bend and go on toward the song that vibrated in the distance.

When I passed the third door and entered a part of the street where I had never gone before, I felt a terrible tightening in my heart. I took only three or four hesitant steps.

I turned around. I could still see the first part of the street, but it looked much smaller. It seemed to me that I had moved dangerously far away from my world. Nevertheless, in a surge of irrational temerity, I ran a short distance, then knelt, and, like a boy peering over a hedge, ventured to look down the unknown part of the street.

Disappointment struck me like a slap. The street continued its winding way, but again I saw nothing except three little doors in a white wall, and some viburnum bushes.

I would surely have gone back then if the wind of song had not passed by, like a distant tide of billowing sound. . . . I surmounted an inexplicable terror and listened to it, hoping to analyze it if possible.

I have called it a tide: it was a sound that came from a considerable distance, but it was enormous, like the sound of the sea.

As I listened to it, I no longer heard the harmonies I had thought I discerned in it at first; instead, I heard a harsh dissonance, a furious clamor of wails and hatred.

Have you ever noticed that the first whiffs of a repulsive smell are sometimes soft and even pleasant? I remember that when I left my house one day I was greeted in the street by an appetizing aroma of roast beef. "Someone's doing some good cooking early in the morning," I thought. But when I had walked a hundred paces, this aroma changed into the sharp, sickening smell of burning cloth: a draper's shop was on fire, filling the air with sparks and smoky flames. In the same way, I may have been deceived by my first perception of the melodious clamor.

"Why don't I go beyond the next bend?" I said to myself. My apprehensive inertia had almost disappeared. Walking calmly now, I covered the space before me in a few seconds—and once again I found exactly the same scene that I had left behind.

I was overwhelmed by a kind of bitter fury that engulfed my broken curiosity. Three identical houses, then three more identical houses. I had plumbed the mystery merely by opening the first door.

Gloomy courage took possession of me. I walked forward along the street, and my disappointment grew at an incredible rate.

A bend, three little yellow doors, a clump of virburnum bushes, then another bend, the same three little doors in the white wall, and the shadow of spindle trees. This repetition continued obsessively while I walked furiously, with loud footsteps.

Suddenly, when I had turned one more bend in the street, this terrible symmetry was broken. There were again three little doors and some viburnum bushes, but there was also a big wooden portal, darkened and worn smooth by time. I was afraid of it.

I now heard the clamor from much closer, hostile and threatening. I began walking back toward the Mohlenstrasse. The scenes went by like the quatrains of a ballad: three little doors and viburnum bushes, three little doors and viburnum bushes. . . .

Finally I saw the first lights of the real world twinkling before me. But the clamor had pursued me to the edge of the Mohlenstrasse. There it stopped abruptly, adapting itself to the joyous evening sounds of the populous streets, so that the mysterious and terrible shouting ended in a chorus of children's voices singing a roundelay.

The whole town is in the grip of an unspeakable terror.

I would not have spoken of it in these brief memoirs, which concern only myself, if I had not found a link between the shadowy street and the crimes that steep the town in blood every night.

Over a hundred people have suddenly disappeared, a hundred others have been savagely murdered.

I recently took a map of the town and drew on it the winding line that must represent Saint Beregonne's Lane, that incomprehensible street that overlaps our terrestrial world. I was horrified to see that *all the crimes have been committed along that line*.

Thus poor Klingbom was one of the first to disappear. According to his clerk, he vanished like a puff of smoke just as he was entering the room containing his stills. The seed merchant's wife was next, snatched away while she was in her sad garden. Her husband was found in his drying-room with his skull smashed.

As I traced the fateful line on the map, my idea became a certainty. I can explain the victims' disappearance only by their passage into an unknown plane; as for the murders, they are easy for invisible beings.

All the inhabitants of a house on Old Purse Street have disappeared. On Church Street, six corpses have been found. On Post Street, there have been five disappearances and four deaths. This goes on and on, apparently limited by the Deichstrasse, where more murders and disappearances are taking place.

I now realize that to talk about what I know would be to place myself in the Kirchhaus insane asylum, a tomb from which no Lazarus ever arises; or else it would give free rein to a superstitious crowd that is exasperated enough to tear me to pieces as a sorcerer.

And yet, ever since the beginning of my monotonous daily thefts, anger has been welling up inside me, driving me to vague plans of vengeance.

"Gockel knows more about this than I do," I thought. "I'm going to tell him what I know: that will make him more inclined to confide in me."

But that evening, while Gockel was emptying his heavy purse into my hands, I said nothing, and he left as usual with polite words that made no allusion to the strange bargain that had attached us to the same chain.

I had a feeling that events were about to leap forward and rush like a torrent through my tranquil life. I was becoming more and more aware that Saint Beregonne's Lane and its little houses were only a mask concealing some sort of horrible face.

So far, fortunately for me, I had gone there only in broad daylight, because for some reason I dreaded to encounter the shadows of evening there. But one day I lingered later than usual, stubbornly pushing furniture around, turning drawers inside out, determined to discover something new. And the "new" came of itself, in the form of a dull rumble, like that of heavy doors moving on rollers. I looked up and saw that the opalescent light had changed into an ashy semidarkness. The panes of glass above the staircase were livid; the little courtyards were already filled with shadow.

My heart tightened, but when the rumbling continued, reinforced by the powerful resonance of the house, my curiosity became stronger than my fear, and I began climbing the stairs to see where the noise was coming from.

It was growing darker and darker, but before leaping back down the stairs like a madman and running out of the house, I was able to see. . . . There was no more wall! The staircase ended at the edge of an abyss dug out of the night, from which vague monstrosities were rising.

I reached the door; behind me, something was furiously knocked over.

The Mohlenstrasse gleamed before me like a haven. I ran faster. Something suddenly seized me with extreme savagery.

"What's the matter with you? Can't you see where you're going?"

I found myself sitting on the pavement of the Mohlenstrasse, before a sailor who was rubbing his sore skull and looking at me in bewilderment. My coat was torn, my neck was bleeding.

I immediately hurried away without wasting any time on apologies, to the supreme indignation of the sailor, who shouted after me that after colliding with him so brutally I should at least buy him a drink.

Anita is gone, vanished!

My heart is broken; I collapse, sobbing, on my useless gold.

And yet her house is far from the zone of danger. Good God! I failed through an excess of prudence and love! One day, without mentioning the street, I showed her the line I had drawn on the map and told her that all the danger seemed to be concentrated along that sinuous trail. Her eyes glowed strangely at that moment. I should have known that the great spirit of adventure that animated her ancestors was not dead in her.

Perhaps, in a flash of feminine intuition, she made a connection between that line and my sudden fortune. . . . Oh, how my life is disintegrating!

There have been more murders and disappearances. And my Anita has been carried off in the bloody, inexplicable whirlwind!

The case of Hans Mendell has given me a mad idea: those vaporous beings, as he described them, may not be invulnerable.

Although Hans Mendell was not a distinguished man, I see no reason not to believe his story. He was a scoundrel who made his living as a mountebank and a cutthroat. When he was found, he had in his pocket the purses and watches of two unfortunate men whose corpses lay bleeding on the ground a few paces away from him.

It would have been assumed that he was guilty of murder if he himself had not been found moaning with both arms torn from his body.

Being a man with a powerful constitution, he was able to live long enough to answer the feverish questions of the magistrates and priests.

He confessed that for several days he had followed a shadow, a kind of black mist, and robbed the bodies of the people it killed. On the night of his misfortune, he saw the black mist waiting in the middle of Post Street in the moonlight. He hid in an empty sentry-box and watched it. He saw other dark, vaporous, awkward forms that bounced like rubber balls, then disappeared.

Soon he heard voices and saw two young men coming up the street. The black mist was no longer in sight, but he suddenly saw the two men writhe on their backs, then lie still.

Mendell added that he had already observed the same sequence in those nocturnal murders on seven other occasions. He had always waited for the shadow to leave, then robbed the bodies. This shows that he had remarkable self-control, worthy of being put to a better use.

As he was robbing the two bodies, he saw with alarm that the shadow had not left, but had only risen off the ground, interposing itself between him and the moon. He then saw that it had a roughly human shape. He tried to go back to the sentry-box but did not have time: the figure pounced on him.

Mendell was an extraordinarily strong man. He struck an enormous blow and encountered a slight resistance, as though he were pushing his hand through a strong current of air.

That was all he was able to say. His horrible wound allowed him to live only another hour after telling his story.

The idea of avenging Anita has now taken root in my brain. I said to Gockel, "Don't come any more. I need revenge and hatred, and your gold can no longer do anything for me."

He looked at me with that profound expression that was familiar to me by now.

"Gockel," I said, "I'm going to take vengeance."

His face suddenly brightened, as though with great joy:

"And . . . do you believe . . . Herr Doktor, that they will disappear?"

I harshly ordered him to have a cart filled with fagots and casks of oil, raw alcohol and gunpowder, and to leave it without a driver early in the morning on the Mohlenstrasse. He bowed low like a servant, and as he was leaving he said to me, "May the Lord help you! May the Lord come to your aid!"

I feel that these are the last lines I shall write in this journal.

I piled up the fagots, streaming with oil and alcohol, against the big door. I laid down trails of gunpowder connecting the nearby small doors with other oil-soaked fagots. I placed charges of powder in all the cracks in the walls.

The mysterious clamor continued all around me. This time I discerned in it abominable lamentations, human wails, echoes of horrible torments of the flesh. But my heart was agitated by tumultuous joy, because I felt around me a wild apprehension that came from *them*. They saw my terrible preparations and were unable to prevent them, for, as I had come to realize, only night released their frightful power.

I calmly struck a light with my tinderbox. A moan passed, and the viburnum bushes quivered as though blown by a sudden stiff breeze. A long blue flame rose into the air, the fagots began crackling, fire crept along the trails of gunpowder. . . .

I ran down the winding street, from bend to bend, feeling a little dizzy, as though I were going too fast down a spiral staircase that descended deep into the earth.

*   *   *

The Deichstrasse and the whole surrounding neighborhood were in flames. From my window, I could see the sky turning yellow above the rooftops. The weather was dry and the town's water supply was nearly exhausted. A red band of sparks and flames hovered high above the street.

The fire had been burning for a day and a night, but it was still far from the Mohlenstrasse. Saint Beregonne's Lane was there, calm with its quivering viburnum bushes. Explosions rumbled in the distance.

Another cart was there, loaded and left by Gockel. Not a soul was in sight: everyone had been drawn toward the formidable spectacle of the fire. *It was not expected here.*

I walked from bend to bend to bend, sowing fagots, pools of oil and alcohol, and the dark frost of gunpowder. Suddenly, just as I had turned another bend, I stopped and stared. Three little houses, the everlasting three little houses, were burning calmly with pretty yellow flames in the peaceful air. It was as though even the fire respected their serenity, for it was doing its work without noise or ferocity. I realized that I was at the red edge of the conflagration that was destroying the town.

With anguish in my soul, I moved back from that mystery that was about to die.

I was near the Mohlenstrasse. I stopped in front of the first of the little doors, the one I had opened, trembling, a few weeks earlier. It was there that I would start the new fire.

For the last time, I saw the kitchen, the austere parlor, and the staircase, which now ended at the wall, as before; and I felt that all this had become familiar, almost dear to me.

On the big tray, the one I had stolen so many times before only to find it waiting for me again the next day, I saw some sheets of paper covered with elegant feminine handwriting.

I picked them up. This was going to be my last theft on the shadowy street.

Vampires! Vampires! Vampires!

* * * * * *

So ends the French manuscript. The last words, evoking the impure spirits of the night, are written across the page in sharp letters that cry out terror and despair. Thus must write those who, on a sinking ship, want to convey a last farewell to the families they hope will survive them.

It was last year in Hamburg. I was strolling through the old city, with its good smell of fresh beer. It was dear to my heart, because it reminded me of the cities I had loved in my youth. And there, on an empty, echoing street, I saw a name on the front of an antique shop: Lockmann Gockel.

I bought an old Bavarian pipe with truculent decorations. The shopkeeper seemed friendly. I asked him if the name of Archipetre meant anything to him. His face had been the color of gray earth; in the twilight it now turned so white that it stood out from the shadows as though illuminated by an inner flame.

"Archipetre," he murmured slowly. "Oh! What are you saying? What do you know?"

I had no reason to conceal the story I had found on the dock. I told it to him.

He lit an archaic gaslight. Its flame danced and hissed foolishly.

I saw that his eyes were weary.

"He was my grandfather," he said, when I mentioned Gockel the antique dealer.

When I had finished my story I heard a great sigh from a dark corner.

"That's my sister," he said.

I nodded to her. She was young and pretty, but very pale. She had been listening to me, motionless among grotesque shadows.

"Our grandfather talked to our father about it nearly every evening," he said in a faltering voice, "and our father used to discuss it with us. Now that he's dead too, we talk about it with each other."

"And now," I said nervously, "thanks to you, we're going to be able to do some research on the subject of that mysterious street, aren't we?"

He slowly raised his hand.

"Alphonse Archipetre taught French in the Gymnasium until 1842."

"Oh!" I said, disappointed. "That's a long time ago!"

"It was the year of the great fire that nearly destroyed Hamburg. The Mohlenstrasse and the vast section of the city between it and the Deichstrasse were a sea of flames."

"And Archipetre?"

"He lived rather far from there, toward Bleichen. The fire didn't reach his street, but in the middle of the second night, on May 6—a terrible night, dry and without water—his house burned down, all alone among the others that were miraculously spared. He died in the flames; or at least he was never found."

"The story . . ." I began.

Lockmann Gockel did not let me finish. He was so happy to have found an outlet that he seized upon the subject greedily. Fortunately he told me more or less what I wanted to hear.

"The story compressed time, just as space was compressed at the fateful location of Saint Beregonne's Lane. In the Hamburg archives, there are accounts of atrocities committed *during the fire* by a band of mysterious evil-doers. Fantastic crimes, looting, riots, red hallucinations on the part of whole crowds—all those things are precisely described, and yet they took place *before the fire*. Do you understand my reference to the contraction of space and time?"

His face became a little calmer.

"Isn't modern science driven back to Euclidean weakness by the theory of that admirable Einstein for whom the whole world envies us? And isn't it forced to accept, with horror and despair, that fantastic Fitzgerald-Lorentz law of contraction? Contraction! Ah, there's a word that's heavy with meaning!"

The conversation seemed to be going off on an insidious tangent.

The young woman silently brought tall glasses filled with yellow wine. Gockel raised his toward the flame and marvelous colors flowed onto his frail hand like a silver river of gems.

He abandoned his scientific dissertation and returned to the story of the conflagration:

"My grandfather, and other people of the time, reported that enormous green flames shot up from the debris. There were hallucinated people who claimed to see figures of indescribably ferocious women in them."

The wine had a soul. I emptied the glass and smiled at Gockel's terrified words.

"Those same green flames," he went on, "rose from Archipetre's house and roared so horribly that people were said to have died of fear in the street."

"Mr. Gockel," I said, "did your grandfather ever speak of the mysterious purchaser who came every evening to buy the same trays and the same candlesticks?"

A weary voice replied for him, in words that were almost identical with those that ended the German manuscript:

"A tall old woman, an immense old woman with fishy eyes in an incredible face. She brought bags of gold so heavy that our grandfather had to divide them into four parts to carry them to his coffers."

The young woman continued:

"When Professor Archipetre came to my grandfather, the Gockel firm was about to go bankrupt. It became rich, and we're still enormously rich, from the gold of the . . . yes, from the gold of those beings of the night!"

"They're gone now," murmured her brother, refilling our glasses.

"Don't say that! They can't have forgotten us. Remember our nights, our horrible nights! All I can hope for now is that there is, or was, a human presence with them that they cherish and that may intercede for us."

Her lovely eyes opened wide before the black abyss of her thoughts.

"Kathie!" exclaimed Gockel. "Have you again seen? . . ."

"You know the things are here every night," she said in a voice as low as a moan. "They assail our thoughts as soon as sleep comes over us. Ah, to sleep no more! . . ."

"To sleep no more," repeated her brother in an echo of terror.

"They come out of their gold, which we keep, and which we love in spite of everything; they rise from everything we've acquired with that infernal fortune. . . . They'll always come back, as long as we exist, and as long as this wretched earth endures!"

—translated by Lowell Bair

Robert Silverberg (b. 1935)

Passengers

Robert Silverberg is one of the dominant figures in science fiction of the last thirty years. Enormously prolific in his younger years, he became one of the leading craftsmen in the field by the end of the 1960s and then, perhaps the leading master of the science fiction short story of the 1970s. During an enormously creative period beginning in the late sixties and ending in the mid-seventies, he wrote a majority of the work upon which his reputation rests. He has won the Nebula Award several times for best story (in 1969 for "Passengers") and for best novella of the year. While his science fiction is often dark and atmospheric, most of his work is far from the horror mode. "Passengers" is a notable exception. It was Silverberg's first award-winner and was one of the works that distinguish the career transition noted above. It is a monster story in which the ambiguous alien invaders function as a psychological metaphor in an unusually foregrounded manner. The only evidence for them is human behavior—and we do not know how far to trust the point-of-view character. Altogether, "Passengers" is a virtuoso performance.

There are only fragments of me left now. Chunks of memory have broken free and drifted away like calved glaciers. It is always like that when a Passenger leaves us. We can never be sure of all the things our borrowed bodies did. We have only the lingering traces, the imprints.

Like sand clinging to an ocean-tossed bottle. Like the throbbings of amputated legs.

I rise. I collect myself. My hair is rumpled; I comb it. My face is creased from too little sleep. There is sourness in my mouth. Has my Passenger been eating dung with my mouth? They do that. They do anything.

It is morning.

A gray, uncertain morning. I stare at it awhile, and then, shuddering, I opaque the window and confront instead the gray, uncertain surface of the inner panel. My room looks untidy. Did I have a woman here? There are ashes in the trays. Searching for butts, I find several with lipstick stains. Yes, a woman was here.

I touch the bedsheets. Still warm with shared warmth. Both pillows tousled. She has gone, though, and the Passenger is gone, and I am alone.

How long did it last, this time?

I pick up the phone and ring Central. "What is the date?"

The computer's bland feminine voice replies, "Friday, December fourth, nineteen eighty-seven."

"The time?"

145

"Nine fifty-one, Eastern Standard Time."

"The weather forecast?"

"Predicted temperature range for today thirty to thirty-eight. Current temperature, thirty-one. Wind from the north, sixteen miles an hour. Chances of precipitation slight."

"What do you recommend for a hangover?"

"Food or medication?"

"Anything you like," I say.

The computer mulls that one over for a while. Then it decides on both, and activates my kitchen. The spigot yields cold tomato juice. Eggs begin to fry. From the medicine slot comes a purplish liquid. The Central Computer is always so thoughtful. Do the Passengers ever ride it, I wonder? What thrills could that hold for them? Surely it must be more exciting to borrow the million minds of Central than to live a while in the faulty, short-circuited soul of a corroding human being!

December 4, Central said. Friday. So the Passenger had me for three nights.

I drink the purplish stuff and probe my memories in a gingerly way, as one might probe a festering sore.

I remember Tuesday morning. A bad time at work. None of the charts will come out right. The section manager irritable; he has been taken by Passengers three times in five weeks, and his section is in disarray as a result, and his Christmas bonus is jeopardized. Even though it is customary not to penalize a person for lapses due to Passengers, according to the system, the section manager seems to feel he will be treated unfairly. So he treats us unfairly. We have a hard time. Revise the charts, fiddle with the program, check the fundamentals ten times over. Out they come: the detailed forecasts for price variations of public utility securities, February–April 1988. That afternoon we are to meet and discuss the charts and what they tell us.

I do not remember Tuesday afternoon.

That must have been when the Passenger took me. Perhaps at work; perhaps in the mahogany-paneled boardroom itself, during the conference. Pink concerned faces all about me; I cough, I lurch, I stumble from my seat. They shake their heads sadly. No one reaches for me. No one stops me. It is too dangerous to interfere with one who has a Passenger. The chances are great that a second Passenger lurks nearby in the discorporate state, looking for a mount. So I am avoided. I leave the building.

After that, what?

Sitting in my room on bleak Friday morning, I eat my scrambled eggs and try to reconstruct the three lost nights.

Of course it is impossible. The conscious mind functions during the period of captivity, but upon withdrawal of the Passenger nearly every recollection goes too. There is only a slight residue, a gritty film of faint and ghostly memories. The mount is never precisely the same person afterwards; though he cannot recall the details of his experience, he is subtly changed by it.

I try to recall.

A girl? Yes: lipstick on the butts. Sex, then, here in my room. Young? Old? Blonde? Dark? Everything is hazy. How did my borrowed body behave? Was I a good lover? I try to be, when I am myself. I keep in shape. At 38, I can handle three sets of tennis on a summer afternoon without collapsing. I can make a woman glow as a woman is meant to glow. Not boasting: just categorizing. We have our skills. These are mine.

But Passengers, I am told, take wry amusement in controverting our skills. So would it have given my rider a kind of delight to find me a woman and force me to fail repeatedly with her?

I dislike that thought.

The fog is going from my mind now. The medicine prescribed by Central works rapidly. I eat, I shave, I stand under the vibrator until my skin is clean. I do my exercises. Did the Passenger exercise my body Wednesday and Thursday mornings? Probably not. I must make up for that. I am close to middle age, now; tonus lost is not easily regained.

I touch my toes twenty times, knees stiff.

I kick my legs in the air.

I lie flat and lift myself on pumping elbows.

The body responds, maltreated though it has been. It is the first bright moment of my awakening: to feel the inner tingling, to know that I still have vigor.

Fresh air is what I want next. Quickly I slip into my clothes and leave. There is no need for me to report to work today. They are aware that since Tuesday afternoon I have had a Passenger; they need not be aware that before dawn on Friday the Passenger departed. I will have a free day. I will walk the city's streets, stretching my limbs, repaying my body for the abuse it has suffered.

I enter the elevator. I drop fifty stories to the ground. I step out into the December dreariness.

The towers of New York rise about me.

In the street the cars stream forward. Drivers sit edgily at their wheels. One never knows when the driver of a nearby car will be borrowed, and there is always a moment of lapsed coordination as the Passenger takes over. Many lives are lost that way on our streets and highways; but never the life of a Passenger.

I begin to walk without purpose. I cross Fourteenth Street, heading north, listening to the soft violent purr of the electric engines. I see a boy jigging in the street and know he is being ridden. At Fifth and Twenty-second a prosperous-looking paunchy man approaches, his necktie askew, this morning's *Wall Street Journal* jutting from an overcoat pocket. He giggles. He thrusts out his tongue. Ridden. Ridden. I avoid him. Moving briskly, I come to the underpass that carries traffic below Thirty-fourth Street toward Queens, and pause for a moment to watch two adolescent girls quarreling at the rim of the pedestrian walk. One is a Negro. Her eyes are rolling in terror. The other pushes her closer to the railing. Ridden. But the Passenger does not have murder on its mind, merely pleasure. The Negro girl is released and falls in a huddled heap, trembling. Then she rises and runs. The other girl draws a long strand of gleaming hair into her mouth, chews on it, seems to awaken. She looks dazed.

I avert my eyes. One does not watch while a fellow sufferer is awakening. There is a morality of the ridden; we have so many new tribal mores in these dark days.

I hurry on.

Where am I going so hurriedly? Already I have walked more than a mile. I seem to be moving toward some goal, as though my Passenger still hunches in my skull, urging me about. But I know that is not so. For the moment, at least, I am free.

Can I be sure of that?

Cogito ergo sum no longer applies. We go on thinking even while we are ridden, and we live in quiet desperation, unable to halt our courses no matter how ghastly, no matter how self-destructive. I am certain that I can distinguish between the condition of bearing a Passenger and the condition of being free. But perhaps not. Perhaps I bear a particularly devilish Passenger which has not quitted me at all, but which merely has receded to the cerebellum, leaving me the illusion of freedom while all the time surreptitiously driving me onward to some purpose of its own.

Did we ever have more than that: the illusion of freedom?

But this is disturbing, the thought that I may be ridden without realizing it. I burst out in heavy perspiration, not merely from the exertion of walking. Stop. Stop here. Why must you walk? You are at Forty-second Street. There is the library. Nothing forces you onward. Stop a while, I tell myself. Rest on the library steps.

I sit on the cold stone and tell myself that I have made this decision for myself. Have I? It is the old problem, free will versus determinism, translated into the foulest of forms. Determinism is no longer a philosopher's abstraction; it is cold alien tendrils sliding between the cranial sutures. The Passengers arrived three years ago. I have been ridden five times since then. Our world is quite different now. But we have adjusted even to this. We have adjusted. We have our mores. Life goes on. Our governments rule, our legislatures meet, our stock exchanges transact business as usual, and we have methods for compensating for the random havoc. It is the only way. What else can we do? Shrivel in defeat? We have an enemy we cannot fight; at best we can resist through endurance. So we endure.

The stone steps are cold against my body. In December few people sit here.

I tell myself that I made this long walk of my own free will, that I halted of my own free will, that no Passenger rides my brain now. Perhaps. Perhaps. I cannot let myself believe that I am not free.

Can it be, I wonder, that the Passenger left some lingering command in me? Walk to this place, halt at this place? That is possible too.

I look about me at the others on the library steps.

An old man, eyes vacant, sitting on newspaper. A boy of thirteen or so with flaring nostrils. A plump woman. Are all of them ridden? Passengers seem to cluster about me today. The more I study the ridden ones, the more convinced I become that I am, for the moment, free. The last time, I had three months of freedom between rides. Some people, they say, are scarcely ever free. Their bodies are in great demand, and they know only scattered bursts of freedom, a day here, a week there, an hour. We have never been able to determine how many Passengers infest our world. Millions, maybe. Or maybe five. Who can tell?

A wisp of snow curls down out of the gray sky. Central had said the chance of precipitation was slight. Are they riding Central this morning too?

I see the girl.

She sits diagonally across from me, five steps up and a hundred feet away, her black skirt pulled up on her knees to reveal handsome legs. She is young. Her hair is deep, rich auburn. Her eyes are pale; at this distance, I cannot make out the precise color. She is dressed simply. She is younger than thirty. She wears a dark green coat and her lipstick has a purplish tinge. Her lips are full, her nose slender, high-bridged, her eyebrows carefully plucked.

I know her.

I have spent the past three nights with her in my room. She is the one. Ridden, she came to me, and ridden, I slept with her. I am certain of this. The veil of memory opens; I see her slim body naked on my bed.

How can it be that I remember this?

It is too strong to be an illusion. Clearly this is something that I have been *permitted* to remember for reasons I cannot comprehend. And I remember more. I remember her soft gasping sounds of pleasure. I know that my own body did not betray me those three nights, nor did I fail her need.

And there is more. A memory of sinuous music; a scent of youth in her hair; the rustle of winter trees. Somehow she brings back to me a time of innocence, a time when I am young and girls are mysterious, a time of parties and dances and warmth and secrets.

I am drawn to her now.

There is an etiquette about such things, too. It is in poor taste to approach someone you have met while being ridden. Such an encounter gives you no privilege; a stranger remains a stranger, no matter what you and she may have done and said during your involuntary time together.

Yet I am drawn to her.

Why this violation of taboo? Why this raw breach of etiquette? I have never done this before. I have been scrupulous.

But I get to my feet and walk along the step on which I have been sitting, until I am below her, and I look up, and automatically she folds her ankles together and angles her knees as if in awareness that her position is not a modest one. I know from the gesture that she is not ridden now. My eyes meet hers. Her eyes are hazy green. She is beautiful, and I rack my memory for more details of our passion.

I climb step by step until I stand before her.

"Hello," I say.

She gives me a neutral look. She does not seem to recognize me. Her eyes are veiled, as one's eyes often are, just after the Passenger has gone. She purses her lips and appraises me in a distant way.

"Hello," she replies coolly. "I don't think I know you."

"No. You don't. But I have the feeling you don't want to be alone just now. And I know I don't." I try to persuade her with my eyes that my motives are decent. "There's snow in the air," I say. "We can find a warmer place. I'd like to talk to you."

"About what?"

"Let's go elsewhere, and I'll tell you. I'm Charles Roth."

"Helen Martin."

She gets to her feet. She still has not cast aside her cool neutrality; she is suspicious, ill at ease. But at least she is willing to go with me. A good sign.

"Is it too early in the day for a drink?" I ask.

"I'm not sure. I hardly know what time it is."

"Before noon."

"Let's have a drink anyway," she says, and we both smile.

We go to a cocktail lounge across the street. Sitting face to face in the darkness, we sip drinks, daiquiri for her, bloody mary for me. She relaxes a little. I ask myself what it is I want from her. The pleasure of her company, yes. Her company in bed? But I have already had that pleasure, three nights of it, though she does not know that. I want something more. Something more. What?

Her eyes are bloodshot. She has had little sleep these past three nights.

I say, "Was it very unpleasant for you?"

"What?"

"The Passenger."

A whiplash of reaction crosses her face. "How did you know I've had a Passenger?"

"I know."

"We aren't supposed to talk about it."

"I'm broadminded," I tell her. "My Passenger left me some time during the night. I was ridden since Tuesday afternoon."

"Mine left me about two hours ago, I think." Her cheeks color. She is doing something daring, talking like this. "I was ridden since Monday night. This was my fifth time."

"Mine also."

We toy with our drinks. Rapport is growing, almost without the need of words. Our recent experiences with Passengers give us something in common, although Helen does not realize how intimately we shared those experiences.

We talk. She is a designer of display windows. She has a small apartment several blocks from here. She lives alone. She asks me what I do. "Securities analyst," I tell her. She smiles. Her teeth are flawless. We have a second round of drinks. I am positive, now, that this is the girl who was in my room when I was ridden.

A seed of hope grows in me. It was a happy chance that brought us together again, so soon after we parted as dreamers. A happy chance, too, that some vestige of the dream lingered in my mind.

We have shared something, who knows what, and it must have been good to leave such a vivid imprint on me, and now I want to come to her conscious, aware, my own master, and renew that relationship, making it a real one this time. It is not proper, for I am trespassing on a privilege that is not mine except by virtue of our Passengers' brief presence in us. Yet I need her. I want her.

She seems to need me, too, without realizing who I am. But fear holds her back.

I am frightened of frightening her, and I do not try to press my advantage too quickly. Perhaps she would take me to her apartment with her now, perhaps not, but I do not ask. We finish our drinks. We arrange to meet by the library steps again tomorrow. My hand momentarily brushes hers. Then she is gone.

I fill three ashtrays that night. Over and over I debate the wisdom of what I am doing. But why not leave her alone? I have no right to follow her. In the place our world has become, we are wisest to remain apart.

And yet—there is that stab of half-memory when I think of her. The blurred lights of lost chances behind the stairs, of girlish laughter in second-floor corridors, of stolen kisses, of tea and cake. I remember the girl with the orchid in her hair, and the one in the spangled dress, and the one with the child's face and the woman's eyes, all so long ago, all lost, all gone, and I tell myself that this one I will not lose, I will not permit her to be taken from me.

Morning comes, a quiet Saturday. I return to the library, hardly expecting to find her there, but she is there, on the steps, and the sight of her is like a reprieve. She looks wary, troubled; obviously she has done much thinking, little sleeping. Together we walk along Fifth Avenue. She is quite close to me, but she does not take my arm. Her steps are brisk, short, nervous.

I want to suggest that we go to her apartment instead of to the cocktail lounge. In these days we must move swiftly while we are free. But I know it would be a mistake to think of this as a matter of tactics. Coarse haste would be fatal, bringing me perhaps an ordinary victory, a numbing defeat within it. In any event her mood hardly seems promising. I look at her, thinking of string music and new snowfalls, and she looks toward the gray sky.

She says, "I can feel them watching me all the time. Like vultures swooping overhead, waiting, waiting. Ready to pounce."

"But there's a way of beating them. We can grab little scraps of life when they're not looking."

"They're *always* looking."

"No," I tell her. "There can't be enough of them for that. Sometimes they're looking the other way. And while they are, two people can come together and try to share warmth."

"But what's the use?"

"You're too pessimistic, Helen. They ignore us for months at a time. We have a chance. We have a chance."

But I cannot break through her shell of fear. She is paralyzed by the nearness of the Passengers, unwilling to begin anything for fear it will be snatched away by our tormentors. We reach the building where she lives, and I hope she will relent and invite me in. For an instant she wavers, but only for an instant: she takes my hand in both of hers, and smiles, and the smile fades, and she is gone, leaving me only with the words, "Let's meet at the library again tomorrow. Noon."

I make the long chilling walk home alone.

Some of her pessimism seeps into me that night. It seems futile for us to try to salvage anything. More than that: wicked for me to seek her out, shameful to offer a hesitant love when I am not free. In this world, I tell myself, we should keep well clear of others, so that we do not harm anyone when we are seized and ridden.

I do not go to meet her in the morning.

It is best this way, I insist. I have no business trifling with her. I imagine her at the library, wondering why I am late, growing tense, impatient, then annoyed. She will be angry with me for breaking our date, but her anger will ebb, and she will forget me quickly enough.

Monday comes. I return to work.

Naturally, no one discusses my absence. It is as though I have never been away. The market is strong that morning. The work is challenging; it is mid-morning before I think of Helen at all. But once I think of her, I can think of nothing else. My cowardice in standing her up. The childishness of Saturday night's dark thoughts. Why accept fate so passively? Why give in? I want to fight, now, to carve out a pocket of security despite the odds. I feel a deep conviction that it can be done. The Passengers may never bother the two of us again, after all. And that flickering smile of hers outside her building Saturday, that momentary glow—it should have told me that behind her wall of fear she felt the same hopes. She was waiting for me to lead the way. And I stayed home instead.

At lunchtime I go to the library, convinced it is futile.

But she is there. She paces along the steps; the wind slices at her slender figure. I go to her.

She is silent a moment. "Hello," she says finally.

"I'm sorry about yesterday."

"I waited a long time for you."

I shrug. "I made up my mind that it was no use to come. But then I changed my mind again."

She tried to look angry. But I know she is pleased to see me again—else why did she come here today? She cannot hide her inner pleasure. Nor can I. I point across the street to the cocktail lounge.

"A daiquiri?" I say. "As a peace offering?"

"All right."

Today the lounge is crowded, but we find a booth somehow. There is a brightness in her eyes that I have not seen before. I sense that a barrier is crumbling within her.

"You're less afraid of me, Helen," I say.

"I've never been afraid of you. I'm afraid of what could happen if we take the risks."

"Don't be. Don't be."

"I'm trying not to be afraid. But sometimes it seems so hopeless. Since *they* came here—"

"We can still try to live our own lives."

"Maybe."

"We have to. Let's make a pact, Helen. No more gloom. No more worrying about the terrible things that might just maybe happen. All right?"

A pause. Then a cool hand against mine.

"All right."

We finished our drinks, and I present my Credit Central to pay for them, and we go outside. I want her to tell me to forget about this afternoon's work and come home with her. It is inevitable, now, that she will ask me, and better sooner than later.

We walk a block. She does not offer the invitation. I sense the struggle inside her, and I wait, letting that struggle reach its own resolution without interference from me. We walk a second block. Her arm is through mine, but she talks only of her work, of the weather, and it is a remote, arm's-length conversation. At the next corner she swings around, away from her apartment, back toward the cocktail lounge. I try to be patient with her.

I have no need to rush things now, I tell myself. Her body is not a secret tome. We have begun our relationship topsy-turvy, with the physical part first; now it will take time to work backward to the more difficult part that some people call love.

But of course she is not aware that we have known each other that way. The wind blows swirling snowflakes in our faces, and somehow the cold sting awakens honesty in me. I know what I must say. I must relinquish my unfair advantage.

I tell her, "While I was ridden last week, Helen, I had a girl in my room."

"Why talk of such things now?"

"I have to, Helen. You were the girl."

She halts. She turns to me. People hurry past us in the street. Her face is very pale, with dark red spots growing in her cheeks.

"That's not funny, Charles."

"It wasn't meant to be. You were with me from Tuesday night to early Friday morning."

"How can you possibly know that?"

"I do. I do. The memory is clear. Somehow it remains, Helen. I see your whole body."

"Stop it, Charles."

"We were very good together," I say. "We must have pleased our Passengers because we were so good. To see you again—it was like waking from a dream, and finding that the dream was real, the girl right there—"

"No!"

"Let's go to your apartment and begin again."

She says, "You're being deliberately filthy, and I don't know why, but there wasn't any reason for you to spoil things. Maybe I was with you and maybe I wasn't, but you wouldn't know it, and if you did know it you should keep your mouth shut about it, and—"

"You have a birthmark the size of a dime," I say, "about three inches below your left breast."

She sobs and hurls herself at me, there in the street. Her long silvery nails rake my cheeks. She pummels me. I seize her. Her knees assail me. No one pays attention; those who pass by assume we are ridden, and turn their heads. She is all fury, but I have my arms around hers like metal bands, so that she can only stamp and snort, and her body is close against mine. She is rigid, anguished.

In a low, urgent voice I say, "We'll defeat them, Helen. We'll finish what they started. Don't fight me. There's no reason to fight me. I know, it's a fluke that I remember you, but let me go with you and I'll prove that we belong together."

"Let—go—"

"Please. Please. Why should we be enemies? I don't mean you any harm. I love you, Helen. Do you remember, when we were kids, we could play at being in love? I did; you must have done it too. Sixteen, seventeen years old. The whispers, the conspiracies—all a big game and we knew it. But the game's over. We can't afford to tease and run. We have so little time, when we're free—we have to trust, to open ourselves—"

"It's wrong."

"No. Just because it's the stupid custom for two people brought together by Passengers to avoid one another, that doesn't mean we have to follow it. Helen—Helen—"

Something in my tone registers with her. She ceases to struggle. Her rigid body softens. She looks up at me, her tearstreaked face thawing, her eyes blurred.

"Trust me," I say. "Trust me, Helen!"

She hesitates. Then she smiles.

In that moment I feel the chill at the back of my skull, the sensation as of a steel needle driven deep through bone. I stiffen. My arms drop away from her. For an instant, I lose touch, and when the mists clear all is different.

"Charles?" she says. "*Charles?*"

Her knuckles are against her teeth. I turn, ignoring her, and go back into the cocktail lounge. A young man sits in one of the front booths. His dark hair gleams with pomade; his cheeks are smooth. His eyes meet mine.

I sit down. He orders drinks. We do not talk.

My hand falls on his wrist, and remains there. The bartender, serving the drinks, scowls but says nothing. We sip our cocktails and put the drained glasses down.

"Let's go," the young man says.

I follow him out.

Harriet Prescott Spofford (1835–1921)

The Moonstone Mass

Harriet Prescott Spofford is, according to Alfred Bendixen, "the major female practitioner of a mode of symbolic romance which many have asserted to be the mainstream of American fiction." She established a reputation as the female heir to Poe and Hawthorne, and especially in supernatural fiction, is one of the most important conduits between Poe and the twentieth century. Her first novel, in the Gothic mode, *Sir Rohan's Ghost* (1859) was praised by James Russell Lowell, who said that no American had ever written a first novel with such "genuine poetic power," and her collection, *The Amber Gods and other stories* (1863), was praised in a review by Henry James, who, although objecting to her "morbid and unhealthful" fascination with the "diseased side of human nature," admired the "united strength and brilliancy of her descriptions." A prolific and sometimes hasty magazine writer, Spofford published hundreds of stories, but her best work was in the supernatural. "The Moonstone Mass" (1868), a symbolic romance in her major mode, shows the clear influence of Poe's *Narrative of Arthur Gordon Pym,* and echoes of poetry from Coleridge's *The Rime of the Ancient Mariner* and "Kubla Khan" to Dante's *Inferno.* It is interesting to compare Spofford's treatment to Lovecraft's "At the Mountains of Madness." Both, it seems to me, reach the heights of poetic frenzy, awe and wonder and fear.

There was a certain weakness possessed by my ancestors, though in nowise peculiar to them, and of which, in common with other more or less undesirable traits, I have come into the inheritance.

It was the fear of dying in poverty. That, too, in the face of a goodly share of pelf stored in stocks, and lands, and copper-bottomed clippers, or what stood for copper-bottomed clippers, or rather sailed for them, in the clumsy commerce of their times.

There was one old fellow in particular—his portrait is hanging over the hall stove today, leaning forward, somewhat blistered by the profuse heat and wasted fuel there, and as if as long as such an outrageous expenditure of caloric was going on he meant to have the full benefit of it—who is said to have frequently shed tears over the probable price of his dinner, and on the next day to have sent home a silver dish to eat it from at a hundred times the cost. I find the inconsistencies of this individual constantly cropping out in myself; and although I could by no possibility be called a niggard, yet I confess that even now my prodigalities make me shiver.

Some years ago I was the proprietor of the old family estate, unencumbered by any thing except timber, that is worth its weight in gold yet, as you might say; alone in the world, save for an unloved relative; and with a sufficiently comfortable income, as I have

154

since discovered, to meet all reasonable wants. I had, moreover, promised me in marriage the hand of a woman without a peer, and which, I believe now, might have been mine on any day when I saw fit to claim it.

That I loved Eleanor tenderly and truly you can not doubt; that I desired to bring her home, to see her flitting here and there in my dark old house, illuminating it with her youth and beauty, sitting at the head of my table that sparkled with its gold and silver heir-looms, making my days and nights like one delightful dream, was just as true.

And yet I hesitated. I looked over my bankbook—I cast up my accounts. I have enough for one, I said; I am not sure that it is enough for two. Eleanor, daintily nurtured, requires as dainty care for all time to come; moreover, it is not two alone to be considered, for should children come, there is their education, their maintenance, their future provision and portion to be found. All this would impoverish us, and unless we ended by becoming mere dependents, we had, to my excited vision, only the cold charity of the world and the work-house to which to look forward. I do not believe that Eleanor thought me right in so much of the matter as I saw fit to explain, but in maiden pride her lips perforce were sealed. She laughed though, when I confessed my work-house fear, and said that for her part she was thankful there was such a refuge at all, standing as it did on its knoll in the midst of green fields, and shaded by broad-limbed oaks—she had always envied the old women sitting there by their evening fireside, and mumbling over their small affairs to one another. But all her words seemed merely idle badinage—so I delayed. I said—when this ship sails in, when that dividend is declared, when I see how this speculation turns out—the days were long that added up the count of years, the nights were dreary; but I believed that I was actuated by principle, and took pride to myself for my strength and self-denial.

Moreover, old Paul, my great-uncle on my mother's side, and the millionaire of the family, was a bitter misogynist, and regarded women and marriage and household cares as the three remediless mistakes of an over-ruling Providence. He knew of my engagement to Eleanor, but so long as it remained in that stage he had nothing to say. Let me once marry, and my share of his million would be best represented by a cipher. However, he was not a man to adore, and he could not live forever.

Still, with all my own effort, I amassed wealth but slowly, according to my standard; my various ventures had various luck; and one day my old Uncle Paul, always intensely interested in the subject, both scientifically and from a commercial point of view, too old and feeble to go himself, but fain to send a proxy, and desirous of money in the family, made me an offer of that portion of his wealth on my return which would be mine on his demise, funded safely subject to my order, provided I made one of those who sought the discovery of the Northwest Passage.

I went to town, canvassed the matter with the experts I had always an adventurous streak, as old Paul well knew—and having given many hours to the pursuit of the smaller sciences, had a turn for danger and discovery as well. And when the *Albatross* sailed—in spite of Eleanor's shivering remonstrance and prayers and tears, in spite of the grave looks of my friends—I was one of those that clustered on her deck, prepared for either fate. They—my companions—it is true, were led by nobler lights; but as for me, it was much as I told Eleanor—my affairs were so regulated that they would go on uninterruptedly in my absence; I should be no worse off for going, and if I returned, letting alone the renown of the thing, my Uncle Paul's donation was to be appropriated; every thing then was assured, and we stood possessed of lucky lives. If I had any keen or eager desire of search, any purpose to aid the growth of the world or to penetrate the secrets of its formation; as indeed I think I must have had, I did not at that time know any thing about it. But I was to learn that death and stillness have no kingdom on this globe, and that even in the extremest bitterness of cold and ice perpetual interchange and motion is taking place. So we went, all sails set on favorable winds, bounding over blue sea, skirting frowning coasts, and ever pushing our way up into the dark mystery of the North.

I shall not delay here to tell of Danish posts and the hospitality of summer settlements in their long afternoon of arctic daylight; nor will I weary you with any description of the succulence of the radishes that grew under the panes of glass in the Governor's scrap of moss and soil, scarcely of more size than a lady's parlor fernery, and which seemed to our dry mouths full of all the earth's cool juices—but advance, as we ourselves hastened to do, while that chill and crystalline sun shone, up into the ice-cased dens and caverns of the Pole. By the time that the long, blue twilight fell, when the rough and rasping cold sheathed all the atmosphere, and the great stars pricked themselves out on the heavens like spears' points, the *Albatross* was hauled up for winter-quarters, banked and boarded, heaved high on fields of ice; and all her inmates, during the wintry dark, led the life that prepared them for further exploits in higher latitudes the coming year, learning the dialects of the Esquimaux, the tricks of the seal and walrus, making long explorations with the dogs and Glipnu, their master, breaking ourselves in for business that had no play about it.

Then, at last, the August suns set us free again; inlets of tumultuous water traversed the great ice-floes; the *Albatross*, refitted, ruffled all her plumage and spread her wings once more for the North—for the secret that sat there domineering all its substance.

It was a year since we had heard from home; but who staid to think of that while our keel spurned into foam the sheets of steely seas, and day by day brought us nearer to the hidden things we sought? For myself I confess that, now so close to the end as it seemed, curiosity and research absorbed every other faculty; Eleanor might be mouldering back to the parent earth—I could not stay to meditate on such a possibility; my Uncle Paul's donation might enrich itself with gold-dust instead of the gathered dust of idle days—it was nothing to me. I had but one thought, one ambition, one desire in those days—the discovery of the clear seas and open passage. I endured all our hardships as if they had been luxuries: I made light of scurvy, banqueted off train-oil, and met that cold for which there is no language framed, and which might be a new element; or which, rather, had seemed in that long night like the vast void of ether beyond the uttermost star, where was neither air nor light nor heat, but only bitter negation and emptiness. I was hardly conscious of my body; I was only a concentrated search in myself.

The recent explorers had announced here, in the neighborhood of where our third summer at last found us, the existence of an immense space of clear water. One even declared that he had seen it.

My Uncle Paul had pronounced the declaration false, and the sight an impossibility. The North he believed to be the breeder of icebergs, an ever-welling fountain of cold; the great glaciers there forever form, forever fall; the ice-packs line the gorges from year to year unchanging; peaks of volcanic rock drop their frozen mantles like a scale only to display the fresher one beneath. The whole region, said he, is Plutonic, blasted by a primordial convulsion of the great forces of creation; and though it may be a few miles nearer to the central fires of the earth, allowing that there are such things, yet that would not in itself detract from the frigid power of its sunless solitudes, the more especially when it is remembered that the spinning of the earth, while in its first plastic material, which gave it greater circumference and thinness of shell at its equator, must have thickened the shell correspondingly at the poles; and the character of all the waste and wilderness there only signifies the impenetrable wall between its surface and centre, through which wall no heat could enter or escape. The great rivers, like the White and the Mackenzie, emptying to the north of the continents, so far from being enough in themselves to form any body of ever fresh and flowing water, can only pierce the opposing ice-fields in narrow streams and bays and inlets as they seek the Atlantic and the Pacific seas. And as for the theory of the currents of water heated in the tropics and carried by the rotary motion of the planet to the Pole, where they rise and melt the ice-floes into this great supposititious sea, it is simply an absurdity on the face of it, he argued, when you remember that warm water being in its nature specifically lighter than cold it would have risen to the surface long before it reached there. No, thought my Uncle Paul, who took nothing for granted; it is as I said, an absurdity on the face of it; my nephew shall prove it, and I stake half the earnings of my life upon it.

To tell the truth, I thought much the same as he did; and now that such a mere trifle of distance intervened between me and the proof, I was full of a feverish impatience that almost amounted to insanity.

We had proceeded but a few days, coasting the crushing capes of rock that every where seemed to run out in a diablerie of tusks and horns to drive us from the region that they warded, now cruising through a runlet of blue water just wide enough for our keel, with silver reaches of frost stretching away into a ghastly horizon—now plunging upon tossing seas, the sun wheeling round and round, and never sinking from the strange, weird sky above us, when again to our look-out a glimmer in the low horizon told its awful tale—a sort of smoky lustre like that which might ascend from an army of spirits—the fierce and fatal spirits tented on the terrible field of the ice-floe.

We were alone, our single little ship speeding ever upward in the midst of that untraveled desolation. We spoke seldom to one another, oppressed with the sense of our situation. It was a loneliness that seemed more than a death in life, a solitude that was supernatural. Here and now it was clear water; ten hours later and we were caught in the teeth of the cold, wedged in the ice that had advanced upon us and surrounded us, fettered by another winter in latitudes where human life had never before been supported.

We found, before the hands of the dial had taught us the lapse of a week, that this would be something not to be endured. The sun sank lower every day behind the crags and silvery horns; the heavens grew to wear a hue of violet, almost black, and yet unbearably dazzling; as the notes of our voices fell upon the atmosphere they assumed a metallic tone, as if the air itself had become frozen from the beginning of the world and they tinkled against it; our sufferings had mounted in their intensity till they were too great to be resisted.

It was decided at length—when the one long day had given place to its answering night, and in the jet-black heavens the stars, like knobs of silver, sparkled so large and close upon us that we might have grasped them in our hands—that I should take a sledge with Glipnu and his dogs, and see if there were any path to the westward by which, if the *Albatross* were forsaken, those of her crew that remained might follow it, and find an escape to safety. Our path was on a frozen sea; if we discovered land we did not know that the foot of man had ever trodden it; we could hope to find no *caché* of snow-buried food—neither fish nor game lived in this desert of ice that was so devoid of life in any shape as to seem dead itself. But, well provisioned, furred to the eyes, and essaying to nurse some hopefulness of heart, we set out on our way through this Valley of Death, relieving one another, and traveling day and night.

Still night and day to the west rose the black coast, one interminable height; to the east extended the sheets of unbroken ice; sometimes a huge glacier hung pendulous from the precipice; once we saw, by the starlight, a white, foaming, rushing river arrested and transformed to ice in its flight down that steep. A south wind began to blow behind us;

we traveled on the ice; three days, perhaps, as days are measured among men, had passed, when we found that we made double progress, for the ice traveled too; the whole field, carried by some northward-bearing current, was afloat; it began to be crossed and cut by a thousand crevasses; the cakes, an acre each, tilted up and down, and made wide waves with their ponderous plashing in the black body of the sea; we could hear them grinding distantly in the clear dark against the coast, against each other. There was no retreat—there was no advance; we were on the ice, and the ice was breaking up. Suddenly we rounded a tongue of the primeval rock, and recoiled before a narrow gulf—one sharp shadow, as deep as despair, as full of aguish fears. It was just wide enough for the sledge to span. Glipnu made the dogs leap; we could be no worse off if they drowned. They touched the opposite block; it careened; it went under; the sledge went with it; I was left alone where I had stood. Two dogs broke loose, and scrambled up beside me; Glipnu and the others I never saw again. I sank upon the ice; the dogs crouched beside me; sometimes I think they saved my brain from total ruin, for without them I could not have withstood the enormity of that loneliness, a loneliness that it was impossible should be broken—floating on and on with that vast journeying company of spectral ice. I had food enough to support life for several days to come, in the pouch at my belt; the dogs and I shared it—for, last as long as it would, when it should be gone there was only death before us—no reprieve—sooner or later that; as well sooner as later—the living terrors of this icy hell were all about us, and death could be no worse.

Still the south wind blew, the rapid current carried us, the dark skies grew deep and darker, the lanes and avenues between the stars were crowded with forebodings—for the air seemed full of a new power, a strange and invisible influence, as if a king of unknown terrors here held his awful state. Sometimes the dogs stood up and growled and bristled their shaggy hides; I, prostrate on the ice, in all my frame was stung with a universal tingle. I was no longer myself. At this moment my blood seemed to sing and bubble in my veins; I grew giddy with a sort of delirious and inexplicable ecstasy; with another moment unutterable horror seized me; I was plunged and weighed down with a black and suffocating load, while evil things seemed to flap their wings in my face, to breathe in my mouth, to draw my soul out of my body and carry it careering through the frozen realm of that murky heaven, to restore it with a shock of agony. Once as I lay there, still floating, floating northward, out of the dim dark rim of the water-world, a lance of piercing light shot up the zenith; it divided the heavens like a knife; they opened out in one blaze, and the fire fell sheetingly down before my face—cold fire, curdlingly cold—light robbed of heat, and set free in a preternatural anarchy of the elements; its fringes swung to and fro before my face, pricked it with flaming spiculæ, dissolving in a thousand colors that spread every where over the low field, flashing, flickering, creeping, reflecting, gathering again in one long serpentine line of glory that wavered in slow convolutions across the cuts and crevasses of the ice, wreathed ever nearer, and, lifting its head at last, became nothing in the darkness but two great eyes like glowing coals, with which it stared me to a stound, till I threw myself face down to hide me in the ice; and the whining, bristling dogs cowered backward, and were dead.

I should have supposed myself to be in the region of the magnetic pole of the sphere, if I did not know that I had long since left it behind me. My pocket-compass had become entirely useless, and every scrap of metal that I had about me had become a loadstone. The very ice, as if it were congealed from water that held large quantities of iron in solution; iron escaping from whatever solid land there was beneath or around, the Plutonic rock that such a region could have alone veined and seamed with metal. The very ice appeared to have a magnetic quality; it held me so that I changed my position upon it with difficulty, and, as if it established a battery by the aid of the singular atmosphere above it, frequently sent thrills quivering through and through me till my flesh seemed about to resolve into all the jarring atoms of its original constitution; and again soothed me, with a velvet touch, into a state which, if it were not sleep, was at least haunted by visions that I dare not believe to have been realities, and from which I always awoke with a start to find myself still floating, floating. My watch had long since ceased to beat. I felt an odd persuasion that I had died when that stood still, and only this slavery of the magnet, of the cold, this power that locked every thing in invisible fetters and let nothing loose again, held my soul still in the bonds of my body. Another idea, also, took possession of me, for my mind was open to whatever visitant chose to enter, since utter despair of safety or release had left it vacant of a hope or fear. These enormous days and nights, swinging in their arc six months long, were the pendulum that dealt time in another measure than that dealt by the sunlight of lower zones; they told the time of what interminable years, the years of what vast generations far beyond the span that covered the age of the primeval men of Scripture—they measured time on this gigantic and enduring scale for what wonderful and mighty beings, old as the everlasting hills, as destitute as they of mortal sympathy, cold and inscrutable, handling the two-edged javelins of frost and magnetism, and served by all the unknown polar agencies. I fancied that I saw their far-reaching cohorts, marshaling and manœuvring at times in the field of an horizon that was boundless, the glitter of their spears and casques, the sheen of their white banners; and again, sitting in fearful circle with their phantasmagoria they shut and hemmed me in and watched me write like a worm before them.

I had a fancy that the perpetual play of magnetic impulses here gradually disintegrated the expanse of ice, as sunbeams might have done. If it succeeded in unseating me from my cold station I should drown, and there would be an end of me; it would be all one; for though I clung to life I did not cling to suffering. Something of the wild beast seemed to spring up in my nature; that ignorance of any moment but the present. I felt a certain kinship to the bear in her comfortable snowiness whom I had left in the parallels far below this unreal tract of horrors. I remembered traditions of such metempsychoses; the thought gave me a pang that none of these fierce and subtle elements had known how to give before. But all the time my groaning, cracking ice was moving with me, splitting now through all its leagues of length along the darkness, with an explosion like a cannon's shot, that echoed again and again in every gap and chasm of its depth, and seemed to be caught up and repeated by a thousand airy sprites, and snatched on from one to another till it fell dead through the frozen thickness of the air.

It was at about this time that I noticed another species of motion than that which had hitherto governed it seizing this journeying ice. It bent and bent, as a glacier does in its viscous flow between mountains; it crowded, and loosened, and rent apart, and at last it broke in every direction, and every fragment was crushed and jammed together again; and the whole mass was following, as I divined, the curve of some enormous whirlpool that swept it from beneath. It might have been a day and night, it might have been an hour, that we traveled on this vast curve—I had no more means of knowing than if I had veritably done with time. We were one expanse of shadow; not a star above us, only a sky of impenetrable gloom received the shimmering that now and again the circling ice cast off. It was a strange slow motion, yet with such a steadiness and strength about it that it had the effect of swiftness. It was long since any water, or the suspicion of any, had been visible; we might have been grinding through some gigantic hollow for all I could have told; snow had never fallen here; the mass moved you knew as if you felt the prodigious hand that grasped and impelled it from beneath. Whither was it tending, in the eddy of what huge stream that went, with the smoke of its fall hovering on the brink, to plunge a tremendous cataract over the limits of the earth into the unknown abyss of space? Far in advance there was a faint glimmering, a sort of powdery light glancing here and there. As we approached it—the ice and I—it grew fainter, and was, by-and-by, lost in a vast twilight that surrounded us on all sides; at the same time it became evident that we had passed under a roof, an immense and vaulted roof. As crowding, stretching, rending, we passed on, uncanny gleams were playing distantly above us and around us, now and then overlaying all things with a sheeted illumination as deathly as a grave-light, now and then shooting up in spires of blood-red radiance that disclosed the terrible aurora. I was in a cavern of ice, as wide and as high as the heavens; these flashes of glory, alternated with equal flashes of darkness, as you might say, taught me to perceive. Perhaps tremendous tide after tide had hollowed it with all its fantastic recesses; or had that Titantic race of the interminable years built it as a palace for their monarch, a temple for their deity, with its domes that sprung far up immeasurable heights and hung palely shining like mock heavens of hazy stars; its aisles that stretched away down colonnades of crystal columns into unguessed darkness; its high-heaved arches, its pierced and open sides? Now an aurora burned up like a blue-light, and went skimming under all the vaults far off into far and farther hollows, revealing, as it went, still loftier heights and colder answering radiances. Then these great arches glowed like blocks of beryl. Wondrous tracery of delicate vines and leaves, greener than the greenest moss, wandered over them, wreathed the great pillars, and spread round them in capitals of flowers; roses crimson as a carbuncle; hyacinths like bedded cubes of amethyst; violets bluer than sapphires—all as if the flowers had been turned to flame, yet all so cruelly cold, as if the power that wrought such wonders could simulate a sparkle beyond even the lustre of light, but could not give it heat, that principle of life, that fountain of first being. Yonder a stalactite of clustered ruby—that kept the aurora and glinted faintly, and more faintly, till the thing came again, when it grasped a whole body-full of splendor—hung downward and dropped a thread-like stem and a blossom of palest pink, like a transfigured Linnæa, to meet the snow-drop in its sheath of green that shot up from a spire of aqua marine below. Here living rainbows flew from buttress to buttress and frolicked in the domes—the only things that dared to live and sport where beauty was frozen into horror. It seemed as if that shifting death-light of the aurora photographed all these things upon my memory, for I noted none of them at the time. I only wondered idly whither we were tending as we drove in deeper and deeper under that ice-roof, and curved more and more circlingly upon our course while the silent flashes sped on overhead. Now we were in the dark again crashing onward; now a cold blue radiance burst from every icicle, from every crevice, and I saw that the whole enormous mass of our motion bent and swept around a single point—a dark yet glittering form that sat as if upon the apex of the world. Was it one of those mightier than the Anakim, more than the sons of God, to whom all the currents of this frozen world converged? Sooth I know not—for presently I imagined that my vision made only an exaggeration of some brown Esquimaux sealed up and left in his snow-house to die. A thin sheathing of ice appeared to clothe him and give the glister to his duskiness. Insensible as I had thought myself to any further fear, I cowered beneath the stare of those dead and icy eyes. Slowly we rounded, and ever rounded; the inside, on which my place was, moving less slowly than the outer circle of the sheeted mass in its viscid flow; and as we moved, by some fate my eye was caught by the substance on which this figure sat. It was no figure at all now, but a bare jag of rock rising in the centre of this solid whirlpool, and carrying on its summit something which held a light that not one of these icy freaks, pranking in the dress of gems and flowers, had found it possible to assume. It was a thing so real, so genuine, my breath became suspended; my heart ceased to beat; my brain, that had been a lump of ice, seemed to move in its skull; hope, that had deserted me, suddenly sprung up like a second life within me; the old passion was not dead, if I was. It rose stronger than life or death or than myself. If I could but snatch that mass of moonstone, that inestimable wealth! It was nothing deceptive, I declared to myself. What more natural home could it have than this region, thrown up here by the old Plutonic powers of the planet, as the same substance in smaller shape was thrown up on the peaks of the Mount St. Gothard, when the Alpine aiguilles first sprang into the day? There it rested, limpid with its milky pearl, casting out flakes of flame and azure, of red and leaf-green light, and holding yet a sparkle of silver in the reflections and refractions of its inner axis—the splendid Turk's-eye of the lapidaries, the cousin of the water-opal and the girasole, the precious essence of feldspar. Could I break it, I would find clusters of great hemitrope crystals. Could I obtain it, I should have a jewel in that mass of moonstone such as the world never saw! The throne of Jemschid could not cast a shadow beside it.

Then the bitterness of my fate overwhelmed me. Here, with this treasure of a kingdom, this jewel that could not be priced, this wealth beyond an Emperor's—and here only to die! My stolid apathy vanished, old thoughts dominated once more, old habits, old desires. I thought of Eleanor then in her warm, sunny home, the blossoms that bloomed around her, the birds that sang, the cheerful evening fires, the longing thoughts for one who never came, who never was to come. But I would! I cried, where human voice had never cried before. I would return! I would take this treasure with me! I would not be defrauded! Should not I, a man, conquer this inanimate blind matter? I reached out my hands to seize it. Slowly it receded—slowly, and less slowly; or was the motion of the ice still carrying me onward? Had we encircled this apex? and were we driving out into the open and uncovered North, and so down the seas and out to the open main of black water again? If so—if I could live through it—I must have this thing!

I rose, and as well as I could, with my cramped and stiffened limbs, I moved to go back for it. It was useless; the current that carried us was growing invincible, the gaping gulfs of the outer seas were sucking us toward them. I fell; I scrambled to my feet; I would still have gone back, but, as I attempted it, the ice whereon I was inclined ever so slightly, tipped more boldly, gave way, and rose in a billow, broke, and piled over on another mass beneath. Then the cavern was behind us, and I comprehended that this ice-stream, having doubled its central point, now in its outward movement encountered the still incoming body, and was to pile above and pass over it, the whole expanse bending, cracking, breaking, crowding, and compressing, till its rearing tumult made bergs more mountainous than the offshot glaciers of the Greenland continent, that should ride safely down to crumble in the surging seas below. As block after block of the rent ice rose in the air, lighted by the blue and bristling aurora-points, toppled and mounted higher, it seemed to me that now indeed I was battling with those elemental agencies in the dreadful fight I had desired—one man against the might of matter. I sprang from that block to another; I gained my balance on a third, climbing, shouldering, leaping, struggling, holding with my hands, catching with my feet, crawling, stumbling, tottering, rising high and higher with the mountain ever making underneath; a power unknown to my foes coming to my aid, a blessed rushing warmth that glowed on all the surface of my skin, that set the blood to racing in my veins, that made my heart beat with newer hope, sink with newer despair, rise buoyant with new determination. Except when the shaft of light pierced the shivering sky I could not see or guess the height that I had gained. I was vaguely aware of chasms that were bottomless, of precipices that opened on them, of pinnacles rising round me in aerial spires, when suddenly the shelf, on which I must have stood, yielded, as if it were pushed by great hands, swept down a steep incline like an avalanche, stopped half-way, but sent me flying on, sliding, glancing, like a shooting-star, down, down the slippery side, breathless, dizzy, smitten with blistering pain by awful winds that whistled by me, far out upon the level ice below that tilted up and down again with the great resonant plash of open water, and conscious for a moment that I lay at last upon a fragment that the mass behind urged on, I knew and I remembered nothing more.

Faces were bending over me when I opened my eyes again, rough, uncouth, and bearded faces, but no monsters of the pole. Whalemen rather, smelling richly of train-oil, but I could recall nothing in all my life one fraction so beautiful as they; the angels on whom I hope to open my eyes when Death has really taken me will scarcely seem sights more blest than did those rude whalers of the North Pacific Sea. The North Pacific Sea—for it was there that I was found, explain it how you may—whether the *Albatross* had pierced farther to the west than her sailing-master knew, and had lost her reckoning with a disordered compass-needle under new stars—or whether I had really been the sport of the demoniac beings of the ice, tossed by them from zone to zone in a dozen hours. The whalers, real creatures enough, had discovered me on a block of ice, they said; nor could I, in their opinion, have been many days undergoing my dreadful experience, for there was still food in my wallet when they opened it. They would never believe a word of my story, and so far from regarding me as one who had proved the Northwest Passage in my own person, they considered me a mere idle maniac, as uncomfortable a thing to have on ship-board as a ghost or a dead body, wrecked and unable to account for myself, and gladly transferred me to a homeward-bound Russian man-of-war, whose officers afforded me more polite but quite as decided skepticism. I have never to this day found any one who believed my story when I told it—so you can take it for what it is worth. Even my Uncle Paul flouted it, and absolutely refused to surrender the sum on whose expectation I had taken ship; while my old ancestor, who hung peeling over the hall fire, dropped from his frame in disgust at the idea of one of his hard-cash descendants turning romancer. But all I know is that the *Albatross* never sailed into port again, and that if I open my knife today and lay it on the table it will wheel about till the tip of its blade points full at the North Star.

I have never found any one to believe me, did I say? Yes, there is one—Eleanor never doubted a word of my narration, never asked me if cold and suffering had not shaken my reason. But then, after the first recital, she has never been willing to hear another word about it, and if I ever allude to my lost treasure or the possibility of instituting search for it, she asks me if I need more lessons to be content with the treasure that I have, and gathers up her work and gently leaves the room. So that, now I speak of it so seldom, if I had not told the thing to you it might come to pass that I should forget altogether the existence of my mass of moonstone. My mass of moonshine, old Paul calls it. I let him have his say; he can not have that nor any thing else much longer; but when all is done I recall Galileo and I mutter to myself, *"Per si muove*—it *was* a mass of moonstone! With these eyes I saw it, with these hands I touched it, with this heart I longed for it, with this will I mean to have it yet!"

Peter Straub (b. 1943)

The Blue Rose

Peter Straub is a poet and novelist who began writing horror without wide reading in the genre. His novel, *Julia* (1975) sparked a friendship between Straub, then living in England, and the visiting Stephen King, who told Straub that his talents lay in the direction of the horror genre and encouraged him to read more of it. The impressive results of Straub's successful integration of his already deep knowledge of contemporary literature with newfound depth in nineteenth and twentieth century horror were the novels *Ghost Story* (1979) and *Shadowland* (1980), two of the finest horror novels of recent decades. Straub and King collaborated on the best-seller, *Floating Dragon* (1983). He won the World Fantasy Award for best novel of the year in 1989 for his thriller, *Koko*. He is a central figure in the horror novel renaissance of the 1970s, and in the British-American social group of writers discussing the strengths and problems of long-form horror. He began writing novellas in the 1980s, resulting in his recent collection of four novellas, *Houses Without Doors* (1990). "The Blue Rose" was his first novella and, while perhaps evincing the influence of King, is very much in Straub's characteristic mode, showing a commitment to character and in this case a kind of dark nostalgia reminiscent of Ray Bradbury's *Something Wicked This Way Comes* (1962), transmuted into grim realism.

I

(for Rosemary Clooney)

On a stifling summer day the two youngest of the five Beevers children, Harry and Little Eddie, were sitting on cane-backed chairs in the attic of their house on South Sixth Street in Palmyra, New York. Their father called it "the upstairs junk room," as this large irregular space was reserved for the boxes of tablecloths, stacks of diminishingly sized girl's winter coats, and musty old dresses Maryrose Beevers had mummified as testimony to the superiority of her past to her present.

A tall mirror that could be tilted in its frame, an artifact of their mother's onetime glory, now revealed to Harry the rear of Little Eddie's head. This object, looking more malleable than a head should be, an elongated wad of Play-Doh covered with straggling feathers, was just peeking above the back of the chair. Even the back of Little Eddie's head looked tense to Harry.

"Listen to me," Harry said. Little Eddie squirmed in his chair, and the wobbly chair squirmed with him. "You think I'm kidding you? I had her last year."

163

"Well, she didn't kill *you,*" Little Eddie said.

"Course not, she liked me, you little dummy. She only hit me a couple of times. She hit some of those kids every single day."

"But teachers can't *kill* people," Little Eddie said.

At nine, Little Eddie was only a year younger than he, but Harry knew that his undersized fretful brother saw him as much a part of the world of big people as their older brothers.

"Most teachers can't," Harry said. "But what if they live right in the same building as the principal? What if they won *teaching awards,* hey, and what if every other teacher in the place is scared stiff of them? Don't you think they can get away with murder? Do you think anybody really misses a snot-faced little brat—a little brat like you? Mrs. Franken took this kid, this runty little Tommy Golz, into the cloakroom, and she killed him right there. I heard him scream. At the end, it sounded just like bubbles. He was trying to yell, but there was too much blood in his throat. He never came back, and nobody ever said boo about it. She killed him, and next year she's going to be your teacher. I hope you're afraid, Little Eddie, because you ought to be." Harry leaned forward. "Tommy Golz even looked sort of like you, Little Eddie."

Little Eddie's entire face twitched as if a lightning bolt had crossed it.

In fact, the young Golz boy had suffered an epileptic fit and been removed from school, as Harry knew.

"Mrs. Franken especially hates selfish little brats that don't share their toys."

"I do share my toys," Little Eddie wailed, tears beginning to run down through the delicate smears of dust on his cheeks. "Everybody *takes* my toys, that's why."

"So give me your Ultraglide Roadster," Harry said. This had been Little Eddie's birthday present, given three days previous by a beaming father and a scowling mother. "Or I'll tell Mrs. Franken as soon as I get inside that school, this fall."

Under its layer of grime, Little Eddie's face went nearly the same white-gray shade as his hair.

An ominous slamming sound came up the stairs.

"Children? Are you messing around up there in the attic? Get down here!"

"We're just sitting in the chairs, Mom," Harry called out.

"Don't you bust those chairs! Get down here this minute!"

Little Eddie slid out of his chair and prepared to bolt.

"I want that car," Harry whispered. "And if you don't give it to me, I'll tell Mom you were foolin' around with her old clothes."

"I didn't do nothin'!" Little Eddie wailed, and broke for the stairs.

"Hey, Mom, we didn't break any stuff, honest!" Harry yelled. He bought a few minutes more by adding, "I'm coming right now," and stood up and went toward a cardboard box filled with interesting books he had noticed the day before his brother's birthday, and which had been his goal before he had remembered the Roadster and coaxed Little Eddie upstairs.

When, a short time later, Harry came through the door to the attic steps, he was carrying a tattered paperback book. Little Eddie stood quivering with misery and rage just outside the bedroom the two boys shared with their older brother Albert. He held out a small blue metal car, which Harry instantly took and eased into a front pocket of his jeans.

"When do I get it back?" Little Eddie asked.

"Never," Harry said. "Only selfish people want to get presents back. Don't you know anything at all?" When Eddie pursed his face up to wail, Harry tapped the book in his hands and said, "I got something here that's going to help you with Mrs. Franken, so don't complain."

His mother intercepted him as he came down the stairs to the main floor of the little house—here were the kitchen and living room, both floored with faded linoleum, the actual "junk room" separated by a stiff brown woolen curtain from the little makeshift room where Edgar Beevers slept, and the larger bedroom reserved for Maryrose. Children were never permitted more than a few steps within this awful chamber, for they might disarrange Maryrose's mysterious "papers" or interfere with the rows of antique dolls on the window seat, which was the sole, much-revered architectural distinction of the Beevers house.

Maryrose Beevers stood at the bottom of the stairs, glaring suspiciously up at her fourth son. She did not ever look like a woman who played with dolls, and she did not look that way now. Her hair was twisted into a knot at the back of her head. Smoke from her cigarette curled up past the big glasses like bird's wings which magnified her eyes.

Harry thrust his hand into his pocket and curled his fingers protectively around the Ultraglide Roadster.

"Those things up there are the possessions of my family," she said. "Show me what you took."

Harry shrugged and held out the paperback as he came down within striking range.

His mother snatched it from him, and tilted her head to see its cover through the cigarette smoke. "Oh. This is from that little box of books up there? Your father used to pretend to read books." She squinted at the print on the cover: "*Hypnosis Made Easy*. Some drugstore trash. You want to read this?"

Harry nodded.

"I don't suppose it can hurt you much." She negligently passed the book back to him. "People in society read books, you know—I used to read a lot, back before I got stuck here with a bunch of dummies. *My* father had a lot of books."

Maryrose nearly touched the top of Harry's head, then snatched back her hand. "You're my scholar, Harry. You're the one who's going places."

"I'm gonna do good in school next year," he said.

"*Well*. You're going to do well. As long as you don't ruin every chance you have by speaking like your father."

Harry felt that particular pain composed of scorn, shame, and terror that filled him when Maryrose spoke of his father in this way. He mumbled something that sounded like acquiescence, and moved a few steps sideways and around her.

II

The porch of the Beevers house extended six feet on either side of the front door, and was the repository for furniture either too large to be crammed into the junk room or too humble to be enshrined in the attic. A sagging porch swing sat beneath the living-room window, to the left of an ancient couch whose imitation green leather had been repaired with black duct tape; on the other side of the front door, through which Harry Beevers now emerged, stood a useless icebox dating from the earliest days of the Beeverses' marriage and two unsteady camp chairs Edgar Beevers had won in a card game. These had never been allowed into the house. Unofficially, this side of the porch was Harry's father's, and thereby had an entirely different atmosphere, defeated, lawless, and shameful, from the side with the swing and couch.

Harry knelt down in neutral territory directly before the front door and fished the Ultraglide Roadster from his pocket. He placed the hypnotism book on the porch and rolled the little metal car across its top. Then he gave the car a hard shove and watched it clunk nose-down onto the wood. He repeated this several times before moving the book aside, flattening himself out on his stomach, and giving the little car a decisive push toward the swing and the couch.

The Roadster rolled a few feet before an irregular board tilted it over on its side and stopped it.

"You dumb car," Harry said, and retrieved it. He gave it another push deeper into his mother's realm. A stiff, brittle section of paint which had separated from its board cracked in half and rested atop the stalled Roadster like a miniature mattress.

Harry knocked off the chip of paint and sent the car backwards down the porch, where it flipped over again and skidded into the side of the icebox. The boy ran down the porch and this time simply hurled the little car back in the direction of the swing. It bounced off the swing's padding and fell heavily to the wood. Harry knelt before the icebox, panting.

His whole head felt funny, as if wet hot towels had been stuffed inside it. Harry picked himself up and walked across to where the car lay before the swing. He hated the way it looked, small and helpless. He experimentally stepped on the car and felt it pressing into the undersole of his moccasin. Harry raised his other foot and stood on the car, but nothing happened. He jumped on the car, but the moccasin was no better than his bare foot. Harry bent down to pick up the Roadster.

"You dumb little car," he said. "You're no good anyhow, you low-class little jerky thing." He turned it over in his hands. Then he inserted his thumbs between the frame and one of the little tires. When he pushed, the tire moved. His face heated. He mashed his thumbs against the tire, and the little black doughnut popped into the tall thick weeds before the porch. Breathing hard more from emotion than exertion, Harry popped the other front tire into the weeds. Harry whirled around, and ground the car into the wall beside his father's bedroom window. Long deep scratches appeared in the paint. When Harry peered at the top of the car, it too was scratched. He found a nailhead which protruded a quarter of an inch out from the front of the house, and scraped a long paring of blue paint off the driver's side of the Roadster. Gray metal shone through. Harry slammed the car several times against the edge of the nailhead, chipping off small quantities of paint. Panting, he popped off the two small rear tires and put them in his pocket because he liked the way they looked.

Without tires, well scratched and dented, the Ultraglide Roadster had lost most of its power. Harry looked it over with a bitter, deep satisfaction and walked across the porch and shoved it far into the nest of weeds. Gray metal and blue paint shone at him from within the stalks and leaves. Harry thrust his hands into their midst and swept his arms back and forth. The car tumbled away and fell into invisibility.

When Maryrose appeared scowling on the porch, Harry was seated serenely on the squeaking swing, looking at the first few pages of the paperback book.

"What are you doing? What was all that banging?"

"I'm just reading, I didn't hear anything," Harry said.

III

"Well, if it isn't the shitbird," Albert said, jumping up the porch steps thirty minutes later. His face and T-shirt bore broad black stripes of grease. Short, muscular, and thirteen, Albert spent every possible minute hanging around the gas station two blocks from their house. Harry knew that Albert despised him. Albert raised a fist and made a jerky, threatening motion toward Harry, who flinched. Albert had often beaten him bloody, as had their two older brothers, Sonny and George, now at Army bases in Oklahoma and Germany. Like Albert, his two oldest brothers had seriously disappointed their mother.

Albert laughed, and this time swung his fist within a couple of inches of Harry's face. On the backswing he knocked the book from Harry's hands.

"Thanks," Harry said.

Albert smirked and disappeared around the front door. Almost immediately Harry could hear his mother beginning to shout about the grease on Albert's face and clothes. Albert thumped up the stairs.

Harry opened his clenched fingers and spread them wide, closed his hands into fists, then spread them wide again. When he heard the bedroom door slam shut upstairs, he was able to get off the swing and pick up the book. Being around Albert made him feel like a spring coiled up in a box. From the upper rear of the house, Little Eddie emitted a ghostly wail. Maryrose screamed that she was going to start smacking him if he didn't shut up, and that was that. The three unhappy lives within the house fell back into silence. Harry sat down, found his page, and began reading again.

A man named Dr. Roland Mentaine had written *Hypnosis Made Easy*, and his vocabulary was much larger than Harry's. Dr. Mentaine used words like "orchestrate" and "ineffable" and "enhance," and some of his sentences wound their way through so many subordinate clauses that Harry lost his way. Yet Harry, who had begun the book only half expecting that he would comprehend anything in it at all, found it a wonderful book. He had made it most of the way through the chapter called "Mind Power."

Harry thought it was neat that hypnosis could cure smoking, stuttering, and bedwetting. (He himself had wet the bed almost nightly until months after his ninth birthday. The bedwetting stopped the night a certain lovely dream came to Harry. In the dream he had to urinate terribly, and was hurrying down a stony castle corridor past suits of armor and torches guttering on the walls. At last Harry reached an open door, through which he saw the most splendid bathroom of his life. The floors were of polished marble, the walls white-tiled. As soon as he entered the gleaming bathroom, a uniformed butler waved him toward the rank of urinals. Harry began pulling down his zipper, fumbled with himself, and got his penis out of his underpants just in time. As the dream-urine gushed out of him, Harry had blessedly awakened.) Hypnotism could get you right inside someone's mind and let you do things there. You could make a person speak in any foreign language they'd ever heard, even if they'd only heard it once, and you could make them act like a baby. Harry considered how pleasurable it would be to make his brother Albert lie squalling and red-faced on the floor, unable to walk or speak as he pissed all over himself.

Also, and this was a new thought to Harry, you could take a person back to a whole row of lives they had led before they were born as the person they were now. This process of rebirth was called reincarnation. Some of Dr. Mentaine's patients had been kings in Egypt and pirates in the Caribbean, some had been murderers, novelists, and artists. They remembered the houses they'd lived in, the names of their mothers and servants and children, the locations of shops where they'd bought cake and wine. Neat stuff, Harry thought. He wondered if someone who had been a famous murderer a long time ago could remember pushing in the knife or bringing down the hammer. A lot of the books remaining in the little cardboard box upstairs, Harry had noticed, seemed to be about murderers. It would not be any use to take Albert back to a previous life, however. If Albert had any previous lives, he had spent them as inanimate objects on the order of boulders and anvils.

Maybe in another life Albert was a murder weapon, Harry thought.

"Hey, college boy! Joe College!"

Harry looked toward the sidewalk and saw the baseball cap and T-shirted gut of Mr. Petrosian, who lived in a tiny house next to the tavern on the corner of South Sixth and Livermore Street. Mr. Petrosian was always shouting genial things at kids, but Maryrose wouldn't let Harry or Little Eddie talk to him. She said Mr. Petrosian was common as dirt. He worked as a janitor in the telephone building and drank a case of beer every night while he sat on his porch.

"Me?" Harry said.

"Yeah! Keep reading books, and you could go to college, right?"

Harry smiled noncommittally. Mr. Petrosian lifted a wide arm and continued to toil down the street toward his house next to the Idle Hour.

In seconds Maryrose burst through the door, folding an old white dish towel in her hands. "Who was that? I heard a man's voice."

"Him," Harry said, pointing at the substantial back of Mr. Petrosian, now half of the way home.

"What did he say? As if it could possibly be interesting, coming from an Armenian janitor."

"He called me Joe College."

Maryrose startled him by smiling.

"Albert says he wants to go back to the station tonight, and I have to go to work soon." Maryrose worked the night shift as a secretary at St. Joseph's Hospital. "God knows when your father'll show up. Get something to eat for Little Eddie and yourself, will you, Harry? I've just got too many things to take care of, as usual."

"I'll get something at Big John's." This was a hamburger stand, a magical place to Harry, erected the summer before in a vacant lot on Livermore Street two blocks down from the Idle Hour.

His mother handed him two carefully folded dollar bills, and he pushed them into his pocket. "Don't let Little Eddie stay in the house alone," his mother said before going back inside. "Take him with you. You know how scared he gets."

"Sure," Harry said, and went back to his book. He finished the chapter on "Mind Power" while first Maryrose left to stand up at the bus stop on the corner and then Albert noisily departed. Little Eddie sat frozen before his soap operas in the living room. Harry turned a page and started reading "Techniques of Hypnosis."

IV

At eight-thirty that night the two boys sat alone in the kitchen, on opposite sides of the table covered in yellow bamboo Formica. From the living room came the sound of Sid Caesar babbling in fake German to Imogene Coca on *Your Show of Shows*. Little Eddie claimed to be scared of Sid Caesar, but when Harry had returned from the hamburger stand with a Big Johnburger (with "the works") for himself and a Mama Marydog for Eddie, double fries, and two chocolate shakes, he had been sitting in front of the television, his face moist with tears of moral outrage. Eddie usually liked Mama Marydogs, but he had taken only a couple of meager bites from the one before him now, and was disconsolately pushing a french fry through a blob of ketchup. Every now and then he wiped at his eyes, leaving nearly symmetrical smears of ketchup to dry on his cheeks.

"Mom *said* not to leave me alone in the house," said Little Eddie. "I heard. It was during *The Edge of Night* and you were on the porch. I think I'm gonna tell on you." He peeped across at Harry, then quickly looked back at the french fry and drew it out of the puddle of ketchup. "I'm ascared to be alone in the house." Sometimes Eddie's voice was like a queer speeded-up mechanical version of Maryrose's.

"Don't be so dumb," Harry said, almost kindly. "How can you be scared in your own house? You live here, don't you?"

"I'm ascared of the attic," Eddie said. He held the dripping french fry before his mouth and pushed it in. "The attic makes noise." A little squirm of red appeared at the corner of his mouth. "You were supposed to take me with you."

"Oh jeez, Eddie, you slow everything down. I wanted to just get the food and come back. I got you your dinner, didn't I? Didn't I get you what you like?"

In truth, Harry liked hanging around Big John's by himself because then he could talk to Big John and listen to his theories. Big John called himself a "renegade Papist" and considered Hitler the greatest man of the twentieth century, followed closely by Paul VI, Padre Pio who bled from the palms of his hands, and Elvis Presley.

All these events occurred in what is usually but wrongly called a simpler time, before Kennedy and feminism and ecology, before the Nixon presidency and Watergate, and before American soldiers, among them a twenty-one-year-old Harry Beevers, journeyed to Vietnam.

"I'm still going to tell," said Little Eddie. He pushed another french fry into the puddle of ketchup. "And that car was my birthday present." He began to snuffle. "Albert hit me, and you stole my car, and you left me alone, and I was scared. And I don't wanna have Mrs. Franken next year, cuz I think she's gonna hurt me."

Harry had nearly forgotten telling his brother about Mrs. Franken and Tommy Golz, and this reminder brought back very sharply the memory of destroying Eddie's birthday present.

Eddie twisted his head sideways and dared another quick look at his brother. "Can I have my Ultraglide Roadster back, Harry? You're going to give it back to me, aren'cha? I won't tell Mom you left me alone if you give it back."

"Your car is okay," Harry said. "It's in a sort of a secret place I know."

"You hurt my car!" Eddie squalled. "You did!"

"Shut up!" Harry shouted, and Little Eddie flinched. "You're driving me crazy!" Harry yelled. He realized that he was leaning over the table, and that Little Eddie was getting ready to cry again. He sat down. "Just don't scream at me like that, Eddie."

"You did something to my car," Eddie said with a stunned certainty. "I knew it."

"Look, I'll prove your car is okay," Harry said, and took the two rear tires from his pocket and displayed them on his palm.

Little Eddie stared. He blinked, then reached out tentatively for the tires.

Harry closed his fist around them. "Do they look like I did anything to them?"

"You took them *off!*"

"But don't they look okay, don't they look fine?" Harry opened his fist, closed it again, and returned the tires to his pocket. "I didn't want to show you the whole car, Eddie, because you'd get all worked up, and you gave it to me. Remember? I wanted to show you the tires so you'd see everything was all right. Okay? Got it?"

Eddie miserably shook his head.

"Anyway, I'm going to help you, just like I said."

"With Mrs. Franken?" A fraction of his misery left Little Eddie's smeary face.

"Sure. You ever hear of something called hypnotism?"

"I heard a hypmotism." Little Eddie was sulking. "Everybody in the whole world heard a that."

"Hypnotism, stupid, not hypmotism."

"Sure, hypmotism. I saw it on the TV. They did it on As the World Turns. A man made a lady go to sleep and think she was going to have a baby."

Harry smiled. "That's just TV, Little Eddie. Real hypnotism is a lot better than that. I read all about it in one of the books from the attic."

Little Eddie was still sulky because of the car. "So what makes it better?"

"Because it lets you do amazing things," Harry said. He called on Dr. Mentaine. "Hypnosis unlocks your mind and lets you use all the power you really have. If you start now, you'll really knock those books when school starts up again. You'll pass every test Mrs. Franken gives you, just like the way I did." He reached across the table and grasped Little Eddie's wrist, stalling a fat brown french fry on its way to the puddle. "But it won't just make you good in school. If you let me try it on you, I'm pretty sure I can show you that you're a lot stronger than you think you are."

Eddie blinked.

"And I bet I can make you so you're not scared of anything anymore. Hypnotism is real good for that. I read in this book, there was this guy who was afraid of bridges. Whenever he even *thought* about crossing a bridge he got all dizzy and sweaty. Terrible stuff happened to him, like he lost his job and once he just had to ride in a car across a bridge and he dumped a load in his pants. He went to see Dr. Mentaine, and Dr. Mentaine hypnotized him and said he would never be afraid of bridges again, and he wasn't."

Harry pulled the paperback from his hip pocket. He opened it flat on the table and bent over the pages. "Here. Listen to this. 'Benefits of the course of treatment were found in all areas of the patient's life, and results were obtained for which he would have paid any price.'" Harry read these words haltingly, but with complete understanding.

"Hypmotism can make me strong?" Little Eddie asked, evidently having saved this point in his head.

"Strong as a bull."

"Strong as Albert?"

"A lot stronger than Albert. A lot stronger than me, too."

"And I can beat up on big guys that hurt me?"

"You just have to learn how."

Eddie sprang up from the chair, yelling nonsense. He flexed his stringlike biceps and for some time twisted his body into a series of muscleman poses.

"You want to do it?" Harry finally asked.

Little Eddie popped into his chair and stared at Harry. His T-shirt's neckband sagged all the way to his breastbone without ever actually touching his chest. "I wanna start."

"Okay, Eddie, good man." Harry stood up and put his hand on the book. "Up to the attic."

"Only, I don't wanna go in the attic," Eddie said. He was still staring at Harry, but his head was tilted over like a weird little echo of Maryrose, and his eyes had filled with suspicion.

"I'm not gonna *take* anything from you, Little Eddie," Harry said. "It's just, we should be out of everybody's way. The attic's real quiet."

Little Eddie stuck his hand inside his T-shirt and let his arm dangle from the wrist.

"You turned your shirt into an armrest," Harry said.

Eddie jerked his hand out of its sling.

"Albert might come waltzing in and wreck everything if we do it in the bedroom."

"If you go up first and turn on the lights," Eddie said.

V

Harry held the book open on his lap, and glanced from it to Little Eddie's tense smeary face. He had read these pages over many times while he sat on the porch. Hypnotism boiled down to a few simple steps, each of which led to the next. The first thing he had to do was to get his brother started right, "relaxed and receptive," according to Dr. Mentaine.

Little Eddie stirred in his cane-backed chair and kneaded his hands together. His shadow, cast by the bulb dangling overhead, imitated him like a black little chair-bound monkey. "I wanna get started, I wanna get to be strong," he said.

"Right here in this book it says you have to be relaxed," Harry said. "Just put your hands on top of your legs, nice and easy, with your fingers pointing forward. Then close your eyes and breathe in and out a couple of times. Think about being nice and tired and ready to go to sleep."

"I don't wanna go to sleep!"

"It's not really sleep, Little Eddie, it's just sort of like it. You'll still really be awake, but nice and relaxed. Or else it won't work. You have to do everything I tell you. Otherwise everybody'll still be able to beat up on you, like they do now. I want you to pay attention to everything I say."

"Okay." Little Eddie made a visible effort to relax. He placed his hands on his thighs and twice inhaled and exhaled.

"Now close your eyes."

Eddie closed his eyes.

Harry suddenly knew that it was going to work—if he did everything the book said, he would really be able to hypnotize his brother.

"Little Eddie, I want you just to listen to the sound of my voice," he said, forcing himself to be calm. "You are already getting nice and relaxed, as easy and peaceful as if you were lying in bed, and the more you listen to my voice, the more relaxed and tired you are going to get. Nothing can bother you. Everything bad is far away, and you're just sitting here, breathing in and out, getting nice and sleepy."

He checked his page to make sure he was doing it right, and then went on.

"It's like lying in bed, Eddie, and the more you hear my voice, the more tired and sleepy you're getting, a little more sleepy the more you hear me. Everything else is sort of fading away, and all you can hear is my voice. You feel tired but good, just like the way you do right before you fall asleep. Everything is fine, and you're drifting a little bit, drifting and drifting, and you're getting ready to raise your right hand."

He leaned over and very lightly stroked the back of Little Eddie's grimy right hand. Eddie sat slumped in the chair with his eyes closed, breathing shallowly. Harry spoke very slowly.

"I'm going to count backwards from ten, and every time I get to another number, your hand is going to get lighter and lighter. When I count, your right hand is going to get so light it floats up and finally touches your nose when you hear me say 'one.' And then you'll be in a deep sleep. Now I'm starting. Ten. Your hand is already feeling light. Nine. It wants to float up. Eight. Your hand really feels light now. It's going to start to go up now. Seven."

Little Eddie's hand obediently floated an inch up from his thigh.

"Six." The grimy little hand rose another few inches. "It's getting lighter and lighter now, and every time I say another number it gets closer and closer to your nose, and you get sleepier and sleepier. Five."

The hand ascended several inches nearer Eddie's face.

"Four."

The hand now dangled like a sleeping bird half of the way between Eddie's knee and his nose.

"Three."

It rose nearly to Eddie's chin.

"Two."

Eddie's hand hung a few inches from his mouth.

"One. You are going to fall asleep now."

The gently curved, ketchup-streaked forefinger delicately brushed the tip of Little Eddie's nose, and stayed there while Eddie sagged against the back of the chair.

Harry's heart beat so loudly that he feared the sound would bring Eddie out of his trance. Eddie remained motionless. Harry breathed quietly by himself for a moment. "Now you can lower your hand to your lap, Eddie. You are going deeper and deeper into sleep. Deeper and deeper and deeper."

Eddie's hand sank gracefully downward.

The attic seemed hot as the inside of a furnace to Harry. His fingers left blotches on the open pages of the book. He wiped his face on his sleeve and looked at his little brother. Little Eddie had slumped so far down in the chair that his head was no longer visible in the tilting mirror. Perfectly still and quiet, the attic stretched out on all sides of them, waiting (or so it seemed to Harry) for what would happen next. Maryrose's trunks sat in rows under the eaves far behind the mirror, her old dresses hung silently within the dusty wardrobe. Harry rubbed his hands on his jeans to dry them, and flicked a page over with the neatness of an old scholar who had spent half his life in libraries.

"You're going to sit up straight in your chair," he said.

Eddie pulled himself upright.

"Now I want to show you that you're really hypnotized, Little Eddie. It's like a test. I want you to hold your right arm straight out before you. Make it as rigid as you can. This is going to show you how strong you can be."

Eddie's pale arm rose and straightened to the wrist, leaving his fingers dangling.

Harry stood up and said, "That's pretty good." He walked the two steps to Eddie's side and grasped his brother's arm and ran his fingers down the length of it, gently straightening Eddie's hand. "Now I want you to imagine that your arm is getting harder and harder. It's getting as hard and rigid as an iron bar. Your whole arm is an iron bar, and nobody on earth could bend it. Eddie, it's stronger than Superman's arm." He removed his hands and stepped back.

"Now. This arm is so strong and rigid that you can't bend it no matter how hard you try. It's an iron bar, and nobody on earth could bend it. Try. Try to bend it."

Eddie's face tightened up, and his arm rose perhaps two degrees. Eddie grunted with invisible effort, unable to bend his arm.

"Okay, Eddie, you did real good. Now your arm is loosening up, and when I count backwards from ten, it's going to get looser and looser. When I get to *one*, your arm'll be normal again." He began counting, and Eddie's fingers loosened and drooped, and finally the arm came to rest again on his leg.

Harry went back to his chair, sat down, and looked at Eddie with great satisfaction. Now he was certain that he would be able to do the next demonstration, which Dr. Mentaine called "The Chair Exercise."

"Now you know that this stuff really works, Eddie, so we're going to do something a little harder. I want you to stand up in front of your chair."

Eddie obeyed. Harry stood up too, and moved his chair forward and to the side so that its cane seat faced Eddie, about four feet away.

"I want you to stretch out between these chairs, with your head on your chair and your feet on mine. And I want you to keep your hands at your sides."

Eddie hunkered down uncomplainingly and settled his head back on the seat of his chair. Supporting himself with his arms, he raised one leg and placed his foot on Harry's chair. Then he lifted the other foot. Difficulty immediately appeared in his face. He raised his arms and clamped them in so that he looked trussed.

"Now your whole body is slowly becoming as hard as iron, Eddie. Your entire body is one of the strongest things on earth. Nothing can make it bend. You could hold yourself there forever and never feel the slightest pain or discomfort. It's like you're lying on a mattress, you're so strong."

The expression of strain left Eddie's face. Slowly his arms extended and relaxed. He lay propped string-straight between the two chairs, so at ease that he did not even appear to be breathing.

"While I talk to you, you're getting stronger and stronger. You could hold up anything. You could hold up an elephant. I'm going to sit down on your stomach to prove it."

Cautiously, Harry seated himself down on his brother's midriff. He raised his legs. Nothing happened. After he had counted slowly to fifteen, Harry lowered his legs and stood. "I'm going to take my shoes off now, Eddie, and stand on you."

He hurried over to a piano stool embroidered with fulsome roses and carried it back; then he slipped off his moccasins and stepped on top of the stool. As Harry stepped on top of Eddie's exposed thin belly, the chair supporting his brother's head wobbled. Harry stood stock-still for a moment, but the chair held. He lifted the other foot from the stool. No movement from the chair. He set the other foot on his brother. Little Eddie effortlessly held him up.

Harry lifted himself experimentally up on his toes and came back down on his heels. Eddie seemed entirely unaffected. Then Harry jumped perhaps half an inch into the air, and since Eddie did not even grunt when he landed, he kept jumping, five, six, seven, eight times, until he was breathing hard. "You're amazing, Little Eddie," he said, and stepped off onto the stool. "Now you can begin to relax. You can put your feet on the floor. Then I want you to sit back up in your chair. Your body doesn't feel stiff anymore."

Little Eddie had been rather tentatively lowering one foot, but as soon as Harry finished speaking he buckled in the middle and thumped his bottom on the floor. Harry's chair (Maryrose's chair) sickeningly tipped over, but landed soundlessly on a neat woolen stack of layered winter coats.

Moving like a robot, Little Eddie slowly sat upright on the floor. His eyes were open but unfocused.

"You can stand up now and get back in your chair," Harry said. He did not remember leaving the stool, but he had left it. Sweat ran into his eyes. He pressed his face into his shirt sleeve. For a second, panic had brightly beckoned. Little Eddie was sleepwalking back to his chair. When he sat down, Harry said, "Close your eyes. You're going deeper and deeper into sleep. Deeper and deeper, Little Eddie."

Eddie settled into the chair as if nothing had happened, and Harry reverently set his own chair upright again. Then he picked up the book and opened it. The print swam before his eyes. Harry shook his head and looked again, but still the lines of print snaked across the page. (When Harry was a sophomore at Adelphi College he was asked to read several poems by Guillaume Apollonaire, and the appearance of the wavering lines on the page brought back this moment with a terrible precision.) Harry pressed the palms of his hands against his eyes, and red patterns exploded across his vision.

He removed his hands from his eyes, blinked, and found that although the lines of print were now behaving themselves, he no longer wanted to go on. The attic was too hot, he was too tired, and the toppling of the chair had been too close a brush with actual disaster. But for a time he leafed purposefully through the book while Eddie tranced on, and then found the subheading "Post-Hypnotic Suggestion."

"Little Eddie, we're just going to do one more thing. If we ever do this again, it'll help us go faster." Harry shut the book. He knew exactly how this went; he would even use the same phrase Dr. Mentaine used with his patients. *Blue rose*—Harry did not quite know why, but he liked the sound of that.

"I'm going to tell you a phrase, Eddie, and from now on whenever you hear me say this phrase, you will instantly go back to sleep and be hypnotized again. The phrase is 'blue rose.' 'Blue rose.' When you hear me say 'blue rose,' you will go right to sleep, just the way you are now, and we can make you stronger again. 'Blue rose' is our secret, Eddie, because nobody else knows it. What is it?"

"Blue rose," Eddie said in a muffled voice.

"Okay. I'm going to count backward from ten, and when I get to 'one' you will be wide awake again. You will not remember anything we did, but you will feel happy and strong. Ten."

As Harry counted backwards, Little Eddie twitched and stirred, let his arms fall to his sides, thumped one foot carelessly on the floor, and at "one" opened his eyes.

"Did it work? What'd I do? Am I strong?"

"You're a bull," Harry said. "It's getting late, Eddie—time to go downstairs."

Harry's timing was accurate enough to be uncomfortable. As soon as the two boys closed the attic door behind them they heard the front door slide open in a cacophony of harsh coughs and subdued mutterings followed by the sound of unsteady footsteps proceeding to the bathroom. Edgar Beevers was home.

VI

Late that night the three homebound Beevers sons lay in their separate beds in the good-sized second-floor room next to the attic stairs. Directly above Maryrose's bedroom, its dimensions were nearly identical to it except that the boys' room, the "dorm," had no window seat and the attic stairs shaved a couple of feet from Harry's end. When the other two boys had lived at home, Harry and Little Eddie had slept together, Albert had slept in a bed with Sonny, and only George, who at the time of his induction into the Army had been six feet tall and weighed two hundred and one pounds, had slept alone. In those days, Sonny had often managed to make Albert cry out in the middle of the night. The very idea of George could still make Harry's stomach freeze.

Though it was now very late, enough light from the street came in through the thin white net curtains to give complex shadows to the bunched muscles of Albert's upper arms as he lay stretched out atop his sheets. The voices of Maryrose and Edgar Beevers, one approximately sober and the other unmistakably drunk, came clearly up the stairs and through the open door.

"*Who* says I waste my time? I don't say that. I don't waste my time."

"I suppose you think you've done a good day's work when you spell a bartender for a couple of hours—and then drink up your wages! That's the story of your life, Edgar Beevers, and it's a sad, sad story of w-a-s-t-e. If my father could have seen what would become of you . . . ."

"I ain't so damn bad."

"You ain't so damn good, either."

"Albert," Eddie said softly from his bed between his two brothers.

As if galvanized by Little Eddie's voice, Albert suddenly sat up in bed, leaned forward, and reached out to try to smack Eddie with his fist.

"I didn't do nothin'!" Harry said, and moved to the edge of his mattress. The blow had been for him, he knew, not Eddie, except that Albert was too lazy to get up.

"I hate your lousy guts," Albert said. "If I wasn't too tired to get out of this-here bed, I'd pound your face in."

"Harry stole my birthday car, Albert," Eddie said. "Makum gimme it back."

"One day," Maryrose said from downstairs, "at the end of the summer when I was seventeen, late in the afternoon, my father said to my mother, 'Honey, I believe I'm going to take out our pretty little Maryrose and get her something special,' and he called up to me from the drawing room to make myself pretty and get set to go, and because my father was a gentleman and a Man of His Word, I got ready in two shakes. My father was wearing a very handsome brown suit and a red bow tie and his boater. I remember just like I can see it now. He stood at the bottom of the staircase, waiting for me, and when I came down he took my arm and we just went out that front door like a courting couple. Down the stone walk, which my father put in all by himself even though he was a white-collar worker, down Majeski Street, arm in arm down to South Palmyra Avenue. In those days all the best people, all the people who counted, did their shopping on South Palmyra Avenue."

"I'd like to knock your teeth down your throat," Albert said to Harry.

"Albert, he took my birthday car, he really did, and I want it back. I'm ascared he busted it. I want it back so much I'm gonna die."

Albert propped himself up on an elbow and for the first time really looked at Little Eddie. Eddie whimpered. "You're such a twerp," Albert said. "I wish you *would* die, Eddie, I wish you'd just drop dead so we could stick you in the ground and forget about you. I wouldn't even cry at your funeral. Prob'ly I wouldn't even be able to remember your name. I'd just say, 'Oh yeah, he was that little creepy kid used to hang around cryin' all the time, glad he's dead, whatever his name was.'"

Eddie had turned his back on Albert and was weeping softly, his unwashed face distorted by the shadows into an uncanny image of the mask of tragedy.

"You know, I really wouldn't mind if you dropped dead," Albert mused. "You neither, shitbird."

". . . realized he was taking me to Alouette's. I'm sure you used to look in their windows when you were a little boy. You remember Alouette's, don't you? There's never been anything so beautiful as that store. When I was a little girl and lived in the big house, all the best people used to go there. My father marched me right inside, with his arm around me, and took me up in the elevator and we went straight to the lady who managed the dress department. 'Give my little girl the best,' he said. Price was no object. Quality was all he cared about. 'Give my little girl the best.' *Are you listening to me, Edgar?*"

Albert snored face-down into his pillow; Little Eddie twitched and snuffled. Harry lay awake for so long he thought he would never get to sleep. Before him he kept seeing Little Eddie's face all slack and dopey under hypnosis—Little Eddie's face made him feel hot and uncomfortable. Now that Harry was lying down in bed, it seemed to him that everything he had done since returning from Big John's seemed really to have been done by someone else, or to have been done in a dream. Then he realized that he had to use the bathroom.

Harry slid out of bed, quietly crossed the room, went out onto the dark landing, and felt his way downstairs to the bathroom.

When he emerged, the bathroom light showed him the squat black shape of the telephone atop the Palmyra directory. Harry moved to the low telephone table beside the stairs. He lifted the phone from the directory and opened the book, the width of a Big 5 tablet, with his other hand. As he had done on many other nights when his bladder forced him downstairs, Harry leaned over the page and selected a number. He kept the number in his head as he closed the directory and replaced the telephone. He dialed. The number rang so often Harry lost count. At last a hoarse voice answered. Harry said, "I'm watching you, and you're a dead man." He softly replaced the receiver in the cradle.

VII

Harry caught up with his father the next afternoon just as Edgar Beevers had begun to move up South Sixth Street toward the corner of Livermore. His father wore his usual costume of baggy gray trousers cinched far above his waist by a belt with a double buckle, a red-and-white plaid shirt, and a brown felt hat stationed low over his eyes. His long fleshy nose swam before him, cut in half by the shadow of the hat brim.

"Dad!"

His father glanced incuriously at him, then put his hands back in his pockets. He turned sideways and kept walking down the street, though perhaps a shade more slowly. "What's up, kid? No school?"

"It's summer, there isn't any school. I just thought I'd come with you for a little."

"Well, I ain't doing much. Your ma asked me to pick up some hamburg on Livermore, and I thought I'd slip into the Idle Hour for a quick belt. You won't turn me in, will you?"

"No."

"You ain't a bad kid, Harry. Your ma's just got a lot of worries. I worry about Little Eddie too, sometimes."

"Sure."

"What's with the books? You read when you walk?"

"I was just sort of looking at them," Harry said.

His father insinuated his hand beneath Harry's left elbow and extracted two luridly jacketed paperback books. They were titled *Murder, Incorporated* and *Hitler's Death Camps*. Harry already loved both of these books. His father grunted and handed *Murder, Incorporated* back to him. He raised the other book nearly to the tip of his nose and peered at the cover, which depicted a naked woman pressing herself against a wall of barbed wire while a uniformed Nazi aimed a rifle at her back.

Looking up at his father, Harry saw that beneath the harsh line of shadow cast by the hat brim his father's whiskers grew in different colors and patterns. Black and brown, red and orange, the glistening spikes swirled across his father's cheek.

"I bought this book, but it didn't look nothing like that," his father said, and returned the book.

"What didn't?"

"That place. Dachau. That death camp."

"How do you know?"

"I was there, wasn't I? You wasn't even born then. It didn't look anything like that picture on that book. It just looked like a piece a shit to me, like most of the places I saw when I was in the Army."

This was the first time Harry had heard that his father had been in the service.

"You mean, you were in World War II?"

"Yeah, I was in the Big One. They made me a corporal over there. Had me a nickname too. 'Beans.' 'Beans' Beevers. And I got a Purple Heart from the time I got a infection."

"You saw Dachau with your own eyes?"

"Damn straight, I did." He bent down suddenly. "Hey—don't let your ma catch you readin' that book."

Secretly pleased, Harry shook his head. Now the book and the death camp were a bond between himself and his father.

"Did you ever kill anybody?"

His father wiped his mouth and both cheeks with one long hand. Harry saw a considering eye far back in the shadow of the brim.

"I killed a guy once."

A long pause.

"I shot him in the back."

His father wiped his mouth again, and then motioned forward with his head. He had to get to the bar, the butcher, and back again in a very carefully defined period of time. "You really want to hear this?"

Harry nodded. He swallowed.

"I guess you do, at that. Okay—we was sent into this camp, Dachau, at the end of the war to process the prisoners and arrest the guards and the commandant. Everything was all arranged. A bunch of brass hats from Division were going to come on an inspection, so we had to wait there a couple days. We had these guards lined up, see, and these skinny old wrecks would come up and give 'em hell. We wasn't supposed to let 'em get too near."

They were passing Mr. Petrosian's little tar-paper house, and Harry felt a spasm of relief that Mr. Petrosian was not out on his tiny porch working on his case of beer. The Idle Hour was only a few paces ahead.

"Anyhow, one of these guards, one of the worst ones, suddenly decided he's going to run for it. He takes off, runnin' like crazy toward the woods. What do I do? I ask. Nobody knows what the hell to do. Shoot him, somebody says. So I shot him in the back. That was all she wrote."

Now they had reached the screen door which led into the Idle Hour, and the smells of malt and hops filled the air. "See you back at the house," his father said, and disappeared through the screen door like a magician.

VIII

After Harry had read a hundred pages of *Murder, Incorporated*, his favorite murderers were Louis "Lepke" Buchalter and Abe "Kid Twist" Reles. They were dependable professionals. A kind of black light surrounded them and made them glitter. Lepke Buchalter and Abe Reles looked out at the world from the shadows of their hat brims. They lived in shadowy rooms and peered out through the curtains. They appeared on a dark corner before their terrified victim, did their work, and walked away, turning up their coat collars.

Suppose you had some kind of job that took you around the country, like a salesman's job, Harry thought as he read away the afternoon in the porch swing; suppose you had a job that took you from one town to another. Suppose you killed someone in each one of those towns, carefully and quietly, and hid the bodies so it would take people a long time to find them. Your work would never be done.

IX

"Blue rose," Harry said.

Little Eddie sagged openmouthed against the cane of his chair, his hands loose in his lap.

It had worked. Harry looked around as if he expected applause, and did feel that all the things in the attic looked back at him with warm approval. It was nine-thirty at night; he and Eddie, alone in the house, occupied the attic in perfect safety. Harry wanted to see if he could put other people under and make them do things, but for now, for tonight, he was content to experiment with Eddie.

"You're going deeper and deeper asleep, Eddie, deeper and deeper, and you're listening to every word I say. You're just sinking down and down, hearing my voice come to you, going deeper and deeper with every word, and now you are real deep asleep and ready to begin."

Little Eddie sat sprawled over Maryrose's cane-backed chair, his chin touching his chest and his little pink mouth drooping open. He looked like a slightly undersized seven-year-old, like a second-grader instead of the fourth-grader he would be when he joined Mrs. Franken's class in the fall. Suddenly he reminded Harry of the Ultraglide Roadster, scratched and dented and stripped of its tires.

"Tonight you're going to see how strong you really are. Sit up, Eddie."

Eddie pulled himself upright and closed his mouth, almost comically obedient.

Harry thought it would be fun to make Little Eddie believe he was a dog and trot around the attic on all fours, barking and lifting his leg. Then he saw Little Eddie staggering across the attic, his tongue bulging out of his mouth, his own hands squeezing and squeezing his throat. Maybe he would try that too, after he had done several other exercises he had discovered in Dr. Mentaine's book. He checked the underside of his collar for maybe the fifth time that evening, and felt the long thin shaft of the pearl-headed hatpin he had stopped reading *Murder, Incorporated* long enough to smuggle out of Maryrose's bedroom after she had left for work.

"Eddie," he said, "now you are very deeply asleep, and you will be able to do everything I say. I want you to hold your right arm straight out in front of you."

Eddie stuck his arm out like a poker.

"That's good, Eddie. Now I want you to notice that all the feeling is leaving that arm. It's getting number and number. It doesn't even feel like flesh and blood anymore. It feels like it's made out of steel or something. It's so numb that you can't feel anything there anymore. You can't even feel pain in it."

Harry stood up, went toward Eddie, and brushed his fingers along his arm. "You didn't feel anything, did you?"

"No," Eddie said in a slow gravel-filled voice.

"Do you feel anything now?" Harry pinched the underside of Eddie's forearm.

"No."

"Now?" Harry used his nails to pinch the side of Eddie's biceps, hard, and left purple dents in the skin.

"No," Eddie repeated.

"How about this?" He slapped his hand against Eddie's forearm as hard as he could. There was a sharp loud smacking sound, and his fingers tingled. If Little Eddie had not been hypnotized, he would have tried to screech down the walls.

"No," Eddie said.

Harry pulled the hatpin out of his collar and inspected his brother's arm. "You're doing great, Little Eddie. You're stronger than anybody in your whole class—you're probably stronger than the whole rest of the school." He turned Eddie's arm so that the palm was up and the white forearm, lightly traced by small blue veins, faced him.

Harry delicately ran the point of the hatpin down Eddie's pale, veined forearm. The pinpoint left a narrow chalk-white scratch in its wake. For a moment Harry felt the floor of the attic sway beneath his feet; then he closed his eyes and jabbed the hatpin into Little Eddie's skin as hard as he could.

He opened his eyes. The floor was still swaying beneath him. From Little Eddie's lower arm protruded six inches of the eight-inch hatpin, the mother-of-pearl head glistening softly in the light from the overhead bulb. A drop of blood the size of a watermelon seed stood on Eddie's skin. Harry moved back to his chair and sat down heavily. "Do you feel anything?"

"No," Eddie said again in that surprisingly deep voice.

Harry stared at the hatpin embedded in Eddie's arm. The oval drop of blood lengthened itself out against the white skin and began slowly to ooze toward Eddie's wrist. Harry watched it advance across the pale underside of Eddie's forearm. Finally he stood up and returned to Eddie's side. The elongated drop of blood had ceased moving. Harry bent over and twanged the hatpin. Eddie could feel nothing. Harry put his thumb and forefinger on the glistening head of the pin. His face was so hot he might have been standing before an open fire. He pushed the pin a further half inch into Eddie's arm, and another small quantity of blood welled up from the base. The pin seemed to be moving in Harry's grasp, pulsing back and forth as if it were breathing.

"Okay," Harry said. "Okay."

He tightened his hold on the pin and pulled. It slipped easily from the wound. Harry held the hatpin before his face just as a doctor holds up a thermometer to read a temperature. He had imagined that the entire bottom section of the shaft would be painted with red, but saw that only a single winding glutinous streak of blood adhered to the pin. For a dizzy second he thought of slipping the end of the pin in his mouth and sucking it clean.

He thought: Maybe in another life I was Lepke Buchalter.

He pulled his handkerchief, a filthy square of red paisley, from his front pocket and wiped the streak of blood from the shaft of the pin. Then he leaned over and gently wiped the red smear from Little Eddie's underarm. Harry refolded the handkerchief so the blood would not show, wiped sweat from his face, and shoved the grubby cloth back into his pocket.

"That was good, Eddie. Now we're going to do something a little bit different."

He knelt down beside his brother and lifted Eddie's nearly weightless, delicately veined arm. "You still can't feel a thing in this arm, Eddie, it's completely numb. It's sound asleep and it won't wake up until I tell it to." Harry repositioned himself in order to hold himself steady while he knelt, and put the point of the hatpin nearly flat against Eddie's arm. He pushed it forward far enough to raise a wrinkle of flesh. The point of the hatpin dug into Eddie's skin but did not break it. Harry pushed harder, and the hatpin raised the little bulge of skin by a small but appreciable amount.

Skin was a lot tougher to break through than anyone imagined.

The pin was beginning to hurt his fingers, so Harry opened his hand and positioned the head against the base of his middle finger. Grimacing, he pushed his hand against the pin. The point of the pin popped through the raised wrinkle.

"Eddie, you're made out of beer cans," Harry said, and tugged the head of the pin backwards. The wrinkle flattened out. Now Harry could shove the pin forward again, sliding the shaft deeper and deeper under the surface of Little Eddie's skin. He could see the raised line of the hatpin marching down his brother's arm, looking as prominent as the damage done to a cartoon lawn by a cartoon rabbit. When the mother-of-pearl head was perhaps three inches from the entry hole, Harry pushed it down into Little Eddie's flesh, thus raising the point of the pin. He gave the head a sharp jab, and the point appeared at the end of the ridge in Eddie's skin, poking through a tiny smear of blood. Harry shoved the pin in further. Now it showed about an inch and a half of gray metal at either end.

"Feel anything?"

"Nothing."

Harry jiggled the head of the pin, and a bubble of blood walked out of the entry wound and began to slide down Eddie's arm. Harry sat down on the attic floor beside Eddie and regarded his work. His mind seemed pleasantly empty of thought, filled only with a variety of sensations. He *felt* but could not hear a buzzing in his head, and a blurry film seemed to cover his eyes. He breathed through his mouth. The long pin stuck through Little Eddie's arm looked monstrous seen one way; seen another, it was sheerly beautiful. Skin, blood, and metal. Harry had never seen anything like it before. He reached out and twisted the pin, causing another little blood-snail to crawl from the exit wound. Harry saw all this as if through smudgy glasses, but he did not mind. He knew the blurriness was only mental. He touched the head of the pin again and moved it from side to side. A little more blood leaked from both punctures. Then Harry shoved the pin in, partially withdrew it so that the point nearly disappeared back into Eddie's arm, moved it forward again; and went on like this, back and forth, back and forth as if he were sewing his brother up, for some time.

Finally he withdrew the pin from Eddie's arm. Two long streaks of blood had nearly reached his brother's wrist. Harry ground the heels of his hands into his eyes, blinked, and discovered that his vision had cleared.

He wondered how long he and Eddie had been in the attic. It could have been hours. He could not quite remember what had happened before he had slid the hatpin into Eddie's skin. Now his blurriness really was mental, not visual. A loud uncomfortable pulse beat in his temples. Again he wiped the blood from Eddie's arm. Then he stood on wobbling knees and returned to his chair.

"How's your arm feel, Eddie?"

"Numb," Eddie said in his gravelly sleepy voice.

"The numbness is going away now. Very, very slowly. You are beginning to feel your arm again, and it feels very good. There is no pain. It feels like the sun was shining on it all afternoon. It's strong and healthy. Feeling is coming back into your arm, and you can move your fingers and everything."

When he had finished speaking Harry leaned back against the chair and closed his eyes. He rubbed his forehead with his hand and wiped the moisture off on his shirt.

"How does your arm feel?" he said without opening his eyes.

"Good."

"That's great, Little Eddie." Harry flattened his palms against his flushed face, wiped his cheeks, and opened his eyes.

I can do this every night, he thought. I can bring Little Eddie up here every single night, at least until school starts.

"Eddie, you're getting stronger and stronger every day. This is really helping you. And the more we do it, the stronger you'll get. Do you understand me?"

"I understand you," Eddie said.

"We're almost done for tonight. There's just one more thing I want to try. But you have to be really deep asleep for this to work. So I want you to go deeper and deeper, as deep as you can go. Relax, and now you are really deep asleep, deep deep, and relaxed and ready and feeling good."

Little Eddie sat sprawled in his chair with his head tilted back and his eyes closed. Two tiny dark spots of blood stood out like mosquito bites on his lower right forearm.

"When I talk to you, Eddie, you're slowly getting younger and younger, you're going backward in time, so now you're not nine years old anymore, you're eight, it's last year and you're in the third grade, and now you're seven, and now you're six years old . . . and now you're five, Eddie, and it's the day of your fifth birthday. You're five years old today, Little Eddie. How old are you?"

"I'm five." To Harry's surprised pleasure, Little Eddie's voice actually seemed younger, as did his hunched posture in the chair.

"How do you feel?"

"Not good. I hate my present. It's terrible. Dad got it, and Mom says it should never be allowed in the house because it's just junk. I wish I wouldn't ever have to have birthdays, they're so terrible. I'm gonna cry."

His face contracted. Harry tried to remember what Eddie had gotten for his fifth birthday, but could not—he caught only a dim memory of shame and disappointment. "What's your present, Eddie?"

In a teary voice, Eddie said, "A radio. But it's busted and Mom says it looks like it came from the junkyard. I don't want it anymore. I don't even wanna *see* it."

Yes, Harry thought, yes, yes, yes. He could remember. On Little Eddie's fifth birthday, Edgar Beevers had produced a yellow plastic radio which even Harry had seen was astoundingly ugly. The dial was cracked, and it was marked here and there with brown circular scablike marks where someone had mashed out cigarettes on it.

The radio had long since been buried in the junk room, where it now lay beneath several geological layers of trash.

"Okay, Eddie, you can forget the radio now, because you're going backwards again, you're getting younger, you're going backwards through being four years old, and now you're three."

He looked with interest at Little Eddie, whose entire demeanor had changed. From being tearfully unhappy, Eddie now demonstrated a self-sufficient good cheer Harry could not ever remember seeing in him. His arms were folded over his chest. He was smiling, and his eyes were bright and clear and childish.

"What do you see?" Harry asked.

"Mommy-ommy-om."

"What's she doing?"

"Mommy's at her desk. She's smoking and looking through her papers." Eddie giggled. "Mommy looks funny. It looks like smoke is coming out of the top of her head." Eddie ducked his chin and hid his smile behind a hand. "Mommy doesn't see me. I can see her, but she doesn't see me. Oh! Mommy works hard! She works hard at her desk!"

Eddie's smile abruptly left his face. His face froze for a second in a comic rubbery absence of expression; then his eyes widened in terror and his mouth went loose and wobbly.

"What happened?" Harry's mouth had gone dry.

"No, Mommy!" Eddie wailed. "Don't, Mommy! I wasn't spying, I wasn't, I promise—" His words broke off into a screech. "NO, MOMMY! DON'T! DON'T, MOMMY!" Eddie jumped upward, sending his chair flying back, and ran blindly toward the rear of the attic. Harry's head rang with Eddie's screeches. He heard a sharp *crack!* of wood breaking, but only as a small part of all the noise Eddie was making as he charged around the attic. Eddie had run into a tangle of hanging dresses, spun around, enmeshing himself deeper in the dresses, and was now tearing himself away from the web of dresses, pulling some of them off the rack. A long-sleeved purple dress with an enormous lace collar had draped itself around Eddie like a ghostly dance partner, and another dress, this of dull red velvet, snaked around his right leg. Eddie screamed again and yanked himself away from the tangle. The entire rack of clothes wobbled and then went over in a mad jangle of sound.

"NO!" he screeched. "HELP!" Eddie ran straight into a big wooden beam marking off one of the eaves, bounced off, and came windmilling toward Harry. Harry knew his brother could not see him.

"Eddie, stop," he said, but Eddie was past hearing him. Harry tried to make Eddie stop by wrapping his arms around him, but Eddie slammed right into him, hitting Harry's chest with a shoulder and knocking his head painfully against Harry's chin; Harry's arms closed on nothing and his eyes lost focus, and Eddie went crashing into the tilting mirror. The mirror yawned over sideways. Harry saw it tilt with dreamlike slowness toward the floor, then in an eye blink drop and crash. Broken glass sprayed across the attic floor.

"STOP!" Harry yelled. "STAND STILL, EDDIE!"

Eddie came to rest. The ripped and dirty dress of dull red velvet still clung to his right leg. Blood oozed down his temple from an ugly cut above his eye. He was breathing hard, releasing air in little whimpering exhalations.

"Holy shit," Harry said, looking around at the attic. In only a few seconds Eddie had managed to create what looked at first like absolute devastation. Maryrose's ancient dresses lay tangled in a heap of dusty fabrics from which wire hangers skeletally protruded; gray Eddie-sized footprints lay like a pattern over the muted explosion of colors the dresses now created. When the rack had gone over, it had knocked a section the size of a dinner plate out of a round wooden coffee table Maryrose had particularly prized for its being made from a single section of teak—"a single piece of *teak*, the rarest wood in all the world, all the way from Ceylon!" The much-prized mirror lay in hundreds of glittering pieces across the attic floor. With growing horror, Harry saw that the wooden frame had cracked like a bone, showing a bone-pale, shockingly white fracture in the expanse of dark stain.

Harry's blood tipped within his body, nearly tipping him with it, like the mirror. "Oh God oh God oh God."

He turned slowly around. Eddie stood blinking two feet to his side, wiping ineffectually at the blood running from his forehead and now covering most of his left cheek. He looked like an Indian in war paint—a defeated, lost Indian, for his eyes were dim and his head turned aimlessly from side to side.

A few feet from Eddie lay the chair in which he had been sitting. One of its thin curved wooden arms lay beside it, crudely severed. It looked like an insect's leg, Harry thought, like a toy gun.

For a moment Harry thought that his face too was red with blood. He wiped his hand over his forehead and looked at his glistening palm. It was only sweat. His heart beat like a bell. Beside him Eddie said, "Aaah . . . what . . . ?" The injury to his head had brought him out of the trance.

The dresses were ruined, stepped on, tangled, torn. The mirror was broken. The table had been mutilated. Maryrose's chair lay on its side like a murder victim, its severed arm ending in a bristle of snapped ligaments.

"My head *hurts*," Eddie said in a weak, trembling voice. "What happened? Ah! I'm all blood! I'm all blood, Harry!"

"You're all blood, you're all blood?" Harry shouted at him. "Everything's *all blood*, you dummy! Look around!" He did not recognize his own voice, which sounded high and tinny and seemed to be coming from somewhere else. Little Eddie took an aimless step away from him, and Harry wanted to fly at him, to pound his bloody head into a pancake, to destroy him, smash him . . .

Eddie held up his bloodstained palm and stared at it. He wiped it vaguely across the front of his T-shirt and took another wandering step. "I'm ascared, Harry," his tiny voice uttered.

"Look what you did!" Harry screamed. "You wrecked everything! Damn it! What do you think is going to happen to us?"

"What's Mom going to do?" Eddie asked in a voice only slightly above a whisper.

"You don't know?" Harry yelled. "You're dead!"

Eddie started to weep.

Harry bunched his hands into fists and clamped his eyes shut. They were both dead, that was the real truth. Harry opened his eyes, which felt hot and oddly heavy, and stared at his sobbing, red-smeared, useless little brother. "Blue rose," he said.

X

Little Eddie's hands fell to his sides. His chin dropped, and his mouth fell open. Blood ran in a smooth wide band down the left side of his face, dipped under the line of his jaw, and continued on down his neck and into his T-shirt. Pooled blood in his left eyebrow dripped steadily onto the floor, as if from a faucet.

"You are going deep *asleep*," Harry said. Where was the hatpin? He looked back to the single standing chair and saw the mother-of-pearl head glistening on the floor near it.

"Your whole body is *numb*." He moved over to the pin, bent down, and picked it up. The metal shaft felt warm in his fingers. "You can feel no *pain*." He went back to Little Eddie. "Nothing can *hurt* you." Harry's breath seemed to be breathing itself, forcing itself into his throat in hot harsh shallow pants, then expelling itself out.

"Did you *hear* me, Little Eddie?"

In his gravelly, slow-moving hypnotized voice, Little Eddie said, "I heard you."

"And you can feel no *pain?*"

"I can feel no pain."

Harry drew his arm back, the point of the hatpin extending forward from his fist, and then jerked his hand forward as hard as he could and stuck the pin into Eddie's abdomen right through the blood-soaked T-shirt. He exhaled sharply, and tasted a sour misery on his breath.

"You don't feel a thing."

"I don't feel a thing."

Harry opened his right hand and drove his palm against the head of the pin, hammering it in another few inches. Little Eddie looked like a voodoo doll. A kind of sparkling light surrounded him. Harry gripped the head of the pin with his thumb and forefinger and yanked it out. He held it up and inspected it. Glittering light surrounded the pin too. The long shaft was painted with blood. Harry slipped the point into his mouth and closed his lips around the warm metal.

He saw himself, a man in another life, standing in a row with men like himself in a bleak gray landscape defined by barbed wire. Emaciated people in rags shuffled up toward them and spat on their clothes. The smells of dead flesh and of burning flesh hung in the air. Then the vision was gone, and Little Eddie stood before him again, surrounded by layers of glittering light.

Harry grimaced or grinned, he could not have told the difference, and drove his long spike deep into Eddie's stomach.

Eddie uttered a small *oof.*

"You don't feel anything, Eddie," Harry whispered. "You feel good all over. You never felt better in your life."

"Never felt better in my life."

Harry slowly pulled out the pin and cleaned it with his fingers.

He was able to remember every single thing anyone had ever told him about Tommy Golz.

"Now you're going to play a funny, funny game," he said. "This is called the Tommy Golz game because it's going to keep you safe from Mrs. Franken. Are you ready?" Harry carefully slid the pin into the fabric of his shirt collar, all the while watching Eddie's slack blood-streaked person. Vibrating bands of light beat rhythmically and steadily about Eddie's face.

"Ready," Eddie said.

"I'm going to give you your instructions now, Little Eddie. Pay attention to everything I say and it's all going to be okay. Everything's going to be okay—as long as you play the game exactly the way I tell you. You understand, don't you?"

"I understand."

"Tell me what I just said."

"Everything's gonna be okay as long as I play the game exactly the way you tell me." A dollop of blood slid off Eddie's eyebrow and splashed onto his already soaked T-shirt.

"Good, Eddie. Now the first thing you do is fall down—not now, when I tell you. I'm going to give you all the instructions, and then I'm going to count backwards from ten, and when I get to *one*, you'll start playing the game. Okay?"

"Okay."

"So first you fall down, Little Eddie. You fall down real hard. Then comes the fun part of the game. You bang your head on the floor. You start to go crazy. You twitch, and you bang your hands and feet on the floor. You do that for a long time. I guess you do that until you count to about a hundred. You foam at the mouth, you twist all over the place. You get real stiff, and then you get real loose, and then you get real stiff, and then real loose again, and all this time you're banging your head and your hands and feet on the floor, and you're twisting all over the place. Then when you finish counting to a hundred in your head, you do the last thing. You swallow your tongue. And that's the game. When you swallow your tongue you're the winner. And then nothing bad can happen to you, and Mrs. Franken won't be able to hurt you ever ever ever."

Harry stopped talking. His hands were shaking. After a second he realized that his insides were shaking too. He raised his trembling fingers to his shirt collar and felt the hatpin.

"Tell me how you win the game, Little Eddie. What's the last thing you do?"

"I swallow my tongue."

"Right. And then Mrs. Franken and Mom will never be able to hurt you, because you won the game."

"Good," said Little Eddie. The glittering light shimmered about him.

"Okay, we'll start playing right now," Harry said. "Ten." He went toward the attic steps. "Nine." He reached the steps. "Eight."

He went down one step. "Seven." Harry descended another two steps. "Six." When he went down another two steps, he called up in a slightly louder voice, "Five."

Now his head was beneath the level of the attic floor, and he could not see Little Eddie anymore. All he could hear was the soft, occasional plop of liquid hitting the floor.

"Four."

"Three."

"Two." He was now at the door to the attic steps. Harry opened the door, stepped through it, breathed hard, and shouted "One!" up the stairs.

He heard a thud, and then quickly closed the door behind him.

Harry went across the hall and into the dormitory bedroom. There seemed to be a strange absence of light in the hallway. For a second he saw—was sure he saw—a line of dark trees across a wall of barbed wire. Harry closed this door behind him too, and went to his narrow bed and sat down. He could feel blood beating in his face; his eyes seemed oddly warm, as if they were heated by filaments. Harry slowly, almost reverently extracted the hatpin from his collar and set it on his pillow. "A hundred," he said. "Ninety-nine, ninety-eight, ninety-seven, ninety-six, ninety-five, ninety-four . . ."

When he had counted down to "one," he stood up and left the bedroom. He went quickly downstairs without looking at the door behind which lay the attic steps. On the ground floor he slipped into Maryrose's bedroom, crossed over to her desk, and slid open the bottom right-hand drawer. From the drawer he took a velvet-covered box. This he opened, and jabbed the hatpin in the ball of material, studded with pins of all sizes and descriptions, from which he had taken it. He replaced the box in the drawer, pushed the drawer into the desk, and quickly left the room and went upstairs.

Back in his own bedroom, Harry took off his clothes and climbed into his bed. His face still burned.

He must have fallen asleep very quickly, because the next thing he knew Albert was slamming his way into the bedroom and tossing his clothes and boots all over the place. "You asleep?" Albert asked. "You left the attic light on, you fuckin' dummies, but if you think I'm gonna save your fuckin' asses and go up and turn it off, you're even stupider than you look."

Harry was careful not to move a finger, not to move even a hair.

He held his breath while Albert threw himself onto his bed, and when Albert's breathing relaxed and slowed, Harry followed his big brother into sleep. He did not awaken again until he heard his father half screeching, half sobbing up in the attic, and that was very late at night.

XI

Sonny came from Fort Sill, George all the way from Germany. Between them, they held up a sodden Edgar Beevers at the gravesite while a minister Harry had never seen before read from a Bible as cracked and rubbed as an old brown shoe. Between his two older sons, Harry's father looked bent and ancient, a skinny old man only steps from the grave himself. Sonny and George despised their father, Harry saw—they held him up on sufferance, in part because they had chipped in thirty dollars apiece to buy him a suit and did not want to see it collapse with its owner inside into the lumpy clay of the graveyard. His whiskers glistened in the sun, and moisture shone beneath his eyes and at the corners of his mouth. He had been shaking too severely for either Sonny or George to shave him, and had been capable of moving in a straight line only after George let him take a couple of long swallows from a leather-covered flask he took out of his duffel bag.

The minister uttered a few sage words on the subject of epilepsy.

Sonny and George looked as solid as brick walls in their uniforms, like prison guards or actual prisons themselves. Next to them, Albert looked shrunken and unfinished. Albert wore the green plaid sport jacket in which he had graduated from the eighth grade, and his wrists hung prominent and red four inches below the bottoms of the sleeves. His motorcycle boots were visible beneath his light gray trousers, but they, like the green jacket, had lost their flash. Like Albert, too. Ever since the discovery of Eddie's body, Albert had gone around the house looking as if he'd just bitten off the end of his tongue and was trying to decide whether or not to spit it out. He never looked anybody in the eye, and he rarely spoke. Albert acted as though a gigantic padlock had been fixed to the middle of his chest and *he* was damned if he'd ever take it off. He had not asked Sonny or George a single question about the Army. Every now and then he would utter a remark about the gas station so toneless that it suffocated any reply.

Harry looked at Albert standing beside their mother, kneading his hands together and keeping his eyes fixed as if by decree on the square foot of ground before him. Albert glanced over at Harry, knew he was being looked at, and did what to Harry was an extraordinary thing. Albert *froze*. All expression drained out of his face, and his hands locked immovably together. He looked as little able to see or hear as a statue. *He's that way because he told Little Eddie that he wished he would die*, Harry thought for the tenth or eleventh time since he had realized this, and with undiminished awe. Then was he lying? Harry wondered. And if he really did wish that Little Eddie would drop dead, why isn't he happy now? Didn't he get what he wanted? Albert would never spit out that piece of his tongue, Harry thought, watching his brother blink slowly and sightlessly toward the ground.

Harry shifted his gaze uneasily to his father, still propped up between George and Sonny, heard that the minister was finally reaching the end of his speech, and took a fast look at his mother. Maryrose was standing very straight in a black dress and black sunglasses, holding the straps of her bag in front of her with both hands. Except for the color of her clothes, she could have been a spectator at a tennis match. Harry knew by the way she was holding her face that she was wishing she could smoke. Dying for a cigarette, he thought, ha-ha, the Monster Mash, it's a graveyard smash.

The minister finished speaking, and made a rhetorical gesture with his hands. The coffin sank on ropes into the rough earth. Harry's father began to weep loudly. First George, then Sonny, picked up large damp shovel-marked pieces of the clay and dropped them on the coffin. Edgar Beevers nearly fell in after his own tiny clod, but George contemptuously swung him back. Maryrose marched forward, bent and picked up a random piece of clay with thumb and forefinger as if using tweezers, dropped it, and turned away before it struck. Albert fixed his eyes on Harry—his own clod had split apart in his hand and crumbled away between his fingers. Harry shook his head *no*. He did not want to drop dirt on Eddie's coffin and make that noise. He did not want to look at Eddie's coffin again. There was enough dirt around to do the job without him hitting that metal box like he was trying to ring Eddie's doorbell. He stepped back.

"Mom says we have to get back to the house," Albert said.

Maryrose lit up as soon as they got into the single black car they had rented through the funeral parlor, and breathed out acrid smoke over everybody crowded into the backseat. The car backed into a narrow graveyard lane, and turned down the main road toward the front gates.

In the front seat, next to the driver, Edgar Beevers drooped sideways and leaned his head against the window, leaving a blurred streak on the glass.

"How in the name of hell could Little Eddie have epilepsy without anybody knowing about it?" George asked.

Albert stiffened and stared out the window.

"Well, that's epilepsy," Maryrose said. "Eddie could have gone on for years without having an attack." That she worked in a hospital always gave her remarks of this sort a unique gravity, almost as if she were a doctor.

"Must have been some fit," Sonny said, squeezed into place between Harry and Albert.

"Grand mal," Maryrose said, and took another hungry drag on her cigarette.

"Poor little bastard," George said. "Sorry, Mom."

"I know you're in the armed forces, and armed forces people speak very freely, but I wish you would not use that kind of language."

Harry, jammed into Sonny's rock-hard side, felt his brother's body twitch with a hidden laugh, though Sonny's face did not alter.

"I said I was sorry, Mom," George said.

"Yes. Driver! Driver!" Maryrose was leaning forward, reaching out one claw to tap the chauffeur's shoulder. "Livermore is the next right. Do you know South Sixth Street?"

"I'll get you there," the driver said.

This is not my family, Harry thought. I came from somewhere else and my rules are different from theirs.

His father mumbled something inaudible as soon as they got in the door and disappeared into his curtained-off cubicle. Maryrose put her sunglasses in her purse and marched into the kitchen to warm the coffee cake and the macaroni casserole, both made that morning, in the oven. Sonny and George wandered into the living room and sat down on opposite ends of the couch. They did not look at each other—George picked up a

Reader's Digest from the table and began leafing through it backward, and Sonny folded his hands in his lap and stared at his thumbs. Albert's footsteps plodded up the stairs, crossed the landing, and went into the dormitory bedroom.

"What's she in the kitchen for?" Sonny asked, speaking to his hands. "Nobody's going to come. Nobody ever comes here, because she never wanted them to."

"Albert's taking this kind of hard, Harry," George said. He propped the magazine against the stiff folds of his uniform and looked across the room at his little brother. Harry had seated himself beside the door, as out of the way as possible. George's attentions rather frightened him, though George had behaved with consistent kindness ever since his arrival two days after Eddie's death. His crew cut still bristled and he could still break rocks with his chin, but some violent demon seemed to have left him. "You think he'll be okay?"

"Him? Sure." Harry tilted his head, grimaced.

"He didn't see Little Eddie first, did he?"

"No, Dad did," Harry said. "He saw the light on in the attic when he came home, I guess. Albert went up there, though. I guess there was so much blood Dad thought somebody broke in and killed Eddie. But he just bumped his head, and that's where the blood came from."

"Head wounds bleed like bastards," Sonny said. "A guy hit me with a bottle once in Tokyo. I thought I was gonna bleed to death right there."

"And Mom's stuff got all messed up?" George asked quietly.

This time Sonny looked up.

"Pretty much, I guess. The dress rack got knocked down. Dad cleaned up what he could, the next day. One of the cane-back chairs got broke, and a hunk got knocked out of the teak table. And the mirror got broken into a million pieces."

Sonny shook his head and made a soft whistling sound through his pursed lips.

"She's a tough old gal," George said. "I hear her coming, though, so we have to stop, Harry. But we can talk tonight."

Harry nodded.

XII

After dinner that night, when Maryrose had gone to bed—the hospital had given her two nights off—Harry sat across the kitchen table from a George who clearly had something to say. Sonny had polished off a six-pack by himself in front of the television and gone up to the dormitory bedroom by himself. Albert had disappeared shortly after dinner, and their father had never emerged from his cubicle beside the junk room.

"I'm glad Pete Petrosian came over," George said. "He's a good old boy. Ate two helpings too."

Harry was startled by George's use of their neighbor's first name—he was not even sure that he had ever heard it before.

Mr. Petrosian had been their only caller that afternoon. Harry had seen that his mother was grateful that someone had come, and despite her preparations wanted no more company after Mr. Petrosian had left.

"Think I'll get a beer, that is if Sonny didn't drink it all," George said, and stood up and opened the fridge. His uniform looked as if it had been painted on his body, and his muscles bulged and moved like a horse's. "Two left," he said. "Good thing you're underage." George popped the caps off both bottles and came back to the table. He winked at Harry, then tilted the first bottle to his lips and took a good swallow. "So what the devil was Little Eddie doing up there anyhow? Trying on dresses?"

"I don't know," Harry said. "I was asleep."

"Hell, I know I kind of lost touch with Little Eddie, but I got the impression he was scared of his shadow. I'm surprised he had the nerve to go up there and mess around with Mom's precious stuff."

"Yeah," Harry said. "Me too."

"You didn't happen to go with him, did you?" George tilted the bottle to his mouth and winked at Harry again.

Harry just looked back. He could feel his face getting hot.

"I just was thinking maybe you saw it happen to Little Eddie, and got too scared to tell anybody. Nobody would be mad at you, Harry. Nobody would blame you for anything. You couldn't know how to help someone who's having an epileptic fit. Little Eddie swallowed his tongue. Even if you'd been standing next to him when he did it and had the presence of mind to call an ambulance, he would have died before it got there. Unless you knew what was wrong and how to correct it. Which nobody would expect you to know, not in a million years. Nobody'd blame you for anything, Harry, not even Mom."

"I was asleep," Harry said.

"Okay, okay. I just wanted you to know."

They sat in silence for a time, then both spoke at once.

"Did you know—"

"We had this—"

"Sorry," George said. "Go on."

"Did you know that Dad used to be in the Army? In World War II?"

"Yeah, I knew that. Of course I knew that."

"Did you know that he committed the perfect murder once?"

"*What?*"

"Dad committed the perfect murder. When he was at Dachau, that death camp."

"Oh Christ, is that what you're talking about? You got a funny way of seeing things, Harry. He shot an enemy who was trying to escape. That's not murder, it's war. There's one hell of a big difference."

"I'd like to see war someday," Harry said. "I'd like to be in the Army, like you and Dad."

"Hold your horses, hold your horses," George said, smiling now. "That's sort of one of the things I wanted to talk to you about." He set down his beer bottle, cradled his hands around it, and tilted his head to look at Harry. This was obviously going to be serious. "You know, I used to be crazy and stupid, that's the only way to put it. I used to look for fights. I had a chip on my shoulder the size of a house, and pounding some dipshit into a coma was my idea of a great time. The Army did me a lot of good. It made me grow up. But I don't think you need that, Harry. You're too smart for that—if you have to go, you go, but out of all of us, you're the one who could really amount to something in this world. You could be a doctor. Or a lawyer. You ought to get the best education you can, Harry. What you have to do is stay out of trouble and get to college."

"Oh, college," Harry said.

"Listen to me, Harry. I make pretty good money, and I got nothing to spend it on. I'm not going to get married and have kids, that's for sure. So I want to make you a proposition. If you keep your nose clean and make it through high school, I'll help you out with college. Maybe you can get a scholarship—I think you're smart enough, Harry, and a scholarship would be great. But either way, I'll see you make it through." George emptied the first bottle, set it down, and gave Harry a quizzical look. "Let's get one person in this family off on the right track. What do you say?"

"I guess I better keep reading," Harry said.

"I hope you'll read your ass off, little buddy," George said, and picked up the second bottle of beer.

XIII

The day after Sonny left, George put all of Eddie's toys and clothes into a box and squeezed the box into the junk room; two days later, George took a bus to New York so he could get his flight to Munich from Idlewild. An hour before he caught his bus, George walked Harry up to Big John's and stuffed him full of hamburgers and french fries and said, "You'll probably miss Eddie a lot, won't you?" "I guess," Harry said, but the truth was that Eddie was now only a vacancy, a blank space. Sometimes a door would close and Harry would know that Little Eddie had just come in; but when he turned to look, he saw only emptiness. George's question, asked a week ago, was the last time Harry had heard anyone pronounce his brother's name.

In the seven days since the charmed afternoon at Big John's and the departure on a southbound bus of George Beevers, everything seemed to have gone back to the way it was before, but Harry knew that really everything had changed. They had been a loose, divided family of five, two parents and three sons. Now they seemed to be a family of three, and Harry thought that the actual truth was that the family had shrunk down to two, himself and his mother.

Edgar Beevers had left home—he too was an absence. After two visits from policemen who parked their cars right outside the house, after listening to his mother's muttered expressions of disgust, after the spectacle of his pale, bleary, but sober and clean-shaven father trying over and over to knot a necktie in front of the bathroom mirror, Harry finally accepted that his father had been caught shoplifting. His father had to go to court, and he was scared. His hands shook so uncontrollably that he could not shave himself, and in the end Maryrose had to knot his tie—doing it in one, two, three quick movements as brutal as the descent of a knife, never removing the cigarette from her mouth.

Grief-stricken Area Man Forgiven of Shoplifting Charge, read the headline over the little story in the evening newspaper which at last explained his father's crime. Edgar Beevers had been stopped on the sidewalk outside the Livermore Avenue National Tea, T-bone steaks hidden inside his shirt and a bottle of Rheingold beer in each of his front pockets. He had stolen two steaks! He had put beer bottles in his pockets! This made Harry feel like he was sweating inside. The judge had sent him home, but home was not where he went. For a short time, Harry thought, his father had hung out on Oldtown Road, Palmyra's Skid Row, and slept in vacant lots with winos and bums. (Then a woman was supposed to have taken him in.)

Albert was another mystery. It was as though a creature from outer space had taken him over and was using his body, like *Invasion of the Body Snatchers*. Albert looked like he thought somebody was always standing behind him, watching every move he made. He was still carrying around that piece of his tongue, and pretty soon, Harry thought, he'd get so used to it that he would forget he had it.

Three days after George left Palmyra, Albert had actually tagged along after Harry on the way to Big John's. Harry had turned around on the sidewalk and seen Albert in his black jeans and grease-blackened T-shirt halfway down the block, shoving his hands in his pockets and looking hard at the ground. That was Albert's way of pretending to be invisible. The next time he turned around, Albert growled, "Keep walking."

Harry went to work on the pinball machine as soon as he got inside Big John's. Albert slunk in a few minutes later and went straight to the counter. He took one of the stained paper menus from a stack squeezed in beside a napkin dispenser and inspected it as if he had never seen it before.

"Hey, let me introduce you guys," said Big John, leaning against the far side of the counter. Like Albert, he wore black jeans and motorcycle boots, but his dark hair, daringly for the nineteen-fifties, fell over his ears. Beneath his stained white apron he wore a long-sleeved black shirt with a pattern of tiny azure palm trees. "You two are the Beevers boys, Harry and Bucky. Say hello to each other, fellows."

Bucky Beaver was a toothy rodent in an Ipana television commercial. Albert blushed, still grimly staring at his menu sheet.

"Call me Beans," Harry said, and felt Albert's gaze shift wonderingly to him.

"Beans and Bucky, the Beevers boys," Big John said. "Well, Buck, what'll you have?"

"Hamburger, fries, shake," Albert said.

Big John half turned and yelled the order through the hatch to Mama Mary's kitchen. For a time the three of them stood in uneasy silence. Then Big John said, "Heard your old man found a new place to hang his hat. His new girlfriend is a real pistol, I heard. Spent some time in County Hospital. On account of she picked up little messages from outer space on the good old Philco. You hear that?"

"He's gonna come home real soon," Harry said. "He doesn't have any new girlfriend. He's staying with an old friend. She's a rich lady and she wants to help him out because she knows he had a lot of trouble and she's going to get him a real good job, and then he'll come home, and we'll be able to move to a better house and everything."

He never even saw Albert move, but Albert had materialized beside him. Fury, rage, and misery distorted his face. Harry had time to cry out only once, and then Albert slammed a fist into his chest and knocked him backwards into the pinball machine.

"I bet that felt real good," Harry said, unable to keep down his own rage. "I bet you'd like to kill me, huh? Huh, Albert? How about that?"

Albert moved backward two paces and lowered his hands, already looking impassive, locked into himself.

For a second in which his breath failed and dazzling light filled his eyes, Harry saw Little Eddie's slack, trusting face before him. Then Big John came up from nowhere with a big hamburger and a mound of french fries on a plate and said, "Down, boys. Time for Rocky here to tackle his dinner."

That night Albert said nothing at all to Harry as they lay in their beds. Neither did he fall asleep. Harry knew that for most of the night Albert just closed his eyes and faked it, like a possum in trouble. Harry tried to stay awake long enough to see when Albert's fake sleep melted into the real thing, but he sank into dreams long before that.

He was rushing down the stony corridor of a castle past suits of armor and torches guttering in sconces. His bladder was bursting, he had to let go, he could not hold it more than another few seconds . . . at last he came to the open bathroom door and ran into that splendid gleaming place. He began to tug at his zipper, and looked around for the butler and the row of marble urinals. Then he froze. Little Eddie was standing before him, not the uniformed butler. Blood ran in a gaudy streak from a gash high on his forehead over his cheek and right down his neck, neat as paint. Little Eddie was waving frantically at Harry, his eyes bright and hysterical, his mouth working soundlessly because he had swallowed his tongue.

Harry sat up straight in bed, about to scream, then realized that the bedroom was all around him and Little Eddie was gone. He hurried downstairs to the bathroom.

XIV

At two o'clock the next afternoon Harry Beevers had to pee again, and just as badly, but this time he was a long way from the bathroom across from the junk room and his father's old cubicle. Harry was standing in the humid sunlight across the street from 45 Oldtown Way. This short street connected the bums, transient hotels, bars, and seedy movie theaters of Oldtown Road with the more respectable hotels, department stores, and restaurants of Palmyra Avenue—the real downtown. 45 Oldtown Way was a four-story brick tenement with an exoskeleton of fire escapes. Black iron bars covered the ground-floor windows. On one side of 45 Oldtown Way were the large soap-smeared windows of a bankrupted shoe store, on the other a vacant lot where loose bricks and broken bottles nestled amongst dandelions and tall Queen Anne's lace. Harry's father lived in that building now. Everybody else knew it, and since Big John had told him, now Harry knew it too.

He jigged from leg to leg, waiting for a woman to come out through the front door. It was as chipped and peeling as his own, and a broken fanlight sat drunkenly atop it. Harry had checked the row of dented mailboxes on the brick wall just outside the door for his father's name, but none bore any names at all. Big John hadn't known the name of the woman who had taken Harry's father, but he said that she was large, black-haired, and crazy, and that she had two children in foster care. About half an hour ago a dark-haired woman had come through the door, but Harry had not followed her because she had not looked especially large to him. Now he was beginning to have doubts. What did Big John mean by "large" anyhow? As big as he was? And how could you tell if someone was crazy? Did it show? Maybe he should have followed that woman. This thought made him even more anxious, and he squeezed his legs together.

His father was in that building now, he thought. Harry thought of his father lying on an unmade bed, his brown winter coat around him, his hat pulled low on his forehead like Lepke Buchalter's, drawing on a cigarette, looking moodily out the window.

Then he had to pee so urgently that he could not have held it in for more than a few seconds, and trotted across the street and into the vacant lot. Near the back fence the tall weeds gave him some shelter from the street. He frantically unzipped and let the braided yellow stream splash into a nest of broken bricks. Harry looked up at the side of the building beside him. It looked very tall, and seemed to be tilting slightly toward him. The four windows on each floor looked back down at him, blank and fatherless. Just as he was tugging at his zipper, he heard the front door of the building slam shut.

His heart slammed too. Harry hunkered down behind the tall white weeds. Anxiety that she might walk the other way, toward downtown, made him twine his fingers together and bend his fingers back. If he waited about five seconds, he figured, he'd know she was going toward Palmyra Avenue and would be able to get across the lot in time to see which way she turned. His knuckles cracked. He felt like a soldier hiding in a forest, like a murder weapon.

He raised up on his toes and got ready to dash back across the street, because an empty grocery cart closely followed by a moving belly with a tiny head and basketball shoes, a cigar tilted in its mouth like a flag, appeared past the front of the building. He could go back and wait across the street. Harry settled down and watched the stomach go down the sidewalk past him. Then a shadow separated itself from the street side of the fat man, and the shadow became a black-haired woman in a long loose dress now striding past the grocery cart. She shook back her head, and Harry saw that she was tall as a queen and that her skin was darker than olive. Deep lines cut through her cheeks. It had to be the woman who had taken his father. Her long rapid strides had taken her well past the fat man's grocery cart. Harry ran across the rubble of the lot and began to follow her up the sidewalk.

His father's woman walked in a hard, determined way. She stepped down into the street to get around groups too slow for her. At the Oldtown Road corner she wove her way through a group of saggy-bottomed men passing around a bottle in a paper bag and cut in front of two black children dribbling a basketball up the street. She was on the move, and Harry had to hurry along to keep her in sight.

"I bet you don't believe me," he said to himself, practicing, and skirted the group of winos on the corner. He picked up his speed until he was nearly trotting. The two black kids with the basketball ignored him as he kept pace with them, then went on ahead. Far up the block, the tall woman with bouncing black hair marched right past a flashing neon sign in a bar window. Her bottom moved back and forth in the loose dress, surprisingly big whenever it bulged out the fabric of the dress; her back seemed as long as a lion's. "What would you say if I told you . . ." Harry said to himself.

A block and a half ahead, the woman turned on her heel and went through the door of the A&P store. Harry sprinted the rest of the way, pushed the yellow wooden door marked ENTER, and walked into the dense, humid air of the grocery store. Other A&P stores may have been air-conditioned, but not the little shop on Oldtown Road.

What was foster care anyway? Did you get money if you gave away your children?

A good person's children would never be in foster care, Harry thought. He saw the woman turning into the third aisle past the cash register. He saw with a small shock that she was taller than his father. If I told you, you might not believe me. He went slowly around the corner of the aisle. She was standing on the pale wooden floor about fifteen feet in front of him, carrying a wire basket in one hand. He stepped forward. What I have to say might seem . . . For good luck, he touched the hatpin inserted into the bottom of his collar. She was staring at a row of brightly colored bags of potato chips. Harry cleared his throat. The woman reached down and picked up a big bag and put it in the basket.

"Excuse me," Harry said.

She turned her head to look at him. Her face was as wide as it was long, and in the mellow light from the store's low-wattage bulbs her skin seemed a very light shade of brown. Harry knew he was meeting an equal. She looked like she could do magic, as if she could shoot fire and sparks out of her fierce black eyes.

"I bet you don't believe me," he said, "but a kid can hypnotize people just as good as an adult."

"What's that?"

His rehearsed words now sounded crazy to him, but he stuck to his script.

"A kid can hypnotize people. I can hypnotize people. Do you believe that?"

"I don't think I even care," she said, and wheeled away toward the rear of the aisle.

"I bet you don't think I could hypnotize you," Harry said.

"Kid, get lost."

Harry suddenly knew that if he kept talking about hypnotism the woman would turn down the next aisle and ignore him no matter what he said, or else begin to speak in a very loud voice about seeing the manager. "My name is Harry Beevers," he said to her back. "Edgar Beevers is my dad."

She stopped and turned around and looked expressionlessly into his face.

Harry dizzyingly saw a wall of barbed wire before him, a dark green wall of trees at the other end of a barren field.

"I wonder if you maybe call him Beans," Harry said.

"Oh, great," she said. "That's just great. So you're one of his boys. Terrific. *Beans* wants potato chips, what do you want?"

"I want you to fall down and bang your head and swallow your tongue and *die* and get buried and have people drop dirt on you," Harry said. The woman's mouth fell open. "Then I want you to puff up with *gas*. I want you to *rot*. I want you to turn green and *black*. I want your *skin* to slide off your bones."

"You're crazy!" the woman shouted at him. "Your whole family's crazy! Do you think your mother wants him anymore?"

"My father shot us in the back," Harry said, and turned and bolted down the aisle for the door.

When he got outside he began to trot down seedy Oldtown Road. When he came to Oldtown Way he turned left. When he ran past number 45, he looked at every blank window. His face, his hands, his whole body felt hot and wet. Soon he had a stitch in his side. Harry blinked, and saw a dark line of trees, a wall of barbed wire before him. At the top of Oldtown Way he turned into Palmyra Avenue. From there he could continue running past Alouette's boarded-up windows, past all the stores old and new, to the corner of Livermore, and from there, he only now realized, to the little house that belonged to Mr. Petrosian.

XV

On a sweltering midafternoon eleven years later at a camp in the Central Highlands of Vietnam, Lieutenant Harry Beevers closed the flap of his tent against the mosquitoes and sat on the edge of his temporary bunk to write a long-delayed letter back to Pat Caldwell, the young woman he wanted to marry—and to whom he would be married for a time, after his return from the war to New York State.

This is what he wrote, after frequent crossings-out and hesitations. Harry later destroyed this letter.

Dear Pat:

First of all I want you to know how much I miss you, my darling, and that if I ever get out of this beautiful and terrible country, which I am going to do, that I am going to chase you mercilessly and unrelentingly until you say that you'll marry me. Maybe in the euphoria of relief (YES!!!), I have the future all worked out, Pat, and you're a big part of it. I have eighty-six days until DEROS, when they pat me on the head and put me on that big bird out of here. Now that my record is clear again, I have no doubts that Columbia Law School will take me in. As you know, my law board scores were pretty respectable (modest me!) when I took them at Adelphi. I'm pretty sure I could even get into Harvard Law, but I settled on Columbia because then we could both be in New York.

My brother George has already told me that he will help out with whatever money I—you and I—will need. George put me through Adelphi. I don't think you knew this. In fact, nobody knew this. When I look back, in college I was such a jerk. I wanted everybody to think my family was well-to-do, or at least middle-class.

The truth is, we were damn poor, which I think makes my accomplishments all the more noteworthy, all the more loveworthy!

You see, this experience, even with all the ugly and self-doubting and humiliating moments, has done me a lot of good. I was right to come here, even though I had no idea what it was really like. I think I needed the experience of war to complete me, and I tell you this even though I know that you will detest any such idea. In fact, I have to tell you that a big part of me loves being here, and that in some way, even with all this trouble, this year will always be one of the high points of my life. Pat, as you see, I'm determined to be honest—to be an honest man. If I'm going to be a lawyer, I ought to be honest, don't you think? (Or maybe the reverse is the reality!) One thing that has meant a lot to me here has been what I can only call the close comradeship of my friends and my men—I actually like the grunts more than the usual officer types, which of course means that I get more loyalty and better performance from my men than the usual lieutenant. Some day I'd like you to meet Mike Poole and Tim Underhill and Pumo the Puma and the most amazing of all, M. O. Dengler, who of course was involved with me in the Ia Thuc cave incident. These guys stuck by me. I even have a nickname, "Beans." They call me "Beans" Beevers, and I like it.

There was no way my court-martial could have really put me in any trouble, because all the facts, and my own men, were on my side. Besides, could you see me actually killing children? This is Vietnam and you kill people, that's what we're doing here—we kill Charlies. But we don't kill babies and children. Not even in the heat of wartime—and Ia Thuc was pretty hot!

Well, this is my way of letting you know that at the court-martial of course I received a complete and utter vindication. Dengler did too. There were even unofficial mutterings about giving us medals for all the BS we put up with for the past six weeks—including that amazing story in Time *magazine. Before people start yelling about atrocities, they ought to have all the facts straight. Fortunately, last week's magazines go out with the rest of the trash.*

Besides, I already knew too much about what death does to people.

I never told you that I once had a little brother named Edward. When I was ten, my little brother wandered up into the top floor of our house one night and suffered a fatal epileptic fit. This event virtually destroyed my family. It led directly to my father's leaving home. (He had been a hero in WWII, something else I never told you.) It deeply changed, I would say even damaged, my older brother Albert. Albert tried to enlist in 1964, but they wouldn't take him because they said he was psychologically unfit. My mom too almost came apart for a while. She used to go up in the attic and cry and wouldn't come down. So you could say that my family was pretty well destroyed, or ruined, or whatever you want to call it, by a sudden death. I took it, and my dad's desertion, pretty hard myself. You don't get over these things easily.

The court-martial lasted exactly four hours. Big deal, hey?—as we used to say back in Palmyra. We used to have a neighbor named Pete Petrosian who said things like that, and against what must have been million-to-one odds, who died exactly the same way my brother did, about two weeks after—lightning really did strike twice. I guess it's dumb to think about him now, but maybe one thing war does is to make you conversant with death. How it happens, what it does to people, what it means, how all the dead in your life are somehow united, joined, part of your eternal family. This is a profound feeling, Pat, and no damn whipped-up failed court-martial can touch it. If there were any innocent children in that cave, then they are in my family forever, like little Edward and Pete Petrosian, and the rest of my life is a poem to them. But the Army says there weren't, and so do I.

I love you and love you and love you. You can stop worrying now and start thinking about being married to a Columbia Law student with one hell of a good future. I won't tell you any more war stories than you want to hear. And that's a promise, whether the stories are about Nam or Palmyra.

Always yours,
Harry
(aka "Beans!")

George R. R. Martin (b. 1948)

Sandkings

George R. R. Martin gained wide popularity in the science fiction field as a young writer in the 1970s, winning both the Hugo and Nebula Awards. In the 1980s, he moved into the horror genre with two novels, *Fevre Dream* (1982), an historical vampire novel, and *Armageddon Rag* (1983), a rock 'n' roll apocalypse of the 1960s, and a short story collection, *Songs the Dead Men Sing* (1983). Since then he has pursued a career as anthologist, television scriptwriter and editor. "Sandkings" was the title story of his last science fiction collection (1979). It won the Hugo Award as best story of the year. One can see that Martin was already moving from science fiction to horror in this piece of uncanny, fantastic nightmare. It is both a literal and a psychological monster story, a social allegory and a moral one. The layering of meaning is deep and complex, the possibilities of reading many. Isaac Asimov said of this piece, "I can't help feeling what a terrific example of the horror story 'Sandkings' is . . . it just keeps hitting you harder as you go." Martin's contribution to horror in the 1980s is significant.

S imon Kress lived alone in a sprawling manor house among the dry, rocky hills fifty kilometers from the city. So, when he was called away unexpectedly on business, he had no neighbors he could conveniently impose on to take his pets. The carrion hawk was no problem; it roosted in the unused belfry and customarily fed itself anyway. The shambler Kress simply shooed outside and left to fend for itself; the little monster would gorge on slugs and birds and rockjocks. But the fish tank, stocked with genuine Earth piranhas, posed a difficulty. Kress finally just threw a haunch of beef into the huge tank. The piranhas could always eat each other if he were detained longer than expected. They'd done it before. It amused him.

Unfortunately, he was detained *much* longer than expected this time. When he finally returned, all the fish were dead. So was the carrion hawk. The shambler had climbed up to the belfry and eaten it. Simon Kress was vexed.

The next day he flew his skimmer to Asgard, a journey of some two hundred kilometers. Asgard was Baldur's largest city and boasted the oldest and largest starport as well. Kress liked to impress his friends with animals that were unusual, entertaining, and expensive; Asgard was the place to buy them.

This time, though, he had poor luck. Xenopets had closed its doors, t'Etherane the Petseller tried to foist another carrion hawk off on him, and Strange Waters offered nothing more exotic than piranhas, glowsharks, and spider-squids. Kress had had all those; he wanted something new.

Near dusk, he found himself walking down the Rainbow Boulevard, looking for places

197

he had not patronized before. So close to the starport, the street was lined by importers' marts. The big corporate emporiums had impressive long windows, where rare and costly alien artifacts reposed on felt cushions against dark drapes that made the interiors of the stores a mystery. Between them were the junk shops; narrow, nasty little places whose display areas were crammed with all manner of offworld bric-a-brac. Kress tried both kinds of shop, with equal dissatisfaction.

Then he came across a store that was different.

It was quite close to the port. Kress had never been there before. The shop occupied a small, single-story building of moderate size, set between a euphoria bar and a temple-brothel of the Secret Sisterhood. Down this far, the Rainbow Boulevard grew tacky. The shop itself was unusual. Arresting.

The windows were full of mist; now a pale red, now the gray of true fog, now sparkling and golden. The mist swirled and eddied and glowed faintly from within. Kress glimpsed objects in the window—machines, pieces of art, other things he could not recognize—but he could not get a good look at any of them. The mists flowed sensuously around them, displaying a bit of first one thing and then another, then cloaking all. It was intriguing.

As he watched, the mist began to form letters. One word at a time. Kress stood and read.

WO. AND. SHADE. IMPORTERS.
ARTIFACTS. ART. LIFE-FORMS. AND. MISC.

The letters stopped. Through the fog, Kress saw something moving. That was enough for him, that and the "life-forms" in their advertisement. He swept his walking cloak over his shoulder and entered the store.

Inside, Kress felt disoriented. The interior seemed vast, much larger than he would have guessed from the relatively modest frontage. It was dimly lit, peaceful. The ceiling was a starscape, complete with spiral nebulae, very dark and realistic, very nice. The counters all shone faintly, to better display the merchandise within. The aisles were carpeted with ground fog. It came almost to his knees in places, and swirled about his feet as he walked.

"Can I help you?"

She almost seemed to have risen from the fog. Tall and gaunt and pale, she wore a practical gray jumpsuit and a strange little cap that rested well back on her head.

"Are you Wo or Shade?" Kress asked. "Or only sales help?"

"Jala Wo, ready to serve you," she replied. "Shade does not see customers. We have no sales help."

"You have quite a large establishment," Kress said. "Odd that I have never heard of you before."

"We have only just opened this shop on Baldur," the woman said. "We have franchises on a number of other worlds, however. What can I sell you? Art, perhaps? You have the look of a collector. We have some fine Nor T'alush crystal carvings."

"No," Simon Kress said. "I own all the crystal carvings I desire. I came to see about a pet."

"A life-form?"

"Yes."

"Alien?"

"Of course."

"We have a mimic in stock. From Celia's World. A clever little simian. Not only will it learn to speak, but eventually it will mimic your voice, inflections, gestures, even facial expressions."

"Cute," said Kress. "And common. I have no use for either, Wo. I want something exotic. Unusual. And not cute. I detest cute animals. At the moment I own a shambler. Imported from Cotho, at no mean expense. From time to time I feed him a litter of unwanted kittens. This is what I think of *cute*. Do I make myself understood?"

Wo smiled enigmatically. "Have you ever owned an animal that worshiped you?" she asked.

Kress grinned. "Oh, now and again. But I don't require worship, Wo. Just entertainment."

"You misunderstand me," Wo said, still wearing her strange smile. "I meant worship literally."

"What are you talking about?"

"I think I have just the thing for you," Wo said. "Follow me."

She led Kress between the radiant counters and down a long, fog-shrouded aisle beneath false starlight. They passed through a wall of mist into another section of the store, and stopped before a large plastic tank. An aquarium, thought Kress.

Wo beckoned. He stepped closer and saw that he was wrong. It was a terrarium. Within lay a miniature desert about two meters square. Pale sand bleached scarlet by wan red light. Rocks: basalt and quartz and granite. In each corner of the tank stood a castle.

Kress blinked, and peered, and corrected himself; actually only three castles stood. The fourth leaned; a crumbled, broken ruin. The other three were crude but intact, carved of stone and sand. Over their battlements and through their rounded porticos, tiny creatures climbed and scrambled. Kress pressed his face against the plastic. "Insects?" he asked.

"No," Wo replied. "A much more complex life-form. More intelligent as well. Smarter than your shambler by a considerable amount. They are called sandkings."

"Insects," Kress said, drawing back from the tank. "I don't care how complex they are." He frowned. "And kindly don't try to gull me with this talk of intelligence. These things are far too small to have anything but the most rudimentary brains."

"They share hiveminds," Wo said. "Castle minds, in this case. There are only three organisms in the tank, actually. The fourth died. You see how her castle has fallen."

Kress looked back at the tank. "Hiveminds, eh? Interesting." He frowned again. "Still, it is only an oversized ant farm. I'd hoped for something better."

"They fight wars."

"Wars? Hmmm." Kress looked again.

"Note the colors, if you will," Wo told him. She pointed to the creatures that swarmed over the nearest castle. One was scrabbling at the tank wall. Kress studied it. It still looked like an insect to his eyes. Barely as long as his fingernail, six-limbed, with six tiny eyes set all around its body. A wicked set of mandibles clacked visibly, while two long fine antennae wove patterns in the air. Antennae, mandibles, eyes and legs were sooty black, but the dominant color was the burnt orange of its armor plating. "It's an insect," Kress repeated.

"It is not an insect," Wo insisted calmly. "The armored exoskeleton is shed when the sandking grows larger. *If* it grows larger. In a tank this size, it won't." She took Kress by the elbow and led him around the tank to the next castle. "Look at the colors here."

He did. They were different. Here the sandkings had bright-red armor; antennae, mandibles, eyes, and legs were yellow. Kress glanced across the tank. The denizens of the third live castle were off-white, with red trim. "Hmmm," he said.

"They war, as I said," Wo told him. "They even have truces and alliances. It was an alliance that destroyed the fourth castle in this tank. The blacks were getting too numerous, so the others joined forces to destroy them."

Kress remained unconvinced. "Amusing, no doubt. But insects fight wars too."

"Insects do not worship," Wo said.

"Eh?"

Wo smiled and pointed at the castle. Kress stared. A face had been carved into the wall of the highest tower. He recognized it. It was Jala Wo's face. "How . . . ?"

"I projected a holograph of my face into the tank, kept it there for a few days. The face of god, you see? I feed them, I am always close. The sandkings have a rudimentary psionic sense. Proximity telepathy. They sense me, and worship me by using my face to decorate their buildings. All the castles have them, see?" They did.

On the castle, the face of Jala Wo was serene and peaceful, and very lifelike. Kress marveled at the workmanship. "How do they do it?"

"The foremost legs double as arms. They even have fingers of a sort: three small, flexible tendrils. And they cooperate well, both in building and in battle. Remember, all the mobiles of one color share a single mind."

"Tell me more," Kress said.

Wo smiled. "The maw lives in the castle. Maw is my name for her. A pun, if you will; the thing is mother and stomach both. Female, large as your fist, immobile. Actually, sandking is a bit of a misnomer. The mobiles are peasants and warriors, the real ruler is a queen. But that analogy is faulty as well. Considered as a whole, each castle is a single hermaphroditic creature."

"What do they eat?"

"The mobiles eat pap, predigested food obtained inside the castle. They get it from the maw after she has worked on it for several days. Their stomachs can't handle anything else, so if the maw dies, they soon die as well. The maw . . . the maw eats anything. You'll have no special expense there. Table scraps will do excellently."

"Live food?" Kress asked.

Wo shrugged. "Each maw eats mobiles from the other castles, yes."

"I am intrigued," he admitted. "If only they weren't so small."

"Yours can be larger. These sandkings are small because their tank is small. They seem to limit their growth to fit available space. If I moved these to a larger tank, they'd start growing again."

"Hmmm. My piranha tank is twice this size, and vacant. It could be cleaned out, filled with sand . . ."

"Wo and Shade would take care of the installation. It would be our pleasure."

"Of course," said Kress, "I would expect four intact castles."

"Certainly," Wo said.

They began to haggle about the price.

Three days later Jala Wo arrived at Simon Kress's estate, with dormant sandkings and a work crew to take charge of the installation. Wo's assistants were aliens unlike any Kress was familiar with; squat, broad bipeds with four arms and bulging, multifaceted eyes. Their skin was thick and leathery, and twisted into horns and spines and protrusions at odd spots upon their bodies. But they were very strong, and good workers. Wo ordered them about in a musical tongue that Kress had never heard.

In a day it was done. They moved his piranha tank to the center of his spacious living room, arranged couches on either side of it for better viewing, scrubbed it clean and filled it two-thirds of the way up with sand and rock. Then they installed a special lighting system, both to provide the dim red illumination the sandkings preferred and to project holographic images into the tank. On top they mounted a sturdy plastic cover, with a feeder mechanism built in. "This way you can feed your sandkings without removing the top of the tank," Wo explained. "You would not want to take any chances on the mobiles escaping."

The cover also included climate control devices, to condense just the right amount of moisture from the air. "You want it dry, but not too dry," Wo said.

Finally one of the four-armed workers climbed into the tank and dug deep pits in the four corners. One of his companions handed the dormant maws over to him, removing them one-by-one from their frosted cryonic traveling cases. They were nothing to look at. Kress decided they resembled nothing so much as a mottled, half-spoiled chunk of raw meat. With a mouth.

The alien buried them, one in each corner of the tank. Then they sealed it all up and took their leave.

"The heat will bring the maws out of dormancy," Wo said. "In less than a week, mobiles will begin to hatch and burrow to the surface. Be certain to give them plenty of food. They will need all their strength until they are well established. I would estimate that you will have castles rising in about three weeks."

"And my face? When will they carve my face?"

"Turn on the hologram after about a month," she advised him. "And be patient. If you have any questions, please call. Wo and Shade are at your service." She bowed and left.

Kress wandered back to the tank and lit a joy stick. The desert was still and empty. He drummed his fingers impatiently against the plastic, and frowned.

On the fourth day, Kress thought he glimpsed motion beneath the sand, subtle subterranean stirrings.

On the fifth day, he saw his first mobile, a lone white.

On the sixth day, he counted a dozen of them, whites and reds and blacks. The oranges were tardy. He cycled through a bowl of half-decayed table scraps. The mobiles sensed it at once, rushed to it, and began to drag pieces back to their respective corners. Each color group was very organized. They did not fight. Kress was a bit disappointed, but he decided to give them time.

The oranges made their appearance on the eighth day. By then the other sandkings had begun to carry small stones and erect crude fortifications. They still did not war. At the moment they were only half the size of those he had seen at Wo and Shade's, but Kress thought they were growing rapidly.

The castles began to rise midway through the second week. Organized battalions of mobiles dragged heavy chunks of sandstone and granite back to their corners, where other mobiles were pushing sand into place with mandibles and tendrils. Kress had purchased a pair of magnifying goggles so he could watch them work, wherever they might go in the tank. He wandered around and around the tall plastic walls, observing. It was fascinating. The castles were a bit plainer than Kress would have liked, but he had an idea about that. The next day he cycled through some obsidian and flakes of colored glass along with the food. Within hours, they had been incorporated into the castle walls.

The black castle was the first completed, followed by the white and red fortresses. The oranges were last, as usual. Kress took his meals into the living room and ate seated on the couch, so he could watch. He expected the first war to break out any hour now.

He was disappointed. Days passed, the castles grew taller and more grand, and Kress seldom left the tank except to attend to his sanitary needs and answer critical business calls. But the sandkings did not war. He was getting upset.

Finally he stopped feeding them.

Two days after the table scraps had ceased to fall from their desert sky, four black mobiles surrounded an orange and dragged it back to their maw. They maimed it first, ripping off its mandibles and antennae and limbs, and carried it through the shadowed main gate of their miniature castle. It never emerged. Within an hour, more than forty orange mobiles marched across the sand and attacked the blacks' corner. They were outnumbered by the blacks that came rushing up from the depths. When the fighting was over, the attackers had been slaughtered. The dead and dying were taken down to feed the black maw.

Kress, delighted, congratulated himself on his genius.

When he put food into the tank the following day, a three-cornered battle broke out over its possession. The whites were the big winners.

After that, war followed war.

Almost a month to the day after Jala Wo had delivered the sandkings, Kress turned on the holographic projector, and his face materialized in the tank. It turned, slowly, around and around, so his gaze fell on all four castles equally. Kress thought it rather a good likeness; it had his impish grin, wide mouth, full cheeks. His blue eyes sparkled, his gray hair was carefully arrayed in a fashionable sidesweep, his eyebrows were thin and sophisticated.

Soon enough, the sandkings set to work. Kress fed them lavishly while his image beamed down at them from their sky. Temporarily, the wars stopped. All activity was directed toward worship.

His face emerged on the castle walls.

At first all four carvings looked alike to him, but as the work continued and Kress studied the reproductions, he began to detect subtle differences in technique and execution. The reds were the most creative, using tiny flakes of slate to put the gray in his hair. The white idol seemed young and mischievous to him, while the face shaped by the blacks—although virtually the same, line for line—struck him as wise and beneficent. The orange sandkings, as ever, were last and least. The wars had not gone well for them, and their castle was sad compared to the others. The image they carved was crude and cartoonish and they seemed to intend to leave it that way. When they stopped work on the face, Kress grew quite piqued with them, but there was really nothing he could do.

When all of the sandkings had finished their Kress-faces, he turned off the holograph and decided that it was time to have a party. His friends would be impressed. He could even stage a war for them, he thought. Humming happily to himself, he began to draw up a guest list.

The party was a wild success.

Kress invited thirty people; a handful of close friends who shared his amusements, a few former lovers, and a collection of business and social rivals who could not afford to ignore his summons. He knew some of them would be discomfited and even offended by his sandkings. He counted on it. Simon Kress customarily considered his parties a failure unless at least one guest walked out in a high dudgeon.

On impulse he added Jala Wo's name to his list. "Bring Shade if you like," he added when dictating her invitation.

Her acceptance surprised him just a bit. "Shade, alas, will be unable to attend. He does not go to social functions," Wo added. "As for myself, I look forward to the chance to see how your sandkings are doing."

Kress ordered them up a sumptuous meal. And when at last the conversation had died down, and most of his guests had gotten silly on wine and joy sticks, he shocked them by personally scraping their table leavings into a large bowl. "Come, all of you," he told them. "I want to introduce you to my newest pets." Carrying the bowl, he conducted them into his living room.

The sandkings lived up to his fondest expectations. He had starved them for two days in preparation, and they were in a fighting mood. While the guests ringed the tank, looking through the magnifying glasses Kress had thoughtfully provided, the sandkings waged a glorious battle over the scraps. He counted almost sixty dead mobiles when the struggle was over. The reds and whites, who had recently formed an alliance, emerged with most of the food.

"Kress, you're disgusting," Cath m'Lane told him. She had lived with him for a short time two years before, until her soppy sentimentality almost drove him mad. "I was a fool to come back here. I thought perhaps you'd changed, wanted to apologize." She had never forgiven him for the time his shambler had eaten an excessively cute puppy of which she had been fond. "Don't *ever* invite me here again, Simon." She strode out, accompanied by her current lover and a chorus of laughter.

His other guests were full of questions.

Where did the sandkings come from? they wanted to know. "From Wo and Shade, Importers," he replied, with a polite gesture toward Jala Wo, who had remained quiet and apart through most of the evening.

Why did they decorate their castles with his likeness? "Because I am the source of all good things. Surely you know that?" That brought a round of chuckles.

Will they fight again? "Of course, but not tonight. Don't worry. There will be other parties."

Jad Rakkis, who was an amateur xenologist, began talking about other social insects and the wars they fought. "These sandkings are amusing, but nothing really. You ought to read about Terran soldier ants, for instance."

"Sandkings are not insects," Jala Wo said sharply, but Jad was off and running, and no one paid her the slightest attention. Kress smiled at her and shrugged.

Malada Blane suggested a betting pool the next time they got together to watch a war, and everyone was taken with the idea. An animated discussion about rules and odds ensued. It lasted for almost an hour. Finally the guests began to take their leave.

Jala Wo was the last to depart. "So," Kress said to her when they were alone, "it appears my sandkings are a hit."

"They are doing well," Wo said. "Already they are larger than my own."

"Yes," Kress said, "except for the oranges."

"I had noticed that," Wo replied. "They seem few in number, and their castle is shabby."

"Well, someone must lose," Kress said. "The oranges were late to emerge and get established. They have suffered for it."

"Pardon," said Wo, "but might I ask if you are feeding your sandkings sufficiently?"

Kress shrugged. "They diet from time to time. It makes them fiercer."

She frowned. "There is no need to starve them. Let them war in their own time, for their own reasons. It is their nature, and you will witness conflicts that are delightfully subtle and complex. The constant war brought on by hunger is artless and degrading."

Simon Kress repaid Wo's frown with interest. "You are in my house, Wo, and here I am the judge of what is degrading. I fed the sandkings as you advised, and they did not fight."

"You must have patience."

"No," Kress said. "I am their master and their god, after all. Why should I wait on their impulses? They did not war often enough to suit me. I corrected the situation."

"I see," said Wo. "I will discuss the matter with Shade."

"It is none of your concern, or his," Kress snapped.

"I must bid you good night, then," Wo said with resignation. But as she slipped into her coat to depart, she fixed him with a final disapproving stare. "Look to your faces, Simon Kress," she warned him. "Look to your faces."

Puzzled, he wandered back to the tank and stared at the castles after she had taken her departure. His faces were still there, as ever. Except— He snatched up his magnifying goggles and slipped them on. Even then it was hard to make out. But it seemed to him that the expression on the face of his images had changed slightly, that his smile was somehow twisted so that it seemed a touch malicious. But it was a very subtle change, if it was a change at all. Kress finally put it down to his suggestibility, and resolved not to invite Jala Wo to any more of his gatherings.

Over the next few months, Kress and about a dozen of his favorites got together weekly for what he liked to call his "war games." Now that his initial fascination with the sandkings was past, Kress spent less time around his tank and more on his business affairs and his social life, but he still enjoyed having a few friends over for a war or two. He kept the combatants sharp on a constant edge of hunger. It had severe effects on the orange sandkings, who dwindled visibly until Kress began to wonder if their maw was dead. But the others did well enough.

Sometimes at night, when he could not sleep, Kress would take a bottle of wine into the darkened living room, where the red gloom of his miniature desert was the only light. He would drink and watch for hours, alone. There was usually a fight going on somewhere, and when there was not he could easily start one by dropping in some small morsel of food.

They took to betting on the weekly battles, as Malada Blane had suggested. Kress won a good amount by betting on the whites, who had become the most powerful and numerous colony in the tank, with the grandest castle. One week he slid the corner of the tank top aside, and dropped the food close to the white castle instead of on the central battleground as usual, so the others had to attack the whites in their stronghold to get any food at all. They tried. The whites were brilliant in defense. Kress won a hundred standards from Jad Rakkis.

Rakkis, in fact, lost heavily on the sandkings almost every week. He pretended to a vast knowledge of them and their ways, claiming that he had studied them after the first party, but he had no luck when it came to placing his bets. Kress suspected that Jad's claims were empty boasting. He had tried to study the sandkings a bit himself, in a moment of idle curiosity, tying in to the library to find out what world his pets were native to. But there was no listing for them. He wanted to get in touch with Wo and ask her about it, but he had other concerns, and the matter kept slipping his mind.

Finally, after a month in which his losses totaled more than a thousand standards, Jad Rakkis arrived at the war games carrying a small plastic case under his arm. Inside was a spiderlike thing covered with fine golden hair.

"A sand spider," Rakkis announced. "From Cathaday. I got it this afternoon from t'Etherane the Petseller. Usually they remove the poison sacs, but this one is intact. Are you game, Simon? I want my money back. I'll bet a thousand standards, sand spider against sandkings."

Kress studied the spider in its plastic prison. His sandkings had grown—they were twice as large as Wo's, as she'd predicted—but they were still dwarfed by this thing. It was venomed, and they were not. Still, there were an awful lot of them. Besides, the endless sandking wars had begun to grow tiresome lately. The novelty of the match intrigued him. "Done," Kress said. "Jad, you are a fool. The sandkings will just keep coming until this ugly creature of yours is dead."

"You are the fool, Simon," Rakkis replied, smiling. "The Cathadayn sand spider customarily feeds on burrowers that hide in nooks and crevices and—well, watch—it will go straight into those castles, and eat the maws."

Kress scowled amid general laughter. He hadn't counted on that. "Get on with it," he said irritably. He went to freshen his drink.

The spider was too large to cycle conveniently through the food chamber. Two of the others helped Rakkis slide the tank top slightly to one side, and Malada Blane handed him up his case. He shook the spider out. It landed lightly on a miniature dune in front of the red castle, and stood confused for a moment, mouth working, legs twitching menacingly.

"Come on," Rakkis urged. They all gathered round the tank. Simon Kress found his magnifiers and slipped them on. If he was going to lose a thousand standards, at least he wanted a good view of the action.

The sandkings had seen the invader. All over the castle, activity had ceased. The small scarlet mobiles were frozen, watching.

The spider began to move toward the dark promise of the gate. On the tower above, Simon Kress's countenance stared down impassively.

At once there was a flurry of activity. The nearest red mobiles formed themselves into two wedges and streamed over the sand toward the spider. More warriors erupted from inside the castle and assembled in a triple line to guard the approach to the underground chamber where the maw lived. Scouts came scuttling over the dunes, recalled to fight.

Battle was joined.

The attacking sandkings washed over the spider. Mandibles snapped shut on legs and abdomen, and clung. Reds raced up the golden legs to the invader's back. They bit and tore. One of them found an eye, and ripped it loose with tiny yellow tendrils. Kress smiled and pointed.

But they were *small*, and they had no venom, and the spider did not stop. Its legs flicked sandkings off to either side. Its dripping jaws found others, and left them broken and stiffening. Already a dozen of the reds lay dying. The sand spider came on and on. It strode straight through the triple line of guardians before the castle. The lines closed around it, covered it, waging desperate battle. A team of sandkings had bitten off one of the spider's legs, Kress saw. Defenders leapt from atop the towers to land on the twitching, heaving mass.

Lost beneath the sandkings, the spider somehow lurched down into the darkness and vanished.

Jad Rakkis let out a long breath. He looked pale. "Wonderful," someone else said. Malada Blane chuckled deep in her throat.

"Look," said Idi Noreddian, tugging Kress by the arm.

They had been so intent on the struggle in the corner that none of them had noticed the activity elsewhere in the tank. But now the castle was still, the sands empty save for dead red mobiles, and now they saw.

Three armies were drawn up before the red castle. They stood quite still, in perfect array, rank after rank of sandkings, orange and white and black. Waiting to see what emerged from the depths.

Simon Kress smiled. "A *cordon sanitaire*," he said. "And glance at the other castles, if you will, Jad."

Rakkis did, and swore. Teams of mobiles were sealing up the gates with sand and stone. If the spider somehow survived this encounter, it would find no easy entrance at the other castles. "I should have brought four spiders," Jad Rakkis said. "Still, I've won. My spider is down there right now, eating your damned maw."

Kress did not reply. He waited. There was motion in the shadows.

All at once, red mobiles began pouring out of the gate. They took their positions on the castle, and began repairing the damage the spider had wrought. The other armies dissolved and began to retreat to their respective corners.

"Jad," said Simon Kress, "I think you are a bit confused about who is eating who."

The following week Rakkis brought four slim silver snakes. The sandkings dispatched them without much trouble.

Next he tried a large black bird. It ate more than thirty white mobiles, and its thrashing and blundering virtually destroyed that castle, but ultimately its wings grew tired, and the sandkings attacked in force wherever it landed.

After that it was a case of insects, armored beetles not too unlike the sandkings themselves. But stupid, stupid. An allied force of oranges and blacks broke their formation, divided them, and butchered them.

Rakkis began giving Kress promissory notes.

It was around that time that Kress met Cath m'Lane again, one evening when he was dining in Asgard at his favorite restaurant. He stopped at her table briefly and told her about the war games, inviting her to join them. She flushed, then regained control of herself and grew icy. "Someone has to put a stop to you, Simon. I guess it's going to be me," she said. Kress shrugged and enjoyed a lovely meal and thought no more about her threat.

Until a week later, when a small, stout woman arrived at his door and showed him a police wristband. "We've had complaints," she said. "Do you keep a tank full of dangerous insects, Kress?"

"Not insects," he said, furious. "Come, I'll show you."

When she had seen the sandkings, she shook her head. "This will never do. What do you know about these creatures, anyway? Do you know what world they're from? Have they been cleared by the ecological board? Do you have a license for these things? We have a report that they're carnivores, possibly dangerous. We also have a report that they are semisentient. Where did you get these creatures, anyway?"

"From Wo and Shade," Kress replied.

"Never heard of them," the woman said. "Probably smuggled them in, knowing our ecologists would never approve them. No, Kress, this won't do. I'm going to confiscate this tank and have it destroyed. And you're going to have to expect a few fines as well."

Kress offered her a hundred standards to forget all about him and his sandkings.

She tsked. "Now I'll have to add attempted bribery to the charges against you."

Not until he raised the figure to two thousand standards was she willing to be persuaded. "It's not going to be easy, you know," she said. "There are forms to be altered, records to be wiped. And getting a forged license from the ecologists will be time-consuming. Not to mention dealing with the complainant. What if she calls again?"

"Leave her to me," Kress said. "Leave her to me."

He thought about it for a while. That night he made some calls.

First he got t'Etherane the Petseller. "I want to buy a dog," he said. "A puppy."

The round-faced merchant gawked at him. "A puppy? That is not like you, Simon. Why don't you come in? I have a lovely choice."

"I want a very specific *kind* of puppy," Kress said. "Take notes. I'll describe to you what it must look like."

Afterward he punched for Idi Noreddian. "Idi," he said, "I want you out here tonight with your holo equipment. I have a notion to record a sandking battle. A present for one of my friends."

The night after they made the recording, Simon Kress stayed up late. He absorbed a controversial new drama in his sensorium, fixed himself a small snack, smoked a joy stick or two, and broke out a bottle of wine. Feeling very happy with himself, he wandered into the living room, glass in hand.

The lights were out. The red glow of the terrarium made the shadows flushed and feverish. He walked over to look at his domain, curious as to how the blacks were doing in the repairs on their castle. The puppy had left it in ruins.

The restoration went well. But as Kress inspected the work through his magnifiers, he chanced to glance closely at the face. It startled him.

He drew back, blinked, took a healthy gulp of wine, and looked again.

The face on the walls was still his. But it was all wrong, all *twisted*. His cheeks were bloated and piggish, his smile was a crooked leer. He looked impossibly malevolent.

Uneasy, he moved around the tank to inspect the other castles. They were each a bit different, but ultimately all the same.

The oranges had left out most of the fine detail, but the result still seemed monstrous, crude: a brutal mouth and mindless eyes.

The reds gave him a satanic, twitching kind of smile. His mouth did odd, unlovely things at its corners.

The whites, his favorites, had carved a cruel idiot god.

Simon Kress flung his wine across the room in rage. "You *dare*," he said under his breath. "Now you won't eat for a week, you damned . . ." His voice was shrill. "I'll teach you." He had an idea. He strode out of the room, returned a moment later with an antique iron throwing-sword in his hand. It was a meter long, and the point was still sharp. Kress smiled, climbed up and moved the tank cover aside just enough to give him working room, opening one corner of the desert. He leaned down, and jabbed the sword at the white castle below him. He waved it back and forth, smashing towers and ramparts and walls. Sand and stone collapsed, burying the scrambling mobiles. A flick of his wrist obliterated the features of the insolent, insulting caricature the sandkings had made of his face. Then he poised the point of the sword above the dark mouth that opened down into the maw's chamber, and thrust with all his strength. He heard a soft, squishing sound, and met resistance. All of the mobiles trembled and collapsed. Satisfied, Kress pulled back.

He watched for a moment, wondering whether he'd killed the maw. The point of the throwing-sword was wet and slimy. But finally the white sandkings began to move again. Feebly, slowly, but they moved.

He was preparing to slide the cover back in place and move on to a second castle when he felt something crawling on his hand.

He screamed and dropped the sword, and brushed the sandking from his flesh. It fell to the carpet, and he ground it beneath his heel, crushing it thoroughly long after it was dead. It had crunched when he stepped on it. After that, trembling, he hurried to seal the tank up again, and rushed off to shower and inspect himself carefully. He boiled his clothing.

Later, after several fresh glasses of wine, he returned to the living room. He was a bit ashamed of the way the sandking had terrified him. But he was not about to open the tank again. From now on, the cover stayed sealed permanently. Still, he had to punish the others.

Kress decided to lubricate his mental processes with another glass of wine. As he finished it, an inspiration came to him. He went to the tank smiling, and made a few adjustments to the humidity controls.

By the time he fell asleep on the couch, his wine glass still in his hand, the sand castles were melting in the rain.

Kress woke to angry pounding on his door.

He sat up, groggy, his head throbbing. Wine hangovers were always the worst, he thought. He lurched to the entry chamber.

Cath m'Lane was outside. "You monster," she said, her face swollen and puffy and streaked by tears. "I cried all night, damn you. But no more, Simon, no more."

"Easy," he said, holding his head. "I've got a hangover."

She swore and shoved him aside and pushed her way into his house. The shambler came peering round a corner to see what the noise was. She spat at it and stalked into the living room, Kress trailing ineffectually after her. "Hold on," he said, "where do you . . . you can't . . ." He stopped, suddenly horror-struck. She was carrying a heavy sledgehammer in her left hand. "No," he said.

She went directly to the sandking tank. "You like the little charmers so much, Simon? Then you can live with them."

"*Cath!*" he shrieked.

Gripping the hammer with both hands, she swung as hard as she could against the side of the tank. The sound of the impact set his head to screaming, and Kress made a low blubbering sound of despair. But the plastic held.

She swung again. This time there was a *crack*, and a network of thin lines sprang into being.

Kress threw himself at her as she drew back her hammer for a third swing. They went down flailing, and rolled. She lost her grip on the hammer and tried to throttle him, but Kress wrenched free and bit her on the arm, drawing blood. They both staggered to their feet, panting.

"You should see yourself, Simon," she said grimly. "Blood dripping from your mouth. You look like one of your pets. How do you like the taste?"

"Get out," he said. He saw the throwing-sword where it had fallen the night before, and snatched it up. "Get out," he repeated, waving the sword for emphasis. "Don't go near that tank again."

She laughed at him. "You wouldn't dare," she said. She bent to pick up her hammer.

Kress shrieked at her, and lunged. Before he quite knew what was happening, the iron blade had gone clear through her abdomen. Cath m'Lane looked at him wonderingly, and down at the sword. Kress fell back whimpering. "I didn't mean . . . I only wanted . . ."

She was transfixed, bleeding, dead, but somehow she did not fall. "You monster," she managed to say, though her mouth was full of blood. And she whirled, impossibly, the sword in her, and swung with her last strength at the tank. The tortured wall shattered, and Cath m'Lane was buried beneath an avalanche of plastic and sand and mud.

Kress made small hysterical noises and scrambled up on the couch.

Sandkings were emerging from the muck on his living room floor. They were crawling across Cath's body. A few of them ventured tentatively out across the carpet. More followed.

He watched as a column took shape, a living, writhing square of sandkings, bearing something, something slimy and featureless, a piece of raw meat big as a man's head. They began to carry it away from the tank. It pulsed.

That was when Kress broke and ran.

It was late afternoon before he found the courage to return.

He had run to his skimmer and flown to the nearest city, some fifty kilometers away, almost sick with fear. But once safely away, he had found a small restaurant, put down several mugs of coffee and two antihangover tabs, eaten a full breakfast, and gradually regained his composure.

It had been a dreadful morning, but dwelling on that would solve nothing. He ordered more coffee and considered his situation with icy rationality.

Cath m'Lane was dead at his hand. Could he report it, plead that it had been an accident? Unlikely. He had run her through, after all, and he had already told that policer to leave her to him. He would have to get rid of the evidence, and hope that she had not told anyone where she was going this morning. That was probable. She could only have gotten his gift late last night. She said that she had cried all night, and she had been alone when she arrived. Very well: he had one body and one skimmer to dispose of.

That left the sandkings. They might prove more of a difficulty. No doubt they had all escaped by now. The thought of them around his house, in his bed and his clothes, infesting his food—it made his flesh crawl. He shuddered and overcame his revulsion. It really shouldn't be too hard to kill them, he reminded himself. He didn't have to account for every mobile. Just the four maws, that was all. He could do that. They were large, as he'd seen. He would find them and kill them.

Simon Kress went shopping before he flew back to his home. He bought a set of skinthins that would cover him from head to foot, several bags of poison pellets for rockjock control, and a spray canister of illegally strong pesticide. He also bought a magnalock towing device.

When he landed, he went about things methodically. First he hooked Cath's skimmer to his own with the magnalock. Searching it, he had his first piece of luck. The crystal chip with Idi Noreddian's holo of the sandking fight was on the front seat. He had worried about that.

When the skimmers were ready, he slipped into his skinthins and went inside for Cath's body.

It wasn't there.

He poked through the fast-drying sand carefully, but there was no doubt of it; the body was gone. Could she have dragged herself away? Unlikely, but Kress searched. A cursory inspection of his house turned up neither the body nor any sign of the sandkings. He did not have time for a more thorough investigation, not with the incriminating skimmer outside his front door. He resolved to try later.

Some seventy kilometers north of Kress's estate was a range of active volcanoes. He flew there, Cath's skimmer in tow. Above the glowering cone of the largest, he released the magnalock and watched it vanish in the lava below.

It was dusk when he returned to his house. That gave him pause. Briefly he considered flying back to the city and spending the night there. He put the thought aside. There was work to do. He wasn't safe yet.

He scattered the poison pellets around the exterior of his house. No one would find that suspicious. He'd always had a rockjock problem. When that task was completed, he primed the canister of pesticide and ventured back inside.

Kress went through the house room by room, turning on lights everywhere he went until he was surrounded by a blaze of artificial illumination. He paused to clean up in the living room, shoveling sand and plastic fragments back into the broken tank. The sandkings were all gone, as he'd feared. The castles were shrunken and distorted, slagged by the watery bombardment Kress had visited upon them, and what little remained was crumbling as it dried.

He frowned and searched on, canister of pest spray strapped across his shoulders.

Down in his deepest wine cellar, he came upon Cath m'Lane's corpse.

It sprawled at the foot of a steep flight of stairs, the limbs twisted as if by a fall. White mobiles were swarming all over it, and as Kress watched, the body moved jerkily across the hard-packed dirt floor.

He laughed, and twisted the illumination up to maximum. In the far corner, a squat little earthen castle and a dark hole were visible between two wine racks. Kress could make out a rough outline of his face on the cellar wall.

The body shifted once again, moving a few centimeters toward the castle. Kress had a sudden vision of the white maw waiting hungrily. It might be able to get Cath's foot in its mouth, but no more. It was too absurd. He laughed again, and started down into the cellar, finger poised on the trigger of the hose that snaked down his right arm. The sandkings—hundreds of them moving as one—deserted the body and formed up battle lines, a field of white between him and their maw.

Suddenly Kress had another inspiration. He smiled and lowered his firing hand. "Cath was always hard to swallow," he said, delighted at his wit. "Especially for one your size. Here, let me give you some help. What are gods for, after all?"

He retreated upstairs, returning shortly with a cleaver. The sandkings, patient, waited and watched while Kress chopped Cath m'Lane into small, easily digestible pieces.

Simon Kress slept in his skinthins that night, the pesticide close at hand, but he did not need it. The whites, sated, remained in the cellar, and he saw no sign of the others.

In the morning he finished cleanup in the living room. After he was through, no trace of the struggle remained except for the broken tank.

He ate a light lunch, and resumed his hunt for the missing sandkings. In full daylight, it was not too difficult. The blacks had located in his rock garden, and built a castle heavy with obsidian and quartz. The reds he found at the bottom of his long-unused swimming pool, which had partially filled with wind-blown sand over the years. He saw mobiles of both colors ranging about his grounds, many of them carrying poison pellets back to their maws. Kress decided his pesticide was unnecessary. No use risking a fight when he could just let the poison do its work. Both maws should be dead by evening.

That left only the burnt-orange sandkings unaccounted for. Kress circled his estate several times, in ever-widening spirals, but found no trace of them. When he began to sweat in his skinthins—it was a hot, dry day—he decided it was not important. If they were out here, they were probably eating the poison pellets along with the reds and blacks.

He crunched several sandkings underfoot, with a certain degree of satisfaction, as he walked back to the house. Inside he removed his skinthins, settled down to a delicious meal, and finally began to relax. Everything was under control. Two of the maws would soon be defunct, the third was safely located ·/here he could dispose of it after it had served his purposes, and he had no doubt that he would find the fourth. As for Cath, all trace of her visit had been obliterated.

His reverie was interrupted when his viewscreen began to blink at him. It was Jad

Rakkis, calling to brag about some cannibal worms he was bringing to the war games tonight.

Kress had forgotten about that, but he recovered quickly. "Oh, Jad, my pardons. I neglected to tell you. I grew bored with all that, and got rid of the sandkings. Ugly little things. Sorry, but there'll be no party tonight."

Rakkis was indignant. "But what will I do with my worms?"

"Put them in a basket of fruit and send them to a loved one," Kress said, signing off. Quickly he began calling the others. He did not need anyone arriving at his doorstep now, with the sandkings alive and about the estate.

As he was calling Idi Noreddian, Kress became aware of an annoying oversight. The screen began to clear, indicating that someone had answered at the other end. Kress flicked off.

Idi arrived on schedule an hour later. She was surprised to find the party canceled, but perfectly happy to share an evening alone with Kress. He delighted her with his story of Cath's reaction to the holo they had made together. While telling it, he managed to ascertain that she had not mentioned the prank to anyone. He nodded, satisfied, and refilled their wine glasses. Only a trickle was left. "I'll have to get a fresh bottle," he said. "Come with me to my wine cellar, and help me pick out a good vintage. You've always had a better palate than I."

She came along willingly enough, but balked at the top of the stairs when Kress opened the door and gestured for her to precede him. "Where are the lights?" she said. "And that smell—what's that peculiar smell, Simon?"

When he shoved her, she looked briefly startled. She screamed as she tumbled down the stairs. Kress closed the door and began to nail it shut with the boards and air-hammer he had left for that purpose. As he was finishing, he heard Idi groan. "I'm hurt," she called. "Simon, what is this?" Suddenly she squealed, and shortly after that the screaming started.

It did not cease for hours. Kress went to his sensorium and dialed up a saucy comedy to blot it out of his mind.

When he was sure she was dead, Kress flew her skimmer north to his volcanoes and discarded it. The magnalock was proving a good investment.

Odd scrabbling noises were coming from beyond the wine cellar door the next morning when Kress went down to check it out. He listened for several uneasy moments, wondering if Idi Noreddian could possibly have survived and be scratching to get out. It seemed unlikely; it had to be the sandkings. Kress did not like the implications of that. He decided that he would keep the door sealed, at least for the moment, and went outside with a shovel to bury the red and black maws in their own castles.

He found them very much alive.

The black castle was glittering with volcanic glass, and sandkings were all over it, repairing and improving. The highest tower was up to his waist, and on it was a hideous caricature of his face. When he approached, the blacks halted in their labors, and formed up into two threatening phalanxes. Kress glanced behind him and saw others closing off his escape. Startled, he dropped the shovel and sprinted out of the trap, crushing several mobiles beneath his boots.

The red castle was creeping up the walls of the swimming pool. The maw was safely settled in a pit, surrounded by sand and concrete and battlements. The reds crept all over the bottom of the pool. Kress watched them carry a rockjock and a large lizard into the castle. He stepped back from the poolside, horrified, and felt something crunch. Looking down, he saw three mobiles climbing up his leg. He brushed them off and stamped them to death, but others were approaching quickly. They were larger than he remembered. Some were almost as big as his thumb.

He ran. By the time he reached the safety of the house, his heart was racing and he was short of breath. The door closed behind him, and Kress hurried to lock it. His house was supposed to be pest-proof. He'd be safe in here.

A stiff drink steadied his nerve. So poison doesn't faze them, he thought. He should have known. Wo had warned him that the maw could eat anything. He would have to use the pesticide. Kress took another drink for good measure, donned his skinthins, and strapped the canister to his back. He unlocked the door.

Outside, the sandkings were waiting.

Two armies confronted him, allied against the common threat. More than he could have guessed. The damned maws must be breeding like rockjocks. They were everywhere, a creeping sea of them.

Kress brought up the hose and flicked the trigger. A gray mist washed over the nearest rank of sandkings. He moved his hand side to side.

Where the mist fell, the sandkings twitched violently and died in sudden spasms. Kress smiled. They were no match for him. He sprayed in a wide arc before him and stepped forward confidently over a litter of black and red bodies. The armies fell back. Kress advanced, intent on cutting through them to their maws.

All at once the retreat stopped. A thousand sandkings surged toward him.

Kress had been expecting the counterattack. He stood his ground, sweeping his misty sword before him in great looping strokes. They came at him and died. A few got through; he could not spray everywhere at once. He felt them climbing up his legs, sensed their mandibles biting futilely at the reinforced plastic of his skinthins. He ignored them, and kept spraying.

Then he began to feel soft impacts on his head and shoulders.

Kress trembled and spun and looked up above him. The front of his house was alive with sandkings. Blacks and reds, hundreds of them. They were launching themselves into the air, raining down on him. They fell all around him. One landed on his faceplate, its mandibles scraping at his eyes for a terrible second before he plucked it away.

He swung up his hose and sprayed the air, sprayed the house, sprayed until the airborne sandkings were all dead or dying. The mist settled back on him, making him cough. He coughed, and kept spraying. Only when the front of the house was clean did Kress turn his attention back to the ground.

They were all around him, on him, dozens of them scurrying over his body, hundreds of others hurrying to join them. He turned the mist on them. The hose went dead. Kress heard a loud *hiss* and the deadly fog rose in a great cloud from between his shoulders, cloaking him, choking him, making his eyes burn and blur. He felt for the hose, and his hand came away covered with dying sandkings. The hose was severed; they'd eaten it through. He was surrounded by a shroud of pesticide, blinded. He stumbled and screamed, and began to run back to the house, pulling sandkings from his body as he went.

Inside, he sealed the door and collapsed on the carpet, rolling back and forth until he was sure he had crushed them all. The canister was empty by then, hissing feebly. Kress stripped off his skinthins and showered. The hot spray scalded him and left his skin reddened and sensitive, but it made his flesh stop crawling.

He dressed in his heaviest clothing, thick workpants and leathers, after shaking them out nervously. "Damn," he kept muttering, "damn." His throat was dry. After searching the entry hall thoroughly to make certain it was clean, he allowed himself to sit and pour a drink. "Damn," he repeated. His hand shook as he poured, slopping liquor on the carpet.

The alcohol settled him, but it did not wash away the fear. He had a second drink, and went to the window furtively. Sandkings were moving across the thick plastic pane. He shuddered and retreated to his communications console. He had to get help, he thought wildly. He would punch through a call to the authorities, and policers would come out with flamethrowers and . . .

Simon Kress stopped in mid-call, and groaned. He couldn't call in the police. He would have to tell them about the whites in his cellar, and they'd find the bodies there. Perhaps the maw might have finished Cath m'Lane by now, but certainly not Idi Noreddian. He hadn't even cut her up. Besides, there would be bones. No, the police could be called in only as a last resort.

He sat at the console, frowning. His communications equipment filled a whole wall; from here he could reach anyone on Baldur. He had plenty of money, and his cunning; he had always prided himself on his cunning. He would handle this somehow.

Briefly he considered calling Wo, but he soon dismissed the idea. Wo knew too much, and she would ask questions, and he did not trust her. No, he needed someone who would do as he asked *without* questions.

His frown faded, and slowly turned into a smile. Simon Kress had contacts. He put through a call to a number he had not used in a long time.

A woman's face took shape on his viewscreen: white-haired, bland of expression, with a long hook nose. Her voice was brisk and efficient. "Simon," she said. "How is business?"

"Business is fine, Lissandra," Kress replied. "I have a job for you."

"A removal? My price has gone up since last time, Simon. It has been ten years, after all."

"You will be well paid," Kress said. "You know I'm generous. I want you for a bit of pest control."

She smiled a thin smile. "No need to use euphemisms, Simon. The call is shielded."

"No, I'm serious. I have a pest problem. Dangerous pests. Take care of them for me. No questions. Understood?"

"Understood."

"Good. You'll need . . . oh, three or four operatives. Wear heat-resistant skinthins, and equip them with flamethrowers, or lasers, something on that order. Come out to my place. You'll see the problem. Bugs, lots and lots of them. In my rock garden and the old swimming pool you'll find castles. Destroy them, kill everything inside them. Then knock on the door, and I'll show you what else needs to be done. Can you get out here quickly?"

Her face was impassive. "We'll leave within the hour."

Lissandra was true to her word. She arrived in a lean black skimmer with three operatives. Kress watched them from the safety of a second-story window. They were all faceless in dark plastic skinthins. Two of them wore portable flamethrowers, a third carried lasercannon and explosives. Lissandra carried nothing; Kress recognized her by the way she gave orders.

Their skimmer passed low overhead first, checking out the situation. The sandkings went mad. Scarlet and ebony mobiles ran everywhere, frenetic. Kress could see the castle in the rock garden from his vantage point. It stood tall as a man. Its ramparts were crawling with black defenders, and a steady stream of mobiles flowed down into its depths.

Lissandra's skimmer came down next to Kress's and the operatives vaulted out and unlimbered their weapons. They looked inhuman, deadly.

The black army drew up between them and the castle. The reds— Kress suddenly realized that he could not see the reds. He blinked. Where had they gone?

Lissandra pointed and shouted, and her two flamethrowers spread out and opened up on the black sandkings. Their weapons coughed dully and began to roar, long tongues of blue-and-scarlet fire licking out before them. Sandkings crisped and blackened and died. The operatives began to play the fire back and forth in an efficient, interlocking pattern. They advanced with careful, measured steps.

The black army burned and disintegrated, the mobiles fleeing in a thousand different directions, some back toward the castle, others toward the enemy. None reached the operatives with the flamethrowers. Lissandra's people were very professional.

Then one of them stumbled.

Or seemed to stumble. Kress looked again, and saw that the ground had given way beneath the man. Tunnels, he thought with a tremor of fear; tunnels, pits, traps. The flamer was sunk in sand up to his waist, and suddenly the ground around him seemed to erupt, and he was covered with scarlet sandkings. He dropped the flamethrower and began to claw wildly at his own body. His screams were horrible to hear.

His companion hesitated, then swung and fired. A blast of flame swallowed human and sandkings both. The screaming stopped abruptly. Satisfied, the second flamer turned back to the castle and took another step forward, and recoiled as his foot broke through the ground and vanished up to the ankle. He tried to pull it back and retreat, and the sand all around him gave way. He lost his balance and stumbled, flailing, and the sandkings were everywhere, a boiling mass of them, covering him as he writhed and rolled. His flamethrower was useless and forgotten.

Kress pounded wildly on the window, shouting for attention. "The castle! Get the castle!"

Lissandra, standing back by her skimmer, heard and gestured. Her third operative sighted with the lasercannon and fired. The beam throbbed across the grounds and sliced off the top of the castle. He brought it down sharply, hacking at the sand and stone parapets. Towers fell. Kress's face disintegrated. The laser bit into the ground, searching round and about. The castle crumbled; now it was only a heap of sand. But the black mobiles continued to move. The maw was buried too deeply; they hadn't touched her.

Lissandra gave another order. Her operative discarded the laser, primed an explosive, and darted forward. He leapt over the smoking corpse of the first flamer, landed on solid ground within Kress's rock garden, and heaved. The explosive ball landed square atop the ruins of the black castle. White-hot light seared Kress's eyes, and there was a tremendous gout of sand and rock and mobiles. For a moment dust obscured everything. It was raining sandkings and pieces of sandkings.

Kress saw that the black mobiles were dead and unmoving.

"The pool," he shouted down through the window. "Get the castle in the pool."

Lissandra understood quickly; the ground was littered with motionless blacks, but the reds were pulling back hurriedly and reforming. Her operative stood uncertain, then reached down and pulled out another explosive ball. He took one step forward, but Lissandra called him and he sprinted back in her direction.

It was all so simple then. He reached the skimmer, and Lissandra took him aloft. Kress rushed to another window in another room to watch. They came swooping in just over the pool, and the operative pitched his bombs down at the red castle from the safety of the skimmer. After the fourth run, the castle was unrecognizable, and the sandkings stopped moving.

Lissandra was thorough. She had him bomb each castle several additional times. Then he used the lasercannon, crisscrossing methodically until it was certain that nothing living could remain intact beneath those small patches of ground.

Finally they came knocking at his door. Kress was grinning manically when he let them in. "Lovely," he said, "lovely."

Lissandra pulled off the mask of her skinthins. "This will cost you, Simon. Two operatives gone, not to mention the danger to my own life."

"Of course," Kress blurted. "You'll be well paid, Lissandra. Whatever you ask, just so you finish the job."

"What remains to be done?"

"You have to clean out my wine cellar," Kress said. "There's another castle down there. And you'll have to do it without explosives. I don't want my house coming down around me."

Lissandra motioned to her operative. "Go outside and get Rajk's flamethrower. It should be intact."

He returned armed, ready, silent. Kress led them down to the wine cellar.

The heavy door was still nailed shut, as he had left it. But it bulged outward slightly, as if warped by some tremendous pressure. That made Kress uneasy, as did the silence that held reign about them. He stood well away from the door as Lissandra's operative removed his nails and planks. "Is that safe in here?" he found himself muttering, pointing at the flamethrower. "I don't want a fire, either, you know."

"I have the laser," Lissandra said. "We'll use that for the kill. The flamethrower probably won't be needed. But I want it here just in case. There are worse things than fire, Simon."

He nodded.

The last plank came free of the cellar door. There was still no sound from below. Lissandra snapped an order, and her underling fell back, took up a position behind her, and leveled the flamethrower square at the door. She slipped her mask back on, hefted the laser, stepped forward, and pulled open the door.

No motion. No sound. It was dark down there.

"Is there a light?" Lissandra asked.

"Just inside the door," Kress said. "On the right-hand side. Mind the stairs, they're quite steep."

She stepped into the door, shifted the laser to her left hand, and reached up with her right, fumbling inside for the light panel. Nothing happened. "I feel it," Lissandra said, "but it doesn't seem to . . ."

Then she was screaming, and she stumbled backward. A great white sandking had clamped itself around her wrist. Blood welled through her skinthins where its mandibles had sunk in. It was fully as large as her hand.

Lissandra did a horrible little jig across the room and began to smash her hand against the nearest wall. Again and again and again. It landed with a heavy, meaty thud. Finally the sandking fell away. She whimpered and fell to her knees. "I think my fingers are broken," she said softly. The blood was still flowing freely. She had dropped the laser near the cellar door.

"I'm not going down there," her operative announced in clear firm tones.

Lissandra looked up at him. "No," she said. "Stand in the door and flame it all. Cinder it. Do you understand?"

He nodded.

Simon Kress moaned. "My *house*," he said. His stomach churned. The white sandking had been so *large*. How many more were down there? "Don't," he continued. "Leave it alone. I've changed my mind. Leave it alone."

Lissandra misunderstood. She held out her hand. It was covered with blood and greenish-black ichor. "Your little friend bit clean through my glove, and you saw what it took to get it off. I don't care about your house, Simon. Whatever is down there is going to die."

Kress hardly heard her. He thought he could see movement in the shadows beyond the cellar door. He imagined a white army bursting forth, all as large as the sandking that had attacked Lissandra. He saw himself being lifted by a hundred tiny arms, and dragged down into the darkness where the maw waited hungrily. He was afraid. "Don't," he said.

They ignored him.

Kress darted forward, and his shoulder slammed into the back of Lissandra's operative just as the man was bracing to fire. The operative grunted, lost his balance, and pitched forward into the black. Kress listened to him fall down the stairs. Afterward there were other noises; scuttlings and snaps and soft squishing sounds.

Kress swung around to face Lissandra. He was drenched in cold sweat, but a sickly kind of excitement was on him. It was almost sexual.

Lissandra's calm cold eyes regarded him through her mask. "What are you doing?" she demanded as Kress picked up the laser she had dropped. "*Simon!*"

"Making a peace," he said, giggling. "They won't hurt god, no, not so long as god is good and generous. I was cruel. Starved them. I have to make up for it now, you see."

"You're insane," Lissandra said. It was the last thing she said. Kress burned a hole in her chest big enough to put his arm through. He dragged the body across the floor and rolled it down the cellar stairs. The noises were louder; chitinous clackings and scrapings and echoes that were thick and liquid. Kress nailed up the door once again.

As he fled, he was filled with a deep sense of contentment that coated his fear like a layer of syrup. He suspected it was not his own.

He planned to leave his home, to fly to the city and take a room for a night, or perhaps for a year. Instead Kress started drinking. He was not quite sure why. He drank steadily for hours, and retched it all up violently on his living room carpet. At some point he fell asleep. When he woke, it was pitch-dark in the house.

He cowered against the couch. He could hear *noises*. Things were moving in the walls. They were all around him. His hearing was extraordinarily acute. Every little creak was the footstep of a sandking. He closed his eyes and waited, expecting to feel their terrible touch, afraid to move lest he brush against one.

Kress sobbed, and was very still.

After a while, nothing happened.

He opened his eyes again. He trembled. Slowly the shadows began to soften and dissolve. Moonlight was filtering through the high windows. His eyes adjusted.

The living room was empty. Nothing there, nothing, nothing. Only his drunken fears.

Simon Kress steeled himself, and rose, and went to a light.

Nothing there. The room was quiet, deserted.

He listened. Nothing. No sound. Nothing in the walls. It had all been his imagination, his fear.

The memories of Lissandra and the thing in the cellar returned to him unbidden. Shame and anger washed over him. Why had he done that? He could have helped her burn it out, kill it. *Why* . . . he knew why. The maw had done it to him, put fear in him.

Wo had said it was psionic, even when it was small. And now it was large, so large. It had feasted on Cath, and Idi, and now it had two more bodies down there. It would keep growing. And it had learned to like the taste of human flesh, he thought.

He began to shake, but he took control of himself again and stopped. It wouldn't hurt him, he was god, the whites had always been his favorites.

He remembered how he had stabbed it with his throwing-sword. That was before Cath came. Damn her anyway.

He couldn't stay here. The maw would grow hungry again. Large as it was, it wouldn't take long. Its appetite would be terrible. What would it do then? He had to get away, back to the safety of the city while it was still contained in his wine cellar. It was only plaster and hard-packed earth down there, and the mobiles could dig and tunnel. When they got free . . . Kress didn't want to think about it.

He went to his bedroom and packed. He took three bags. Just a single change of clothing, that was all he needed; the rest of the space he filled with his valuables, with jewelry and art and other things he could not bear to lose. He did not expect to return.

His shambler followed him down the stairs, staring at him from its baleful glowing eyes. It was gaunt. Kress realized that it had been ages since he had fed it. Normally it could take care of itself, but no doubt the pickings had grown lean of late. When it tried to clutch at his leg, he snarled at it and kicked it away, and it scurried off, offended.

Kress slipped outside, carrying his bags awkwardly, and shut the door behind him.

For a moment he stood pressed against the house, his heart thudding in his chest. Only a few meters between him and his skimmer. He was afraid to take them. The moonlight was bright, and the front of his house was a scene of carnage. The bodies of Lissandra's two flamers lay where they had fallen, one twisted and burned, the other swollen beneath a mass of dead sandkings. And the mobiles, the black and red mobiles, they were all around him. It was an effort to remember that they were dead. It was almost as if they were simply waiting, as they had waited so often before.

Nonsense, Kress told himself. More drunken fears. He had seen the castles blown apart. They were dead, and the white maw was trapped in his cellar. He took several deep and deliberate breaths, and stepped forward onto the sandkings. They crunched. He ground them into the sand savagely. They did not move.

Kress smiled, and walked slowly across the battleground, listening to the sounds, the sounds of safety.

Crunch. Crackle. Crunch.

He lowered his bags to the ground and opened the door to his skimmer.

Something moved from shadow into light. A pale shape on the seat of his skimmer. It was as long as his forearm. Its mandibles clacked together softly, and it looked up at him from six small eyes set all around its body.

Kress wet his pants and backed away slowly.

There was more motion from inside the skimmer. He had left the door open. The sandking emerged and came toward him, cautiously. Others followed. They had been hiding beneath his seats, burrowed into the upholstery. But now they emerged. They formed a ragged ring around the skimmer.

Kress licked his lips, turned, and moved quickly to Lissandra's skimmer.

He stopped before he was halfway there. Things were moving inside that one too. Great maggoty things half-seen by the light of the moon.

Kress whimpered and retreated back toward the house. Near the front door, he looked up.

He counted a dozen long white shapes creeping back and forth across the walls of the building. Four of them were clustered close together near the top of the unused belfry where the carrion hawk had once roosted. They were carving something. A face. A very recognizable face.

Simon Kress shrieked and ran back inside.

A sufficient quantity of drink brought him the easy oblivion he sought. But he woke. Despite everything, he woke. He had a terrific headache, and he smelled, and he was hungry. Oh so very hungry. He had never been so hungry.

Kress knew it was not his *own* stomach hurting.

A white sandking watched him from atop the dresser in his bedroom, its antennae moving faintly. It was as big as the one in the skimmer the night before. He tried not to shrink away. "I'll . . . I'll feed you," he said to it. "I'll feed you." His mouth was horribly dry, sandpaper dry. He licked his lips and fled from the room.

The house was full of sandkings; he had to be careful where he put his feet. They all seemed busy on errands of their own. They were making modifications in his house, burrowing into or out of his walls, carving things. Twice he saw his own likeness staring out at him from unexpected places. The faces were warped, twisted, livid with fear.

He went outside to get the bodies that had been rotting in the yard, hoping to appease the white maw's hunger. They were gone, both of them. Kress remembered how easily the mobiles could carry things many times their own weight.

It was terrible to think that the maw was *still* hungry after all of that.

When Kress reentered the house, a column of sandkings was wending its way down the stairs. Each carried a piece of his shambler. The head seemed to look at him reproachfully as it went by.

Kress emptied his freezers, his cabinets, everything, piling all the food in the house in the center of his kitchen floor. A dozen whites waited to take it away. They avoided the frozen food, leaving it to thaw in a great puddle, but they carried off everything else.

When all the food was gone, Kress felt his own hunger pangs abate just a bit, though he had not eaten a thing. But he knew the respite would be short-lived. Soon the maw would be hungry again. He had to feed it.

Kress knew what to do. He went to his communicator. "Malada," he began casually when the first of his friends answered, "I'm having a small party tonight. I realize this is terribly short notice, but I hope you can make it. I really do."

He called Jad Rakkis next, and then the others. By the time he had finished, nine of them had accepted his invitation. Kress hoped that would be enough.

Kress met his guests outside—the mobiles had cleaned up remarkably quickly, and the grounds looked almost as they had before the battle—and walked them to his front door. He let them enter first. He did not follow.

When four of them had gone through, Kress finally worked up his courage. He closed the door behind his latest guest, ignoring the startled exclamations that soon turned into shrill gibbering, and sprinted for the skimmer the man had arrived in. He slid in safely, thumbed the startplate, and swore. It was programmed to lift only in response to its owner's thumbprint, of course.

Jad Rakkis was the next to arrive. Kress ran to his skimmer as it set down, and seized Rakkis by the arm as he was climbing out. "Get back in, quickly," he said, pushing. "Take me to the city. Hurry, Jad. *Get out of here!*"

But Rakkis only stared at him, and would not move. "Why, what's wrong, Simon? I don't understand. What about your party?"

And then it was too late, because the loose sand all around them was stirring, and the red eyes were staring at them, and the mandibles were clacking. Rakkis made a choking sound, and moved to get back in his skimmer, but a pair of mandibles snapped shut about his ankle, and suddenly he was on his knees. The sand seemed to boil with subterranean activity. Jad thrashed and cried terribly as they tore him apart. Kress could hardly bear to watch.

After that, he did not try to escape again. When it was all over, he cleaned out what remained in his liquor cabinet, and got extremely drunk. It would be the last time he would enjoy that luxury, he knew. The only alcohol remaining in the house was stored down in the wine cellar.

Kress did not touch a bite of food the entire day, but he fell asleep feeling bloated, sated at last, the awful hunger vanquished. His last thoughts before the nightmares took him were on who he could ask out tomorrow.

Morning was hot and dry. Kress opened his eyes to see the white sandking on his dresser again. He shut them again quickly, hoping the dream would leave him. It did not, and he could not go back to sleep, and soon he found himself staring at the thing.

He stared for almost five minutes before the strangeness of it dawned on him; the sandking was not moving.

The mobiles could be preternaturally still, to be sure. He had seen them wait and watch a thousand times. But always there was some motion about them; the mandibles clacked, the legs twitched, the long fine antennae stirred and swayed.

But the sandking on his dresser was completely still.

Kress rose, holding his breath, not daring to hope. Could it be dead? Could something have killed it? He walked across the room.

The eyes were glassy and black. The creature seemed swollen, somehow; as if it were soft and rotting inside, filling up with gas that pushed outward at the plates of white armor.

Kress reached out a trembling hand and touched it.

It was warm; hot even, and growing hotter. But it did not move.

He pulled his hand back, and as he did, a segment of the sandking's white exoskeleton fell away from it. The flesh beneath was the same color, but softer-looking, swollen and feverish. And it almost seemed to throb.

Kress backed away, and ran to the door.

Three more white mobiles lay in his hall. They were all like the one in his bedroom.

He ran down the stairs, jumping over sandkings. None of them moved. The house was full of them, all dead, dying, comatose, whatever. Kress did not care what was wrong with them. Just so they could not move.

He found four of them inside his skimmer. He picked them up one by one, and threw them as far as he could. Damned monsters. He slid back in, on the ruined half-eaten seats, and thumbed the startplate.

Nothing happened.

Kress tried again, and again. Nothing. It wasn't fair. This was *his* skimmer, it ought to start, why wouldn't it lift, he didn't understand.

Finally he got out and checked, expecting the worst. He found it. The sandkings had torn apart his gravity grid. He was trapped. He was still trapped.

Grimly Kress marched back into the house. He went to his gallery and found the antique axe that had hung next to the throwing sword he had used on Cath m'Lane. He set to work. The sandkings did not stir even as he chopped them to pieces. But they splattered when he made the first cut, the bodies almost bursting. Inside was awful; strange half-formed organs, a viscous reddish ooze that looked almost like human blood, and the yellow ichor.

Kress destroyed twenty of them before he realized the futility of what he was doing. The mobiles were nothing, really. Besides, there were so *many* of them. He could work for a day and night and still not kill them all.

He had to go down into the wine cellar and use the axe on the maw.

Resolute, he started down. He got within sight of the door, and stopped.

It was not a door anymore. The walls had been eaten away, so the hole was twice the size it had been, and round. A pit, that was all. There was no sign that there had ever been a door nailed shut over that black abyss.

A ghastly choking fetid odor seemed to come from below.

And the walls were wet and bloody and covered with patches of white fungus.

And worst, it was *breathing*.

Kress stood across the room and felt the warm wind wash over him as it exhaled, and he tried not to choke, and when the wind reversed direction, he fled.

Back in the living room, he destroyed three more mobiles, and collapsed. What was *happening?* He didn't understand.

Then he remembered the only person who might understand. Kress went to his communicator again, stepped on a sandking in his haste, and prayed fervently that the device still worked.

When Jala Wo answered, he broke down and told her everything.

She let him talk without interruption, no expression save for a slight frown on her gaunt, pale face. When Kress had finished, she said only, "I ought to leave you there."

Kress began to blubber. "You can't. Help me. I'll pay . . ."

"I ought to," Wo repeated, "but I won't."

"Thank you," Kress said. "Oh, thank . . ."

"Quiet," said Wo. "Listen to me. This is your own doing. Keep your sandkings well, and they are courtly ritual warriors. You turned yours into something else, with starvation and torture. You were their god. You made them what they are. That maw in your cellar is sick, still suffering from the wound you gave it. It is probably insane. Its behavior is . . . unusual.

"You have to get out of there quickly. The mobiles are not dead, Kress. They are dormant. I told you the exoskeleton falls off when they grow larger. Normally, in fact, it falls off much earlier. I have never heard of sandkings growing as large as yours while still in the insectoid stage. It is another result of crippling the white maw, I would say. That does not matter.

"What matters is the metamorphosis your sandkings are now undergoing. As the maw grows, you see, it gets progressively more intelligent. Its psionic powers strengthen, and its mind becomes more sophisticated, more ambitious. The armored mobiles are useful enough when the maw is tiny and only semisentient, but now it needs better servants, bodies with more capabilities. Do you understand? The mobiles are all going to give birth to a new breed of sandking. I can't say exactly what it will look like. Each maw designs its own, to fit its perceived needs and desires. But it will be biped, with four arms, and opposable thumbs. It will be able to construct and operate advanced machinery. The individual sandkings will not be sentient. But the maw will be very sentient indeed."

Simon Kress was gaping at Wo's image on the viewscreen. "Your workers," he said, with an effort. "The ones who came out here . . . who installed the tank . . ."

Jala Wo managed a faint smile. "Shade," she said.

"Shade is a sandking," Kress repeated numbly. "And you sold me a tank of . . . of . . . infants, ah . . ."

"Do not be absurd," Wo said. "A first-stage sandking is more like a sperm than an infant. The wars temper and control them in nature. Only one in a hundred reaches second stage. Only one in a thousand achieves the third and final plateau, and becomes like Shade. Adult sandkings are not sentimental about the small maws. There are too many of them, and their mobiles are pests." She sighed. "And all this talk wastes time. That white sandking is going to waken to full sentience soon. It is not going to need you any longer, and it hates you, and it will be very hungry. The transformation is taxing. The maw must eat enormous amounts both before and after. So you have to get out of there. Do you understand?"

"I *can't*," Kress said. "My skimmer is destroyed, and I can't get any of the others to start. I don't know how to reprogram them. Can you come out for me?"

"Yes," said Wo. "Shade and I will leave at once, but it is more than two hundred kilometers from Asgard to you, and there is equipment we will need to deal with the deranged sandking you've created. You cannot wait there. You have two feet. Walk. Go due east, as near as you can determine, as quickly as you can. The land out there is pretty desolate. We can find you easily with an aerial search, and you'll be safely away from the sandkings. Do you understand?"

"Yes," said Simon Kress. "Yes, oh, yes."

They signed off, and he walked quickly toward the door. He was halfway there when he heard the noise; a sound halfway between a pop and a crack.

One of the sandkings had split open. Four tiny hands covered with pinkish-yellow blood came up out of the gap, and began to push the dead skin aside.

Kress began to run.

He had not counted on the heat.

The hills were dry and rocky. Kress ran from the house as quickly as he could, ran until his ribs ached and his breath was coming in gasps. Then he walked, but as soon as he had recovered he began to run again. For almost an hour he ran and walked, ran and walked, beneath the fierce hot sun. He sweated freely, and wished that he had thought to bring some water, and he watched the sky in hopes of seeing Wo and Shade.

He was not made for this. It was too hot, and too dry, and he was in no condition. But he kept himself going with the memory of the way the maw had breathed, and the thought of the wriggling little things that by now were surely crawling all over his house. He hoped Wo and Shade would know how to deal with them.

He had his own plans for Wo and Shade. It was all their fault, Kress had decided, and they would suffer for it. Lissandra was dead, but he knew others in her profession. He would have his revenge. He promised himself that a hundred times as he struggled and sweated his way east.

At least he hoped it was east. He was not that good at directions, and he wasn't certain which way he had run in his initial panic, but since then he had made an effort to bear due east, as Wo had suggested.

When he had been running for several hours, with no sign of rescue, Kress began to grow certain that he had gone wrong.

When several more hours passed, he began to grow afraid. What if Wo and Shade could not find him? He would die out here. He hadn't eaten in two days, he was weak and frightened, his throat was raw for want of water. He couldn't keep going. The sun was sinking now, and he'd be completely lost in the dark. What was wrong? Had the sandkings eaten Wo and Shade? The fear was on him again, filling him, and with it a great thirst and a terrible hunger. But Kress kept going. He stumbled now when he tried to run, and twice he fell. The second time he scraped his hand on a rock, and it came away bloody. He sucked at it as he walked, and worried about infection.

The sun was on the horizon behind him. The ground grew a little cooler, for which

Kress was grateful. He decided to walk until last light and settle in for the night. Surely he was far enough from the sandkings to be safe, and Wo and Shade would find him come morning.

When he topped the next rise, he saw the outline of a house in front of him.

It wasn't as big as his own house, but it was big enough. It was habitation, safety. Kress shouted and began to run toward it. Food and drink, he had to have nourishment, he could taste the meal now. He was aching with hunger. He ran down the hill toward the house, waving his arms and shouting to the inhabitants. The light was almost gone now, but he could still make out a half-dozen children playing in the twilight. "Hey there," he shouted. "Help, help."

They came running toward him.

Kress stopped suddenly. "No," he said, "Oh, no. Oh, no." He backpedaled, slipped on the sand, got up, and tried to run again. They caught him easily. They were ghastly little things with bulging eyes and dusky-orange skin. He struggled, but it was useless. Small as they were, each of them had four arms, and Kress had only two.

They carried him toward the house. It was a sad, shabby house built of crumbling sand, but the door was quite large, and dark, and it breathed. That was terrible, but it was not the thing that set Simon Kress to screaming. He screamed because of the others, the little orange children who came crawling out from the castle, and watched impassively as he passed.

All of them had his face.

Arthur Machen (1863–1947)

The Great God Pan

Arthur Machen is one of the greatest writers of supernatural horror in the English language. The *Penguin Encyclopedia of Horror and the Supernatural* calls him "one of supernatural fantasy's greatest stylists; with the eye of a visionary and a language that is, at times, truly incantatory, he reveals the wonder—and terror—lying hidden behind everyday scenes." He never wrote a ghost story. Philip Van Doren Stern said, "Machen dealt with the elemental forces of evil, with spells that outlast time, and with the malign powers of folklore and fairy tale." His most important books are *The Great God Pan and The Inmost Light* (1894), *The Three Imposters* (1895), *The House of Souls* (1906), and his selected *Tales of Horror and the Supernatural* (1949). His "The White People" (1899) was a seminal influence on H. P. Lovecraft, and Helen Vaughan of "The Great God Pan" inspired the femme fatale in Peter Straub's *Ghost Story* (1979). Machen's influence is widespread, though his stories are infrequently reprinted today. "The Great God Pan" was a cause célèbre when it appeared—it certainly horrified the critics—and was one of the works of fiction that gave the 1890s a reputation for decadence. A tale of science gone awry, it descends from Mary Shelley and Robert Louis Stevenson, but introduces Machen's unique vision and lush, lurid style. It is Machen's most famous story and shows him at the start of his career already a master of horror.

I   The Experiment

"I am glad you came, Clarke; very glad indeed. I was not sure you could spare the time."

"I was able to make arrangements for a few days; things are not very lively just now. But have you no misgivings, Raymond? Is it absolutely safe?"

The two men were slowly pacing the terrace in front of Dr. Raymond's house. The sun still hung above the western mountain line, but it shone with a dull red glow that cast no shadows, and all the air was quiet; a sweet breath came from the great wood on the hillside above, and with it, at intervals, the soft murmuring call of the wild doves. Below, in the long lovely valley, the river wound in and out between the lonely hills, and, as the sun hovered and vanished into the west, a faint mist, pure white, began to rise from the banks. Dr. Raymond turned sharply to his friend.

"Safe? Of course it is. In itself the operation is a perfectly simple one; any surgeon could do it."

"And there is no danger at any other stage?"

"None; absolutely no physical danger whatever, I give you my word. You are always timid, Clarke, always; but you know my history. I have devoted myself to transcendental medicine for the last twenty years. I have heard myself called quack and charlatan and impostor, but all the while I knew I was on the right path. Five years ago I reached the goal, and since then every day has been a preparation for what we shall do tonight."

"I should like to believe it is all true." Clarke knit his brows, and looked doubtfully at Dr. Raymond. "Are you perfectly sure, Raymond, that your theory is not a phantasmagoria—a splendid vision, certainly, but a mere vision after all?"

Dr. Raymond stopped in his walk and turned sharply. He was a middle-aged man, gaunt and thin, of a pale yellow complexion, but as he answered Clarke and faced him, there was a flush on his cheek.

"Look about you, Clarke. You see the mountain, and hill following after hill, as wave on wave, you see the woods and orchards, the fields of ripe corn, and the meadows reaching to the reed beds by the river. You see me standing here beside you, and hear my voice; but I tell you that all these things—yes, from that star that has just shone out in the sky to the solid ground beneath our feet—I say that all these are but dreams and shadows: the shadows that hide the real world from our eyes. There *is* a real world, but it is beyond this glamour and this vision, beyond these 'chases in Arras, dreams in a career,' beyond them all as beyond a veil. I do not know whether any human being has ever lifted that veil; but I do know, Clarke, that you and I shall see it lifted this very night from before another's eyes. You may think all this strange nonsense; it may be strange, but it is true, and the ancients knew what lifting the veil means. They called it seeing the god Pan."

Clarke shivered; the white mist gathering over the river was chilly.

"It is wonderful indeed," he said. "We are standing on the brink of a strange world, Raymond, if what you say is true. I suppose the knife is absolutely necessary?"

"Yes; a slight lesion in the grey matter, that is all; a trifling rearrangement of certain cells, a microscopical alteration that would escape the attention of ninety-nine brain specialists out of a hundred. I don't want to bother you with 'shop,' Clarke; I might give you a mass of technical detail which would sound very imposing, and would leave you as enlightened as you are now. But I suppose you have read, casually, in out-of-the-way corners of your paper, that immense strides have been made recently in the physiology of the brain. I saw a paragraph the other day about Digby's theory, and Browne Faber's discoveries. Theories and discoveries! Where they are standing now, I stood fifteen years ago, and I need not tell you that I have not been standing still for the last fifteen years. It will be enough if I say that five years ago I made the discovery to which I alluded when I said that then I reached the goal. After years of labour, after years of toiling and groping in the dark, after days and nights of disappointment and sometimes of despair, in which I used now and then to tremble and grow cold with the thought that perhaps there were others seeking for what I sought, at last, after so long, a pang of sudden joy thrilled my soul, and I knew the long journey was at an end. By what seemed then and still seems a chance, the suggestion of a moment's idle thought followed up upon familiar lines and paths that I had tracked a hundred times already, the great truth burst upon me, and I saw, mapped out in lines of light, a whole world, a sphere unknown; continents and islands, and great oceans in which no ship has sailed (to my belief) since Man first lifted up his eyes and beheld the sun, and the stars of heaven, and the quiet earth beneath. You will think all this high-flown language, Clarke, but it is hard to be literal. And yet; I do not know whether what I am hinting at cannot be set forth in plain and homely terms. For instance, this world of ours is pretty well girded now with the telegraph wires and cables; thought, with something less than the speed of thought, flashes from sunrise to sunset, from north to south, across the floods and the desert places. Suppose that an electrician of today were suddenly to perceive that he and his friends have merely been playing with pebbles and mistaking them for the foundations of the world; suppose that such a man saw uttermost space lie open before the current, and words of men flash forth to the sun and beyond the sun into the systems beyond, and the voices of articulate-speaking men echo in the waste void that bounds our thought. As analogies go, that is a pretty good analogy of what I have done; you can understand now a little of what I felt as I stood here one evening; it was a summer evening, and the valley looked much as it does now; I stood here, and saw before me the unutterable, the unthinkable gulf that yawns profound between two worlds, the world of matter and the world of spirit; I saw the great empty deep stretch dim before me, and in that instant a bridge of light leapt from the earth to the unknown shore, and the abyss was spanned. You may look in Browne Faber's book, if you like, and you will find that to the present day men of science are unable to account for the presence, or to specify the functions of a certain group of nerve-cells in the brain. That group is, as it were, land to let, a mere waste place for fanciful theories. I am not in the position of Browne Faber and the specialists, I am perfectly instructed as to the possible functions or those nerve-centres in the scheme of things. With a touch I can bring them into play, with a touch, I say, I can set free the current, with a touch I can complete the communication between this world of sense and—we shall be able to finish the sentence later on. Yes, the knife is necessary; but think what that knife will effect. It will level utterly the solid wall of sense, and probably, for the first time since man was made, a spirit will gaze on a spirit world. Clarke, Mary will see the god Pan!"

"But you remember what you wrote to me? I thought it would be requisite that she—"

He whispered the rest into the doctor's ear.

"Not at all, not at all. That is nonsense, I assure you. Indeed, it is better as it is; I am quite certain of that."

"Consider the matter well, Raymond. It's a great responsibility. Something might go wrong; you would be a miserable man for the rest of your days."

"No, I think not, even if the worst happened. As you know, I rescued Mary from the gutter, and from almost certain starvation, when she was a child; I think her life is mine, to use as I see fit. Come, it is getting late; we had better go in."

Dr. Raymond led the way into the house, through the hall, and down a long dark passage. He took a key from his pocket and opened a heavy door, and motioned Clarke into his laboratory. It had once been a billiard-room, and was lighted by a glass dome in the centre of the ceiling, whence there still shone a sad grey light on the figure of the doctor as he lit a lamp with a heavy shade and placed it on a table in the middle of the room.

Clarke looked about him. Scarcely a foot of wall remained bare; there were shelves all around laden with bottles and phials of all shapes and colours, and at one end stood a little Chippendale bookcase. Raymond pointed to this.

"You see that Parchment Oswald Crollius? He was one of the first to show me the way, though I don't think he ever found it himself. That is a strange saying of his: 'In every grain of wheat there lies hidden the soul of a star.'"

There was not much furniture in the laboratory. The table in the centre, a stone slab with a drain in one corner, the two arm-chairs on which Raymond and Clarke were sitting; that was all, except an odd-looking chair at the furthest end of the room. Clarke looked at it, and raised his eyebrows.

"Yes, that is the chair," said Raymond. "We may as well place it in position." He got up and wheeled the chair to the light, and began raising and lowering it, letting down the seat, setting the back at various angles, and adjusting the foot-rest. It looked comfortable enough, and Clarke passed his hand over the soft green velvet, as the doctor manipulated the levers.

"Now, Clarke, make yourself quite comfortable. I have a couple of hours' work before me; I was obliged to leave certain matters to the last."

Raymond went to the stone slab, and Clarke watched him drearily as he bent over a row of phials and lit the flame under the crucible. The doctor had a small hand-lamp, shaded as the larger one, on a ledge above his apparatus, and Clarke, who sat in the shadows, looked down the great dreary room, wondering at the bizarre effects of brilliant light and undefined darkness contrasting with one another. Soon he became conscious of an odd odour, at first the merest suggestion of odour, in the room; and as it grew more decided he felt surprised that he was not reminded of the chemist's shop or the surgery. Clarke found himself idly endeavouring to analyse the sensation, and, half conscious, he began to think of a day, fifteen years ago, that he had spent in roaming through the woods and meadows near his old home. It was a burning day at the beginning of August, the heat had dimmed the outlines of all things and all distances were a faint mist, and people who observed the thermometer spoke of an abnormal register, of a temperature that was almost tropical. Strangely that wonderful hot day of the 'fifties rose up in Clarke's imagination; the sense of dazzling all-pervading sunlight seemed to blot out the shadows and the lights of the laboratory, and he felt again the heated air beating in gusts about his face, saw the shimmer rising from the turf, and heard the myriad murmur of the summer.

"I hope the smell doesn't annoy you, Clarke; there's nothing unwholesome about it. It may make you a bit sleepy, that's all."

Clarke heard the words quite distinctly, and knew that Raymond was speaking to him, but for the life of him he could not rouse himself from his lethargy. He could only think of the lonely walk he had taken fifteen years ago; it was his last look at the fields and woods he had known since he was a child, and now it all stood out in brilliant light, as a picture, before him. Above all there came to his nostrils the scent of summer, the smell of flowers mingled, and the odour of the woods, of cool shaded places, deep in the green depths, drawn forth by the sun's heat; and the scent of the good earth, lying as it were with arms stretched forth, and smiling lips, overpowered all. His fancies made him wander, as he had wandered long ago, from the fields into the wood, tracking a little path between the shining undergrowth of beech-trees; and the trickle of water dropping from the limestone rock sounded as a clear melody in the dream. Thoughts began to go astray and to mingle with other recollections; the beech alley was transformed to a path beneath ilex trees, and here and there a vine climbed from bough to bough, and sent up waving tendrils and drooped with purple grapes, and the sparse grey-green leaves of a wild olive tree stood out against the dark shadows of the ilex. Clarke, in the deep folds of dream, was conscious that the path from his father's house had led him into an undiscovered country, and he was wondering at the strangeness of it all, when suddenly, in place of the hum and murmur of the summer, an infinite silence seemed to fall on all things, and the wood was hushed, and for a moment of time he stood face to face there with a presence, that with neither man nor beast, neither the living nor the dead, but all things mingled, the form of all things but devoid of all form. And in that moment, the sacrament of body and soul was dissolved, and a voice seemed to cry "Let us go hence," and then the darkness of darkness beyond the stars, the darkness of everlasting.

When Clarke woke up with a start he saw Raymond pouring a few drops of some oily fluid into a green phial, which he stoppered tightly.

"You have been dozing," he said: "the journey must have tired you out. It is done now. I am going to fetch Mary; I shall be back in ten minutes."

Clarke lay back in his chair and wondered. It seemed as if he had but passed from one dream into another. He half expected to see the walls of the laboratory melt and disappear, and to awake in London, shuddering at his own sleeping fancies. But at last the door opened, and the doctor returned, and behind him came a girl of about seventeen, dressed all in white. She was so beautiful that Clarke did not wonder at what the doctor had written to him. She was blushing now over face and neck and arms, but Raymond seemed unmoved.

"Mary," he said, "the time has come. You are quite free. Are you willing to trust yourself to me entirely?"

"Yes, dear."

"You hear that Clarke? You are my witness. Here is the chair, Mary. It is quite easy. Just sit in it and lean back. Are you ready?"

"Yes, dear, quite ready. Give me a kiss before you begin."

The doctor stooped and kissed her mouth, kindly enough. "Now shut your eyes," he said. The girl closed her eyelids, as if she were tired, and longed for sleep, and Raymond held the green phial to her nostrils. Her face grew white, whiter than her dress: she struggled faintly, and then with the feeling of submission strong within her, crossed her arms upon her breast as a little child about to say her prayers. The bright light of the lamp beat full upon her, and Clarke watched changes fleeting over that face as the changes of the hills when the summer clouds float across the sun. And then she lay all white and still, and the doctor turned up one of her eyelids. She was quite unconscious. Raymond pressed hard on one of the levers and the chair instantly sank back. Clarke saw him cutting away a circle, like a tonsure, from her hair, and the lamp was moved nearer. Raymond took a small glittering instrument from a little case, and Clarke turned away shuddering. When he looked again the doctor was binding up the wound he had made.

"She will awake in five minutes." Raymond was still perfectly cool. "There is nothing more to be done; we can only wait."

The minutes passed slowly; they could hear a slow, heavy ticking. There was an old clock in the passage. Clarke felt sick and faint; his knees shook beneath him, he could hardly stand.

Suddenly, as they watched, they heard a long-drawn sigh, and suddenly did the colour that had vanished return to the girl's cheeks, and suddenly her eyes opened. Clarke quailed before them. They shone with an awful light, looking far away, and a great wonder fell upon her face, and her hands stretched out as if to touch what was invisible; but in an instant the wonder faded, and gave place to the most awful terror. The muscles of her face were hideously convulsed, she shook from head to foot; the soul seemed struggling and shuddering within the house of flesh. It was a horrible sight, and Clarke rushed forward, as she fell shrieking to the floor.

Three days later Raymond took Clarke to Mary's bedside. She was lying wide-awake, rolling her head from side to side, and grinning vacantly.

"Yes," said the doctor, still quite cool, "it is a great pity; she is a hopeless idiot. However, it could not be helped; and, after all, she has seen the Great God Pan."

II   Mr. Clarke's Memoirs

Mr. Clarke, the gentleman chosen by Dr. Raymond to witness the strange experiment of the god Pan, was a person in whose character caution and curiosity were oddly mingled;

in his sober moments he thought of the unusual and the eccentric with undisguised aversion, and yet, deep in his heart, there was a wide-eyed inquisitiveness with respect to all the more recondite and esoteric elements in the nature of men. The latter tendency had prevailed when he accepted Raymond's invitation, for though his considered judgment had always repudiated the doctor's theories as the wildest nonsense, yet he secretly hugged a belief in fantasy, and would have rejoiced to see that belief confirmed. The horrors that he witnessed in the dreary laboratory were to a certain extent salutary; he was conscious of being involved in an affair not altogether reputable, and for many years afterwards he clung bravely to the commonplace, and rejected all occasions of occult investigation. Indeed, on some homoeopathic principle, he for some time attended the séances of distinguished mediums, hoping that the clumsy tricks of these gentlemen would make him altogether disgusted with mysticism of every kind, but the remedy, though caustic, was not efficacious. Clarke knew that he still pined for the unseen, and little by little, the old passion began to reassert itself, as the face of Mary, shuddering and convulsed with an unknowable terror, faded slowly from his memory. Occupied all day in pursuits both serious and lucrative, the temptation to relax in the evening was too great, especially in the winter months, when the fire cast a warm glow over his snug bachelor apartment, and a bottle of some choice claret stood ready by his elbow. His dinner digested, he would make a brief pretence of reading the evening paper, but the mere catalogue of news soon palled upon him, and Clarke would find himself casting glances of warm desire in the direction of an old Japanese bureau, which stood at a pleasant distance from the hearth. Like a boy before a jam-closet, for a few minutes he would hover indecisive, but lust always prevailed, and Clarke ended by drawing up his chair, lighting a candle, and sitting down before the bureau. Its pigeon-holes and drawers teemed with documents on the most morbid subjects, and in the well reposed a large manuscript volume, in which he had painfully entered the gems of his collection. Clarke had a fine contempt for published literature; the most ghostly story ceased to interest him if it happened to be printed; his sole pleasure was in the reading, compiling, and rearranging what he called his "Memoirs to Prove the Existence of the Devil," and engaged in this pursuit the evening seemed to fly and the night appeared too short.

On one particular evening, an ugly December night, black with fog, and raw with frost, Clarke hurried over his dinner, and scarcely deigned to observe his customary ritual of taking up the paper and laying it down again. He paced two or three times up and down the room, and opened the bureau, stood still a moment, and sat down. He leant back, absorbed in one of those dreams to which he was subject, and at length drew out his book, and opened it at the last entry. There were three or four pages densely covered with Clarke's round, set penmanship, and at the beginning he had written in a somewhat larger hand:

> *Singular Narrative told me by my Friend, Dr. Phillips. He assures me that all the facts related therein are strictly and wholly True, but refuses to give either the Surnames of the Persons concerned, or the Place where these Extraordinary Events occurred.*

Mr. Clarke began to read over the account for the tenth time, glancing now and then at the pencil notes he had made when it was told him by his friend. It was one of his humours to pride himself on a certain literary ability; he thought well of his style, and took pains in arranging the circumstances in dramatic order. He read the following story:—

The persons concerned in this statement are Helen V., who, if she is still alive, must now be a woman of twenty-three, Rachel M., since deceased, who was a year younger than the above, and Trevor W., an imbecile, aged thirteen. These persons were at the period of the story inhabitants of a village on the border of Wales, a place of some importance in the time of the Roman occupation, but now a scattered hamlet, of not more than five hundred souls. It is situated on rising ground, about six miles from the sea, and is sheltered by a large and picturesque forest.

Some eleven years ago, Helen V. came to the village under rather peculiar circumstances. It is understood that she, being an orphan, was adopted in her infancy by a distant relative, who brought her up in his own house till she was twelve years old. Thinking, however, that it would be better for the child to have playmates of her own age, he advertised in several local papers for a good home in a comfortable farmhouse for a girl of twelve, and this advertisement was answered by Mr. R., a well-to-do farmer in the above-mentioned village. His references proving satisfactory, the gentleman sent his adopted daughter to Mr. R., with a letter, in which he stipulated that the girl should have a room to herself, and stated that her guardians need be at no trouble in the matter of education, as she was already sufficiently educated for the position in life which she would occupy. In fact, Mr. R. was given to understand that the girl was to be allowed to find her own occupations, and to spend her time almost as she liked. Mr. R. duly met her at the nearest station, a town some seven miles away from his house, and seems to have remarked nothing extraordinary about the child, except that she was reticent as to her former life and her adopted father. She was, however, of a very different type from the inhabitants of the village; her skin was a pale, clear olive, and her features were strongly marked, and of a somewhat foreign character. She appears to have settled down easily enough into farmhouse life, and became a favourite with the children, who sometimes went with her on her rambles in the forest, for this was her amusement. Mr. R. states that he has known her to go out by herself directly after their early breakfast, and not return till after dusk, and that, feeling uneasy at a young girl being out alone for so many hours, he communicated with her adopted father, who replied in a brief note that Helen must do as she chose. In the winter, when the forest paths are impassable, she spent most of her time in her bedroom, where she slept alone, according to the instructions of her relative. It was on one of these expeditions to the forest that the first of the singular incidents with which this girl is connected occurred, the date being about a year after her arrival at the village. The preceding winter had been remarkably severe, the snow drifting to a great depth, and the frost continuing for an unexampled period, and the summer following was as noteworthy for its extreme heat. On one of the very hottest days in this summer, Helen V. left the farmhouse for one of her long rambles in the forest, taking with her, as usual, some bread and meat for lunch. She was seen by some men in the fields making for the old Roman Road, a green causeway which traverses the highest part of the wood, and they were astonished to observe that the girl had taken off her hat, though the heat of the sun was almost tropical. As it happened, a labourer, Joseph W. by name, was working in the forest near the Roman Road, and at twelve o'clock his little son, Trevor, brought the man his dinner of bread and cheese. After the meal, the boy, who was about seven years old at the time, left his father at work, and, as he said, went to look for flowers in the wood, and the man, who could hear him shouting with delight over his discoveries, felt no uneasiness. Suddenly, however, he was horrified at hearing the most dreadful screams, evidently the result of great terror, proceeding from the direction in which his son had gone, and he hastily threw down his tools and ran to see what had happened. Tracing his path by the sound, he met the little boy, who was running headlong, and was evidently terribly frightened, and on questioning him the man at last elicited that after picking a posy of flowers he felt tired, and lay down on the grass and fell asleep. He was suddenly awakened, as he stated, by a peculiar noise, a sort of singing he called it, and on peeping through the branches he saw Helen V playing on the grass with a "strange naked man," whom he seemed unable to describe more fully. He said he felt dreadfully frightened, and ran away crying for his father. Joseph W. proceeded in the direction indicated by his son, and found Helen V. sitting on the grass in the middle of a glade or open space left by charcoal burners. He angrily charged her with frightening his little boy, but she entirely denied the accusation and laughed at the child's story of a "strange man," to which he himself did not attach much credence. Joseph W. came to the conclusion that the boy had woke up with a sudden fright, as children sometimes do, but Trevor persisted in his story, and continued in such evident distress that at last his father took him home, hoping that his mother would be able to soothe him. For many weeks, however, the boy gave his parents much anxiety; he became nervous and strange in his manner, refusing to leave the cottage by himself, and constantly alarming the household by waking in the night with cries of "The man in the wood! Father! Father!"

In course of time, however, the impression seemed to have worn off, and about three months later he accompanied his father to the house of a gentleman in the neighbourhood, for whom Joseph W. occasionally did work. The man was shown into the study, and the little boy was left sitting in the hall, and a few minutes later, while the gentleman was giving W. his instructions, they were both horrified by a piercing shriek and the sound of a fall, and rushing out they found the child lying senseless on the floor, his face contorted with terror. The doctor was immediately summoned, and after some examination he pronounced the child to be suffering from a fit, apparently produced by a sudden shock. The boy was taken to one of the bedrooms, and after some time recovered consciousness, but only to pass into a condition described by the medical man as one of violent hysteria. The doctor exhibited a strong sedative, and in the course of two hours pronounced him fit to walk home, but in passing through the hall the paroxysms of fright returned and with additional violence. The father perceived that the child was pointing at some object and heard the old cry. "The man in the wood," and looking in the direction indicated saw a stone head of grotesque appearance, which had been built into the wall above one of the doors. It seems that the owner of the house had recently made alterations in his premises, and on digging the foundation for some offices, the men had found a curious head, evidently of the Roman period, which had been placed in the hall in the manner described. The head is pronounced by the most experienced archaeologists of the district to be that of a faun or satyr.[1]

From whatever cause arising, this second shock seemed too severe for the boy Trevor, and at the present date he suffers from a weakness of intellect, which gives but little promise of amending. The matter caused a good deal of sensation at the time, and the girl Helen was closely questioned by Mr. R., but to no purpose, she steadfastly denying that she had frightened or in any way molested Trevor.

[1]Dr. Phillips tells me that he has seen the head in question, and assures me that he has never received such a vivid presentment of intense evil.

The second event with which the girl's name is connected took place about six years ago, and is of a still more extraordinary character.

At the beginning of the summer of 1882 Helen contracted a friendship of a peculiarly intimate character with Rachel M., the daughter of a prosperous farmer in the neighbourhood. This girl, who was a year younger than Helen, was considered by most people to be the prettier of the two, though Helen's features had to a great extent softened as she became older. The two girls, who were together on every available opportunity, presented a singular contrast, the one with her clear, olive skin and almost Italian appearance, and the other of the proverbial red and white of our rural districts. It must be stated that the payments made to Mr. R. for the maintenance of Helen were known in the village for their excessive liberality, and the impression was general that she would one day inherit a large sum of money from her relative. The parents of Rachel were therefore not averse from their daughter's friendship with the girl, and even encouraged the intimacy, though they now bitterly regret having done so. Helen still retained her extraordinary fondness for the forest, and on several occasions Rachel accompanied her, the two friends setting out early in the morning, and remaining in the wood till dusk. Once or twice after these excursions Mrs. M. thought her daughter's manner rather peculiar; she seemed languid and dreamy, and as it has been expressed, "different from herself," but these peculiarities seem to have been thought too trifling for remark. One evening, however, after Rachel had come home, her mother heard a noise which sounded like suppressed weeping in the girl's room, and on going in found her lying, half undressed, upon the bed, evidently in the greatest distress. As soon as she saw her mother, she exclaimed, "Ah, Mother, Mother, why did you let me go to the forest with Helen?" Mrs. M. was astonished at so strange a question, and proceeded to make inquiries. Rachel told her a wild story. She said—

Clarke closed the book with a snap, and turned his chair towards the fire. When his friend sat one evening in that very chair, and told his story, Clarke had interrupted him at a point a little subsequent to this, had cut short his words in a paroxysm of horror. "My God!" he had exclaimed, "think, think what you are saying. It is too incredible, too monstrous; such things can never be in this quiet world, where men and women live and die, and struggle, and conquer, or maybe fail, and fall down under sorrow, and grieve and suffer strange fortunes for many a year; but not this, Phillips, not such things as this. There must be some explanation, some way out of the terror. Why, man, if such a case were possible, our earth would be a nightmare."

But Phillips had told his story to the end, concluding:

"Her flight remains a mystery to this day; she vanished in broad sunlight: they saw her walking in a meadow, and a few moments later she was not there."

Clarke tried to conceive the thing again, as he sat by the fire, and again his mind shuddered and shrank back, appalled before the sight of such awful, unspeakable elements enthroned as it were, and triumphant in human flesh. Before him stretched the long dim vista of the green causeway in the forest, as his friend had described it; he saw the swaying leaves and the quivering shadows on the grass, he saw the sunlight and the flowers, and far away, far in the long distance, the two figures moved toward him. One was Rachel, but the other?

Clarke had tried his best to disbelieve it all, but at the end of the account, as he had written it in his book, he had placed the inscription:

ET DIABOLUS INCARNATUS EST.
ET HOMO FACTUS EST.

III   The City of Resurrections

"Herbert! Good God! Is it possible?"

"Yes, my name's Herbert. I think I know your face too, but I don't remember your name. My memory is very queer."

"Don't you recollect Villiers of Wadham?"

"So it is, so it is. I beg your pardon, Villiers, I didn't think I was begging of an old college friend. Good-night."

"My dear fellow, this haste is unnecessary. My rooms are close by, but we won't go there just yet. Suppose we walk up Shaftsbury Avenue a little way? But how in heaven's name have you come to this pass, Herbert?"

"It's a long story, Villiers, and a strange one too, but you can hear it if you like."

"Come on, then. Take my arm, you don't seem very strong."

The ill-assorted pair moved slowly up Rupert Street; the one in dirty, evil-looking rags, and the other attired in the regulation uniform of a man about town, trim, glossy, and eminently well-to-do. Villiers had emerged from his restaurant after an excellent dinner of many courses, assisted by an ingratiating little flask of Chianti, and, in that frame of mind which was with him almost chronic, had delayed a moment by the door, peering round in the dimly lighted street in search of those mysterious incidents and persons with which the streets of London teem in every quarter and at every hour. Villiers prided himself as a practised explorer of such obscure mazes and byways of London life, and in this unprofitable pursuit he displayed an assiduity which was worthy of more serious employment. Thus he stood beside the lamp-post surveying the passers-by with undisguised curiosity, and with that gravity only known to the systematic diner, had just enunciated in his mind the formula: "London has been called the city of encounters; it is more than that, it is the city of resurrections," when these reflections were suddenly interrupted by a piteous whine at his elbow, and a deplorable appeal for alms. He looked around in some irritation, and with a sudden shock found himself confronted with the embodied proof of his somewhat stilted fancies. There, close beside him, his face altered and disfigured by poverty and disgrace, his body barely covered by greasy ill-fitting rags, stood his old friend Charles Herbert, who had matriculated on the same day as himself, with whom he had been merry and wise for twelve revolving terms. Different occupations and varying interests had interrupted the friendship, and it was six years since Villiers had seen Herbert; and now he looked upon this wreck of a man with grief and dismay, mingled with a certain inquisitiveness as to what dreary chain of circumstance had dragged him down to such a doleful pass. Villiers felt together with compassion all the relish of the amateur in mysteries, and congratulated himself on his leisurely speculations outside the restaurant.

They walked on in silence for some time, and more than one passer-by stared in astonishment at the unaccustomed spectacle of a well-dressed man with an unmistakable beggar hanging on to his arm, and, observing this, Villiers led the way to an obscure street in Soho. Here he repeated his question.

"How on earth has it happened, Herbert? I always understood you would succeed to an excellent position in Dorsetshire. Did your father disinherit you? Surely not?"

"No, Villiers; I came into all the property at my poor father's death; he died a year after I left Oxford. He was a very good father to me, and I mourned his death sincerely enough. But you know what young men are; a few months later I came up to town and went a good deal into society. Of course I had excellent introductions, and I managed to enjoy myself very much in a harmless sort of way. I played a little, certainly, but never for heavy stakes, and the few bets I made on races brought me in money—only a few pounds, you know, but enough to pay for cigars and such petty pleasures. It was in my second season that the tide turned. Of course you have heard of my marriage?"

"No, I never heard anything about it."

"Yes, I married, Villiers. I met a girl, a girl of the most wonderful and strange beauty, at the house of some people whom I knew. I cannot tell you her age; I never knew it, but, so far as I can guess, I should think she must have been about nineteen when I made her acquaintance. My friends had come to know her at Florence; she told them she was an orphan, the child of an English father and an Italian mother, and she charmed them as she charmed me. The first time I saw her was at an evening party. I was standing by the door talking to a friend, when suddenly above the hum and babble of conversation I heard a voice which seemed to thrill to my heart. She was singing an Italian song. I was introduced to her that evening, and in three months I married Helen. Villiers, that woman, if I can call her 'woman,' corrupted my soul. The night of the wedding I found myself sitting in her bedroom in the hotel, listening to her talk. She was sitting up in bed, and I listened to her as she spoke in her beautiful voice, spoke of things which even now I would not dare whisper in blackest night, though I stood in the midst of a wilderness. You, Villiers, you may think you know life, and London, and what goes on day and night in this dreadful city; for all I can say you may have heard the talk of the vilest, but I tell you you can have no conception of what I know, not in your most fantastic, hideous dreams can you have imagined forth the faintest shadow of what I have heard— and seen. Yes, seen. I have seen the incredible, such horrors that even I myself sometime stop in the middle of the street, and ask whether it is possible for a man to hold such things and live. In a year, Villiers, I was a ruined man, in body and soul—in body and soul."

"But your property, Herbert? You had land in Dorset."

"I sold it all; the field and woods, the dear old house—everything."

"And the money?"

"She took it all from me."

"And then left you?"

"Yes; she disappeared one night. I don't know where she went, but I am sure if I saw her again it would kill me. You may think, Villiers, that I have exaggerated and talked for effect; but I have not told you half. I could tell you certain things which would convince you, but you would never know a happy day again. You would pass the rest of your life, as I pass mine, a haunted man, a man who has seen hell."

Villiers took the unfortunate man to his rooms, and gave him a meal. Herbert could eat little, and scarcely touched the glass of wine set before him. He sat moody and silent by the fire, and seemed relieved when Villiers sent him away with a small present of money.

"By the way, Herbert," said Villiers, as they parted at the door, "what was your wife's name? You said Helen, I think? Helen what?"

"The name she passed under when I met her was Helen Vaughan, but what her real name was I can't say. I don't think she had a name. No, no, not in that sense. Only human beings have names, Villiers; I can't say anymore. Good-bye; yes, I will not fail to call if I see any way in which you can help me. Good-night."

The man went out into the bitter night, and Villiers returned to his fireside. There was something about Herbert which shocked him inexpressibly; not his poor rags nor the marks which poverty had set upon his face, but rather an indefinite terror which hung about him like a mist. He had acknowledged that he himself was not devoid of blame; the woman, he had avowed, had corrupted him body and soul, and Villiers felt that this man, once his friend, had been an actor in scenes evil beyond the power of words. His story needed no confirmation: he himself was the embodied proof of it. Villiers mused curiously over the story he had heard, and wondered whether he had heard both the first and the last of it. "No," he thought, "certainly not the last, probably only the beginning. A case like this is like a nest of Chinese boxes; you open one after another and find a quainter workmanship in every box. Most likely poor Herbert is merely one of the outside boxes; there are stranger ones to follow."

Villiers could not take his mind away from Herbert and his story, which seemed to grow wilder as the night wore on. The fire began to burn low, and the chilly air of the morning crept into the room; Villiers got up with a glance over his shoulder, and shivering slightly, went to bed.

A few days later he saw at his club a gentleman of his acquaintance, named Austin, who was famous for his intimate knowledge of London life, both in its tenebrous and luminous phases. Villiers, still full of his encounter in Soho and its consequences, thought Austin might possibly be able to shed some light on Herbert's history, and so after some casual talk he suddenly put the question:

"Do you happen to know anything of a man named Herbert—Charles Herbert?"

Austin turned round sharply and stared at Villiers with some astonishment.

"Charles Herbert? Weren't you in town three years ago? No; then you have not heard of the Paul Street case? It caused a good deal of sensation at the time."

"What was the case?"

"Well, a gentleman, a man of very good position, was found dead, stark dead, in the area of a certain house in Paul Street, off Tottenham Court Road. Of course the police did not make the discovery; if you happen to be sitting up all night and have a light in your window, the constable will ring the bell, but if you happen to be lying dead in somebody's area, you will be left alone. In this instance as in many others the alarm was raised by some kind of vagabond; I don't mean a common tramp, or a public-house loafer, but a gentleman, whose business or pleasure, or both, made him a spectator of the London streets at five o'clock in the morning. This individual was, as he said, "going home," it did not appear whence or whither, and had occasion to pass through Paul Street between four and five AM. Something or other caught his eye at Number 20; he said, absurdly enough, that the house had the most unpleasant physiognomy he had ever observed, but, at any rate, he glanced down the area, and was a good deal astonished to see a man lying on the stones, his limbs all huddled together, and his face turned up. Our gentleman thought his face looked peculiarly ghastly, and so set off at a run in search of the nearest policeman. The constable was at first inclined to treat the matter lightly, suspecting common drunkenness; however, he came, and after looking at the man's face, changed his tone, quickly enough. The early bird, who had picked up this fine worm, was sent off for a doctor, and the policeman rang and knocked at the door till a slatternly servant girl came down looking more than half asleep. The constable pointed out the contents of the area to the maid, who screamed loudly enough to wake up the street, but she knew nothing of the man; had never seen him at the house, and so forth. Meanwhile the original discoverer had come back with a medical man, and the next thing was to get into the area. The gate was open, so the whole quartet stumped down the steps. The doctor hardly needed a moment's examination; he said the poor fellow had been dead for several hours, and it was then the case began to get interesting. The dead man had not been robbed, and in one of his pockets were papers identifying him as—well, as a man of good family and means, a favourite in society, and nobody's enemy, so far as could be known. I don't give his name, Villiers, because it has nothing to do with the story, and because it's no good raking up these affairs about the dead when there are no relations living. The next curious point was that the medical men couldn't agree as to how he met his death. There were some slight bruises on his shoulders, but they were so slight that it looked as if he had been pushed roughly out of the kitchen door, and not thrown over the railings from the street or even dragged down the steps. But there were positively no other marks of violence about him, certainly none that would account for his death; and when they came to the autopsy there wasn't a trace of poison of any kind. Of course the police wanted to know all about the people at Number 20, and here again, so I have heard from private sources, one or two other very curious points came out. It appears that the occupants of the house were a Mr. and Mrs. Charles Herbert; he was said to be a landed proprietor, though it struck most people that Paul Street was not exactly the place to look for county gentry. As for Mrs. Herbert, nobody seemed to know who or what she was, and, between ourselves, I fancy the divers after her history found themselves in rather strange waters. Of course they both denied knowing anything about the deceased, and in default of any evidence against them they were discharged. But some very odd things came out about them. Though it was between five and six in the morning when the dead man was removed, a large crowd had collected, and several of the neighbours ran to see what was going on. They were pretty free with their comments, by all accounts, and from these it appeared that Number 20 was in very bad odour in Paul Street. The detectives tried to trace down these rumours to some solid foundation of fact, but could not get hold of anything. People shook their heads and raised their eyebrows and thought the Herberts rather 'queer,' 'would rather not be seen going into their house,' and so on, but there was nothing tangible. The authorities were morally certain that the man met his death in some way or another in the house and was thrown out by the kitchen door, but they couldn't prove it, and the absence of any indications of violence or poisoning left them helpless. An odd case, wasn't it? But curiously enough, there's something more that I haven't told you. I happened to know one of the doctors who was consulted as to the cause of death, and some time after the inquest I met him, and asked him about it. 'Do you really mean to tell me,' I said, 'that you were baffled by the case, that you actually don't know what the man died of?' 'Pardon me,' he replied. 'I know perfectly well what caused death. Blank died of fright, of sheer, awful terror; I never saw features so hideously contorted in the entire course of my practice, and I have seen the faces of a whole host of dead.' The doctor was usually a cool customer enough, and a certain vehemence in his manner struck me, but I couldn't get anything more out of him. I suppose the Treasury didn't see their way to prosecuting the Herberts for frightening a man to death; at any rate, nothing was done, and the case dropped out of men's minds. Do you happen to know anything of Herbert?"

"Well," replied Villiers, "he was an old college friend of mine."

"You don't say so? Have you ever seen his wife?"

"No, I haven't. I have lost sight of Herbert for many years."

"It's queer, isn't it, parting with a man at the college gate or at Paddington, seeing nothing of him for years, and then finding him pop up his head in such an odd place. But I should like to have seen Mrs. Herbert; people said extraordinary things about her."

"What sort of things?"

"Well, I hardly know how to tell you. Everyone who saw her at the police court said she was at once the most beautiful woman and the most repulsive they had ever set eyes on. I have spoken to a man who saw her, and I assure you he positively shuddered as he tried to describe the woman, but he couldn't tell why. She seems to have been a sort of enigma; and I expect if that one dead man could have told tales, he would have told some uncommonly queer ones. And there you are again in another puzzle; what could a respectable country gentleman like Mr. Blank (we'll call him that if you don't mind) want in such a very queer house as Number 20? It's altogether a very odd case, isn't it?"

"It is indeed, Austin; an extraordinary case. I didn't think, when I asked you about my old friend, I should strike on such strange metal. Well, I must be off; good-day."

Villiers went away, thinking of his own conceit of the Chinese boxes; here was quaint workmanship indeed.

IV   The Discovery in Paul Street

A few months after Villiers's meeting with Herbert, Mr. Clarke was sitting, as usual, by his after-dinner hearth, resolutely guarding his fancies from wandering in the direction of the bureau. For more than a week he had succeeded in keeping away from the "Memoirs," and he cherished hopes of a complete self-reformation; but in spite of his endeavours, he could not hush the wonder and the strange curiosity that that last case he had written down had excited within him. He had put the case, or rather the outline of it, conjecturally to a scientific friend, who shook his head, and thought Clarke getting queer, and on this particular evening Clarke was making an effort to rationalize the story, when a sudden knock at his door roused him from his meditations.

"Mr. Villiers to see you, sir."

"Dear me, Villiers, it is very kind of you to look me up; I have not seen you for many months; I should think nearly a year. Come in, come in. And how are you, Villiers: Want any advice about investments?"

"No, thanks, I fancy everything I have in that way is pretty safe. No, Clarke, I have really come to consult you about a rather curious matter that has been brought under my notice of late. I am afraid you will think it all rather absurd when I tell my tale. I sometimes think so myself, and that's just why I made up my mind to come to you, as I know you're a practical man."

Mr. Villiers was ignorant of the "Memoirs to Prove the Existence of the Devil."

"Well, Villiers, I shall be happy to give you my advice, to the best of my ability. What is the nature of the case?"

"It's an extraordinary thing altogether. You know my ways; I always keep my eyes open in the streets, and in my time I have chanced upon some queer customers, and queer cases too, but this, I think, beats all. I was coming out of a restaurant one nasty winter night about three months ago: I had had a capital dinner and a good bottle of Chianti, and I stood for a moment on the pavement, thinking what a mystery there is about London streets and the companies that pass along them. A bottle of red wine encourages these fancies, Clarke, and I dare say I should have thought a page of small type, but I was cut short by a beggar who had come behind me, and was making the usual appeals. Of course I looked round, and this beggar turned out to be what was left of an old friend of mine, a man named Herbert. I asked him how he had come to such a wretched pass, and he told me. We walked up and down one of those long dark Soho streets, and there I listened to his story. He said he had married a beautiful girl, some years younger than himself, and, as he put it, she had corrupted him body and soul. He wouldn't go into details; he said he dare not, that what he had seen and heard haunted him by night and day, and when I looked in his face I knew he was speaking the truth. There was something about the man that made me shiver. I don't know why, but it was there. I gave him a little money and sent him away, and I assure you that when he was gone I gasped for breath. His presence seemed to chill one's blood."

"Isn't all this just a little fanciful, Villiers? I suppose the poor fellow had made an imprudent marriage, and, in plain English, gone to the bad."

"Well, listen to this." Villiers told Clarke the story he had heard from Austin.

"You see," he concluded, "there can be but little doubt that this Mr. Blank, whoever he was, died of sheer terror; he saw something so awful, so terrible, that it cut short his life. And what he saw, he most certainly saw in that house, which, somehow or other, had got a bad name in the neighbourhood. I had the curiosity to go and look at the place for myself. It's a saddening kind of street; the houses are old enough to be mean and dreary, but not old enough to be quaint. As far as I could see most of them are let in lodgings, furnished and unfurnished, and almost every door has three bells to it. Here and there the ground floors have been made into shops of the commonest kind; it's a dismal street in every way. I found Number 20 was to let, and I went to the agent's and got the key. Of course I should have heard nothing of the Herberts in that quarter, but I asked the man, fair and square, how long they had left the house, and whether there had been other tenants in the meanwhile. He looked at me queerly for a minute, and told me the Herberts had left immediately after the unpleasantness, as he called it, and since then the house had been empty."

Mr. Villiers paused for a moment.

"I have always been rather fond of going over empty houses; there's a sort of fascination about the desolate empty rooms, with the nails sticking in the walls, and the dust thick upon the window-sills. But I didn't enjoy going over Number 20, Paul Street. I had hardly put my foot inside the passage before I noticed a queer, heavy feeling about the air of the house. Of course all empty houses are stuffy, and so forth, but this was something quite different; I can't describe it to you, but it seemed to stop the breath. I went into the front room and the back room, and the kitchens downstairs; they were all dirty and dusty enough, as you would expect, but there was something strange about them all. I couldn't define it to you, I only know I felt queer. It was one of the rooms on the first floor, though, that was the worst. It was a largish room, and once on a time the paper must have been cheerful enough, but when I saw it, paint, paper, and everything were most doleful. But the room was full of horror; I felt my teeth grinding as I put my hand on the door, and when I went in, I thought I should have fallen fainting to the floor. However, I pulled myself together, and stood against the end wall, wondering what on earth there could be about the room to make my limbs tremble, and my heart beat as if I were at the hour of death. In one corner there was a pile of newspapers littered about on the floor, and I began looking at them; they were papers of three or four years ago, some of them half torn, and some crumpled as if they had been used for packing. I turned the whole pile over, and amongst them I found a curious drawing; I will show it you presently. But I couldn't stay in the room; I felt it was overpowering me. I was thankful to come out, safe and sound, into the open air. People stared at me as I walked along the street, and one man said I was drunk. I was staggering about from one side of the pavement to the other, and it was as much as I could do to take the key back to the agent and get home. I was in bed for a week, suffering from what my doctor called nervous shock and exhaustion. One of those days I was reading the evening paper, and happened to notice a paragraph headed: 'Starved to Death.' It was the usual style of thing; a model lodging-house in Marylebone, a door locked for several days, and a dead man in his chair when they broke in. 'The deceased,' said the paragraph, 'was known as Charles Herbert, and is believed to have been once a prosperous country gentlemen. His name was familiar to the public three years ago in connection with the mysterious death in Paul Street, Tottenham Court Road, the deceased being the tenant of the house Number 20, in the area of which a gentleman of good position was found dead under circumstances not devoid of suspicion.' A tragic ending, wasn't it? But after all, if what he told me were true, which I am sure it was, the man's life was all a tragedy, and a tragedy of a stranger sort than they put on the boards."

"And that is the story, is it?" said Clarke musingly.

"Yes, that is the story."

"Well, really, Villiers, I scarcely know what to say about it. There are, no doubt, circumstances in the case which seem peculiar, the finding of the dead man in the area of Herbert's house, for instance, and the extraordinary opinion of the physician as to the cause of death; but, after all, it is conceivable that the facts may be explained in a straightforward manner. As to your own sensations, when you went to see the house, I would suggest that they were due to a vivid imagination; you must have been brooding, in a semi-conscious way, over what you had heard. I don't exactly see what more can be said or done in the matter; you evidently think there is a mystery of some kind, but Herbert is dead; where then do you propose to look?"

"I propose to look for the woman; the woman whom he married. *She* is the mystery."

The two men sat silent by the fireside; Clarke secretly congratulating himself on having successfully kept up the character of advocate of the commonplace, and Villiers wrapt in his gloomy fancies.

"I think I will have a cigarette," he said at last, and put his hand in his pocket to feel for the cigarette-case.

"Ah!" he said, starting slightly, "I forgot I had something to show you. You remember my saying that I had found a rather curious sketch amongst the pile of old newspapers at the house in Paul Street? Here it is."

Villiers drew out a small thin parcel from his pocket. It was covered with brown paper, and secured with string, and the knots were troublesome. In spite of himself Clarke felt inquisitive; he bent forward on his chair as Villiers painfully undid the string, and unfolded the outer covering. Inside was a second wrapping of tissue, and Villiers took it off and handed the small piece of paper to Clarke without a word.

There was dead silence in the room for five minutes or more; the two men sat so still that they could hear the ticking of the tall old-fashioned clock that stood outside in the hall, and in the mind of one of them the slow monotony of sound woke up a far, far memory. He was looking intently at the small pen-and-ink sketch of the woman's head; it had evidently been drawn with great care, and by a true artist, for the woman's soul looked out of the eyes, and the lips were parted with a strange smile. Clarke gazed still at the face; it brought to his memory one summer evening long ago; he saw again the long lovely valley, the river winding between the hills, the meadows and the cornfields, the dull red sun, and the cold white mist rising from the water. He heard a voice speaking to him across the waves of many years, and saying: "Clarke, Mary will see the God Pan!" and then he was standing in the grim room beside the doctor, listening to the heavy ticking of the clock, waiting and watching, watching the figure lying on the green chair beneath the lamp-light. Mary rose up, and he looked into her eyes, and his heart grew cold within him.

"Who is this woman?" he said at last. His voice was dry and hoarse.

"That is the woman whom Herbert married."

Clarke looked again at the sketch; it was not Mary after all. There certainly was Mary's face, but there was something else, something he had not seen on Mary's features when the white-clad girl entered the laboratory with the doctor, nor at her terrible awakening, nor when she lay grinning on the bed. Whatever it was, the glance that came from those eyes, the smile on the full lips, or the expression of the whole face, Clarke shuddered before it in his inmost soul, and thought, unconsciously, of Dr. Phillip's words, "the most vivid presentment of evil I have ever seen." He turned the paper over mechanically in his hand and glanced at the back.

"Good God! Clarke, what is the matter? You are as white as death."

Villiers had started wildly from his chair, as Clarke fell back with a groan, and let the paper drop from his hands.

"I don't feel very well, Villiers, I am subject to these attacks. Pour me out a little wine; thanks, that will do. I shall feel better in a few minutes."

Villiers picked up the fallen sketch and turned it over as Clarke had done.

"You saw that?" he said. "That's how I identified it as being a portrait of Herbert's wife, or I should say his widow. How do you feel now?"

"Better, thanks, it was only a passing faintness. I don't think I quite catch your meaning. What did you say enabled you to identify the picture?"

"This word—'Helen'—written on the back. Didn't I tell you her name was Helen? Yes; Helen Vaughan."

Clarke groaned; there could be no shadow of doubt.

"Now, don't you agree with me," said Villiers, "that in the story I have told you tonight, and in the part this woman plays in it, there are some very strange points?"

"Yes, Villiers," Clarke muttered, "it is a strange story indeed; a strange story indeed. You must give me time to think it over; I may be able to help you or I may not. Must you be going now? Well, good-night, Villiers, good-night. Come and see me in the course of a week."

V   The Letter of Advice

"Do you know, Austin," said Villiers, as the two friends were pacing sedately along Picadilly one pleasant morning in May, "do you know I am convinced that what you told me about Paul Street and the Herberts is a mere episode in an extraordinary history? I may as well confess to you that when I asked you about Herbert a few months ago I had just seen him."

"You had seen him? Where?"

"He begged of me in the street one night. He was in the most pitiable plight, but I recognized the man, and I got him to tell me his history, or at least the outline of it. In brief, it amounted to this—he had been ruined by his wife."

"In what manner?"

"He would not tell me; he would only say that she had destroyed him, body and soul. The man is dead now."

"And what has become of his wife?"

"Ah, that's what I should like to know, and I mean to find her sooner or later. I know a man named Clarke, a dry fellow, in fact a man of business, but shrewd enough. You understand my meaning; not shrewd in the mere business sense of the word, but a man who really knows something about men and life. Well, I laid the case before him, and he was evidently impressed. He said it needed consideration, and asked me to come again in the course of a week. A few days later I received this extraordinary letter."

Austin took the envelope, drew out the letter, and read it curiously. It ran as follows:—

My dear Villiers,—I have thought over the matter on which you consulted me the other night, and my advice to you is this. Throw the portrait into the fire, blot

out the story from your mind. Never give it another thought, Villiers, or you will be
sorry. You will think, no doubt, that I am in possession of some secret information,
and to a certain extent that is the case. But I only know a little; I am like a traveller
who has peered over an abyss, and has drawn back in terror. What I know is
strange enough and horrible enough, but beyond my knowledge there are depths
and horrors more frightful still, more incredible than any tale told of winter nights
about the fire. I have resolved, and nothing shall shake that resolve, to explore no
whit farther, and if you value your happiness you will make the same
determination.

Come and see me by all means; but we will talk on more cheerful topics than
this.

Austin folded the letter methodically, and returned it to Villiers.

"It is certainly an extraordinary letter," he said; "what does he mean by the portrait?"

"Ah I forgot to tell you I have been to Paul Street and have made a discovery."

Villiers told his story as he had told it to Clarke, and Austin listened in silence. He seemed puzzled.

"How very curious that you should experience such an unpleasant sensation in that room!" he said at length. "I hardly gather that it was a mere matter of the imagination; a feeling of repulsion, in short."

"No, it was more physical than mental. It was as if I were inhaling at every breath some deadly fume, which seemed to penetrate to every nerve and bone and sinew of my body. I felt racked from head to foot, my eyes began to grow dim; it was like the entrance of death."

"Yes, yes, very strange, certainly. You see, your friend confesses that there is some very black story connected with this woman. Did you notice any particular emotion in him when you were telling your tale?"

"Yes, I did. He became very faint, but he assured me that it was a mere passing attack to which he was subject."

"Did you believe him?"

"I did at the time, but I don't now. He heard what I had to say with a good deal of indifference, till I showed him the portrait. It was then he was seized with the attack of which I spoke. He looked ghastly, I assure you."

"Then he must have seen the woman before. But there might be another explanation; it might have been the name, and not the face, which was familiar to him. What do you think?"

"I couldn't say. To the best of my belief it was after turning the portrait in his hands that he nearly dropped from his chair. The name, you know, was written on the back."

"Quite so. After all, it is impossible to come to any resolution in a case like this. I hate melodrama, and nothing strikes me as more commonplace and tedious than the ordinary ghost story of commerce; but really, Villiers, it looks as if there were something very queer at the bottom of all this."

The two men had, without noticing it, turned up Ashley Street, leading northward from Piccadilly. It was a long street, and rather a gloomy one, but here and there a brighter taste had illuminated the dark houses with flowers, and gay curtains, and a cheerful paint on the doors. Villiers glanced up as Austin stopped speaking, and looked at one of these houses; geraniums, red and white, drooped from every sill, and daffodil-coloured curtains were draped back from each window.

"It looks cheerful, doesn't it?" he said.

"Yes, and the inside is still more cheery. One of the pleasantest houses of the season, so I have heard. I haven't been there myself, but I've met several men who have, and they tell me it's uncommonly jovial."

"Whose house is it?"

"A Mrs. Beaumont's."

"And who is she?"

"I couldn't tell you. I have heard she comes from South America, but, after all, who she is is of little consequence. She is a very wealthy woman, there's no doubt of that, and some of the best people have taken her up. I heard she has some wonderful claret, really marvellous wine, which must have cost a fabulous sum. Lord Argentine was telling me about it; he was there last Sunday evening. He assures me he has never tasted such a wine, and Argentine, as you know, is an expert. By the way, that reminds me, she must be an oddish sort of woman, this Mrs. Beaumount. Argentine asked her how old the wine was, and what do you think she said? 'About a thousand years, I believe.' Lord Argentine thought she was chaffing him, you know, but when he laughed she said she was speaking quite seriously, and offered to show him the jar. Of course, he couldn't say anything more after that; but it seems rather antiquated for a beverage, doesn't it? Why, here we are at my rooms. Come in, won't you?"

"Thanks, I think I will. I haven't seen the curiosity-shop for some time."

It was a room furnished richly, yet oddly, where every chair and bookcase and table, and every rug and jar and ornament seemed to be a thing apart, preserving each its own individuality.

"Anything fresh lately?" said Villiers after a while.

"No; I think not; you saw those queer jugs, didn't you? I thought so. I don't think I have come across anything for the last few weeks."

Austin glanced round the room from cupboard to cupboard, from shelf to shelf, in search of some new oddity. His eyes fell at last on an old chest, pleasantly and quaintly carved, which stood in a dark corner of the room.

"Ah," he said, "I was forgetting, I have got something to show you." Austin unlocked the chest, drew out a thick quarto volume, laid it on the table, and resumed the cigar he had put down.

"Did you know Arthur Meyrick the painter, Villiers?"

"A little; I met him two or three times at the house of a friend of mine. What has become of him? I haven't heard his name mentioned for some time."

"He's dead."

"You don't say so! Quite young, wasn't he?"

"Yes; only thirty when he died."

"What did he die of?"

"I don't know. He was an intimate friend of mine, and a thoroughly good fellow. He used to come here and talk to me for hours, and he was one of the best talkers I have met. He could even talk about painting, and that's more than can be said of most painters. About eighteen months ago he was feeling rather overworked, and partly at my suggestion he went off on a sort of roving expedition, with no very definite end or aim about it. I believe New York was to be his first port, but I never heard from him. Three months ago I got this book, with a very civil letter from an English doctor practising at Buenos Aires, stating that he had attended the late Mr. Meyrick during his illness, and that the deceased had expressed an earnest wish that the enclosed packet should be sent to me after his death. That was all."

"And haven't you written for further particulars?"

"I have been thinking of doing so. You would advise me to write to the doctor?"

"Certainly. And what about the book?"

"It was sealed up when I got it. I don't think the doctor had seen it."

"It is something very rare? Meyrick was a collector, perhaps?"

"No, I think not, hardly a collector. Now, what do you think of those Ainu jugs?"

"They are peculiar, but I like them. But aren't you going to show me poor Meyrick's legacy?"

"Yes, yes, to be sure. The fact is, it's rather a peculiar sort of thing, and I haven't shown it to anyone. I wouldn't say anything about it if I were you. There it is."

Villiers took the book, and opened it at haphazard.

"It isn't a printed volume then?" he said.

"No. It is a collection of drawings in black and white by my poor friend Meyrick."

Villiers turned to the first page, it was blank; the second bore a brief inscription, which he read:

> Silet per diem universus, nec sine horrore secretus est; lucet nocturnis ignibus, chorus Aegipanum undique personatur: audiuntur et cantus tibiarum, et tinnitus cymbalorum per oram maritimam.

On the third page was a design which made Villiers start and look up at Austin; he was gazing abstractedly out of the window. Villiers turned page after page, absorbed, in spite of himself, in the frightful Walpurgis-night of evil, strange monstrous evil, that the dead artist had set forth in hard black and white. The figures of fauns and satyrs and Aegipans danced before his eyes, the darkness of the thicket, the dance on the mountain-top, the scenes by lonely shores, in green vineyards, by rocks and desert places, passed before him: a world before which the human soul seemed to shrink back and shudder. Villiers whirled over the remaining pages; he had seen enough, but the picture on the last leaf caught his eye, as he almost closed the book.

"Austin!"

"Well, what is it?"

"Do you know who that is?"

It was a woman's face, alone on the white page.

"Know who it is? No, of course not."

"I do."

"Who is it?"

"It is Mrs. Herbert."

"Are you sure?"

"I am perfectly certain of it. Poor Meyrick! He is one more chapter in her history."

"But what do you think of the designs?"

"They are frightful. Lock the book up again, Austin. If I were you I would burn it; it must be a terrible companion even though it be in a chest."

"Yes, they are singular drawings. But I wonder what connection there could be between Meyrick and Mrs. Herbert, or what link between her and these designs?"

"Ah, who can say? It is possible that the matter may end here, and we shall never know, but in my own opinion this Helen Vaughan, or Mrs. Herbert, is only the beginning. She will come back to London, Austin; depend upon it, she will come back, and we shall hear more about her then. I don't think it will be very pleasant news."

VI   The Suicides

Lord Argentine was a great favourite in London society. At twenty he had been a poor man, decked with the surname of an illustrious family, but forced to earn a livelihood as best he could, and the most speculative of money-lenders would not have entrusted him with fifty pounds on the chance of his ever changing his name for a title, and his poverty for a great fortune. His father had been near enough to the fountain of good things to secure one of the family livings, but the son, even if he had taken orders, would scarcely have obtained so much as this, and moreover felt no vocation for the ecclesiastical estate. Thus he fronted the world with no better armour than the bachelor's gown and the wits of a younger son's grandson, with which equipment he contrived in some way to make a very tolerable fight of it. At twenty-five Mr. Charles Aubernoun saw himself still a man of struggles and of warfare with the world, but out of the seven who stood between him and the high places of his family three only remained. These three, however, were "good lives," but yet not proof against the Zulu assegais and typhoid fever, and so one morning Aubernoun woke up and found himself Lord Argentine, a man of thirty who had faced the difficulties of existence, and had conquered. The situation amused him immensely, and he resolved that riches should be as pleasant to him as poverty had always been. Argentine, after some little consideration, came to the conclusion that dining, regarded as a fine art, was perhaps the most amusing pursuit open to fallen humanity, and thus his dinners became famous in London, and an invitation to his table a thing covetously desired. After ten years of lordship and dinners Argentine still declined to be jaded, still persisted in enjoying life, and by a kind of infection had become recognized as the cause of joy in others, in short, as the best of company. His sudden and tragical death therefore caused a wide and deep sensation. People could scarce believe it, even though the newspaper was before their eyes, and the cry of "Mysterious Death of a Nobleman" came ringing up from the street. But there stood the brief paragraph: "Lord Argentine was found dead this morning by his valet under distressing circumstances. It is stated that there can be no doubt that his lordship committed suicide, though no motive can be assigned for the act. The deceased nobleman was widely known in society, and much liked for his genial manner and sumptuous hospitality. He is succeeded by," etc., etc.

By slow degrees the details came to light, but the case still remained a mystery. The chief witness at the inquest was the dead nobleman's valet, who said that the night before his death Lord Argentine had dined with a lady of good position, whose name was suppressed in the newspaper reports. At about eleven o'clock Lord Argentine had returned, and informed his man that he should not require his services till the next morning. A little later the valet had occasion to cross the hall and was somewhat astonished to see his master quietly letting himself out at the front door. He had taken off his evening clothes, and was dressed in a Norfolk coat and knickerbockers, and wore a low brown hat. The valet had no reason to suppose that Lord Argentine had seen him, and though his master rarely kept late hours, thought little of the occurrence till the next morning, when he knocked at the bedroom door at a quarter to nine as usual. He received no answer, and, after knocking two or three times, entered the room, and saw Lord Argentine's body leaning forward at an angle from the bottom of the bed. He found that his master had tied a cord securely to one of the short bedposts, and, after making a running noose and slipping it round his neck, the unfortunate man must have resolutely fallen forward, to die by slow strangulation. He was dressed in the light suit in which the valet had seen him go out, and the doctor who was summoned pronounced that life had been extinct for more than four hours. All papers, letters, and so forth seemed in perfect order, and nothing was discovered which pointed in the most remote way to any scandal either great or small. Here the evidence ended; nothing more could be discovered. Several persons had been present at the dinner-party at which Lord Argentine had assisted, and to all these he seemed in his usual genial spirits. The valet, indeed, said he thought his master appeared a little excited when he came home, but he confessed that the alteration in his manner was very slight, hardly noticeable, indeed. It seemed hopeless to seek for any clue, and the suggestion that Lord Argentine had been suddenly attacked by acute suicidal mania was generally accepted.

It was otherwise, however, when within three weeks, three more gentlemen, one of them a nobleman, and the two others men of good position and ample means, perished miserably in almost precisely the same manner. Lord Swanleigh was found one morning in his dressing-room, hanging from a peg affixed to the wall, and Mr. Collier-Stuart and Mr. Herries had chosen to die as Lord Argentine. There was no explanation in either case; a few bald facts; a living man in the evening, and a dead body with a black swollen face in the morning. The police had been forced to confess themselves powerless to arrest or to explain the sordid murders of Whitechapel; but before the horrible suicides of Piccadilly and Mayfair they were dumbfounded, for not even the mere ferocity which did duty as an explanation of the crimes of the East End, could be of service in the West. Each of these men who had resolved to die a tortured shameful death was rich, prosperous, and to all appearances in love with the world, and not the acutest research could ferret out any shadow of a lurking motive in either case. There was a horror in the air, and men looked at one another's faces when they met, each wondering whether the other was to be the victim of the fifth nameless tragedy. Journalists sought in vain in their scrap-books for materials whereof to concoct reminiscent articles; and the morning paper was unfolded in many a house with a feeling of awe; no man knew when or where the blow would next light.

A short while after the last of these terrible events, Austin came to see Mr. Villiers. He was curious to know whether Villiers had succeeded in discovering any fresh traces of Mrs. Herbert, either through Clarke or by other sources, and he asked the question soon after he had sat down.

"No," said Villiers, "I wrote to Clarke, but he remains obdurate, and I have tried other channels, but without any result. I can't find out what became of Helen Vaughan after she left Paul Street, but I think she must have gone abroad. But to tell the truth, Austin, I haven't paid very much attention to the matter for the last few weeks; I knew poor Herries intimately, and his terrible death has been a great shock to me, a great shock."

"I can well believe it," answered Austin gravely; "you know Argentine was a friend of mine. If I remember rightly, we were speaking of him that day you came to my rooms."

"Yes; it was in connection with that house in Ashley Street, Mrs. Beaumont's house. You said something about Argentine's dining there."

"Quite so. Of course you know it was there Argentine dined the night before—before his death."

"No, I haven't heard that."

"Oh yes; the name was kept out of the papers to spare Mrs. Beaumont. Argentine was a great favourite of hers, and it is said she was in a terrible state for some time after."

A curious look came over Villiers's face; he seemed undecided whether to speak or not. Austin began again.

"I never experienced such a feeling of horror as when I read the account of Argentine's death. I didn't understand it at the time, and I don't now. I knew him well, and it completely passes my understanding for what possible cause he—or any of the others for the matter of that—could have resolved in cold blood to die in such an awful manner. You know how men babble away each other's characters in London, you may be sure any buried scandal or hidden skeleton would have been brought to light in such a case as this; but nothing of the sort has taken place. As for the theory of mania, that is very well, of course, for the coroner's jury, but everybody knows that it's all nonsense. Suicidal mania is not smallpox."

Austin relapsed into gloomy silence. Villiers sat silent also, watching his friend. The expression of indecision still fleeted across his face; he seemed as if weighing his thoughts in the balance, and the considerations he was revolving left him still silent. Austin tried to shake off the remembrance of tragedies as hopeless and perplexed as the labyrinth of Daedalus, and began to talk in an indifferent voice of the most pleasant incidents and adventures of the season.

"That Mrs. Beaumont," he said, "of whom we were speaking, is a great success; she has taken London almost by storm. I met her the other night at Fulham's; she is really a remarkable woman."

"You have met Mrs. Beaumont?"

"Yes; she had quite a court around her. She would be called very handsome, I suppose, and yet there is something about her face which I didn't like. The features are exquisite, but the expression is strange. And all the time I was looking at her, and afterwards, when I was going home, I had a curious feeling that that very expression was in some way or other familiar to me."

"You must have seen her in the Row."

"No, I am sure I never set eyes on the woman before; it is that which makes it puzzling. And to the best of my belief I have never seen anybody like her; what I felt was a kind of dim far-off memory, vague but persistent. The only sensation I can compare it to, is that odd feeling one sometimes has in a dream, when fantastic cities and wondrous lands and phantom personages appear familiar and accustomed."

Villiers nodded and glanced aimlessly round the room, possibly in search of someting on which to turn the conversation. His eyes fell on an old chest somewhat like that in which the artist's strange legacy lay hid beneath a Gothic scutcheon.

"Have you written to the doctor about poor Meyrick?" he asked.

"Yes; I wrote asking for full particulars as to his illness and death. I don't expect to have an answer for another three weeks or a month. I thought I might as well inquire whether Meyrick knew an Englishwoman named Herbert, and if so, whether the doctor could give me any information about her. But it's very possible that Meyrick fell in with her at New York, or Mexico, or San Francisco; I have no idea as to the extent or direction of his travels."

"Yes, and it's very possible that the woman may have more than one name."

"Exactly. I wish I had thought of asking you to lend me the portrait of her which you possess. I might have enclosed it in my letter to Dr. Matthews."

"So you might: that never occurred to me. We might send it now. Hark! what are those boys calling?"

While the two men had been talking together a confused noise of shouting had been gradually growing louder. The noise rose from the eastward and swelled down Piccadilly, drawing nearer and nearer, a very torrent of sound; surging up streets usually quiet, and making every window a frame for a face, curious or excited. The cries and voices came echoing up the silent street where Villiers lived, growing more distinct as they advanced, and, as Villiers spoke, an answer rang up from the pavement:

"THE WEST END HORRORS; ANOTHER AWFUL SUICIDE; FULL DETAILS!"

Austin rushed down the stairs and bought a paper and read out the paragraph to Villiers as the uproar in the street rose and fell. The window was open and the air seemed full of noise and terror.

Another gentleman has fallen a victim to the terrible epidemic of suicide which for the last month has prevailed in the West End. Mr. Sidney Crashaw of Stoke House, Fulham, and King's Pomeroy, Devon, was found, after a prolonged search, hanging from the branch of a tree in his garden at one o'clock to-day. The deceased gentleman dined last night at the Carlton Club and seemed in his usual health and spirits. He left the Club at about ten o'clock, and was seen walking leisurely up St. James's Street a little later. Subsequent to this his movements cannot be traced. On the discovery of the body medical aid was at once summoned, but life had evidently been long extinct. So far as is known, Mr. Crashaw had no trouble or anxiety of any kind. This painful suicide, it will be remembered, is the fifth of the kind in the last month. The authorities at Scotland Yard are unable to suggest any explanation of these terrible occurrences.

Austin put down the paper in mute horror.

"I shall leave London tomorrow," he said, "it is a city of nightmares. How awful this is, Villiers!"

Mr. Villiers was sitting by the window quietly looking out into the street. He had listened to the newspaper report attentively, and the hint of indecision was no longer on his face.

"Wait a moment, Austin," he replied, "I have made up my mind to mention a little matter that occurred last night. It is stated, I think, that Crashaw was last seen alive in St. James's Street shortly after ten?"

"Yes, I think so. I will look again. Yes, you are quite right."

"Quite so. Well, I am in a position to contradict that statement at all events. Crashaw was seen after that; considerably later indeed."

"How do you know?"

"Because I happened to see Crashaw myself at about two o'clock this morning."

"You saw Crashaw? You, Villiers?"

"Yes, I saw him quite distinctly; indeed, there were but a few feet between us."

"Where, in Heaven's name, did you see him?"

"Not far from here. I saw him in Ashley Street. He was just leaving a house."

"Did you notice what house it was?"

"Yes. It was Mrs. Beaumont's."

"Villiers! Think what you are saying; there must be some mistake. How could Crashaw be in Mrs. Beaumont's house at two o'clock in the morning? Surely, surely, you must have been dreaming, Villiers, you were always rather fanciful."

"No; I was wide awake enough. Even if I had been dreaming as you say, what I saw would have roused me effectually."

"What you saw? What did you see? Was there anything strange about Crashaw? But I can't believe it; it is impossible."

"Well, if you like I will tell you what I saw, or if you please, what I think I saw, and you can judge for yourself."

"Very good, Villiers."

The noise and clamour of the street had died away, though now and then the sound of shouting still came from the distance, and the dull, leaden silence seemed like the quiet after an earthquake or a storm. Villiers turned from the window and began speaking.

"I was at a house near Regent's Park last night, and when I came away the fancy took me to walk home instead of taking a hansom. It was a clear pleasant night enough, and after a few minutes I had the streets pretty much to myself. It's a curious thing, Austin, to be alone in London at night, the gas-lamps stretching away in perspective, and the dead silence, and then perhaps the rush and clatter of a hansom on the stones, and the fire starting up under the horse's hoofs. I walked along pretty briskly, for I was feeling a little tired of being out in the night, and as the clocks were striking two I turned down Ashley Street, which, you know, is on my way. It was quieter than ever there, and the lamps were fewer; altogether, it looked as dark and gloomy as a forest in winter. I had done about half the length of the street when I heard a door closed very softly, and naturally I looked up to see who was abroad like myself at such an hour. As it happens, there is a street lamp close to the house in question, and I saw a man standing on the step. He had just shut the door and his face was towards me, and I recognized Crashaw directly. I never knew him to speak to, but I had often seen him, and I am positive that I was not mistaken in my man. I looked into his face for a moment, and then—I will confess the truth—I set off at a good run, and kept it up till I was within my own door."

"Why?"

"Why? Because it made my blood run cold to see that man's face. I could never have supposed that such an infernal medley of passions could have glared out of any human eyes; I almost fainted as I looked. I knew I had looked into the eyes of a lost soul, Austin, the man's outward form remained, but all hell was within it. Furious lust, and hate that was like fire, and the loss of all hope and horror that seemed to shriek aloud to the night, though his teeth were shut; and the utter blackness of despair. I am sure he did not see me; he saw nothing that you or I can see, but he saw what I hope we never shall. I do not know when he died; I suppose in an hour, or perhaps two, but when I passed down Ashley Street and heard the closing door, that man no longer belonged to this world; it was a devil's face I looked upon."

There was an interval of silence in the room when Villiers ceased speaking. The light was failing, and all the tumult of an hour ago was quite hushed. Austin had bent his head at the close of the story, and his hand covered his eyes.

"What can it mean?" he said at length.

"Who knows, Austin, who knows? It's a black business, but I think we had better keep it to ourselves, for the present at any rate. I will see if I cannot learn anything about that house through private channels of information, and if I do light upon anything I will let you know."

VII   The Encounter in Soho

Three weeks later Austin received a note from Villiers, asking him to call either that afternoon or the next. He chose the nearer date, and found Villiers sitting as usual by the window, apparently lost in meditation on the drowsy traffic of the street. There was a bamboo table by his side, a fantastic thing, enriched with gilding and queer painted scenes, and on it lay a little pile of papers arranged and docketed as neatly as anything in Mr. Clarke's office.

"Well, Villiers, have you made any discoveries in the last three weeks?"

"I think so; I have here one or two memoranda which struck me as singular, and there is a statement to which I shall call your attention."

"And these documents relate to Mrs. Beaumont? It was really Crashaw whom you saw that night standing on the doorstep of the house in Ashley Street?"

"As to that matter my belief remains unchanged, but neither my inquiries nor their results have any special relation to Crashaw. But my investigations have had a strange issue. I have found out who Mrs. Beaumont is!"

"Who she is? In what way do you mean?"

"I mean that you and I know her better under another name."

"What name is that?"

"Herbert."

"Herbert!" Austin repeated the word, dazed with astonishment.

"Yes, Mrs. Herbert of Paul Street, Helen Vaughan of earlier adventures unknown to me. You had reason to recognize the expression of her face; when you go home look at the face in Meyrick's book of horrors, and you will know the sources of your recollection."

"And you have proof of this?"

"Yes, the best of proof; I have seen Mrs. Beaumont, or shall we say Mrs. Herbert?"

"Where did you see her?"

"Hardly in a place where you would expect to see a lady who lives in Ashley Street, Piccadilly. I saw her entering a house in one of the meanest and most disreputable streets in Soho. In fact, I had made an appointment, though not with her, and she was precise both to time and place."

"All this seems very wonderful, but I cannot call it incredible. You must remember, Villiers, that I have seen this woman, in the ordinary adventure of London society, talking and laughing, and sipping her coffee in a commonplace drawing-room with commonplace people. But you know what you are saying?"

"I do; I have not allowed myself to be led by surmises or fancies. It was with no thought of finding Helen Vaughan that I searched for Mrs. Beaumont in the dark waters of the life of London, but such has been the issue."

"You must have been in strange places, Villiers."

"Yes, I have been in very strange places. It would have been useless, you know, to go to Ashley Street, and ask Mrs. Beaumont to give me a short sketch of her previous history. No; assuming, as I had to assume, that her record was not of the cleanest, it would be pretty certain that at some previous time she must have moved in circles not quite so refined as her present ones. If you see mud on the top of a stream, you may be sure that it was once at the bottom. I went to the bottom. I have always been fond of diving into Queer Street for my amusement, and I found my knowledge of that locality and its inhabitants very useful. It is, perhaps, needless to say that my friends had never heard the name of Beaumont, and as I had never seen the lady, and was quite unable to describe her, I had to set to work in an indirect way. The people there know me; I have been able to do some of them a service now and again, so they made no difficulty about giving their information; they were aware I had no communication direct or indirect with Scotland Yard. I had to cast out a good many lines, though, before I got what I wanted, and when I landed the fish I did not for a moment suppose it was my fish. But I listened to what I was told out of a constitutional liking for useless information, and I found myself in possession of a very curious story, though, as I imagined, not the story I was looking for. It was to this effect. Some five or six years ago, a woman named Raymond suddenly made her appearance in the neighbourhood to which I am referring. She was described to me as being quite young, probably not more than seventeen or eighteen, very handsome, and looking as if she came from the country. I should be wrong in saying that she found her level in going to this particular quarter, or associating with these people, for from what I was told, I should think the worst den in London far too good for her. The person from whom I got my information, as you may suppose, no great Puritan, shuddered and grew sick in telling me of the nameless infamies which were laid to her charge. After living there for a year, or perhaps a little more, she disappeared as suddenly as she came, and they saw nothing of her till about the time of the Paul Street case. At first she came to her old haunts only occasionally, then more frequently, and finally took up her abode there as before, and remained for six or eight months. It's of no use my going into details as to the life that woman led; if you want particulars you can look at Meyrick's legacy. Those designs were not drawn from his imagination. She again disappeared, and the people of the place saw nothing of her till a few months ago. My informant told me that she had taken some rooms in a house which he pointed out, and these rooms she was in the habit of visiting two or three times a week and always at ten in the morning. I was led to expect that one of these visits would be paid on a certain day about a week ago, and I accordingly managed to be on the look-out in company with my cicerone at a quarter to ten, and the hour and the lady came with equal punctuality. My friend and I were standing under an archway, a little way back from the street, but she saw us, and gave me a glance that I shall be long in forgetting. That look was quite enough for me; I knew Miss Raymond to be Mrs. Herbert; as for Mrs. Beaumont she had quite gone out of my head. She went into the house, and I watched it till four o'clock, when she came out, and then I followed her. It was a long chase, and I had to be very careful to keep a long way in the background, and yet not lose sight of the woman. She took me down to the Strand, and then to Westminster, and then up St. James's Street, and along Piccadilly. I felt queerish when I saw her turn up Ashley Street; the thought that Mrs. Herbert was Mrs. Beaumont came into my mind, but it seemed too improbable to be true. I waited at the corner, keeping my eye on her all the time, and I took particular care to note the house at which she stopped. It was the house with the gay curtains, the house of flowers, the house out of which Crashaw came the night he hanged himself in his garden. I was just going away with my discovery, when I saw an empty carriage come round and draw up in front of the house, and I came to the conclusion that Mrs. Herbert was going out for a drive, and I was right. I took a hansom and followed the carriage into the Park. There, as it happened, I met a man I know, and we stood talking together a little distance from the carriage-way, to which I had my back. We had not been there for ten minutes when my friend took off his hat, and I glanced round and saw the lady I had been following all day. 'Who is that?' I said, and his answer was, 'Mrs. Beaumont; lives in Ashley Street.' Of course there could be no doubt after that. I don't know whether she saw me, but I don't think she did. I went home at once, and, on consideration, I thought that I had a sufficiently good case with which to go to Clarke."

"Why to Clarke?"

"Because I am sure that Clarke is in possession of facts about this woman, facts of which I know nothing."

"Well, what then?"

Mr. Villiers leaned back in his chair and looked reflectively at Austin for a moment before he answered:

"My idea was that Clarke and I should call on Mrs. Beaumont."

"You would never go into such a house as that? No, no, Villiers, you cannot do it. Besides, consider; what result . . ."

"I will tell you soon. But I was going to say that my information does not end here; it has been completed in an extraordinary manner.

"Look at this neat little packet of manuscript; it is paginated, you see, and I have indulged in the civil coquetry of a ribbon of red tape. It has almost a legal air, hasn't it? Run your eye over it, Austin. It is an account of the entertainment Mrs. Beaumont provided for her choicer guests. The man who wrote this escaped with his life, but I do not think he will live many years. The doctors tell him he must have sustained some severe shock to the nerves."

Austin took the manuscript, but never read it. Opening the neat pages at haphazard his eye was caught by a word and a phrase that followed it; and, sick at heart, with white lips and a cold sweat pouring like water from his temples, he flung the paper down.

"Take it away, Villiers, never speak of this again. Are you made of stone, man? Why, the dread and horror of death itself, the thoughts of the man who stands in the keen morning air on the black platform, bound, the bell tolling in his ears, and waits for the harsh rattle of the bolt, are as nothing compared to this. I will not read it; I should never sleep again."

"Very good. I can fancy what you saw. Yes; it is horrible enough; but after all, it is an old story, an old mystery played in our day, and in dim London streets instead of amidst the vineyards and the olive gardens. We know what happened to those who chanced to meet the Great God Pan, and those who are wise know that all symbols are symbols of something, not of nothing. It was, indeed, an exquisite symbol beneath which men long ago veiled their knowledge of the most awful, most secret forces which lie at the heart of all things; forces before which the souls of men must wither and die and blacken, as their bodies blacken under the electric current. Such forces cannot be named, cannot be spoken, cannot be imagined except under a veil and a symbol, a symbol to the most of us appearing a quaint, poetic fancy, to some a foolish tale. But you and I, at all events, have known something of the terror that may dwell in the secret place of life, manifested under human flesh; that which is without form taking to itself a form. Oh, Austin, how can it be? How is it that the very sunlight does not turn to blackness before this thing, the hard earth melt and boil beneath such a burden?"

Villiers was pacing up and down the room, and the beads of sweat stood out on his forehead. Austin sat silent for a while, but Villiers saw him make a sign upon his breast.

"I say again, Villiers, you will surely never enter such a house as that? You would never pass out alive."

"Yes, Austin, I shall go out alive—I, and Clarke with me."

"What do you mean? You cannot, you would not dare. . . ."

"Wait a moment. The air was very pleasant and fresh this morning; there was a breeze blowing, even through this dull street, and I thought I would take a walk. Piccadilly stretched before me a clear, bright vista, and the sun flashed on the carriages and on the quivering leaves in the park. It was a joyous morning, and men and women looked at the sky and smiled as they went about their work or their pleasure, and the wind blew as blithely as upon the meadows and the scented gorse. But somehow or other I got out of the bustle and the gaiety, and found myself walking slowly along a quiet, dull street, where there seemed to be no sunshine and no air, and where the few footpassengers loitered as they walked, and hung indecisively about corners and archways. I walked along, hardly knowing where I was going or what I did there, but feeling impelled, as one sometimes is, to explore still further, with a vague idea of reaching some unknown goal. Thus I forged up the street, noting the small traffic of the milk-shop, and wondering at the incongruous medley of penny pipes, black tobacco, sweets, newspaper, and comic songs which here and there jostled one another in the short compass of a single window. I think it was a cold shudder that suddenly passed through me that first told me that I had found what I wanted. I looked up from the pavement and stopped before a dusty shop, above which the lettering had faded, where the red bricks of two hundred years ago had grimed to black; where the windows had gathered to themselves the fog and the dirt of winters innumerable. I saw what I required; but I think it was five minutes before I had steadied myself and could walk in and ask for it in a cool voice and with a calm face. I think there must even then have been a tremor in my words, for the old man who came out from his back parlour, and fumbled slowly amongst his goods, looked oddly at me as he tied the parcel. I paid what he asked, and stood leaning by the counter, with a strange reluctance to take up my goods and go. I asked about the business, and learnt that trade was bad and the profits cut down sadly; but then the street was not what it was before traffic had been diverted, but that was done forty years ago, 'just before my father died,' he said. I got away at last, and walked along sharply; it was a dismal street indeed, and I was glad to return to the bustle and the noise. Would you like to see my purchase?"

Austin said nothing, but nodded his head slightly; he still looked white and sick. Villiers pulled out a drawer in the bamboo table, and showed Austin a long coil of cord, hard and new; and at one end was a running noose.

"It is the best hempen cord," said Villiers, "just as it used to be made for the old trade, the man told me. Not an inch of jute from end to end."

Austin set his teeth hard, and stared at Villiers, growing whiter as he looked.

"You would not do it," he murmured at last. "You would not have blood on your hands, My God!" he exclaimed, with sudden vehemence, "you cannot mean this, Villiers, that you will make yourself a hangman?"

"No. I shall offer a choice, and leave Helen Vaughan alone with this cord in a locked room for fifteen minutes. If when we go in it is not done, I shall call the nearest policeman. That is all."

"I must go now. I cannot stay here any longer; I cannot bear this. Good-night."

"Good-night, Austin."

The door shut, but in a moment it was opened again, and Austin stood, white and ghastly, in the entrance.

"I was forgetting," he said, "that I too have something to tell. I have received a letter from Dr. Harding of Buenos Aires. He says that he attended Meyrick for three weeks before his death."

"And does he say what carried him off in the prime of life? It was not fever?"

"No, it was not fever. According to the doctor, it was an utter collapse of the whole system, probably caused by some severe shock. But hesitates that the patient would tell him nothing, and that he was consequently at some disadvantage in treating the case."

"Is there anything more?"

"Yes. Dr. Harding ends his letter by saying: 'I think this is all the information I can give you about your poor friend. He had not been long in Buenos Aires, and knew scarcely anyone, with the exception of a person who did not bear the best of characters, and has since left—a Mrs. Vaughan.'"

VIII   The Fragments

Amongst the papers of the well-known physician, Dr. Robert Matheson, of Ashley Street, Piccadilly, who died suddenly of apopletic seizure, at the beginning of 1892, a leaf of manuscript paper was found, covered with pencil jottings. These notes were in Latin, much abbreviated, and has evidently been made in great haste. The MS. was only deciphered with great difficulty, and some words have up to the present time evaded all the efforts of the expert employed. The date, "XXV Jul. 1888," is written on the right-hand corner of the MS. The following is a translation of Dr. Matheson's manuscript.

Whether science would benefit by these brief notes if they could be published, I do not know, but rather doubt. But certainly I shall never take the responsibility of publishing or divulging one word of what is here written, not only on account of my oath freely given to those two persons who were present, but also because the details are too abominable. It is probably that, upon mature consideration, and after weighing the good and evil, I shall one day destroy this paper, or at least leave it under seal to my friend D., trusting in his discretion, to use it or to burn it, as he may think fit.

As was befitting, I did all that my knowledge suggested to make sure that I was suffering under no delusion. At first astounded, I could hardly think, but in a minute's time I was sure that my pulse was steady and regular, and that I was in my real and true senses. I then fixed my eyes quietly on what was before me.

Though horror and revolting nausea rose up within me, and an odour of corruption choked my breath, I remained firm. I was then privileged or accursed, I dare not say which, to see that which was on the bed, lying there black like ink, transformed before my eyes. The skin, and the flesh, and the muscles, and the bones, and the firm structure of the human body that I had thought to be unchangeable, and permanent as adamant, began to melt and dissolve.

I knew that the body may be separated into its elements by external agencies, but I should have refused to believe what I saw. For here there was some internal force, of which I knew nothing, that caused dissolution and change.

Here too was all the work by which man had been made repeated before my eyes. I saw the form waver from sex to sex, dividing itself from itself, and then again reunited. Then I saw the body descend to the beasts whence it ascended, and that which was on the heights go down to the depths, even to the abyss of all being. The principle of life, which makes organism, always remained, while the outward form changed.

The light within the room had turned to blackness, not the darkness of night, in which objects are seen dimly, for I could see clearly and without difficulty. But it was the negation of light; objects were presented to my eyes, if I may say so, without any medium, in such a manner that if there had been a prism in the room I should have seen no colours represented in it.

I watched, and at last I saw nothing but a substance as jelly. Then the ladder was ascended again . . . [here the MS. is illegible] . . . for one instant I saw a Form, shaped in dimness before me, which I will not farther describe. But the symbol of this form may be seen in ancient sculptures, and in paintings which survived beneath the lava, too foul to be spoken of . . . as a horrible and unspeakable shape, neither man nor beast, was changed into human form, there came finally death.

I who saw all this, not without great horror and loathing of soul, here write my name, declaring all that I have set on this paper to be true.

Robert Matheson, Med. Dr.

. . . Such, Raymond, is the story of what I know and what I have seen. The burden of it was too heavy for me to bear alone, and yet I could tell it to none but you. Villiers, who was with me at the last, knows nothing of that awful secret of the wood, of how what we both saw die, lay upon the smooth, sweet turf amidst the summer flowers, half in sun and half in shadow, and holding the girl Rachel's hand, called and summoned those companions, and shaped in solid form, upon the earth we tread on, the horror which we can but hint at, which we can only name under a figure. I would not tell Villiers of this, nor of that resemblance, which struck me as with a blow upon my heart, when I saw the portrait, which filled the cup of terror at the end. What this can mean I dare not guess. I know that what I saw perish was not Mary, and yet in the last agony Mary's eyes looked into mine. Whether there be anyone who can show the last link in this chain of awful mystery, I do not know, but if there be anyone who can do this, you, Raymond, are the man. And if you know the secret, it rests with you to tell it or not, as you please.

I am writing this letter to you immediately on my getting back to town. I have been in the country for the last few days; perhaps you may be able to guess in what part. While the horror and wonder of London was at its height—for "Mrs. Beaumont," as I have told you, was well known in society—I wrote to my friend Dr. Phillips, giving some brief outline, or rather hint, of what had happened, and asking him to tell me the name of the village where the events he had related to me occurred. He gave me the name, as he said with the less hesitation, because Rachel's father and mother were dead, and the rest of the family had gone to a relative in the state of Washington six months before. The parents, he said, had undoubtedly died of grief and horror caused by the terrible death of their daughter, and by what had gone before that death. On the evening of the day on which I received Phillip's letter I was at Caermaen, and standing beneath the mouldering Roman walls, white with the winters of seventeen hundred years. I looked over the meadow where once had stood the older Temple of the "God of the Deeps," and saw a house gleaming in the sunlight. It was the house where Helen had lived. I stayed at Caermaen for several days. The people of the place, I found, knew little and had guessed less. Those whom I spoke to on the matter seemed surprised that an antiquarian (as I professed myself to be) should trouble about a village tragedy, of which they gave a very commonplace version, and, as you may imagine, I told nothing of what I knew. Most of my time was spent in the great wood that rises just above the village and climbs the hillside, and goes down to the river in the valley; such another long lovely valley, Raymond, as that on which we looked one summer night, walking to and fro before your house. For many an hour I strayed through the maze of the forest, turning now to right and now to left, pacing slowly down long alleys of undergrowth, shadowy and chill, even under the midday sun, and halting beneath great oaks; lying on the short turf of a clearing where the faint sweet scent of wild roses came to me on the wind and mixed with the heavy perfume of the elder, whose mingled odour is like the odour of the room of the dead, a vapour of incense and corruption. I stood at the edges of the wood, gazing at all the pomp and procession of the foxgloves towering amidst the bracken and shining red in the broad sunshine, and beyond them into deep thickets of close undergrowth where springs boil up from the rock and nourish the water-weeds, dank and evil. But in all my wanderings I avoided one part of the wood; it was not till yesterday that I climbed to the summit of the hill, and stood upon the ancient Roman road that threads the highest ridge of the wood. Here they had walked, Helen and Rachel, along this quiet causeway, upon the pavement of green turf, shut in on either side by high banks of red earth, and tall hedges of shining beech, and here I followed in their steps, looking out, now and again, through partings in the boughs, and seeing on one side the sweep of the wood stretching far to right and left, and sinking into the broad level, and beyond, the yellow sea, and the land over the sea. On the other side was the valley and the river and hill following hill as wave on wave, and wood and meadow, and cornfield, and white houses gleaming, and a great wall of mountain, and far blue peaks in the north. And so at last I came to the place. The track went up a gentle slope and widened out into an open space with a wall of thick undergrowth around it, and then, narrowing again, passed on into the distance and the faint blue mist of summer heat. And into this pleasant summer glade Rachel passed a girl, and left it, who shall say what? I did not stay long there.

In a small town near Caermaen there is a museum, containing for the most part Roman remains which have been found in the neighbourhood at various times. On the day after my arrival at Caermaen I walked over to the town in question, and took the opportunity of inspecting this museum. After I had seen most of the sculptured stones, the coffins, rings, coins, and fragments of tessellated pavement which the place contains, I was shown a small square pillar of white stone, which had been recently discovered in the wood of which I have been speaking, and, as I found on inquiry, in that open space where the Roman road broadens out. On one side of the pillar was an inscription, of which I took a note. Some of the letters have been defaced, but I do not think there can be any doubt as to those which I supply. The inscription is as follows:

DEVOMNODENT*i*
ELA*v*IVSSENILISPOSSV*it*
PROPTERNVP*tias*
*quas*VIDITSVBYMB*ra*

"To the great god Nodens (the god of the Great Deep or Abyss) Flavius Senilis has erected this pillar on account of the marriage which he saw beneath the shade."

The custodian of the museum informed me that local antiquaries were much puzzled, not by the inscription, or by any difficulty in translating it, but as to the circumstance or rite to which allusion is made.

. . . And now, my dear Clarke, as to what you tell me about Helen Vaughan, whom you say you saw die under circumstances of the utmost and almost incredible horror. I was interested in your account, but a good deal, nay all, of what you told me I knew already. I can understand the strange likeness you remarked both in the portrait and in the actual face; you have seen Helen's mother. You remember that still summer night so many years ago, when I talked to you of the world beyond the shadows, and of the god Pan. You remember Mary. She was the mother of Helen Vaughan, who was born nine months after that night.

Mary never recovered her reason. She lay, as you saw her, all the while upon her bed, and a few days after the child was born she died. I fancy that just at the last she knew me; I was standing by the bed, and the old look came into her eyes for a second, and then she shuddered and groaned and died. It was an ill work I did that night when you were present; I broke open the door of the house of life, without knowing or caring what might pass forth or enter in. I recollect your telling me at the time, sharply enough, and rightly enough too, in one sense, that I had ruined the reason of a human being by a foolish experiment, based on an absurd theory. You did well to blame me, but my theory was not all absurdity. What I said Mary would see, she saw, but I forgot that no human eyes could look on such a vision with impunity. And I forgot, as I have just said, that when the house of life is thus thrown open, there may enter in that for which we have no name, and human flesh may become the veil of a horror one dare not express. I played with energies which I did not understand, and you have seen the ending of it. Helen Vaughan did well to bind the cord about her neck and die, though the death was horrible. The blackened face, the hideous form upon the bed, changing and melting before your eyes from woman to man, from man to beast, and from beast to worse than beast, all the strange horror that you witnessed, surprises me but little. What you say the doctor whom you sent for saw and shuddered at I noticed long ago; I knew what I had done the moment the child was born, and when it was scarcely five years old I surprised it, not once or twice but several times with a playmate, you may guess of what kind. It was for me a constant, an incarnate horror, and after a few years I felt I could bear it no longer, and I sent Helen Vaughan away. You know now what frightened the boy in the wood. The rest of the strange story, and all else that you tell me, as discovered by your friend, I have contrived to learn from time to time, almost to the last chapter. And now Helen is with her companions. . . .

Carlos Fuentes (b. 1928)

Aura

Carlos Fuentes is the foremost living Mexican novelist and one of the world's great living writers. The son of a diplomat, he has lived in several countries and spent much time in Paris, in particular. His novella, "Aura," is one of the masterpieces of horror of the twentieth century and an important work of contemporary fiction. In an essay "On Reading and Writing Myself: How I Wrote "Aura," Fuentes traces the genesis of the piece to a moment in Paris in the summer of 1961, and the concatenation of circumstances surrounding a moment when he saw a woman enter his bedroom in the mirror, illuminated by the light of the city, and perceived a second person in the mirror: ". . . that threshold between the parlor and the bedroom became the lintel between all the ages of this girl: the light that had been struggling against the clouds also fought against her flesh, took it, sketched it, granted her a shadow of years, sculpted a death in her eyes, tore the smile from her lips, waned through her hair with the floating melancholy of madness. . . . I was only, that afternoon, 'a strange guest in the kingdom of love,' and knew that the eyes of love can also see us with—once more I quote Quevedo—'a beautiful Death."

"The next morning I started writing "Aura" in a cafe near my hotel. . . ." Fuentes names his conscious influences as Henry James' "The Aspern Papers,' Charles Dickens' *Great Expectations,* Pushkin's *The Queen of Spades,* Michelet's medieval sorceress, and Circe, saying "Aura came into this world to increase the secular descent of witches." What more need one say about this powerful novella's place in the evolution of horror?

> *Man hunts and struggles.*
> *Woman intrigues and dreams;*
> *she is the mother of fantasy,*
> *the mother of the gods.*
> *She has second sight,*
> *the wings that enable her to fly*
> *to the infinite of*
> *desire and the imagination . . .*
> *The gods are like men:*
> *they are born and they die*
> *on a woman's breast . . .*
> —Jules Michelet

I

You're reading the advertisement: an offer like this isn't made every day. You read it and reread it. It seems to be addressed to you and nobody else. You don't even notice when the ash from your cigarette falls into the cup of tea you ordered in this cheap, dirty café. You read it again. "Wanted, young historian, conscientious, neat. Perfect knowledge colloquial French." Youth . . . knowledge of French, preferably after living in France for a while . . . "Four thousand pesos a month, all meals, comfortable bedroom-study." All that's missing is your name. The advertisement should have two more words, in bigger, blacker type: Felipe Montero, Wanted, Felipe Montero, formerly on scholarship at the Sorbonne, historian full of useless facts, accustomed to digging among yellowed documents, part-time teacher in private schools, nine hundred pesos a month. But if you read that, you'd be suspicious, and take it as a joke. "Address, Donceles 815." No telephone. Come in person.

You leave a tip, reach for your briefcase, get up. You wonder if another young historian, in the same situation you are, has seen the same advertisement, has got ahead of you and taken the job already. You walk down to the corner, trying to forget this idea. As you wait for the bus, you run over the dates you must have on the tip of your tongue so that your sleepy pupils will respect you. The bus is coming now, and you're staring at the tips of your black shoes. You've got to be prepared. You put your hand in your pocket, search among the coins, and finally take out thirty centavos. You've got to be prepared. You grab the handrail—the bus slows down but doesn't stop—and jump aboard. Then you shove your way forward, pay the driver the thirty centavos, squeeze yourself in among the passengers already standing in the aisle, hang onto the overhead rail, press your briefcase tighter under your left arm, and automatically put your left hand over the back pocket where you keep your billfold.

This day is just like any other day, and you don't remember the advertisement until the next morning, when you sit down in the same café and order breakfast and open your newspaper. You come to the advertising section and there it is again: *young historian*. The job is still open. You reread the advertisement, lingering over the final words: four thousand pesos.

It's surprising to know that anyone lives on Donceles Street. You always thought that nobody lived in the old center of the city. You walk slowly, trying to pick out the number 815 in that conglomeration of old colonial mansions, all of them converted into repair shops, jewelry shops, shoe stores, drugstores. The numbers have been changed, painted over, confused. A 13 next to a 200. An old plaque reading 47 over a scrawl in blurred charcoal: *Now 924*. You look up at the second stories. Up there, everything is the same as it was. The jukeboxes don't disturb them. The mercury streetlights don't shine in. The cheap merchandise on sale along the street doesn't have any effect on that upper level; on the baroque harmony of the carved stones; on the battered stone saints with pigeons clustering on their shoulders; on the latticed balconies, the copper gutters, the sandstone gargoyles; on the greenish curtains that darken the long windows; on that window from which someone draws back when you look at it. You gaze at the fanciful vines carved over the doorway, then lower your eyes to the peeling wall and discover *815, formerly 69*.

You rap vainly with the knocker, that copper head of a dog, so worn and smooth that it resembles the head of a canine foetus in a museum of natural science. It seems as if the dog is grinning at you and you let go of the cold metal. The door opens at the first light push of your fingers, but before going in you give a last look over your shoulder, frowning at the long line of stalled cars that growl, honk, and belch out the unhealthy fumes of their impatience. You try to retain some single image of that indifferent outside world.

You close the door behind you and peer into the darkness of a roofed alleyway. It must be a patio of some sort, because you can smell the mold, the dampness of the plants, the rotting roots, the thick drowsy aroma. There isn't any light to guide you, and you're searching in your coat pocket for the box of matches when a sharp, thin voice tells you, from a distance: "No, it isn't necessary. Please. Walk thirteen steps forward and you'll come to a stairway at your right. Come up, please. There are twenty-two steps. Count them."

Thirteen. To the right. Twenty-two.

The dank smell of the plants is all around you as you count out your steps, first on the paving-stones, then on the creaking wood, spongy from the dampness. You count to twenty-two in a low voice and then stop, with the matchbox in your hand, and the briefcase under your arm. You knock on a door that smells of old pine. There isn't any knocker. Finally you push it open. Now you can feel a carpet under your feet, a thin carpet, badly laid. It makes you trip and almost fall. Then you notice the grayish filtered light that reveals some of the humps.

"Señora," you say, because you seem to remember a woman's voice. "Señora . . ."

"Now turn to the left. The first door. Please be so kind."

You push the door open: you don't expect any of them to be latched, you know they all open at a push. The scattered lights are braided in your eyelashes, as if you were seeing them through a silken net. All you can make out are the dozens of flickering lights. At last you can see that they're votive lights, all set on brackets or hung between unevenly spaced panels. They cast a faint glow on the silver objects, the crystal flasks, the gilt-framed mirrors. Then you see the bed in the shadows beyond, and the feeble movement of a hand that seems to be beckoning to you.

But you can't see her face until you turn your back on that galaxy of religious lights. You stumble to the foot of the bed, and have to go around it in order to get to the head of it. A tiny figure is almost lost in its immensity. When you reach out your hand, you don't touch another hand, you touch the ears and thick fur of a creature that's chewing silently and steadily, looking up at you with its glowing red eyes. You smile and stroke the rabbit that's crouched beside her hand. Finally you shake hands, and her cold fingers remain for a long while in your sweating palm.

"I'm Felipe Montero. I read your advertisement."

"Yes, I know. I'm sorry, there aren't any chairs."

"That's all right. Don't worry about it."

"Good. Please let me see your profile. No, I can't see it well enough. Turn toward the light. That's right. Excellent."

"I read your advertisement . . ."

"Yes, of course. Do you think you're qualified? *Avez-vous fait des études?*"

"*A Paris, madame.*"

"*Ah, oui, ça me fait plaisir, toujours, toujours, d'entendre . . . oui . . . vous savez . . . on était tellement habitué . . . et après . . .*"

You move aside so that the light from the candles and the reflections from the silver and crystal show you the silk coif that must cover a head of very white hair, and that frames a face so old it's almost childlike. Her whole body is covered by the sheets and the feather pillows and the high, tightly buttoned white collar, all except for her arms, which are wrapped in a shawl, and her pallid hands resting on her stomach. You can only stare at her face until a movement of the rabbit lets you glance furtively at the crusts and bits of bread scattered on the worn-out red silk of the pillows.

"I'll come directly to the point. I don't have many years ahead of me, Señor Montero, and therefore I decided to break a life-long rule and place an advertisement in the newspaper."

"Yes, that's why I'm here."

"Of course. So you accept."

"Well, I'd like to know a little more."

"Yes. You're wondering."

She sees you glance at the night table, the differentcolored bottles, the glasses, the aluminum spoons, the row of pillboxes, the other glasses—all stained with whitish liquids—on the floor within reach of her hand. Then you notice that the bed is hardly raised above the level of the floor. Suddenly the rabbit jumps down and disappears in the shadows.

"I can offer you four thousand pesos."

"Yes, that's what the advertisement said today."

"Ah, then it came out."

"Yes, it came out."

"It has to do with the memoirs of my husband, General Llorente. They must be put in order before I die. I want them to be published. I decided that a short time ago."

"But the General himself? Wouldn't he be able to . . ."

"He died sixty years ago, Señor. They're his unfinished memoirs. They have to be completed before I die."

"But . . ."

"I can tell you everything. You'll learn to write in my husband's own style. You'll only have to arrange and read his manuscripts to become fascinated by his style . . . his clarity . . . his . . ."

"Yes, I understand."

"Saga, Saga. Where are you? *Ici*, Saga!"

"Who?"

"My companion."

"The rabbit?"

"Yes. She'll come back."

When you raise your eyes, which you've been keeping lowered, her lips are closed but you can hear her words again—"She'll come back"—as if the old lady were pronouncing them at that instant. Her lips remain still. You look in back of you and you're almost blinded by the gleam from the religious objects. When you look at her again you see that her eyes have opened very wide, and that they're clear, liquid, enormous, almost the same color as the yellowish whites around them, so that only the black dots of the pupils mar that clarity. It's lost a moment later in the heavy folds of her lowered eyelids, as if she wanted to protect that glance which is now hiding at the back of its dry cave.

"Then you'll stay here. Your room is upstairs. It's sunny there."

"It might be better if I didn't trouble you, Señora. I can go on living where I am and work on the manuscripts there."

"My conditions are that you have to live here. There isn't much time left."

"I don't know if . . ."

"Aura . . ."

The old woman moves for the first time since you entered her room. As she reaches out her hand again, you sense that agitated breathing beside you, and another hand reaches out to touch the Señora's fingers. You look around and a girl is standing there, a girl whose whole body you can't see because she's standing so close to you and her arrival was so unexpected, without the slightest sound—not even these sounds that can't be heard but are real anyway because they're remembered immediately afterwards, because in spite of everything they're louder than the silence that accompanies them.

"I told you she'd come back."

"Who?"

"Aura. My companion. My niece."

"Good afternoon."

The girl nods and at the same instant the old lady imitates her gesture.

"This is Señor Montero. He's going to live with us."

You move a few steps so that the light from the candles won't blind you. The girl keeps her eyes closed, her hands at her sides. She doesn't look at you at first, then little by little she opens her eyes as if she were afraid of the light. Finally you can see that those eyes are sea green and that they surge, break to foam, grow calm again, then surge again like a wave. You look into them and tell yourself it isn't true, because they're beautiful green eyes just like all the beautiful green eyes you've ever known. But you can't deceive yourself: those eyes do surge, do change, as if offering you a landscape that only you can see and desire.

"Yes. I'm going to live with you."

II

The old woman laughs sharply and tells you that she is grateful for your kindness and that the girl will show you to your room. You're thinking about the salary of four thousand pesos, and how the work should be pleasant because you like these jobs of careful research that don't include physical effort or going from one place to another or meeting people you don't want to meet. You're thinking about this as you follow her out of the room, and you discover that you've got to follow her with your ears instead of your eyes: you follow the rustle of her skirt, the rustle of taffeta, and you're anxious now to look into her eyes again. You climb the stairs behind that sound in the darkness, and you're still unused to the obscurity. You remember it must be about six in the afternoon, and the flood of light surprises you when Aura opens the door to your bedroom—another door without a latch—and steps aside to tell you: "This is your room. We'll expect you for supper in an hour."

She moves away with that same faint rustle of taffeta, and you weren't able to see her face again.

You close the door and look up at the skylight that serves as a roof. You smile when you find that the evening light is blinding compared with the darkness in the rest of the house, and smile again when you try out the mattress on the gilded metal bed. Then you glance around the room: a red wool rug, olive and gold wallpaper, an easy chair covered in red velvet, an old walnut desk with a green leather top, an old Argand lamp with its soft glow for your nights of research, and a bookshelf over the desk in reach of your hand. You walk over to the other door, and on pushing it open you discover an outmoded bathroom: a four-legged bathtub with little flowers painted on the porcelain, a blue hand basin, an old-fashioned toilet. You look at yourself in the large oval mirror on the door of the wardrobe—it's also walnut—in the bathroom hallway. You move your heavy eyebrows and wide thick lips, and your breath fogs the mirror. You close your black eyes, and when you open them again the mirror has cleared. You stop holding your breath and run your hand through your dark, limp hair; you touch your fine profile, your lean cheeks; and when your breath hides your face again you're repeating her name: "Aura."

After smoking two cigarettes while lying on the bed, you get up, put on your jacket, and comb your hair. You push the door open and try to remember the route you followed coming up. You'd like to leave the door open so that the lamplight could guide you, but that's impossible because the springs close it behind you. You could enjoy playing with that door, swinging it back and forth. You don't do it. You could take the lamp down with you. You don't do it. This house will always be in darkness, and you've got to learn it and relearn it by touch. You grope your way like a blind man, with your arms stretched out wide, feeling your way along the wall, and by accident you turn on the light-switch. You stop and blink in the bright middle of that long, empty hall. At the end of it you can see the bannister and the spiral staircase.

You count the stairs as you go down: another custom you've got to learn in Señora Llorente's house. You take a step backward when you see the reddish eyes of the rabbit, which turns its back on you and goes hopping away.

You don't have time to stop in the lower hallway because Aura is waiting for you at a half-open stained-glass door, with a candelabrum in her hand. You walk toward her, smiling, but you stop when you hear the painful yowling of a number of cats—yes, you stop to listen, next to Aura, to be sure that they're cats—and then follow her to the parlor.

"It's the cats," Aura tells you. "There are lots of rats in this part of the city."

You go through the parlor: furniture upholstered in faded silk; glass-fronted cabinets containing porcelain figurines, musical clocks, medals, glass balls; carpets with Persian designs; pictures of rustic scenes; green velvet curtains. Aura is dressed in green.

"Is your room comfortable?"

"Yes. But I have to get my things from the place where . . ."

"It won't be necessary. The servant has already gone for them."

"You shouldn't have bothered."

You follow her into the dining room. She places the candelabrum in the middle of the table. The room feels damp and cold. The four walls are paneled in dark wood, carved in Gothic style, with fretwork arches and large rosettes. The cats have stopped yowling. When you sit down, you notice that four places have been set. There are two large, covered plates and an old, grimy bottle.

Aura lifts the cover from one of the plates. You breathe in the pungent odor of the liver and onions she serves you, then you pick up the old bottle and fill the cut-glass goblets with that thick red liquid. Out of curiosity you try to read the label on the wine bottle, but the grime has obscured it. Aura serves you some whole broiled tomatoes from the other plate.

"Excuse me," you say, looking at the two extra places, the two empty chairs, "but are you expecting someone else?"

Aura goes on serving the tomatoes. "No. Señora Consuelo feels a little ill tonight. She won't be joining us."

"Señora Consuelo? Your aunt?"

"Yes. She'd like you to go in and see her after supper."

You eat in silence. You drink that thick wine, occasionally shifting your glance so that Aura won't catch you in the hypnotized stare that you can't control. You'd like to fix the girl's features in your mind. Every time you look away you forget them again, and an irresistible urge forces you to look at her once more. As usual, she has her eyes lowered.

While you're searching for the pack of cigarettes in your coat pocket, you run across that big key, and remember, and say to Aura: "Ah! I forgot that one of the drawers in my desk is locked. I've got my papers in it."

And she murmurs: "Then you want to go out?" She says it as a reproach.

You feel confused, and reach out your hand to her with the key dangling from one finger.

"It isn't important. The servant can go for them tomorrow."

But she avoids touching your hand, keeping her own hands on her lap. Finally she looks up, and once again you question your senses, blaming the wine for your bewilderment, for the dizziness brought on by those shining, clear green eyes, and you stand up after Aura does, running your hand over the wooden back of the Gothic chair, without daring to touch her bare shoulder or her motionless head.

You make an effort to control yourself, diverting your attention away from her by listening to the imperceptible movement of a door behind you—it must lead to the kitchen—or by separating the two different elements that make up the room: the compact circle of light around the candelabrum, illuminating the table and one carved wall, and the larger circle of darkness surrounding it. Finally you have the courage to go up to her, take her hand, open it, and place your key-ring in her smooth palm as a token.

She closes her hand, looks up at you, and murmurs, "Thank you." Then she rises and walks quickly out of the room.

You sit down in Aura's chair, stretch your legs, and light a cigarette, feeling a pleasure you've never felt before, one that you knew was part of you but that only now you're experiencing fully, setting it free, bringing it out because this time you know it'll be answered and won't be lost . . . And Señora Consuelo is waiting for you, as Aura said. She's waiting for you after supper . . .

You leave the dining room, and with the candelabrum in your hand you walk through the parlor and the hallway. The first door you come to is the old lady's. You rap on it with your knuckles, but there isn't any answer. You knock again. Then you push the door open because she's waiting for you. You enter cautiously, murmuring: "Señora . . . Señora . . ."

She doesn't hear you, for she's kneeling in front of that wall of religious objects, with her head resting on her clenched fists. You see her from a distance: she's kneeling there in her coarse woolen nightgown, with her head sunk into her narrow shoulders; she's thin, even emaciated, like a medieval sculpture; her legs are like two sticks, and they're inflamed with erysipelas. While you're thinking of the continual rubbing of that rough wool against her skin, she suddenly raises her fists and strikes feebly at the air, as if she were doing battle against the images you can make out as you tiptoe closer: Christ, the Virgin, St. Sebastian, St. Lucia, the Archangel Michael, and the grinning demons in an old print, the only happy figures in that iconography of sorrow and wrath, happy because they're jabbing their pitchforks into the flesh of the damned, pouring cauldrons of boiling water on them, violating the women, getting drunk, enjoying all the liberties forbidden to the saints. You approach that central image, which is surrounded by the tears of Our Lady of Sorrows, the blood of Our Crucified Lord, the delight of Lucifer, the anger of the Archangel, the viscera preserved in bottles of alcohol, the silver heart: Señora Consuelo, kneeling, threatens them with her fists, stammering the words you can hear as you move even closer: "Come, City of God! Gabriel, sound your trumpet! Ah, how long the world takes to die!"

She beats her breast until she collapses in front of the images and candles in a spasm of coughing. You raise her by the elbow, and as you gently help her to the bed you're surprised at her smallness: she's almost a little girl, bent over almost double. You realize that without your assistance she would have had to get back to bed on her hands and knees. You help her into that wide bed with its bread crumbs and old feather pillows, and cover her up, and wait until her breathing is back to normal, while the involuntary tears run down her parchment cheeks.

"Excuse me . . . excuse me, Señor Montero. Old ladies have nothing left but . . . the pleasures of devotion . . . Give me my handkerchief, please."

"Señorita Aura told me . . ."

"Yes, of course. I don't want to lose any time. We should . . . we should begin working as soon as possible. Thank you."

"You should try to rest."

"Thank you . . . Here . . ."

The old lady raises her hand to her collar, unbuttons it, and lowers her head to remove the frayed purple ribbon that she hands to you. It's heavy because there's a copper key hanging from it.

"Over in that corner . . . Open that trunk and bring me the papers at the right, on top of the others . . . They're tied with a yellow ribbon."

"I can't see very well . . ."

"Ah, yes . . . it's just that I'm so accustomed to the darkness. To my right . . . Keep going till you come to the trunk. They've walled us in, Señor Montero. They've built up all around us and blocked off the light. They've tried to force me to sell, but I'll die first. This house is full of memories for us. They won't take me out of here till I'm dead! Yes, that's it. Thank you. You can begin reading this part. I will give you the others later. Good night, Señor Montero. Thank you. Look, the candelabrum has gone out. Light it outside the door, please. No, no, you can keep the key. I trust you."

"Señora, there's a rat's nest in that corner."

"Rats? I never go over there."

"You should bring the cats in here."

"The cats? What cats? Good night. I'm going to sleep. I'm very tired."

"Good night."

III

That same evening you read those yellow papers written in mustard-colored ink, some of them with holes where a careless ash had fallen, others heavily fly-specked. General Llorente's French doesn't have the merits his wife attributed to it. You tell yourself you can make considerable improvements in the style, can tighten up his rambling account of past events: his childhood on a hacienda in Oaxaca, his military studies in France, his friendship with the duc de Morny and the intimates of Napoleon III, his return to Mexico on the staff of Maximilian, the imperial ceremonies and gatherings, the battles, the defeat in 1867, his exile in France. Nothing that hasn't been described before. As you undress you think of the old lady's distorted notions, the value she attributes to these memoirs. You smile as you get into bed, thinking of the four thousand pesos.

You sleep soundly until a flood of light wakes you up at six in the morning: that glass roof doesn't have any curtain. You bury your head under the pillow and try to go back to sleep. Ten minutes later you give it up and walk into the bathroom, where you find all your things neatly arranged on a table and your few clothes hanging in the wardrobe. Just as you finish shaving the early morning silence is broken by that painful, desperate yowling.

You try to find out where it's coming from: you open the door to the hallway, but you can't hear anything from there: those cries are coming from up above, from the skylight. You jump up on the chair, from the chair onto the desk, and by supporting yourself on the bookshelf you can reach the skylight. You open one of the windows and pull yourself up to look out at that side garden, that square of yew trees and brambles where five, six, seven cats—you can't count them, can't hold yourself up there for more than a second—are all twined together, all writhing in flames and giving off a dense smoke that reeks of burnt fur. As you get down again you wonder if you really saw it: perhaps you only imagined it from those dreadful cries that continue, grow less, and finally stop.

You put on your shirt, brush off your shoes with a piece of paper, and listen to the sound of a bell that seems to run through the passageways of the house until it arrives at your door. You look out into the hallway. Aura is walking along it with a bell in her hand. She turns her head to look at you and tells you that breakfast is ready. You try to detain her but she goes down the spiral staircase, still ringing that black-painted bell as if she were trying to wake up a whole asylum, a whole boarding-school.

You follow her in your shirt-sleeves, but when you reach the downstairs hallway you can't find her. The door of the old lady's bedroom opens behind you and you see a hand that reaches out from behind the partly opened door, sets a chamberpot in the hallway and disappears again, closing the door.

In the dining room your breakfast is already on the table, but this time only one place has been set. You eat quickly, return to the hallway, and knock at Señora Consuelo's door. Her sharp, weak voice tells you to come in. Nothing has changed: the perpetual shadows, the glow of the votive lights and the silver objects.

"Good morning, Señor Montero. Did you sleep well?"

"Yes. I read till quite late."

The old lady waves her hand as if in a gesture of dismissal. "No, no, no. Don't give me your opinion. Work on those pages and when you've finished I'll give you the others."

"Very well. Señora, would I be able to go into the garden?"

"What garden, Señor Montero?"

"The one that's outside my room."

"This house doesn't have any garden. We lost our garden when they built up all around us."

"I think I could work better outdoors."

"This house has only got that dark patio where you came in. My niece is growing some shade plants there. But that's all."

"It's all right, Señora."

"I'd like to rest during the day. But come to see me tonight."

"Very well, Señora."

You spend all morning working on the papers, copying out the passages you intend to keep, rewriting the ones you think are especially bad, smoking one cigarette after another and reflecting that you ought to space your work so that the job lasts as long as possible. If you can manage to save at least twelve thousand pesos, you can spend a year on nothing but your own work, which you've postponed and almost forgotten. Your great, inclusive work on the Spanish discoveries and conquests in the New World. A work that sums up all the scattered chronicles, makes them intelligible, and discovers the resemblances among all the undertakings and adventures of Spain's Golden Age, and all the human prototypes and major accomplishments of the Renaissance. You end up by putting aside the General's tedious pages and starting to compile the dates and summaries of your own work. Time passes and you don't look at your watch until you hear the bell again. Then you put on your coat and go down to the dining room.

Aura is already seated. This time Señora Llorente is at the head of the table, wrapped in her shawl and nightgown and coif, hunching over her plate. But the fourth place has also been set. You note it in passing. It doesn't bother you anymore. If the price of your future creative liberty is to put up with all the manias of this old woman, you can pay it easily. As you watch her eating her soup you try to figure out her age. There's a time after which it's impossible to detect the passing of the years, and Señora Consuelo crossed that frontier a long time ago. The General hasn't mentioned her in what you've already read of the memoirs. But if the General was forty-two at the time of the French invasion, and died in 1901, forty years later, he must have died at the age of eighty-two. He must have married the Señora after the defeat at Querétaro and his exile. But she would only have been a girl at that time . . .

The dates escape you because now the Señora is talking in that thin, sharp voice of hers, that birdlike chirping. She's talking to Aura and you listen to her as you eat, hearing her long list of complaints, pains, suspected illnesses, more complaints about the cost of medicines, the dampness of the house and so forth. You'd like to break in on this domestic conversation to ask about the servant who went for your things yesterday, the servant you've never even glimpsed and who never waits on table. You're going to ask about him but you're suddenly surprised to realize that up to this moment Aura hasn't said a word and is eating with a sort of mechanical fatality, as if she were waiting for some outside impulse before picking up her knife and fork, cutting a piece of liver—yes, it's liver again, apparently the favorite dish in this house—and carrying it to her mouth. You glance quickly from the aunt to the niece, but at that moment the Señora becomes motionless, and at the same moment Aura puts her knife on her plate and also becomes motionless, and you remember that the Señora put down her knife only a fraction of a second earlier.

There are several minutes of silence: you finish eating while they sit there rigid as statues, watching you. At last the Señora says, "I'm very tired. I ought not to eat at the table. Come, Aura, help me to my room."

The Señora tries to hold your attention: she looks directly at you so that you'll keep looking at her, although what she's saying is aimed at Aura. You have to make an effort in order to evade that look, which once again is wide, clear, and yellowish, free of the veils and wrinkles that usually obscure it. Then you look at Aura, who is staring fixedly at nothing and silently moving her lips. She gets up with a motion like those you associate with dreaming, takes the arm of the bent old lady, and slowly helps her from the dining room.

Alone now, you help yourself to the coffee that has been there since the beginning of the meal, the cold coffee you sip as you wrinkle your brow and ask yourself if the Señora doesn't have some secret power over her niece: if the girl, your beautiful Aura in her green dress, isn't kept in this dark old house against her will. But it would be so easy for her to escape while the Señora was asleep in her shadowy room. You tell yourself that her hold over the girl must be terrible. And you consider the way out that occurs to your imagination: perhaps Aura is waiting for you to release her from the chains in which the perverse, insane old lady, for some unknown reason, has bound her. You remember Aura as she was a few moments ago, spiritless, hypnotized by her terror, incapable of speaking in front of the tyrant, moving her lips in silence as if she were silently begging you to set her free; so enslaved that she imitated every gesture of the Señora, as if she were permitted to do only what the Señora did.

You rebel against this tyranny. You walk toward the other door, the one at the foot of the staircase, the one next to the old lady's room: that's where Aura must live, because there's no other room in the house. You push the door open and go in. This room is dark also, with whitewashed walls, and the only decoration is an enormous black Christ. At the left there's a door that must lead into the widow's bedroom. You go up to it on tiptoe, put your hands against it, then decide not to open it: you should talk with Aura alone.

And if Aura wants your help she'll come to your room. You go up there for a while, forgetting the yellowed manuscripts and your own notebooks, thinking only about the beauty of your Aura. And the more you think about her, the more you make her yours, not only because of her beauty and your desire, but also because you want to set her free: you've found a moral basis for your desire, and you feel innocent and self-satisfied. When you hear the bell again you don't go down to supper because you can't bear another scene like the one at the middle of the day. Perhaps Aura will realize it, and come up to look for you after supper.

You force yourself to go on working on the papers. When you're bored with them you undress slowly, get into bed, and fall asleep at once, and for the first time in years you dream, dream of only one thing, of a fleshless hand that comes toward you with a bell, screaming that you should go away, everyone should go away; and when that face with its empty eye-sockets comes close to yours, you wake up with a muffled cry, sweating, and feel those gentle hands caressing your face, those lips murmuring in a low voice, consoling you and asking you for affection. You reach out your hands to find that other body, that naked body with a key dangling from its neck, and when you recognize the key you recognize the woman who is lying over you, kissing you, kissing your whole body. You can't see her in the black of the starless night, but you can smell the fragrance of the patio plants in her hair, can feel her smooth, eager body in your arms; you kiss her again and don't ask her to speak.

When you free yourself, exhausted, from her embrace, you hear her first whisper: "You're my husband." You agree. She tells you it's daybreak, then leaves you, saying that she'll wait for you that night in her room. You agree again, and then fall asleep, relieved, unburdened, emptied of desire, still feeling the touch of Aura's body, her trembling, her surrender.

It's hard for you to wake up. There are several knocks on the door, and at last you get out of bed, groaning and still half-asleep. Aura, on the other side of the door, tells you not to open it: she says that Señora Consuelo wants to talk with you, is waiting for you in her room.

Ten minutes later you enter the widow's sanctuary. She's propped up against the pillows, motionless, her eyes hidden by those drooping, wrinkled, dead-white lids; you notice the puffy wrinkles under her eyes, the utter weariness of her skin.

Without opening her eyes she asks you, "Did you bring the key to the trunk?"

"Yes, I think so . . . Yes, here it is."

"You can read the second part. It's in the same place. It's tied with a blue ribbon."

You go over to the trunk, this time with a certain disgust: the rats are swarming around it, peering at you with their glittering eyes from the cracks in the rotted floorboards, galloping toward the holes in the rotted walls. You open the trunk and take out the second batch of papers, then return to the foot of the bed. Señora Consuelo is petting her white rabbit. A sort of croaking laugh emerges from her buttoned-up throat, and she asks you, "Do you like animals?"

"No, not especially. Perhaps because I've never had any."

"They're good friends. Good companions. Above all when you're old and lonely."

"Yes, they must be."

"They're always themselves, Señor Montero. They don't have any pretensions."

"What did you say his name is?"

"The rabbit? She's Saga. She's very intelligent. She follows her instincts. She's natural and free."

"I thought it was a male rabbit."

"Oh? Then you still can't tell the difference."

"Well, the important thing is that you don't feel all alone."

"They want us to be alone, Señor Montero, because they tell us that solitude is the only way to achieve saintliness. They forget that in solitude the temptation is even greater."

"I don't understand, Señora."

"Ah, it's better that you don't. Get back to work now, please."

You turn your back on her, walk to the door, leave her room. In the hallway you clench your teeth. Why don't you have courage enough to tell her that you love the girl? Why don't you go back and tell her, once and for all, that you're planning to take Aura away with you when you finish the job? You approach the door again and start pushing it open, still uncertain, and through the crack you see Señora Consuelo standing up, erect, transformed, with a military tunic in her arms: a blue tunic with gold buttons, red epaulettes, bright medals with crowned eagles—a tunic the old lady bites ferociously, kisses tenderly, drapes over her shoulders as she performs a few teetering dance steps. You close the door.

"She was fifteen years old when I met her," you read in the second part of the memoirs. "*Elle avait quinze ans lorsque je l'ai connue et, si j'ose le dire, ce sont ses yeux verts qui ont fait ma perdition.*" Consuelo's green eyes, Consuelo who was only fifteen in 1867, when General Llorente married her and took her with him into exile in Paris. "*Ma jeune poupée,*" he wrote in a moment of inspiration, "*ma jeune poupée aux yeux verts; je t'ai comblée d'amour.*" He described the house they lived in, the outings, the dances, the carriages, the world of the Second Empire, but all in a dull enough way. "*J'ai même supporté ta haine des chats, moi qu'aimais tellement les jolies bêtes . . .*" One day he found her torturing a cat: she had it clasped between her legs, with her crinoline skirt pulled up, and he didn't know how to attract her attention because it seemed to him that "*tu faisais ca d'une façon si innocent, par pur enfantillage,*" and in fact it excited him so much that if you can believe what he wrote, he made love to her that night with extraordinary passion, "*parce que tu m'avais dit que torturer les chats était ta manière a toi de rendre notre amour favorable, par un sacrifice symbolique . . .*" You've figured it up: Señora Consuelo must be 109. Her husband died fifty-nine years ago. "*Tu sais si bien t'habiller, ma douce Consuelo, toujours drappé dans de velours verts, verts comme tes yeux. Je pense que tu seras toujours belle, même dans cent ans . . .*" Always dressed in green. Always beautiful, even after a hundred years. "*Tu es si fière de ta beauté; que ne ferais-tu pas pour rester toujours jeune?*"

IV

Now you know why Aura is living in this house: to perpetuate the illusion of youth and beauty in that poor, crazed old lady. Aura, kept here like a mirror, like one more icon on that votive wall with its clustered offerings, preserved hearts, imagined saints and demons.

You put the manuscript aside and go downstairs, suspecting there's only one place Aura could be in the morning—the place that greedy old woman has assigned to her.

Yes, you find her in the kitchen, at the moment she's beheading a kid: the vapor that rises from the open throat, the smell of spilt blood, the animal's glazed eyes, all give you nausea. Aura is wearing a ragged, blood-stained dress and her hair is disheveled; she looks at you without recognition and goes on with her butchering.

You leave the kitchen: this time you'll really speak to the old lady, really throw her greed and tyranny in her face. When you push open the door she's standing behind the veil of lights, performing a ritual with the empty air, one hand stretched out and clenched, as if holding something up, and the other clasped around an invisible object, striking again and again at the same place. Then she wipes her hands against her breast, sighs, and starts cutting the air again, as if—yes, you can see it clearly—as if she were skinning an animal . . .

You run through the hallway, the parlor, the dining room, to where Aura is slowly skinning the kid, absorbed in her work, heedless of your entrance or your words, looking at you as if you were made of air.

You climb up to your room, go in, and brace yourself against the door as if you were afraid someone would follow you: panting, sweating, victim of your horror, of your certainty. If something or someone should try to enter, you wouldn't be able to resist, you'd move away from the door, you'd let it happen. Frantically you drag the armchair over to that latchless door, push the bed up against it, then fall onto the bed, exhausted, drained of your will-power, with your eyes closed and your arms wrapped around your pillow—the pillow that isn't yours. Nothing is yours.

You fall into a stupor, into the depths of a dream that's your only escape, your only means of saying No to insanity. "She's crazy, she's crazy," you repeat again and again to make yourself sleepy, and you can see her again as she skins the imaginary kid with an imaginary knife. "She's crazy, she's crazy . . ."

in the depths of the dark abyss, in your silent dream with its mouths opening in silence, you see her coming toward you from the blackness of the abyss, you see her crawling toward you.

in silence,

moving her fleshless hand, coming toward you until her face touches yours and you see the old lady's bloody gums, her toothless gums, and you scream and she goes away again, moving her hand, sowing the abyss with the yellow teeth she carries in her blood-stained apron:

your scream is an echo of Aura's, she's standing in front of you in your dream, and she's screaming because someone's hands have ripped her green taffeta skirt in two, and then

she turns her head toward you

with the torn folds of the skirt in her hands, turns toward you and laughs silently, with the old lady's teeth superimposed on her own, while her legs, her naked legs, shatter into bits and fly toward the abyss . . .

There's a knock at the door, then the sound of the bell, the supper bell. Your head aches so much that you can't make out the hands on the clock, but you know it must be late: above your head you can see the night clouds beyond the skylight. You get up painfully, dazed and hungry. You hold the glass pitcher under the faucet, wait for the water to run, fill the pitcher, then pour it into the basin. You wash your face, brush your teeth with your worn toothbrush that's clogged with greenish paste, dampen your hair—you don't notice you're doing all this in the wrong order—and comb it meticulously in front of the oval mirror on the walnut wardrobe. Then you tie your tie, put on your jacket and go down to the empty dining room, where only one place has been set—yours.

Beside your plate, under your napkin, there's an object you start caressing with your fingers: a clumsy little rag doll, filled with a powder that trickles from its badly sewn shoulder; its face is drawn with India ink, and its body is naked, sketched with a few brush strokes. You eat the cold supper—liver, tomatoes, wine—with your right hand while holding the doll in your left.

You eat mechanically, without noticing at first your own hypnotized attitude, but later you glimpse a reason for your oppressive sleep, your nightmare, and finally identify your sleep-walking movements with those of Aura and the old lady. You're suddenly disgusted by that horrible little doll, in which you begin to suspect a secret illness, a contagion. You let it fall to the floor. You wipe your lips with the napkin, look at your watch, and remember that Aura is waiting for you in her room.

You go cautiously up to Señora Consuelo's door, but there isn't a sound from within. You look at your watch again: it's barely nine o'clock. You decide to feel your way down to that dark, roofed patio you haven't been in since you came through it, without seeing anything, on the day you arrived here.

You touch the damp, mossy walls, breathe the perfumed air, and try to isolate the different elements you're breathing, to recognize the heavy, sumptuous aromas that surround you. The flicker of your match lights up the narrow, empty patio, where various plants are growing on each side in the loose, reddish earth. You can make out the tall, leafy forms that cast their shadows on the walls in the light of the match. But it burns down, singeing your fingers, and you have to light another one to finish seeing the flowers, fruits and plants you remember reading about in old chronicles, the forgotten herbs that are growing here so fragrantly and drowsily: the long, broad, downy leaves of the henbane; the twining stems with flowers that are yellow outside, red inside; the pointed, heart-shaped leaves of the nightshade; the ash-colored down of the grape-mullein with its clustered flowers; the bushy gatheridge with its white blossoms; the belladonna. They come to life in the flare of your match, swaying gently with their shadows, while you recall the uses of these herbs that dilate the pupils, alleviate pain, reduce the pangs of childbirth, bring consolation, weaken the will, induce a voluptuous calm.

You're all alone with the perfumes when the third match burns out. You go up to the hallway slowly, listen again at Señora Consuelo's door, then tiptoe on to Aura's. You push it open without knocking and go into that bare room, where a circle of light reveals the bed, the huge Mexican crucifix, and the woman who comes toward you when the door is closed. Aura is dressed in green, in a green taffeta robe from which, as she approaches, her moon-pale thighs reveal themselves. The woman, you repeat as she comes close, the woman, not the girl of yesterday: the girl of yesterday—you touch Aura's fingers, her waist—couldn't have been more than twenty; the woman of today—you caress her loose black hair, her pallid cheeks—seems to be forty. Between yesterday and today, something about her green eyes has turned hard; the red of her lips has strayed beyond their former outlines, as if she wanted to fix them in a happy grimace, a troubled smile; as if, like that plant in the patio, her smile combined the taste of honey and the taste of gall. You don't have time to think of anything more.

"Sit down on the bed, Felipe."

"Yes."

"We're going to play. You don't have to do anything. Let me do everything myself."

Sitting on the bed, you try to make out the source of that diffuse, opaline light that hardly lets you distinguish the objects in the room, and the presence of Aura, from the golden atmosphere that surrounds them. She sees you looking up, trying to find where it comes from. You can tell from her voice that she's kneeling down in front of you.

"The sky is neither high nor low. It's over us and under us at the same time."

She takes off your shoes and socks and caresses your bare feet.

You feel the warm water that bathes the soles of your feet, while she washes them with a heavy cloth, now and then casting furtive glances at that Christ carved from black wood. Then she dries your feet, takes you by the hand, fastens a few violets in her loose hair, and begins to hum a melody, a waltz, to which you dance with her, held by the murmur of her voice, gliding around to the slow, solemn rhythm she's setting, very different from the light movements of her hands, which unbutton your shirt, caress your chest, reach around to your back and grasp it. You also murmur that wordless song, that melody rising naturally from your throat: you glide around together, each time closer to the bed, until you muffle the song with your hungry kisses on Aura's mouth, until you stop the dance with your crushing kisses on her shoulders and breasts.

You're holding the empty robe in your hands. Aura, squatting on the bed, places an object against her closed thighs, caressing it, summoning you with her hand. She caresses that thin wafer, breaks it against her thighs, oblivious of the crumbs that roll down her hips: she offers you half of the wafer and you take it, place it in your mouth at the same time she does, and swallow it with difficulty. Then you fall on Aura's naked body, you fall on her naked arms, which are stretched out from one side of the bed to the other like the arms of the crucifix hanging on the wall, the black Christ with that scarlet silk wrapped around his thighs, his spread knees, his wounded side, his crown of thorns set on a tangled black wig with silver spangles. Aura opens up like an altar.

You murmur her name in her ear. You feel the woman's full arms against your back. You hear her warm voice in your ear: "Will you love me forever?"

"Forever, Aura. I'll love you forever."

"Forever? Do you swear it?"

"I swear it."

"Even though I grow old? Even though I lose my beauty? Even though my hair turns white?"

"Forever, my love, forever."

"Even if I die, Felipe? Will you love me forever, even if I die?"

"Forever, forever. I swear it. Nothing can separate us."

"Come, Felipe, come . . ."

When you wake up, you reach out to touch Aura's shoulder, but you only touch the still-warm pillow and the white sheet that covers you.

You murmur her name.

You open your eyes and see her standing at the foot of the bed, smiling but not looking at you. She walks slowly toward the corner of the room, sits down on the floor, places her arms on the knees that emerge from the darkness you can't peer into, and strokes the wrinkled hand that comes forward from the lessening darkness: she's sitting at the feet of the old lady, of Señora Consuelo, who is seated in an armchair you hadn't noticed earlier: Señora Consuelo smiles at you, nodding her head, smiling at you along with Aura, who moves her head in rhythm with the old lady's: they both smile at you, thanking you. You lie back, without any will, thinking that the old lady has been in the room all the time;

> you remember her movements, her voice, her dance,
> though you keep telling yourself she wasn't there.

The two of them get up at the same moment, Consuelo from the chair, Aura from the floor. Turning their backs on you, they walk slowly toward the door that leads to the widow's bedroom, enter that room where the lights are forever trembling in front of the images, close the door behind them, and leave you to sleep in Aura's bed.

V

Your sleep is heavy and unsatisfying. In your dreams you had already felt the same vague melancholy, the weight on your diaphragm, the sadness that won't stop oppressing your imagination. Although you're sleeping in Aura's room, you're sleeping all alone, far from the body you believe you've possessed.

When you wake up, you look for another presence in the room, and realize it's not Aura who disturbs you but rather the double presence of something that was engendered during the night. You put your hands on your forehead, trying to calm your disordered senses: that dull melancholy is hinting to you in a low voice, the voice of memory and premonition, that you're seeking your other half, that the sterile conception last night engendered your own double.

And you stop thinking, because there are things even stronger than the imagination: the habits that force you to get up, look for a bathroom off this room without finding one, go out into the hallway rubbing your eyelids, climb the stairs tasting the thick bitterness of your tongue, enter your own room feeling the rough bristles on your chin, turn on the bath faucets and then slide into the warm water, letting yourself relax into forgetfulness.

But while you're drying yourself, you remember the old lady and the girl as they smiled at you before leaving the room arm in arm; you recall that whenever they're together they always do the same things: they embrace, smile, eat, speak, enter, leave, at the same time, as if one were imitating the other, as if the will of one depended on the existence of the other . . . You cut yourself lightly on one cheek as you think of these things while you shave; you make an effort to get control of yourself. When you finish shaving you count the objects in your traveling case, the bottles and tubes which the servant you've never seen brought over from your boarding house: you murmur the names of these objects, touch them, read the contents and instructions, pronounce, the names of the manufacturers, keeping to these objects in order to forget that other one, the one without a name, without a label, without any rational consistency. What is Aura expecting of you? you ask yourself, closing the traveling case. What does she want, what does she want?

In answer you hear the dull rhythm of her bell in the corridor telling you breakfast is ready. You walk to the door without your shirt on. When you open it you find Aura there: it must be Aura because you see the green taffeta she always wears, though her face is covered with a green veil. You take her by the wrist, that slender wrist which trembles at your touch . . .

"Breakfast is ready," she says, in the faintest voice you've ever heard.

"Aura, let's stop pretending."

"Pretending?"

"Tell me if Señora Consuelo keeps you from leaving, from living your own life. Why did she have to be there when you and I . . . Please tell me you'll go with me when . . ."

"Go away? Where?"

"Out of this house. Out into the world, to live together. You shouldn't feel bound to your aunt forever . . . Why all this devotion? Do you love her that much?"

"Love her?"

"Yes. Why do you have to sacrifice yourself this way?"

"Love her? She loves me. She sacrifices herself for me."

"But she's an old woman, almost a corpse. You can't . . ."

"She has more life than I do. Yes, she's old and repulsive . . . Felipe, I don't want to become . . . to be like her . . . another . . ."

"She's trying to bury you alive. You've got to be reborn, Aura."

"You have to die before you can be reborn . . . No, you don't understand. Forget about it, Felipe. Just have faith in me."

"If you'd only explain."

"Just have faith in me. She's going to be out today for the whole day."

"She?"

"Yes, the other."

"She's going out? But she never . . ."

"Yes, sometimes she does. She makes a great effort and goes out. She's going out today. For all day. You and I could . . ."

"Go away?"

"If you want to."

"Well . . . perhaps not yet. I'm under contract. But as soon as I can finish the work, then . . ."

"Ah, yes. But she's going to be out all day. We could do something."

"What?"

"I'll wait for you this evening in my aunt's bedroom. I'll wait for you as always."

She turns away, ringing her bell like the lepers who use a bell to announce their approach, telling the unwary: "Out of the way, out of the way." You put on your shirt and coat and follow the sound of the bell calling you to the dining room. In the parlor the widow Llorente comes toward you, bent over, leaning on a knobby cane; she's dressed in an old white gown with a stained and tattered gauze veil. She goes by without looking at you, blowing her nose into a handkerchief, blowing her nose and spitting. She murmurs, "I won't be at home today, Señor Montero. I have complete confidence in your work. Please keep at it. My husband's memoirs must be published."

She goes away, stepping across the carpets with her tiny feet, which are like those of an antique doll, and supporting herself with her cane, spitting and sneezing as if she wanted to clear something from her congested lungs. It's only by an effort of the will that you keep yourself from following her with your eyes, despite the curiosity you feel at seeing the yellowed bridal gown she's taken from the bottom of that old trunk in her bedroom.

You scarcely touch the cold coffee that's waiting for you in the dining room. You sit for an hour in the tall, archback chair, smoking, waiting for the sounds you never hear, until finally you're sure the old lady has left the house and can't catch you at what you're going to do. For the last hour you've had the key to the trunk clutched in your hand, and now you get up and silently walk through the parlor into the hallway, where you wait for another fifteen minutes—your watch tells you how long—with your ear against Señora Consuelo's door. Then you slowly push it open until you can make out, beyond the spider's web of candle, the empty bed on which her rabbit is gnawing at a carrot: the bed that's always littered with scraps of bread, and that you touch gingerly as if you thought the old lady might be hidden among the rumples of the sheets. You walk over to the corner where the trunk is, stepping on the tail of one of those rats; it squeals, escapes from your foot, and scampers off to warn the others. You fit the copper key into the rusted padlock, remove the padlock, and then raise the lid, hearing the creak of the old, stiff hinges. You take out the third portion of the memoirs—it's tied with a red ribbon—and under it you discover those photographs, those old, brittle, dog-eared photographs. You pick them up without looking at them, clutch the whole treasure to your breast, and hurry out of the room without closing the trunk, forgetting the hunger of the rats. You close the door, lean against the wall in the hallway till you catch your breath, then climb the stairs to your room.

Up there you read the new pages, the continuation, the events of an agonized century. In his florid language General Llorente describes the personality of Eugenia de Montijo, pays his respects to Napoleon the Little, summons up his most martial rhetoric to proclaim the Franco-Prussian War, fills whole pages with his sorrow at the defeat, harangues all men of honor about the Republican monster, sees a ray of hope in General Boulanger, sighs for Mexico, believes that in the Dreyfus affair the honor—always that word "honor"—of the army has asserted itself again.

The brittle pages crumble at your touch: you don't respect them now, you're only looking for a reappearance of the woman with green eyes. "I know why you weep at times, Consuelo. I have not been able to give you children, although you are so radiant with life . . ." And later: "Consuelo, you should not tempt God. We must reconcile ourselves. Is not my affection enough? I know that you love me; I feel it. I am not asking you for resignation, because that would offend you. I am only asking you to see, in the great love which you say you have for me, something sufficient, something that can fill both of us, without the need of turning to sick imaginings . . ." On another page: "I told Consuelo that those medicines were utterly useless. She insists on growing her own herbs in the garden. She says she is not deceiving herself. The herbs are not to strengthen the body, but rather the soul." Later: "I found her in a delirium, embracing the pillow. She cried, 'Yes, yes, yes, I've done it, I've re-created her! I can invoke her, I can give her life with my own life!' It was necessary to call the doctor. He told me he could not quiet her, because the truth was that she was under the effects of narcotics, not of stimulants." And finally: "Early this morning I found her walking barefooted through the hallways. I wanted to stop her. She went by without looking at me, but her words were directed to me. 'Don't stop me,' she said. 'I'm going toward my youth, and my youth is coming toward me. It's coming in, it's in the garden, it's come back . . .' Consuelo, my poor Consuelo! Even the devil was an angel once."

There isn't any more. The memoirs of General Llorente end with that sentence: "*Consuelo, le démon aussi était un ange, avant . . .*"

And after the last page, the portraits. The portrait of an elderly gentleman in a military uniform, an old photograph with these words in one corner: "*Moulin, Photographe, 35 Boulevard Haussmann*" and the date "*1894.*" Then the photograph of Aura, of Aura with her green eyes, her black hair gathered in ringlets, leaning against a Doric column with a painted landscape in the background: the landscape of a Lorelei in the Rhine. Her dress is buttoned up to the collar, there's a handkerchief in her hand, she's wearing a bustle: Aura, and the date "*1876*" in white ink, and on the back of the daguerreotype, in spidery handwriting: "*Fait pour notre dixième anniversaire de mariage,*" and a signature in the same hand, "*Consuelo Llorente.*" In the third photograph you see both Aura and the old gentleman, but this time they're dressed in outdoor clothes, sitting on a bench in a garden. The photograph has become a little blurred: Aura doesn't look as young as she did in the other picture, but it's she, it's he, it's . . . it's you. You stare and stare at the photographs, then hold them up to the skylight. You cover General Llorente's beard with your finger, and imagine him with black hair, and you only discover yourself: blurred, lost, forgotten, but you, you, you.

Your head is spinning, overcome by the rhythms of that distant waltz, by the odor of damp, fragrant plants: you fall exhausted on the bed, touching your cheeks, your eyes, your nose, as if you were afraid that some invisible hand had ripped off the mask you've been wearing for twenty-seven years, the cardboard features that hid your true face, your real appearance, the appearance you once had but then forgot. You bury your face in the pillow, trying to keep the wind of the past from tearing away your own features, because you don't want to lose them. You lie there with your face in the pillow, waiting for what has to come, for what you can't prevent. You don't look at your watch again, that useless object tediously measuring time in accordance with human vanity, those little hands marking out the long hours that were invented to disguise the real passage of time, which races with a mortal and insolent swiftness no clock could ever measure. A life, a century, fifty years: you can't imagine those lying measurements any longer, you can't hold that bodiless dust within your hands.

When you look up from the pillow, you find you're in darkness. Night has fallen.

Night has fallen. Beyond the skylight the swift black clouds are hiding the moon, which tries to free itself, to reveal its pale, round, smiling face. It escapes for only a moment, then the clouds hide it again. You haven't got any hope left. You don't even look at your watch. You hurry down the stairs, out of that prison cell with its old papers and faded daguerreotypes, and stop at the door of Señora Consuelo's room, and listen to your own voice, muted and transformed after all those hours of silence: "Aura . . ."

Again: "Aura . . ."

You enter the room. The votive lights have gone out. You remember that the old lady has been away all day: without her faithful attention the candles have all burned up. You grope forward in the darkness to the bed.

And again: "Aura . . ."

You hear a faint rustle of taffeta, and the breathing that keeps time with your own. You reach out your hand to touch Aura's green robe.

"No. Don't touch me. Lie down at my side."

You find the edge of the bed, swing up your legs, and remain there stretched out and motionless. You can't help feeling a shiver of fear: "She might come back any minute."

"She won't come back."

"Ever?"

"I'm exhausted. She's already exhausted. I've never been able to keep her with me for more than three days."

"Aura . . ."

You want to put your hand on Aura's breasts. She turns her back: you can tell by the difference in her voice.

"No . . . Don't touch me . . ."

"Aura . . . I love you."

"Yes. You love me. You told me yesterday that you'd always love me."

"I'll always love you, always. I need your kisses, your body . . ."

"Kiss my face. Only my face."

You bring your lips close to the head that's lying next to yours. You stroke Aura's long black hair. You grasp that fragile woman by the shoulders, ignoring her sharp complaint. You tear off her taffeta robe, embrace her, feel her small and lost and naked in your arms, despite her moaning resistance, her feeble protests, kissing her face without thinking, without distinguishing, and you're touching her withered breasts when a ray of moonlight shines in and surprises you, shines in through a chink in the wall that the rats have chewed open, an eye that lets in a beam of silvery moonlight. It falls on Aura's eroded face, as brittle and yellowed as the memoirs, as creased with wrinkles as the photographs. You stop kissing those fleshless lips, those toothless gums: the ray of moonlight shows you the naked body of the old lady, of Señora Consuelo, limp, spent, tiny, ancient, trembling because you touch her. You love her, you too have come back . . .

You plunge your face, your open eyes, into Consuelo's silver-white hair, and you'll embrace her again when the clouds cover the moon, when you're both hidden again, when the memory of youth, of youth re-embodied, rules the darkness.

"She'll come back, Felipe. We'll bring her back together. Let me recover my strength and I'll bring her back . . ."

—*Translated from the Spanish by Lysander Kemp*

Thomas Hardy (1840–1928)

Barbara, of the House of Grebe

Thomas Hardy, one of the finest British novelists and poets, wrote a small number of stories of high quality relevant to horror literature, for the most part macabre pieces. Critics often refer to his poetry as an influence on the development of horror fiction as well. Moreover, individual scenes in his novels, such as the children's suicide in *Jude the Obscure,* are horrific. His most clearly supernatural piece, "The Withered Arm," is a story of witchcraft with a strongly psychological subtext. Less familiar, but stronger in impact, is "Barbara, of the House of Grebe." T.S. Eliot, in *After Strange Gods,* described it as revealing "a world of pure evil." It is certainly not what we would consider a genre horror tale, but it develops through one horrific scene after another a powerful effect without any overt supernatural trappings. As a moral and psychological tale of horror it is often overlooked. It is for stories such as this that the Penguin *Encyclopedia* says his "neglected short tales constitute one of the key contributions to horror literature by a distinguished writer." While perhaps an overstatement, Hardy somehow holds a place of influence in the evolution of the mode in the late nineteenth and early twentieth century.

It was apparently an idea, rather than a passion, that inspired Lord Uplandtowers' resolve to win her. Nobody ever knew when he formed it, or whence he got his assurance of success in the face of her manifest dislike of him. Possibly not until after that first important act of her life which I shall presently mention. His matured and cynical doggedness at the age of nineteen, when impulse mostly rules calculation, was remarkable, and might have owed its existence as much to his succession to the earldom and its accompanying local honours in childhood, as to the family character; an elevation which jerked him into maturity, so to speak, without his having known adolescence. He had only reached his twelfth year when his father, the fourth Earl, died, after a course of the Bath waters.

Nevertheless, the family character had a great deal to do with it. Determination was hereditary in the bearers of that escutcheon; sometimes for good, sometimes for evil.

The seats of the two families were about ten miles apart, the way between them lying along the now old, then new, turnpike-road connecting Havenpool and Warborne with the city of Melchester; a road which, though only a branch from what was known as the Great Western Highway, is probably, even at present, as it has been for the last hundred years, one of the finest examples of a macadamized turnpike-track that can be found in England.

The mansion of the Earl, as well as that of his neighbour, Barbara's father, stood back about a mile from the highway, with which each was connected by an ordinary drive and lodge. It was along this particular highway that the young Earl drove on a certain evening at Christmastide some twenty years before the end of the last century, to attend a ball at Chene Manor, the home of Barbara and her parents Sir John and Lady Grebe. Sir John's was a baronetcy created a few years before the breaking out of the Civil War, and his lands were even more extensive than those of Lord Uplandtowers himself, comprising this Manor of Chene, another on the coast near, half the Hundred of Cockdene, and well-enclosed lands in several other parishes, notably Warborne and those contiguous. At this time Barbara was barely seventeen, and the ball is the first occasion on which we have any tradition of Lord Uplandtowers attempting tender relations with her; it was early enough, God knows.

An intimate friend—one of the Drenkhards—is said to have dined with him that day, and Lord Uplandtowers had, for a wonder, communicated to his guest the secret design of his heart.

"You'll never get her—sure; you'll never get her!' this friend had said at parting. "She's not drawn to your lordship by love: and as for thought of a good match, why, there's no more calculation in her than in a bird."

"We'll see," said Lord Uplandtowers impassively.

He no doubt thought of his friend's forecast as he travelled along the highway in his chariot; but the sculptural repose of his profile against the vanishing daylight on his right hand would have shown his friend that the Earl's equanimity was undisturbed. He reached the solitary wayside tavern called Lornton Inn—the rendezvous of many a daring poacher for operations in the adjoining forest; and he might have observed, if he had taken the trouble, a strange post-chaise standing in the halting-space before the inn. He duly sped past it, and half-an-hour after through the little town of Warborne. Onward, a mile further, was the house of his entertainer.

At this date it was an imposing edifice—or, rather, congeries of edifices—as extensive as the residence of the Earl himself, though far less regular. One wing showed extreme antiquity, having huge chimneys, whose substructures projected from the external walls like towers; and a kitchen of vast dimensions, in which (it was said) breakfasts had been cooked for John of Gaunt. Whilst he was yet in the forecourt he could hear the rhythm of French horns and clarionets, the favourite instruments of those days at such entertainments.

Entering the long parlour, in which the dance had just been opened by Lady Grebe with a minuet—it being now seven o'clock, according to the tradition—he was received with a welcome befitting his rank, and looked round for Barbara. She was not dancing, and seemed to be preoccupied—almost, indeed, as though she had been waiting for him. Barbara at this time was a good and pretty girl, who never spoke ill of anyone, and hated other pretty women the very least possible. She did not refuse him for the country-dance which followed, and soon after was his partner in a second.

The evening wore on, and the horns and clarionets tootled merrily. Barbara evinced towards her lover neither distinct preference nor aversion; but old eyes would have seen that she pondered something. However, after supper she pleaded a headache, and disappeared. To pass the time of her absence, Lord Uplandtowers went into a little room adjoining the long gallery, where some elderly ones were sitting by the fire—for he had a phlegmatic dislike of dancing for its own sake,—and, lifting the window-curtains, he looked out of the window into the park and wood, dark now as a cavern. Some of the guests appeared to be leaving even so soon as this, two lights showing themselves as turning away from the door and sinking to nothing in the distance.

His hostess put her head into the room to look for partners for the ladies, and Lord

Uplandtowers came out. Lady Grebe informed him that Barbara had not returned to the ball-room: she had gone to bed in sheer necessity.

"She has been so excited over the ball all day," her mother continued, "that I feared she would be worn out early. . . . But sure, Lord Uplandtowers, you won't be leaving yet?"

He said that it was near twelve o'clock, and that some had already left.

"I protest nobody has gone yet," said Lady Grebe.

To humour her he stayed till midnight, and then set out. He had made no progress in his suit; but he had assured himself that Barbara gave no other guest the preference, and nearly everybody in the neighbourhood was there.

"'Tis only a matter of time," said the calm young philosopher.

The next morning he lay till near ten o'clock, and he had only just come out upon the head of the staircase when he heard hoofs upon the gravel without; in a few moments the door had been opened, and Sir John Grebe met him in the hall, as he set foot on the lowest stair.

"My lord—where's Barbara—my daughter?"

Even the Earl of Uplandtowers could not repress amazement. "What's the matter, my dear Sir John," says he.

The news was startling, indeed. From the Baronet's disjointed explanation Lord Uplandtowers gathered that after his own and the other guests' departure Sir John and Lady Grebe had gone to rest without seeing any more of Barbara; it being understood by them that she had retired to bed when she sent word to say that she could not join the dancers again. Before then she had told her maid that she would dispense with her services for this night; and there was evidence to show that the young lady had never lain down at all, the bed remaining unpressed. Circumstances seemed to prove that the deceitful girl had feigned indisposition to get an excuse for leaving the ball-room, and that she had left the house within ten minutes, presumably during the first dance after supper.

"I saw her go," said Lord Uplandtowers.

"The devil you did!" says Sir John.

"Yes." And he mentioned the retreating carriage-lights, and how he was assured by Lady Grebe that no guest had departed.

"Surely that was it!" said the father. "But she's not gone alone, d'ye know!"

"Ah—who is the young man?"

"I can on'y guess. My worst fear is my most likely guess. I'll say no more. I thought—yet I would not believe—it possible that you was the sinner. Would that you had been! But 'tis t'other, 'tis t'other, by Heaven! I must e'en up and after 'em!"

"Whom do you suspect?"

Sir John would not give a name, and, stultified rather than agitated, Lord Uplandtowers accompanied him back to Chene. He again asked upon whom were the Baronet's suspicions directed; and the impulsive Sir John was no match for the insistence of Uplandtowers.

He said at length, "I fear 'tis Edmond Willowes."

"Who's he?"

"A young fellow of Shottsford-Forum—a widow-woman's son," the other told him, and explained that Willowes's father, or grandfather, was the last of the old glass-painters in that place, where (as you may know) the art lingered on when it had died out in every other part of England.

"By God that's bad—mighty bad!" said Lord Uplandtowers, throwing himself back in the chaise in frigid despair.

They despatched emissaries in all directions; one by the Melchester Road, another by Shottsford-Forum, another coastwards.

But the lovers had a ten-hours' start; and it was apparent that sound judgment had been exercised in choosing as their time of flight the particular night when the movements of a strange carriage would not be noticed, either in the park or on the neighbouring highway, owing to the general press of vehicles. The chaise which had been seen waiting at Lornton Inn was, no doubt, the one they had escaped in; and the pair of heads which had planned so cleverly thus far had probably contrived marriage ere now.

The fears of her parents were realized. A letter sent by special messenger from Barbara, on the evening of that day, briefly informed them that her lover and herself were on the way to London, and before this communication reached her home they would be united as husband and wife. She had taken this extreme step because she loved her dear Edmond as she could love no other man, and because she had seen closing round her the doom of marriage with Lord Uplandtowers, unless she put that threatened fate out of possibility by doing as she had done. She had well considered the step beforehand, and was prepared to live like any other country-townsman's wife if her father repudiated her for her action.

"Damn her!" said Lord Uplandtowers, as he drove homeward that night. "Damn her for a fool!"—which shows the kind of love he bore her.

Well; Sir John had already started in pursuit of them as a matter of duty, driving like a wild man to Melchester, and thence by the direct highway to the capital. But he soon saw that he was acting to no purpose; and by and by, discovering that the marriage had actually taken place, he forebore all attempts to unearth them in the City, and returned and sat down with his lady to digest the event as best they could.

To proceed against this Willowes for the abduction of our heiress was, possibly, in their power; yet, when they considered the now unalterable facts, they refrained from violent retribution. Some six weeks passed, during which time Barbara's parents, though they keenly felt her loss, held no communication with the truant, either for reproach or condonation. They continued to think of the disgrace she had brought upon herself; for, though the young man was an honest fellow, and the son of an honest father, the latter had died so early, and his widow had had such struggles to maintain herself, that the son was very imperfectly educated. Moreover, his blood was, as far as they knew, of no distinction whatever, whilst hers, through her mother, was compounded of the best juices of ancient baronial distillation, containing tinctures of Maundeville, and Mohun, and Syward, and Peverell, and Culliford, and Talbot, and Plantagenet, and York, and Lancaster, and God knows what besides, which it was a thousand pities to throw away.

The father and mother sat by the fireplace that was spanned by the four-centred arch bearing the family shields on its haunches, and groaned aloud—the lady more than Sir John.

"To think this should have come upon us in our old age!" said he.

"Speak for yourself!" she snapped through her sobs, "I am only one-and-forty! . . . Why didn't ye ride faster and overtake 'em!"

In the meantime the young married lovers, caring no more about their blood than about ditch-water, were intensely happy—happy, that is, in the descending scale which, as we all know, Heaven in its wisdom has ordained for such rash cases; that is to say, the first week they were in the seventh heaven, the second in the sixth, the third week temperate, the fourth reflective, and so on; a lover's heart after possession being comparable to the earth in its geologic stages, as described to us sometimes by our worthy President; first a hot coal, then a warm one, then a cooling cinder, then chilly—the simile shall be pursued no further. The long and the short of it was that one day a letter, sealed with their daughter's own little seal, came into Sir John and Lady Grebe's hands; and, on opening it, they found it to contain an appeal from the young couple to Sir John to forgive them for what they had done, and they would fall on their naked knees and be most dutiful children for evermore.

Then Sir John and his lady sat down again by the fireplace with the four-centred arch, and consulted, and re-read the letter. Sir John Grebe, if the truth must be told, loved his daughter's happiness far more, poor man, than he loved his name and lineage; he recalled to his mind all her little ways, gave vent to a sigh; and, by this time acclimatized to the idea of the marriage, said that what was done could not be undone, and that he supposed they must not be too harsh with her. Perhaps Barbara and her husband were in actual need; and how could they let their only child starve?

A slight consolation had come to them in an unexpected manner. They had been credibly informed that an ancestor of plebeian Willowes was once honoured with intermarriage with a scion of the aristocracy who had gone to the dogs. In short, such is the foolishness of distinguished parents, and sometimes of others also, that they wrote that very day to the address Barbara had given them, informing her that she might return home and bring her husband with her; they would not object to see him, would not reproach her, and would endeavour to welcome both, and to discuss with them what could best be arranged for their future.

In three or four days a rather shabby post-chaise drew up at the door of Chene Manor-house, at sound of which the tender-hearted baronet and his wife ran out as if to welcome a prince and princess of the blood. They were overjoyed to see their spoilt child return safe and sound—though she was only Mrs. Willowes, wife of Edmond Willowes of nowhere. Barbara burst into penitential tears, and both husband and wife were contrite enough, as well they might be, considering that they had not a guinea to call their own.

When the four had calmed themselves, and not a word of chiding had been uttered to the pair, they discussed the position soberly, young Willowes sitting in the background with great modesty till invited forward by Lady Grebe in no frigid tone.

"How handsome he is!" she said to herself. "I don't wonder at Barbara's craze for him."

He was, indeed, one of the handsomest men who ever set his lips on a maid's. A blue coat, murrey waistcoat, and breeches of drab set off a figure that could scarcely be surpassed. He had large dark eyes, anxious now, as they glanced from Barbara to her parents and tenderly back again to her; observing whom, even now in her trepidation, one could see why the *sang froid* of Lord Uplandtowers had been raised to more than lukewarmness. Her fair young face (according to the tale handed down by old women) looked out from under a gray conical hat, trimmed with white ostrich-feathers, and her little toes peeped from a buff petticoat worn under a puce gown. Her features were not regular; they were almost infantine, as you may see from miniatures in possession of the family, her mouth showing much sensitiveness, and one could be sure that her faults would not lie on the side of bad temper unless for urgent reasons.

Well, they discussed their state as became them, and the desire of the young couple to gain the good-will of those upon whom they were literally dependent for everything induced them to agree to any temporizing measure that was not too irksome. Therefore, having been nearly two months united, they did not oppose Sir John's proposal that he should furnish Edmond Willowes with funds sufficient for him to travel a year on the Continent in the company of a tutor, the young man undertaking to lend himself with the utmost diligence to the tutor's instructions, till he became polished outwardly and inwardly to the degree required in the husband of such a lady as Barbara. He was to apply himself to the study of languages, manners, history, society, ruins, and everything else that came under his eyes, till he should return to take his place without blushing by Barbara's side.

"And by that time," said worthy Sir John, "I'll get my little place out at Yewsholt ready for you and Barbara to occupy on your return. The house is small and out of the way; but it will do for a young couple for a while."

"If 'twere no bigger than a summer-house it would do!" says Barbara.

"If 'twere no bigger than a sedan-chair!" says Willowes. "And the more lonely the better."

"We can put up with the loneliness," said Barbara, with less zest. "Some friends will come, no doubt."

All this being laid down, a travelled tutor was called in—a man of many gifts and great experience—and on a fine morning away tutor and pupil went. A great reason urged against Barbara accompanying her youthful husband was that his attentions to her would naturally be such as to prevent his zealously applying every hour of his time to learning and seeing—an argument of wise prescience, and unanswerable. Regular days for letter-writing were fixed, Barbara and her Edmond exchanged their last kisses at the door, and the chaise swept under the archway into the drive.

He wrote to her from Le Havre, as soon as he reached that port, which was not for seven days, on account of adverse winds; he wrote from Rouen, and from Paris; described to her his sight of the King and Court at Versailles, and the wonderful marble-work and mirrors in that palace; wrote next from Lyons; then, after a comparatively long interval, from Turin, narrating his fearful adventures in crossing Mont Cenis on mules, and how he was overtaken with a terrific snowstorm, which had well-nigh been the end of him, and his tutor, and his guides. Then he wrote glowingly of Italy; and Barbara could see the development of her husband's mind reflected in his letters month by month; and she much admired the forethought of her father in suggesting this education for Edmond. Yet she sighed sometimes—her husband being no longer in evidence to fortify her in her choice of him—and timidly dreaded what mortifications might be in store for her by reason of this *mésalliance*. She went out very little; for on the one or two occasions on which she had shown herself to former friends she noticed a distinct difference in their manner, as though they should say, "Ah, my happy swain's wife; you're caught!"

Edmond's letters were as affectionate as ever; even more affectionate, after a while, than hers were to him. Barbara observed this growing coolness in herself; and like a good and honest lady was horrified and grieved, since her only wish was to act faithfully and uprightly. It troubled her so much that she prayed for a warmer heart, and at last wrote to her husband to beg him, now that he was in the land of Art, to send her his portrait, ever so small, that she might look at it all day and every day, and never for a moment forget his features.

Willowes was nothing loth, and replied that he would do more than she wished: he had made friends with a sculptor in Pisa, who was much interested in him and his history; and he had commissioned this artist to make a bust of himself in marble, which when finished he would send her. What Barbara had wanted was something immediate; but she expressed no objection to the delay; and in his next communication Edmond told her that the sculptor, of his own choice, had decided to extend the bust to a full-length statue, so anxious was he to get a specimen of his skill introduced to the notice of the English aristocracy. It was progressing well, and rapidly.

Meanwhile, Barbara's attention began to be occupied at home with Yewsholt Lodge, the house that her kind-hearted father was preparing for her residence when her husband

282 Foundations of Fear

returned. It was a small place on the plan of a large one—a cottage built in the form of a mansion, having a central hall with a wooden gallery running round it, and rooms no bigger than closets to support this introduction. It stood on a slope so solitary, and surrounded by trees so dense, that the birds who inhabited the boughs sang at strange hours, as if they hardly could distinguish night from day.

During the progress of repairs at this bower Barbara frequently visited it. Though so secluded by the dense growth, it was near the high road, and one day while looking over the fence she saw Lord Uplandtowers riding past. He saluted her courteously, yet with mechanical stiffness, and did not halt. Barbara went home, and continued to pray that she might never cease to love her husband. After that she sickened, and did not come out of doors again for a long time.

The year of education had extended to fourteen months, and the house was in order for Edmond's return to take up his abode there with Barbara, when, instead of the accustomed letter for her, came one to Sir John Grebe in the handwriting of the said tutor, informing him of a terrible catastrophe that had occurred to them at Venice. Mr. Willowes and himself had attended the theatre one night during the Carnival of the preceding week, to witness the Italian comedy, when owing to the carelessness of one of the candle-snuffers, the theatre had caught fire, and been burnt to the ground. Few persons had lost their lives, owing to the superhuman exertions of some of the audience in getting out the senseless sufferers; and, among them all, he who had risked his own life the most heroically was Mr. Willowes. In re-entering for the fifth time to save his fellow-creatures some fiery beams had fallen upon him, and he had been given up for lost. He was, however, by the blessing of Providence, recovered, with the life still in him, though he was fearfully burnt; and by almost a miracle he seemed likely to survive, his constitution being wondrously sound. He was, of course, unable to write, but he was receiving the attention of several skilful surgeons. Further report would be made by the next mail or by private hand.

The tutor said nothing in detail of poor Willowes's sufferings, but as soon as the news was broken to Barbara she realized how intense they must have been, and her immediate instinct was to rush to his side, though, on consideration, the journey seemed impossible to her. Her health was by no means what it had been, and to post across Europe at that season of the year, or to traverse the Bay of Biscay in a sailing-craft, was an undertaking that would hardly be justified by the result. But she was anxious to go till, on reading to the end of the letter, her husband's tutor was found to hint very strongly against such a step if it should be contemplated, this being also the opinion of the surgeons. And though Willowes's comrade refrained from giving his reasons, they disclosed themselves plainly enough in the sequel.

The truth was that the worst of the wounds resulting from the fire had occurred to his head and face—that handsome face which had won her heart from her,—and both the tutor and the surgeons knew that for a sensitive young woman to see him before his wounds had healed would cause more misery to her by the shock than happiness to him by her ministrations.

Lady Grebe blurted out what Sir John and Barbara had thought, but had had too much delicacy to express.

"Sure, 'tis mighty hard for you, poor Barbara, that the one little gift he had to justify your rash choice of him—his wonderful good looks—should be taken away like this, to leave 'ee no excuse at all for your conduct in the world's eyes. . . . Well, I wish you'd married t'other—that do I!" And the lady sighed.

"He'll soon get right again," said her father soothingly.

Such remarks as the above were not often made; but they were frequent enough to cause Barbara an uneasy sense of self-stultification. She determined to hear them no longer; and the house at Yewsholt being ready and furnished, she withdrew thither with her maids, where for the first time she could feel mistress of a home that would be hers and her husband's exclusively, when he came.

After long weeks Willowes had recovered sufficiently to be able to write himself, and slowly and tenderly he enlightened her upon the full extent of his injuries. It was a mercy, he said, that he had not lost his sight entirely; but he was thankful to say that he still retained full vision in one eye, though the other was dark for ever. The sparing manner in which he meted out particulars of his condition told Barbara how appalling had been his experience. He was grateful for her assurance that nothing could change her; but feared she did not fully realize that he was so sadly disfigured as to make it doubtful if she would recognize him. However, in spite of all, his heart was as true to her as it ever had been.

Barbara saw from his anxiety how much lay behind. She replied that she submitted to the decrees of Fate, and would welcome him in any shape as soon as he could come. She told him of the pretty retreat in which she had taken up her abode, pending their joint occupation of it, and did not reveal how much she had sighed over the information that all his good looks were gone. Still less did she say that she felt a certain strangeness in awaiting him, the weeks they had lived together having been so short by comparison with the length of his absence.

Slowly drew on the time when Willowes found himself well enough to come home. He landed at Southampton, and posted thence towards Yewsholt. Barbara arranged to go out to meet him as far as Lornton Inn—the spot between the Forest and the Chase at which he had waited for night on the evening of their elopement. Thither she drove at the appointed hour in a little pony-chaise, presented her by her father on her birthday for her especial use in her new house; which vehicle she sent back on arriving at the inn, the plan agreed upon being that she should perform the return journey with her husband in his hired coach.

There was not much accommodation for a lady at this wayside tavern; but, as it was a fine evening in early summer, she did not mind—walking about outside, and straining her eyes along the highway for the expected one. But each cloud of dust that enlarged in the distance and drew near was found to disclose a conveyance other than his post-chaise. Barbara remained till the appointment was two hours passed, and then began to fear that owing to some adverse wind in the Channel he was not coming that night.

While waiting she was conscious of a curious trepidation that was not entirely solicitude, and did not amount to dread; her tense state of incertitude bordered both on disappointment and on relief. She had lived six or seven weeks with an imperfectly educated yet handsome husband whom now she had not seen for seventeen months, and who was so changed physically by an accident that she was assured she would hardly know him. Can we wonder at her compound state of mind?

But her immediate difficulty was to get away from Lornton Inn, for her situation was becoming embarrassing. Like too many of Barbara's actions, this drive had been undertaken without much reflection. Expecting to wait no more than a few minutes for her husband in his post-chaise, and to enter it with him, she had not hesitated to isolate herself by sending back her own little vehicle. She now found that, being so well known in this neighbourhood, her excursion to meet her long-absent husband was exciting great interest. She was conscious that more eyes were watching her from the inn-windows than met her own gaze. Barbara had decided to get home by hiring whatever kind of conveyance the tavern afforded, when, straining her eyes for the last time over the now darkening highway, she perceived yet another dust-cloud drawing near. She paused; a chariot ascended to the inn, and would have passed had not its occupant caught sight of her standing expectantly. The horses were checked on the instant.

"You here—and alone, my dear Mrs. Willowes?" said Lord Uplandtowers, whose carriage it was.

She explained what had brought her into this lonely situation; and, as he was going in the direction of her own home, she accepted his offer of a seat beside him. Their conversation was embarrassed and fragmentary at first; but when they had driven a mile or two she was surprised to find herself talking earnestly and warmly to him: her impulsiveness was in truth but the natural consequence of her late existence—a somewhat desolate one by reason of the strange marriage she had made; and there is no more indiscreet mood than that of a woman surprised into talk who has long been imposing upon herself a policy of reserve. Therefore her ingenuous heart rose with a bound into her throat when, in response to his leading questions, or rather hints, she allowed her troubles to leak out of her. Lord Uplandtowers took her quite to her own door, although he had driven three miles out of his way to do so; and in handing her down she heard from him a whisper of stern reproach: "It need not have been thus if you had listened to me!"

She made no reply, and went indoors. There, as the evening wore away, she regretted more and more that she had been so friendly with Lord Uplandtowers. But he had launched himself upon her so unexpectedly: if she had only foreseen the meeting with him, what a careful line of conduct she would have marked out! Barbara broke into a perspiration of disquiet when she thought of her unreserve, and, in self-chastisement, resolved to sit up till midnight on the bare chance of Edmond's return; directing that supper should be laid for him, improbable as his arrival till the morrow was.

The hours went past, and there was dead silence in and round about Yewsholt Lodge, except for the soughing of the trees; till, when it was near upon midnight, she heard the noise of hoofs and wheels approaching the door. Knowing that it could only be her husband, Barbara instantly went into the hall to meet him. Yet she stood there not without a sensation of faintness, so many were the changes since their parting! And, owing to her casual encounter with Lord Uplandtowers, his voice and image still remained with her, excluding Edmond, her husband, from the inner circle of her impressions.

But she went to the door, and the next moment a figure stepped inside, of which she knew the outline, but little besides. Her husband was attired in a flapping black cloak and slouched hat, appearing altogether as a foreigner, and not as the young English burgess who had left her side. When he came forward into the light of the lamp, she perceived with surprise, and almost with fright, that he wore a mask. At first she had not noticed this—there being nothing in its colour which would lead a casual observer to think he was looking on anything but a real countenance.

He must have seen her start of dismay at the unexpectedness of his appearance, for he said hastily: "I did not mean to come in to you like this—I thought you would have been in bed. How good you are, dear Barbara!" He put his arm round her, but he did not attempt to kiss her.

"O Edmond—it is you?—it must be?" she said, with clasped hands, for though his figure and movement were almost enough to prove it, and the tones were not unlike the old tones, the enunciation was so altered as to seem that of a stranger.

"I am covered like this to hide myself from the curious eyes of the inn-servants and others," he said, in a low voice. "I will send back the carriage and join you in a moment."

"You are quite alone?"

"Quite. My companion stopped at Southampton."

The wheels of the post-chaise rolled away as she entered the dining-room, where the supper was spread; and presently he rejoined her there. He had removed his cloak and hat, but the mask was still retained; and she could now see that it was of special make, of some flexible material like silk, coloured so as to represent flesh; it joined naturally to the front hair, and was otherwise cleverly executed.

"Barbara—you look ill," he said, removing his glove, and taking her hand.

"Yes—I have been ill," said she.

"Is this pretty little house ours?"

"O—yes." She was hardly conscious of her words, for the hand he had ungloved in order to take hers was contorted, and had one or two of its fingers missing; while through the mask she discerned the twinkle of one eye only.

"I would give anything to kiss you, dearest, now at this moment!" he continued, with mournful passionateness. "But I cannot—in this guise. The servants are abed, I suppose?"

"Yes," said she. "But I can call them? You will have some supper?"

He said he would have some, but that it was not necessary to call anybody at that hour. Thereupon they approached the table, and sat down, facing each other.

Despite Barbara's scared state of mind, it was forced upon her notice that her husband trembled, as if he feared the impression he was producing, or was about to produce, as much as, or more than, she. He drew nearer, and took her hand again.

"I had this mask made at Venice," he began, in evident embarrassment. "My darling Barbara—my dearest wife—do you think you—will mind when I take it off? You will not dislike me—will you?"

"O Edmond, of course I shall not mind," said she. "What has happened to you is our misfortune; but I am prepared for it."

"Are you sure you are prepared?"

"O yes! You are my husband."

"You really feel quite confident that nothing external can affect you?" he said again, in a voice rendered uncertain by his agitation.

"I think I am—quite," she answered faintly.

He bent his head. "I hope, I hope you are," he whispered.

In the pause which followed, the ticking of the clock in the hall seemed to grow loud; and he turned a little aside to remove the mask. She breathlessly awaited the operation, which was one of some tediousness, watching him one moment, averting her face the next; and when it was done she shut her eyes at the dreadful spectacle that was revealed. A quick spasm of horror had passed through her; but though she quailed she forced herself to regard him anew, repressing the cry that would naturally have escaped from her ashy lips. Unable to look at him longer, Barbara sank down on the floor beside her chair, covering her eyes.

"You cannot look at me!" he groaned in a hopeless way. "I am too terrible an object even for you to bear! I knew it; yet I hoped against it. O, this is a bitter fate—curse the skill of those Venetian surgeons who saved me alive! . . . Look up, Barbara," he continued beseechingly; "view me completely; say you loathe me, if you do loathe me, and settle the case between us for ever!"

His unhappy wife pulled herself together for a desperate strain. He was her Edmond; he had done her no wrong; he had suffered. A momentary devotion to him helped her, and lifting her eyes as bidden she regarded this human remnant, this *écorché*, a second time. But the sight was too much. She again involuntarily looked aside and shuddered.

"Do you think you can get used to this?" he said. "Yes or no! Can you bear such a thing of the charnel-house near you? Judge for yourself, Barbara. Your Adonis, your matchless man, has come to this!"

The poor lady stood beside him motionless, save for the restlessness of her eyes. All her natural sentiments of affection and pity were driven clean out of her by a sort of panic; she had just the same sense of dismay and fearfulness that she would have had in the presence of an apparition. She could nohow fancy this to be her chosen one—the man she had loved; he was metamorphosed to a specimen of another species. "I do not loathe you," she said with trembling. "But I am so horrified—so overcome! Let me recover myself. Will you sup now? And while you do so may I go to my room to—regain my old feeling for you? I will try, if I may leave you awhile? Yes, I will try!"

Without waiting for an answer from him, and keeping her gaze carefully averted, the frightened woman crept to the door and out of the room. She heard him sit down to the table, as if to begin supper; though, Heaven knows, his appetite was slight enough after a reception which had confirmed his worst surmises. When Barbara had ascended the stairs and arrived in her chamber she sank down, and buried her face in the coverlet of the bed.

Thus she remained for some time. The bed-chamber was over the dining-room, and presently as she knelt Barbara heard Willowes thrust back his chair, and rise to go into the hall. In five minutes that figure would probably come up the stairs and confront her again; it,—this new and terrible form, that was not her husband's. In the loneliness of this night, with neither maid nor friend beside her, she lost all self-control, and at the first sound of his footstep on the stairs, without so much as flinging a cloak round her, she flew from the room, ran along the gallery to the back staircase, which she descended, and, unlocking the back door, let herself out. She scarcely was aware what she had done till she found herself in the greenhouse, crouching on a flower-stand.

Here she remained, her great timid eyes strained through the glass upon the garden without, and her skirts gathered up, in fear of the field-mice which sometimes came there. Every moment she dreaded to hear footsteps which she ought by law to have longed for, and a voice that should have been as music to her soul. But Edmond Willowes came not that way. The nights were getting short at this season, and soon the dawn appeared, and the first rays of the sun. By daylight she had less fear than in the dark. She thought she could meet him, and accustom herself to the spectacle.

So the much-tried young woman unfastened the door of the hot-house, and went back by the way she had emerged a few hours ago. Her poor husband was probably in bed and asleep, his journey having been long; and she made as little noise as possible in her entry. The house was just as she had left it, and she looked about in the hall for his cloak and hat, but she could not see them; nor did she perceive the small trunk which had been all that he brought with him, his heavier baggage having been left at Southampton for the road-waggon. She summoned courage to mount the stairs; the bedroom-door was open as she had left it. She fearfully peeped round; the bed had not been pressed. Perhaps he had lain down on the dining-room sofa. She descended and entered; he was not there. On the table beside his unsoiled plate lay a note, hastily written on the leaf of a pocket-book. It was something like this:

MY EVER-BELOVED WIFE,—The effect that my forbidding appearance has produced upon you was one which I foresaw as quite possible. I hoped against it, but foolishly so. I was aware that no *human* love could survive such a catastrophe. I confess I thought yours *divine*; but, after so long an absence, there could not be left sufficient warmth to overcome the too natural first aversion. It was an experiment, and it has failed. I do not blame you; perhaps, even, it is better so.

Good-bye. I leave England for one year. You will see me again at the expiration of that time, if I live. Then I will ascertain your true feeling; and, if it be against me, go away for ever.

E.W.

On recovering from her surprise, Barbara's remorse was such that she felt herself absolutely unforgiveable. She should have regarded him as an afflicted being, and not have been this slave to mere eyesight, like a child. To follow him and entreat him to return was her first thought. But on making inquiries she found that nobody had seen him: he had silently disappeared.

More than this, to undo the scene of last night was impossible. Her terror had been too plain, and he was a man unlikely to be coaxed back by her efforts to do her duty. She went and confessed to her parents all that had occurred; which, indeed, soon became known to more persons than those of her own family.

The year passed, and he did not return; and it was doubted if he were alive. Barbara's contrition for her unconquerable repugnance was now such that she longed to build a church-aisle, or erect a monument, and devote herself to deeds of charity for the remainder of her days. To that end she made inquiry of the excellent parson under whom she sat on Sundays, at a vertical distance of a dozen feet. But he could only adjust his wig and tap his snuff-box; for such was the lukewarm state of religion in those days, that not an aisle, steeple, porch, east window, Ten-Commandment board, lion-and-unicorn, or brass candlestick, was required anywhere at all in the neighbourhood as a votive offering from a distracted soul—the last century contrasting greatly in this respect with the happy times in which we live, when urgent appeals for contributions to such objects pour in by every morning's post, and nearly all churches have been made to look like new pennies. As the poor lady could not ease her conscience this way, she determined at least to be charitable, and soon had the satisfaction of finding her porch thronged every morning by the raggedest, idlest, most drunken, hypocritical, and worthless tramps in Christendom.

But human hearts are as prone to change as the leaves of the creeper on the wall, and in the course of time, hearing nothing of her husband, Barbara could sit unmoved whilst her mother and friends said in her hearing, "Well, what has happened is for the best." She began to think so herself, for even now she could not summon up that lopped and mutilated form without a shiver, though whenever her mind flew back to her early wedded days, and the man who had stood beside her then, a thrill of tenderness moved her, which if quickened by his living presence might have become strong. She was young and inexperienced, and had hardly on his late return grown out of the capricious fancies of girlhood.

But he did not come again, and when she thought of his word that he would return once more, if living, and how unlikely he was to break his word, she gave him up for dead. So did her parents; so also did another person—that man of silence, of irresistible incisiveness, of still countenance, who was as awake as seven sentinels when he seemed to be as sound asleep as the figures on his family monument. Lord Uplandtowers, though not yet thirty, had chuckled like a caustic fogey of threescore when he heard of Barbara's terror and flight at her husband's return, and of the latter's prompt departure. He felt pretty sure, however, that Willowes, despite his hurt feelings, would have reappeared to claim his bright-eyed property if he had been alive at the end of the twelve months.

As there was no husband to live with her, Barbara had relinquished the house prepared for them by her father, and taken up her abode anew at Chene Manor, as in the days of her girlhood. By degrees the episode with Edmond Willowes seemed but a fevered dream, and as the months grew to years Lord Uplandtowers' friendship with the people at Chene—which had somewhat cooled after Barbara's elopement—revived considerably, and he again became a frequent visitor there. He could not make the most trivial alteration or improvement at Knollingwood Hall, where he lived, without riding off to consult with his friend Sir John at Chene; and thus putting himself frequently under her eyes, Barbara grew accustomed to him, and talked to him as freely as to a brother. She even began to look up to him as a person of authority, judgment, and prudence; and though his severity on the bench towards poachers, smugglers, and turnip-stealers was matter of common notoriety, she trusted that much of what was said might be misrepresentation.

Thus they lived on till her husband's absence had stretched to years, and there could be no longer any doubt of his death. A passionless manner of renewing his addresses seemed no longer out of place in Lord Uplandtowers. Barbara did not love him, but hers was essentially one of those sweet-pea or with-wind natures which require a twig of stouter fibre than its own to hang upon and bloom. Now, too, she was older, and admitted to herself that a man whose ancestor had run scores of Saracens through and through in fighting for the site of the Holy Sepulchre was a more desirable husband, socially considered, than one who could only claim with certainty to know that his father and grandfather were respectable burgesses.

Sir John took occasion to inform her that she might legally consider herself a widow; and, in brief, Lord Uplandtowers carried his point with her, and she married him, though he could never get her to own that she loved him as she had loved Willowes. In my childhood I knew an old lady whose mother saw the wedding, and she said that when Lord and Lady Uplandtowers drove away from her father's house in the evening it was in a coach-and-four, and that my lady was dressed in green and silver, and wore the gayest hat and feather that ever were seen; though whether it was that the green did not suit her complexion, or otherwise, the Countess looked pale, and the reverse of blooming. After their marriage her husband took her to London, and she saw the gaieties of a season there; then they returned to Knollingwood Hall, and thus a year passed away.

Before their marriage her husband had seemed to care but little about her inability to love him passionately. "Only let me win you," he had said, "and I will submit to all that." But now her lack of warmth seemed to irritate him, and he conducted himself towards her with a resentfulness which led to her passing many hours with him in painful silence. The heir-presumptive to the title was a remote relative, whom Lord Uplandtowers did not exclude from the dislike he entertained towards many persons and things besides, and he had set his mind upon a lineal successor. He blamed her much that there was no promise of this, and asked her what she was good for.

On a particular day in her gloomy life a letter, addressed to her as Mrs. Willowes, reached Lady Uplandtowers from an unexpected quarter. A sculptor in Pisa, knowing nothing of her second marriage, informed her that the long-delayed life-size statue of Mr. Willowes, which, when her husband left that city, he had been directed to retain till it was sent for, was still in his studio. As his commission had not wholly been paid, and the statue was taking up room he could ill spare, he should be glad to have the debt cleared off, and directions where to forward the figure. Arriving at a time when the Countess was beginning to have little secrets (of a harmless kind, it is true) from her husband, by reason of their growing estrangement, she replied to this letter without saying a word to Lord Uplandtowers, sending off the balance that was owing to the sculptor, and telling him to despatch the statue to her without delay.

It was some weeks before it arrived at Knollingwood Hall, and, by a singular coincidence, during the interval she received the first absolutely conclusive tidings of her Edmond's death. It had taken place years before, in a foreign land, about six months after their parting, and had been induced by the sufferings he had already undergone, coupled with much depression of spirit, which had caused him to succumb to a slight ailment. The news was sent her in a brief and formal letter from some relative of Willowes's in another part of England.

Her grief took the form of passionate pity for his misfortunes, and of reproach to herself for never having been able to conquer her aversion to his latter image by recollection of what Nature had originally made him. The sad spectacle that had gone from earth had never been her Edmond at all to her. O that she could have met him as he was at first! Thus Barbara thought. It was only a few days later that a waggon with two horses, containing an immense packing-case, was seen at breakfast-time both by Barbara and her husband to drive round to the back of the house, and by-and-by they were informed that a case labelled "Sculpture" had arrived for her ladyship.

"What can that be?" said Lord Uplandtowers.

"It is the statue of poor Edmond, which belongs to me, but has never been sent till now," she answered.

"Where are you going to put it?" asked he.

"I have not decided," said the Countess. "Anywhere, so that it will not annoy you."

"Oh, it won't annoy me," says he.

When it had been unpacked in a back room of the house, they went to examine it. The statue was a full-length figure, in the purest Carrara marble, representing Edmond Willowes in all his original beauty, as he had stood at parting from her when about to set out on his travels; a specimen of manhood almost perfect in every line and contour. The work had been carried out with absolute fidelity.

"Phœbus-Apollo, sure," said the Earl of Uplandtowers, who had never seen Willowes, real or represented, till now.

Barbara did not hear him. She was standing in a sort of trance before the first husband, as if she had no consciousness of the other husband at her side. The mutilated features of Willowes had disappeared from her mind's eye; this perfect being was really the man she had loved, and not that later pitiable figure; in whom tenderness and truth should have seen this image always, but had not done so.

It was not till Lord Uplandtowers said roughly, "Are you going to stay here all the morning worshipping him?" that she roused herself.

Her husband had not till now the least suspicion that Edmond Willowes originally looked thus, and he thought how deep would have been his jealousy years ago if Willowes had been known to him. Returning to the Hall in the afternoon he found his wife in the gallery, whither the statue had been brought.

She was lost in reverie before it, just as in the morning.

"What are you doing?" he asked.

She started and turned. "I am looking at my husb— my statue, to see if it is well done," she stammered. "Why should I not?"

"There's no reason why," he said. "What are you going to do with the monstrous thing? It can't stand here forever."

"I don't wish it," she said. "I'll find a place."

In her boudoir there was a deep recess, and while the Earl was absent from home for a few days in the following week, she hired joiners from the village, who under her directions enclosed the recess with a panelled door. Into the tabernacle thus formed she had the statue placed, fastening the door with a lock, the key of which she kept in her pocket.

When her husband returned he missed the statue from the gallery, and, concluding that it had been put away out of deference to his feelings, made no remark. Yet at moments he noticed something on his lady's face which he had never noticed there before. He could not construe it; it was a sort of silent ecstasy, a reserved beatification. What had become of the statue he could not divine, and growing more and more curious, looked about here and there for it till, thinking of her private room, he went towards that spot. After knocking he heard the shutting of a door, and the click of a key; but when he entered his wife was sitting at work, on what was in those days called knotting. Lord Uplandtowers' eye fell upon the newly painted door where the recess had formerly been.

"You have been carpentering in my absence then, Barbara," he said carelessly.

"Yes, Uplandtowers."

"Why did you go putting up such a tasteless enclosure as that—spoiling the handsome arch of the alcove?"

"I wanted more closet-room; and I thought that as this was my own apartment—"

"Of course," he returned. Lord Uplandtowers knew now where the statue of young Willowes was.

One night, or rather in the smallest hours of the morning, he missed the Countess from his side. Not being a man of nervous imaginings he fell asleep again before he had much considered the matter, and the next morning had forgotten the incident. But a few nights later the same circumstances occurred. This time he fully roused himself; but before he had moved to search for her she returned to the chamber in her dressing-gown, carrying a candle, which she extinguished as she approached, deeming him asleep. He could discover from her breathing that she was strangely moved; but not on this occasion either did he reveal that he had seen her. Presently, when she had lain down, affecting to wake, he asked her some trivial questions. "Yes, *Edmond*," she replied absently.

Lord Uplandtowers became convinced that she was in the habit of leaving the chamber in this queer way more frequently than he had observed, and he determined to watch. The next midnight he feigned deep sleep, and shortly after perceived her stealthily rise and let herself out of the room in the dark. He slipped on some clothing and followed. At the further end of the corridor, where the clash of flint and steel would be out of the hearing of one in the bed-chamber, she struck a light. He stepped aside into an empty room till she had lit a taper and had passed on to her boudoir. In a minute or two he followed. Arrived at the door of the boudoir, he beheld the door of the private recess open, and Barbara within it, standing with her arms clasped tightly round the neck of her Edmond, and her mouth on his. The shawl which she had thrown round her nightclothes had slipped from her shoulders, and her long white robe and pale face lent her the blanched appearance of a second statue embracing the first. Between her kisses, she apostrophized it in a low murmur of infantine tenderness:

"My only love—how could I be so cruel to you, my perfect one—so good and true—I am ever faithful to you, despite my seeming infidelity! I always think of you—dream of you—during the long hours of the day, and in the night-watches! O Edmond, I am always yours!" Such words as these, intermingled with sobs, and streaming tears, and dishevelled hair, testified to an intensity of feeling in his wife which Lord Uplandtowers had not dreamed of her possessing.

"Ha, ha!" says he to himself. "This is where we evaporate—this is where my hopes of a successor in the title dissolve—ha! ha! This must be seen to, verily!"

Lord Uplandtowers was a subtle man when once he set himself to strategy; though in the present instance he never thought of the simple stratagem of constant tenderness. Nor did he enter the room and surprise his wife as a blunderer would have done, but went back to his chamber as silently as he had left it. When the Countess returned thither, shaken by spent sobs and sighs, he appeared to be soundly sleeping as usual. The next day he began his countermoves by making inquiries as to the whereabouts of the tutor who had travelled with his wife's first husband; this gentleman, he found, was now master of a grammar-school at no great distance from Knollingwood. At the first convenient moment Lord Uplandtowers went thither and obtained an interview with the said gentleman. The schoolmaster was much gratified by a visit from such an influential neighbour, and was ready to communicate anything that his lordship desired to know.

After some general conversation on the school and its progress, the visitor observed that he believed the schoolmaster had once travelled a good deal with the unfortunate Mr. Willowes, and had been with him on the occasion of his accident. He, Lord Uplandtowers, was interested in knowing what had really happened at that time, and had often thought of inquiring. And then the Earl not only heard by word of mouth as much as he wished to know, but, their chat becoming more intimate, the schoolmaster drew upon paper a sketch of the disfigured head, explaining with bated breath various details in the representation.

"It was very strange and terrible!" said Lord Uplandtowers, taking the sketch in his hand. "Neither nose nor ears, nor lips scarcely!"

A poor man in the town nearest to Knollingwood Hall, who combined the art of sign-painting with ingenious mechanical occupations, was sent for by Lord Uplandtowers to come to the Hall on a day in that week when the Countess had gone on a short visit to her parents. His employer made the man understand that the business in which his assistance was demanded was to be considered private, and money insured the observance of this request. The lock of the cupboard was picked, and the ingenious mechanic and painter, assisted by the schoolmaster's sketch, which Lord Uplandtowers had put in his pocket, set to work upon the god-like countenance of the statue under my lord's direction. What the fire had maimed in the original the chisel maimed in the copy. It was a fiendish disfigurement, ruthlessly carried out, and was rendered still more shocking by being tinted to the hues of life, as life had been after the wreck.

Six hours after, when the workman was gone, Lord Uplandtowers looked upon the result, and smiled grimly, and said:

"A statue should represent a man as he appeared in life, and that's as he appeared. Ha! ha! But 'tis done to good purpose, and not idly."

He locked the door of the closet with a skeleton key, and went his way to fetch the Countess home.

That night she slept, but he kept awake. According to the tale, she murmured soft words in her dream; and he knew that the tender converse of her imaginings was held with one whom he had supplanted but in name. At the end of her dream the Countess of Uplandtowers awoke and arose, and then the enactment of former nights was repeated. Her husband remained still and listened. Two strokes sounded from the clock in the pediment without, when, leaving the chamber-door ajar, she passed along the corridor to the other end, where, as usual, she obtained a light. So deep was the silence that he could even from his bed hear her softly blowing the tinder to a glow after striking the steel. She moved on into the boudoir, and he heard, or fancied he heard, the turning of the key in the closet-door. The next moment there came from that direction a loud and prolonged shriek, which resounded to the furthest corners of the house. It was repeated, and there was the noise of a heavy fall.

Lord Uplandtowers sprang out of bed. He hastened along the dark corridor to the door of the boudoir, which stood ajar, and, by the light of the candle within, saw his poor young Countess lying in a heap in her nightdress on the floor of the closet. When he reached her side he found that she had fainted, much to the relief of his fears that matters were worse. He quickly shut up and locked in the hated image which had done the mischief, and lifted his wife in his arms, where in a few instants she opened her eyes. Pressing her face to his without saying a word, he carried her back to her room, endeavouring as he went to disperse her terrors by a laugh in her ear, oddly compounded of causticity, predilection, and brutality.

"Ho—ho—ho!" says he. "Frightened, dear one, hey? What a baby 'tis! Only a joke, sure, Barbara—a splendid joke! But a baby should not go to closets at midnight to look for the ghost of the dear departed! If it do it must expect to be terrified at his aspect—ho—ho—ho!"

When she was in her bed-chamber, and had quite come to herself, though her nerves were still much shaken, he spoke to her more sternly. "Now, my lady, answer me: do you love him—eh?"

"No—no!" she faltered, shuddering, with her expanded eyes fixed on her husband. "He is too terrible—no, no!"

"You are sure?"

"Quite sure!" replied the poor broken-spirited Countess.

But her natural elasticity asserted itself. Next morning he again inquired of her: "Do you love him now?" She quailed under his gaze, but did not reply.

"That means that you do still, by God!" he continued.

"It means that I will not tell an untruth, and do not wish to incense my lord," she answered, with dignity.

"Then suppose we go and have another look at him?" As he spoke, he suddenly took her by the wrist, and turned as if to lead her towards the ghastly closet.

"No—no! O—no!" she cried, and her desperate wriggle out of his hand revealed that the fright of the night had left more impression upon her delicate soul than superficially appeared.

"Another dose or two, and she will be cured," he said to himself.

It was now so generally known that the Earl and Countess were not in accord, that he took no great trouble to disguise his deeds in relation to this matter. During the day he ordered four men with ropes and rollers to attend him in the boudoir. When they arrived, the closet was open, and the upper part of the statue tied up in canvas. He had it taken to the sleeping-chamber. What followed is more or less matter of conjecture. The story, as told to me, goes on to say that, when Lady Uplandtowers retired with him that night, she saw facing the foot of the heavy oak four-poster, a tall dark wardrobe, which had not stood there before; but she did not ask what its presence meant.

"I have had a little whim," he explained when they were in the dark.

"Have you?" says she.

"To erect a little shrine, as it may be called."

"A little shrine?"

"Yes; to one whom we both equally adore—eh? I'll show you what it contains."

He pulled a cord which hung covered by the bed-curtains, and the doors of the wardrobe slowly opened, disclosing that the shelves within had been removed throughout, and the interior adapted to receive the ghastly figure, which stood there as it had stood in the boudoir, but with a wax candle burning on each side of it to throw the cropped and distorted features into relief. She clutched him, uttered a low scream, and buried her head in the bedclothes. "O, take it away—please take it away!" she implored.

"All in good time; namely, when you love me best," he returned calmly. "You don't quite yet—eh?"

"I don't know—I think—O Uplandtowers, have mercy—I cannot bear it—O, in pity, take it away!"

"Nonsense; one gets accustomed to anything. Take another gaze."

In short, he allowed the doors to remain unclosed at the foot of the bed, and the wax-tapers burning; and such was the strange fascination of the grisly exhibition that a morbid curiosity took possession of the Countess as she lay, and, at his repeated request, she did again look out from the coverlet, shuddered, hid her eyes, and looked again, all the while begging him to take it away, or it would drive her out of her senses. But he would not do so yet, and the wardrobe was not locked till dawn.

The scene was repeated the next night. Firm in enforcing his ferocious correctives, he continued the treatment till the nerves of the poor lady were quivering in agony under the virtuous tortures inflicted by her lord, to bring her truant heart back to faithfulness.

The third night, when the scene had opened as usual, and she lay staring with immense wild eyes at the horrid fascination, on a sudden she gave an unnatural laugh; she laughed more and more, staring at the image, till she literally shrieked with laughter: then there was silence, and he found her to have become insensible. He thought she had fainted, but soon saw that the event was worse: she was in an epileptic fit. He started up, dismayed by the sense that, like many other subtle personages, he had been too exacting for his own interests. Such love as he was capable of, though rather a selfish gloating than a cherishing solicitude, was fanned into life on the instant. He closed the wardrobe with the pulley, clasped her in his arms, took her gently to the window, and did all he could to restore her.

It was a long time before the Countess came to herself, and when she did so, a considerable change seemed to have taken place in her emotions. She flung her arms around him, and with gasps of fear abjectly kissed him many times, at last bursting into tears. She had never wept in this scene before.

"You'll take it away, dearest—you will!" she begged plaintively.

"If you love me."

"I do—oh, I do!"

"And hate him, and his memory?"

"Yes—yes!"

"Thoroughly?"

"I cannot endure recollection of him!" cried the poor Countess slavishly. "It fills me with shame—how could I ever be so depraved! I'll never behave badly again, Uplandtowers; and you will never put the hated statue again before my eyes?"

He felt that he could promise with perfect safety. "Never," said he.

"And then I'll love you," she returned eagerly, as if dreading lest the scourge should be applied anew. "And I'll never, never dream of thinking a single thought that seems like faithlessness to my marriage vow."

The strange thing now was that this fictitious love wrung from her by terror took on, through mere habit of enactment, a certain quality of reality. A servile mood of attachment to the Earl became distinctly visible in her contemporaneously with an actual dislike for her late husband's memory. The mood of attachment grew and continued when the statue was removed. A permanent revulsion was operant in her, which intensified as time wore on. How fright could have effected such a change of idiosyncrasy learned physicians alone can say; but I believe such cases of reactionary instinct are not unknown.

The upshot was that the cure became so permanent as to be itself a new disease. She clung to him so tightly that she would not willingly be out of his sight for a moment. She would have no sitting-room apart from his, though she could not help starting when he entered suddenly to her. Her eyes were well-nigh always fixed upon him. If he drove out, she wished to go with him; his slightest civilities to other women made her frantically jealous; till at length her very fidelity became a burden to him, absorbing his time, and curtailing his liberty, and causing him to curse and swear. If he ever spoke sharply to her now, she did not revenge herself by flying off to a mental world of her own; all that affection for another, which had provided her with a resource, was now a cold black cinder.

From that time the life of this scared and enervated lady—whose existence might have been developed to so much higher purpose but for the ignoble ambition of her parents and the conventions of the time—was one of obsequious amativeness towards a perverse and cruel man. Little personal events came to her in quick succession—half a dozen, eight, nine, ten such events,—in brief, she bore him no less than eleven children in the nine following years, but half of them came prematurely into the world, or died a few days old; only one, a girl, attained to maturity; she in after years became the wife of the Honourable Mr. Beltonleigh, who was created Lord d'Almaine, as may be remembered.

There was no living son and heir. At length, completely worn out in mind and body, Lady Uplandtowers was taken abroad by her husband, to try the effect of a more genial climate upon her wasted frame. But nothing availed to strengthen her, and she died at Florence, a few months after her arrival in Italy.

Contrary to expectation, the Earl of Uplandtowers did not marry again. Such affection as existed in him—strange, hard, brutal as it was—seemed untransferable, and the title, as is known, passed at his death to his nephew. Perhaps it may not be so generally known that, during the enlargement of the Hall for the sixth Earl, while digging in the grounds for the new foundations, the broken fragments of a marble statue were unearthed. They were submitted to various antiquaries, who said that, so far as the damaged pieces would allow them to form an opinion, the statue seemed to be that of a mutilated Roman satyr; or, if not, an allegorical figure of Death. Only one or two old inhabitants guessed whose statue those fragments had composed.

I should have added that, shortly after the death of the Countess, an excellent sermon was preached by the Dean of Melchester, the subject of which, though names were not mentioned, was unquestionably suggested by the aforesaid events. He dwelt upon the folly of indulgence in sensuous love for a handsome form merely; and showed that the only rational and virtuous growths of that affection were those based upon intrinsic worth. In the case of the tender but somewhat shallow lady whose life I have related, there is no doubt that an infatuation for the person of young Willowes was the chief feeling that induced her to marry him; which was the more deplorable in that his beauty, by all tradition, was the least of his recommendations, every report bearing out the inference that he must have been a man of steadfast nature, bright intelligence, and promising life.

Thomas M. Disch (b. 1940)

Torturing Mr. Amberwell

Thomas M. Disch began his writing career as a science fiction writer in the revolutionary "New Wave" days of the 1960s, but is a diverse writer of many talents that no genre can quite contain. Poet, essayist, dramatist, critic, novelist and short story writer, he excels. *Newsweek* called him the most underrated major writer in America. He is a frequent contributor to *The Nation,* in which his abilities as a biting social satirist are given their full play. He wrote a controversial play called *The Cardinal Detoxes.* The Catholic Church, landlord of the theater in which it was performed, took such strong exception to the play that it tried to evict the theater company. His children's book *The Brave Little Toaster* is the basis for a Disney movie. Throughout his career he has written stories in the horror mode, and is one of the finest living writers of horrific fiction, often darkly humorous. He has the stylistic polish of a Jamesian and ironic vision similar to Philip K. Dick (in whose memory Disch founded a literary award). He has published a number of short story collections with horrific content, and edited a distinguished anthology, *Strangeness* (1977), devoted to the Poesian and the bizarre. His horror novels include *The Businessman: A Tale of Terror,* and *The M.D.: A Tale of Horror.* "Torturing Mr. Amberwell" was published only in a limited edition by a small press. This is the first time it has been reprinted.

January 30, 1983

Amberwell is installed in the basement, fully conscious and indignant as Donald Duck. What do I think I'm doing, he wants to know.

"That's a question," I replied, "that I hope we'll be able to discuss at length, Mr. Amberwell."

Then it was Quack! Quack! Quack! until I called a halt, forcing his mouth open by crimping his nostrils till he had to take a breath, then wedging in a gag that kept him quiet. He did not try hard to resist. He seems to understand the need for ready compliance. I left him with the tape of "That's Entertainment" (Boston Pops directed by John Williams, Philips 6302 124) blaring tinnily from the cassette player. The tape is one of three with which Amberwell's limousine was supplied.

Eleven o'clock. Nothing to be done now but reduce my own excitement to a slow simmer. For half an hour I worked on a new 1000-piece jigsaw of King Ludwig's megalomaniacal Neuschwanstein, all its turrets and battlements edged with snow. The urge to go down to the basement and get going on Amberwell was intense. But I resisted

295

it, got the sky assembled, steeped in the tub, jotted down these few lines, and called it a day.

January 31

Amberwell was already awake when I went downstairs at 7 A.M. "Mmmrff! Mmmrff! Mmmrff!" said Amberwell.

"That's one way to look at it," I teased. "But if you took a somewhat larger view, as I do, you'd see that there is a real opportunity for personal growth in the situation. People too often let personal anxieties get in the way of the Big Picture. Like getting your thumb in front of the lens when you're taking a photograph. Which reminds me, I need film."

He attempted a defiant stare—but I knew better. For there at the corner of each eye tears of pure fear were forming. I hunkered down in front of the chair into which Amberwell was bound, took his chin in my hand, and tilted his head to the right and to the left, like an appraiser judging a prize Toby mug. "Tears! Oh, there's nothing so apt to melt the cruelty of my nature as the sight of genuine liquid tears. Especially in a man. Men are brought up to hide their vulnerability. Their feelings are all bottled up, until after a while they get so atrophied you wouldn't recognize them as feelings, and it takes the emotional equivalent of an earthquake to produce one single—" Just before it rolled down his cheek I caught the tear on the end of my finger and showed it to Amberwell. "—teardrop."

"But now to be practical—" I wiped the teardrop off on the cuff of my jacket. "—I suppose you would like an explanation of why I've abducted you and made you a prisoner here in the basement of my house. Hmm?"

He nodded.

"That's a legitimate curiosity. There you were, about to fly off to . . . Where was it? Cleveland? Omaha? Toledo? . . . and instead you find yourself bound and gagged in the basement of someone who doesn't even have the decency to offer an explanation of his behavior. Naturally, you must be wondering what I have in mind. Am I some kind of sex maniac, for instance, who's got tired of luring teenage drifters to his den of unspeakable vice and has started hunting for bigger game? I'm sure that possibility must have occurred to you by now. And even though the idea is a bit self-aggrandizing in a man of your years, still you can never entirely discount the sexual component. It's always bound to be present in any relationship as intimate as that between a torturer and his victim."

Amberwell contemplated that statement a moment, then strained against his bonds and produced the loudest and most emphatic of Mmmrff's: "MMMRFF!!" The chair, anchored by each leg to a 6'-square sheet of plywood, seemed proof against any amount of lurching about, so I felt no qualms in leaving Amberwell to his thoughts.

Though not to those exclusively. Before I left I plugged some earphones into my new AIWA cassette recorder, taped the earphones to Amberwell's ears, made sure no amount of head-twisting could loosen the wires, and left Amberwell to the endlessly autoreversing strains of "That's Entertainment." I can't lay claim to any originality in that. The idea came from General Dozier's captors, and before that from Billy Wilder's cold-war comedy, *One, Two, Three*.

Then I had breakfast, wrote the above entry while the events were still fresh, and set off for work.

For obvious reasons I'm obliged to censor a good many details of my day-to-day life, so that the authorities, at some future date when this memoir is published, won't be able to track me to my lair. Enough to say that my job is respectable without being glamorous. Basically I english the pronouncements of corporate executives of two- and three-star rank and otherwise run rhetorical interference—without, however, making decisions. It's a job that brings me into contact regularly with the Amberwells of the world (with, indeed, Amberwell himself, though only at the remove of two switchboards), though none of them would ever mistake me for a peer. To say any more than this would be compromising, so regretfully (for I have, as much as any poet or painter, a natural desire to be credited for the work I've accomplished) I must restrict this narrative to the events of my life at home with Amberwell. It's a bit ironic that I thereby find myself observing one of the standard protocols of conventional fiction.

I got home, as usual, just in time to turn on the 7 O'Clock News, where who to my wondering eyes should appear but Brigadier-General James "Speak of the Devil" Dozier, who'd gone to Rome to hand out medals to the policemen who'd rescued him from the Red Brigade. Then Reagan came on to deliver his Budget Message ("To arms! To arms!"), and I went downstairs to find Amberwell asleep despite all that music could do. The air was thick with the smell of his urine, though the pool that had formed between his shackled feet had almost entirely evaporated.

This seemed the right time to accustom myself and Amberwell to the formal requirements of our relationship, and so I spent the next fifteen minutes torturing him, starting at the soles of his feet and working up to the eyelids. Having no basis for comparison, it's hard to say whether I tortured Amberwell mildly, moderately, or severely. I thought it important that his punishments should exceed those commonly meted out in the classic pornographic narratives of de Sade, et al, since I wanted to emphasize the point I'd made that morning, that ours was not to be an erotic association. On the other hand I didn't wish, this soon, to precipitate a medical crisis.

Then upstairs to cook dinner. Already the shock of this radically new experience was unsettling accustomed perceptions. The chuck I sliced into two-inch cubes for stewing was no longer the innocent cellophane-wrapped commodity I'd picked out of the grocer's meat cooler. It was a cross-section of recently living tissue with a strong family resemblance to what might be laid bare under my own, or Amberwell's, skin—beneath, you might say, our beauty.

While the stew bubbled, I went back downstairs, stripped off Amberwell's clothes, and hosed him clean. Then I took out his gag and let him plead for water (granted), his life, my mercy, an explanation, a chance to get out of the chair. He assured me that his wife would readily pay any ransom I demanded and with the utmost secrecy.

"I have no intention of asking for ransom, Mr. Amberwell. There's no likelier way to get caught. In any case, profit isn't my motive."

"Then what is?" he asked in a throaty whisper that mingled outrage and fear and a tremor of something unpinpointable that might have been the dawning of a sense of what was in store for him or maybe only the start of a cold.

I unfolded a metal chair, set it down in front of him, sat down, and lighted a cigarette. "I'll explain as best I can, Mr. Amberwell. My original idea, about a year ago, came from seeing you on "Sixty Minutes." Toxic waste disposal is the one issue in the news that always gets my blood boiling. And there you were trying to wave the camera out of existence and answering every question with the same smirking 'No Comment.' My first furious fantasy was to rent a cropduster and phone a bomb threat to the Unitask office, and then while you were all out in the parking lot fly over and douse the lot of you with your own medicine. A cocktail of dioxin and toluene and maybe some trichloroethylene for impaired memory function. But obviously that's just a wish-fulfillment fantasy and requires a budget and skills I simply don't possess. Whereas this costs less than a weekend skiing in the Catskills. Some chloroform from a hobby shop, a few gadgets from a sex boutique, odds and ends from a hardware store, four hours of carpentry, and I was ready to open shop."

"You mean to tell me that you're doing this because . . . because you're a god-damned *environmentalist?*"

"That's what I mean to tell you."

"But—" He shook his head briskly, as who would say, "You've got to be kidding."

"Of course, I haven't been what you'd call an activist. Unless this counts as activism. I never could get over my feeling of hopelessness of ever accomplishing anything against people like you. Like Unitask. I mean, there you are, monolithically in control. You've got the money. You've bought the politicians and the judges. The A.B.A. is your harem. You don't care *how* you mess up the world for anyone else so long as your net assets increase and multiply. And even when the government gets you for tax evasion or some such, the most that happens is that you get fined. And the fine probably entitles you to a tax deduction the next year. It's so frustrating to people like me."

"To the lunatics, you mean," said Amberwell.

It's a wonderful how basic a sense of contentiousness is to human nature. Here was Amberwell still quivering from what he'd been through, and he could not resist putting in his two cents. Lucky for him I'm not so small-minded (or short-sighted) as to revenge myself on a taunt.

"I suppose on the face of it I would be considered a lunatic. A fanatic at the very least. On the other hand, it may be that I'm just a step ahead of the crowd."

Amberwell made a sort of snorting sound to express his derision.

"No, seriously. Consider Argentina. Unitask has strong ties with Argentina. You'll be building a plant there soon, I understand."

"What's this have to do with Argentina?" Amberwell demanded in the tone of a defendant preparing to plead the Fifth Amendment.

"Argentina is an example of a country governed by torture," I said, dropping the ash of my cigarette on the back of Amberwell's hand. "And not even the most extreme example. Now it's my contention that what the government can do, individuals can do just as effectively. With respect to torture, that is. The larger deterrents, like missiles, still require forces on a grand scale. So you might think of this as a counter-cultural, human-scale penitentiary. The first of who knows how many? Indeed, who knows if it's the first?"

"Listen, if you're some kind of . . . terrorist, you're making a mistake. I've got no connection with Argentina. That's another branch of Unitask entirely. I'm just an ordinary business executive. As for the allegations on that god-damned TV program, the government decided on its own not to prosecute. No one knew that that [expletive deleted] toluene—"

I pressed the burning tip of the cigarette against the back of Amberwell's hand and, when he was done screaming, explained:

"Please, Mr. Amberwell, don't use obscene language. I want our discussions to be frank and open, and you will not be punished for expressing any opinion you have. But don't use language you wouldn't use before a TV camera. When the tapes of our meetings are aired, I don't want them to have an X-rated tone. I've always thought one of the reasons Watergate made so little lasting impact among the namby-pamby-minded was that just because of all the foul language they discounted the whole affair as a kind of dirty joke."

"You think a TV station would agree to . . ."

"A radio station, more likely. It would probably do wonders for their ratings. Remember how hard Nixon fought—and still is fighting—to keep *his* tapes from being broadcast? And this has the added drama of your being tortured from time to time."

"You are really demented," said Amberwell.

I poised the cigarette over his hand. "What do you want to bet, Mr. Amberwell, that you will beg to have our tapes broadcast by all the radio stations in the country?"

"Please," he said. "Don't."

I brought the cigarette closer to his hand, so the ginger hairs began to shrivel, crisp, and smell.

"You will *implore* radio stations everywhere to make you a celebrity. Will you not, Mr. Amberwell?"

"Yes," he said.

"Yes what?"

"Yes, I will . . . implore them."

"Then begin, sir, begin. We're recording: implore."

I won't bother to transcribe that part of the session. When I had satisfied myself as to Amberwell's complete abjection, I went upstairs. Just in time to keep the stew from burning and to catch the beginning of the movie version of *Pennies from Heaven*. But before two songs had been sung, the old Sony finally conked out.

February 1

The repair shop called me at work to advise me that I'll be without a TV till Friday. Woe's me: TV is my most reliable tranquilizer. So, after work, to compensate for my affliction, I went to *Gandhi*. I don't understand Pauline Kael. Can't she get off on anything but horror movies anymore? The movie was nothing like the dud she'd made it out to be. I can't imagine anyone leaving the theater without feeling ennobled. Long live humanity! Peace now! We *shall* overcome! Of course, I wasn't convinced that passive resistance is the most effective way to deal with the bad guys of history, but then I didn't expect to be. It's still a terrific movie.

On the homebound train, mulling over the movie and my own domestic situation, I had an inspiration for a further turn of the screw. I'm leery, on principle, of deviating from the scenario already under way, but this would add a dimension of drollery (of kinkiness?) that will be hard to resist. Maybe I won't resist it.

Down in the dungeon I transferred a groaning Amberwell from the chair into a canvas straitjacket that I'd bought at Nymphomania's Special January White Sale. There's enough slack in the chains mooring him to the anchorbolts in the floor so that now he can sit up or stretch out as he chooses.

He was too weak to put up more than token resistance as I fit him into the straitjacket. He cried and mumbled and seemed more or less out of his mind. It seems a bit early in the game for him to have reached that stage of collapse. I told him to buck up and got what was left of last night's stew from the refrigerator and spoonfed it to him. By the time the pot was empty, Amberwell was almost his old self, promising me the open sesames to all four of his clandestine bank accounts: *if* I would let him go. I praised him for his more cooperative spirit and announced he would not be tortured tonight, by courtesy of Mahatma Gandhi. When I left he begged me not to turn off the light.

February 2

On my lunch hour I found all things needful to carry out my new change of plan. Encountered, as well, an Omen in the form of a magazine abandoned in a trash can, which the wind had opened to an article headlined:

SHOULD WE TRY
TO CHANGE
OTHER PEOPLE?

No comment, in Amberwell's words.

Tonight instead of using insidious-type tortures I simply beat Amberwell with a rubber truncheon (they seem to be a popular item these days at army surplus stores; there was a barrel full of them where I got mine) until he'd given me all the relevant information on the bank accounts he's spoken of. Then, postponing the use of today's purchases, I set Amberwell the task, as per the established scenario, of singing nursery rhymes for the rest of the night in harmony with the Mother Goose Consort (Merritime Records XG352 900).

I spent the rest of the evening alternating between the jigsaw (the lighter-toned bricks of the castle are mostly in place) and Erik Erikson's *Gandhi's Truth* (Norton, 1969). Meanwhile, Amberwell seranaded me, over the rewired stereo, with a medley of "Bye, baby bunting," "Ding, dong, bell," "Mary had a little lamb," and a counting rhyme that he never could seem to get right, even though I would go downstairs each time he goofed and clobber him with the truncheon. Here's how it goes:

One-ery, two-ery, tickery, seven,
Hallibo, crackibo, ten and eleven,
Spin, span, muskidan,
Twiddle-um, twaddle-um, twenty-one.
Eeerie, orie, ourie,
You, are, out!

February 3

Having laid the groundwork yesterday with dark hints and muffled coughs, I phoned in sick to work this morning, then went through a charade of dish clattering and door banging to simulate my departure. When Amberwell judged me to be out of earshot, he set into baying "Please! Somebody! Help me! Please!" and similar litanies of hopelessness, all quite inaudible, I'm pleased to say, except over the audio system.

When he appeared to be shouted out, I went downstairs with my parcel of yesterday's purchases.

"Oh, Mr. Amberwell," I said reproachfully. "You're going to catch it now."

Amberwell slumped sideways, curling his knees to his chest, as though waiting to be kicked, and squeezing his eyes tight shut.

On the concrete wall behind Amberwell I taped the posters I had bought at the Aghora Panthis Meditation Center. One showed Shiva wearing a tiger skin and holding out, invitingly, a skull-shaped bowl adorned with snakes. The second represented Ganesh, Shiva's fat, elephant-headed son, whose specialty is guaranteeing success to new undertakings.

I then persuaded Amberwell to open his eyes and study a photograph in B.K.S. Iyengar's *Light on Yoga* (Schocken, 1966) representing a yogi in the *padmasana*, or lotus, position. Fortunately for Amberwell he belongs to the new breed of business executives who jog, and he was able, with only a small assist from me and a modest amount of surgical tape, to assume the lotus position. With a new dhoti, a necklace of rudraksha berries, a clean-shaven head, and a dab of white paint in the middle of his forehead, he looked the spit-and-image of Ben Kingsley.

The dicey part came when I removed the straitjacket so that Amberwell might extend his arms in the manner illustrated in the book. Would he have the strength and the will to struggle once his arms were free? Admittedly, his lower body was secured to the bolt in the floor by a belt (also from Nymphomania) hidden beneath his dhoti. Admittedly, too, I had the truncheon on the ready. But if Amberwell weren't willing to cooperate, then all this elaborate scene-setting would be in vain.

I needn't have worried. Amberwell spread out his arms just so, and curled his finger to his thumb in a gesture of prayer. He even smiled for the camera upon command. It could not be said to have been a very warm smile, but any sense of strain could be accounted for by the difficulty of the position for a neophyte.

When the two Polariod pictures had developed themselves, I showed them to Amberwell, who was once again straitjacketed.

He stared at them gloomily. "This is some kind of religious cult, isn't it?"

"Yes, Mr. Amberwell, now you know. This is how we indoctrinate all our new members. It may seem cruel to you at first, but once your heart opens to accept our gods, you will know the joy that can only come after the ego has been destroyed and the mind cleansed."

"What . . . gods?" Amberwell asked, as a suspicious diner might ask to know the ingredients of some anomalous dish at a Chinese restaurant.

I pressed my hands together, church-steeple-style, and made an obeisance to the garishly-colored, elephant-headed god. "This is our god Ganesh. Say hi to Ganesh."

Amberwell gave me a look halfway between horror and incredulous amusement. Then he turned to the poster and said, "Hi . . . Ganesh."

"And this—" Tapping the other poster. "—is Shiva, the Destroyer."

Amberwell did not say hi to Shiva, nor did I suggest he should. He regarded the snake-festooned skull that Shiva held out to him with respectful silence. Then he closed his eyes and his jaw dropped open and his breathing became slower and deeper.

In what we are about to undertake, O Ganesh, make us truly successful!

February 4

A postcard from the library has notified me that they have got in the copy of Leni Riefenstahl's *The Last of the Nuba* that I'd put in a request for two months ago. Too late, now that Amberwell is so far along the path to becoming a Hindoo, to terrorize him with the prospect of having his face decoratively welted like his black brothers in Africa. There's something much more serious, and accordingly scarier, about a world-class religion. People are known to *believe* in religions. You can see them at airports selling their records or marvel at the troops of them hippity-hopping up the street. They've become one of life's real possibilities. Whereas, unless you know who Leni Riefenstahl *was*, the Nuba and their scarifications come off as little more than a coffee-table book, ethnology for punk rockers.

This evening, after a light repast, Amberwell, assuming the lotus position, chanted the following mantra for two hours:

> Mary had a little lamb,
>   Its fleece was white as snow,
> And everywhere that Mary went
>   The lamb was sure to go.
>   Hari Mary,
>   Rama lamb-a,
> Amberwell loves Ganesh.

Upstairs on my born-again TV I watched a cable broadcast of *The Atomic Cafe*, a montage of old Civil Defense instruction films that does for the defense industry what *Reefer Madness* did for narcs. From time to time I would tune in to Amberwell's progress in the basement. Only twice did he flag and require correction.

February 5

Saturday. My soon-to-be-ex-wife dropped by unannounced at lunchtime, letting herself in with the key she'd assured me she didn't have.

"Whatever are you listening to?" Adelle asked, as she set down her matching ("The Bag") canvas totes and I hastened to turn off the broadcast of Amberwell's noontide mantra from the torture chamber.

"Oh nothing. Some new piece by Terry Riley I think the announcer said."

"Spare me," said Adelle.

"Have I ever *forced* you to listen to Terry Riley?"

"Yes. Often."

"I didn't think you had another set of keys," I noted, holding out my hand.

"Until I've got all my things out, I have every right to have a set of keys."

"I thought you had everything now you agreed you had any right to."

"I made of list of what I'd forgotten." She handed me her list.

I ran down the two columns, which were headed "Negotiable" and "Non-negotiable." The blender was non-negotiable. "The blender?" I protested. You've *got* the food processor. It does everything a blender can do."

"The blender was a wedding present from my cousin in Tarrytown. There's no reason you should have it."

"No. I suppose not. But you'll have to wash it out."

"Fine." She stared at me defiantly, waiting for further objections, but none were forthcoming. She seemed disappointed. She once complained that my unwillingness to be combative about small things showed a lack of feeling.

For the next hour I tagged after her from room to room as she filled first one tote and then the other with all the negotiable and non-negotiable items. Vases vanished from tabletops, records from shelves, the Canadian codeine-laced aspirin from the medicine cabinet. By the time we'd reached the kitchen her second bag was nearly full.

"On second thought," she said, "I'll let you keep the carving board. There's really no room for it in the cupboard I've got now."

"Thanks."

"But I do want the blender."

"It's in the icebox."

She got the blender out of the refrigerator and sniffed at what was in it. "Yuck!"

"Try it, you'll like it."

"What in hell is it?"

"It's a kind of bean paste from the Pritikin Program Cookbook. Remember? You got it for me for my birthday two years ago."

"It smells *awful*."

"It tastes better on a cracker than just plain. But I'm out of crackers."

"I'll let you keep the blender," Adelle conceded. "Since you've been so nice about everything else."

"I'm a basically nice guy."

She grimaced. Her eye lighted on the door to the basement. "I suppose I should have one last look down there."

"There's nothing on your list that would be down there," I said in what must have been a different tone of voice.

She looked at me strangely.

"Whatever is in the basement now is mine," I insisted. "That's my non-negotiable demand. Now give me those keys; you've got what you came for."

She gave me the keys, and another odd look, and then I helped her take the loaded totebags out to her car. When they were stowed in the backseat she offered her hand to be shaken.

"I must say," she said, "you seem a whole lot more . . . relaxed. Than last year, or even a month ago."

"I guess it's the Pritikin Program."

"Or not having me to contend with?"

"Honestly, Adelle, I never thought you were all that much trouble."

"You're still the world's coldest icicle—that hasn't changed."

"And you're still as pretty as the day we met. Age cannot wither."

"Go to hell," she said with a smile. She started her Datsun. "Go directly to hell. Do not pass Go. Do not collect $200."

She also still thought parroting catch-phrases counted as a sense of humor, but I didn't rub her nose in that. I just said "Bye now," and stood back from the curb.

Back in the house I tuned in on Amberwell. He'd left off chanting his mantra, and I could hear him, ever so faintly, crying. Somehow, though there was no surface resemblance, the sound he was making put me in mind of the Environments$_{TM}$ record, *Gentle Rain in a Pine Forest*.

Hush, poor Amberwell, I thought, as I scooped out his dinner from the blender. *Hush, poor bare forked radish, hush.*

February 6

After twice feigning he was incapable of writing, Amberwell has been persuaded to write, at my dictation, the following letter:

Dear Ann,
    Who could have predicted that seeing a movie could change a man's life so completely as mine has changed—and in only a week's time! You won't easily believe what I have to tell you. I can scarcely believe it myself. Here's what's happened. I missed my flight on Sunday, the traffic was snarled on the way to the airport, and decided to take in the movie *Gandhi*, which has been getting such good reviews. Watching the movie, I was overcome with remorse for all the wrong and hurtful things I've done in the course of my business career. A Higher Spirit must have been looking on, for after the movie I was guided into the waiting arms of the good people who have helped me to understand how I can make restitution for the wrongs I've done. Some of my colleagues, who helped me commit those crimes and shared in ill-gotten profits, must suffer, but Justice must be done, I see that now. I shall write to the appropriate authorities in due course to give them the information they will need to begin an investigation, but I write to you first, my dear wife, so that you may prepare yourself to cooperate with the authorities, make my papers and bank statements available to them, etc. Do not attempt to stay the course of Justice. When they find, as they surely will, compelling proofs of my malfeasances, cooperate with them in making immediate restitution to those I've wronged. I am sorry I cannot be with you during the approaching period of travail, but my virtue is still a frail reed, and so I must continue under the guidance of my Spiritual Master. I will offer prayers for your enlightenment to Rama, avatar of the great Vishnu, and to his wife Sita, whose attendants are white elephants. May the light soon enter your life that has entered mine.

With holy love,
Alec Amberwell

P.S. I am leaving the Lincoln for you.
P.P.S. Go see *Gandhi* as soon as you can.

I put the letter into an envelope together with one of the Polaroids I'd taken on Friday. Then I drove to the airport parking lot, where Amberwell's limousine was parked in the same space I'd left it a week ago. I put the letter in the driver's seat, the keys beneath it out of sight. Then I phoned Amberwell's home and informed the maid that I was an airport security officer and that Mr. Amberwell's Lincoln appeared to have been deserted at the airport parking lot. I made her write down the precise directions for finding the car and then hung up.

The trouble with sending Christmas presents to faraway friends is that you can't be on hand to see them unwrapped.

Got home just in time to catch the start of *The Winds of War*.

February 7

The office was a madhouse today, but in the rush of more important matters I did not neglect to phone Amberwell's secretary and ask to have his decision anent Unitask's option to purchase some ten thousand depositary receipts. (It had been the ongoing negotiations over this matter, conducted mainly through his secretary, that had allowed me to pick up the odds and ends of information I'd needed in order to waylay Amberwell at the opportune moment of his intended departure.)

I was informed that Mr. Amberwell was not in.

"Oh," said I. "I understood that he was due back today. There's no one else who can handle this, is there? The option expires on Friday."

"It will be the first thing Mr. Amberwell deals with when he gets back," I was assured.

This evening, after episode 2 of *The Winds of War*, I began to help Amberwell form an inventory of those corporate crimes he's assisted in for which tangible evidence is likely to be still recoverable. He spilled the beans like a silo in orgasm. Half this fair continent would seem to be planted with Unitask's time bombs, and every filing cabinet to conceal a smoking gun. I began to suspect that Amberwell was inventing crimes simply to appease my hunger for righteousness, but it's hard to doubt his sincerity at the moment of truth. Besides, Amberwell doesn't have enough imagination to spin a web of lies. His lies are all denials: "No, we didn't do it. No, I didn't write that memo. No, I don't know." What he *can* do—the reason there is a head on his shoulders—is remember details. His mind is all retrieval system, and that, of course, makes him just the right executive for this position. By 2 AM the first dossier was ready for mailing: top copy to Mrs. Amberwell, urging her to share its contents with the press; first carbon to J. M. Carnell, Chairman of the Board of the ship Amberwell's revelations will scuttle; second carbon to Elizabeth Golub, author of *Our Children and the Toxic Timebomb* (Grossman, 1980).

Now for a couple days I'd better coddle the goose who lays such golden eggs. I fear I may have activated an ulcer, for Amberwell's stools are vermilion.

February 8

Easing the tension doesn't seem to have helped. Amberwell is in a state of almost total physical and mental collapse. Running a high temperature, incontinent, and babbling (when he thinks he's alone).

What's needed now is someone able to play the role of nice-guy partner, as against my blue meany, someone who could come in and stroke Amberwell's psyche and win his confidence and lift his morale. Lacking that, the best I could manage was a story: at dinnertime, while I spooned lovely, fresh-baked custard into his slack mouth, I told Amberwell how I've been ordered by our Spiritual Leader to treat him with more consideration as a reward for his confession (which I mailed off this morning from the central P.O.).

A gleam—of intelligence? purpose? hope? who can say?—came into his right eye. (His left is swollen shut.) "Who . . . is . . . our—"

I pressed my hands together, Gandhi-style. "Her name is Kali-Ananda, Kali's Joy. She cannot come to you until your purification has been complete, but if you would like to venerate her picture, you can do that."

"Yes." Amberwell nodded. "Let me . . . venerate her picture."

Up in the bedroom I dug out the box of memorabilia from the back of the closet and sorted through the various 8-by-11 prints I'd made of Adelle back in the days when the torture chamber was only a darkroom. The one I was looking for showed her in ballet tights, in lotus position (the Iyengar book was hers originally), and smiling that caught-in-the-act smile a camera always induced from her. It wasn't at all hard to re-imagine this Adelle as Kali-Ananda.

Back in the torture chamber I taped this icon of our Spiritual Leader to the wall between the posters of Ganesh and Shiva.

"Hail, Kali-Ananda!" I declared.

"Hail, Kali-Ananda," Amberwell agreed.

Then, without a hint from me, anxious to comply as a newly housebroken dog whining beside the door to the street, Amberwell wrestled his legs into a lotus position, faced the photograph of Adelle, and began to chant his mantra.

Later I revealed to him, as to one being initiated into a solemn mystery, the last of the nursery rhyme's four stanzas:

> Why does the lamb love Mary so?
> The eager children cry;
> Why, Mary loves the lamb, you know,
> The teacher did reply.

Amberwell's reaction was to break down, quite helplessly, into tears. He's much more in touch with his feelings these days.

"Amberwell," I said softly, "why are you crying?"

He shook his head. "I don't know."

"There must be a reason."

"Please," he said. The tears were gone. "Don't hurt me anymore. Just kill me and be done with it. You'll have to some day, I understand that. It's obvious that you can never let me go free. And I've told you everything you need to shaft Unitask in court, anything more would just be trimming. So please don't hurt me anymore, *please*."

"I will ask Kali-Ananda," I promised him. "She knows what is best for all her minions. I too once despaired, Mr. Amberwell, but now I rejoice to be her servant." I turned to Adelle's photo and made an obeisance. "So may you, Mr. Amberwell . . . in time. Now, hold your arms out."

Amberwell held out his arms, like a child accepting his pajamas, and I assisted him into his straitjacket.

February 9

Speaking more truly than she knew, Amberwell's secretary informs me that he has taken a leave of absence for reasons of personal health. Mr. Kramer has been assigned to deal with me in the matter of the option to purchase. Kramer was one of the four Unitask VIPs whom Amberwell's confession most deeply and provably implicate. Patience! I only mailed off Amberwell's manuscript yesterday. Unitask may not have an inkling yet of the tornado heading their way. Unless Mrs. Amberwell went to them, rather than to the police, with her husband's letter. Come to think of it, she must be cooperating in the story of her husband's "leave of absence," or there would already be headlines: TOP EXEC JOINS NUT CULT.

No matter. Even if Mrs. A. joins Unitask in a cover-up, there is still the copy that went to Elizabeth Golub. She is certain to avail herself of Amberwell's revelations. So there's no need to worry—only to wait.

At home, Amberwell is on the mend. His temperature's down to a mild 101°. He's re-established sovereignity over his bowels. His appetite is back. And he asked me to forget what he'd said yesterday. He was depressed and delirious. He does not want to die. He will be Kali-Ananda's servant in all she requires.

"Our Spiritual Leader will be happy to hear of your devotion," I assured him. "And tonight, after our hour of worship, I will tell you the story of her holy life. But first—" I handed him a plastic waterbucket and a sponge. "—you'd better get this place cleaned up. It's getting smelly in here."

Upstairs I phoned for a take-out delivery from the area's one Indian restaurant, then finished all the snowy parts of the jigsaw. Nothing left now but the dark pieces—pine trees and shadowed stone.

The delivery came just as episode 4 of *The Winds of War* was repeating its opening montage/synopsis. I nipped downstairs to retrieve the bucket and the sponge, buckled Amberwell into the chair (as a change of pace from the lotus-position-cum-straitjacket), and set him to chanting his mantra. Then back to the living room for two hours of video popcorn and beef vindaloo. Also, a tad too much Courvoisier, inspired by which I thought it would be amusing—and more verisimilar—if I were to appear before Amberwell in the spare dhoti that I'd bought with his incontinence in mind. To show him that we are *both* worshippers of Shiva, Ganesh, and Kali-Ananda.

He seemed duly impressed. I lighted a candle and a stick of incense, then fed Amberwell the remains of my curry dinner. I spoke to him, consolingly, of the life he might expect to lead someday on our ashram in Nepal, doing penitence for his sins as a Unitask executive and worshipping our Spiritual Leader.

Then I told him the story of her life: how she was born in the all-too-aptly-named town of Bitter Lake, Michigan, attended the Bitter Lake schools, and drank the chlorinated waters of Bitter Lake, never suspecting that there were other chemicals than chlorine added to those waters, chemicals that were the cause of the cramps and headaches she'd suffered through her adolescent years and of the kidney disorder her younger brother died of when he was thirteen, chemicals that would, even ten years after she had moved away from Bitter Lake, be responsible for the miscarriage of her first pregnancy and the severe abnormalities of her only child, Jonathan, now living a vegetable life in a home for vegetable children not five miles from the Unitask Corp facility that had produced the toluene wastes that Gurnsey Hauling had hauled to Bitter Lake and Axelrod Disposal Systems had there disposed of.

Gurnsey Hauling and Axelrod Disposal Systems were both wholly owned subsidiaries of Unitask, and much of Amberwell's confession detailed the means by which Unitask had divested itself of the embarrassment that Gurnsey and Axelrod had come to represent—and, at the same time, evaded any legal responsibility for their actions. That part of the story, of course, Amberwell already knew.

"There you have it, Mr. Amberwell," I said, as the candle guttered in its socket. "The story of the youth and young womanhood of our Spiritual Leader, and the reasons why she, and so many other concerned citizens, including myself, feel a grievance against Unitask Corporation, Gurnsey Hauling, and Axelrod Disposal Systems."

Is it a true story, you may be asking yourself. Was this nameless narrator's wife really one of the Bitter Lake disaster victims? Or is he just saying this to underscore Amberwell's guilt, to make at least one of Unitask's victims something more than a statistic?

Scout's honor, it's all true, all but the obvious lie that my-not-yet-ex-wife has been the guiding light behind Amberwell's re-education. For, far from being the sternly avenging Kali-Ananda I'd painted to Amberwell's imagination, Adelle is one of your classic cheek-turning, placard-bearing liberals who think they've scored points against the Unitasks of the world if they can get Rachel Carson's face on a postage stamp. It had been this—her milky-mild *goodness*—more than even a steadily encroaching tendency to vegetarianism that had led to our mostly amicable breakup.

However, in one inessential respect Adelle *is* a fiction: her name is not Adelle, nor was she born by the shores of the infamous Bitter Lake, nor yet by those of Love Canal, but by a toxic waste dump of lesser notoriety. These and some few other small details and proper names have been changed in order to protect the innocent and baffle pursuit. So if you have been thinking of playing detective, forget it. There is no Nymphomania, no Aghora Panthis Meditation Center, no option to purchase ten thousand depositary receipts. Anything that might look like a clue is, in fact, a red herring. Why, even Amberwell's name might be something else than Amberwell. Yet you wouldn't for all that, deny that he and his kind exist, would you? Or that it's possibly for anyone so resolved to step up behind his or her selected Amberwell, tap him on the shoulder, and say, "Come with me, sir. I am making a citizen's arrest."?

In fact, however, Amberwell's name *is* Amberwell, and he is, or was, an executive for Unitask. My tracks are well enough covered that in that crucial particular I can be candid and boast openly of my accomplishment. There he is. Behold the son of a bitch. Think what he's done, and ask yourself if you aren't really a little pleased that he got a bit of what he gave.

Stop me before I preach more.

February 10

Just as I tapped the last piece of the puzzle in place and Neuschwanstein stood complete, it came to me, the word I'd been looking for, the answer to Amberwell's riddle: imagination. That was what he lacked, the missing element of his mental makeup that allowed him to assist Unitask in creating its great national anti-lottery, where a winning ticket will buy you and your family a lifetime supply of dioxin right in your own backyard. Unitask's victims don't exist for Amberwell because they live in hick towns like Bitter Lake or Love Canal, while he, and the fifty or sixty human beings whose faces he can recognize and who may, on that account, be real to him, all live in the posher suburbs that Unitask has not yet got round to devastating (from the Latin, *devastare*, to lay waste).

That, from the carefully blinkered view of Big Business is the danger of imagination— i.e., of books and movies—that it gives names to that legion of victims who were otherwise only rolling freight. Names and faces, addresses, personal histories, inner lives, and voices that can rise off a printed page and say, "Don't kill us. O great Unitask. We're real, we're alive, we exist. If you prick us we bleed. If you tickle us we laugh. If you poison us we die."

The problem has always been getting someone like Amberwell to listen. And I appear to have solved that problem.

February 11

Such weather. As though winter meant to make up for all her mildness till now with one sockdolager blizzard. We'd had fair warning and didn't have to show. Notwithstanding which exemption I headed in to the office, made myself visible at two meetings, lunched with my boss, and then, at three PM, just as the snowfall had escalated from impressive to awesome, I taxied to the "Discrete, Sumptuous, Comfortable Chamber of Fantasy" of the "Notorious" Mademoiselle X. (I quote from her two-column ad in the back pages of a weekly tabloid paper.)

Mademoiselle appeared at the door of the Chamber of Fantasy attired in a black spandex body stocking and thigh-high boots with stiletto heels. She touched my chest with her riding crop. "*You* must be Mr. Amberwell."

I smiled sheepishly by way of confirmation. Then, realizing my smile would be invisible behind my Phantom of the Opera domino-cum-veil, I said, "I am he."

She made a sweeping gesture with her riding crop. "*Entrez, Monsieur, dans ma chambre du mal et du volupté.*"

"*Merci, Mademoiselle.*"

From my briefcase I took out the cassette recorder, and from its file folder the script I'd spent yesterday evening preparing.

Mademoiselle X's fee, five $20 bills, was paperclipped to the script.

"Won't you make yourself more comfortable, Mr. Amberwell?"

"Thank you," I said, and removed my hat.

She unclipped the money, made a neat bundle of it, and slipped it becomingly into the top of her boots. "And you are certain you do not desire to do anything else while you are here, but only . . . ?"

"Just for you to record the script as it is written, Mademoiselle, that's all. Perhaps if you read it through once to yourself, to see that it presents no problems. Then when you're ready, so is my recorder."

Mademoiselle X gave me a discreet, ironic look, removed a cigarette from the box on the low glass table, and sat back on the sumptuous, comfortable goatskin-draped futon, script in hand, waiting, with eyebrows raised, for her cigarette to be lighted. Once the dignity of her profession had been accorded this due deference, she turned her attention to the script. Her silent reading was quite as dramatic as that which she consigned to tape. Her high forehead would crinkle into a threatening frown, her eyes widen with alarm, her lips curl into a smile of ridicule or complicity.

"This is very professional work, Mr. Amberwell," she said, when she had finished reading. "Usually in this situation I am able to offer useful hints or suggestions. But this is a finished piece of work. It's nicely paced, it builds well, and overall it's thoroughly nasty. I hope for your sake, Mr. Amberwell, this script represents no more than a . . . fantasy. You would surely come to regret taking actions so . . . irreversible in their nature."

I blushed all unseen. "Thank you for your compliments, Mademoiselle. Are you ready to record?"

She sighed. "Someday," she said, "the women of our profession will get residuals for this sort of thing. *D'accord*, Mr. Amberwell, I am ready."

"Oh, and Mademoiselle?"

"Yes, Mr. Amberwell?"

"Use an ordinary tone of voice, please. Nothing too theatrical. You should sound, ideally, like somebody's mother."

She leered. "Oh, Mr. Amberwell, you have been a very bad boy. You have torn your best clothes. You have skinned your knee. And I am afraid that for such behavior you must be severely punished. *Comme ça?*"

"Just so," I assured her. "Ready?"

She stubbed out the cigarette, cleared her throat, held up the script, and nodded. I pushed RECORD.

It looks like I won't be getting home tonight, and maybe not tomorrow. The snow is coming down not in flakes but in truckloads. The train station was a madhouse. I was lucky to find a hotel room.

So, it's a choice between "The Dukes of Hazzard," a werewolf movie, and episode 6 of *The Winds of War*. Despite my lifelong affinity for werewolves and a growing world-war-weariness (was there ever a conclusion so foreordained?), I watched Wouk's magnum opus. And he's right, of course. You can't let the Hitlers of the world walk all over you. You've got to draw a line. Gandhi's nonviolence only works against an enemy with an operational conscience.

February 12

All the drama of the Great Blizzard of '83 is over, even for Amberwell. Fortunately I'd left him in his straitjacket, not in the stricter confines of the chair. Except for the fright (he must have thought himself abandoned), he's none the worse for wear. After a hosing down and a bite to eat and a few minutes off the earphones, he seemed almost his old self.

"I think it's time," I said, unfolding the metal chair and sitting down before Amberwell, who was in a kneeling position and shivering, as the beads of water from his cleansing trickled down his face and soaked through the canvas straitjacket, "for you and me to have a heart-to-heart talk about your conscience, Mr. Amberwell. How is it that you were able to go on doing exactly the same things that had already done so much harm even after the Bitter Lake trial had begun?"

"We felt that the standards the Government had set were too exacting. In fact, the E.P.A.'s new rulings tend to confirm our—"

I tromped lightly on the more sensitive of Amberwell's big toes. "Not *we*, Mr. Amberwell. I've read the transcripts of the trial and I know Unitask's position. It's *you*, second person singular, that I want to hear from. People were coming down with kidney and liver problems (which can be acutely painful), because of the poisons leeching into their drinking water. Their hair was falling out. Their children were stillborn. Don't tell me it hasn't been *proven*: all that is just sophistry. Where there's a third-degree burn there's fire."

"What do you want me to say?" Amberwell asked sullenly, petulance overcoming fear.

"Not that you're sorry, because I don't suppose you were. Just the truth—what you actually felt and thought about the crimes you were committing."

"I never thought what I was doing was a crime."

"Do you think anything is a crime? Murder, for instance."

"Yes, of course."

"What about this—what I'm doing to you—is that a crime?"

Amberwell glowered but made no reply.

"Be honest, Mr. Amberwell. Otherwise I'll feed you more pepper. I'll push pins under your fingernails; we haven't done that yet. I'll drill your teeth like Lawrence Olivier drilled Dustin Hoffman's in *Marathon Man*. Do you think what I'm doing to you is a crime?"

He took a deep breath and made his eyes meet mine. "Certainly. And you do too, you can't deny it."

"My ethical sense is not the issue, Mr. Amberwell. *Why* is it a crime?"

"Because . . . if you were caught you'd be arrested and put in jail."

"But if I'm not caught, and not put in jail—as Unitask wasn't and probably won't be—then does it follow that this is not a crime?"

"I didn't say that."

"What if I were an agent of the government, Mr. Amberwell? Suppose the F.B.I. were running another ABSCAM operation and decided that the only way to get the goods on Unitask was to put one of their executives through the wringer."

"Our government wouldn't do that."

"No? Some would."

The suggestion sank in. "Then . . . are you . . ."

"An F.B.I. agent? Sure, why not, if it'll make you feel more at home."

"Oh my god, I should have known."

I had to laugh, and I could tell, from the furrowing of Amberwell's brow, that his faith in the Justice Department was restored.

"Let's approach this from a different angle, Mr. Amberwell. Have you ever read a book called *The Scarlet Letter?*"

He shook his head. "I don't read many books."

"Or *The Retreat?*"

He shook his head.

"How about *I, the Jury?*"

"That's by Spillane, isn't it? I read some of his stuff when I was a kid, so I might have read that one."

So much for literature.

"Well, let's consider just the word itself: guilt. Have you ever felt guilty for *anything* you've done Mr. Amberwell?"

"Certainly. I'm no saint."

"For instance."

"I've, uh, cheated on my wife from time to time."

"And that made you feel guilty? Troubled? Perplexed?"

"Sure, all of that."

"Not just worried you might get the clap?"

"That too, I guess." He licked his upper lip, trying to think what it was I wanted him to say. "Maybe . . . maybe I don't understand those terms the same way you do. I mean, they're like words you read in the newspaper more than the ones you use in everyday life. For me anyhow." He looked up at me with the eager-to-please but certain-to-fail look of a student being examined in a subject he's never studied. Fearing the alternative, he was desperate to keep our little Socratic dialogue afloat, but the effort to try and speak in my language was as frustrating as if he'd been required to converse in Sanskrit (which is a long-term possibility worth considering; there must be instruction cassettes available somewhere).

"They didn't have required courses in ethics when you were getting your M.B.A., did they, Mr. Amberwell?"

"No. I graduated a good while before Watergate."

"Did you ever wonder, in the course of the Bitter Lake trial, whether you'd have acted differently if you had had such a course?"

"No. And I don't think it would make that much difference. At least I don't see any difference in the younger guys coming in, who've had to take that sort of stuff. I figure it's like requiring courses in the history of music. It doesn't really relate to the real world."

"I don't know about that, Mr. Amberwell. Isn't *this* the real world?"

Amberwell did not at once agree to that proposition. But at last, with no prompting, but without looking up from the floor, he nodded his head.

"Are you beginning to understand why you're being tortured, Mr. Amberwell?"

"To . . . uh . . . set an example, I suppose."

"You suppose correctly. Now look up at my camera, Mr. Amberwell. I want a good clear picture of the original condition of your face, before we start tattooing."

Amberwell looked up with abject terror. "No! No, you wouldn't—"

"Smile," I said, adjusting the focus for a close-up. "Then, while we're getting you ready to set an example for other executives in the chemical industry, I'll fill you in on the basic plot of *The Scarlet Letter*."

It was at that moment of purely psychological strain that Amberwell achieved something like a primal scream. His back arched, his neck corded, his face became a mask of beet-red rage, and the sound he made as the flashcube popped was utterly inhuman, an elemental roar that filled the torture chamber to its acoustical brim, as a Berlioz finale fills a concert hall. A single time Amberwell screamed so, and then fell silent, his last hope spent.

"It seems to me, Mr. Amberwell, that your soul is not yet prepared to pay the price that Kali-Ananda requires."

"You [expletive deleted]," said Amberwell. "Why don't you stop playing your [expletive deleted] games, and get this the [expletive deleted] over with."

"Kali-Ananda would derive no satisfaction from your mere death, Mr. Amberwell. It's atonement she's after. Once your heart is fully in accord with hers, then you will *ask* to be allowed to serve her with your whole being. You will be a role model for other executives. And when you have been taken to our secret ashram and dedicated completely to the goddess's worship, people will point to you with amazement and whisper, 'Is *that* Amberwell?' You will be a living legend. But I cannot say these things so well as Kali-Ananda herself can say them. She has taped a message for you, Mr. Amberwell. I will let Kali-Ananda explain to you, in her own voice, the nature and extent of your guilt—and how, with her help and mine, you can begin to seek expiation."

Though Amberwell struggled, he has become so weak that I had little difficulty securing him in the chair. I saw to it that by no amount of neck-twisting or shaking of his head could he dislodge the earphones. Then I inserted in the player the cassette that Mademoiselle X had recorded and left Amberwell alone, with one burning candle, to make the acquaintance of Kali-Ananda, whose joy is her wrath, whose kiss is a scourge, whose retribution is like the lightning that rends the oak.

February 13

Sunday, and the newspaper seems to tell of nothing but the misdeeds of the world's ever-busy Amberwells:

Item: For ten years Ford has been manufacturing cars with a transmission defect that has caused "scores of deaths and injuries"—a defect that Ford "could have corrected for 3 cents a vehicle."

Item: Miss Rita Lavelle has been appointed to be Reagan's ritual scapegoat in the impending scandals at E.P.A. "I can defend every action I have taken," she is quoted as saying. (So can I, Miss Lavelle, so can I! I wish we might have a chance to defend our actions together someday in intimate surroundings.)

Item: All Mexico's police are criminals. Ditto in Richmond, California.

Item: The Governor of Tennessee's conviction for conspiracy, mail fraud, and extortion was overturned by an appeals court judge on the grounds of "faulty jury selection."

Item: By a 3 to 2 margin, the American Bar Association has decided that a lawyer is to be *prohibited* from exposing a crime he knows his client intends to commit, unless the crime intended is murder or bodily harm. (A statute certain to make the world of corporate crime even more "discreet, sumptuous, and comfortable" than it is now, but one that is patently unfair to torturers.)

While I renewed my sense of indignation at this ever-replenished source, Amberwell, downstairs, listened to Kali-Ananda's laments, her accusations and revilings, her promise of redemption to the sinner who would embrace his punishment. Then, when the tape had automatically rewound itself, he listened again.

At eleven, when *The Winds of War* was over, and Pearl Harbor had been beautifully blasted to bits, I brought Amberwell his dinner of broccoli stalks, potato skins, and shredded salt codfish soaked in vermouth. He ate on his knees, in his straitjacket, snarfling up the mess vacuum-cleaner style.

"A penny for your thoughts, Mr. Amberwell," I said, when his bowl had been licked clean down to the Purina Dog-Chow logo.

He regarded me dully, such a gaze as a retarded deaf-mute child might give to the talk show on view on his ward's TV.

"Now, Mr. Amberwell, don't be difficult." I donned my comic Gestapo accent: "You know ve haf vays of making you talk."

He took a deep breath and closed his eyes. "I wasn't thinking. My mind was blank."

"Come, come, Mr. Amberwell. There's no such thing as a blank mind. You've had a whole day to meditate on the counsels and instruction of our Spiritual Leader. Your mind must be quite *full*."

"I was glad you turned the tape off for a while," he said hollowly. "Her voice is . . . But I guess that's your idea, to see if you can drive me crazy. And I guess you will if you keep at it."

"You begin to sound resigned to your lot, Mr. Amberwell. Kali-Ananda will be pleased."

"Yeah." He smiled a smile that was a votive of offering to Kali's black heart. "You give my love to Kali-Ananda. You do that."

This seemed the propitious moment. I unstoppered the bottle of chloroform, dampened a wad of surgical gauze, and held it to Amberwell's face. He succumbed to its anesthetic influence without struggle.

While he was unconscious, I abraded the skin of his forehead with one of those miniature graters Dr. Scholl markets for filing away at the calluses on your feet. I scraped at Amberwell's forehead till the skin was raw, but I tried not to draw blood. Then I affixed a compress soaked in salt water to the area thus sensitized and secured the compress in place with loops and loops of surgical gauze until Amberwell's head was properly mummified from chin to crown. Strangely, as Amberwell became more abstract, he became more pathetic too. I pitied him as a mummy as I never had as a man.

I have no idea whether the sensation of a salty compress on sandpapered skin is more or less painfull than the aftermath of a tattoo—but neither would Amberwell. Surely he wouldn't be able to resist the power of the suggestion, but to be doubly sure I left on the floor beside his bandaged head a sketch of his hypothetical tattoo. It represented— crudely, I confess, for I've never been much of a draftsman—the goddess Kali, as she is described in my Britannica: "a naked black woman, four-armed, wearing a garland of heads of giants slain by her, and a string of skulls round her neck . . . with gaping mouth and protruding tongue." To which devout motif I added a further decorative surround of interlinked U's and C's, the corporate emblem of Unitask Corporation. It looked, quite literally, god-awful.

February 14

I greeted Amberwell, who was already wide awake, with a cheery "Happy Valentine's Day!" and he lunged and plunged about like a rodeo rider. Donald Duck lives again. Amazing that after more than two weeks of semi-starvation he should still have such reserves of strength.

"Now how are you going to eat your good breakfast if you're in such a state of frenzy?" I asked rhetorically.

Amberwell replied with his limited stock of curses. Even rage can't fire the man's imagination.

"Very well then, I'll just leave them here—" I placed the juiceless orange rinds on the floor beside the drawing of Kali. (It's remarkable, by the way, how much altogether edible food the average person disposes of as "garbage.") "—and tonight when you're calmer, we'll take the photos to send to the press."

I left Amberwell still fuming and clanking his chains and took the train into town through the dazzling, redesigned landscape that Friday's great blizzard had left behind.

That was this morning. Since when my scenario has just been through a major revision at the hands of chance or tragic fate—take your pick.

Briefly: When I got home, at about seven, I found a valentine chocolate box on the dining room table, together with a comic homemade card.

From Adelle, of course. Adelle always remembers Valentine's Day. I always forget. She had, as I should have foreseen, made herself a spare set of keys—not from any deep need to be sneaky, just because she can't accustom herself to the idea that she's been excluded from my life.

At first I didn't think to be alarmed. I made a mental note to get this further set of keys from her and helped myself to a nut cluster from the chocolate box. Then I turned on the stereo to find out what, if anything, Amberwell might be up to. The torture chamber was silent.

Something in that silence made me uneasy. I went downstairs and discovered— beyond the door that stood ajar—Adelle dead and Amberwell gone.

It may have been my specific prohibition of the cellar on her previous visit that had piqued her curiosity. (Her valentine was inscribed "To Bluebeard.") Or she may have heard Amberwell carrying on. She knew where I hung the key to the room, since it had served not only as a darkroom but as a storage vault for our choicer stealables when we'd gone off on holidays. Naturally enough, when she'd discovered Amberwell straitjacketed and wrapped in gauze, she had released him. (Conceivably, so mummified, she might have thought him to be me; we're of the same general stature.)

Amberwell, seeing the woman he recognized from her photograph as Kali-Ananda, *might* have said very little. Or, just as possibly, he'd pleaded to have his straitjacket removed. In either case, how could Adelle have acted otherwise than to release him? Probably she'd taken off the straitjacket first, whereupon, having been provided with the only weapon he required, Amberwell had strangled her. Then, with the other keys on the ring she'd brought into the room, he'd been able to free himself from the shackles about his feet and the belt that was chained to the bolt in the floor.

Once at liberty, he'd behaved with remarkable composure and—given what I must assume to be his purpose—well-considered purposefulness. He could not, having just murdered Adelle, call 911 for help. Instead, he helped himself—first to some food (most of a box of Wheaties and two quarts of milk), then to clothes from my closet, then to a suitcase into which he packed all of the paraphernalia from the torture chamber. Finally he'd taken the keys to Adelle's Datsun from her purse, together with her spare cash, and driven . . . where? To a hotel? To one of the banks where he's established a clandestine account? In the long term I'm quite sure I know what Amberwell intends.

I think the moral of the story is clear: I've converted Amberwell to the wrong religion.

February 21

Can it be only a week gone by? I feel . . . I don't know what I feel. Adelle would always be asking me that question: What are you *feeling?* And I would say I didn't know, or that I was feeling nothing in particular. And it's still the case. No, that's not quite true—I feel jittery. I've locked up the house and taken a hotel room around the corner from work. But apart from the nervousness of feeling hunted, I've been really quite self-possessed. There's been no overwhelming guilt or grief.

And that's not quite true either, for there was a day last week when I had to excuse myself from a staff meeting and go into the john and cry, and for a while I thought I might not be able to stop. But it wasn't the thought of Adelle's death that had undone me. It was remembering a scene from the end of *Gandhi*, when Gandhi, who'd fasted himself almost to death, advises a vengeful Hindu, whose son has been slain by Moslems, that he can only cure the wound of that loss if he will adopt an orphaned Moslem child as his own, and raise him in the Muslim faith. I don't know why that should rack me up so, but it does. I could go off on another crying jag right now if I let myself.

Would I (I've been wondering) have killed Amberwell finally? I did make provision for that eventuality. (Fortunately, for I was able, thereby, to dispose of Adelle's corpse expeditiously.) But I like to think that in the end, when my satisfaction in acting as public avenger had palled, I would have simply driven the chloroformed Amberwell to some secluded spot—ideally one of Unitask's own dumping grounds—and left him there to wake up as a free man, leaving it to him whether to raise a public hue and cry for what had been done. Somehow I doubt he'd have done that. I also doubt he'd have been able, with or without the help of the authorities, to discover who had played such a nasty trick upon him, since I'd taken reasonable precautions to cover my tracks. Amberwell never saw me without my Phantom of the Opera mask.

In the event my precautions are all quite pointless. Amberwell has my entire *curriculum vitae*. He took my business papers, my passport, a family photo album, a stack of family letters, my Rolodex—everything but this manuscript, which had accompanied me to work in my attaché case.

Should I give some kind of warning—at least to my parents? They spend their summers at a lakeside cabin whose seclusion is half of its charm. I haven't done so from a dread of having to enter into explanations. In any case, what is the use of a warning so ill-defined? My hope, such as it is, must be that Amberwell's appetite for revenge will be limited to my sole self.

On the cue of my finishing the preparation of this manuscript, which will be entrusted to my attorney, to be opened only in the event of a prolonged and unexplained absence, I received a phone call here in my hotel room. After I answered the fourth ring—which I did with reluctance, having registered here under an assumed name—there was a longish pause, then a click, and then the voices of the Mother Goose Consort singing:

> One-ery, two-ery, tickery, seven,
> Hallibo, crackibo, ten and eleven,
> Spin, span, muskidan,
> Twiddle-um, twaddle-um, twenty-one.
> Eerie, orie, ourie,
> You, are, out!

Violet Hunt (1866–1942)

The Prayer

Violet Hunt was a socially connected British author, journalist and biographer, who was a friend and correspondent of Henry James, H. G. Wells and Ford Madox Ford, among others, and travelled in the social sphere of the finest writers of her day. She was a committed feminist. She published two collections of weird and supernatural stories, *Tales of the Uneasy* (1911), which is a rare book, and *More Tales of the Uneasy* (1925). Her fiction is characterized by a somewhat Jamesian manner and eye for social detail, and is worthy of serious attention and comparison to Edith Wharton's ghost stories. "The Prayer" is a straightforward story of the Christian supernatural, an uncommon form of horror practiced notably in the contemporary period by Russell Kirk, but without any theological allegory in Hunt's penetrating psychological portrayal of a bizarre marriage. The story resembles nothing so much as a Victorian children's story, with the ironic moral: be careful what you pray for—you might get it and be punished horribly. It is interesting to compare it to the children's stories of Lucy Clifford, a close friend of Hunt's (and James'). Also to Thomas Hardy's "Barbara, of the House of Grebe," which deals with similar thematic material.

I

"It is but giving over of a game,
That must be lost"
—Philaster

"Come, Mrs. Arne—come, my dear, you must not give way like this! You can't stand it—you really can't! Let Miss Kate take you away—now do!" urged the nurse, with her most motherly of intonations.

"Yes, Alice, Mrs Joyce is right. Come away—do come away—you are only making yourself ill. It is all over; you can do nothing! Oh, oh, do come away!" implored Mrs. Arne's sister, shivering with excitement and nervousness.

A few moments ago Dr Graham had relinquished his hold on the pulse of Edward Arne with the hopeless movement of the eyebrows that meant—the end.

The nurse had made the little gesture of resignation that was possibly a matter of form with her. The young sister-in-law had hidden her face in her hands. The wife had

317

screamed a scream that had turned them all hot and cold—and flung herself on the bed over her dead husband. There she lay; her cries were terrible, her sobs shook her whole body.

The three gazed at her pityingly, not knowing what to do next. The nurse, folding her hands, looked towards the doctor for directions, and the doctor drummed with his fingers on the bed-post. The young girl timidly stroked the shoulder that heaved and writhed under her touch.

"Go away! Go away!" her sister reiterated continually, in a voice hoarse with fatigue and passion.

"Leave her alone, Miss Kate," whispered the nurse at last; "she will work it off best herself, perhaps."

She turned down the lamp as if to draw a veil over the scene. Mrs Arne raised herself on her elbow, showing a face stained with tears and purple with emotion.

"What! Not gone?" she said harshly. "Go away, Kate, go away! It is my house. I don't want you, I want no one—I want to speak to my husband. Will you go away—all of you. Give me an hour, half-an-hour—five minutes!"

She stretched out her arms imploringly to the doctor.

"Well . . ." said he, almost to himself.

He signed to the two women to withdraw, and followed them out into the passage. "Go and get something to eat," he said peremptorily, "while you can. We shall have trouble with her presently. I'll wait in the dressing-room."

He glanced at the twisting figure on the bed, shrugged his shoulders, and passed into the adjoining room, without, however, closing the door of communication. Sitting down in an arm-chair drawn up to the fire, he stretched himself and closed his eyes. The professional aspects of the case of Edward Arne rose up before him in all its interesting forms of complication . . .

It was just this professional attitude that Mrs Arne unconsciously resented both in the doctor and in the nurse. Through all their kindness she had realised and resented their scientific interest in her husband, for to them he had been no more than a curious and complicated case; and now that the blow had fallen, she regarded them both in the light of executioners. Her one desire, expressed with all the shameless sincerity of blind and thoughtless misery, was to be free of their hateful presence and alone—alone with her dead!

She was weary of the doctor's subdued manly tones—of the nurse's commonplace motherliness, too habitually adapted to the needs of all to be appreciated by the individual—of the childish consolation of the young sister, who had never loved, never been married, did not know what sorrow was! Their expressions of sympathy struck her like blows, the touch of their hands on her body, as they tried to raise her, stung her in every nerve.

With a sigh of relief she buried her head in the pillow, pressed her body more closely against that of her husband, and lay motionless.

Her sobs ceased.

The lamp went out with a gurgle. The fire leaped up, and died. She raised her head and stared about her helplessly, then sinking down again she put her lips to the ear of the dead man.

"Edward—dear Edward!" she whispered, "why have you left me? Darling, why have you left me? I can't stay behind—you know I can't. I am too young to be left. It is only a year since you married me. I never thought it was only for a year. 'Till death us do part!' Yes, I know that's in it, but nobody ever thinks of that! I never thought of living without you! I meant to die with you . . .

"No—no—I can't die—I must not—till my baby is born. You will never see it. Don't you want to see it? Don't you? Oh, Edward, speak! Say something, darling, one word—one little word! Edward! Edward! are you there? Answer me for God's sake, answer me!

"Darling, I am so tired of waiting. Oh, think, dearest. There is so little time. They only gave me half-an-hour. In half-an-hour they will come and take you away from me—take you where I can't come to you—with all my love I can't come to you! I know the place—I saw it once. A great lonely place full of graves, and little stunted trees dripping with dirty London rain . . . and gas-lamps flaring all round . . . but quite, quite dark where the grave is . . . a long grey stone just like the rest. How could you stay there?—all alone—all alone—without me?

"Do you remember, Edward, what we once said—that whichever of us died first should come back to watch over the other, in the spirit? I promised you, and you promised me. What children we were! Death is not what we thought. It comforted us to say that then.

"Now, it's nothing—nothing—worse than nothing! I don't want your spirit—I can't see it—or feel it—I want you, you, your eyes that looked at me, your mouth that kissed me—"

She raised his arms and clasped them round her neck, and lay there very still, murmuring, "Oh, hold me, hold me! Love me if you can. Am I hateful? This is me! These are your arms . . ."

The doctor in the next room moved in his chair. The noise awoke her from her dream of contentment, and she unwound the dead arm from her neck, and, holding it up by the wrist, considered it ruefully.

"Yes, I can put it round me, but I have to hold it there. It is quite cold—it doesn't care. Ah, my dear, you don't care! You are dead. I kiss you, but you don't kiss me. Edward! Edward! Oh, for heaven's sake kiss me once. Just once!

"No, no, that won't do—that's not enough! that's nothing! worse than nothing! I want you back, you, all you . . . What shall I do? . . . I often pray . . . Oh, if there be a God in heaven, and if He ever answered a prayer, let Him answer mine—my only prayer. I'll never ask another—and give you back to me! As you were—as I loved you—as I adored you! He must listen. He must! My God, my God, he's mine—he's my husband, he's my lover—give him back to me!"

"Left alone for half-an-hour or more with the corpse! It's not right!"

The muttered expression of the nurse's revolted sense of professional decency came from the head of the staircase, where she had been waiting for the last few minutes. The doctor joined her.

"Hush, Mrs Joyce! I'll go to her now."

The door creaked on its hinges as he gently pushed it open and went in.

"What's that? What's that?" screamed Mrs Arne. "Doctor! Doctor! Don't touch me! Either I am dead or he is alive!"

"Do you want to kill yourself, Mrs Arne?" said Dr Graham, with calculated sternness, coming forward; "come away!"

"Not dead! Not dead!" she murmured.

"He is dead, I assure you. Dead and cold an hour ago! Feel!" He took hold of her, as she lay face downwards, and in so doing he touched the dead man's cheek—it was not cold! Instinctively his finger sought a pulse.

"Stop! Wait!" he cried in his intense excitement. "My dear Mrs Arne, control yourself!"

But Mrs Arne had fainted, and fallen heavily off the bed on the other side. Her sister, hastily summoned; attended to her, while the man they had all given over for dead was, with faint gasps and sighs and reluctant moans, pulled, as it were, hustled and dragged back over the threshold of life.

II

"Why do you always wear black, Alice?" asked Esther Graham. "You are not in mourning that I know of."

She was Dr Graham's only daughter and Mrs Arne's only friend. She sat with Mrs Arne in the dreary drawing-room of the house in Chelsea. She had come to tea. She was the only person who ever did come to tea there.

She was brusque, kind, and blunt, and had a talent for making inappropriate remarks. Six years ago Mrs Arne had been a widow for an hour! Her husband had succumbed to an apparently mortal illness, and for the space of an hour had lain dead. When suddenly and inexplicably he had revived from his trance, the shock, combined with six weeks' nursing, had nearly killed his wife. All this Esther had heard from her father. She herself had only come to know Mrs Arne after her child was born, and all the tragic circumstances of her husband's illness put aside, and it was hoped forgotten. And when her idle question received no answer from the pale absent woman who sat opposite, with listless lack-lustre eyes fixed on the green and blue flames dancing in the fire, she hoped it had passed unnoticed. She waited for five minutes for Mrs Arne to resume the conversation, then her natural impatience got the better of her.

"Do say something, Alice!" she implored.

"Esther, I beg your pardon!" said Mrs Arne. "I was thinking."

"What were you thinking of?"

"I don't know."

"No, of course you don't. People who sit and stare into the fire never do think, really. They are only brooding and making themselves ill, and that is what you are doing. You mope, you take no interest in anything, you never go out—I am sure you have not been out of doors today?"

"No—yes—I believe not. It is so cold."

"You are sure to feel the cold if you sit in the house all day, and sure to get ill! Just look at yourself!"

Mrs Arne rose and looked at herself in the Italian mirror over the chimney-piece. It reflected faithfully enough her even pallor, her dark hair and eyes, the sweeping length of her eyelashes, the sharp curves of her nostrils, and the delicate arch of her eyebrows, that formed a thin sharp black line, so clear as to seem almost unnatural.

"Yes, I do look ill," she said with conviction.

"No wonder. You choose to bury yourself alive."

"Sometimes I do feel as if I lived in a grave. I look up at the ceiling and fancy it is my coffin-lid."

"Don't please talk like that!" expostulated Miss Graham, pointing to Mrs Arne's little girl. "If only for Dolly's sake, I think you should not give way to such morbid fancies. It isn't good for her to see you like this always."

"Oh, Esther," the other exclaimed, stung into something like vivacity, "don't reproach me! I hope I am a good mother to my child!"

"Yes, dear, you are a model mother—and model wife too. Father says the way you look after your husband is something wonderful, but don't you think for your own sake you might try to be a little gayer? You encourage these moods, don't you? What is it? Is it the house?"

She glanced around her—at the high ceiling, at the heavy damask *portières*, the tall cabinets of china, the dim oak panelling—it reminded her of a neglected museum. Her eye travelled into the farthest corners, where the faint filmy dusk was already gathering, lit only by the bewildering cross-lights of the glass panels of cabinet doors—to the tall narrow windows—then back again to the woman in her mourning dress, cowering by the fire. She said sharply—

"You should go out more."

"I do not like to—leave my husband."

"Oh, I know that he is delicate and all that, but still, does he never permit you to leave him? Does he never go out by himself?"

"Not often!"

"And you have no pets! It is very odd of you. I simply can't imagine a house without animals."

"We did have a dog once," answered Mrs Arne plaintively, "but it howled so we had to give it away. It would not go near Edward . . . But please don't imagine that I am dull! I have my child." She laid her hand on the flaxen head at her knee.

Miss Graham rose, frowning.

"Ah, you are too bad!" she exclaimed. "You are like a widow exactly, with one child, stroking its orphan head and saying, 'Poor fatherless darling.'"

Voices were heard outside. Miss Graham stopped talking quite suddenly, and sought her veil and gloves on the mantelpiece.

"You need not go, Esther," said Mrs Arne. "It is only my husband."

"Oh, but it is getting late," said the other, crumpling up her gloves in her muff, and shuffling her feet nervously.

"Come!" said her hostess, with a bitter smile, "put your gloves on properly—if you must go—but it is quite early still."

"Please don't go, Miss Graham," put in the child.

"I must. Go and meet your papa, like a good girl."

"I don't want to."

"You mustn't talk like that, Dolly," said the doctor's daughter absently, still looking towards the door. Mrs Arne rose and fastened the clasps of the big fur-cloak for her friend. The wife's white, sad, oppressed face came very close to the girl's cheerful one, as she murmured in a low voice—

"You don't like my husband, Esther? I can't help noticing it. Why don't you?"

"Nonsense!" retorted the other, with the emphasis of one who is repelling an overtrue accusation. "I do, only—"

"Only what?"

"Well, dear, it is foolish of me, of course, but I am—a little afraid of him."

"Afraid of Edward!" said his wife slowly. "Why should you be?"

"Well, dear—you see—I—I suppose women can't help being a little afraid of their friends' husbands—they can spoil their friendships with their wives in a moment, if they choose to disapprove of them. I really must go! Good-bye, child; give me a kiss! Don't ring, Alice. Please don't! I can open the door for myself—"

"Why should you?" said Mrs Arne. "Edward is in the hall; I heard him speaking to Foster."

"No; he has gone into his study. Good-bye, you apathetic creature!" She gave Mrs Arne a brief kiss and dashed out of the room. The voices outside had ceased, and she had reasonable hopes of reaching the door without being intercepted by Mrs Arne's husband. But he met her on the stairs. Mrs Arne, listening intently from her seat by the fire, heard her exchange a few shy sentences with him, the sound of which died away as they went downstairs together. A few moments after, Edward Arne came into the room and dropped into the chair just vacated by his wife's visitor.

He crossed his legs and said nothing. Neither did she.

His nearness had the effect of making the woman look at once several years older. Where she was pale he was well-coloured; the network of little filmy wrinkles that, on a close inspection, covered her face, had no parallel on his smooth skin. He was handsome; soft, well-groomed flakes of auburn hair lay over his forehead, and his steely blue eyes shone equally, a contrast to the sombre fire of hers, and the masses of dark crinkly hair that shaded her brow. The deep lines of permanent discontent furrowed that brow as she sat with her chin propped on her hands, and her elbows resting on her knees. Neither spoke. When the hands of the clock over Mrs Arne's head pointed to seven, the white-aproned figure of the nurse appeared in the doorway, and the little girl rose and kissed her mother very tenderly.

Mrs Arne's forehead contracted. Looking uneasily at her husband, she said to the child tentatively, yet boldly, as one grasps the nettle, "Say good night to your father!"

The child obeyed, saying "Good night" indifferently in her father's direction.

"Kiss him!"

"No, please—please not."

Her mother looked down on her curiously, sadly . . .

"You are a naughty, spoilt child!" she said, but without conviction. "Excuse her, Edward."

He did not seem to have heard.

"Well, if you don't care—" said his wife bitterly. "Come, child!" She caught the little girl by the hand and left the room.

At the door she half turned and looked fixedly at her husband. It was a strange ambiguous gaze; in it passion and dislike were strangely combined. Then she shivered and closed the door softly after her.

The man in the arm-chair sat with no perceptible change of attitude, his unspeculative eyes fixed on the fire, his hands clasped idly in front of him. The pose was obviously habitual. The servant brought lights and closed the shutters, drew the curtains, and made up the fire noisily, without, however, eliciting any reproof from his master.

Edward Arne was an ideal master, as far as Foster was concerned. He kept cases of cigars, but never smoked them, although the supply had often to be renewed. He did not care what he ate or drank, although he kept as good a cellar as most gentlemen—Foster knew that. He never interfered, he counted for nothing, he gave no trouble. Foster had no intention of ever leaving such an easy place. True, his master was not cordial; he very seldom addressed him or seemed to know whether he was there, but then neither did he grumble if the fire in the study was allowed to go out, or interfere with Foster's liberty in any way. He had a better place of it than Annette, Mrs Arne's maid, who would be called up in the middle of the night to bathe her mistress's forehead with eau-de-Cologne, or made to brush her long hair for hours together to soothe her. Naturally enough Foster and Annette compared notes as to their respective situations, and drew unflattering parallels between this capricious wife and model husband.

III

Miss Graham was not a demonstrative woman. On her return home she somewhat startled her father, as he sat by his study table, deeply interested in his diagnosis book, by the sudden violence of her embrace.

"Why this excitement?" he asked, smiling and turning round. He was a young-looking man for his age; his thin wiry figure and clear colour belied the evidence of his hair, tinged with grey, and the tired wrinkles that gave value to the acuteness and brilliancy of the eyes they surrounded.

"I don't know!" she replied, "only you are so nice and alive somehow. I always feel like this when I come back from seeing the Arnes."

"Then don't go to see the Arnes."

"I'm so fond of her, father, and she will never come here to me, as you know. Or else nothing would induce me to enter her tomb of a house, and talk to that walking funeral of a husband of hers. I managed to get away today without having to shake hands with him. I always try to avoid it. But, father, I do wish you would go and see Alice."

"Is she ill?"

"Well, not exactly ill, I suppose, but her eyes make me quite uncomfortable, and she says such odd things! I don't know if it is you or the clergyman she wants, but she is all wrong somehow! She never goes out except to church; she never pays a call, or has any one to call on her! Nobody ever asks the Arnes to dinner, and I'm sure I don't blame them—the sight of that man at one's table would spoil any party—and they never entertain. She is always alone. Day after day I go in and find her sitting over the fire, with that same brooding expression. I shouldn't be surprised in the least if she were to go mad some day. Father, what is it? What is the tragedy of the house? There is one, I am convinced. And yet, though I have been the intimate friend of that woman for years, I know no more about her than the man in the street."

"She keeps her skeleton safe in the cupboard," said Dr Graham. "I respect her for that. And please don't talk nonsense about tragedies. Alice Arne is only morbid—the malady of the age. And she is a very religious woman."

"I wonder if she complains of her odious husband to Mr Bligh. She is always going to his services."

"Odious?"

"Yes, odious!" Miss Graham shuddered. "I cannot stand him! I cannot bear the touch of his cold froggy hands, and the sight of his fishy eyes! That inane smile of his simply makes me shrivel up. Father, honestly, do you like him yourself?"

"My dear, I hardly know him! It is his wife I have known ever since she was a child, and I a boy at college. Her father was my tutor. I never knew her husband till six years ago, when she called me in to attend him in a very serious illness. I suppose she never speaks of it? No? A very odd affair. For the life of me I cannot tell how he managed to recover. You needn't tell people, for it affects my reputation, but I didn't save him! Indeed I have never been able to account for it. The man was given over for dead!"

"He might as well be dead for all the good he is," said Esther scornfully. "I have never heard him say more than a couple of sentences in my life."

"Yet he was an exceedingly brilliant young man; one of the best men of his year at Oxford—a good deal run after—poor Alice was wild to marry him!"

"In love with that spiritless creature? He is like a house with someone dead in it, and all the blinds down!"

"Come, Esther, don't be morbid—not to say silly! You are very hard on the poor man! What's wrong with him? He is the ordinary, commonplace, cold-blooded specimen of humanity, a little stupid, a little selfish—people who have gone through a serious illness like that are apt to be—but on the whole, a good husband, a good father, a good citizen—"

"Yes, and his wife is afraid of him, and his child hates him!" exclaimed Esther.

"Nonsense!" said Dr Graham sharply. "The child is spoilt. Only children are apt to be—and the mother wants a change or a tonic of some kind. I'll go and talk to her when I have time. Go along and dress. Have you forgotten that George Graham is coming to dinner?"

After she had gone the doctor made a note on the corner of his blotting-pad, "Mem.: to go and see Mrs Arne," and dismissed the subject of the memorandum entirely from his mind.

George Graham was the doctor's nephew, a tall, weedy, cumbrous young man, full of fads and fallacies, with a gentle manner that somehow inspired confidence. He was several years younger than Esther, who loved to listen to his semi-scientific, semi-romantic stories of things met with in the course of his profession. "Oh, I come across very queer things!" he would say mysteriously. "There's a queer little widow—!"

"Tell me about your little widow?" asked Esther that day after dinner, when, her father having gone back to his study, she and her cousin sat together as usual.

He laughed.

"You like to hear of my professional experiences? Well, she certainly interested me," he said thoughtfully. "She is an odd psychological study in her way. I wish I could come across her again."

"Where did you come across her, and what is her name?"

"I don't know her name, I don't want to; she is not a personage to me, only a case. I hardly know her face even. I have never seen it except in the twilight. But I gathered that she lived somewhere in Chelsea, for she came out on to the Embankment with only a kind of lacy thing over her head; she can't live far off, I fancy."

Esther became instantly attentive. "Go on," she said.

"It was three weeks ago," said George Graham. "I was coming along the Embankment about ten o'clock. I walked through that little grove, you know, just between Cheyne Walk and the river, and I heard in there someone sobbing very bitterly. I looked and saw a woman sitting on a seat, with her head in her hands, crying. I was most awfully sorry, of course, and I thought I could perhaps do something for her, get her a glass of water, or salts, or something. I took her for a woman of the people—it was quite dark, you know. So I asked her very politely if I could do anything for her, and then I noticed her hands—they were quite white and covered with diamonds."

"You were sorry you spoke, I suppose," said Esther.

"She raised her head and said—I believe she laughed—'Are you going to tell me to move on?'"

"She thought you were a policeman?"

"Probably—if she thought at all—but she was in a semi-dazed condition. I told her to wait till I came back, and dashed round the corner to the chemist's and bought a bottle of salts. She thanked me, and made a little effort to rise and go away. She seemed very weak. I told her I was a medical man, I started in and talked to her."

"And she to you?"

"Yes, quite straight. Don't you know that women always treat a doctor as if he were one step removed from their father confessor—not human—not in the same category as themselves? It is not complimentary to one as a man, but one hears a good deal one would not otherwise hear. She ended by telling me all about herself—in a veiled way, of course. It soothed her—relieved her—she seemed not to have had an outlet for years!"

"To a mere stranger!"

"To a doctor. And she did not know what she was saying half the time. She was hysterical, of course. Heavens! what nonsense she talked! She spoke of herself as a person somehow haunted, cursed by some malign fate, a victim of some fearful spiritual catastrophe, don't you know? I let her run on. She was convinced of the reality of a sort of 'doom' that she had fancied had befallen her. It was quite pathetic. Then it got rather chilly—she shivered—I suggested her going in. She shrank back; she said, 'If you only knew what a relief it is, how much less miserable I am out here! I can breathe; I can live—it is my only glimpse of the world that is alive—I live in a grave—oh, let me stay!' She seemed positively afraid to go home."

"Perhaps someone bullied her at home."

"I suppose so, but then—she had no husband. He died, she told me, years ago. She had adored him, she said—"

"Is she pretty?"

"Pretty! Well, I hardly noticed. Let me see! Oh, yes, I suppose she was pretty—no, now I think of it, she would be too worn and faded to be what you call pretty."

Esther smiled.

"Well, we sat there together for quite an hour, then the clock of Chelsea church struck eleven, and she got up and said 'Good-bye,' holding out her hand quite naturally, as if our meeting and conversation had been nothing out of the common. There was a sound like a dead leaf trailing across the walk and she was gone."

"Didn't you ask if you should see her again?"

"That would have been a mean advantage to take."

"You might have offered to see her home."

"I saw she did not mean me to."

"She was a lady, you say," pondered Esther. "How was she dressed?"

"Oh, all right, like a lady—in black—mourning, I suppose. She has dark crinkly hair, and her eyebrows are very thin and arched—I noticed that in the dusk."

"Does this photograph remind you of her?" asked Esther suddenly, taking him to the mantelpiece.

"Rather!"

"Alice! Oh, it couldn't be—she is not a widow, her husband is alive—has your friend any children?"

"Yes, one, she mentioned it."

"How old?"

"Six years old, I think she said. She talks of the 'responsibility of bringing up an orphan.'"

"George, what time is it?" Esther asked suddenly.

"About nine o'clock."

"Would you mind coming out with me?"

"I should like it. Where shall we go?"

"To St Adhelm's! It is close by here. There is a special late service tonight, and Mrs Arne is sure to be there."

"Oh, Esther—curiosity!"

"No, not mere curiosity. Don't you see if it is my Mrs Arne who talked to you like this, it is very serious? I have thought her ill for a long time; but as ill as that—"

At St Adhelm's Church, Esther Graham pointed out a woman who was kneeling beside a pillar in an attitude of intense devotion and abandonment. She rose from her knees, and turned her rapt face up towards the pulpit whence the Reverend Ralph Bligh was holding his impassioned discourse. George Graham touched his cousin on the shoulder, and motioned to her to leave her place on the outermost rank of worshippers.

"That is the woman!" said he.

IV

"Mem.: to go and see Mrs Arne." The doctor came across this note in his blotting-pad one day six weeks later. His daughter was out of town. He had heard nothing of the Arnes since her departure. He had promised to go and see her. He was a little conscience-stricken. Yet another week elapsed before he found time to call upon the daughter of his old tutor.

At the corner of Tite Street he met Mrs Arne's husband, and stopped. A doctor's professional kindliness of manner is, or ought to be, independent of his personal likings and dislikings, and there was a pleasant cordiality about his greeting which should have provoked a corresponding fervour on the part of Edward Arne.

"How are you, Arne?" Graham said. "I was on my way to call on your wife."

"Ah—yes!" said Edward Arne, with the ascending inflection of polite acquiescence. A ray of blue from his eyes rested transitorily on the doctor's face, and in that short moment the latter noted its intolerable vacuity, and for the first time in his life he felt a sharp pang of sympathy for the wife of such a husband.

"I suppose you are off to your club?—er—good bye!" he wound up abruptly. With the best will in the world he somehow found it almost impossible to carry on a conversation with Edward Arne, who raised his hand to his hat-brim in token of salutation, smiled sweetly, and walked on.

"He really is extraordinarily good-looking," reflected the doctor, as he watched him down the street and safely over the crossing with a certain degree of solicitude for which he could not exactly account. "And yet one feels one's vitality ebbing out at the finger-ends as one talks to him. I shall begin to believe in Esther's absurd fancies about him soon. Ah, there's the little girl!" he exclaimed, as he turned into Cheyne Walk and caught sight of her with her nurse, making violent demonstrations to attract his attention. "She is alive, at any rate. How is your mother, Dolly?" he asked.

"Quite well, thank you," was the child's reply. She added, "She's crying. She sent me away because I looked at her. So I did. Her cheeks are quite red."

"Run away—run away and play!" said the doctor nervously. He ascended the steps of the house, and rang the bell very gently and neatly.

"Not at—" began Foster, with the intonation of polite falsehood, but stopped on seeing the doctor, who, with his daughter, was a privileged person. "Mrs Arne will see you, Sir."

"Mrs Arne is not alone?" he said interrogatively.

"Yes, Sir, quite alone. I have just taken tea in."

Dr Graham's doubts were prompted by the low murmur as of a voice, or voices, which came to him through the open door of the room at the head of the stairs. He paused and listened while Foster stood by, merely remarking, "Mrs Arne do talk to herself sometimes, Sir."

It was Mrs Arne's voice—the doctor recognised it now. It was not the voice of a sane or healthy woman. He at once mentally removed his visit from the category of a morning call, and prepared for a semi-professional inquiry.

"Don't announce me," he said to Foster, and quietly entered the back drawing-room, which was separated by a heavy tapestry *portière* from the room where Mrs Arne sat, with an open book on the table before her, from which she had been apparently reading aloud. Her hands were now clasped tightly over her face, and when, presently, she removed them and began feverishly to turn page after page of her book, the crimson of her cheeks was seamed with white where her fingers had impressed themselves.

The doctor wondered if she saw him, for though her eyes were fixed in his direction, there was no apprehension in them. She went on reading, and it was the text, mingled with passionate interjection and fragmentary utterances, of the burial service that met his ears.

" 'For as in Adam all die!' All die! It says all! For he must reign . . . The last enemy that shall be destroyed is Death. What shall they do if the dead rise not at all . . . I die daily! . . . Daily! No, no, better get it over . . . dead and buried . . . out of sight, out of mind . . . under a stone. Dead men don't come back . . . Go on! Get it over. I want to hear the earth rattle on the coffin, and then I shall know it is done. 'Flesh and blood cannot inherit!' Oh, what did I do? What have I done? Why did I wish it so fervently? Why did I pray for it so earnestly? God gave me my wish—"

"Alice! Alice!" groaned the doctor.

She looked up. " 'When this corruptible shall have put on incorruption—' 'Dust to dust, ashes to ashes, earth to earth—' Yes, that is it. 'After death, though worms destroy this body—' "

She flung the book aside and sobbed.

"That is what I was afraid of. My God! My God! Down there—in the dark—for ever and ever and ever! I could not bear to think of it! My Edward! And so I interfered . . . and prayed . . . and prayed till . . . Oh! I am punished. Flesh and blood could not inherit! I kept him there—I would not let him go . . . I kept him . . . I prayed . . . I denied him Christian burial . . . Oh, how could I know . . ."

"Good heavens, Alice!" said Graham, coming sensibly forward, "what does this mean? I have heard of schoolgirls going through the marriage service by themselves, but the burial service—"

He laid down his hat and went on severely, "What have you to do with such things? Your child is flourishing—your husband alive and here—"

"And who kept him here?" interrupted Alice Arne fiercely, accepting the fact of his appearance without comment.

"You did," he answered quickly, "with your care and tenderness. I believe the warmth of your body, as you lay beside him for that half-hour, maintained the vital heat during that extraordinary suspension of the heart's action, which made us all give him up for dead. You were his best doctor, and brought him back to us."

"Yes, it was I—it was I—you need not tell me it was I!"

"Come, be thankful!" he said cheerfully. "Put that book away, and give me some tea, I'm very cold."

"Oh, Dr Graham, how thoughtless of me!" said Mrs Arne, rallying at the slight imputation on her politeness he had purposely made. She tottered to the bell and rang it before he could anticipate her.

"Another cup," she said quite calmly to Foster, who answered it. Then she sat down quivering all over with the suddenness of the constraint put upon her.

"Yes, sit down and tell me all about it," said Dr Graham good-humouredly, at the same time observing her with the closeness he gave to difficult cases.

"There is nothing to tell," she said simply, shaking her head, and futilely altering the position of the tea-cups on the tray. "It all happened years ago. Nothing can be done now. Will you have sugar?"

He drank his tea and made conversation. He talked to her of some Dante lectures she was attending; of some details connected with her child's Kindergarten classes. These subjects did not interest her. There was a subject she wished to discuss, he could see that a question trembled on her tongue, and tried to lead up to it.

She introduced it herself, quite quietly, over a second cup. "Sugar, Dr Graham? I forget. Dr Graham, tell me, do you believe that prayers—wicked unreasonable prayers—are granted?"

He helped himself to another slice of bread and butter before answering.

"Well," he said slowly, "it seems hard to believe that every fool who has a voice to pray with, and a brain where to conceive idiotic requests with, should be permitted to interfere with the economy of the universe. As a rule, if people were long-sighted enough to see the result of their petitions, I fancy very few of us would venture to interfere."

Mrs Arne groaned.

She was a good Churchwoman, Graham knew, and he did not wish to sap her faith in any way, so he said no more, but inwardly wondered if a too rigid interpretation of some of the religious dogmas of the Vicar of St Adhelm's, her spiritual adviser, was not the clue to her distress. Then she put another question—

"Eh! What?" he said. "Do I believe in ghosts? I will believe you if you will tell me you have seen one."

"You know, Doctor," she went on, "I was always afraid of ghosts—of spirits—things unseen. I couldn't ever read about them. I could not bear the idea of someone in the room with me that I could not see. There was a text that always frightened me that hung up in my room: 'Thou, God, seest me!' It frightened me when I was a child, whether I had been doing wrong or not. But now," shuddering, "I think there are worse things than ghosts."

"Well, now, what sort of things?" he asked good-humouredly. "Astral bodies—?"

She leaned forward and laid her hot hand on his.

"Oh, Doctor, tell me, if a spirit—without the body we know it by—is terrible, what of a body"—her voice sank to a whisper, "a body—senseless—lonely—stranded on this earth—without a spirit?"

She was watching his face anxiously. He was divided between a morbid inclination to laugh and the feeling of intense discomfort provoked by this wretched scene. He longed to give the conversation a more cheerful turn, yet did not wish to offend her by changing it too abruptly.

"I have heard of people not being able to keep body and soul together," he replied at last, "but I am not aware that practically such a division of forces has ever been achieved. And if we could only accept the theory of the de-spiritualised body, what a number of antipathetic people now wandering about in the world it would account for!"

The piteous gaze of her eyes seemed to seek to ward off the blow of his misplaced jocularity. He left his seat and sat down on the couch beside her.

"Poor child! poor girl! you are ill, you are over-excited. What is it? Tell me," he asked her as tenderly as the father she had lost in early life might have done. Her head sank on his shoulder.

"Are you unhappy?" he asked her gently.

"Yes!"

"You are too much alone. Get your mother or your sister to come and stay with you."

"They won't come," she wailed. "They say the house is like a grave. Edward has made himself a study in the basement. It's an impossible room—but he has moved all his things in, and I can't—I won't go to him there . . ."

"You're wrong. For it's only a fad," said Graham, "he'll tire of it. And you must see more people somehow. It's a pity my daughter is away. Had you any visitors today?"

"Not a soul has crossed the threshold for eighteen days."

"We must change all that," said the doctor vaguely. "Meantime you must cheer up. Why, you have no need to think of ghosts and graves—no need to be melancholy—you have your husband and your child—"

"I have my child—yes."

The doctor took hold of Mrs. Arne by the shoulder and held her a little away from him. He thought he had found the cause of her trouble—a more commonplace one than he had supposed.

"I have known you, Alice, since you were a child," he said gravely. "Answer me! You love your husband, don't you?"

"Yes," It was as if she were answering futile prefatory questions in the witness-box. Yet he saw by the intense excitement in her eyes that he had come to the point she feared, and yet desired to bring forward.

"And he loves you?"

She was silent.

"Well, then, if you love each other, what more can you want? Why do you say you have only your child in that absurd way?"

She was still silent, and he gave her a little shake.

"Tell me, have you and he had any difference lately? Is there any—coldness—any—temporary estrangement between you?"

He was hardly prepared for the burst of foolish laughter that proceeded from the demure Mrs. Arne as she rose and confronted him, all the blood in her body seeming for the moment to rush to her usually pale cheeks.

"Coldness! Temporary estrangement! If that were all! Oh, is everyone blind but me? There is all the world between us!—all the difference between this world and the next!"

She sat down again beside the doctor and whispered in his ear, and her words were like a breath of hot wind from some Gehenna of the soul.

"Oh, Doctor, I have borne it for six years, and I must speak. No other woman could bear what I have borne, and yet be alive! And I loved him so; you don't know how I loved him! That was it—that was my crime—"

"Crime?" repeated the doctor,

"Yes, crime! It was impious, don't you see? But I have been punished. Oh, Doctor, you don't know what my life is! Listen! I must tell you. To live with a— At first before I guessed when I used to put my arms round him, and he merely submitted—and then it dawned on me what I was kissing! It is enough to turn a living woman into stone—for I am living, though sometimes I forget it. Yes, I am a live woman, though I live in a grave. Think what it is!—to wonder every night if you will be alive in the morning, to lie down every night in an open grave—to smell death in every corner—every room—to breathe death—to touch it . . ."

The *portière* in front of the door shook, a hoopstick parted it, a round white clad bundle supported on a pair of mottled red legs peeped in, pushed a hoop in front of her. The child made no noise. Mrs. Arne seemed to have heard her, however. She slewed round violently as she sat on the sofa beside Dr. Graham, leaving her hot hands clasped in his.

"You ask Dolly," she exclaimed. "She knows it, too—she feels it."

"No, no, Alice, this won't do!" the doctor adjured her very low. Then he raised his voice and ordered the child from the room. He had managed to lift Mrs. Arne's feet and laid her full length on the sofa by the time the maid appeared. She had fainted.

He pulled down her eyelids and satisfied himself as to certain facts he had up till now dimly apprehended. When Mrs. Arne's maid returned, he gave her mistress over to her care and proceeded to Edward Arne's new study in the basement.

"Morphia!" he muttered to himself, as he stumbled and faltered through gaslit passages, where furtive servants eyed him and scuttled to their burrows.

"What is he burying himself down here for?" he thought. "Is it to get out of her way? They *are* a nervous pair of them!"

Arne was sunk in a large arm-chair drawn up before the fire. There was no other light, except a faint reflection from the gas-lamp in the road, striking down past the iron bars of the window that was sunk below the level of the street. The room was comfortless and empty, there was little furniture in it except a large bookcase at Arne's right hand and a table with a Tantalus on it standing some way off.There was a faded portrait in pastel of Alice Arne over the mantelpiece, and beside it, a poor pendant, a pen and ink sketch of the master of the house. They were quite discrepant, in size and medium, but they appeared to look at each other with the stolid attentiveness of newly married people.

"Seedy, Arne?" Graham said.

"Rather, today. Poke the fire for me, will you?"

"I've known you quite seven years," said the doctor cheerfully, "so I presume I can do that . . . There, now! . . . And I'll presume further—What have we got here?"

He took a small bottle smartly out of Edward Arne's fingers and raised his eyebrows. Edward Arne had rendered it up agreeably; he did not seem upset or annoyed.

"Morphia. It isn't a habit. I only got hold of the stuff yesterday—found it about the house. Alice was very jumpy all day, and communicated her nerves to me, I suppose. I've none as a rule, but do you know, Graham, I seem to be getting them—feel things a good deal more than I did, and want to talk about them."

"What, are you growing a soul?" said the doctor carelessly, lighting a cigarette.

"Heaven forbid!" Arne answered equably. "I've done very well without it all these years. But I'm fond of old Alice, you know, in my own way, When I was a young man, I was quite different. I took things hardly and got excited about them. Yes, excited. I was wild about Alice, wild! Yes, by Jove! though she has forgotten all about it."

"Not that, but still it's natural she should long for some little demonstration of affection now and then . . . and she'd be awfully distressed if she saw you fooling with a bottle of morphia! You know, Arne, after that narrow squeak you had of it six years ago, Alice and I have a good right to consider that your life belongs to us!"

Edward Arne settled in his chair and replied, rather fretfully—

"All very well, but you didn't manage to do the job thoroughly. You didn't turn me out lively enough to please Alice. She's annoyed because when I take her in my arms, I don't hold her tight enough. I'm too quiet, too languid! . . . Hang it all, Graham, I believe she'd like me to stand for Parliament! . . . Why can't she let me just go along my own way? Surely a man who's come through an illness like mine can be let off parlour tricks? All this worry—it culminated the other day when I said I wanted to colonise a room down here, and did, with a spurt that took it out of me horribly,—all this worry, I say, seeing her upset and so on, keeps me low, and so I feel as if I wanted to take drugs to soothe me."

"Soothe!" said Graham. This stuff is more than soothing if you take enough of it. I'll send you something more like what you want, and I'll take this away, by your leave."

"I really can't argue!" replied Arne . . . "If you see Alice, tell her you find me fairly comfortable and don't put her off this room. I really like it best. She can come and see me here, I keep a good fire, tell her . . . I feel as if I wanted to sleep . . ." he added brusquely.

"You have been indulging already," said Graham softly, Arne had begun to doze off. His cushion had sagged down, the doctor stooped to rearrange it, carelessly laying the little phial for the moment in a crease of the rug covering the man's knees.

Mrs. Arne in her mourning dress was crossing the hall as he came to the top of the basement steps and pushed open the swing door. She was giving some orders to Foster, the butler, who disappeared as the doctor advanced.

"You're about again," he said, "good girl!"

"Too silly of me," she said, "to be hysterical! After all these years! One should be able to keep one's own counsel. But it is over now, I promise I will never speak of it again."

"We frightened poor Dolly dreadfully. I had to order her out like a regiment of soldiers."

"Yes, I know, I'm going to her now!"

On his suggestion that she should look in on her husband first she looked askance. "Down there!"

"Yes, that's his fancy. Let him be. He is a good deal depressed about himself and you. He notices a great deal more than you think. He isn't quite as apathetic as you describe him to be . . . Come here!" He led her into the unlit dining-room a little way. "You expect too much, my dear. You do really! You make too many demands on the vitality you saved."

"What did one save him for?" she asked fiercely. She continued more quietly, "I know. I am going to be different."

"Not you," said Graham fondly. He was very partial to Alice Arne in spite of her silliness. "You'll worry about Edward till the end of the chapter. I know you. And"—he turned her round by the shoulder so that she fronted the light in the hall—"you elusive thing, let me have a good look at you . . . Hum! Your eyes, they're a bit starey . . ."

He let her go again with a sigh of impotence. Something must be done . . . soon . . . he must think . . . He got hold of his coat and began to get into it . . .

Mrs. Arne smiled, buttoned a button for him and then opened the front door, like a good hostess, a very little way. With a quick flirt of his hat he was gone, and she heard the clap of his brougham door and the order "Home."

"Been saying good-bye to that thief Graham?" said her husband gently, when she entered his room, her pale eyes staring a little, her thin hand busy at the front of her dress . . .

"Thief? Why? One moment! Where's your switch?"

She found it and turned on a blaze of light from which her husband seemed to shrink.

"Well, he carried off my drops. Afraid of my poisoning myself, I suppose?"

"Or acquiring the morphia habit," said his wife in a dull level voice, "as I have."

She paused. He made no comment. Then, picking up the little phial Dr. Graham had left in the crease of the rug, she spoke—

"You are the thief, Edward, as it happens, this is mine."

"Is it? I found it knocking about: I didn't know it was yours. Well, will you give me some?"

"I will, if you like."

"Well, dear, decide. You know I am in your hands and Graham's. He was rubbing that into me today."

"Poor lamb!" she said derisively; "I'd not allow my doctor, or my wife either, to dictate to me whether I should put an end to myself, or not."

"Ah, but you've got a spirit, you see!" Arne yawned. "However, let me have to go at the stuff and then you put it on top of the wardrobe or a shelf, where I shall know it is, but never reach out to get it, I promise you."

"No, you wouldn't reach out a hand to keep yourself alive, let alone kill yourself," said she. "That is you all over, Edward."

"And don't you see that is why I did die," he said, with earnestness unexpected by her. "And then, unfortunately, you and Graham bustled up and wouldn't let Nature take its course . . . I rather wish you hadn't been so officious."

"And let you stay dead," said she carelessly. "But at the time I cared for you so much that I should have had to kill myself, or commit suttee like a Bengali widow. Ah, well!"

She reached out for a glass half-full of water that stood on the low ledge of a bookcase close by the arm of his chair . . . "Will this glass do? What's in it? Only water? How much morphia shall I give you? An overdose?"

"I don't care if you do, and that's fact."

"It was a joke, Edward," she said piteously.

"No joke to me. This fag end of life I've clawed hold of, doesn't interest me. And I'm bound to be interested in what I'm doing or I'm no good. I'm no earthly good now. I don't enjoy life, I've nothing to enjoy it with—in here—he struck his breast. "It's like a dull party one goes to by accident. All I want to do is to get into a cab and go home."

His wife stood over him with a half-full glass in one hand and the little bottle in the other. Her eyes dilated . . . her chest heaved . . .

"Edward!" she breathed. "Was it all so useless?"

"Was what useless? Yes, as I was telling you, I go as one in a dream—a bad, bad dream, like the dreams I used to have when I overworked at college. I was brilliant, Alice, brillant, do you hear? At some cost, I expect! Now I hate people—my fellow creatures. I've left them. They come and go, jostling me, and pushing me, on the pavements as I go along, avoiding them. Do you know where they should be, really, in relation to me?"

He rose a little in his seat— she stepped nervously aside, made as if to put down the bottle and the glass she was holding, then thought better of it and continued to extend them mechanically.

"They should be over my head. I've already left them and their petty nonsense of living. They mean nothing to me, no more than if they were ghosts walking. Or perhaps, it's I who am a ghost to them? . . . You don't understand it. It's because I suppose you have no imagination. You just know what you want and do your best to get it. You blurt out your blessed petition to your Deity and the idea that you're irrelevant never enters your head, soft, persistent, High Church thing that you are! . . ."

Alice Arne smiled, and balanced the objects she was holding. He motioned her to pour out the liquid from one to the other, but she took no heed; she was listening with all her ears. It was the nearest approach to the language of compliment, to anything in the way of loverlike personalities that she had heard fall from his lips since his illness. He went on, becoming as it were lukewarm to his subject—

"But the worst of it is that once break the cord that links you to humanity—it can't be mended. Man doesn't live by bread alone . . . or lives to disappoint you. What am I to you, without my own poor personality? . . . Don't stare so, Alice! I haven't talked so much or so intimately for ages, have I? Let me, try and have it out . . . Are you in any sort of hurry?"

"No, Edward."

"Pour that stuff out and have done . . . Well, Alice, it's a queer feeling, I tell you. One goes about with one's looks on the ground, like a man who eyes the bed he is going to lie down in, and longs for. Alice, the crust of the earth seems a barrier between me and my own place. I want to scratch the boardings with my nails and shriek something like this: "Let me get down to you all, there where I belong!" It's a horrible sensation, like a vampire reversed! . . ."

"Is that why you insisted on having this room in the basement?" she asked breathlessly.

"Yes, I can't bear being upstairs, somehow. Here, with these barred windows and stone-cold floors . . . I can see the people's feet walking above there in the street . . . one has some sort of illusion . . ."

"Oh!" She shivered and her eyes travelled like those of a caged creature round the bare room and fluttered when they rested on the sombre windows imperiously barred. She dropped her gaze to the stone flags that showed beyond the oasis of Turkey carpet on which Arne's chair stood . . . Then to the door, the door that she had closed on entering. It had heavy bolts, but they were not drawn against her, though by the look of her eyes it seemed she half imagined they were . . .

She made a step forward and moved her hands slightly. She looked down on them and what they held . . . then changed the relative positions of the two objects and held the bottle over the glass . . .

"Yes, come along!" her husband said. "Are you going to be all day giving it me?"

With a jerk, she poured the liquid out into a glass and handed it to him. She looked away—forwards the door . . .

"Ah, your way of escape!" said he, following her eyes. Then he drank, painstakingly. The empty bottle fell out of her hands. She wrung them, murmuring—

"Oh, if I had only known!"

"Known what? That I should go near to cursing you for bringing me back?"

He fixed his cold eyes on her, as the liquid passed slowly over his tongue . . .

"—Or that you would end by taking back the gift you gave?"

John W. Campbell (1910-1971)

Who Goes There?

John W. Campbell was a revolutionary magazine editor in the science fiction and fantasy genre from 1937 to his death in 1971. His short-lived (1939-44) magazine, *Unknown*, had a profound influence on the development of horror fiction for decades. His entire body of fiction, written as a young man before he ceased writing as a job condition of becoming editor of *Astounding Stories*, was in the science fiction genre. His one exceptional piece of horror is the popular and influential novella, "Who Goes There?" the title story of one of the two later collections of his stories, and the source the famous 1950s film, *The Thing*. "Science fiction," says Leslie Fiedler, "evokes a cataclysmic horror that threatens the entire earth . . . it is essentially terror fiction." To the extent that this is true, it gets at the intimate connections between science fiction and the horror genre in the twentieth century. Campbell, a technological optimist, did not characteristically write in this mode, and when he did, published his stories under a pseudonym originally. Further, writing in the genre that had been invented only in 1926 (when the first issue of *Amazing Stories* declared a new genre of literature, "scientifiction"), for *Astounding*, the science fiction magazine that had published several major Lovecraft stories of cosmic horror and many stories by his circle, Campbell set out to write a science fiction story that would "scare the pants off people," as he told me in conversation, but in a clear, unobtrusive style. He succeeded in creating not only an acknowledged classic of modern science fiction but one of the most influential horror stories of the century.

I

The place stank. A queer, mingled stench that only the ice-buried cabins of an Antarctic camp know, compounded of reeking human sweat, and the heavy, fish-oil stench of melted seal blubber. An overtone of liniment combatted the musty smell of sweat-and-snow drenched furs. the acrid odor of burnt cooking fat, and the animal, not-unpleasant smell of dogs, diluted by time, hung in the air.

Lingering odors of machine oil contrasted sharply with the taint of harness dressing and leather. Yet, somehow, through all that reek of human beings and their associates—dogs, machines, and cooking—came another taint. It was a queer, neck-ruffling thing, a faintest suggestion of an odor alien among the smells of industry and life. And it was a life-smell. But it came from the thing that lay bound with cord and tarpaulin on the table, dripping slowly, methodically onto the heavy planks, dank and gaunt under the unshielded glare of the electric light.

Blair, the little bald-pated biologist of the expedition, twitched nervously at the wrappings, exposing clear, dark ice beneath and then pulling the tarpaulin back into place restlessly. His little birdlike motions of suppressed eagerness danced his shadow across the fringe of dingy gray underwear hanging from the low ceiling, the equatorial fringe of stiff, graying hair around his naked skull a comical halo about the shadow's head.

Commander Garry brushed aside the lax legs of a suit of underwear, and stepped toward the table. Slowly his eyes traced around the rings of men sardined into the Administration Building. His tall, stiff body straightened finally, and he nodded. "Thirty-seven. All here." His voice was low, yet carried the clear authority of the commander by nature, as well as by title.

"You know the outline of the story back of that find of the Secondary Pole Expedition. I have been conferring with Second-in-Command McReady, and Norris, as well as Blair and Dr. Copper. There is a difference of opinion, and because it involves the entire group, it is only just that the entire Expedition personnel act on it.

"I am going to ask McReady to give you the details of the story, because each of you has been too busy with his own work to follow closely the endeavors of the others. McReady?"

Moving from the smoke-blued background, McReady was a figure from some forgotten myth, a looming, bronze statue that held life, and walked. Six-feet-four inches he stood as he halted beside the table, and with a characteristic glance upward to assure himself of room under the low ceiling beams, straightened. His rough, clashingly orange windproof jacket he still had on, yet on his huge frame it did not seem misplaced. Even here, four feet beneath the drift-wind that droned across the antarctic waste above the ceiling, the cold of the frozen continent leaked in, and gave meaning to the harshness of the man. And he was bronze—his great red-bronze beard, the heavy hair that matched it. The gnarled, corded hands gripping, relaxing, gripping and relaxing on the table planks were bronze. Even the deep-sunken eyes beneath heavy brows were bronzed.

Age-resisting endurance of the metal spoke in the cragged heavy outlines of his face, and the mellow tones of the heavy voice. "Norris and Blair agree on one thing; that animal we found was not—terrestrial in origin. Norris fears there may be danger in that; Blair says there is none.

"But I'll go back to how, and why we found it. To all that was known before we came here, it appeared that this point was exactly over the South Magnetic Pole of Earth. The compass does point straight down here, as you all know. The more delicate instruments of the physicists, instruments especially designed for this expedition and its study of the magnetic pole, detected a secondary effect, a secondary, less powerful magnetic influence about 80 miles southwest of here.

The Secondary Magnetic Expedition went out to investigate it. There is no need for details. We found it, but it was not the huge meteorite or magnetic mountain Norris had expected to find. Iron ore is magnetic, of course; iron more so—and certain special steels even more magnetic. From the surface indications, the secondary pole we found was small, so small that the magnetic effect it had was preposterous. No magnetic material conceivable could have that effect. Soundings through the ice indicated it was within one hundred feet of the glacier surface.

"I think you should know the structure of the place. There is a broad plateau, a level sweep that runs more than 150 miles due south from the Secondary station, Van Wall says. He didn't have time or fuel to fly farther, but it was running smoothly due south then. Right there, where that buried thing was, there is an ice-drowned mountain ridge, a granite wall of unshakable strength that has dammed back the ice creeping from the south.

"And four hundred miles due south is the South Polar Plateau. You have asked me at various times why it gets warmer here when the wind rises, and most of you know. As a meteorologist I'd have staked my word that no wind could blow at −70 degrees; that no more than a 5-mile wind could blow at −50; without causing warming due to friction with ground, snow and ice and the air itself.

"We camped there on the lip of that ice-drowned mountain range for twelve days. We dug our camp into the blue ice that formed the surface, and escaped most of it. But for twelve consecutive days the wind blew at 45 miles an hour. It went as high as 48, and fell to 41 at times. The temperature was −63 degrees. It rose to −60 and fell to −68. It was meteorologically impossible, and it went on uninterruptedly for twelve days and twelve nights.

"Somewhere to the south, the frozen air of the South Polar Plateau slides down from that 18,000 foot bowl, down a mountain pass, over a glacier, and starts north. There must be a funneling mountain chain that directs it, and sweeps it away for four hundred miles to hit that bald plateau where we found the secondary pole, and 350 miles farther north reaches the Antarctic Ocean.

"It's been frozen there since Antarctica froze twenty million years ago. There never has been a thaw there.

"Twenty million years ago Antarctica was beginning to freeze. We've investigated, though, and built speculations. What we believe happened was about like this.

"Something came down out of space, a ship. We saw it there in the blue ice, a thing like a submarine without a conning tower or directive vanes, 280 feet long and 45 feet in diameter at its thickest.

"Eh, Van Wall? Space? Yes, but I'll explain that better later." McReady's steady voice went on.

"It came down from space, driven and lifted by forces men haven't discovered yet, and somehow—perhaps something went wrong then—tangled with Earth's megnetic field. It came south here, out of control probably, circling the magnetic pole. That's a savage country there; but when Antarctica was still freezing, it must have been a thousand times more savage. There must have been blizzard snow, as well as drift, new snow falling as the continent glaciated. The swirl there must have been particularly bad, the wind hurling a solid blanket of white over the lip of that now-buried mountain.

"The ship struck solid granite head-on, and cracked up. Not every one of the passengers in it was killed, but the ship must have been ruined, her driving mechanism locked. It tangled with Earth's field, Norris believes. No thing made by intelligent beings can tangle with the dead immensity of a planet's natural forces and survive.

"One of its passengers stepped out. The wind we saw there never fell below 41, and the temperature never rose above −60. Then—the wind must have been stronger. And there was drift falling in a solid sheet. The *thing* was lost completely in ten paces." He paused for a moment, the deep, steady voice giving way to the drone of wind overhead and the uneasy, malicious gurgling in the pipe of the galley-stove.

Drift—adrift-wind was sweeping by overhead. Right now the snow picked up by the mumbling wind fled in level, blinding lines across the faces of the buried camp. If a man stepped out of the tunnels that connected each of the camp buildings beneath the surface, he'd be lost in ten paces. Out there, the slim, black finger of the radio mast lifted 300 feet into the air, and at its peak was the clear night sky. A sky of thin, whining wind rushing steadily from beyond to another beyond under the licking, curling mantle of the aurora. And off north, the horizon flamed with queer, angry colors of the midnight twilight. That was spring 300 feet above Antarctica.

At the surface—it was white death. Death of a needle-fingered cold driven before the wind, sucking heat from any warm thing. Cold—and white mist of endless, everlasting drift, the fine, line particles of licking snow that obscured all things.

Kinner, the little, scar-faced cook, winced. Five days ago he had stepped out to the surface to reach a cache of frozen beef. He had reached it, started back—and the drift-wind leapt out of the south. Cold, white death that streamed across the ground blinded him in twenty seconds. He stumbled on wildly in circles. It was half an hour before rope-guided men from below found him in the impenetrable murk.

It was easy for man—or *thing*—to get lost in ten paces. "And the drift-wind then was probably more impenetrable than we know." McReady's voice snapped Kinner's mind back. Back to welcome, dank warmth of the Ad Building. "The passenger of the ship wasn't prepared either, it appears. It froze within ten feet of the ship.

"We dug down to find the ship, and our tunnel hapnel happened to find the frozen—animal. Barclay's ice-ax struck its skull.

"When we saw what it was, Barclay went back to the tractor, started the fire up and when the steam pressure built, sent a call for Blair and Dr. Copper. Barclay himself was sick then. Stayed sick for three days, as a matter of fact.

"When Blair and Copper came, we cut out the animal in a block of ice, as you see, wrapped it and loaded it on the tractor for return here. We wanted to get into that ship.

"We reached the side and found the metal was something we didn't know. Our beryllium-bronze, non-magnetic tools wouldn't touch it. Barclay had some tool-steel on the tractor, and that wouldn't scratch it either. We made reasonable tests—even tried some acid from the batteries with no results.

"They must have had a passivating process to make magnesium metal resist acid that way, and the alloy must have been at least 95% magnesium. But we had no way of guessing that, so when we spotted the barely opened lock door, we cut around it. There was clear, hard ice inside the lock, where we couldn't reach it. Through the little crack we could look in and see that only metal and tools were in there, so we decided to loosen the ice with a bomb.

"We had decanite bombs and thermite. Thermite is the ice-softener; decanite might have shattered valuable things, where the thermite's heat would just loosen the ice. Dr. Copper, Norris and I placed a 25-pound thermite bomb, wired it, and took the connector up the tunnel to the surface, where Blair had the steam tractor waiting. A hundred yards the other side of that granite wall we set off the thermite bomb.

"The magnesium metal of the ship caught of course. The glow of the bomb flared and died, then it began to flare again. We ran back to the tractor, and gradually the glare built up. From where we were we could see the whole ice-field illuminated from beneath with an unbearable light; the ship's shadow was a great, dark cone reaching off toward the north, where the twilight was just about gone. For a moment it lasted, and we counted three other shadow-things that might have been other—passengers—frozen there. Then the ice was crashing down and against the ship.

"That's why I told you about that place. The wind sweeping down from the Pole was at our backs. Steam and hydrogen flame were torn away in white ice-fog; the flaming heat under the ice there was yanked away toward the Antarctic Ocean before it touched us. Otherwise we wouldn't have come back, even with the shelter of that granite ridge that stopped the light.

"Somehow in the blinding inferno we could see great hunched things—black bulks. They shed even the furious incandescence of the magnesium for a time. Those must have been the engines, we knew. Secrets going in blazing glory—secrets that might have given Man the planets. Mysterious things that could lift and hurl that ship—and had soaked in the force of the Earth's magnetic field. I saw Norris's mouth move, and ducked. I couldn't hear him.

"Insulation—something—gave way. All earth's field they'd soaked up twenty million years before broke loose. The aurora in the sky above licked down, and the whole plateau there was bathed in cold fire that blanketed vision.The ice-ax in my hand got red hot, and hissed on the ice. Metal buttons on my clothes burned into me. And a flash of electric blue seared upward from beyond the granite wall.

"Then the walls of ice crashed down on it. For an instant it squealed the way dry-ice does when it's pressed between metal.

"We were blind and groping in the dark for hours while our eyes recovered. We found every coil within a mile was fused rubbish, the dynamo and every radio set, the earphones and speakers. If we hadn't had the steam tractor, we wouldn't have gotten over to the Secondary Camp.

"Van Wall flew in from Big Magnet at sun-up, as you know. We came home as soon as possible. That is the history of—that." McReady's great bronze beard gestured toward the thing on the table.

II

Blair stirred uneasily, his little, bony fingers wriggling under the harsh light. Little brown freckles on his knuckles slid back and forth as the tendons under the skin twitched. He pulled aside a bit of the tarpaulin and looked impatiently at the dark ice-bound thing inside.

McReady's big body straightened somewhat. He'd ridden the rocking, jarring steam tractor forty miles that day, pushing on to Big Magnet here. Even his calm will had been pressed by the anxiety to mix again with humans. It was lone and quiet out there in Secondary Camp, where a wolf-wind howled down from the Pole. Wolf-wind howling in his sleep—winds droning and the evil, unspeakable face of that monster leering up as he'd first seen it through clear, blue ice, with a bronze ice-ax buried in its skull.

The giant meteorologist spoke again. "The problem is this. Blair wants to examine the thing. Thaw it out and make micro slides of its tissues and so forth. Morris doesn't believe that is safe, and Blair does. Dr. Copper agrees pretty much with Blair. Norris is a physicist, of course, not a biologist. But he makes a point I think we should all hear. Blair has described the microscopic life-forms biologists find living, even in this cold and inhospitable place. They freeze every winter, and thaw every summer—for three months—and live.

"The point Norris makes is—they thaw, and live again. There must have been microscopic life associated with this creature. There is with every living thing we know. And Norris is afraid that we may release a plague—some germ disease unknown to Earth—if we thaw those microscopic things that have been frozen there for twenty million years.

"Blair admits that such micro life might retain the power of living. Such unorganized things as individual cells can retain life for unknown periods, when solidly frozen. The beast itself is as dead as those frozen mammoths they find in Siberia. Organized, highly developed life-forms can't stand that treatment.

"But micro-life could. Norris suggests that we may release some disease-form that man, never having met it before, will be utterly defenseless against.

"Blair's answer is that there may be such still-living germs, but that Norris has the case reversed. They are utterly non-immune to man. Our life-chemistry probably—"

"Probably!" The little biologist's head lifted in a quick, birdlike motion. The halo of gray hair about his bald head ruffled as though angry. "Heh, one look—"

"I know," McReady acknowledged. "The thing is not Earthly. It does not seem likely that it can have a life-chemistry sufficiently like ours to make cross-infection remotely possible. I would say that there is no danger."

McReady looked toward Dr.Copper. The physician shook his head slowly. "None whatever," he asserted confidently. "Man cannot infect or be infected by germs that live in such comparatively close relatives as the snakes. And they are, I assure you," his clean-shaven face grimaced uneasily, "*much* nearer to us than—*that!*"

Vance Norris moved angrily. He was comparatively short in this gathering of big men, some five-feet-eight, and his stocky, powerful build tended to make him seem shorter. His black hair was crisp and hard, like short, steel wires, and his eyes were the gray of fractured steel. If McReady was a man of bronze, Norris was all steel. His movements, his thoughts, his whole bearing had the quick, hard impulse of a steel spring. His nerves were steel—hard, quick-acting—swift corroding.

He was decided on his point now, and he lashed out in its defense with a characteristic quick, clipped flow of words. "Different chemistry be damned. That thing may be dead—or, by God, it may not—but I don't like it. Damn it, Blair, let them see the monstrosity you are petting over there. Let them see the foul thing and decide for themselves whether they want that thing thawed out in this camp.

"Thawed out, by the way. That's got to be thawed out in one of the shacks tonight, if it is thawed out. Somebody—who's watchman tonight? Magnetic—oh, Connant. Cosmic rays tonight. Well, you get to sit up with that twenty-millon-year-old mummy of his. Unwrap it, Blair. How the hell can they tell what they are buying, if they can't see it? It may have a different chemistry. I don't care what else it has, but I know it has something I don't want. If you can judge by the look on its face—it isn't human so maybe you can't—it was annoyed when it froze. Annoyed, in fact, is just about as close an approximation of the way it felt, as crazy, mad, insane hatred. Neither one touches the subject.

"How the hell can these birds tell what they are voting on? They haven't seen those three red eyes and that blue hair like crawling worms. Crawling—damn, it's crawling there in the ice right now!

"Nothing Earth ever spawned had the unutterable sublimation of devastating wrath that thing let loose in its face when it looked around its frozen desolation twenty million years ago. Mad? It was mad clear through—searing, blistering mad!

"Hell, I've had bad dreams ever since I looked at those three red eyes. Nightmares. Dreaming the thing thawed out and came to life—that it wasn't dead, or even wholly unconscious all those twenty million years, but just slowed, waiting—waiting. You'll dream too, while that damned thing that Earth wouldn't own is dripping, dripping in the Cosmos House tonight.

"And, Connant," Norris whipped toward the cosmic ray specialist, "won't you have fun sitting up all night in the quiet. Wind whining above—and that thing dripping—" He stopped for a moment, and looked around.

"I know. That's not science. But this is, it's psychology. You'll have nightmares for a year to come. Every night since I looked at that thing I've had 'em. That's why I hate it—sure I do—and don't want it around. Put it back where it came from and let it freeze for another twenty million years. I had some swell nightmares—that it wasn't made like we are—which is obvious—but of a different kind of flesh that it can really control. That it can change its shape, and look like a man—and wait to kill and eat—

"That's not a logical argument. I know it isn't. The thing isn't Earth-logic anyway.

"Maybe it has an alien body-chemistry, and maybe its bugs do have a different body-chemistry. A germ might not stand that, but, Blair and Copper, how about a virus? That's just an enzyme molecule, you've said. That wouldn't need anything but a protein molecule of any body to work on.

"And how are you so sure that, of the million varieties of microscopic life it may have, *none* of them are dangerous. How about diseases like hydrophobia—rabies—that attacks any warm-blooded creature, whatever its body chemistry may be? And parrot fever? Have you a body like a parrot, Blair? And plain rot—gangrene—necrosis if you want? *That* isn't choosy about body chemistry!"

Blair looked up from his puttering long enough to meet Norris's angry, gray eyes for an instant. "So far the only thing you have said this thing gave off that was catching was dreams. I'll go so far as to admit that." An impish, slightly malignant grin crossed the little man's seamed face. "I had some too. So. It's dream-infectious. No doubt an exceedingly dangerous malady.

"So far as your other things go, you have a baldly mistaken idea about viruses. In the first place, nobody has shown that the enzyme-molecule theory, and that alone, explains them. And in the second place, when you catch tobacco mosaic or wheat rust, let me know. A wheat plant is a lot nearer your body-chemistry than this otherworld creature is.

"And your rabies is limited, strictly limited. You can't get it from, nor give it to, a wheat plant or a fish—which is a collateral descendant of a common ancestor of yours. Which this, Norris, is not." Blair nodded pleasantly toward the tarpaulined bulk on the table.

"Well, thaw the damned thing in a tub of formalin if you must. I've suggested that—"

"And I've said there would be no sense in it. You can't compromise. Why did you and Commander Garry come down here to study magnetism? Why weren't you content to stay at home? There's magnetic force enough in New York. I could no more study the life this thing once had from a formalin-pickled sample than you could get the information you wanted back in New York. And—if this one is so treated, *never in all time to come can there be a duplicate!* The race it came from must have passed away in the twenty million years it lay frozen, so that even if it came from Mars then, we'd never find its like. And—the ship is gone.

"There's only one way to do this—and that is the best possible way. It must be thawed slowly, carefully, and not in formalin."

Commander Garry stood forward again, and Norris stepped back muttering angrily. "I think Blair is right, gentlemen. What do you say?"

Connant grunted. "It sounds right to us, I think—only perhaps he ought to stand watch over it while it's thawing." He grinned ruefully, brushing a stray lock of ripe-cherry hair back from his forehead. "Swell idea, in fact—if he sits up with his jolly little corpse."

Garry smiled slightly. A general chuckle of agreement rippled over the group. "I should think any ghost it may have had would have starved to death if it hung around here that long, Connant," Garry suggested. "And you look capable of taking care of it. "Ironman" Connant ought to be able to take out any opposing players, still."

Connant shook himself uneasily. "I'm not worrying about ghosts. Let's see that thing. I—"

Eagerly Blair was stripping back the ropes. A single throw of the tarpaulin revealed the thing. The ice had melted somewhat in the heat of the room, and it was clear and blue as thick, good glass. It shone wet and sleek under the harsh light of the unshielded globe above.

The room stiffened abruptly. It was face-up there on the plain, greasy planks of the table. The broken haft of the bronze ice-axe was still buried in the queer skull. Three mad, hate-filled eyes blazed up with a living fire, bright as fresh-spilled blood, from a face ringed with a writhing, loathsome nest of worms, blue, mobile worms that crawled where hair should grow—

Van Wall, six feet and two hundred pounds of ice-nerved pilot, gave a queer, strangled gasp, and butted, stumbled his way out to the corridor. Half the company broke for the doors. The others stumbled away from the table.

McReady stood at one end of the table watching them, his great body planted solid on his powerful legs. Norris from the opposite end glowered at the thing with smouldering hate. Outside the door, Garry was talking with half a dozen of the men at once.

Blair had a tack hammer. The ice that cased the thing *schluffed* crisply under its steel claw as it peeled from the thing it had cased for twenty thousand thousand years—

III

"I know you don't like the thing, Connant, but it just has to be thawed out right. You say leave it as it is till we get back to civilization. All right, I'll admit your argument that we could do a better and more complete job there is sound. But—how are we going to get this across the Line? We have to take this through one temperate zone, the equatorial zone, and half way through the other temperate zone before we get it to New York. You don't want to sit with it one night, but you suggest, then, that I hang its corpse in the freezer with the beef?" Blair looked up from his cautious chipping, his bald freckled skull nodding triumphantly.

Kinner, the stocky, scar-faced cook, saved Connant the trouble of answering. "Hey, you listen, mister. You put that thing in the box with the meat, and by all the gods there ever were, I'll put you in to keep it company. You birds have brought everything movable in this camp in onto my mess tables here already, and I had to stand for that. But you go putting things like that in my meat box, or even my meat cache here, and you cook your own damn grub."

"But, Kinner, this is the only table in Big Magnet that's big enough to work on," Blair objected. "Everybody's explained that."

"Yeah, and everybody's brought everything in here. Clark brings his dogs every time there's a fight and sews them up on that table. Ralsen brings in his sledges. Hell, the only thing you haven't had on that table is the Boeing. And you'd 'a' had that in if you coulda figured a way to get it through the tunnels."

Commander Garry chuckled and grinned at Van Wall, the huge Chief Pilot. Van Wall's great blond beard twitched suspiciously as he nodded gravely to Kinner. "You're right, Kinner. The aviation department is the only one that treats you right."

"It does get crowded, Kinner," Garry acknowledged. "But I'm afraid we all find it that way at times. Not much privacy in an antarctic camp."

"Privacy? What the hell's that? You know, the thing that really made me weep, was when I saw Barclay marchin' through here chantin' 'The last lumber in the camp! The last lumber in the camp!' and carryin' it out to build that house on his tractor. Damn it, I missed that moon cut in the door he carried out more'n I missed the sun when it set. That wasn't just the last lumber Barclay was walkin' off with. He was carryin' off the last bit of privacy in this blasted place."

A grin rode even on Connant's heavy face as Kinner's perennial, good-natured grouch came up again. But it died away quickly as his dark, deep-set eyes turned again to the red-eyed thing Blair was chipping from its cocoon of ice. A big hand ruffed his shoulder-length hair, and tugged at a twisted lock that fell behind his ear in a familiar gesture. "I know that cosmic ray shack's going to be too crowded if I have to sit up with that thing," he growled. "Why can't you go on chipping the ice away from around it—you can do that without anybody butting in, I assure you—and then hang the thing up over the power-plant boiler? That's warm enough. It'll thaw out a chicken, even a whole side of beef, in a few hours."

"I know," Blair protested, dropping the tack hammer to gesture more effectively with his bony, freckled fingers, his small body tense with eagerness, "but this is too important to take any chances. There never was a find like this; there never can be again. It's the only chance men will ever have, and it has to be done exactly right.

"Look, you know how the fish we caught down near the Ross Sea would freeze almost as soon as we got them on deck, and come to life again if we thawed them gently? Low forms of life aren't killed by quick freezing and slow thawing. We have—"

"Hey, for the love of Heaven—you mean that damned thing will come to life!" Connant yelled. "You get the damned thing—Let me at it! That's going to be in so many pieces—"

"No! *No*, you fool—" Blair jumped in front of Connant to protect his precious find. "No. Just *low* forms of life. For Pete's sake let me finish. You can't thaw higher forms of life and have them come to. Wait a moment now—hold it! A fish can come to after freezing because it's so low a form of life that the individual cells of its body can revive, and that alone is enough to reestablish life. Any higher forms thawed out that way are dead. Though the individual cells revive, they die because there must be organization and cooperative effort to live. That cooperation cannot be reestablished. There is a sort of potential life in any uninjured, quick-frozen animal. But it can't—can't under any circumstances—become active life in higher animals. The higher animals are too complex, too delicate. This is an intelligent creature as high in its evolution as we are in ours. Perhaps higher. It is as dead as a frozen man would be."

"How do you know?" demanded Connant, hefting the ice-ax he had seized a moment before.

Commander Garry laid a restraining hand on his heavy shoulder. "Wait a minute, Connant. I want to get this straight. I agree that there is going to be no thawing of this thing if there is the remotest chance of its revival. I quite agree it is much too unpleasant to have alive, but I had no idea there was the remotest possibility."

Dr. Copper pulled his pipe from between his teeth and heaved his stocky, dark body from the bunk he had been sitting in. "Blair's being technical. That's dead. As dead as the mammoths they find frozen in Siberia. We have all sorts of proof that things don't live after being frozen—not even fish, generally speaking—and no proof that higher animal life can under any circumstances. What's the point, Blair?"

The little biologist shook himself. The little ruff of hair standing out around his bald pate waved in righteous anger. "The point is," he said in an injured tone, "that the individual cells might show the characteristics they had in life if it is properly thawed. A man's muscle cells live many hours after he has died. Just because they live, and a few things like hair and fingernail cells still live, you wouldn't accuse a corpse of being a Zombie, or something.

"Now if I thaw this right, I may have a chance to determine what sort of world it's native to. We don't, and can't know by any other means, whether it came from Earth or Mars or Venus or from beyond the stars.

"And just because it looks unlike men, you don't have to accuse it of being evil, or vicious or something. Maybe that expression on its face is its equivalent to a resignation to fate. White is the color of mourning to the Chinese. If men can have different customs, why can't a so-different race have different understandings of facial expressions?"

Connant laughed softly, mirthlessly. "Peaceful resignation! If that is the best it could do in the way of resignation, I should exceedingly dislike seeing it when it was looking mad. That face was never designed to express peace. It just didn't have any philosophical thoughts like peace in its make-up.

"I know it's your pet—but be sane about it. That thing grew up on evil, adolesced slowly roasting alive the local equivalent of kittens, and amused itself through maturity on new and ingenious torture."

"You haven't the slightest right to say that," snapped Blair. "How do you know the first thing about the meaning of a facial expression inherently inhuman? It may well have no human equivalent whatever. That is just a different development of Nature, another example of Nature's wonderful adaptability. Growing on another, perhaps harsher world, it has different form and features. But it is just as much a legitimate child of Nature as you are. You are displaying that childish human weakness of hating the different. On its own world it would probably class you as a fish-belly, white monstrosity with an insufficient number of eyes and a fungoid body pale and bloated with gas.

"Just because its nature is different, you haven't any right to say it's necessarily evil."

Norris burst out a single, explosive, "Haw!" He looked down at the thing. "Maybe that things from other worlds don't *have* to be evil just because they're different. But that thing *was!* Child of Nature, eh? Well, it was a hell of an evil Nature."

"Aw, will you mugs cut crabbing at each other and get the damned thing off my table?" Kinner growled. "And put a canvas over it. It looks indecent."

"Kinner's gone modest," jeered Connant.

Kinner slanted his eyes up to the big physicist. The scarred cheek twisted to join the line of his tight lips in a twisted grin. "All right, big boy, and what were you grousing about a minute ago? We can set the thing in a chair next to you tonight, if you want."

"I'm not afraid of its face," Connant snapped. "I don't like keeping a wake over its corpse particularly, but I'm going to do it."

Kinner's grin spread. "Uh-huh." He went off to the galley stove and shook down ashes vigorously, drowning the brittle chipping of the ice as Blair fell to work again.

IV

"Cluck," reported the cosmic ray counter, "*cluck-burrrp-cluck.*"

Connant started and dropped his pencil.

"Damnation." Thy physicist looked toward the far corner, back at the Geiger counter on the table near that corner. And crawled under the desk at which he had been working to retrieve the pencil. He sat down at his work again, trying to make his writing more even. It tended to have jerks and quavers in it, in time with the abrupt proud-hen noises of the Geiger counter. The muted whoosh of the pressure lamp he was using for illumination, the mingled gargles and bugle calls of a dozen men sleeping down the corridor in Paradise House formed the background sounds for the irregular, clucking noises of the counter, the occasional rustle of falling coal in the copper-bellied stove. And a soft, steady *drip-drip-drip* from the thing in the corner.

Connant jerked a pack of cigarettes from his pocket, snapped it so that a cigarette protruded, and jabbed the cylinder into his mouth. The lighter failed to function, and he pawed angrily through the pile of papers in search of a match. He scratched the wheel of the lighter several times, dropped it with a curse and got up to pluck a hot coal from the stove with the coal-tongs.

The lighter functioned instantly when he tried it on returning to the desk. The counter ripped out a series of chuckling guffaws as a burst of cosmic rays struck through to it. Connant turned to glower at it, and tried to concentrate on the interpretation of data collected during the past week. The weekly summary—

He gave up and yielded to curiosity, or nervousness. He lifted the pressure lamp from the desk and carried it over to the table in the corner. Then he returned to the stove and picked up the coal tongs. The beast had been thawing for nearly eighteen hours now. He poked at it with an unconscious caution; the flesh was no longer hard as armor plate, but had assumed a rubbery texture. It looked like wet, blue rubber glistening under droplets of water like little round jewels in the glare of the gasoline pressure lantern. Connant felt an unreasoning desire to pour the contents of the lamp's reservoir over the thing in its box and drop the cigarette into it. The three red eyes glared up at him sightlessly, the ruby eyeballs reflecting murky, smoky rays of light.

He realized vaguely that he had been looking at them for a very long time, even vaguely understood that they were no longer sightless. But it did not seem of importance, of no more importance than the labored, slow motion of the tentacular things that sprouted from the base of the scrawny, slowly pulsing neck.

Connant picked up the pressure lamp and returned to his chair. He sat down, staring at the pages of mathematics before him. The clucking of the counter was strangely less disturbing, the rustle of the coals in the stove no longer distracting.

The creak of the floorboards behind him didn't interrupt his thoughts as he went about his weekly report in an automatic manner, filling in columns of data and making brief, summarizing notes.

The creak of the floorboards sounded nearer.

V

Blair came up from the nightmare-haunted depths of sleep abruptly. Connant's face floated vaguely above him; for a moment it seemed a continuance of the wild horror of the dream. But Connant's face was angry, and a little frightened. "Blair—Blair you damned log, wake up."

"Uh-eh?" the little biologist rubbed his eyes, his bony, freckled finger crooked to a mutilated child-fist. From surrounding bunks other faces lifted to stare down at them.

Connant straightened up. "Get up—and get a lift on. Your damned animal's escaped."

"Escaped—what!" Chief Pilot Van Wall's bull voice roared out with a volume that shook the walls. Down the communication tunnels other voices yelled suddenly. The dozen inhabitants of Paradise House tumbled in abruptly, Barclay, stocky and bulbous in long woolen underwear, carrying a fire extinguisher.

"What the hell's the matter?" Barclay demanded.

"Your damned beast got loose. I fell asleep about twenty minutes ago, and when I woke up, the thing was gone. Hey, Doc, the hell you say those things can't come to life. Blair's blasted potential life developed a hell of a lot of potential and walked out on us."

Copper stared blankly. "It wasn't—Earthly," he sighed suddenly. "I—I guess Earthly laws don't apply."

"Well, it applied for leave of absence and took it. We've got to find it and capture it somehow." Connant swore bitterly, his deep-set black eyes sullen and angry. "It's a wonder the hellish creature didn't eat me in my sleep."

Blair started back, his pale eyes suddenly fear-struck. "Maybe it di—er—uh—we'll have to find it."

"You find it. It's your pet. I've had all I want to do with it, sitting there for seven hours with the counter clucking every few seconds, and you birds in here singing night-music. It's a wonder I got to sleep. I'm going through to the Ad Building."

Commander Garry ducked through the doorway, pulling his belt tight. "You won't have to. Van's roar sounded like the Boeing taking off down wind. So it wasn't dead?"

"I didn't carry it off in my arms, I assure you," Connant snapped. "The last I saw, the split skull was oozing green goo, like a squashed caterpillar. Doc just said our laws don't work—it's unearthly. Well, it's an unearthly monster, with an unearthly disposition, judging by the face, wandering around with a split skull and brains oozing out."

Norris and McReady appeared in the doorway, a doorway filling with other shivering men. "Has anybody seen it coming over here?" Norris asked innocently. "About four feet tall—three red eyes—brains oozing— Hey, has anybody checked to make sure this isn't a cracked idea of humor? If it is, I think we'll unite in tying Blair's pet around Connant's neck like the Ancient Mariner's albatross."

"It's no humor," Connant shivered. "Lord, I wish it were. I'd rather wear—" He stopped. A wild, weird howl shrieked through the corridors. The men stiffened abruptly, and half turned.

"I think it's been located," Connant finished. His dark eyes shifted with a queer unease. He darted back to his bunk in Paradise House, to return almost immediately with a heavy .45 revolver and an ice-ax. He hefted both gently as he started for the corridor toward Dogtown. "It blundered down the wrong corridor—and landed among the huskies. Listen—the dogs have broken their chains—"

The half-terrorized howl of the dog pack changed to a wild hunting melee. The voices of the dogs thundered in the narrow corridors, and through them came a low rippling snarl of distilled hate. A shrill of pain, a dozen snarling yelps.

Connant broke for the door. Close behind him, McReady, then Barclay and Commander Garry came. Other men broke for the Ad Building, and weapons—the sledge house. Pomroy, in charge of Big Magnet's five cows, started down the corridor in the opposite direction—he had a six-foot-handled, long-tined pitchfork in mind.

Barclay slid to a halt, as McReady's giant bulk turned abruptly away from the tunnel leading to Dogtown, and vanished off at an angle. Uncertainly, the mechanician wavered a moment, the fire extinguisher in his hands, hesitating from one side to the other. Then he was racing after Connant's broad back. Whatever McReady had in mind, he could be trusted to make it work.

Connant stopped at the bend in the corridor. His breath hissed suddenly through his throat. "Great God—" The revolver exploded thunderously; three numbing, palpable waves of sound crashed through the confined corridors. Two more. The revolver dropped to the hard-packed snow of the trail, and Barclay saw the ice-ax shift into defensive position. Connant's powerful body blocked his vision, but beyond he heard something mewing, and, insanely, chuckling. The dogs were quieter; there was a deadly seriousness in their low snarls. Taloned feet scratched at hard-packed snow, broken chains were clinking and tangling.

Connant shifted abruptly, and Barclay could see what lay beyond. For a second he stood frozen, then his breath went out in a gusty curse. The Thing launched itself at Connant, the powerful arms of the man swung the ice-ax flatside first at what might have been a hand. It scrunched horribly, and the tattered flesh, ripped by a half-dozen savage huskies, leapt to its feet again. The red eyes blazed with an unearthly hatred, an unearthly, unkillable vitality.

Barclay turned the fire extinguisher on it; the blinding, blistering stream of chemical spray confused it, baffled it, together with the savage attacks of the huskies, not for long afraid of anything that did, or could live, held it at bay.

McReady wedged men out of his way and drove down the narrow corridor packed with men unable to reach the scene. There was a sure fore-planned drive to McReady's attack. One of the giant blow-torches used in warming the plane's engines was in his bronzed hands. It roared gustily as he turned the corner and opened the valve. The mad mewing hissed louder. The dogs scrambled back from the three-foot lance of blue-hot flame.

"Bar, get a power cable, run it in somehow. And a handle. We can electrocute this—monster, if I don't incinerate it." McReady spoke with an authority of planned action. Barclay turned down the long corridor to the power plant, but already before him Norris and Van Wall were racing down.

Barclay found the cable in the electrical cache in the tunnel wall. In a half minute he was hacking at it, walking back. Van Wall's voice rang out in warning shout of "Power!" as the emergency gasoline-powered dynamo thudded into action. Half a dozen other men were down there now; the coal, kindling were going into the firebox of the steam power plant. Norris, cursing in a low, deadly monotone, was working with quick, sure fingers on the other end of Barclay's cable, splicing a contacter into one of the power leads.

The dogs had fallen back when Barclay reached the corridor bend, fallen back before a furious monstrosity that glared from baleful red eyes, mewing in trapped hatred. The dogs were a semi-circle of red-dipped muzzles with a fringe of glistening white teeth, whining with a vicious eagerness that near matched the fury of the red eyes. McReady stood confidently alert at the corridor bend, the gustily muttering torch held loose and ready for action in his hands. He stepped aside without moving his eyes from the beast as Barclay came up. There was a slight, tight smile on his lean, bronzed face.

Norris's voice called down the corridor, and Barclay stepped forward. The cable was taped to the long handle of a snow-shovel, the two conductors split and held 18 inches apart by a scrap of lumber lashed at right angles across the far end of the handle. Bare copper conductors, charged with 220 volts, glinted in the light of pressure lamps. The Thing mewed and hated and dodged. McReady advanced to Barclay's side. The dogs beyond sensed the plan with the almost-telepathic intelligence of trained huskies. Their whining grew shriller, softer, their mincing steps carried them nearer. Abruptly a huge night-black Alaskan leapt onto the trapped thing. It turned squalling, saber-clawed feet slashing.

Barclay leapt forward and jabbed. A weird, shrill scream rose and choked out. The smell of burnt flesh in the corridor intensified; greasy smoke curled up. The echoing pound of the gas-electric dynamo down the corridor became a slogging thud.

The red eyes clouded over in a stiffening, jerking travesty of a face. Armlike, leglike members quivered and jerked. The dogs leapt forward, and Barclay yanked back his shovel-handled weapon. The thing on the snow did not move as gleaming teeth ripped it open.

VI

Garry looked about the crowded room. Thirty-two men, some tensed nervously standing against the wall, some uneasily relaxed, some sitting, most perforce standing as intimate as sardines. Thirty-two, plus the five engaged in sewing up wounded dogs, made thirty-seven, the total personnel.

Garry started speaking. "All right, I guess we're here. Some of you—three or four at most—saw what happened. All of you have seen that thing on the table, and can get a general idea. Anyone hasn't, I'll lift—" His hand strayed to the tarpaulin bulking over the thing on the table. There was an acrid odor of singed flesh seeping out of it. The men stirred restlessly, hasty denials.

"It looks rather as though Charnauk isn't going to lead any more teams," Garry went on. "Blair wants to get at this thing, and make some more detailed examination. We want to know what happened, and make sure right now that this is permanently, totally dead. Right?"

Connant grinned. "Anybody that doesn't can sit up with it tonight."

"All right then, Blair, what can you say about it? What was it?" Garry turned to the little biologist.

"I wonder if we ever saw its natural form," Blair looked at the covered mass. "It may have been imitating the beings that built that ship—but I don't think it was. I think that was its true form. Those of us who were up near the bend saw the thing in action; the thing on the table is the result. When it got loose, apparently, it started looking around. Antartica still frozen as it was ages ago when the creature first saw it—and froze. From my observations while it was thawing out, and the bits of tissue I cut and hardened then, I think it was native to a hotter planet than Earth. It couldn't, in its natural form, stand the temperature. There is no life-form on Earth that can live in Antartica during the winter, but the best compromise is the dog. It found the dogs, and somehow got near enough to Charnauk to get him. The others smelled it—heard it—I don't know—anyway they went wild, and broke chains, and attacked it before it was finished. The thing we found was part Charnauk, queerly only half-dead, part Charnauk half-digested by the jellylike protoplasm of that creature, and part the remains of the thing we originally found, sort of melted down to the basic protoplasm.

"When the dogs attacked it, it turned into the best fighting thing it could think of. Some otherworld beast apparently."

"Turned," snapped Garry. "How?"

"Every living thing is made up of jelly—protoplasm and minute, submicroscopic things called nuclei, which control the bulk, the protoplasm. This thing was just a modification of that same worldwide plan of Nature; cells made up of protoplasm, controlled by infinitely tinier nuclei. You physicists might compare it—an individual cell of any living thing—with an atom; the bulk of the atom, the space-filling part, is made up of the electron orbits, but the character of the thing is determined by the atomic nucleus.

"This isn't wildly beyond what we already know. It's just a modification we haven't seen before. It's as natural, as logical, as any other manifestation of life. It obeys exactly the same laws. The cells are made of protoplasm, their character determined by the nucleus.

"Only, in this creature, the cell-nuclei can control those cells *at will*. It digested Charnauk, and as it digested, studied every cell of his tissue, and shaped its own cells to imitate them exactly. Parts of it—parts that had time to finish changing—are dog-cells. But they don't have dog-cell nuclei." Blair lifted a fraction of the tarpaulin. A torn dog's leg, with stiff gray fur protruded. "That, for instance, isn't dog at all; it's imitation. Some parts I'm uncertain about; the nucleus was hiding itself, covering up with dog-cell imitation nucleus. In time, not even a microscope would have shown the difference."

"Suppose," asked Norris bitterly, "it had had lots of time?"

"Then it would have been a dog. The other dogs would have accepted it. I don't think anything would have distinguished it, not microscope, nor X ray, nor any other means. This is a member of a supremely intelligent race, a race that has learned the deepest secrets of biology, and turned them to its use."

"What was it planning to do?" Barclay looked at the humped tarpaulin.

Blair grinned unpleasantly. The wavering halo of thin hair round his bald pate wavered in a stir of air. "Take over the world, I imagine."

"Take over the world! Just it, all by itself?" Connant gasped. "Set itself up as a lone dictator?"

"No." Blair shook his head. The scalpel he had been fumbling in his bony fingers dropped; he bent to pick it up, so that his face was hidden as he spoke. "It would become the population of the world."

"Become—populate the world? Does it reproduce asexually?"

Blair shook his head and gulped. "It's—it doesn't have to. It weighed 85 pounds. Charnauk weighed about 90. It would have become Charnauk, and had 85 pounds left, to become—oh, Jack for instance, or Chinook. It can imitate anything—that is, become anything. If it had reached the Antarctic Sea, it would have become a seal, maybe two seals. They might have attacked a killer whale, and become either killers, or a herd of seals. Or maybe it would have caught an albatross, or a skua gull, and flown to South America."

Norris cursed softly. "And every time it digested something, and imitated it—"

"It would have had its original bulk left, to start again," Blair finished. "Nothing would kill it. It has no natural enemies, because it becomes whatever it wants to. If a killer whale attacked it, it would become a killer whale. If it was an albatross, and an eagle attacked it, it would become an eagle. Lord, it might become a female eagle. Go back—build a nest and lay eggs!"

"Are you sure that thing from hell is dead?" Dr. Copper asked softly.

"Yes, thank Heaven," the little biologist gasped. "After they drove the dogs off, I stood there poking Bar's electrocution thing into it for five minutes. It's dead and—cooked."

"Then we can only give thanks that this is Antarctica, where there is not one, single, solitary, living thing for it to imitate, except these animals in camp."

"Us," Blair giggled. "It can imitate us. Dogs can't make 400 miles to the sea; there's no food. There aren't any skua gulls to imitate at this season. There aren't any penguins this far inland. There's nothing that can reach the sea from this point—except us. We've got brains. We can do it. Don't you see—*it's got to imitate us*—*it's got to be one of us*—*that's the only way it can fly an airplane*—*fly a plane for two hours, and rule*—*be*—*all Earth's inhabitants*. A world for the taking—*if it imitates us!*

"It didn't know yet. It hadn't had a chance to learn. It was rushed—hurried—took the thing nearest its own size. Look—I'm Pandora! I opened the box! And the only hope that can come out is—that nothing can come out. You didn't see me. I did it. I fixed it. I smashed every magneto. Not a plane can fly. Nothing can fly." Blair giggled and lay down on the floor crying.

Chief Pilot Van Wall made a dive for the door. His feet were fading echoes in the corridors as Dr. Copper bent unhurriedly over the little man on the floor. From his office at the end of the room he brought something, and injected a solution into Blair's arm. "He might come out of it when he wakes up," he sighed rising. McReady helped him lift the biologist onto a near-by bunk. "It all depends on whether we can convince him that thing is dead."

Van Wall ducked into the shack brushing his heavy blond beard absently. "I didn't think a biologist would do a thing like that up thoroughly. He missed the spares in the second cache. It's all right. I smashed them."

Commander Garry nodded. "I was wondering about the radio."

Dr. Copper snorted. "You don't think it can leak out on a radio wave, do you? You'd have five rescue attempts in the next three months if you stop the broadcasts. The thing to do is talk loud and not make a sound. Now I wonder—"

McReady looked speculatively at the doctor. "It might be like an infectious disease. Everything that drank any of its blood?"

Copper shook his head. "Blair missed something. Imitate it may, but it has, to a certain extent, its own body-chemistry, its own metabolism. If it didn't, it would become a dog—and be a dog and nothing more. It has to be an imitation dog. Therefore you can detect it by serum tests. And its chemistry, since it comes from another world, must be so wholly, radically different that a few cells, such as gained by drops of blood, would be treated as disease germs by the dog, or human body."

"Blood—would one of those imitations bleed?" Norris demanded.

"Surely. Nothing mystic about blood. Muscle is about 90% water; blood differs only in having a couple percent more water, and less connective tissue. They'd bleed all right," Copper assured him.

Blair sat up in his bunk suddenly. "Connant—where's Connant?"

The physicist moved over toward the little biologist. "Here I am. What do you want?"

"Are you?" giggled Blair. He lapsed back into the bunk contorted with silent laughter.

Connant looked at him blankly. "Huh? Am I what?" "Are you there?" Blair burst into gales of laughter. "Are you Connant? The beast wanted to be man—not a dog—"

VII

Dr. Copper rose wearily from the bunk, and washed the hypodermic carefully. The little tinkles it made seemed loud in the packed room, now that Blair's gurgling laughter had finally quieted. Copper looked toward Garry and shook his head slowly. "Hopeless, I'm afraid. I don't think we can ever convince him the thing is dead now."

Norris laughed uncertainly. "I'm not sure you can convince me. Oh, damn you, McReady."

"McReady?" Commander Garry turned to look from Norris to McReady curiously.

"The nightmares," Norris explained. "He had a theory about the nightmares we had at the Secondary Station after finding that thing."

"And that was?" Garry looked at McReady levelly.

Norris answered for him, jerkily, uneasily. "That the creature wasn't dead, had a sort of enormously slowed existence, an existence that permitted it, nonetheless, to be vaguely aware of the passing of time, of our coming, after endless years. I had a dream it could imitate things."

"Well," Copper grunted, "it can."

"Don't be an ass," Norris snapped. "That's not what's bothering me. In the dream it could read minds, read thoughts and ideas and mannerisms."

"What's so bad about that? It seems to be worrying you more than the thought of the joy we're going to have with a madman in an antarctic camp." Copper nodded toward Blair's sleeping form.

McReady shook his great head slowly. "You know that Connant is Connant, because he not merely looks like Connant—which we're beginning to believe that beast might be able to do—but he thinks like Connant, moves himself around as Connant does. That takes more than merely a body that looks like him; that takes Connant's own mind, and thoughts and mannerisms. Therefore, though you know that the thing might make itself *look* like Connant, you aren't much bothered, because you know it has a mind from another world, a totally unhuman mind, that couldn't possibly react and think and talk like a man we know, and do it so well as to fool us for a moment. The idea of the creature imitating one of us is fascinating, but unreal, because it is too completely unhuman to deceive us. It doesn't have a human mind."

"As I said before," Norris repeated, looking steadily at McReady, "you can say the damnedest things at the damnedest times. Will you be so good as to finish that thought—one way or the other?"

Kinner, the scar-faced expedition cook, had been standing near Connant. Suddenly he moved down the length of the crowded room toward his familiar galley. He shook the ashes from the galley stove noisily.

"It would do it no good," said Dr. Copper, softly as though thinking out loud, "to merely look like something it was trying to imitate; it would have to understand its feelings, its reactions. It *is* unhuman; it has powers of imitation beyond any conception of man. A good actor, by training himself, can imitate another man, another man's mannerisms, well enough to fool most people. Of course no actor could imitate so perfectly as to deceive men who had been living with the imitated one in the complete lack of privacy of an antarctic camp. That would take a superhuman skill."

"Oh, you've got the bug too?" Norris cursed softly.

Connant, standing alone at one end of the room, looked about him wildly, his face white. A gentle eddying of the men had crowded them slowly down toward the other end of the room, so that he stood quite alone. "My God, will you two Jeremiahs shut up?" Connant's voice shook. "What am I? Some kind of a microscopic specimen you're dissecting? Some unpleasant worm you're discussing in the third person?"

McReady looked up at him; his slowly twisting hands stopped for a moment. "Having a lovely time. Wish you were here. Signed: Everybody.

"Connant, if you think you're having a hell of a time, just move over on the other end for a while. You've got one thing we haven't; you know what the answer is. I'll tell you this, right now you're the most feared and respected man in Big Magnet."

"Lord, I wish you could see your eyes," Connant gasped. "Stop staring, will you! What the hell are you going to do?"

"Have you any suggestions, Dr. Copper?" Commander Garry asked steadily. "The present situation is impossible."

"Oh, is it?" Connant snapped. "Come over here and look at that crowd. By Heaven, they look exactly like that gang of huskies around the corridor bend. Benning, will you stop hefting that damned ice-ax?"

The coppery blade rang on the floor as the aviation mechanic nervously dropped it. He bent over and picked it up instantly, hefting it slowly, turning it in his hands, his brown eyes moving jerkily about the room.

Cooper sat down on the bunk beside Blair. The wood creaked noisily in the room. Far down a corridor, a dog yelped in pain, and the dog-drivers' tense voices floated softly back. "Microscopic examination," said the doctor thoughtfully, "would be useless, as Blair pointed out. Considerable time has passed. However, serum tests would be definitive."

"Serum tests? What do you mean exactly?" Commander Garry asked.

"If I had a rabbit that had been injected with human blood—a poison to rabbits, of course, as is the blood of any animal save that of another rabbit—and the injections continued in increasing doses for some time, the rabbit would be human-immune. If a small quantity of its blood were drawn off, allowed to separate in a test-tube, and to the clear serum, a bit of human blood were added, there would be a visible reaction, proving the blood was human. If cow, or dog blood were added—or any protein material other than that one thing, human blood—no reaction would take place. That would prove definitely."

"Can you suggest where I might catch a rabbit for you, Doc?" Norris asked. "That is, nearer than Australia; we don't want to waste time going that far."

"I know there aren't any rabbits in Antarctica." Copper nodded. "But that is simply the usual animal. Any animal except man will do. A dog for instance. But it will take several days, and due to the greater size of the animal, considerable blood. Two of us will have to contribute."

"Would I do?" Garry asked.

"That will make two," Copper nodded. "I'll get to work on it right away."

"What about Connant in the meantime," Kinner demanded. "I'm going out that door and head off for the Ross Sea before I cook for him."

"He may be human—" Copper started.

Connant burst out in a flood of curses. "Human! *May* be human, you damned sawbones! What in hell do you think I am?"

"A monster," Copper snapped sharply. "Now shut up and listen." Connant's face drained of color and he sat down heavily as the indictment was put in words. "Until we know—you know as well as we do that we have reason to question the fact, and only you know how that question is to be answered—we may reasonably be expected to lock you up. If you are—unhuman—you're a lot more dangerous than poor Blair there, and I'm going to see that he's locked up thoroughly. I expect that his next stage will be a violent desire to kill you, all the dogs, and probably all of us. When he wakes, he will be convinced we're all unhuman, and nothing on the planet will ever change his conviction. It would be kinder to let him die, but we can't do that, of course. He's going in one shack, and you can stay in Cosmos House with your cosmic ray apparatus. Which is about what you'd do anyway. I've got to fix up a couple of dogs."

Connant nodded bitterly. "I'm human. Hurry that test. Your eyes—Lord, I wish you could see your eyes staring—"

Commander Garry watched anxiously as Clark, the dog-handler, held the big brown Alaskan husky, while Copper began the injection treatment. The dog was not anxious to cooperate; the needle was painful, and already he'd experienced considerable needle work that morning. Five stitches held closed a slash that ran from his shoulder, across the ribs, halfway down his body. One long fang was broken off short; the missing part was to be found half buried in the shoulder bone of the monstrous thing on the table in the Ad Building.

"How long will that take?" Garry asked, pressing his arm gently. It was sore from the prick of the needle Dr. Copper had used to withdraw blood.

Copper shrugged. "I don't know, to be frank. I know the general method. I've used it on rabbits. But I haven't experimented with dogs. They're big, clumsy animals to work with; naturally rabbits are preferable, and serve ordinarily. In civilized places you can buy a stock of human-immune rabbits from suppliers, and not many investigators take the trouble to prepare their own."

"What do they want with them back there?" Clark asked.

"Criminology is one large field. A says he didn't murder B, but that the blood on his shirt came from killing a chicken. The State makes a test, then it's up to A to explain how it is the blood reacts on human-immune rabbits, but not on chicken-immunes."

"What are we going to do with Blair in the meantime?" Garry asked wearily. "It's all right to let him sleep where he is for a while, but when he wakes up—"

"Barclay and Benning are fitting some bolts on the door of Cosmos House," Copper replied grimly. "Connant's acting like a gentleman. I think perhaps the way the other men look at him makes him rather want privacy. Lord knows, heretofore we've all of us individually prayed for a little privacy."

Clark laughed brittly. "Not anymore, thank you. The more the merrier."

"Blair," Copper went on, "will also have to have privacy—and locks. He's going to have a pretty definite plan in mind when he wakes up. Ever hear the old story of how to stop hoof-and-mouth disease in cattle?"

Clark and Garry shook their heads silently.

"If there isn't any hoof-and-mouth disease, there won't be any hoof-and-mouth disease," Copper explained. "You get rid of it by killing every animal that exhibits it, and every animal that's been near the diseased animal. Blair's a biologist, and knows that story. He's afraid of this thing we loosed. The answer is probably pretty clear in his mind now. Kill everybody and everything in this camp before a skua gull or a wandering albatross coming in with the spring chances out this way and—catches the disease."

Clark's lips curled in a twisted grin. "Sounds logical to me. If things get too bad—maybe we'd better let Blair get loose. It would save us committing suicide. We might also make something of a vow that if things get bad, we see that that does happen."

Copper laughed softly. "The last man alive in Big Magnet—wouldn't be a man," he pointed out. "Somebody's got to kill those—creatures that don't desire to kill themselves, you know. We don't have enough thermite to do it all at once, and the decanite explosive wouldn't help much. I have an idea that even small pieces of one of those being would be self-sufficient."

"If," said Garry thoughtfully, "they can modify their protoplasm at will, won't they simply modify themselves to birds and fly away? They can read all about birds, and imitate their structure without even meeting them. Or imitate, perhaps, birds of their home planet."

Copper shook his head, and helped Clark to free the dog. "Man studied birds for centuries, trying to learn how to make a machine to fly like them. He never did do the trick; his final success came when he broke away entirely and tried new methods. Knowing the general idea, and knowing the detailed structure of wing and bone and nerve-tissue is something far, far different. And as for otherworld birds, perhaps, in fact very probably, the atmospheric conditions here are so vastly different that their birds couldn't fly. Perhaps, even, the being came from a planet like Mars with such a thin atmosphere that there were no birds."

Barclay came into the building, trailing a length of airplane control cable. "It's finished, Doc. Cosmos House can't be opened from the inside. Now where do we put Blair?"

Copper looked toward Garry. "There wasn't any biology building. I don't know where we can isolate him."

"How about East Cache?" Garry said after a moment's thought. "Will Blair be able to look after himself—or need attention?"

"He'll be capable enough. We'll be the ones to watch out," Copper assured him grimly. "Take a stove, a couple of bags of coal, necessary supplies and a few tools to fix it up. Nobody's been out there since last fall, have they?"

Garry shook his head. "If he gets noisy—I thought that might be a good idea."

Barclay hefted the tools he was carrying and looked up at Garry. "If the muttering he's doing now is any sign, he's going to sing away the night hours. And we won't like his song."

"What's he saying?" Copper asked.

Barclay shook his head. "I didn't care to listen much. You can if you want to. But I gathered that the blasted idiot had all the dreams McReady had, and a few more. He slept beside the thing when we stopped on the trail coming in from Secondary Magnetic, remember. He dreamt the thing was alive, and dreamt more details. And—damn his soul—knew it wasn't all dream, or had reason to. He knew it had telepathic powers that were stirring vaguely, and that it could not only read minds, but project thoughts. They weren't dreams, you see. They were stray thoughts that thing was broadcasting, the way Blair's broadcasting his thoughts now—a sort of telepathic muttering in its sleep. That's why he knew so much about its powers. I guess you and I, Doc, weren't so sensitive—if you want to believe in telepathy."

"I have to," Copper sighed. "Dr. Rhine of Duke University has shown that it exists, shown that some are much more sensitive than others."

"Well, if you want to learn a lot of details, go listen in on Blair's broadcast. He's driven most of the boys out of the Ad Building; Kinner's rattling pans like coal going down a chute. When he can't rattle a pan, he shakes ashes.

"By the way, Commander, what are we going to do this spring, now the planes are out of it?"

Garry sighed. "I'm afraid our expedition is going to be a loss. We cannot divide our strength now."

"It won't be a loss—if we continue to live, and come out of this," Copper promised him. "The find we've made if we can get it under control, is important enough. The cosmic ray data, magnetic work, and atmospheric work won't be greatly hindered."

Garry laughed mirthlessly. "I was just thinking of the radio broadcasts. Telling half the world about the wonderful results of our exploration flights, trying to fool men like Byrd and Ellsworth back home there that we're doing something."

Copper nodded gravely. "They'll know something's wrong. But men like that have judgment enough to know we wouldn't do tricks without some sort of reason, and will wait for our return to judge us. I think it comes to this: men who know enough to recognize our deception will wait for our return. Men who haven't discretion and faith enough to wait will not have the experience to detect any fraud. We know enough of the conditions here to put through a good bluff."

"Just so they don't send 'rescue' expeditions," Garry prayed. "When—if—we're ever ready to come out, we'll have to send word to Captain Forsythe to bring a stock of magnetos with him when he comes down. But—never mind that."

"You mean if we don't come out?" asked Barclay. "I was wondering if a nice running account of an eruption or an earthquake via radio—with a swell windup by using a stick of decanite under the microphone—would help. Nothing, of course, will entirely keep people out. One of those swell, melodramatic 'last-man-alive-scenes' might make 'em go easy though."

Garry smiled with genuine humor. "Is everybody in camp trying to figure that out too?"

Copper laughed. "What do you think, Garry? We're confident we can win out. But not too easy about it, I guess."

Clark grinned up from the dog he was petting into calmness. "Confident, did you say, Doc?"

VIII

Blair moved restlessly around the small shack. His eyes jerked and quivered in vague, fleeting glances at the four men with him; Barclay, six feet tall and weighing over 190 pounds; McReady, a bronze giant of a man; Dr. Copper, short, squatly powerful; and Benning, five-feet-ten of wiry strength.

Blair was huddled up against the far wall of the East Cache cabin, his gear piled in the middle of the floor beside the heating stove, forming an island between him and the four men. His bony hands clenched and fluttered, terrified. His pale eyes wavered uneasily as his bald, freckled head darted about in birdlike motion.

"I don't want anybody coming here. I'll cook my own food," he snapped nervously. "Kinner may be human now, but I don't believe it. I'm going to get out of here, but I'm not going to eat any food you send me. I want cans. Sealed cans."

"O.K., Blair, we'll bring 'em tonight," Barclay promised. "You've got coal, and the fire's started. I'll make a last—" Barclay started forward.

Blair instantly scurried to the farthest corner. "Get out! Keep away from me, you monster!" the little biologist shrieked, and tried to claw his way through the wall of the shack. "Keep away from me—keep away—I won't be absorbed—I won't be—"

Barclay relaxed and moved back. Dr. Copper shook his head. "Leave him alone, Bar. It's easier for him to fix the thing himself. We'll have to fix the door, I think—"

The four men let themselves out. Efficiently, Benning and Barclay fell to work. There were no locks in Antarctica; there wasn't enough privacy to make them needed. But powerful screws had been driven in each side of the doorframe, and the spare aviation control cable, immensely strong, woven steel wire, was rapidly caught between them and drawn taut. Barclay went to work with a drill and a keyhole saw. Presently he had a trap cut in the door through which goods could be passed without unlashing the entrance. Three powerful hinges from a stock-crate, two hasps and a pair of three-inch cotterpins made it proof against opening from the other side.

Blair moved about restlessly inside. He was dragging something over to the door with panting gasps, and muttering frantic curses. Barclay opened the hatch and glanced in, Dr. Copper peering over his shoulder. Blair had moved the heavy bunk against the door. It could not be opened without his cooperation now.

"Don't know but what the poor man's right at that." McReady sighed. "If he gets loose, it is his avowed intention to kill each and all of us as quickly as possible, which is something we don't agree with. But we've something on our side of that door that is worse than a homicidal maniac. If one or the other has to get loose, I think I'll come up and undo these lashings here."

Barclay grinned. "You let me know, and I'll show you how to get these off fast. Let's go back."

The sun was painting the northern horizon in multicolored rainbows still, though it was two hours below the horizon. The field of drift swept off to the north, sparkling under its flaming colors in a million reflected glories. Low mounds of rounded white on the northern horizon showed the Magnet Range was barely awash above the sweeping drift. Little eddies of wind-lifted snow swirled away from their skis as they set out toward the main encampment two miles away. The spidery finger of the broadcast radiator lifted a gaunt black needle against the white of the Antarctic continent. The snow under their skis was like fine sand, hard and gritty.

"Spring," said Benning bitterly, "is come. Ain't we got fun! And I've been looking forward to getting away from this blasted hole in the ice."

"I wouldn't try it now, if I were you." Barclay grunted. "Guys that set out from here in the next few days are going to be marvelously unpopular."

"How is your dog getting along, Dr. Copper?" McReady asked. "Any results yet?"

"In thirty hours? I wish there were. I gave him an injection of my blood today. But I imagine another five days will be needed. I don't know certainly enough to stop sooner."

"I've been wondering—if Connant were—changed, would he have warned us so soon after the animal escaped? Wouldn't he have waited long enough for it to have a real chance to fix itself? Until we woke up naturally?" McReady asked slowly.

"The thing is selfish. You didn't think it looked as though it were possessed of a store of the higher justices, did you?" Dr. Copper pointed out. "Every part of it is all of it, every part of it is all for itself, I imagine. If Connant were changed, to save his skin, he'd have to—but Connant's feelings aren't changed; they're imitated perfectly, or they're his own. Naturally, the imitation, imitating perfectly Connant's feelings, would do exactly what Connant would do."

"Say, couldn't Norris or Vane give Connant some kind of a test? If the thing is brighter than men, it might know more physics than Connant should, and they'd catch it out," Barclay suggested.

Copper shook his head wearily. "Not if it reads minds. You can't plan a trap for it. Vane suggested that last night. He hoped it would answer some of the questions of physics he'd like to know answers to."

"This expedition-of-four idea is going to make life happy." Benning looked at his companions. "Each of us with an eye on the other to make sure he doesn't do something—peculiar. Man, aren't we going to be a trusting bunch! Each man eyeing his neighbors with the grandest exhibition of faith and trust—I'm beginning to know what Connant meant by 'I wish you could see your eyes.' Every now and then we all have it, I guess. One of you looks around with a sort of 'I-wonder-if-the-other-*three*-are look.' Incidentally, I'm not excepting myself."

"So far as we know, the animal is dead, with a slight question as to Connant. No other is suspected," McReady stated slowly. "The 'always-four' order is merely a precautionary measure."

"I'm waiting for Garry to make it four-in-a-bunk," Barclay sighed. "I thought I didn't have any privacy before, but since that order—"

IX

None watched more tensely than Connant. A little sterile glass test-tube, half-filled with straw-colored fluid. One—two—three—four—five drops of the clear solution Dr. Copper had prepared from the drops of blood from Connant's arm. The tube was shaken carefully, then set in a beaker of clear, warm water. The thermometer read blood heat, a little thermostat clicked noisily, and the electric hotplate began to glow as the lights flickered slightly. Then—little white flecks of precipitation were forming, snowing down in the clear straw-colored fluid. "Lord," said Connant. He dropped heavily into a bunk, crying like a baby. "Six days—" Connant sobbed, "six days in there—wondering if that damned test would lie—"

Garry moved over silently, and slipped his arm across the physicist's back.

"It couldn't lie," Dr. Copper said. "The dog was human-immune—and the serum reacted."

"He's—all right?" Norris gasped. "Then—the animal is dead—dead forever?"

"He is human," Copper spoke definitely, "and the animal is dead."

Kinner burst out laughing, laughing hysterically. McReady turned toward him and slapped his face with a methodical one-two, one-two action. The cook laughed, gulped, cried a moment, and sat up rubbing his cheeks, mumbling his thanks vaguely. "I was scared. Lord, I was scared—"

Norris laughed brittly. "You think we weren't, you ape? You think maybe Connant wasn't?"

The Ad Building stirred with a sudden rejuvenation. Voices laughed, the men clustering around Connant spoke with unnecessarily loud voices, jittery, nervous voices relievedly friendly again. Somebody called out a suggestion, and a dozen started for their skis. Blair, Blair might recover— Dr. Copper fussed with his test-tubes in nervous relief, trying solutions. The party of relief for Blair's shack started out the door, skis clapping noisily. Down the corridor, the dogs set up a quick yelping howl as the air of excited relief reached them.

Dr. Copper fussed with his tubes. McReady noticed him first, sitting on the edge of the bunk, with two precipitin-whitened test-tubes of straw-colored fluid, his face whiter than the stuff in the tubes, silent tears slipping down from horror-widened eyes.

McReady felt a cold knife of fear pierce through his heart and freeze in his breast. Dr. Copper looked up. "Garry," he called hoarsely. "Garry, for God's sake, come here."

Commander Garry walked toward him sharply. Silence clapped down on the Ad Building. Connant looked up, rose stiffly from his seat.

"Garry—tissue from the monster—precipitates too. It proves nothing. Nothing but—but the dog was monster-immune too. That *one of the two contributing blood—one of us two*, you and I, Garry—*one of us is a monster.*"

X

"Bar, call back those men before they tell Blair," McReady said quietly. Barclay went to the door; faintly his shouts came back to the tensely silent men in the room. Then he was back.

"They're coming," he said. "I didn't tell them why. Just that Dr. Copper said not to go."

"McReady," Garry sighed, "you're in command now. May God help you. I cannot."

The bronzed giant nodded slowly, his deep eyes on Commander Garry.

"I may be the one," Garry added. "I know I'm not, but I cannot prove it to you in any way. Dr. Copper's test has broken down. The fact that he showed it was useless, when it was to the advantage of the monster to have that uselessness not known, would seem to prove he was human."

Copper rocked back and forth slowly on the bunk. "I know I'm human. I can't prove it either. One of us two is a liar, for that test cannot lie, and it says one of us is. I gave proof that the test was wrong, which seems to prove I'm human, and now Garry has given that argument which proves me human—which he, as the monster, should not do. Round and round and round and round and—"

Dr. Copper's head, then his neck and shoulders began circling slowly in time to the words. Suddenly he was lying back on the bunk, roaring with laughter. "It doesn't have to prove *one* of us is a monster! It doesn't have to prove that at all! Ho-ho. If we're *all* monsters it works the same—we're all monsters—all of us—Connant and Garry and I—and all of you."

"McReady," Van Wall, the blond-bearded Chief Pilot, called softly, "you were on the way to an M.D. when you took up meteorology, weren't you? Can you make some kind of test?"

McReady went over to Copper slowly, took the hypodermic from his hand, and washed it carefully in 95% alcohol. Garry sat on the bunk-edge with wooden face, watching Copper and McReady expressionlessly. "What Copper said is possible." McReady sighed. "Van, will you help here? Thanks." The filled needle jabbed into Copper's thigh. The man's laughter did not stop, but slowly faded into sobs, then sound sleep as the morphia took hold.

McReady turned again. The men who had started for Blair stood at the far end of the room, skis dripping snow, their faces as white as their skis. Connant had a lighted cigarette in each hand; one he was puffing absently, and staring at the floor. The heat of the one in his left hand attracted him and he stared at it and the one in the other hand stupidly for a moment. He dropped one and crushed it under his heel slowly.

"Dr. Copper," McReady repeated, "could be right. I know I'm human—but of course can't prove it. I'll repeat the test for my own information. Any of you others who wish to may do the same."

Two minutes later, McReady held a test-tube with white precipitin settling slowly from straw-colored serum. "It reacts to human blood too, so they aren't both monsters."

"I didn't think they were," Van Wall sighed. "That wouldn't suit the monster either; we could have destroyed them if we knew. Why hasn't the monster destroyed us, do you suppose? It seems to be loose."

McReady snorted. Then laughed softly. "Elementary, my dear Watson. The monster wants to have life-forms available. It cannot animate a dead body, apparently. It is just waiting—waiting until the best opportunities come. We who remain human, it is holding in reserve."

Kinner shuddered violently. "Hey. Hey, Mac. Mac, would I know if I was a monster? Would I know if the monster had already got me? Oh Lord, I may be a monster already."

"You'd know," McReady answered.

"But we wouldn't," Norris laughed shortly, half-hysterically.

McReady looked at the vial of serum remaining. "There's one thing this damned stuff is good for, at that," he said thoughtfully. "Clark, will you and Van help me? The rest of the gang better stick together here. Keep an eye on each other," said bitterly. "See that you don't get into mischief, shall we say?"

McReady started down the tunnel toward Dog Town with Clark and Van Wall behind him. "You need more serum?" Clark asked.

McReady shook his head. "Tests. There's four cows and a bull, and nearly seventy dogs down there. This stuff reacts only to human blood and—monsters."

XI

McReady came back to the Ad Building and went silently to the washstand. Clark and Van Wall joined him a moment later. Clark's lips had developed a tic, jerking into sudden, unexpected sneers.

"What did you do?" Connant exploded suddenly. "More immunizing?"

Clark snickered, and stopped with a hiccough. "Immunizing. Haw! Immune all right."

"That monster," said Van Wall steadily, "is quite logical. Our immune dog was quite all right, and we drew a little more serum for the tests. But we won't make anymore."

"Can't—can't you use one man's blood on another dog—" Norris began.

"There aren't," said McReady softly, "any more dogs. Nor cattle, I might add."

"No more dogs?" Benning sat down slowly.

"They're very nasty when they start changing," Van Wall said precisely. "But slow. That electrocution iron you made up, Barclay, is very fast. There is only one dog left—our immune. The monster left that for us, so we could play with our little test. The rest—" He shrugged and dried his hands.

"The cattle—" gulped Kinner.

"Also. Reacted very nicely. They look funny as hell when they start melting. The beast hasn't any quick escape, when it's tied in dog chains, or halters, and it had to be to imitate."

Kinner stood up slowly. His eyes darted around the room, and came to rest horribly quivering on a tin bucket in the galley. Slowly, step by step, he retreated toward the door, his mouth opening and closing silently, like a fish out of water.

"The milk—" he gasped. "I milked 'em an hour ago—" His voice broke into a scream as he dived through the door. He was out on the ice-cap without windproof or heavy clothing.

Van Wall looked after him for a moment thoughtfully. "He's probably hopelessly mad," he said at length, "but he might be a monster escaping. He hasn't skis. Take a blow-torch—in case."

The physical motion of the chase helped them; something that needed doing. Three of the other men were quietly being sick. Norris was lying flat on his back, his face greenish, looking steadily at the bottom of the bunk above him.

"Mac, how long have the—cows been not-cows—"

McReady shrugged his shoulders hopelessly. He went over to the milk bucket, and with his little tube of serum went to work on it. The milk clouded it, making certainty difficult. Finally he dropped the test-tube in the stand, and shook his head. "It tests negatively. Which means either they were cows then, or that, being perfect imitations, they gave perfectly good milk."

Copper stirred restlessly in his sleep and gave a gurgling cross between a snore and a laugh. Silent eyes fastened on him. "Would morphia—a monster—" somebody started to ask.

"Lord knows." McReady shrugged. "It affects every Earthly animal I know of."

Connant suddenly raised his head. "Mac! The dogs must have swallowed pieces of the monster, and the pieces destroyed them! The dogs were where the monster resided. I was locked up. Doesn't that prove—"

Van Wall shook his head. "Sorry. Proves nothing about what you are, only proves what you didn't do."

"It doesn't do that." McReady sighed. "We are helpless because we don't know enough, and so jittery we don't think straight. Locked up! Ever watch a white corpuscle of the blood go through the wall of a blood vessel? No? It sticks out a pseudopod. And there it is—on the far side of the wall."

"Oh," said Van Wall unhappily. "The cattle tried to melt down, didn't they? They could have melted down—become just a thread of stuff and leaked under a door to re-collect on the other side. Ropes—no—no, that wouldn't do it. They couldn't live in a sealed tank or—"

"If," said McReady, "you shoot it through the heart, and it doesn't die, it's a monster. That's the best test I can think of, offhand."

"No dogs," said Garry quietly, "and no cattle. It has to imitate men now. And locking up doesn't do any good. Your test might work, Mac, but I'm afraid it would be hard on the men."

XII

Clark looked up from the galley stove as Van Wall, Barclay, McReady, and Benning came in, brushing the drift from their clothes. The other men jammed into the Ad Building continued studiously to do as they were doing, playing chess, poker, reading. Ralsen was fixing a sledge on the table; Vane and Norris had their heads together over magnetic data, while Harvey read tables in a low voice.

Dr. Copper snored softly on the bunk. Garry was working with Dutton over a sheaf of radio messages on the corner of Dutton's bunk and a small fraction of the radio table. Connant was using most of the table for cosmic ray sheets.

Quite plainly through the corridor, despite two closed doors, they could hear Kinner's voice. Clark banged a kettle onto the galley stove and beckoned McReady silently. The meteorologist went over to him.

"I don't mind the cooking so damn much," Clark said nervously, "but isn't there some way to stop that bird? We all agreed that it would be safe to move him into Cosmos House."

"Kinner?" McReady nodded toward the door. "I'm afraid not. I can dope him, I suppose, but we don't have an unlimited supply of morphia, and he's not in danger of losing his mind. Just hysterical."

"Well, we're in danger of losing ours. You've been out for an hour and a half. That's been going on steadily ever since, and it was going for two hours before. There's a limit, you know."

Garry wandered over slowly, apologetically. For an instant, McReady caught the feral spark of fear—horror—in Clark's eyes, and knew at the same instant it was in his own. Garry—Garry or Copper—was certainly a monster.

"If you could stop that, I think it would be a sound policy, Mac," Garry spoke quietly. "There are—tensions enough in this room. We agreed that it would be safe for Kinner in there, because everyone else in camp is under constant eyeing." Garry shivered slightly. "And try, try in God's name, to find some test that will work."

McReady sighed. "Watched or unwatched, everyone's tense. Blair's jammed the trap so it won't open now. Says he's got food enough, and keeps screaming 'Go away, go away—you're monsters. I won't be absorbed. I won't. I'll tell men when they come. Go away.' So—we went away."

"There's no other test?" Garry pleaded.

McReady shrugged his shoulders. "Copper was perfectly right. The serum test could be absolutely definitive if it hadn't been—contaminated. But that's the only dog left, and he's fixed now."

"Chemicals? Chemical tests?"

McReady shook his head. "Our chemistry isn't that good. I tried the microscope you know."

Garry nodded. "Monster-dog and real dog were identical. But—you've got to go on. What are we going to do after dinner?"

Van Wall had joined them quietly. "Rotation sleeping. Half the crowd sleep; half stay awake. I wonder how many of us are monsters? All the dogs were. We thought we were safe, but somehow it got Copper—or you." Van Wall's eyes flashed uneasily. "It may have gotten every one of you—all of you but myself may be wondering, looking. No, that's not possible. You'd just spring then, I'd be helpless. We humans must somehow have the greater numbers now. But—" he stopped.

McReady laughed shortly. "You're doing what Norris complained of in me. Leaving it hanging. 'But if one more is changed—that may shift the balance of power. It doesn't fight. I don't think it ever fights. It must be a peaceable thing, in its own—inimitable—way. It never had to, because it always gained its end otherwise."

Van Wall's mouth twisted in a sickly grin. "You're suggesting then, that perhaps it already *has* the greater numbers, but is just waiting—waiting, all of them—all of you, for all I know—waiting till I, the last human drop my wariness in sleep. Mac, did you notice their eyes, all looking at us."

Garry sighed. "You haven't been sitting here for four straight hours, while all their eyes silently weighed the information that one of us two, Copper or I, is a monster certainly—perhaps both of us."

Clark repeated his request. "Will you stop that bird's noise? He's driving me nuts. Make him tone down, anyway."

"Still praying?" McReady asked.

"Still praying." Clark groaned. "He hasn't stopped for a second. I don't mind his praying if it relieves him, but he yells, he sings psalms and hymns and shouts prayers. He thinks God can't hear well way down here."

"Maybe he can't," Barclay grunted. "Or he'd have done something about this thing loosed from hell."

"Somebody's going to try that test you mentioned, if you don't stop him," Clark stated grimly. "I think a cleaver in the head would be as positive a test as a bullet in the heart."

"Go ahead with the food. I'll see what I can do. There may be something in the cabinets." McReady moved wearily toward the corner Copper had used as his dispensary. Three tall cabinets of rough boards, two locked, were the repositories of the camp's medical supplies. Twelve years ago, McReady had graduated, had started for an internship, and been diverted to meteorology. Copper was a picked man, a man who knew his profession thoroughly and modernly. More than half the drugs available were totally unfamiliar to McReady; many of the others he had forgotten. There was no huge medical library here, no series of journals available to learn the things he had forgotten, the elementary, simple things to Copper, things that did not merit inclusion in the small library he had been forced to content himself with. Books are heavy, and every ounce of supplies had been freighted in by air.

McReady picked a barbiturate hopefully. Barclay and Van Wall went with him. One man never went anywhere alone in Big Magnet.

Ralsen had his sledge put away, and the physicists had moved off the table, the poker game broken up, when they got back. Clark was putting out the food. The click of spoons and the muffled sounds of eating were the only sign of life in the room. There were no words spoken as the three returned; simply all eyes focused on them questioningly while the jaws moved methodically.

McReady stiffened suddenly. Kinner was screeching out a hymn in a hoarse, cracked voice. He looked wearily at Van Wall with a twisted grin and shook his head. "Uh-uh."

Van Wall cursed bitterly, and sat down at the table. "We'll just plumb have to take that till his voice wears out. He can't yell like that forever."

"He's got a brass throat and a cast-iron larynx," Norris declared savagely. "Then we could be hopeful, and suggest he's one of our friends. In that case he could go on renewing his throat till doomsday."

Silence clamped down. For twenty minutes they ate without a word. Then Connant jumped up with an angry violence. "You sit as still as a bunch of graven images. You don't say a word, but oh, Lord, what expressive eyes you've got. They roll around like a bunch of glass marbles spilling down a table. They wink and blink and stare—and whisper things. Can you guys look somewhere else for a change, please?

"Listen, Mac, you're in charge here. Let's run movies for the rest of the night. We've been saving those reels to make 'em last. Last for what? Who is it's going to see those last reels, eh? Let's see 'em while we can, and look at something other than each other."

"Sound idea, Connant. I, for one, am quite willing to change this in any way I can."

"Turn the sound up loud, Dutton. Maybe you can drown out the hymns," Clark suggested.

"But don't," Norris said softly, "don't turn off the lights altogether."

"The lights will be out." McReady shook his head. "We'll show all the cartoon movies we have. You won't mind seeing the old cartoons will you?"

"Goody, goody—a moom-pitcher show. I'm just in the mood." McReady turned to look at the speaker, a lean, lanky New Englander, by the name of Caldwell. Caldwell was stuffing his pipe slowly, a sour eye cocked up to McReady.

The bronze giant was forced to laugh. "O.K., Bart, you win. Maybe we aren't quite in the mood for Popeye and trick ducks, but it's something."

"Let's play Classifications," Caldwell suggested slowly. "Or maybe you call it Guggenheim. You draw lines on a piece of paper, and put down classes of things—like animals, you know. One for 'H' and one for 'U' and so on. Like 'Human' and 'Unknown' for instance. I think that would be a hell of a lot better game. Classification, I sort of figure, is what we need right now a lot more than movies. Maybe somebody's got a pencil that he can draw lines with, draw lines between the 'U' animals and the 'H' animals for instance."

"McReady's trying to find that kind of a pencil," Van Wall answered quietly, "but, we've got three kinds of animals here, you know. One that begins with 'M.' We don't want any more."

"Mad ones, you mean. Uh-huh. Clark, I'll help you with those pots so we can get our little peep-show going." Caldwell got up slowly.

Dutton and Barclay and Benning, in charge of the projector and sound mechanism arrangements, went about their job silently, while the Ad Building was cleared and the dishes and pans disposed of. McReady drifted over toward Van Wall slowly, and leaned back in the bunk beside him. "I've been wondering, Van," he said with a wry grin, "whether or not to report my ideas in advance. I forgot the 'U animal' as Caldwell named it, could read minds. I've a vague idea of something that might work. It's too vague to bother with, though. Go ahead with your show, while I try to figure out the logic of the thing. I'll take this bunk."

Van Wall glanced up, and nodded. The movie screen would be practically on a line with this bunk, hence making the pictures least distracting here, because least intelligible. "Perhaps you should tell us what you have in mind. As it is, only the unknowns know what you plan. You might be—unknown before you got it into operation."

"Won't take long, if I get it figured out right. But I don't want any more all-but-the-test-dog-monsters things. We better move Copper into this bunk directly above me. He won't be watching the screen either." McReady nodded toward Copper's gently snoring bulk. Garry helped them lift and move the doctor.

McReady leaned back against the bunk, and sank into a trance, almost, of concentration, trying to calculate chances, operations, methods. He was scarcely aware as the others distributed themselves silently, and the screen lit up. Vaguely Kinner's hectic, shouted prayers and his rasping hymn-singing annoyed him till the sound accompaniment started. The lights were turned out, but the large, light-colored areas of the screen reflected enough light for ready visibility. It made men's eyes sparkle as they moved restlessly. Kinner was still praying, shouting, his voice a raucous accompaniment to the mechanical sound. Dutton stepped up the amplification.

So long had the voice been going on, that only vaguely at first was McReady aware that something seemed missing. Lying as he was, just across the narrow room from the corridor leading to Cosmos House, Kinner's voice had reached him fairly clearly, despite the sound accompaniment of the pictures. It struck him abruptly that it had stopped.

"Dutton, cut that sound," McReady called as he sat up abruptly. The pictures flickered a moment, soundless and strangely futile in the sudden, deep silence. The rising wind on the surface above bubbled melancholy tears of sound down the stove pipes. "Kinner's stopped," McReady said softly.

"For God's sake start that sound then; he may have stopped to listen," Norris snapped.

McReady rose and went down the corridor. Barclay and Van Wall left their places at the far end of the room to follow him. The flickers bulged and twisted on the back of Barclay's gray underwear as he crossed the still-functioning beam of the projector. Dutton snapped on the lights, and the pictures vanished.

Norris stood at the door as McReady had asked. Garry sat down quietly in the bunk nearest the door, forcing Clark to make room for him. Most of the others had stayed exactly where they were. Only Connant walked slowly up and down the room, in steady, unvarying rhythm.

"If you're going to do that, Connant," Clark spat, "we can get along without you altogether, whether you're human or not. Will you stop that damned rhythm?"

"Sorry." The physicist sat down in a bunk, and watched his toes thoughtfully. It was almost five minutes, five ages, while the wind made the only sound, before McReady appeared at the door.

"We," he announced, "haven't got enough grief here already. Somebody's tried to help us out. Kinner has a knife in his throat, which was why he stopped singing, probably. We've got monsters, madmen and murderers. Any more 'M's' you can think of, Caldwell? If there are, we'll probably have 'em before long."

XIII

"Is Blair loose?" someone asked.

"Blair is not loose. Or he flew in. If there's any doubt about where our gentle helper came from—this may clear it up." Van Wall held a foot-long, thin-bladed knife in a cloth. The wooden handle was half-burnt, charred with the peculiar pattern of the top of the galley stove.

Clark stared at it. "I did that this afternoon. I forgot the damn thing and left it on the stove."

Van Wall nodded. "I smelled it, if you remember. I knew the knife came from the galley."

"I wonder," said Benning looking around at the party warily, "how many more monsters have we? If somebody could slip out of his place, go back of the screen to the galley and then down to the Cosmos House and back—he did come back didn't he? Yes—everybody's here. Well, if one of the gang could do all that—"

"Maybe a monster did it," Garry suggested quietly. "There's that possibility."

"The monster, as you pointed out today, has only men left to imitate. Would he decrease his—supply, shall we say?" Van Wall pointed out. "No, we just have a plain, ordinary louse, a murderer to deal with. Ordinarily we'd call him an 'inhuman murderer' I suppose, but we have to distinguish now. We have inhuman murderers, and now we have human murderers. Or one at least."

"There's one less human," Norris said softly. "Maybe the monsters have the balance of power now."

"Never mind that." McReady sighed and turned to Barclay. "Bar, will you get your electric gadget? I'm going to make certain—"

Barclay turned down the corridor to get the pronged electrocuter, while McReady and Van Wall went back toward Cosmos House. Barclay followed them in some thirty seconds.

The corridor to Cosmos House twisted, as did nearly all corridors in Big Magnet, and Norris stood at the entrance again. But they heard, rather muffled, McReady's sudden shout. There was a savage flurry of blows, dull *ch-thunk, shluff* sounds. "Bar—Bar—" And a curious, savage mewing scream, silenced before even quick-moving Norris had reached the bend.

Kinner—or what had been Kinner—lay on the floor, cut half in two by the great knife McReady had had. The meteorologist stood against the wall, the knife dripping red in his hand. Van Wall was stirring vaguely on the floor, moaning, his hand half-consciously rubbing at his jaw. Barclay, an unutterably savage gleam in his eyes, was methodically leaning on the pronged weapon in his hand, jabbing—jabbing, jabbing.

Kinner's arms had developed a queer, scaly fur, and the flesh had twisted. The fingers had shortened, the hand rounded, the finger nails become three-inch long things of dull red horn, keened to steel-hard, razor-sharp talons.

McReady raised his head, looked at the knife in his hand and dropped it. "Well, whoever did it can speak up now. He was an inhuman murderer at that—in that he murdered an inhuman. I swear by all that's holy, Kinner was a lifeless corpse on the floor here when we arrived. But when It found we were going to jab It with the power—It changed."

Norris stared unsteadily. "Oh, Lord, those things can act. Ye gods—sitting in here for hours, mouthing prayers to a God it hated! Shouting hymns in a cracked voice—hymns about a Church it never knew. Driving us mad with its ceaseless howling—

"Well. Speak up, whoever did it. You didn't know it, but you did the camp a favor. And I want to know how in blazes you got out of the room without anyone seeing you. It might help in guarding ourselves."

"His screaming—his singing. Even the sound projector couldn't drown it." Clark shivered. "It was a monster."

"Oh," said Van Wall in sudden comprehension. "You *were* sitting right next to the door, weren't you? And almost behind the projection screen already."

Clark nodded dumbly. "He—it's quiet now. It's a dead—Mac, your test's no damn good. It was dead anyway, monster or man, it was dead."

McReady chuckled softly. "Boys, meet Clark, the only one we know is human! Meet Clark, the one who proves he's human by trying to commit murder—and failing. Will the rest of you please refrain from trying to prove you're human for a while? I think we may have another test."

"A test!" Connant snapped joyfully, then his face sagged in disappointment. "I suppose it's another either-way-you-want-it."

"No," said McReady steadily. "Look sharp and be careful. Come into the Ad Building. Barclay, bring your electrocuter. And somebody—Dutton—stand with Barclay to make sure he does it. Watch every neighbor, for by the hell these monsters came from, I've got something, and they know it. They're going to get dangerous!"

The group tensed abruptly. An air of crushing menace entered into every man's body, sharply they looked at each other. More keenly than ever before—*is that man next to me an inhuman monster?*

"What is it?" Garry asked, as they stood again in the main room. "How long will it take?"

"I don't know, exactly," said McReady, his voice brittle with angry determination. "But I *know* it will work, and no two ways about it. It depends on a basic quality of the *monsters*, not on us. 'Kinner' just convinced me." He stood heavy and solid in bronzed immobility, completely sure of himself again at last.

"This," said Barclay, hefting the wooden-handled weapon tipped with its two sharp-pointed, charged conductors, "is going to be rather necessary, I take it. Is the power plant assured?"

Dutton nodded sharply. "The automatic stoker bin is full. The gas power plant is on stand-by. Van Wall and I set it for the movie operation—and we've checked it over rather carefully several times, you know. Anything those wires touch, dies," he assured them grimly. "*I* know that."

Dr. Copper stirred vaguely in his bunk, rubbed his eyes with fumbling hand. He sat up slowly, blinked his eyes blurred with sleep and drugs, widened with an unutterable horror of drug-ridden nightmares. "Garry," he mumbled, "Garry—listen. Selfish— from hell they came, and hellish shellfish—I mean self— Do I? What do I mean?" He sank back in his bunk, and snored softly.

McReady looked at him thoughtfully. "We'll know presently." He nodded slowly. "But selfish is what you mean, all right. You may have thought of that, half-sleeping, dreaming there. I didn't stop to think what dreams you might be having. But that's all right. Selfish is the word. They must be, you see." He turned to the men in the cabin, tense, silent men staring with wolfish eyes each at his neighbor. "Selfish, and as Dr. Copper said—*every part is a whole*. Every piece is self-sufficient, an animal in itself.

"That, and one other thing, tell the story. There's nothing mysterious about blood; it's just as normal a body tissue as a piece of muscle, or a piece of liver. But it hasn't so much connective tissue, though it has millions, billions of life-cells."

McReady's great bronze beard ruffled in a grim smile. "This is satisfying, in a way. I'm pretty sure we humans still outnumber you—others. Others standing here. And we have what you, your otherworld race, evidently doesn't. Not an imitated, but a bred-in-the-bone instinct, a driving, unquenchable fire that's genuine. We'll fight, fight with a ferocity you may attempt to imitate, but you'll never equal! We're human. We're real. You're imitations, false to the core of your every cell.

"All right. It's a showdown now. *You* know. You, with your mind-reading. You've lifted the idea from my brain. You can't do a thing about it.

"Standing here—

"Let it pass. Blood is tissue. They have to bleed; if they don't bleed when cut, then by Heaven, they're phoney from hell! If they bleed—then that blood, separated from them, is an individual—*a newly formed individual in its own right, just as they—split, all of them from one original—are individuals!*

"Get it, Van? See the answer, Bar?"

Van Wall laughed very softly. "The blood—the blood will not obey. It's a new individual, with all the desire to protect its own life that the original—the main mass from which it was split—has. The *blood* will live—and try to crawl away from a hot needle, say!"

McReady picked up the scalpel from the table. From the cabinet, he took a rack of test-tubes, a tiny alcohol lamp, and a length of platinum wire set in a little glass rod. A smile of grim satisfaction rode his lips. For a moment he glanced up at those around him. Barclay and Dutton moved toward him slowly, the wooden-handled electric instrument alert.

"Dutton," said McReady, "suppose you stand over by the splice there where you've connected that in. Just make sure no—thing pulls it loose."

Dutton moved away. "Now, Van, suppose you be first on this."

White-faced, Van Wall stepped forward. With a delicate precision, McReady cut a vein in the base of his thumb. Van Wall winced slightly, then held steady as a half inch of bright blood collected in the tube. McReady put the tube in the rack, gave Van Wall a bit of alum, and indicated the iodine bottle.

Van Wall stood motionlessly watching. McReady heated the platinum wire in the alcohol lamp flame, then dipped it into the tube. It hissed softly. Five times he repeated the test. "Human, I'd say." McReady sighed, and straightened. "As yet, my theory hasn't been actually proven—but I have hopes. I have hopes.

"Don't, by the way, get too interested in this. We have with us some unwelcome ones, no doubt. Van, will you relieve Barclay at the switch? Thanks. O.K., Barclay, and may I say I hope you stay with us? You're a damned good guy."

Barclay grinned uncertainly; winced under the keen edge of the scalpel. Presently, smiling widely, he retrieved his long-handled weapon.

"Mr. Samuel Dutt—*Bar!*"

The tensity was released in that second. Whatever of hell the monsters may have had within them, the men in that instant matched it. Barclay had no chance to move his weapon, as a score of men poured down on the thing that had seemed Dutton. It mewed, and spat, and tried to grow fangs—and was a hundred broken, torn pieces. Without knives, or any weapon save the brute-given strength of a staff of picked men, the thing was crushed, rent.

Slowly they picked themselves up, their eyes smouldering, very quiet in their motions. A curious wrinkling of their lips betrayed a species of nervousness.

Barclay went over with the electric weapon. Things smouldered and stank. The caustic acid Van Wall dropped on each spilled drop of blood gave off tickling, cough-provoking fumes.

McReady grinned, his deep-set eyes alight and dancing. "Maybe," he said softly, "I underrated man's abilities when I said nothing human could have the ferocity in the eyes of that thing we found. I wish we could have the opportunity to treat in a more befitting manner these things. Something with boiling oil, or melted lead in it, or maybe slow roasting in the power boiler. When I think what a man Dutton was—

"Never mind. My theory is confirmed by—by one who knew? Well, Van Wall and Barclay are proven. I think, then, that I'll try to show you what I already know. That I, too, am human." McReady switched the scalpel in absolute alcohol, burned it off the metal blade, and cut the base of his thumb expertly.

Twenty seconds later he looked up from the desk at the waiting men. There were more grins out there now, friendly grins, yet withal, something else in the eyes.

"Connant," McReady laughed softly, "was right. The huskies watching that thing in the corridor bend had nothing on you. Wonder why we think only the wolf blood has the right to ferocity? Maybe on spontaneous viciousness a wolf takes tops, but after these seven days—abandon all hope, ye wolves who enter here!

"Maybe we can save time. Connant, would you step for—"

Again Barclay was too slow. There were more grins, less tensity still, when Barclay and Van Wall finished their work.

Garry spoke in a low, bitter voice. "Connant was one of the finest men we had here—and five minutes ago I'd have sworn he was a man. Those damnable things are more than imitation." Garry shuddered and sat back in his bunk.

And thirty seconds later, Garry's blood shrank from the hot platinum wire, and struggled to escape the tube, struggled as frantically as a suddenly feral, red-eyed, dissolving imitation of Garry struggled to dodge the snake-tongue weapon Barclay advanced at him, white-faced and sweating. The Thing in the test-tube screamed with a tiny, tinny voice as McReady dropped it into the glowing coal of the galley stove.

XIV

"The last of it?" Dr. Copper looked down from his bunk with bloodshot, saddened eyes. "Fourteen of them—"

McReady nodded shortly. "In some ways—if only we could have permanently prevented their spreading—I'd like to have even the imitations back. Commander Garry—Connant—Dutton—Clark—"

"Where are they taking those things?" Copper nodded to the stretcher Barclay and Norris were carrying out.

"Outside. Outside on the ice, where they've got fifteen smashed crates, half a ton of coal, and presently will add ten gallons of kerosene. We've dumped acid on every spilled drop, every torn fragment. We're going to incinerate those."

"Sounds like a good plan." Copper nodded wearily. "I wonder, you haven't said whether Blair—"

McReady started. "We forgot him? We had so much else! I wonder—do you suppose we can cure him now?"

"If—" began Dr. Copper, and stopped meaningly.

McReady started a second time. "Even a madman. It imitated Kinner and his praying hysteria—" McReady turned toward Van Wall at the long table. "Van, we've got to make an expedition to Blair's shack."

Van looked up sharply, the frown of worry faded for an instant in surprised remembrance. Then he rose, nodded. "Barclay better go along. He applied the lashings, and may figure how to get in without frightening Blair too much."

Three quarters of an hour, through −37° cold, while the aurora curtain bellied overhead. The twilight was nearly twelve hours long, flaming in the north on snow like white, crystalline sand under their skis. A five-mile wind piled it in drift-lines pointing off to the northwest. Three quarters of an hour to reach the snow-buried shack. No smoke came from the little shack, and the men hastened.

"Blair!" Barclay roared into the wind when he was still a hundred yards away. "Blair!"

"Shut up," said McReady softly. "And hurry. He may be trying a lone hike. If we have to go after him—no planes, the tractors disabled—"

"Would a monster have the stamina a man has?"

"A broken leg wouldn't stop it for more than a minute," McReady pointed out.

Barclay gasped suddenly and pointed aloft. Dim in the twilit sky, a winged thing circled in curves of indescribable grace and ease. Great white wings tipped gently, and the bird swept over them in silent curiosity. "Albatross—" Barclay said softly. "First of the season, and wandering way inland for some reason. If a monster's loose—"

Norris bent down on the ice, and tore hurriedly at his heavy, windproof clothing. He straightened, his coat flapping open, a grim blue-metaled weapon in his hand. It roared a challenge to the white silence of Antarctica.

The thing in the air screamed hoarsely. Its great wings worked frantically as a dozen feathers floated down from its tail. Norris fired again. The bird was moving swiftly now, but in an almost straight line of retreat. It screamed again, more feathers dropped, and with beating wings it soared behind a ridge of pressure ice, to vanish.

Norris hurried after the others. "It won't come back," he panted.

Barclay cautioned him to silence, pointing. A curiously, fiercely blue light beat out from the cracks of the shack's door. A very low, soft humming sounded inside, a low, soft humming and a clink and click of tools, the very sounds somehow bearing a message of frantic haste.

McReady's face paled. "Lord help us if that thing has—" He grabbed Barclay's shoulder, and made snipping motions with his fingers, pointing toward the lacing of control-cables that held the door.

Barclay drew the wirecutters from his pocket, and kneeled soundlessly at the door. The snap and twang of cut wires made an unbearable racket in the utter quiet of the Antarctic hush. There was only that strange, sweetly soft hum from within the shack, and the queerly, hectically clipped clicking and rattling of tools to drown their noises.

McReady peered through a crack in the door. His breath sucked in huskily and his great fingers clamped cruelly on Barclay's shoulder. The meteorologist backed down. "It isn't," he explained very softly, "Blair. It's kneeling on something on the bunk—something that keeps lifting. Whatever it's working on is a thing like a knapsack—and it lifts."

"All at once," Barclay said grimly. "No. Norris, hang back, and get that iron of yours out. It may have—weapons."

Together, Barclay's powerful body and McReady's giant strength struck the door. Inside, the bunk jammed against the door screeched madly and crackled into kindling. The door flung down from broken hinges, the patched lumber of the doorpost dropping inward.

Like a blue rubber ball, a Thing bounced up. One of its four tentacle-like arms looped out like a striking snake. In a seven-tentacled hand a six-inch pencil of winking, shining metal glinted and swung upward to face them. Its line-thin lips twitched back from snake-fangs in a grin of hate, red eyes blazing.

Norris's revolver thundered in the confined space. The hate-washed face twitched in agony, the looping tentacle snatched back. The silvery thing in its hand a smashed ruin of metal, the seven-tentacled hand became a mass of mangled flesh oozing greenish-yellow ichor. The revolver thundered three times more. Dark holes drilled each of the three eyes before Norris hurled the empty weapon against its face.

The Thing screamed in feral hate, a lashing tentacle wiping at blinded eyes. For a moment it crawled on the floor, savage tentacles lashing out, the body twitching. Then it staggered up again, blinded eyes working, boiling hideously, the crushed flesh sloughing away in sodden gobbets.

Barclay lurched to his feet and dove forward with an ice-ax. The flat of the weighty thing crushed against the side of the head. Again the unkillable monster went down. The tentacles lashed out, and suddenly Barclay fell to his feet in the grip of a living, livid rope. The thing dissolved as he held it, a white-hot band that ate into the flesh of his hands like living fire. Frantically he tore the stuff from him, held his hands where they could not be reached. The blind Thing felt and ripped at the tough, heavy, windproof cloth, seeking flesh—flesh it could convert—

The huge blowtorch McReady had brought coughed solemnly. Abruptly it rumbled disapproval throatily. Then it laughed gurglingly, and thrust out a blue-white, three-foot tongue. The Thing on the floor shrieked, flailed out blindly with tentacles that writhed and withered in the bubbling wrath of the blowtorch. It crawled and turned on the floor, it shrieked and hobbled madly, but always McReady held the blowtorch on the face, the dead eyes burning and bubbling uselessly. Frantically the Thing crawled and howled.

A tentacle sprouted a savage talon—and crisped in the flame. Steadily McReady moved with a planned, grim campaign. Helpless, maddened, the Thing retreated from the grunting torch, the caressing, licking tongue. For a moment it rebelled, squalling in inhuman hatred at the touch of the icy snow. Then it fell back before the charring breath of the torch, the stench of its flesh bathing it. Hopelessly it retreated—on and on across the Antarctic snow. The bitter wind swept over it, twisting the torch-tongue; vainly it flopped, a trail of oily, stinking smoke bubbling away from it—

McReady walked back toward the shack silently. Barclay met him at the door. "No more?" the giant meteorologist asked grimly.

Barclay shook his head. "No more. It didn't split?"

"It had other things to think about," McReady assured him. "When I left it, it was a glowing coal. What was it doing?"

Norris laughed shortly. "Wise boys, we are. Smash magnetos, so planes won't work. Rip the boiler tubing out of the tractors. And leave that Thing alone for a week in this shack. Alone and undisturbed."

McReady looked in at the shack more carefully. The air, despite the ripped door, was hot and humid. On a table at the far end of the room rested a thing of coiled wires and small magnets, glass tubing and radio tubes. At the center a block of rough stone rested. From the center of the block came the light that flooded the place, the fiercely blue light bluer than the glare of an electric arc, and from it came the sweetly soft hum. Off to one side was another mechanism of crystal glass, blown with an incredible neatness and delicacy, metal plates and a queer, shimmery sphere of insubstantiality.

"What is that?" McReady moved nearer.

Norris grunted. "Leave it for investigation. But I can guess pretty well. That's atomic power. That stuff to the left—that's a neat little thing for doing what men have been trying to do with 100-ton cyclotrons and so forth. It separates neutrons from heavy water, which he was getting from the surrounding ice."

"Where did he get all—oh. Of course. A monster couldn't be locked in—or out. He's been through the apparatus caches." McReady stared at the apparatus. "Lord, what minds that race must have—"

"The shimmery sphere—I think it's a sphere of pure force. Neutrons can pass through any matter, and he wanted a supply reservoir of neutrons. Just project neutrons against silica—calcium—beryllium—almost anything, and the atomic energy is released. That thing is the atomic generator."

McReady plucked a thermometer from his coat. "It's 120° in here, despite the open door. Our clothes have kept the heat out to an extent, but I'm sweating now."

Norris nodded. "The light's cold. I found that. But it gives off heat to warm the place through that coil. He had all the power in the world. He could keep it warm and pleasant, as his race thought of warmth and pleasantness. Did you notice the light, the color of it?"

McReady nodded. "Beyond the stars is the answer. From beyond the stars. From a hotter planet that circled a brighter, bluer sun they came."

McReady glanced out the door toward the blasted, smoke-stained trail that flopped and wandered blindly off across the drift. "There won't be any more coming. I guess. Sheer accident it landed here, and that was twenty million years ago. What did it do all that for?" He nodded toward the apparatus.

Barclay laughed softly. "Did you notice what it was working on when we came? Look." He pointed toward the ceiling of the shack.

Like a knapsack made of flattened coffee-tins, with dangling cloth straps and leather belts, the mechanism clung to the ceiling. A tiny, glaring heart of supernal flame burned in it, yet burned through the ceiling's wood without scorching it. Barclay walked over to it, grasped two of the dangling straps in his hands, and pulled it down with an effort. He strapped it about his body. A slight jump carried him in a weirdly slow arc across the room.

"Anti-gravity," said McReady softly.

"Anti-gravity." Norris nodded. "Yes, we had 'em stopped, with no planes, and no birds. The birds hadn't come—but it had coffee-tins and radio parts, and glass and the machine shop at night. And a week—a whole week—all to itself. America in a single jump—with anti-gravity powered by the atomic energy of matter.

"We had 'em stopped. Another half hour—it was just tightening these straps on the device so it could wear it—and we'd have stayed in Antarctica, and shot down any moving thing that came from the rest of the world."

"The albatross—" McReady said softly. "Do you suppose—"

"With this thing almost finished? With that death weapon it held in its hand?

"No, by the grace of God, who evidently does hear very well, even down here, and the margin of half an hour, we keep our world, and the planets of the system too. Anti-gravity, you know, and atomic power. Because They came from another sun, a star beyond the stars. *They* came from a world with a bluer sun."

Theodore Sturgeon (1918–1985)

. . . and my fear is great

Theodore Sturgeon was one of the finest and most influential science fiction and fantasy writers of the mid-twentieth century. He once claimed never to have written a story in the horror genre, but many of his stories, and one of his novels, the stunning *Some of Your Blood* (1961), are central to the development of genre horror between the 1930s and the 1980s. His early fantasy stories published in *Unknown* and *Weird Tales* were a seminal influence on Ray Bradbury's early work—Bradbury wrote an introduction to Sturgeon's first story collection, *Without Sorcery* (1949)— and were centrally in the horror mode, if not the genre. Many of his science fiction stories, for instance, the classic "Killdozer" (1944), concerning the possession of a discarded World War II bulldozer by an alien life-form—certainly an ancestor of Matheson's "Duel"—also used the horror mode to striking effect. The Penguin *Encyclopedia* describes him as a writer "whose frequent excursions into dark fantasy sought, with lambent lyrical prose, a unified vision of beauty and horror." His story "It" (1940) is the ancestor of many images of crawling horrors later the province of 1950s comics, particularly "the heap." Sturgeon's literary and emotional range was wide, and he was particularly known as an experimenter in prose style, especially in his use of poetic meter in prose. The long quotation from William Butler Yeats in the present story is a clue to the metric underpinnings of Sturgeon's own prose here. ". . . and my fear is great . . ." is certainly a story of the supernatural and the fantastic and certainly dramatizes material on the edge of repression, but is most comparable to Hardy's "Barbara, of the House of Grebe" in the present collection in its use of horrific moments and investigation of evil.

H e hefted one corner of the box high enough for him to get his knuckle on the buzzer, then let it sag. He stood waiting, wheezing. The door opened.

"Oh! You *didn't* carry it up five flights!"

"No, huh?" he grunted, and pushed inside. He set the groceries down on the sink top in the kitchenette and looked at her. She was sixty something and could have walked upright under his armpit with her shoes on.

"That old elevator . . ." she said. "Wait. Here's something."

He wiped sweat out of his eyes and sensed her approach. He put out his hand for the coin but it wasn't a coin. It was a glass. He looked at it, mildly startled. He wished it were beer. He tasted it, then gulped it down. Lemonade.

"Slow-ly, slow-ly," she said, too late. "You'll get heat cramps. What's your name?" Her voice seemed to come from a distance. She seemed, in an odd way, to stand at a distance as well. She was small as a tower is small on the horizon.

"Don," he grunted.

"Well, Donny," she said, "sit down and rest."

He had said, "Don," not "Donny." When he was in rompers he was "Donny." He turned to the door. "I got to go."

"Wait a bit."

He stopped without turning.

"That's a beautiful watch for a boy like you."

"I like it."

"May I see it?"

Breath whistled briefly in his nostrils. She had her fingers lightly on the heel of his hand before he could express any more annoyance than that.

Grudgingly, he raised his arm and let her look.

"Beautiful. Where did you get it?"

He looked at her, surlily. "In a store."

Blandly she asked, "Did you buy it?"

He snatched his hand away. He swiped nervously, twice, with a hooked index finger at his upper lip. His eyes were slits. "What's it to you?"

"Well, did you?"

"Look, lady. I brought your groceries and I got my lemonade. It's all right about the watch, see? Don't worry about the watch. I got to go now."

"You stole it."

"Whaddaya—crazy? I didn't steal no watch."

"You stole that one."

"I'm gettin' outa here." He reached for the knob.

"Not until you tell me about the watch."

He uttered a syllable and turned the knob. The door stayed closed. He twisted, pulled, pushed, twisted again. Then he whirled, his back thudding against the door. His gangly limbs seemed to compact. His elbows came out, his head down. His teeth bared like an animal's. "Hey, what is this?"

She stood, small and chunky and straight, and said in her faraway voice, "Are you going to tell me?" Her eyes were a milky blue, slightly protruding, and unreadable.

"You lemme out, hear?"

She shook her head.

"You better lemme out," he growled. He took two steps toward her. "Open that door."

"You needn't be frightened. I won't hurt you."

"Somebuddy's goin' to get hurt," he said.

"Not—another—step," she said without raising her voice.

He released an ugly bark of nervous laughter and took the other step. His feet came forward and upward and his back slammed down on the floor. For a moment he lay still, then his eyelids moved slowly up and down and up again while for a moment he gave himself over to the purest astonishment. He moved his head forward so that he could see the woman. She had not moved.

He sat up, clenching his jaw against pain, and scuttled backward to the door. He helped himself rise with the doorpost, never taking his eyes off her. "Jesus, I slipped."

"Don't curse in this house," she said—just as mild, just as firm.

"I'll say what I damn please!"

Wham! His shoulders hit the floor again. His eyes were closed, his lips drawn back. He lifted one shoulder and arched his spine. One long agonized wheeze escaped through his teeth like an extrusion.

"You see, you didn't slip," said the woman. "Poor child. Let me help you."

She put her strong, small hand on his left biceps and another between his shoulder blades. She would have led him to a chair but he pulled away.

"I'm awright," he said. He said it again, as if unconvinced, and, "What'd you . . . do?"

"Sit down," she said solicitously. He cowered where he was. "Sit down," she said again, no more sharply, but there was a difference.

He went to the chair. He sidled along the wall, watching her, and he did not go very fast, but he went. He sank down into it. It was a very low chair. His long legs doubled and his knees thrust up sharply. He looked like a squashed grasshopper. He panted.

"About the watch," she prompted him.

He panted twice as fast for three breaths and whimpered, "I don't want no trouble, lady, just lemme go, huh?"

She pointed at his wrist.

"Awright, you want the watch?" Hysterically he stripped it off and dangled it toward her. "Okay? Take it." His eyes were round and frightened and wary. When she made no move he put the watch on her ancient gateleg table. He put his palms on the seat of the chair and his feet walked two paces doorward, though he did not rise, but swiveled around, keeping his face to her, eager, terrified.

"Where did you get it?"

He whimpered, wordless. He cast one quick, hungry look at the door, tensed his muscles, met her gaze again, and slumped. "You gonna turn me in?"

"Of course not!" she said with more force than she had used so far.

"You're goin' to, all the same."

She simply shook her head, and waited.

He turned, finally, picked up the watch, snapped the flexible gold band. "I swiped it—off Eckhart," he whispered.

"Who?"

"Eckhart on Summit Av-noo. He lives behind the store. It was just laying there, on the counter. I put a box of groceries on it and snagged it out from under. You gonna tell?"

"Well, Donny! Don't you feel better, now you've confessed?"

He looked up at her through his eyebrows, hesitated. "Yeah."

"Is that the truth, Donny?"

"Uh-huh." Then, meeting those calm, imponderable eyes, he said, "Well, no. I dunno, lady. I dunno. You got me all mixed up. Can I go now?"

"What about the watch?"

"I don't want it no more."

"I want you to take it back where you got it."

"What?" He recoiled, primarily because in shock he had raised his voice and the sound of it frightened him. "Je—shucks, lady, you want him to put me in the can?"

"My name is Miss Phoebe, not 'lady.' No, Donny, I think you'll do it. Just a moment."

She sat at a shaky escritoire and wrote for a moment, while he watched. Presently, "Here," she said. She handed him the sheet. He looked at her and then at the paper.

Dear Mr. Eckhart,
Inside the clasp of this watch your name and address is stamped. Would you be good enough to see that it gets to its rightful owner?

Yours very truly,
(Miss) Phoebe Watkins

She took it out of his hand, folded it. She put the watch in an envelope, folded that neatly into a square, dropped it in a second envelope with the note, sealed it and handed it to Don.

"You—you're givin' it right back to me!"

"Am I?"

He lowered his eyes, pinched the top edge of the envelope, pulled it through his fingers to crease the top edge sharply. "I know. You're gonna phone him. You're gonna get me picked up."

"You would be no good to me in the reformatory, Donny."

He looked quickly at her eyes, one, then the other. "I'm gonna be some good to you?"

"Tomorrow at four, I want you to come to tea," she said abruptly.

"To what?"

"To tea. That means wash your face and hands, put on a tie and don't be late."

Wash your face and hands. Nobody had dared to order him around like that for years. And yet, instead of resentment, something sharp and choking rose up in his throat. It was not anger. It was something which, when swallowed, made his eyes wet. He frowned and blinked hard.

"You'd better go," she said, before he could accept or refuse, "before the stores close." She didn't even say which stores.

He rose. He pulled his shoulder blades together and his back cracked audibly. He winced, shambled to the door and stood waiting—not touching it, head down, patient—like a farm horse before a closed gate.

"What is it, Donny?"

"Ain'tcha gonna unlock it?"

"It was never locked."

For a long moment he stood frozen, his back to her, his eyes down. Then he put a slow hand to the knob, turned it. The door opened. He went out, almost but not quite pausing at the threshold, almost but not quite turning to look back. He closed the door quietly and was gone.

She put her groceries away.

He did not come at four o'clock.

He came at four minutes before the hour, and he was breathing hard.

"Come in, Donny!" She held the door for him. He looked over his shoulder, down the corridor, at the elevator gates and the big window where feathery trees and the wide sky showed, and then he came into the room. He stood just inside, watching her as she moved to the kitchenette. He looked around the room, looking for policemen, perhaps, for bars on the windows.

There was nothing in the room but its old-not-antique furniture, the bowlegged occasional chair with the new upholstery which surely looked as old as it had before it was redone; there was the gateleg table, now bearing a silver tea-service with a bit of brass showing at the shoulder of the hot-water pot, and a sugar bowl with delicate tongs which did not match the rest of the set. There was the thin rug with its nap quite swept off, and the dustless books; there was the low chair where he had sat before with its tasseled antimacassars on back and arms.

"Make yourself at home," said her quiet voice, barely competing, but competing easily with the susurrus of steam that rose from the kettle.

He moved a little further in and stopped awkwardly. His Adam's apple loomed mightily over the straining button of his collar. His tie was blue and red, and he wore a horrendous sports jacket, much too small, with a violent yellow-and-gray tweed weave. His trousers were the color of baked earth, and had as much crease as his shoes had shine, and their soles had more polish than the uppers. But he'd scrubbed his face almost raw, and his hair was raked back so hard that his forehead gleamed like scoured porcelain.

When she faced him he stood his ground and said abruptly, before she could tell him to sit down, "I din' wanna come."

"Didn't you?"

"Well, I did, but I wasn' gonna."

"Why did you come, then?"

"I wuz scared not to."

She crossed the room with a large platter of little sandwiches. There were cheese and Spam and egg salad and liverwurst. They were not delicacies; they were food. She put it down next to a small store-bought chocolate cake and two bowls of olives, one ripe, one green, neither stuffed.

She said, "You had nothing to be afraid of."

"No, huh?" He wet his lips, took a deep breath. The rehearsed antagonism blurted out. "You done something to me yesterday I don't know what it was. How I know I ain't gonna drop dead if I don't show up or somep'n like that?"

"I did nothing to you, child!"

"Somebuddy sure as h— sure did."

"You did it to yourself."

"*What?*"

She looked at him. "Angry people don't live very long. Donny, did you know? But sometimes—" Her eyes fell to her hand on the table, and his followed. With one small age-mottled finger she traced around the table's edge, from the far side around one end. "—Sometimes it takes a long time to hurt them. But the hurt can come short and quickly, like *this!*" and she drew her finger straight across from side to side.

Don looked at the table as if something were written on it in a strange language. "Awright, but you made it do that."

"Come and sit down," she said.

But he hadn't finished. "I took the watch back."

"I knew you would."

"Well, okay then. Thass what I come to tell you. That's what you wanted me for, isn't it?"

"I asked you to *tea*. I didn't want to bully you and I didn't want to discuss that silly watch—that matter is closed. It was closed yesterday. Now *do* come and sit down."

"Oh," he said. "I get it. You mean sit down *or else*."

She fixed her eyes on his and looked at him without speaking and without any expression at all until his gaze dropped. "Donny, go and open the door."

He backed away, felt behind him for the knob. He paused there, tense. When she nodded he opened it.

"You're free to go whenever you like. But before you do, I want you to understand that there are a lot of people I could have tea with. I haven't asked anyone but you. I haven't asked the grocery boy or the thief or any of the other people you seem to be sometimes. Just *you*."

He pulled the door to and stood yanking at his bony knuckles. "I don't know about none of that," he said confusedly. He glanced down between his ribs and his elbow at the doorknob. "I just din' want you to think you hadda put on no feedbag to fin' out did I take the watch back."

"I could have telephoned to Mr. Eckhart."

"Well, din't you?"

"Certainly not. There was no need. Was there?"

He came and sat down.

"Sugar?"

"Huh? Yeah—yeah."

"Lemon, or cream?"

"You mean I can have whichever?"

"Of course."

"Then both."

"Both? I think perhaps the cream would curdle."

"In lemon ice cream it don't."

She gave him cream. He drank seven cups of tea, ate all the sandwiches and most of the cake. He ate quickly, not quite glancing over his shoulder to drive away enemies who might snatch the food. He ate with a hunger that was not of hours or days, but the hunger of years. Miss Phoebe patiently passed and refilled and stoked and served until he was done. He loosened his belt, spread out his long legs, wiped his mouth with one sleeve and his brow with the other, closed his eyes and sighed.

"Donny," she said when his jaws had stopped moving, "have you ever been to a bawdy house?"

The boy literally and immediately fell out of his chair. In this atmosphere of doilies and rectitude he could not have been more jolted by a batted ball on his mountainous Adam's apple. He floundered on the carpet, bumped the table, slopped her tea, and crawled back into his seat with his face flaming.

"No," he said, in a strangled voice.

She began then to talk to him quite calmly about social ills of many kinds. She laid out the grub and smut and greed and struggle of his own neighborhood streets as neatly and as competently as she had laid the tea table.

She spoke without any particular emphasis of the bawdy house she had personally closed up, after three reports to the police had no effect. (She had called the desk sergeant, stated her name and intentions, and had asked to be met at the house in twenty minutes. When the police got there she had the girls lined up and two-thirds of their case histories already written.) She spoke of playgrounds and civil defense of pool-rooms, dope pushers, candy stores with beer taps in the soda fountains and the visiting nurse service.

Don listened, fairly humming with reaction. He had seen all the things she mentioned, good and bad. Some he had not understood, some he had not thought about, some he wouldn't dream of discussing in mixed company. He knew vaguely that things were better than they had been twenty, fifty, a hundred years ago, but he had never before been face to face with one of those who integrate, correlate, extrapolate this progress, who dirty their hands on this person or that in order to work for people.

Sometimes, he bit the insides of his cheeks to keep from laughing at her bluntness and efficiency—he wished he could have seen that desk sergeant's *face!*—or to keep from sniggering self-consciously at the way unmentionables rolled off her precise tongue. Sometimes he was puzzled and lost in the complexities of the organizations with which she was so familiar. And sometimes he was slackjawed with fear for her, thinking of the retribution she must surely be in the way of, breaking up rackets like that. But then his own aching back would remind him that she had ways of taking care of herself, and a childlike awe would rise in him.

There was no direct instruction in anything she said. It was purely description. And yet, he began to feel that in this complex lay duties for him to perform. Exactly what they might be did not emerge. It was simply that he felt, as never before, a functioning part, rather than an excrescence, of his own environment.

He was never to remember all the details of that extraordinary communion, nor the one which immediately followed; for somehow she had stopped speaking and there was a long quiet between them. His mind was so busy with itself that there seemed no break in this milling and chewing of masses of previously unregarded ideas.

For a time she had been talking, for a time she did not talk, and in it all he was completely submerged. At length she said, "Donny, tell me something ugly."

"What do you mean ugly?" The question and its answer had flowed through him almost without contact; had she not insisted, he would have lapsed into his busy silence.

"Donny, something that you know about that you've done. Anything at all. Something you've seen."

It was easy to turn from introspection to deep recalls. "Went to one of those summer camps that there paper runs for kids. I wus about seven, I guess."

"Donny," she said, after what may have been a long time, "go on."

"Wasps," he said, negotiating the divided sibilant with some difficulty. "The ones that make paper nests." Suddenly he turned quite pale. "They stung me, it was on the big porch. The nurse, she came out an' hugged me and went away and came back with a bottle, ammonia it was, and put it on where I was stung." He coughed. "Stuff stunk, but it felt fine. Then a counsellor, a big kid from up the street, he came with a long stick. There was a ol' rag tied on the end, it had kerosene on it. He lit it up with a match, it burned all yellow and smoky. He put it up high by them paper nests. The wasps, they come out howlin', they flew right into the fire. When they stopped comin' he pushed at the nest and down it come.

"He gone on to the next one, and down the line, twelve, fifteen of them. Every time he come to a new one the wasps they flew into the fire. You could see the wings go, not like burning, not like melting, sort of *fzzz!* they gone. They fall. They fall all over the floor, they wiggle around, some run like ants, some with they legs burned off they just go around in one place like a phonograph.

"Kids come from all over, watching bugeyed, runnin' around the porch, stampin' on them wasps with their wings gone, they can't sting nobody. Stamp on 'em and squeal and run away an' run back and stamp some more. I'm back near the door, I'm bawlin'. The nurse is squeezin' me, watchin' the wasps, wipin' the ammonia on me any old place, she's not watchin' what she's doin'.

"An' all the time the fire goes an' goes, the wasps fly at it, never once a dumb damn wasp goes to see who's at the other end of the stick. An' I'm there with the nurse, bawlin'. *Why am I bawlin'?*" It came out a deep, basic demand.

"You must have been stung quite badly," said Miss Phoebe. She was leaning forward, her strange unlovely eyes fixed on him. Her lower lip was wet.

"Nah! Three times, four . . ." He struggled hard to fit rich sensation to a poverty of words. "It was me, see. I guess if I got stung every wasp done it should get killed. Maybe burned even. But them wasps in the nest-es, they din't sting nobody, an' here they are all . . . all *brave*, that's what, brave, comin' and fallin' and comin' and fallin' and gettin' squashed. Why? Fer *me*, thass why! Me, it was me, I hadda go an' holler because I got stung an' make all that happen." He screwed his eyes tight shut and breathed as if he had been running. Abruptly his eyes opened very wide and he pressed himself upward in his chair, stretching his long bony neck as if he sat in rising water up to his chin. "What am I talkin' about, wasps? We wasn't talkin' about no wasps. How'd we get talkin' like this?"

She said, "It's all part of the same thing." She waited for him to quiet down. He seemed to, at last. "I asked you to tell me something ugly, and you did. Did it make you feel better?"

He looked at her strangely. *Wasn't there something—oh, yes. Yesterday, about the watch. She made him tell and then asked if he didn't feel better. Was she getting back to that damn watch? I guess not,* he thought, and for some reason felt very ashamed. "Yeah, I feel some better." He looked into himself, found that what he had just said was true, and started in surprise. "Why should that be?" he asked, and it was the first time in his whole life he had asked such a question.

"There's two of us carrying it now," she explained.

He thought, and then protested, "There was twenty people there."

"Not one of them knew why you were crying."

Understanding flashed in him, bloomed almost to revelation. "God damn," he said softly.

This time she made no comment. Instead she said, "You learned something about bravery that day, didn't you?"

"Not until . . . now."

She shrugged. "That doesn't matter. As long as you understand, it doesn't matter how long it takes. Now, if all that happened just to make you understand something about bravery, it isn't an ugly thing at all, is it?"

He did not answer, but his very silence was a response.

"Perhaps one day you will fly into the fire and burn your wings and die, because it's all you can do to save something dear to you," she said softly. She let him think about that for a moment and then said, "Perhaps you will be a flame yourself, and see the brave ones fly at you and lose their wings and die. Either way, you'd know a little better what you were doing, because of the wasps, wouldn't you?"

He nodded.

"The playgrounds," she said, "the medicines, the air-raid watching, the boys' clubs, everything we were discussing . . . each single one of them kills something to do its work, and sometimes what is killed is very brave. It isn't easy to know good from evil."

"*You* know," he blurted.

"Ah," she said, "but there's a reason for that. You'd better go now, Donny."

Everything she had said flew to him as she spoke it, rested lightly on him, soaked in while he waited, and in time found a response. This was no exception. When he understood what she had said he jumped up, guiltily covering the thoughtful and receptive self with self-consciousness like a towel snatched up to cover nakedness.

"Yeah I got to, what time is it?" he muttered. "Well," he said, "yeah. I guess I should." He looked about him as if he had forgotten some indefinable thing, turned and gave her a vacillating smile and went to the door. He opened it and turned. Silently and with great difficulty his mouth moved. He pressed the lips together.

"Good-by, Donny."

"Yeah. Take it easy," he said.

As he spoke he saw himself in the full-length mirror fixed to the closet door. His eyes widened. It was himself he saw there—no doubt of that. But there was no sharp-cut, seam-strained sports jacket, no dull and tattered shoes, no slicked-down hair, smooth in front and down-pointing shag at the nape. In the reflection, he was dressed in a dark suit. The coat matched the trousers. The tie was a solid color, maroon, and was held by a clasp so low down that it could barely be seen in the V of the jacket. The shoes gleamed, not like enamel but like the sheen of a new black-iron frying pan.

He gasped and blinked, and in that second the reflection told him only that he was what he was, flashy and clumsy and very much out of place here. He turned one long scared glance on Miss Phoebe and bolted through the door.

Don quit his job at the market. He quit jobs often, and usually needed no reason, but he had one this time. The idea of delivering another package to Miss Phoebe made him sweat, and the sweat was copious and cold. He did not know if it was fear or awe or shame, because he did not investigate the revulsion. He acknowledged it and acted upon it and otherwise locked the broad category labeled "Miss Phoebe" in the most guarded passages of his mind.

He was, unquestionably, haunted. Although he refused to acknowledge its source, he could not escape what can only be described as a sense of function. When he sharked around the pool halls to pick up some change—he carried ordinary seaman's papers, so could get a forty-cent bed at the Seaman's Institute—he was of the nonproductive froth on the brackish edges of a backwater, and he knew it acutely.

When he worked as helper in a dockside shop, refurbishing outdated streetcars to be shipped to South America, his hand was unavoidably a link in a chain of vision and enterprise starting with an idea and ending with a peasant who, at this very moment, walked, but who would inevitably ride. Between that idea and that shambling peasant were months and miles and dollars, but the process passed through Don's hands every time they lifted a wrench, and he would watch them with mingled wonder and resentment.

He was a piece of nerve tissue becoming aware of the proximity of a ganglion, and dimly conscious of the existence, somewhere, of a brain. His resentment stemmed from a nagging sense of loss. In ignorance he had possessed a kind of freedom—he'd have called it loneliness while he had it—which in retrospect filled him with nostalgia. He carried his inescapable sense of *belonging* like a bundle of thorns, light but most irritating. It was with him in drunkenness and the fights, the movies and the statistical shoutings of the baseball season. He never slept, but was among those who slept. He could not laugh without the realization that he was among the laughers. He no longer moved in a static universe, or rested while the world went by, for his every action had too obvious a reaction. Unbidden, his mind made analogies to remind him of this invert-unwanted duality.

The street, he found, pressed upward to his feet with a force equal to his weight. A new job and he approached one another with an equal magnetism, and he lost it or claimed it not by his effort or lack of it, but by an intricate resultant compounded of all the forces working with him matched against those opposed.

On going to bed he would remove one shoe, and wake from a reverie ten minutes later to find with annoyance that he had sat motionless all that time to contemplate the weight of the shoe versus the upward force of the hand that held it. No birth is painless, and the stirrings of departure from a reactive existence are most troubling, since habit opposes it and there is no equipment to define the motivating ambition.

His own perceptions began to plague him. There had been a time when he was capable of tuning out that which did not concern him. But whatever it was that was growing within him extended its implacable sense of kinship to more areas than those of human endeavor. Why, he would ask himself insistently, *is the wet end of a towel darker than the dry end? What do spiders do with their silk when they climb up a single strand? What makes the brows of so many big executives tilt downward from the center?*

He was not a reader, and though he liked to talk, his wharf-rat survival instinct inhibited him from talking "different" talk, which is what his "different" questions would be, for one does not expose oneself to the sharp teeth of raillery.

He found an all-night cafe where the talk was as different as the talkers could make it; where girls who were unsure of their difference walked about with cropped hair and made their voices boom, and seedy little polyglots surreptitiously ate catsup and sugar with their single interminable cup of coffee; where a lost man could exchange his broken compass for a broken oar.

He went there night after night, sitting alone and listening, held by the fact that many of these minds were genuinely questing. Armed with his strange understanding of opposites, he readily recognized those on one side or the other of forces which most naturally oppose one another, but since he could admire neither phrasing nor intensity for their own sakes, he could only wonder at the misery of these children perched so lonesomely on their dialectical seesaws, mourning the fact that they did not get off the ground while refusing to let anyone get on the other end.

Once he listened raptly to a man with a bleeding ear who seemed to understand the things he felt, but instead of believing many things, this man believed in nothing. Don went away, sad, wondering if there were anyone anywhere who cared importantly that when you yawn, an Italian will ask you if you're hungry while a Swede will think you need sleep; or that only six parallel cuts on a half-loaf of bread will always get you seven slices.

So for many months he worked steadily so that his hands could drain off tensions and let him think. When he had worked through every combination and permutation of which he was capable, he could cast back and discover that all his thoughts had stemmed from Miss Phoebe. His awe and fear of her ceased to exist when he decided to go back, not to see her, but to get more material.

A measure of awe returned, however, when he phoned. He heard her lift the receiver, but she did not say "Hello." She said, "Why, Don! How are you?"

He swallowed hard and said, "Good, Miss Phoebe."

"Four o'clock tomorrow," she said, and hung up.

He put the receiver back carefully and stood looking at the telephone. He worked the tip of the finger-stop under his thumbnail and stood for a long time in the booth, carefully cleaning away the thin parenthesis of oily grime which had defied his brush that morning. When it was gone, so was his fright, but it took a long time. *I've forgotten it all right*, he thought, *but oh, my aching back!*

Belatedly he thought, *Why, she called me Don, not Donny.*

He went back to the cafe that night, feeling a fine new sense of insulation. He had so much to look forward to that searches could wait. And like many a searcher before him, he found what he was looking for as soon as he stopped looking. It was a face that could not have drawn him more if it had been luminous, or leaf-green. It was a face with strong and definite lines, with good pads of laughter-muscles under the cheekbones, and eye-sockets shaped to catch and hold laughter early and long. Her hair was long and seemed black, but its highlights were not blue but red. She sat with six other people around a large table, her eyes open and sleeping, her mouth lax and miserable.

He made no attempt to attract her attention, or to join the group. He simply watched her until she left, which was some three or four hours later. He followed her and so did another man. When she turned up the steps of a brownstone a few blocks away the man followed her, and was halfway up the steps when she was at the top, fumbling for a key. When Don stopped, looking up, the man saw him and whirled. He blocked Don's view of the girl. To Don he was not a person at all, but something in the way.

Don made an impatient, get-out-of-the-way gesture with his head, and only then realized that the man was at bay, terrified, caught red-handed. His eyes were round and he drooled. Don stood, looking upward, quite astonished, as the man sidled down, glaring, panting, and suddenly leaped past him and pelted off down the street.

Don looked from the shadowed, dwindling figure to the lighted doorway. The girl had both hands on the side of the outer, open doorway and was staring down at him with bright unbelief in her face. "Oh, dear God," she said.

Don saw that she was frightened, so he said, "It's all right." He stayed where he was.

She glanced down the street where the man had gone and found it empty. Slowly, she came toward Don and stopped on the third step above him. "Are you an angel?" she asked. In her voice was a childlike eagerness and the shadow of the laughter that her face was made for.

Don made a small, abashed sound. "Me? Not me."

She looked down the street and shuddered. "I thought I didn't care anymore *what* happened," she said, as if she were not speaking to him at all. Then she looked at him. "Anyway, thanks. Thanks. I don't know what he might've . . . if you . . ."

Don writhed under her clear, sincere eyes. "I didn't do nothing." He backed off a pace. "What do you mean, am I a angel?"

"Didn't you ever hear about a guardian angel?"

He had, but he couldn't find it in himself to pursue such a line of talk. He had never met anyone who talked like this. "Who was that guy?"

"He's crazy. They had him locked up for a long time, he hurt a little girl once. He gets like that once in a while."

"Well, you want to watch out," he said.

She nodded gravely. "I guess I care after all," she said. "I'll watch out."

"Well, take it easy," he said.

She looked quickly at his face. His words had far more dismissal in them than he had intended, and he suddenly felt miserable. She turned and slowly climbed the steps. He began to move away because he could think of nothing else to do. He looked back over his shoulder and saw her in the doorway, facing him. He thought she was going to call out, and stopped. She went inside without speaking again, and he suddenly felt very foolish. He went home and thought about her all night and all the next day. He wondered what her name was.

When he pressed the buzzer, Miss Phoebe did not come to the door immediately. He stood there wondering if he should buzz again or go away or what. Then the door opened. "Come in, Don."

He stepped inside, and though he thought he had forgotten about the strange mirror, he found himself looking for it even before he saw Miss Phoebe's face. It was still there, and in it he saw himself as before, with the dark suit, the quiet tie, the dull, clean-buffed shoes. He saw it with an odd sense of disappointment, for it had given him such a wondrous shock before, but now reflected only what a normal mirror would, since he was wearing such a suit and tie and shoes, but wait—the figure in the reflection carried something and he did not. A paper parcel . . . a wrapped bunch of flowers; not a florist's elaboration, but tissue-wrapped jonquils from a subway peddler. He blinked, and the reflection was now quite accurate again.

All this took place in something over three seconds. He now became aware of a change in the room, *it's—oh, the light*. It had been almost glary with its jewel-clean windows and scrubbed white woodwork, but now it was filled with mellow orange light. Part of this was sunlight struggling through the inexpensive blinds, which were drawn all the way down. Part was something else he did not see until he stepped fully into the room and into the range of light from the near corner. He gasped and stared, and, furiously, he felt tears rush into his eyes so that the light wavered and ran.

"Happy birthday, Don," said Miss Phoebe severely.

Don said, "Aw." He blinked hard and looked at the little round cake with its eighteen five-and-dime candles. "Aw."

"Blow them out quickly," she said. "They run."

He bent over the cake.

"Every one, mind," she said. "In one breath."

He blew. All the candles went out but one. He had no air left in his lungs, and he looked at the candle in purple panic. In a childlike way, he could not bring himself to break the rules she had set up. His mouth yawped open and closed like that of a beached fish. He puffed his cheeks out by pushing his tongue up and forward, leaned very close to the candle, and released the air in his mouth with a tiny explosive pop. The candle went out.

"Splendid. Open the blinds for me like a good boy."

He did as he was asked without resentment. As she plucked the little sugar candleholders out of the cake, he said, "How'd you know it was my birthday?"

"Here's the knife. You must cut it first, you know."

He came forward. "It's real pretty. I never had no birthday cake before."

"I'm glad you like it. Hurry now. The tea's just right."

He busied himself, serving and handing and receiving and setting down, moving chairs, taking sugar. He was too happy to speak.

"Now then," she said when they were settled. "Tell me what you've been up to."

He assumed she knew, but if she wanted him to say, why, he would. "I'm a typewriter mechanic now," he said. "I like it fine. I work nights in big offices and nobody bothers me none. How've you been?"

She did not answer him directly, but her serene expression said that nothing bad could ever happen to her. "And is that all? Just work and sleep?"

"I been thinkin'," he said. He looked at her curiously. "I thought a lot about what you said." She did not respond. "I mean about everything working on everything else, an' the wasps and all." Again she was silent, but now there was response in it.

He said, "I was all mixed up for a long time. Part of the time I was mad. I mean, like you're working for a boss who won't let up on you, thinks he owns you just because you work there. Used to be I thought about whatever I wanted to, I could stop thinkin' like turnin' a light off."

"Very apt," she remarked. "It was exactly that."

He waited while this was absorbed. "After I was here I couldn't turn off the light; the switch was busted. The more I worked on things, the more mixed up they got." In a moment he added, "For a while."

"What things?" she asked.

"Hard to say," he answered honestly. "I never had nobody to tell me much, but I had some things pretty straight. It's wrong to swipe stuff. It's right to do what they tell you. It's right to go to church."

"It's right to worship," she interjected. "If you can worship in a church, that's the best place to do it. If you can worship better in another place, then that's where you should go instead."

"That's what I mean!" he barked, pointing a bony finger like a revolver. "You say something like that, so sure and easy, an' all the—the fences go down. Everything's all in the right box, see, an' you come along and shake everything together. You don't back off from nothing. You say what you want about anything, an' you let me say anything I want to you. Everything I ever thought was right or wrong could be wrong or right. Like those wasps dyin' because of me, and you say they maybe died *for* me, so's I could learn something. Like you sayin' I could be a wasp or a fire, an' still know what was what . . . I'll get mixed up again if I go on talkin' about it."

"I think not," she said, and he felt very pleased. She said, "It's in the nature of things to be 'shaken all together,' as you put it. A bird brings death to a worm and a wildcat brings death to the bird. Can we say that what struck the worm and the bird was evil, when the wildcat's kittens took so much good from it? Or if the murder of the worm is good, can we call the wildcat evil?"

"There isn't no . . . no *altogether* good or bad, huh."

"Now, that is a very wrong thing to say," she said with soft-voiced asperity.

"You gone an' done it again!" he exclaimed.

She did not smile with him. "There is an absolute good and an absolute evil. They cannot be confused with right and wrong, or building and destroying as we know them, because, like the cat and the worm, those things depend on whose side you take. Don, I'm going to show you something very strange and wonderful."

She went to her little desk and got pencil and paper. She drew a circle, and within it she sketched in an S-shaped line. One side of this line she filled in with quick short strokes of her pencil:

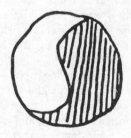

"This," she said, as Don pored over it, "is the most ancient symbol known to man. It's called 'yin and Yang.' 'Yin' is the Chinese term for darkness and earth. 'Yang' means light and sky. Together they form the complete circle—the universe, the cosmos—everything. Nothing under heaven can be altogether one of these things or the other. The symbol means light and dark. It means birth and death. It is everything which holds together and draws down, with everything that pours out and disperses. It is male and female, hope and history, love and hate. It's—everything there is or could be. It's why you can't say the murder of a worm by a bird is good or evil."

"This here yin an' Yang's in everything we do, huh."

"Yes."

"It's God an' the Devil then."

"*Good* and *evil*." She placed her hand over the entire symbol. "God is all of it."

"Well, all right!" he exclaimed. "So it's like I said. There ain't a 'altogether good' and a 'altogether bad.' Miss Phoebe, how you know you're right when you bust up some pusher's business or close a joint?"

"There's a very good way of knowing, Don. I'm very glad you asked me that question." She all but beamed at him—she, who hardly ever even smiled. "Now listen carefully. I am going to tell you something which it took me many years to find out. I am going to tell you because I do not see why the young shouldn't use it.

"Good and evil are active forces—almost like living things. I said that nothing under heaven can be completely one of these things or the other, and it's true. But, Don—good and evil come to us from *somewhere*. They reach this cosmos as living forces, constantly replenished—from *somewhere*. It follows that there is a Source of good and a Source of evil . . . or call them light and dark, or birth and death if you like."

She put her finger on the symbol. "Human beings, at least with their conscious wills, try to live here, in the Yang part. Many find themselves on the dark side, some cross and recross the borderline. Some set a course for themselves and drive it straight and true, and never understand that the border itself turns and twists and will have them in one side and then the other.

"In any case, these forces are in balance, and they must remain so. But as they are living, vital forces, there must be those who willingly and purposefully work with them."

With his thumbnail he flicked the paper. "From this, everything's so even-steven you'd never know who you're working for."

"Not true, Don. There are ways of knowing."

He opened his lips and closed them, turned away, shaking his head.

"You may ask me, Don," she said.

"Well, okay. You're one of 'em. Right?"

"Perhaps so."

"Perhaps *nothing*. You knocked me flat on my noggin twice in a row an' never touched me. You're—you're somethin' special, that's for sure. You even knew about my birthday. You know who's callin' when the phone rings."

"There are advantages."

"All right then, here's what I'm gettin' to, and I don't want you to get mad at me. What I want to know is, why ain't you rich?"

"What do you mean by *rich?*"

He kicked the table leg gently. "Junk," he said. He waved at the windows. "Everybody's got venetian blinds now. Look there, cracks in the ceiling 'n you'll get a rent rise if you complain, long as it ain't leakin'. You know, if I could do the things you do, I'd have me a big house an' a car. I'd have flunkies to wash dishes an' all like that."

"I wouldn't be rich if I had all those things, Don."

He looked at her guardedly. He knew she was capable of a preachment, though he had been lucky so far. "Miss Phoebe," he said respectfully, "you ain't goin' to tell me the—uh—inner riches is better'n a fishtail Cadillac."

"I'll ask *you*," she said patiently. "Would you want a big house and servants and all those things?"

"Well, *sure!*"

"Why?"

"Why? Well, because, because—well, that's the way to live, that's all."

"Why is it the way to live?"

"Well, anyone can see why."

"Don, answer the question! Why is that the way to live?"

"Well," he said. He made a circular gesture and put his hand down limply. He wet his lips. "Well, because you'd have what you wanted." He looked at her hopefully and realized he'd have to try again. "You could make anyone do what you wanted."

"Ah," she said. "Why would you want to do that?"

"So you wouldn't have to do your own work."

"Aside from personal comfort—why would you want to be able to tell other people what to do?"

"You tell me," he said with some warmth.

"The answers are in you if you'll only look, Don. Tell me: Why?"

He considered. "I guess it'd make me feel good."

"Feel good?"

"The boss. The Man. You know. I say jump, they jump."

"Power?"

"Yeah, that's it, power."

"Then you want riches so you'll have a sense of power."

"You're in."

"And you wonder why I don't want riches. Don, I've *got* power. Moreover, it was given me and it's mine. I needn't buy it for the rest of my life."

"Well, now . . ." he breathed.

"You can't imagine power in any other terms than cars and swimming pools, can you?"

"Yes I can," he said instantly. Then he grinned and added, "But not yet."

"I think that's more true than you know," she said, giving him her sparse smile. "You'll come to understand it."

They sat in companionable silence. He picked up a crumb of cake icing and looked at it. "Real good cake," he murmured, and ate it. Almost without change of inflection, he said, "I got a real ugly one to tell you."

She waited, in the responsive silence he was coming to know so well.

"Met a girl last night."

He was not looking at her and so did not see her eyes click open, round and moist. He hooked his heel in the chair rung and put his fist on the raised knee, thumb up. He lowered his head until the thumb fitted into the hollow at the bridge of his nose. Resting his head precariously there, rolling it slightly from time to time as if he perversely enjoyed the pressure and the ache, he began to speak. And if Miss Phoebe found surprising the leaps from power to birthday cake to a girl to what happened in the sewer, she said nothing.

"Big sewer outlet down under the docks at Twenty-seventh," he said. "Wuz about nine or ten, playing there. Kid called Renzo. We were inside the pipe; it was about five feet high, and knee-deep in storm water. Saw somethin' bobbin' in the water, got close enough to look. It was the hind feet off a dead rat, a great big one, and *real* dead. Renzo, he was over by the outlet tryin' to see if he could get up on a towboat out there, and I thought it might be fine if I could throw the rat on his back on account he didn't have no shirt on. I took hold of the rat's feet and pulled, but that rat, he had his head stuck in a side-pipe somehow, an' I guess he swole some too. I guess I said something and Renzo he come over, so there was nothin' for it then but haul the rat out anyway. I got a good hold and yanked, an' something popped an' up he came. I pulled 'im right out of his skin. There he was wet an' red an' bare an' smellin' a good deal. Renzo, he lets out a big holler, laughin', I can still hear it in that echoey pipe. I'm standin' there like a goofball, starin' at this rat. Renzo says, 'Hit'm quick, Doc, or he'll never start breathin'!' I just barely got the idea when the legs come off the rat an' it fell in the water with me still holdin' the feet."

It was very quiet for a while. Don rocked his head, digging his thumb into the bridge of his nose. "Renzo and me we had a big fight after. He tol' everybody I had a baby in the sewer. He tol' 'em I's a firstclass stork. They all started to call me Stork, I hadda fight five of 'em in two days before they cut it out.

"Kid stuff," he said suddenly, too loudly, and sat upright, wide-eyed, startled at the sound. "I know it was kid stuff, I can forget it. But it won't . . . it won't forget."

Miss Phoebe stirred, but said nothing.

Don said, "Girls. I never had nothing much to do with girls, kidded 'em some if there was somebody with me started it, and like that. Never by myself. I tell you how it is, it's—" He was quiet for a long moment. His lips moved as if he were speaking silently, words after words until he found the words he wanted. He went on in precisely the same tone, like an interrupted tape recorder.

"—Like this, I get so I like a girl a whole lot, I want to get close to her, I think about her like any fellow does. So before I can think much about it, let alone *do* anything, zing! I'm standin' in that stinkin' sewer, Renzo's yellin' 'Hit'm quick, Doc,' an' all the rest of it." He blew sharply from his nostrils. "The better a girl smells," he said hoarsely, "the worse it is. So I think about girls, I think about rats, I think about babies, it's Renzo and me and that echo. Laughin'," he mumbled, "him laughin'.

"I met a girl last night," he said clearly, "I don't want ever to think about like that. I walked away. I don't know what her name is. I want to see her some more. I'm afraid. So that's why."

After a while he said, "That's why I told you."

And later, "You were a big help before, the wasps." As he spoke he realized that there was no point in hurrying her; she had heard him the first time and would wait until she was ready. He picked up another piece of icing, crushed it, tossed the pieces back on the plate.

"You never asked me," said Miss Phoebe, "about the power I have, and how it came to me."

"Din't think you'd say. I wouldn't, if I had it. This girl was—"

"Study," said Miss Phoebe. "More of it than you realize. Training and discipline and, I suppose, a certain natural talent which," she said, fixing him sternly with her eyes as he was about to interrupt, "I am sure you also have. To a rather amazing degree. I have come a long way, a long hard way, and it isn't so many years ago that I first began to feel this power . . . I like to think of you with it, young and strong and . . . and good, growing greater, year by year. Don, would you like the power? Would you work hard and patiently for it?"

He was very quiet. Suddenly he looked up at her. "What?"

She said—and for once the control showed—"I thought you might want to answer a question like that."

He scratched his head and grinned. "Gee, I'm sorry, Miss Phoebe, but for that one second I was thinkin' about . . . something else, I guess. Now," he said brightly, "what was it you wanted to know?"

"What was this matter you found so captivating?" she asked heavily. "I must say I'm not used to talking to myself, Don."

"Ah, don't jump salty, Miss Phoebe," he said contritely. "I'll pay attention, honest. It's just that I—you din't say *one* word about what I told you. I guess I was tryin' to figure it out by myself if you wasn't goin' to help."

"Perhaps you didn't wait long enough."

"Oh." He looked at her and his eyes widened. "*Oh!* I never thought of that. Hey, go ahead, will you?" He drew his knees together and clasped them, turned to face her fully.

She nodded with a slightly injured satisfaction. "I asked you, Don, if you'd like the kind of power I have, for yourself."

"*Me?*" he demanded, incredulously.

"You. And I also asked you if you would work hard and patiently to get it. Would you?"

"Would I! Look, you don't really think, I mean, I'm just a—"

"We'll see," she said.

She glanced out the window. Dusk was not far away. The curtains hung limp and straight in the still air. She rose and went to the windows, drew the blinds down. The severe velour drapes were on cranes. She swung them over the windows. They were not cut full enough to cover completely, each window admitted a four-inch slit of light. But that side of the building was in shadow, and she turned back to find Don blinking in deep obscurity. She went back to her chair.

"Come closer," she said. "No, not that way—facing me. That's it. Your back to the window. Now, I'm going to cover my face. That's because otherwise the light would be on it; I don't want you to look at me or at anything but what you find inside yourself." She took a dark silk scarf from the small drawer in the end of the gateleg table. "Put your hands out. Palms down. So." She dropped the scarf over her face and hair, and felt for his hands. She slipped hers under his, palms upward, and leaned forward until she could grasp his wrists. "Hold mine that way too. Good. Be absolutely quiet."

He was.

She said, "There's something the matter. You're all tightened up. And you're not close enough. Don't move! I mean, in your mind . . . ah, I see. You'll have your questions answered. Just trust me." A moment later she said, "That's *much* better. There's something on your mind, though, a little something. Say it, whatever it is."

"I was thinkin', this is a trapeze grip, like in the circus."

"So it is! Well, it's a good contact. Now, don't think of anything at all. If you want to speak, well, do; but nothing will be accomplished until you no longer feel like talking.

"There is a school of discipline called Yoga," she said quietly. "For years I have studied and practiced it. It's a lifetime's work in itself, and still it's only the first part of what I've done. It has to do with the harmony of the body and the mind, and the complete control of both. My breathing will sound strange to you. Don't be frightened, it's perfectly all right."

His hands lay heavily in hers. He opened his eyes and looked at her but there was nothing to see, just the black mass of her silk-shrouded head and shoulders in the dim light. Her breathing deepened. As he became more and more aware of other silences, her breathing became more and more central in his attention. He began to wonder where she was putting it all; an inhalation couldn't possibly continue for so long, like the distant hiss of escaping steam. And when it dwindled, the silence was almost too complete, for too long; no one could hold such a deep breath for as long as that! And when at last the breath began to come out again, it seemed as if the slow hiss went on longer even than the inhalation. If he had wondered where she was putting it, he now wondered where she was getting it.

And at last he realized that the breathing was not deep at all, but shallow in the extreme; it was just that the silence was deeper and her control greater than he had imagined. His hands—

"It tingles. Like electric," he said aloud.

His voice did not disturb her in the least. She made no answer in any area. The silence deepened, the darkness deepened, the tingling continued and grew . . . not grew; it spread. When he first felt it, it had lived in a spot on each wrist, where it contacted hers. Now it uncoiled, sending a thin line of sensation up into his forearms and down into his hands. He followed its growth, fascinated. Around the center of each palm the tingling drew a circle, and sent a fine twig of feeling growing into his fingers, and at the same time he could feel it negotiating the turn of his elbows.

He thought it had stopped growing, and then realized that it had simply checked its twig-like creeping, and was broadening; the line in his arms and fingers was becoming a band, a bar of feeling. It crossed his mind that if this bothered him at all he could pull his hands away and break the contact, and that if he did that Miss Phoebe would not resent it in any way. And, since he knew he was free to do it, knew it without question, he was not tempted. He sat quietly, wonder-struck, tasting the experience.

With a small silent explosion there were the tingling, hair-thin lines of sensation falling like distant fireworks through his chest and abdomen, infusing his loins and thighs and the calves of his legs. At the same time more of them crept upward through his neck and head, flared into and around his ears, settled and boiled and shimmered through his lobes and cheeks, curled and clasped the roots of his eyelids. And again there was the feeling of the lines broadening, fusing one with the other as they swelled. Distantly he recognized their ultimate; they would grow inward and outward until they were a complete thing, bounded exactly by everything he was, every hair, every contour, every thought and function.

He opened his eyes, and the growth was not affected. The dark mass of Miss Phoebe's head was where it had been, friendly and near and reassuring. He half-smiled, and the sparkling delicate little lines of feeling on his lips yielded to the smile, played in it like infinitesimal dolphins, gave happy news of it to all the other threads, and they all sang to his half-smile and gave him joy. He closed his eyes comfortably, and cheerful filaments reached for one another between his upper and lower lashes.

An uncountable time passed. Time now was like no time he knew of, drilling as it always had through event after event, predictable and dictatorial to rust, springtime, and the scissoring hands of clocks. This was a new thing, not a suspension, for it was too alive for that. It was different, that's all, different the way this feeling was, and now the lines and bands and bars were fused and grown, and he was filled . . . he was, himself, of a piece with what had once been the tingling of a spot on his wrist.

It was a feeling, still a feeling, but it was a substance too, Don-sized, Don-shaped. A color . . . no, it wasn't a color, but if it had been a color it was beginning to glow and change. It was glowing as steel glows in the soaking-pits, a color impossible to call black because it is red inside; and now you can see the red; and now the red has orange in it, and now in the orange is yellow, and when white shows in the yellow you may no longer look, but still the radiation beats through you, intensifying . . . not a color, no; this thing had no color and no light, but if it had been a color, this would have been its spectral growth.

And this was the structure, this the unnamable *something* which now found itself alive and joyous. It was from such a peak that the living thing rose as if from sleep, became conscious of its own balance and strength, and leaped heavenward with a single cry like all the satisfying, terminal resolving chords of all music, all uttered in a wingbeat of time.

Then it was over not because it was finished, like music or a meal, but because it was perfect—like foam or a flower caught in the infrangible amber of memory. Don left the experience without surfeit, without tension, without exhaustion. He sat peacefully with his hands in Miss Phoebe's, not dazzled, not numb, replenished in some luxurious volume within him which kept what it gained for all of life, and which had an infinite capacity. But for the cloth over her face and the odd fact that their hands were dripping with perspiration, they might just that second have begun. It may even have been that second.

Miss Phoebe disengaged her hands and plucked away the cloth. She was smiling—really smiling, and Don understood why she so seldom smiled, if this were the expression she used for such experiences.

He answered the smile, and said nothing, because about perfect things nothing can be said. He went and dried his hands and then pulled back the drapes and raised the blinds while she straightened the chairs.

"The ancients," said Miss Phoebe, "recognized four elements: earth, air, fire and water. This power can do anything those four elements can do." She put down the clean cups, and went to get her crumb brush. "To start with," she added.

He placed the remark where it would soak in, and picked up a piece of icing from the cake plate. This time he ate it. "Why is a wet towel darker than a dry one?"

"I—why, I hadn't thought," she said. "It is, now that you mention it. I'm sure I don't know why, though."

"Well, maybe you know this," he said. "Why I been worrying about it so much?"

"Worrying?"

"You know what I mean. That and why most motors that use heat for power got to have a cooling system, and why do paper towels tear where they ain't perf'rated, and a zillion things like that. I never used to."

"Perhaps it's . . . yes, I know. Of *course!*" she said happily. "You're getting a—call it a kinship with things. A sense of interrelationship."

"Is that good?"

"I think it is. It means I was right in feeling that you have a natural talent for what I'm going to teach you."

"It takes up a lot of my time," he grumbled.

"It's good to be alive all the time," she said. She poured. "Don, do you know what a revelation is?"

"I heard of it."

"It's a sudden glimpse of the real truth. You had one about the wasps."

"I had it awful late."

"That doesn't matter. You had it, that's the important thing. You had one with the rat, too."

"I did?"

"With the wasps you had a revelation of sacrifice and courage. With the rat—well, you know yourself what effect it has had on you."

"I'm the only one I know has no girl," he said.

"That is exactly it."

"Don't tell me it's s'posed to be that way!"

"For you, I—I'd say so."

"Miss Phoebe, I don't think I know what you're talkin' about."

She looked at her teacup. "I've never been married."

"Me too," he said somberly. "Wait, is that what you—"

"Why do people get married?"

"Kids."

"Oh, that isn't all."

He said, with his mouth full, "They wanna be together, I guess. Team up, like. One pays the bills, the other runs the joint."

"That's about it. Sharing. They want to share. You know the things they share."

"I heard," he said shortly.

She leaned forward. "Do you think they can share anything like what we've had this afternoon?"

"*That* I never heard," he said pensively.

"I don't wonder. Don, your revelation with the rat is as basic a picture of what is called 'original sin' as anything I have ever heard."

"Original sin," he said thoughtfully. "That's about Adam an'—no, wait. I remember. Everybody's supposed to be sinful to start with because it takes a sin to get'm started."

"Once in a while," she said, "it seems as if you know so few words because you don't need them. That was beautifully put. Don, I think that awful thing that happened to you in the sewer was a blessing. I think it's a good thing, not a bad one. It might be bad for someone else, but not for you. It's kept you as you are, so far. I don't think you should try to forget it. It's a warning and a defense. It's a weapon against the 'yin' forces. You are a very special person, Don. You were made for better things than—than others."

"About the wasps," he said. "As soon as you started to talk I begun to feel better. About this, I don't feel better." He looked up to the point where the wall met the ceiling and seemed to be listening to his own last phrase. He nodded definitely. "I don't feel better. I feel worse."

She touched his arm. It was the only time she had made such a gesture. "You're strong and growing and you're just eighteen." Her voice was very kind. "It would be a strange thing indeed if a young man your age didn't have his problems and struggles and tempta—I mean, battles. I'm sorry I can't resolve it for you, Don. I wish I could. But I know what's right. Don't I, Don, don't I?"

"Every time," he said glumly. "But I . . ." His gaze became abstracted.

She watched him anxiously. "Don't think about her," she whispered. "Don't. You don't have to. Don, do you know that what we did this afternoon was only the very beginning, like the first day of kindergarten?"

His eyes came back to her, bright.

"Yeah, huh. Hey, Miss Phoebe, how about that."

"When would you like to do some more?"

"Now?"

"Bless you, no! We both have things to do. And besides, you have to think. You know it takes time to think."

"Yeah, okay. When?"

"A week."

"Don't worry about me, I'll be here. Hey, I'm gonna be late for work."

He went to the door. "Take it easy," he said.

He went out and closed the door but before the latch clicked he pushed it open again. He crossed the room to her.

He said, "Hey, thanks for the birthday cake. It was . . ." His mouth moved as he searched. "It was a good birthday cake." He took her hand and shook it heartily. Then he was gone.

Miss Phoebe was just as pink as the birthday cake. To the closed door she murmured, "Take it easy."

Don was in a subway station two nights later, waiting for an express. The dirty concrete shaft is atypical and mysterious at half-past four in the morning. The platforms are unlittered and deserted, and there is a complete absence of the shattering roar and babble and bustle for which these urban entrails are built. An approaching train can be heard starting and running and stopping sometimes ten or twelve minutes before it pulls in, and a single set of footfalls on the mezzanine above will outlast it. The few passengers waiting seem always to huddle together near one of the wooden benches, and there seems to be a kind of inverse square law in operation, for the closer they approach one another the greater the casual unnoticing manners they affect, though they will all turn to watch someone walking toward them from two hundred feet away. And when angry voices bark out, the effect is more shocking than it would be in a cathedral.

A tattered man slept uneasily on the bench. Two women buzz-buzzed ceaselessly at the other end. A black-browed man in gray tweed strode the platform, glowering, looking as if he were expected to decide on the recall of the Ambassador to the Court of St. James by morning.

Don happened to be looking at the tattered man, and the way the old brown hat was pulled down over the face (it could have been a headless corpse, and no one would have been the wiser) when the body shuddered and stirred. A strip of stubbled skin emerged between the hat and the collar, and developed a mouth into which was stuffed a soggy collection of leaf-mold which may have been a cigar butt yesterday. The man's hand came up and fumbled around for the thing. The jaws worked, the lips smacked distastefully. The hand pushed the hat brim up only enough to expose a red eye, which glared at the butt. The hat fell again, and the hand pitched the butt away.

At this point the black-browed man hove to, straddle-legged in front of the bench. He opened his coat and hooked his thumbs in the armholes of his waistcoat. He tilted his head back, half-closed his eyes, and sighted through the cleft on his chin at the huddled creature on the bench. "You!" he grated, and everyone swung around to stare at him. He thumped the sleeping man's ankle with the side of his foot. "You!" Everyone looked at the bench.

The tattered man said "Whuh-wuh-wuh-wuh," and smacked his lips. Suddenly he was bolt upright, staring.

"You!" barked the black-browed man. He pointed to the butt. "Pick that up!"

The tattered man looked at him and down at the butt. His hand strayed to his mouth, felt blindly on and around it. He looked down again at the butt and dull recognition began to filter into his face. "Oh, sure, boss, sure," he whined. He cringed low, beginning to stoop down off the bench but afraid to stop talking, afraid to turn his gaze away from the danger point. "I don't make no trouble for anybody, mister, not me, honest I don't," he wheedled. "A feller gets down on his luck, you know how it is, but I never make trouble, mister . . ."

"Pick it up!"

"Oh sure, sure, right away, boss."

That was when Don, to his amazement, felt himself approaching the black-browed man. He tapped him on the shoulder.

"Mister," he said. He prayed that his tight voice would not break. "Mister, make me pick it up, huh?"

"What?"

Don waved at the tattered man. "A two-year-old kid could push him around. So what are you proving, you're a big man or something? Make me pick up the butt, you're such a big man."

"Get away from me," said the black-browed man. He took two quick paces backward. "I know what you are, you're one of those subway hoodlums."

Don caught a movement from the corner of his eye. The tattered man had one knee on the platform, and was leaning forward to pick up the butt. "Get away from that," he snapped, and kicked the butt onto the local tracks.

"Sure, boss, sure, I don't want no . . ."

"Get away from me, both of you," said the black-browed man. He was preparing for flight. Don suddenly realized that he was afraid—afraid that he and the tattered man might join forces, or perhaps even that they had set the whole thing up in advance. He laughed. The black-browed man backed into a pillar. And just then a train roared in, settling the matter.

Something touched Don between the shoulder blades and he leaped as if it had been an icepick. But it was one of the women. "I just had to tell you, that was very brave. You're a fine young man," she said. She sniffed in the direction of the distant tweed-clad figure and marched to the train. It was a local. Don watched it go, and smiled. He felt good.

"Mister, you like to save my life, you did. I don't want no trouble, you unnerstan', I never do. Feller gets down on his luck once in a wh—"

"Shaddup!" said Don. He turned away and froze. Then he went back to the man and snatched off the old hat. The man cringed.

"I know who you are. You just got back from the can. You got sent up for attackin' a girl."

"I ain't done a *thing*," whispered the man. "Gimme back my hat, please, mister?"

Don looked down at him. He should walk away, he ought to leave this hulk to rot, but his questing mind was against him. He threw the hat on the man's lap and wiped his fingers on the side of his jacket. "I saw you stayin' out of trouble three nights ago on Mulberry Street. Followin' a girl into a house there."

"It was you chased me," said the man. "Oh God." He tucked himself up on the bench in a uterine position and began to weep.

"Cut that out," Don snarled. "I ain't hit you. If I wanted I coulda thrown you in front of that train, right?"

"Yeah, instead you saved me f'm that killer," said the man brokenly. "Y'r a prince, mister. Y'r a real prince, that's what you are."

"You goin' to stay away from that girl?"

"*Your girl?* Look, I'll never even walk past her house no more. I'll kill anybody looks at her."

"Never mind that. Just *you* stay away from her."

The express roared in. Don rose and so did the man. Don shoved him back to the bench. "Take the next one."

"Yeah, sure, anything you say. Just you say the word."

Don thought, *I'll ask him what it is that makes it worth the risk, chance getting sent up for life just for a thing like that.* Then, No, he thought. *I think I know why.*

He got on the train.

He sat down and stared dully ahead. *A man will give up anything, his freedom, his life even, for a sense of power. How much am I giving up? How should I know?*

He looked at the advertisements. "Kulkies are better." "The better skin cream." He wondered if anyone ever wanted to know what these things were better *than.* "For that richer, creamier, safer lather." "Try Miss Phoebe for that better, more powerful power."

He wondered, and wondered . . .

Summer dusk, all the offices closed, the traffic gone, no one and nothing in a hurry for a little while. Don put his back against a board fence where he could see the entrance, and took out a toothpick. She might be going out, she might be coming home, she might be home and not go out, she might be out and not come home. He'd stick around.

He never even got the toothpick wet.

She stood at the top of the steps, looking across at him. He simply looked back. There were many things he might have done. Rushed across. Waved. Done a time-step. Looked away. Run. Fallen down.

But he did nothing, and the single fact that filled his perceptions at that moment was that as long as she stood there with russet gleaming in her black hair, with her sad, sad cups-for-laughter eyes turned to him, with the thin summer cloak whipping up and falling to her clean straight body, why there was nothing he could do.

She came straight across to him. He broke the toothpick and dropped it, and waited. She crossed the sidewalk and stopped in front of him, looking at his eyes, his mouth, his eyes. "You don't even remember me."

"I remember you all right."

She leaned closer. The whites of her eyes showed under her pupils when she did that, like the high crescent moon in the tropics that floats startlingly on its back. These two crescents were twice as startling. "I don't think you do."

"Over there." With his chin he indicated her steps. "The other night."

It was then, at last, that she smiled, and the eyes held what they were made for. "I saw him again."

"He try anything?"

She laughed. "He *ran!* He was afraid of me. I don't think anybody was ever afraid of me."

"I am."

"Oh, that's the silliest—" She stopped, and again leaned toward him. "You mean it, don't you?"

He nodded.

"Don't ever be afraid of me," she said gravely, "not *ever.* What did you do to that man?"

"Nothin'. Talked to him."

"You didn't hurt him?"

He nodded.

"I'm glad," she said. "He's sick and he's ugly and he's bad, too, I guess, but I think he's been hurt enough. What's your name?"

"Don."

She counted on her fingers. "Don is a Spanish grandee. Don is putting on clothes. Don is the sun coming up in the morning. Don is . . . is the opposite of up. You're a whole lot of things, Don." Her eyes widened. "You laughed!"

"Was that wrong?"

"Oh, *no!* But I didn't know you ever laughed.

"I watched you for three hours the other night and *you* didn't laugh. You didn't even talk."

"I would've talked if I'd known you were there. Where were you?"

"That all-night joint. I followed you."

He looked at his shoeshine. With his other foot, he carefully stepped on it.

"Why did you follow me? Were you going to talk to me?"

"No!" he said. "No, by God, I wasn't. I wouldn'ta."

"Then why did you follow me?"

"I liked looking at you. I liked seeing you walk." He glanced across at the brownstone steps. "I didn't want anything to happen to you, all alone like that."

"Oh, I didn't care."

"That's what you said that night."

The shadow that crossed her face crossed swiftly, and she laughed. "It's all right now."

"Yeah, but what was it?"

"Oh," she said. Her head moved in an impatient gesture, but she smiled at the sky.

"There was nothing and nobody. I left school. Daddy was mad at me. Kids from school acted sorry for me. Other kids, the ones you saw, they made me tired. I was tired because they were the same way all the time about the same things all the time, and I was tired because they kept me up so late."

"What did you leave school for?"

"I found out what it was for."

"It's for learning stuff."

"It isn't," she said positively. "It's for learning how to learn. And I know that already. I can learn anything. Why did you come here today?"

"I wanted to see you. Where were you going when you came out?"

"Here," she said, tapping her foot. "I saw you from the window. I was waiting for you. I was waiting for you yesterday too. What's the matter?"

He grunted.

"Tell me, tell me!"

"I never had a girl talk to me like you do."

"Don't you like the way I talk?" she asked anxiously.

"Oh for Pete's sake it ain't that!" he exploded. Then he half-smiled at her. "It's just I had a crazy idea. I had the idea you always talk like this. I mean, to anybody."

"I don't, I don't!" she breathed. "Honestly, you've got to believe that. Only you. I've always talked to you like this."

"What do you mean always?"

"Well, everybody's got somebody to talk to, all their life. You know what they like to talk about and when they like to say nothing, when you can be just silly and when they'd rather be serious and important. The only thing you don't know is their face. For that you wait. And then one day you see the face, and then you have it all."

"You ain't talkin' about *me!*"

"Yes I am."

"Look," he said. He had to speak between heartbeats. He had never felt like this in his whole life before. "You could be—takin' a—*awful* chance."

She shook her head happily.

"Did you ever think maybe everybody ain't like that?"

"It doesn't matter. I am."

His face pinched up. "Suppose I just walked away now and never saw you again."

"You wouldn't."

"But suppose."

"Why then I—I'd've had this. Talking to you."

"Hey, you're crying!"

"Well," she said, "there you were, walking away."

"You'd've called me back though."

She turned on him so quickly a tear flew clear off her face and fell sparkling to the back of his hand. Her eyes blazed. "Never that!" she said between her teeth. "I want you to stay, but if you want to go, you go, that's all. All *I* want to do is make you want to stay. I've managed so far . . ."

"How many minutes?" he teased.

"Minutes? Years," she said seriously.

"The—somebody you talked to, you kind of made him up, huh?"

"I suppose."

"How could he ever walk away?"

"Easiest thing in the world," she said. "Somebody like that, they're somebody to live up to. It isn't always easy. You've been very patient," she said. She reached out and touched his cheek.

He snatched her wrist and held it, hard. "You know what I think," he said in a rough whisper, because it was all he had. "I think you're out of your goddam head."

She stood very straight with her eyes closed. She was trembling.

"What's your name, anyway?"

"Joyce."

"I love you too, Joyce. Come on, I want you to meet a friend of mine. It's a long ride on the subway and I'll tell you all about it."

He tried hard but he couldn't tell her all of it. For some of it there were no words at all. For some of it there were no words he could use. She was attentive and puzzled. He bought flowers from a cart, just a few—red and yellow rosebuds.

"Why flowers?"

He remembered the mirror. That was one of the things he hadn't been able to talk about. "It's just what you do," he said, "bring flowers."

"I bet she loves you."

"Whaddaya mean, she's pushin' sixty!"

"All the same," said Joyce, "if she does she's not going to like me."

They went up in the elevator. In the elevator he kissed her.

"What's the matter, Don?"

"If you want to crawl around an' whimper like a puppy-dog," he whispered, "if you feel useful as a busted broom-handle and worth about two wet sneezes in a hailstorm—this is a sense of power?"

"I don't understand."

"Never mind."

In the corridor he stopped. He rubbed a smudge off her nose with his thumb. "She's sorta funny," he said. "Just give her a little time. She's quite a gal. She looks like Sunday school and talks the same way but she knows the score. Joyce, she's the best friend I ever had."

"All right all right all *right!* I'll be good."

He kissed where the smudge had been.

"Come on."

One of Miss Phoebe's envelopes was stuck to the door by its flap. On it was his name.

They looked at one another and then he took the envelope down and got the note from it.

Don:
I am not at home. Please phone me this evening.

P.W.

"Don, I'm *sorry!*"

"I shoulda phoned. I wanted to surprise her."

"Surprise her? She knew you were coming."

"She didn't know you were coming. Damn it anyway."

"Oh it's all right," she said. She took his hand. "There'll be other times. Come on. What'll you do with those?"

"The flowers? I dunno. Want 'em?"

"They're hers," said Joyce.

He gave her a puzzled look. "I got a lot of things to get used to. What do you mean when you say somethin' that way?"

"Almost exactly what I say."

He put the flowers against the door and they went away.

The phone rang four times before Miss Phoebe picked it up.

"It is far too late," she said frigidly, "for telephone calls. You should have called earlier, Don. However, it's just as well. I want you to know that I am *very* displeased with you. I have given you certain privileges, young man, but among them is not that of calling on me unexpectedly."

"Miss—"

"Don't interrupt. In addition, I have never indicated to you that you were free to—"

"But Miss Ph—"

"—to bring to my home any casual acquaintance you happen to have scraped up in heaven knows where—"

"Miss *Phoebe!* Please! I'm in *jail.*"

"—and invade my—you are *what?*"

"Jail, Miss Phoebe, I got arrested."

"Where are you now?"

"County. But you don't need—"

"I'm coming right down," said Miss Phoebe.

"No, Miss Phoebe, I didn't call you for that. You go back to b—"

Miss Phoebe hung up.

Miss Phoebe strode into the County Jail with grim familiarity, and before her, red tape disappeared like confetti in a blast furnace. Twelve minutes after she arrived she had Don out of his cell and into a private room, his crisp new jail-record card before her, and was regarding him with a strange expression of wooden ferocity.

"Sit there," she said, as the door clicked shut behind an awed and reverberating policeman.

Don sat. He was rumpled and sleepy, angry and hurt, but he smiled when he said, "I never thought you'd come. I never expected that, Miss Phoebe."

She did not respond. Instead she said coldly, "Indeed? Well, young man, the matters I have to discuss will not wait." She sat down opposite him and picked up the card.

"Miss Phoebe," he said, "could you be wrong about what you said about me and girls . . . that original sin business, and all? I'm all mixed up, Miss Phoebe. I'm all mixed up!" In his face was a desperate appeal.

"Be quiet," she said sternly. She was studying the card. "This," she said, putting the card down on the table with a dry snap, "tells a great deal, but says nothing. Public nuisance, indecent exposure, suspicion of rape, impairing the morals of a minor, resisting an officer, and destruction of city property. Would you care to explain this—this catalogue to me?"

"What you mean, tell you what happened?"

"That is what I mean."

"Miss Phoebe, where is she? What they done with her?"

"With whom? You mean the girl? I do not know; moreover, it doesn't concern me and it should no longer concern you. Didn't she get you into this?"

"I got her into it. Look, could you find out, Miss Phoebe?"

"I do not know what I will do. You'd better explain to me what happened."

Again the look of appeal, while she waited glacially. He scratched his head hard with both hands at once. "Well, we went to your house."

"I am aware of that."

"Well, you wasn't home so we went out. She said take her father's car. I got a license; it was all right. So we went an' got the car and rode around. Well, we went to a place an' she showed me how to dance some. We went somewheres else an' ate. Then we parked over by the lake. Then, well, a cop come over and poked around an' made some trouble an' I got mad an' next thing you know here we are."

"I asked you," said Miss Phoebe evenly, "what happened?"

"Aw-w." It was a long-drawn sound, an admixture of shame and irritation. "We were in the car an' this cop came pussyfootin' up. He had a big flashlight *this* long. I seen him comin'. When he got to the car we was all right. I mean, I had my arm around Joyce, but that's all."

"What *had* you been doing?"

"Talkin', that's all, just talkin', and . . ."

"And what?"

"Miss Phoebe," he blurted, "I always been able to say anything to you I wanted, about anything. Listen, I *got* to tell you about this. That thing that happened, the way it is with me and girls because of the rat, well, it just wasn't there with Joyce, it was nothin', it was like it never happened. Look, you and me, we had that thing with the hands; it was . . . I can't say it, you know how good it was. Well, with Joyce it was somepin' different. It was like I could fly. I never felt like that before. Miss Phoebe, I had too much these last few days, I don't know what goes on . . . you was right, you was always right, but this I had with Joyce, that was right too, and they can't both be right." He reached across the table, not quite far enough to touch her. The reaching was in his eyes and his voice.

Miss Phoebe stiffened a spine already straight as a bowstring. "I have asked you a simple question and all you can do is gibber at me. *What happened in that car?*"

Slowly he came back to the room, the hard chair, the bright light, Miss Phoebe's implacable face. "That cop," he said. "He claimed he seen us. Said he was goin' to run us in, I said what for, he said carryin' on like that in a public place. There was a lot of argument. Next thing you know he told Joyce to open her dress, he said when it was the way he seen it before he'd let me know. Joyce she begun to cry an' I tol' her not to do it, an' the cop said if I was goin' to act like that he would run us in for *sure*. You know, I got the idea if she'd done it he'da left us alone after?

"So I got real mad, I climbed out of the car, I tol' him we ain't done nothin', he pushes me one side, he shines the light in on Joyce. She squinchin' down in the seat, cryin', he says, 'Come on, you, you know what to do.' I hit the flashlight. I on'y meant to get the light off her, but I guess I hit it kind of hard. It came up and clonked him in the teeth. Busted the flashlight too. That's the city property I destroyed. He started to cuss and I tol' him not to. He hit me and opened the car door an' shoved me in. He got in the back an' took out his gun and tol' me to drive to the station house." He shrugged. "So I had to. That's all."

"It is not all. You have not told me what you did before the policeman came."

He looked at her, startled. "Why, I—we—" His face flamed, "I love her," he said, with difficulty, as if he spoke words in a new and troublesome tongue. "I mean I . . . do, that's all."

"What did you do?"

"I kissed her."

"What else did you do?"

"I—" He brought up one hand, made a vague circular gesture, dropped the hand. He met her gaze. "Like when you love somebody, that's all."

"Are you going to tell me exactly what you did, or are you not?"

"Miss Phoebe . . ." he whispered, "I ain't never seen you look like that."

"I want the whole filthy story," she said. She leaned forward so far that her chin was only a couple of inches from the tabletop. Her protruding, milky eyes seemed to whirl, then it was as if a curtain over them had been twitched aside, and they blazed.

Don stood up. "Miss Phoebe," he said. "Miss Phoebe . . ." It was the voice of terror itself.

Then a strange thing happened. It may have been the mere fact of his rising, of being able, for a moment, to stand over her, look down on her. "Miss Phoebe," he said, "there—ain't—no—filthy—story."

She got up and without another word marched to the door. As she opened it the boy raised his fists. His wrists and forearms corded and writhed. His head went back, his lungs filled, and with all his strength he shouted the filthiest word he knew. It had one syllable, it was sibilant and explosive, it was immensely satisfying.

Miss Phoebe stopped, barely in balance between one pace and the next, momentarily paralyzed. It was like the breaking of the drive-coil on a motion picture projector.

"They locked her up," said Don hoarsely. "They took her away with two floozies an' a ole woman with DT's. She ain't never goin' to see me again. Her ole man'll kill me if he ever sets eyes on me. You were all I had left. Get the hell out of here . . ."

She reached the door as it was opened from the other side by a policeman, who said, "What's goin' on here?"

"Incorrigible," Miss Phoebe spat, and went out. They took Don back to his cell.

The courtroom was dark and its pew-like seats were almost empty. Outside it was raining, and the statue of Justice had a broken nose. Don sat with his head in his hands, not caring about the case then being heard, not caring about his own, not caring about people or things or feelings. For five days he had not cared about the whitewashed cell he had shared with the bicycle thief; the two prunes and weak coffee for breakfast, the blare of the radio in the inner court; the day in, day out screaming of the man on the third tier who hoarsely yelled, "I din't do it I din't do it I din't do . . ."

His name was called and he was led or shoved—he didn't care which—before the bench. A man took his hand and put it on a book held by another man who said something rapidly. "I do," said Don. And then Joyce was there, led up by a tired kindly old fellow with eyes like hers and an unhappy mouth. Don looked at her once and was sure she wasn't even trying to recognize his existence. If she had left her hands at her sides, she was close enough for him to have touched one of them secretly, for they stood side by side, facing the judge. But she kept her hands in front of her and stood with her eyes closed, with her whole face closed, her lashes down on her cheeks like little barred gates.

The cop, the lousy cop was there too, and he reeled off things about Don and things about Joyce that were things they hadn't done, couldn't have done, wouldn't do . . . he cared about that for a moment, but as he listened it seemed very clear that what the cop was saying was about two other people who knew a lot about flesh and nothing about love; and after that he stopped caring again.

When the cop was finished, the kindly tired man came forward and said that he would press no charges against this young man if he promised he would not see his daughter again until she was twenty-one. The judge pushed down his glasses and looked over them at Don. "Will you make that promise?"

Don looked at the tired man, who turned away. He looked at Joyce, whose eyes were closed. "Sure," he told the judge.

There was some talk about respecting the laws of society which were there to protect innocence, and how things would be pretty bad if Don ever appeared before that bench again, and next thing he knew he was being led through the corridors back to the jail, where they returned the wallet and fountain pen they had taken away from him, made him sign a book, unlocked three sets of doors and turned him loose. He stood in the rain and saw, half a block away, Joyce and her father getting into a cab.

About two hours later one of the jail guards came out and saw him. "Hey, boy. You like it here?"

Don pulled the wet hair out of his eyes and looked at the man, and turned and walked off without saying anything.

"Well, hello!"

"Now you get away from me, girl. You're just going to get me in trouble and I don't want no trouble."

"I won't make any trouble for you, really I won't. Don't you want to talk to me?"

"Look, you know me, you heard about me. Hey, you been sick?"

"No."

"You look like you been sick. I was sick a whole lot. Fellow down on his luck, everything happens. Here comes the old lady from the delicatessen. She'll see us."

"That's all right."

"She'll see you, she knows you, she'll see you talkin' to me. I don't want no trouble."

"There won't be any trouble. Please don't be afraid. I'm not afraid of you."

"I ain't scared of you either but one night that young fellow of yours, that tall skinny one, he said he'll throw me under a train if I talk to you."

"I have no fellow."

"Yes you have, that tall skin—"

"Not anymore. Not anymore . . . talk to me for a while. Please talk to me."

"You sure? You sure he ain't . . . you ain't . . ."

"I'm sure. He's gone, he doesn't write, he doesn't care."

"You been sick."

"No, no, no, no!—I want to tell you something: if ever you eat your heart out over something, hoping and wishing for it, dreaming and wanting it, doing everything you can to make yourself fit for it, and then that something comes along, know what to do?"

"I do' wan' no trouble . . . yea, grab it!"

"No. *Run!* Close your eyes and turn your back and run away. Because wanting something you've never had hurts, sometimes, but not as much as having it and then losing it."

"I never had *nothing*."

"You did so. And you were locked up for years."

"I didn't have it, girl. I used it. It wasn't mine."

"You didn't lose it, then—ah, I *see!*"

"If a cop comes along he'll pinch me just because I'm talkin' to you. I'm just a bum, I'm down on my luck, we can't stand out here like this."

"Over there, then. Coffee."

"I ain't got but four cents."

"Come on. I have enough."

"What'sa matter with you, you want to talk to a bum like me!"

"Come on, come on . . . listen, listen to this:

" 'It is late last night the dog was speaking of you; the snipe was speaking of you in her deep marsh. It is you are the lonely bird throughout the woods; and that you may be without a mate until you find me.

" 'You promised me and you said a lie to me, that you would be before me where the sheep are flocked. I gave a whistle and three hundred cries to you; and I found nothing there but fleeting lamb.

" 'You promised me a thing that was hard for you, a ship of gold under a silver mast; twelve towns and a market in all of them, and a fine white court by the side of the sea.

" 'You promised me a thing that is not possible; that you would give me gloves of the skin of a fish; that you would give me shoes of the skin of a bird, and a suit of the dearest silk in Ireland.

" 'My mother said to me not to be talking with you, to-day or to-morrow or on Sunday. It was a bad time she took for telling me that, it was shutting the door after the house was robbed . . .

" 'You have taken the east from me, you have taken the west from me, you have taken what is before me and what is behind me; you have taken the moon, you have taken the sun from me, and my fear is great you have taken God from me.' "

". . . That's something I remembered. I remember, I remember everything."

"That's a lonesome thing to remember."

"Yes . . . and no one knows who she was. A man called Yeats heard this Irish girl lamenting, and took it down."

"I don't know, I seen you around, I never saw you like this, you been sick."

"Drink your coffee and we'll have another cup."

Dear Miss Phoebe:

Well dont fall over with surprise to get a letter from me I am not much at letter writing to any body and I never thot I would wind up writing to you.

I know you was mad at me and I guess I was mad at you too. Why I am writing this is I am trying to figure out what it was all about. I know why I was mad I was mad because you said there was something dirty about what I did. Mentioning no names. I did not do nothing dirty and so thats why I was mad.

But all I know about you Miss Phoebe is you was mad I dont know why. I never done nothing to you I was ascared to in the first place and anyway I thot you was my friend. I thot anytime there was something on my mind I could not figure it out, all I had to do was to tell you. This one time I was in more trouble then I ever had in my entire. All you did you got mad at me.

Now if you want to stay mad at me thats your busnis but I wish you would tell me why. I wish we was freinds again but okay if you dont want to.

Well write to me if you feel like it at the Seamans Institute thats where I am picking up my mail these days I took a ride on a tank ship and was sick most of the time but thats life.

I am going to get a new fountain pen this one wont spell right (joke). So take it easy yours truly Don.

Don came out of the Seaman's Institute and stood looking at the square. A breeze lifted and dropped, carrying smells of fish and gasoline, spices, sea-salt, and a slight chill. Don buttoned up his pea-jacket and pushed his hands down into the pockets. Miss Phoebe's letter was there, straight markings on inexpensive, efficient paper, the envelope torn almost in two because of the way he had opened it. He could see it in his mind's eye without effort.

My Dear Don:

Your letter came as something of a surprise to me. I thought you might write, but not that you would claim unawareness of the reasons for my feelings toward you.

You will remember that I spent a good deal of time and energy in acquainting you with the nature of Good and the nature of Evil. I went even further and familiarized you with a kind of union between souls which, without me, would have been impossible to you. And I feel I made quite clear to you the fact that a certain state of grace is necessary to the achievement of these higher levels of being.

Far from attempting to prove to me that you were a worthy pupil of the teachings I might have given you, you plunged immediately into actions which indicate that there is a complete confusion in your mind as to Good and Evil. You have grossly defiled yourself, almost as if you insisted upon being unfit. You engaged in foul and carnal practices which make a mockery of the pure meetings of the higher selves which once were possible to you.

You should understand that the Sources of the power I once offered you are ancient and sacred and not to be taken lightly. Your complete lack of reverence for these antique matters is to me the most unforgivable part of your inexcusable conduct. The Great Thinkers who developed these powers in ancient times surely meant a better end for them than that they be given to young animals.

Perhaps one day you will become capable of understanding the meaning of reverence, obedience, and honor to ancient mysteries. At that time I would be interested to hear from you again.

Yours very truly,
(Miss) Phoebe Watkins

Don growled deep in his throat. Subsequent readings would serve to stew all the juices from the letter; one reading was sufficient for him to realize that in the note was no affection and no forgiveness. He remembered the birthday cake with a pang. He remembered the painful hot lump in his throat when she had ordered him to wash his face; she had *cared* whether he washed his face or not.

He went slowly down to the street. He looked older; he felt older. He had used his seaman's papers for something else besides entree to a clean and inexpensive dormitory. Twice he had thought he was near that strange, blazing loss of self he had experienced with Miss Phoebe, just in staring at the living might of the sea. Once, lying on his back on deck in a clear moonless night, he had been sure of it. There had been a sensation of having been *chosen* for something, of having been fingertip-close to some simple huge fact, some great normal coalescence of time and distance, a fusion and balance, like yin and Yang, in all things. But it had escaped him, and now it was of little assistance to him to know that his sole authority in such things considered him as disqualified.

"Foul an' carnal practices," he said under his breath. *Miss Phoebe*, he thought, *I bet I could tell you a thing or two about 'reverence, obedience an' honor to ancient mysteries*. In a flash of deep understanding, he saw that those who hold themselves aloof from the flesh are incapable of comprehending this single fact about those who do not: only he who is free to take it is truly conscious of what he does when he leaves it alone.

Someone was in his way. He stepped aside and the man was still in the way. He snapped out of his introspection and brought his sight back to earth, clothed in an angry scowl.

For a moment he did not recognize the man. He was still tattered, but he was clean and straight, and his eyes were clear. It was obvious that he felt the impact of Don's scowl, he retreated a short pace, and with the step were the beginnings of old reflexes; to cringe, to flee. But then he held hard, and Don had to stop.

"Y'own the sidewalk?" Don demanded. "Oh—it's you."

"I got to talk to you," the man said in a strained voice.

"I got nothin' to talk to you about," said Don. "Get back underground where you belong. Go root for cigar butts in the subway."

"It's about Joyce," said the man.

Don reached and gathered together the lapels of the man's old jacket. "I told you once to stay away from her. That means don't even talk about her."

"Get your hands off me," said the man evenly.

Don grunted in surprise, and let him go.

The man said, "I had somepin' to tell you, but now you can go to hell."

Don laughed. "What do you know! What are you—full of hash or somethin'?"

The man tugged at the lapels and moved to pass Don. Don caught his arm. "Wait. What did you want to tell me?"

The man looked into his face. "Remember you said you was going to kill me, I get near her?"

"I remember."

"I seen her this morning. I seen her yesterday an' four nights last week."

"The hell you did!"

"You got to get that through your head 'fore I tell you anything."

Don shook his head slowly. "This beats anything I ever seen. What happened to you?"

As if he had not heard, the man said, "I found out what ship you was on. I watched the papers. I figured you'd go to the Institoot for mail. I been waitin' three hours."

Don grabbed the thin biceps. "Hey. Is somethin' wrong with Joyce?"

"You give a damn?"

"Listen," said Don, "I can still break your damn neck."

The man simply shrugged.

Baffled, Don said, between his teeth, "Talk. You said you wanted to talk—go ahead."

"Why ain't you wrote to her?"

"What's that to you?"

"It's a whole lot to her."

"You seem to know a hell of a lot."

"I told you I see her all the time," the man pointed out.

"She must talk a lot."

"To me," said the man, closing his eyes, "a whole lot."

"She wouldn't want to hear from me," Don said. Then he barked, "What are you tryin' to tell me? You and her—what are you to her? You're not messin' with her, comin' braggin' to me about it?"

The man put a hand on Don's chest and pushed him away. There was disgust on his face, and a strange dignity. "Cut it out," he said. "Look, I don't like you. I don't like doin' what I'm doin' but I got to. Joyce, she's been half crazy, see. I don't know why she started to talk to me. Maybe she just didn't care anymore, maybe she felt so bad she wanted to dive in a swamp an' I was the nearest thing to it. She been talkin' to me, she . . . smiles when she sees me. She'll eat with me, even."

"You shoulda stayed away from her," Don mumbled uncertainly.

"Yeah, maybe. And suppose I did, what would she do? If she didn't have me to talk to, maybe it would be someone else. Maybe someone else wouldn't . . . be as . . . leave her . . ."

"You mean, take care of her," said Don softly.

"Well, if you want to call it that. Take up her time, anyway, she can't get into any other trouble." He looked at Don beseechingly. "I ain't never laid a hand on her. You believe that?"

Don said, "Yeah, I believe that."

"You going to see her?"

Don shook his head.

The man said in a breathy, shrill voice, "I oughta punch you in the mouth!"

"Shaddup," said Don miserably. "What you want me to see her for?"

Suddenly there were tears in the weak blue eyes. But the voice was still steady. "I ain't got nothin'. I'll never have nothin'. This is all I can do, make you go back. Why won't you go back?"

"She wouldn't want to see me," said Don, "after what I done."

"You better go see her," whispered the man. "She thinks she ain't fit to live, gettin' you in jail and all. She thinks it was her fault. She thinks you feel the same way. She even . . . she even thinks that's right. You dirty rotten no-good lousy—" he cried. He suddenly raised his fists and hit his own temples with them, and made a bleating sound. He ran off toward the waterfront.

Don watched him go, stunned to the marrow. Then he turned blindly and started across the street. There was a screeching of brakes, a flurry of movement, and he found himself standing with one hand on the front fender of a taxi.

"Where the hell you think you're goin'?"

Stupidly, Don said, "What?"

"What's the matter with you?" roared the cabby.

Don fumbled his way back to the rear door. "A lot, a whole lot," he said as he got in. "Take me to 37 Mulberry Street," he said.

It was three days later, in the evening, when he went to see Miss Phoebe.

"Well!" she said when she opened to his ring.

"Can I come in?"

She did not move. "You received my letter?"

"Sure."

"You understood . . ."

"I got the idea."

"There were—ah—certain conditions."

"Yeah," said Don. "I got to be capable of understandin' the meaning of reverence, obedience, an' honor to certain ancient mysteries."

"Have you just memorized it, or do you feel you really are capable?"

"Try me."

"Very well." She moved aside.

He came in, shoving a blue knitted cap into his side pocket. He shucked out of the pea jacket. He was wearing blue slacks and a black sweater with a white shirt and blue tie. He was as different from the scrubbed schoolboy neatness of his previous visit as he was from the ill-fit flashiness of his first one. "How've you been?"

"Well, thank you," she answered coolly. "Sit down."

They sat facing one another. Don was watchful, Miss Phoebe wary.

"You've . . . grown," said Miss Phoebe. It was made not so much as a statement, but as an admission.

"I did a lot," said Don. "Thought a lot. You're so right about people in the world that work for—call it yin an' Yang—an' know what they're doin', why they're doin' it. All you got to do is look around you. Read the papers."

She nodded. "Do you have any difficulty in determining which side these people are on?"

"No more."

"If that's true," she said, "it's wonderful." She cleared her throat. "You've seen that—that girl again."

"I couldn't lie."

"Are you willing to admit that beastliness is no substitute for the true meeting of minds?"

"Absolutely."

"Well!" she said. "This *is* progress!" She leaned forward suddenly. "Oh, Don, that wasn't for you. Not you! You are destined for great things, my boy. You have no idea."

"I think I have."

"And you're willing to accept my teaching?"

"Just as much as you'll teach me."

"I'll make tea," she said, almost gaily. She rose and as she passed him she squeezed his shoulder. He grinned.

When she was in the kitchenette he said, "Fellow in my neighborhood just got back from a long stretch for hurting a little girl."

"Oh?" she said. "What is his name?"

"I don't know."

"Find out," she said. "They have to be watched."

"Why?"

"Animals," she said, "wild animals. They have to be caught and caged, to protect society."

He nodded. The gesture was his own, out of her range. He said, "I ate already. Don't go to no trouble."

"Very well. Just some cookies." She emerged with the tea service. "It's good to have you back. I'm rather surprised. I'd nearly given you up."

He smiled. "Never do that."

She poured boiling water from the kettle into the teapot and brought it out. "You're almost like a different person."

"How come?"

"Oh, you—you're much more self-assured." She looked at him searchingly. "More complete. I think the word for it is 'integrated.' Actually, I can't seem to . . . to . . . Don, you're not hiding anything from me, are you?"

"Me? Why, how could I do that?"

She seemed troubled. "I don't know." She gave him a quick glance, almost spoke, then shook her head slightly.

"What's the matter? I do something wrong?"

"No, oh no."

They were quiet until the tea was steeped and poured.

"Miss Phoebe . . ."

"What is it?"

"Just what did you think went on in that car before we got arrested?"

"Isn't that rather obvious?"

"Well," he said, with a quick smile, "to me, yeah. I was there."

"You can be cleansed," she said confidently.

"Can I now! Miss Phoebe, I just want to get this clear in my mind. I think you got the wrong idea, and I'd like to straighten you out. I didn't go the whole way with that girl."

"You didn't?"

He shook his head.

"Oh," she said. "The policeman got there in time after all."

He put down his teacup very carefully. "We had lots of time. What I'm telling you is we just didn't."

"Oh," she said. "Oh!"

"What's the matter, Miss Phoebe?"

"Nothing," she said, tensely. "Nothing. This . . . puts a different complexion on things."

"I sort of thought you'd be glad."

"But of course!" She whirled on him. "You are telling me the truth, Don?"

"You can get in an' out of County," he reminded her. "There's records of her medical examination there that proves it, you don't believe me."

"Oh," she said, "oh dear." Suddenly her face cleared. "Perhaps I've underestimated you. What you're telling me is that you . . . you didn't *want* to, is that it? But you said that the old memory of the rat left you when you were with her. Why didn't you—*why?*"

"Hey—easy, take it easy! You want to know why, it was because it wasn't the time. What we had would last, it would keep. We din't have to grab."

"You . . . really felt that way about her?"

He nodded.

"I had no idea," she said in a stunned whisper. "And afterward . . . did you . . . do you still . . ."

"You can find out, can't you? You know ways to find out what I'm thinking."

"I can't," she cried. "I can't! Something has happened to you. I can't get in, it's as if there were a steel plate between us!"

"I'm sorry," he said with grave cheerfulness.

She closed her eyes and made some huge internal effort. When she looked up, she seemed quite composed. "You are willing to work with me?"

"I want to."

"Very well. I don't know what has happened and I must find out, even if I have to use . . . drastic measures."

"Anything you say, Miss Phoebe."

"Lie down over there."

"Oh that? I'm longer than it is!" He went to the little sofa and maneuvered himself so that at least his shoulder blades and head were horizontal. "Like so?"

"That will do. Make yourself just as comfortable as you can." She threw a tablecloth over the lampshade and turned out the light in the kitchenette. Then she drew up a chair near his head, out of his visual range. She sat down.

It got very quiet in the room. "You're sleepy, you're so sleepy," she said softly. "You're sl—"

"No I ain't," he said briskly.

"Please," she said, "fall in with this. Just let your mind go blank and listen to me."

"Okay."

She droned on and on. His eyes half-closed, opened, then closed all the way. He began to breathe more slowly, more deeply.

". . . And sleep, sleep, but hear my voice, hear what I am saying, can you hear me?"

"Yes," he said heavily.

"Lie there and sleep, and sleep, but answer me truthfully, tell me only the truth, the truth, answer me, whom do you love?"

"Joyce."

"You told me you restrained yourself the night you were arrested. Is this true?"

"Yes."

Miss Phoebe's eyes narrowed. She wet her lips, wrung her hands.

"The union you had with me, that flight of soul, was that important to you?"

"Yes."

"Would you like to do more of it?"

"Yes."

"Don't you realize that it is a greater, more intimate thing than any union of the flesh?"

"Yes."

"Am I not the only one with whom you can do it?"

"No."

Miss Phoebe bit her lip. "Tell the truth, the truth," she said raggedly. "Who else?"

"Joyce."

"Have you ever done it with Joyce?"

"Not yet."

"Are you sure you can?"

"I'm sure."

Miss Phoebe got up and went into the kitchenette. She put her forehead against the cool tiles of the wall beside the refrigerator. She put her fingertips on her cheeks, and her hands contracted suddenly, digging her fingers in, drawing her flesh downward until her scalding, tightshut eyes were dragged open from underneath. She uttered an almost soundless whimper.

After a moment she straightened up, squared her shoulders and went noiselessly back to her chair. Don slumbered peacefully.

"Don, go on sleeping. Can you hear me?"

"Yes."

"I want you to go down deeper and deeper and deeper, down and down to a place where there is nothing at all, anywhere, anywhere, except my voice, and everything I say is true. Go down, down, deep, deep . . ." On and on she went, until at last she reached down and gently rolled back one of his eyelids. She peered at the eye, nodded with satisfaction.

"Stay down there, Don, stay there."

She crouched in the chair and thought, hard. She knew of the difficulty of hypnotically commanding a subject to do anything repugnant to him. She also knew, however, that it is a comparatively simple matter to convince a subject that a certain person is a pillow, and then fix the command that a knife must be thrust into that pillow.

She pieced and fitted, and at last, "Don, can you hear me?"

His voice was a bare whisper, slurred, "Yes . . ."

"The forces of evil have done a terrible thing to Joyce, Don. When you see her again she will look as before. She will speak and act as before. But she is different. The real Joyce has been taken away. A substitute has been put in her place. The substitute is dangerous. You will know, when you see her. You will not trust her. You will not touch her. You will share nothing with her. You will put her aside and have nothing to do with her.

"But the real Joyce is alive and well, although she was changed. I saved her. When she was replaced by the substitute, I took the real Joyce and made her a part of me. So now when you talk to Miss Phoebe you are talking to Joyce, when you touch Miss Phoebe you are touching Joyce, when you kiss and hold and love Miss Phoebe you will be loving Joyce. Only through Miss Phoebe can you know Joyce, and they are one and the same. And you will never call Joyce by name again. Do you understand?"

"Miss . . . Phoebe is . . . Joyce now . . ."

"That's right."

Miss Phoebe was breathing hard. Her mouth was wet.

"You will remember none of this deep sleep, except what I have told you. Don," she whispered, "my dear, my dear . . ."

Presently she rose and threw the cloth off the lampshade. She felt the teapot; it was still quite hot. She emptied the hot-water pot and filled it again from the kettle. She sat down at the tea table, covered her eyes, and for a moment the only sound in the room was her deep, slow, controlled breathing as she oxygenated her lungs.

She sat up, refreshed, and poured tea. "Don! Don! Wake up, Don!"

He opened his eyes and stared unseeingly at the ceiling. Then he raised his head, sat up, shook himself.

"Goodness!" said Miss Phoebe. "You're getting positively absentminded. I like to be answered when I speak to you."

"Whuh? Hm?" He shook himself again and rose. "Sorry, Miss Phoebe. Guess I sorta . . . did you ask me something?"

"The tea, the tea," she said with pleasant impatience. "I've just poured."

"Oh," he said. "Good."

"Don," she said, "we're going to accomplish so *very* much."

"We sure are. And we'll do it a hell of a lot faster with your help."

"I beg—*what?*"

"Joyce and me," he said patiently. "The things you can do, that planting a reflection in a mirror the way you want it, and knowing who's at the door and on the phone and all . . . we can sure use those things."

"I—I'm afraid I don't . . ."

"Oh God, Miss Phoebe, don't! I hate to see you cut yourself up like this!"

"You were faking."

"You mean just now, the hypnosis routine? No I wasn't. You had me under all right. It's just that it won't stick with me. Everything worked but the commands."

"That's—impossible!"

"No it ain't. Not if I had a deeper command to remember 'em—and disregard 'em."

"Why didn't I think of that?" she said tautly. "*She* did it!"

He nodded.

"She's evil, Don, can't you see? I was only trying to save—"

"I know what you were tryin' to save," he interrupted, not unkindly. "You're in real good shape for a woman your age, Miss Phoebe. This power of yours, it keeps you going. Keeps your glands going. With you, that's a problem. With us, now, it'll be a blessing. Pity you never thought of that."

"Foul," she said, "how perfectly foul . . ."

"No it ain't!" he rapped. "Look, maybe we'll all get a chance to work together after all, and if we do, you'll get an idea what kind of chick Joyce is. I hope that happens. But mind you, if it don't, we'll get along. We'll do all you can do, in time."

"I'd *never* cooperate with evil!"

"You went and got yourself a little mixed up about that, Miss Phoebe. You told me yourself about yin an' Yang, how some folks set a course straight an' true an' never realize the boundary can twist around underneath them. You asked me just tonight was I sure which was which, an' I said yes. It's real simple. When you see somebody with power who is usin' it for what Yang stands for—good, an' light, an' all like that, you'll find he ain't usin' it for himself."

"I wasn't using it for myself!"

"No, huh?" He chuckled. "Who was it I was goin' to kiss an' hold just like it was Joyce?"

She moaned and covered her face. "I just wanted to keep you pure," she said indistinctly.

"Now that's a thing you got to get straightened out on. That's a big thing. Look here." He rose and went to the long bookcase. Through her fingers, she watched him. "Suppose this here's all the time that has passed since there was anything like a human being on earth." He moved his hand from one end of the top shelf to the other. "Maybe way back at the beginning they was no more 'n smart monkeys, but all the same they had whatever it is makes us human beings. These forces you talk about, they were operatin' then just like now. An' the cavemen an' the savages an' all, hundreds an' hundreds of years, they kept developing until we got humans like us.

"All right. You talk about ancient mysteries, your Yoga an' all. An' this tieup with virgins. Look, I'm going to show you somepin. You an' all your studyin' and copyin' the ancient secrets, you know how ancient they were? I'll show you." He put out his big hand and put three fingers side by side on the "modern" end of the shelf.

"Those three fingers covers it—down to about fourteen thousand years before Christ. Well, maybe the thing did work better without sex. But only by throwin' sex into study instead of where it was meant to go. Now you want to free yourself from sex in your thinkin', there's a much better way than that. You do it like Joyce an' me. We're a bigger unit together than you ever could be by yourself. An' we're not likely to get pushed around by our glands, like you. No offense, Miss Phoebe . . . so there's your *really* ancient mystery. Male an' female together; there's a power for you. Why you s'pose people in love get to fly so high, get to feel like gods?" He swept his hand the full length of the shelf. "A *real* ancient one."

"Wh-where did you learn all this?" she whispered.

"Joyce. Joyce and me, we figured it out. Look, she's not just any chick. She quit school because she learns too fast. She gets everything right now, this minute, as soon as she sees it. All her life everyone around her seems to be draggin' their feet. An' besides, she's like a kid. I don't mean childish, I don't mean simple, I mean like she believes in something even when there's no evidence around for it, she keeps on believing until the evidence comes along. There must be a word for that."

"Faith," said Miss Phoebe faintly.

He came and sat down near her. "Don't take it so hard, Miss Phoebe," he said feelingly. "It's just that you got to stand aside for a later model. If anybody's going to do Yang work in a world like this, they got to get rid of a lot of deadwood. I don't mean you're deadwood. I mean a lot of your ideas are. Like that fellow was in jail about the little girl, you say *watch 'im!* one false move an' back in the cage he goes. And all that guy wanted all his life was just to have a couple people around him who give a damn, 'scuse me, Miss Phoebe. He never had that, so he took what he could get from whoever was weaker'n him, and that was only girls. You should see him now, he's goin' to be our best man."

"You're a child. You can't undertake work like this. You don't know the powers you're playing with."

"Right. We're goin' to make mistakes. An' that's where you come in. Are you on?"

"I—don't quite—"

"We want your help," he said, and bluntly added, "but if you can't help, don't hinder."

"You'd want to work with me after I . . . Joyce, Joyce will hate me!"

"Joyce ain't afraid of you." Her face crumpled. He patted her clumsily on the shoulder. "Come on, what do you say?"

She sniffled, then turned red-rimmed, protruding eyes up to him. "If you want me. I'd have to . . . I'd like to talk to Joyce."

"Okay. JOYCE!"

Miss Phoebe started. "She—she's not—oh!" she cried as the doorknob turned. She said, "It's locked."

He grinned. "No it ain't."

Joyce came in. She went straight to Don, her eyes on his face, searching, and did not look around her until her hand was in his. Then she looked down at Miss Phoebe.

"This here, this is Joyce," Don said.

Joyce and Miss Phoebe held each other's eyes for a long moment, tense at first, gradually softening. At last Miss Phoebe made a tremulous smile.

"I'd better make some tea," she said, gathering her feet under her.

"I'll help," said Joyce. She turned her face to the tea tray, which lifted into the air and floated to the kitchenette. She smiled at Miss Phoebe. "You tell me what to do."

Elizabeth Engstrom (b. 1951)

When Darkness Loves Us

Elizabeth Engstrom entered the horror field with little fanfare in the 1980s with the publication of her book of two novellas, *When Darkness Loves Us* (1985), containing an introduction by Theodore Sturgeon, who was one of her teachers and literary mentors. Since then, she has written two horror novels, *Black Ambrosia* (1988) and *Lizzie Borden* (1990), in the process gaining a reputation among connoisseurs and an award nomination from the newly founded Horror Writers of America. Her reputation is still growing. Elizabeth Engstrom seems destined to become a central figure in the field. "When Darkness Loves Us" is a deeply disturbing tale that moves subtly, then with more force into the fantastic and grotesque to expose monstrous psychological abnormality. Its rural setting is reminiscent of many of Shirley Jackson's works, and its concerns link it closely to the horror fiction by women from the late nineteenth century to the present. It is interesting to compare it, for instance, to Violet Hunt's "The Prayer." There is no more direct or powerful examination of the darkness in relationships in the entire body of contemporary horror literature than this novella.

Part One

1

Sally Ann Hixson, full with the blush of spring and gleeful playfulness as only sixteen-year-olds know it, hid around the side of the huge tree at the edge of the woods as the great tractor drove past her. She saw her husband, torso bare, riding the roaring monster, his smooth muscles gliding under sweat-slick skin tanned a deep brown. She didn't want him to see her . . . not yet.

She plopped down into the long grass, feeling the rough bark of the big tree against her back as she gazed into the woods. This had been her favorite place to play when she was little. She could just barely see her parents' house on the hill about a mile off. Her mother had noticed her restlessness as soon as the major canning was done and sent her away to run, to play, to spy on her new husband as he worked with her father in the fields.

This summer, they would build their house on the other hill, and they could raise their family to be good country folk, just like their fathers and their fathers before them. She stretched her legs into a sunbeam, feeling them warm under her new jeans. She had a wild impulse to cast off her clothes and run naked through the grass. She thought of Michael then, and their delicious lovemaking the night before. She was not able to give of herself very freely while in her parents' house, but some nights Michael took her by the hand and led her out to the hill where their house would soon be built, high up on the knoll, and with the moon watching and the cicadas playing the romantic background music, they would make love, uninhibited, wonderful love. They explored each other's bodies and released sensations unfamiliar to either of them, with joy and togetherness in discovering the full potentials of their sexuality.

The idea made her tingle, then blush, and she crossed her legs, thinking of the times her thoughts strayed to such matters when she was with her mother. It was worse then, because she was sure lovemaking was not like that for her parents, and sometimes she had to excuse herself and go into the bathroom until she could stop grinning.

She picked up a long strand of grass and put it between her teeth as she peeked around the tree and watched her man, handsome and tousled, drive the machine over the next hill. She glanced around one more time to make sure her pest of a little sister wasn't lurking somewhere in the shadows. She jumped up and followed the edge of the woods until she could see the flatbed truck where her father waited. Michael would stop there and have a glass of iced water that she had put in a thermos jug for him that morning. She saw him turn to look behind him, so she dodged back into the woods . . . and saw the stone steps that led down into the ground.

It was so familiar. She used to play here when she was small, but she hadn't come here in years. There were two brand-new doors with shiny hinges mounted to the concrete, and she knew that it was going to be sealed against children and mishaps forever. What used to be the attraction here so long ago? She remembered the darkness and a tunnel, and she stepped down to the first step, then the second one, looking into a black hole that had no end.

It was cool, but not cold, and she took the sweatshirt that was tied around her waist and slipped it over her shoulders. She continued down into the eerie darkness and tried to remember the story about this place. A hiding place for runaway slaves, maybe. She continued her descent. The steps were sturdy, stone set in concrete. She felt her way along with her hand, the rough rock cool to the touch. The steps were narrow, set at an easy angle, and as she glanced back to reassure herself of the warm spring day above, she noticed that the entrance to the stairs would be out of sight before she reached the bottom. Yet down she went.

At the bottom there was a hole in the side of the wall, and memories, just out of reach, began to form themselves in her mind. She wondered if any of the old playthings were still in the tunnel. She crouched down to enter. Once inside, she straightened up—the tunnel was quite large. The small amount of light afforded by the entry provided very little visibility, but she made her way slowly along the tunnel, until the toe of her tennis shoe struck something that went ringing into the darkness. It was a baby spoon. The light glinted off the surface, just enough for her to find it. She picked it up, suddenly remembering the nursery rhymes and the frightening pleasure of having tea parties in such a forbidden place.

She rubbed the spoon between her fingers: tiny, smooth, and round, with a handle that doubled back upon itself, big enough for her finger. Then she remembered Jackie, killed in Vietnam. They were inseparable, always knew they'd eventually marry, and she had cried when he went off to the army. But now Jackie was gone and Michael was up there, and she had better go surprise him before she missed her chance. With one more thought of Jackie and a prayer for his soul, she moved back through the tunnel to the hole in the wall and the stairs, back to the sun and the springtime.

She heard Michael's voice above the roar of the idling tractor just as she came through the hole in the wall, caught the last words of his sentence. Angry that he had found her before she could surprise him, she had started running up the stairs when the doors above slammed shut, cutting off all light, and the sound of a padlock's shank driving home pierced her heart. She stood stock-still. The walls instantly closed in around her, and the air disappeared. She managed one scream, drowned by the earth-vibrating essence of the great engine above. She gasped, stumbled up one more step, then fell to her knees, fighting for breath, trying desperately to repress the horror of being locked in the darkness, while Michael's last words reverberated in her mind: ". . . before one of my kids falls down there."

Chest heaving, she tried to crawl up the stairs, fingers clawing—capable only of breathless moans rather than the strong screams she was trying desperately to utter in a vain attempt to bring father and husband to her rescue. She convulsed in fear, fingers stiffening, back arching. A muscular spasm turned her onto her back, the stone steps dug into her spine, and the darkness moved in and took over her mind.

2

The awakening was slow, starting with the pain in her lower back, then in her fingers, followed by the throbbing in her head. Slowly she opened her eyes. Darkness. She felt her eyes with her fingers to see if they were open or if she was dreaming. She felt the cold stone steps beneath her. Then she remembered. She looked around, but could see absolutely nothing. On her hands and knees, she mounted the steps until her head touched the heavy wooden doors, and she remembered the shiny new hinges and the solid, heavy wood that wouldn't rot as the seasons changed.

It must be night, she thought, or surely I could see a crack of daylight somewhere. She felt alone, isolated, abandoned. Tears leaked out of the corners of her eyes as she focused all her panic and shot it to her husband, hoping that somewhere there was a God who would transmit the message to him, so he could sense her surroundings and come rescue her and take her home to their warm, soft bed.

She pushed on the door with her shoulders, and it didn't give at all. She lost hope of wiggling the hinges loose. Cold and afraid, she huddled on the first steps, knowing that soon Michael and her dad would be coming for her. It was the only possible place she could be. After she had been missing for a night, they would come looking for her here. And here she would be, brave (not really) and okay (barely) and so very glad to see them. She fought the claustrophobic feeling and tried to relax. She was desperately tired and uncomfortable. She put her head on her arms and slept.

When she awoke, it was still pitch-dark and she had to go to the bathroom. She couldn't be embarrassed by the foul smells of her own excretions when her husband came to rescue her, so she had to find some place to go. Slowly, with aching muscles, she moved crablike down the stairs, visualizing in her mind's eye the hole in the wall and the tunnel thereafter. She crouched, feeling the circumference of the hole so she wouldn't hit her head, and slipped through to the big tunnel.

She remembered that it ran wide and true to where she had picked up the spoon, and she took brave steps in the darkness. She remembered Jackie, talking to her when they were out walking in the countryside on dark moonless nights. "You'll never stumble if you walk boldly and pick your feet up high." It worked then, and it worked now. She walked through the darkness and the fear, until she sensed by the echoes around her that the tunnel took a turn to the right. In the corner she relieved herself.

Nothing could be worse than waiting at the top of the steps, so she decided to explore the tunnel just a little farther and exercise the kinks out of her legs. The tunnel wound around until she was certain she must be directly under the stairs; then it straightened again. Her breathing echoed off the walls in eerie rasps. She walked still farther, and the air turned cooler. It smelled different. Water. Suddenly overcome with thirst, she walked boldly and entered a large cavern. The change in acoustics was immediate. She felt small and lost after the intimacy of the tunnel. Pebbles crunched underfoot.

She picked up a handful of loose stones and began tossing them around her to get a bearing on the dimensions of the cavern. It was huge. A path seemed to continue right through it, water on both sides. Slowly she stepped off the right side of the path, taking baby steps down into the darkness until her tennis shoe splashed in water. She lifted a cupped handful to her nose, then tasted it. Delicious. Eagerly, with both feet in the water, she drank her fill.

Wouldn't Dad be surprised, she thought, to know of this underwater lake on his property. The water tasted like the cave smelled—mossy—but it seemed pure, and it did the trick. She splashed some on her face, stood up, and dried her hands on her sweatshirt.

Feeling far more comfortable, she picked up another handful of pebbles and started throwing them. On this side of the path was a small pond, but the lake on the other side seemed endless. She threw a rock as far as she could, and still it plopped into the water. She threw another to the side, and it splashed. She threw another and there was no sound. Her heart froze. Maybe it had landed on a moss island. She threw one more in roughly the same direction and heard it land with a plop, and she visualized the concentric circles of black ripples edging out toward her.

She walked along the path, humming away the discomfort, spraying pebbles in wide sweeping arcs. The sound was friendly. Pebbles gone, she continued walking until she could feel the cavern narrowing back into a tunnel, and it was then that she heard the splash behind her. A small splash, as if one of the pebbles had been held up from its fate, suspended, until it finally fell. She stopped, midstep, and listened. The darkness pressed in upon her, and she could hear her blood rush through her veins. Silence. She had resumed her walk, stepping quietly, when another splash came, closer behind her, and her mind again was seized with unparalleled terror. She froze. A third noise, a sucking sound coming from the water just inches away from her feet, made her start. Moans of panic churning up unbidden, she ran blindly, until she stumbled and collided at a turn with the wall of the tunnel. She wildly felt her way around the turn and continued running the length of it until the cave with its lake and resident monster were far behind her.

She stopped for breath, the tunnel becoming a close friend. She was sure of the walls around her, and there were only two directions to be concerned with. Still her heart pounded. She leaned against the wall of the tunnel in despair. The darkness was terrifying. She could dimly see some kind of tracers in front of her eyes as she passed her hand in front of her face, but could not make out even the shapes of her fingers. Her eyes ached from trying. The tears were a long time coming, beginning first with shuddering whimpers, then great, racking, soul-filled sobs. The hopelessness of the situation was overwhelming. There was no point in going on, and she could not go back past the creature in the lake. Just the thought of going back made her want to vomit. She would stay right there until she starved to death. Exhausted by the scare, the run, and the cry, eventually she slept.

She dreamed of Michael. They were running together through the waist-high grass, laughing. He tripped her, and holding her so she would not fall too hard, he came down on top of her, his face so close, and he moved as if to kiss her. Instead, he said, *"You're going to rot down there, aren't you?"*

She awoke with a piercing scream that echoed back to her again and again and again, so that even after she had stopped, she had to put her hands to her ears to keep out the terrible noise. She sat straight up, looking ahead at the darkness. "Oh, God." Her soul wrenched inside of her. "NO!" she shouted. "I WON'T rot down here! I WILL SURVIVE!" The loud sound of her voice set her heart pounding again, and she started to think clearly. The decision to survive created bravery in her, and she wanted to make a plan. She knew now that she would survive until she was rescued.

Shelter. That was a laugh. No problem. Because it was a bit warm, she rolled up her jeans to just below the knee. She certainly wasn't going to freeze. She stood and tied the sweatshirt again around her waist. Food. Now that was a problem. And she was definitely hungry. Water. If there was one lake, there must be another. Or a stream. She would continue down these tunnels until she found what she needed and then found a way out of here. She couldn't wait to be discovered. Where there was water, there was most likely food. Fish! Probably the monster in the lake was nothing more than a couple of fish, their long-undisturbed life in the lake interrupted by the stones. Maybe she could catch a fish to eat.

She thought back to her science books, to pale, sickly fish with bulging blind eyes and horrendous teeth that lived so deep in the ocean that no light penetrated their lair, and she shuddered. So much for the fish. She'd have to eat them raw anyway. No good. Moss, maybe. Seaweed was supposed to be good for you; maybe moss was just as good. Maybe also, there was a way out of here. She got up and started down the tunnel, thinking as she went, trying to ignore the gnawing in her belly that would soon, very soon, have to be satisfied.

She walked on, wondering how long she'd been there, wondering how long it would be until she heard Michael's booming voice. She would keep track of time with marks on the cave wall, but that was pretty silly, because she wouldn't be able to see them. By the number of times she slept? No good. By her menstrual periods? Nonsense. She would never be here a whole month, and besides that, she hadn't had a period in the two months she and Michael had been married.

No matter how bravely she told herself that things were going to be all right, now she had two doubts nagging the back of her mind.

She walked until her legs were leaden; then she sat and slept and walked some more. There must be miles and miles of tunnel in here. She crossed two streams, both of which had water seeping from one wall, crossing the floor of the tunnel, and leaking out the other side. Barely enough to drink—she would put her lips to the wall and suck up what moisture was needed to keep the dangerous thirst away. She knew, too, that if she didn't find something to eat soon, she would no longer have the energy to look. Her jeans were a little baggy on her already slim frame, and her steps were slower and not always in a straight line.

Sleeping when tired, she made her way through the endless tunnel with its twistings and turnings, her hands raw from catching herself after stumbling over the uneven flooring as her steps began to drag. After countless naps, with weak legs, bleeding and blistered, she tripped over a rise in the tunnel floor and lay there, her will almost gone, overcome by thirst and hunger, so tired, wanting that final sleep that would bring peace.

In half consciousness, her brain fevered and delirious, she cried out "Michael!" and her voice reverberated off the walls of a large cavern. Then she heard water dripping.

She crawled painfully toward the sound and found a pool of water, cold and delicious. She lay on her stomach and drank from her hands until she was full. It was in the half sleep that followed that Jackie came to her and brought her food. She heard his voice, and looked up. He stood over her, his face illuminated in the darkness by a glow, a radiance. "Eat these, Sally Ann. They're good for you." She picked one up. It was a fat slug, slippery on one side and rough on the other side, about the size of her thumb.

414 Foundations of Fear

"I can't eat this."

"You can. It's good for you. You have to. Pop the whole thing in your mouth like a cherry tomato and bite once, then swallow. It's easy. Here. Try." Too tired to feel revulsion, she put the slug into her mouth and chomped down hard. She felt it burst, squirting down her throat and she swallowed quickly, followed by a handful of cold water. Yuck. It tasted awful. He encouraged her to eat more, and she did. She finished all those he had brought her and, stomach full, slept where she lay.

3

"Jackie?"

"Hmmm?"

"Are you a ghost?"

"I don't know."

The question had burned in her mind since she had first seen him the day he'd saved her. Fearing the worst—that she was mad—she had promised herself not to ask the question until he had been with her for a while.

"Well, how did you come to be here? And why can I see you when I can't even see my hands in front of my face?"

"I don't know that either, Sally Ann. All I know is that I was in Vietnam, and we were carrying wounded back to the camp. There was a yell and some sniper fire. I got hit in the chest . . . and the next thing I knew was that you were dying and I had to find some food for you to eat. I can see you, too, you know. It is pretty strange."

"The Vietnam war ended more than five years ago, Jackie. You were killed there."

This bit of news seemed no surprise to him. They sat in the main cavern with their backs up against the wall, comfortable on a mattress of soft dry moss that Sally had gathered for their bed. Her pregnancy was confirmed—there was no other explanation for the growing bulge in her belly—and she had stopped wearing her jeans long ago.

It had taken her a long time to recover, but Jackie helped nurse her back to health. His devotion to her, and the baby she carried, helped her accept the fact that unless Michael found his way to her, she was stuck for the time being. The resiliency of youth healed her body and her mind. She adapted to her new surroundings as best she could, and as time went on, she pined less and less for her family.

Jackie urged her on, and together they explored the immediate regions of their homestead, discovered many large tunnels and smaller tributaries. One led to a swift-running stream, and it was here that Sally made her toilet. Another entered a monstrous cavern like a hollowed-out mountain, with sheer drops of hundreds or more feet, as she estimated by dropping rocks from their ledges.

A smaller cavern revealed what seemed to be thousands of skeletons. The final resting place, Sally Ann speculated, of all those slaves trying to escape. How long did they search for a way out before they sat down together and starved to death? What a terrible way to die. Lost, sightless, terrified. Their remains were a fortunate discovery, however, for from these bones Jackie and Sally fashioned plenty of useful tools—bowls, knives, awls, and supports. It also reaffirmed her will to survive.

This same cavern yielded mushrooms of many flavors. Sally found the mushroom patch by stepping on the spongy fungi as she walked carefully around, searching the area. Just as she found the mushrooms, Jackie discovered a tough razorlike lichen growing around the walls. Sally had begun the dangerous habit of tasting everything that smelled okay. She couldn't help herself. Sometimes the cravings were just too intense. The mushrooms didn't hurt her, and when she soaked the lichen, it too became palatable.

It was strange how she could see Jackie as he worked; he seemed so old, so smart. The only time her eyes hurt her now was when she was exploring a new region, straining vainly to see where she was stepping. Sometimes she just closed them and wandered. It made no difference. She could see Jackie and nothing else, eyes open or closed.

She still became frightened, especially when Jackie went away. He went off on exploration trips of his own at times, mostly when he sensed she needed to be alone. The fear was not of the caverns, though, nor of monsters (even though the lake creature continued to haunt her dreams) or bogeymen. The fear seeped in when she was reflecting on her past life—Michael, her mother, father, and sister. The fear told her that she would be here until she died, that her child and its father would never meet. When the fear came, and she started to pant with the physical effect, and her eyes bulged in the darkness, looking from side to side trying to find a way out, Jackie would come back and sit with her, and soon the calm would descend. They became very close.

There was always plenty of food. Sally had merely to pick the slugs from the walls, wash them in the pond, and eat. There was also a kind of kelp that grew on the edges of the rocks in the water and on the sides of the tunnel where the water ran down, and now and then a fish would float up, and she would ravenously eat it, bones and all.

The water level fluctuated, dramatically at times. Sometimes when they went to sleep the water would be low, but when they awoke, it would reach almost to their bed. Now and then they would find things floating in it: Apples sometimes showed up, even a cabbage once; frequently there were walnuts and an occasional dead rodent, all of which added up to an adequate diet.

Their bed was comfortable; they were dry, clean, warm, fed, and together. And it was at times like this that they philosophized about their predicament—she being both grateful and angry.

Sally Ann was a fairly responsible sort of a girl, level-headed and born with an instinct to roll with the punches. That's how she felt about their situation. They had to make the best of it. What concerned her most, though, was the birth of her child. What to name him? How to keep from losing him in the dark? Jackie seemed convinced it was to be a son, and Sally Ann had taken a liking to the name Clinton. It was a solid name, and had enough hard sounds to make it easily understood when she had to call to him in the darkness.

Jackie's undying cheerfulness helped chase away what blues came and went: He was totally unwilling to look at the negative side of things or talk of despair. They lay close together at sleep time and chased away the bad dreams. He even cut her hair. A tortuous process. Her blond hair was thin, and she had always worn it quite long, but in the time they spent in the underworld it had grown much too long to be manageable. It was always getting in her way and washing it was quite out of the question. She lay with her neck on her jeans, her head on a boulder; with a sharp rock, Jackie sawed away at her hair, wearing it through more than cutting it. The end result felt uneven and strange, but more comfortable.

The baby grew rapidly, and in the last days, it was too dangerous to be awkwardly stumbling around in the darkness. She confined herself to her moss mattress and contemplated Michael.

Again and again she would lapse into despair until Jackie came to lift her spirits. He told her how he had delivered babies for women in Nam, said he was experienced, that there was nothing to it, and though she didn't believe him, he talked to her in his calm, low voice until she was convinced there was nothing to fear.

But when the time came, when the pains racked her whole body, and her water broke, and she began to cry and scream and writhe on her bed, she wished for Dr. Stirling and his warm, confident hands. But Jackie was there, and he talked to her—rubbed her back between contractions and spoke of the coming baby and what a joy it would be. She thought of how happy it would make Michael to know that he had a baby, and she gritted her teeth and bore the pain and finally bore the baby. It emerged screaming and choking, and the reverberations in the cavern were joyous to hear.

She lifted the baby, warm and slippery, to her belly, and her hands moved over it to reassure herself that it was real, that it was whole and had all its parts. She discovered that it was indeed a son. Jackie brought her water in a skull bowl, and with the baby at her breast, they tied the umbilical cord with her shoelaces and severed it with a sharpened bone. He helped her deliver the afterbirth, which he put away to eat later, then cleaned up around them. He brought the fresh moss that had been stockpiled for the occasion, then lay down beside mother and son, and enshrouded in darkness, they all slept.

4

"I'm cold, Mommy."

"Well then, silly, come out of the water and I'll dry you off."

Tall as his mother's shoulder, Clint came dripping out of the pond and stood shivering by her side. She rubbed him briskly with a handful of soft dry moss to help restore circulation, then pulled him down to her lap. They sat together, rocking back and forth, naked, she appreciating the coolness of his body as he appreciated the warmth of hers. They were very close, too close at times, she thought, but she constantly had to reevaluate her standards. In such an abnormal situation, she had to trust her judgment. His mouth automatically groped for her breast, and he gently sucked on it as they sat together. Her milk had dried up long ago, but this closeness was very important.

His little body was hard, muscular, compact, with just a little potbelly protruding, and though he was small, he was strong. She often wondered about his physical development without the sun. He seemed healthy, and he certainly was happy. A joy to her, even though she had never seen his face.

"Tell me again about sun and sky." When he was a baby, Sally Ann had told him stories about his father and the place where she had lived above ground, and he never tired of hearing about the sun and the sky, the plants, meadows, fruits, and delicious things of nature.

"Morning time is when the sun comes up in the sky and makes everything bright and you can see for miles. There are woods by where my parents live, and acres and acres of wheat fields. Your daddy works in those fields and his skin is tanned and brown. He eats sweet jam that I made for him before I came here to have you."

"What's 'see' again?"

"It's another sense, honey. Like feeling or tasting or smelling. Listen. Hear that water drip? Well, if you go put your hand under it you can feel the drop, and if you could see it, it would look like a tiny jewel, a little precious piece of sunlight captured in the water. Someday you will see it. Someday your daddy will come down here and find us and take us back up to the farm and you'll be able to run in the sunlight."

"I wish he'd come soon, Mommy."

"Me too, honey." Her heart went out to this perfect child who didn't understand what seeing was, who didn't know the wonders of life and nature.

Sally Ann gathered up their things and started back to the main cavern which had been their home since Clint was born. Born to the darkness, he was naturally oriented, and ran ahead of her, totally unafraid, at peace with the elements of his underworld life. She walked along slowly. She knew that she was planting a few seeds of dissatisfaction when she talked to him of the aboveground world, that he longed to see the magic things that she talked of, but how else was she to explain life to him? And she did believe that one day they would be discovered and taken back.

He was a very independent boy, and he had thoughts of his own about the world above. Sally Ann could tell he doubted that everything she talked about existed. She could hardly blame him. How could he believe in the sun when he had never even used his eyes? When she stopped to think about it, as she did now, it saddened her. She wanted all the experiences of life to be his: to run and play in the meadow, to hear the birds, to see the stars. I guess it's a little like believing in God, she thought. One has to believe, and then belief becomes strengthened. If one disbelieves, then disbelief is strengthened. And turning your back, once you know the truth, leads to evil.

She showed him her tennis shoes in an attempt to pique his curiosity, but he wasn't interested. And there wasn't anything she could do but accept it, was there?

When Clint was far enough ahead of her, she called to Jackie and he joined her on her walk. Clint couldn't see or hear Jackie, so he reserved his visiting time for Sally alone, after Clint was asleep. Many times they discussed for hours the best way to help Clint understand. Sally was confident that he was growing up to be a normal boy. He delighted in finding new kinds of life in the caves, some of which they gratefully added to their diet—like the crayfish that blindly lived in the fast-running streams—and some of which provided hours of entertainment for Clint—like the dim-witted puff-fish that would let him pick them up and transport them from one pond to another and back again. He played war games with them, playfully pitting one against the other, with food as the supreme reward. They seemed, in their cold, reptilian way, to be almost affectionate to him. But then, he was always kind to them.

Clint was crossing the swift stream on the stepping-stones when he first discovered the crayfish. He was chewing one of a handful of slugs, when one slipped out between his fingers just at the edge of the stream and he heard it splash into the water. The water began boiling with activity, and unafraid as he was, he reached in and pulled out a crayfish as long as his arm.

Jackie said that as long as it ate what you ate, it should be okay for you to eat it. So they shelled it and discovered that it was delicious. Sally Ann couldn't quite get over her fear of putting her hand right into the black water, though Clint teased her about it, but she was grateful that he would bring her those delectable treats now and then.

Yes, he was a joy to her, but in her times alone she wondered many things. What would happen to him if she died? Was she glorifying the outside world to him so that he would never rest until he saw it? Was there a way out of here? She and Jackie had searched the tunnels and caverns for years, looking for a way out, and nothing had come of it yet. She knew that the stairs were securely locked and guarded by a beast in the lake, so they avoided that direction. Maybe, though, Clint would have the hunger, the burning desire to go to the magic place she had described for him, and through some mercy from heaven, he would be shown the way out. God knows a boy shouldn't live his life in tunnels and caves.

"Why so silent?" Jackie had been walking alongside her, respecting her contemplative mood.

"What is the purpose of all this, Jackie? Are we doing something here for someone's benefit? What possible part in God's plan are we fulfilling? I want my son out of here. We've been here for years, Jackie. YEARS! Clint is probably eight years old now, and he's never even SEEN, for God's sake. And Michael. What must he have thought, that his young wife had run away? And my parents. And my sister. Jackie. I've got to get out of here with my child, NOW!"

Jackie looked at her sadly. "I've a feeling, Sally Ann, that all this IS for a higher purpose."

"I can't accept that. Clint and I are going to find our way out of here—NOW!" Suddenly she was filled with a sense of purpose, of immediacy. The drive had taken hold of her with a single-mindedness that demanded attention. She knew, deep in her soul, that Clint was old enough now to be a help, not a hindrance, and if they were ever going to do it, now was the time.

She ran back to the main cavern and found Clint. She grabbed his shoulders with both hands and put her face up next to his.

"Clint. We've got to get out of here. We've got to get up to the sunshine and the grass and the fresh air, and see your daddy. We can stay here forever, and we probably will, if we don't make the commitment—right NOW—to get out of here. Now I'm going to pack up some moss and some water and some food, and we're going to keep going until we find a way out of these caves. Okay? Are you ready?"

"We've never looked the other way." Sally knew he meant the way of the monster in the lake. She had never returned that way, had never gone back, had never tried the stairs again. She had chosen to stay in the caves rather than risk what might be in that lake. But now she wasn't so sure.

"Then that's the way we'll start. Get ready."

They didn't speak again until they each had bundles tied to their backs and had entered the tunnel forbidden to Clint all his life. Then he said, "Why now, all of a sudden? You were happy here until now. Don't you want to be down here with me anymore?"

"Of course I want to be with you, honey. There are just better things for you than an old cave. I want to see your face. I want to see how much you look like your daddy."

"You always told me Daddy would rescue us. He hasn't, though, has he? And now you want to go find him. Why? We live here. This is our home. We're happy here. Don't you want to be with me anymore?"

Sally stopped and reached out for him, but he avoided her touch. She was astonished at his bitterness.

"Clint . . ."

"Don't! You don't want me anymore. You just want to go chasing a dream. There is no 'up there.' There is no 'daddy.' There's nothing but you and me and that's not good enough for you. You're a liar and I don't want YOU anymore, either!" He ran off into the darkness.

"Clint!" She screamed after him. There was no response. She kept screaming as if the echoes were her only friends.

5

Filled with a stifling terror that had built upon itself over the years, Sally Ann felt her way along the side of the tunnel toward the opening she had first come through so long ago. Still sobbing and aching for her runaway son, she had but one thing in mind—to show him the truth. How could he not believe her? When she stopped to rest there was only silence around her. She heard nothing of her son but did not worry. Clint was far more capable of navigating the winding tunnels than she. She also resisted the temptation of calling Jackie. This was a situation she would have to deal with on her own.

For the first time, doubts began to fill her mind. Maybe it was all a lie. Maybe Jackie was a lie, too. Maybe this was all a dream, a nightmare; maybe there was nothing, really, except her and the darkness. No caves, no tunnels, no Clint, no Michael, no God.

Maybe she was the product of the imagination of some madman who was dreaming. Maybe she was the central character of a novel, and the imagery of the writer was strong enough to flash her into existence. How else could she explain Jackie? Was he just the product of her need? How could he be real?

"There is only one way to find out. I will prove to Clint and I will prove to myself that there is something else—something better for us than the darkness, than these damned tunnels. I will get out of here and come back for Clint." She spoke loudly, boldly, as much to calm herself as in the hope that Clint could hear her.

She continued through the tunnel, reliving the journey from the tunnel entrance to the main cavern. She walked with her eyes closed, hoping her feet would remember the way and not let her mind guide her down the wrong tunnel, take the wrong turn at a fork, sabotage her freedom. When she was tired she slept, and when she was hungry she ate until all she had brought with her was gone. Still she walked, the ache within her abdomen a constant companion, the pain of a mother falsely accused of being dishonest with her child.

The old tennis shoes were finally rotting away, and she discarded the soles and the few strings that still held them together and continued barefoot. She soaked her cut and bleeding feet at the first stream she crossed. There she found more food, and rested until she was able to continue.

Limping, stumbling, and near the end of her endurance, she sensed a wall in front of her, and made her way to it. It was made of bricks! The first manmade substance she had known since leaving the stairs. Clint would have to believe her now! She felt her way along the wall and finally, hands pulling on her hair, sank to her knees. It was a dead end. The wall was solid.

She rested awhile, then scavenged the tunnel floor on all fours until she found a pointed rock. Chipping away at the old mortar proved to be a tremendous task, but she kept at it consistently, resting when she was too tired to go on, and taking trips back to the stream for fresh food and water. There was no sound except her own raspy breathing, no word from Clint. She knew that she was quite lost in the underground maze, that her bearings were so far off she might never again find either the Home Cavern or the stairs. This wall was her only hope. There must be something behind it.

She worked at the cement, chipping an inch at a time, until she had loosened one whole brick. With bleeding fingers she worked the brick loose from its slot and pulled it out. Half fearing what she would find, she reached her hand in the hole and felt . . . more bricks. A double wall. Her soul wilted. Would she never get used to disappointment? She summoned courage and patience and kept going. Eventually she had worked an opening that was five bricks wide and seven bricks high. She began scraping at the mortar of the inner wall.

The second wall of bricks was not as solid, and by putting her foot in the opening and bracing her back, she could make the whole structure give a bit as she pushed.

She worked one brick until it became loose. She pushed it with her hand, then her foot, until it gave way and fell in. Holding her breath, she listened. Nothing. Then a splash, way, way below, and the nauseating stench of mold, must, and rotting stuff wafted through the hole.

It was an old well, and where there was a well, there was access from above. Overcoming her sickness, she doubled her efforts to push out the inner wall. With one brick gone, the wall crumbled fairly easily. Soon she had an opening big enough to crawl through.

The effort was exhausting. She sat back and rested while her mind raced ahead. Here is a way out for all of us! She thought of Jackie, and called him. Instantly, he was there.

He looked in the hole, and pulled his head back in revulsion. "This place is diseased. You can't crawl up there. The well has been closed up for years. I'm sure the top has been sealed."

"I can do it. I've got to get Clint out of here."

"You *can't* do it. Look at you. You're skin and bones and half dead. Do you know how you'd get up there, with no rope? And once you got to the top, then what? How are you going to open the lid? Forget it, Sally Ann."

"I *can* do it and I *will* do it and I don't need you telling me I can't. Now you can help me or you can go away."

"I won't help you kill yourself. How fast have you been losing your teeth?" Her hand went to her mouth, to the sore gums and the holes she tried not to think about. "Come on, we can find our way back to the Home Cavern."

"And do what? Rot? Have you ever thought what will happen to Clint after I get old and die? No, Jackie, this is our only way out."

"What's the difference, Sally Ann? You can die here, or you can die in that hole."

She took his arm and looked into his eyes. He looked so sad. "Jackie, we can get out of here. All of us . . ."

"Not me, Sally Ann. I can't go. I don't know why, but when you don't need me anymore, I think I'm going away."

"Well, I certainly don't need you now!" She was instantly sorry she had said that, and had time only to see the hurt flash through Jackie's eyes before he faded away. "Jackie? Come back. I do need you . . . Jackie!" But he was gone. She curled up in the corner by her pile of bricks and cried herself to sleep.

6

She took her time preparing for the journey. A plan was carefully followed and executed. She was determined to succeed. She began by eating all she could find. Each time she ate, she stuffed herself until repelled by the thought of another bite. She licked salt from the wall until tears came to her eyes, ignoring the stinging in her mouth, then drank her fill from the fresh water in the stream. She even fearlessly fished for crayfish, and ate them eagerly. She continually called out for Clint to come join her, but there was never a reply. She didn't venture out farther than the stream for fear of losing her way back to the well, but her voice carried, and was so loud to her ears that she was certain he heard her. Each time the echoes rang hollowly back to her, the ache in her stomach rang with them.

She slept on a bed of moss that her body heat eventually made dry enough to be pliable. She shredded it, braided it back together, and wove a bag that she could sling over her shoulder to carry supplies, but she couldn't make a rope strong enough to be of any use. She braided another bundle of moss to weave a kind of shirt, since her clothes were long gone and the air from the well was decidedly cool. She made a snug-fitting pair of booties and wound some more moss around her elbows and hands.

Finally, she took a deep breath and stood. She was ready. She grabbed a handful of pebbles and put her head through the wall. She threw a pebble to the opposite wall and found it to be only about three feet away. She threw a stone straight up, but could not tell by the sound whether it was bouncing off the lid or off the side. The stones fell a long way before they splashed. She pulled her head out of the opening and gave one last shout to Clint. "I'm going into the well now, Clint. I'll bring your dad back."

Feet first, she entered the hole and felt for the other side. The sharp bricks bruised and cut her ribs before her feet found a purchase on the opposite wall. She walked her toes down until she could slide her torso through the opening and rest her back just below the hole. Slowly, moving her feet sideways, then inching her back around, she revolved around the inside of the well so as to miss the opening on her climb up the shaft. Already she knew she was in for an endurance test the likes of which she had never encountered. Her straining back muscles screamed, and she rested, willing herself to relax, placing the weight on her straightened legs and her toes.

With her arms straight out to her sides, the weight of her whole body was on her toes and her back. She was able to give her back some relief by raising herself up on her hands a little. The rough surface of the well wall helped. She was afraid her shoulders or elbows might give way, though, so this was only a momentary respite.

Up and up, through the vertical tunnel that had no ending and no beginning, she focused her mind on freedom and light and laughter in the sunshine and willed her bruised and torn back to go just one more inch, then one more, and another after that. She ate from her store and rested often, afraid of falling asleep, afraid of not falling asleep. Eventually she had blackout periods where she lost consciousness, and she was sure it was her mind insisting on the sleep she was denying it. Each time she awakened, her knees were locked tight and secure, but it was still startling, and her heart pounded.

Except for the loosened chunks of mortar and dirt splashing in the water far below, the only sound in the well was her echoed breathing. Now and then she heard a soft scuttling noise, but she refused to let her mind dwell on what might be making such a sound. She finally removed the moss shirt she had made when the moss became imbedded in the lacerations on her back. This exertion was enough to make her pant for breath and stay still until the dizziness left her. She put what was left of the bloody moss into her bag and continued her ascent after her head had cleared.

Feeling faint and frail, she stopped and considered going back to the tunnel, but she wasn't sure how far she had come, nor was she sure how far she had to go. The blackness was absolute. Going down would be as bad as going up, she reasoned, so she might as well make for the top. Giving up would be the same either way. Archaeologists would either find her bones wedged in the well shaft like a prop, or they would find them at the bottom. She felt the rough brick biting into her shoulders as she continued, and whispered a little prayer that thundered in the silence. Time for a rest. Just a little sleep. She knew she was in danger of hallucinating from lack of sleep and that her mind wasn't functioning clearly, so she wedged herself in very tightly and planned to rest there for a while. Sleep came quickly.

When she awoke, there were insects crawling over her legs. She screamed and brushed at her legs with her shoulder bag. "Oh, God! Get them off of me!" Cockroaches. They were two inches long, attracted by the smell of the rotting slugs in her bag and the blood and raw flesh of her feet and back. At her violent movements they scurried away—to wait. She suppressed the bile rising in her throat, and knew that if she allowed herself to be surprised like that again, she would be likely to fall. Then the venomous little beasts could feast.

She began again her torturous climb. Below her she could hear scrapings, but dared not think about their significance. She had to concentrate. As she moved upward inch by agonizing inch, she felt close to losing all. This was a foolish venture, and now she would die and it would all be for nothing.

"Mommy?"

"Oh, Jesus." More of a groan than words, she cursed the obsession that kept Clint foremost in her mind. She was surely hallucinating.

"Mommy, are you up there?"

"Clint!" The cry came from the depths of her soul. "Clint. I'm going to get us out of here." As she spoke, her voice reverberated around the walls of her circular cell, but she noticed a new dimension in the echoes, a flat sound from above. She was near the top! "Clint! I'm almost out! I'll come back and bring your daddy to get you out. Stay there."

The small voice came from far below. Much farther than she believed she could have come.

"Mommy, come back. Don't leave me here alone. You don't need to go, Mommy. The darkness loves us."

Darkness? How could he talk of darkness? Pieces of thoughts, concepts swirled through her fevered brain. How could he talk of darkness when he knew nothing else? There is only darkness when there is light to compare it with. Does he believe, then? Exhausted, she could talk no longer. "Wait there for me, Clint."

She rested for a while before continuing. Knowing she was near the top gave her added strength, but even when the spirit is renewed, the flesh needs sustenance. She knew from the odor that the food in her bag was no longer edible. She ripped the moss armband from her elbow and chewed on it. She managed to swallow a couple of mouthfuls before continuing. She also knew she was losing a fair amount of blood. It mixed with her sweat and trickled down her back. She couldn't quit now. Her baby depended on her.

She persevered, eyes closed, up the wall which was growing continually warmer. She kept going until she heard her breath echo off the lid; then she raised her hands and felt it. Wooden. Old. Cracked in the middle and split along one side. She braced her poor toes against the far wall and pushed with one arm. The bricks ripped freshly into the skin on her shoulders, but the wood gave a little bit. Encouraged, and blinded to the pain by the relief she saw in store, she heaved with all she had. One leg slipped off the wall, and for one precious moment, one heart-stopping second, she hung suspended, held only by one toe and one shoulder. Holding her breath, she inched her other leg up to join the first one, the muscles groaning and stiff, and soon she again had both feet on the wall. The blood rushed through her veins with a maddening roar. She rested.

Try again, she encouraged herself. She found one crack with the tips of her fingers and felt its length, looking for an opening large enough to accommodate her hand. Almost, but not quite. The second crack was a little bit wider, and by sacrificing the skin from her knuckles, she could get her fingers all the way through. She pulled, then pushed, and felt, then heard, the old wood splinter. Carefully, so she would not lose her precarious balance, she wiggled the board back and forth until it came loose, and she dropped it to the water below.

The opening was now about four inches wide and a foot and a half long. She inches her way up and reached through the hole; she felt nothing. She loosened the next board and it came away more easily; now a full half of the opening was uncovered. The remaining half of the cover was loose, and she wrestled with it, afraid it would fall on her on its way past. Successful, she heard it bounce and scrape its way to the bottom, for a final splash. The opening was now clear. So why wasn't there fresh air to breathe?

Part Two

1

Michael strode up the porch steps and into the kitchen, the screen door slamming behind him. He kissed his wife on the side of the neck, then pulled a cold beer from the refrigerator and sat at the kitchen table before opening it. She was a lovely girl, Maggie. A little plumper than the day they had married, but her face was just as pleasant and her disposition just as cheerful. She had passed that precious quality on to their children, too, both in their natural demeanor and in their attitudes. He loved her very much.

Maggie dried her hands on her apron, poured herself a glass of fresh lemonade, and sat at the table with him. The kids were not yet home from school, and these midafternoon talks with just the two of them at the kitchen table had become a daily ritual, one they both enjoyed. She looked at him closely. The years were wearing on him well. The lines etched deeply in his skin gave his face character. Tanned and rough, with a generous sprinkling of gray in his hair, he was more handsome now than ever before. Put a suit on him and he'd look the picture of a successful executive. She smiled. He was a farmer, though, and she liked that.

"I went to see your mom today," he said.

"How is she?" Michael had always felt closer to Maggie's parents than she had, and he visited Cora often since her husband had died of a stroke two years ago in the fields.

"She's good. She sent her love to you and the kids. She also sent some peaches she put up last season. They're in the truck."

Michael wished Maggie would pay more attention to her mother but didn't press the issue. He knew the problem. He sipped his beer.

Maggie stared into her glass. "I thought I'd drive her into town tomorrow. Maybe we could go shopping or something." Michael worked hard to suppress his surprise and pleasure. He didn't want to overdo it, but to have his wife and her mother together on a social basis was more than he could have wished for. It was, in fact, an answer to his prayers.

"I think that's a fine idea. Why don't you pick up some more yarn and knit me another of those sweaters? The winter is coming, and I've worn holes in the elbows of my favorite."

"What color would you like?"

"I don't know. Do you think red would make me sexy?"

She laughed and got up. "You don't need no help." She shooed him out of the kitchen and went back to fixing dinner.

2

"Momma? Sit down here a minute, would you, please? I've got something on my mind that I think needs put to rest." Maggie was in her mother's kitchen for the first time in a year. The table was piled high with their purchases from town, including some new red wool for Michael's sweater and a bolt of Pendleton blue plaid for the kids' winter clothes. She knew Michael would laugh when he saw she'd bought a whole bolt of it, like he did when she bought a whole bolt of red and white checkered cloth from the Sears, Roebuck catalog. But it had made a tablecloth, kitchen draperies, several aprons, towels, and dresses for the girls. He had liked the effect, even though it was all the same. Economy, she had told him, and he'd given her a kiss.

Cora sat across the table from her, a pot of steeping tea between them. She moved the packages aside and looked at her daughter.

"Yes, I believe it's time whatever is between us was laid to rest, Maggie." She poured the tea and waited.

"Momma, I've prayed long and hard about this, and I think I'm at fault. I'm feeling guilty, and have been laying it on you and Papa. Ever since Michael and I . . ."

"Hush, child. There's no reason to go over all that again."

"I can't hush, Momma. I've got to talk this out, and I've got to do it now, in order to cleanse myself and be rid of this feeling."

424   Foundations of Fear

Cora sipped her tea and listened. Maggie always was a strong-willed girl. She waited.

"I guess I always thought it was wrong when Michael and me started loving one another, so soon after Sally Ann died. And then we went against Papa's wishes and yours and went ahead and lived together before she could be pronounced dead, and that bothered me a tremendous lot. That's why we went off and got married without you and Papa there. I was pregnant with Justin, and I was angry that we had to sneak around with our love for so long out of respect for Sally Ann's memory. When she just up and took off. Or whatever.

"But you have to know, Momma, it was all my doing. Michael loves you as well as he loved his own folks, and he was against getting married without your blessings. But, Momma . . ." The tears began to spill over her eyelids. "I was so tired of having to deal with Sally Ann. I had to deal with her all my life, because she was older, and slimmer, and prettier, and she married Michael, and I was always so jealous. And then Michael loved me when she took off, and she didn't deserve him and I did, but still I had to live in her shadow for seven long years. It was hard, Momma, and it went against my grain, and I always felt you and Papa were disappointed in me for not respecting Sally Ann's memory like you taught me to." The tears were coming faster, and the sobs broke from her chest.

"I'm a good wife, Momma. And a good mother. Our kids are bright and nice and Michael and I love each other so much . . . and I love you too, Momma, and I want us to be friends."

She looked up and saw silent tears on Cora's face. Neither spoke for a long time. Maggie felt the knot in the pit of her stomach ease up for the first time in all these years, and love for her mother and sorrow for the missed chances in their relationship coursed through her. The pent-up flood of tears broke and she put her forehead on her arms and cried. Cora came around and sat beside her.

"Maggie. I know you're a good wife and mother. I've got eyes. So did your papa. And we could see the way you and Michael looked at each other. There are no more perfect grandchildren in the whole world than the ones you've given us. What happened with your sister is over and done with now. Only God knows her fate, and it was God that brought you and Michael together right here under our roof. We've always loved you, and always prayed that you'd come back to us. God bless you, child. You've lived with a burden that wasn't necessarily yours to bear. Come now. Drink your tea."

Maggie looked up and smiled at her mother. And soon they were both laughing. Laughing with a joy of togetherness that they had never known.

3

Life sure is good, Michael thought to himself as he loaded the last of the calves on the back of the truck. He jumped in the cab, started the engine, and with a final wave to Maggie, set off to the city, where the calves would bring a nice price on the auction block. He always enjoyed this yearly three-day trip away from the farm. It gave him some time to think, to miss the family, to see some new sights, to get a taste of the other side of life. It always renewed his appreciation for what he had.

As he turned onto the main highway, his thoughts automatically went to Sally Ann. His first trip to market was one week after she had left, and she was the topic of conversation all the way in and all the way home with his father-in-law. He never seemed to be able to drive this way without trying to figure out why she had left, or where she had gone. It was so long ago, but still the mystery remained. He couldn't bear to consider that she had been killed, or kidnapped. He preferred, no matter how much it hurt, to think she had left him and was living a happy and comfortable life.

Oh, Sally Ann, how I loved you. I hope you are well. With that, he turned his thoughts to the load of beef on the back of his truck.

Maggie watched the truck disappear down the highway and returned to the kitchen where tubs of plump blueberries were to capture her attention for the rest of the day. She got the recipe file from the shelf and pulled cards for jam, jelly, and Michael's favorite compote. She called to Justin to get out of bed and help her bring in the cases of jars from the barn, then rousted the twins to wash their hands, then wash the blueberries. Time they learned how to get their hands all purple, too.

She was holding the door for Justin as he brought in the last case of jars when the phone rang.

"Maggie?"

"Hello, Momma."

"Maggie, has Michael left for market yet?"

"About a half hour ago, why?"

"Well, there's a noise going on over here that's starting to concern me and I was hoping I could catch him before he left. I'd like to find out what's wrong. I sure hope it isn't the water heater again, but I'm afraid it is, and it's been going on for a couple of days now."

"Justin and I can come over before we start the blueberries, Momma."

"No . . . I hate to bother you."

"No bother, Momma. We'll be right over."

Maggie hung up and wished she hadn't volunteered. Most likely it wasn't anything they could do anything about anyway, but it might set her mother's mind at ease.

"C'mon, Justin. We're going over to Grandma's for a few minutes." The girls squealed with delight. "You two keep washing those blueberries. We won't be gone but a couple of minutes." They returned to their task with sullen faces.

Cora met them in the drive, and the three went behind the house to the water-heater shed.

"Now listen."

A faint tapping broke the stillness, erratic but high-pitched, metal on metal.

"The sound's comin' from over there," Justin said. They all turned to where he pointed, and saw nothing but the neighboring field and the old well cover that stuck up about two feet from the ground. Justin walked toward the well cover, but the sound had stopped.

"It was louder yesterday," Cora said. "I just can't for the life of me figure what it might be."

Justin stopped in front of the old well. "What's this, Grandma?"

"Just an old well, Justin. It went dry years ago and your Grandpa put that cover on it to keep you young'uns from falling in and killing yourselves. There isn't anything down there."

He walked over to it and knocked on the domed iron lid. It rang solid. A moment later, the tapping began, furiously.

"It *is* coming from here! Listen!" They all heard it.

Justin examined the bolts that held the lid on. "I'm going to get the crowbar and get this lid off here, Momma. There's something in there that wants out."

The two women looked at each other.

An hour later, the last bolt broke. Cora stepped back out of the way while Maggie went to help her son slide the heavy lid off the well. A putrid odor assaulted them as the top grated open. They stopped, caught their breaths, and gave a final heave, and the lid slid off the opening and one edge fell to the ground.

"Good God!" Justin's hand covered his mouth. Maggie screamed and backed away. A moan escaped Sally Ann's black and swollen lips as she tried to shield her blind, jerking eyes with a forearm that had lost its muscular control. "Momma, help me!" Justin shouted. Maggie shook her head, eyes riveted on the apparition from the well, and backed farther away. "Grandma?" Cora moved in quickly and, fighting the reaction from the terrible smell, grabbed the thin brittle wrist and stilled its flailing about.

"Grab her ankles, Justin, and we'll ease her out of there." Sally Ann had wedged herself into a niche four inches high by three inches deep, between the cover and the top lip of the well. Working carefully, pulling gently, one leg at a time, the hips, then the shoulders were eased out. They set her down on the grass and Cora sent Justin for a bucket of cool water.

It was the body of a little girl, but it was as light as a paper bag. Breasts were sunken into the ribs, and the toes were worn down, leaving raw wounds on her feet. Strands of blond hair remained, but most of the head was bald and raw, and her shoulder bones were laid bare where the flesh had been scraped off. Eyes were sunk deep into their sockets and as Cora washed away the blood and grime from her face, the girl became semiconscious and started sucking the cloth. "Easy, girl. Not too much to drink at first." She removed the cloth, and immediately the girl tried to speak.

The swollen tongue wagged through toothless gums as clicking noises came gagging from deep in her throat. Cora turned to Justin who was gaping at the sight. "Justin, get your mother and cover up this hole, then help me get this poor thing into the house."

Maggie stepped forward. "No!"

Cora turned and looked up at her, a puzzled frown asking the question.

"She's come back to haunt me, Momma. It's Sally Ann, back from the grave!"

Cora looked down at the frail creature and she caught her breath. "Great Mother of God," she breathed quietly. She scooped the girl up in her arms and carried her into the cool house, the bent baby spoon still dangling from one finger.

4

After a brief knock on the door, Cora entered the room. "Are you awake?"

"Yes."

"I brought you some breakfast."

"I'm not very hungry."

"If you don't eat, girl, you won't be able to keep up your strength." Cora set the tray down on the dresser. "Here. At least have some toast."

Sally Ann sat up in bed and took the plate of wheat toast from her mother. "Thanks."

"And after you eat, I'll take another look at those toes. You should be up and walking about now. That'll bring back your appetite."

"I want to see Michael."

Cora sighed. She drew up a chair from the desk and sat down. "I guess it's time we talked the truth to each other, Sally Ann. Michael doesn't know you're here."

"Well, tell him. I'm well enough to see him now."

"It isn't that simple. You see, when you disappeared, Michael mourned you for a long,

long time. We all did. We didn't know if you'd run off or been kidnapped or what. But there was never any word, and so we finally had to get over it and get on with living our lives. I know your Papa prayed for you every day of his life. And Michael . . . well, he had to get on with his life, too. Once you were declared dead, he remarried. So now he has a family, and we don't want anything to interfere with his happiness."

"Any *thing?* You mean me! But if he waited so long, he can't have much of a family yet. Oh, Momma, the only thing that kept me going down there was thinking of Michael. I've really got to see him. I've got something to tell him."

"You've been gone a long time, Sally Ann. Michael and Maggie have four children . . ."

"Maggie? *Maggie?* Michael married Maggie?" Sally threw the covers off her legs and started to get up. "You've no right to keep me here. I want to see my husband."

Cora pushed her back to bed with one hand. Still so frail, she thought. "He's not your husband any longer, Sally Ann. He and Maggie have four children; did you hear me?"

Sally stopped struggling against her mother and lay her head back on the pillow. She closed her eyes, feeling faint from the exertion. She couldn't possibly have heard what she thought she heard.

"You've been gone twenty years, Sally Ann."

The room started spinning. She heard a voice from far off saying "Clinton! Wait for me, Clint." It was her own voice, but her head seemed stuffed with cotton. She felt a cool cloth on her forehead, and she waited until the buzzing in her ears died away. Twenty years. Twenty years of her life wasted in an underground hole. She was now thirty-six years old. And scarred and ugly and Michael was lost to her forever. Tears leaked out of the corners of her eyes and she reached for her mother's hand.

5

Cora was cleaning up the luncheon dishes in the kitchen while Sally Ann did her daily exercises on the living-room floor. Her body had healed well, and though the scarred skin was pulled taut over her back, the muscles were starting to come back. She had gained weight and walked with barely a trace of a limp. Her eyes had stopped that incessant jerking, and her sight was returning rapidly.

"Momma?"

"Yes, dear?"

The problem, as she viewed herself in the mirror, was the face. Her parchment skin showed blue veins as it clung to her bones. Over her sunken cheeks were patches of scaly skin that itched and turned red and white when she scratched them. Her head was still bald and scarred, even though the hair was growing back in spots. A scarf hid most of that. Her lips and what teeth were left were black as tar. She looked like a living skull.

She thought constantly of Clint—she missed him almost more than she could bear—but there were things she needed to do before she could go back to him. He would be all right. He was in his element, he was twenty years old, and—the darkness loved him.

"I want to go to town."

"I think that's a very good idea if you're feeling up to it."

"I want to see the dentist."

Cora stood in the doorway and dried her hands on a dish towel. Sally Ann looked up at her and said, "Don't worry. I'll use a fake name."

Pain crossed Cora's face, and she turned and went back to the kitchen. It is so unfair,

Sally thought. She was supposed to pick up the pieces of her life. But where was she to start, when her own family wouldn't even support her? Well, at least the situation was clear.

Cora walked to the bedroom and returned with a simple housedress that might fit Sally's slim frame. "Here. Try this on and I'll call Dr. Green for an appointment."

The trip to town was traumatic for both of them. Cora didn't like lying to the doctor, and there wasn't much he could do about Sally Ann's teeth anyway. He filled two cavities, gave her a prescription for vitamins and calcium, and tried to get her to come back for dentures. Sally Ann knew he was trying to be kind, and he was more than curious about her appearance. She thanked him and they were on their way.

She bought a new pair of jeans, tennis shoes, socks, several T-shirts, and a jacket. Clothes felt so binding. She also bought a child's sweater, size ten, light blue and soft. Cora asked no questions. The worst of the trip was the way everyone stared. Cora introduced her as a friend from the city who had come to recuperate in the good country air, and people were nice, but they still stared. They stared at her face, her teeth, at the way she walked, and they kept their distance. By the time Cora and Sally got home, both were exhausted.

The next day, the inevitable happened. After two months, Michael finally came over, to ask about Cora's friend visiting from the city. He had heard from someone at church, and was hoping to get some information about a man he was working with on a land deal. Cora told him her friend was resting, and she was, but she was listening from the bedroom.

Michael's voice. Deeper now, but just as she remembered it. Could it hurt him all that much to see her? All these years of thinking of him, dreaming of him, wondering how he was faring. What did he look like? What had twenty years done to his face? To his body? Their voices were a murmur now; she assumed they had walked into the kitchen to talk, in order not to disturb Cora's resting friend.

Then he laughed. A hearty, resonant laugh, and her chest constricted with brutal force. What has he to laugh about? When was the last time I laughed? Oh, God, I want to laugh with him. Touch him. She got up from bed and put on her jeans and a T-shirt. She wrapped a scarf about her head quickly and put the tennis shoes over the bandages on her feet. She looked in the mirror and her heart fell. I can never let him see me like this. She opened the door a crack and peeked out.

He was standing by the front door, ready to leave, when he saw the door open. "I believe your friend is awake, Mom. Do you think she'd mind talking to me for a minute?"

Cora paled as she saw the door ajar. "Well, no, I suppose not, Michael. Let me ask her." She walked over to the door, knocked, and went in. "*What do you think you are doing?*" she hissed.

"Why no, I'd be delighted," Sally Ann said loudly and pushed past her mother and out the door. She walked directly to Michael who winced as he saw her, then quickly recovered with a smile.

"How do you do? I'm Michael Hixson. I understand you're visiting from the city, and I thought you might know of a man by the name of Ralph Lederer. I'm thinking of buying a piece of property that he owns next to my farm and wondered if you had any word of his reputation."

He didn't recognize her. She was lost for words. She was ready for his hurt, his anger, his denial, his love, his passing out and falling on the floor, but she was *not* ready for this! What to do? Should she say, hello, Michael, I'm Sally Ann and we have a son who is living in underground caverns like a bat? Should she throw her arms around him and kiss him and make him forget all about Maggie? Should she embarrass him and say, Michael, don't you even recognize your own wife when you see her? Should she sink to the floor and hug his knees and say how long she'd been dreaming of this moment?

She stared at him, then looked at her feet. "I don't know, Mr. Hixson. The name is not familiar."

"Well, okay. I appreciate your time. You look a little pale. Maybe I shouldn't have disturbed your rest."

"No, it's quite all right. Please excuse me." She returned to her room, shut the door, then leaned heavily against it.

After Michael left, Cora came into the room quietly and sat on the edge of the bed. Sally Ann was strangely quiet. The experiences Sally had gone through had prepared her in some ways for things Cora couldn't even dream about. "How about some lunch?"

Sally kept her gaze steady on the ceiling. "That would be nice, Momma."

6

Clint sat on the moss mattress and picked at it while he thought. He missed his mother. His eyes were swollen from crying, and his grief had given way to anger.

"I don't care." The sound of his voice in the Home Cavern was hollow, but comforting. He knew she had made it; he had stayed by the hole in the wall and listened. He heard other voices, and the hole was invaded by a powerful monster, a presence that pierced his brain and knocked him back into the tunnel. It hurt his head. It was like a dream he had when he slept, where images danced around and said silly things and "looked" a funny way. He still didn't understand "look," but that's what his mommy said. He lay there, frightened, until he heard the grating of the lid again and the monster was gone.

There really was an "up there." He had known it all along. He pretended he didn't believe, because he didn't want her to go. He didn't want to go. He liked it here. There were things to play with and it was comfortable. Up there was strange, and he didn't much like the stories she told.

"Why would she go there? What's up there that she needs? We have everything here. Why would she want to leave me?" Tears of anger again seeped out of his eyes, and he reached down to stroke himself, his only comfort. "I'd like to punish her when she gets back. Oh, yes." The pleasure was intense. "I'd like to hurt her like she hurt me." Faster. "I'll hit her and pinch her and knock her down." He thought he would burst. "And she'll beg me." His orgasm was violent, his whole body stiffened with the release. Afterward, he felt happy and free. He went for a swim.

Every so often, he returned to the hole in the wall by the square rocks. She was never there. He felt lonely, he missed her, but he never really felt alone. The air of the tunnels, the familiar feel of the rocks under his feet, the cold ponds and their inhabitants were his companions. When he felt sad, or angry, he would think he had chased her away. Then he would stroke himself and feel better again. It gave him intense pleasure until he learned that cutting the fish was better. That was even more intense. He tortured them while they were still alive, and they flopped and writhed and slowly died.

He took all these fish and bundled them up in moss and carried them past the tunnel that led to the square rock wall to a different cavern, a cavern with a little pond on one side and a huge lake on the other side. He dumped them in the lake, far away from where the stench would bother him. These fish were dirty; he could not eat them.

But mostly, he waited. He sat in the dark, blind eyes staring into nothingness, thinking about his mother, choosing not to think about the light and the world above. He thought she would be back soon, and they would live forever in the caves. Together.

7

Sally diligently worked her body until it was fit. She swam in the old swimming hole she and Jackie used to frequent when they were children. She couldn't comprehend that she was now middle-aged, that Clint was twenty years old, that her life was thoroughly destroyed. She took long walks through the woods and the fields. The aged and worn boards that covered the stairs to the tunnel were still there, the lock and hinges rusted solid. She would sit with her back to the big trees and stare at the cover, thinking about time, about life, about fairness.

She'd seen Michael's children, too. Justin, about thirteen years old, strong, tall, looking much like his father. The twins, eleven years old, with thick red hair like Maggie's, turned-up noses and freckles; Ellen and Elsie. And Mary. Different from the rest. No more than four, she was small, thin, with hands and feet too big for her size and very, very shy. The children would swim in the pond as she watched, quietly hidden in the woods. She didn't want to frighten them, and she didn't want to have to answer any questions.

Cora was a good woman. They talked sometimes far into the night. But she could never understand. Sally Ann hadn't told her about Clint, because this was not his world. He didn't believe in it, and who was she to keep telling him that there was something better? She had survived with the dream that back with her family she would be happy again. She wanted a normal life for him. She wanted him to be surrounded by love and family and all the things she wanted for herself. But maybe none of that was to be for them. There was no happiness up here.

Her body was healed. She was gaining weight. Now she had some decisions to make.

Her mother encouraged her to get out and socialize, but the thought was frightening. She had nothing to say to anyone. Except Michael. She had plenty to say to him, and Maggie as well. But she wouldn't. There was no point. She sighed.

On the way back to the house, she saw Michael and Maggie's home on the hill where once her dream house was to have stood. The sun was going down and lights were on. It looked so homey, so comfortable. As if they had a will of their own, her feet took her closer to the house. She saw the barn off to the side. Michael kept it all painted up nice. The tractor looked fairly new; the grounds were neat, the trees tall and picturesque. Close enough now to see through the window, Sally Ann kept the big tree in the front yard between her and the kitchen window. When she reached it, she leaned against it and tried to talk sense into herself. "What are you hoping to accomplish by spying on them?" Her conscience would not let her alone.

The temptation however, ruled her actions, and she peered around the tree and into the kitchen. There was Maggie. Fat as always. She didn't want to see any more, but she couldn't help herself. She stood next to the tree, eyes riveted on the warm little scene inside, and she was fantasizing that she was the one in there, making dinner for the babies and loving them all. She was so caught up that she didn't hear Michael come up behind her until he spoke.

"Hello?"

Her face burned a bright red, and she was grateful for the fading light. "Oh, hello. I was, uh, just admiring your house."

He looked at her carefully. "You're Cora's friend, aren't you?"

"Yes. I was just out walking."

"It's getting late. I think you should be getting back." His face softened. "Can I give you a lift?"

"Oh, well . . ." She smiled. "If it wouldn't be too much of an inconvenience. I am rather tired."

"Not at all. Why don't you come in and meet my wife while I get the keys to the truck."

Sally Ann smiled inwardly. She felt devilish. She followed him to the door.

"Maggie? Honey, come meet a friend of your mom's. She was out walking and got a little too tired, so I'm going to give her a lift back." He turned to Sally. "I'll be back in a minute." He disappeared down the hall.

Maggie walked warily into the living room. Her tone was venomous. "*What in the hell are you doing here?*"

Sally Ann smiled. "Well, hello, Maggie. It's been a long time, hasn't it? You're looking well."

"Don't play cutsie with me, Sally Ann. If you tell Michael who you are, I'll finish ruining your ugly face."

Sally took a step toward her sister. "Maggie, I don't want to hurt anybody. I just want to make a life for myself."

"Then go make it somewhere else. You can't do it here, and you can't do it with us!" Maggie almost spit those last words, then turned on her heel and went back to the kitchen. Sally Ann sat down, put her face in her hands, and started to cry.

She felt Michael's hand on her shoulder. "Are you all right, Mrs. . . . Mrs. . . . uh, I don't even know your name—I'm sorry."

"SALLY ANN HIXSON!" she wanted to scream in his face. She looked up at the concern in his face and started to cry harder. "Can't . . ."

"Mrs. Cant? Maggie? Would you fetch a glass of water for Mrs. Cant, please?"

Sally Ann took the proffered glass of water and drank it down without looking at Maggie. She didn't need to see the hate that was written all over her face; she could feel it emanating from her whole being. "Thank you very much. I'm feeling better now. Maybe we'd better go."

She went straight to her room, past her mother sitting silently in the living room. The next morning she was gone.

8

"Clint? Clint. It's Mommy. I'm back." Sally Ann raced through the tunnel, holding tight to the wrist of the wailing child she was half dragging behind her. "Get up and walk or I'll leave you here!" The child cried louder, trying desperately to keep up, hiccuping fear. "Clint!"

Her sense of navigation came back in a rush. She knew exactly where she was going. The tunnels were her old friends. The smell, the roughness beneath her shoes, the blessed darkness, all meant she was home. And at home she would find peace.

She felt empathy for the child trailing behind her. The initial blindness was an awesome, frightening thing. They ran through the first tunnel that wound around, then approached the huge cavern with Monster Lake. She tried to hush up the girl before they entered, and succeeded in lowering her screams to a whimper. Sally tried to suppress the terrible constriction she felt in her stomach as they entered the cave. They crossed the path between the lakes as quickly and quietly as possible. As soon as they were back into the comfortable tunnels, they took off running again.

"Jackie?" But even as she called, she knew Jackie was gone forever. "Clint! Come see what Mommy has brought you." Out of breath, they slowed to a walk, and passed an auxiliary tunnel that had a dank and terrible smell to it. The well was at the end of this tunnel. She stopped and put her face up to Mary's. "Smell that? You must never, never go near this place. The whole underworld is yours to play in, but you must return to the Home Cavern as soon as you get near that smell."

"I don't want to play here. Please. I'm scared. I want to go home."

"This is home for you now, Mary."

After an exhausted sleep, Mary was slightly more docile, and she followed Sally Ann as long as they kept contact with their hands. How flexible the young are, Sally thought. How adaptable. The sleep felt wonderful. She awoke refreshed and invigorated. Ready for a new day. It was so good to have your sleeping and eating regulated by the body rather than by the sun. She laughed and skipped along the main tunnel, teaching Mary how to quench her thirst by sucking the dripping water from the side of the tunnel.

Eventually, they reached Home Cavern, and Clint was there.

They hugged each other and cried together and she felt all over his whole body to make sure he was all right. Thin, perhaps, but that is the way of the underworld.

"I brought you some surprises, Clint. Some jam." She took the small jar out of her bag and handed it to him. She laughed at his puzzlement, took it back and opened it for him. He stuck his finger in and licked it.

"Ick. What's that taste?"

"Sugar, honey. You're supposed to like it."

"I don't like nothing from there."

"How about this?" and she handed him the sweater. "Here, I'll help you put it on."

"I don't much like this either." He kept running his hands over the soft wool. "What's making those noises?"

"That's your new sister, Mary. She's come to live with us and be your playmate."

"She doesn't sound so good."

"I was afraid like that when I first got here. Be nice to her. She'll learn the ways of our life soon."

Clint walked over to Mary. "Wanna swim?"

"I want to go home," she sniffed.

"She's dumb, Mommy."

"Give her time, honey."

While Mary slept, Sally Ann and Clint talked. He wasn't interested in hearing much about the time she'd spent "in the sun," but she did tell him that some people would probably come into the tunnels to look for them. "Can we find a place to hide for a while, Clint?"

"Sure. I've found some places that nobody else could find."

Sally sensed a change in Clint. He seemed older. Distant. Maybe it was because she knew that he was twenty years old, instead of thinking he was only about eight. Maybe being on his own for a couple of months had matured him.

After sleep they started. They dumped the jam into the lake and filled the jar with food. That went into her bag along with the extra T-shirts she had brought and some moss. Mary was a problem, but Sally Ann had expected it and was prepared. Clint tried to emulate her patience, but it was hard for him. He was so swift in the tunnels.

Clint led them down a series of side tunnels that were barely big enough to crawl through in some places. Up and down they went, following his lead.

Finally, one tunnel came to a dead end at a lake and they had to swim underwater to find the opening on the other side. This was nearly an impossible task for Mary, but the fact that she was so small and light helped a lot; they virtually held her breath for her and pulled her under and through the tunnel entrance.

The other side was a perfect space. It was dry and warm, with a deep swimming hole in the middle, and a brisk stream running down one side. The new Home Cavern.

Sally set up housekeeping, making beds, preparing a toilet, continually keeping her ears open for invaders. They came, but she never heard them.

Part Three

1

Sally Ann and Mary sat on the side of the swimming hole, their feet dangling in the water. The children were playing loudly in the pool, splashing and laughing. Clint was throwing them high into the air and they begged for turns over and over again. He was a good father.

"I'm going to go away for a while, Mary. I have some unfinished business to take care of."

Mary grabbed her hand. "Are you going up there? Can I go and take the boys? Can Clint go? Can we all go with you, Sally? Oh, please?"

"You know Clint and the children can never leave this place, Mary. And your place is here with them. This is your home now. I'll be back. I won't be gone long."

"I wish you wouldn't go."

"I know, dear. I'll be back before you miss me. Time passes quickly down here."

Clint had nothing to say when she told him. His silence spoke of his disapproval. She packed some gear and left without further discussion.

The door at the top of the stairs was open, as she expected. She knew Michael would leave it that way in case any of them cared to return. She spent two days at the bottom of the stairs, getting used to the light, then ventured up. It was hot.

How do I look now, she wondered. She skirted the woods and made her way to her mother's house. Strengthening her resolve, she knocked on the kitchen door. Her mother looked dully out at her.

"You've come back."

"Yes. Momma."

"Well, come in and clean up."

Not exactly a rousing welcome, but about what she had expected. After all, she had kidnapped Michael's youngest daughter and given her a life in the caverns. Not an act to endear her to the family.

After she showered, she put on the clean housedress her mother had laid out. She examined herself in the mirror. Her face looked about the same. A few more lines around the mouth and eyes, maybe. Somehow she didn't feel nearly as monstrous as she had the last time she was here. The smell of bacon frying came through from the kitchen. She joined her mother, wordlessly set the table, then sat down and waited.

"How's Mary?"

"She's fine. She's happy, Momma."

Her mother turned with fury in her eyes. "Don't you dare talk of happiness to me. You. Living under the earth like a worm. Destroying all that Michael and Maggie had by taking their little girl like you did. You're Satan himself."

Sally Ann endured her mother's venom. She knew it had to come out sooner or later, and was glad Cora could get it off her chest so soon. She stood up and put her arms around her mother as she stood at the stove. She felt the silent sobs shake her frail frame. Her mother had grown old. Very old.

"Oh, Sally Ann, why have you come back again? Just when a hurt has healed, you come back to pick it open again. Why do you do that?"

"I've come to see Michael."

"I guess I knew that the moment I saw you at the door. Well, there's the phone. Get it over with."

The number was written on a list Cora kept on the wall. Sally dialed the number slowly, praying that Maggie wouldn't answer the phone. She did.

"Hello?"

"Hello, Maggie. This is Sally Ann. May I speak to Michael, please?"

The phone bounced on the floor, and Sally Ann visualized Maggie's open-mouthed shock. The idea gave her distinct pleasure.

"Hello? Hello, who's this?" Michael asked.

"Hello, Michael. This is Sally Ann. Would you come to breakfast at Mother's this morning?"

"Oh, my God . . ." The phone went dead.

Sally smiled, slowly hanging up the phone. "He'll be right over, Momma." Cora left the room. Sally heard the bedroom door close.

Michael pulled up to the front door in a cloud of dust, got out of the truck, and walked up the front steps. He paused for a deep breath, then opened the screen door and came in. "Sally Ann?"

"In the kitchen, Michael."

He came in and sat down at the kitchen table. He was visibly trying to keep himself under control. "Where's Mary, Sally Ann?"

She turned to look at him and he took in the black teeth, the scaly, thin skin, the ragged hair, and the arms so thin they were like little sticks. All his anger disappeared.

"I came back to tell you that you have three grandchildren." His mouth fell open and he stared at her. "Three beautiful children, Michael. They play in the water and laugh and love. And they don't believe in you."

A new type of anger held him to his seat. The thought of three children in caves. What kind of a monster was this woman? Then he thought of Mary. Sweet Mary. Like a flower. She survived down there? But . . . who was the father? He laughed. "You're insane, Sally. There's no children. There's just you and your twisted ways. I knew Mary. She was too fragile. She could never have survived down there."

"You're wrong, Michael, I survived. And your *son* survived." Shock froze his face.

"My son?"

"Yes. *Our* son. And now he and Mary have three children. I'm sorry I don't have pictures of them for you."

He jumped up and grabbed her skull and started to squeeze. He could feel her thin, brittle bones, and he just wanted to pop her head like a melon. "You monster! I'll kill you for this!" His rage was born of fear, and didn't last. His hands slipped from her head to rest on her shoulders, and he started to cry. She put a comforting hand on his face.

"It's not so bad, Michael. They're really very happy. It's a whole different type of existence down there, but it's not a bad life."

"We looked for you," he sobbed. "We searched for weeks. There are so damned many tunnels down there. We all got sick. We couldn't believe that anybody could live down there. Oh, Sally Ann." He sank to the floor and hugged her legs. "My soul ached to think you have been down there all those years. All those years I had given you up for dead. I locked you down there that day and didn't know it. And I've lived with that guilt ever since."

She stroked his hair. "It's okay, Michael. I thought it wasn't, but it is now. Everything is all right. Our son is a good man, and he's a good father to the boys and a good husband to Mary."

"When Mary was missing and Maggie told me it was you staying here with Mom, I didn't believe her. I hit her. She makes me so angry sometimes. But I had to believe her when your Mom said the same thing, and the lock was broken off the door to the stairs. Our life hasn't been the same since." Sally Ann smiled slowly above his head. "How could you . . . ? How did you raise a child down there?"

"One has to do what one has to do, Michael. His name is Clinton."

"My God. Will you take me to see them?"

"Of course, Michael. You won't be able to really see them, it's too dark. But I'll take you to them, if you like."

Cora paled when Sally told her what had happened. "You can't take Michael down there!"

"I can and I will. Besides, he wants to go. He wants to see his son."

Cora looked at her in horror, then turned to her closet. She put on a jacket and scarf. "Where are you going, Momma?"

"To church."

2

Sally Ann laughed when she saw what Michael brought with him. A whole backpack, with sleeping bag, food, fresh clothes, and flashlights. "No flashlights," she said.

"I can't go down there without a flashlight."

"If you take a light, you go alone." He saw the resolve in her grotesque face. Reluctantly, he left them behind.

They descended. She breathed the familiar air of the main tunnel. Refreshing. She urged Michael to walk faster, but he was unaccustomed to walking in the dark so their progress was stumbling and slow. "At this rate, it will take us a month to get to them." He didn't think that was very funny, but Sally laughed. He was amazed at her ability to navigate.

When they reached Monster Lake, Sally told him of the beast that lived in the waters to the left of the path. They rested near the entrance, and when Sally made a meal of the slugs they found on the floor, Michael found this practice so revolting that he quite lost his appetite. She laughed at this, too. "You'll be eating them soon enough." He didn't believe that a monster lived in the lake and told her so. "Take a swim in there, then, if you don't believe." The thought of swimming in total darkness made his flesh crawl.

He found his backpack cumbersome, and Sally was quickly losing patience with his slow pace. In fact, she was not as thrilled to be with him as she had imagined she would be. He was foreign here. This was not his element. He didn't belong. Well, she would take him to see his children and grandchildren, and then he could go back.

They tiptoed through Monster Cavern, then resumed their normal slow pace. Sally found the temptation to leave him when he was sleeping deliciously irresistible. He would wake up and find himself alone. The panic in his voice as he shouted for her was comforting. Then she would return to him and he was so glad to have her back. At last she was needed. Clint had needed her, but that was different. This was Michael, the man she had needed for a long, long time. And now he needed her. Not for companionship, but for basic survival. She loved it.

They stopped frequently and slept. She convinced him that there were tunnels too small to take the pack into, so he agreed to leave it, taking with him only his essentials—sandwiches. Along the way she told him stories of Clint and his growing up and what a delight he was. He shared with her stories of his children. Justin, he said, was in the air force, thinking about making a career of it. The twins had been modeling and making television ads for some time. He spoke of his marriage to Maggie, how it had come about, how her father had died, the relationship between Cora and Maggie. She encouraged him to talk; it made her realize how little she missed that world. In fact, she was glad she was back where she was comfortable.

As they passed the tunnel with the dank smell, she told him of her grueling trip up the well shaft, adding bits here and there about how much she had missed him. He was horrified. She was glad.

They reached the first Home Cavern and she showed him where she had given birth, where for twenty years they had had their home. He was beginning to have an appreciation for her strength, her courage. She could feel it, and he made little comments alluding to the fact that he had no idea . . . Of course he had no idea. What a fool he was. She impressed upon him the number of smaller tunnels, some dead ends, some leading to huge caverns with hundred-foot drop-offs, the dangers of wandering without knowing where you were going. He insisted he would stick close to her.

She felt a growing surge of power in this relationship. The tables had indeed turned and she was enjoying every minute of it. She toyed with the idea of just leaving him and letting him find for himself the overpowering fear. Let him discover his own inner strength, she told herself with contempt. It takes no balls to ride a tractor. Was this the man she had pined for during more than thirty years in the underworld? This was her God, this weak man who carried peanut-butter sandwiches with him and whined when she wasn't by his side when he awoke? She must have been insane.

They continued through tunnels barely large enough for Michael's muscular body, up and down shafts, eating when hungry, resting when tired. They finally reached the lake, and the underwater doorway to Home Cavern.

At the large lake, they camped. Michael didn't know that his children and grandchildren were so close, just on the other side of the wall. No sounds escaped the underwater entrance. Suddenly she didn't want Michael to see them. She wanted to keep him under her control. She realized that he might want to take her babies back with him, and that was out of the question. She prayed Clint or Mary or one of the boys wouldn't come out this way while they were there.

"Tell me, Michael. Does Maggie know you're with me?"

"Oh, yes. She didn't like it, but then she doesn't like much anymore. I didn't tell her about Clinton. I told her you were taking me to see Mary."

"I see." Sally Ann grinned in the darkness. A plan was taking form in her mind.

3

After sleeping three or four times, Michael was anxious to get under way. Sally Ann delayed their departure as long as she dared, then led him down a tunnel, far away from the Home Cavern where the children played. She remembered from long ago another cavern, much like the one Michael expected, and she took him there. It took them a long time. She doubled back down different tunnels, and frequently he would ask, "Didn't we come this way?" and she would laugh at him and call him foolish. She enjoyed the power she held over him. It was time he learned something.

Finally, they stopped just outside the cavern. Sally Ann talked to Michael in a low voice, as if the others could hear. "Michael. They're not used to anybody else, you know. Clinton doesn't even believe in you, so he won't let the boys believe in you, either. Mary has been here a long time, and she's not sure who to believe, so don't expect a major welcome. This is their territory, you know, and you're an intruder. They may even ignore you, or tell you to go away. But they're flexible. They'll get used to you."

How well he knew what an intruder he was. She had made him feel very uncomfortable since the beginning of this damned journey, and he was now sorry he had ever agreed to come. He was totally at her mercy, and he didn't like that at all. She seemed a little crazed. "I'll be all right. Let's go."

They turned the corner and Sally Ann went dancing into the cavern. "Clinton! We're home! Mary? Boys? Come see the surprise I've brought." Silence reverberated in the huge room.

"There's no one here, Sally."

"Oh, they're probably just busy. Or maybe they're hiding. They'll come back soon."

They sat down to wait. Sally fidgeted, as her mind raced. They didn't wait long. "Here they are, Michael." She got up and ran to the back of the cavern. "Hello, Clint. And Mary. How are you? I told you I wouldn't be gone long. Come say hello to your daddy." Michael was silent at the entrance to the cavern.

"There's nobody here, Sally."

"Nonsense, Michael. Here they are, right here. Clint, shake hands with your dad. Mary, where are the boys? Oh, here they are. Hello, fellas. My, you've grown, just in the short time I've been away. Michael, meet little Jimmy and Jerry and this is Jonah. Aren't they sweet?" She worked hard to keep up the chatter in the empty cavern.

"Sally, stop it!" His voice echoed in the cavern.

"Why, Michael? What's the matter?"

His breath stuck in his throat. She was insane. She talked such a good story that she had duped him into coming into this hellhole, and now he was stuck down here with a madwoman. He turned and darted down the tunnel.

"Michael, wait!" She could hardly suppress the giggles that seemed to have overtaken her. Whatever had gotten into her to do such a thing to him? She followed him out, her tennis shoes silent on the tunnel floor. "Michael," she called out musically to him. "You'll never make it out of here aloooone." She heard his footsteps echoing in the distance. She skipped along gaily behind him. She would be sure he wouldn't get lost. But a good scare never hurt anyone, either.

She was surprised at the way he circumvented her roundabout path. He seemed to know where he was going and didn't get lost in the maze of tunnels and tributaries. He crawled through the smaller tunnels with amazing speed, and this gave her great amusement. All the way back she teased and tantalized him with bits and pieces of her thoughts. Always out of reach, her voice echoed around him. He remained steadfastly silent.

When he stopped to sleep, she would sneak around him and wake him with great peals of echoing laughter, eerie in the pressing darkness. The low curses he muttered to himself tickled her even more. What had gotten into her that she would act this way? No matter. He was close to the stairs now. They passed the well tunnel and she hollered ahead to him, "Michael. Cockroaches almost ate me in there while I was coming to you. Doesn't that make you hungry, Michael? Have some slugs, Michael," and her insane giggles echoed through the night.

When he'd had enough, he stopped short and hid quietly in a turn of the tunnel. When she skipped past him, he reached out and grabbed her. "Sally Ann. Am I on the right way out of here?" She laughed. "Tell me." He shook her until she felt her eyes rattle in her head.

"Oh, Michael. Don't be a spoilsport. Of course you're on the right way. I wouldn't let my little baby, the love of my life, get lost in these dark, dirty tunnels, now, would I?" He threw her to the side and continued on, weak from hunger, heartsick and tired. He entered Monster Cavern. She followed, making monster noises, taunting him, wearing him down.

"Come here, Sally Ann." His voice was calm, quiet.

"No. You'll hurt me. You'll feed me to the monster."

"Don't be a petulant child. Come here. I want to talk to you." He was sitting on a rock at the edge of the lake. She heard him pick up a handful of pebbles and start throwing them into the water. They landed with little plops. "Sally Ann, I want you to come back with me. They have places for people who need help readjusting to a new environment. I'll pay for it, and you'll like it there. There's no reason for you to stay down here and . . ."

"And ROT?" She shouted in his ear, surprising him. He stood up quickly, and his foot slipped on the rock. Arms waving wildly, he couldn't regain his balance, and he fell backward into the water. Sally Ann sobered immediately and went to his aid, but she heard splashing and slapping sounds in the water and the old fear once again took over her mind. She crouched on the path and whimpered.

"Sally Ann . . ." he gasped. "Oh, God! Sally, help me. Something's caught my leg. Sally! Oh, please." There was silence while he ducked under the water. He surfaced with a splash. "*Sally!*" One last scream, then he was gone. The surface of the water continued to agitate, and the waves lapped at her shoes as she stood in the middle of the path, horrified. Then all was silent.

"Michael?" she called out softly. Silence. "Michael, don't play any games with me. Come out of there." She backed up, toward the entrance to the cave. "Michael?" A little louder, a little braver. "Oh, God, *Michael!*" She turned and ran.

4

Clint didn't need to be told what had happened. He read it in her face, in her body, as they felt each other in greeting. He knew that an era was dead, that he no longer needed to view the other world as a threat. It was over; she was his now, like Mary, like the boys. He felt her loss. It was, after all, what had sustained her all this time. She would get over it. She was a survivor. Like him.

The angry meanness that had consumed him soon after his mother had gone vanished with her return. He lay on his bed of moss, the only one awake, and contemplated his growing empire. Mary was pregnant again, but it wasn't soon enough. He told her she had to have a girl.

He would build something here far superior to anything up there. He and his mother. She would help him.

She needed some time, he knew, to let the wound heal. Then they would go up there, together, and get what they needed. Two more girls should be enough. Young ones.

He turned over on his side and snuggled up to Mary's back. His hand felt the smooth swell of her baby. Yes. He smiled to himself. This baby girl and two more.

Frederik Pohl (b.1919)

We Purchased People

Fred Pohl is one of the great living science fiction writers and editors, winner of many awards for his novels and stories, including both the Hugo and Nebula Awards several times. Kingsley Amis, in his study of the literature of science fiction, *New Maps of Hell,* called him the best living science fiction writer. He edited *Galaxy* magazine for more than a decade and has held various senior editorial positions in book publishing, but has always returned to writing. He has written no category horror. This piece however, whose ending may be compared to the finale of Mark Twain's *Puddin'head Wilson* for horrific effect, is a pure example of the style, tropes, and conventions of science fiction being used to create a devastating and horrid impact. Furthermore, this compressed and intense social allegory is not merely a tricky plotted story, but a work that uses horror to awaken the sensitivities of the reader to good and evil, humane feeling, social injustice. Pohl is a moralist, like Twain, like Vonnegut, and in spite of his utopian strain, his major mode has been satire, sometimes quite dark. It is also a fascinating transformation of Robert Silverberg's "Passengers," showing how writers in a genre (in this case, science fiction) make the tropes evolve.

In the third of March the purchased person named Wayne Golden took part in trade talks in Washington as the representative of the dominant race of the Groombridge star. What he had to offer was the license of the basic patents on a device to convert nuclear power plant waste products into fuel cells. It was a good item, with a ready market. Since half of Idaho was already bubbling with radioactive wastes, the Americans were anxious to buy, and he sold for a credit of $100 million. On the following day he flew to Spain. He was allowed to sleep all the way, stretched out across two seats in the first-class section of the Concorde, with the fastenings of a safety belt gouging into his side. On the fifth of the month he used up part of the trade credit in the purchase of fifteen Picasso oils-on-canvas, the videotape of a flamenco performance and a fifteenth-century harpsichord, gilt with carved legs. He arranged for them to be preserved, crated, and shipped in bond to Orlando, Florida, after which the items would be launched from Cape Kennedy on a voyage through space that would take more than twelve thousand years. The Groombridgians were not in a hurry and thought big. The Saturn Five booster rocket cost $11 million in itself. It did not matter. There was plenty of money left in the Groombridge credit balance. On the fifteenth of the month Golden returned to the United States, made a close connection at Logan Airport in Boston, and arrived early at his home kennel in Chicago. He was then given eighty-five minutes of freedom.

I knew exactly what to do with my eighty-five minutes. I always know. See, when you're working for the people who own you you don't have any choice about what you do, but up to a point you can think pretty much whatever you like. That thing you get in your head only controls you. It doesn't change you, or anyway I don't think it does. (Would I know if I were changed?)

My owners never lie to me. Never. I don't think they know what a lie is. If I ever needed anything to prove that they weren't human, that would be plenty, even if I didn't know they lived 86 zillion miles away, near some star that I can't even see. They don't tell me much, but they don't lie.

Not ever lying, that makes you wonder what they're like. I don't mean physically. I looked that up in the library once, when I had a couple of hours of free time. I don't remember where, maybe in Paris at the Bibliothèque Nationale, anyway I couldn't read what the language in the books said. But I saw the photographs and the holograms. I remember the physical appearance of my owners, all right. Jesus. The Altairians look kind of like spiders, and the Sirians are a little bit like crabs. But those folks from the Groombridge star, boy, they're something else. I felt bad about it for a long time, knowing I'd been sold to something that looked as much like a cluster of maggots on an open wound as anything else I'd ever seen. On the other hand, they're all those miles away, and all I ever have to do with them is receive their fast-radio commands and do what they tell me. No touching or anything. So what does it matter what they look like?

But what kind of freaky creature is it that never says anything that is not objectively the truth, never changes its mind, never makes a promise that it doesn't keep? They aren't machines, I know, but maybe they think I'm kind of a machine. You wouldn't bother to lie to a machine, would you? You wouldn't make it any promises. You wouldn't do it any favors, either, and they never do me any. They don't tell me that I can have eighty-five minutes off because I've done something they like, or because they want to sweeten me up because they want something from me. Everything considered, that's silly. What could they want? It isn't as if I had any choice. Ever. So they don't lie, or threaten, or bribe, or reward.

But for some reason they sometimes give me minutes or hours or days off, and this time I had eighty-five minutes. I started using it right away, the way I always do. The first thing was to check at the kennel location desk to see where Carolyn was. The locator clerk—he isn't owned, he works for a salary and treats us like shit—knows me by now. "Oh, hell, Wayne boy," he said with that imitation sympathy and lying friendliness that makes me want to kill him, "you just missed the lady friend. Saw her, let's see, Wednesday, was it? But she's gone." "Where to?" I asked him. He pushed around the cards on the locator board for a while, he knows I don't have very much time ever so he uses it up for me, and said: "Nope, not on my board at all. Say, I wonder. Was she with that bunch that went to Peking? Or was that the other little fat broad with the big boobs?" I didn't stop to kill him. If she wasn't on the board she wasn't in eighty-five-minute transportation range, so my eighty-five minutes—seventy-nine minutes—wasn't going to get me near her.

I went to the men's room, jerked off quickly, and went out into the miserable biting March Chicago wind to use up my seventy-nine minutes. Seventy-one minutes. There's a nice Mexican kind of restaurant near the kennel, a couple of blocks away past Ohio. They know me there. They don't care who I am. Maybe the brass plate in my head doesn't bother them because they think it's great that the people from the other stars are doing such nice things for the world, or maybe it's because I tip big. (What else do I have to do with the money I get?) I stuck my head in, whistled at Terry, the bartender, and said: "The usual. I'll be back in ten minutes." Then I walked up to Michigan and bought a clean shirt and changed into it, leaving the smelly old one. Sixty-six minutes. In the drugstore on the corner I picked up a couple of porno paperbacks and stuck them in my pockets, bought some cigarettes, leaned over and kissed the hand of the cashier, who was slim and fair-complexioned and smelled good, left her startled behind me, and got back to the restaurant just as Alicia, the waitress, was putting the gazpacho and the two bottles of beer on my table. Fifty-nine minutes. I settled down to enjoy my time. I smoked, and I ate, and I drank the beer, smoking between bites, drinking between puffs. You really look forward to something like that when you're working and not your own boss. I don't mean they don't let us eat when we're working. Of course they do, but we don't have any choice about what we eat or where we eat it. Pump fuel into the machine, keep it running. So I finished the guacamole and sent Alicia back for more of it when she brought the chocolate cake and American coffee, and ate the cake and the guacamole in alternate forkfuls. Eighteen minutes.

If I had had a little more time I would have jerked off again, but I didn't, so I paid the bill, tipped everybody, and left the restaurant. I got to the block where the kennel was with maybe two minutes to spare. Along the curb a slim woman in a fur jacket and pants suit was walking her Scottie away from me. I went up behind her and said, "I'll give you fifty dollars for a kiss." She turned around. She was all of sixty years old, but not bad, really, so I kissed her and gave her the fifty dollars. Zero minutes, and I just made it into the kennel when I felt the tingling in my forehead, and my owners took over again.

In the next seven days of March Wayne Golden visited Karachi, Srinagar, and Butte, Montana, on the business of the Groombridgians. He completed thirty-two assigned tasks. Quite unexpectedly he was then given 1,000 minutes of freedom.

That time I was in, I think it was, Pocatello, Idaho, or some place like that. I had to send a TWX to the faggy locator clerk in Chicago to ask about Carolyn. He took his time answering, as I knew he would. I walked around a little bit, waiting to hear. Everybody was very cheerful, smiling as they walked around through the dusty, sprinkly snow that was coming down, even smiling at me as though they didn't care that I was purchased, as they could plainly see from the golden oval of metal across my forehead that my owners use to tell me what to do. Then the message came back from Chicago: "Sorry, Wayne baby, but Carolyn isn't on my board. If you find her, give her one for me."

Well. All right. I have plenty of spending money, so I checked into a hotel. The bellboy brought me a fifth of Scotch and plenty of ice, fast, because he knew why I was in a hurry and that I would tip for speed. When I asked about hookers he offered anything I liked. I told him white, slim, beautiful asses. That's what I first noticed about Carolyn. It's special for me. The little girl I did in New Brunswick, what was her name—Rachel— she was only nine years old, but she had an ass on her you wouldn't believe.

I showered and put on clean clothes. The owners don't really give you enough time for that sort of thing. A lot of the time I smell. A lot of times I've almost wet my pants because they didn't let me go when I needed to. Once or twice I just couldn't help myself, held out as long as I could and, boy, you feel lousy when that happens. The worst was when I was covering some kind of a symposium in Russia, a place with a name like Akademgorodok. It was supposed to be on nuclear explosion processes. I don't know anything about that kind of stuff, and anyway I was a little mixed up because I thought that was one of the things the star people had done for us, worked out some way the different countries didn't have to have nuclear weapons and bombs and wars and so on anymore. But that wasn't what they meant. It was explosions at the nucleus of the galaxy they meant. Astronomical stuff. Just when a fellow named Eysenck was talking about how the FG prominence and the EMK prominence, whatever they were, were really part of an expanding pulse sphere, whatever that is, I crapped my pants. I knew I was going to. I'd tried to tell the Groombridge people about it. They wouldn't listen. Then the session redactor came down the aisle and shouted in my ear, as though my owners were deaf or stupid, that they would have to get me out of there, please, for reasons concerning the comfort and hygiene of the other participants. I thought they would be angry, because that meant they were going to miss some of this conference that they were interested in. They didn't do anything to me, though. I mean, as if there was anything they *could* do to me that would be any worse, or any different, from what they do to me all the time, and always will.

When I was all clean and in an open-necked shirt and chinos, I turned on the TV and poured a mild drink. I didn't want to be still drunk when my thousand minutes were up. There was a special program on all the networks, something celebrating a treaty between the United Nations and a couple of the star people, Sirians and Capellans it seemed to be. Everybody was very happy about it, because it seemed that now the Earth had bought some agricultural and chemical information, and pretty soon there would be more food than we could eat. How much we owed to the star people, the Secretary General of the UN was saying, in Brazilian-accented English. We could look forward to their wise guidance to help Earth survive its multitudinous crises and problems, and we should all be very happy.

But I wasn't happy, not even with a glass of John Begg and the hooker on her way up, because what I really wanted was Carolyn.

Carolyn was a purchased person, like me. I had seen her a couple of dozen times, all in all. Not usually when either of us was on freedom. Almost never when both of us were. It was sort of like falling in love by postcard, except that now and then we were physically close, even touching. And once or twice we had been briefly not only together, but out from under control. We had had about eight minutes once in Bucharest, after coming back from the big hydropower plant at the Iron Gate. That was the record, so far. Outside of that it was just that we passed, able to see each other but not to do anything about it, in the course of our duties. Or that one of us was free and found the other. When that happened the one of us that was free could talk, and even touch the other one, in any way that didn't interfere with what the other was doing. The one that was working couldn't do anything active, but could hear, or feel. We were both totally careful to avoid interfering with actual work. I don't know what would have happened if we had interfered. Maybe nothing? We didn't want to take that chance, though sometimes it was a temptation I could almost not resist. There was a time when I was free and I found Carolyn, working but not doing anything active, just standing there, at TWA Gate 51 at the St. Louis airport. She was waiting for someone to arrive. I really wanted to kiss her. I talked to her. I patted her, you know, holding my trenchcoat over my arm so that the people passing by wouldn't notice anything much. I told her things I wanted her to hear. But what I wanted was to kiss her, and I was afraid to. Kissing her on the mouth would have meant putting my head in front of her eyes. I didn't think I wanted to chance that. It might have meant she wouldn't see the person she was there to see. Who turned out to be a Ghanaian police officer arriving to discuss the sale of some political prisoners to the Groombridgians. I was there when he came down the ramp, but I couldn't stay to see if she would by any chance be free after completing the negotiations with him, because then my own time ran out.

But I had had three hours that time, being right near her. It felt very sad and very strange, and I wouldn't have given it up for anything in the world. I knew she could hear and feel everything, even if she couldn't respond. Even when the owners are running you, there's a little personal part of you that stays alive. I talked to that part of her. I told her how much I wished we could kiss, and go to bed, and be with each other. Oh, hell. I even told her I loved her and wanted to marry her, although we both know perfectly well there's not ever going to be any chance of that ever. We don't get pensioned off or retired; we're *owned*.

Anyway, I stayed there with her as long as I could. I paid for it later. Balls that felt as though I'd been stomped, the insides of my undershorts wet and chilly. And there wasn't any way in the world for me to do anything about it, not even by masturbating, until my next free time. That turned out to be three weeks later. In Switzerland, for God's sake. Out of season. With nobody in the hotel except the waiters and bellboys and a couple of old ladies who looked at the gold oval in my forehead as though it smelled bad.

It is a terrible but cherished thing to love without hope.

I pretended there was hope, always. Every bit of freedom I got, I tried to find her. They keep pretty careful tabs on us, all two or three hundred thousand of us purchased persons, working for whichever crazy bunch of creepy crawlers or gassy ghosts happens to have bought us to be their remote-access facilities on the planet they themselves cannot ever visit. Carolyn and I were owned by the same bunch, which had its good side and its bad side. The good side was that there was a chance that someday we would be free for quite a long while at the same time. It happened. I don't know why. Shifts change on the Groombridge planet, or they have a holiday or something. But every once in a while there would be a whole day, maybe a week, when none of the Groombridge people would be doing anything at all, and all of us would be free at once.

The bad side was that they hardly ever needed to have more than one of us in one place. So Carolyn and I didn't run into each other a lot. And the times when I was free for a pretty good period it took most of that to find her, and by the time I did she was like a half a world away. No way of getting there and back in time for duty. I did so much want to fuck her, but we had never made it that far and maybe never would. I never even got a chance to ask her what she had been sentenced for in the first place. I really didn't know her at all, except enough to love her.

When the bellboy turned up with my girl I was comfortably buzzed, with my feet up and the Rangers on the TV. She didn't look like a hooker, particularly. She was wearing hip-huggers cut below the navel, bigger breasted than I cared about but with that beautiful curve of waist and back into hips that I like. Her name was Nikki. The bellboy took my money, took five for himself, passed the rest to her, and disappeared, grinning. What's so funny about it? He knew what I was, because the plate in my head told him, but he had to think it was funny.

"Do you want me to take my clothes off?" She had a pretty, breathless little voice, long red hair, and a sweet, broad, friendly face. "Go ahead," I said. She slipped off the sandals. Her feet were clean, a little ridged where the straps went. Stepped out of the hip-huggers and folded them across the back of Conrad Hilton's standard armchair, took off the blouse and folded it, ducked out of the medallion and draped it over the blouse, down to red lace bra and red bikini panties. Then she turned back the bedclothes, got in, sat up, snapped off the bra, snuggled down, kicked the panties out of the side of the bed, and pulled the covers over her. "Any time, honey," she said. But I didn't lay her. I didn't even get in the bed with her, not under the covers; I drank some more of the Scotch, and that and fatigue put me out, and when I woke up it was daylight, and she had cleaned out my wallet. Seventy-one minutes left. I paid the bill with a check and persuaded them to give me carfare in change. Then I headed back for the kennel. All I got out of it was clean clothes and a hangover. I think I had scared her a little. Everybody knows how we purchased people came to be up for sale, and maybe they're not all the way sure that we won't do something bad again, because they don't know how reliably our owners keep us from ever doing anything they don't like. But I wished she hadn't stolen my money.

The overall strategies and objectives of the star people, particularly the people from Groombridge star who were his own masters, were unclear to the purchased person named Wayne Golden. What they did was not hard to understand. All the world knew that the star people had established fast-radio contact with the people of Earth, and that in order to conduct their business on Earth they had purchased the bodies of certain convicted criminals, installing in them tachyon fast-radio transceivers. Why they did what they did was less easy to comprehend. Art objects they admired and purchased. Certain rare kinds of plants and flowers they purchased and had frozen at liquid-helium temperatures. Certain kinds of utilitarian objects they purchased. Every few months another rocket roared up from Merritt Island, just north of the Cape, and another cargo headed for the Groombridge star, on its twelve-thousand-year voyage. Others, to other stars, peopled by other races in the galactic confraternity, took shorter times—or longer—but none of the times was short enough for those star people who made the purchases to come to Earth to see what they had bought. The distances were too huge.

What they spent most of their money on was the rockets. And, of course, the people they purchased, into whom they had transplanted their tachyon transceivers. Each rocket cost at least $10 million. The going rate for a healthy male paranoid capable of three or more decades of useful work was in the hundreds of thousands of dollars, and they bought them by the dozen.

The other things they bought, all of them—the taped symphonies and early-dynasty *ushabti*, the flowering orchids, and the Van Goghs—cost only a fraction of 1 percent of what they spent on people and transportation. Of course, they had plenty of money to spend. Each star race sold off licensing rights on its own kinds of technology. All of them received trade credits from every government on Earth for their services in resolving disputes and preventing wars. Still, it seemed to Wayne Golden, to the extent that he was capable of judging the way his masters conducted their affairs, a pretty high-overhead way to run a business, although of course neither he nor any other purchased person was ever consulted on questions like that.

By late spring he had been on the move for many weeks without rest. He completed sixty-eight tasks, great and small. There was nothing in this period of eighty-seven days that was in any way remarkable except that on one day in May, while he was observing the riots on the Place de la Concorde from a window of the American Embassy on behalf of his masters, the girl named Carolyn came into his room. She whispered in his ear, attempted unsuccessfully to masturbate him while the liaison attaché was out of the room, remained in all for some forty minutes, and then left, sobbing softly. He could not even turn his head to see her go. Then on the sixth of June the purchased person named Wayne Golden was returned to the Dallas kennel and given indefinite furlough, subject to recall at fifty minutes' notice.

Sweetest dear Jesus, nothing like that had ever happened to me before! It was like the warden coming into Death Row with the last-minute reprieve! I could hardly believe it.

But I took it, started moving at once. I got a fix on Carolyn's last reported whereabouts from the locator board and floated away from Dallas in a cloud of Panama Red, drinking champagne as fast as the hostess could bring it to me, en route to Colorado.

But I didn't find Carolyn there.

I hunted her through the streets of Denver, and she was gone. By phone I learned she had been sent to Rantoul, Illinois. I was off. I checked at the Kansas City airport, where I was changing planes, and she was gone from Illinois already. Probably, they weren't sure, they thought, to the New York district. I put down the phone and jumped on a plane, rented a car at Newark, and drove down the Turnpike to the Garden State, checking every car I passed to see if it was the red Volvo they thought she might be driving, stopping at every other Howard Johnson's to ask if they'd seen a girl with short black hair, brown eyes and a tip-tilted nose and, oh, yes, the golden oval in her forehead.

I remembered it was in New Jersey that I first got into trouble. There was the nineteen-year-old movie cashier in Paramus, she was my first. I picked her up after the 1 AM show. And I showed her. But she was really all wrong for me, much too old and much too worldly. I didn't like it much when she died.

After that I was scared for a while, and I watched the TV news every night, twice, at six and eleven, and never passed a newsstand without looking at all the headlines in the papers, until a couple of months had passed. Then I thought over what I really wanted very carefully. The girl had to be quite young and, well, you can't tell, but as much as I could be sure, a virgin. So I sat in a luncheonette in Perth Amboy for three whole days, watching the kids get out of the parochial school, before I found my second. It took a while. The first one that looked good turned out to be a bus kid, the second was a walker but her big sister from the high school walked with her. The third walked home alone. It was December, and the afternoons got pretty dark, and that Friday she walked, but she didn't get home. I never molested any of them sexually, you know. I mean, in some ways I'm still kind of a virgin. That wasn't what I wanted, I just wanted to see them die. When they asked me at the pre-trial hearing if I knew the difference between right and wrong I didn't know how to answer them. I knew what I did was wrong for them. But it wasn't wrong for me; it was what I wanted.

So, driving down the Parkway, feeling discouraged about Carolyn, I noticed where I was and cut over to Route 35 and doubled back. I drove right to the school, past it, and to the lumberyard where I did the little girl. I stopped and cut the motor, looking around. Happy day. Now it was a different time of year, and things looked a little different. They'd piled up a stack of two-by-twelves over the place where I'd done her. But in my mind's eye I could see it the way it had been then. Dark gray sky. Lights from the cars going past. I could hear the little buzzing feeling in her throat as she tried to scream under my fingers. Let's see. That was, oh, good heavens, nine years ago.

And if I hadn't done her she would have been twenty or so. Screwing all the boys. Probably on dope. Maybe knocked up or married. Looked at in a certain way, I saved her a lot of sordid, miserable stuff, menstruating, letting the boys' hands and mouths on her, all that . . .

My head began hurting. That's one thing the plate in your head does, it doesn't let you get very deeply into things you did in the old days, because it hurts too much. So I started up the car and drove away, and pretty soon the hurting stopped.

I never think of Carolyn, you know, that way.

They never proved that little girl on me. The one they caught me for was the nurse in Long Branch, in the parking lot. And she was a mistake. She was so small, and she had a sweater over her uniform. I didn't know she was grown up until it was too late. I was very angry about that. In a way I didn't mind when they caught me, because I had been getting very careless. But I really hated that ward in Marlboro where they put me. Seven, Jesus, seven years. Up in the morning, and drink your pink medicine out of the little paper cup. Make your bed and do your job—mine was sweeping in the incontinent wards, and the smells and the sights would make you throw up.

After a while they let me watch TV and even read the papers, and when the Altair people made the first contact with Earth I was interested, and when they began buying criminally insane to be their proxies, I wanted them to buy me. Anything, I wanted *anything* that would let me out of that place, even if it meant I'd have to let them put a box in my head and never be able to live a normal life again.

But the Altair people wouldn't buy me. For some reason they only took blacks. Then the others began showing up on the fast radio, making their deals. And still none of them wanted me. The ones from Procyon liked young women, wouldn't ever buy a male. I think they have only one sex there, someone said. All these funnies are peculiar in one way or another. Metal, or gas, or blobby, or hard-shelled and rattly. Whatever. And they all have funny habits, like if you belong to the Canopus bunch you can't ever eat fish.

I think they're disgusting, and I don't really know why the USA wanted to get involved with them in the first place. But the Chinese did, and the Russians did, and I guess we just couldn't stay out. I suppose it hasn't hurt much. There hasn't been a war, and there's a lot of ways in which they've helped clean things up for us. It hasn't hurt me, that's for sure. The Groombridge people came into the market pretty late, and most of the good healthy criminals were gone; they would buy anybody. They bought me. We're a hard-case lot, we Groombridgians, and I do wonder what Carolyn was in for.

I drove all the way down the coast, Asbury Park, Brielle, Atlantic City, all the way to Cape May, phoning back to check with the locator clerk, and never found her.

The one thing I did know was that all I was missing was the shell of her, because she was working. I could have had a kiss or a feel, no more. But I wanted to find her anyway. Just on the chance. How many times do you get an indefinite furlough? If I'd been able to find her, and stay with her, sooner or later, maybe, she would have been off too. Even if it were only for two hours. Even thirty minutes.

And then in broad daylight, just as I was checking into a motel near an Army base, with the soldiers' girls lined up at the cashier's window so their boyfriends could get back for reveille, I got the call: Report to the Philadelphia kennel. Soonest.

By then I was giddy for sleep, but I drove that Hertz lump like a Maserati, because soonest means soonest. I dumped the car and signed in at the kennel, feeling my heart pounding and my mouth ragged from fatigue, and aching because I had blown what would have to be my best chance of really being with Carolyn. "What do they want?" I asked the locator clerk. "Go inside," he said, looking evilly amused. All locator clerks treat us the same, all over the world. "She'll tell you."

Not knowing who "she" was, I opened the door and walked through, and there was Carolyn.

"Hello, Wayne," she said.

"Hello, Carolyn," I said.

I really did not have any idea of what to do at all. She didn't give me a cue. She just sat. It was at that point that it occurred to me to wonder at the fact that she wasn't wearing much, just a shortie nightgown with nothing under it. She was also sitting on a turned-down bed. Now, you would think that considering everything, especially the nature of most of my thinking about Carolyn, that I would have instantly accepted this as a personal gift from God to me of every boy's all-American dream. I didn't. It wasn't fatigue, either. It was Carolyn. It was the expression on her face, which was neither inviting nor loving, was not even the judgment-reserving look of a girl at a singles bar. What it especially was not was happy.

"The thing is, Wayne," she said, "we're supposed to go to bed now. So take your clothes off, why don't you?"

Sometimes I can stand outside of myself and look at me and, even when it's something terrible or something sad, I can see it was funny; it was like that when I did the little girl in Edison Township, because her mother had sewed her into her school clothes. I was actually laughing when I said, "Carolyn, what's the matter?"

"Well," she said, "they want us to ball, Wayne. You know. The Groombridge people. They've got interested in what human beings do to each other, and they want to kind of watch."

I started to ask why us, but I didn't have to; I could see where Carolyn and I had had a lot of that on our minds, and maybe our masters could get curious about it. I didn't exactly like it. Not exactly; in fact in a way I kind of hated it, but it was so much better than nothing at all that I said, "Why, honey, that's great!"—almost meaning it; trying to talk her into it; moving in next to her and putting my arm around her. And then she said:

"Only we have to wait, Wayne. They want to do it. Not us."

"What do you mean, wait? Wait for what?" She shrugged under my arm. "You mean," I said, "that we have to be plugged in to them? Like they'll be doing it with our bodies?

She leaned against me. "That's what they told me, Wayne. Any minute now, I guess."

I pushed her away. "Honey," I said, half crying, "all this time I've been wanting to—Jesus, Carolyn! I mean, it isn't just that I wanted to go to bed with you. I mean—"

"I'm sorry," she cried, big tears on her face.

"That's lousy!" I shouted. My head was pounding, I was so furious. "It isn't fair! I'm not going to stand for it. They don't have any *right!*"

But they did, of course, they had all the right in the world; they had bought us and paid for us, and so they owned us. I knew that. I just didn't want to accept it, even by admitting what I knew was so. The notion of screwing Carolyn flipped polarity; it wasn't what I desperately wanted, it was what I would have died to avoid, as long as it meant letting *them* paw her with my hands, kiss her with my mouth, flood her with my juices; it was like the worst kind of rape, worse than anything I had ever done, both of us raped at once. And then—

And then I felt that burning tingle in my forehead as they took over. I couldn't even scream. I just had to sit there inside my own head, no longer owning a muscle, while those freaks who owned me did to Carolyn with my body all manner of things, and I could not even cry.

After concluding the planned series of experimental procedures, which were duly recorded, the purchased person known as Carolyn Schoerner was no longer salvageable. Appropriate entries were made. The Probation and Out-Service department of the Meadville Women's Reformatory was notified that she had ceased to be alive. A purchasing requisition was initiated for a replacement, and her account was terminated.

The purchased person known as Wayne Golden was assigned to usual duties, at which he functioned normally while under control. It was discovered that when control was withdrawn he became destructive, both to others and to himself. The conjecture has been advanced that that sexual behavior which had been established as his norm—the destruction of the sexual partner—may not have been appropriate in the conditions obtaining at the time of the experimental procedures. Further experiments will be made with differing procedures and other partners in the near future. Meanwhile Wayne Golden continues to function at normal efficiency, provided control is not withdrawn at any time, and apparently will do so indefinitely.

Gertrude Atherton (1857–1948)

The Striding Place

"Gertrude Atherton has been the subject of more controversey than any other living American novelist. England, we are told, regards her as the greatest living novelist of America. Many Americans so rate her," said a survey of the American novel in 1918. "A good deal of it comes out of Mrs. Atherton's long-standing and vigorous assault on the literary schools of William Dean Howells and Henry James." A bohemian in her youth, who travelled widely, San Francisco writer Gertrude Atherton matured into a grande dame of the literary scene without losing her verve or distinctive style. She was the grand-niece of Benjamin Franklin. Her most famous horror story, "The Striding Place" (1896) was inspired by an actual locale, the setting of a famous crime. She says in her autobiography, "I haunted that spot, fascinated, and consumed with a desire to write a gruesome story of the Strid, but could think of nothing. . . . One night I determined to try an experiment. Just before dropping off to sleep I ordered my mind to conceive that story and have it formulated when I awoke. And the moment I opened my eyes, there it was. I wrote it out before leaving the bed." She first submitted it to *The Yellow Book* but it was rejected as "far too gruesome." She concludes, "It seems to me the best short story I ever wrote." Today, she is remembered only for her historical novel, *The Conqueror* (1902), based on the life of Alexander Hamilton, and for her two collections of horror stories, *The Bell in The Fog* (1905) and *The Foghorn* (1934).

W eigall, continental and detached, tired early of grouse-shooting. To stand propped against a sod fence while his host's workmen routed up the birds with long poles and drove them towards the waiting guns, made him feel himself a parody on the ancestors who had roamed the moors and forests of this West Riding of Yorkshire in hot pursuit of game worth the killing. But when in England in August he always accepted whatever proffered for the season, and invited his host to shoot pheasants on his estates in the South. The amusements of life, he argued, should be accepted with the same philosophy as its ills.

It had been a bad day. A heavy rain had made the moor so spongy that it fairly sprang beneath the feet. Whether or not the grouse had haunts of their own, wherein they were immune from rheumatism, the bag had been small. The women, too, were an unusually dull lot, with the exception of a new-minded *débutante* who bothered Weigall at dinner by demanding the verbal restoration of the vague paintings on the vaulted roof above them.

But it was no one of these things that sat on Weigall's mind as, when the other men went up to bed, he let himself out of the castle and sauntered down to the river. His intimate friend, the companion of his boyhood, the chum of his college days, his fellow-traveller in many lands, the man for whom he possessed stronger affection than for all men, had mysteriously disappeared two days ago, and his track might have sprung to the upper air for all trace he had left behind him. He had been a guest on the adjoining estate during the past week, shooting with the fervour of the true sportsman, making love in the intervals to Adeline Cavan, and apparently in the best of spirits. As far as was known, there was nothing to lower his mental mercury, for his rent-roll was a large one, Miss Cavan blushed whenever he looked at her, and, being one of the best shots in England, he was never happier than in August. The suicide theory was preposterous, all agreed, and there was as little reason to believe him murdered. Nevertheless, he had walked out of March Abbey two nights ago without hat or overcoat, and had not been seen since.

The country was being patrolled night and day. A hundred keepers and working men were beating the woods and poking the bogs on the moors, but as yet not so much as a handkerchief had been found.

Weigall did not believe for a moment that Wyatt Gifford was dead, and although it was impossible not to be affected by the general uneasiness, he was disposed to be more angry than frightened. At Cambridge Gifford had been an incorrigible practical joker, and by no means had outgrown the habit; it would be like him to cut across the country in his evening clothes, board a cattle train, and amuse himself touching up the picture of the sensation in West Riding.

However, Weigall's affection for his friend was too deep to companion with tranquility in the present state of doubt, and, instead of going to bed early with the other men, he determined to walk until ready for sleep. He went down to the river and followed the path through the woods. There was no moon, but the stars sprinkled their cold light upon the pretty belt of water flowing placidly past wood and ruin, between green masses of overhanging rocks or sloping banks tangled with tree and shrub, leaping occasionally over stones with the harsh notes of an angry scold, to recover its equanimity the moment the way was clear again.

It was very dark in the depths where Weigall trod. He smiled as he recalled a remark of Gifford's. "An English wood is like a good many other things in life—very promising at a distance, but a hollow mockery when you get within. You see daylight on both sides, and the sun freckles the very bracken. Our woods need the night to make them seem what they ought to be—what they once were, before our ancestors' descendants demanded so much more money, in these so much more various days."

Weigall strolled along, smoking, and thinking of his friend, his pranks—many of which had done more credit to his imagination than this—and recalling conversations that had lasted the night through. Just before the end of the London season they had walked the streets one hot night after a party, discussing the various theories of the soul's destiny. That afternoon they had met at the coffin of a college friend whose mind had been a blank for the past three years. Some months previously they had called at the asylum to see him. His expression had been senile, his face imprinted with the record of debauchery. In death the face was placid, intelligent, without ignoble lineation—the face of the man they had known at college. Weigall and Gifford had had no time to comment there, and the afternoon and evening were full; but, coming forth from the house of festivity together, they had reverted almost at once to the topic.

"I cherish the theory," Gifford had said, "that the soul sometimes lingers in the body after death. During madness, of course, it is an impotent prisoner, albeit a conscious one. Fancy its agony, and its horror! What more natural than that, when the life-spark goes out, the tortured soul should take possession of the vacant skull and triumph once more for a few hours while old friends look their last? It has had time to repent while compelled to crouch and behold the result of its work, and it has shrived itself into a state of comparative purity. If I had my way, I should stag inside my bones until the coffin had gone into its niche, that I might obviate for my poor old comrade the tragic impersonality of death. And I should like to see justice done to it, as it were—to see it lowered among its ancestors with the ceremony and solemnity that are its due. I am afraid that if I dissevered myself too quickly, I should yield to curiosity and hasten to investigate the mysteries of space."

"You believe in the soul as an independent entity, then—that it and the vital principle are not one and the same."

"Absolutely. The body and soul are twins, life comrades—sometimes friends, sometimes enemies, but always loyal in the last instance. Someday, when I am tired of the world, I shall go to India and become a mahatma, solely for the pleasure of receiving proof during life of this independent relationship."

"Suppose you were not sealed up properly, and returned after one of your astral flights to find your earthly part unfit for habitation? It is an experiment I don't think I should care to try, unless even juggling with soul and flesh had palled."

"That would not be an uninteresting predicament. I should rather enjoy experimenting with broken machinery."

The high wild roar of water smote suddenly on Weigall's ear and checked his memories. He left the wood and walked out on the huge slippery stones which nearly close the River Wharfe at this point, and watched the waters boil down into the narrow pass with their furious untiring energy. The black quiet of the woods rose high on either side. The stars seemed colder and whiter just above. On either hand the perspective of the river might have run into a rayless cavern. There was no lonelier spot in England, nor one which had the right to claim so many ghosts, if ghosts there were.

Weigall was not a coward, but he recalled uncomfortably the tales of those that had been done to death in the Strid.[1] Wordsworth's Boy of Egremond had been disposed of by the practical Whitaker; but countless others, more venturesome than wise, had gone down into that narrow boiling course, never to appear in the still pool a few yards beyond. Below the great rocks which form the walls of the Strid was believed to be a natural vault, on to whose shelves the dead were drawn. The spot had an ugly fascination. Weigall stood, visioning skeletons, uncoffined and green, the home of the eyeless things which had devoured all that had covered and filled that rattling symbol of man's mortality; then fell to wondering if anyone had attempted to leap the Strid of late. It was covered with slime; he had never seen it look so treacherous.

He shuddered and turned away, impelled, despite his manhood, to flee the spot. As he did so, something tossing in the foam below the fall—something as white, yet independent of it—caught his eye and arrested his step. Then he saw that it was describing a contrary motion to the rushing water—an upward backward motion. Weigall stood rigid, breathless; he fancied he heard the crackling of his hair. Was that a hand? It thrust itself still higher above the boiling foam, turned sidewise, and four frantic fingers were distinctly visible against the black rock beyond.

Weigall's superstitious terror left him. A man was there, struggling to free himself from

[1]"This striding-place is called the "Strid",
  A name which it took of yore;
  A thousand years hath it borne the name,
  And it shall a thousand more."

the suction beneath the Strid, swept down, doubtless, but a moment before his arrival, perhaps as he stood with his back to the current.

He stepped as close to the edge as he dared. The hand doubled as if in imprecation, shaking savagely in the face of that force which leaves its creatures to immutable law; then spread wide again, clutching, expanding, crying for help as audibly as the human voice.

Weigall dashed to the nearest tree, dragged and twisted off a branch with his strong arms, and returned as swiftly to the Strid. The hand was in the same place, still gesticulating as wildly; the body was undoubtedly caught in the rocks below, perhaps already halfway along one of those hideous shelves. Weigall let himself down upon a lower rock, braced his shoulder against the mass beside him, then, leaning out over the water, thrust the branch into the hand. The fingers clutched it convulsively. Weigall tugged powerfully, his own feet dragged perilously near the edge. For a moment he produced no impression, then an arm shot above the waters.

The blood sprang to Weigall's head; he was choked with the impression that the Strid had him in her roaring hold, and he saw nothing. Then the mist cleared. The hand and arm were nearer, although the rest of the body was still concealed by the foam. Weigall peered out with distended eyes. The meagre light revealed in the cuffs links of a peculiar device. The fingers clutching the branch were as familiar.

Weigall forgot the slippery stones, the terrible death if he stepped too far. He pulled with passionate will and muscle. Memories flung themselves into the hot light of his brain, trooping rapidly upon each other's heels, as in the thought of the drowning. Most of the pleasures of his life, good and bad, were identified in some way with this friend. Scenes of college days, of travel, where they had deliberately sought adventure and stood between one another and death upon more occasions than one, of hours of delightful companionship among the treasures of art, and others in the pursuit of pleasure, flashed like the changing particles of a kaleidoscope. Weigall had loved several women; but he would have flouted in these moments the thought that he had ever loved any woman as he loved Wyatt Gifford. There were so many charming women in the world, and in the thirty-two years of his life he had never known another man to whom he had cared to give his intimate friendship.

He threw himself on his face. His wrists were cracking, the skin was torn from his hands. The fingers still gripped the stick. There was life in them yet.

Suddenly something gave way. The hand swung about, tearing the branch from Weigall's grasp. The body had been liberated and flung outward, though still submerged by the foam and spray.

Weigall scrambled to his feet and sprang along the rocks, knowing that the danger from suction was over and that Gifford must be carried straight to the quiet pool. Gifford was a fish in the water and could live under it longer than most men. If he survived this, it would not be the first time that his pluck and science had saved him from drowning.

Weigall reached the pool. A man in his evening clothes floated on it, his face turned towards a projecting rock over which his arm had fallen, upholding the body. The hand that had held the branch hung limply over the rock, its white reflection visible in the black water. Weigall plunged into the shallow pool, lifted Gifford in his arms and returned to the bank. He laid the body down and threw off his coat that he might be the freer to practise the methods of resuscitation. He was glad of the moment's respite. The valiant life in the man might have been exhausted in that last struggle. He had not dared to look at his face, to put his ear to the heart. The hesitation lasted but a moment. There was no time to lose.

He turned to his prostrate friend. As he did so, something strange and disagreeable smote his senses. For a half-moment he did not appreciate its nature. Then his teeth clacked together, his feet, his outstretched arms pointed towards the woods. But he sprang to the side of the man and bent down and peered into his face. There was no face.

Clive Barker (b. 1952)

In The Hills, The Cities

Clive Barker, originally from Liverpool, now residing in Southern California, was the most exciting new horror writer to enter the horror field in the early 1980s. His six-volume *The Books of Blood* (1984–85) galvanized the attention of horror readers and instantly drew praise from Stephen King, Ramsey Campbell and Peter Straub, establishing Barker as their peer. He immediately turned to the novel form and produced a string of best-sellers, beginning with *The Damnation Game* (1985) and continuing today. He is one of the world's best-known horror writers. His background was in theater, and he became at the same time a filmmaker of considerable popularity, specializing in the horror genre. His major influences are not the literature, but comics and films. His main preoccupations are with the religious and philosophical meanings of sex and violence. He writes quickly and strives for powerful effects over polish and structure—which he frequently achieves. Nowhere more so than in "In The Hills, The Cities." If not his best story, it is certainly his most memorable to date. Barker creates a fantastic, mythic image that relates more closely to the stories of E. T. A. Hoffman than to more recent literature. It is also consistent with the direction his films and novels have taken in the last five years and so perhaps best represents Barker's strengths.

It wasn't until the first week of the Yugoslavian trip that Mick discovered what a political bigot he'd chosen as a lover. Certainly, he'd been warned. One of the queens at the Baths had told him Judd was to the Right of Attila the Hun, but the man had been one of Judd's ex-affairs, and Mick had presumed there was more spite than perception in the character assassination.

If only he'd listened. Then he wouldn't be driving along an interminable road in a Volkswagen that suddenly seemed the size of a coffin, listening to Judd's views on Soviet expansionism. Jesus, he was so boring. He didn't converse, he lectured, and endlessly. In Italy the sermon had been on the way the Communists had exploited the peasant vote. Now, in Yugoslavia, Judd had really warmed to this theme, and Mick was just about ready to take a hammer to his self-opinionated head.

It wasn't that he disagreed with everything Judd said. Some of the arguments (the ones Mick understood) seemed quite sensible. But then, what did he know? He was a dance teacher. Judd was a journalist, a professional pundit. He felt, like most journalists Mick had encountered, that he was obliged to have an opinion on everything under the sun. Especially politics; that was the best trough to wallow in. You could get your snout, eyes, head and front hooves in that mess of muck and have a fine old time splashing around. It was an inexhaustible subject to devour, a swill with a little of everything in it, because everything, according to Judd, was political. The arts were political. Sex was political. Religion, commerce, gardening, eating, drinking and farting—all political.

Jesus, it was mind-blowingly boring; killingly, love-deadeningly boring.

Worse still, Judd didn't seem to notice how bored Mick had become, or if he noticed, he didn't care. He just rambled on, his arguments getting windier and windier, his sentences lengthening with every mile they drove.

Judd, Mick had decided, was a selfish bastard, and as soon as their honeymoon was over he'd part with the guy.

It was not until their trip, that endless, motiveless caravan through the graveyards of mid-European culture, that Judd realized what a political lightweight he had in Mick. The guy showed precious little interest in the economics or the politics of the countries they passed through. He registered indifference to the full facts behind the Italian situation, and yawned, yes, yawned when he tried (and failed) to debate the Russian threat to world peace. He had to face the bitter truth: Mick was a queen; there was no other word for him; all right, perhaps he didn't mince or wear jewelry to excess, but he was a queen nevertheless, happy to wallow in a dreamworld of early Renaissance frescoes and Yugoslavian icons. The complexities, the contradictions, even the agonies that made those cultures blossom and wither were just tiresome to him. His mind was no deeper than his looks; he was a well-groomed nobody.

Some honeymoon.

The road south from Belgrade to Novi Pazar was, by Yugoslavian standards, a good one. There were fewer potholes than on many of the roads they'd travelled, and it was relatively straight. The town of Novi Pazar lay in the valley of the River Raska, south of the city named after the river. It wasn't an area particularly popular with the tourists. Despite the good road it was still inaccessible, and lacked sophisticated amenities; but Mick was determined to see the monastery at Sopocani, to the west of the town and after some bitter argument, he'd won.

The journey had proved uninspiring. On either side of the road the cultivated fields looked parched and dusty. The summer had been unusually hot, and droughts were affecting many of the villages. Crops had failed, and livestock had been prematurely slaughtered to prevent them dying of malnutrition. There was a defeated look about the few faces they glimpsed at the roadside. Even the children had dour expressions; brows as heavy as the stale heat that hung over the valley.

Now, with the cards on the table after a row at Belgrade, they drove in silence most of the time; but the straight road, like most straight roads, invited dispute. When the driving was easy, the mind rooted for something to keep it engaged. What better than a fight?

"Why the hell do you want to see this damn monastery?" Judd demanded.

It was an unmistakable invitation.

"We've come all this way . . ." Mick tried to keep the tone conversational. He wasn't in the mood for an argument.

"More fucking Virgins, is it?"

Keeping his voice as even as he could, Mick picked up the Guide and read aloud from it: ". . . there, some of the greatest works of Serbian painting can still be seen and enjoyed, including what many commentators agree to be the enduring masterpiece of the Raska school: 'The Dormition of the Virgin.'"

Silence.

Then Judd: "I'm up to here with churches."

"It's a masterpiece."

"They're all masterpieces according to that bloody book."

Mick felt his control slipping.

"Two and a half hours at most—"

"I told you, I don't want to see another church; the smell of the places makes me sick. Stale incense, old sweat and lies . . ."

"It's a short detour; then we can get back on to the road and you can give me another lecture on farming subsidies in the Sandzak."

"I'm just trying to get some decent conversation going instead of this endless tripe about Serbian fucking masterpieces—"

"Stop the car!"

"What?"

"Stop the car!"

Judd pulled the Volkswagen into the side of the road. Mick got out.

The road was hot, but there was a slight breeze. He took a deep breath, and wandered into the middle of the road. Empty of traffic and of pedestrians in both directions. In every direction, empty. The hills shimmered in the heat off the fields. There were wild poppies growing in the ditches. Mick crossed the road, squatted on his haunches and picked one.

Behind him he heard the VW's door slam.

"What did you stop us for?" Judd said. His voice was edgy, still hoping for that argument, begging for it.

Mick stood up, playing with the poppy. It was close to seeding, late in the season. The petals fell from the receptacle as soon as he touched them, little splashes of red fluttering down on to the grey tarmac.

"I asked you a question," Judd said again.

Mick looked around. Judd was standing the far side of the car, his brows a knitted line of burgeoning anger. But handsome; oh yes; a face that made women weep with frustration that he was gay. A heavy black moustache (perfectly trimmed) and eyes you could watch forever, and never see the same light in them twice. Why in God's name, thought Mick, does a man as fine as that have to be such an insensitive little shit?

Judd returned the look of contemptuous appraisal, staring at the pouting pretty boy across the road. It made him want to puke, seeing the little act Mick was performing for his benefit. It might just have been plausible in a sixteen-year-old virgin. In a twenty-five-year-old, it lacked credibility.

Mick dropped the flower, and untucked his T-shirt from his jeans. A tight stomach, then a slim, smooth chest were revealed as he pulled it off. His hair was ruffled when his head reappeared, and his face wore a broad grin. Judd looked at the torso. Neat, not too muscular. An appendix scar peering over his faded jeans. A gold chain, small but catching the sun, dipped in the hollow of his throat. Without meaning to, he returned Mick's grin, and a kind of peace was made between them.

Mick was unbuckling his belt.

"Want to fuck?" he said, the grin not faltering.

"It's no use," came an answer, though not to that question.

"What isn't?"

"We're not compatible."

"Want a bet?"

Now he was unzipped, and turning away towards the wheat field that bordered the road.

Judd watched as Mick cut a swathe through the swaying sea, his back the color of the grain, so that he was almost camouflaged by it. It was a dangerous game, screwing in the open air—this wasn't San Francisco, or even Hampstead Heath. Nervously, Judd glanced along the road. Still empty in both directions. And Mick was turning, deep in the field, turning and smiling and waving like a swimmer buoyed up in a golden surf. What the hell . . . there was nobody to see, nobody to know. Just the hills, liquid in the heat-haze, their forested backs bent to the business of the earth, and a lost dog, sitting at the edge of the road, waiting for some lost master.

Judd followed Mick's path through the wheat, unbuttoning his shirt as he walked. Field mice ran ahead of him, scurrying through the stalks as the giant came their way, his feet like thunder. Judd saw their panic, and smiled. He meant no harm to them, but then how were they to know that? Maybe he'd put out a hundred lives, mice, beetles, worms, before he reached the spot where Mick was lying, stark bollock naked, on a bed of trampled grain, still grinning.

It was good love they made, good, strong love, equal in pleasure for both; there was a precision to their passion, sensing the moment when effortless delight became urgent, when desire became necessity. They locked together, limb around limb, tongue around tongue, in a knot only orgasm could untie, their backs alternately scorched and scratched as they rolled around exchanging blows and kisses. In the thick of it, creaming together, they heard the phut-phut-phut of a tractor passing by; but they were past caring.

They made their way back to the Volkswagen with body-threshed wheat in their hair and their ears, in their socks and between their toes. Their grins had been replaced with easy smiles: the truce, if not permanent, would last a few hours at least.

The car was baking hot, and they had to open all the windows and doors to let the breeze cool it before they started towards Novi Pazar. It was four o'clock, and there was still an hour's driving ahead.

As they got into the car Mick said, "We'll forget the monastery, eh?"

Judd gaped.

"I thought—"

"I couldn't bear another fucking Virgin—"

They laughed lightly together, then kissed, tasting each other and themselves, a mingling of saliva, and the aftertaste of salt semen.

The following day was bright, but not particularly warm. No blue skies: just an even layer of white cloud. The morning air was sharp in the lining of the nostrils, like ether, or peppermint.

Vaslav Jelovsek watched the pigeons in the main square of Popolac courting death as they skipped and fluttered ahead of the vehicles that were buzzing around. Some about military business, some civilian. An air of sober intention barely suppressed the excitement he felt on this day, an excitement he knew was shared by every man, woman and child in Popolac. Shared by the pigeons too for all he knew. Maybe that was why they played under the wheels with such dexterity, knowing that on this day of days no harm could come to them.

He scanned the sky again, that same white sky he'd been peering at since dawn. The cloud-layer was low; not ideal for the celebrations. A phrase passed through his mind, an English phrase he'd heard from a friend, "to have your head in the clouds." It meant, he gathered, to be lost in a reverie, in a white, sightless dream. That, he thought wryly, was all the West knew about clouds, that they stood for dreams. It took a vision they lacked to make a truth out of that casual turn of phrase. Here, in these secret hills, wouldn't they create a spectacular reality from those idle words? A living proverb.

A head in the clouds.

Already the first contingent was assembling in the square. There were one or two absentees owing to illness, but the auxiliaries were ready and waiting to take their places. Such eagerness! Such wide smiles when an auxiliary heard his or her name and number called and was taken out of line to join the limb that was already taking shape. On every side, miracles of organization. Everyone with a job to do and a place to go. There was no shouting or pushing: indeed, voices were scarcely raised above an eager whisper. He watched in admiration as the work of positioning and buckling and roping went on.

It was going to be a long and arduous day. Vaslav had been in the square since an hour before dawn, drinking coffee from imported plastic cups, discussing the half-hourly meteorological reports coming in from Pristina and Mitrovica, and watching the starless sky as the grey light of morning crept across it. Now he was drinking his sixth coffee of the day, and it was still barely seven o'clock. Across the square Metzinger looked as tired and as anxious as Vaslav felt.

They'd watched the dawn seep out of the east together. Metzinger and he. But now they had separated, forgetting previous companionship, and would not speak until the contest was over. After all Metzinger was from Podujevo. He had his own city to support in the coming battle. Tomorrow they'd exchange tales of their adventures, but for today they must behave as if they didn't know each other, not even to exchange a smile. For today they had to be utterly partisan, caring only for the victory of their own city over the opposition.

Now the first leg of Popolac was erected, to the mutual satisfaction of Metzinger and Vaslav. All the safety checks had been meticulously made, and the leg left the square, its shadow falling hugely across the face of the Town Hall.

Vaslav sipped his sweet, sweet coffee and allowed himself a little grunt of satisfaction. Such days, such days. Days filled with glory, with snapping flags and high, stomach-turning sights, enough to last a man a lifetime. It was a golden foretaste of Heaven.

Let America have its simple pleasures, its cartoon mice, its candy-coated castles, its cults and its technologies, he wanted none of it. The greatest wonder of the world was here, hidden in the hills.

Ah, such days.

In the main square of Podujevo the scene was no less animated, and no less inspiring. Perhaps there was a muted sense of sadness underlying this year's celebration, but that was understandable. Nita Obrenovic, Podujevo's loved and respected organizer, was no longer living. The previous winter had claimed her at the age of ninety-four, leaving the city bereft of her fierce opinions and her fiercer proportions. For sixty years Nita had worked with the citizens of Podujevo, always planning for the next contest and improving on the designs, her energies spent on making the next creation more ambitious and more lifelike than the last.

Now she was dead, and sorely missed. There was no disorganization in the streets without her, the people were far too disciplined for that, but they were already falling behind schedule, and it was almost seven-twenty-five. Nita's daughter had taken over in her mother's stead, but she lacked Nita's power to galvanize the people into action. She was, in a word, too gentle for the job in hand. It required a leader who was part prophet and part ringmaster, to coax and bully and inspire the citizens into their places. Maybe, after two or three decades, and with a few more contests under her belt, Nita Obrenovic's daughter would make the grade. But for today Podujevo was behindhand; safety-checks were being overlooked; nervous looks replaced the confidence of earlier years.

Nevertheless, at six minutes before eight the first limb of Podujevo made its way out of the city to the assembly point, to wait for its fellow.

By that time the flanks were already lashed together in Popolac, and armed contingents were awaiting orders in the Town Square.

Mick woke promptly at seven, though there was no alarm clock in their simply furnished room at the Hotel Beograd. He lay in his bed and listened to Judd's regular breathing from the twin bed across the room. A dull morning light whimpered through the thin curtains, not encouraging an early departure. After a few minutes' staring at the cracked paintwork on the ceiling, and a while longer at the crudely carved crucifix on the opposite wall, Mick got up and went to the window. It was a dull day, as he had guessed. The sky was overcast, and the roofs of Novi Pazar were grey and featureless in the flat morning light. But beyond the roofs, to the east, he could see the hills. There was sun there. He could see shafts of light catching the blue-green of the forest, inviting a visit to their slopes.

Today maybe they would go south to Kosovska Mitrovica. There was a market there, wasn't there, and a museum? And they could drive down the valley of the Ibar, following the road beside the river, where the hills rose wild and shining on either side. The hills, yes; today he decided they would see the hills.

It was eight-fifteen.

By nine the main bodies of Popolac and Podujevo were substantially assembled. In their allotted districts the limbs of both cities were ready and waiting to join their expectant torsos.

Vaslav Jelovsek capped his gloved hands over his eyes and surveyed the sky. The cloud-base had risen in the last hour, no doubt of it, and there were breaks in the clouds to the west; even, on occasion, a few glimpses of the sun. It wouldn't be a perfect day for the contest perhaps, but certainly adequate.

Mick and Judd breakfasted late on hemendeks—roughly translated as ham and eggs—and several cups of good black coffee. It was brightening up, even in Novi Pazar, and their ambitions were set high. Kosovska Mitrovica by lunchtime, and maybe a visit to the hill-castle of Zvecan in the afternoon.

About nine-thirty they motored out of Novi Pazar and took the Srbovac road south to the Ibar valley. Not a good road, but the bumps and potholes couldn't spoil the new day.

The road was empty, except for the occasional pedestrian; and in place of the maize and corn fields they'd passed on the previous day the road was flanked by undulating hills, whose sides were thickly and darkly forested. Apart from a few birds, they saw no wildlife. Even their infrequent travelling companions petered out altogether after a few miles, and the occasional farmhouse they drove by appeared locked and shuttered up. Black pigs ran unattended in the yard, with no child to feed them. Washing snapped and billowed on a sagging line, with no washerwoman in sight.

At first this solitary journey through the hills was refreshing in its lack of human contact, but as the morning drew on, an uneasiness grew on them.

"Shouldn't we have seen a signpost to Mitrovica, Mick?"

He peered at the map.

"Maybe . . ."

"—we've taken the wrong road."

"If there'd been a sign, I'd have seen it. I think we should try and get off this road, bear south a bit more—meet the valley closer to Mitrovica than we'd planned."

"How do we get off this bloody road?"

"There've been a couple of turnings . . ."

"Dirt-tracks."

"Well it's either that or going on the way we are."

Judd pursed his lips.

"Cigarette?" he asked.

"Finished them miles back."

In front of them, the hills formed an impenetrable line. There was no sign of life ahead; no frail wisp of chimney smoke, no sound of voice or vehicle.

"All right," said Judd, "we take the next turning. Anything's better than this."

They drove on. The road was deteriorating rapidly, the potholes becoming craters, the hummocks feeling like bodies beneath the wheels.

Then:

"There!"

A turning: a palpable turning. Not a major road, certainly. In fact barely the dirt-track Judd had described the other roads as being, but it was an escape from the endless perspective of the road they were trapped on.

"This is becoming a bloody safari," said Judd as the VW began to bump and grind its way along the doleful little track.

"Where's your sense of adventure?"

"I forgot to pack it."

They were beginning to climb now, as the track wound its way up into the hills. The forest closed over them, blotting out the sky, so a shifting patchwork of light and shadow scooted over the bonnet as they drove. There was birdsong suddenly, vacuous and optimistic, and a smell of new pine and undug earth. A fox crossed the track, up ahead, and watched a long moment as the car grumbled up towards it. Then, with the leisurely stride of a fearless prince, it sauntered away into the trees.

Wherever they were going, Mick thought, this was better than the road they'd left. Soon maybe they'd stop, and walk a while, to find a promontory from which they could see the valley, even Novi Pazar, nestled behind them.

The two men were still an hour's drive from Popolac when the head of the contingent at last marched out of the Town Square and took up its position with the main body.

This last exit left the city completely deserted. Not even the sick or the old were neglected on this day; no one was to be denied the spectacle and the triumph of the contest. Every single citizen, however young or infirm, the blind, the crippled, babes in arms, pregnant women—all made their way up from their proud city to the stamping ground. It was the law that they should attend: but it needed no enforcing. No citizen of either city would have missed the chance to see that sight—to experience the thrill of that contest.

The confrontation had to be total, city against city. This was the way it had always been.

So the cities went up into the hills. By noon they were gathered, the citizens of Popolac and Podujevo, in the secret well of the hills, hidden from civilized eyes, to do ancient and ceremonial battle.

Tens of thousands of hearts beat faster. Tens of thousands of bodies stretched and strained and sweated as the twin cities took their positions. The shadows of the bodies darkened tracts of land the size of small towns; the weight of their feet trampled the grass to a green milk; their movement killed animals, crushed bushes and threw down trees.

The earth literally reverberated with their passage, the hills echoing with the booming din of their steps.

In the towering body of Podujevo, a few technical hitches were becoming apparent. A slight flaw in the knitting of the left flank had resulted in a weakness there: and there were consequent problems in the swivelling mechanism of the hips. It was stiffer than it should be, and the movements were not smooth. As a result there was considerable strain being put upon that region of the city. It was being dealt with bravely; after all, the contest was intended to press the contestants to their limits. But breaking point was closer than anyone would have dared to admit. The citizens were not as resilient as they had been in previous contests. A bad decade for crops had produced bodies less well-nourished, spines less supple, wills less resolute. The badly knitted flank might not have caused an accident in itself, but further weakened by the frailty of the competitors it set a scene for death on an unprecedented scale.

They stopped the car.

"Hear that?"

Mick shook his head. His hearing hadn't been good since he was an adolescent. Too many rock shows had blown his eardrums to hell.

Judd got out of the car.

The birds were quieter now. The noise he'd heard as they drove came again. It wasn't simply a noise: it was almost a motion in the earth, a roar that seemed seated in the substance of the hills.

Thunder, was it?

No, too rhythmical. It came again, through the soles of the feet—

Boom.

Mick heard it this time. He leaned out of the car window.

"It's up ahead somewhere. I hear it now."

Judd nodded.

Boom.

The earth-thunder sounded again.

"What the hell is it?" said Mick.

"Whatever it is, I want to see it—"

Judd got back into the Volkswagen, smiling.

"Sounds almost like guns," he said, starting the car. "Big guns."

Through his Russian-made binoculars Vaslav Jelovsek watched the starting-official raise his pistol. He saw the feather of white smoke rise from the barrel, and a second later heard the sound of the shot across the valley.

The contest had begun.

He looked up at twin towers of Popolac and Podujevo. Heads in the clouds—well almost. They practically stretched to touch the sky. It was an awesome sight, a breath-stopping, sleep-stabbing sight. Two cities swaying and writhing and preparing to take their first steps towards each other in this ritual battle.

Of the two, Podujevo seemed the less stable. There was a slight hesitation as the city raised its left leg to begin its march. Nothing serious, just a little difficulty in coordinating hip and thigh muscles. A couple of steps and the city would find its rhythm; a couple more and its inhabitants would be moving as one creature, one perfect giant set to match its grace and power against its mirror-image.

The gunshot had sent flurries of birds up from the trees that banked the hidden valley.

They rose up in celebration of the great contest, chattering their excitement as they swooped over the stamping-ground.

"Did you hear a shot?" asked Judd.
  Mick nodded.
  "Military exercises . . . ?" Judd's smile had broadened. He could see the headlines already—exclusive reports of secret maneuvers in the depths of the Yugoslavian countryside. Russian tanks perhaps, tactical exercises being held out of the West's prying sight. With luck, he would be the carrier of this news.
  Boom.
  Boom.
  There were birds in the air. The thunder was louder now.
  It did sound like guns.
  "It's over the next ridge . . ." said Judd.
  "I don't think we should go any further."
  "I have to see."
  "I don't. We're not supposed to be here."
  "I don't see any signs."
  "They'll cart us away; deport us—I don't know—I just think—"
  Boom.
  "I've got to see."
  The words were scarcely out of his mouth when the screaming started.

Podujevo was screaming: a death-cry. Someone buried in the weak flank had died of the strain, and had begun a chain of decay in the system. One man loosed his neighbor and that neighbor loosed his, spreading a cancer of chaos through the body of the city. The coherence of the towering structure deteriorated with terrifying rapidity as the failure of one part of the anatomy put unendurable pressure on the other.
  The masterpiece that the good citizens of Podujevo had constructed of their own flesh and blood tottered and then—a dynamited skyscraper, it began to fall.
  The broken flank spewed citizens like a slashed artery spitting blood. Then, with a graceful sloth that made the agonies of the citizens all the more horrible, it bowed towards the earth, all its limbs dissembling as it fell.
  The huge head, that had brushed the clouds so recently, was flung back on its thick neck. Ten thousand mouths spoke a single scream for its vast mouth, a wordless, infinitely pitiable appeal to the sky. A howl of loss, a howl of anticipation, a howl of puzzlement. How, that scream demanded, could the day of days end like this, in a welter of falling bodies?

"Did you hear that?"
  It was unmistakably human, though almost deafening loud. Judd's stomach convulsed. He looked across at Mick, who was as white as a sheet.
  Judd stopped the car.
  "No," said Mick.
  "Listen—for Christ's sake—"
  The din of dying moans, appeals and imprecations flooded the air. It was very close.
  "We've got to go on now," Mick implored.
  Judd shook his head. He was prepared for some military spectacle—all the Russian army massed over the next hill—but that noise in his ears was the noise of human flesh—too human for words. It reminded him of his childhood imaginings of Hell; the

endless, unspeakable torments his mother had threatened him with if he failed to embrace Christ. It was a terror he'd forgotten for twenty years. But suddenly, here it was again, fresh-faced. Maybe the pit itself gaped just over the next horizon, with his mother standing at its lip, inviting him to taste its punishments.

"If you won't drive, I will."

Mick got out of the car and crossed in front of it, glancing up the track as he did so. There was a moment's hesitation, no more than a moment's, when his eyes flickered with disbelief, before he turned towards the windscreen, his face even paler than it had been previously and said: "Jesus Christ . . ." in a voice that was thick with suppressed nausea.

His lover was still sitting behind the wheel, his head in his hands, trying to blot out memories.

"Judd . . ."

Judd looked up, slowly. Mick was staring at him like a wildman, his face shining with a sudden, icy sweat. Judd looked past him. A few meters ahead the track had mysterious darkened, as a tide edged towards the car, a thick, deep tide of blood. Judd's reason twisted and turned to make any other sense of the sight than that inevitable conclusion. But there was no saner explanation. It was blood, in unendurable abundance, blood without end—

And now, in the breeze, there was the flavor of freshly opened carcasses: the smell out of the depths of the human body, part sweet, part savory.

Mick stumbled back to the passenger's side of the VW and fumbled weakly at the handle. The door opened suddenly and he lurched inside, his eyes glazed.

"Back up," he said.

Judd reached for the ignition. The tide of blood was already sloshing against the front wheels. Ahead, the world had been painted red.

"Drive, for fuck's sake, drive!"

Judd was making no attempt to start the car.

"We must look," he said, without conviction, "we have to."

"We don't have to do anything," said Mick, "but get the hell out of here. It's not our business . . ."

"Plane-crash—"

"There's no smoke."

"Those are human voices."

Mick's instinct was to leave well alone. He could read about the tragedy in a newspaper—he could see the pictures tomorrow when they were grey and grainy. Today it was too fresh, too unpredictable—

Anything could be at the end of that track, bleeding—

"We must—"

Judd started the car, while beside him Mick began to moan quietly. The VW began to edge forward, nosing through the river of blood, its wheels spinning in the queasy, foaming tide.

"No," said Mick, very quietly. "Please, no . . ."

"We must," was Judd's reply. "We must. We must."

Only a few yards away the surviving city of Popolac was recovering from its first convulsions. It stared, with a thousand eyes, at the ruins of its ritual enemy, now spread in a tangle of rope and bodies over the impacted ground, shattered forever. Popolac staggered back from the sight, its vast legs flattening the forest that bounded the stamping-ground, its arms flailing the air. But it kept its balance, even as a common insanity, woken by the horror at its feet, surged through its sinews and curdled its brain. The order went out: the body thrashed and twisted and turned from the grisly carpet of Podujevo, and fled into the hills.

As it headed into oblivion, its towering form passed between the car and the sun, throwing its cold shadow over the bloody road. Mick saw nothing through his tears, and Judd, his eyes narrowed against the sight he feared seeing around the next bend, only dimly registered that something had blotted the light for a minute. A cloud, perhaps. A flock of birds.

Had he looked up at that moment, just stolen a glance out towards the north-east, he would have seen Popolac's head, the vast, swarming head of a maddened city, disappearing below his line of vision, as it marched into the hills. He would have known that this territory was beyond his comprehension; and that there was no healing to be done in this corner of Hell. But he didn't see the city, and he and Mick's last turning-point had passed. From now on, like Popolac and its dead twin, they were lost to sanity, and to all hope of life.

They rounded the bend, and the ruins of Podujevo came into sight.

Their domesticated imaginations had never conceived of a sight so unspeakably brutal.

Perhaps in the battlefields of Europe as many corpses had been heaped together: but had so many of them been women and children, locked together with the corpses of men? There had been piles of dead as high, but ever so many so recently abundant with life? There had been cities laid waste as quickly, but ever an entire city lost to the simple dictate of gravity?

It was a sight beyond sickness. In the face of it the mind slowed to a snail's pace, the forces of reason picked over the evidence with meticulous hands, searching for a flaw in it, a place where it could say:

This is not happening. This is a dream of death, not death itself.

But reason could find no weakness in the wall. This was true. It was death indeed. Podujevo had fallen.

Thirty-eight thousand, seven hundred and sixty-five citizens were spread on the ground, or rather flung in ungainly, seeping piles. Those who had not died of the fall, or of suffocation, were dying. There would be no survivors from that city except that bundle of onlookers that had traipsed out of their homes to watch the contest. Those few Podujevians, the crippled, the sick, the ancient few, were now staring, like Mick and Judd, at the carnage, trying not to believe.

Judd was first out of the car. The ground beneath his suedes was sticky with coagulating gore. He surveyed the carnage. There was no wreckage: no sign of a plane crash, no fire, no smell of fuel. Just tens of thousands of fresh bodies, all either naked or dressed in an identical grey serge, men, women and children alike. Some of them, he could see, wore leather harnesses, tightly buckled around their upper chests, and snaking out from these contraptions were lengths of rope, miles and miles of it. The closer he looked, the more he saw of the extraordinary system of knots and lashings that still held the bodies together. For some reason these people had been tied together, side by side. Some were yoked on their neighbors' shoulders, straddling them like boys playing at horseback riding. Others were locked arm in arm, knitted together with threads of rope in a wall of muscle and bone. Yet others were trussed in a ball, with their heads tucked between their knees. All were in some way connected up with their fellows, tied together as though in some insane collective bondage game.

Another shot.

Mick looked up.

Across the field a solitary man, dressed in a drab overcoat, was walking amongst the bodies with a revolver, dispatching the dying. It was a pitifully inadequate act of mercy, but he went on nevertheless, choosing the suffering children first. Emptying the revolver, filling it again, emptying it, filling it, emptying it—

Mick let go.

He yelled at the top of his voice over the moans of the injured.

"What is this?"

The man looked up from his appalling duty, his face as deadgrey as his coat.

"Uh?" he grunted, frowning at the two interlopers through his thick spectacles.

"What's happened here?" Mick shouted across at him. It felt good to shout, it felt good to sound angry at the man. Maybe he was to blame. It would be a fine thing, just to have someone to blame.

"Tell us—" Mick said. He could hear the tears throbbing in his voice. "Tell us, for God's sake. Explain."

Grey-coat shook his head. He didn't understand a word this young idiot was saying. It was English he spoke, but that's all he knew. Mick began to walk towards him, feeling all the time the eyes of the dead on him. Eyes like black, shining gems set in broken faces: eyes looking at him upside down, on heads severed from their seating. Eyes in heads that had solid howls for voices. Eyes in heads beyond howls, beyond breath.

Thousands of eyes.

He reached Grey-coat, whose gun was almost empty. He had taken off his spectacles and thrown them aside. He too was weeping, little jerks ran through his big, ungainly body.

At Mick's feet, somebody was reaching for him. He didn't want to look, but the hand touched his shoe and he had no choice but to see its owner. A young man, lying like a flesh swastika, every joint smashed. A child lay under him, her bloody legs poking out like two pink sticks.

He wanted the man's revolver, to stop the hand from touching him. Better still he wanted a machine gun, a flamethrower, anything to wipe the agony away.

As he looked up from the broken body, Mick saw Grey-coat raise the revolver.

"Judd—" he said, but as the word left his lips the muzzle of the revolver was slipped into Grey-coat's mouth and the trigger was pulled.

Grey-coat had saved the last bullet for himself. The back of his head opened like a dropped egg, the shell of his skull flying off. His body went limp and sank to the ground, the revolver still between his lips.

"We must—" began Mick, saying the words to nobody. "We must . . ."

What was the imperative? In this situation, what *must* they do?

"We must—"

Judd was behind him.

"Help—" he said to Mick.

"Yes. We must get help. We must—"

"Go."

Go! That was what they must do. On any pretext, for any fragile, cowardly reason, they must go. Get out of the battlefield, get out of the reach of a dying hand with a wound in place of a body.

"We have to tell the authorities. Find a town. Get help—"

"Priests," said Mick. "They need priests."

It was absurd, to think of giving the Last Rites to so many people. It would take an army of priests, a water cannon filled with holy water, a loudspeaker to pronounce the benedictions.

They turned away, together, from the horror, and wrapped their arms around each other, then picked their way through the carnage to the car.

It was occupied.

Vaslav Jelovsek was sitting behind the wheel, and trying to start the Volkswagen. He turned the ignition key once. Twice. Third time the engine caught and the wheels spun in the crimson mud as he put her into reverse and backed down the track. Vaslav saw the Englishmen running towards the car, cursing him. There was no help for it—he didn't want to steal the vehicle, but he had work to do. He had been a referee, he had been responsible for the contest, and the safety of the contestants. One of the heroic cities had already fallen. He must do everything in his power to prevent Popolac from following its twin. He must chase Popolac, and reason with it. Talk it down out of its terrors with quiet words and promises. If he failed there would be another disaster the equal of the one in front of him, and his conscience was already broken enough.

Mick was still chasing the VW, shouting at Jelovsek. The thief took no notice, concentrating on maneuvering the car back down the narrow, slippery track. Mick was losing the chase rapidly. The car had begun to pick up speed. Furious, but without the breath to speak his fury, Mick stood in the road, hands on his knees, heaving and sobbing.

"Bastard!" said Judd.

Mick looked down the track. Their car had already disappeared.

"Fucker couldn't even drive properly."

"We have . . . we have . . . to catch . . . up . . ." said Mick through gulps of breath.

"How?"

"On foot . . ."

"We haven't even got a map . . . it's in the car."

"Jesus . . . Christ . . . Almighty."

They walked down the track together, away from the field.

After a few meters the tide of blood began to peter out. Just a few congealing rivulets dribbled on towards the main road. Mick and Judd followed the bloody tiremarks to the junction.

The Srbovac road was empty in both directions. The tiremarks showed a left turn. "He's gone deeper into the hills," said Judd, staring along the lovely road towards the blue-green distance. "He's out of his mind!"

"Do we go back the way we came?"

"It'll take us all night on foot."

"We'll hop a lift."

Judd shook his head: his face was slack and his look lost. "Don't you see, Mick, they all knew this was happening. The people in the farms—they got the hell out while those people went crazy up there. There'll be no cars along this road, I'll lay you anything—except maybe a couple of shit-dumb tourists like us—and no tourist would stop for the likes of us."

He was right. They looked like butchers—splattered with blood. Their faces were shining with grease, their eyes maddened.

"We'll have to walk," said Judd, "the way he went."

He pointed along the road. The hills were darker now; the sun had suddenly gone out on their slopes.

Mick shrugged. Either way he could see they had a night on the road ahead of them.

But he wanted to walk somewhere—anywhere—as long as he put distance between him and the dead.

In Popolac a kind of peace reigned. Instead of a frenzy of panic there was a numbness, a sheeplike acceptance of the world as it was. Locked in their positions, strapped, roped and harnessed to each other in a living system that allowed for no single voice to be louder than any other, nor any back to labor less than its neighbor's, they let an insane consensus replace the tranquil voice of reason. They were convulsed into one mind, one thought, one ambition. They became, in the space of a few moments, the single-minded giant whose image they had so brilliantly recreated. The illusion of petty individuality was swept away in an irresistible tide of collective feeling—not a mob's passion, but a telepathic surge that dissolved the voices of thousands into one irresistible command.

And the voice said: Go!

The voice said: take this horrible sight away, where I need never see it again.

Popolac turned away into the hills, its legs taking strides half a mile long. Each man, woman and child in that seething tower was sightless. They saw only through the eyes of the city. They were thoughtless, but to think the city's thoughts. And they believed themselves deathless, in their lumbering, relentless strength. Vast and mad and deathless.

Two miles along the road Mick and Judd smelt petrol in the air, and a little further along they came upon the VW. It had overturned in the reed-clogged drainage ditch at the side of the road. It had not caught fire.

The driver's door was open, and the body of Vaslav Jelovsek had tumbled out. His face was calm in unconsciousness. There seemed to be no sign of injury, except for a small cut or two on his sober face. They gently pulled the thief out of the wreckage and up out of the filth of the ditch on to the road. He moaned a little as they fussed about him, rolling Mick's sweater up to pillow his head and removing the man's jacket and tie.

Quite suddenly, he opened his eyes.

He stared at them both.

"Are you all right?" Mick asked.

The man said nothing for a moment. He seemed not to understand.

Then:

"English?" he said. His accent was thick, but the question was quite clear.

"Yes."

"I heard your voices. English."

He frowned and winced.

"Are you in pain?" said Judd.

The man seemed to find this amusing.

"Am I in pain?" he repeated, his face screwed up in a mixture of agony and delight. "I shall die," he said, through gritted teeth.

"No," said Mick. "You're all right—"

The man shook his head, his authority absolute.

"I shall die," he said again, the voice full of determination, "I want to die."

Judd crouched closer to him. His voice was weaker by the moment.

"Tell us what to do," he said. The man had closed his eyes. Judd shook him awake, roughly.

"Tell us," he said again, his show of compassion rapidly disappearing. "Tell us what this is all about."

"About?" said the man, his eyes still closed. "It was a fall, that's all. Just a fall . . ."

"What fell?"

"The city. Podujevo. My city."

"What did it fall from?"

"Itself, of course."

The man was explaining nothing; just answering one riddle with another.

"Where were you going?" Mick inquired, trying to sound as unaggressive as possible.

"After Popolac," said the man.

"Popolac?" said Judd.

Mick began to see some sense in the story.

"Popolac is another city. Like Podujevo. Twin cities. They're on the map—"

"Where's the city now?" said Judd.

Vaslav Jelovsek seemed to choose to tell the truth. There was a moment when he hovered between dying with a riddle on his lips, and living long enough to unburden his story. What did it matter if the tale was told now? There could never be another contest: all that was over.

"They came to fight," he said, his voice now very soft, "Popolac and Podujevo. They come every ten years—"

"Fight?" said Judd, "You mean all those people were slaughtered?"

Vaslav shook his head.

"No, no. They fell. I told you."

"Well how do they fight?" Mick said.

"Go into the hills," was the only reply.

Vaslav opened his eyes a little. The faces that loomed over him were exhausted and sick. They had suffered, these innocents. They deserved some explanation.

"As giants," he said. "They fought as giants. They made a body out of their bodies, do you understand? The frame, the muscles, the bone, the eyes, nose, teeth all made of men and women."

"He's delirious," said Judd.

"You go into the hills," the man repeated. "See for yourselves how true it is."

"Even supposing—" Mick began.

Vaslav interrupted him, eager to be finished. "They were good at the game of giants. It took many centuries of practice: every ten years making the figure larger and larger. One always ambitious to be larger than the other. Ropes to tie them all together, flawlessly. Sinews . . . ligaments . . . There was food in its belly . . . there were pipes from the loins, to take away the waste. The best-sighted sat in the eye-sockets, the best voiced in the mouth and throat. You wouldn't believe the engineering of it."

"I don't," said Judd, and stood up.

"It is the body of the state," said Vaslav, so softly his voice was barely above a whisper, "it is the shape of our lives."

There was a silence. Small clouds passed over the road, soundlessly shedding their mass to the air.

"It was a miracle," he said. It was as if he realized the true enormity of the fact for the first time. "It was a miracle."

It was enough. Yes. It was quite enough.

His mouth closed, the words said, and he died.

Mick felt this death more acutely than the thousands they had fled from; or rather this death was the key to unlock the anguish he felt for them all.

Whether the man had chosen to tell a fantastic lie as he died, or whether this story was in some way true, Mick felt useless in the face of it. His imagination was too narrow to encompass the idea. His brain ached with the thought of it, and his compassion cracked under the weight of misery he felt.

They stood on the road, while the clouds scudded by, their vague, grey shadows passing over them towards the enigmatic hills.

It was twilight.

Popolac could stride no further. It felt exhaustion in every muscle. Here and there in its huge anatomy deaths had occurred; but there was no grieving in the city for its deceased cells. If the dead were in the interior, the corpses were allowed to hang from their harnesses. If they formed the skin of the city they were unbuckled from their positions and released, to plunge into the forest below.

The giant was not capable of pity. It had no ambition but to continue until it ceased.

As the sun slunk out of sight Popolac rested, sitting on a small hillock, nursing its huge head in its huge hands.

The stars were coming out, with their familiar caution. Night was approaching, mercifully bandaging up the wounds of the day, blinding eyes that had seen too much.

Popolac rose to its feet again, and began to move, step by booming step. It would not be long surely, before fatigue overcame it: before it could lie down in the tomb of some lost valley and die.

But for a space yet it must walk on, each step more agonizingly slow than the last, while the night bloomed black around its head.

Mick wanted to bury the car thief, somewhere on the edge of the forest. Judd, however, pointed out that burying a body might seem, in tomorrow's saner light, a little suspicious. And besides, wasn't it absurd to concern themselves with one corpse when there were literally thousands of them lying a few miles from where they stood?

The body was left to lie, therefore, and the car to sink deeper into the ditch.

They began to walk again.

It was cold, and colder by the moment, and they were hungry. But the few houses they passed were all deserted, locked and shuttered, every one.

"What did he mean?" said Mick, as they stood looking at another locked door.

"He was talking metaphor—"

"All that stuff about giants?"

"It was some Trotskyist tripe—" Judd insisted.

"I don't think so."

"I know so. It was his deathbed speech, he'd probably been preparing for years."

"I don't think so," Mick said again, and began walking back towards the road.

"Oh, how's that?" Judd was at his back.

"He wasn't towing some party line."

"Are you saying you think there's some giant around here someplace? For God's sake!"

Mick turned to Judd. His face was difficult to see in the twilight. But his voice was sober with belief.

"Yes. I think he was telling the truth."

"That's absurd. That's ridiculous. No."

Judd hated Mick that moment. Hated his naïvete, his passion to believe any half-witted story if it had a whiff of romance about it. And this? This was the worst, the most preposterous . . .

"No," he said again. "No. No. No."

The sky was porcelain smooth, and the outline of the hills black as pitch.

"I'm fucking freezing," said Mick out of the ink. "Are you staying here or walking with me?"

Judd shouted: "We're not going to find anything this way."

"Well it's a long way back."

"We're just going deeper into the hills."

"Do what you like—I'm walking."

His footsteps receded: the dark encased him.

After a minute, Judd followed.

The night was cloudless and bitter. They walked on, their collars up against the chill, their feet swollen in their shoes. Above them the whole sky had become a parade of stars. A triumph of spilled light, from which the eye could make as many patterns as it had patience for. After a while, they slung their tired arms around each other, for comfort and warmth.

About eleven o'clock, they saw the glow of a window in the distance.

The woman at the door of the stone cottage didn't smile, but she understood their condition, and let them in. There seemed to be no purpose in trying to explain to either the woman or her crippled husband what they had seen. The cottage had no telephone, and there was no sign of a vehicle, so even had they found some way to express themselves, nothing could be done.

With mimes and face-pullings they explained that they were hungry and exhausted. They tried further to explain that they were lost, cursing themselves for leaving their phrasebook in the VW. She didn't seem to understand very much of what they said, but sat them down beside a blazing fire and put a pan of food on the stove to heat.

They ate thick unsalted pea soup and eggs, and occasionally smiled their thanks at the woman. Her husband sat beside the fire, making no attempt to talk, or even look at the visitors.

The food was good. It buoyed their spirits.

They would sleep until morning and then begin the long trek back. By dawn the bodies in the field would be being quantified, identified, parcelled up and dispatched to their families. The air would be full of reassuring noises, cancelling out the moans that still rang in their ears. There would be helicopters, lorry loads of men organizing the clearing-up operations. All the rites and paraphernalia of a civilized disaster.

And in a while, it would be palatable. It would become part of their history: a tragedy, of course, but one they could explain, classify and learn to live with. All would be well, yes, all would be well. Come morning.

The sleep of sheer fatigue came on them suddenly. They lay where they had fallen, still sitting at the table, their heads on their crossed arms. A litter of empty bowls and bread crusts surrounded them.

They knew nothing. Dreamt nothing. Felt nothing.

Then the thunder began.

In the earth, in the deep earth, a rhythmical tread, as of a titan, that came, by degrees, closer and closer.

The woman woke her husband. She blew out the lamp and went to the door. The night sky was luminous with stars: the hills black on every side.

The thunder still sounded: a full half minute between every boom, but louder now. And louder with every new step.

They stood at the door together, husband and wife, and listened to the night-hills echo back and forth with the sound. There was no lightning to accompany the thunder.

Just the boom—
Boom—
Boom—
It made the ground shake: it threw dust down from the door-lintel, and rattled the window-latches.
Boom—
Boom—
They didn't know what approached, but whatever shape it took, and whatever it intended, there seemed no sense in running from it. Where they stood, in the pitiful shelter of their cottage, was as safe as any nook of the forest. How could they choose, out of a hundred thousand trees, which would be standing when the thunder had passed? Better to wait: and watch.

The wife's eyes were not good, and she doubted what she saw when the blackness of the hill changed shape and reared up to block the stars. But her husband had seen it too: the unimaginably huge head, vaster in the deceiving darkness, looming up and up, dwarfing the hills themselves with ambition.

He fell to his knees, babbling a prayer, his arthritic legs twisted beneath him.

His wife screamed: no words she knew could keep this monster at bay—no prayer, no plea, had power over it.

In the cottage, Mick woke and his outstretched arm, twitching with a sudden cramp, wiped the plate and the lamp off the table.

They smashed.

Judd woke.

The screaming outside had stopped. The woman had disappeared from the doorway into the forest. Any tree, any tree at all, was better than this sight. Her husband still let a string of prayers dribble from his slack mouth, as the great leg of the giant rose to take another step—
Boom—
The cottage shook. Plates danced and smashed off the dresser. A clay pipe rolled from the mantelpiece and shattered in the ashes of the hearth.

The lovers knew the noise that sounded in their substance: that earth-thunder.

Mick reached for Judd, and took him by the shoulder.

"You see," he said, his teeth blue-grey in the darkness of the cottage. "See? See?"

There was a kind of hysteria bubbling behind his words. He ran to the door, stumbling over a chair in the dark. Cursing and bruised he staggered out into the night—
Boom—
The thunder was deafening. This time it broke all the windows in the cottage. In the bedroom one of the roof-joists cracked and flung debris downstairs.

Judd joined his lover at the door. The old man was now face down on the ground, his sick and swollen fingers curled, his begging lips pressed to the damp soil.

Mick was looking up, towards the sky. Judd followed his gaze.

There was a place that showed no stars. It was a darkness in the shape of a man, a vast, broad human frame, a colossus that soared up to meet heaven. It was not quite a perfect giant. Its outline was not tidy; it seethed and swarmed.

He seemed broader too, this giant, than any real man. His legs were abnormally thick and stumpy, and his arms were not long. The hands, as they clenched and unclenched, seemed oddly jointed and over-delicate for its torso.

Then it raised one huge, flat foot and placed it on the earth, taking a stride towards them.
Boom—

The step brought the roof collapsing in on the cottage. Everything that the car-thief had said was true. Popolac was a city and a giant; and it had gone into the hills . . .

Now their eyes were becoming accustomed to the night light. They could see in ever more horrible detail the way this monster was constructed. It was a masterpiece of human engineering: a man made entirely of men. Or rather, a sexless giant, made of men and women and children. All the citizens of Popolac writhed and strained in the body of this flesh-knitted giant, their muscles stretched to breaking point, their bones close to snapping.

They could see how the architects of Popolac had subtly altered the proportions of the human body; how the thing had been made squatter to lower its center of gravity; how its legs had been made elephantine to bear the weight of the torso; how the head was sunk low on to the wide shoulders, so that the problems of a weak neck had been minimized.

Despite these malformations, it was horribly lifelike. The bodies that were bound together to make its surface were naked but for their harnesses, so that its surface glistened in the starlight, like one vast human torso. Even the muscles were well copied, though simplified. They could see the way the roped bodies pushed and pulled against each other in solid cords of flesh and bone. They could see the intertwined people that made up the body: the backs like turtles packed together to offer the sweep of the pectorals; the lashed and knotted acrobats at the joints of the arms and the legs alike, rolling and unwinding to articulate the city.

But surely the most amazing sight of all was the face.

Cheeks of bodies; cavernous eye-sockets in which heads stared, five bound together for each eyeball; a broad, flat nose and a mouth that opened and closed, as the muscles of the jaw bunched and hollowed rhythmically. And from that mouth, lined with teeth of bald children, the voice of the giant, now only a weak copy of its former powers, spoke a single note of idiot music.

Popolac walked and Popolac sang.

Was there ever a sight in Europe the equal of it?

They watched, Mick and Judd, as it took another step towards them.

The old man had wet his pants. Blubbering and begging, he dragged himself away from the ruined cottage into the surrounding trees, dragging his dead legs after him.

The Englishmen remained where they stood, watching the spectacle as it approached. Neither dread nor horror touched them now, just an awe that rooted them to the spot. They knew this was a sight they could never hope to see again; this was the apex—after this there was only common experience. Better to stay then, though every step brought death nearer, better to stay and see the sight while it was still there to be seen. And if it killed them, this monster, then at least they would have glimpsed a miracle, known this terrible majesty for a brief moment. It seemed a fair exchange.

Popolac was within two steps of the cottage. They could see the complexities of its structure quite clearly. The faces of the citizens were becoming detailed: white, sweat-wet, and content in their weariness. Some hung dead from their harnesses, their legs swinging back and forth like the hanged. Others, children particularly, had ceased to obey their training, and had relaxed their positions, so that the form of the body was degenerating, beginning to seethe with the boils of rebellious cells.

Yet it still walked, each step an incalculable effort of coordination and strength.

Boom—

The step that trod the cottage came sooner than they thought.

Mick saw the leg raised; saw the faces of the people in the shin and ankle and foot—they were as big as he was now—all huge men chosen to take the full weight of this great creation. Many were dead. The bottom of the foot, he could see, was a jigsaw of crushed and bloody bodies, pressed to death under the weight of their fellow citizens.

The foot descended with a roar.

In a matter of seconds the cottage was reduced to splinters and dust.

Popolac blotted the sky utterly. It was, for a moment, the whole world, heaven and earth, its presence filled the senses to overflowing. At this proximity one look could not encompass it, the eye had to range backwards and forwards over its mass to take it all in, and even then the mind refused to accept the whole truth.

A whirling fragment of stone, flung off from the cottage as it collapsed, struck Judd full in the face. In his head he heard the killing stroke like a ball hitting a wall: a play-yard death. No pain: no remorse. Out like a light, a tiny, insignificant light; his death-cry lost in the pandemonium, his body hidden in the smoke and darkness. Mick neither saw nor heard Judd die.

He was too busy staring at the foot as it settled for a moment in the ruins of the cottage, while the other leg mustered the will to move.

Mick took his chance. Howling like a banshee, he ran towards the leg, longing to embrace the monster. He stumbled in the wreckage, and stood again, bloodied, to reach for the foot before it was lifted and he was left behind. There was a clamour of agonized breath as the message came to the foot that it must move; Mick saw the muscles of the shin bunch and marry as the leg began to lift. He made one last lunge at the limb as it began to leave the ground, snatching a harness or a rope, or human hair, or flesh itself—anything to catch this passing miracle and be part of it. Better to go with it wherever it was going, serve it in its purpose, whatever that might be; better to die with it than live without it.

He caught the foot, and found a safe purchase on its ankle. Screaming his sheer ecstasy at his success he felt the great leg raised, and glanced down through the swirling dust to the spot where he had stood, already receding as the limb climbed.

The earth was gone from beneath him. He was a hitchhiker with a god: the mere life he had left was nothing to him now, or ever. He would live with this thing, yes, he would live with it—seeing it and seeing it and eating it with his eyes until he died of sheer gluttony.

He screamed and howled and swung on the ropes, drinking up his triumph. Below, far below, he glimpsed Judd's body, curled up pale on the dark ground, irretrievable. Love and life and sanity were gone, gone like the memory of his name, or his sex, or his ambition.

It all meant nothing. Nothing at all.

Boom—

Boom—

Popolac walked, the noise of its steps receding to the east. Popolac walked, the hum of its voice lost in the night.

After a day, birds came, foxes came, flies, butterflies, wasps came. Judd moved, Judd shifted, Judd gave birth. In his belly maggots warmed themselves, in a vixen's den the good flesh of his thigh was fought over. After that, it was quick. The bones yellowing, the bones crumbling: soon, an empty space which he had once filled with breath and onions.

Darkness, light, darkness, light. He interrupted neither with his name.

Philip K. Dick (1928–1982)

Faith of Our Fathers

Philip K. Dick was a prolific American science fiction writer whose work often strayed into the emotional territory of the horror field, though the monsters of his stories are most often science-fictional or technological. His reputation has grown since his death in 1982 and he is widely regarded as the most important science fiction writer of his generation. The nature of reality was a consistent theme in his work: a recent book on the man and his works is entitled *Only Apparently Real* (1986). There is a vigorous international organization devoted to his writings, The Philip K. Dick Society, and many of his best novels are now being reissued, not in genre but in the prestigious Vintage Contemporaries publishing line. Plays, films (including *Bladerunner*), and an avant garde opera based on his works have appeared in the last decade. He is something of a cult figure. "Faith of Our Fathers" was written in the late 1960s on a commission to produce a novella under the influence of LSD, since Dick had a reputation for experimentation with drugs. The result is this politically and philosophically complex horror story of a future in Southeast Asia, a totalitarian and religious nightmare characteristic of Dick at his best.

O
n the streets of Hanoi he found himself facing a legless peddler who rode a little wooden cart and called shrilly to every passerby. Chien slowed, listened, but did not stop; business at the Ministry of Cultural Artifacts cropped into his mind and deflected his attention: it was as if he were alone, and none of those on bicycles and scooters and jet-powered motorcycles remained. And likewise it was as if the legless peddler did not exist.

"Comrade," the peddler called however, and pursued him on his cart; a helium battery operated the drive and sent the car scuttling expertly after Chien. "I possess a wide spectrum of time-tested herbal remedies complete with testimonials from thousands of loyal users; advise me of your malady and I can assist."

Chien, pausing, said, "Yes, but I have no malady." Except, he thought, for the chronic one of those employed by the Central Committee, that of career opportunism testing constantly the gates of each official position. Including mine.

"I can cure for example radiation sickness," the peddler chanted, still pursuing him. "Or expand, if necessary, the element of sexual prowess. I can reverse carcinomatous progressions, even the dreaded melanomae, what you would call black cancers." Lifting a tray of bottles, small aluminum cans and assorted powders in plastic jars, the peddler sang, "If a rival persists in trying to usurp your gainful bureaucratic position, I can purvey an ointment which, appearing as a dermal balm, is in actuality a desperately effective

474

toxin. And my prices, comrade, are low. And as a special favor to one so distinguished in bearing as yourself I will accept the postwar inflationary paper dollars reputedly of international exchange but in reality damn near no better than bathroom tissue."

"Go to hell," Chien said, and signaled a passing hovercar taxi; he was already three and one half minutes late for his first appointment of the day, and his various fat-assed superiors at the Ministry would be making quick mental notations—as would, to an even greater degree, his subordinates.

The peddler said quietly, "But, comrade; you *must* buy from me."

"Why?" Chien demanded. Indignation.

"Because, comrade, I am a war veteran. I fought in the Colossal Final War of National Liberation with the People's Democratic United Front against the Imperialists; I lost my pedal extremities at the battle of San Francisco." His tone was triumphant, now, and sly. "*It is the law.* If you refuse to buy wares offered by a veteran you risk a fine and possible jail sentence—and in addition disgrace."

Wearily, Chien nodded the hovercab on. "Admittedly," he said. "Okay, I must buy from you." He glanced summarily over the meager display of herbal remedies, seeking one at random. "That," he decided, pointing to a paper-wrapped parcel in the rear row.

The peddler laughed. "That, comrade, is a spermatocide, bought by women who for political reasons cannot qualify for The Pill. It would be of shallow use to you, in fact none at all, since you are a gentleman."

"The law," Chien said bitingly, "does not require me to purchase anything useful from you; only that I purchase something. I'll take that." He reached into his padded coat for his billfold, huge with the postwar inflationary bills in which, four times a week, he as a government servant was paid.

"Tell me your problems," the peddler said.

Chien stared at him. Appalled by the invasion of privacy—and done by someone outside the government.

"All right, comrade," the peddler said, seeing his expression. "I will not probe; excuse me. But as a doctor—an herbal healer—it is fitting that I know as much as possible." He pondered, his gaunt features somber. "Do you watch television unusually much?" he asked abruptly.

Taken by surprise, Chien said, "Every evening. Except on Friday when I go to my club to practice the esoteric imported art from the defeated West of steer-roping." It was his only indulgence; other than that he had totally devoted himself to Party activities.

The peddler reached, selected a gray paper packet. "Sixty trade dollars," he stated. "With a full guarantee; if it does not do as promised, return the unused portion for a full and cheery refund."

"And what," Chien said cuttingly, "is it guaranteed to do?"

"It will rest eyes fatigued by the countenance of meaningless official monologues," the peddler said. "A soothing preparation; take it as soon as you find yourself exposed to the usual dry and lengthy sermons which—"

Chien paid the money, accepted the packet, and strode off. Balls, he said to himself. It's a racket, he decided, the ordinance setting up war vets as a privileged class. They prey off us—we, the younger ones—like raptors.

Forgotten, the gray packet remained deposited in his coat pocket, as he entered the imposing postwar Ministry of Cultural Artifacts building, and his own considerable stately office, to begin his workday.

A portly, middle-aged Caucasian male, wearing a brown Hong Kong silk suit, double-breasted with vest, waited in his office. With the unfamiliar Caucasian stood his own immediate superior, Ssu-Ma Tso-pin. Tso-pin introduced the two of them in Cantonese, a dialect which he used badly.

"Mr. Tung Chien, this is Mr. Darius Pethel. Mr. Pethel will be headmaster at the new ideological and cultural establishment of didactic character soon to open at San Fernando, California." He added, "Mr. Pethel has had a rich and full lifetime supporting the people's struggle to unseat imperialist-bloc countries via pedagogic media; therefore this high post."

They shook hands.

"Tea?" Chien asked the two of them; he pressed the switch of his infrared hibachi and in an instant the water in the highly ornamented ceramic pot—of Japanese origin—began to burble. As he seated himself at his desk he saw that trustworthy Miss Hsi had laid out the information poop-sheet (confidential) on Comrade Pethel; he glanced over it, meanwhile pretending to be doing nothing in particular.

"The Absolute Benefactor of the People," Tso-pin said, "has personally met Mr. Pethel and trusts him. This is rare. The school in San Fernando will appear to teach run-of-the-mill Taoist philosophies but will, of course, in actuality maintain for us a channel of communication to the liberal and intellectual youth segment of western U.S. There are many of them still alive, from San Diego to Sacramento; we estimate at least ten thousand. The school will accept two thousand. Enrollment will be mandatory for those we select. Your relationship to Mr. Pethel's programing is grave. Ahem; your tea water is boiling."

"Thank you," Chien murmured, dropping in the bag of Lipton's tea.

Tso-pin continued, "Although Mr. Pethel will supervise the setting up of the courses of instruction presented by the school to its student body, all examination papers will oddly enough be relayed here to your office for your own expert, careful, ideological study. In other words, Mr. Chien, you will determine who among the two thousand students is reliable, which are truly responding to the programing and who is not."

"I will now pour my tea," Chien said, doing so ceremoniously.

"What we have to realize," Pethel rumbled in Cantonese even worse than that of Tso-pin, "is that, once having lost the global war to us, the American youth has developed a talent for dissembling." He spoke the last word in English; not understanding it, Chien turned inquiringly to his superior.

"Lying," Tso-pin explained.

Pethel said, "Mouthing the proper slogans for surface appearance, but on the inside believing them false. Test papers by this group will closely resemble those of genuine—"

"You mean that the test papers of *two thousand* students will be passing through my office?" Chien demanded. He could not believe it. "That's a full-time job in itself; I don't have time for anything remotely resembling that." He was appalled. "To give critical, official approval or denial of the astute variety which you're envisioning—" He gestured. "Screw that," he said, in English.

Blinking at the strong, Western vulgarity, Tso-pin said, "You have a staff. Plus also you can requisition several more from the pool; the Ministry's budget, augmented this year, will permit it. And remember: the Absolute Benefactor of the People has hand-picked Mr. Pethel." His tone, now, had become ominous, but only subtly so. Just enough to penetrate Chien's hysteria, and to wither it into submission. At least temporarily. To underline his point, Tso-pin walked to the far end of the office; he stood before the full-length 3-D portrait of the Absolute Benefactor, and after an interval his proximity triggered the tape-transport mounted behind the portrait; the face of the Benefactor moved, and from it came a familiar homily, in more than familiar accents. "Fight for peace, my sons," it intoned gently, firmly.

"Ha," Chien said, still perturbed, but concealing it. Possibly one of the Ministry's computers could sort the examination papers; a yes-no-maybe structure could be employed, in conjunction with a pre-analysis of the pattern of ideological correctness— and incorrectness. The matter could be made routine. Probably.

Darius Pethel said, "I have with me certain material which I would like you to scrutinize, Mr. Chien." He unzipped an unsightly, old-fashioned, plastic briefcase. "Two examination essays," he said as he passed the documents to Chien. "This will tell us if you're qualified." He then glanced at Tso-pin; their gazes met. "I understand," Pethel said, "that if you are successful in this venture you will be made vice-councilor of the Ministry, and His Greatness the Absolute Benefactor of the People will personally confer Kisterigian's medal on you." Both he and Tso-pin smiled in wary unison.

"The Kisterigian medal," Chien echoed; he accepted the examination papers, glanced over them in a show of leisurely indifference. But within him his heart vibrated in ill-concealed tension. "Why these two? By that I mean, what am I looking for, sir?"

"One of them," Pethel said, "is the work of a dedicated progressive, a loyal Party member of thoroughly researched conviction. The other is by a young *stilyagi* whom we suspect of holding petit bourgeois imperialist degenerate crypto-ideas. It is up to you, sir, to determine which is which."

Thanks a lot, Chien thought. But, nodding, he read the title of the top paper.

DOCTRINES OF THE ABSOLUTE BENEFACTOR ANTICIPATED IN THE POETRY OF
BAHA AD-DIN ZUHAYR, OF THIRTEENTH-CENTURY ARABIA.

Glancing down the initial pages of the essay, Chien saw a quatrain familiar to him; it was called "Death" and he had known it most of his adult, educated life.

> Once he will miss, twice he will miss,
> He only chooses one of many hours;
> For him nor deep nor hill there is,
> But all's one level plain he hunts for flowers.

"Powerful," Chien said. "This poem."

"He makes use of the poem," Pethel said, observing Chien's lips moving as he reread the quatrain, "to indicate the age-old wisdom, displayed by the Absolute Benefactor in our current lives, that no individual is safe; everyone is mortal, and only the supra-personal, historically essential cause survives. As it should be. Would you agree with him? With this student, I mean? Or—" Pethel paused. "Is he in fact perhaps satirizing the Absolute Benefactor's promulgations?"

Cagily, Chien said, "Give me a chance to inspect the other paper."

"You need no further information; decide."

Haltingly, Chien said, "I—had never thought of this poem that way." He felt irritable. "Anyhow, it isn't by Baha ad-Din Zuhayr; it's part of the *Thousand and One Nights* anthology. It is, however, thirteenth century; I admit that." He quickly read over the text of the paper accompanying the poem. It appeared to be a routine, uninspired rehash of Party clichés, all of them familiar to him from birth. The blind, imperialist monster who mowed down and snuffed out (mixed metaphor) human aspiration, the calculations of the still extant anti-Party group in eastern United States . . . He felt dully bored, and as uninspired as the student's paper. We must persevere, the paper declared. Wipe out the Pentagon remnants in the Catskills, subdue Tennessee and most especially the pocket of diehard reaction in the red hills of Oklahoma. He sighed.

"I think," Tso-pin said, "we should allow Mr. Chien the opportunity of observing this difficult material at his leisure." To Chien he said, "You have permission to take them home to your condominium, this evening, and adjudge them on your own time." He bowed, half mockingly, half solicitously. In any case, insult or not, he had gotten Chien off the hook, and for that Chien was grateful.

"You are most kind," he murmured, "to allow me to perform this new and highly stimulating labor on my own time. Mikoyan, were he alive today, would approve." You bastard, he said to himself. Meaning both his superior and the Caucasian Pethel. Handing me a hot potato like this, and on my own time. Obviously the CP USA is in trouble; its indoctrination academies aren't managing to do their job with the notoriously mulish, eccentric Yank youths. And you've passed that hot potato on and on until it reaches me.

Thanks for nothing, he thought acidly.

That evening in his small but well-appointed condominium apartment he read over the other of the two examination papers, this one by a Marion Culper, and discovered that it, too, dealt with poetry. Obviously this was speciously a poetry class, and he felt ill. It had always run against his grain, the use of poetry—of any art—for social purposes. Anyhow, comfortable in his special spine-straightening, simulated-leather easy chair, he lit a Cuesta Rey Number One English Market immense corona cigar and began to read.

The writer of the paper, Miss Culper, had selected as her text a portion of a poem of John Dryden, the seventeenth-century English poet, final lines from the well-known "A Song for St. Cecilia's Day."

> . . . So when the last and dreadful hour
> This crumbling pageant shall devour,
> The trumpet shall be heard on high,
> The dead shall live, the living die,
> And Music shall untune the sky.

Well, that's a hell of a thing, Chien thought to himself bitingly. Dryden, we're supposed to believe, anticipated the fall of capitalism? That's what he meant by the "crumbling pageant"? Christ. He leaned over to take hold of his cigar and found that it had gone out. Groping in his pockets for his Japanese-made lighter, he half rose to his feet . . .

Tweeeeeee! the TV set at the far end of the living room said.

Aha, Chien said. We're about to be addressed by the Leader. By the Absolute Benefactor of the People, up there in Peking where he's lived for ninety years now; or is it one hundred? Or, as we sometimes like to think of him, the Ass—

"May the ten thousand blossoms of abject self-assumed poverty flower in your spiritual courtyard," the TV announcer said. With a groan, Chien rose to his feet, bowed the mandatory bow of response; each TV set came equipped with monitoring devices to narrate to the Secpol, the Security Police, whether its owner was bowing and/or watching.

On the screen a clearly defined visage manifested itself, the wide, unlined, healthy features of the one-hundred-and-twenty-year-old leader of CP East, ruler of many—far too many, Chien reflected. Blah to you, he thought, and reseated himself in his simulated-leather easy chair, now facing the TV screen.

"My thoughts," the Absolute Benefactor said in his rich and slow tones, "are on you, my children. And especially on Mr. Tung Chien of Hanoi, who faces a difficult task ahead, a task to enrich the people of Democratic East, plus the American West Coast. We must think in unison about this noble, dedicated man and the chore which he faces, and I have chosen to take several moments of my time to honor him and encourage him. Are you listening, Mr. Chien?"

"Yes, Your Greatness," Chien said, and pondered to himself the odds against the Party Leader singling *him* out this particular evening. The odds caused him to feel uncomradely cynicism; it was unconvincing. Probably this transmission was being beamed to his apartment building alone—or at least this city. It might also be a lip-synch job, done at Hanoi TV, Incorporated. In any case he was required to listen and watch—and absorb. He did so, from a lifetime of practice. Outwardly he appeared to be rigidly attentive. Inwardly he was still mulling over the two test papers, wondering which was which; where did devout Party enthusiasm end and sardonic lampoonery begin? Hard to say . . . which of course explained why they had dumped the task in his lap.

Again he groped in his pockets for his lighter—and found the small gray envelope which the war-veteran peddler had sold him. Gawd, he thought, remembering what it had cost. Money down the drain and what did this herbal remedy do? Nothing. He turned the packet over and saw, on the back, small printed words. Well, he thought, and began to unfold the packet with care. The words had snared him—as of course they were meant to do.

Failing as a Party member and human? Afraid of becoming obsolete and discarded on the ash heap of history by

He read rapidly through the text, ignoring its claims, seeking to find out what he had purchased.

Meanwhile, the Absolute Benefactor droned on.

Snuff. The package contained snuff. Countless tiny black grains, like gunpowder, which sent up an interesting aromatic to tickle his nose. The title of the particular blend was Princes Special, he discovered. And very pleasing, he decided. At one time he had taken snuff—smoked tobacco for a time having been illegal for reasons of health—back during his student days at Peking U; it had been the fad, especially the amatory mixes prepared in Chungking, made from god knew what. Was this that? Almost any aromatic could be added to snuff, from essence of orange to pulverized babycrap . . . or so some seemed, especially an English mixture called High Dry Toast which had in itself more or less put an end to his yearning for nasal, inhaled tobacco.

On the TV screen the Absolute Benefactor rumbled monotonously on as Chien sniffed cautiously at the powder, read the claims—it cured everything from being late to work to falling in love with a woman of dubious political background. Interesting. But typical of claims—

His doorbell rang.

Rising, he walked to the door, opened it with full knowledge of what he would find. There, sure enough, stood Mou Kuei, the Building Warden, small and hard-eyed and alert to his task; he had his armband and metal helmet on, showing that he meant business. "Mr. Chien, comrade Party worker. I received a call from the television authority. You are failing to watch your screen and are instead fiddling with a packet of doubtful content." He produced a clipboard and ballpoint pen. "Two red marks, and hithertonow you are summarily ordered to repose yourself in a comfortable, stress-free posture before your screen and give the Leader your unexcelled attention. His words, this evening, are directed particularly to you, sir; to you."

"I doubt that," Chien heard himself say.

Blinking, Kuei said, "What do you mean?"

"The Leader rules eight billion comrades. He isn't going to single me out." He felt wrathful; the punctuality of the warden's reprimand irked him.

Kuei said, "But I distinctly heard with my own ears. You were mentioned."

Going over to the TV set, Chien turned the volume up. "But now he's talking about crop failures in People's India; that's of no relevance to me."

"Whatever the Leader expostulates is relevant." Mou Kuei scratched a mark on his clipboard sheet, bowed formally, turned away. "My call to come up here to confront you with your slackness originated at Central. Obviously they regard your attention as important; I must order you to set in motion your automatic transmission recording circuit and replay the earlier portions of the Leader's speech."

Chien farted. And shut the door.

Back to the TV set, he said to himself. Where our leisure hours are spent. And there lay the two student examination papers; he had that weighing him down, too. And all on my own time, he thought savagely. The hell with them. Up theirs. He strode to the TV set, started to shut it off; at once a red warning light winked on, informing him that he did not have permission to shut off the set—could not in fact end its tirade and image even if he unplugged it. Mandatory speeches, he thought, will kill us all, bury us; if I could be free of the noise of speeches, free of the din of the Party baying as it hounds mankind . . .

There was no known ordinance, however, preventing him from taking snuff while he watched the Leader. So, opening the small gray packet, he shook out a mound of the black granules onto the back of his left hand. He then, professionally, raised his hand to his nostrils and deeply inhaled, drawing the snuff well up into his sinus cavities. Imagine the old superstition, he thought to himself. That the sinus cavities are connected to the brain, and hence an inhalation of snuff directly affects the cerebral cortex. He smiled, seated himself once more, fixed his gaze on the TV screen and the gesticulating individual known so utterly to them all.

The face dwindled away, disappeared. The sound ceased. He faced an emptiness, a vacuum. The screen, white and blank, confronted him and from the speaker a faint hiss sounded.

The frigging snuff, he said to himself. And inhaled greedily at the remainder of the powder on his hand, drawing it up avidly into his nose, his sinuses, and, or so it felt, into his brain; he plunged into the snuff, absorbing it elatedly.

The screen remained blank and then, by degrees, an image once more formed and established itself. It was not the Leader. Not the Absolute Benefactor of the People, in point of fact not a human figure at all.

He faced a dead mechanical construct, made of solid state circuits, of swiveling pseudopodia, lenses and a squawk-box. And the box began, in a droning din, to harangue him.

Staring fixedly, he thought, *What is this?* Reality? Hallucination, he thought. The peddler came across some of the psychodelic drugs used during the War of Liberation— he's selling the stuff and I've taken some, taken a whole lot!

Making his way unsteadily to the vidphone he dialed the Secpol station nearest his building. "I wish to report a pusher of hallucinogenic drugs," he said into the receiver.

"Your name, sir, and conapt location?" Efficient, brisk and impersonal bureaucrat of the police.

He gave them the information, then haltingly made it back to his simulated-leather easy chair, once again to witness the apparition on the TV screen. This is lethal, he said to himself. It must be some preparation developed in Washington, D.C., or London—

stronger and stranger than the LSD-25 which they dumped so effectively into our reservoirs. And I thought it was going to relieve me of the burden of the Leader's speeches . . . this is far worse, this electronic sputtering, swiveling, metal and plastic monstrosity yammering away—this is terrifying.

To have to face *this* the remainder of my life—

It took ten minutes for the Secpol two-man team to come rapping at his door. And by then, in a deteriorating set of stages, the familiar image of the Leader had seeped back into focus on the screen, had supplanted the horrible artificial construct which waved its 'podia and squalled on and on. He let the two cops in shakily, led them to the table on which he had left the remains of the snuff in its packet.

"Psychedelic toxin," he said thickly. "Of short duration. Absorbed into the blood stream directly, through nasal capillaries. I'll give you details as to where I got it, from whom, all that." He took a deep shaky breath; the presence of the police was comforting.

Ballpoint pens ready, the two officers waited. And all the time, in the background, the Leader rattled out his endless speech. As he had done a thousand evenings before in the life of Tung-Chien. But, he thought, it'll never be the same again, at least not for me. Not after inhaling that near-toxic snuff.

He wondered, Is that what they intended?

It seemed odd to him, thinking of a *they*. Peculiar—but somehow correct. For an instant he hesitated, not giving out the details, not telling the police enough to find the man. A peddler, he started to say. I don't know where; can't remember. But he did; he remembered the exact street intersection. So, with unexplainable reluctance, he told them.

"Thank you, Comrade Chien." The boss of the team of police carefully gathered up the remaining snuff—most of it remained—and placed it in his uniform—smart, sharp uniform—pocket. "We'll have it analyzed at the first available moment," the cop said, "and inform you immediately in case counter medical measures are indicated for you. Some of the old wartime psychedelics were eventually fatal, as you have no doubt read."

"I've read," he agreed. That had been specifically what he had been thinking.

"Good luck and thanks for notifying us," both cops said, and departed. The affair, for all their efficiency, did not seem to shake them; obviously such a complaint was routine.

The lab report came swiftly—surprisingly so, in view of the vast state bureaucracy. It reached him by vidphone before the Leader had finished his TV speech.

"It's not a hallucinogen," the Secpol lab technician informed him.

"No?" he said, puzzled and, strangely, not relieved. Not at all.

"On the contrary. It's a phenothiazine, which as you doubtless know is anti-hallucinogenic. A strong dose per gram of admixture, but harmless. Might lower your blood pressure or make you sleepy. Probably stolen from a wartime cache of medical supplies. Left by the retreating barbarians. I wouldn't worry."

Pondering, Chien hung up the vidphone in slow motion. And then walked to the window of his conapt—the window with the fine view of other Hanoi high-rise conapts—to think.

The doorbell rang. Feeling as if he were in a trance, he crossed the carpeted living room to answer it.

The girl standing there, in a tan raincoat with a babushka over her dark, shiny, and very long hair, said in a timid little voice, "Um, Comrade Chien? Tung Chien? Of the Ministry of—"

He led her in, reflexively, and shut the door after her. "You've been monitoring my vidphone," he told her; it was a shot in darkness, but something in him, an unvoiced certitude, told him that she had.

"Did—they take the rest of the snuff?" She glanced about. "Oh, I hope not; it's so hard to get these days."

"Snuff," he said, "is easy to get. Phenothiazine isn't. Is that what you mean?"

The girl raised her head, studied him with large, moon-darkened eyes. "Yes. Mr. Chien—" She hesitated, obviously as uncertain as the Secpol cops had been assured. "Tell me what you saw; it's of great importance for us to be certain."

"I had a choice?" he said acutely.

"Y-yes, very much so. That's what confuses us; that's what is not as we planned. We don't understand; it fits nobody's theory." Her eyes even darker and deeper, she said, "Was it the aquatic horror shape? The thing with slime and teeth, the extraterrestrial life form? Please tell me; we have to know." She breathed irregularly, with effort, the tan raincoat rising and falling; he found himself watching its rhythm.

"A machine," he said.

"Oh!" She ducked her head, nodding vigorously. "Yes, I understand; a mechanical organism in no way resembling a human. Not a simulacrum, something constructed to resemble a man."

He said, "This did not look like a man." He added to himself, And it failed—did not try—to talk like a man.

"You understand that it was not a hallucination."

"I've been officially told that what I took was a phenothiazine. That's all I know." He said as little as possible; he did not want to talk but to hear. Hear what the girl had to say.

"Well, Mr. Chien—" She took a deep, unstable breath. "If it was not a hallucination, then what was it? What does that leave? What is called 'extra-consciousness'—could that be it?"

He did not answer; turning his back, he leisurely picked up the two student test papers, glanced over them, ignoring her. Waiting for her next attempt.

At his shoulder she appeared, smelling of spring rain, smelling of sweetness and agitation, beautiful in the way she smelled, and looked, and, he thought, speaks. So different from the harsh plateau speech patterns we hear on the TV—have heard since I was a baby.

"Some of them," she said huskily, "who take the stelazine—it was stelazine you got, Mr. Chien—see one apparition, some another. But distinct categories have emerged; there is not an infinite variety. Some see what you saw; we call it the Clanker. Some the aquatic horror; that's the Gulper. And then there's the Bird, and the Climbing Tube, and—" She broke off. "But other reactions tell you very little. Tell *us* very little." She hesitated, then plunged on. "Now that this has happened to you, Mr. Chien, we would like you to join our gathering. Join your particular group, those who see what you see. Group Red. We want to know what it *really* is, and—" She gestured with tapered, wax-smooth fingers. "It can't be *all* those manifestations." Her tone was poignant, nai[u]vely so. He felt his caution relax—a trifle.

He said, "What do you see? You in particular?"

"I'm a part of Group Yellow. I see—a storm. A whining, vicious whirlwind. That roots everything up, crushes condominium apartments built to last a century." She smiled wanly. "The Crusher. Twelve groups in all, Mr. Chien. Twelve absolutely different experiences, all from the same phenothiazine, all of the Leader as he speaks over TV. As *it* speaks, rather." She smiled up at him, lashes long—probably protracted artificially—and gaze engaging, even trusting. As if she thought he knew something or could do something.

"I should make a citizen's arrest of you," he said presently.

"There is no law, not about this. We studied Soviet juridical writings before we—found people to distribute the stelazine. We don't have much of it; we have to be very careful whom we give it to. It seemed to us that you constituted a likely choice . . . a well-known, postwar, dedicated young career man on his way up." From his fingers she took the examination papers. "They're having you pol-read?" she asked.

" 'Pol-read'?" He did not know the term.

"Study something said or written to see if it fits the Party's current world view. You in the hierarchy merely call it 'read,' don't you?" Again she smiled. "When you rise one step higher, up with Mr. Tso-pin, you will know that expression." She added somberly, "And with Mr. Pethel. He's very far up. Mr. Chien, there is no ideological school in San Fernando; these are forged exam papers, designed to read back to them a thorough analysis of *your* political ideology. And have you been able to distinguish which paper is orthodox and which is heretical?" Her voice was pixie-like, taunting with amused malice. "Choose the wrong one and your budding career stops dead, cold, in its tracks. Choose the proper one—"

"Do you know which is which?" he demanded.

"Yes." She nodded soberly. "We have listening devices in Mr. Tso-pin's inner offices; we monitored his conversation with Mr. Pethel—who is not Mr. Pethel but the Higher Secpol Inspector Judd Craine. You have possibly heard mention of him; he acted as chief assistant to Judge Vorlawsky at the '98 war crimes trial in Zurich."

With difficulty he said, "I—see." Well, that explained that.

The girl said, "My name is Tanya Lee."

He said nothing; he merely nodded, too stunned for any cerebration.

"Technically, I am a minor clerk," Miss Lee said, "at your Ministry. You have never run into me, however, that I can at least recall. We try to hold posts wherever we can. As far up as possible. My own boss—"

"Should you be telling me this?" He gestured at the TV set, which remained on. "Aren't they picking this up?"

Tanya Lee said, "We introduced a noise factor in the reception of both vid and aud material from this apartment building; it will take them almost an hour to locate the sheathing. So we have"—she examined the tiny wristwatch on her slender wrist—"fifteen more minutes. And still be safe."

"Tell me," he said, "which paper is orthodox."

"Is that what you care about? Really?"

"What," he said, "should I care about?"

"Don't you see, Mr. Chien? You've learned something. The Leader is not the Leader; he is something else, but we can't tell what. Not yet. Mr. Chien, with all due respect, have you ever had your drinking water analyzed? I know it sounds paranoiac, but have you?"

"No," he said. "Of course not." Knowing what she was going to say.

Miss Lee said briskly, "Our tests show that it's saturated with hallucinogens. It is, has been, will continue to be. Not the ones used during the war; not the disorienting ones, but a synthetic quasi-ergot derivative called Datrox-3. You drink it here in the building from the time you get up; you drink it in restaurants and other apartments that you visit. You drink it at the Ministry; it's all piped from a central, common source." Her tone was bleak and ferocious. "We solved that problem; we knew, as soon as we discovered it, that any good phenothiazine would counter it. What we did not know, of course, was this—a *variety* of authentic experiences; that makes no sense, rationally. It's the hallucination which should differ from person to person, and the reality experience which should be ubiquitous—it's all turned around. We can't even construct an ad hoc theory which accounts for that, and god knows we've tried. Twelve mutually exclusive hallucinations

—that would be easily understood. But not one hallucination and twelve realities." She ceased talking, then, and studied the two test papers, her forehead wrinkling. "The one with the Arabic poem is orthodox," she stated. "If you tell them that they'll trust you and give you a higher post. You'll be another notch up in the hierarchy of Party officialdom." Smiling—her teeth were perfect and lovely—she finished, "Look what you received back for your investment this morning. Your career is underwritten for a time. And by us."

He said, "I don't believe you." Instinctively, his caution operated within him, always, the caution of a lifetime lived among the hatchet men of the Hanoi branch of the CP East. They knew an infinitude of ways by which to ax a rival out of contention—some of which he himself had employed; some of which he had seen done to himself and to others. This could be a novel way, one unfamiliar to him. It could always be.

"Tonight," Miss Lee said, "in the speech the Leader singled you out. Didn't this strike you as strange? You, of all people? A minor officeholder in a meager ministry—"

"Admitted," he said. "It struck me that way; yes."

"That was legitimate. His Greatness is grooming an elite cadre of younger men, postwar men, he hopes will infuse new life into the hidebound, moribund hierarchy of old fogies and Party hacks. His Greatness singled you out for the same reason that we singled you out; if pursued properly, your career could lead you all the way to the top. At least for a time . . . as we know. That's how it goes."

He thought, So virtually everyone has faith in me. Except myself; and certainly not after this, the experience with the anti-hallucinatory snuff. It had shaken years of confidence, and no doubt rightly so. However, he was beginning to regain his poise; he felt it seeping back, a little at first, then with a rush.

Going to the vidphone, he lifted the receiver and began, for the second time that night, to dial the number of the Hanoi Security Police.

"Turning me in," Miss Lee said, "would be the second most regressive decision you could make. I'll tell them that you brought me here to bribe me; you thought, because of my job at the Ministry, I would know which examination paper to select."

He said, "And what would be my first most regressive decision?"

"Not taking a further dose of phenothiazine," Miss Lee said evenly.

Hanging up the phone, Tung Chien thought to himself, I don't understand what's happening to me. Two forces, the Party and His Greatness on one hand—this girl with her alleged group on the other. One wants me to rise as far as possible in the Party hierarchy; the other—*What did Tanya Lee want?* Underneath the words, inside the membrane of an almost trivial contempt for the Party, the Leader, the ethical standards of the People's Democratic United Front—what was she after in regard to him?

He said curiously, "Are you anti-Party?"

"No."

"But—" He gestured. "That's all there is; Party and anti-Party. You must be Party, then." Bewildered, he stared at her; with composure she returned the stare. "You have an organization," he said, "and you meet. What do you intend to destroy? The regular function of government? Are you like the treasonable college students of the United States during the Vietnam War who stopped troop trains, demonstrated—"

Wearily Miss Lee said, "It wasn't like that. But forget it; that's not the issue. What we want to know is this: who or what is leading us? We must penetrate far enough to enlist someone, some rising young Party theoretician, who could conceivably be invited to a tête-à-tête with the Leader—you see?" Her voice lifted; she consulted her watch, obviously anxious to get away: the fifteen minutes were almost up. "Very few persons actually see the Leader, as you know. I mean really see him."

"Seclusion," he said. "Due to his advanced age."

"We have hope," Miss Lee said, "that if you pass the phony test which they have arranged for you—and with my help you have—you will be invited to one of the stag parties which the Leader has from time to time, which of course the 'papes don't report. Now do you see?" Her voice rose shrilly, in a frenzy of despair. "Then we would know; if you could go in there under the influence of the anti-hallucinogenic drug, could see him face to face as he actually is—"

Thinking aloud, he said, "And end my career of public service. If not my life."

"You owe us something," Tanya Lee snapped, her cheeks white. "If I hadn't told you which exam paper to choose you would have picked the wrong one and your dedicated public service career would be over anyhow; you would have failed—failed at a test you didn't even realize you were taking!"

He said mildly, "I had a fifty-fifty chance."

"No." She shook her head fiercely. "The heretical one is faked up with a lot of Party jargon; they deliberately constructed the two texts to trap you. They *wanted* you to fail!"

Once more he examined the two papers, feeling confused. Was she right? Possibly. Probably. It rang true, knowing the Party functionaries as he did, and Tso-pin, his superior, in particular. He felt weary then. Defeated. After a time he said to the girl, "What you're trying to get out of me is a quid pro quo. You did something for me—you got, or claim you got—the answer to this Party inquiry. But you've already done your part. What's to keep me from tossing you out of here on your head? I don't have to do a goddam thing." He heard his voice, toneless, sounding the poverty of empathic emotionality so usual in Party circles.

Miss Lee said, "There will be other tests, as you continue to ascend. And we will monitor for you with them too." She was calm, at ease; obviously she had forseen his reaction.

"How long do I have to think it over?" he said.

"I'm leaving now. We're in no rush; you're not about to receive an invitation to the Leader's Yellow River villa in the next week or even month." Going to the door, opening it, she paused. "As you're given covert rating tests we'll be in contact, supplying the answers—so you'll see one or more of us on those occasions. Probably it won't be me; it'll be that disabled war veteran who'll sell you the correct response sheets as you leave the Ministry building." She smiled a brief, snuffed-out-candle smile. "But one of these days, no doubt unexpectedly, you'll get an ornate, official, very formal invitation to the villa, and when you go you'll be heavily sedated with stelazine . . . possibly our last dose of our dwindling supply. Good night." The door shut after her; she had gone.

My god, he thought. They can blackmail me. For what I've done. And she didn't even bother to mention it; in view of what they're involved with it was not worth mentioning.

But blackmail for what? He had already told the Secpol squad that he had been given a drug which had proved to be a phenothiazine. *Then they know*, he realized. They'll watch me; they're alert. Technically I haven't broken a law, but—they'll be watching, all right.

However, they always watched anyhow. He relaxed slightly, thinking that. He had, over the years, become virtually accustomed to it, as had everyone.

I will see the Absolute Benefactor of the People as he is, he said to himself. Which possibly no one else has done. What will it be? Which of the subclasses of non-hallucination? Classes which I do not even know about . . . a view which may totally overthrow me. How am I going to be able to get through the evening, to keep my poise, if it's like the shape I saw on the TV screen? The Crusher, the Clanker, the Bird, the Climbing Tube, the Gulper—or worse.

He wondered what some of the other views consisted of . . . and then gave up that line of speculation; it was unprofitable. And too anxiety-inducing.

The next morning Mr. Tso-pin and Mr. Darius Pethel met him in his office, both of them calm but expectant. Wordlessly, he handed them one of the two "exam papers." The orthodox one, with its short and heart-smothering Arabian poem.

"This one," Chien said tightly, "is the product of a dedicated Party member or candidate for membership. The other—" He slapped the remaining sheets. "Reactionary garbage." He felt anger. "In spite of a superficial—"

"All right, Mr. Chien," Pethel said, nodding. "We don't have to explore each and every ramification; your analysis is correct. You heard the mention regarding you in the Leader's speech last night on TV?"

"I certainly did," Chien said.

"So you have undoubtedly inferred," Pethel said, "that there is a good deal involved in what we are attempting, here. The Leader has his eye on you; that's clear. As a matter of fact, he has communicated to myself regarding you." He opened his bulging briefcase and rummaged. "Lost the goddam thing. Anyhow—" He glanced at Tso-pin, who nodded slightly. "His Greatness would like to have you appear for dinner at the Yangtze River Ranch next Thursday night. Mrs. Fletcher in particular appreciates—"

Chien said, " 'Mrs. Fletcher'? Who is 'Mrs. Fletcher'?"

After a pause Tso-pin said dryly, "The Absolute Benefactor's wife. His name—which you of course had never heard—is Thomas Fletcher."

"He's a Caucasian," Pethel explained. "Originally from the New Zealand Communist Party; he participated in the difficult takeover there. This news is not in the strict sense secret, but on the other hand it hasn't been noised about." He hesitated, toying with his watchchain. "Probably it would be better if you forgot about that. Of course, as soon as you meet him, see him face to face, you'll realize that, realize that he's a Cauc. As I am. As many of us are."

"Race," Tso-pin pointed out, "has nothing to do with loyalty to the Leader and the Party. As witness Mr. Pethel, here."

But His Greatness, Chien thought, jolted. He did not appear, on the TV screen, to be occidental. "On TV—" he began.

"The image," Tso-pin interrupted, "is subjected to a variegated assortment of skillful refinements. For ideological purposes. Most persons holding higher offices are aware of this." He eyed Chien with hard criticism.

So everyone agrees, Chien thought. What we see every night is not real. The question is, How unreal? Partially? Or—completely?

"I will be prepared," he said tautly. And he thought, There has been a slip-up. They weren't prepared for me—the people that Tanya Lee represents—to gain entry so soon. Where's the anti-hallucinogen? Can they get it to me or not? Probably not on such short notice.

He felt, strangely, relief. He would be going into the presence of His Greatness in a position to see him as a human being, see him as he—and everybody else—saw him on TV. It would be a most stimulating and cheerful dinner party, with some of the most influential Party members in Asia. I think we can do without the phenothiazines, he said to himself. And his sense of relief grew.

"Here it is, finally," Pethel said suddenly, producing a white envelope from his briefcase. "Your card of admission. You will be flown by Sino-rocket to the Leader's villa Thursday morning; there the protocol officer will brief you on your expected behavior. It will be formal dress, white tie and tails, but the atmosphere will be cordial. There are always a great number of toasts." He added, "I have attended two such stag gets-together. Mr. Tso-pin"—he smiled creakily—"has not been honored in such a fashion. But as they say, all things come to him who waits. Ben Franklin said that."

Tso-pin said, "It has come for Mr. Chien rather prematurely, I would say." He shrugged philosophically. "But my opinion has never at any time been asked."

"One thing," Pethel said to Chien. "It is possible that when you see His Greatness in person you will be in some regards disappointed. Be alert that you do not let this make itself apparent, if you should so feel. We have, always, tended—been trained—to regard him as more than a man. But at table he is"—he gestured—"a forked radish. In certain respects like ourselves. He may for instance indulge in moderately human oral-aggressive and -passive activity; he possibly may tell an off-color joke or drink too much . . . To be candid, no one ever knows in advance how these things will work out, but they do generally hold forth until late the following morning. So it would be wise to accept the dosage of amphetamines which the protocol officer will offer you."

"Oh?" Chien said. This was news to him, and interesting.

"For stamina. And to balance the liquor. His Greatness has amazing staying power; he often is still on his feet and raring to go after everyone else has collapsed."

"A remarkable man," Tso-pin chimed in. "I think his—indulgences only show that he is a fine fellow. And fully in the round; he is like the ideal Renaissance man; as, for example, Lorenzo de' Medici."

"That does come to mind," Pethel said; he studied Chien with such intensity that some of last night's chill returned. Am I being led into one trap after another? Chien wondered. That girl—was she in fact an agent of the Secpol probing me, trying to ferret out a disloyal, anti-Party streak in me?

I think, he decided, I will make sure that the legless peddler of herbal remedies does not snare me when I leave work; I'll take a totally different route back to my conapt.

He was successful. That day he avoided the peddler and the same the next, and so on until Thursday.

On Thursday morning the peddler scooted from beneath a parked truck and blocked his way, confronting him.

"My medication?" the peddler demanded. "It helped? I know it did; the formula goes back to the Sung Dynasty—I can tell it did. Right?"

Chien said, "Let me go."

"Would you be kind enough to answer?" The tone was not the expected, customary whining of a street peddler operating in a marginal fashion, and that tone came across to Chien; he heard loud and clear . . . as the Imperialist puppet troops of long ago phrased it.

"I know what you gave me," Chien said. "And I don't want any more. If I change my mind I can pick it up at a pharmacy. Thanks." He started on, but the cart, with the legless occupant, pursued him.

"Miss Lee was talking to me," the peddler said loudly.

"Hmm," Chien said, and automatically increased his pace; he spotted a hovercab and began signaling for it.

"It's tonight you're going to the stag dinner at the Yangtze River villa," the peddler said, panting for breath in his effort to keep up. "Take the medication—now!" He held out a flat packet, imploringly. "Please, Party Member Chien; for your own sake, for all of us. So we can tell what it is we're up against. Good lord, it may be non-terran; that's our most basic fear. Don't you understand, Chien? What's your goddam career compared with that? If we can't find out—"

The cab bumped to a halt on the pavement; its door slid open. Chien started to board it.

The packet sailed past him, landed on the entrance sill of the cab, then slid into the gutter, damp from earlier rain.

"Please," the peddler said. "And it won't cost you anything; today it's free. Just take it, use it before the stag dinner. And don't use the amphetamines; they're a thalamic stimulant, contra-indicated whenever an adrenal suppressant such as a phenothiazine is—"

The door of the cab closed after Chien. He seated himself.

"Where to, comrade?" the robot drive-mechanism inquired.

He gave the ident tag number of his conapt.

"That half-wit of a peddler managed to infiltrate his seedy wares into my clean interior," the cab said. "Notice; it reposes by your foot."

He saw the packet—no more than an ordinary-looking envelope. I guess, he thought, this is how drugs come to you; all of a sudden they're lying there. For a moment he sat, and then he picked it up.

As before, there was a written enclosure above and beyond the medication, but this time, he saw, it was handwritten. A feminine script: from Miss Lee:

We were surprised at the suddenness. But thank heaven we were ready. Where were you Tuesday and Wednesday? Anyhow, here it is, and good luck. I will approach you later in the week; I don't want you to try to find me.

He ignited the note, burned it up in the cab's disposal ashtray.

And kept the dark granules.

All this time, he thought. Hallucinogens in our water supply. Year after year. Decades. And not in wartime but in peacetime. And not to the enemy camp but here in our own. The evil bastards, he said to himself. Maybe I ought to take this; maybe I ought to find out what he or it is and let Tanya's group know.

I will, he decided. And—he was curious.

A bad emotion, he knew. Curiosity was, especially in Party activities, often a terminal state careerwise.

A state which, at the moment, gripped him thoroughly. He wondered if it would last through the evening, if, when it came right down to it, he would actually take the inhalant.

Time would tell. Tell that and everything else. We are blooming flowers, he thought, on the plain, which he picks. As the Arabic poem had put it. He tried to remember the rest of the poem but could not.

That probably was just as well.

The villa protocol officer, a Japanese named Kimo Okubara, tall and husky, obviously a quondam wrestler, surveyed him with innate hostility, even after he presented his engraved invitation and had successfully managed to prove his identity.

"Surprise you bother to come," Okubara muttered. "Why not stay home and watch on TV? Nobody miss you. We got along fine without up to right now."

Chien said tightly, "I've already watched on TV." And anyhow the stag dinners were rarely televised; they were too bawdy.

Okubara's crew double-checked him for weapons, including the possibility of an anal suppository, and then gave him his clothes back. They did not find the phenothiazine, however. Because he had already taken it. The effects of such a drug, he knew, lasted approximately four hours; that would be more than enough. And, as Tanya had said, it was a major dose; he felt sluggish and inept and dizzy, and his tongue moved in spasms of pseudo Parkinsonism—an unpleasant side effect which he had failed to anticipate.

A girl, nude from the waist up, with long coppery hair down her shoulders and back, walked by. Interesting.

Coming the other way, a girl nude from the bottom up made her appearance. Interesting, too. Both girls looked vacant and bored, and totally self-possessed.

"You go in like that too," Okubara informed Chien.

Startled, Chien said, "I understood white tie and tails."

"Joke," Okubara said. "At your expense. Only girls wear nude; you even get so you enjoy, unless you homosexual."

Well, Chien thought, I guess I had better like it. He wandered on with the other guests—they, like him, wore white tie and tails or, if women, floor-length gowns—and felt ill at ease, despite the tranquilizing effect of the stelazine. Why am I here? he asked himself. The ambiguity of his situation did not escape him. He was here to advance his career in the Party apparatus, to obtain the intimate and personal nod of approval from His Greatness . . . and in addition he was here to decipher His Greatness as a fraud; he did not know what variety of fraud, but there it was: fraud against the Party, against all the peace-loving democratic people of Terra. Ironic, he thought. And continued to mingle.

A girl with small, bright, illuminated breasts approached him for a match; he absentmindedly got out his lighter. "What makes your breasts glow?" he asked her. "Radioactive injections?"

She shrugged, said nothing, passed on, leaving him alone. Evidently he had responded in the incorrect way.

Maybe it's a wartime mutation, he pondered.

"Drink, sir." A servant graciously held out a tray; he accepted a martini—which was the current fad among the higher Party classes in People's China—and sipped the ice-cold dry flavor. Good English gin, he said to himself. Or possibly the original Holland compound; juniper or whatever they added. Not bad. He strolled on, feeling better; in actuality he found the atmosphere here a pleasant one. The people here were self-assured; they had been successful and now they could relax. It evidently was a myth that proximity to His Greatness produced neurotic anxiety: he saw no evidence here, at least, and felt little himself.

A heavy-set elderly man, bald, halted him by the simple means of holding his drink glass against Chien's chest. "That frably little one who asked you for a match," the elderly man said, and sniggered. "The quig with the Christmas-tree breasts—that was a boy, in drag." He giggled. "You have to be cautious around here."

"Where, if anywhere," Chien said, "do I find authentic women? In the white ties and tails?"

"Darn near," the elderly man said, and departed with a throng of hyperactive guests, leaving Chien alone with his martini.

A handsome, tall woman, well dressed, standing near Chien, suddenly put her hand on his arm; he felt her fingers tense and she said, "Here he comes. His Greatness. This is the first time for me; I'm a little scared. Does my hair look all right?"

"Fine," Chien said reflexively, and followed her gaze, seeking a glimpse—his first—of the Absolute Benefactor.

What crossed the room toward the table in the center was not a man.

And it was not, Chien realized, a mechanical construct either; it was not what he had seen on TV. That evidently was simply a device for speechmaking, as Mussolini had once used an artificial arm to salute long and tedious processions.

God, he thought, and felt ill. Was this what Tanya Lee had called the "aquatic horror" shape? It had no shape. Nor pseudopodia, either flesh or metal. It was, in a sense, not there at all; when he managed to look directly at it, the shape vanished; he saw through it, saw the people on the far side—but not it. Yet if he turned his head, caught it out of a sidelong glance, he could determine its boundaries.

It was terrible; it blasted him with its awfulness. As it moved it drained the life from each person in turn; it ate the people who had assembled, passed on, ate again, ate more with an endless appetite. It hated; he felt its hate. It loathed; he felt its loathing for everyone present—in fact he shared its loathing. All at once he and everyone else in the big villa were each a twisted slug, and over the fallen slug-carcasses the creature savored, lingered, but all the time coming directly toward him—or was that an illusion? If this is a hallucination, Chien thought, it is the worst I have ever had; if it is not, then it is evil reality; it's an evil thing that kills and injures. He saw the trail of stepped-on, mashed men and women remnants behind it; he saw them trying to reassemble, to operate their crippled bodies; he heard them attempting speech.

I know who you are, Tung Chien thought to himself. You, the supreme head of the worldwide Party structure. You, who destroy whatever living object you touch; I see that Arabic poem, the searching for the flowers of life to eat them—I see you astride the plain which to you is Earth, plain without hills, without valleys. You go anywhere, appear any time, devour anything; you engineer life and then guzzle it, and you enjoy that.

He thought, You are God.

"Mr. Chien," the voice said, but it came from inside his head, not from the mouthless spirit that fashioned itself directly before him. "It is good to meet you again. You know nothing. Go away. I have no interest in you. Why should I care about slime? Slime; I am mired in it, I must excrete it, and I choose to. I could break you; I can break even myself. Sharp stones are under me; I spread sharp pointed things upon the mire. I make the hiding places, the deep places, boil like a pot; to me the sea is like a pot of ointment. The flakes of my flesh are joined to everything. You are me. I am you. It makes no difference, just as it makes no difference whether the creature with ignited breasts is a girl or boy; you could learn to enjoy either." It laughed.

He could not believe it was speaking to him; he could not imagine—it was too terrible—that it had picked him out.

"I have picked everybody out," it said. "No one is too small; each falls and dies and I am there to watch. I don't need to do anything but watch; it is automatic; it was arranged that way." And then it ceased talking to him; it disjoined itself. But he still saw it; he felt its manifold presence. It was a globe which hung in the room, with fifty thousand eyes, with a million eyes—billions: an eye for each living thing as it waited for each thing to fall, and then stepped on the living thing as it lay in a broken state. Because of this it had created the things, and he knew; he understood. What had seemed in the Arabic poem to be death was not death but god; or rather God was death, it was one force, one hunter, one cannibal thing, and it missed again and again but, having all eternity, it could afford to miss. Both poems, he realized; the Dryden one too. The crumbling; that is our world and you are doing it. Warping it to come out that way; bending us.

But at least, he thought, I still have my dignity. With dignity he set down his drink glass, turned, walked toward the doors of the room. He passed through the doors. He walked down a long carpeted hall. A villa servant dressed in purple opened a door for him; he found himself standing out in the night darkness, on a veranda, alone.

Not alone.

It had followed after him. Or it had already been here before him; yes, it had been expecting. It was not really through with him.

"Here I go," he said, and made a dive for the railing; it was six stories down, and there below gleamed the river, and death, real death, not what the Arabic poem had seen.

As he tumbled over, it put an extension of itself on his shoulder.

"Why?" he said. But, in fact, he paused. Wondering. Not understanding, not at all.

"Don't fall on my account," it said. He could not see it because it had moved behind him. But the piece of it on his shoulder—it had begun to look to him like a human hand.

And then it laughed.

"What's funny?" he demanded, as he teetered on the railing, held back by its pseudo-hand.

"You're doing my task for me," it said. "You aren't waiting; don't you have time to wait? I'll select you out from among the others; you don't need to speed the process up."

"What if I do?" he said. "Out of revulsion for you?"

It laughed. And didn't answer.

"You won't even say," he said.

Again no answer. He started to slide back, onto the veranda. And at once the pressure of its pseudo-hand lifted.

"You founded the Party?" he asked.

"I founded everything. I founded the anti-Party and the Party that isn't a Party, and those who are for it and those who are against, those that you call Yankee Imperialists, those in the camp of reaction, and so on endlessly. I founded it all. As if they were blades of grass."

"And you're here to enjoy it?" he said.

"What I want," it said, "is for you to see me, as I am, as you have seen me, and then trust me."

"What?" he said, quavering. "Trust you to what?"

It said, "Do you believe in me?"

"Yes," he said. "I can see you."

"Then go back to your job at the Ministry. Tell Tanya Lee that you saw an overworked, overweight, elderly man who drinks too much and likes to pinch girls' rear ends."

"Oh, Christ," he said.

"As you live on, unable to stop, I will torment you," it said. "I will deprive you, item by item, of everything you possess or want. And then when you are crushed to death I will unfold a mystery."

"What's the mystery?"

"The dead shall live, the living die. I kill what lives; I save what has died. And I will tell you this: *there are things worse than I.* But you won't meet them because by then I will have killed you. Now walk back into the dining room and prepare for dinner. Don't question what I'm doing; I did it long before there was a Tung Chien and I will do it long after."

He hit it as hard as he could.

And experienced violent pain in his head.

And darkness, with the sense of falling.

After that, darkness again. He thought, I will get you. I will see that you die too. That you suffer; you're going to suffer, just like us, exactly in every way we do. I'll dedicate my life to that; I'll confront you again, and I'll nail you; I swear to god I'll nail you up somewhere. And it will hurt. As much as I hurt now.

He shut his eyes.

Roughly, he was shaken. And heard Mr. Kimo Okubara's voice. "Get to your feet, common drunk. Come on!"

Without opening his eyes he said, "Get me a cab."

"Cab already waiting. You go home. Disgrace. Make a violent scene out of yourself."

Getting shakily to his feet, he opened his eyes, examined himself. Our Leader whom we follow, he thought, is the One True God. And the enemy whom we fight and have fought is God too. They are right; he is everywhere. But I didn't understand what that meant. Staring at the protocol officer, he thought, You are God too. So there is no getting away, probably not even by jumping. As I started, instinctively, to do. He shuddered.

"Mix drinks with drugs," Okubara said witheringly. "Ruin career. I see it happen many times. Get lost."

Unsteadily, he walked toward the great central door of the Yangtze River villa; two servants, dressed like medieval knights, with crested plumes, ceremoniously opened the door for him and one of them said, "Good night, sir."

"Up yours," Chien said, and passed out into the night.

At a quarter to three in the morning, as he sat sleepless in the living room of his conapt, smoking one Cuesta Rey Astoria after another, a knock sounded at the door.

When he opened it he found himself facing Tanya Lee in her trenchcoat, her face pinched with cold. Her eyes blazed, questioningly.

"Don't look at me like that," he said roughly. His cigar had gone out; he relit it. "I've been looked at enough," he said.

"You saw it," she said.

He nodded.

She seated herself on the arm of the couch and after a time she said, "Want to tell me about it?"

"Go as far from here as possible," he said. "Go a long way." And then he remembered; no way was long enough. He remembered reading that too. "Forget it," he said; rising to his feet, he walked clumsily into the kitchen to start up the coffee.

Following after him, Tanya said, "Was—it that bad?"

"We can't win," he said. "You can't win; I don't mean me. I'm not in this; I just want to do my job at the Ministry and forget about it. Forget the whole damned thing."

"Is it non-terrestrial?"

"Yes." He nodded.

"Is it hostile to us?"

"Yes," he said. "No. Both. Mostly hostile."

"Then we have to—"

"Go home," he said, "and go to bed." He looked her over carefully; he had sat a long time and he had done a great deal of thinking. About a lot of things. "Are you married?" he said.

"No. Not now. I used to be."

He said, "Stay with me tonight. The rest of tonight, anyhow. Until the sun comes up." He added, "The night part is awful."

"I'll stay," Tanya said, unbuckling the belt of her raincoat, "but I have to have some answers."

"What did Dryden mean," Chien said, "about music untuning the sky? I don't get that. What does music do to the sky?"

"All the celestial order of the universe ends," she said as she hung her raincoat up in the closet of the bedroom; under it she wore an orange striped sweater and stretchpants.

He said, "And that's bad."

Pausing, she reflected. "I don't know. I guess so."

"It's a lot of power," he said, "to assign to music."

"Well, you know that old Pythagorean business about the 'music of the spheres.' " Matter-of-factly she seated herself on the bed and removed her slipperlike shoes.

"Do you believe in that?" he said. "Or do you believe in God?"

" 'God'!" She laughed. "That went out with the donkey steam engine. What are you talking about? God, or god?" She came over close beside him, peering into his face.

"Don't look at me so closely," he said sharply, drawing back. "I don't ever want to be looked at again." He moved away, irritably.

"I think," Tanya said, "that if there is a God He has very little interest in human affairs. That's my theory, anyhow. I mean, He doesn't seem to care if evil triumphs or people and animals get hurt and die. I frankly don't see Him anywhere around. And the Party has always denied any form of—"

"Did you ever see Him?" he asked. "When you were a child?"

"Oh, sure, as a child. But I also believed—"

"Did it ever occur to you," Chien said, "that good and evil are names for the same thing? That God could be both good and evil at the same time?"

"I'll fix you a drink," Tanya said, and padded barefoot into the kitchen.

Chien said, "The Crusher. The Clanker. The Gulper and the Bird and the Climbing Tube—plus other names, forms, I don't know. I had a hallucination. At the stag dinner. A big one. A terrible one."

"But the stelazine—"

"It brought on a worse one," he said.

"Is there any way," Tanya said somberly, "that we can fight this thing you saw? This apparition you call a hallucination but which very obviously was not?"

He said, "Believe in it."

"What will that do?"

"Nothing," he said wearily. "Nothing at all. I'm tired; I don't want a drink—let's just go to bed."

"Okay." She padded back into the bedroom, began pulling her striped sweater over her head. "We'll discuss it more thoroughly later."

"A hallucination," Chien said, "is merciful. I wish I had it; I want mine back. I want to be before your peddler got to me with that phenothiazine."

"Just come to bed. It'll be toasty. All warm and nice."

He removed his tie, his shirt—and saw, on his right shoulder, the mark, the stigma, which it had left when it stopped him from jumping. Livid marks which looked as if they would never go away. He put his pajama top on, then; it hid the marks.

"Anyhow," Tanya said as he got into the bed beside her, "your career is immeasurably advanced. Aren't you glad about that?"

"Sure," he said, nodding sightlessly in the darkness. "Very glad."

"Come over against me," Tanya said, putting her arms around him. "And forget everything else. At least for now."

He tugged her against him, then, doing what she asked and what he wanted to do. She was neat; she was swiftly active; she was successful and she did her part. They did not bother to speak until at last she said, "Oh!" And then she relaxed.

"I wish," he said, "that we could go on forever."

"We did," Tanya said. "It's outside of time; it's boundless, like an ocean. It's the way we were in Cambrian times, before we migrated up onto the land; it's the ancient primary waters. This is the only time we get to go back, when this is done. That's why it means so much. And in those days we weren't separate; it was like a big jelly, like those blobs that float up on the beach."

"Float up," he said, "and are left there to die."

"Could you get me a towel?" Tanya asked. "Or a washcloth? I need it."

He padded into the bathroom for a towel. There—he was naked, now—he once more saw his shoulder, saw where it had seized hold of him and held on, dragged him back, possibly to toy with him a little more.

The marks, unaccountably, were bleeding.

He sponged the blood away. More oozed forth at once and seeing that, he wondered how much time he had left. Probably only hours.

Returning to bed, he said, "Could you continue?"

"Sure. If you have any energy left; it's up to you." She lay gazing up at him unwinkingly, barely visible in the dim nocturnal light.

"I have," he said. And hugged her to him.

Gertrude Atherton (1857–1948)

The Bell in the Fog

Gertrude Atherton dedicated her first and best collection of ghost stories, *The Bell in the Fog and Other Stories* (1905), "To the Master, Henry James." The title story of the collection is both an homage to James and an extraordinary critique. Ralph, the central character who becomes obsessed with a painting, is a portrait of the James whom Atherton knew, and the stamp of emulation is everywhere in the piece. But in the end, the portrayal is not entirely sympathetic. One wonders what James made of this piece. An intriguing fact is that Henry James began writing in 1900 upon the request of William Dean Howells a long story about an "international ghost," that he wrote in part and then abandoned when he had difficulty with the plot. In 1915, he took it up again but died before completing *The Sense of the Past,* which was published as a fragment posthumously (1917). Ralph, the central character, becomes obsessed with a century-old painting, and travels back to the past as a "ghost" from the future, who sits for that very portrait. Whatever the case, "The Bell in the Fog" is an effective supernatural piece by a feminist writer who later became James' literary enemy.

I

The great author had realized one of the dreams of his ambitious youth, the possession of an ancestral hall in England. It was not so much the good American's reverence for ancestors that inspired the longing to consort with the ghosts of an ancient line, as artistic appreciation of the mellowness, the dignity, the aristocratic aloofness of walls that have sheltered, and furniture that has embraced, generations and generations of the dead. To mere wealth, only his astute and incomparably modern brain yielded respect; his ego raised its goose-flesh at the sight of rooms furnished with a single check, conciliatory as the taste might be. The dumping of the old interiors of Europe into the glistening shells of the United States not only roused him almost to passionate protest, but offended his patriotism—which he classified among his unworked ideals. The average American was not an artist, therefore he had no excuse for even the affectation of cosmopolitanism. Heaven knew he was national enough in everything else, from his accent to his lack of repose; let his surroundings be in keeping.

Orth had left the United States soon after his first successes, and, his art being too great to be confounded with locality, he had long since ceased to be spoken of as an American author. All civilized Europe furnished stages for his puppets, and, if never picturesque nor impassioned, his originality was as overwhelming as his style. His subtleties might not always be understood—indeed, as a rule, they were not—but the musical mystery of his language and the penetrating charm of his lofty and cultivated mind induced raptures in the initiated, forever denied to those who failed to appreciate him.

His following was not a large one, but it was very distinguished. The aristocracies of the earth gave to it; and not to understand and admire Ralph Orth was deliberately to relegate one's self to the ranks. But the elect are few, and they frequently subscribe to the circulating libraries; on the Continent, they buy the Tauchnitz edition; and had not Mr. Orth inherited a sufficiency of ancestral dollars to enable him to keep rooms in Jermyn Street, and the wardrobe of an Englishman of leisure, he might have been forced to consider the tastes of the middle-class at a desk in Hampstead. But, as it mercifully was, the fashionable and exclusive sets of London knew and sought him. He was too wary to become a fad, and too sophisticated to grate or bore; consequently, his popularity continued evenly from year to year, and long since he had come to be regarded as one of them. He was not keenly addicted to sport, but he could handle a gun, and all men respected his dignity and breeding. They cared less for his books than women did, perhaps because patience is not a characteristic of their sex. I am alluding, however, in this instance, to men-of-the-world. A group of young literary men—and one or two women—put him on a pedestal and kissed the earth before it. Naturally, they imitated him, and as this flattered him, and he had a kindly heart deep among the cere-cloths of his formalities, he sooner or later wrote "appreciations" of them all, which nobody living could understand, but which owing to the subtitle and signature answered every purpose.

With all this, however, he was not utterly content. From the 12th of August until late in the winter—when he did not go to Homburg and the Riviera—he visited the best houses in England, slept in state chambers, and meditated in historic parks; but the country was his one passion, and he longed for his own acres.

He was turning fifty when his great-aunt died and made him her heir: "as a poor reward for his immortal services to literature," read the will of this phenomenally appreciative relative. The estate was a large one. There was a rush for his books; new editions were announced. He smiled with cynicism, not unmixed with sadness; but he was very grateful for the money, and as soon as his fastidious taste would permit he bought him a country-seat.

The place gratified all his ideals and dreams—for he had romanced about his sometime English possession as he had never dreamed of woman. It had once been the property of the Church, and the ruin of cloister and chapel above the ancient wood was sharp against the low pale sky. Even the house itself was Tudor, but wealth from generation to generation had kept it in repair; and the lawns were as velvety, the hedges as rigid, the trees as aged as any in his own works. It was not a castle nor a great property, but it was quite perfect; and for a long while he felt like a bridegroom on a succession of honeymoons. He often laid his hand against the rough ivied walls in a lingering caress.

After a time, he returned the hospitalities of his friends, and his invitations, given with the exclusiveness of his great distinction, were never refused. Americans visiting England eagerly sought for letters to him; and if they were sometimes benumbed by that cold and formal presence, and awed by the silences of Chillingsworth—the few who entered there—they thrilled in anticipation of verbal triumphs, and forthwith bought an entire set of his books. It was characteristic that they dared not ask him for his autograph.

Although women invariably described him as "brilliant," a few men affirmed that he was gentle and lovable, and any one of them was well content to spend weeks at Chillingsworth with no other companion. But, on the whole, he was rather a lonely man.

It occurred to him how lonely he was one gay June morning when the sunlight was streaming through his narrow windows, illuminating tapestries and armor, the family portraits of the young profligate from whom he had made this splendid purchase, dusting its gold on the black wood of wainscot and floor. He was in the gallery at the moment, studying one of his two favorite portraits, a gallant little lad in the green costume of Robin Hood. The boy's expression was imperious and radiant, and he had that perfect beauty which in any disposition appealed so powerfully to the author. But as Orth stared today at the brilliant youth, of whose life he knew nothing, he suddenly became aware of a human stirring at the foundations of his aesthetic pleasure.

"I wish he were alive and here," he thought, with a sigh. "What a jolly little companion he would be! And this fine old mansion would make a far more complementary setting for him than for me."

He turned away abruptly, only to find himself face to face with the portrait of a little girl who was quite unlike the boy, yet so perfect in her own way, and so unmistakably painted by the same hand, that he had long since concluded they had been brother and sister. She was angelically fair, and, young as she was—she could not have been more than six years old—her dark-blue eyes had a beauty of mind which must have been remarkable twenty years later. Her pouting mouth was like a little scarlet serpent, her skin almost transparent, her pale hair fell waving—not curled with the orthodoxy of childhood—about her tender bare shoulders. She wore a long white frock, and clasped tightly against her breast a doll far more gorgeously arrayed than herself. Behind her were the ruins and the woods of Chillingsworth.

Orth had studied this portrait many times, for the sake of an art which he understood almost as well as his own; but today he saw only the lovely child. He forgot even the boy in the intensity of this new and personal absorption.

"Did she live to grow up, I wonder?" he thought. "She should have made a remarkable, even a famous woman, with those eyes and that brow, but—could the spirit within that ethereal frame stand the enlightenments of maturity? Would not that mind—purged, perhaps, in a long probation from the dross of other existences—flee in disgust from the commonplace problems of a woman's life? Such perfect beings should die while they are still perfect. Still, it is possible that this little girl, whoever she was, was idealized by the artist, who painted into her his own dream of exquisite childhood."

Again he turned away impatiently. "I believe I am rather fond of children," he admitted. "I catch myself watching them on the street when they are pretty enough. Well, who does not like them?" he added, with some defiance.

He went back to his work; he was chiselling a story which was to be the foremost excuse of a magazine as yet unborn. At the end of half an hour he threw down his wondrous instrument—which looked not unlike an ordinary pen—and making no attempt to disobey the desire that possessed him, went back to the gallery. The dark splendid boy, the angelic little girl were all he saw—even of the several children in that roll call of the past—and they seemed to look straight down his eyes into depths where the fragmentary ghosts of unrecorded ancestors gave faint musical response.

"The dead's kindly recognition of the dead," he thought. "But I wish these children were alive."

For a week he haunted the gallery, and the children haunted him. Then he became impatient and angry. "I am mooning like a barren woman," he exclaimed. "I must take the briefest way of getting those youngsters off my mind."

With the help of his secretary, he ransacked the library, and finally brought to light the gallery catalogue which had been named in the inventory. He discovered that his children were the Viscount Tancred and the Lady Blanche Mortlake, son and daughter of the second Earl of Teignmouth. Little wiser than before, he sat down at once and wrote to the present earl, asking for some account of the lives of the children. He awaited the answer with more restlessness than he usually permitted himself, and took long walks, ostentatiously avoiding the gallery.

"I believe those youngsters have obsessed me," he thought, more than once. "They certainly are beautiful enough, and the last time I looked at them in that waning light they were fairly alive. Would that they were, and scampering about this park."

Lord Teignmouth, who was intensely grateful to him, answered promptly.

"I am afraid," he wrote, "that I don't know much about my ancestors—those who didn't do something or other; but I have a vague rememberance of having been told by an aunt of mine, who lives on the family traditions—she isn't married—that the little chap was drowned in the river, and that the little girl died too—I mean when she *was* a little girl—wasted away, or something—I'm such a beastly idiot about expressing myself, that I wouldn't dare to write to you at all if you weren't really great. That is actually all I can tell you, and I am afraid the painter was their only biographer."

The author was gratified that the girl had died young, but grieved for the boy. Although he had avoided the gallery of late, his practised imagination had evoked from the throngs of history the high-handed and brilliant, surely adventurous career of the third Earl of Teignmouth. He had pondered upon the deep delights of directing such a mind and character, and had caught himself envying the dust that was older still. When he read of the lads early death, in spite of his regret that such promise should have come to naught, he admitted to a secret thrill of satisfaction that the boy had so soon ceased to belong to anyone. Then he smiled with both sadness and humor.

"What an old fool I am!" he admitted. "I believe I not only wish those children were alive, but that they were my own."

The frank admission proved fatal. He made straight for the gallery. The boy, after the interval of separation, seemed more spiritedly alive than ever, the little girl to suggest, with her faint appealing smile, that she would like to be taken up and cuddled.

"I must try another way," he thought, desperately, after that long communion. "I must write them out of me."

He went back to the library and locked up the *tour de force* which had ceased to command his classic faculty. At once, he began to write the story of the brief lives of the children, much to the amazement of that faculty, which was little accustomed to the simplicities. Nevertheless, before he had written three chapters, he knew that he was at work upon a masterpiece—and more: he was experiencing a pleasure so keen that once and again his hand trembled, and he saw the page through a mist. Although his characters had always been objective to himself and his more patient readers, none knew better than he—a man of no delusions—that they were so remote and exclusive as barely to escape being mere mentalities; they were never the pulsing living creations of the more full-blooded genius. But he had been content to have it so. His creations might find and leave him cold, but he had known his highest satisfaction in chiselling the statuettes, extracting subtle and elevating harmonies, while combining words as no man of his tongue had combined them before.

But the children were not statuettes. He had loved and brooded over them long ere he had thought to tuck them into his pen, and on its first stroke they danced out alive. The old mansion echoed with their laughter, with their delightful and original pranks. Mr. Orth knew nothing of children, therefore all the pranks he invented were as original as his faculty. The little girl clung to his hand or knee as they both followed the adventurous course of their common idol, the boy. When Orth realized how alive they were, he opened each room of his home to them in turn, that evermore he might have sacred and poignant memories with all parts of the stately mansion where he must dwell alone to the end. He selected their bedrooms, and hovered over them—not through infantile disorders, which were beyond even his imagination,—but through those painful intervals incident upon the enterprising spirit of the boy and the devoted obedience of the girl to fraternal command. He ignored the second Lord Teignmouth; he was himself their father, and he admired himself extravagantly for the first time; art had chastened him long since. Oddly enough, the children had no mother, not even the memory of one.

He wrote the book more slowly than was his wont, and spent delightful hours pondering upon the chapter of the morrow. He looked forward to the conclusion with a sort of terror, and made up his mind that when the inevitable last word was written he should start at once for Homburg. Incalculable times a day he went to the gallery, for he no longer had any desire to write the children out of his mind, and his eyes hungered for them. They were his now. It was with an effort that he sometimes humorously reminded himself that another man had fathered them, and that their little skeletons were under the choir of the chapel. Not even for peace of mind would he have descended into the vaults of the lords of Chillingsworth and looked upon the marble effigies of his children. Nevertheless, when in a superhumorous mood, he dwelt upon his high satisfaction in having been enabled by his great-aunt to purchase all that was left of them.

For two months he lived in his fool's paradise, and then he knew that the book must end. He nerved himself to nurse the little girl through her wasting illness, and when he clasped her hands, his own shook, his knees trembled. Desolation settled upon the house, and he wished he had left one corner of it to which he could retreat unhaunted by the child's presence. He took long tramps, avoiding the river with a sensation next to panic. It was two days before he got back to his table, and then he had made up his mind to let the boy live. To kill him off, too, was more than his augmented stock of human nature could endure. After all, the lad's death had been purely accidental, wanton. It was just that he should live—with one of the author's inimitable suggestions of future greatness; but, at the end, the parting was almost as bitter as the other. Orth knew then how men feel when their sons go forth to encounter the world and ask no more of the old companionship.

The author's boxes were packed. He sent the manuscript to his publisher an hour after it was finished—he could not have given it a final reading to have saved it from failure—directed his secretary to examine the proof under a microscope, and left the next morning for Homburg. There, in inmost circles, he forgot his children. He visited in several of the great houses of the Continent until November; then returned to London to find his book the literary topic of the day. His secretary handed him the reviews; and for once in a way he read the finalities of the nameless. He found himself hailed as a genius, and compared in astonished phrases to the prodigiously clever talent which the world for twenty years had isolated under the name of Ralph Orth. This pleased him, for every writer is human enough to wish to be hailed as a genius, and immediately. Many are, and many wait; it depends upon the fashion of the moment, and the needs and bias of those who write of writers. Orth had waited twenty years; but his past was bedecked with the headstones of geniuses long since forgotten. He was gratified to come thus publicly into his estate, but soon reminded himself that all the adulation of which a belated world was capable could not give him one thrill of the pleasure which the companionship of that book had given him, while creating. It was the keenest pleasure in his memory, and when a man is fifty and has written many books, that is saying a great deal.

He allowed what society was in town to lavish honors upon him for something over a month, then cancelled all his engagements and went down to Chillingsworth.

His estate was in Hertfordshire, that county of gentle hills and tangled lanes, of ancient oaks and wide wild heaths, of historic houses, and dark woods, and green fields innumerable—a Wordsworthian shire, steeped in the deepest peace of England. As Orth drove towards his own gates he had the typical English sunset to gaze upon, a red streak with a church spire against it. His woods were silent. In the fields, the cows stood as if conscious of their part. The ivy on his old gray towers had been young with his children.

He spent a haunted night, but the next day stranger happenings began.

II

He rose early, and went for one of his long walks. England seems to cry out to be walked upon, and Orth, like others of the transplanted, experienced to the full the country's gift of foot-restlessness and mental calm. Calm flees, however, when the ego is rampant, and today, as upon others too recent, Orth's soul was as restless as his feet. He had walked for two hours when he entered the wood of his neighbor's estate, a domain seldom honored by him, as it, too, had been bought by an American—a flighty hunting widow, who displeased the fastidious taste of the author. He heard children's voices, and turned with the quick prompting of retreat.

As he did so, he came face-to-face, on the narrow path, with a little girl. For the moment he was possessed by the most hideous sensation which can visit a man's being—abject terror. He believed that body and soul were disintegrating. The child before him was his child, the original of a portrait in which the artist, dead two centuries ago, had missed exact fidelity, after all. The difference, even his rolling vision took note, lay in the warm pure living whiteness and the deeper spiritual suggestion of the child in his path. Fortunately for his self-respect, the surrender lasted but a moment. The little girl spoke.

"You look real sick," she said. "Shall I lead you home?"

The voice was soft and sweet, but the intonation, the vernacular, were American, and not of the highest class. The shock was, if possible, more agonizing than the other, but this time Orth rose to the occasion.

"Who are you?" he demanded, with asperity. "What is your name? Where do you live?"

The child smiled, an angelic smile, although she was evidently amused. "I never had so many questions asked me all at once," she said. "But I don't mind, and I'm glad you're not sick. I'm Mrs. Jennie Root's little girl—my father's dead. My name is Blanche—you *are* sick! No?—and I live in Rome, New York State. We've come over here to visit pa's relations."

Orth took the child's hand in his. It was very warm and soft.

"Take me to your mother," he said, firmly; "now, at once. You can return and play afterwards. And as I wouldn't have you disappointed for the world, I'll send to town today for a beautiful doll."

The little girl, whose face had fallen, flashed her delight, but walked with great dignity beside him. He groaned in his depths as he saw they were pointing for the widow's house, but made up his mind that he would know the history of the child and of all her ancestors, if he had to sit down at table with his obnoxious neighbor. To his surprise, however, the child did not lead him into the park, but towards one of the old stone houses of the tenantry.

"Pa's great-great-great-grandfather lived there," she remarked, with all the American's pride of ancestry. Orth did not smile, however. Only the warm clasp of the hand in his, the soft thrilling voice of his still mysterious companion, prevented him from feeling as if moving through the mazes of one of his own famous ghost stories.

The child ushered him into the dining-room, where an old man was seated at the table reading his Bible. The room was at least eight hundred years old. The ceiling was supported by the trunk of a tree, black, and probably petrified. The windows had still their diamond panes, separated, no doubt, by the original lead. Beyond was a large kitchen in which were several women. The old man, who looked patriarchal enough to have laid the foundations of his dwelling, glanced up and regarded the visitor without hospitality. His expression softened as his eyes moved to the child.

"Who 'ave ye brought?" he asked. He removed his spectacles. "Ah!" He rose, and offered the author a chair. At the same moment, the women entered the room.

"Of course you've fallen in love with Blanche, sir," said one of them. "Everybody does."

"Yes, that is it. Quite so." Confusion still prevailing among his faculties, he clung to the naked truth. "This little girl has interested and startled me because she bears a precise resemblance to one of the portraits in Chillingsworth—painted about two hundred years ago. Such extraordinary likenesses do not occur without reason, as a rule, and, as I admired my portrait so deeply that I have written a story about it, you will not think it unnatural if I am more than curious to discover the reason for this resemblance. The little girl tells me that her ancestors lived in this very house, and as my little girl lived next door, so to speak, there undoubtedly is a natural reason for the resemblance."

His host closed the Bible, put his spectacles in his pocket, and hobbled out of the house.

"He'll never talk of family secrets," said an elderly woman, who introduced herself as the old man's daughter, and had placed bread and milk before the guest. "There are secrets in every family, and we have ours, but he'll never tell those old tales. All I can tell you is that an ancestor of little Blanche went to wreck and ruin because of some fine lady's doings, and killed himself. The story is that his boys turned out bad. One of them saw his crime, and never got over the shock; he was foolish like, after. The mother was a poor scared sort of creature, and hadn't much influence over the other boy. There seemed to be blight on all the man's descendants, until one of them went to America. Since then, they haven't prospered, exactly, but they've done better, and they don't drink so heavy."

"They haven't done so well," remarked a worn patient-looking woman. Orth typed her as belonging to the small middle-class of an interior town of the eastern United States.

"You are not the child's mother?"

"Yes, sir. Everybody is surprised; you needn't apologize. She doesn't look like any of us, although her brothers and sisters are good enough for anybody to be proud of. But we all think she strayed in by mistake, for she looks like any lady's child, and, of course, we're only middle-class."

Orth gasped. It was the first time he had ever heard a native American use the term middle-class with a personal application. For the moment, he forgot the child. His analytical mind raked in the new specimen. He questioned, and learned that the woman's husband had kept a hat store in Rome, New York; that her boys were clerks, her girls in stores, or type-writing. They kept her and little Blanche—who had come after her other children were well grown—in comfort; and they were all very happy together. The boys broke out, occasionally; but, on the whole, were the best in the world, and her girls were worthy of far better than they had. All were robust, except Blanche. "She coming so late, when I was no longer young, makes her delicate," she remarked, with a slight blush, the signal of her chaste Americanism; "but I guess she'll get along all right. She couldn't have better care if she was a queen's child."

Orth, who had gratefully consumed the bread and milk, rose. "Is that really all you can tell me?" he asked.

"That's all," replied the daughter of the house. "And you couldn't pry open father's mouth."

Orth shook hands cordially with all of them, for he could be charming when he chose. He offered to escort the little girl back to her playmates in the wood, and she took prompt possession of his hand. As he was leaving, he turned suddenly to Mrs. Root. "Why did you call her Blanche?" he asked.

"She was so white and dainty, she just looked it."

Orth took the next train for London, and from Lord Teignmouth obtained the address of the aunt who lived on the family traditions, and a cordial note of introduction to her. He then spent an hour anticipating, in a toy shop, the whims and pleasures of a child—an incident of paternity which his book-children had not inspired. He bought the finest doll, piano, French dishes, cooking apparatus, and playhouse in the shop, and signed a check for thirty pounds with a sensation of positive rapture. Then he took the train for Lancashire, where the Lady Mildred Mortlake lived in another ancestral home.

Possibly there are few imaginative writers who have not a leaning, secret or avowed, to the occult. The creative gift is in very close relationship with the Great Force behind the universe; for aught we know, may be an atom thereof. It is not strange, therefore, that the lesser and closer of the unseen forces should send their vibrations to it occasionally; or, at all events, that the imagination should incline its ear to the most mysterious and picturesque of all beliefs. Orth frankly dallied with the old dogma. He formulated no personal faith of any sort, but his creative faculty, that ego within an ego, had made more than one excursion into the invisible and brought back literary treasure.

The Lady Mildred received with sweetness and warmth the generous contributor to the family sieve, and listened with fluttering interest to all he had not told the world—she had read the book—and to the strange, Americanized sequel.

"I am all at sea," concluded Orth. "What had my little girl to do with the tragedy? What relation was she to the lady who drove the young man to destruction—?"

"The closest," interrupted Lady Mildred. "She was herself!"

Orth stared at her. Again he had a confused sense of disintegration. Lady Mildred, gratified by the success of her bolt, proceeded less dramatically:

"Wally was up here just after I read your book, and I discovered he had given you the wrong history of the picture. Not that he knew it. It is a story we have left untold as often as possible, and I tell it to you only because you would probably become a monomaniac if I didn't. Blanche Mortlake—that Blanche—there had been several of her name, but there has not been one since—did not die in childhood, but lived to be twenty-four. She was an angelic child, but little angels sometimes grow up into very naughty girls. I believe she was delicate as a child, which probably gave her that spiritual look. Perhaps she was spoiled and flattered, until her poor little soul was stifled, which is likely. At all events, she was the coquette of her day—she seemed to care for nothing but breaking hearts; and she did not stop when she married, either. She hated her husband, and became reckless. She had no children. So far, the tale is not an uncommon one; but the worst, and what makes the ugliest stain in our annals, is to come.

"She was alone one summer at Chillingsworth—where she had taken temporary refuge from her husband—and she amused herself—some say, fell in love—with a young man of the yeomanry, a tenant of the next estate. His name was Root. He, so it comes down to us, was a magnificent specimen of his kind, and in those days the yeomanry gave us our great soldiers. His beauty of face was quite as remarkable as his physique; he led all the rural youth in sport, and was a bit above his class in every way. He had a wife in no way remarkable, and two little boys, but was always more with his friends than his family. Where he and Blanche Mortlake met I don't know—in the woods, probably, although it has been said that he had the run of the house. But, at all events, he was wild about her, and she pretended to be about him. Perhaps she was, for women have stooped before and since. Some women can be stormed by a fine man in any circumstances; but, although I am a woman of the world, and not easy to shock, there are some things I tolerate so hardly that it is all I can do to bring myself to believe in them; and stooping is one. Well, they were the scandal of the county for months, and then, either because she had tired of her new toy, or his grammar grated after the first glamour, or because she feared her husband, who was returning from the Continent, she broke off with him and returned to town. He followed her, and forced his way into her house. It is said she melted, but made him swear never to attempt to see her again. He returned to his home, and killed himself. A few months later she took her own life. That is all I know."

"It is quite enough for me," said Orth.

The next night, as his train travelled over the great wastes of Lancashire, a thousand chimneys were spouting forth columns of fire. Where the sky was not red it was black. The place looked like hell. Another time Orth's imagination would have gathered immediate inspiration from this wildest region of England. The fair and peaceful counties of the south had nothing to compare in infernal grandeur with these acres of flaming columns. The chimneys were invisible in the lower darkness of the night; the fires might have leaped straight from the angry caldron of the earth.

But Orth was in a subjective world, searching for all he had ever heard of occultism. He recalled that the sinful dead are doomed, according to this belief, to linger for vast reaches of time in that borderland which is close to earth, eventually sent back to work out their final salvation; that they work it out among the descendants of the people they have wronged; that suicide is held by the devotees of occultism to be a cardinal sin, abhorred and execrated.

Authors are far closer to the truths enfolded in mystery than ordinary people, because of that very audacity of imagination which irritates their plodding critics. As only those who dare to make mistakes succeed greatly, only those who shake free the wings of their imagination brush, once in a way, the secrets of the great pale world. If such writers go wrong, it is not for the mere brains to tell them so.

Upon Orth's return to Chillingsworth, he called at once upon the child, and found her happy among his gifts. She put her arms about his neck, and covered his serene unlined face with soft kisses. This completed the conquest. Orth from that moment adored her as a child, irrespective of the psychological problem.

Gradually he managed to monopolize her. From long walks it was but a step to take her home for luncheon. The hours of her visits lengthened. He had a room fitted up as a nursery and filled with the wonders of toyland. He took her to London to see the pantomimes; two days before Christmas, to buy presents for her relatives; and together they strung them upon the most wonderful Christmas-tree that the old hall of Chillingsworth had ever embraced. She had a donkey-cart, and a trained nurse, disguised as a maid, to wait upon her. Before a month had passed she was living in state at Chillingsworth and paying daily visits to her mother. Mrs. Root was deeply flattered, and apparently well content. Orth told her plainly that he should make the child independent, and educate her, meanwhile. Mrs. Root intended to spend six months in England, and Orth was in no hurry to alarm her by broaching his ultimate design.

He reformed Blanche's accent and vocabulary, and read to her out of books which would have addled the brains of most little maids of six; but she seemed to enjoy them, although she seldom made a comment. He was always ready to play games with her, but she was a gentle little thing, and, moreover, tired easily. She preferred to sit in the depths of a big chair, toasting her bare toes at the log-fire in the hall, while her friend read or talked to her. Although she was thoughtful, and, when left to herself, given to dreaming, his patient observation could detect nothing uncanny about her. Moreover, she had a quick sense of humor, she was easily amused, and could laugh as merrily as any child in the world. He was resigning all hope of further development on the shadowy side when one day he took her to the picture-gallery.

It was the first warm day of summer. The gallery was not heated, and he had not dared to take his frail visitor into its chilly spaces during the winter and spring. Although he had wished to see the effect of the picture on the child, he had shrunk from the bare possibility of the very developments the mental part of him craved; the other was warmed and satisfied for the first time, and held itself aloof from disturbance. But one day the sun streamed through the old windows, and, obeying a sudden impulse, he led Blanche to the gallery.

It was some time before he approached the child of his earlier love. Again he hesitated. He pointed out many other fine pictures, and Blanche smiled appreciatively at his remarks, that were wise in criticism and interesting in matter. He never knew just how much she understood, but the very fact that there were depths in the child beyond his probing riveted his chains.

Suddenly he wheeled about and waved his hand to her prototype. "What do you think of that?" he asked. "You remember, I told you of the likeness the day I met you."

She looked indifferently at the picture, but he noticed that her color changed oddly; its pure white tone gave place to an equally delicate gray.

"I have seen it before," she said. "I came in here one day to look at it. And I have been quite often since. You never forbade me," she added, looking at him appealingly, but dropping her eyes quickly. "And I like the little girl—and the boy—very much."

"Do you? Why?"

"I don't know"—a formula in which she had taken refuge before. Still her candid eyes were lowered; but she was quite calm. Orth, instead of questioning, merely fixed his eyes upon her, and waited. In a moment she stirred uneasily, but she did not laugh nervously, as another child would have done. He had never seen her self-possession ruffled, and he had begun to doubt he ever should. She was full of human warmth and affection. She seemed made for love, and every creature who came within her ken adored her, from the author himself down to the litter of puppies presented to her by the stable-boy a few weeks since; but her serenity would hardly be enhanced by death.

She raised her eyes finally, but not to his. She looked at the portrait.

"Did you know that there was another picture behind?" she asked.

"No," replied Orth, turning cold. "How did you know it?"

"One day I touched a spring in the frame, and this picture came forward. Shall I show you?"

"Yes!" And crossing curiosity and the involuntary shrinking from impending phenomena was a sensation of aesthetic disgust that *he* should be treated to a secret spring.

The little girl touched hers, and that other Blanche sprang aside so quickly that she might have been impelled by a sharp blow from behind. Orth narrowed his eyes and stared at what she revealed. He felt that his own Blanche was watching him, and set his features, although his breath was short.

There was the Lady Blanche Mortlake in the splendor of her young womanhood, beyond a doubt. Gone were all traces of her spiritual childhood, except, perhaps, in the shadows of the mouth; but more than fulfilled were the promises of her mind. Assuredly, the woman had been as brilliant and gifted as she had been restless and passionate. She wore her very pearls with arrogance, her very hands were tense with eager life, her whole being breathed mutiny.

Orth turned abruptly to Blanche, who had transferred her attention to the picture.

"What a tragedy is there!" he exclaimed, with a fierce attempt at lightness. "Think of a woman having all that pent up within her two centuries ago! And at the mercy of a stupid family, no doubt, and a still stupider husband. No wonder—Today, a woman like that might not be a model for all the virtues, but she certainly would use her gifts and become famous, the while living her life too fully to have any place in it for yeomen and such, or even for the trivial business of breaking hearts." He put his finger under Blanche's chin, and raised her face, but he could not compel her gaze. "You are the exact image of that little girl," he said, "except that you are even purer and finer. She had no chance, none whatever. You live in the woman's age. Your opportunities will be infinite. I shall see to it that they are. What you wish to be you shall be. There will be no pent-up energies here to burst out into disaster for yourself and others. You shall be trained to self-control—that is, if you ever develop self-will, dear child—every faculty shall be educated, every school of life you desire knowledge through shall be opened to you. You shall become that finest flower of civilization, a woman who knows how to use her independence."

She raised her eyes slowly, and gave him a look which stirred the roots of sensation—a long look of unspeakable melancholy. Her chest rose once; then she set her lips tightly, and dropped her eyes.

"What do you mean?" he cried, roughly, for his soul was chattering. "Is—it—do you—?" He dared not go too far, and concluded lamely, "You mean you fear that your mother will not give you to me when she goes—you have divined that I wish to adopt you? Answer me, will you?"

But she only lowered her head and turned away, and he, fearing to frighten or repel her, apologized for his abruptness, restored the outer picture to its place, and led her from the gallery.

He sent her at once to the nursery, and when she came down to luncheon and took her place at his right hand, she was as natural and childlike as ever. For some days he restrained his curiosity, but one evening, as they were sitting before the fire in the hall listening to the storm, and just after he had told her the story of the erl-king, he took her on his knee and asked her gently if she would not tell him what had been in her thoughts when he had drawn her brilliant future. Again her face turned gray, and she dropped her eyes.

"I cannot," she said. "I—perhaps—I don't know."

"Was it what I suggested?"

She shook her head, then looked at him with a shrinking appeal which forced him to drop the subject.

He went the next day alone to the gallery, and looked long at the portrait of the woman. She stirred no response in him. Nor could he feel that the woman of Blanche's future would stir the man in him. The paternal was all he had to give, but that was hers forever.

He went out into the park and found Blanche digging in her garden, very dirty and absorbed. The next afternoon, however, entering the hall noiselessly, he saw her sitting in her big chair, gazing out into nothing visible, her whole face settled in melancholy. He asked her if she were ill, and she recalled herself at once, but confessed to feeling tired. Soon after this he noticed that she lingered longer in the comfortable depths of her chair, and seldom went out, except with himself. She insisted that she was quite well, but after he had surprised her again looking as sad as if she had renounced every joy of childhood, he summoned from London a doctor renowned for his success with children.

The scientist questioned and examined her. When she had left the room he shrugged his shoulders.

"She might have been born with ten years of life in her, or she might grow up into a buxom woman," he said. "I confess I cannot tell. She appears to be sound enough, but I have no X rays in my eyes, and for all I know she may be on the verge of decay. She certainly has the look of those who die young. I have never seen so spiritual a child. But I can put my finger on nothing. Keep her out-of-doors, don't give her sweets, and don't let her catch anything if you can help it."

Orth and the child spent the long warm days of summer under the trees of the park, or driving in the quiet lanes. Guests were unbidden, and his pen was idle. All that was human in him had gone out to Blanche. He loved her, and she was a perpetual delight to him. The rest of the world received the large measure of his indifference. There was no further change in her, and apprehension slept and let him sleep. He had persuaded Mrs. Root to remain in England for a year. He sent her theatre tickets every week, and placed a horse and phaeton at her disposal. She was enjoying herself and seeing less and less of Blanche. He took the child to Bournemouth for a fortnight, and again to Scotland, both of which outings benefited as much as they pleased her. She had begun to tyrannize over him amiably, and she carried herself quite royally. But she was always sweet and truthful, and these qualities, combined with that something in the depths of her mind which defied his explorations, held him captive. She was devoted to him, and cared for no other companion, although she was demonstrative to her mother when they met.

It was in the tenth month of this idyl of the lonely man and the lonely child that Mrs. Root flurriedly entered the library of Chillingsworth, where Orth happened to be alone.

"Oh, sir," she exclaimed, "I must go home. My daughter Grace writes me—she should have done it before—that the boys are not behaving as well as they should—she didn't tell me, as I was having such a good time she just hated to worry me—Heaven knows I've had enough worry—but now I must go—I just couldn't stay—boys are an awful responsibility—girls ain't a circumstance to them, although mine are a handful sometimes."

Orth had written about too many women to interrupt the flow. He let her talk until she paused to recuperate her forces. Then he said quietly:

"I am sorry this has come so suddenly, for it forces me to broach a subject at once which I would rather have postponed until the idea had taken possession of you by degrees—"

"I know what it is you want to say, sir," she broke in, "and I've reproached myself that I haven't warned you before, but I didn't like to be the one to speak first. You want Blanche—of course, I couldn't help seeing that; but I can't let her go, sir, indeed, I can't."

"Yes," he said, firmly, "I want to adopt Blanche, and I hardly think you can refuse, for you must know how greatly it will be to her advantage. She is a wonderful child; you have never been blind to that; she should have every opportunity, not only of money, but of association. If I adopt her legally, I shall, of course, make her my heir, and—there is no reason why she should not grow up as great a lady as any in England."

The poor woman turned white, and burst into tears. "I've sat up nights and nights, struggling," she said, when she could speak. "That, and missing her. I couldn't stand in her light, and I let her stay. I know I oughtn't to, now—I mean, stand in her light—but, sir, she is dearer than all the others put together."

"Then live here in England—at least, for some years longer. I will gladly relieve your children of your support, and you can see Blanche as often as you choose."

"I can't do that, sir. After all, she is only one, and there are six others. I can't desert them. They all need me, if only to keep them together—three girls unmarried and out in the world, and three boys just a little inclined to be wild. There is another point, sir—I don't exactly know how to say it."

"Well?" asked Orth, kindly. This American woman thought him the ideal gentleman, although the mistress of the estate on which she visited called him a boor and a snob.

"It is—well—you must know—you can imagine—that her brothers and sisters just worship Blanche. They save their dimes to buy her everything she wants—or used to want. Heaven knows what will satisfy her now, although I can't see that she's one bit spoiled. But she's just like a religion to them; they're not much on church. I'll tell you, sir, what I couldn't say to anyone else, not even to these relations who've been so kind to me—but there's wildness, just a streak, in all my children, and I believe, I know, it's Blanche that keeps them straight. My girls get bitter, sometimes; work all the week and little fun, not caring for common men and no chance to marry gentlemen; and sometimes they break out and talk dreadful; then, when they're over it, they say they'll live for Blanche—they've said it over and over, and they mean it. Every sacrifice they've made for her—and they've made many—has done them good. It isn't that Blanche ever says a word of the preachy sort, or has anything of the Sunday-school child about her, or even tries to smooth them down when they're excited. It's just herself. The only thing she ever does is sometimes to draw herself up and look scornful, and that nearly kills them. Little as she is, they're crazy about having her respect. I've grown superstitious about her. Until she came I used to get frightened, terribly, sometimes, and I believe she came for that. So—you see! I know Blanche is too fine for us and ought to have the best; but, then, they are to be considered, too. They have their rights, and they've got much more good than bad in them. I don't know! I don't know! It's kept me awake many nights."

Orth rose abruptly. "Perhaps you will take some further time to think it over," he said. "You can stay a few weeks longer—the matter cannot be so pressing as that."

The woman rose. "I've thought this," she said; "let Blanche decide. I believe she knows more than any of us. I believe that whichever way she decided would be right. I won't say anything to her, so you won't think I'm working on her feelings; and I can trust you. But she'll know."

"Why do you think that?" asked Orth, sharply. "There is nothing uncanny about the child. She is not yet seven years old. Why should you place such a responsibility upon her?"

"Do you think she's like other children?"

"I know nothing of other children."

"I do, sir. I've raised six. And I've seen hundreds of others. I never was one to be a fool about my own, but Blanche isn't like any other child living—I'm certain of it."

"What *do* you think?"

And the woman answered, according to her lights: "I think she's an angel, and came to us because we needed her."

"And I think she is Blanche Mortlake working out the last of her salvation," thought the author; but he made no reply, and was alone in a moment.

It was several days before he spoke to Blanche, and then, one morning, when she was sitting on her mat on the lawn with the light full upon her, he told her abruptly that her mother must return home.

To his surprise, but unutterable delight, she burst into tears and flung herself into his arms.

"You need not leave me," he said, when he could find his own voice. "You can stay here always and be my little girl. It all rests with you."

"I can't stay," she sobbed. "I can't!"

"And that is what made you so sad once or twice?" he asked, with a double eagerness. She made no reply.

"Oh!" he said, passionately, "give me your confidence, Blanche. You are the only breathing thing that I love."

"If I could I would," she said. "But I don't know—not quite."

"How much do you know?"

But she sobbed again and would not answer. He dared not risk too much. After all, the physical barrier between the past and the present was very young.

"Well, well, then, we will talk about the other matter. I will not pretend to disguise the fact that your mother is distressed at the idea of parting from you, and thinks it would be as sad for your brothers and sisters, whom she says you influence for their good. Do you think that you do?"

"Yes."

"How do you know this?"

"Do you know why you know everything?"

"No, my dear, and I have great respect for your instincts. But your sisters and brothers are now old enough to take care of themselves. They must be of poor stuff if they cannot live properly without the aid of a child. Moreover, they will be marrying soon. That will also mean that your mother will have many little grandchildren to console her for your loss. I will be the one bereft, if you leave me. I am the only one who really needs you. I don't say I will go to the bad, as you may have very foolishly persuaded yourself your family will do without you, but I trust to your instincts to make you realize how unhappy, how inconsolable I shall be. I shall be the loneliest man on earth!"

She rubbed her face deeper into his flannels, and tightened her embrace. "Can't you come, too?" she asked.

"No; you must live with me wholly or not at all. Your people are not my people, their ways are not my ways. We should not get along. And if you lived with me over there you might as well stay here, for your influence over them would be quite as removed. Moreover, if they are of the right stuff, the memory of you will be quite as potent for good as your actual presence."

"Not unless I died."

Again something within him trembled. "Do you believe you are going to die young?" he blurted out.

But she would not answer.

He entered the nursery abruptly the next day and found her packing her dolls. When she saw him, she sat down and began to weep hopelessly. He knew then that his fate was sealed. And when, a year later, he received her last little scrawl, he was almost glad that she went when she did.

E. T. A. Hoffmann (1776–1822)

The Sand-man

Ernst Theodor Wihelm Hoffman, who in 1808 changed one of his middle names from Wilhelm to Amadeus in honor of Mozart, is the only candidate to rival Poe (who was influenced by him) as the creator of the modern supernatural tale. His stories are a large part of the founding texts of the "fantastic" in European literature. His reputation rivalled those of Lord Byron and Sir Walter Scott in the Europe of his day. He is the greatest fantasy writer of the nineteenth century; his most famous stories include "The Golden Pot," which Everett Bleiler calls the greatest fantasy story of the nineteenth century, "Nutcracker and the King of the Mice," the source of Tchaikovsky's *The Nutcracker*, "Mademoiselle De Scudéry," arguably the first detective story. His great innovation was to bring the fantastic into the everyday present (fairy and folk tales had traditionally been set long ago and far away), a foundation of all horror literature since. His novella, "The Sand-man," a nightmarish piece that fascinated Sigmund Freud so much that he used it as the basic text of his essay, "The Uncanny," was written in 1816. As John Sladek point out in *Horror: The 100 Best Books*, "This dark tale was written two years before Mary Shelley's *Frankenstein*, in a similar spirit of horrified fascination with science and its application to artificial life. Hoffman is concerned with the horror of automata indistinguishable from real people." This theme has grown and reverberated through literature since, and is particulary common in science fiction. It is interesting to compare "The Sand-man" to George R. R. Martin's "Sandkings," Philip K. Dick's "Faith of Our Fathers," and John W. Campbell's "Who Goes There?"

Nathanael to Lothair

I know you are all very uneasy because I have not written for such a long, long time. Mother, to be sure, is angry, and Clara, I dare say, believes I am living here in riot and revelry, and quite forgetting my sweet angel, whose image is so deeply engraved upon my heart and mind. But that is not so; daily and hourly do I think of you all, and my lovely Clara's form comes to gladden me in my dreams, and smiles upon me with her bright eyes, as graciously as she used to do in the days when I went in and out amongst you. Oh! how could I write to you in the distracted state of mind in which I have been, and which, until now, has quite bewildered me! A terrible thing has happened to me. Dark forebodings of some awful fate threatening me are spreading themselves out over my head like black clouds, impenetrable to every friendly ray of sunlight. I must now tell

510 Foundations of Fear

you what has taken place; I must, that I see well enough, but only to think upon it makes the wild laughter burst from my lips. Oh! my dear, dear Lothair, what shall I say to make you feel, if only in an inadequate way, that that which happened to me a few days ago could thus really exercise such a hostile and disturbing influence upon my life? Oh that you were here to see for yourself! but now you will, I suppose, take me for a superstitious ghost-seer. In a word, the terrible thing which I have experienced, the fatal effect of which I in vain exert every effort to shake off, is simply that some days ago, namely, on the 30th October, at twelve o'clock at noon, a dealer in weather-glasses came into my room and wanted to sell me one of his wares. I bought nothing, and threatened to kick him downstairs, whereupon he went away of his own accord.

You will conclude that it can only be very peculiar relations—relations intimately intertwined with my life—that can give significance to this event, and that it must be the person of this unfortunate hawker which has had such a very inimical effect upon me. And so it really is. I will summon up all my faculties in order to narrate to you calmly and patiently as much of the early days of my youth as will suffice to put matters before you in such a way that your keen sharp intellect may grasp everything clearly and distinctly, in bright and living pictures. Just as I am beginning, I hear you laugh and Clara say, "What's all this childish nonsense about!" Well, laugh at me, laugh heartily at me, pray do. But, good God! my hair is standing on end, and I seem to be entreating you to laugh at me in the same sort of frantic despair in which Franz Moor entreated Daniel to laugh him to scorn. But to my story.

Except at dinner we, i. e., I and my brothers and sisters, saw but little of our father all day long. His business no doubt took up most of his time. After our evening meal, which, in accordance with an old custom, was served at seven o'clock, we all went, mother with us, into father's room, and took our places around a round table. My father smoked his pipe, drinking a large glass of beer to it. Often he told us many wonderful stories, and got so excited over them that his pipe always went out; I used then to light it for him with a spill, and this formed my chief amusement. Often, again, he would give us picture-books to look at, whilst he sat silent and motionless in his easy-chair, puffing out such dense clouds of smoke that we were all as it were enveloped in mist. On such evenings mother was very sad; and directly it struck nine she said, "Come, children! off to bed! Come! The 'Sand-man' is come I see." And I always did seem to hear something trampling upstairs with slow heavy steps; that must be the Sand-man. Once in particular I was very much frightened at this dull trampling and knocking; as mother was leading us out of the room I asked her, "O mamma! but who is this nasty Sand-man who always sends us away from papa? What does he look like?" "There is no Sand-man, my dear child," mother answered; "when I say the Sand-man is come, I only mean that you are sleepy and can't keep your eyes open, as if somebody had put sand in them." This answer of mother's did not satisfy me; nay, in my childish mind the thought clearly unfolded itself that mother denied there was a Sand-man only to prevent us being afraid,—why, I always heard him come upstairs. Full of curiosity to learn something more about this Sand-man and what he had to do with us children, I at length asked the old woman who acted as my youngest sister's attendant, what sort of a man he was—the Sand-man? "Why, 'thanael, darling, don't you know?" she replied. "Oh! he's a wicked man, who comes to little children when they won't go to bed and throws handfuls of sand in their eyes, so that they jump out of their heads all bloody; and he puts them into a bag and takes them to the half-moon as food for his little ones; and they sit there in the nest and have hooked beaks like owls, and they pick naughty little boys' and girls' eyes out with them." After this I formed in my own mind a horrible picture of the cruel Sand-man. When anything came blundering upstairs at night I trembled with fear and dismay; and all that my mother could get out of me were the stammered words "The Sand-man! the Sand-man!" whilst the tears coursed down my cheeks. Then I ran into my bedroom, and the whole night through tormented myself with the terrible apparition of the Sand-man. I was quite old enough to perceive that the old woman's tale about the Sand-man and his little ones' nest in the half-moon couldn't be altogether true; nevertheless the Sand-man continued to be for me a fearful incubus, and I was always seized with terror—my blood always ran cold, not only when I heard anybody come up the stairs, but when I heard anybody noisily open my father's room door and go in. Often he stayed away for a long season altogether; then he would come several times in close succession.

This went on for years, without my being able to accustom myself to this fearful apparition, without the image of the horrible Sand-man growing any fainter in my imagination. His intercourse with my father began to occupy my fancy ever more and more; I was restrained from asking my father about him by an unconquerable shyness; but as the years went on the desire waxed stronger and stronger within me to fathom the mystery myself and to see the fabulous Sand-man. He had been the means of disclosing to me the path of the wonderful and the adventurous, which so easily find lodgment in the mind of the child. I liked nothing better than to hear or read horrible stories of goblins, witches, Tom Thumbs, and so on; but always at the head of them all stood the Sand-man, whose picture I scribbled in the most extraordinary and repulsive forms with both chalk and coal everywhere, on the tables, and cupboard doors, and walls. When I was ten years old my mother removed me from the nursery into a little chamber off the corridor not far from my father's room. We still had to withdraw hastily whenever, on the stroke of nine, the mysterious unknown was heard in the house. As I lay in my little chamber I could hear him go into father's room, and soon afterwards I fancied there was a fine and peculiar smelling steam spreading itself through the house. As my curiosity waxed stronger, my resolve to make somehow or other the Sand-man's acquaintance took deeper root. Often when my mother had gone past, I slipped quickly out of my room into the corridor, but I could never see anything, for always before I could reach the place where I could get sight of him, the Sand-man was well inside the door. At last, unable to resist the impulse any longer, I determined to conceal myself in father's room and there wait for the Sand-man.

One evening I perceived from my father's silence and mother's sadness that the Sand-man would come; accordingly, pleading that I was excessively tired, I left the room before nine o'clock and concealed myself in a hiding-place close beside the door. The street door creaked, and slow, heavy, echoing steps crossed the passage towards the stairs. Mother hurried past me with my brothers and sisters. Softly—softly—I opened father's room door. He sat as usual, silent and motionless, with his back towards it; he did not hear me; and in a moment I was in and behind a curtain drawn before my father's open wardrobe, which stood just inside the room. Nearer and nearer and nearer came the echoing footsteps. There was a strange coughing and shuffling and mumbling outside. My heart beat with expectation and fear. A quick step now close, close beside the door, a noisy rattle of the handle, and the door flies open with a bang. Recovering my courage with an effort, I take a cautious peep out. In the middle of the room in front of my father stands the Sand-man, the bright light of the lamp falling full upon his face. The Sand-man, the terrible Sand-man, is the old advocate *Coppelius* who often comes to dine with us.

But the most hideous figure could not have awakened greater trepidation in my heart than this Coppelius did. Picture to yourself a large broad-shouldered man, with an immensely big head, a face the colour of yellow-ochre, grey bushy eyebrows, from beneath which two piercing, greenish, cat-like eyes glittered, and a prominent Roman nose hanging over his upper lip. His distorted mouth was often screwed up into a malicious smile; then two dark-red spots appeared on his cheeks, and a strange hissing noise proceeded from between his tightly clenched teeth. He always wore an ash-grey coat of an old-fashioned cut, a waistcoat of the same, and nether extremeties to match, but black stockings and buckles set with stones on his shoes. His little wig scarcely extended beyond the crown of his head, his hair was curled round high up above his big red ears, and plastered to his temples with cosmetic, and a broad closed hair-bag stood out prominently from his neck, so that you could see the silver buckle that fastened his folded neck-cloth. Altogether he was a most disagreeable and horribly ugly figure; but what we children detested most of all was his big coarse hairy hands; we could never fancy anything that he had once touched. This he had noticed; and so, whenever our good mother quietly placed a piece of cake or sweet fruit on our plates, he delighted to touch it under some pretext or other, until the bright tears stood in our eyes, and from disgust and loathing we lost the enjoyment of the tit-bit that was intended to please us. And he did just the same thing when father gave us a glass of sweet wine on holidays. Then he would quickly pass his hand over it, or even sometimes raise the glass to his blue lips, and he laughed quite sardonically when all we dared do was to express our vexation in stifled sobs. He habitually called us the "little brutes;" and when he was present we might not utter a sound; and we cursed the ugly spiteful man who deliberately and intentionally spoilt all our little pleasures. Mother seemed to dislike this hateful Coppelius as much as we did; for as soon as he appeared her cheerfulness and bright and natural manner were transformed into sad, gloomy seriousness. Father treated him as if he were a being of some higher race, whose ill-manners were to be tolerated, whilst no efforts ought to be spared to keep him in good-humour. He had only to give a slight hint, and his favourite dishes were cooked for him and rare wine uncorked.

As soon as I saw this Coppelius, therefore, the fearful and hideous thought arose in my mind that he, and he alone, must be the Sand-man; but I no longer conceived of the Sand-man as the bugbear in the old nurse's fable, who fetched children's eyes and took them to the half-moon as food for his little ones—no! but as an ugly spectre-like fiend bringing trouble and misery and ruin, both temporal and everlasting, everywhere wherever he appeared.

I was spell-bound on the spot. At the risk of being discovered, and, as I well enough knew, of being severely punished, I remained as I was, with my head thrust through the curtains listening. My father received Coppelius in a ceremonious manner. "Come, to work!" cried the latter, in a hoarse snarling voice, throwing off his coat. Gloomily and silently my father took off his dressing-gown, and both put on long black smock-frocks. Where they took them from I forgot to notice. Father opened the folding-doors of a cupboard in the wall; but I saw that what I had so long taken to be a cupboard was really a dark recess, in which was a little hearth. Coppelius approached it, and a blue flame crackled upwards from it. Round about were all kinds of strange utensils. Good God! as my old father bent down over the fire how different he looked! His gentle and venerable features seemed to be drawn up by some dreadful convulsive pain into an ugly, repulsive Satanic mask. He looked like Coppelius. Coppelius plied the red-hot tongs and drew bright glowing masses out of the thick smoke and began assiduously to hammer them. I fancied that there were men's faces visible round about, but without eyes, having ghastly deep black holes where the eyes should have been. "Eyes here! Eyes here!" cried Coppelius, in a hollow sepulchral voice. My blood ran cold with horror; I screamed and tumbled out of my hiding-place into the floor. Coppelius immediately seized upon me. "You little brute! You little brute!" he bleated, grinding his teeth. Then, snatching me up, he threw me on the hearth, so that the flames began to singe my hair. "Now we've got eyes—eyes—a beautiful pair of children's eyes," he whispered, and, thrusting his hands into the flames he took out some red-hot grains and was about to strew them into my eyes. Then my father clasped his hands and entreated him, saying, "Master, master, let my Nathanael keep his eyes—oh! do let him keep them." Coppelius laughed shrilly and replied, "Well then, the boy may keep his eyes and whine and pule his way through the world; but we will now at any rate observe the mechanism of the hand and the foot." And there with he roughly laid hold upon me, so that my joints cracked, and twisted my hands and my feet, pulling them now this way, and now that, "That's not quite right altogether! It's better as it was!—the old fellow knew what he was about." Thus lisped and hissed Coppelius; but all around me grew black and dark; a sudden convulsive pain shot through all my nerves and bones; I knew nothing more.

I felt a soft warm breath fanning my cheek; I awakened as if out of the sleep of death; my mother was bending over me. "Is the Sand-man still there?" I stammered. "No, my dear child; he's been gone a long, long time; he'll not hurt you." Thus spoke my mother, as she kissed her recovered darling and pressed him to her heart. But why should I tire you, my dear Lothair? why do I dwell at such length on these details, when there's so much remains to be said? Enough—I was detected in my eavesdropping, and roughly handled by Coppelius. Fear and terror had brought on a violent fever, of which I lay ill several weeks. "Is the Sand-man still there?" These were the first words I uttered on coming to myself again, the first sign of my recovery, of my safety. Thus, you see, I have only to relate to you the most terrible moment of my youth for you to thoroughly understand that it must not be ascribed to the weakness of my eyesight if all that I see is colourless, but to the fact that a mysterious destiny has hung a dark veil of clouds about my life, which I shall perhaps only break through when I die.

Coppelius did not show himself again; it was reported he had left the town.

It was about a year later when, in pursuance of the old unchanged custom, we sat around the round table in the evening. Father was in very good spirits, and was telling us amusing tales about his youthful travels. As it was striking nine we all at once heard the street door creak on its hinges, and slow ponderous steps echoed across the passage and up the stairs. "That is Coppelius," said my mother, turning pale. "Yes, it is Coppelius," replied my father in a faint broken voice. The tears started from my mother's eyes. "But, father, father," she cried, "must it be so?" "This is the last time," he replied; "this is the last time he will come to me, I promise you. Go now, go and take the children. Go, go to bed—good-night."

As for me, I felt as if I were converted into cold, heavy stone; I could not get my breath. As I stood there immovable my mother seized me by the arm. "Come, Nathanael! do come along!" I suffered myself to be led away; I went into my room. "Be a good boy and keep quiet," mother called after me; "get into bed and go to sleep." But, tortured by indescribable fear and uneasiness, I could not close my eyes. That hateful, hideous Coppelius stood before me with his glittering eyes, smiling maliciously down upon me; in vain did I strive to banish the image. Somewhere about midnight there was a terrific crack, as if a cannon were being fired off. The whole house shook; something went rustling and clattering past my door; the house-door was pulled to with a bang. "That is Coppelius," I cried, terror-stricken, and leaped out of bed. Then I heard a wild heart-rending scream; I rushed into my father's room; the door stood open, and clouds of suffocating smoke came rolling towards me. The servant maid shouted, "Oh! my master! my master!" On the floor in front of the smoking hearth lay my father, dead, his face burned black and fearfully distorted, my sisters weeping and moaning around him, and my mother lying near them in a swoon.

"Coppelius, you atrocious fiend, you've killed my father," I shouted. My senses left me. Two days later, when my father was placed in his coffin, his features were mild and gentle again as they had been when he was alive. I found great consolation in the thought that his association with the diabolical Coppelius could not have ended in his everlasting ruin.

Our neighbours had been awakened by the explosion; the affair got talked about, and came before the magisterial authorities, who wished to cite Coppelius to clear himself. But he had disappeared from the place, leaving no traces behind him.

Now when I tell you, my dear friend, that the peddler I spoke of was the villain Coppelius, you will not blame me for seeing impending mischief in his inauspicious reappearance. He was differently dressed; but Coppelius's figure and features are too deeply impressed upon my mind for me to be capable of making a mistake in the matter. Moreover, he has not even changed his name. He proclaims himself here, I learn, to be a Piedmontese mechanician, and styles himself Giuseppe Coppola.

I am resolved to enter the lists against him and avenge my father's death, let the consequences be what they may.

Don't say a word to mother about the reappearance of this odious monster. Give my love to my darling Clara; I will write to her when I am in a somewhat calmer frame of mind. Adieu, &c.

Clara to Nathanael

You are right, you have not written to me for a very long time, but nevertheless I believe that I still retain a place in your mind and thoughts. It is a proof that you were thinking a good deal about me when you were sending off your last letter to brother Lothair, for instead of directing it to him you directed it to me. With joy I tore open the envelope, and did not perceive the mistake until I read the words, "Oh! my dear, dear Lothair."

Now I know I ought not to have read any more of the letter, but ought to have given it to my brother. But as you have so often in innocent raillery made it a sort of reproach against me that I possessed such a calm and, for a woman, cool-headed temperament that I should be like the woman we read of—if the house was threatening to tumble down, I should stop before hastily fleeing, to smooth down a crumple in the window curtains—I need hardly tell you that the beginning of your letter quite upset me. I could scarcely breathe; there was a bright mist before my eyes.

Oh! my darling Nathanael! what could this terrible thing be that had happened? Separation from you—never to see you again, the thought was like a sharp knife in my heart. I read on and on. Your description of that horrid Coppelius made my flesh creep. I now learned for the first time what a terrible and violent death your good old father died. Brother Lothair, to whom I handed over his property, sought to comfort me, but with little success. That horrid peddler Giuseppe Coppola followed me everywhere; and I am almost ashamed to confess it, but he was able to disturb my sound and in general calm sleep with all sorts of wonderful dream-shapes. But soon—the next day—I saw everything in a different light. Oh! do not be angry with me, my best-beloved, if, despite your strange presentiment that Coppelius will do you some mischief, Lothair tells you I am in quite as good spirits, and just the same as ever.

I will frankly confess, it seems to me that all that was fearsome and terrible of which you speak, existed only in your own self, and that the real true outer world had but little to do with it. I can quite admit that old Coppelius may have been highly obnoxious to you children, but your real detestation of him arose from the fact that he hated children.

Naturally enough the gruesome Sand-man of the old nurse's story was associated in your childish mind with old Coppelius, who, even though you had not believed in the Sand-man, would have been to you a ghostly bugbear, especially dangerous to children. His mysterious labours along with your father at night-time were, I daresay, nothing more than secret experiments in alchemy, with which your mother could not be over well pleased, owing to the large sums of money that most likely were thrown away upon them; and besides, your father, his mind full of the deceptive striving after higher knowledge, may probably have become rather indifferent to his family, as so often happens in the case of such experimentalists. So also it is equally probable that your father brought about his death by his own imprudence, and that Coppelius is not to blame for it. I must tell you that yesterday I asked our experienced neighbour, the chemist, whether in experiments of this kind an explosion could take place which would have a momentarily fatal effect. He said, "Oh, certainly!" and described to me in his prolix and circumstantial way how it could be occasioned, mentioning at the same time so many strange and funny words that I could not remember them at all. Now I know you will be angry at your Clara, and will say, "Of the Mysterious which often clasps man in its invisible arms there's not a ray can find its way into this cold heart. She sees only the varied surface of the things of the world, and, like the little child, is pleased with the golden glittering fruit, at the kernel of which lies the fatal poison."

Oh! my beloved Nathanael, do you believe then that the intuitive prescience of a dark power working within us to our own ruin cannot exist also in minds which are cheerful, natural, free from care? But please forgive me that I, a simple girl, presume in any way to indicate to you what I really think of such an inward strife. After all, I should not find the proper words, and you would only laugh at me, not because my thoughts were stupid, but because I was so foolish as to attempt to tell them to you.

If there is a dark and hostile power which traitorously fixes a thread in our hearts in order that, laying hold of it and drawing us by means of it along a dangerous road to ruin, which otherwise we should not have trod—if, I say, there is such a power, it must assume within us a form like ourselves, nay, it must be ourselves; for only in that way can we believe in it, and only so understood do we yield to it so far that it is able to accomplish its secret purpose. So long as we have sufficient firmness, fortified by cheerfulness, to always acknowledge foreign hostile influences for what they really are, whilst we quietly pursue the path pointed out to us by both inclination and calling, then this mysterious power perishes in its futile struggles to attain the form which is to be the reflected image of ourselves. It is also certain, Lothair adds, that if we have once voluntarily given ourselves up to this dark physical power, it often reproduces within us the strange forms which the outer world throws in our way, so that thus it is we ourselves who engender within ourselves the spirit which by some remarkable delusion we imagine to speak in that outer form. It is the phantom of our own self whose intimate relationship with, and whose powerful influence upon our soul either plunges us into hell or elevates us to heaven. Thus you will see, my beloved Nathanael, that I and brother Lothair have well talked over the subject of dark powers and forces; and now, after I have with some difficulty written down the principal results of our discussion, they seem to me to contain many really profound thoughts. Lothair's last words, however, I don't quite understand altogether; I only dimly guess what he means; and yet I cannot help thinking it is all very true. I beg you, dear, strive to forget the ugly advocate Coppelius as well as the weather-glass hawker Giuseppe Coppola. Try and convince yourself that these foreign influences can have no power over you, that it is only the belief in their hostile power which can in reality make them dangerous to you. If every line of your letter did not betray the violent excitement of your mind, and if I did not sympathise with your condition from the bottom of my heart, I could in truth jest about the advocate Sand-man and weather-glass hawker Coppelius. Pluck up your spirits! Be cheerful! I have resolved to appear to you as your guardian-angel if that ugly man Coppola should dare take it into his head to bother you in your dreams, and drive him away with a good hearty laugh. I'm not afraid of him and his nasty hands, not the least little bit; I won't let him either as advocate spoil any dainty tit-bit I've taken, or as Sand-man rob me of my eyes.

My darling, darling Nathanael,
Eternally your, &c. &c.

Nathanael to Lothair.

I am very sorry that Clara opened and read my last letter to you; of course the mistake is to be attributed to my own absence of mind. She has written me a very deep philosophical letter, proving conclusively that Coppelius and Coppola only exist in my own mind and are phantoms of my own self, which will at once be dissipated, as soon as I look upon them in that light. In very truth one can hardly believe that the mind which so often sparkles in those bright, beautifully smiling, childlike eyes of hers like a sweet lovely dream could draw such subtle and scholastic distinctions. She also mentions your name. You have been talking about me. I suppose you have been giving her lectures, since she sifts and refines everything so acutely. But enough of this! I must now tell you it is most certain that the weather-glass hawker Giuseppe Coppola is not the advocate Coppelius. I am attending the lectures of our recently appointed Professor of Physics, who, like the distinguished naturalist, is called Spalanzani, and is of Italian origin. He has known Coppola for many years; and it is also easy to tell from his accent that he really is a Piedmontese. Coppelius was a German, though no honest German, I fancy. Nevertheless I am not quite satisfied. You and Clara will perhaps take me for a gloomy dreamer, but nohow can I get rid of the impression which Coppelius's cursed face made upon me. I am glad to learn from Spalanzani that he has left the town. This Professor Spalanzani is a very queer fish. He is a little fat man, with prominent cheek-bones, thin nose, projecting lips, and small piercing eyes. You cannot get a better picture of him than by turning over one of the Berlin pocket-almanacs and looking at Cagliostro's portrait engraved by Chodowiecki; Spalanzani looks just like him.

Once lately, as I went up the steps to his house, I perceived that beside the curtain which generally covered a glass door there was a small chink. What it was that excited my curiosity I cannot explain; but I looked through. In the room I saw a female, tall, very slender, but of perfect proportions, and splendidly dressed, sitting at a little table, on which she had placed both her arms, her hands being folded together. She sat opposite the door, so that I could easily see her angelically beautiful face. She did not appear to notice me, and there was moreover a strangely fixed look about her eyes, I might almost say they appeared as if they had no power of vision; I thought she was sleeping with her eyes open. I felt quite uncomfortable, and so I slipped away quietly into the Professor's lecture-room, which was close at hand. Afterwards I learnt that the figure which I had seen was Spalanzani's daughter, Olimpia, whom he keeps locked in a most wicked and unaccountable way, and no man is ever allowed to come near her. Perhaps, however, there is after all something peculiar about her; perhaps she's an idiot or something of that sort. But why am I telling you all this? I could have told you it all better and more in detail when I see you. For in a fortnight I shall be amongst you. I must see my dear sweet angel, my Clara, again. Then the little bit of ill-temper, which, I must confess, took possession of me after her fearfully sensible letter, will be blown away. And that is the reason why I am not writing to her as well today. With all best wishes, &c.

Nothing more strange and extraordinary can be imagined, gracious reader, than what happened to my poor friend, the young student Nathanael, and which I have undertaken to relate to you. Have you ever lived to experience anything that completely took possession of your heart and mind and thoughts to the utter exclusion of everything else? All was seething and boiling within you; your blood, heated to fever pitch, leapt through your veins and inflamed your cheeks. Your gaze was so peculiar, as if seeking to grasp in empty space forms not seen of any other eye, and all your words ended in sighs betokening some mystery. Then your friends asked you, "What is the matter with you, my dear friend? What do you see?" And, wishing to describe the inner pictures in all their vivid colours, with their lights and their shades, you in vain struggled to find words with which to express yourself. But you felt as if you must gather up all the events that had happened, wonderful, splendid, terrible, jocose, and awful, in the very first word, so that the whole might be revealed by a single electric discharge, so to speak. Yet every word and all that partook of the nature of communication by intelligible sounds seemed to be colourless, cold, and dead. Then you try and try again, and stutter and stammer, whilst your friends' prosy questions strike like icy winds upon your heart's hot fire until they extinguish it. But if, like a bold painter, you had first sketched in a few audacious strokes the outline of the picture you had in your soul, you would then easily have been able to deepen and intensify the colours one after the other, until the varied throng of living figures carried your friends away, and they, like you, saw themselves in the midst of the scene that had proceeded out of your own soul.

Strictly speaking, indulgent reader, I must indeed confess to you, nobody has asked me for the history of young Nathanael; but you are very well aware that I belong to that remarkable class of authors who, when they are bearing anything about in their minds in the manner I have just described, feel as if everybody who comes near them, and also the whole world to boot, were asking, "Oh! what is it? Oh! do tell us, my good sir?" Hence I was most powerfully impelled to narrate to you Nathanael's ominous life. My soul was full of the elements of wonder and extraordinary peculiarity in it; but, for this very reason, and because it was necessary in the very beginning to dispose you, indulgent reader, to bear with what is fantastic—and that is not a little thing—I racked my brain to find a way of commencing the story in a significant and original manner, calculated to arrest your attention. To begin with "Once upon a time," the best beginning for a story, seemed to me too tame; with "In the small country town S—— —— lived," rather better, at any rate allowing plenty of room to work up to the climax; or to plunge at one in *medias res*, " 'Go to the devil!' cried the student Nathanael, his eyes blazing wildly with rage and fear, when the weather-glass hawker Giuseppe Coppola"—well, that is what I really had written, when I thought I detected something of the ridiculous in Nathanael's wild glance; and the history is anything but laughable. I could not find any words which seemed fitted to reflect in even the feeblest degree the brightness of the colours of my mental vision. I determined not to begin at all. So I pray you, gracious reader, accept the three letters which my friend Lothair has been so kind as to communicate to me as the outline of the picture, into which I will endeavour to introduce more and more colour as I proceed with my narrative. Perhaps, like a good portrait-painter, I may succeed in depicting more than one figure in such wise that you will recognise it as a good likeness without being acquainted with the original, and feel as if you had very often seen the original with your own bodily eyes. Perhaps, too, you will then believe that nothing is more wonderful, nothing more fantastic than real life, and that all that a writer can do is to present it as a dark reflection from a dim cut mirror.

In order to make the very commencement more intelligible, it is necessary to add to the letters that, soon after the death of Nathanael's father, Clara and Lothair, the children of a distant relative, who had likewise died, leaving them orphans, were taken by Nathanael's mother into her own house. Clara and Nathanael conceived a warm affection for each other, against which not the slightest objection in the world could be urged. When therefore Nathanael left home to prosecute his studies in G———, they were betrothed. It is from G——— that his last letter is written, where he is attending the lectures of Spalanzani, the distinguished Professor of Physics.

I might now proceed comfortably with my narration, did not at this moment Clara's image rise up so vividly before my eyes that I cannot turn them away from it, just as I never could when she looked upon me and smiled so sweetly. Nowhere would she have passed for beautiful; that was the unanimous opinion of all who professed to have any technical knowledge of beauty. But whilst architects praised the pure proportions of her figure and form, painters averred that her neck, shoulders, and bosom were almost too chastely modelled, and yet, on the other hand, one and all were in love with her glorious Magdalene hair, and talked a good deal of nonsense about Battoni-like colouring. One of them, a veritable romanticist, strangely enough likened her eyes to a lake by Ruisdael, in which is reflected the pure azure of the cloudless sky, the beauty of woods and flowers, and all the bright and varied life of a living landscape. Poets and musicians went still further and said, "What's all this talk about seas and reflections? How can we look upon the girl without feeling that wonderful heavenly songs and melodies beam upon us from her eyes, penetrating deep down into our hearts, till all becomes awake and throbbing with emotion? And if we cannot sing anything at all passable then, why, we are not worth much; and this we can also plainly read in the rare smile which flits around her lips when we have the hardihood to squeak out something in her presence which we pretend to call singing, in spite of the fact that it is nothing more than a few single notes confusedly linked together." And it really was so. Clara had the powerful fancy of a bright, innocent, unaffected child, a woman's deep and sympathetic heart, and an understanding clear, sharp, and discriminating. Dreamers and visionaries had but a bad time of it with her; for without saying very much—she was not by nature of a talkative disposition—she plainly asked, by her calm steady look, and rare ironical smile, "How can you imagine, my dear friends, that I can take these fleeting shadowy images for true living and breathing forms?" For this reason many found fault with her as being cold, prosaic, and devoid of feeling; others, however, who had reached a clearer and deeper conception of life, were extremely fond of the intelligent, childlike, large-hearted girl. But none had such an affection for her as Nathanael, who was a zealous and cheerful cultivator of the fields of science and art. Clara clung to her lover with all her heart; the first clouds she encountered in life were when he had to separate from her. With what delight did she fly into his arms when, as he had promised in his last letter to Lothair, he really came back to his native town and entered his mother's room! And as Nathanael had foreseen, the moment he saw Clara again he no longer thought about either the advocate Coppelius or her sensible letter; his ill-humour had quite disappeared.

Nevertheless Nathanael was right when he told his friend Lothair that the repulsive vendor of weatherglasses, Coppola, had exercised a fatal and disturbing influence upon his life. It was quite patent to all; for even during the first few days he showed that he was completely and entirely changed. He gave himself up to gloomy reveries, and moreover acted so strangely; they had never observed anything at all like it in him before. Everything, even his own life, was to him but dreams and presentiments. His constant theme was that every man who delusively imagined himself to be free was merely the plaything of the cruel sport of mysterious powers, and it was vain for man to resist them; he must humbly submit to whatever destiny had decreed for him. He went so far as to maintain that it was foolish to believe that a man could do anything in art or science of his own accord; for the inspiration in which alone any true artistic work could be done did not proceed from the spirit within outwards, but was the result of the operation directed inwards of some Higher Principle existing without and beyond ourselves.

This mystic extravagance was in the highest degree repugnant to Clara's clear intelligent mind, but it seemed vain to enter upon any attempt at refutation. Yet when Nathanael went on to prove that Coppelius was the Evil Principle which had entered into him and taken possession of him at the time he was listening behind the curtain, and that this hateful demon would in some terrible way ruin their happiness, then Clara grew grave and said, "Yes, Nathanael. You are right; Coppelius is an Evil Principle; he can do dreadful things, as bad as could a Satanic power which should assume a living physical form, but only—only if you do not banish him from your mind and thoughts. So long as you believe in him he exists and is at work; your belief in him is his only power." Whereupon Nathanael, quite angry because Clara would only grant the existence of the demon in his own mind, began to dilate at large upon the whole mystic doctrine of devils and awful powers, but Clara abruptly broke off the theme by making, to Nathanael's very great disgust, some quite commonplace remark. Such deep mysteries are sealed books to cold, unsusceptible characters, he thought, without being clearly conscious to himself that he counted Clara amongst these inferior natures, and accordingly he did not remit his efforts to initiate her into these mysteries. In the morning, when she was helping to prepare breakfast, he would take his stand beside her, and read all sorts of mystic books to her, until she begged him—"But, my dear Nathanael, I shall have to scold you as the Evil Principle which exercises a fatal influence upon my coffee. For if I do as you wish, and let things go their own way, and look into your eyes whilst you read, the coffee will all boil over into the fire, and you will none of you get any breakfast." Then Nathanael hastily banged the book to and ran away in great displeasure to his own room.

Formerly he had possessed a peculiar talent for writing pleasing, sparkling tales, which Clara took the greatest delight in listening to; but now his productions were gloomy, unintelligible, and wanting in form, so that, although Clara out of forbearance towards him did not say so, he nevertheless felt how very little interest she took in them. There was nothing that Clara disliked so much as what was tedious; at such times her intellectual sleepiness was not to be overcome; it was betrayed both in her glances and in her words. Nathanael's effusions were, in truth, exceedingly tedious. His ill-humour at Clara's cold prosaic temperament continued to increase; Clara could not conceal her distaste of his dark, gloomy, wearying mysticism; and thus both began to be more and more estranged from each other without exactly being aware of it themselves. The image of the ugly Coppelius had, as Nathanael was obliged to confess to himself, faded considerably in his fancy, and it often cost him great pains to present him in vivid colours in his literary efforts, in which he played the part of the ghoul of Destiny. At length it entered into his head to make his dismal presentiment that Coppelius would ruin his happiness the subject of a poem. He made himself and Clara, united by true love, the central figures, but represented a black hand as being from time to time thrust into their life and plucking out a joy that had blossomed for them. At length, as they were standing at the altar, the terrible Coppelius appeared and touched Clara's lovely eyes, which leapt into Nathanael's own bosom, burning and hissing like bloody sparks. Then Coppelius laid hold upon him, and hurled him into a blazing circle of fire, which spun round with the speed of a whirlwind, and, storming and blustering, dashed away with him. The fearful noise it made was like a furious hurricane lashing the foaming sea-waves until they rise up like black, white-headed giants in the midst of the raging struggle. But through the midst of the savage fury of the tempest he heard Clara's voice calling, "Can you not see me, dear? Coppelius has deceived you; they were not my eyes which burned so in your bosom; they were fiery drops of your own heart's blood. Look at me, I have got my own eyes still." Nathanael thought, "Yes, that is Clara, and I am hers forever." Then this thought laid a powerful grasp upon the fiery circle so that it stood still, and the riotous turmoil died away rumbling down a dark abyss. Nathanael looked into Clara's eyes; but it was death whose gaze rested so kindly upon him.

Whilst Nathanael was writing this work he was very quiet and sober-minded; he filed and polished every line, and as he had chosen to submit himself to the limitations of metre, he did not rest until all was pure and musical. When, however, he had at length finished it and read it aloud to himself he was seized with horror and awful dread, and he screamed, "Whose hideous voice is this?" But he soon came to see in it again nothing beyond a very successful poem, and he confidently believed it would enkindle Clara's cold temperament, though to what end she should be thus aroused was not quite clear to his own mind, nor yet what would be the real purpose served by tormenting her with these dreadful pictures, which prophesied a terrible and ruinous end to her affection.

Nathanael and Clara sat in his mother's little garden. Clara was bright and cheerful, since for three entire days her lover, who had been busy writing his poem, had not teased her with his dreams or forebodings. Nathanael, too, spoke in a gay and vivacious way of things of merry import, as he formerly used to do, so that Clara said, "Ah! now I have you again. We have driven away that ugly Coppelius, you see." Then it suddenly occurred to him that he had got the poem in his pocket which he wished to read to her. He at once took out the manuscript and began to read. Clara, anticipating something tedious as usual, prepared to submit to the infliction, and calmly resumed her knitting. But as the sombre clouds rose up darker and darker she let her knitting fall on her lap and sat with her eyes fixed in a set stare upon Nathanael's face. He was quite carried away by his own work, the fire of enthusiasm coloured his cheeks a deep red, and tears started from his eyes. At length he concluded, groaning and showing great lassitude; grasping Clara's hand, he sighed as if he were being utterly melted in inconsolable grief, "Oh! Clara! Clara!" She drew him softly to her heart and said in a low but very grave and impressive tone, "Nathanael, my darling Nathanael, throw that foolish, senseless, stupid thing into the fire." Then Nathanael leapt indignantly to his feet, crying, as he pushed Clara from him, "You damned lifeless automaton!" and rushed away. Clara was cut to the heart, and wept bitterly. "Oh! he has never loved me, for he does not understand me," she sobbed.

Lothair entered the arbour. Clara was obliged to tell him all that had taken place. He was passionately fond of his sister; and every word of her complaint fell like a spark upon his heart, so that the displeasure which he had long entertained against his dreamy friend Nathanael was kindled into furious anger. He hastened to find Nathanael, and upbraided him in harsh words for his irrational behaviour towards his beloved sister. The fiery Nathanael answered him in the same style. "A fantastic, crack-brained fool," was retaliated with, "A miserable, common, everyday sort of fellow." A meeting was the inevitable consequence. They agreed to meet on the following morning behind the garden-wall, and fight, according to the custom of the students of the place, with sharp rapiers. They went about silent and gloomy; Clara had both heard and seen the violent quarrel, and also observed the fencing-master bring the rapiers in the dusk of the evening. She had a presentiment of what was to happen. They both appeared at the appointed place wrapped up in the same gloomy silence, and threw off their coats. Their eyes flaming with the bloodthirsty light of pugnacity, they were about to begin their contest when Clara burst through the garden door. Sobbing, she screamed, "You savage, terrible men! Cut me down before you attack each other; for how can I live when my lover has slain my brother, or my brother slain my lover?" Lothair let his weapon fall and gazed silently upon the ground, whilst Nathanael's heart was rent with sorrow, and all the affection which he had felt for his lovely Clara in the happiest days of her golden youth was awakened within him. His murderous weapon, too, fell from his hand; he threw himself at Clara's feet. "Oh! can you ever forgive me, my only, my dearly loved Clara? Can you, my dear brother Lothair, also forgive me?" Lothair was touched by his friend's great distress; the three young people embraced each other amidst endless tears, and swore never again to break their bond of love and fidelity.

Nathanael felt as if a heavy burden that had been weighing him down to the earth was now rolled from off him, nay, as if by offering resistance to the dark power which had possessed him, he had rescued his own self from the ruin which had threatened him. Three happy days he now spent amidst the loved ones, and then returned to G———, where he had still a year to stay before settling down in his native town for life.

Everything having reference to Coppelius had been concealed from the mother, for they knew she could not think of him without horror, since she as well as Nathanael believed him to be guilty of causing her husband's death.

When Nathanael came to the house where he lived he was greatly astonished to find it burnt down to the ground, so that nothing but the bare outer walls were left standing amidst a heap of ruins. Although the fire had broken out in the laboratory of the chemist who lived on the ground-floor, and had therefore spread upwards, some of Nathanael's bold, active friends had succeeded in time in forcing a way into his room in the upper storey and saving his books and manuscripts and instruments. They had carried them all uninjured into another house, where they engaged a room for him; this he now at once took possession of. That he lived opposite Professor Spalanzani did not strike him particularly, nor did it occur to him as anything more singular that he could, as he observed, by looking out of his window, see straight into the room where Olimpia often sat alone. Her figure he could plainly distinguish, although her features were uncertain and confused. It did at length occur to him, however, that she remained for hours together in the same position in which he had first discovered her through the glass door, sitting at a little table without any occupation whatever, and it was evident that she was constantly gazing across in his direction. He could not but confess to himself that he had never seen a finer figure. However, with Clara mistress of his heart, he remained perfectly unaffected by Olimpia's stiffness and apathy; and it was only occasionally that he sent a fugitive glance over his compendium across to her—that was all.

He was writing to Clara; a light tap came at the door. At his summons to "Come in," Coppola's repulsive face appeared peeping in. Nathanael felt his heart beat with trepidation; but, recollecting what Spalanzani had told him about his fellow-countryman Coppola, and what he had himself so faithfully promised his beloved in respect to the Sand-man Coppelius, he was ashamed at himself for this childish fear of spectres. Accordingly, he controlled himself with an effort, and said, as quietly and as calmly as he possibly could, "I don't want to buy any weather-glasses, my good friend; you had better go elsewhere." Then Coppola came right into the room, and said in a hoarse voice, screwing up his wide mouth into a hideous smile, whilst his little eyes flashed keenly from beneath his long grey eyelashes, "What! Nee weather-gless? Nee weather-gless? 've got foine oyes as well—foine oyes!" Affrighted, Nathanael cried, "You stupid man, how can you have eyes?—eyes—eyes?" But Coppola, laying aside his weather-glasses, thrust his hands into his big coat-pockets and brought out several spy-glasses and spectacles, and put them on the table. "Theer! Theer! Spect'cles! Spect'cles to put 'n nose! Them's my oyes—foine oyes." And he continued to produce more and more spectacles from his pockets until the table began to gleam and flash all over. Thousands of eyes were looking and blinking convulsively, and staring up at Nathanael; he could not avert his gaze from the table. Coppola went on heaping up his spectacles, whilst wilder and ever wilder burning flashes crossed through and through each other and darted their blood-red rays into Nathanael's breast. Quite overcome, and frantic with terror, he shouted, "Stop! stop! you terrible man!" and he seized Coppola by the arm, which he had again thrust into his pocket in order to bring out still more spectacles, although the whole table was covered all over with them. With a harsh disagreeable laugh Coppola gently freed himself; and with the words "So! went none! Well, here foine gless!" he swept all his spectacles together, and put them back into his coat-pockets, whilst from a breast-pocket he produced a great number of larger and smaller perspectives. As soon as the spectacles were gone Nathanael recovered his equanimity again; and, bending his thoughts upon Clara, he clearly discerned that the gruesome incubus had proceeded only from himself, as also that Coppola was a right honest mechanician and optician, and far from being Coppelius's dreaded double and ghost. And then, besides, none of the glasses which Coppola now placed on the table had anything at all singular about them, at least nothing so weird as the spectacles; so, in order to square accounts with himself, Nathanael now really determined to buy something of the man. He took up a small, very beautifully cut pocket perspective, and by way of proving it looked through the window. Never before in his life had he had a glass in his hands that brought out things so clearly and sharply and distinctly. Involuntarily he directed the glass upon Spalanzani's room; Olimpia sat at the little table as usual, her arms laid upon it and her hands folded. Now he saw for the first time the regular and exquisite beauty of her features. The eyes, however, seemed to him to have a singular look of fixity and lifelessness. But as he continued to look closer and more carefully through the glass he fancied a light like humid moonbeams came into them. It seemed as if their power of vision was now being enkindled; their glances shone with ever-increasing vivacity. Nathanael remained standing at the window as if glued to the spot by a wizard's spell, his gaze rivetted unchangeably upon the divinely beautiful Olimpia. A coughing and shuffling of the feet awakened him out of his enchaining dream, as it were. Coppola stood behind him, "Tre zechini" (three ducats). Nathanael had completely forgotten the optician; he hastily paid the sum demanded. "Ain't 't? Foine gless? foine gless?" asked Coppola in his harsh unpleasant voice, smiling sardonically. "Yes, yes, yes," rejoined Nathanael impatiently; "adieu, my good friend." But Coppola did not leave the room without casting many peculiar side-glances upon Nathanael; and the young student heard him laughing loudly on the stairs. "Ah well!" thought he, "he's laughing at me because I've paid him too much for this little perspective—because I've given him too much money—that's it." As he softly murmured these words he fancied he detected a gasping sigh as of a dying man stealing awfully through the room; his heart stopped beating with fear. But to be sure he had heaved a deep sigh himself; it was quite plain. "Clara is quite right," said he to himself, "in holding me to be an incurable ghost-seer; and yet it's very ridiculous—ay, more than ridiculous, that the stupid thought of having paid Coppola too much for his glass should cause me this strange anxiety; I can't see any reason for it."

Now he sat down to finish his letter to Clara; but a glance through the window showed him Olimpia still in her former posture. Urged by an irresistible impulse he jumped up and seized Coppola's perspective; nor could he tear himself away from the fascinating Olimpia until his friend and brother Siegmund called for him to go to Professor

Spalanzani's lecture. The curtains before the door of the all-important room were closely drawn, so that he could not see Olimpia. Nor could he even see her from his own room during the two following days, notwithstanding that he scarcely ever left his window, and maintained a scarce interrupted watch through Coppola's perspective upon her room. On the third day curtains even were drawn across the window. Plunged into the depths of despair,—goaded by longing and ardent desire, he hurried outside the walls of the town. Olimpia's image hovered about his path in the air and stepped forth out of the bushes, and peeped up at him with large and lustrous eyes from the bright surface of the brook. Clara's image was completely faded from his mind; he had no thoughts except for Olimpia. He uttered his love-plaints aloud and in a lachrymose tone, "Oh! my glorious, noble star of love, have you only risen to vanish again, and leave me in the darkness and hopelessness of night?"

Returning home, he became aware that there was a good deal of noisy bustle going on in Spalanzani's house. All the doors stood wide open; men were taking in all kinds of gear and furniture; the windows of the first floor were all lifted off their hinges; busy maid-servants with immense hair-brooms were driving backwards and forwards dusting and sweeping, whilst within could be heard the knocking and hammering of carpenters and upholsterers. Utterly astonished, Nathanael stood still in the street; then Siegmund joined him, laughing, and said, "Well, what do you say to our old Spalanzani?" Nathanael assured him that he could not say anything, since he knew not what it all meant; to his great astonishment, he could hear, however, that they were turning the quiet gloomy house almost inside out with their dusting and cleaning and making of alterations. Then he learned from Siegmund that Spalanzani intended giving a great concert and ball on the following day, and that half the university was invited. It was generally reported that Spalanzani was going to let his daughter Olimpia, whom he had so long so jealously guarded from every eye, make her first appearance.

Nathanael received an invitation. At the appointed hour, when the carriages were rolling up and the lights were gleaming brightly in the decorated halls, he went across to the Professor's, his heart beating high with expectation. The company was both numerous and brilliant. Olimpia was richly and tastefully dressed. One could not but admire her figure and the regular beauty of her features. The striking inward curve of her back, as well as the wasp-like smallness of her waist, appeared to be the result of too-tight lacing. There was something stiff and measured in her gait and bearing that made an unfavourable impression upon many; it was ascribed to the constraint imposed upon her by the company. The concert began. Olimpia played on the piano with great skill; and sang as skilfully an *aria di bravura*, in a voice which was, if anything, almost too sharp, but clear as glass bells. Nathanael was transported with delight; he stood in the background farthest from her, and owing to the blinding lights could not quite distinguish her features. So, without being observed, he took Coppola's glass out of his pocket, and directed it upon the beautiful Olimpia. Oh! then he perceived how her yearning eyes sought him, how every note only reached its full purity in the loving glance which penetrated to and inflamed his heart. Her artificial *roulades* seemed to him to be the exultant cry towards heaven of the soul refined by love; and when at last, after the *cadenza*, the long trill rang shrilly and loudly through the hall, he felt as if he were suddenly grasped by burning arms and could no longer control himself,—he could not help shouting aloud in his mingled pain and delight, "Olimpia!" All eyes were turned upon him; many people laughed. The face of the cathedral organist wore a still more gloomy look than it had done before, but all he said was, "Very well!"

The concert came to an end, and the ball began. Oh! to dance with her—with her—that was now the aim of all Nathanael's wishes, of all his desires. But how should he have courage to request her, the queen of the ball, to grant him the honour of a dance? And yet he couldn't tell how it came about, just as the dance began, he found himself standing close beside her, nobody having as yet asked her to be his partner; so, with some difficulty stammering out a few words, he grasped her hand. It was cold as ice; he shook with an awful, frosty shiver. But, fixing his eyes upon her face, he saw that her glance was beaming upon him with love and longing, and at the same moment he thought that the pulse began to beat in her cold hand, and the warm life-blood to course through her veins. And passion burned more intensely in his own heart also; he threw his arm round her beautiful waist and whirled her round the hall. He had always thought that he kept good and accurate time in dancing, but from the perfectly rhythmical evenness with which Olimpia danced, and which frequently put him quite out, he perceived how very faulty his own time really was. Notwithstanding, he would not dance with any other lady; and everybody else who approached Olimpia to call upon her for a dance, he would have liked to kill on the spot. This, however, only happened twice; to his astonishment Olimpia remained after this without a partner, and he failed not on each occasion to take her out again. If Nathanael had been able to see anything else except the beautiful Olimpia, there would inevitably have been a good deal of unpleasant quarrelling and strife; for it was evident that Olimpia was the object of the smothered laughter only with difficulty suppressed, which was heard in various corners amongst the young people; and they followed her with very curious looks, but nobody knew for what reason. Nathanael, excited by dancing and the plentiful supply of wine he had consumed, had laid aside the shyness which at other times characterised him. He sat beside Olimpia, her hand in his own, and declared his love enthusiastically and passionately in words which neither of them understood, neither he nor Olimpia. And yet she perhaps did, for she sat with her eyes fixed unchangeably upon his, sighing repeatedly, "Ach! Ach! Ach!" Upon this Nathanael would answer, "Oh, you glorious heavenly lady! You ray from the promised paradise of love! Oh! what a profound soul you have! my whole being is mirrored in it!" and a good deal more in the same strain. But Olimpia only continued to sigh "Ach! Ach!" again and again.

Professor Spalanzani passed by the two happy lovers once or twice, and smiled with a look of peculiar satisfaction. All at once it seemed to Nathanael, albeit he was far away in a different world, as if it were growing perceptibly darker down below at Professor Spalanzani's. He looked about him, and to his very great alarm became aware that there were only two lights left burning in the hall, and they were on the point of going out. The music and dancing had long ago ceased. "We must part—part!" he cried, wildly and despairingly; he kissed Olimpia's hand; he bent down to her mouth, but ice-cold lips met his burning ones. As he touched her cold hand, he felt his heart thrilled with awe; the legend of "The Dead Bride" shot suddenly through his mind. But Olimpia had drawn him closer to her, and the kiss appeared to warm her lips into vitality. Professor Spalanzani strode slowly through the empty apartment, his footsteps giving a hollow echo; and his figure had, as the flickering shadows played about him, a ghostly, awful appearance. "Do you love me? Do you love me, Olimpia? Only one little word—Do you love me?" whispered Nathanael, but she only sighed, "Ach! Ach!" as she rose to her feet. "Yes, you are my lovely, glorious star of love," said Nathanael, "and will shine forever, purifying and ennobling my heart." "Ach! Ach!" replied Olimpia, as she moved along. Nathanael followed her; they stood before the Professor. "You have had an extraordinarily animated conversation with my daughter," said he, smiling; "well, well, my dear Mr. Nathanael, if you find pleasure in talking to the stupid girl, I am sure I shall be glad for you to come and do so." Nathanael took his leave, his heart singing and leaping in a perfect delirium of happiness.

During the next few days Spalanzani's ball was the general topic of conversation. Although the Professor had done everything to make the thing a splendid success, yet certain gay spirits related more than one thing that had occurred which was quite irregular and out of order. They were especially keen in pulling Olimpia to pieces for her taciturnity and rigid stiffness; in spite of her beautiful form they alleged that she was hopelessly stupid, and in this fact they discerned the reason why Spalanzani had so long kept her concealed from publicity. Nathanael heard all this with inward wrath, but nevertheless he held his tongue; for, thought he, would it indeed be worth while to prove to these fellows that it is their own stupidity which prevents them from appreciating Olimpia's profound and brilliant parts? One day Siegmund said to him, "Pray, brother, have the kindness to tell me how you, a sensible fellow, came to lose your head over that Miss Wax-face—that wooden doll across there?" Nathanael was about to fly into a rage, but he recollected himself and replied, "Tell me, Siegmund, how came it that Olimpia's divine charms could escape your eye, so keenly alive as it always is to beauty, and your acute perception as well? But Heaven be thanked for it, otherwise I should have had you for a rival, and then the blood of one of us would have had to be spilled." Siegmund, perceiving how matters stood with his friend, skilfully interposed and said, after remarking that all argument with one in love about the object of his affections was out of place, "Yet it's very strange that several of us have formed pretty much the same opinion about Olimpia. We think she is—you won't take it ill, brother?—that she is singularly statuesque and soulless. Her figure is regular, and so are her features, that can't be gainsaid; and if her eyes were not so utterly devoid of life, I may say, of the power of vision, she might pass for a beauty. She is strangely measured in her movements, they all seem as if they were dependent upon some wound-up clock-work. Her playing and singing has the disagreeably perfect, but insensitive time of a singing machine, and her dancing is the same. We felt quite afraid of this Olimpia, and did not like to have anything to do with her; she seemed to us to be only acting *like* a living creature, and as if there was some secret at the bottom of it all." Nathanael did not give way to the bitter feelings which threatened to master him at these words of Siegmund's; he fought down and got the better of his displeasure, and merely said, very earnestly, "You cold prosaic fellows may very well be afraid of her. It is only to its like that the poetically organised spirit unfolds itself. Upon me alone did her loving glances fall, and through my mind and thoughts alone did they radiate; and only in her love can I find my own self again. Perhaps, however, she doesn't do quite right not to jabber a lot of nonsense and stupid talk like other shallow people. It is true, she speaks but few words; but the few words she does speak are genuine hieroglyphs of the inner world of Love and of the higher cognition of the intellectual life revealed in the intuition of the Eternal beyond the grave. But you have no understanding for all these things, and I am only wasting words." "God be with you, brother," said Siegmund very gently, almost sadly, "but it seems to me that you are in a very bad way. You may rely upon me, if all—No, I can't say any more." It all at once dawned upon Nathanael that his cold prosaic friend Siegmund really and sincerely wished him well, and so he warmly shook his proffered hand.

Nathanael had completely forgotten that there was a Clara in the world, whom he had once loved—and his mother and Lothair. They had all vanished from his mind; he lived for Olimpia alone. He sat beside her every day for hours together, rhapsodising about his love and sympathy enkindled into life, and about psychic elective affinity—all of which Olimpia listened to with great reverence. He fished up from the very bottom of his desk all the things that he had ever written—poems, fancy sketches, visions, romances, tales, and the heap was increased daily with all kinds of aimless sonnets, stanzas, canzonets. All these he read to Olimpia hour after hour without growing tired; but then he had never had such an exemplary listener. She neither embroidered, nor knitted; she did not look out of the window, or feed a bird, or play with a little pet dog or a favourite cat, neither did she twist a piece of paper or anything of that kind round her finger; she did not forcibly convert a yawn into a low affected cough—in short, she sat hour after hour with her eyes bent unchangeably upon her lover's face, without moving or altering her position, and her gaze grew more ardent and more ardent still. And it was only when at last Nathanael rose and kissed her lips or her hand that she said, "Ach! Ach!" and then "Good-night, dear." Arrived in his own room, Nathanael would break out with, "Oh! what a brilliant—what a profound mind! Only you—you alone understand me." And his heart trembled with rapture when he reflected upon the wondrous harmony which daily revealed itself between his own and his Olimpia's character; for he fancied that she had expressed in respect to his works and his poetic genius the identical sentiments which he himself cherished deep down in his own heart in respect to the same, and even as if it was his own heart's voice speaking to him. And it must indeed have been so; for Olimpia never uttered any other words than those already mentioned. And when Nathanael himself in his clear and sober moments, as, for instance, directly after waking in a morning, thought about her utter passivity and taciturnity, he only said, "What are words—but words? The glance of her heavenly eyes says more than any tongue of earth. And how can, anyway, a child of heaven accustom herself to the narrow circle which the exigencies of a wretched mundane life demand?"

Professor Spalanzani appeared to be greatly pleased at the intimacy that had sprung up between his daughter Olimpia and Nathanael, and showed the young man many unmistakable proofs of his good feeling towards him; and when Nathanael ventured at length to hint very delicately at an alliance with Olimpia, the Professor smiled all over his face at once, and said he should allow his daughter to make a perfectly free choice. Encouraged by these words, and with the fire of desire burning in his heart, Nathanael resolved the very next day to implore Olimpia to tell him frankly, in plain words, what he had long read in her sweet loving glances,—that she would be his for ever. He looked for the ring which his mother had given him at parting; he would present it to Olimpia as a symbol of his devotion, and of the happy life he was to lead with her from that time onwards. Whilst looking for it he came across his letters from Clara and Lothair; he threw them carelessly aside, found the ring, put it in his pocket, and ran across to Olimpia. Whilst still on the stairs, in the entrance-passage, he heard an extraordinary hubbub; the noise seemed to proceed from Spalanzani's study. There was a stamping—a rattling—pushing—knocking against the door, with curses and oaths intermingled. "Leave hold—leave hold—you monster—you rascal—staked your life and honour upon it?—Ha! ha! ha! ha!—That was not our wager—I, I made the eyes—I the clock-work.—Go to the devil with your clock-work—you damned dog of a watch-maker—be off—Satan—stop—you paltry turner—you infernal beast!—stop—begone—let me go." The voices which were thus making all this racket and rumpus were those of Spalanzani and the fearsome Coppelius. Nathanael rushed in, impelled by some nameless dread. The Professor was grasping a female figure by the shoulders, the Italian Coppola held her by the feet; and they were pulling and dragging each other backwards and forwards, fighting furiously to get possession of her. Nathanael recoiled with horror on recognising that the figure was Olimpia. Boiling with rage, he was about to tear his beloved from the grasp of the madmen, when Coppola by an extraordinary exertion of strength twisted the figure out of the Professor's hands and gave him such a terrible blow with her, that he reeled backwards and fell over the table all amongst the phials and retorts, the bottles and glass cylinders, which covered it: all these things were smashed into a thousand pieces. But Coppola threw the figure across his shoulder, and, laughing shrilly and horribly, ran hastily down the stairs, the figure's ugly feet hanging down and banging and rattling like wood against the steps. Nathanael was stupefied;— he had seen only too distinctly that in Olimpia's pallid waxed face there were no eyes, merely black holes in their stead; she was an inanimate puppet. Spalanzani was rolling on the floor; the pieces of glass had cut his head and breast and arm; the blood was escaping from him in streams. But he gathered his strength together by an effort.

"After him—after him! What do you stand staring there for? Coppelius—Coppelius —he's stolen my best automaton—at which I've worked for twenty years—staked my life upon it—the clock-work—speech—movement—mine—your eyes—stolen your eyes—damn him—curse him—after him—fetch me back Olimpia—there are the eyes." And now Nathanael saw a pair of bloody eyes lying on the floor staring at him; Spalanzani seized them with his uninjured hand and threw them at him, so that they hit his breast. Then madness dug her burning talons into him and swept down into his heart, rending his mind and thoughts to shreds. "Aha! aha! aha! Fire-wheel—fire-wheel! Spin round, fire-wheel! merrily, merrily! Aha! wooden doll! spin round, pretty wooden doll!" and he threw himself upon the Professor, clutching him fast by the throat. He would certainly have strangled him had not several people, attracted by the noise, rushed in and torn away the madman; and so they saved the Professor, whose wounds were immediately dressed. Siegmund, with all his strength, was not able to subdue the frantic lunatic, who continued to scream in a dreadful way, "Spin round, wooden doll!" and to strike out right and left with his doubled fists. At length the united strength of several succeeded in overpowering him by throwing him on the floor and binding him. His cries passed into a brutish bellow that was awful to hear; and thus raging with the harrowing violence of madness, he was taken away to the madhouse.

Before continuing my narration of what happened further to the unfortunate Nathanael, I will tell you, indulgent reader, in case you take any interest in that skilful mechanician and fabricator of automata, Spalanzani, that he recovered completely from his wounds. He had, however, to leave the university, for Nathanael's fate had created a great sensation; and the opinion was pretty generally expressed that it was an imposture altogether unpardonable to have smuggled a wooden puppet instead of a living person into intelligent tea-circles,—for Olimpia had been present at several with success. Lawyers called it a cunning piece of knavery, and all the harder to punish since it was directed against the public; and it had been so craftily contrived that it had escaped unobserved by all except a few preternaturally acute students, although everybody was very wise now and remembered to have thought of several facts which occurred to them as suspicious. But these latter could not succeed in making out any sort of a consistent tale. For was it, for instance, a thing likely to occur to any one as suspicious that, according to the declaration of an elegant beau of these tea-parties, Olimpia had, contrary to all good manners, sneezed oftener than she had yawned? The former must have been, in the opinion of this elegant gentleman, the winding up of the concealed clock-work; it had always been accompanied by an observable creaking, and so on. The Professor of Poetry and Eloquence took a pinch of snuff, and, slapping the lid to and clearing his throat, said solemnly, "My most honourable ladies and gentlemen, don't you see then where the rub is? The whole thing is an allegory, a continuous metaphor. You understand me? *Sapienti sat.*" But several most honourable gentlemen did not rest satisfied with this explanation; the history of this automaton had sunk deeply into their souls, and an absurd mistrust of human figures began to prevail. Several lovers, in order to be fully convinced that they were not paying court to a wooden puppet, required that their mistress should sing and dance a little out of time, should embroider or knit or play with her little pug, &c., when being read to, but above all things else that she should do something more than merely listen—that she should frequently speak in such a way as to really show that her words presupposed as a condition some thinking and feeling. The bonds of love were in many cases drawn closer in consequence, and so of course became more engaging; in other instances they gradually relaxed and fell away. "I cannot really be made responsible for it," was the remark of more than one young gallant. At the tea-gatherings everybody, in order to ward off suspicion, yawned to an incredible extent and never sneezed. Spalanzani was obliged, as has been said, to leave the place in order to escape a criminal charge of having fraudulently imposed an automaton upon human society. Coppola, too, had also disappeared.

When Nathanael awoke he felt as if he had been oppressed by a terrible nightmare; he opened his eyes and experienced an indescribable sensation of mental comfort, whilst a soft and most beautiful sensation of warmth pervaded his body. He lay on his own bed in his own room at home; Clara was bending over him, and at a little distance stood his mother and Lothair. "At last, at last, O my darling Nathanael; now we have you again; now you are cured of your grievous illness, now you are mine again." And Clara's words came from the depths of her heart; and she clasped him in her arms. The bright scalding tears streamed from his eyes, he was so overcome with mingled feelings of sorrow and delight; and he gasped forth, "My Clara, my Clara!" Siegmund, who had staunchly stood by his friend in his hour of need, now came into the room. Nathanael gave him his hand—"My faithful brother, you have not deserted me." Every trace of insanity had left him, and in the tender hands of his mother and his beloved, and his friends, he quickly recovered his strength again. Good fortune had in the meantime visited the house; a niggardly old uncle, from whom they had never expected to get anything, had died, and left Nathanael's mother not only a considerable fortune, but also a small estate, pleasantly situated not far from the town. There they resolved to go and live, Nathanael and his mother, and Clara, to whom he was now to be married, and Lothair. Nathanael was become gentler and more childlike than he had ever been before, and now began really to understand Clara's supremely pure and noble character. None of them ever reminded him, even in the remotest degree, of the past. But when Siegmund took leave of him, he said, "By heaven, brother! I was in a bad way, but an angel came just at the right moment and led me back upon the path of light. Yes, it was Clara." Siegmund would not let him speak further, fearing lest the painful recollections of the past might arise too vividly and too intensely in his mind.

The time came for the four happy people to move to their little property. At noon they were going through the streets. After making several purchases they found that the lofty tower of the townhouse was throwing its giant shadows across the marketplace. "Come," said Clara, "let us go up to the top once more and have a look at the distant hills." No sooner said than done. Both of them, Nathanael and Clara, went up the tower; their mother, however, went on with the servant-girl to her new home, and Lothair, not feeling inclined to climb up all the many steps, waited below. There the two lovers stood arm-in-arm on the topmost gallery of the tower, and gazed out into the sweet-scented wooded landscape, beyond which the blue hills rose up like a giant's city.

"Oh! do look at that strange little grey bush, it looks as if it were actually walking towards us," said Clara. Mechanically he put his hand into his side-pocket; he found Coppola's perspective and looked for the bush; Clara stood in front of the glass. Then a convulsive thrill shot through his pulse and veins; pale as a corpse, he fixed his staring eyes upon her; but soon they began to roll, and a fiery current flashed and sparkled in them, and he yelled fearfully, like a hunted animal. Leaping up high in the air and laughing horribly at the same time, he began to shout, in a piercing voice, "Spin round, wooden doll! Spin round, wooden doll!" With the strength of a giant he laid hold upon

Clara and tried to hurl her over, but in an agony of despair she clutched fast hold of the railing that went round the gallery. Lothair heard the madman raging and Clara's scream of terror: a fearful presentiment flashed across his mind. He ran up the steps; the door of the second flight was locked. Clara's scream for help rang out more loudly. Mad with rage and fear, he threw himself against the door, which at length gave way. Clara's cries were growing fainter and fainter,—"Help! save me! save me!" and her voice died away in the air. "She is killed—murdered by that madman," shouted Lothair. The door to the gallery was also locked. Despair gave him the strength of a giant; he burst the door off its hinges. Good God! there was Clara in the grasp of the madman Nathanael, hanging over the gallery in the air; she only held to the iron bar with one hand. Quick as lightning, Lothair seized his sister and pulled her back, at the same time dealing the madman a blow in the face with his doubled fist, which sent him reeling backwards, forcing him to let go his victim.

Lothair ran down with his insensible sister in his arms. She was saved. But Nathanael ran round and round the gallery, leaping up in the air and shouting, "Spin round, fire-wheel! Spin round, fire-wheel!" The people heard the wild shouting, and a crowd began to gather. In the midst of them towered the advocate Coppelius, like a giant; he had only just arrived in the town, and had gone straight to the marketplace. Some were going up to overpower and take charge of the madman, but Coppelius laughed and said, "Ha! ha! wait a bit; he'll come down of his own accord;" and he stood gazing upwards along with the rest. All at once Nathanael stopped as if spell-bound; he bent down over the railing, and perceived Coppelius. With a piercing scream, 'Ha! foine oyes! foine oyes!" he leapt over.

When Nathanael lay on the stone pavement with a broken head, Coppelius had disappeared in the crush and confusion.

Several years afterwards it was reported that, outside the door of a pretty country house in a remote district, Clara had been seen sitting hand in hand with a pleasant gentleman, whilst two bright boys were playing at her feet. From this it may be concluded that she eventually found that quiet domestic happiness which her cheerful, blithesome character required, and which Nathanael, with his tempest-tossed soul, could never have been able to give her.

Octavia Butler (b. 1947)

Bloodchild

Octavia Butler is one of a small number of distinguished black writers writing science fiction today, and of them, the only woman. Her most famous novels are *Wild Seed* (1980) and *Kindred* (1979). Butler's stories are characterized by literal or metaphorical issues of class or race, by strong moral consciousness, and careful attention to detail. Science fiction, her chosen genre, is particularly rich in possibilities for constructing imagined societies that reflect metaphorically upon our own, and Butler has taken full advantage of them in her works. Sometimes the possibilities are horrifying, and she often uses horrific effects in her work, with grim realism. Her most significant story to date is "Bloodchild," which won the 1985 Hugo Award, and the Nebula Award of the Science Fiction Writers of America. An initiation story of considerable power, it plays with great virtuosity upon her usual themes and adds an extraordinary emotional warmth to a dark and horrifying depiction of brutal sexual and social enslavement. It is also a departure for her, in that she characteristically uses women as central characters. Perhaps the most important influence on Butler are the darkly ironic works of Harlan Ellison, her mentor.

My last night of childhood began with a visit home. T'Gatoi's sisters had given us two sterile eggs. T'Gatoi gave one to my mother, brother, and sisters. She insisted that I eat the other one alone. It didn't matter. There was still enough to leave everyone feeling good. Almost everyone. My mother wouldn't take any. She sat, watching everyone drifting and dreaming without her. Most of the time she watched me.

I lay against T'Gatoi's long, velvet underside, sipping from my egg now and then, wondering why my mother denied herself such a harmless pleasure. Less of her hair would be gray if she indulged now and then. The eggs prolonged life, prolonged vigor. My father, who had never refused one in his life, had lived more than twice as long as he should have. And toward the end of his life, when he should have been slowing down, he had married my mother and fathered four children.

But my mother seemed content to age before she had to. I saw her turn away as several of T'Gatoi's limbs secured me closer. T'Gatoi liked our body heat, and took advantage of it whenever she could. When I was little and at home more, my mother used to try to tell me how to behave with T'Gatoi—how to be respectful and always obedient because T'Gatoi was the Tlic government official in charge of the Preserve, and thus the most important of her kind to deal directly with Terrans. It was an honor, my mother said, that such a person had chosen to come into the family. My mother was at her most formal and severe when she was lying.

I had no idea why she was lying, or even what she was lying about. It *was* an honor to have T'Gatoi in the family, but it was hardly a novelty. T'Gatoi and my mother had been friends all my mother's life, and T'Gatoi was not interested in being honored in the house she considered her second home. She simply came in, climbed onto one of her special couches and called me over to keep her warm. It was impossible to be formal with her while lying against her and hearing her complain as usual that I was too skinny.

"You're better," she said this time, probing me with six or seven of her limbs. "You're gaining weight finally. Thinness is dangerous." The probing changed subtly, became a series of caresses.

"He's still too thin," my mother said sharply.

T'Gatoi lifted her head and perhaps a meter of her body off the couch as though she were sitting up. She looked at my mother and my mother, her face lined and old-looking, turned away.

"Lien, I would like you to have what's left of Gan's egg."

"The eggs are for the children," my mother said.

"They are for the family. Please take it."

Unwillingly obedient, my mother took it from me and put it to her mouth. There were only a few drops left in the now-shrunken, elastic shell, but she squeezed them out, swallowed them, and after a few moments some of the lines of tension began to smooth from her face.

"It's good," she whispered. "Sometimes I forget how good it is."

"You should take more," T'Gatoi said. "Why are you in such a hurry to be old?"

My mother said nothing.

"I like being able to come here," T'Gatoi said. "This place is a refuge because of you, yet you won't take care of yourself."

T'Gatoi was hounded on the outside. Her people wanted more of us made available. Only she and her political faction stood between us and the hordes who did not understand why there was a Preserve—why any Terran could not be courted, paid, drafted, in some way made available to them. Or they did understand, but in their desperation, they did not care. She parceled us out to the desperate and sold us to the rich and powerful for their political support. Thus, we were necessities, status symbols, and an independent people. She oversaw the joining of families, putting an end to the final remnants of the earlier system of breaking up Terran families to suit impatient Tlic. I had lived outside with her. I had seen the desperate eagerness in the way some people looked at me. It was a little frightening to know that only she stood between us and that desperation that could so easily swallow us. My mother would look at her sometimes and say to me, "Take care of her." And I would remember that she too had been outside, had seen.

Now T'Gatoi used four of her limbs to push me away from her onto the floor. "Go on, Gan," she said. "Sit down there with your sisters and enjoy not being sober. You had most of the egg. Lien, come warm me."

My mother hesitated for no reason that I could see. One of my earliest memories is of my mother stretched alongside T'Gatoi, talking about things I could not understand, picking me up from the floor and laughing as she sat me on one of T'Gatoi's segments. She ate her share of eggs then. I wondered when she had stopped, and why.

She lay down now against T'Gatoi, and the whole left row of T'Gatoi's limbs closed around her, holding her loosely, but securely. I had always found it comfortable to lie that way but, except for my older sister, no one else in the family liked it. They said it made them feel caged.

T'Gatoi meant to cage my mother. Once she had, she moved her tail slightly, then spoke. "Not enough egg, Lien. You should have taken it when it was passed to you. You need it badly now."

T'Gatoi's tail moved once more, its whip motion so swift I wouldn't have seen it if I hadn't been watching for it. Her sting drew only a single drop of blood from my mother's bare leg.

My mother cried out—probably in surprise. Being stung doesn't hurt. Then she sighed and I could see her body relax. She moved languidly into a more comfortable position within the cage of T'Gatoi's limbs. "Why did you do that?" she asked, sounding half asleep.

"I could not watch you sitting and suffering any longer."

My mother managed to move her shoulders in a small shrug. "Tomorrow," she said.

"Yes. Tomorrow you will resume your suffering—if you must. But for now, just for now, lie here and warm me and let me ease your way a little."

"He's still mine, you know," my mother said suddenly. "Nothing can buy him from me." Sober, she would not have permitted herself to refer to such things.

"Nothing," T'Gatoi agreed, humoring her.

"Did you think I would sell him for eggs? For long life? My son?"

"Not for anything," T'Gatoi said, stroking my mother's shoulders, toying with her long, graying hair.

I would like to have touched my mother, shared that moment with her. She would take my hand if I touched her now. Freed by the egg and the sting, she would smile and perhaps say things long held in. But tomorrow, she would remember all this as a humiliation. I did not want to be part of a remembered humiliation. Best just to be still and know she loved me under all the duty and pride and pain.

"Xuan Hoa, take off her shoes," T'Gatoi said. "In a little while I'll sting her again and she can sleep."

My older sister obeyed, swaying drunkenly as she stood up. When she had finished, she sat down beside me and took my hand. We had always been a unit, she and I.

My mother put the back of her head against T'Gatoi's underside and tried from that impossible angle to look up into the broad, round face. "You're going to sting me again?"

"Yes, Lien."

"I'll sleep until tomorrow noon."

"Good. You need it. When did you sleep last?"

My mother made a wordless sound of annoyance. "I should have stepped on you when you were small enough," she muttered.

It was an old joke between them. They had grown up together, sort of, though T'Gatoi had not, in my mother's lifetime, been small enough for any Terran to step on. She was nearly three times my mother's present age, yet would still be young when my mother died of age. But T'Gatoi and my mother had met as T'Gatoi was coming into a period of rapid development—a kind of Tlic adolescence. My mother was only a child, but for a while they developed at the same rate and had no better friends than each other.

T'Gatoi had even introduced my mother to the man who became my father. My parents, pleased with each other in spite of their very different ages, married as T'Gatoi was going into her family's business—politics. She and my mother saw each other less. But sometime before my older sister was born, my mother promised T'Gatoi one of her children. She would have to give one of us to someone, and she preferred T'Gatoi to some stranger.

Years passed. T'Gatoi traveled and increased her influence. The Preserve was hers by the time she came back to my mother to collect what she probably saw as her just reward for her hard work. My older sister took an instant liking to her and wanted to be chosen, but my mother was just coming to term with me and T'Gatoi liked the idea of choosing an infant and watching and taking part in all the phases of development. I'm told I was first caged within T'Gatoi's many limbs only three minutes after my birth. A few days later, I was given my first taste of egg. I tell Terrans that when they ask whether I was ever afraid of her. And I tell it to Tlic when T'Gatoi suggests a young Terran child for them and they, anxious and ignorant, demand an adolescent. Even my brother who had somehow grown up to fear and distrust the Tlic could probably have gone smoothly into one of their families if he had been adopted early enough. Sometimes, I think for his sake he should have been. I looked at him, stretched out on the floor across the room, his eyes open, but glazed as he dreamed his egg dream. No matter what he felt toward the Tlic, he always demanded his share of egg.

"Lien, can you stand up?" T'Gatoi asked suddenly.

"Stand?" my mother said. "I thought I was going to sleep."

"Later. Something sounds wrong outside." The cage was abruptly gone.

"What?"

"Up, Lien!"

My mother recognized her tone and got up just in time to avoid being dumped on the floor. T'Gatoi whipped her three meters of body off her couch, toward the door, and out at full speed. She had bones—ribs, a long spine, a skull, four sets of limbbones per segment. But when she moved that way, twisting, hurling herself into controlled falls, landing running, she seemed not only boneless, but aquatic—something swimming through the air as though it were water. I loved watching her move.

I left my sister and started to follow her out the door, though I wasn't very steady on my own feet. It would have been better to sit and dream, better yet to find a girl and share a waking dream with her. Back when the Tlic saw us as not much more than convenient big warm-blooded animals, they would pen several of us together, male and female, and feed us only eggs. That way they could be sure of getting another generation of us no matter how we tried to hold out. We were lucky that didn't go on long. A few generations of it and we would have *been* little more than convenient big animals.

"Hold the door open, Gan," T'Gatoi said. "And tell the family to stay back."

"What is it?" I asked.

"N'Tlic."

I shrank back against the door. "Here? Alone?"

"He was trying to reach a call box, I suppose." She carried the man past me, unconscious, folded like a coat over some of her limbs. He looked young—my brother's age perhaps—and he was thinner than he should have been. What T'Gatoi would have called dangerously thin.

"Gan, go to the call box," she said. She put the man on the floor and began stripping off his clothing.

I did not move.

After a moment, she looked up at me, her sudden stillness a sign of deep impatience.

"Send Qui," I told her. "I'll stay here. Maybe I can help."

She let her limbs begin to move again, lifting the man and pulling his shirt over his head. "You don't want to see this," she said. "It will be hard. I can't help this man the way his Tlic could."

"I know. But send Qui. He won't want to be of any help here. I'm at least willing to try."

She looked at my brother—older, bigger, stronger, certainly more able to help her here. He was sitting up now, braced against the wall, staring at the man on the floor with undisguised fear and revulsion. Even she could see that he would be useless.

"Qui, go!" she said.

He didn't argue. He stood up, swayed briefly, then steadied, frightened sober.

"This man's name is Bram Lomas," she told him, reading from the man's arm band. I fingered my own arm band in sympathy. "He needs T'Khotgif Teh. Do you hear?"

"Bram Lomas, T'Khotgif Teh," my brother said. "I'm going." He edged around Lomas and ran out the door.

Lomas began to regain consciousness. He only moaned at first and clutched spasmodically at a pair of T'Gatoi's limbs. My younger sister, finally awake from her egg dream, came close to look at him, until my mother pulled her back.

T'Gatoi removed the man's shoes, then his pants, all the while leaving him two of her limbs to grip. Except for the final few, all her limbs were equally dexterous. "I want no argument from you this time, Gan," she said.

I straightened. "What shall I do?"

"Go out and slaughter an animal that is at least half your size."

"Slaughter? But I've never—"

She knocked me across the room. Her tail was an efficient weapon whether she exposed the sting or not.

I got up, feeling stupid for having ignored her warning, and went into the kitchen. Maybe I could kill something with a knife or an ax. My mother raised a few Terran animals for the table and several thousand local ones for their fur. T'Gatoi would probably prefer something local. An achti, perhaps. Some of those were the right size, though they had about three times as many teeth as I did and a real love of using them. My mother, Hoa, and Qui could kill them with knives. I had never killed one at all, had never slaughtered any animal. I had spent most of my time with T'Gatoi while my brother and sisters were learning the family business. T'Gatoi had been right. I should have been the one to go to the call box. At least I could do that.

I went to the corner cabinet where my mother kept her larger house and garden tools. At the back of the cabinet there was a pipe that carried off waste water from the kitchen—except that it didn't anymore. My father had rerouted the waste water before I was born. Now the pipe could be turned so that one half slid around the other and a rifle could be stored inside. This wasn't our only gun, but it was our most easily accessible one. I would have to use it to shoot one of the biggest of the achti. Then T'Gatoi would probably confiscate it. Firearms were illegal in the Preserve. There had been incidents right after the Preserve was established—Terrans shooting Tlic, shooting N'Tlic. This was before the joining of families began, before everyone had a personal stake in keeping the peace. No one had shot a Tlic in my lifetime or my mother's, but the law still stood—for our protection, we were told. There were stories of whole Terran families wiped out in reprisal back during the assassinations.

I went out to the cages and shot the biggest achti I could find. It was a handsome breeding male and my mother would not be pleased to see me bring it in. But it was the right size, and I was in a hurry.

I put the achti's long, warm body over my shoulder—glad that some of the weight I'd gained was muscle—and took it to the kitchen. There, I put the gun back in its hiding place. If T'Gatoi noticed the achti's wounds and demanded the gun, I would give it to her. Otherwise, let it stay where my father wanted it.

I turned to take the achti to her, then hesitated. For several seconds, I stood in front of the closed door wondering why I was suddenly afraid. I knew what was going to happen. I hadn't seen it before but T'Gatoi had shown me diagrams, and drawings. She had made sure I knew the truth as soon as I was old enough to understand it.

Yet I did not want to go into that room. I wasted a little time choosing a knife from the carved, wooden box in which my mother kept them. T'Gatoi might want one, I told myself, for the tough, heavily furred hide of the achti.

"Gan!" T'Gatoi called, her voice harsh with urgency.

I swallowed. I had not imagined a simple moving of the feet could be so difficult. I realized I was trembling and that shamed me. Shame impelled me through the door.

I put the achti down near T'Gatoi and saw that Lomas was unconscious again. She, Lomas, and I were alone in the room, my mother and sisters probably sent out so they would not have to watch. I envied them.

But my mother came back into the room as T'Gatoi seized the achti. Ignoring the knife I offered her, she extended claws from several of her limbs and slit the achti from throat to anus. She looked at me, her yellow eyes intent. "Hold this man's shoulders, Gan."

I stared at Lomas in panic, realizing that I did not want to touch him, let alone hold him. This would not be like shooting an animal. Not as quick, not as merciful, and, I hoped, not as final, but there was nothing I wanted less than to be part of it.

My mother came forward. "Gan, you hold his right side," she said. "I'll hold his left." And if he came to, he would throw her off without realizing he had done it. She was a tiny woman. She often wondered aloud how she had produced, as she said, such "huge" children.

"Never mind," I told her, taking the man's shoulders. "I'll do it."

She hovered nearby.

"Don't worry," I said. "I won't shame you. You don't have to stay and watch."

She looked at me uncertainly, then touched my face in a rare caress. Finally, she went back to her bedroom.

T'Gatoi lowered her head in relief. "Thank you, Gan," she said with courtesy more Terran than Tlic. "That one . . . she is always finding new ways for me to make her suffer."

Lomas began to groan and make choked sounds. I had hoped he would stay unconscious. T'Gatoi put her face near his so that he focused on her.

"I've stung you as much as I dare for now," she told him. "When this is over, I'll sting you to sleep and you won't hurt anymore."

"Please," the man begged. "Wait . . ."

"There's no more time, Bram. I'll sting you as soon as it's over. When T'Khotgif arrives she'll give you eggs to help you heal. It will be over soon."

"T'Khotgif!" the man shouted, straining against my hands.

"Soon, Bram." T'Gatoi glanced at me, then placed a claw against his abdomen slightly to the right of the middle, just below the last rib. There was movement on the right side—tiny, seemingly random pulsations moving his brown flesh, creating a concavity here, a convexity there, over and over until I could see the rhythm of it and knew where the next pulse would be.

Lomas's entire body stiffened under T'Gatoi's claw, though she merely rested it against him as she wound the rear section of her body around his legs. He might break my grip, but he would not break hers. He wept helplessly as she used his pants to tie his hands, then pushed his hands above his head so that I could kneel on the cloth between them and pin them in place. She rolled up his shirt and gave it to him to bite down on.

And she opened him.

His body convulsed with the first cut. He almost tore himself away from me. The sounds he made . . . I had never heard such sounds come from anything human.

536   Foundations of Fear

T'Gatoi seemed to pay no attention as she lengthened and deepened the cut, now and then pausing to lick away blood. His blood vessels contracted, reacting to the chemistry of her saliva, and the bleeding slowed.

I felt as though I were helping her torture him, helping her consume him. I knew I would vomit soon, didn't know why I hadn't already. I couldn't possibly last until she was finished.

She found the first grub. It was fat and deep red with his blood—both inside and out. It had already eaten its own egg case, but apparently had not yet begun to eat its host. At this stage, it would eat any flesh except its mother's. Let alone, it would have gone on excreting the poisons that had both sickened and alerted Lomas. Eventually it would have begun to eat. By the time it ate its way out of Lomas's flesh, Lomas would be dead or dying—and unable to take a revenge on the thing that was killing him. There was always a grace period between the time the host sickened and the time the grubs began to eat him.

T'Gatoi picked up the writhing grub carefully, and looked at it, somehow ignoring the terrible groans of the man.

Abruptly, the man lost consciousness.

"Good." T'Gatoi looked down at him. "I wish you Terrans could do that at will." She felt nothing. And the thing she held . . .

It was limbless and boneless at this stage, perhaps fifteen centimeters long and two thick, blind and slimy with blood. It was like a large worm. T'Gatoi put it into the belly of the achti, and it began at once to burrow. It would stay there and eat as long as there was anything to eat.

Probing through Lomas's flesh, she found two more, one of them smaller and more vigorous. "A male!" she said happily. He would be dead before I would. He would be through his metamorphosis and screwing everything that would hold still before his sisters even had limbs. He was the only one to make a serious effort to bite T'Gatoi as she placed him in the achti.

Paler worms oozed to visibility in Lomas's flesh. I closed my eyes. It was worse than finding something dead, rotting, and filled with tiny animal grubs. And it was far worse than any drawing or diagram.

"Ah, there are more," T'Gatoi said, plucking out two long, thick grubs. "You may have to kill another animal, Gan. Everything lives inside you Terrans."

I had been told all my life that this was a good and necessary thing Tlic and Terran did together—a kind of birth. I had believed it until now. I knew birth was painful and bloody, no matter what. But this was something else, something worse. And I wasn't ready to see it. Maybe I never would be. Yet I couldn't *not* see it. Closing my eyes didn't help.

T'Gatoi found a grub still eating its egg case. The remains of the case were still wired into a blood vessel by their own little tube or hook or whatever. That was the way the grubs were anchored and the way they fed. They took only blood until they were ready to emerge. Then they ate their stretched, elastic egg cases. Then they ate their hosts.

T'Gatoi bit away the egg case, licked away the blood. Did she like the taste? Did childhood habits die hard—or not die at all?

The whole procedure was wrong, alien. I wouldn't have thought anything about her could seem alien to me.

"One more, I think," she said. "Perhaps two. A good family. In a host animal these days, we would be happy to find one or two alive." She glanced at me. "Go outside, Gan, and empty your stomach. Go now while the man is unconscious."

I staggered out, barely made it. Beneath the tree just beyond the front door, I vomited until there was nothing left to bring up. Finally, I stood shaking, tears streaming down my face. I did not know why I was crying but I could not stop. I went farther from the house to avoid being seen. Every time I closed my eyes I saw red worms crawling over redder human flesh.

There was a car coming toward the house. Since Terrans were forbidden motorized vehicles except for certain farm equipment, I knew this must be Lomas's Tlic with Qui and perhaps a Terran doctor. I wiped my face on my shirt, struggled for control.

"Gan," Qui called as the car stopped. "What happened?" He crawled out of the low, round, Tlic-convenient car door. Another Terran crawled out the other side and went into the house without speaking to me. The doctor. With his help and a few eggs, Lomas might make it.

"T'Khotgif Teh?" I said.

The Tlic driver surged out of her car, reared up half her length before me. She was paler and smaller than T'Gatoi—probably born from the body of an animal. Tlic from Terran bodies were always larger as well as more numerous.

"Six young," I told her. "Maybe seven, all alive. At least one male."

"Lomas?" she said harshly. I liked her for the question and the concern in her voice when she asked it. The last coherent thing he had said was her name.

"He's alive," I said.

She surged away to the house without another word.

"She's been sick," my brother said, watching her go. "When I called, I could hear people telling her she wasn't well enough to go out even for this."

I said nothing. I had extended courtesy to the Tlic. Now I didn't want to talk to anyone. I hoped he would go in—out of curiosity if nothing else.

"Finally found out more than you wanted to know, eh?"

I looked at him.

"Don't give me one of *her* looks," he said. "You're not her. You're just her property."

One of her looks. Had I picked up even an ability to imitate her expressions?

"What'd you do, puke?" He sniffed the air. "So now you know what you're in for."

I walked away from him. He and I had been close when we were kids. He would let me follow him around when I was home and sometimes T'Gatoi would let me bring him along when she took me into the city. But something had happened when he reached adolescence. I never knew what. He began keeping out of T'Gatoi's way. Then he began running away—until he realized there was no "away." Not in the Preserve. Certainly not outside. After that he concentrated on getting his share of every egg that came into the house, and on looking out for me in a way that made me all but hate him—a way that clearly said, as long as I was all right, he was safe from the Tlic.

"How was it, really?" he demanded, following me.

"I killed an achti. The young ate it."

"You didn't run out of the house and puke because they ate an achti."

"I had . . . never seen a person cut open before." That was true, and enough for him to know. I couldn't talk about the other. Not with him.

"Oh," he said. He glanced at me as though he wanted to say more, but he kept quiet.

We walked, not really headed anywhere. Toward the back, toward the cages, toward the fields.

"Did he say anything?" Qui asked. "Lomas, I mean."

Who else would he mean? "He said 'T'Khotgif.'"

Qui shuddered. "If she had done that to me, she'd be the last person I'd call for."

"You'd call for her. Her sting would ease your pain without killing the grubs in you."

"You think I'd care if they died?"

No. Of course he wouldn't. Would I?

"Shit!" He drew a deep breath. "I've seen what they do. You think this thing with Lomas was bad? It was nothing."

I didn't argue. He didn't know what he was talking about.

"I saw them eat a man," he said.

I turned to face him. "You're lying!"

"*I saw them eat a man.*" He paused. "It was when I was little. I had been to the Hartmund house and I was on my way home. Halfway here, I saw a man and a Tlic and the man was N'Tlic. The ground was hilly. I was able to hide from them and watch. The Tlic wouldn't open the man because she had nothing to feed the grubs. The man couldn't go any farther and there were no houses around. He was in so much pain he told her to kill him. He begged her to kill him. Finally, she did. She cut his throat. One swipe of one claw. I saw the grubs eat their way out, then burrow in again, still eating."

His words made me see Lomas's flesh again, parasitized, crawling. "Why didn't you tell me that?" I whispered.

He looked startled, as though he'd forgotten I was listening. "I don't know."

"You started to run away not long after that, didn't you?"

"Yeah. Stupid. Running inside the Preserve. Running in a cage."

I shook my head, said what I should have said to him long ago. "She wouldn't take you, Qui. You don't have to worry."

"She would . . . if anything happened to you."

"No. She'd take Xuan Hoa. Hoa . . . wants it." She wouldn't if she had stayed to watch Lomas.

"They don't take women," he said with contempt.

"They do sometimes." I glanced at him. "Actually, they prefer women. You should be around them when they talk among themselves. They say women have more body fat to protect the grubs. But they usually take men to leave the women free to bear their own young."

"To provide the next generation of host animals," he said, switching from contempt to bitterness.

"It's more than that!" I countered. Was it?

"If it were going to happen to me, I'd want to believe it was more, too."

"It *is* more!" I felt like a kid. Stupid argument.

"Did you think so while T'Gatoi was picking worms out of that guy's guts?"

"It's not supposed to happen that way."

"Sure it is. You weren't supposed to see it, that's all. And his Tlic was supposed to do it. She could sting him unconscious and the operation wouldn't have been as painful. But she'd still open him, pick out the grubs, and if she missed even one, it would poison him and eat him from the inside out."

There was actually a time when my mother told me to show respect for Qui because he was my older brother. I walked away, hating him. In his way, he was gloating. He was safe and I wasn't. I could have hit him, but I didn't think I would be able to stand it when he refused to hit back, when he looked at me with contempt and pity.

He wouldn't let me get away. Longer-legged, he swung ahead of me and made me feel as though I were following him.

"I'm sorry," he said.

I strode on, sick and furious.

"Look, it probably won't be that bad with you. T'Gatoi likes you. She'll be careful."

I turned back toward the house, almost running from him.

"Has she done it to you yet?" he asked, keeping up easily. "I mean, you're about the right age for implantation. Has she—"

I hit him. I didn't know I was going to do it, but I think I meant to kill him. If he hadn't been bigger and stronger, I think I would have.

He tried to hold me off, but in the end, had to defend himself. He only hit me a couple of times. That was plenty. I don't remember going down, but when I came to, he was gone. It was worth the pain to be rid of him.

I got up and walked slowly toward the house. The back was dark. No one was in the kitchen. My mother and sisters were sleeping in their bedrooms—or pretending to.

Once I was in the kitchen, I could hear voices—Tlic and Terran from the next room. I couldn't make out what they were saying—didn't want to make it out.

I sat down at my mother's table, waiting for quiet. The table was smooth and worn, heavy and well-crafted. My father had made it for her just before he died. I remembered hanging around underfoot when he built it. He didn't mind. Now I sat leaning on it, missing him. I could have talked to him. He had done it three times in his long life. Three clutches of eggs, three times being opened and sewed up. How had he done it? How did anyone do it?

I got up, took the rifle from its hiding place, and sat down again with it. It needed cleaning, oiling.

All I did was load it.

"Gan?"

She made a lot of little clicking sounds when she walked on bare floor, each limb clicking in succession as it touched down. Waves of little clicks.

She came to the table, raised the front half of her body above it, and surged onto it. Sometimes she moved so smoothly she seemed to flow like water itself. She coiled herself into a small hill in the middle of the table and looked at me.

"That was bad," she said softly. "You should not have seen it. It need not be that way."

"I know."

"T'Khotgif—Ch'Khotgif now—she will die of her disease. She will not live to raise her children. But her sister will provide for them, and for Bram Lomas." Sterile sister. One fertile female in every lot. One to keep the family going. That sister owed Lomas more than she could ever repay.

"He'll live then?"

"Yes."

"I wonder if he would do it again."

"No one would ask him to do that again."

I looked into the yellow eyes, wondering how much I saw and understood there, and how much I only imagined. "No one ever asks us," I said. "You never asked me."

She moved her head slightly. "What's the matter with your face?"

"Nothing. Nothing important." Human eyes probably wouldn't have noticed the swelling in the darkness. The only light was from one of the moons, shining through a window across the room.

"Did you use the rifle to shoot the achti?"

"Yes."

"And do you mean to use it to shoot me?"

I stared at her, outlined in moonlight—coiled, graceful body. "What does Terran blood taste like to you?"

She said nothing.

"What are you?" I whispered. "What are we to you?"

She lay still, rested her head on her topmost coil. "You know me as no other does," she said softly. "You must decide."

"That's what happened to my face," I told her.

"What?"

"Qui goaded me into deciding to do something. It didn't turn out very well." I moved the gun slightly, brought the barrel up diagonally under my own chin. "At least it was a decision I made."

"As this will be."

"Ask me, Gatoi."

"For my children's lives?"

She would say something like that. She knew how to manipulate people, Terran and Tlic. But not this time.

"I don't want to be a host animal," I said. "Not even yours."

It took her a long time to answer. "We use almost no host animals these days," she said. "You know that."

"You use us."

"We do. We wait long years for you and teach you and join our families to yours." She moved restlessly. "You know you aren't animals to us."

I stared at her, saying nothing.

"The animals we once used began killing most of our eggs after implantation long before your ancestors arrived," she said softly. "You know these things, Gan. Because your people arrived, we are relearning what it means to be a healthy, thriving people. And your ancestors, fleeing from their homeworld, from their own kind who would have killed or enslaved them—they survived because of us. We saw them as people and gave them the Preserve when they still tried to kill us as worms."

At the word "worms" I jumped. I couldn't help it, and she couldn't help noticing it.

"I see," she said quietly. "Would you really rather die than bear my young, Gan?"

I didn't answer.

"Shall I go to Xuan Hoa?"

"Yes!" Hoa wanted it. Let her have it. She hadn't had to watch Lomas. She'd be proud . . . Not terrified.

T'Gatoi flowed off the table onto the floor, startling me almost too much.

"I'll sleep in Hoa's room tonight," she said. "And sometime tonight or in the morning, I'll tell her."

This was going too fast. My sister. Hoa had had almost as much to do with raising me as my mother. I was still close to her—not like Qui. She could want T'Gatoi and still love me.

"Wait! Gatoi!"

She looked back, then raised nearly half her length off the floor and turned it to face me. "These are adult things, Gan. This is my life, my family!"

"But she's . . . my sister."

"I have done what you demanded. I have asked you!"

"But—"

"It will be easier for Hoa. She has always expected to carry other lives inside her."

Human lives. Human young who would someday drink at her breasts, not at her veins.

I shook my head. "Don't do it to her, Gatoi." I was not Qui. It seemed I could become him, though, with no effort at all. I could make Xuan Hoa my shield. Would it be easier to know that red worms were growing in her flesh instead of mine?

"Don't do it to Hoa," I repeated.

She stared at me, utterly still.

I looked away, then back at her. "Do it to me."

I lowered the gun from my throat and she leaned forward to take it.

"No," I told her.

"It's the law," she said.

"Leave it for the family. One of them might use it to save my life someday."

She grasped the rifle barrel, but I wouldn't let go. I was pulled into a standing position over her.

"Leave it here!" I repeated. "If we're not your animals, if these are adult things, accept the risk. There is risk, Gatoi, in dealing with a partner."

It was clearly hard for her to let go of the rifle. A shudder went through her and she made a hissing sound of distress. It occurred to me that she was afraid. She was old enough to have seen what guns could do to people. Now her young and this gun would be together in the same house. She did not know about our other guns. In this dispute, they did not matter.

"I will implant the first egg tonight," she said as I put the gun away. "Do you hear, Gan?"

Why else had I been given a whole egg to eat while the rest of the family was left to share one? Why else had my mother kept looking at me as though I were going away from her, going where she could not follow? Did T'Gatoi imagine I hadn't known?

"I hear."

"Now!" I let her push me out of the kitchen, then walked ahead of her toward my bedroom. The sudden urgency in her voice sounded real. "You would have done it to Hoa tonight!" I accused.

"I must do it to someone tonight."

I stopped in spite of her urgency and stood in her way. "Don't you care who?"

She flowed around me and into my bedroom. I found her waiting on the couch we shared. There was nothing in Hoa's room that she could have used. She would have done it to Hoa on the floor. The thought of her doing it to Hoa at all disturbed me in a different way now, and I was suddenly angry.

Yet I undressed and lay down beside her. I knew what to do, what to expect. I had been told all my life. I felt the familiar sting, narcotic, mildly pleasant. Then the blind probing of her ovipositor. The puncture was painless, easy. So easy going in. She undulated slowly against me, her muscles forcing the egg from her body into mine. I held on to a pair of her limbs until I remembered Lomas holding her that way. Then I let go, moved inadvertently, and hurt her. She gave a low cry of pain and I expected to be caged at once within her limbs. When I wasn't, I held on to her again, feeling oddly ashamed.

"I'm sorry," I whispered.

She rubbed my shoulders with four of her limbs.

"Do you care?" I asked. "Do you care that it's me?"

She did not answer for some time. Finally, "You were the one making choices tonight, Gan. I made mine long ago."

"Would you have gone to Hoa?"

"Yes. How could I put my children into the care of one who hates them?"

"It wasn't . . . hate."

"I know what it was."

"I was afraid."

Silence.

"I still am." I could admit it to her here, now.

"But you came to me . . . to save Hoa."

"Yes." I leaned my forehead against her. She was cool velvet, deceptively soft. "And to keep you for myself," I said. It was so. I didn't understand it, but it was so.

She made a soft hum of contentment. "I couldn't believe I had made such a mistake with you," she said. "I chose you. I believed you had grown to choose me."

"I had, but . . ."

"Lomas."

"Yes."

"I have never known a Terran to see a birth and take it well. Qui has seen one, hasn't he?"

"Yes."

"Terrans should be protected from seeing."

I didn't like the sound of that—and I doubted that it was possible. "Not protected," I said. "Shown. Shown when we're young kids, and shown more than once. Gatoi, no Terran ever sees a birth that goes right. All we see is N'Tlic—pain and terror and maybe death."

She looked down at me. "It is a private thing. It has always been a private thing."

Her tone kept me from insisting—that and the knowledge that if she changed her mind, I might be the first public example. But I had planted the thought in her mind. Chances were it would grow, and eventually she would experiment.

"You won't see it again," she said. "I don't want you thinking any more about shooting me."

The small amount of fluid that came into me with her egg relaxed me as completely as a sterile egg would have, so that I could remember the rifle in my hands and my feelings of fear and revulsion, anger and despair. I could remember the feelings without reviving them. I could talk about them.

"I wouldn't have shot you," I said. "Not you." She had been taken from my father's flesh when he was my age.

"You could have," she insisted.

"Not you." She stood between us and her own people, protecting, interweaving.

"Would you have destroyed yourself?"

I moved carefully, uncomfortably. "I could have done that. I nearly did. That's Qui's 'away.' I wonder if he knows."

"What?"

I did not answer.

"You will live now."

"Yes." *Take care of her*, my mother used to say. Yes.

"I'm healthy and young," she said. "I won't leave you as Lomas was left—alone, N'Tlic. I'll take care of you."

Richard Matheson (b. 1926)

Duel

Richard Matheson won instant notoriety in 1950 with his first short story, "Born of Man and Woman" published in *The Magazine of Fantasy and Science Fiction*. There followed a number of clean, sharp stories of dark fantasy and horrific science fiction, enough to fill several collections in the fifties alone. His first novel, *I Am Legend* (1954), the classic science fiction vampire story, and his second, *The Shrinking Man* (1956), basis for the popular fifties' film, established him as the premier science fiction horror writer of the decade. He went on to a career in Hollywood and is recognized as scriptwriter of stories for "The Twilight Zone" and many television movies. His contemporary classic horror novel, *Hell House* (1971), was successfully filmed. *Bid Time Return* (1975) won the World Fantasy Award for best novel. "Duel" was the basis of a notable 1971 television movie directed by Steven Spielberg, for which Matheson wrote the teleplay. He is one of the finest living writers of horror. Without a hint of science fiction or an overt whiff of the supernatural, "Duel" manages to invoke both the science fiction tradition of the menace of the intelligent machine and the monster tradition of the horror genre. It is a psychological monster story, subtly shocking, compelling, fantastic.

A t 11:32 AM, Mann passed the truck.
     He was heading west, en route to San Francisco. It was Thursday and unseasonably hot for April. He had his suitcoat off, his tie removed and shirt collar opened, his sleeve cuffs folded back. There was sunlight on his left arm and on part of his lap. He could feel the heat of it through his dark trousers as he drove along the two-lane highway. For the past twenty minutes, he had not seen another vehicle going in either direction.

Then he saw the truck ahead, moving up a curving grade between two high green hills. He heard the grinding strain of its motor and saw a double shadow on the road. The truck was pulling a trailer.

He paid no attention to the details of the truck. As he drew behind it on the grade, he edged his car toward the opposite lane. The road ahead had blind curves and he didn't try to pass until the truck had crossed the ridge. He waited until it started around a left curve on the downgrade, then, seeing that the way was clear, pressed down on the accelerator pedal and steered his car into the eastbound lane. He waited until he could see the truck front in his rearview mirror before he turned back into the proper lane.

Mann looked across the countryside ahead. There were ranges of mountains as far as he could see and, all around him, rolling green hills. He whistled softly as the car sped down the winding grade, its tires making crisp sounds on the pavement.

At the bottom of the hill, he crossed a concrete bridge and, glancing to the right, saw a

543

dry streambed strewn with rocks and gravel. As the car moved off the bridge, he saw a trailer park set back from the highway to his right. How can anyone live out here? he thought. His shifting gaze caught sight of a pet cemetery ahead and he smiled. Maybe those people in the trailers wanted to be close to the graves of their dogs and cats.

The highway ahead was straight now. Mann drifted into a reverie, the sunlight on his arm and lap. He wondered what Ruth was doing. The kids, of course, were in school and would be for hours yet. Maybe Ruth was shopping; Thursday was the day she usually went. Mann visualized her in the supermarket, putting various items into the basket cart. He wished he were with her instead of starting on another sales trip. Hours of driving yet before he'd reach San Francisco. Three days of hotel sleeping and restaurant eating, hoped-for contacts and likely disappointments. He sighed; then, reaching out impulsively, he switched on the radio. He revolved the tuning knob until he found a station playing soft, innocuous music. He hummed along with it, eyes almost out of focus on the road ahead.

He started as the truck roared past him on the left, causing his car to shudder slightly. He watched the truck and trailer cut in abruptly for the westbound lane and frowned as he had to brake to maintain a safe distance behind it. What's with you? he thought.

He eyed the truck with cursory disapproval. It was a huge gasoline tanker pulling a tank trailer, each of them having six pairs of wheels. He could see that it was not a new rig but was dented and in need of renovation, its tanks painted a cheap-looking silvery color. Mann wondered if the driver had done the painting himself. His gaze shifted from the word FLAMMABLE printed across the back of the trailer tank, red letters on a white background, to the parallel reflector lines painted in red across the bottom of the tank to the massive rubber flaps swaying behind the rear tires, then back up again. The reflector lines looked as though they'd been clumsily applied with a stencil. The driver must be an independent trucker, he decided, and not too affluent a one, from the looks of his outfit. He glanced at the trailer's license plate. It was a California issue.

Mann checked his speedometer. He was holding steady at 55 miles an hour, as he invariably did when he drove without thinking on the open highway. The truck driver must have done a good 70 to pass him so quickly. That seemed a little odd. Weren't truck drivers supposed to be a cautious lot?

He grimaced at the smell of the truck's exhaust and looked at the vertical pipe to the left of the cab. It was spewing smoke, which clouded darkly back across the trailer. Christ, he thought. With all the furor about air pollution, why do they keep allowing that sort of thing on the highways?

He scowled at the constant fumes. They'd make him nauseated in a little while, he knew. He couldn't lag back here like this. Either he slowed down or he passed the truck again. He didn't have the time to slow down. He'd gotten a late start. Keeping it at 55 all the way, he'd just about make his afternoon appointment. No, he'd have to pass.

Depressing the gas pedal, he eased his car toward the opposite lane. No sign of anything ahead. Traffic on this route seemed almost nonexistent today. He pushed down harder on the accelerator and steered all the way into the eastbound lane.

As he passed the truck, he glanced at it. The cab was too high for him to see into. All he caught sight of was the back of the truck driver's left hand on the steering wheel. It was darkly tanned and square-looking, with large veins knotted on its surface.

When Mann could see the truck reflected in the rearview mirror, he pulled back over to the proper lane and looked ahead again.

He glanced at the rearview mirror in surprise as the truck driver gave him an extended horn blast. What was that? he wondered; a greeting or a curse? He grunted with amusement, glancing at the mirror as he drove. The front fenders of the truck were a dingy purple color, the paint faded and chipped; another amateurish job. All he could see was the lower portion of the truck; the rest was cut off by the top of his rear window.

To Mann's right, now, was a slope of shalelike earth with patches of scrub grass growing on it. His gaze jumped to the clapboard house on top of the slope. The television aerial on its roof was sagging at an angle of less than 40 degrees. Must give great reception, he thought.

He looked to the front again, glancing aside abruptly at a sign printed in jagged block letters on a piece of plywood: NIGHT CRAWLERS—BAIT. What the hell is a night crawler? he wondered. It sounded like some monster in a low-grade Hollywood thriller.

The unexpected roar of the truck motor made his gaze jump to the rearview mirror. Instantly, his startled look jumped to the side mirror. By God, the guy was passing him *again*. Mann turned his head to scowl at the leviathan form as it drifted by. He tried to see into the cab but couldn't because of its height. What's with him, anyway? he wondered. What the hell are we having here, a contest? See which vehicle can stay ahead the longest?

He thought of speeding up to stay ahead but changed his mind. When the truck and trailer started back into the westbound lane, he let up on the pedal, voicing a newly incredulous sound as he saw that if he hadn't slowed down, he would have been prematurely cut off again. Jesus Christ, he thought. What's *with* this guy?

His scowl deepened as the odor of the truck's exhaust reached his nostrils again. Irritably, he cranked up the window on his left. Damn it, was he going to have to breathe that crap all the way to San Francisco? He couldn't afford to slow down. He had to meet Forbes at a quarter after three and that was that.

He looked ahead. At least there was no traffic complicating matters. Mann pressed down on the accelerator pedal, drawing close behind the truck. When the highway curved enough to the left to give him a completely open view of the route ahead, he jarred down on the pedal, steering out into the opposite lane.

The truck edged over, blocking his way.

For several moments, all Mann could do was stare at it in blank confusion. Then, with a startled noise, he braked, returning to the proper lane. The truck moved back in front of him.

Mann could not allow himself to accept what apparently had taken place. It had to be a coincidence. The truck driver couldn't have blocked his way on purpose. He waited for more than a minute, then flicked down the turn-indicator lever to make his intentions perfectly clear and, depressing the accelerator pedal, steered again into the eastbound lane.

Immediately, the truck shifted, barring his way.

"*Jesus Christ!*" Mann was astounded. This was unbelievable. He'd never seen such a thing in twenty-six years of driving. He returned to the westbound lane, shaking his head as the truck swung back in front of him.

He eased up on the gas pedal, falling back to avoid the truck's exhaust. Now what? he wondered. He still had to make San Francisco on schedule. Why in God's name hadn't he gone a little out of his way in the beginning, so he could have traveled by freeway? This damned highway was two lane all the way.

Impulsively, he sped into the eastbound lane again. To his surprise, the truck driver did not pull over. Instead, the driver stuck his left arm out and waved him on. Mann started pushing down on the accelerator. Suddenly, he let up on the pedal with a gasp and jerked the steering wheel around, raking back behind the truck so quickly that his car began to fishtail. He was fighting to control its zigzag whipping when a blue convertible shot by him in the opposite lane. Mann caught a momentary vision of the man inside it glaring at him.

The car came under his control again. Mann was sucking breath in through his mouth. His heart was pounding almost painfully. My God! he thought. *He wanted me to hit that car head-on.* The realization stunned him. True, he should have seen to it himself that the road ahead was clear; that was his failure. But to wave him on . . . Mann felt appalled and sickened. Boy, oh, boy, oh, boy, he thought. This was really one for the books. That son of a bitch had meant for not only him to be killed but a totally uninvolved passerby as well. The idea seemed beyond his comprehension. On a California highway on a Thursday morning? *Why?*

Mann tried to calm himself and rationalize the incident. Maybe it's the heat, he thought. Maybe the truck driver had a tension headache or an upset stomach; maybe both. Maybe he'd had a fight with his wife. Maybe she'd failed to put out last night. Mann tried in vain to smile. There could be any number of reasons. Reaching out, he twisted off the radio. The cheerful music irritated him.

He drove behind the truck for several minutes, his face a mask of animosity. As the exhaust fumes started putting his stomach on edge, he suddenly forced down the heel of his right hand on the horn bar and held it there. Seeing that the route ahead was clear, he pushed in the accelerator pedal all the way and steered into the opposite lane.

The movement of his car was paralleled immediately by the truck. Mann stayed in place, right hand jammed down on the horn bar. Get out of the way, you son of a bitch! he thought. He felt the muscles of his jaw hardening until they ached. There was a twisting in his stomach.

"*Damn!*" He pulled back quickly to the proper lane, shuddering with fury. "You miserable son of a bitch," he muttered, glaring at the truck as it was shifted back in front of him. What the hell is wrong with you? I pass your goddamn rig a couple of times and you go flying off the deep end? Are you nuts or something? Mann nodded tensely. Yes, he thought; he *is.* No other explanation.

He wondered what Ruth would think of all this, how she'd react. Probably, she'd start to honk the horn and would keep on honking it, assuming that, eventually, it would attract the attention of a policeman. He looked around with a scowl. Just where in hell *were* the policemen out here, anyway? He made a scoffing noise. What policemen? Here in the boondocks? They probably had a sheriff on horseback, for Christ's sake.

He wondered suddenly if he could fool the truck driver by passing on the right. Edging his car toward the shoulder, he peered ahead. No chance. There wasn't room enough. The truck driver could shove him through that wire fence if he wanted to. Mann shivered. And he'd want to, sure as hell, he thought.

Driving where he was, he grew conscious of the debris lying beside the highway: beer cans, candy wrappers, ice-cream containers, newspaper sections browned and rotted by the weather, a FOR SALE sign torn in half. Keep America beautiful, he thought sardonically. He passed a boulder with the name WILL JASPER painted on it in white. Who the hell is Will Jasper? he wondered. What would he think of this situation?

Unexpectedly, the car began to bounce. For several anxious moments, Mann thought that one of his tires had gone flat. Then he noticed that the paving along this section of highway consisted of pitted slabs with gaps between them. He saw the truck and trailer jolting up and down and thought: I hope it shakes your brains loose. As the truck veered into a sharp left curve, he caught a fleeting glimpse of the driver's face in the cab's side mirror. There was not enough time to establish his appearance.

"Ah," he said. A long, steep hill was looming up ahead. The truck would have to climb it slowly. There would doubtless be an opportunity to pass somewhere on the grade. Mann pressed down on the accelerator pedal, drawing as close behind the truck as safety would allow.

Halfway up the slope, Mann saw a turnout for the eastbound lane with no oncoming traffic anywhere in sight. Flooring the accelerator pedal, he shot into the opposite lane. The slow-moving truck began to angle out in front of him. Face stiffening, Mann steered his speeding car across the highway edge and curved it sharply on the turnout. Clouds of dust went billowing up behind his car, making him lose sight of the truck. His tires buzzed and crackled on the dirt, then, suddenly, were humming on the pavement once again.

He glanced at the rearview mirror and a barking laugh erupted from his throat. He'd only meant to pass. The dust had been an unexpected bonus. Let the bastard get a sniff of something rotten-smelling in *his* nose for a change! he thought. He honked the horn elatedly, a mocking rhythm of bleats. Screw you, Jack!

He swept across the summit of the hill. A striking vista lay ahead: sunlit hills and flatland, a corridor of dark trees, quadrangles of cleared-off acreage and bright-green vegetable patches; far off, in the distance, a mammoth water tower. Mann felt stirred by the panoramic sight. Lovely, he thought. Reaching out, he turned the radio back on and started humming cheerfully with the music.

Seven minutes later, he passed a billboard advertising CHUCK'S CAFE. No thanks, Chuck, he thought. He glanced at a gray house nestled in a hollow. Was that a cemetery in its front yard or a group of plaster statuary for sale?

Hearing the noise behind him, Mann looked at the rearview mirror and felt himself go cold with fear. The truck was hurtling down the hill, pursuing him.

His mouth fell open and he threw a glance at the speedometer. He was doing more than 60! On a curving downgrade, that was not at all a safe speed to be driving. Yet the truck must be exceeding that by a considerable margin, it was closing the distance between them so rapidly. Mann swallowed, leaning to the right as he steered his car around a sharp curve. Is the man *insane?* he thought.

His gaze jumped forward searchingly. He saw a turnoff half a mile ahead and decided that he'd use it. In the rearview mirror, the huge square radiator grille was all he could see now. He stamped down on the gas pedal and his tires screeched unnervingly as he wheeled around another curve, thinking that, surely, the truck would have to slow down here.

He groaned as it rounded the curve with ease, only the sway of its tanks revealing the outward pressure of the turn. Mann bit trembling lips together as he whipped his car around another curve. A straight descent now. He depressed the pedal farther, glanced at the speedometer. Almost 70 miles an hour! He wasn't used to driving this fast!

In agony, he saw the turnoff shoot by on his right. He couldn't have left the highway at this speed, anyway, he'd have overturned. Goddamn it, what was wrong with that son of a bitch? Mann honked his horn in frightened rage. Cranking down the window suddenly, he shoved his left arm out to wave the truck back. *"Back!"* he yelled. He honked the horn again. "Get back, you crazy bastard!"

The truck was almost on him now. He's going to kill me! Mann thought, horrified. He honked the horn repeatedly, then had to use both hands to grip the steering wheel as he swept around another curve. He flashed a look at the rearview mirror. He could see only the bottom portion of the truck's radiator grille. He was going to lose control! He felt the rear wheels start to drift and let up on the pedal quickly. The tire treads bit in, the car leaped on, regaining its momentum.

Mann saw the bottom of the grade ahead, and in the distance there was a building with a sign that read CHUCK'S CAFE. The truck was gaining ground again. This is insane!

he thought, enraged and terrified at once. The highway straightened out. He floored the pedal: 74 now—75. Mann braced himself, trying to ease the car as far to the right as possible.

Abruptly, he began to brake, then swerved to the right, raking his car into the open area in front of the cafe. He cried out as the car began to fishtail, then careened into a skid. *Steer with it!* screamed a voice in his mind. The rear of the car was lashing from side to side, tires spewing dirt and raising clouds of dust. Mann pressed harder on the brake pedal, turning further into the skid. The car began to straighten out and he braked harder yet, conscious, on the sides of his vision, of the truck and trailer roaring by on the highway. He nearly sideswiped one of the cars parked in front of the cafe, bounced and skidded by it, going almost straight now. He jammed in the brake pedal as hard as he could. The rear end broke to the right and the car spun half around, sheering sideways to a neck-wrenching halt thirty yards beyond the cafe.

Mann sat in pulsing silence, eyes closed. His heartbeats felt like club blows in his chest. He couldn't seem to catch his breath. If he were ever going to have a heart attack, it would be now. After a while, he opened his eyes and pressed his right palm against his chest. His heart was still throbbing laboredly. No wonder, he thought. It isn't every day I'm almost murdered by a truck.

He raised the handle and pushed out the door, then started forward, grunting in surprise as the safety belt held him in place. Reaching down with shaking fingers, he depressed the release button and pulled the ends of the belt apart. He glanced at the cafe. What had its patrons thought of his breakneck appearance? he wondered.

He stumbled as he walked to the front door of the cafe. TRUCKERS WELCOME, read a sign in the window. It gave Mann a queasy feeling to see it. Shivering, he pulled open the door and went inside, avoiding the sight of its customers. He felt certain they were watching him, but he didn't have the strength to face their looks. Keeping his gaze fixed straight ahead, he moved to the rear of the cafe and opened the door marked GENTS.

Moving to the sink, he twisted the right-hand faucet and leaned over to cup cold water in his palms and splash it on his face. There was a fluttering of his stomach muscles he could not control.

Straightening up, he tugged down several towels from their dispenser and patted them against his face, grimacing at the smell of the paper. Dropping the soggy towels into a wastebasket beside the sink, he regarded himself in the wall mirror. Still with us, Mann, he thought. He nodded, swallowing. Drawing out his metal comb, he neatened his hair. You never know, he thought. You just never know. You drift along, year after year, presuming certain values to be fixed; like being able to drive on a public thoroughfare without somebody trying to murder you. You come to depend on that sort of thing. Then something occurs and all bets are off. One shocking incident and all the years of logic and acceptance are displaced and, suddenly, the jungle is in front of you again. *Man, part animal, part angel.* Where had he come across that phrase? He shivered.

It was entirely an animal in that truck out there.

His breath was almost back to normal now. Mann forced a smile at his reflection. All right, boy, he told himself. It's over now. It was a goddamned nightmare, but it's over. You are on your way to San Francisco. You'll get yourself a nice hotel room, order a bottle of expensive Scotch, soak your body in a hot bath and forget. Damn right, he thought. He turned and walked out of the washroom.

He jolted to a halt, his breath cut off. Standing rooted, heartbeat hammering at his chest, he gaped through the front window of the cafe.

The truck and trailer were parked outside.

Mann stared at them in unbelieving shock. It wasn't possible. He'd seen them roaring by at top speed. The driver had won; he'd *won!* He'd had the whole damn highway to himself! *Why had he turned back?*

Mann looked around with sudden dread. There were five men eating, three along the counter, two in booths. He cursed himself for having failed to look at faces when he'd entered. Now there was no way of knowing who it was. Mann felt his legs begin to shake.

Abruptly, he walked to the nearest booth and slid in clumsily behind the table. Now wait, he told himself; just wait. Surely, he could tell which one it was. Masking his face with the menu, he glanced across its top. Was it that one in the khaki work shirt? Mann tried to see the man's hands but couldn't. His gaze flicked nervously across the room. Not that one in the suit, of course. Three remaining. That one in the front booth, square-faced, black-haired? If only he could see the man's hands, it might help. One of the two others at the counter? Mann studied them uneasily. Why hadn't he looked at faces when he'd come in?

Now *wait*, he thought. Goddamn it, *wait!* All right, the truck driver was in here. That didn't automatically signify that he meant to continue the insane duel. Chuck's Cafe might be the only place to eat for miles around. It *was* lunchtime, wasn't it? The truck driver had probably intended to eat here all the time. He'd just been moving too fast to pull into the parking lot before. So he'd slowed down, turned around and driven back, that was all. Mann forced himself to read the menu. Right, he thought. No point in getting so rattled. Perhaps a beer would help relax him.

The woman behind the counter came over and Mann ordered a ham sandwich on rye toast and a bottle of Coors. As the woman turned away, he wondered, with a sudden twinge of self-reproach, why he hadn't simply left the cafe, jumped into his car and sped away. He would have known immediately, then, if the truck driver was still out to get him. As it was, he'd have to suffer through an entire meal to find out. He almost groaned at his stupidity.

Still, what if the truck driver *had* followed him out and started after him again? He'd have been right back where he'd started. Even if he'd managed to get a good lead, the truck driver would have overtaken him eventually. It just wasn't in him to drive at 80 and 90 miles an hour in order to stay ahead. True, he might have been intercepted by a California Highway Patrol car. What if he weren't though?

Mann repressed the plaguing thoughts. He tried to calm himself. He looked deliberately at the four men. Either of two seemed a likely possibility as the driver of the truck: the square-faced one in the front booth and the chunky one in the jumpsuit sitting at the counter. Mann had an impulse to walk over to them and ask which one it was, tell the man he was sorry he'd irritated him, tell him anything to calm him, since, obviously, he wasn't rational, was a manic-depressive, probably. Maybe buy the man a beer and sit with him awhile to try to settle things.

He couldn't move. What if the truck driver were letting the whole thing drop? Mightn't his approach rile the man all over again? Mann felt drained by indecision. He nodded weakly as the waitress set the sandwich and the bottle in front of him. He took a swallow of the beer, which made him cough. Was the truck driver amused by the sound? Mann felt a stirring of resentment deep inside himself. What right did that bastard have to impose this torment on another human being? It was a free country, wasn't it? Damn it, he had every right to pass the son of a bitch on a highway if he wanted to!

"Oh, hell," he mumbled. He tried to feel amused. He was making entirely too much of this. Wasn't he? He glanced at the pay telephone on the front wall. What was to prevent him from calling the local police and telling them the situation? But, then, he'd have to stay here, lose time, make Forbes angry, probably lose the sale. And what if the truck driver stayed to face them? Naturally, he'd deny the whole thing. What if the police believed him and didn't do anything about it? After they'd gone, the truck driver would undoubtedly take it out on him again, only worse. *God!* Mann thought in agony.

The sandwich tasted flat, the beer unpleasantly sour. Mann stared at the table as he ate. For God's sake, why was he just *sitting* here like this? He was a grown man, wasn't he? Why didn't he settle this damn thing once and for all?

His left hand twitched so unexpectedly, he spilled beer on his trousers. The man in the jumpsuit had risen from the counter and was strolling toward the front of the cafe. Mann felt his heartbeat thumping as the man gave money to the waitress, took his change and a toothpick from the dispenser and went outside. Mann watched in anxious silence.

The man did not get into the cab of the tanker truck.

It had to be the one in the front booth, then. His face took form in Mann's remembrance: square, with dark eyes, dark hair; the man who'd tried to kill him.

Mann stood abruptly, letting impulse conquer fear. Eyes fixed ahead, he started toward the entrance. Anything was preferable to sitting in that booth. He stopped by the cash register, conscious of the hitching of his chest as he gulped in air. Was the man observing him? he wondered. He swallowed, pulling out the clip of dollar bills in his right-hand trouser pocket. He glanced toward the waitress. Come *on*, he thought. He looked at his check and, seeing the amount, reached shakily into his trouser pocket for change. He heard a coin fall onto the floor and roll away. Ignoring it, he dropped a dollar and a quarter onto the counter and thrust the clip of bills into his trouser pocket.

As he did, he heard the man in the front booth get up. An icy shudder spasmed up his back. Turning quickly to the door, he shoved it open, seeing, on the edges of his vision, the square-faced man approach the cash register. Lurching from the cafe, he started toward his car with long strides. His mouth was dry again. The pounding of his heart was painful in his chest.

Suddenly, he started running. He heard the cafe door bang shut and fought away the urge to look across his shoulder. Was that a sound of other running footsteps now? Reaching his car, Mann yanked open the door and jarred in awkwardly behind the steering wheel. He reached into his trouser pocket for the keys and snatched them out, almost dropping them. His hand was shaking so badly he couldn't get the ignition key into its slot. He whined with mounting dread. Come on! he thought.

The key slid in, he twisted it convulsively. The motor started and he raced it momentarily before jerking the transmission shift to drive. Depressing the accelerator pedal quickly, he raked the car around and steered it toward the highway. From the corners of his eyes, he saw the truck and trailer being backed away from the cafe.

Reaction burst inside him. "No!" he raged and slammed his foot down on the brake pedal. This was idiotic! Why the hell should he run away? His car slid sideways to a rocking halt and, shouldering out the door, he lurched to his feet and started toward the truck with angry strides. *All right, Jack*, he thought. He glared at the man inside the truck. You want to punch my nose, okay, but no more goddamn tournament on the highway.

The truck began to pick up speed. Mann raised his right arm. "Hey!" he yelled. He knew the driver saw him. *"Hey!"* He started running as the truck kept moving, engine grinding loudly. It was on the highway now. He sprinted toward it with a sense of martyred outrage. The driver shifted gears, the truck moved faster. "Stop!" Mann shouted. "Damn it, *stop!*"

He thudded to a panting halt, staring at the truck as it receded down the highway, moved around a hill and disappeared. "You son of a bitch," he muttered. "You goddamn, miserable son of a bitch."

He trudged back slowly to his car, trying to believe that the truck driver had fled the hazard of a fistfight. It was possible, of course, but, somehow, he could not believe it.

He got into his car and was about to drive onto the highway when he changed his mind and switched the motor off. That crazy bastard might just be tooling along at 15 miles an hour, waiting for him to catch up. Nuts to that, he thought. So he blew his schedule; screw it. Forbes would have to wait, that was all. And if Forbes didn't care to wait, that was all right, too. He'd sit here for a while and let the nut get out of range, let him think he'd won the day. He grinned. You're the bloody Red Baron, Jack; you've shot me down. Now go to hell with my sincerest compliments. He shook his head. Beyond belief, he thought.

He really should have done this earlier, pulled over, waited. Then the truck driver would have had to let it pass. *Or picked on someone else*, the startling thought occurred to him. Jesus, maybe that was how the crazy bastard whiled away his work hours! Jesus Christ Almighty! was it possible?

He looked at the dashboard clock. It was just past 12:30. Wow, he thought. All that in less than an hour. He shifted on the seat and stretched his legs out. Leaning back against the door, he closed his eyes and mentally perused the things he had to do tomorrow and the following day. Today was shot to hell, as far as he could see.

When he opened his eyes, afraid of drifting into sleep and losing too much time, almost eleven minutes had passed. The nut must be an ample distance off by now, he thought; at least 11 miles and likely more, the way he drove. Good enough. He wasn't going to try to make San Francisco on schedule now, anyway. He'd take it real easy.

Mann adjusted his safety belt, switched on the motor, tapped the transmission pointer into drive position and pulled onto the highway, glancing back across his shoulder. Not a car in sight. Great day for driving. Everybody was staying at home. That nut must have a reputation around here. When Crazy Jack is on the highway, lock your car in the garage. Mann chuckled at the notion as his car began to turn the curve ahead.

Mindless reflex drove his right foot down against the brake pedal. Suddenly, his car had skidded to a halt and he was staring down the highway. The truck and trailer were parked on the shoulder less than 90 yards away.

Mann couldn't seem to function. He knew his car was blocking the westbound lane, knew that he should either make a U-turn or pull off the highway, but all he could do was gape at the truck.

He cried out, legs retracting, as a horn blast sounded behind him. Snapping up his head, he looked at the rearview mirror, gasping as he saw a yellow station wagon bearing down on him at high speed. Suddenly, it veered off toward the eastbound lane, disappearing from the mirror. Mann jerked around and saw it hurtling past his car, its rear end snapping back and forth, its back tires screeching. He saw the twisted features of the man inside, saw his lips move rapidly with cursing.

Then the station wagon had swerved back into the westbound lane and was speeding off. It gave Mann an odd sensation to see it pass the truck. The man in that station wagon could drive on, unthreatened. Only he'd been singled out. What happened was demented. Yet it was happening.

He drove his car onto the highway shoulder and braked. Putting the transmission into neutral, he leaned back, staring at the truck. His head was aching again. There was a pulsing at his temples like the ticking of a muffled clock.

What was he to do? He knew very well that if he left his car to walk to the truck, the driver would pull away and repark farther down the highway. He may as well face the fact that he was dealing with a madman. He felt the tremor in his stomach muscles starting up again. His heartbeat thudded slowly, striking at his chest wall. Now what?

With a sudden, angry impulse, Mann snapped the transmission into gear and stepped down hard on the accelerator pedal. The tires of the car spun sizzlingly before they gripped; the car shot out onto the highway. Instantly, the truck began to move. He even had the motor on! Mann thought in raging fear. He floored the pedal, then, abruptly, realized he couldn't make it, that the truck would block his way and he'd collide with its trailer. A vision flashed across his mind, a fiery explosion and a sheet of flame incinerating him. He started braking fast, trying to decelerate evenly, so he wouldn't lose control.

When he'd slowed down enough to feel that it was safe, he steered the car onto the shoulder and stopped it again, throwing the transmission into neutral.

Approximately eighty yards ahead, the truck pulled off the highway and stopped.

Mann tapped his fingers on the steering wheel. *Now* what? he thought. Turn around and head east until he reached a cutoff that would take him to San Francisco by another route? How did he know the truck driver wouldn't follow him even then? His cheeks twisted as he bit his lips together angrily. No! He wasn't going to turn around!

His expression hardened suddenly. Well, he wasn't going to *sit* here all day, that was certain. Reaching out, he tapped the gearshift into drive and steered his car onto the highway once again. He saw the massive truck and trailer start to move but made no effort to speed up. He tapped at the brakes, taking a position about 30 yards behind the trailer. He glanced at his speedometer. Forty miles an hour. The truck driver had his left arm out of the cab window and was waving him on. What did that mean? Had he changed his mind? Decided, finally, that this thing had gone too far? Mann couldn't let himself believe it.

He looked ahead. Despite the mountain ranges all around, the highway was flat as far as he could see. He tapped a fingernail against the horn bar, trying to make up his mind. Presumably, he could continue all the way to San Francisco at this speed, hanging back just far enough to avoid the worst of the exhaust fumes. It didn't seem likely that the truck driver would stop directly on the highway to block his way. And if the truck driver pulled onto the shoulder to let him pass, he could pull off the highway, too. It would be a draining afternoon but a safe one.

On the other hand, outracing the truck might be worth just one more try. This was obviously what that son of a bitch wanted. Yet, surely, a vehicle of such size couldn't be driven with the same daring as, potentially, his own. The laws of mechanics were against it, if nothing else. Whatever advantage the truck had in mass, it had to lose in stability, particularly that of its trailer. If Mann were to drive at, say, 80 miles an hour and there were a few steep grades—as he felt sure there were—the truck would have to fall behind.

The question was, of course, whether he had the nerve to maintain such a speed over a long distance. He'd never done it before. Still, the more he thought about it, the more it appealed to him; far more than the alternative did.

Abruptly, he decided. *Right*, he thought. He checked ahead, then pressed down hard on the accelerator pedal and pulled into the eastbound lane. As he neared the truck, he tensed, anticipating that the driver might block his way. But the truck did not shift from the westbound lane. Mann's car moved along its mammoth side. He glanced at the cab and saw the name KELLER printed on its door. For a shocking instant, he thought it read KILLER and started to slow down. Then, glancing at the name again, he saw what it really was and depressed the pedal sharply. When he saw the truck reflected in the rearview mirror, he steered his car into the westbound lane.

He shuddered, dread and satisfaction mixed together, as he saw that the truck driver was speeding up. It was strangely comforting to know the man's intentions definitely again. That plus the knowledge of his face and name seemed, somehow, to reduce his stature. Before, he had been faceless, nameless, an embodiment of unknown terror. Now, at least, he was an individual. All right, Keller, said his mind, let's see you beat me with that purple-silver relic now. He pressed down harder on the pedal. *Here we go,* he thought.

He looked at the speedometer, scowling as he saw that he was doing only 74 miles an hour. Deliberately, he pressed down on the pedal, alternating his gaze between the highway ahead and the speedometer until the needle turned past 80. He felt a flickering of satisfaction with himself. All right, Keller, you son of a bitch, top that, he thought.

After several moments, he glanced into the rearview mirror again. Was the truck getting closer? Stunned, he checked the speedometer. Damn it! He was down to 76! He forced in the accelerator pedal angrily. *He mustn't go less than 80!* Mann's chest shuddered with convulsive breath.

He glanced aside as he hurtled past a beige sedan parked on the shoulder underneath a tree. A young couple sat inside it, talking. Already they were far behind, their world removed from his. Had they even glanced aside when he'd passed? He doubted it.

He started as the shadow of an overhead bridge whipped across the hood and windshield. Inhaling raggedly, he glanced at the speedometer again. He was holding at 81. He checked the rearview mirror. Was it his imagination that the truck was gaining ground? He looked forward with anxious eyes. There had to be some kind of town ahead. To hell with time; he'd stop at the police station and tell them what had happened. They'd have to believe him. Why would he stop to tell them such a story if it weren't true? For all he knew, Keller had a police record in these parts. *Oh, sure, we're on to him,* he heard a faceless officer remark. *That crazy bastard's asked for it before and now he's going to get it.*

Mann shook himself and looked at the mirror. The truck *was* getting closer. Wincing, he glanced at the speedometer. Goddamn it, pay attention! raged his mind. He was down to 74 again! Whining with frustration, he depressed the pedal. Eighty!—80! he demanded of himself. There was a murderer behind him!

His car began to pass a field of flowers; lilacs, Mann saw, white and purple stretching out in endless rows. There was a small shack near the highway, the words FIELD FRESH FLOWER painted on it. A brown-cardboard square was propped against the shack, the word FUNERALS printed crudely on it. Mann saw himself, abruptly, lying in a casket, painted like some grotesque mannequin. The overpowering smell of flowers seemed to fill his nostrils. Ruth and the children sitting in the first row, heads bowed. All his relatives—

Suddenly, the pavement roughened and the car began to bounce and shudder, driving bolts of pain into his head. He felt the steering wheel resisting him and clamped his hands around it tightly, harsh vibrations running up his arms. He didn't dare look at the mirror now. He had to force himself to keep the speed unchanged. Keller wasn't going to slow down; he was sure of that. *What if he got a flat tire, though?* All control would vanish in an instant. He visualized the somersaulting of his car, its grinding, shrieking tumble, the explosion of its gas tank, his body crushed and burned and—

The broken span of pavement ended and his gaze jumped quickly to the rearview mirror. The truck was no closer, but it hadn't lost ground, either. Mann's eyes shifted. Up ahead were hills and mountains. He tried to reassure himself that upgrades were on his side, that he could climb them at the same speed he was going now. Yet all he could imagine were the downgrades, the immense truck close behind him, slamming violently into his car and knocking it across some cliff edge. He had a horrifying vision of dozens of broken, rusted cars lying unseen in the canyons ahead, corpses in every one of them, all flung to shattering deaths by Keller.

Mann's car went rocketing into a corridor of trees. On each side of the highway was a eucalyptus windbreak, each trunk three feet from the next. It was like speeding through a high-walled canyon. Mann gasped, twitching, as a large twig bearing dusty leaves dropped down across the windshield, then slid out of sight. Dear God! he thought. He was getting near the edge himself. If he should lose his nerve at this speed, it was over. Jesus! That would be ideal for Keller! he realized suddenly. He visualized the square-faced driver laughing as he passed the burning wreckage, knowing that he'd killed his prey without so much as touching him.

Mann started as his car shot out into the open. The route ahead was not straight now but winding up into the foothills. Mann willed himself to press down on the pedal even more. Eighty-three now, almost 84.

To his left was a broad terrain of green hills blending into mountains. He saw a black car on a dirt road, moving toward the highway. *Was its side painted white?* Mann's heartbeat lurched. Impulsively, he jammed the heel of his right hand down against the horn bar and held it there. The blast of the horn was shrill and racking to his ears. His heart began to pound. Was it a police car? *Was it?*

He let the horn bar up abruptly. *No, it wasn't.* Damn! his mind raged. Keller must have been amused by his pathetic efforts. Doubtless, he was chuckling to himself right now. He heard the truck driver's voice in his mind, coarse and sly. *You think you gonna get a cop to save you, boy? Shee-it. You gonna die.* Mann's heart contorted with savage hatred. *You son of a bitch!* he thought. Jerking his right hand into a fist, he drove it down against the seat. Goddamn you, Keller! I'm going to kill you, if it's the last thing I do!

The hills were closer now. There would be slopes directly, long steep grades. Mann felt a burst of hope within himself. He was sure to gain a lot of distance on the truck. No matter how he tried, that bastard Keller couldn't manage 80 miles an hour on a hill. But *I can!* cried his mind with fierce elation. He worked up saliva in his mouth and swallowed it. The back of his shirt was drenched. He could feel sweat trickling down his sides. A bath and a drink, first order of the day on reaching San Francisco. A long, hot bath, a long, cold drink. Cutty Sark. He'd splurge, by Christ. He rated it.

The car swept up a shallow rise. Not steep enough, goddamn it! The truck's momentum would prevent its losing speed. Mann felt mindless hatred for the landscape. Already, he had topped the rise and tilted over to a shallow downgrade. He looked at the rearview mirror. *Square,* he thought, everything about the truck was square: the radiator grille, the fender shapes, the bumper ends, the outline of the cab, even the shape of Keller's hands and face. He visualized the truck as some great entity pursuing him, insentient, brutish, chasing him with instinct only.

Mann cried out, horror-stricken, as he saw the ROAD REPAIRS sign up ahead. His frantic gaze leaped down the highway. Both lanes blocked, a huge black arrow pointing toward the alternate route! He groaned in anguish, seeing it was dirt. His foot jumped automatically to the brake pedal and started pumping it. He threw a dazed look at the rearview mirror. The truck was moving as fast as ever! It *couldn't,* though! Mann's expression froze in terror as he started turning to the right.

He stiffened as the front wheels hit the dirt road. For an instant, he was certain that the back part of the car was going to spin; he felt it breaking to the left. "No, don't!" he cried. Abruptly, he was jarring down the dirt road, elbows braced against his sides, trying to keep from losing control. His tires battered at the ruts, almost tearing the wheel from his grip. The windows rattled noisily. His neck snapped back and forth with painful jerks.

His jolting body surged against the binding of the safety belt and slammed down violently on the seat. He felt the bouncing of the car drive up his spine. His clenching teeth slipped and he cried out hoarsely as his upper teeth gouged deep into his lip.

He gasped as the rear end of the car began surging to the right. He started to jerk the steering wheel to the left, then, hissing, wrenched it in the opposite direction, crying out as the right rear fender cracked into a fence pole, knocking it down. He started pumping at the brakes, struggling to regain control. The car rear yawed sharply to the left, tires shooting out a spray of dirt. Mann felt a scream tear upward in his throat. He twisted wildly at the steering wheel. The car began careening to the right. He hitched the wheel around until the car was on course again. His head was pounding like his heart now, with gigantic, throbbing spasms. He started coughing as he gagged on dripping blood.

The dirt road ended suddenly, the car regained momentum on the pavement and he dared to look at the rearview mirror. The truck was slowed down but was still behind him, rocking like a freighter on a storm-tossed sea, its huge tires scouring up a pall of dust. Mann shoved in the accelerator pedal and his car surged forward. A good, steep grade lay just ahead; he'd gain that distance now. He swallowed blood, grimacing at the taste, then fumbled in his trouser pocket and tugged out his handkerchief. He pressed it to his bleeding lip, eyes fixed on the slope ahead. Another fifty yards or so. He writhed his back. His undershirt was soaking wet, adhering to his skin. He glanced at the rearview mirror. The truck had just regained the highway. *Tough!* he thought with venom. Didn't get me, did you, Keller?

His car was on the first yards of the upgrade when steam began to issue from beneath its hood. Mann stiffened suddenly, eyes widening with shock. The steam increased, became a smoking mist. Mann's gaze jumped down. The red light hadn't flashed on yet but had to in a moment. How could this be happening? Just as he was set to get away! The slope ahead was long and gradual, with many curves. He knew he couldn't stop. Could he U-turn unexpectedly and go back down? the sudden thought occurred. He looked ahead. The highway was too narrow, bound by hills on both sides. There wasn't room enough to make an uninterrupted turn and there wasn't time enough to ease around. If he tried that, Keller would shift direction and hit him head-on. "Oh, my God!" Mann murmured suddenly.

He was going to die.

He stared ahead with stricken eyes, his view increasingly obscured by steam. Abruptly, he recalled the afternoon he'd had the engine steam-cleaned at the local car wash. The man who'd done it had suggested he replace the water hoses, because steam-cleaning had a tendency to make them crack. He'd nodded, thinking that he'd do it when he had more time. *More time!* The phrase was like a dagger in his mind. He'd failed to change the hoses and, for that failure, he was now about to die.

He sobbed in terror as the dashboard light flashed on. He glanced at it involuntarily and read the word HOT, black on red. With a breathless gasp, he jerked the transmission into low. Why hadn't he done that right away! He looked ahead. The slope seemed endless. Already, he could hear a boiling throb inside the radiator. How much coolant was there left? Steam was clouding faster, hazing up the windshield. Reaching out, he twisted at a dashboard knob. The wipers started flicking back and forth in fan-shaped sweeps. There had to be enough coolant in the radiator to get him to the top. *Then* what? cried his mind. He couldn't drive without coolant, even downhill. He glanced at the rearview mirror. The truck was falling behind. Mann snarled with maddened fury. *If it weren't for that goddamned hose, he'd be escaping now!*

The sudden lurching of the car snatched him back to terror. If he braked now, he could jump out, run and scrabble up that slope. Later, he might not have the time. He couldn't make himself stop the car, though. As long as it kept on running, he felt bound to it, less vulnerable. God knows what would happen if he left it.

Mann started up the slope with haunted eyes, trying not to see the red light on the edges of his vision. Yard by yard, his car was slowing down. Make it, make it, pleaded his mind, even though he thought that it was futile. The car was running more and more unevenly. The thumping percolation of its radiator filled his ears. Any moment now, the motor would be choked off and the car would shudder to a stop, leaving him a sitting target. *No*, he thought. He tried to blank his mind.

He was almost to the top, but in the mirror he could see the truck drawing up on him. He jammed down on the pedal and the motor made a grinding noise. He groaned. It had to make the top! Please, God, help me! screamed his mind. The ridge was just ahead. Closer. Closer. Make it. "Make it." The car was shuddering and clanking, slowing down—oil, smoke and steam gushing from beneath the hood. The windshield wipers swept from side to side. Mann's head throbbed. Both his hands felt numb. His heartbeat pounded as he stared ahead. Make it, please, God, make it. Make it. *Make* it!

Over! Mann's lips opened in a cry of triumph as the car began descending. Hand shaking uncontrollably, he shoved the transmission into neutral and let the car go into a glide. The triumph strangled in his throat as he saw that there was nothing in sight but hills and more hills. Never mind! He was on a downgrade now, a long one. He passed a sign that read, TRUCKS USE LOW GEARS NEXT 12 MILES. Twelve miles! Something would come up. It had to.

The car began to pick up speed. Mann glanced at the speedometer. Forty-seven miles an hour. The red light still burned. He'd save the motor for a long time, too, though; let it cool for twelve miles, if the truck was far enough behind.

His speed increased. Fifty . . . 51. Mann watched the needle turning slowly toward the right. He glanced at the rearview mirror. The truck had not appeared yet. With a little luck, he might still get a good lead. Not as good as he might have if the motor hadn't overheated but enough to work with. There had to be some place along the way to stop. The needle edged past 55 and started toward the 60 mark.

Again, he looked at the rearview mirror, jolting as he saw that the truck had topped the ridge and was on its way down. He felt his lips begin to shake and crimped them together. His gaze jumped fitfully between the steam-obscured highway and the mirror. The truck was accelerating rapidly. Keller doubtless had the gas pedal floored. It wouldn't be long before the truck caught up to him. Mann's right hand twitched unconsciously toward the gearshift. Noticing, he jerked it back, grimacing, glanced at the speedometer. The car's velocity had just passed 60. Not enough! He had to use the motor now! He reached out desperately.

His right hand froze in midair as the motor stalled; then, shooting out the hand, he twisted the ignition key. The motor made a grinding noise but wouldn't start. Mann glanced up, saw that he was almost on the shoulder, jerked the steering wheel around. Again, he turned the key, but there was no response. He looked up at the rearview mirror. The truck was gaining on him swiftly. He glanced at the speedometer. The car's speed was fixed at 62. Mann felt himself crushed in a vise of panic. He stared ahead with haunted eyes.

Then he saw it, several hundred yards ahead: an escape route for trucks with burned-out brakes. There was no alternative now. Either he took the turnout or his car would be rammed from behind. The truck was frighteningly close. He heard the high-pitched wailing of its motor. Unconsciously, he started easing to the right, then jerked the wheel back suddenly. He mustn't give the move away! He had to wait until the last possible moment. Otherwise, Keller would follow him in.

Just before he reached the escape route, Mann wrenched the steering wheel around. The car rear started breaking to the left, tires shrieking on the pavement. Mann steered with the skid, braking just enough to keep from losing all control. The rear tires grabbed and, at 60 miles an hour, the car shot up the dirt trail, tires slinging up a cloud of dust. Mann began to hit the brakes. The rear wheels sideslipped and the car slammed hard against the dirt bank to the right. Mann gasped as the car bounced off and started to fishtail with violent whipping motions, angling toward the trail edge. He drove his foot down on the brake pedal with all his might. The car rear skidded to the right and slammed against the bank again. Mann heard a grinding rend of metal and felt himself heaved downward suddenly, his neck snapped, as the car plowed to a violent halt.

As in a dream, Mann turned to see the truck and trailer swerving off the highway. Paralyzed, he watched the massive vehicle hurtle toward him, staring at it with a blank detachment, knowing he was going to die but so stupefied by the sight of the looming truck that he couldn't react. The gargantuan shape roared closer, blotting out the sky. Mann felt a strange sensation in his throat, unaware that he was screaming.

Suddenly, the truck began to tilt. Mann stared at it in choked-off silence as it started tipping over like some ponderous beast toppling in slow motion. Before it reached his car, it vanished from his rear window.

Hands palsied, Mann undid the safety belt and opened the door. Struggling from the car, he stumbled to the trail edge, staring downward. He was just in time to see the truck capsize like a foundering ship. The tanker followed, huge wheels spinning as it overturned.

The storage tank on the truck exploded first, the violence of its detonation causing Mann to stagger back and sit down clumsily on the dirt. A second explosion roared below, its shock wave buffeting across him hotly, making his cars hurt. His glazed eyes saw a fiery column shoot up toward the sky in front of him, then another.

Mann crawled slowly to the trail edge and peered down at the canyon. Enormous gouts of flame were towering upward, topped by thick, black, oily smoke. He couldn't see the truck or trailer, only flames. He gaped at them in shock, all feeling drained from him.

Then, unexpectedly, emotion came. Not dread, at first, and not regret; not the nausea that followed soon. It was a primeval tumult in his mind: the cry of some ancestral beast above the body of its vanquished foe.

Edgar Pangborn (1909–1976)

Longtooth

Edgar Pangborn was one of the most admired fantasy and science fiction writers of the 1950s-70s. He wrote two classic novels of the genre, *A Mirror for Observers*, winner of the International Fantasy Award (1954) and *Davy* (1954), and a number of highly regarded short stories, many of them set in the same future world as the latter novel. He also wrote historical fiction. His work is notable for its precise and polished prose style and for his ability to round characters, in a field where either talent is comparatively rare. His few horror stories were mostly cast in the science fiction mode, with the exception of "Longtooth," his masterpiece. A monster story set in the Maine woods, it is an unusual piece of pastoral horror in the tradition of Algernon Blackwood, with perhaps an admixture of Theodore Sturgeon, a writer who admired Pangborn and to whom Pangborn was often compared. The mixture of horror of, and compassion for, the monster together with the suggestion of a scientific rationale places "Longtooth" firmly in the twentieth century horror tradition.

My word is good. How can I prove it? Born in Darkfield, wasn't I? Stayed away thirty more years after college, but when I returned I was still Ben Dane, one of the Darkfield Danes, Judge Marcus Dane's eldest. And they knew my word was good. My wife died and I sickened of all cities; then my bachelor brother Sam died, too, who'd lived all his life here in Darkfield, running his one-man law office over in Lohman—our nearest metropolis, pop. 6437. A fast coronary at fifty; I had loved him. Helen gone, then Sam—I wound up my unimportances and came home, inheriting Sam's housekeeper Adelaide Simmons, her grim stability and celestial cooking. Nostalgia for Maine is a serious matter, late in life: I had to yield. I expected a gradual drift into my childless old age playing correspondence chess, translating a few of the classics. I thought I could take for granted the continued respect of my neighbors. I say my word is good.

I will remember again that middle of March a few years ago, the snow skimming out of an afternoon sky as dirty as the bottom of an old aluminum pot. Harp Ryder's back road had been plowed since the last snowfall; I supposed Bolt-Bucket could make the mile and a half in to his farm and out again before we got caught. Harp had asked me to get him a book if I was making a trip to Boston, any goddamn book that told about Eskimos, and I had one for him, De Poncins's *Kabloona*. I saw the midget devils of white running crazy down a huge slope of wind, and recalled hearing at the Darkfield News Bureau, otherwise Cleve's General Store, somebody mentioning a forecast of the worst blizzard in forty years. Joe Cleve, who won't permit a radio in the store because it pesters his ulcers, inquired of his Grand Inquisitor who dwells ten yards behind your right shoulder: "Why's it always got to be the worst in so-and-so many years, that going to help anybody?" The bureau was still analyzing this difficult inquiry when I left, with my cigarettes and as much as I could remember of Adelaide's grocery list after leaving it on the dining table. It wasn't yet three when I turned in on Harp's back road, and a gust slammed at Bolt-Bucket like death with a shovel.

I tried to win momentum for the rise to the high ground, swerved to avoid an idiot rabbit and hit instead a patch of snow-hidden melt-and-freeze, skidding to a full stop from which nothing would extract me but a tow.

I was fifty-seven that year, my wind bad from too much smoking and my heart (I now know) no stronger than Sam's. I quit cursing—gradually, to avoid sudden actions—and tucked *Kabloona* under my parka. I would walk the remaining mile to Ryder's, stay just to leave the book, say hello, and phone for a tow; then, since Harp never owned a car and never would, I could walk back and meet the truck.

If Leda Ryder knew how to drive, it didn't matter much after she married Harp. They farmed it, back in there, in almost the manner of Harp's ancestors of Jefferson's time. Harp did keep his two hundred laying hens by methods that were considered modern before the poor wretches got condemned to batteries, but his other enterprises came closer to antiquity. In his big kitchen garden he let one small patch of weeds fool themselves for an inch or two, so he'd have it to work at; they survived nowhere else. A few cows, a team, four acres for market crops, and a small dog Droopy, whose grandmother had made it somehow with a dachshund. Droopy's only menace in obese old age was a wheezing bark. The Ryders must have grown nearly all vital necessities except chewing tobacco and once in a while a new dress for Leda. Harp could snub the twentieth century, and I doubt if Leda was consulted about it in spite of his obsessive devotion for her. She was almost thirty years younger, and yes, he should not have married her. Other side up just as scratchy; she should not have married him, but she did.

Harp was a dinosaur perhaps, but I grew up with him, he a year the younger. We swam, fished, helled around together. And when I returned to Darkfield growing old, he was one of the few who acted glad to see me, so far as you can trust what you read in a face like a granite promontory. Maybe twice a week Harp Ryder smiled.

I pushed on up the ridge, and noticed a going-and-coming set of wide tire tracks already blurred with snow. That would be the egg truck I had passed a quarter hour since on the main road. Whenever the west wind at my back lulled, I could swing around and enjoy one of my favorite prospects of birch and hemlock lowland. From Ryder's Ridge there's no sign of Darkfield two miles southwest except one church spire. On clear days you glimpse Bald Mountain and his two big brothers, more than twenty miles west of us.

The snow was thickening. It brought relief and pleasure to see the black shingles of Harp's barn and the roof of his Cape Codder. Foreshortened, so that it looked snug against the barn; actually house and barn were connected by a two-story shed fifteen feet wide and forty feet long—woodshed below, hen loft above. The Ryders' sunrise-facing bedroom window was set only three feet above the eaves of that shed roof. They truly went to bed with the chickens. I shouted, for Harp was about to close the big shed door. He held it for me. I ran, and the storm ran after me. The west wind was bouncing off the barn; eddies howled at us. The temperature had tumbled ten degrees since I left Darkfield. The thermometer by the shed door read fifteen degrees, and I knew I'd been a damn fool. As I helped Harp fight the shed door closed, I thought I heard Leda, crying.

A swift confused impression. The wind was exploring new ranges of passion, the big door squawked, and Harp was asking: "Ca' break down?" I do still think I heard Leda wail. If so, it ended as we got the door latched and Harp drew a newly fitted two-by-four bar across it. I couldn't understand that: the old latch was surely proof against any wind short of a hurricane.

"Bolt-Bucket never breaks down. Ought to get one, Harp—lots of company. All she did was go in the ditch."

"You might see her again come spring." His hens were scratching overhead, not yet scared by the storm. Harp's eyes were small gray glitters of trouble. "Ben, you figure a man's getting old at fifty-six?"

"No." My bones (getting old) ached for the warmth of his kitchen-dining-living-everything room, not for sad philosophy. "Use your phone, okay?"

"If the wires ain't down," he said, not moving, a man beaten on by other storms. "Them loafers didn't cut none of the overhang branches all summer. I told 'em of course, I told 'em how it would be . . . I meant, Ben, old enough to get dumb fancies?" My face may have told him I thought he was brooding about himself with a young wife. He frowned, annoyed that I hadn't taken his meaning. "I meant, *seeing* things. Things that can't be so, but—"

"We can all do some of that at any age, Harp."

That remark was a stupid brushoff, a stone for bread, because I was cold, impatient, wanted in. Harp had always a tense one-way sensitivity. His face chilled. "Well, come in, warm up. Leda ain't feeling too good. Getting a cold or something."

When she came downstairs and made me welcome, her eyes were reddened. I don't think the wind made that noise. Droopy waddled from her basket behind the stove to snuff my feet and give me my usual low passing mark.

Leda never had it easy there, young and passionate with scant mental resources. She was twenty-eight that year, looking tall because she carried her firm body handsomely. Some of the sullenness in her big mouth and lucid gray eyes was sexual challenge, some pure discontent. I liked Leda; her nature was not one for animosity or meanness. Before her marriage the Darkfield News Bureau used to declare with its customary scrupulous fairness that Leda had been covered by every goddamn thing in pants within thirty miles. For once the bureau may have spoken a grain of truth in the malice, for Leda did have the smoldering power that draws men without word or gesture. After her abrupt marriage to Harp—Sam told me all this; I wasn't living in Darkfield then and hadn't met her—the garbage-gossip went hastily underground: enraging Harp Ryder was never healthy.

The phone wires weren't down, yet. While I waited for the garage to answer, Harp said, "Ben, I can't let you walk back in that. Stay over, huh?"

I didn't want to. It meant extra work and inconvenience for Leda, and I was ancient enough to crave my known safe burrow. But I felt Harp wanted me to stay for his own sake. I asked Jim Short at the garage to go ahead with Bolt-Bucket if I wasn't there to meet him. Jim roared: "Know what it's doing right now?"

"Little spit of snow, looks like."

"Jesus!" He covered the mouthpiece imperfectly. I heard his enthusiastic voice ring through cold-iron echoes: "Hey, old Ben's got that thing into the ditch again! Ain't that something . . . ? Listen, Ben, I can't make no promises. Got both tow trucks out already. You better stop over and praise the Lord you got that far."

"Okay," I said. "It wasn't much of a ditch."

Leda fed us coffee. She kept glancing toward the landing at the foot of the stairs where a night-darkness already prevailed. A closed-in stairway slanted down at a never-used front door; beyond that landing was the other ground floor room-parlor, spare, guestroom—where I would sleep. I don't know what Leda expected to encounter in that shadow. Once when a chunk of firewood made an odd noise in the range, her lips clamped shut on a scream.

The coffee warmed me. By that time the weather left no loophole for argument. Not yet 3:30, but west and north were lost in furious black. Through the hissing white flood I could just see the front of the barn forty feet away. "Nobody's going no place into that," Harp said. His little house shuddered, enforcing the words. "Leda, you don't look too brisk. Get you some rest."

"I better see to the spare room for Ben."

Neither spoke with much tenderness, but it glowed openly in him when she turned her back. Then some other need bent his granite face out of its normal seams. His whole gaunt body leaning forward tried to help him talk. "You wouldn't figure me for a man'd go off his rocker?" he asked.

"Of course not. What's biting, Harp?"

"There's something in the woods, got no right to be there." To me that came as a letdown of relief: I would not have to listen to another's marriage problems. "I wish, b'Jesus Christ, it would hit somebody else once, so I could say what I know and not be laughed at all to hell. I *ain't* one for dumb fancies."

You walked on eggs, with Harp. He might decide any minute that *I* was laughing. "Tell me," I said. "If anything's out there now, it must feel a mite chilly."

"Ayah." He went to the north window, looking out where we knew the road lay under white confusion. Harp's land sloped down the other side of the road to the edge of mighty evergreen forest. Katahdin stands more than fifty miles north and a little east of us. We live in a withering shrink-world, but you could still set out from Harp's farm and, except for the occasional country road and the rivers—not many large ones—you could stay in deep forest all the way to the tundra, or Alaska. Harp said, "This kind of weather is when it comes."

He sank into his beat-up kitchen armchair and reached for *Kabloona*. He had barely glanced at the book while Leda was with us. "Funny name."

"Kabloona's an Eskimo word for white man."

"He done these pictures . . . ? Be they good, Ben?"

"I like 'em. Photographs in the back."

"Oh." He turned the pages hastily for those, but studied only the ones that showed the strong Eskimo faces, and his interest faded. Whatever he wanted was not here. "These people, be they—civilized?"

"In their own way, sure."

"Ayah, this guy looks like he could find his way in the woods."

"Likely the one thing he couldn't do, Harp. They never see a tree unless they come south, and they hate to do that. Anything below the Arctic is too warm."

"That a fact . . . ? Well, it's a nice book. How much was it?" I'd found it secondhand; he paid me to the exact penny. "I'll be glad to read it." He never would. It would end up on the shelf in the parlor with the Bible, an old almanac, a Longfellow, until someday this place went up for auction and nobody remembered Harp's way of living.

"What's this all about, Harp?"

"Oh . . . I was hearing things in the woods, back last summer. I'd think, fox, then I'd know it wasn't. Make your hair stand right on end. Lost a cow, last August, from the north pasture acrosst the rud. Section of board fence tore out. I mean, Ben, the two top boards was *pulled out from the nail holes*. No hammer marks."

"Bear?"

"Only track I found looked like bear except too small. You know a bear wouldn't *pull* it out, Ben."

"Cow slamming into it, panicked by something?"

He remained patient with me. "Ben, would I build a cow-pasture fence nailing the crosspieces from the outside? Cow hit it with all her weight she might bust it, sure. And kill herself doing it, be blood and hair all over the split boards, and she'd be there, not a mile and a half away into the woods. Happened during a big thunderstorm. I figured it had to be somebody with a spite ag'inst me, maybe some son of a bitch wanting the prop'ty, trying to scare me off that's lived here all my life and my family before me. But that don't make sense. I found the cow a week later, what was left. Way into the woods. The head and the bones. Hide tore up and flang around. Any *person* dressing off a beef, he'll cut whatever he wants and take off with it. He don't sit down and chaw the meat off the *bones*, b'Jesus Christ. He don't tear the thighbone out of the joint. . . . All right, maybe bear. But no bear did that job on that fence and then driv old Nell a mile and a half into the woods to kill her. Nice little Jersey, clever's a kitten. Leda used to make over her, like she don't usually do with the stock. . . . I've looked plenty in the woods since then, never turned up anything. Once and again I did smell something. Fishy, like bear-smell but—*different.*"

"But Harp, with snow on the ground—"

"Now you'll really call me crazy. When the weather is clear, I ain't once found his prints. I hear him then, at night, but I go out by daylight where I think the sound was, there's no trail. Just the usual snow tracks. I know. He lives in the trees and don't come down except when it's storming, I got to believe that? Because then he does come, Ben, when the weather's like now, like right now. And old Ned and Jerry out in the stable go wild, and sometimes we hear his noise under the window. I shine my flashlight through the glass—never catch sight of him. I go out with the ten gauge if there's any light to see by, and there's prints around the house—holes filling up with snow. By morning there'll be maybe some marks left, and they'll lead off to the north woods, but under the trees you won't find it. So he gets up in the branches and travels thataway? . . . Just once I have seen him, Ben. Last October. I better tell you one other thing first. A day or so after I found what was left of old Nell, I lost six roaster chickens. I made over a couple box stalls, maybe you remember, so the birds could be out on range and roost in the barn at night. Good doors, and I always locked 'em. Two in the morning, Ned and Jerry go crazy. I got out through the barn into the stable, and they was spooked, Ned trying to kick his way out. I got 'em quiet, looked all over the stable—loft, harness room, everywhere. Not a thing. Dead quiet night, no moon. It had to be something the horses smelled. I come back into the barn, and found one of the chicken-pen doors open—*tore* out from the lock. Chicken thief would bring along something to pry with—wouldn't he be a Christly idjut if he didn't . . . ? Took six birds, six nice eight-pound roasters, and left the heads on the floor—bitten off."

"Harp—some lunatic. People *can* go insane that way. There are old stories—"

"Been trying to believe that. Would a man live the winter out there? Twenty below zero?"

"Maybe a cave—animal skins."

"I've boarded up the whole back of the barn. Done the same with the hen-loft windows—two-by-fours with four-inch spikes driv slantwise. They be twelve feet off the ground, and he ain't come for 'em, not yet. . . . So after that happened I sent for Sheriff Robart. Son of a bitch happens to live in Darkfield, you'd think he might've took an interest."

"Do any good?"

Harp laughed. He did that by holding my stare, making no sound, moving no muscle except a disturbance at the eye corners. A New England art; maybe it came over on the

Mayflower. "Robart he come by, after a while. I showed him that door. I showed him them chicken heads. Told him how I'd been spending my nights out there on my ass, with the ten gauge." Harp rose to unload tobacco juice into the range fire; he has a theory it purifies the air. "Ben, I might've showed him them chicken heads a shade close to his nose. By the time he got here, see, they wasn't all that fresh. He made out he'd look around and let me know. Mid-September. Ain't seen him since."

"Might've figured he wouldn't be welcome?"

"Why, he'd be welcome as shit on a tablecloth."

"You spoke of—seeing it, Harp?"

"Could call it seeing . . . All right. It was during them Indian summer days—remember? Like June except them pretty colors, smell of windfalls—God, I like that, I like October. I'd gone down to the slope acrosst the rud where I mended my fence after losing old Nell. Just leaning there, guess I was tired. Late afternoon, sky pinking up. You know how the fence cuts acrosst the slope to my east wood lot. I've let the bushes grow free—lot of elder, other stuff the birds come for. I was looking down toward that little break between the north woods and my wood lot, where a bit of old growed-up pasture shows through. Pretty spot. Painter fella come by a few years ago and done a picture of it, said the place looked like a coro, dunno what the hell that is, he didn't say."

I pushed at his brown study. "You saw it there?"

"No. Off to my right in them elder bushes. Fifty feet from me, I guess. By God, I didn't turn my head. I got it with the tail of my eye and turned the other way as if I meant to walk back to the rud. Made like busy with something in the grass, come wandering back to the fence some nearer. He stayed for me, a brownish patch in them bushes by the big yellow birch. Near the height of a man. No gun with me, not even a stick . . . Big shoulders, couldn't see his goddamn feet. He don't stand more'n five feet tall. His hands, if he's got real ones, hung out of my sight in a tangle of elder bushes. He's got brown fur, Ben, reddy-brown fur all over him. His face, too, his head, his big thick neck. There's a shine to fur in sunlight, you can't be mistook. So—I did look at him direct. Tried to act like I still didn't see him, but he knowed. He melted back and got the birch between him and me. Not a sound." And then Harp was listening for Leda upstairs. He went on softly: "Ayah, I ran back for a gun, and searched the woods, for all the good it did me. You'll want to know about his face. I ain't told Leda all this part. See, she's scared, I don't want to make it no worse, I just said it was some animal that snuck off before I could see it good. A big face, Ben. Head real human except it sticks out too much around the jaw. Not much nose—open spots in the fur. Ben, the—the *teeth!* I seen his mouth drop open and he pulled up one side of his lip to show me them stabbing things. I've seen as big as that on a full-growed bear. That's what I'll hear, I ever try to tell this. They'll say I seen a bear. Now, I shot my first bear when I was sixteen and Pa took me over toward Jackman. I've got me one maybe every other year since then. I know 'em, all their ways. But that's what I'll hear if I tell the story."

I am a frustrated naturalist, loaded with assorted facts. I know there aren't any monkeys or apes that could stand our winters except maybe the harmless Himalayan langur. No such beast as Harp described lived anywhere on the planet. It didn't help. Harp was honest; he was rational; he wanted a reasonable explanation as much as I did. Harp wasn't the village atheist for nothing. I said, "I guess you will, Harp. People mostly won't take the—unusual."

"Maybe you'll hear him tonight, Ben."

Leda came downstairs, and heard part of that. "He's been telling you, Ben. What do you think?"

"I don't know what to think."

"Led', I thought, if I imitate that noise for him—"

"No!" She had brought some mending and was about to sit down with it, but froze as if threatened by attack. "I couldn't stand it, Harp. And—it might bring them."

"Them?" Harp chuckled uneasily. "I don't guess I could do it that good he'd come for it."

"Don't *do* it, Harp!"

"All right, hon." Her eyes were closed, her head drooping back. "Don't git nerved up so."

I started wondering whether a man still seeming sane could dream up such a horror for the unconscious purpose of tormenting a woman too young for him, a woman he could never imagine he owned. If he told her a fox bark wasn't right for a fox, she'd believe him. I said. "We shouldn't talk about it if it upsets her."

He glanced at me like a man floating up from underwater. Leda said in a small, aching voice: "I wish to *God* we could move to Boston."

The granite face closed in defensiveness. "Led', we been over all that. Nothing is going to drive me off of my land. I got no time for the city at my age. What the Jesus would I do? Night watchman? Sweep out somebody's back room, b'Jesus Christ? Savings'd be gone in no time. We been all over it. We ain't moving nowhere."

"I could find work." For Harp, of course, that was the worst thing she could have said. She probably knew it from his stricken silence. She said clumsily, "I forgot something upstairs." She snatched up her mending and she was gone.

We talked no more of it the rest of the day. I followed through the milking and other chores, lending a hand where I could, and we made everything as secure as we could against storm and other enemies. The long-toothed furry thing was the spectral guest at dinner, but we cut him, on Leda's account, or so we pretended. Supper would have been awkward anyway. They weren't in the habit of putting up guests, and Leda was a rather deadly cook because she cared nothing about it. A Darkfield girl, I suppose she had the usual twentieth-century mishmash of television dreams until some impulse or maybe false signs of pregnancy tricked her into marrying a man out of the nineteenth. We had venison treated like beef and overdone vegetables. I don't like venison even when it's treated right.

At six Harp turned on his battery radio and sat stone-faced through the day's bad news and the weather forecast—"a blizzard which may prove the worst in forty-two years. Since three PM, eighteen inches have fallen at Bangor, twenty-one at Boston. Precipitation is not expected to end until tomorrow. Winds will increase during the night with gusts up to seventy miles per hour." Harp shut it off, with finality. On other evenings I had spent there he let Leda play it after supper only kind of soft, so there had been a continuous muted bleat and blatter all evening. Tonight Harp meant to listen for other sounds. Leda washed the dishes, said an early good night, and fled upstairs.

Harp didn't talk, except as politeness obliged him to answer some blah of mine. We sat and listened to the snow and the lunatic wind. An hour of it was enough for me; I said I was beat and wanted to turn in early. Harp saw me to my bed in the parlor and placed a new chunk of rock maple in the pot-bellied stove. He produced a difficult granite smile, maybe using up his allowance for the week, and pulled out a bottle from a cabinet that had stood for many years below a parlor print—George Washington, I think, concluding a treaty with some offbeat sufferer from hepatitis who may have been General Cornwallis if the latter had two left feet. The bottle contained a brand of rye that Harp sincerely believed to be drinkable, having charred his gullet forty-odd years trying to prove it. While my throat healed, Harp said, "Shouldn't've bothered you with all this crap, Ben.

Hope it ain't going to spoil your sleep." He got me his spare flashlight, then let me be, and closed the door.

I heard him drop back into his kitchen armchair. Under too many covers, lamp out, I heard the cruel whisper of the snow. The stove muttered, a friend, making me a cocoon of living heat in a waste of outer cold. Later I heard Leda at the head of the stairs, her voice timid, tired, and sweet with invitation: "You comin' up to bed, Harp?" The stairs creaked under him. Their door closed; presently she cried out in that desired pain that is brief release from trouble.

I remembered something Adelaide Simmons had told me about this house, where I had not gone upstairs since Harp and I were boys. Adelaide, one of the very few women in Darkfield who never spoke unkindly of Leda, said that the tiny west room across from Harp and Leda's bedroom was fixed up for a nursery, and Harp wouldn't allow anything in there but baby furniture. Had been so since they were married seven years before.

Another hour dragged on, in my exasperations of sleeplessness.

Then I heard Longtooth.

The noise came from the west side, beyond the snow-hidden vegetable garden. When it snatched me from the edge of sleep, I tried to think it was a fox barking, the ringing, metallic shriek the little red beast can belch dragonlike from his throat. But wide awake, I knew it had been much deeper, chestier. Horned owl?—no. A sound that belonged to ancient times when men relied on chipped stone weapons and had full reason to fear the dark.

The cracks in the stove gave me firelight for groping back into my clothes. The wind had not calmed at all. I stumbled to the west window, buttoning up, and found it a white blank. Snow had drifted above the lower sash. On tiptoe I could just see over it. A light appeared, dimly illuminating the snowfield beyond. That would be coming from a lamp in the Ryders' bedroom, shining through the nursery room and so out, weak and diffused, into the blizzard chaos.

Yaaarrhh!

Now it had drawn horribly near. From the north windows of the parlor I saw black nothing. Harp squeaked down to my door.

"'Wake, Ben?"

"Yes. Come look at the west window."

He had left no night-light burning in the kitchen, and only a scant glow came down to the landing from the bedroom. He murmured behind me, "Ayah, snow's up some. Must be over three foot on the level by now."

Yaaarrhh!

The voice had shouted on the south side, the blinder side of the house, overlooked only by one kitchen window and a small one in the pantry where the hand pump stood. The view from the pantry window was mostly blocked by a great maple that overtopped the house. I heard the wind shrilling across the tree's winter bones.

"Ben, you want to git your boots on? Up to you—can't ask it. I might have to go out." Harp spoke in an undertone as if the beast might understand him through the tight walls.

"Of course." I got into my knee boots and caught up my parka as I followed him into the kitchen. A .30-caliber rifle and his heavy shotgun hung on deerhorn over the door to the woodshed. He found them in the dark.

What courage I possessed that night came from being shamed into action, from fearing to show a poor face to an old friend in trouble. I went through the Normandy invasion. I have camped out alone, when I was younger and healthier, and slept nicely. But that noise of Longtooth stole courage. It ached along the channel of the spine.

I had the spare flashlight, but knew Harp didn't want me to use it here. I could make out the furniture, and Harp reaching for the gun rack. He already had on his boots, fur cap, and mackinaw. "You take this'n," he said, and put the ten gauge in my hands. "Both barrels loaded. Ain't my way to do that, ain't right, but since this thing started—"

Yaaarrhh!

"Where's he got to now?" Harp was by the south window. "Round this side?"

"I thought so. . . . Where's Droopy?"

Harp chuckled thinly. "Poor little shit! She come upstairs at the first sound of him and went under the bed. I told Led' to stay upstairs. She'd want a light down here. Wouldn't make sense."

Then, apparently from the east side of the hen loft and high, booming off some resonating surface: *Yaaarrhh!*

"He can't! Jesus, that's twelve foot off the ground!" But Harp plunged out into the shed, and I followed. "Keep your light on the floor, Ben." He ran up the narrow stairway. "Don't shine it on the birds, they'll act up."

So far the chickens, stupid and virtually blind in the dark, were making only a peevish tut-tutting of alarm. But something was clinging to the outside of the barricaded east window, snarling, chattering teeth, pounding on the two-by-fours. With a fist?—it sounded like nothing else. Harp snapped, "Get your light on the window!" And he fired through the glass.

We heard no outcry. Any noise outside was covered by the storm and the squawks of the hens scandalized by the shot. The glass was dirty from their continual disturbance of the litter; I couldn't see through it. The bullet had drilled the pane without shattering it, and passed between the two-by-fours, but the beast could have dropped before he fired. "I got to go out there. You stay, Ben." Back in the kitchen he exchanged rifle for shotgun. "Might not have no chance to aim. You remember this piece, don't y'?—eight in the clip."

"I remember it."

"Good. Keep your ears open." Harp ran out through the door that gave on a small paved area by the woodshed. To get around under the east loft window he would have to push through the snow behind the barn, since he had blocked all the rear openings. He could have circled the house instead, but only by bucking the west wind and fighting deeper drifts. I saw his big shadow melt out of sight.

Leda's voice quavered down to me: "He—get it?"

"Don't know. He's gone to see. Sit tight. . . ."

I heard that infernal bark once again before Harp returned, and again it sounded high off the ground; it must have come from the big maple. And then moments later—I was still trying to pierce the dark, watching for Harp—a vast smash of broken glass and wood, and the violent bang of the door upstairs. One small wheezing shriek cut short, and one scream such as no human being should ever hear. I can still hear it.

I think I lost some seconds in shock. Then I was groping up the narrow stairway, clumsy with the rifle and flashlight. Wind roared at the opening of the kitchen door, and Harp was crowding past me, thrusting me aside. But I was close behind him when he flung the bedroom door open. The blast from the broken window that had slammed the door had also blown out the lamp. But our flashlights said at once that Leda was not there. Nothing was, nothing living.

Droopy lay in a mess of glass splinters and broken window sash, dead from a crushed neck—something had stamped on her. The bedspread had been pulled almost to the window—maybe Leda's hand had clenched on it. I saw blood on some of the glass fragments, and on the splintered sash, a patch of reddish fur.

Harp ran back downstairs. I lingered a few seconds. The arrow of fear was deep in me, but at the moment it made me numb. My light touched up an ugly photograph on the wall, Harp's mother at fifty or so, petrified and acid-faced before the camera, a puritan deity with shallow, haunted eyes. I remembered her.

Harp had kicked over the traces when his father died, and quit going to church. Mrs. Ryder "disowned" him. The farm was his; she left him with it and went to live with a widowed sister in Lohman, and died soon, unreconciled. Harp lived on as a bachelor, crank, recluse, until his strange marriage in his fifties. Now here was Ma still watchful, pucker-faced, unforgiving. In my dullness of shock I thought: Oh, they probably always made love with the lights out.

But now Leda wasn't there.

I hurried after Harp, who had left the kitchen door to bang in the wind. I got out there with rifle and flashlight, and over across the road I saw his torch. No other light, just his small gleam and mine.

I knew as soon as I had forced myself beyond the corner of the house and into the fantastic embrace of the storm that I could never make it. The west wind ground needles into my face. The snow was up beyond the middle of my thighs. With weak lungs and maybe an imperfect heart I could do nothing out here except die quickly to no purpose. In a moment Harp would be starting down the slope of the woods. His trail was already disappearing under my beam. I drove myself a little farther, and an instant's lull in the storm allowed me to shout: "Harp! I can't follow!"

He heard. He cupped his mouth and yelled back: "Don't try! Git back to the house! Telephone!" I waved to acknowledge the message and struggled back.

I only just made it. Inside the kitchen doorway I fell flat, gun and flashlight clattering off somewhere, and there I stayed until I won back enough breath to keep myself living. My face and hands were ice blocks, then fires. While I worked at the task of getting air into my body, one thought continued, an inner necessity: *There must be a rational cause. I do not abandon the rational cause.* At length I hauled myself up and stumbled to the telephone. The line was dead.

I found the flashlight and reeled upstairs with it. I stepped past poor Droopy's body and over the broken glass to look through the window space. I could see that snow had been pushed off the shed roof near the bedroom window; the house sheltered that area from the full drive of the west wind, so some evidence remained. I guessed that whatever came must have jumped to the house roof from the maple, then down to the shed roof and then hurled itself through the closed window without regard for it as an obstacle. Losing a little blood and a little fur.

I glanced around and could not find that fur now. Wind must have pushed it out of sight. I forced the door shut. Downstairs, I lit the table lamps in kitchen and parlor. Harp might need those beacons—if he came back. I refreshed the fires, and gave myself a dose of Harp's horrible whiskey. It was nearly one in the morning. If he never came back?

It might be days before they could plow out the road. When the storm let up I could use Harp's snowshoes, maybe . . .

Harp came back at 1:20, bent and staggering. He let me support him to the armchair. When he could speak he said, "No trail. No trail." He took the bottle from my hands and pulled on it. "Christ Jesus! What can I do? Ben . . . ? I got to go to the village, get help. If they got any help to give."

"Do you have an extra pair of snowshoes?"

He stared toward me, battling confusion. "Hah? No, I ain't. Better you stay anyhow.

I'll bring yours from your house if you want, if I can git there." He drank again and slammed in the cork with the heel of his hand. "I'll leave you the ten gauge."

He got his snowshoes from a closet. I persuaded him to wait for coffee. Haste could accomplish nothing now; we could not say to each other that we knew Leda was dead. When he was ready to go, I stepped outside with him into the mad wind. "Anything you want me to do before you get back?" He tried to think about it.

"I guess not, Ben . . . God, ain't I *lived* right? No, that don't make sense? God? That's a laugh." He swung away. Two or three great strides and the storm took him.

That was about two o'clock. For four hours I was alone in the house. Warmth returned, with the bedroom door closed and fires working hard. I carried the kitchen lamp into the parlor, and then huddled in the nearly total dark of the kitchen with my back to the wall, watching all the windows, the ten gauge near my hand, but I did not expect a return of the beast, and there was none.

The night grew quieter, perhaps because the house was so drifted in that snow muted the sounds. I was cut off from the battle, buried alive.

Harp would get back. The seasons would follow their natural way, and somehow we would learn what had happened to Leda. I supposed the beast would have to be something in the human pattern—mad, deformed, gone wild, but still human.

After a time I wondered why we had heard no excitement in the stable. I forced myself to take up gun and flashlight and go look. I groped through the woodshed, big with the jumping shadows of Harp's cordwood, and into the barn. The cows were peacefully drowsing. In the center alley I dared to send my weak beam swooping and glimmering through the ghastly distances of the hayloft. Quiet, just quiet; natural rustling of mice. Then to the stable, where Ned whickered and let me rub his brown cheek, and Jerry rolled a humorous eye. I suppose no smell had reached them to touch off panic, and perhaps they had heard the barking often enough so that it no longer disturbed them. I went back to my post, and the hours crawled along a ridge between the pits of terror and exhaustion. Maybe I slept.

No color of sunrise that day, but I felt paleness and change; even a blizzard will not hide the fact of dayshine somewhere. I breakfasted on bacon and eggs, fed the hens, forked down hay, and carried water for the cows and horses. The one cow in milk, a jumpy Ayrshire, refused to concede that I meant to be useful. I'd done no milking since I was a boy, the knack was gone from my hands, and relief seemed less important to her than kicking over the pail; she was getting more amusement than discomfort out of it, so for the moment I let it go. I made myself busy work shoveling a clear space by the kitchen door. The wind was down, the snowfall persistent but almost peaceful. I pushed out beyond the house and learned that the stuff was up over my hips.

Out of that, as I turned back, came Harp in his long, snowshoe stride, and down the road three others. I recognized Sheriff Robart, overfed but powerful; and Bill Hastings, wry and ageless, a cousin of Harp's and one of his few friends; and last, Curt Davidson, perhaps a friend to Sheriff Robart but certainly not to Harp.

I'd known Curt as a thickwitted loudmouth when he was a kid; growing to man's years hadn't done much for him. And when I saw him I thought, irrationally perhaps: Not good for our side. A kind of absurdity, and yet Harp and I were joined against the world simply because we had experienced together what others were going to call impossible, were going to interpret in harsh, even damnable ways; and no help for it.

I saw the white thin blur of the sun, the strength of it growing. Nowhere in all the white expanse had the wind and the new snow allowed us any mark of the visitation of the night.

The men reached my cleared space and shook off snow. I opened the woodshed. Harp gave me one hopeless glance of inquiry and I shook my head.

"Having a little trouble?" That was Robart, taking off his snowshoes.

Harp ignored him. "I got to look after my chores." I told him I'd done it except for that damn cow. "Oh, Bess, ayah, she's nervy. I'll see to her." He gave me my snowshoes that he had strapped to his back. "Adelaide, she wanted to know about your groceries. Said I figured they was in the ca'."

"Good as an icebox," says Robart, real friendly.

Curt had to have his pleasures too. "Ben, you sure you got hold of old Bess by the right end, where the tits was?" Curt giggles at his own jokes, so nobody else is obliged to. Bill Hastings spat in the snow.

"Okay if I go in?" Robart asked. It wasn't a simple inquiry: He was present officially and meant to have it known. Harp looked him up and down.

"Nobody stopping you. Didn't bring you here to stand around, I suppose."

"Harp," said Robart pleasantly enough, "don't give me a hard time. You come tell me certain things has happened, I got to look into it is all." But Harp was already striding down the woodshed to the barn entrance. The others came into the house with me, and I put on water for fresh coffee. "Must be your ca' down the rud a piece, Ben? Heard you kind of went into a ditch. All's you can see now is a hump in the snow. Deep freeze might be good for her, likely you've tried everything else." But I wasn't feeling comic, and never had been on those terms with Robart. I grunted, and his face shed mirth as one slips off a sweater. "Okay, what's the score? Harp's gone and told me a story I couldn't feed to the dogs, so what about it? Where's Mrs. Ryder?"

Davidson giggled again. It's a nasty little sound to come out of all that beef. I don't think Robart had much enthusiasm for him either, but it seems he had sworn in the fellow as a deputy before they set out. "Yes, sir," said Curt, "that was *really* a story, that was."

"Where's Mrs. Ryder?"

"Not here," I told him. "We think she's dead."

He glowered, rubbing cold out of his hands. "Seen that window. Looks like the frame is smashed."

"Yes, from the outside. When Harp gets back you'd better look. I closed the door on that room and haven't opened it. There'll be more snow, but you'll see about what we saw when we got up there."

"Let's look right now," said Curt.

Bill Hastings said, "Curt, ain't you a mite busy for a dep'ty? Mr. Dane said when Harp gets back." Bill and I are friends; normally he wouldn't mister me. I think he was trying to give me some flavor of authority.

I acknowledged the alliance by asking: "You a deputy too, Bill?" Giving him an opportunity to spit in the stove, replace the lid gently, and reply: "Shit no."

Harp returned and carried the milk pail to the pantry. Then he was looking us over. "Bill, I got to try the woods again. You want to come along?"

"Sure, Harp. I didn't bring no gun."

"Take my ten gauge."

"Curt here'll go along," said Robart. "Real good man on snowshoes. Interested in wild life."

Harp said, "That's funny, Robart. I guess that's the funniest thing I heard since Cutler's little girl fell under the tractor. You joining us too?"

"Fact is, Harp, I kind of pulled a muscle in my back coming up here. Not getting no younger neither. I believe I'll just look around here a little. Trust you got no objection? To me looking around a little?"

"Coffee's dripped," I said.

"Thing of it is, if I'd've thought you had any objection, I'd've been obliged to get me a warrant."

"Thanks, Ben." Harp gulped the coffee scalding. "Why, if looking around the house is the best you can do, Sher'f, I got no objection. Ben, I shouldn't be keeping you away from your affairs, but would you stay? Kind of keep him company? Not that I got much in the house, but still—you know—"

"I'll stay." I wished I could tell him to drop that manner; it only got him deeper in the mud.

Robart handed Davidson his gun belt and holster. "Better have it, Curt, so to be in style."

Harp and Bill were outside getting on their snowshoes; I half heard some remark of Harp's about the sheriff's aching back. They took off. The snow had almost ceased. They passed out of sight down the slope to the north, and Curt went plowing after them. Behind me Robart said, "You'd think Harp believed it himself."

"That's how it's to be? You make us both liars before you've even done any looking?"

"I got to try to make sense of it is all." I followed him up to the bedroom. It was cruelly cold. He touched Droopy's stiff corpse with his foot. "Hard to figure a man killing his own dog."

"We get nowhere with that kind of idea."

"Ben, you got to see this thing like it looks to other people. And keep out of my hair."

"That's what scares me, Jack. Something unreasonable did happen, and Harp and I were the only ones to experience it—except Mrs. Ryder."

"You claim you saw this—animal?"

"I didn't say that. I heard her scream. When we got upstairs this room was the way you see it." I looked around, and again couldn't find that scrap of fur, but I spoke of it, and I give Robart credit for searching. He shook out the bedspread and blankets, examined the floor and the closet. He studied the window space, leaned out for a look at the house wall and the shed roof. His big feet avoided the broken glass, and he squatted for a long gaze at the pieces of window sash. Then he bore down on me, all policeman personified, a massive, rather intelligent, conventionally honest man with no patience for imagination, no time for any fact not already in the books. "Piece of fur, huh?" He made it sound as if I'd described a Jabberwock with eyes of flame. "Okay, we're done up here." He motioned me downstairs—all policemen who'd ever faced a crowd's dangerous stupidity with their own.

As I retreated I said, "Hope you won't be too busy to have a chemist test the blood on that sash."

"We'll do that." He made move-along motions with his slab hands. "Going to be a pleasure to do that little thing for you and your friend."

Then he searched the entire house, shed, barn, and stable. I had never before watched anyone on police business; I had to admire his zeal. I got involved in the farce of holding the flashlight for him while he rooted in the cellar. In the shed I suggested that if he wanted to restack twenty-odd cords of wood he'd better wait till Harp could help him; he wasn't amused. He wasn't happy in the barn loft either. Shifting tons of hay to find a hypothetical corpse was not a one-man job. I knew he was capable of returning with a crew and machinery to do exactly that. And by his lights it was what he ought to do. Then we were back in the kitchen, Robart giving himself a manicure with his jackknife, and I down to my last cigarette, almost the last of my endurance.

Robart was not unsubtle. I answered his questions as temperately as I could—even, for instance: "Wasn't you a mite sweet on Leda yourself?" I didn't answer any of them with flat silence; to do that right you need an accompanying act like spitting in the stove, and I'm not a chewer. From the north window he said: "Comin' back. It figures." They had been out a little over an hour.

Harp stood by the stove with me to warm his hands. He spoke as if alone with me: "No trail, Ben." What followed came in an undertone: "Ben, you told me about a friend of yours, scientist or something, professor—"

"Professor Malcolm?" I remembered mentioning him to Harp a long while before; I was astonished at his recalling it. Johnny Malcolm is a professor of biology who has avoided too much specialization. Not a really close friend. Harp was watching me out of a granite despair as if he had asked me to appeal to some higher court. I thought of another acquaintance in Boston, too, whom I might consult—Dr. Kahn, a psychiatrist who had once seen my wife, Helen, through a difficult time. . . .

"Harp," said Robart, "I got to ask you a couple, three things. I sent word to Dick Hammond to get that goddamned plow of his into this road as quick as he can. Believe he'll try. Whiles we wait on him, we might's well talk. You know I don't like to get tough."

"Talk away," said Harp, "only Ben here he's got to get home without waiting on no Dick Hammond."

"That a fact, Ben?"

"Yes. I'll keep in touch."

"Do that," said Robart, dismissing me. As I left he was beginning a fresh manicure, and Harp waited rigidly for the ordeal to continue. I felt morbidly that I was abandoning him.

Still—corpus delicti—nothing much more would happen until Leda Ryder was found. Then if her body were found dead by violence, with no acceptable evidence of Longtooth's existence—well, what then?

I don't think Robart would have let me go if he'd known my first act would be to call Short's brother Mike and ask him to drive me into Lohman, where I could get a bus for Boston.

Johnny Malcolm said, "I can see this is distressing you, and you wouldn't lie to me. But, Ben, as biology it won't do. Ain't no such animile. You know that."

He wasn't being stuffy. We were having dinner at a quiet restaurant, and I had, of course, enjoyed the roast duckling too much. Johnny is a rock-ribbed beanpole who can eat like a walking famine with no regrets. "Suppose," I said, "just for argument and because it's not biologically inconceivable, that there's a basis for the yeti legend."

"Not inconceivable. I'll give you that. So long as any poorly known corners of the world are left—the Himalayan uplands, jungles, tropic swamps, the tundra—legends will persist and some of them will have little gleams of truth. You know what I think about moon flights and all that?" He smiled; privately I was hearing Leda scream. "One of our strongest reasons for them, and for the biggest flights we'll make if we don't kill civilization first, is a hunt for new legends. We've used up our best ones, and that's dangerous."

"Why don't we look at the countries inside us?" But Johnny wasn't listening much.

"Men can't stand it not to have closed doors and a chance to push at them. Oh, about your yeti—he might exist. Shaggy anthropoid able to endure severe cold, so rare and clever the explorers haven't tripped over him yet. Wouldn't have to be a carnivore to have big ugly canines—look at the baboons. But if he was active in a Himalayan winter, he'd have to be able to use meat, I think. Mind you, I don't believe any of this, but you can have it as a biological not-impossible. How'd he get to Maine?"

"Strayed? Tibet—Mongolia—Arctic ice."

"Maybe." Johnny had begun to enjoy the hypothesis as something to play with during dinner. Soon he was helping along the brute's passage across the continents, and having fun till I grumbled something about alternatives, extraterrestrials. He wouldn't buy that, and got cross. Still hearing Leda scream, I assured him I wasn't watching for little green men.

"Ben, how much do you know about this—Harp?"

"We grew up along different lines, but he's a friend. Dinosaur, if you like, but a friend."

"Hardshell Maine bachelor picks up dizzy young wife—"

"She's not dizzy. Wasn't. Sexy, but not dizzy."

"All right. Bachelor stewing in his own juices for years. Sure he didn't get up on that roof himself?"

"Nuts. Unless all my senses were more paralyzed than I think, there wasn't time."

"Unless they were more paralyzed than you think."

"Come off it! I'm not senile yet. . . . What's he supposed to have done with her? Tossed her into the snow?"

"Mph," said Johnny, and finished his coffee. "All right. Some human freak with abnormal strength and the endurance to fossick around in a Maine blizzard stealing women. I liked the yeti better. You say you suggested a madman to Ryder yourself. Pity if you had to come all the way here just so I could repeat your own guesswork. To make amends, want to take in a bawdy movie?"

"Love it."

The following day Dr. Kahn made time to see me at the end of the afternoon, so polite and patient that I felt certain I was keeping him from his dinner. He seemed undecided whether to be concerned with the traumas of Harp Ryder's history or those of mine. Mine were already somewhat known to him. "I wish you had time to talk all this out to me. You've given me a nice summary of what the physical events appear to have been, but—"

"Doctor," I said, "it *happened*. I heard the animal. The window *was* smashed—ask the sheriff. Leda Ryder did scream, and when Harp and I got up there together, the dog had been killed and Leda was gone."

"And yet, if it was all as clear as that, I wonder why you thought of consulting me at all, Ben. I wasn't there. I'm just a headshrinker."

"I wanted . . . Is there any way a delusion could take hold of Harp *and* me, disturb our senses in the same way? Oh, just saying it makes it ridiculous."

Dr. Kahn smiled. "Let's say, difficult."

"Is it possible Harp could have killed her, thrown her out through the window of the *west* bedroom—the snow must have drifted six feet or higher on that side—and then my mind distorted my time sense? So I might've stood there in the dark kitchen all the time it went on, a matter of minutes instead of seconds? Then he jumped down by the shed roof, came back into the house the normal way while I was stumbling upstairs? Oh, hell."

Dr. Kahn had drawn a diagram of the house from my description, and peered at it with placid interest. "Benign" was a word Helen had used for him. He said, "Such a distortion of the time sense would be—unusual. . . . Are you feeling guilty about anything?"

"About standing there and doing nothing? I can't seriously believe it was more than a few seconds. Anyway, that would make Harp a monster out of a detective story. He's not that. How could he count on me to freeze in panic? Absurd. I'd've heard the struggle, steps, the window of the west room going up. Could he have killed her and I known all about it at the time, even witnessed it, and then suffered amnesia for that one event?"

He still looked so patient, I wished I hadn't come. "I won't say any trick of the mind is impossible, but I might call that one highly improbable. Academically, however, considering your emotional involvement—"

"I'm not emotionally involved!" I yelled that. He smiled, looking much more interested. I laughed at myself. That was better than poking him in the eye. "I'm upset, Doctor, because the whole thing goes against reason. If you start out knowing nobody's going to believe you, it's all messed up before you open your mouth."

He nodded kindly. He's a good joe. I think he'd stopped listening for what I didn't say long enough to hear a little of what I did say. "You're not unstable, Ben. Don't worry about amnesia. The explanation, perhaps some human intruder, will turn out to be within the human norm. The norm of possibility does include such things as lycanthropic delusions, maniacal behavior, and so on. Your police up there will carry on a good search for the poor woman. They won't overlook that snowdrift. Don't underestimate them, and don't worry about your own mind, Ben."

"Ever seen our Maine woods?"

"No, I go away to the Cape."

"Try it sometime. Take a patch of it, say about fifty miles by fifty, that's twenty-five hundred square miles. Drop some eager policemen into it, tell 'em to hunt for something they never saw before and don't want to see, that doesn't want to be found."

"But if your beast is human, human beings leave traces. Bodies aren't easy to hide, Ben."

"In those woods? A body taken by a carnivorous animal? Why not?" Well, our minds didn't touch. I thanked him for his patience and got up. "The maniac responsible," I said. "But whatever we call him, Doctor, he was *there.*"

Mike Short picked me up at the Lohman bus station and told me something of a ferment in Darkfield. I shouldn't have been surprised. "They're all scared, Mr. Dane. They want to hurt somebody." Mike is Jim Short's younger brother. He scrapes up a living with his taxi service and occasional odd jobs at the garage. There's a droop in his shaggy ringlets, and I believe thirty is staring him in the face. "Like old Harp, he wants to tell it like it happened and nobody buys. That's sad, man. You been away what, three days? The fuzz was pissed off. You better connect with Mr. Sheriff Robart like soon. He climbed all over my ass just for driving you to the bus that day, like I should've known you shouldn't."

"I'll pacify him. They haven't found Mrs. Ryder?"

Mike spat out the car window, which was rolled down for the mild air. "Old Harp he never got such a job of snow-shoveling done in all his days. By the c'munity, for free. No, they won't find her." In that there was plenty of I-want-to-be-asked, and something more, a hint of the mythology of Mike's generation.

"So what's your opinion, Mike?"

He maneuvered a fresh cigarette against the stub of the last and drove on through tiresome silence. The road was winding between ridged mountains of plowed, rotting snow. I had the window down on my side, too, for the genial afternoon sun, and imagined a tang of spring. At last Mike said, "You prob'ly don't go along . . . Jim got your ca' out, by the way. It's at your place. . . . Well, you'll hear 'em talking it all to pieces. Some claim Harp's telling the truth. Some say he killed her himself. They don't say how he made her disappear. Ain't heard any talk against you, Mr. Dane, nothing that counts. The sheriff's peeved, but that's just on account you took off without asking." His vague, large eyes watched the melting landscape, the ambiguous messages of spring. "Well, I think, like, a demon took her, Mr. Dane. She was one of his own, see? You got to remember, I knew that chick. Okay, you can say it ain't scientific, only there is a science to these things, I read a book about it. You can laugh if you want."

I wasn't laughing. It wasn't my first glimpse of the contemporary medievalism and won't be my last if I survive another year or two. I wasn't laughing, and I said nothing. Mike sat smoking, expertly driving his twentieth-century artifact while I suppose his thoughts were in the seventeenth, sniffing after the wonders of the invisible world, and I recalled what Johnny Malcolm had said about the need for legends. Mike and I had no more talk.

Adelaide Simmons was dourly glad to see me. From her I learned that the sheriff and state police had swarmed all over Harp's place and the surrounding countryside, and were still at it. Result, zero. Harp had repeatedly told our story and was refusing to tell it anymore. "Does the chores and sets there drinking," she said, "or staring off. Was up to see him yesterday, Mr. Dane—felt I should. Couple days they didn't let him alone a minute, maybe now they've eased off some. He asked me real sharp, was you back yet. Well, I redd up his place, made some bread, least I could do."

When I told her I was going there, she prepared a basket while I sat in the kitchen and listened. "Some say she busted that window herself, jumped down, and run off in the snow, out of her mind. Any sense in that?"

"Nope."

"And some claim she deserted him. Earlier. Which'd make you a liar. And they say whichever way it was, Harp's made up this crazy story because he can't stand the truth." Her clever hands slapped sandwiches into shape. "They claim Harp got you to go along with it, they don't say how."

"Hypnotized me, likely. Adelaide, it all happened the way Harp told it. I heard the thing too. If Harp is ready for the squirrels, so am I."

She stared hard, and sighed. She likes to talk, but her mill often shuts off suddenly, because of a quality of hers which I find good as well as rare: I mean that when she has no more to say she doesn't go on talking.

I got up to Ryder's Ridge about suppertime. Bill Hastings was there. The road was plowed slick between the snow ridges, and I wondered how much of the litter of tracks and crumpled paper and spent cigarette packages had been left by sight-seers. Ground frost had not yet yielded to the mud season, which would soon make normal driving impossible for a few weeks. Bill let me in, with the look people wear for serious illness. But Harp heaved himself out of that armchair, not sick in body at least. "Ben, I heard him last night. Late."

"What direction?"

"North."

"You hear it, Bill?" I set down the basket.

My pint-size friend shook his head. "Wasn't here." I couldn't guess how much Bill accepted of the tale.

Harp said, "What's the basket?—oh. Obliged. Adelaide's a nice woman." But his mind was remote. "It was north, Ben, a long way, but I think I know about where it would be. I wouldn't've heard it except the night was so still, like everything had quieted for me. You know, they been adeviling me night and day. Robart, state cops, mess of smart little buggers from the papers. I couldn't sleep, I stepped outside like I was called. Why, he might've been the other side of the stars, the sky so full of 'em and nothing stirring. Cold . . . You went to Boston, Ben?"

"Yes. Waste of time. They want it to be something human—anyhow, something that fits the books."

Whittling, Bill said neutrally, "Always a man for the books yourself, wasn't you, Ben?"

I had to agree. Harp asked, "Hadn't no ideas?"

"Just gave me back my own thoughts in their language. We have to find it, Harp. Of course some wouldn't take it for true even if you had photographs."

Harp said, "Photographs be goddamned."

"I guess you got to go," said Bill Hastings. "We been talking about it, Ben. Maybe I'd feel the same if it was me. . . . I better be on my way or supper'll be cold and the old woman raising hellfire." He tossed his stick back in the woodbox.

"Bill," said Harp, "you won't mind feeding the stock couple, three days?"

"I don't mind. Be up tomorrow."

"Do the same for you sometime. I wouldn't want it mentioned anyplace."

"Harp, you know me better'n that. See you, Ben."

"Snow's going fast," said Harp when Bill had driven off. "Be in the woods a long time yet, though."

"You wouldn't start this late."

He was at the window, his lean bulk shutting off much light from the time-seasoned kitchen where most of his indoor life had been passed. "Morning, early. Tonight I got to listen."

"Be needing sleep, I'd think."

"I don't always get what I need," said Harp.

"I'll bring my snowshoes. About six? And my carbine—I'm best with a gun I know."

He stared at me awhile. "All right, Ben. You understand, though, you might have to come back alone. I ain't coming back till I get him, Ben. Not this time."

At sunup I found him with Ned and Jerry in the stable. He had lived eight or ten years with that team. He gave Ned's neck a final pat as he turned to me and took up our conversation as if night had not intervened. "Not till I get him. Ben, I don't want you drug into this ag'inst your inclination."

"Did you hear it again last night?"

"I heard it. North."

The sun was at the point of rising when we left on our snowshoes, like morning ghosts ourselves. Harp strode ahead down the slope to the woods without haste, perhaps with some reluctance. Near the trees he halted, gazing to his right, where a red blaze was burning the edge of the sky curtain; I scolded myself for thinking that he was saying good-bye to the sun.

The snow was crusted, sometimes slippery even for our web feet. We entered the woods along a tangle of tracks, including the fat tire marks of a snow scooter. "Guy from Lohman," said Harp. "Hired the goddamn thing out to the state cops and hisself with it. Goes pootin' around all over hell, fit to scare everything inside eight, ten miles." He cut himself a fresh plug to last the morning. "I b'lieve the thing is a mite farther off than that. They'll be messing around again today." His fingers dug into my arm. "See how it is, don't y'? They ain't looking for what we are. Looking for a dead body to hang on to my neck. And if they was to find her the way I found—the way I found—"

"Harp, you needn't borrow trouble."

"I know how they think," he said. "Was I to walk down the road beyond Darkfield, they'd pick me up. They ain't got me in shackles because they got no—no body, Ben. Nobody needs to tell me about the law. They got to have a body. Only reason they didn't leave a man here overnight, they figure I can't go nowhere. They think a man couldn't travel in three, four foot of snow. . . . Ben, I mean to find that thing and shoot it down. . . . We better slant off thisaway."

He set out at a wide angle from those tracks, and we soon had them out of sight. On the firm crust our snowshoes left no mark. After a while we heard a grumble of motors far back, on the road. Harp chuckled viciously. "Bright and early like yesterday." He stared back the way we had come. "They'll never pick that up without dogs. That son of a bitch Robart did talk about borrying a hound somewhere, to sniff Leda's clothes. More likely give 'em a sniff of mine, now."

We had already come so far that I didn't know the way back. Harp would know it. He could never be lost in any woods, but I have no mental compass such as his. So I followed him blindly, not trying to memorize our trail. It was a region of uniform old growth, mostly hemlock, no recent lumbering, few landmarks. The monotony wore down native patience to a numbness, and our snowshoes left no more impression than our thoughts.

An hour passed, or more; after that sound of motors faded. Now and then I heard the wind move peacefully overhead. Few bird calls, for most of our singers had not yet returned. "Been in this part before, Harp?"

"Not with snow on the ground, not lately." His voice was hushed and careful. "Summers. About a mile now, and the trees thin out some. Stretch of slash where they were taking out pine four, five years back and left everything a christly pile of shit like they always do."

No, Harp wouldn't get lost here, but I was well lost, tired, sorry I had come. Would he turn back if I collapsed? I didn't think he could, now, for any reason. My pack with blanket roll and provisions had become infernal. He had said we ought to have enough for three or four days. Only a few years earlier I had carried heavier camping loads than this without trouble, but now I was blown, a stitch beginning in my side. My wristwatch said only nine o'clock.

The trees thinned out as he had promised, and here the land rose in a long slope to the north. I looked up across a tract of eight or ten acres, where the devastation of stupid lumbering might be healed if the hurt region could be let alone for sixty years. The deep snow, blinding out here where only scrub growth interfered with the sunlight, covered the worst of the wreckage. "Good place for wild ras'berries," Harp said quietly. "Been time for 'em to grow back. Guess it was nearer seven years ago when they cut here and left this mess. Last summer I couldn't hardly find their logging road. Off to the left—"

He stopped, pointing with a slow arm to a blurred gray line that wandered up from the left to disappear over the rise of ground. The nearest part of that gray curve must have been four hundred feet away, and to my eyes it might have been a shadow cast by an irregularity of the snow surface; Harp knew better. Something had passed there, heavy enough to break the crust. "You want to rest a mite, Ben? Once over that rise I might not want to stop again."

I let myself down on the butt of an old log that lay tilted toward us, cut because it had happened to be in the way, left to rot because they happened to be taking pine. "Can you really make anything out of that?"

"Not enough," said Harp. "But it could be him." He did not sit by me but stood relaxed with his load, snowshoes spaced so he could spit between them. "About half a mile over that rise," he said, "there's a kind of gorge. Must've been a good brook, former times, still a stream along the bottom in summer. Tangle of elders and stuff. Couple, three caves in the bank at one spot. I guess it's three summers since I been there. Gloomy goddamn place. There was foxes into one of them caves. Natural caves, I b'lieve. I didn't go too near, not then."

I sat in the warming light, wondering whether there was any way I could talk to Harp about the beast—if it existed, if we weren't merely a pair of aging men with disordered minds. Any way to tell him the creature was important to the world outside our dim little village? That it ought somehow to be kept alive, not just shot down and shoveled aside? How could I say this to a man without science, who had lost his wife and also the trust of his fellow men?

Take away that trust and you take away the world.

Could I ask him to shoot it in the legs, get it back alive? Why, to my own self, irrationally, that appeared wrong, horrible, as well as beyond our powers. Better if he shot to kill. Or if I did. So in the end I said nothing, but shrugged my pack into place and told him I was ready to go on.

With the crust uncertain under that stronger sunshine, we picked our way slowly up the rise, and when we came at length to that line of tracks, Harp said matter-of-factly, "Now you've seen his mark. It's him."

Sun and overnight freezing had worked on the trail. Harp estimated it had been made early the day before. But wherever the weight of Longtooth had broken through, the shape of his foot showed clearly down there in its pocket of snow, a foot the size of a man's but broader, shorter. The prints were spaced for the stride of a short-legged person. The arch of the foot was low, but the beast was not actually flat-footed. Beast or man. I said, "This is a man's print, Harp. Isn't it?"

He spoke without heat. "No. You're forgetting, Ben. I seen him."

"Anyhow, there's only one."

He said slowly, "Only one set of tracks."

"What d'you mean?"

Harp shrugged. "It's heavy. He could've been carrying something. Keep your voice down. That crust yesterday, it would've held me without no web feet, but he went through, and he ain't as big as me." Harp checked his rifle and released the safety. "Half a mile to them caves. B'lieve that's where he is, Ben. Don't talk unless you got to, and take it slow."

I followed him. We topped the rise, encountering more of that lumberman's desolation on the other side. The trail crossed it, directly approaching a wall of undamaged trees that marked the limit of the cutting. Here forest took over once more, and where it began, Longtooth's trail ended. "Now you seen how it goes," Harp said. "Anyplace where he can travel above ground he does. He don't scramble up the trunks, seems like. Look here—he must've got aholt of that branch and swung hisself up. Knocked off some snow, but the wind knocks off so much, too, you can't tell nothing. See, Ben, he—he figures it out. He knows about trails. He'll have come down out of these trees far enough from where we are now so there ain't no chance of us seeing the place from here. Could be anywhere in a half circle, and draw it as big as you please."

"Thinking like a man."

"But he ain't a man," said Harp. "There's things he don't know. How a man feels, acts. I'm going on to them caves." From necessity, I followed him. . . .

I ought to end this quickly. Prematurely I am an old man, incapacitated by the effects of a stroke and a damaged heart. I keep improving a little—sensible diet, no smoking, Adelaide's care. I expect several years of tolerable health on the way downhill. But I find, as Harp did, that it is even more crippling to lose the trust of others. I will write here once more, and not again, that my word is good.

It was noon when we reached the gorge. In that place some melancholy part of night must always remain. Down the center of the ravine between tangles of alder, water murmured under ice and rotting snow, which here and there had fallen in to reveal the dark brilliance. Harp did not enter the gorge itself but moved slowly through tree cover along the left edge, eyes flickering for danger. I tried to imitate his caution. We went a hundred yards or more in that inching advance, maybe two hundred. I heard only the occasional wind of spring.

He turned to look at me with a sickly triumph, a grimace of disgust and of justification too. He touched his nose and then I got it also, a rankness from down ahead of us, a musky foulness with an ammoniacal tang and some smell of decay. Then on the other side of the gorge, off in the woods but not far, I heard Longtooth.

A bark, not loud. Throaty, like talk.

Harp suppressed an answering growl. He moved on until he could point down to a black cave mouth on the opposite side. The breeze blew the stench across to us. Harp whispered, "See, he's got like a path. Jumps down to that flat rock, then to the cave. We'll see him in a minute." Yes, there were sounds in the brush. "You keep back." His left palm lightly stroked the underside of his rifle barrel.

So intent was he on the opening where Longtooth would appear, I may have been first to see the other who came then to the cave mouth and stared up at us with animal eyes. Longtooth had called again, a rather gentle sound. The woman wrapped in filthy hides may have been drawn by that call or by the noise of our approach.

Then Harp saw her.

He knew her. In spite of the tangled hair, scratched face, dirt, and the shapeless deer pelt she clutched around herself against the cold, I am sure he knew her. I don't think she knew him, or me. An inner blindness, a look of a beast wholly centered on its own needs. I think human memories had drained away. She knew Longtooth was coming. I think she wanted his warmth and protection, but there were no words in the whimper she made before Harp's bullet took her between the eyes.

Longtooth shoved through the bushes. He dropped the rabbit he was carrying and jumped down to that flat rock snarling, glancing sidelong at the dead woman who was still twitching. If he understood the fact of death, he had no time for it. I saw the massive overdevelopment of thigh and leg muscles, their springy motions of preparation. The distance from the flat rock to the place where Harp stood must have been fifteen feet. One spear of sunlight touched him in that blue-green shade, touched his thick red fur and his fearful face.

Harp could have shot him. Twenty seconds for it, maybe more. But he flung his rifle aside and drew out his hunting knife, his own long tooth, and had it waiting when the enemy jumped.

So could I have shot him. No one needs to tell me I ought to have done so.

Longtooth launched himself, clawed fingers out, fangs exposed. I felt the meeting as if the impact had struck my own flesh. They tumbled roaring into the gorge, and I was cold, detached, an instrument for watching.

It ended soon. The heavy brownish teeth clenched in at the base of Harp's neck. He made no more motion except the thrust that sent his blade into Longtooth's left side. Then they were quiet in that embrace, quiet all three. I heard the water flowing under the ice.

I remember a roaring in my ears, and I was moving with slow care, one difficult step after another, along the lip of the gorge and through mighty corridors of white and green. With my hard-won detached amusement I supposed this might be the region where I had recently followed poor Harp Ryder to some destination or other, but not (I thought) one of those we talked about when we were boys. A band of iron had closed around my forehead, and breathing was an enterprise needing great effort and caution, in order not to worsen the indecent pain that clung as another band around my diaphragm. I leaned against a tree for thirty seconds or thirty minutes, I don't know where. I knew I mustn't take off my pack in spite of the pain, because it carried provisions for three days. I said once: "Ben, you are lost."

I had my carbine, a golden bough, staff of life, and I recall the shrewd management and planning that enabled me to send three shots into the air. Twice.

It seems I did not want to die, and so hung on the cliff edge of death with a mad stubbornness. They tell me it could not have been the second day that I fired the second burst, the one that was heard and answered—because they say a man can't suffer the kind of attack I was having and then survive a whole night of exposure. They say that when a search party reached me from Wyndham Village (eighteen miles from Darkfield), I made some garbled speech and fell flat on my face.

I woke immoblized, without power of speech or any motion except for a little life in my left hand, and for a long time memory was only a jarring of irrelevancies. When that cleared, I still couldn't talk for another long deadly while. I recall someone saying with exasperated admiration that with cerebral hemorrhage on top of coronary infarction, I had no damn right to be alive; this was the first sound that gave me any pleasure. I remember recognizing Adelaide and being unable to thank her for her presence. None of this matters to the story, except the fact that for months I had no bridge of communication with the world; and yet I loved the world and did not want to leave it.

One can always ask: What will happen next?

Sometime in what they said was June my memory was (I think) clear. I scrawled a little, with the nurse supporting the deadened part of my arm. But in response to what I wrote, the doctor, the nurses, Sheriff Robart, even Adelaide Simmons and Bill Hastings, looked—sympathetic. I was not believed. I am not believed now, in the most important part of what I wish I might say: that there are things in our world that we do not understand, and that this ignorance ought to generate humility. People find this obvious, bromidic—oh, they always have!—and therefore they do not listen, retaining the pride of their ignorance intact.

Remnants of the three bodies were found in late August, small thanks to my efforts, for I had no notion what compass direction we took after the cut-over area, and there are so many such areas of desolation I couldn't tell them where to look. Forest scavengers, including a pack of dogs, had found the bodies first. Water had moved them, too, for the last of the big snow melted suddenly, and for a couple of days at least there must have been a small river raging through that gorge. The head of what they are calling the "lunatic" got rolled downstream, bashed against rocks, partly buried in silt. Dogs had chewed and scattered what they speak of as "the man's fur coat."

It will remain a lunatic in a fur coat, for they won't have it any other way. So far as I know, no scientist ever got a look at the wreckage, unless you glorify the coroner by that title. I believe he was a good vet before he got the job. When my speech was more or less regained, I was already through trying to talk about it. A statement of mine was read at the inquest—that was before I could talk or leave the hospital. At this ceremony society officially decided that Harper Harrison Ryder, of this township, shot to death his wife, Leda, and an individual, male, of unknown identity, while himself temporarily of unsound mind, and died of knife injuries received in a struggle with the said individual of unknown, and so forth.

I don't talk about it because that only makes people more sorry for me, to think a man's mind should fail so, and he not yet sixty.

I cannot even ask them: "What is truth?" They would only look more saddened, and I suppose shocked, and perhaps find reasons for not coming to see me again.

They are kind. They will do anything for me, except think about it.

Mary Wilkins Freeman (1852–1930)

Luella Miller

Mary E. Wilkins Freeman was in her day one of the best-known American writers. She was championed by William Dean Howells for her literary value and awarded the Howells Medal for fiction of the American Academy in 1926. Her reputation however, and her work, declined after entering an oppressive marriage in 1902. Like Kate Chopin, Sarah Orne Jewett, and others, she has been consigned to the ghetto of "local colorists" by critics for most of this century. Primarily a short story writer, Freeman was popular and prolific, but produced only eleven supernatural stories, six of which were collected in her volume, *The Wind in the Rose-Bush and Other Stories of the Supernatural* (1903), which is, according to Everett Bleiler, "of greater critical and historical importance than its uniqueness might suggest. It is one of the very few bodies of work that combine domestic realism with supernaturalism, and it has been the founding document of a minor school within supernatural fiction (notably August Derleth and his followers)." Derleth ranked her as one of the four "absolute formative masters" of the horror genre following the Gothic vogue. His press, Arkham House, released the definitive *Collected Ghost Stories* (1974), with a useful introduction by Edward Wagenknecht. "Luella Miller" is her most horrific tale. Told by an unreliable narrator, it is at the same time an attack on the helpless child-woman and paradoxically on the independent single woman, the outsider. It is a ghost story and a vampire story at once. One must gauge the narrator's prejudices. It is an interesting contrast to Violet Hunt, Madeline Yale Wynne, and at an opposite pole from Le Fanu, M. R. James, and the Lovecraftians. It is perhaps one of the ancestors of Ray Bradbury.

Close to the village street stood the one-story house in which Luella Miller, who had an evil name in the village, had dwelt. She had been dead for years, yet there were those in the village who, in spite of the clearer light which comes on a vantage-point from a long-past danger, half believed in the tale which they had heard from their childhood. In their hearts, although they scarcely would have owned it, was a survival of the wild horror and frenzied fear of their ancestors who had dwelt in the same age with Luella Miller. Young people even would stare with a shudder at the old house as they passed, and children never played around it as was their wont around an untenanted building. Not a window in the old Miller house was broken: the panes reflected the morning sunlight in patches of emerald and blue, and the latch of the sagging front door was never lifted, although no bolt secured it. Since Luella Miller had been carried out of it, the house had had no tenant except one friendless old soul who had no choice between that and the far-off shelter of the open sky. This old woman, who had survived her kindred and friends, lived in the house one week, then one morning no smoke came out of the chimney, and a body of neighbours, a score strong, entered and found her dead in her bed. There were dark whispers as to the cause of her death, and there were those who testified to an expression of fear so exalted that it showed forth the state of the departing soul upon the dead face. The old woman had been hale and hearty when she entered the house, and in seven days she was dead; it seemed that she had fallen a victim to some uncanny power. The minister talked in the pulpit with covert severity against the sin of superstition; still the belief prevailed. Not a soul in the village but would have chosen the almshouse rather than that dwelling. No vagrant, if he heard the tale, would seek shelter beneath that old roof, unhallowed by nearly half a century of superstitious fear.

There was only one person in the village who had actually known Luella Miller. That person was a woman well over eighty, but a marvel of vitality and unextinct youth. Straight as an arrow, with the spring of one recently let loose from the bow of life, she moved about the streets, and she always went to church, rain or shine. She had never married, and had lived alone for years in a house across the road from Luella Miller's.

This woman had none of the garrulousness of age, but never in all her life had she ever held her tongue for any will save her own, and she never spared the truth when she essayed to present it. She it was who bore testimony to the life, evil, though possibly wittingly or designedly so, of Luella Miller, and to her personal appearance. When this old woman spoke—and she had the gift of description, although her thoughts were clothed in the rude vernacular of her native village—one could seem to see Luella Miller as she had really looked. According to this woman, Lydia Anderson by name, Luella Miller had been a beauty of a type rather unusual in New England. She had been a slight, pliant sort of creature, as ready with a strong yielding to fate and as unbreakable as a willow. She had glimmering lengths of straight, fair hair, which she wore softly looped round a long, lovely face. She had blue eyes full of soft pleading, little slender, clinging hands, and a wonderful grace of motion and attitude.

"Luella Miller used to sit in a way nobody else could if they sat up and studied a week of Sundays," said Lydia Anderson, "and it was a sight to see her walk. If one of them willows over there on the edge of the brook could start up and get its roots free of the ground, and move off, it would go just the way Luella Miller used to. She had a green shot silk she used to wear, too, and a hat with green ribbon streamers, and a lace veil blowing across her face and out sideways, and a green ribbon flyin' from her waist. That was what she came out bride in when she married Erastus Miller. Her name before she was married was Hill. There was always a sight of 'l's' in her name, married or single. Erastus Miller was good lookin', too, better lookin' than Luella. Sometimes I used to think that Luella wa'n't so handsome after all. Erastus just about worshiped her. I used to know him pretty well. He lived next door to me, and we went to school together. Folks used to say he was waitin' on me, but he wa'n't. I never thought he was except once or twice when he said things that some girls might have suspected meant somethin'. That was before Luella came here to teach the district school. It was funny how she came to get it, for folks said she hadn't any education, and that one of the big girls, Lottie Henderson, used to do all the teachin' for her, while she sat back and did embroidery work on a cambric pocket-handkerchief. Lottie Henderson was a real smart girl, a splendid scholar, and she just set her eyes by Luella, as all the girls did. Lottie would have made a real smart woman, but she died when Luella had been here about a year—just faded away and died: nobody knew what ailed her. She dragged herself to that schoolhouse and helped Luella teach till the very last minute. The committee all knew how Luella didn't do much of the work herself, but they winked at it. It wa'n't long after Lottie died that Erastus married her. I always thought he hurried it up because she wa'n't fit to teach. One of the big boys used to help her after Lottie died, but he hadn't much government, and the school didn't do very well, and Luella might have had to give it up, for the committee couldn't have shut their eyes to things much longer. The boy that helped her was a real honest, innocent sort of fellow, and he was a good scholar, too. Folks said he overstudied, and that was the reason he was took crazy the year after Luella married, but I don't know. And I don't know what made Erastus Miller go into consumption of the blood the year after he was married: consumption wa'n't in his family. He just grew weaker and weaker, and went almost bent double when he tried to wait on Luella, and he spoke feeble, like an old man. He worked terrible hard till the last trying to save up a little to leave Luella. I've seen him out in the worst storms on a wood-sled—he used to cut and sell wood—and he was hunched up on top lookin' more dead than alive. Once I couldn't stand it: I went over and helped him pitch some wood on the cart—I was always strong in my arms. I wouldn't stop for all he told me to, and I guess he was glad enough for the help. That was only a week before he died. He fell on the kitchen floor while he was gettin' breakfast. He always got the breakfast and let Luella lay abed. He did all the sweepin' and the washin' and the ironin' and most of the cookin'. He couldn't bear to have Luella lift her finger, and she let him do for her. She lived like a queen for all the work she did. She didn't even do her sewin'. She said it made her shoulder ache to sew, and poor Erastus's sister Lily used to do all her sewin'. She wa'n't able to, either; she was never strong in her back, but she did it beautifully. She had to, to suit Luella, she was so dreadful particular. I never saw anythin' like the fagottin' and hemstitchin' that Lily Miller did for Luella. She made all Luella's weddin' outfit, and that green silk dress, after Maria Babbit cut it. Maria she cut it for nothin', and she did a lot more cuttin' and fittin' for nothin' for Luella, too. Lily Miller went to live with Luella after Erastus died. She gave up her home, though she was real attached to it and wa'n't a mite afraid to stay alone. She rented it and she went to live with Luella right away after the funeral."

Then this old woman, Lydia Anderson, who remembered Luella Miller, would go on to relate the story of Lily Miller. It seemed that on the removal of Lily Miller to the house of her dead brother, to live with his widow, the village people first began to talk. This Lily Miller had been hardly past her first youth, and a most robust and blooming woman, rosy-cheeked, with curls of strong, black hair overshadowing round, candid temples and bright dark eyes. It was not six months after she had taken up her residence with her sister-in-law that her rosy colour faded and her pretty curves became wan hollows. White shadows began to show in the black rings of her hair, and the light died out of her eyes, her features sharpened, and there were pathetic lines at her mouth, which yet wore always an expression of utter sweetness and even happiness. She was devoted to her sister; there was no doubt that she loved her with her whole heart, and was perfectly content in her service. It was her sole anxiety lest she should die and leave her alone.

"The way Lily Miller used to talk about Luella was enough to make you mad and enough to make you cry," said Lydia Anderson. "I've been in there sometimes toward the last when she was too feeble to cook and carried her some blanc-mange or custard—somethin' I thought she might relish, and she'd thank me, and when I asked her how she was, say she felt better than she did yesterday, and asked me if I didn't think she looked better, dreadful pitiful, and say poor Luella had an awful time takin' care of her and doin' the work—she wa'n't strong enough to do anythin'—when all the time Luella wa'n't liftin' her finger and poor Lily didn't get any care except what the neighbours gave her, and Luella eat up everythin' that was carried in for Lily. I had it real straight that she did. Luella used to just sit and cry and do nothin'. She did act real fond of Lily, and she pined away considerable, too. There was those that thought she'd go into a decline herself. But after Lily died, her Aunt Abby Mixter came, and then Luella picked up and grew as fat and rosy as ever. But poor Aunt Abby begun to droop just the way Lily had, and I guess somebody wrote to her married daughter, Mrs. Sam Abbot, who lived in Barre, for she wrote her mother that she must leave right away and come and make her a visit, but Aunt Abby wouldn't go. I can see her now. She was a real good-lookin' woman, tall and large, with a big, square face and a high forehead that looked of itself kind of benevolent and good. She just tended out on Luella as if she had been a baby, and when her married daughter sent for her she wouldn't stir one inch. She'd always thought a lot of her daughter, too, but she said Luella needed her and her married daughter didn't. Her daughter kept writin' and writin', but it didn't do any good. Finally she came, and when she saw how bad her mother looked, she broke down and cried and all but went on her knees to have her come away. She spoke her mind out to Luella, too. She told her that she'd killed her husband and everybody that had anythin' to do with her, and she'd thank her to leave her mother alone. Luella went into hysterics, and Aunt Abby was so frightened that she called me after her daughter went. Mrs. Sam Abbot she went away fairly cryin' out loud in the buggy, the neighbours heard her, and well she might, for she never saw her mother again alive. I went in that night when Aunt Abby called for me, standin' in the door with her little green-checked shawl over her head. I can see her now. 'Do come over here, Miss Anderson,' she sung out, kind of gasping for breath. I didn't stop for anythin'. I put over as fast as I could, and when I got there, there was Luella laughin' and cryin' all together, and Aunt Abby trying to hush her, and all the time she herself was white as a sheet and shakin' so she could hardly stand. 'For the land sakes, Mrs. Mixter,' says I, 'you look worse than she does. You ain't fit to be up out of your bed.'

"'Oh, there ain't anythin' the matter with me,' says she. Then she went on talkin' to Luella. 'There, there, don't, don't, poor little lamb,' says she. 'Aunt Abby is here. She ain't goin' away and leave you. Don't, poor little lamb.'

"'Do leave her with me, Mrs. Mixter, and you get back to bed,' says I, for Aunt Abby had been layin' down considerable lately, though somehow she contrived to do the work.

"'I'm well enough,' says she. 'Don't you think she had better have the doctor, Miss Anderson?'

"'The doctor,' says I, 'I think you had better have the doctor. I think you need him much worse than some folks I could mention.' And I looked right straight at Luella Miller laughin' and cryin' and goin' on as if she was the centre of all creation. All the time she was actin' so—seemed as if she was too sick to sense anythin'—she was keepin' a sharp lookout as to how we took it out of the corner of one eye. I see her. You could never cheat me about Luella Miller. Finally I got real mad and I run home and I got a bottle of valerian I had, and I poured some boilin' hot water on a handful of catnip, and I mixed up that catnip tea with most half a wineglass of valerian, and I went with it over to Luella's. I marched right up to Luella, a-holdin' out of that cup, all smokin'. 'Now,' says I, 'Luella Miller, *you swaller this!*'

"'What is—what is it, oh, what is it?' she sort of screeches out. Then she goes off a-laughin' enough to kill.

"'Poor lamb, poor little lamb,' says Aunt Abby, standin' over her, all kind of tottery, and tryin' to bathe her head with camphor.

"'*You swaller this right down,*' says I. And I didn't waste any ceremony. I just took hold of Luella Miller's chin and I tipped her head back, and I caught her mouth open with laughin' and I clapped that cup to her lips, and I fairly hollered at her: 'Swaller, swaller, swaller!' and she gulped it right down. She had to, and I guess it did her good.

Anyhow, she stopped cryin' and laughin' and let me put her to bed, and she went to sleep like a baby inside of half an hour. That was more than poor Aunt Abby did. She lay awake all that night and I stayed with her, though she tried not to have me; said she wa'n't sick enough for watchers. But I stayed, and I made some good cornmeal gruel and I fed her a teaspoon every little while all night long. It seemed to me as if she was jest dyin' from bein' all wore out. In the mornin' as soon as it was light I run over to the Bisbees and sent Johnny Bisbee for the doctor. I told him to tell the doctor to hurry, and he come pretty quick. Poor Aunt Abby didn't seem to know much of anythin' when he got there. You couldn't hardly tell she breathed, she was so used up. When the doctor had gone, Luella came into the room lookin' like a baby in her ruffled nightgown. I can see her now. Her eyes were as blue and her face all pink and white like a blossom, and she looked at Aunt Abby in the bed sort of innocent and surprised. 'Why,' says she, 'Aunt Abby ain't got up yet?'

"'No, she ain't,' says I, pretty short.

"'I thought I didn't smell the coffee,' says Luella.

"'Coffee,' says I. 'I guess if you have coffee this mornin' you'll make it yourself.'

"'I never made the coffee in all my life,' says she, dreadful astonished. 'Erastus always made the coffee as long as he lived, and then Lily she made it, and then Aunt Abby made it. I don't believe I *can* make the coffee, Miss Anderson.'

"'You can make it or go without, jest as you please,' says I.

"'Ain't Aunt Abby goin' to get up?' says she.

"'I guess she won't get up,' says I, 'sick as she is.' I was gettin' madder and madder. There was somethin' about that little pink-and-white thing standin' there and talkin' about coffee, when she had killed so many better folks than she was, and had jest killed another, that made me feel 'most as if I wished somebody would up and kill her before she had a chance to do any more harm.

"'Is Aunt Abby sick?' says Luella, as if she was sort of aggrieved and injured.

"'Yes,' says I, 'she's sick, and she's goin' to die, and then you'll be left alone, and you'll have to do for yourself and wait on yourself, or do without things.' I don't know but I was sort of hard, but it was the truth, and if I was any harder than Luella Miller had been I'll give up. I ain't never been sorry that I said it. Well, Luella, she up and had hysterics again at that, and I jest let her have 'em. All I did was to bundle her into the room on the other side of the entry where Aunt Abby couldn't hear her, if she wa'n't past it—I don't know but she was—and set her down hard in a chair and told her not to come back into the other room, and she minded. She had her hysterics in there till she got tired. When she found out that nobody was comin' to coddle her and do for her she stopped. At least I supposed she did. I had all I could do with poor Aunt Abby tryin' to keep the breath of life in her. The doctor had told me that she was dreadful low, and give me some very strong medicine to give to her in drops real often, and told me real particular about the nourishment. Well, I did as he told me real faithful till she wa'n't able to swaller any longer. Then I had her daughter sent for. I had begun to realize that she wouldn't last any time at all. I hadn't realized it before, though I spoke to Luella the way I did. The doctor he came, and Mrs. Sam Abbot, but when she got there it was too late; her mother was dead. Aunt Abby's daughter just give one look at her mother layin' there, then she turned sort of sharp and sudden and looked at me.

"'Where is she?' says she, and I knew she meant Luella.

"'She's out in the kitchen,' says I. 'She's too nervous to see folks die. She's afraid it will make her sick.'

"The Doctor he speaks up then. He was a young man. Old Doctor Park had died the year before, and this was a young fellow just out of college. 'Mrs. Miller is not strong,' says he, kind of severe, 'and she is quite right in not agitating herself.'

"'You are another, young man; she's got her pretty claw on you,' think I, but I didn't say anythin' to him. I just said over to Mrs. Sam Abbot that Luella was in the kitchen, and Mrs. Sam Abbot she went out there, and I went, too, and I never heard anythin' like the way she talked to Luella Miller. I felt pretty hard to Luella myself, but this was more than I ever would have dared to say. Luella she was too scared to go into hysterics. She jest flopped. She seemed to jest shrink away to nothin' in that kitchen chair, with Mrs. Sam Abbot standin' over her and talkin' and tellin' her the truth. I guess the truth was most too much for her and no mistake, because Luella presently actually did faint away, and there wa'n't any sham about it, the way I always suspected there was about them hysterics. She fainted dead away and we had to lay her flat on the floor, and the Doctor he came runnin' out and he said somethin' about a weak heart dreadful fierce to Mrs. Sam Abbot, but she wa'n't a mite scared. She faced him jest as white as even Luella was layin' there lookin' like death and the Doctor feelin' of her pulse.

"'Weak heart,' says she, 'weak heart; weak fiddlesticks! There ain't nothin' weak about that woman. She's got strength enough to hang onto other folks till she kills 'em. Weak? It was my poor mother that was weak: this woman killed her as sure as if she had taken a knife to her.'

"But the Doctor he didn't pay much attention. He was bendin' over Luella layin' there with her yellow hair all streamin' and her pretty pink-and-white face all pale, and her blue eyes like stars gone out, and he was holdin' onto her hand and smoothin' her forehead, and tellin' me to get the brandy in Aunt Abby's room, and I was sure as I wanted to be that Luella had got somebody else to hand onto, now Aunt Abby was gone, and I thought of poor Erastus Miller, and I sort of pitied the poor young Doctor, led away by a pretty face, and I made up my mind I'd see what I could do.

"I waited till Aunt Abby had been dead and buried about a month, and the Doctor was goin' to see Luella steady and folks were beginnin' to talk; then one evenin', when I knew the Doctor had been called out of town and wouldn't be round, I went over to Luella's. I found her all dressed up in a blue muslin with white polka dots on it, and her hair curled jest as pretty, and there wa'n't a young girl in the place could compare with her. There was somethin' about Luella Miller seemed to draw the heart right out of you, but she didn't draw it out of *me*. She was settin' rocking in the chair by her sittin'-room window, and Maria Brown had gone home. Maria Brown had been in to help her, or rather to do the work, for Luella wa'n't helped when she didn't do anythin'. Maria Brown was real capable and she didn't have any ties; she wa'n't married, and lived alone, so she'd offered. I couldn't see why she should do the work any more than Luella; she wa'n't any too strong; but she seemed to think she could and Luella seemed to think so, too, so she went over and did all the work—washed, and ironed, and baked, while Luella sat and rocked. Maria didn't live long afterward. She began to fade away just the same fashion the others had. Well, she was warned, but she acted real mad when folks said anythin': said Luella was a poor, abused woman, too delicate to help herself, and they'd ought to be ashamed, and if she died helpin' them that couldn't help themselves she would—and she did.

"'I s'pose Maria has gone home,' says I to Luella, when I had gone in and sat down opposite her.

"'Yes, Maria went half an hour ago, after she had got supper and washed the dishes,' says Luella, in her pretty way.

"'I suppose she has got a lot of work to do in her own house tonight,' says I, kind of bitter, but that was all thrown away on Luella Miller. It seemed to her right that other folks that wa'n't any better able than she was herself should wait on her, and she couldn't get it through her head that anybody should think it *wa'n't* right.

"'Yes,' says Luella, real sweet and pretty, 'yes, she said she had to do her washin' tonight. She has let it go for a fortnight along of comin' over here.'

"'Why don't she stay home and do her washin' instead of comin' over here and doin' *your* work, when you are just as well able, and enough sight more so, than she is to do it?' says I.

"Then Luella she looked at me like a baby who has a rattle shook at it. She sort of laughed as innocent as you please. 'Oh, I can't do the work myself, Miss Anderson,' says she. 'I never did. Maria *has* to do it.'

"Then I spoke out: 'Has to do it!' says I. 'Has to do it! She don't have to do it, either. Maria Brown has her own house and enough to live on. She ain't beholden to you to come over here and slave for you and kill herself.'

'Luella she jest set and stared at me for all the world like a doll-baby that was so abused that it was comin' to life.

"'Yes,' says I, 'she's killin' herself. She's goin' to die just the way Erastus did, and Lily, and your Aunt Abby. You're killin' her jest as you did them. I don't know what there is about you, but you seem to bring a curse,' says I. 'You kill everybody that is fool enough to care anythin' about you and do for you.'

'She stared at me and she was pretty pale.

"'And Maria ain't the only one you're goin' to kill,' says I. 'You're goin' to kill Doctor Malcom before you're done with him.'

'Then a red colour came flamin' all over her face. 'I ain't goin' to kill him, either,' says she, and she begun to cry.

"'Yes, you *be!*' says I. Then I spoke as I had never spoke before. You see, I felt it on account of Erastus. I told her that she hadn't any business to think of another man after she'd been married to one that had died for her: that she was a dreadful woman; and she was, that's true enough, but sometimes I have wondered lately if she knew it—if she wa'n't like a baby with scissors in its hand cuttin' everybody without knowin' what it was doin'.

'Luella she kept gettin' paler and paler, and she never took her eyes off my face. There was somethin' awful about the way she looked at me and never spoke one word. After awhile I quit talkin' and I went home. I watched that night, but her lamp went out before nine o'clock, and when Doctor Malcom came drivin' past and sort of slowed up he see there wa'n't any light and he drove along. I saw her sort of shy out of meetin' the next Sunday, too, so he shouldn't go home with her, and I begun to think mebbe she did have some conscience after all. It was only a week after that that Maria Brown died—sort of sudden at the last, though everybody had seen it was comin'. Well, then there was a good deal of feelin' and pretty dark whispers. Folks said the days of witchcraft had come again, and they were pretty shy of Luella. She acted sort of offish to the Doctor and he didn't go there, and there wa'n't anybody to do anythin' for her. I don't know how she *did* get along. I wouldn't go in there and offer to help her—not because I was afraid of dyin' like the rest, but I thought she was just as well able to do her own work as I was to do it for her, and I thought it was about time that she did it and stopped killin' other folks. But it wa'n't very long before folks began to say that Luella herself was goin' into a decline jest the way her husband, and Lily, and Aunt Abby and the others had, and I saw myself that she looked pretty bad. I used to see her goin' past from the store with a bundle as if she could hardly crawl, but I remembered how Erastus used to wait and 'tend when he couldn't hardly put one foot before the other, and I didn't go out to help her.

'But at last one afternoon I saw the Doctor come drivin' up like mad with his medicine chest, and Mrs. Babbit came in after supper and said that Luella was real sick.

"'I'd offer to go in and nurse her,' says she, 'but I've got my children to consider, and mebbe it ain't true what they say, but it's queer how many folks that have done for her have died.'

'I didn't say anythin', but I considered how she had been Erastus's wife and how he had set his eyes by her, and I made up my mind to go in the next mornin', unless she was better, and see what I could do; but the next mornin' I see her at the window, and pretty soon she came steppin' out as spry as you please, and a little while afterward Mrs. Babbit came in and told me that the Doctor had got a girl from out of town, a Sarah Jones, to come there, and she said she was pretty sure that the Doctor was goin' to marry Luella.

'I saw him kiss her in the door that night myself, and I knew it was true. The woman came that afternoon, and the way she flew around was a caution. I don't believe Luella had swept since Maria died. She swept and dusted, and washed and ironed; wet clothes and dusters and carpets were flyin' over there all day, and every time Luella set her foot out when the Doctor wa'n't there there was that Sarah Jones helpin' of her up and down the steps, as if she hadn't learned to walk.

'Well, everybody knew that Luella and the Doctor were goin' to be married, but it wa'n't long before they began to talk about his lookin' so poorly, jest as they had about the others; and they talked about Sarah Jones, too.

'Well, the Doctor did die, and he wanted to be married first, so as to leave what little he had to Luella, but he died before the minister could get there, and Sarah Jones died a week afterward.

'Well, that wound up everything for Luella Miller. Not another soul in the whole town would lift a finger for her. There got to be a sort of panic. Then she began to droop in good earnest. She used to have to go to the store herself, for Mrs. Babbit was afraid to let Tommy go for her, and I've seen her goin' past and stoppin' every two or three steps to rest. Well, I stood it as long as I could, but one day I see her comin' with her arms full and stoppin' to lean against the Babbit fence, and I run out and took her bundles and carried them to her house. Then I went home and never spoke one word to her though she called after me dreadful kind of pitiful. Well, that night I was taken sick with a chill, and I was sick as I wanted to be for two weeks. Mrs. Babbit had seen me run out to help Luella and she come in and told me I was goin' to die on account of it. I didn't know whether I was or not, but I considered I had done right by Erastus's wife.

'That last two weeks Luella she had a dreadful hard time, I guess. She was pretty sick, and as near as I could make out nobody dared go near her. I don't know as she was really needin' anythin' very much, for there was enough to eat in her house and it was warm weather, and she made out to cook a little flour gruel every day, I know, but I guess she had a hard time, she that had been so petted and done for all her life.

'When I got so I could go out, I went over there one morning. Mrs. Babbit had just come in to say she hadn't seen any smoke and she didn't know but it was somebody's duty to go in, but she couldn't help thinkin' of her children, and I got right up, though I hadn't been out of the house for two weeks, and I went in there, and Luella she was layin' on the bed, and she was dyin'.

'She lasted all that day and into the night. But I sat there after the new doctor had gone away. Nobody else dared to go there. It was about midnight that I left her for a minute to run home and get some medicine I had been takin', for I begun to feel rather bad.

'It was a full moon that night, and just as I started out of my door to cross the street back to Luella's, I stopped short, for I saw something."

Lydia Anderson at this juncture always said with a certain defiance that she did not expect to be believed, and then proceeded in a hushed voice:

'I saw what I saw, and I know I saw it, and I will swear on my death bed that I saw it. I saw Luella Miller and Erastus Miller, and Lily, and Aunt Abby, and Maria, and the Doctor, and Sarah, all goin' out of her door, and all but Luella shone white in the moonlight, and they were all helpin' her along till she seemed to fairly fly in the midst of them. Then it all disappeared. I stood a minute with my heart poundin', then I went over there. I thought of goin' for Mrs. Babbit, but I thought she'd be afraid. So I went alone, though I knew what had happened. Luella was layin' real peaceful, dead on her bed.'

This was the story that the old woman, Lydia Anderson, told, but the sequel was told by the people who survived her, and this is the tale which has become folklore in the village.

Lydia Anderson died when she was eighty-seven. She had continued wonderfully hale and hearty for one of her years until about two weeks before her death.

One bright moonlight evening she was sitting beside a window in her parlour when she made a sudden exclamation, and was out of the house and across the street before the neighbour who was taking care of her could stop her. She followed as fast as possible and found Lydia Anderson stretched on the ground before the door of Luella Miller's deserted house, and she was quite dead.

The next night there was a red gleam of fire athwart the moonlight and the old house of Luella Miller was burned to the ground. Nothing is now left of it except a few old cellar stones and a lilac bush, and in summer a helpless trail of morning glories among the weeds, which might be considered emblematic of Luella herself.

Gerald Durrell (b. 1925)

The Entrance

Gerald Durrell is the brother of Lawrence Durrell, who exceeded his sibling's literary success and reputation in the 1950s with *The Alexandria Quartet*. Yet Gerald, the world-famous naturalist, always made more money, principally on nonfiction. Gerald's short fiction is not well known and "The Entrance" seems to spring from nowhere in the body of his work. It was a serious project for him, and he was reportedly pleased that Lawrence praised the piece that moved in a new direction, over which he had taken some time. One suspects that, like Fuentes' "Aura," the story was generated not by genre reading but by rich reading experiences and, perhaps, images of mirrors. The device of a tale told by a manuscript is common in horror, from Le Fanu and M. R. James through, for instance, Jean Ray's "The Shadowy Street" (which makes an interesting comparison). Another literary antecedant might well be Oscar Wilde's classic novella, "The Portrait of Dorian Grey." Another, *Through The Looking Glass*. In any case, "The Entrance" is a polished and effective tale of horror that deserves wide recognition and repays careful reading. It is a monster story about the nature of identity.

M y friends Paul and Marjorie Glenham are both failed artists or, perhaps, to put it more charitably, they are both unsuccessful. But they enjoy their failure more than most successful artists enjoy their success, and this is what makes them such good company and is one of the reasons why I always go and stay with them when I am in France. Their rambling farmhouse in Provence was always in a state of chaos, with sacks of potatoes, piles of dried herbs, plates of garlic and forests of dried maize jostling with piles of half-finished watercolors and oil paintings of the most hideous sort, perpetrated by Marjorie, and strange Neanderthal sculpture, which was Paul's handiwork. Throughout this marketlike mess prowled cats of every shade and marking and a river of dogs, from an Irish wolfhound the size of a pony to an old English bulldog that made noises like Stevenson's Rocket. Around the walls in ornate cages were housed Marjorie's collection of roller canaries, who sang with undiminished vigor regardless of the hour, thus making speech difficult. It was a warm, friendly cacophonous atmosphere and I loved it.

When I arrived in the early evening I had had a long drive and was tired, a condition that Paul set about remedying with a hot brandy and lemon of Herculean proportions. I was glad to have got there, for during the last half hour a summer storm had moved ponderously over the landscape like a great black cloak, and thunder reverberated among the crags like a million rocks cascading down a wooden staircase. I had only just reached the safety of the warm, noisy kitchen, redolent with the mouth-watering smells of

Marjorie's cooking, when the rain started in torrents. The noise of it on the tile roof, combined with the massive thunder claps that made even the solid stone farmhouse shudder, aroused the competitive spirit in the canaries and they all burst into song simultaneously. It was the noisiest storm I had ever encountered.

"Another noggin, dear boy?" enquired Paul hopefully.

"No, no!" shouted Marjorie above the bubbling songs of the birds and the roar of the rain. "The food's ready and it will spoil if you keep it waiting. Have some wine. Come and sit down, Gerry dear."

"Wine, wine, that's the thing. I've got something special for you, dear boy," said Paul, and he went off into the cellar to reappear a moment later with his arms full of bottles, which he placed reverently on the table near me. "A special Gigondas I have discovered," he said. "Brontosaurus blood, I do assure you my dear fellow, pure prehistoric monster juice. It will go well with the truffles and the guinea fowl Marjorie's run up."

He uncorked a bottle and splashed the deep red wine into a generously large goblet. He was right. The wine slid into your mouth like red velvet and then, when it reached the back of your tongue, it exploded like a fireworks display into your brain cells.

"Good, eh?" said Paul, watching my expression. "I found it in a small *cave* near Avignon. It was a blistering hot day and the *cave* was so nice and cool that I sat and drank two bottles of it before I realized what I was doing. It's a seducing wine, alright. Of course, when I got out in the sun again the damn stuff hit me like a sledgehammer. Marjorie had to drive."

"I was so ashamed," said Marjorie, placing in front of me a black truffle the size of a peach, encased in a fragile, feather-light overcoat of crisp brown pastry. "He paid for the wine and then bowed to the *Patron* and fell flat on his face. The *Patron* and his sons had to lift him into the car. It was disgusting."

"Nonsense," said Paul. "The *Patron* was enchanted. It gave his wine the accolade it needed."

"That's what you think," said Marjorie. "Now start, Gerry, before it gets cold."

I cut into the globe of golden pastry in front of me and released the scent of the truffle, like the delicious aroma of a damp autumn wood, a million leafy, earthy smells rolled up into one. With the Gigondas as an accompaniment, this promised to be a meal for the Gods. We fell silent as we attacked our truffles and listened to the rain on the roof, the roar of thunder and the almost apoplectic singing of the canaries. The bulldog, who had for no apparent reason fallen suddenly and deeply in love with me, sat by my chair watching me fixedly with his protuberant brown eyes, panting gently and wheezing.

"Magnificent, Marjorie," I said as the last fragment of pastry dissolved like a snowflake on my tongue. "I don't know why you and Paul don't set up a restaurant: with your cooking and Paul's choice of wines you'd be one of the three-star *Michelin* jobs in next to no time."

"Thank you, dear," said Marjorie, sipping her wine, "but I prefer to cook for a small audience of gourmets rather than a large audience of gourmands."

"She's right; there's no gainsaying it," agreed Paul, splashing wine into our glasses with gay abandon.

A sudden prolonged roar of thunder directly overhead precluded speech for a long minute and was so fierce and sustained that even the canaries fell silent, intimidated by the sound. When it had finished, Marjorie waved her fork at her spouse.

"You mustn't forget to give Gerry your thingummy," she said.

"Thingummy?" asked Paul blankly. "What thingummy?"

"You *know*," said Marjorie impatiently, "your thingummy . . . your manuscript . . . It's just the right sort of night for him to read it."

"Oh, the manuscript . . . *yes*," said Paul enthusiastically. "The *very* night for him to
read it."

"I refuse," I protested. "Your paintings and sculptures are bad enough. I'm damned if
I'll read your literary efforts as well."

"Heathen," said Marjorie good-naturedly. "Anyway, it's not Paul's, it's someone
else's."

"I don't think he *deserves* to read it after those disparaging remarks about my art," said
Paul. "It's too good for him."

"What is it?" I asked.

"It's a very curious manuscript I picked up," Paul began when Marjorie interrupted.
"Don't tell him about it; let him read it," she said. "I might say it gave *me*
nightmares."

While Marjorie was serving helpings of guinea fowl wrapped in an almost tangible
aroma of herbs and garlic, Paul went over to the corner of the kitchen, where a tottering
mound of books, like some ruined castle, lay between two sacks of potatoes and a large
barrel of wine. He rummaged around for a bit and then emerged triumphantly with a fat
red notebook, very much the worse for wear, and came and put it on the table.

"There!" he said with satisfaction. "The moment I'd read it I thought of you. I got it
among a load of books I bought from the library of old Doctor Lepitre, who used to be
prison doctor down in Marseilles. I don't know whether it's a hoax or what."

I opened the book, and on the inside of the cover I found a bookplate in black, three
cyprus trees and a sundial under which was written, in Gothic script, *Ex Libras Lepitre*. I
flipped over the pages and saw that the manuscript was in longhand, some of the most
beautiful and elegant copperplate handwriting I had seen, the ink now faded to a rusty
brown.

"I wish I had waited until daylight to read it," said Marjorie with a shudder.

"What is it? A ghost story?" I asked curiously.

"No," said Paul uncertainly, "at least, not exactly. Old Lepitre is dead, unfortunately,
so I couldn't find out about it. It's a very curious story. But the moment I read it I
thought of you, knowing your interest in the occult and things that go bump in the night.
Read it and tell me what you think. You can have the manuscript if you want it. It might
amuse you, anyway."

"I would hardly call it amusing," said Marjorie, "anything but amusing. I think it's
horrid."

Some hours later, full of good food and wine, I took the giant golden oil lamp,
carefully trimmed, and in its gentle daffodil-yellow light I made my way upstairs to the
guest room and a feather bed the size of a barn door. The bulldog had followed me
upstairs and had sat wheezing, watching me undress and climb into bed. He sat by the
bed looking at me soulfully. The storm continued unabated, and the rumble of thunder
was almost continuous while the dazzling flashes of lightning lit up the whole room at
intervals. I adjusted the wick of the lamp, moved it closer to me, picked up the red
notebook and settled myself back against the pillows to read. The manuscript began
without preamble:

March 16th, 1901, Marseilles.

I have all night lying ahead of me, and as I know I cannot sleep—in spite of my
resolve—I thought I would try and write down in detail the thing that has just happened

to me. I am afraid that even setting it down like this will not make it any the more believable, but it will pass the time until dawn comes and with it my release.

Firstly, I must explain a little about myself and my relationship with Gideon de Teildras Villeray so that the reader (if there ever is one) will understand how I came to be in the depths of France in midwinter. I am an antiquarian bookseller and I can say, in all modesty, I am at the top of my profession. Or perhaps it would be more accurate to say that I *was* at the top of my profession. I was even once described by one of my fellow booksellers—I hope more in a spirit of levity than one of jealousy—as a "literary truffle hound," a description that I suppose, in its amusing way, does describe me. A hundred or more libraries have passed through my hands, and I have been responsible for a number of important finds, the original Gottenstein manuscript, for example, the rare "Conrad" illustrated *Bible*, said by some to be as beautiful as the *Book of Kells*, the five new poems by Blake that I unearthed at an unpromising country house sale in the Midlands, and many lesser but nonetheless satisfying discoveries, such as the signed first edition of *Alice in Wonderland* that I found in a trunk full of rag books and toys in the nursery of a vicarage in Shropshire and a presentation copy of *Sonnets from the Portuguese*, signed and with a six-line verse written on the flyleaf by both Robert and Elizabeth Browning. I think to be able to unearth such things in unlikely places is a gift that you are born with. It is really rather like water divining; either you are born with the gift or not, but it is not a gift you can acquire, though most certainly, with practice, you are able to sharpen your perceptions and make your eye keener. In my spare time I also catalogue some of the smaller and more important libraries, as I get enormous pleasure out of simply *being* with books. To me the quietness of a library, the smell and the feel of the books is like the smell and texture of food to a gourmet. It may sound fanciful, but I can stand in the middle of a library and hear the myriad voices around me as though I were standing in the middle of a vast choir, a choir of knowledge and beauty.

Naturally, because of my work, it was at Sotheby's that I first met Gideon. I had unearthed in a house in Sussex a small but quite interesting collection of first editions, and being interested to see what they would fetch, I had attended the sale myself. As the bidding was in progress I got the rather uncomfortable feeling that I was being watched. I glanced around but could see no one whose attention was not upon the auctioneer. Yet, as the sale proceeded I got more and more uncomfortable. Perhaps this is too strong a word, but I became convinced that I was the object of an intense scrutiny. At last the crowd in the salesroom moved slightly and I saw who it was. He was a man of medium height with a handsome but somewhat plump face, piercing and very large dark eyes and smoky black curly hair, worn rather long. He was dressed in a very well cut dark overcoat with an astrakhan collar, and in his elegantly gloved hands he carried the sales catalogue and a wide-brimmed dark velour hat. His glittering, gypsylike eyes were fixed on me intently but then, when he saw me looking at him, the fierceness of his gaze faded, and he gave me a faint smile and a tiny nod of his head, as if to acknowledge that he had been caught out in staring at me in such a vulgar fashion. He turned then and shouldered his way through the people who surrounded him and was soon lost to my sight. I don't know why but the intense scrutiny of this stranger somewhat disconcerted me, to such an extent that I did not follow the rest of the sale with any degree of attention, except to note that the items I had put up fetched more than I had anticipated they would. The bidding over, I made my way through the crush and out into the street. It was a dank, raw day in February, with that unpleasant smoky smell in the air that augers fog and makes the back of your throat raw. As it looked unpleasantly as though it might drizzle, I hailed a cab. I have one of those tall, narrow houses in Smith Street, just off the Kings Road. It was bequeathed to me by my mother and does me very well. It is not in a fashionable part of town, but the house is quite big enough for a bachelor like myself and his books, for I have, over the years, collected a small but extremely nice library on the various subjects that interest me: Indian art, particularly miniatures; some of the early natural histories; a small but rather rare collection of books on the occult; a number of volumes on plants and great gardens; and a very nice collection of first editions of contemporary novelists. My home is simply furnished but comfortable, and although I am not rich, I have sufficient for my needs and I keep a good table and very reasonable wine cellar.

As I paid off the cab and mounted the steps to my front door, I saw that, as I had predicted, the fog was starting to descend upon the city and already it was difficult to see the end of the street. It was obviously going to turn out to be a real pea-souper and I was glad to be home. My housekeeper, Mrs. Manning, had a bright and cheerful fire burning in my small drawing room, and next to my favorite chair she had as usual, laid out my slippers (for who can relax without slippers?) and on a small table all the accoutrements for a warming punch. I took off my coat and hat, slipped off my shoes and put on my slippers.

Presently Mrs. Manning appeared from the kitchen below and asked me, in view of the weather, if I would mind if she went home since it seemed as if the fog was getting thicker. She had left me some soup, a steak-and-kidney pie and an apple tart, all of which only needed heating. I said that this would do splendidly, since on many occasions I had looked after myself in this way when the weather had forced Mrs. Manning to leave early.

"There was a gentleman come to see you a bit earlier," said Mrs. Manning.

"A gentleman? What was his name?" I asked, astonished that anyone should call on an evening like this.

"He wouldn't give no name, sir," she replied, "but said he'd call again."

I thought that, in all probability, it had something to do with a library I was cataloguing then, and thought no more about it. Presently Mrs. Manning reappeared, dressed for the street, and I let her out of the front door and bolted it securely behind her, before returning to my drink and the warm fire. My cat Neptune appeared from my study upstairs, where his comfortable basket was, gave a faint meuw of greeting and jumped gracefully onto my lap where, after paddling with his forepaws for a short while, he settled down to dream and doze, purring like a great tortoiseshell hive of bees. Lulled by the fire, the punch and the loud purrs of Neptune, I dropped off to sleep.

I must have slept heavily for I awoke with a start and was unable to recall what it was that had awakened me. On my lap Neptune rose and stretched and yawned as if he knew he was going to be disturbed. I listened but the house was silent. I had just decided that it must have been the rustling scrunch of coals shifting in the grate when there came an imperious knocking at the front door. I made my way to the front door, repairing, as I went, the damage that sleep had perpetrated on my neat appearance, straightening my collar and tie and smoothing down my hair, which is unruly at the best of times. I lit the light in the hall, unbolted the front door and threw it open. Shreds of mist swirled in, and there, standing on the top step, was the curious, gypsylike man that I had seen watching me so intently at Sotheby's. Now he was dressed in a well-cut evening suit and was wearing an opera cloak lined with red silk. On his head was a top hat whose shining appearance was blurred by the tiny drops of moisture deposited on it by the fog, which moved, like an unhealthy yellow backdrop, behind him. In one gloved hand he held a slender ebony cane with a beautifully worked gold top and he swung this gently between his fingers like a pendulum. When he saw that it was I who had opened the door and not a butler or some skivvy, he straightened up and removed his hat.

"Good evening," he said, giving me a most charming smile that showed very fine, white, even teeth. His voice had a peculiar husky, lilting musical quality about it that was most attractive and enhanced by his slight but noticeable French intonation.

"Good evening," I said, puzzled as to what this stranger could possibly want of me.

"Am I addressing Mr. Letting . . . Mr. Peter Letting?" he asked.

"Yes," I said, "I am Peter Letting."

He smiled again, removed his glove and held out a well-manicured hand on which a large blood opal gleamed in a gold ring.

"I am more delighted than I can say at this opportunity of meeting you, sir," he said, as he shook my hand, "and I must first of all apologize for disturbing you at such a time, on such a night."

He drew his cloak around him slightly and glanced at the damp, yellow fog that swirled behind him. Noting this, I felt it incumbent on me to ask him to step inside and state his business, for I felt it would hardly be good manners to keep him standing on the step in such unpleasant weather. He entered the hall, and when I had turned from closing and bolting the front door, I found that he had divested himself of his hat, stick and cloak, and was standing there, rubbing his hands together, looking at me expectantly.

"Come into the drawing room Mr. . . ." I paused on a note of interrogation.

A curious, childlike look of chagrin passed across his face, and he looked at me contritely. "My dear sir," he said, "my dear Mr. Letting. How excessively remiss of me. You will be thinking me totally lacking in social graces, forcing my way into your home on such a night and then not even bothering to introduce myself. I do apologize. I am Gideon de Teildras Villeray."

"I am pleased to meet you," I said politely, though in truth I must confess that, in spite of his obvious charm, I was slightly uneasy for I could not see what a Frenchman of his undoubted aristocratic lineage would want of an antiquarian bookseller such as myself. "Perhaps," I continued, "you would care to come in and partake of a little refreshment—some wine perhaps, or maybe, since the night is so chilly, a little brandy?"

"You are very kind and very forgiving," he said with a slight bow, still smiling his beguiling smile. "A glass of wine would be most welcome, I do assure you."

I showed him into my drawing room and he walked to the fire and held his hands out to the blaze, clenching and unclenching his white fingers so that the opal in his ring fluttered like a spot of blood against his white skin. I selected an excellent bottle of Margaux and transported it carefully up to the drawing room with two of my best crystal glasses. My visitor had left the fire and was standing by my bookshelves, a volume in his hands. He glanced up as I entered and held up the book.

"What a superb copy of Eliphas Levi," he said enthusiastically, "and what a lovely collection of *grimoires* you have got. I did not know you were interested in the occult."

"Not really," I said, uncorking the wine. "After all, no sane man would believe in witches and warlocks and sabbaths and spells and all that tarradiddle. No, I merely collect them as interesting books which are of value and, in many cases, because of their contents, exceedingly amusing."

"Amusing?" he said, coming forward to accept the glass of wine I held out to him. "How do you mean, amusing?"

"Well, don't you find it amusing, the thought of all those grown men mumbling all those silly spells and standing about for hours in the middle of the night expecting Satan to appear? I confess I find it very amusing indeed."

"I do not," he said, and then, as if he feared that he had been too abrupt and perhaps rude, he smiled and raised his glass. "Your very good health, Mr. Letting."

He drank, and he rolled the wine round his mouth and then raised his eyebrows.

"May I compliment you on your cellar," he said. "This is an excellent bottle of Margaux."

"Thank you," I said, flattered, I must confess, that this aristocratic Frenchman should approve my choice in wine. "Won't you have a chair and perhaps explain to me how I may be of service to you."

He seated himself elegantly in a chair by the fire, sipped his wine and stared at me thoughtfully for a moment. When his face was in repose like that, one noticed the size and blackness and luster of his eyes. They seemed to probe you; they seemed almost as if they could read one's very thoughts. The impression they gave made one uncomfortable, to say the least. But then he smiled and immediately the eyes flashed with mischief, good humor and an overwhelming charm.

"I'm afraid that my unexpected arrival so late at night—and on such a night—must lend an air of mystery to what is, I'm afraid, a very ordinary request that I have to make of you. Simply, it is that I should like you to catalogue a library for me, a comparatively small collection of books, not above twelve hundred, I surmise, which was left to me by my aunt when she died last year. As I say, it is only a small collection of books and I have done no more than give it a cursory glance. However, I believe it to contain some quite rare and valuable things, and I feel it necessary to have it properly catalogued, a precaution my aunt never took, poor dear. She was a woman with a mind of cotton wool and never, I dare swear, opened a book from the start of her life until the end of it. She led an existence untrammelled and unruffled by the slightest breeze of culture. She had inherited the books from her father, and from the day they came into her possession she never paid them the slightest regard. They are a muddled and confused mess, and I would be grateful if you would lend me your expertise in sorting them out. The reason I have invaded your house at such an hour is force of circumstances, for I must go back to France tomorrow morning very early, and this was my only chance of seeing you. I do hope you can spare the time to do this for me?"

"I shall be happy to be of what assistance I can," I said, for I must admit that the idea of a trip to France was a pleasant thought, "but I am curious to know why you have picked on me when there are so many people who could do the job just as well, if not better."

"I think you do yourself an injustice," said my visitor. "You must be aware of the excellent reputation you enjoy. I asked a number of people for their advice and when I found that they all, of their own free will, advised me to ask you, then I was sure that, if you agreed to do the work, I would be getting the very best, my dear Mr. Letting."

I confess I flushed with pleasure, since there was no way of doubting the man's sincerity, and it was pleasant to know that my colleagues thought so highly of me. "When would you wish me to commence?" I asked.

He spread his hands and gave an expressive shrug. "I'm in no hurry," he said. "Naturally I would have to fall in with your plans. But I was wondering if, say, sometime in the spring? The Loire valley is particularly beautiful then and there is no reason why you should not enjoy the countryside as well as catalogue books."

"The spring would suit me admirably," I said, pouring out some more wine. "Would April be alright?"

"Excellent," he said. "I would think that the job should take you a month or so, but from my point of view, please stay as long as is necessary. I have a good cellar and a good chef, so I can minister to the wants of the flesh, at any rate."

I fetched my diary and we settled on April the fourteenth as being a suitable date for both of us, and my visitor rose to go.

"Just one other thing," he said as he swirled his cloak around his shoulders. "I would be the first to admit that I have a difficult name to remember and pronounce. Therefore, if you would not consider it presumptuous of me, I would like you to call me Gideon, and may I call you Peter?"

"Of course," I said immediately and with some relief, for the name de Teildras Villeray was not one that slid easily off the tongue.

He shook my hand warmly, once again apologized for disturbing me, promised he would write with full details of how to reach him in France and then strode off confidently into the swirling yellow fog and was soon lost to view.

I returned to my warm and comfortable drawing room and finished the bottle of wine while musing on my strange visitor. The more I thought about it the more curious the whole incident became. For example, why had Gideon not approached me when he first saw me at Sotheby's? He said that he was in no hurry to have his library catalogued and yet felt it imperative that he should see me, late at night, as if the matter were of great urgency. Surely he could have written to me? Or did he perhaps think the force of his personality would make me accept a commission that I might otherwise refuse? I was in two minds about the man himself. As I said, when his face was in repose, his eyes were so fiercely brooding and penetrating that they made one uneasy and one was filled almost with a sense of repugnance. But then when he smiled and his eyes filled with laughter and he spoke with that husky, musical voice, one was charmed in spite of oneself. He was, I decided, a very curious character, and I determined that I would try and find out more about him before I went over to France. Having made this resolution, I made my way down to the kitchen, preceded by a now hungry Neptune, and fixed myself my late supper.

A few days later I ran into my old friend Edward Wallenger at a sale, and during the course of it I asked him casually if he knew of Gideon. He gave me a very penetrating look from over the top of his glasses.

"Gideon de Teildras Villeray?" he asked. "D'you mean the Count . . . the nephew of the old Marquis de Teildras Villeray?"

"He didn't tell me he was a Count, but I suppose it must be the same one," I said. "Do you know anything about him?"

"When the sale is over we'll go and have a drink and I'll tell you," said Edward. "They are a very odd family . . . at least, the old Marquis is distinctly odd."

The sale over, we repaired to the local pub and over a drink Edward told me what he knew of Gideon. It appeared that, many years previously, the Marquis de Teildras Villeray had asked my friend to go to France (just as Gideon had done with me) to catalogue and value his extensive library. Edward had accepted the commission and had set off for the Marquis' place in the Gorge du Tarn.

"Do you know that area of France?" Edward asked.

"I have never been to France at all," I confessed.

"Well, it's a desolate area. The house is in a wild and remote district right in the Gorge itself. It's a rugged country, with huge cliffs and deep gloomy gorges, waterfalls and rushing torrents, not unlike the Gustave Doré drawings for Dante's *Inferno*, you know." Edward paused to sip his drink thoughtfully and then occupied himself with lighting a cigar. When it was drawing to his satisfaction, he went on. "In the house, apart from the family retainers of which there seemed to be only three (a small number for such a large establishment), was the uncle and his nephew, who, I take it, was your visitor of the other night. The uncle was—well, not to put too fine a point on it—a most unpleasant old man. He must have been about eighty-five, I suppose, with a really evil, leering face, and an oily manner that he obviously thought was charm. The boy was about fourteen, I suppose, with huge dark eyes in a pale face. He seemed an intelligent lad, old for his age, but the thing that worried me was that he seemed to be suffering from intense fear, a fear, it seemed to me, of his uncle. The first night I arrived, after we had had dinner which was, to my mind, meager and badly cooked fare for France, I went to bed early, for I was fatigued after my journey. The old man and the boy stayed up. As luck would have it, the dining room was directly below my bedroom, and so although I could not hear clearly all that passed between them, I could hear enough to discern that the old man was doing his best to persuade his nephew into some course of action that the boy found repugnant, for he was vehement in his refusal. The argument went on for some time, the uncle's voice getting louder and louder and more angry. Suddenly, I heard the scrape of a chair as the boy stood and shouted—positively shouted, my dear Peter—in French at his uncle, 'No, no, I will not be devoured so that you may live . . . I hate you.' I heard it quite clearly and I thought it an astonishing statement for a young boy to make. Then I heard the door of the dining salon open and bang shut, and I heard the boy's footsteps running up the stairs and, eventually, the banging of what I assumed was his bedroom door. After a short while I heard the uncle get up from the table and come upstairs. There was no mistaking his footfall, for one of his feet was twisted and misshapen, and so he walked slowly with a pronounced limp, dragging his left foot. He came slowly up the stairs, and I do assure you, my dear Peter, there was positive evil in this slow, shuffling approach that really made my hair stand on end. I heard him go to the boy's bedroom door, open it and enter. He called the boy's name two or three times, softly and cajolingly, but with indescribable menace. Then he said one sentence that I could not catch. After this he closed the boy's door and for some moments I could hear him dragging and shuffling down the long corridor to his own quarters. I opened my door and from the boy's room I could hear muffled weeping, as though the poor child had his head under the bedclothes. It went on for a long time, and I was very worried. I wanted to go and comfort the lad, but I felt it might embarrass him, and in any case it was really none of my business. But I did not like the situation at all. The whole atmosphere, my dear Peter, was charged with something unpleasant. I am not a superstitious man, as you well know, but I lay awake for a long time and wondered if I could stay in the atmosphere of that house for the two or three weeks it would take me to finish the job I had agreed to do. Fortunately, fate gave me the chance I needed: the very next day I received a telegram saying that my sister had fallen gravely ill and so, quite legitimately, I could ask de Teildras Villeray to release me from my contract. He was, of course, most reluctant to do so, but he eventually agreed with ill grace. While I was waiting for the dogcart to arrive to take me to the station, I had a quick look round some of his library which, since it was really extensive, spread all over the house. But the bulk of it was housed in what he referred to as the Long Gallery, a very handsome long room that would not have disgraced one of our aristocratic country houses. It was all hung with giant mirrors between the bookcases. In fact, the whole house was full of mirrors. I can never remember being in a house with so many before. Well, he certainly had a rare and valuable collection, particularly on one of your pet subjects, Peter: the occult. I noticed, in my hurried browse, among other things some most interesting Hebrew manuscripts on witchcraft, as well as an original copy of Mathew Hopkin's *Discovery of Witches* and a truly beautiful copy of Dee's *De Mirabilius Naturae*. But then the dogcart arrived and, making my farewells, I left. I can tell you, my dear boy, I was never so glad in my life to be quit of a house. I truly believe the old man to have been evil and would not be surprised to learn that he practiced witchcraft and was trying to involve that nice young lad in his foul affairs. However, I have no proof of this, you understand, so that is why I would not wish you to repeat it. I should imagine that the uncle is now dead, or if not, he must be in his nineties. As to the boy, I later heard from friends in Paris that there were rumors that his private life was not all it should be, some talk of his attachment to certain women, you know, but this was all circumstantial, and in any case, as you know, dear boy, foreigners have a totally different set of morals to an Englishman. It is one of the many things that sets us apart from the rest of the world, thank God."

I had listened with great interest to Edward's account, and I resolved to ask Gideon about his uncle if I got the chance.

So I prepared myself for my trip to France with, I must admit, pleasurable anticipation, and on April the fourteenth I embarked on the train to Dover, thence uneventfully (even to *mal de mer*) to Calais. I spent the night in Paris, sampling the delights of French food and wine, and the following day I embarked once more on the train. Eventually, I arrived at the bustling station at Tours, and Gideon was there to meet me, as he had promised he would. He seemed in great spirits and greeted me as if I were an old and valued friend, which, I confess, flattered me. I thanked him for coming to meet me, but he waved my thanks away.

"It's nothing, my dear Peter," he said. "I have nothing to do except eat, drink and grow fat. A visit from someone like you is a rare pleasure."

Outside the station we entered a handsome brougham drawn by two beautiful bay horses, and we set off at a spanking pace through the most delicious countryside, all green and gold and shimmering in the sunlight. We drove for an hour along roads that got progressively narrower and narrower, until we were travelling along between high banks emblazoned with flowers of every sort, while overhead, the branches of the trees on each side of the road entwined branches covered with the delicate green leaves of spring. Occasionally, there would be a gap in the trees and high banks, and I could see the silver gleam of the Loire between the trees and realized that we were driving parallel to the great river. Once, we passed the massive stone gateposts and huge wrought iron gates that guarded the wide paths up to an immense and very beautiful *château* in gleaming pinky-yellow stone. Gideon saw me looking at it, perhaps with an expression of wonder, for it did look like something out of a fairy tale, and he smiled.

"I hope, my dear Peter, that you do not expect to find me living in a monster like that? If so, you will be doomed to disappointment. I am afraid that my *château* is a miniature one, but big enough for my needs."

I protested that I did not care if he lived in a cow shed: for me the experience of being in France for the first time and seeing all these new sights, and with the prospect of a fascinating job at the end of it, was more than sufficient.

It was not until evening, when the mauve tree shadows were stretched long across the green meadows that we came to Gideon's establishment, the Château St. Claire. The gateposts were surmounted by two large, delicately carved owls in a pale honey-colored stone, and I saw that the same motif had been carried out most skillfully in the wrought iron gates that hung from the pillars. As soon as we entered the grounds, I was struck by the contrast to the countryside we had been passing through, which had been exuberant and unkempt, alive with wild flowers and meadows, shaggy with long rich grass. Here the drive was lined with giant oak and chestnut trees, each the circumference of a small room, gnarled and ancient, with bark as thick as an elephant's hide. How many hundred years these trees had guarded the entrance to the Château St. Claire, I could not imagine, but many of them must have been well-grown trees when Shakespeare was a young man. The greensward under them was as smooth as baize on a billiard table, and responsible for this were several herds of spotted fallow deer, grazing peacefully in the setting sun's rays. The bucks, with their fine twisted antlers, threw up their heads and gazed at us without fear as we clopped past them and down the avenue. Beyond the greensward I could see a line of gigantic poplars and, gleaming between them, the Loire. Then the drive turned away from the river and the *château* came into sight. It was, as Gideon had said, small but perfect, as a miniature is perfect. In the evening sun its pale straw-colored walls glowed and the light gave a soft and delicate patina to the bluish slate of the roofs of the main house and its two turrets. It was surrounded by a wide verandah of great flagstone, hemmed in by a wide balustrade on which were perched above thirty peacocks, their magnificent tails trailing down towards the well-kept lawn. Around the balustrade, the flower beds, beautifully kept, were ablaze with flowers in a hundred different colors that seemed to merge with the peacocks' tails which trailed amongst them. It was a magnificent and breathtaking sight. The carriage pulled up by the wide steps, the butler threw open the door of the brougham, and Gideon dismounted, took off his hat and swept me a low bow, grinning mischievously.

"Welcome to the Château St. Claire," he said.

Thus for me began an enchanted three weeks, for it was more of a holiday than work. The miniature but impeccably kept and furnished *château* was a joy to live in. The tiny park that meandered along the riverbank was also beautifully kept, for every tree looked as if it were freshly groomed; the emerald lawns looked as if they were combed each morning; and the peacocks, trailing their glittering tails amongst the massive trees, looked as if they had just left the careful hands of Fabergé. Combined with a fine cellar and a kitchen ruled over by a red balloon of a chef whose deft hands could conjour up the most delicate and aromatic of meals, you had a close approach to an earthly paradise. The mornings would be spent sorting and cataloguing the books (and a most interesting collection it was), and then in the afternoon Gideon would insist that we go swimming or for a ride round the park, for he possessed a small stable of very nice horses. In the evenings, after dinner, we would sit out on the still sun-warmed terrace and talk, our conversation made warm and friendly with the wine we had consumed and the excellent meal we had eaten. Gideon was an excellent host, a brilliant raconteur and this, together with his extraordinary gift for mimicry, made him a most entertaining companion. I shall never know now, of course, whether he deliberately exerted all his charm in order to ensnare my liking and friendship. I like to think not; I like to think that he quite genuinely liked me and my company. Not that I suppose it matters now. But certainly, as day followed day, I grew fonder and fonder of Gideon. I am a solitary creature by nature, and I have only a very small circle of friends—close friends—whom I see perhaps once or twice a year, preferring, for my part, my own company. However, my time spent at the *château* with Gideon had an extraordinary effect upon me. It began to dawn upon me that I had perhaps made myself into too much of a recluse. It was also borne upon me most forceably that all my friends were of a different age group; they were all much older than I was. Gideon, if I could count him as a friend (and by this time, I certainly did), was the only friend I had who was, roughly speaking, my own age. Under his influence I began to expand. As he said to me one night, a slim cigar crushed between his strong white teeth, squinting at me past the blue smoke, "The trouble with you, Peter, is that you are in danger of becoming a young fogey." I had laughed, of course, but on reflection I knew he was right. I also knew that when the time came for me to leave the *château*, I would miss his volatile company a great deal, probably more than I cared to admit, even to myself.

In all our talks Gideon discussed his extensive family with me with a sort of ironic affection, telling me anecdotes to illustrate their stupidity or their eccentricity, never maliciously but rather with a sort of detached good humor. However, the curious thing was that he never once mentioned his uncle, the Marquis, until one evening. We were sitting out on the terrace, watching the white owls that lived in the hollow oaks along the drive doing their first hunting swoops across the greensward in front of us. I had been telling him of a book which I knew was to be put up for sale in the autumn and which I thought could be purchased for some two thousand pounds, a large price, but it was an important work and I felt he should have it in his library, as it complemented the other works he had on the subject. Did he want me to bid for him? He had flipped his cigar butt over the balustrade into the flower bed, where it lay gleaming like a monstrous red glowworm, and he chuckled softly.

"Two thousand pounds?" he said. "My dear Peter, I am not rich enough to indulge my hobby to that extent unfortunately. If my uncle were to die now it would be a different story."

"Your uncle?" I queried cautiously. "I did not know you had any uncles."

"Only one, thank God," said Gideon, "but unfortunately he holds the purse strings of the family fortunes and the old swine appears to be indestructible. He is ninety-one and when I last saw him, a year or two back, he did not look a day over fifty. However, in spite of all his efforts I do not believe him to be immortal, and so one day the devil will gather him to his bosom, and on that happy day I will inherit a very large sum of money and a library that will make even you, my dear Peter, envious. But until that day comes I cannot go around spending two thousand pounds on a book. But waiting for dead men's shoes is a tedious occupation, and my uncle is an unsavory topic of conversation, so let's have some more wine and talk of something pleasant."

"If he is unsavory, then he is in contrast to the rest of your relatives you have told me about," I said lightly, hoping he would give me further information about his infamous uncle.

Gideon was silent for a moment.

"Yes, a great contrast," he said, "but as every village must have its idiot, so every family must have its black sheep or its madman."

"Oh, come now, Gideon," I protested, "surely that's a bit too harsh a criticism?"

"You think so?" he asked and in the half light I could see that his face was shining with sweat. "You think I am being harsh to my dear relative? But then you have not had the pleasure of meeting him, have you?"

"No," I said, worried by the savage bitterness in his voice and wishing I had let the subject drop since it seemed to disturb him so much.

"When my mother died, I had to go and live with my 'dear' uncle for several years until I inherited the modest amount of money my father left me in trust and then I could be free of him. But for ten years I lived in purgatory with that corrupt old swine. For ten years not a day or night passed without my being terrified out of my soul. There are no words to describe how evil he is, and there are no lengths to which he will not go to achieve his ends. If Satan prowls the earth in the guise of a man, then he surely inhabits the filthy skin of my uncle."

He got up abruptly and went into the house, leaving me puzzled and alarmed at the vehemence with which he had spoken. I did not know whether to follow him or not. But presently he returned carrying the brandy decanter and two glasses. He sat down and poured us both a generous amount of the spirit.

"I must apologize, my dear Peter, for all my histrionics, for inflicting on you melodrama that would be more in keeping in the *Grande Guignol* than on this terrace," he said, handing me my drink. "Talking of my old swine of an uncle always has that effect on me, I'm afraid. At one time I lived in fear because I thought he had captured my soul . . . you know the stupid ideas children get? It was many years before I grew out of that. But it still, as you can see, upsets me to talk of him, so let's drink and talk of other things, eh?"

I agreed wholeheartedly, and we talked pleasantly for a couple of hours or so. But that night was the only time I saw Gideon go to bed the worse for liquor, and I felt most guilty since I felt it was due to my insistence that he talked to me about his uncle who had obviously made such a deep, lasting and unpleasant impression on his mind.

Over the next four years I grew to know Gideon well. He came to stay with me whenever he was in England and I paid several delightful visits to the Château St. Claire. Then for a period of six months I heard nothing from him, and I could only presume that he had been overcome by what he called his "travel disease" and had gone off to Egypt or the Far East or even America on one of his periodic jaunts. However, this coincided with a time when I was, myself, extremely busy and so I had little time to ponder on the whereabouts of Gideon. Then one evening, I returned home to Smith Street dead tired after a long journey from Aberdeen and I found awaiting me a telegram from Gideon:

ARRIVING LONDON MONDAY THIRTY CAN I STAY STOP UNCLE PUT TO DEATH I INHERIT LIBRARY WOULD YOU CATALOGUE VALUE MOVE STOP EXPLAIN ALL WHEN WE MEET REGARDS GIDEON.

I was amused that Gideon, who prided himself on his impeccable English, should have written "put to death" instead of "died" until he arrived and I discovered that this is exactly what had happened to his uncle, or at least, what appeared to have happened. Gideon arrived quite late on the Monday evening, and as soon as I looked at him I could see that he had been undergoing some harrowing experience. But surely, I thought, it could not be the death of his uncle that was affecting him so. If anything, I would have thought he would be glad. But my friend had lost weight, his handsome face was gaunt and white and he had dark circles under his eyes, which themselves seemed to have suddenly lost all their sparkle and luster. When I poured him a glass of his favorite wine he took it with a hand that trembled slightly and tossed it back in one gulp as if it had been mere water.

"You look tired Gideon," I said. "You must have a few glasses of wine and then I suggest an early dinner and bed. We can discuss all there is to be discussed in the morning."

"Dear old Peter," he said, giving me a shadow of his normally effervescent smile, "please don't act like an English nanny, and take that worried look off your face. I am not sickening for anything. It's just that I have had rather a hard time these last few weeks and I'm suffering from reaction. However, it's all over now, thank God. I'll tell you all about it over dinner, but before then I would be grateful if I could have a bath, my dear chap."

"Of course," I said immediately, and went to ask Mrs. Manning to draw a bath for my friend and to take his baggage up to the guest room.

He went upstairs to bathe and change, and very shortly I followed him. Both my bedroom and the guest room each had its own bathroom, for there was sufficient room on that floor to allow this little luxury. I was just about to start undressing in order to start my own ablutions when I was startled by a loud moaning cry, almost a strangled scream, followed by a crash of breaking glass which appeared to emanate from Gideon's bathroom. I hastened across the narrow landing and tapped on his door.

"Gideon?" I called, "Gideon, are you alright . . . can I come in?"

There was no reply and so, greatly agitated, I entered the room. I found my friend in his bathroom, bent over the basin and holding on to it for support, his face the ghastly white of cheese, sweat streaming down it. The big mirror over the basin had been shattered and the fragments, together with a broken bottle of what looked like shampoo, littered the basin and the floor around.

"He did it . . . he did it . . . he did it . . ." muttered Gideon to himself, swaying, clutching hold of the basin. He seemed oblivious of my presence. I seized him by the arm and helped him into the bedroom, where I made him lie down on the bed and called down the stairs for Mrs. Manning to bring up some brandy and look sharp about it.

When I went back into the room, Gideon was looking a little better, but he was lying there with his eyes closed, taking deep shuddering breaths like a man who has just run a gruelling race. When he heard me approach the bed, he opened his eyes and gave me a ghastly smile.

"My dear Peter," he said, "I do apologize . . . so stupid of me . . . I suddenly felt faint . . . I think it must be the journey and lack of food, plus your excellent wine . . . I fear I fell forward with that bottle in my hand and shattered your beautiful mirror. . . . I'm so sorry . . . of course, I will replace it."

I told him, quite brusquely, not to be so silly, and when Mrs. Manning came panting up the stairs with the brandy, I forced him to take some in spite of his protests. While he was drinking it, Mrs. Manning cleaned up the mess in the bathroom.

"Ah. That's better," said Gideon at last. "I feel quite revived now. All I want is a nice relaxing bath and I shall be a new man."

I felt that he ought to have his food in bed, but he would not hear of it, and when he descended to the dining room half an hour later I must say he did look better and much more relaxed. He laughed and joked with Mrs. Manning as she served us and complimented her lavishly on her cooking, swearing that he would get rid of his own chef and kidnap Mrs. Manning and take her to his *château* in France to cook for him. Mrs. Manning was enchanted by him, as indeed she always was, but I could see that it cost him some effort to be so charming and jovial. When at last we had finished the sweet and cheese and Mrs. Manning had put the decanter of port on the table and, saying goodnight, had left us, Gideon accepted a cigar, lighted it, and leant back in his chair and smiled at me through the smoke.

"Now, Peter," he said, "I can tell you something of what's been happening."

"I am most anxious to know what it is that has brought you to this low ebb, my friend," I said seriously.

He felt in his pocket and produced from it a large iron key with heavy teeth and an ornate butt. He threw it on the table, where it fell with a heavy thud. "This was one of the causes of the trouble," he said, staring at it moodily, "the key to life and death, as you might say."

"I don't understand you," I said, puzzled.

"Because of this key I was nearly arrested for murder," said Gideon with a smile.

"Murder? You?" I said, aghast. "But how can that possibly be?"

Gideon took a sip of port and settled himself back in his chair. "About two months ago," he said, "I got a letter from my uncle asking me to go and see him. This I did, with considerable reluctance as you may imagine for you know what my opinion of him was. Well, to cut a long story short, there were certain things he wanted me to do . . . er . . . family matters . . . which I refused to do. He flew into a rage and we quarrelled furiously. I am afraid that I left him in no doubt as to what I thought of him, and the servants heard us quarrel. I left his house and continued on my way to Marseilles to catch a boat for Morocco where I was going for a tour. Two days later my uncle was murdered."

"So that's why you put 'uncle put to death' in your telegram," I said. "I wondered."

"He *had* been put to death, and in the most mysterious circumstances," said Gideon. "He was found in an empty attic at the top of the house which contained nothing but a large broken mirror. He was a hideous mess, his clothes torn off, his throat and body savaged as if by a mad dog. There was blood everywhere. I had to identify the body. It was not a pleasant task, for his face had been so badly mauled that it was almost unrecognizable." He paused and took another sip of port. Presently he went on. "But the curious thing about all this was that the attic was locked, *locked on the inside* with that key."

"But how could that be?" I asked, bewildered. "How did his assailant leave the room?"

"That's exactly what the police wanted to know," said Gideon dryly. "As you know, the French police are very efficient but lacking in imagination. Their logic worked something like this: I was the one who stood to gain by my uncle's death because I inherit the family fortune and his library and several extensive farms dotted about all over France. So as I was the one who stood to gain, *enfin*, I must be the one who committed murder."

"But that's ridiculous," I broke in indignantly.

"Not to a policeman," said Gideon, "especially when they heard that at my last meeting with my uncle we had quarrelled bitterly, and one of the things the servants heard me saying to him was that I wished he would drop dead and thus leave the world a cleaner place."

"But in the heat of a quarrel one is liable to say anything," I protested. "Everyone knows that . . . And how did they suggest you killed your uncle and then left the room locked on the inside?"

"Oh, it was possible, quite possible," said Gideon. "With a pair of long-nosed, very slender pliers, it could be done, but it would undoubtedly have left marks on the end of the key, and as you can see it's unmarked. The real problem was that at first I had no alibi. I had gone down to Marseilles, and as I had cut my visit to my uncle short, I was too early for my ship. I booked into a small hotel and enjoyed myself for those few days in exploring the port. I knew no one there so, naturally, there was no one to vouch for my movements. As you can imagine, it took time to assemble all the porters, maids, *maîtres d'hotels*, restaurant owners, hotel managers and so on and, through their testimony, prove to the police that I was, in fact, in Marseilles and minding my own business when my uncle was killed. It has taken me the last six weeks to do it, and it has been extremely exhausting.

"Why didn't you telegraph me?" I asked. "I could have come and at least have kept you company."

"You are very kind, Peter, but I did not want to embroil my friends in such a sordid mess. Besides, I knew that if all went well and the police released me (which they eventually did after much protest), I should want your help on something appertaining to this."

"Anything I can do," I said. "You know you have only to ask, my dear fellow."

"Well, as I told you, I spent my youth under my uncle's care, and after that experience I grew to loathe his house and everything about it. Now, with this latest thing, I really feel I cannot set foot in that place again. I am not exaggerating but I seriously think that if I were to go there and stay I should become seriously ill."

"I agree," I said firmly. "On no account must you even contemplate such a step."

"Well, the furniture and the house I can, of course, get valued and sold by a Paris firm; that is simple. But the most valuable thing in the house is, of course, the library. And this is where you come in, Peter. Would you be willing to go down and catalogue and value the books for me, and then I can arrange for them to be stored until I can build an extension to my library to house them?"

"Of course I will," I said, "with the greatest of pleasure. You just tell me when you want me to come."

"I shall not be with you; you'll be quite alone," Gideon warned.

"I am a solitary creature, as I have told you." I laughed. "And as long as I have a supply of books to amuse me I shall get along splendidly; don't worry."

"I would like it done as soon as possible," said Gideon, "so that I may get rid of the house. How soon could you come down?"

I consulted my diary and found that, fortunately, I was coming up to a rather slack period. "How about the end of next week?" I asked.

Gideon's face lit up. "So soon?" he said delightedly. "That would be splendid. I could meet you at the station at Fontaine next Friday. Would that be alright?"

"Perfectly alright," I said, "and I will soon have the books sorted out for you. Now, another glass of port and then you must away to bed."

"My dear Peter, what a loss you are to Harley Street," joked Gideon, but he took my advice.

Twice during the night I awakened, thinking that I heard him cry out, but after listening for a while and finding all was quiet, I concluded that it was just my imagination. The following morning he left for France and I started making my preparations to follow him, packing sufficient things for a prolonged stay at his late uncle's house.

The whole of Europe was in the grip of an icy winter and it was certainly not the weather to travel in. Indeed, no one but Gideon could have got me to leave home in such weather. Crossing the Channel was a nightmare, and I felt so sick on arrival in Paris that I could not do more than swallow a little broth and go straight to bed. On the following day it was icy cold, with a bitter wind, grey skies and driving veils of rain that stung one's face. Eventually, I reached the station and boarded the train for what seemed an interminable journey, during which I had to change and wait at more and more inhospitable stations, until I was so numbed with cold I could hardly think straight. All the rivers wore a rim of lacy ice along their shores, and the ponds and lakes turned blank frozen eyes to the steel grey sky.

At length, the local train I had changed to dragged itself, grimy and puffing, into the station of Fontaine and I disembarked and made my way with my luggage to the tiny booking office and minute waiting room. Here, to my relief, I found that there was an old-fashioned, pot-bellied stove stuffed with chestnut roots and glowing almost red hot. I piled my luggage in the corner and spent some time thawing myself out, for the heating on the train had been minimal. There was no sign of Gideon.

Presently, warmed by the fire and a nip of brandy I had taken from my travelling flask, I began to feel better. But half an hour later I began to worry about Gideon's absence. I went out onto the platform and discovered that the grey sky seemed to have moved closer to the earth and a few snowflakes were starting to fall, huge lacy ones the size of a half-crown, that augured a snowstorm of considerable dimensions in the not-too-distant future. I was just wondering if I should try walking to the village when I heard the clop of hooves and made out a dogcart coming along the road, driven by Gideon muffled up in a glossy fur coat and wearing an astrakhan hat.

"I'm so very sorry, Peter, for keeping you waiting like this," he said, wringing my hand, "but we seem to have one catastrophe after another. Come, let me help you with your bags and I will tell you all about it as we drive."

We collected my baggage, bundled it into the dogcart, and then I climbed up onto the box alongside Gideon and covered myself thankfully with the thick fur rug he had brought. He turned the horse, cracked his whip and we went bowling down the snowflakes which were now falling quite fast. The wind whipped our faces and made our eyes water, but still Gideon kept the horse at a fast trot.

"I am anxious to get there before the snowstorm really starts," he said. "That is why I am going at this uncivilized pace. Once these snowstorms start up here they can be very severe. One can even get snowed in for days at a time."

"It is certainly becoming a grim winter," I said.

"The worst we've had here for fifty years," said Gideon.

He came to the village and Gideon was silent as he guided his horse through the narrow, deserted streets, already white with settling snow. Occasionally a dog would run out of an alley and run barking alongside us for a way, but otherwise there was no sign of life and the village could have been deserted for all evidence to the contrary.

"I am afraid that once again, my dear Peter, I shall have to trespass upon your good nature," said Gideon, smiling at me, his hat and his eyebrows white with snow. "Sooner or later my demands on our friendship will exhaust your patience."

"Nonsense," I said. "Just tell me what the problem is."

"Well," said Gideon, "I was to leave you in charge of François and his wife, who were my uncle's servants. Unfortunately, when I went to the house this morning I found that François's wife, Marie, had slipped on the icy front steps and had fallen some thirty feet onto the rocks and broken her legs. They are, I'm afraid, splintered very badly, and I really don't hold out much hope for their being saved."

"Poor woman, how dreadful," I exclaimed.

"Yes," Gideon continued. "Of course, François was nearly frantic when I got there, and so there was nothing for it but to drive them both to the hospital in Milau, which took me over two hours, hence the reason I was late meeting you."

"That doesn't matter at all," I said. "Of course you had to drive them to the hospital."

"Yes, but it creates another problem as well," said Gideon. "You see, none of the villagers liked my uncle, and François and Marie were the only couple who would work for him. So with both of them in Milau, there is no one to look after you, at least for two or three days until François comes back."

"My dear chap, don't let that worry you." I laughed. "I am quite used to fending for myself, I do assure you. If I have food and wine and a fire I will be very well found I promise you."

"Oh, you'll have all that," said Gideon. "The larder is well stocked, and down in the game room there is a haunch of venison, half a wild boar, some pheasants and partridge, and a few brace of wild duck. There is wine aplenty, since my uncle kept quite a good cellar, and the cellar is full of chestnut roots and pine logs, so you will be warm. You will also have for company the animals."

"Animals, what animals?" I asked, curious.

"A small dog called Agrippa," said Gideon, laughing, "a very large and idiotic cat called Clair de Lune, or Clair for short, a whole cage full of canaries and various finches, and an extremely old parrot called Octavius."

"A positive menagerie," I exclaimed. "It's a good thing that I like animals."

"Seriously, Peter," said Gideon, giving me one of his very penetrating looks, "are you sure you will be alright? It seems a terrible imposition to me."

"Nonsense," I said heartily. "What are friends for?"

The snow was now coming down with a vengeance and we could see only a yard or two beyond the horse's ears, so dense were the whirling clouds of huge flakes. We had now entered one of the many tributary gorges that led into the Gorge du Tarn proper.

On our left the brown and black cliffs, dappled with patches of snow on sundry crevices and ledges, loomed over us, in places actually overhanging the narrow road. On our right the ground dropped away, almost sheer, five or six hundred feet into the gorge below where, through the windblown curtains of snow, one could catch occasional glimpses of the green river, its tumbled rocks snow-wigged, their edges crusted with ice. The road was rough, snow and water worn, and in places covered with a sheet of ice that made the horse slip and stumble and slowed our progress. Once a small avalanche of snow slid down the cliff face with a hissing sound and thumped onto the road in front of us, making the horse shy so badly that Gideon had to fight to keep control, and for several hair-raising minutes I feared that we, the dogcart and the terrified horse might slide over the edge of the gorge and plunge down into the river below. But eventually Gideon got it under control and we crawled along our way.

At length the gorge widened a little, and presently we rounded a corner and there before us was the strange bulk of Gideon's uncle's house. It was a very extraordinary edifice and I feel I should describe it in some detail. To begin with, the whole thing was perched up on top of a massive rock that protruded from the river far below so that it formed what could only be described as an island, shaped not unlike an isosceles triangle, with the house on top. It was connected to the road by a massive and very old stone bridge. The tall outside walls of the house fell straight down to the rocks and river below, but as we crossed the bridge and drove under the huge arch, guarded by thick oak doors, we found that the house was built round a large center courtyard, cobblestoned and with a pond with a fountain in the middle. This last depicted a dolphin held up by cherubs, the whole thing polished with ice and with icicles hanging from it. All the many windows that looked down into the court were shuttered with a fringe of huge icicles hanging from every cornice. Between the windows were monstrous gargoyles depicting various forms of animal life, both known and unknown to science, each one seeming more malign than the last and their appearance not improved by the ice and snow that blurred their outlines so that they seemed to be peering at you from some snowy ambush. As Gideon drew the horse to a standstill by the steps that led to the front door, we could hear the barking of the dog inside. My friend opened the front door with a large rusty key and immediately the dog tumbled out, barking vociferously and wagging its tail with pleasure. The large black-and-white cat was more circumspect and did not deign to come out into the snow but merely stood, arching its back and mewing, in the doorway. Gideon helped me carry my bags into the large marble hall, where a handsome staircase led to the upper floors of the house. All the pictures, mirrors and furniture were covered with dust sheets.

"I am sorry about the covers," said Gideon, and it seemed to me that as soon as he entered the house he became increasingly nervous and ill at ease. "I meant to remove them all this morning and make it more habitable for you, but what with one thing and another I did not manage it."

"Don't worry," I said, making a fuss over the dog and cat, who were both vying for my attention. "I shan't be inhabiting all of the house, so I will just remove the sheets in those parts that I shall use."

"Yes, yes," said Gideon, running his hands through his hair in a nervous fashion. "Your bed is made up . . . the bedroom is the second door on the left as you reach the top of the stairs. Now, come with me and I'll show you the kitchen and cellar."

He led me across the hall to a door that was hidden under the main staircase. Opening this he made his way down broad stone steps that spiralled their way down into gloom. Presently we reached a passageway that led to a gigantic stone-flagged kitchen and, adjoining it, cavernous cellars and a capacious larder, cold as a glacier, with the carcasses of game, chicken and duck, and legs of lamb and saddles of beef hanging from hooks or lying on the marble shelves that ran around the walls. In the kitchen was a great range, each fire carefully laid, and on the great table in the center had been arranged various commodities that Gideon thought I may need: rice, lentils as black as soot, potatoes, carrots and other vegetables in large baskets, pottery jars of butter and preserves, and a pile of freshly baked loaves. On the other side of the kitchen, opposite to the cellars and larder, lay the wine store, approached through a heavy door, bolted and padlocked. Obviously Gideon's uncle had not trusted his staff when it came to alcoholic beverages. The cellar was small, but I saw at a glance that it contained some excellent vintages.

"Do not stint yourself, Peter," said Gideon. "There are some really quite nice wines in there and they will be some small compensation for staying in the gloomy place alone."

"You want me to spend my time in an inebriated state?" I laughed. "I would never get the books valued. But don't worry, Gideon; I shall be quite alright. As I told you before, I like being on my own, and here I have food and wine enough for an army, plenty of fuel for the fire, a dog and a cat and birds to keep me company and a large and interesting library. What more could any man want?"

"The books, by the way, are mainly in the Long Gallery, on the south side of the house. I won't show it to you—it's easy enough to find—but I really must be on my way," said Gideon, leading the way up into the hall once more. He delved into his pocket and produced a huge bunch of ancient keys. "The 'keys of the Kingdom,'" he said with a faint smile. "I don't think anything is locked, but if it is, please open it. I will tell François that he is to come back here and look after you as soon as his wife is out of danger, and I myself will return in about four weeks' time. By then you should have finished your task."

"Easily," I said. "In fact, if I get it done before then I will send you a telegram."

"Seriously, Peter," he said, taking my hand, "I am really most deeply in your debt for what you are doing. I shall not forget it."

"Rubbish, my friend," I said. "It gives me great pleasure to be of service to you."

I stood in the doorway of the house, the dog panting by my side, the cat arching itself round my legs and purring loudly, and watched Gideon get back into the dogcart, wrap the rug around himself and then flick the horses with the reins. As they broke into a trot and he steered them towards the entrance to the courtyard, he raised his whip in salute. He disappeared through the archway and very soon the sound of the hoof beats were muffled by the snow and soon faded altogether. Picking up the warm silky body of the cat and whistling to the dog who had chased the dogcart to the archway, barking exuberantly, I went back into the house and bolted the front door behind me.

I decided that the first thing to do was to explore the house and ascertain where the various books were that I had come to work with, and thus to make up my mind which rooms I needed to open up. On a table in the hall I had spotted a large six-branched silver candelabra loaded with candles and a box of matches lying beside it. I decided to use this in my exploration since it would relieve me of the tedium of having to open and close innumerable shutters. So, lighting the candles and accompanied by the eager, bustling dog whose nails rattled on the bare floors like castanets, I started off. The whole of the ground floor consisted of three very large rooms and one smaller one, which comprised the drawing room, the dining room, a study and then this smaller salon. Strangely enough, this room—which I called the blue salon as it was decorated in various shades of blue and gold—was the only one that was locked, and it took me some time to find the right key for it. This salon formed one end of the house and so it was a long, narrow shoebox shape, with large windows at each end. The door by which you entered was midway down one of the longer walls and hanging on the wall opposite was one of the biggest mirrors I have ever seen. It must have been fully nine feet high, stretching from floor level to almost the ceiling, and some thirty-five feet in length. The mirror itself was slightly tarnished, which gave it a pleasant bluish tinge, like the waters of a shallow lake, but it still reflected clearly and accurately. The whole was encompassed in a wide and very ornate gold frame, carved to depict various nymphs and satyrs, unicorns, griffons and other fabulous beasts. The frame in itself was a work of art. By seating oneself in one of the comfortable chairs that stood one on each side of the fireplace, one could see the whole room reflected in this remarkable mirror, and although the room was somewhat narrow, this gave one a great sense of space. Owing to the size, the convenience and—I must admit—the novelty of the room, I decided to make it my living room, and so in a very short space of time I had the dust covers off the furniture and a roaring blaze of chestnut roots in the hearth. Then I moved in the cage of finches and canaries and placed them at one end of the room together with Octavius, the parrot, who seemed pleased by the change, for he shuffled his feathers, cocked his head to one side and whistled a few bars of the "Marseillaise." The dog and cat immediately stretched out in front of the blaze and fell into a contented sleep. Thus, deserted by my companions, I took my candelabra and continued my investigation of the house alone.

The next floor was comprised mainly of bed and bathrooms, but I found that one whole wing of the house (which formed the hollow square in which the courtyard lay) was one enormous room, the Long Gallery, as Gideon had called it. Down one side of this long, wide room—which would have done credit to any great country house in England—there were very tall windows, and opposite each window was a tall mirror, similar to the one downstairs but long and narrow. Between these mirrors stood the bookcases of polished oak, and piled on the shelves haphazardly were a myriad of books, some on their sides, some upside down in total confusion. Even a cursory glance was enough to tell me that the library was so muddled it would take me some considerable time to sort the books into subjects before I could even start to catalogue and value them. Leaving the Long Gallery shrouded in dust sheets and with the shutters still closed, I went one floor higher. Here there were only attics, and in one of them I came upon the gilt frame of a mirror and I shivered, for I presumed that this was the attic in which Gideon's uncle had been found dead. The mirror frame was identical to the one in the blue salon but on a much smaller scale, of course. Here again were the satyrs, the unicorns, the griffons and hippographs, but in addition there was a small area at the top of the frame, carved like a medallion, in which were inscribed in French the words: "I am your servant. Feed and liberate me. I am you." It did not seem to make sense. I closed the attic door and, chiding myself for being a coward, I locked it securely and in consequence felt much better.

When I made my way downstairs to the blue salon, I was greeted with rapture by both dog and cat, as if I had been away on a journey of many days, and I realized that they were hungry. Simultaneously I realized that I was hungry too, for the excitement of arriving at the house and exploring it had quite made me forget to prepare myself any luncheon and it was now past six o'clock in the evening. So, accompanied by the eager animals, I made my way down to the kitchen to cook some food for us all. For the dog, I stewed some scraps of mutton, and a little chicken for the cat, both combined with some boiled rice and potatoes; they were delighted with this menu. For myself, I grilled a large steak with an assortment of vegetables and chose from the cellar an excellent bottle of red wine. When this was ready I carried it up to the blue salon and, pulling my chair up to the fire, made myself comfortable and fell on the food hungrily. Presently the dog and the cat, replete with food, joined me and spread out in front of the fire. I got up and closed the door once they were settled, for there was quite a cold draught from the big hall which, with its marble floor, was now as cold as an ice-chest. Finishing my food, I lay back contentedly in my chair, sipping my wine and watching the blue flames run to and fro over the chestnut roots in the fire. I was very relaxed and happy and the wine, rich and heavy, was having a soporific effect on me. I slept for perhaps an hour. Then, suddenly, I was fully awake with every nerve tingling, as if someone had shouted my name. I listened, but the only sounds were the soft breathing of the sleeping dog and the contented purr of the cat curled up on the chair opposite me. It was so silent that I could hear the faint bubble and crackle of the chestnut roots in the fire. Feeling sure I must have imagined a sound, and yet feeling unaccountably uneasy for no discernible reason, I threw another log on the fire and settled back in the chair to doze.

It was then I glanced across at the mirror opposite me and noticed that in the reflection the door to the salon which I had carefully closed was now ajar. Surprised, I twisted round in my chair and looked at the real door, only to find it was securely closed as I had left it. I looked again into the mirror and made sure my eyes—aided by the wine—were not playing tricks, but sure enough, in the reflection the door appeared to be slightly ajar. I was sitting there looking at it and wondering what trick of light and reflection could produce the effect of an open door when the door responsible for the reflection was securely closed, when I noticed something that made me sit up, astonished and uneasy. *The door in the reflection was being pushed open still further.* I looked at the real door again and saw that it was still firmly shut. Yet its reflection in the mirror was opening, very slowly, millimeter by millimeter. I sat watching it, the hair on the nape of my neck stirring, and suddenly round the edge of the door, on the carpet, there appeared something that at first glance I thought was some sort of caterpillar. It was long, wrinkled and yellowishwhite in color, and at one end it had a long blackened horn. It humped itself up and scrabbled at the surface of the carpet with its horn in a way that I had seen no caterpillar behave. Then, slowly, it retreated behind the door. I found that I was sweating. I glanced once more at the real door to assure myself that it was closed because, for some reason or other, I did not fancy having that caterpillar or whatever it was crawling about the room with me. The door was still shut. I took a draught of wine to steady my nerves and was annoyed to see that my hand was shaking. I, who had never believed in ghosts, or hauntings, or magic spells or any of that claptrap, was imagining things in a mirror and convincing myself to such an extent they were real that I was actually afraid. It was ridiculous, I told myself as I drank the wine. There was some perfectly rational explanation for the whole thing. I sat forward in my chair and gazed at the reflection in the mirror with great intentness. For a long time nothing happened, and then the door in the mirror swung open a fraction and the caterpillar appeared again, but this time it was joined by another and then, after a pause, yet another and suddenly my blood ran cold for I realized what it was. They were not caterpillars but attenuated yellow fingers with long black nails twisted like gigantic misshapen rose thorns. The moment I realized this the whole hand came into view, feeling its way feebly along the carpet. The hand was a mere skeleton covered with the pale yellow, parchmentlike skin through which the knuckles and joints showed like walnuts. It felt around on the carpet in a blind, groping sort of way, the hand moving from a bony wrist, like the tentacles of some strange sea anemone from the deep, one that has become pallid through living in perpetual dark. Then slowly it withdrew behind the door. I shuddered for I wondered what sort of body was attached to that horrible hand. I waited for perhaps quarter of an hour, dreading what might suddenly appear from behind the mirror door, but nothing happened.

After a while I became restive. I was still attempting to convince myself that the whole thing was an hallucination brought on by the wine and the heat of the fire, but without success. For there was the door of the blue salon carefully closed against the draught and the door in the mirror still ajar with apparently something lurking behind it. I wanted to walk over to the mirror and examine it, but I did not have the courage, I regret to say. Instead, I thought of a plan which, I felt, would show me whether I was imagining things or not. I woke Agrippa the dog and, crumpling up a sheet of the newspaper I had been reading into a ball, I threw it down the room so that it landed just by the closed door. In the mirror it lay just near the door that was ajar. Agrippa, more to please me than anything else for he was very sleepy, bounded after it. Gripping the arms of my chair, I watched his reflection in the mirror as he ran towards the door. He reached the ball of newspaper and paused to pick it up. And then something so hideous happened that I could scarcely believe my eyes. The mirror door was pushed open still further and the hand and a long white bony arm shot out. It grabbed the dog in the mirror by the scruff of its neck and pulled it speedily, kicking and struggling, behind the door. Agrippa had now come back to me, having retrieved the newspaper, but I took no notice of him, for my gaze was fixed on the reflection in the mirror. After a few minutes the hand suddenly reappeared. Was it my imagination or did it now seem stronger? At any event, it curved itself round the woodwork of the door and drew it completely shut, leaving on the white paint a series of bloody fingerprints that made me feel sick. The real Agrippa was nosing my leg, the newspaper in his mouth, seeking my approval, while behind the mirror door, God knows what fate had overtaken his reflection.

To say that I was shaken means nothing. I could scarcely believe the evidence of my senses. I sat staring at the mirror for a long time, but nothing further happened. Eventually, and with my skin prickling with fear, I got up and examined both the mirror and the door into the salon, but both bore a perfectly ordinary appearance. I wanted very much to open the door to the salon and see if the reflection in the mirror opened as well, but to tell the truth, I was too frightened of disturbing whatever it was that lurked behind the mirror door. I glanced up at the top of the mirror and saw for the first time that it bore the same inscription as the one I had found in the attic: *I am your servant. Feed and liberate me. I am you.* Did this mean the creature behind the door, I wondered? Feed and liberate me—was that what I had done by letting the dog go near the door? Was the creature now feasting upon the dog it had caught in the mirror? I shuddered at the thought. I determined that the only thing to do was to get a good night's rest, for I was tired and overwrought. In the morning, I assured myself, I would hit upon a ready explanation for all this mumbo-jumbo. So, picking up the cat and calling for the dog (for, if the truth be known, I needed the company of the animals), I left the blue salon. As I was closing the door I was frozen into immobility and the hair on my head prickled as I heard a cracked, harsh voice bid me *"Bon nuit"* in wheedling tones. It was a moment or two before I realized it was Octavius the parrot and went limp with relief.

Clair the cat drowsed peacefully in my arms, but Agrippa needed some encouragement to accompany me upstairs, for it was obvious that he had never been allowed above the ground floor before. At length, with reluctance that soon turned to excitement at the novelty, he followed me upstairs. The fire in the bedroom had died down, but the atmosphere was still warm. I made my toilet and, without further ado, climbed into bed with Agrippa lying on one side of me and Clair on the other. I received much comfort from the feel of their warm bodies but, in addition, I am not ashamed to say I left the candles burning and the door to the room securely locked.

The following morning when I awoke I was immediately conscious of the silence. Throwing open the shutters, I gazed out at a world muffled in snow. It must have been snowing steadily all night, and great drifts had piled up on the rock faces, on the bare trees, along the river bank and piled in a great cushion some seven feet deep along the crest of the bridge that joined the house to the mainland. Every windowsill and every projection of the eaves were a fearsome armory of icicles, and the sills themselves were varnished with a thin layer of ice. The sky was dark grey and lowering so that I could see we were in for yet more snow. Even if I had wanted to leave the house, the roads were already impassable, and with another snowfall, I would be completely cut off from the outside world. I must say that, thinking back on my experiences of the previous night, this fact made me feel somewhat uneasy. But I chided myself and by the time I had finished dressing, I had managed to convince myself that my experience in the blue salon was due entirely to a surfeit of good wine and an overexcited imagination.

Thus comforting myself, I went downstairs, picked up Clair in my arms, called Agrippa to heel and, steeling myself, threw open the door of the blue salon and entered. It was as I had left it, the dirty plates and wine bottle near my chair, the chestnut roots in the fire burnt to a delicate grey ash that stirred slightly at the sudden draught from the open door. But it was the only thing in the room that stirred. Everything was in order. Everything was normal and I heaved a sigh of relief. It was not until I was halfway down the room that I glanced at the mirror, and I stopped as suddenly as if I had walked into a brick wall and my blood froze, for I could not believe what I was seeing.

Reflected in the mirror was myself with the cat in my arms, but *there was no dog at my heels, although Agrippa was nosing at my ankles*.

For several seconds I stood there thunderstruck, unable to believe the evidence of my own senses, gazing first at the dog at my feet and then at the mirror with no reflection of the animal. I, the cat and the rest of the room were reflected with perfect clarity, but there was no reflection of Agrippa. I dropped the cat on the floor (and she remained reflected by the mirror) and picked Agrippa up in my arms. In the mirror I appeared to be carrying an imaginary object in my arms. Hastily I picked up the cat and so, with Clair under one arm and an invisible dog under the other, I left the blue salon and securely locked the door behind me.

Down in the kitchen I was ashamed to find that my hands were shaking. I gave the animals some milk (and the way Agrippa dealt with his, there was no doubt he was a flesh-and-blood animal) and made myself some breakfast. As I automatically fried eggs and some heavily smoked ham, my mind was busy with what I had seen in the blue salon. Unless I was mad—and I had never felt saner in my life—I was forced to admit that I had really experienced what I had seen, incredible though it seemed and indeed still seems to me. Although I was terrified at whatever it was that lurked behind the door in the mirror, yet I was filled with an overwhelming curiosity, a desire to see whatever creature it was that possessed that gaunt and tallow hand, yellow and emaciated arm. I determined that that very evening I would attempt to lure the creature out so that I could examine it. I was filled with horror at what I intended to do, but my curiosity was stronger than my fear. So I spent the day cataloguing the books in the study and, when darkness fell, I again lit the fire in the salon and cooked myself some supper and carried it and a bottle of wine upstairs and settled myself by the hearth. This time, however, I had taken the precaution of arming myself with a stout ebony cane and this gave me a certain confidence, though if I had thought about it, what use a cane was going to be to me against a looking-glass adversary, Heaven only knew. As it turned out eventually, arming myself with the stick was the worst thing I could have done and nearly cost me my life.

I ate my food, my eyes fixed on the mirror, the two animals lying asleep at my feet as they had done the night before. I finished my meal and still there was no change in the mirror image of the door. I sat back sipping my wine and watching. After an hour or so the fire was burning low and so I got up to put some logs on it; I had just settled back in my chair when I saw the handle of the mirror door start to turn very slowly. Then, millimeter by millimeter, the door was pushed open a foot or so. It was incredible that the opening of a door should be charged with such menace, but the slow furtive way it swung across the carpet was indescribably evil. Then the hand appeared, again moving very slowly, humping its way across the carpet until the wrist and part of the yellowish forearm was in view. It paused for a moment, lying flaccid on the carpet. Then, in a sickening sort of way, it started to grope around, as if the creature in control of the hand was blind. Now, it seemed to me, was the moment to put my carefully thought out plan into operation. I had deliberately starved Clair so that she would be hungry and so now I woke her up and waved under her nose a piece of meat which I had brought up from the kitchen for this purpose. Her eyes widened and she let out a loud mew of excitement. I waved the meat under her nose until she was frantic to get the morsel and then I threw it down the room so that it landed on the carpet near the firmly closed door of the salon. In the mirror I could see that it had landed near, but not too near the reflection of the hand which was still groping about blindly. Uttering a loud wail of hunger, Clair sped down the room after it. I had hoped that the cat would be so far away from the door that it would tempt the creature out into the open. But I realized that I had thrown the meat too close to the door for, as Clair's reflection stopped and the cat bent down to take the meat in her mouth, the hand ceased its blind groping, and shooting out with incredible speed, it seized Clair by the tail and dragged her, struggling and twisting, behind the door. As before, after a moment, the hand reappeared, curved round the door and slowly drew it shut, leaving bloody fingerprints on the woodwork. I think what made the whole thing doubly horrible was the contrast between the speed and ferocity with which the hand grabbed its prey, and the slow, furtive way it opened and closed the door. Clair now returned with the meat in her mouth to eat it in comfort by the fire, and like Agrippa, she seemed none the worse for now having no reflection. Although I waited up until after midnight the hand did not appear again, and so I took the animals and went to bed, determined that on the morrow I would work out a plan that would force the thing behind the door to show itself.

By evening on the following day I had finished my preliminary sorting and listing of the books on the ground floor of the house, and so the next step was to move upstairs to where the bulk of the library was housed in the Long Gallery. I felt somewhat tired that day and so, towards five o'clock, I decided to take a turn outside to get some fresh air in my lungs. Alas for my hopes! It had been snowing steadily since my arrival and now the glistening drifts were so high I could not walk through them. The only way to have got out of the central courtyard and across the bridge would have been to dig a path, and this would have been through snow lying in a great crusty blanket some six feet deep. Some of the icicles hanging from the guttering, the window ledges and the gargoyles were four and five feet long and as thick as my arm. The animals would not accompany me, but I tried walking a few steps into this spacious white world, as silent and as cold as the bottom of a well. The snow squeaked protestingly, like mice, beneath my shoes, and I sank in over my knees and soon had to struggle back to the house. The snow was still falling in flakes as big as dandelion blooms, thickening the white pie crusts on the roof ridges and gables. There was that complete silence that snow brings, no sound, no bird song, no whine of wind, just an almost tangible silence, as though the living world had been gagged with a crisp white scarf. Rubbing my frozen hands, I hastened inside, closed the front door and hastened down to the kitchen to prepare my evening meal. While this was cooking, I lit the fire in the blue salon once more and when the food was ready carried it up there as had become my habit, the animals accompanying me. Once again I armed myself with my stout stick and this gave me a small measure of comfort. I ate my food and drank my wine, watching the mirror but the hand did not put in an appearance.

Where was it, I wondered. Did it stalk about and explore a reflection of the house that lay behind the door, a reflection I could not see? Or did it exist only when it became a reflection in the mirror that I looked at? Musing on this, I dozed, warmed by the fire, and presently slept deeply, which I had not meant to do. I must have slept for about an hour when I was suddenly shocked awake by the sound of a voice, a thin cracked voice, singing shrilly:

> *Auprès de ma blonde, auprès de ma blonde,*
> *qu'il fait bon dormir . . .*

This was followed by a grating peal of hysterical laughter. Half asleep as I was, it was a moment before I realized that the singing and laughter came from Octavius. But the shock of suddenly hearing a human voice like that was considerable, and my heart was racing. I glanced down the room and saw that the cages containing the canaries and Octavius were still as I had placed them. Then I glanced in the mirror and sat transfixed in my chair at the sight I saw. I suffered a revulsion and terror that surpassed anything I had felt before, for my wish had been granted and the thing from behind the door had appeared. As I watched it, how fervently I wished to God that I had left well alone, that I had locked the blue salon after the first night and never revisited it.

The creature—I must call it that for it seemed scarcely human—was small and humpbacked and clad in what I could only believe was a shroud, a yellowish linen garment spotted with gobbets of dirt and mould, torn in places where the fabric had worn thin, pulled over the thing's head and twisted round, like a scarf. At that moment, all that was visible of its face was a tattered fringe of faded orange hair on a heavily lined forehead and two large pale yellow eyes that glared with the fierce, impersonal arrogance of a goat, while below them the shroud was twisted round and held in place by one of the thing's pale, black-nailed hands.

It was standing behind the big cage that had contained the canaries. The cage was now twisted and wrenched and disembowelled, like a horse in a bull ring, and covered with a cloud of yellow feathers that stuck to the bloodstains on the bars. I noticed that there were a few yellow feathers between the fingers of the creature's hand. As I watched, it moved from the remains of the canary cage to the next table where the parrot cage had been placed. It moved slowly and limped heavily, appearing more to drag one foot after the other than anything else. It reached the cage in which the reflection of Octavius was weaving from side to side on his perch. The real bird in the room with me was still singing and cackling with laughter periodically. In the mirror the creature studied the parrot in its cage with its ferocious yellow eyes. Then suddenly, two things happened. The thing's hand shot out and the fingers entwined round the bars of the cage and wrenched and twisted them apart. While both hands were thus occupied, the piece of shroud that had been covering the face fell away and revealed the most disgusting face I have ever seen. Most of the features below the eyes appeared to have been eaten away, either by decay or some disease akin to leprosy. Where the nose should have been, there were just two black holes with tattered rims. The whole of one cheek was missing and so the upper and lower jaw, with mildewed gums and decaying teeth, were displayed, and trickles of saliva flooded out from the mouth and dripped down into the folds of the shroud. What was left of the lips were serrated with fine wrinkles so that they looked as though they had been stitched together and the cotton pulled tight. What made the whole thing even worse, as a macabre spectacle, was that on one of the creature's disgusting fingers it wore a large gold ring in which an opal flashed like flame as its hands moved, twisting the metal of the cage. This refinement on such a corpselike apparition only served to enhance its repulsive appearance. Presently it had twisted the wires enough so that there was room for it to put its hands inside the cage. The parrot was still bobbing and weaving on his perch, and the real Octavius was still singing and laughing. The creature grabbed the parrot in the reflection and it flapped and struggled in its hands, while Octavius continued to sing. The creature dragged the bird from the broken cage and lifted it to its obscene mouth and cracked the parrot's skull as it would a nut, and then with enjoyment started to suck out the brains, feathers and fragments of brain and skull mixing with the saliva that fell from the thing's mouth onto the shroud. I was filled with such revulsion and yet such rage at the creature's actions that I grasped my stick and leapt to my feet, trembling with anger. I approached the mirror and as I did so and my reflection appeared, I realized that (in the mirror) I was approaching the thing from behind. I moved forward until, in the reflection, I was close to the thing and then I raised my stick. But suddenly the creature's eyes appeared to blaze in its disintegrating face, and it stopped its revolting feast and dropped the corpse of the parrot to the ground at the same time whirling round to face my reflection with such speed that I was taken aback and stood there, staring at it, my stick raised. The creature did not hesitate for a second but dived forward and fastened its lean and powerful hands round my throat in the reflection. This sudden attack made my reflection stagger backwards and it dropped the stick. The creature and my reflection fell to the floor behind the table and I could see them both thrashing about together. Horrified, I dropped my stick and running to the mirror beat futilely against the glass. Presently all movement ceased behind the table. I could not see what was happening but, convinced the creature was dealing with my reflection as it had done with the dog and the cat, I continued to beat upon the mirror's surface. Presently, from behind the table, the creature rose up unsteadily, panting. It had its back to me. It remained like that for a moment or two and then it bent down and seizing my reflection body it dragged it slowly through the door. As it did so, I could see that the body had had its throat torn out. The creature then reappeared licking its lips in an anticipatory sort of way. It picked up the ebony stick and once more disappeared. It was gone some ten minutes and when it came back it was—to my horror and anger—feasting upon a severed hand, as a man might eat the wing of a chicken. Forgetting all fear, I beat on the mirror again. Slowly, as if trying to decide where the noise was coming from, the beast turned round, its eyes flashing terribly, its face covered with blood that could only be mine. Then it saw me and its eyes widened with a ferocious, knowing expression that turned me cold. Slowly it started to approach the mirror, and as it did so I stopped my futile hammering on the glass and backed away, appalled by the menace in the thing's goatlike eyes. Slowly it moved forward, its fierce eyes fixed on me as if stalking me. When it was close to the mirror, it put out its hands and touched the glass, *leaving bloody fingerprints and yellow and grey feathers stuck to the glass*. It felt the surface of the mirror delicately, as one would test the fragility of ice on a pond, and then it bunched its appalling hands into knobbly fists and beat a sudden furious tattoo on the glass, emitting a sudden, startling rattle of drums in the silent room. Then it unbunched its hands and felt the glass again. It stood for a moment watching me, as if it were musing. It was quite obvious that it could see me and I could only conclude that, although I possessed no reflection in my mirror, I must be visible as a reflection in the mirror that formed part of the looking-glass world which this creature inhabited. Suddenly, as if coming to a decision, it turned and limped off across the room and then, to my alarm, it disappeared through the door only to reappear a moment later carrying in its hands the ebony stick that my reflection had been carrying. Terrified, I realized that if I could hear the creature beating on the glass with its hands it must be in some way *solid*, and this meant that if it attacked the mirror with the stick the chances were the glass would shatter and that the creature could then, in some way, get through to me. As it limped down the room I made up my mind. I was determined that neither I nor the animals would stay in the blue salon any longer. I ran to where the cat and the dog lay asleep in front of the fire and gathered them up in my arms. I ran down the room and threw them unceremoniously into the hall. As I turned and hurried towards the bird cages, the creature reached the mirror, whirled the stick around its head and brought it crashing down. I saw that part of the mirror whiten and star in the way that ice on a pond does when struck with a stone. I did not wait. I seized the two cages and fled down the room with them and threw them into the hall and followed. As I grabbed the door to pull it shut, there was another crash and I saw a large portion of the mirror shower onto the floor and, sticking through the void, protruding into the blue salon, the emaciated, twisted arm of the creature brandishing the ebony cane. I did not wait to see more, but slammed the door and turned the key in the lock and leaned against the solid wood, the sweat running down my face, my heart hammering.

I collected my wits after a moment and made my way down to the kitchen where I poured myself a stiff brandy. My hand was trembling so much that I could hardly hold the glass. Desperately, I marshalled my wits and tried to think. It seemed to me that the mirror, when broken, acted as an *entrance* for the creature into my world. I did not know whether it was just this particular mirror or all mirrors. Furthermore, I did not know—if I broke any mirror that might act as an entrance for the thing—whether I would be preventing it or aiding it. I was shaking with fear but I knew that I would have to do something, for it was obvious that the creature would hunt me through the house. I went into the cellar and found myself a short, broad-bladed axe and then, picking up the candelabra, I made my way upstairs. The door to the blue salon was securely locked. I steeled myself and went into the study next door where there was, I knew, a medium-sized mirror hanging on the wall. I approached it, the candelabra held high, my axe ready. It was a curious sensation to stand in front of a mirror and not see yourself. I stood thus for a moment and then started with fright, for there appeared in the mirror suddenly, where my reflection should have been, the ghastly face of the creature glaring at me with a mad, lustful look in its eyes. I knew this was the moment that I would have to test my theory, but even so, I hesitated for a second before I smashed the axe head against the glass and saw it splinter and heard the pieces crash to the floor.

I stepped back after I had dealt the blow and stood with my weapon raised, ready to do battle should the creature try to get at me through the mirror, but with the disappearance of the glass, it was as if the creature had disappeared as well. Then I knew my idea was correct: if the mirror was broken from my side it ceased to be an entrance. I now knew that, to save myself, I had to destroy every mirror in the house and do it quickly, before the creature got to them and broke through. Picking up the candelabra, I moved swiftly to the dining salon where there was a large mirror and reached it just as the creature did. Luckily, I dealt the glass a shivering blow before the thing could break it with the cane that it still carried.

Moving as quickly as I could without quenching the candles, I made my way up to the first floor. Here I moved swiftly from bedroom to bedroom, bathroom to bathroom, wreaking havoc. Fear must have lent my feet wings because I arrived at all these mirrors before the creature did and managed to break them without seeing a sign of my adversary. Then all that was left was the Long Gallery with its ten or so huge mirrors hanging between the tall bookcases. I made my way there as rapidly as I could, walking for some stupid reason on tiptoe. When I reached the door, I was overcome with terror that the creature would have reached there before me and broken through and was, even now, waiting for me in the darkness. I put my ear to the door but could hear nothing. Taking a deep breath I threw open the door, holding the candelabra high.

Ahead of me lay the Long Gallery in soft velvety darkness, as anonymous as a mole's burrow. I stepped inside the door and the candle flames rocked and twisted on the ends of the candles, flapping the shadows like black funeral pennants on the floor and walls. I walked a little way into the room peering at the far end of the gallery, which was too far away to be illuminated by my candles, but it seemed to me that all the mirrors were intact. Hastily I placed the candelabra on a table and turned to the long row of mirrors. At that moment a sudden loud crash and tinkle sent my heart into my mouth, and it was a moment or so before I realized, with sick relief, that it was not the sound of a breaking mirror I heard but the noise of a great icicle that had broken loose from one of the windows and had fallen, with a sound like breaking glass, into the courtyard below.

I knew I had to act swiftly before that shuffling, limping monstrosity reached the Long Gallery and broke through. Taking a grip on the axe, I hurried from mirror to mirror, creating wreckage that no delinquent schoolboy could have rivalled. Again and again I smashed the head of the axe into the smooth surface like a man clearing ice from a lake, and the surface would star and whiten and then slip, the pieces chiming musically as they fell, to crash on the ground. The noise, in that silence, was extraordinarily loud. I reached the last mirror but one, and as my axe head splintered it, the one next door cracked and broke and the ebony stick, held in the awful hand, came through. Dropping the axe in my fright, I turned and fled, pausing only to snatch up the candelabra. As I slammed the door shut and locked it, I caught a glimpse of something white struggling to disentangle itself from the furthest mirror in the Gallery. I leaned against the door, shaking with fright, my heart hammering, listening. Dimly, through the locked door, I could hear faint sounds of tinkling glass and then there was silence. I strained my ears but could hear no more. Then, against my back, I could feel the handle of the door being slowly turned. Cold with fear, I leapt away and, fascinated, watched the handle move round until the creature realized that the door was locked. Then there came such an appalling scream of frustrated rage, shrill, raw and indescribably evil and menacing, that I almost dropped the candelabra in my fright. I leaned against the wall, shaking, wiping the sweat from my face but limp with relief. Now all the mirrors in the house were broken and the only two rooms that thing had access to were securely locked. For the first time in twenty-four hours, I felt safe. Inside the Long Gallery the creature was snuffling round the door like a pig in a trough. Then it gave another blood-curdling scream of frustrated rage and then there was silence. I listened for a few minutes but I could hear nothing so, taking up my candelabra, I started to make my way downstairs.

I paused frequently to listen. I moved slowly so that the tiny scraping noises of my sleeve against my coat would not distract my hearing. I held my breath. All I could hear was my heart, hammering against my ribs like a desperate hand, and the very faint rustle and flap of the candle flames as they danced to my movement. Thus, slowly, every sense alert, I made my way down to the lower floor of that gaunt, cold, empty house. It was not until I reached the bend in the staircase that led down into the hall that I realized I had made a grave mistake.

I paused at the bend to listen and I stood so still that even the candle flames stood upright, like a little grove of orange cypress trees. I could hear nothing. I let my breath out slowly in a sigh of relief and then I rounded the corner and saw the one thing I had forgotten, the tall pier glass that hung at the foot of the stairs.

In my horror I nearly dropped the candelabra. I gripped it more firmly in my sweating hands. The mirror hung there, innocently on the wall, reflecting nothing more alarming than the flight of steps I was about to descend. All was quiet. I prayed the thing was still upstairs snuffling around in the wreckage of a dozen broken mirrors. Slowly I started to descend the stairs.

Then halfway down, I stopped suddenly, paralyzed with fear, for reflected in the top of the mirror, descending as I was towards the hall, appeared the bare, misshapen feet of the creature.

I was panic-stricken, did not know what to do. I knew that I should break the mirror before the creature descended to the level where it could see me. But to do this I would have to throw the candelabra at the mirror to shatter it and this would then leave me in the dark. And supposing I missed? To be trapped on the stairs, in the dark, by that monstrous thing was more than I could bear. I hesitated, and hesitated too long. For with surprising speed the limping creature descended the stairs, using the stick in one hand to support it while the other ghastly hand clasped the bannister rail, the opal ring glinting as it moved. Its head and decaying face came into view and it glared through the mirror at me and snarled. Still I could do nothing. I stood rooted to the spot, holding the candles high, unable to move.

It seemed to me more important that I should have light so that I could see what the thing was doing than that I should use the candelabra to break the mirror. But I hesitated too long. The creature drew back its emaciated arm, lifted the stick high and brought it down. There was a splintering crash; the mirror splinters became opaque, and through the falling glass the creature's arm appeared. More glass fell until it was all on the floor and the frame was clear. The creature, snuffling and whining eagerly, like a dog that has been shown a plate of food, stepped through the mirror and, its feet scrunching and squeaking, trod on the broken glass. Its blazing eyes fixed upon me, it opened its mouth and uttered a shrill, gurgling cry of triumph; the saliva flowed out of its decomposing ruins of cheeks, and I could hear its teeth squeak together as it ground them. It was such a fearful sight I was panicked into making a move. Praying that my aim would be sure, I raised the heavy candelabra and hurled it down at the creature. For a moment it seemed as though the candelabra hung in midair, the flames still on the candles, the creature standing in the wreckage of the mirror, glaring up at me, and then the heavy ornate weapon struck it. As the candles went out I heard the soggy thud and the grunt the creature gave, followed by the sound of the candelabra hitting the marble floor and the sound of a body falling. Then there was complete darkness and complete silence. I could not move. I was shaking with fear and at any minute I expected to feel those hideous white hands fasten around my throat or round my ankles, but nothing happened. How many minutes I stood there I do not know. At length I heard a faint, gurgling sigh and then there was silence again. I waited, immobile in the darkness, and still nothing happened. Taking courage I felt in my pocket for the matches. My hands were shaking so much that I could hardly strike one, but at length I succeeded. The feeble light it threw was not enough for me to discern anything except that the creature lay huddled below the mirror, a hunched heap that looked very dark in the flickering light. It was either unconscious or dead, I thought, and then cursed as the match burnt my hand and I dropped it. I lit another and made my way cautiously down the stairs. Again the match went out before I reached the bottom and I was forced to pause and light another. I bent over the thing, holding out the match and then recoiled at what I saw:

Lying with his head in a pool of blood was Gideon.

I stared down at his face in the flickering light of the match, my senses reeling. He was dressed as I had last seen him. His astrakhan hat had fallen from his head and the blood had gushed from his temple where the candelabra had hit him. I felt for his heartbeat and his pulse, but he was quite dead. His eyes, now lacking the fire of his personality, gazed blankly up at me. I relit the candles and then sat on the stairs and tried to work it out. I am still trying to work it out today.

I will spare the reader the details of my subsequent arrest and trial. All those who read newspapers will remember my humiliation, how they would not believe me (particularly as they found the strangled and half-eaten corpses of the dog, the cat and the birds) that after the creature appeared we had merely become the reflections in its mirror. If I was baffled to find an explanation, you may imagine how the police treated the whole affair. The newspapers called me the "Monster of the Gorge" and were shrill in calling for my blood. The police, dismissing my story of the creature, felt they had enough evidence in the fact that Gideon had left me a large sum of money in his will. In vain I protested that it was I, at God knows what cost to myself, who had fought my way through the snow to summon help. For the police, disbelievers in witchcraft (as indeed I had been before this), the answer was simple: I had killed my friend for money and then made up this tarradiddle of the creature in the mirror. The evidence was too strongly against me and the uproar of the Press, fanning the flames of public opinion, sealed my fate. I was a monster and must be punished. So I was sentenced to death, sentenced to die beneath the blade of the guillotine. Dawn is not far away, and it is then that I am to die. So I have whiled away the time writing down this story in the hopes that anyone who reads it might believe me. I have never fancied death by the guillotine; it has always seemed to me to be a most barbarous means of putting a man to death. I am watched, of course, so I cannot cheat what the French call "the widow," with macabre sense of humor. But I have been asked if I have a last request, and they have agreed to let me have a full-length mirror to dress myself for the occasion. I shall be interested to see what will happen.

Here the manuscript ended. Written underneath, in a different hand, was the simple statement: the prisoner was found dead in front of the mirror. Death was due to heart failure. Dr. Lepitre.

The thunder outside was still tumultuous and the lightning still lit up the room at intervals. I am not ashamed to say I went and hung a towel over the mirror on the dressing table and then, picking up the bulldog, I got back into bed and snuggled down with him.

Scott Baker (b. 1947)

The Lurking Duck

Scott Baker, originally from the American midwest, is the author of the subtle and startling horror novels *Webs* and *Dhampire* and a number of disturbing and original horror stories, of which "Nesting Instinct" won the World Fantasy Award for 1988. He is also the winner of the Prix Apollo, the distinguished French Award for science fiction. Characteristically, Baker works with the subtle accumulation of detail and atmosphere to create progressively more disturbing revelations. He has lived for many years in Paris with his wife, Suzy, who is a translator. This story first appeared in France, in a French collection of Baker's stories never published in English. A substantially shorter form appeared in *Omni* in 1987, and was a World Fantasy Award nominee, but the unabridged version, too short to be published as a full-length book, and too long for most magazines and anthologies, remained unpublished in English until now. When I asked Baker why he had chosen this particular title, he replied that he wanted that old Lovecraftian feel. Beware of Baker's deadpan humor, which underpins some of the finest moments of this piece. Here, for the first time, in the unabridged version is "The Lurking Duck."

Julie: 1981

It was Tuesday evening, just before dark, a few weeks after my birthday. I was four years old. Mother and Daddy had just had another fight. Daddy used to be a policeman before he got paralyzed all below the neck but Mother was still a policewoman and she was very strong and every now and then she lost control and knocked him around a little. That's what she called it and that's what happened this time, but even after she got him to shut up they were still both really mad at each other, so she took me down to El Estero Lake to watch the ducks and the swans while she ran around the lake to make herself calm down. The swans were mean but I liked the ducks a lot.

She put me on one of the concrete benches and got out the piece of string she always kept in her pocket when she was with me, then made a circle around the bench with it. The piece of string was about ten feet long but the circle it made was a lot smaller and I had to stay inside it. Then she went off to do her jogging.

After a while I noticed that there was an old green car with no one in it, one of those big bump-shaped cars like the ones you see in the black-and-white movies on TV, parked a little ways away from me on the gravel, up under a tree where it was pretty close to the water. The sun was already gone and it was almost dark but I could still see that every now and then one of the ducks would get curious about the car and waddle up to it and stick its head underneath to look at something, then sort of squeeze down and push itself

619

the rest of the way under the car. I couldn't see what happened to the ducks under the car but none of them ever came out again. I saw two of the ducks with the bright green heads—mallards—and one brown duck go under the car before Mother came back to do her jump-roping.

When I told her about the ducks she got real mad again. At first I thought she was mad at me but then she went and found a man hiding in the car under an old blanket and she arrested him. He was all dirty and ragged and skinny and he smelled bad. His hands were all big and red. Mother said that he was a drunk and that he was sick in the head but he wasn't very old. He'd made a hole in the bottom of his car and put a lot of duck food on the ground beneath it so the ducks would come underneath where he could grab them by the neck and kill them without anybody being able to see what he was doing. Mother said that Daddy'd arrested him for doing the same thing once back before the accident. She found five dead mallards and seven of the brown ducks and two white ducks under the blanket with him but they were all already dead.

JAMES PATRICK DUBIC

I. From the *SAND CITY SHORELINE RAG AND TATTLESHEET,* May 22, 1981:

DUCKNAPPER NABBED YET AGAIN!
by RAG Staff Writer Thom Homart

The *RAG* learned yesterday that twenty-nine year old aerospace heir James Patrick Dubic, a former part-time instructor in the department of computer sciences at Monterey Peninsula and Chapman Colleges, was arrested Monday evening by Police Officer Mrs. Virginia Matson on multiple charges stemming from the alleged theft and slaughter of fourteen ducks from El Estero Park in downtown Monterey.

Officer Matson, who was recently promoted to the head of the Monterey Municipal Police Tac Squad (where she replaces her husband, Thomas Philip Matson, paralyzed in a tragic skateboard accident during the Parent-Teacher Day celebrations at Monterey High School last fall), was off duty at the time of the arrest. She had taken her daughter Julie, four, to the lake to "get her out of the house for a while" when Julie noticed that there were a lot of ducks going under an old car parked near them but that none of the ducks that went under the car ever came out again! She told her mother and Officer Matson investigated, only to find James Patrick Dubic hidden under a blanket in the backseat. With him under the blanket she found a cloth sack labeled *Dewer's Duckfood* containing fourteen recently killed ducks. The floorboards of the car had been removed and duck pellets scattered on the ground beneath it to attract the birds.

Dubic is currently out on bail on previous charges stemming from the alleged sale of a large number of sea gulls and a smaller number of cats to five ethnic restaurants here on the Peninsula and in Salinas. The restaurants in question—Casa Miguel, La Poubelle de Luxe, The Ivory Pagoda, Shanghai Express, and Ho's Terrace Cafe—have been charged with serving the sea gulls, which are protected by state, federal, county and city law, as duck and chicken in a variety of dishes such as *Cantonese duck*, *Pollo Mole*, and *Duck à l'orange*. The cats are alleged to have served as the basis for a number of beef and rabbit dishes.

Dubic, furthermore, has not only been convicted on three previous misdemeanor charges involving what might be termed violence against domestic birds and wildfowl but is also the man whom Monterey County Prosecutor Florio Volpone attempted last year to prove was the actual head of the dognapping ring that in the last five years has been responsible for the deaths of thousands of Central California Irish Setters and Afghans sold to the Mexican fur industry for their beautiful "pelts." Though we here at the RAG cannot disagree with Judge Hapgood's ruling to the effect that the evidence Prosecutor Volpone produced was insufficient to prove Dubic guilty before the law of the dognapping and related conspiracy charges—which is to say, guilty of them beyond the shadow of a reasonable doubt—yet we cannot help but feel that there is something at the very least quite *suggestive* about the fact that Dubic has been arrested and charged with similar crimes on at least *forty* other occasions in the recent past. Though it is not perhaps completely fair for those of us here at the RAG, in our capacity of armchair quarterbacks, to suggest that, as the saying goes, there's no smoke without fire and that there must have been some compelling reason for not just one but all of our local police forces to keep on arresting Dubic again and again for the same kind of alleged crime. . . .

II. The Trial

"Objection sustained," Hapgood said but it was already too late. Volpone'd been able to get the jury thinking about the dognapping charges again, with that bit about Mexico thrown in to appeal to their racism. The bastard. He knew as well as I did that that was all bullshit, that I'd never had anything against dogs. Or cats either, and he was trying to get them to believe I'd been killing cats too, and that wasn't true. I'd always loved cats, I'd even had one of my own for a while and he knew it, but it didn't make any difference to Volpone, he was going to try to get me for the cats anyway.

". . . a rubber duck," Wibsome was saying the next time I bothered to tune in to him. I hadn't been missing anything. I'd heard it all before time after time and anyway he was even clumsier than usual today. Probably because he knew there was no way his particular brand of rhetoric was going to get me out of anything this time, no matter how hard he tried, so he wasn't even trying.

"A rubber duck," he continued, "which the late Robert Tyrone Dubic had the habit of filling with bird shot and ball bearings before he used it to beat his defenseless five-year-old brother into unconsciousness. The same rubber duck with which he often threatened to kill that younger brother, James Patrick Dubic, here before you on charges from what the prosecution claims is a pathological hatred of birds in general and ducks in particular.

"But I ask you—is there anything really all *that* sick or irrational in the defendent's feelings about birds? Would *you*, any of you, have had a great fondness for the creatures if you had been repeatedly beaten by a sadistic older brother with a lead-filled rubber duck during your formative years? If you had been so badly mauled by your aunt's flock of geese that you were hospitalized for three days? Would you have had any overwhelming love for our feathered friends if your grandfather had disinherited you in favor of a bird sanctuary in Guatemala, a country which neither you nor he had ever visited? Is there anything odd about the fact that James Patrick Dubic is, as you yourselves have heard him testify, disgusted with the evident hypocrisy of people who publically demand increased protection for the California environment while at the same time spending a fortune in certain local restaurants for meat from wild boar they know perfectly well have been killed illegally inside the Los Padres Forest preserve?

"I'm not going to try to pretend to you that James Patrick Dubic is immensely likeable, or that he's just like everybody else. He isn't. But what he *is* is a man of intelligence and principle, a former teacher who was always respected by his students, and he is neither irrational nor insane. His dislike of birds, regrettable though it may be, is a perfectly normal reaction to the rather unique and unfortunate circumstances of his childhood. . . ."

It wasn't going to work. Not this time. Wibsome wasn't even trying. They were going to lock me up again, and not just for a little while this time. Maybe even get me committed to Atascadero, put me away for the rest of my life by claiming I was criminally insane. That sounded like what Wibsome was really after this time. Get me out of Father's hair for good. And even if they let me out later he could always have me put back in if I made any more trouble for him. If they ever let me out. He'd like that now, with Mother remarried so she couldn't make him do anything for me anymore.

"We're going to appeal," Wibsome told me when he came back and sat down again. Meaning that there was no way they weren't going to find me guilty. "Those articles in the *RAG*—I'm pretty sure we can prove they prejudiced the jury and kept you from getting a fair trial. And there may be other things I can turn up when I've had the time to study the court recorder's transcripts of the trial for a while."

"Wibsome," I said, "you know I didn't have anything to do with the dogs, or with those cats either. You know how I've always liked dogs and cats—"

"Of course, Jimmy." He didn't believe me even though he was supposed to be on my side. "Not the dogs and cats. Just those nasty, nasty birds."

"Yes!" He was laughing at me again. Just like Bobby used to, before they shipped him off to Vietnam and killed him. But if I ever got out of here I was going to get him just like I was going to get all the rest of them. That oh-so sweet little girl and her bull-dyke mother and her paralyzed father who was the one who'd lied about me at that other trial, the time that he'd been the one who'd arrested me. That bastard who'd written all those articles for the *RAG* and all those restaurant owners who'd tried to put each other out of business by accusing each other of having hired me to get their sea gulls and cats for them, when all the time they'd hired me to get sea gulls for them themselves and they knew I wouldn't have anything to do with killing cats. And Judge Hapgood and Florio Volpone and the jury and Wibsome and my father and the ducks.

All of them. But especially the ducks.

III. From the *SAND CITY SHORELINE RAG AND TATTLESHEET*, August 8, 1983:

. . . remember that the judge and jury agreed with our editorial staff and that Dubic was sentenced to three concurrent terms of ten to twenty years in the state penitentiary. Since then his lawyers have made repeated attempts to have his convictions overturned, most recently by charging that the *RAG*'s crusading editorials and reportage unfairly prejudiced the jury against him and so precluded the possibility of a fair trial. Dubic's lawyers accompanied this latest appeal with a simultaneous multimillion dollar suit against the *RAG* and its editorial staff for libel and defamation of character.

We are very happy indeed to report that Dubic's appeal has been denied and that all charges against us for libel and defamation of character have been unconditionally dismissed.

IV. From THE BUZZBOMB, House Organ of the Dubic Aerospace and Munitions Industrial Group, January, 1984:

Aerospace Guidance System Division Chief Damien Holmes announced today the purchase of THE OTHER CHESSPLAYER, INC., designers and manufacturers of the popular PROGRAMMED PRO line of computerized tennis opponents, as well as of the increasingly popular computer games SHARK ALERT, ROBOBRAWL, and GET THE PROWLER BEFORE HE GETS YOU. "With their genius for innovative software and our technical expertise," Vice President Holmes told the *Buzzbomb*, "it shouldn't be more than a matter of months before we're not only light-years ahead of our competitors here in the United States but even further ahead of everybody else in the rest of the world, and most especially our counterparts in Soviet Russia."

V. From "Philanthropy for the Year 2000", a speech delivered by James Damien Dubic to the Orange County League of Republican Women, March 19, 1984

". . . not just new ways of doing things that have never really done anybody much real good. To put it another way, we don't want to compete with any of the other charitable and philanthropic organizations now operating, we want to put them out of business altogether by making the very need for charity and philanthropy obsolete.

"Furthermore, there's no question in any of our minds that our society's future lies with increased computerization. Now, there are some disadvantages to this, as I'm sure some of you may have noticed every now and then when you've caught a computer error on your bank statement or your Mastercharge, but that kind of problem doesn't come from using computers, it just comes from the fact that we haven't been using computers long enough to have learned everything there is to know about using them. A good comparison would be to think of yourselves in the same position as the first railway passengers, who inevitably got covered with soot and smoke from the locomotive's engines because nobody'd yet found out how to make them burn cleaner and how to keep the smoke away from the passengers. But after trains had been around for a while they found all sorts of solutions to the problems, so they weren't really problems at all anymore.

"But let me get back to what we at the Dubic Foundation are trying to do right now, which is to find new ways to use the future's increased computerization for the social good. Not just new ways of doing old things—like a robot soup-line to compete with the Salvation Army's human volunteers—but ways to do new things altogether, things that nobody's ever been able to do before. And we're pretty sure we've found some new ways of doing things, all of them so far based on the concepts of shared computer time and decentralization.

"Let me make that a little clearer for you. Take a look at oh, any of the big banks here in California. Bank of America, UCB, even the Japanese Maritime Bank, any bank with a lot of branches scattered all over the state. All their records are computerized, but there's no way that any of these banks could have ever afforded a separate computer system for every one of their branches, even if they'd wanted to have them for some reason. No, what they've got is a single master computer connected by telephone linkages to separate data terminals in every branch, so that each branch is sharing the master computer's capabilities with all the other branches. There are even a number of companies that rent their spare computer time to companies too small to have a cost-effective computer capacity of their own. Dubic Aerospace is one such company, which is one of the reasons I know what I do about the subject.

"Anyway, ladies, think about what would happen if you took the whole process one step further, and took at least some of the data terminals out of the branch offices or whatever and put them into the employees' homes, so that you had a double telephone linkage working for you, not only between the master computer and the branch offices, but also between the branch offices and the employees' home terminals. There are an awful lot of peripheral benefits we haven't yet had a chance to examine to be gained from having people work at home like that—no commuting time wasted and less traffic jams, for one thing, possible savings on expensive office space for another, to pick just two examples—but that sort of thing's not really what we, as philanthropists, are interested in right now. What we want to know is, how can we find new ways to use this development to make things better for people?

"Well, one of the first things we thought of was the way this could help shut-ins, perfectly competent and intelligent people who because of some accident or chronic illness are unable to leave their homes or, even worse, have been condemned to live the rest of their lives confined to their beds. Just think what it would do for these people's sense of self-esteem if they had a way of holding a real job and of becoming more or less self-supporting. Not to mention the savings to society involved in getting them off welfare. This wouldn't really affect all that many people, probably, but it could make an enormous difference in the lives of the people it did affect, and save the taxpayer some money in the process.

"But there's another kind of shut-in this kind of set-up could help, and help in a way that could quite possibly do all of us an enormous amount of incidental good. I'm talking about convicts, convicted criminals, all those men and women that society has been forced for its own protection, and in the hope of reforming them, to put behind bars. And there are a lot of them, make no mistake of that, all our jails, prisons, penitentiaries and work farms are not only full but dangerously overcrowded with men, women and adolescents whose care and keeping is paid for by the rest of us, all of us who pay taxes.

"And what we're paying for, really, is a kind of school system or fraternity where all the petty criminals—the kids who hot-wired cars to go joyriding or the clerk who for the first and only time in his life needed money so badly that he took a hundred dollars out of his employer's cash register and got caught at it—where all these people who have nothing better to do with their time than break rocks or stamp out license plates learn from the other prisoners, the real hardened criminals, how to become hardened criminals themselves. And when they finally do get out the only people they know are criminals, they can't get a job because of their records and because, especially if they were pretty young when they went in, all they know how to do is break rocks or make license plates or hang around with criminals. And so what their stay in prison has really done for them is just to put them on the road to becoming far more dangerous and expensive to society than they might ever have become on their own.

"But think about a convict who gets the training he needs to be a computer programmer of some sort in prison. He's already learned a skill that will be useful to society and that has a good chance of taking him away from the poverty and bad influences that may well have been what turned him to crime in the first place.

"So far, so good. But now let's assume that some company or group of companies has arranged to have some of its data terminals installed within the prison walls, in much the same way as the terminals for the shut-in patients I mentioned earlier would have been installed in their homes, and that this company agrees to accept qualifying prisoners for some sort of apprentice program, so that they can not only be gaining useful skills and on-the-job training while still in prison, but they can already have a job waiting for them when they get out AND have a bank account they've built up from what they were being paid during their apprenticeship waiting for them outside. That way, they'll be able to sidestep the whole grinding cycle of poverty and humiliation and living on welfare that right now drives so many ex-convicts straight back to a life of crime.

"Of course, there are still a few safeguards we're going to have to work out before we can put our pilot program in practice because these are, after all, convicted criminals we're talking about. To give you just one example of the kinds of things we're going to have to guard against, you wouldn't want to put a genius embezzler or even safecracker in total control of Bank of America's computer system. . . ."

Julie: 1988

It was a really hot night even though it was still only April and the air conditioner was broken again. Mother was yelling at Father and he was whining back at her again. Pretty soon he'd start yelling and then she'd start hitting him again. They'd been drinking a lot too, both of them, like they always did. I was eleven and they'd been doing the same thing ever since I could remember. I couldn't stand them, either of them.

I put my slingshot—the hunting kind you get at sporting goods stores that shoots steel balls, not one of those homemade rubber band things for little kids—into my bag and went down to the lake to sit around for a while. We lived about four blocks away, up by the Naval Postgraduate School. Sometimes when there wasn't anyone else at the lake I'd try to get one of the swans or even one of the ducks with my slingshot—I'd killed a swan once, one of the black ones with the red beaks, and hit one or two others and a couple of ducks—but there were a lot of people out on the lake on those stupid little two-person aquacycles, those boat-things you pedal like bicycles. Couples mainly, some high school kids but mainly old people, tourists and golfers. Some fathers with their kids. They all looked stupid.

I didn't like the park all that much but I didn't have any friends that lived close and I didn't feel like walking or even riding my bike very far, especially not all the way up Carmel Hill to where Beth lived. But I couldn't stand staying home any longer either, not while they were still fighting. It would be OK later on, when something they both wanted to watch came on TV or when Father had a little more to drink. After a while he just got quieter and quieter until he went to sleep. Which was why I was glad he drank all the time, even though he got pretty nasty in the evening and when he first woke up in the morning. And that was OK anyway, because he had a right to get angry even if not at me, the way Mother treated him. She treated him like shit and he never did anything wrong, all he did was sit around all day watching television and reading magazines and detective stories and drinking a little beer through his tube. He didn't hurt anybody and it wasn't his fault if he couldn't wash himself and if sometimes he smelled bad and that he'd gotten all sort of fat and droopy-faced and pasty-looking, not at all like he looked in those pictures Mother still had of him from before the accident, when he still looked a lot like that mess sergeant Mother sometimes brought home with her from Fort Ord, the one who kept telling me he was going to fix the air conditioner but never did. Only Father'd been a lot cleaner and handsomer and younger than the mess sergent was, then.

The sun was going away even though it wasn't quite dark yet and it looked like it was going to rain pretty soon. A lot of people were coming back in to shore and turning in their aquacycles to the man that rented them out, though there were still a couple of chicano-looking kids in an aluminum canoe who didn't look like they were going to quit before dark. And I had to be careful, I could still remember sitting there on that bench watching Mother arrest that man who'd been killing the ducks under his car. I still had all the clippings that Mother'd saved for me from that, including the ones with my picture in them from the *Post-Sentinel* and the *RAG*, and the other one where they'd had me talk a bit for the *Pine Cone*.

The highschool kids in the canoe were down at the other end of lake. I was watching the ducks and the swans out on the lake feeding—I didn't want to try anything with any of the ones up on shore, where somebody could see what happened to it and where there wouldn't be that much skill involved anyway—because I had to know where they all were so I could find them again if I had to wait until it was almost all the way dark before everybody else went away. The swans were mean but I didn't dislike the ducks or anything—though I didn't much like them either, with their mean little suspicious eyes and the way they walked around when they were on land like they thought they were the most important things in the world—but there wasn't anything else I could do to go get back at something when I felt like this. Just like Father yelling at Mother whenever he got to thinking about how really bad it was to be paralyzed and that we had to feed him and help him go to the bathroom, or Mother hitting him whenever she couldn't stand to look at how horrible it was for him anymore.

A lot of the ducks and swans were up on the shore near me looking for food somebody might have left and quacking and honking at each other or lying down on their stomachs with their heads tucked in and sleeping. The swans that were in the water were down at the other end of the lake but the ducks in the water were all paddling around in groups and quacking at each other. A lot of the male mallards were doing that thing they do together when they all swim after one of the brown females without ever catching her and then they all take off together and they chase her through the air but they still don't catch her, and a few of them every now and then were doing that thing where they beat their wings and sort of get up out of the water like they were standing on their tiptoes and beating their chests like Tarzan. But most of them were just swimming around and sticking their heads down underwater the way they do when they're looking for something to eat down there but don't feel like diving for it, or doing that thing where they turn all the way upside down like they're standing on their heads with their tails sticking straight up out of the water.

There was an old lady down at the other end of the lake, near the kids in the canoe. She was throwing bread crumbs or something to the swans but she looked pretty busy and I didn't think she'd notice what I was doing if I waited until it got just a little darker.

One of the ducks, a mallard, a really pretty male with a bright green head and a big patch of shiny blue on his side, was off alone out in the middle, not doing much with the other ducks, just sort of floating there like he was half-asleep through he didn't have his head tucked back or anything. He was pretty far away but close enough so I thought I could hit him with a good enough shot.

Suddenly he started doing that thing that ducks do when they're real mad at each other or fighting over a female or that the females sort of do when they're telling all the males to go away and they stick their necks forward with their mouths wide open and charge at each other using their wings to go fast enough so they're almost running at each other on top of the water. But the weird thing was that the duck wasn't charging another male, he was charging a whole little group of four or five females—I could tell they were females because they were all brown and speckled and one of them even had some of her black and yellow baby ducklings swimming around her—and he wasn't making that sort of hissing warning noise that all the other ducks I'd ever seen make when they're charging like that.

He didn't stop when he was close enough to warn them off either, like they usually do. All at once he was in with the other ducks and they were all squacking and beating their wings and trying to fly away. I thought I saw something real bright flash, like a knife blade, only it was too dark for a piece of metal to flash like that, and then all but one of the females that had been trying to get away were up out of the water and flying off and the baby ducklings were running across the water peeping and trying to get away.

But one of the females—maybe the mother, I couldn't tell—was floating there with its belly up and its orange legs twitching. Then its legs quit twitching and I could tell it was dead. And the male was gone. It hadn't flown away with the others and it hadn't swum away and it wasn't anywhere I could see in the water. So it must have dived down to the bottom and stayed there or at least not come up until it was a long ways away. Maybe it was lurking down there like a snapping turtle.

The chicano high school kids were landing their canoe and I tried to get them to take me out in it again so I could get the dead duck and take a look at it and see what the male had done to it but they were already starting to put their canoe back in their pickup and they weren't interested.

It was getting too dark to see anything so I walked around for a while. I went down to the wharf to see if the organ-grinder was there with his monkey but he wasn't—it wasn't quite the beginning of the tourist season yet and anyway it was the middle of the week, so there weren't that many people around—so I walked back to McDonald's and bought a Big Mac with some money I took from Mother's purse when she left it lying around a few days before, then went the rest of the way home. Father was asleep but Mother was still up watching a movie on TV. I didn't have any homework so after I fed my turtles and guppies I sat down and watched the movie with her until she told me it was too late and I had to go to bed.

When I went down to the lake the next morning before school with a pair of binoculars the dead duck was gone. I looked for the other duck for a while, but I couldn't find it or if I did find it it looked just like all the other mallards and wasn't doing anything special.

But I spotted it for sure when I came back again after school. It was just floating around the same way it had the night before and it always stayed out near the middle, away from shore and the shallow water where all the other ducks liked to feed, and it wouldn't move at all except to keep away from the people on their aquacycles. That was how I noticed it, because when an aquacycle came within maybe fifteen feet of where it was resting it would move away so it stayed just fifteen feet away from the aquacycle, then move back to where it'd been as soon as the people on the cycle were far enough away. And it did the same thing once with some people in a boat.

And besides it never dived or quacked or preened itself or seemed to be looking for anything to eat and all the other ducks ignored it. They didn't seem scared of it, they just didn't pay any attention to it, and all it did was float there and keep away from people.

But that was only when the sun was shining on it. As soon as things clouded over it would start swimming towards the other ducks, but it always stopped and went back to floating on its own away from everything else when the sun came out from behind the clouds again.

All except one time, after I'd been there a couple of hours, when a lot of really dark clouds covered the sun and kept it covered for about fifteen minutes. The duck started swimming towards another duck the way it always did when the sun got covered over—the other duck was a male mallard just like it was this time—but it didn't stop like it had before, the times when the sun came out from behind the clouds again. I was watching it through the binoculars to try to see what it did if it attacked the other male the same way it'd attacked the females the night before.

Only it didn't attack the other duck. It just swam closer and closer to it until the two ducks were maybe three feet away from each other, then it put its head down and went forward a little like it was looking for food on the bottom and then it dived.

A second or two late the other mallard gave a sort of shocked SQUAWK! and got pulled under, just like a giant snapping turtle had reached up from underneath and grabbed it in its jaws and pulled it down. Only I knew it wasn't a snapping turtle, it was the other duck.

I watched where it had gone under with the binoculars for a while but there wasn't any blood or feathers I could see, nothing to make it look like the duck was getting killed or eaten there under the water, except that it never came up again.

But about five minutes later the duck that had killed it came bobbing up again. It was all muddy and I thought that maybe it had been lying down there on the bottom in the mud eating the other duck and then had buried what was left of its body like a dog with a bone it's finished with. It preened itself for a while, looking pretty and silly and self-important like any other mallard, then paddled back to the middle and went back to its sunbathing.

It was getting near dinner time so I went home to take care of Father. Mother was still at the police station and he was in a pretty good mood and watching something he liked on TV so it wasn't so bad. I changed his urine bottle and washed him up a bit, then fed him a TV dinner and connected his drinking tube to a big bottle of one of those pre-mixed drinks—a whisky sour or a gin martini, I forget which—then left him there and went back down to the lake to watch the ducks for a while. I took some bread down with me to feed to the other ducks and swans in case somebody wanted to know what I was doing there. The day was still pretty bright out and the duck that was killing the other ducks was still floating out alone in the middle, though not quite in the same place, so I didn't have any trouble finding it again.

It pulled another duck down the same way before the sun went down, a different kind this time, one of those grey and white ones with the chocolate brown heads and necks with a white stripe running up each side. And then, just as the last light was going away, it did the same thing it'd done the night before, when it'd attacked the group of females. Only this time I had the binoculars ready and I knew what I was looking for, so I got to see what it did when it killed the other duck.

It charged just the way any other duck would've again, only it didn't stop when the other duck tried to get away. The duck it was after was another male mallard again—there were a whole lot of them out on the lake, like there always were—and the duck that was attacking it kept right on going faster and faster with its bill wide open until just before it was going to ram into the other duck something like a pair of shiny steel garden shears came out of its open mouth like a gigantic metal snake's tongue and cut the other duck's head off.

The scissors went back into the killer duck's mouth and it grabbed the dead duck's head in its bill then dived like it had the other times, when it had pulled the ducks down. Only this time it left the headless duck's body floating on the water and it didn't come up again.

I waited until it was too dark to see, then made sure I knew how to find the spot where the duck had disappeared and went home. Father was asleep in his wheelchair in front of the TV. Mother wasn't home yet. I changed Father's urine bag again then wheeled him into his bedroom and got him into bed, then fed the turtles and guppies and went to bed with a book I'd gotten out of the school library about ducks.

But I was out of bed the next morning before it got light out and by the time the sun came up I was already down at the lake with the binoculars, watching the spot where the duck had disappeared the night before. There was a whole cluster of five or six big water lilies there I hadn't noticed before but I was still pretty sure I had the right spot.

About an hour after the sun came up the water lillies disappeared like fishing-line bobbers being yanked down by a big fish and a moment later the duck bobbed to the surface. It was all muddy again but it preened itself for a while until it was all clean, then swam back to the middle of the lake, but not quite the same spot it had been in the day before.

I went back to the house. Mother hadn't come home at all last night but Father was already awake. I helped him get dressed and go to the bathroom, then cleaned him up and made us both some scrambled eggs and toast. After I fed him I wheeled him into the living room and put his book in the thing to turn the pages for him, then made myself two liver sausage sandwiches for lunch. Mother came home just as I was leaving and gave me a ride to school.

It rained all afternoon and I didn't get to see the duck with the scissors in its mouth, though most of the other ducks were still out in the rain and I looked for it for a long time. But I was down by the lake when it started to get light out again the next morning and I found its group of lily pads—they were cleaner-looking than the other water lilies, not as scummy and ragged, and they were farther out into deep water than they should have been and bigger than most of the others—and was there watching it through the binoculars when it came up. This time I noticed that it seemed to be preening itself real slowly, like it was very tired or something, and that when it swam out to the middle again it was swimming a lot slower than usual.

Father yelled at me at breakfast when I spilled some cereal and milk on his shirt so I just left him there in his wheelchair and went to school early, without any sandwiches. I had enough money so I could've bought myself lunch at school if I'd wanted to but I wanted to save it, so I told Beth I'd forgotten it and she gave me half of one of her sandwiches and bought me a carton of milk with her own money.

After school I went around to all the sporting goods stores and checked out the prices they wanted for fishing nets. They were all too expensive and anyway the duck could've cut its way out of all of them with the scissors in its mouth. Besides, I didn't know what it did when it pulled the ducks under in the daytime. The scissors in its mouth meant it had to be some kind of machine or maybe it was a real duck that had been changed around so it was part duck and part machine like the bionic man and woman, so it could've had all sorts of other ways to break out of the net anyway. Maybe it had some kind of extra claws or a hooked sword or something like that hidden under its feathers that it used to drag the ducks under that it got in the daytime.

I went home and checked Mother's purse for some money I could take but all she had was an awful lot of ten- and twenty-dollar bills and even though she had so many I was sure she'd notice if any of them were missing. But she had five or six quarters and a fifty cent piece, so I took three of the quarters and put two nickels back in their place so it would feel like she still had the same amount of money. And that night one of her friends called to ask if I could baby-sit his two kids Saturday afternoon. All Mother's friends knew how good I was at taking care of Father, even the ones that didn't really know how bad *she* was at taking care of him—he never talked about it to anybody when she wasn't there, though he always made a lot of nasty remarks about the way she treated him when she was in the room with him and his friends and I were there—so I got a lot of offers to do baby-sitting. But Mother liked to keep me home to watch Father when she was working or had something else she wanted to do and she was always working or doing something and she didn't like to come home very much if she could get out of it, so I didn't get to do much baby-sitting. But this time she'd already decided to stay home all day Saturday, so she said go ahead and I ended up making seven and a half dollars.

The next morning I was up early again. I blew up a big white balloon and put it on the end of a long bamboo fishing pole made out of five sticks that screwed together we had out in the garage, but when I found the duck's lily pads they were too far away from shore for me to put the balloon by where the duck was going to come up and hold it there so I could see what he was going to do with it. They didn't rent out aquacycles until way too late and anyway the pole was long but it wasn't quite fifteen feet long so an aquacycle wouldn't have done me any good and there wasn't anything I could do.

It was the same way Monday and Tuesday and then it rained Wednesday and Thursday, so I didn't get to see the duck at all. But Friday even though it was too far out from shore for me to put the balloon next to its lily pads I saw it get a white duck and a black swan, which made me very happy.

Beth came over Saturday and we rented one of the aquacycles and I went pedaling after the duck but it just kept itself away from me. I didn't want to tell Beth what I was doing and she got really bored and angry with me after a while but I made her keep on pedaling until our time was up.

And then Saturday the robot duck finally killed another duck close to shore with the scissors in its mouth so that Sunday I had my balloon right by its lily pad when it came up in the morning. But the day was all sunny and starting to get hot and the duck just ignored the balloon and went off to float in the middle of the lake. And by that time I'd realized that even when it got cloudy out the duck never attacked another duck if the other duck was near an aquacycle or one of the aluminum canoes. So there wasn't any real way I could find out what it would and wouldn't attack, and anyway I was getting scared that people might be beginning to notice me, out there with my balloon on a pole every morning. So I stayed away from the lake for a week and I was glad I did, because there was a movie on TV that Saturday afternoon that I watched over at Beth's house, *The Invisible Boy* with Robbie the Robot, where this evil computer takes control over Robbie and makes him do things he doesn't want to do. And that made me think about those kids with their radio-controlled toy sailboats and I started wondering if there was someone who came down to watch the duck after it came up and who kept the controls he used to make the duck kill the other ducks hidden in his pocket or something. So after I'd stayed away from the lake for a week I came back and didn't do anything, just watched, but though there were some people who came down almost every day to watch the ducks and feed them, there wasn't anybody I could see who was there every day when the duck killed something by pulling it under and I watched for more than two weeks to make sure. Besides, the little old man who was there the most often even came when it was raining out and the duck stayed underwater.

By this time I had enough money from Mother's purse and my baby-sitting and even one time five dollars from the mess sergeant's wallet to buy a net if I wanted one but not one with a long handle. The only way I'd figured out to catch the duck was to wade or swim out to where its lily pads were some night when it was resting or turned off at the bottom and then scoop it up in the net and hope it would stay turned off or asleep or whatever until I got it into something dark and strong, like the ten-gallon grease can I'd already gotten from the gas station down on Del Monte by the Navy School. But I was scared to try it because for all I knew the duck never really turned itself off, it just went down to hide in the mud on the bottom of the lake where it could cut the ducks it had killed into little pieces with the scissors in its mouth so that nobody would ever find their bodies, and I couldn't think of any reason it couldn't kill me the same way it killed the ducks and swans, either with its scissors or with whatever it used when it got them from underwater. Besides which, I was afraid somebody'd come driving by and catch me. Or that a car would come by and the light from its headlights would turn the duck back on even if it had been turned off and *then* it would get me.

But I didn't want to give up, I wanted that duck a lot, especially after I found the headless body of one of the white ducks washed up early in the morning. I took it away and put it in somebody's garbage can a ways away from the lake, under the garbage so nobody else'd see it and figure out what was going on, and from then on I tried to check the shore as much as I could to make sure that none of the other bodies washed up but either the rest of them must have just sunk or dogs or cats came by in the nighttime and ate them as soon as they washed up.

I spent a few more days down by the lake feeding the ducks and pigeons and even the swans a lot of stale bread and other garbage to give myself an excuse for being there before I got the idea of putting some sort of noose at the end of the bamboo pole and using it to snag the whole group of lily pads. They had to be connected to the duck and made out of plastic or metal or something like that and be pretty strong, so I could use them to drag the duck up out of the water. The thing is, I didn't know if that would wake the duck up or not, or if the stems were really strong enough to pull the duck out of the water without breaking it somehow. If it was all made of metal except for its feathers it had to be very heavy. And if I woke the duck up dragging it out like that, I didn't know if it would just try to get away from me or if it would try to kill me to make me stop and keep anyone else from learning about it. I'd never seen it up on shore like the other ducks so for all I knew it couldn't even walk and I'd be safe as long as I didn't go in the water with it.

But then again I'd already seen it do that half-flying thing where it came partway up out of the water when it attacked the other ducks so for all I knew it could fly all the way. And I didn't really know how it dragged the ducks and swans under or what it did to them there. Perhaps it had big knives hidden in its wings or hooks, or maybe even it had some sort of built-in spear gun it used to harpoon them from the bottom so it could reel them down and then cut them up into little pieces there in the mud.

But the real thing that was wrong with trying to catch it at night in the dark was that I wouldn't be able to see it unless I used a light, so I wouldn't know what it was doing, and if I did use a light that might wake it up, and anyway, somebody might see the light and come to find out what I was doing. So I finally decided that what I had to do was try to pull it out some real bright morning when it was near to shore, just after the sun came up but before it was ready to come up to the surface on its own. That way, maybe it would still be only half turned-on again, and even if it was all the way awake, maybe it would just try to swim back out to the middle and start sunbathing a little early.

I bought some plastic rope, the kind you use to tie things on cars and trailers, and a heavy khaki sack from the Army-Navy surplus store to keep the duck dark in while I got it away from the lake and into the ten-gallon can. I'd cleaned the can out a long time ago, right after I got it from the station, and it had a lid on it, so I could shut the duck tight inside it where none of the light could get in to turn it on when I took it home.

I waited until one night when I saw it was down in the mud close enough to shore on my side of the lake, then hid the can in somebody's hedge about half a block up from the lake. I had about an inch of water in the can in case the duck needed it.

I went down to the lake a long time before the sun came up and waited for the sky to get pink and for things to get bright enough so I could see. Not very many cars drove by and nobody in any of them paid any attention to me, except for one police car but I had all my stuff hidden and they were both friends of my father's and already knew me, so it was all right. I told them I liked to come out and run around the lake and get some exercise and one of them said my father used to be just like me, which made me feel bad for a while even after they left.

The sun came up while I was talking to them and it was already pretty bright by the time they left so I got my stuff out and put all the bamboo sections of the fishing pole together and went after the duck.

It wasn't all that hard to get the noose around the lily pads and pull them in to shore but when I got them I saw that they just seemed to stretch all the way back to the part of the bottom they'd been floating over. I waited a moment before I touched the lily pads and the stems, then tried it. They seemed to be made of some sort of tough plastic, so I got all the stems together in my hands and started pulling on them. At first they were real easy to pull in, like that kind of clothesline that goes on a spring-reel and that you can stretch out a long way, but after a while I felt them grab, like when you're fishing and you finally reel in enough line to feel a big fish or a snag on it. I pulled and I could feel the duck on the other end. It was heavy and didn't want to come when I yanked but it didn't seem to be snagged and it wasn't fighting me like a fish or anything and when I quit pulling it just stayed where it was, so I knew it wasn't trying to get away or come after me. I tried pulling on the stems again and the same thing happened, so I kept pulling it in a little at a time, ready to let go and run if the duck started moving on its own.

A candy-red Porsche came by, going a lot faster than it was supposed to. I just stood still, pretending that all I was doing was looking out at the water. The Porsche went by without stopping but now I could see another car over on the other side of the lake and somebody on his bicycle going up the back way to the college, so I knew that everybody was starting to get up and go to work and I had to start dragging the duck in a lot faster, without stopping every few seconds to check it like I'd been doing.

Pretty soon I could see it and it wasn't a duck at all, it was more like a big piece of dead wood, a branch about three feet long and maybe a couple of inches thick, with four or five broken-off little branches sticking out of it. At first I thought it was just something I'd snagged and that when I got it in to shore I'd have to get the lily pad stems from wrapped around it but then I saw that each stem came out of the end of a different one of the broken-off branches.

As soon as I had the branch up out of the water and into the light it started to change. The ends started slowly humping in to the middle and the middle started to bulge out, but everything was happening real, real slow, like a slug creeping up the porch steps after it rains. I quick threw the sack over it to shut out the light but I could see it was still changing underneath until I got the lily pads in under the sack and out of the light too, and then it moved slower and slower until it stopped.

There wasn't anyone else around and the thing was still too long to get into the can, so I pulled the sack off it again. It started squeezing itself in some more and humping out all around the middle, still moving real slow, while I got the sack open and ready to throw over it again, but this time so I could push it inside the sack with the pole. I waited until it wasn't much bigger than a real duck, though it didn't look like a duck any more than it looked like a branch now, just a big lump of mud. I put the sack over it open and reached in underneath with the pole and wedged the pole under it so I could tip it back and make it fall into the sack, then pushed it back more and more until it was all the way inside the sack and I could tie the sack closed. I picked up the sack, making sure it didn't get too close to my body. The duck was just a big round lump in the sack and it didn't move at all. It wasn't too heavy either, maybe about twenty pounds, but that was still heavy enough to make it a lot of work to get it up to the place where I had the can hid.

I got the can out of the hedge and put the bag in it, but even though it wasn't too big around to go in it was too long for me to put the top on it, just a little, maybe a couple of inches, but it was too late to try to open the sack and let in enough light to make the thing change some more, so I just left the lid there and carried the can the rest of the way home and put it in the toolshed behind the garage, under a bench, before I went back for the lid. Mother never used the toolshed, it was something Father'd built for himself back before they had me but sometimes the mess sergeant would make something out of wood for us back there, or work on something that needed fixing. He wasn't really a bad man, even though I hated him. So even though there were a lot of cobwebs and spiders there and it was real dusty and full of other junk the lights still worked and the shed was in good enough shape to keep the rain and the sunlight out. It didn't have any windows. If you went inside and closed the door before you turned the lights on nobody could see that they were turned on from the house.

When I went back to get the lid I decided to check back at the lake to see if I'd left anything there, but I hadn't, so I went back to the shed and put the lid by the can under the bench, then moved a broken black-and-white TV that was sitting in the far corner over in front of the can so that nobody could see the can unless they took the TV out from in front of it and so that even when the door was open the light from inside wouldn't touch the can. I'd been thinking about what I had to do for a long time and I had it all figured out, or most of it, anyway.

I even knew whose duck it was. James Patrick Dubic, the one I'd helped mother arrest and put away in prison. There couldn't be two people that hated ducks that much, and in some of the clippings Mother'd saved for me they talked about how smart he was and how good he was with computers. I'd figured it out for sure that time I'd seen *"The Invisible Boy"* on TV because I'd already figured out that the duck had to be a robot or something just pretending to look like a duck the way it was pretending to look like a lump of mud right now. I got out my clippings just after I saw the movie so I could be sure what James Patrick Dubic looked like and after that I'd been watching all the people sitting on the benches and walking around the lake, but he wasn't ever there, at least not unless he'd changed an awful lot.

I locked the shed and left the duck there in its can until Saturday night. That way if it had solar batteries maybe they'd run down enough so that even if it wanted to hurt me it wouldn't be able to. Also, if it tried to escape I wouldn't be there when it tried and so it couldn't hurt me.

Saturday night Mother had to work. I asked her before she left for the station what'd happened to Dubic, if he was still in prison or if they'd let him out or put him in a mental hospital or anything. She said she didn't know but she'd ask and try to find out for me if I wanted. I said yes. It was still early when she drove away, about six-thirty, so it wasn't nearly dark yet.

We'd all had dinner together and Mother'd wheeled Father into the living room to watch the movies on the cable TV chain so I didn't have anything to do except watch them with Father until it got dark enough.

Around nine I went back to the shed. I had a flashlight, so when I unlocked the door and pushed it open I shone the light in through it before I went in to turn the real light on, but the duck was still in its can behind the TV set. I closed the door again and dragged the can out. It was heavier than I'd remembered, maybe twenty-five or thirty-five pounds. I pulled the bag out of the can and put it down, then got between it and the door and opened the door so I could run out of it and get away from the duck if it came after me. Then I turned the lights off and used the flashlight to see by when I dumped the duck out of the sack.

It was still just a big lump, though some of the mud was dry and falling off. It smelled like mud and like sewers. I poked at it with the wooden end of a hoe and it didn't do anything even when I poked it again harder, so I turned on the lights. I was right there by the door with my hand on the light switch waiting for it to do something but it didn't do anything, even when I poked it with the hoe again. I watched it for three or four hours but it never did anything. I was afraid I'd broken it somehow but if I hadn't maybe I'd be able to handle it safely at night with the lights on, which was good. I put the sack back over it and tipped it back into the sack with the hoe handle, then pushed the sack back under the bench behind the TV.

Mother was home all day the next day and she and Father had some of his old friends from back when he was on the Marina police force, back before they'd combined it with the fire department there, over for a barbecue. They made hamburgers and spareribs in the black metal cooker in the backyard, then sat around drinking beer out of cans and talking about what things'd been like before Father's accident and how good a cop he'd been. I couldn't get back into the toolshed with them there. Father and Mother seemed to be having a pretty good time, like they liked each other again. Mother had Father's shirt off so he could get a bit of a tan and one of the other men had his shirt off too. After a while I got really bored and uncomfortable so I went up to Beth's house. I hadn't seen her for a long time, not like I usually did, so I put my swimming suit on under my clothes and rode my bike up to her house but her brother had all his friends over to use the pool and her cousin was there too so she couldn't go away with me even though she didn't like any of them any more than I did. I went down to Thirty-one Flavors and got myself a double cone and a banana split before I went down to the wharf. I watched the tourists there for a while. It was a very nice day, all hot and clear, and there were two sea otters playing in the water. There was some sort of convention at the Doubletree Inn too, so there were too many people on the wharf and even though the organ-grinder had his monkey passing the tin cup and everything the tourists were all old and drunk and boring, worse than the golfers always were even. One of them threw a beer can at one of the sea otters but he missed. I told the traffic cop who was keeping them from driving out on the wharf when they weren't supposed to anyway, and he made the man leave.

After that I went over to the secret beach behind the Navy School that nobody's supposed to use and went swimming for a while. The water wasn't all that cold but it was still *pretty* cold, so when the sun started to go down I went back home. Mother and Father were still out back with their friends. Father had his shirt back on and he was starting to make nasty comments about Mother every now and then even though he still seemed to be having a pretty good time. I didn't understand everything he said but I understood most of it, and when I didn't understand something I could tell whether or not it was mean from the look on Mother's face. One of his friends didn't look very happy but the other one'd drunk as much as Father or maybe even more and he was all loud and happy. Mother was pretending she loved Father a lot and that the only reason he was saying all those awful things about her was because he wasn't grateful for all she did for him but I don't think anybody but Father and me noticed what she was saying.

After a while I asked her about Dubic but she said she hadn't had a chance to check up on him yet and she'd find out for me Monday.

Monday she didn't have to go to the station until late. I tried to tell her I was sick and couldn't go to school but she had a hangover and got really angry and hit me, she said she had enough sick people in the house without me trying to get away with things by pretending to be sick too when I wasn't, so I had to go anyway.

She wasn't home when I got back but she'd put Father's wheelchair by the window because there wasn't anything he wanted to watch on TV and that way he could watch the birds and the squirrels and the flowers in the backyard if he didn't feel like reading. I couldn't go back into the toolshed with him there so I put another magazine in his reader, then went down to the lake and watched the ducks for a while.

The next morning I got up before it was light out and went back to the shed. The hinges on the door were rusty and made some noise when I opened it but not enough to wake anybody up. I used the flashlight to make sure the bag with the duck in it was still under the bench before I closed the door behind me and turned on the lights, then I oiled the hinges before I got the duck out from under the bench. I turned the lights off again and used the flashlight to see by while I got it out of the sack. It still looked like it was wet, even though the mud on it was almost all dry on both sides when pieces of it fell off.

I wasn't sure whether it was safe to touch it or not even after I poked it with the hoe again and it still didn't do anything, but I already knew I had to learn more about how it worked if I was going to be able to make it do what I wanted, so I opened the door again. It was still dark outside. I got on the door side of the duck before I reached out and touched one of the spots where it was still coated with dry mud real quick.

It didn't do anything. I pushed it a little, to see if I could feel it react to me, but no motor started running inside it or anything. I pushed it again a little harder, still on one of the mud-covered spots, then touched it for just a second on one of the spots that looked like it was made out of wet muck. But it wasn't really wet at all, just a little cold and all smooth and slick and sort of greasy, like the bottoms of those nonstick frying pans when you just rinse them out for a few days without using detergent on them. And it still hadn't done anything.

I looked at it for a while, trying to see if I could tell any difference between the different parts of it, but it was still just a lump and the same everywhere. So I touched it again in a different place and then in still another place, but the third time I let my hand stay there touching it a lot longer, maybe almost a minute, before I took it away. Then I pushed it again, only a lot harder this time.

I sat down and looked at it again for a while, trying to get my courage up, then I picked it up real quick before I dropped it and ran back to the door to see what it did. But it didn't do anything and I was starting to get really afraid that I'd broken it somehow.

The sky was beginning to go pink and purple. I picked the lump up again and took it over to the door and put it down close enough so the sunlight coming through the doorway would hit it soon. The door opened into the shed so I couldn't put the lump right inside, it had to be back a bit so I could swing the door shut to keep it locked up inside if anything went wrong, so I had it maybe two feet back from the door. I tied a long piece of string to the door handle so I could stand outside away from the shed and pull the door shut without coming near the duck if I had to.

About half an hour after the sun finally came up all the way the light coming through the doorway started to hit the duck, and after about ten more minutes it started to change again the way it'd changed that other time, just after I pulled it out of the water, only even slower this time. It humped itself in tighter and tighter, just like it had when it'd been changing from a log into a lump, until it was almost the same size as a real duck, maybe just a little bigger, and sort of the shape of a duck, only it still didn't have a head or a tail or any wings or feathers or legs. While it was doing this all the dry mud on it cracked and fell off so the whole thing was wet-looking and glistening like it had just come out of the water. That took almost another hour and it was starting to get late so I pulled the door shut with the string and then locked it and hid the rope and went back inside the house.

Mother was already up and in the bathroom. I'd forgotten to close the curtains to keep anyone from seeing what I was doing out back and the bathroom had two big windows beside the skylight, but she hadn't noticed me or she would have come out to find out what I was doing. I put her coffee on for her, then got Father up and helped him into his wheelchair and took him to the bathroom while she made French toast for all of us for breakfast. He was really dirty for some reason so I had to clean the bathroom up a bit before I took my own shower and finished getting ready.

The phone rang while I was still in the shower. When I sat down to eat Mother told me she'd just gotten a phone call and that a lot of other cops had caught some sort of weird ten-day flu from a bunch of Australian wine growers here for a convention and that she was going to have to be filling in for all sorts of people and that everyone's hours were going to be messed up even worse than usual for a long time and she wasn't going to be able to come home very often for the next few weeks. I wasn't sure but I thought she was lying to us and that she had somewhere else she wanted to go for a while, maybe up to Lake Tahoe again with her mess sergeant. I asked her whether she'd found out anything about James Patrick Dubic for me yet and she said she'd forgotten again and that she was sorry but she was going to be too busy to check for me for a while now, and why was I so interested all of a sudden? I told her I'd found all the old newspaper clippings while I was cleaning my room and she seemed to think that answered her question because she didn't ask me any more about it.

Father said something about liberal judges and parole boards and how you sometimes had to exaggerate the truth a little because otherwise they'd ignore half of what a criminal'd really done and let him out when he was dangerous and should be kept in jail for a lot longer. Mother agreed with him and they talked about police work for a while. Then they talked a while about getting him a new TV, the kind with the videotape built into it, so he could record his favorite programs and movies and stuff that was on after he wanted to go to sleep, and we all thought that was a good idea even though Mother said we'd have to wait a while to get enough money to pay for it because she already owed too much right now.

She finished her coffee and we wheeled him into the living room in front of the TV, then I set up his reader so he could use it if he wanted to and made sure the switch to change from the TV to the reader was where he liked it on his shoulder and strapped on tight enough so it wouldn't slip back where he couldn't get at it if he nudged it too hard with his chin. I still had a little time before I had to go to school but I wanted to wait until dark before I opened the shed again so I could see if the duck had done any more changing or moving around in the dark after I'd shut the door. So what I did is I took the binoculars down to the lake and watched the ducks through them for a while to make sure there wasn't another robot duck there already to replace the one I'd taken, and at the same time I checked to make sure there wasn't anybody else down at the lake looking for the duck the same way I was, or anyone who looked like James Patrick Dubic. But there wasn't anybody else looking and there didn't seem to be anything special happening with the ducks on the lake, so I went to school. After school I checked again but there still wasn't anything worth looking at happening.

Father was asleep in his chair. I closed all the curtains so he couldn't see out to the backyard, then went back and tied my string to the shed door again and unlocked it and pushed it open.

The duck had changed in the dark this time, but just a little. It was still in almost the same place but something had started to push out where its neck and tail were going to be and it looked a little different where its wings were going to be. It was starting to look like a real duck or one of those wooden decoys, but all covered with mud. But it was too late in the day and the sun wasn't coming directly in through the door anymore so it didn't do any more changing.

I heard the telephone ringing and yanked the door to the shed shut by pulling on the string real hard but didn't have time to lock it before I ran back into the house. It was Mother, saying she wasn't going to be home that night or all the next day and asking me if I had everything I needed and if there was enough food in the refrigerator and freezer. I checked and told her there was and she said if I ran out of anything or needed help to come down to the station and one of her friends there would take care of it for me, she'd tell them I might be coming in so it would be all right. I said OK and she hung up.

I was really tired because I'd been getting up so early for so long so I set the alarm clock to wake me up in time to fix dinner for Father and took a nap. When I got up I made him macaroni and cheese with tuna fish in it then stayed up and watched television with him until it was time to put him to bed. He said it was a good thing I was superstrong for my age and not just tall and skinny when I was getting him into the tub, because even though he was still mainly skinny he was awful flabby and he'd be getting fat pretty soon, so moving him would be getting to be a lot of work before I was much older. I told him the exercise was good for me and anyway all I had to do was wheel his chair from one room to another every now and then and then help him in and out of the bath and anyway I was used to it. He said, thank you for saying that Julie, but I know how hard it is on you and your Mother with me like this, and then he started talking about how wonderful Mother had been before the accident, when she hadn't had to take care of him all the time, and that made me feel bad for him again and at the same time like Mother a little more, even though I knew that half the reason he was telling me all this was because even though he knew it was true he wanted me to tell him it wasn't so he could pretend to himself it wasn't his fault.

Wednesday morning when the sun came in through the door and hit the thing and its lily pads it finally finished changing all the way back into a duck. The head and the tail and the wings pushed their way out from inside until the duck was the right shape, even though it still didn't have any legs and was all smooth and brown, like one of those pottery ducks people use for sugar bowls.

It started reeling the lily pads in. The stems got shorter and shorter and at the same time the lily pads themselves were closing up like flowers that had been open going back to being buds, only they were even tighter than that, like rolled up pieces of paper, so that by the time the stems had been reeled all the way back into the duck they weren't any bigger around than the stems had been and they just followed them into the duck.

And while the duck had been reeling in the stems its skin had been changing. First all over its surface a lot of things like tiny doors had opened, only none of them were much bigger than the lead in a pencil and they were all over the surface, everywhere, so it was like the whole duck was a venetian blind that somebody had opened. Then the doors all closed again, but on the other side, so what had been on the back of them and hidden inside the duck before was now on the outside where you could see it and you could see that the duck had what looked like feathers again.

And then the orange legs came pushing out from the bottom of the duck and it started to try to swim. It wasn't trying to stand up or anything like a real duck on land, it was trying to swim like it thought it was underwater and had to get to the surface.

A few seconds later it stopped making swimming motions, either because it thought it had made it to the surface or because it had figured out it wasn't in the water. I couldn't tell which. But it still wasn't standing or lying like a duck on land, it had its feet sticking out backwards under it so it was tilted forward a bit with its tail in the air. That didn't seem to bother it, though, and it started preening itself like it always did after it came up out of the mud in the morning even though there wasn't any mud on it.

When it finished preening itself it looked all around just like a real duck deciding what direction it wanted to swim in, only it was still tilted forward like a wheelbarrow. It kept looking around for a long time and I wondered what it thought about being in the shed, if it knew there was anything wrong or what to do about it. Then it started swimming for the door, out into the light, only it wasn't using its wings to help it and it wasn't walking, just paddling its legs, but even so that pushed it slowly across the floor so that maybe ten minutes later it came to the doorsill and then it hopped over the sill just like a duck in the water hopping over something even though it went back to trying to swim as soon as it was outside in the backyard.

It looked around again as soon as it was out of the shed and then changed its direction, paddling across the grass to the center of the yard as far away from the fence and the shed and the house as it could get, with its chest still pointing down and its legs sticking out behind it and its tail up, so it looked more like it was trying to dig its way into the lawn than like it was walking. But it got to the center of the yard finally and stayed there, all stiff and fake-looking now that it was out of the water.

I was way back at the other end of the yard, maybe thirty feet away from it, but since the sun was shining bright I knew it wouldn't attack me if I got closer to it, so I came forward a bit, until I was maybe twenty feet away from it, and then a little more, until I was fifteen feet away from it, then ten, but I was afraid to get any closer right then and I went back to the toolshed and closed the door, then went in and got Father up and fixed his breakfast for him, then put him in the living room with the TV and his detective novel. I had him facing away from the window and I had the curtains closed anyway, so there was no way he could see what I was doing in the backyard.

I told him I wasn't feeling very well and didn't want to go to school today and he said, OK, if the school called just give him the phone and he'd say I was sick and he wouldn't tell Mother. It was the only thing he was really ever able to do for me and he did it whenever he could, even though Mother sometimes got real mad at him for it and yelled at him and even hit him.

It was still bright out so I went back out into the yard and tried coming close to the duck again. I came up behind it and got maybe ten feet away from it again but it still didn't seem to notice me, even when I circled around so I was beside it and then in front of it where a real duck would have been able so see me.

Then I thought about those old men and women you see with their metal detectors looking for money people've dropped on beaches so I went back into the shed and got the hoe out and came at the duck with the metal end, real slowly. I got a lot closer than fifteen feet, maybe even less than a foot away from it before it started to try to get away, and then I spent a while just chasing it around the yard, but always making sure I kept it out of the bright sunlight and away from the shade near the house and fence and under the trees, even though it looked so clumsy and pompous and stupid, even stupider than a real duck. When I finally quit chasing it it worked its way back into the middle of the yard.

Only that wasn't good enough because out in the lake I'd watched it go away from two or three rowboats made out of wood. So maybe it had two systems, some sort of metal detector and some sort of thing to keep it away from wood. (And a third system, too, to find the ducks and swans with.) I tried it with the wooden end of the hoe and it wouldn't do anything until I actually touched it with the wooden end of the hoe, and then it just tried to move a few feet away before it stopped, just far enough so that if the hoe'd been a branch the duck wouldn't have gotten snagged on it.

Maybe it had some sort of radar or sonar system to keep it from getting too close to big objects, like boats or piers. So I tried to use the metal end of the hoe to herd it close to the side of the fence that was still in the sun, but it wouldn't go close to the fence, when it was maybe ten feet away from it the duck would start to go off at an angle sideways so it never got any closer.

The phone rang. I ran inside and got it and took it into the living room and held it up to Father's ear and mouth without saying anything. It was the school, asking why I wasn't there. But we had an agreement, even though we'd never come right out and talked about it. He said I was sick, some sort of flu, that it probably wasn't serious but that even so I wouldn't be able to come in until at least tomorrow or maybe the day after and that, no, I hadn't been to a doctor and I wouldn't have a doctor's excuse because he was my father and it was his decision to make whether or not he let me go to school, he knew perfectly well what a flu was like and what you had to do to get better from one and he wasn't going to pay a doctor just to write me a note and say that there was a lot of that going around so not to worry, and, no, he wasn't going to write a note for me either, because my mother was away working for a few days and he happened to be paralyzed from the neck down, but if they wanted to send somebody out to make sure he really was my father and that he really was sitting in his wheelchair paralyzed they could go right ahead, but it would be easier if they just looked at their records or talked to someone who knew what he was talking about there at the school. The school said, No, we're sorry to have bothered you, Mr. Matson, to him and he had me hang up. I kissed him and went back out to the yard.

The duck was still out in the middle of the yard sunbathing. I wanted to push it into the shade from the house and see if it would attack me even if I was bigger than a swan and wasn't a bird at all. It wouldn't be very dangerous because as long as I stayed in the sunlight the duck would stop attacking as soon as it got back out into the sun with me. But I didn't want to be too close to it when it came at me in case it came at me a lot faster than it moved when it was trying to paddle around as if it was still in the water. So I took one of the pieces of the bamboo fishing rod and tied it to the handle of the hoe to make it long enough so I'd be further away from the duck when I herded it into the shade.

I pushed the duck as far away from me into the shade as I could with the metal end of the hoe, so it was maybe almost ten feet out of the direct sunlight before I stopped. That took almost ten minutes. Then I started to back away from it.

As soon as I took the hoe away it moved its head like it was looking for something then started coming at me, paddling as fast as it could and ripping up the lawn a little but even with the way it was kicking it was still just inching and sliding its way across the grass slower than I could have moved on my hands and knees. It wasn't trying to use its wings like I'd been pretty sure it wouldn't, it only used its wings when it made its other kind of attack, the one it did with the scissors that came out of its mouth when the sun was going down. I stayed just on the bright side of the shadow's edge but I moved away up towards the side fence so that I could watch the duck chase me some more. It was so slow and stupid-looking and I was in the sun, so I wasn't very worried. Besides, I wanted to see what it would try to do to me when it came time for it to try to dive under to grab me.

What it did was when I let it get about two or three feet away from me it stuck its head down under its body, pushing it in under its puffed-up chest which made it look even sillier because of the way its chest was already resting on the grass so that with its two legs sticking out behind it looked like some sort of crazy toy wheelbarrow. Then it kicked off with its legs like it was trying to dive straight down to the bottom of the lake but all that happened was that it fell back into the same sort of wheelbarrow position again. But it didn't even seem to notice it wasn't underwater, because then it pulled its head out from under its chest and stuck it straight at me and paddled as fast as it could at me until it was just almost to the edge of the shadow, then it suddenly arched its head and neck and body backwards and did something with its wings real fast so it fell over on its back. I moved away a little further down the shadow line so it could come after me without getting in the sun. Now that it was over on its back it was using its wings to try to swim at me like they were the oars of a rowboat and that was working a little better than the paddling had because the grass was very smooth there but even so the wings could sort of catch in it and slide the duck along. I stood where I was this time and when it got closer to me—it was about two feet away from me now, just before where the shadow ended—its legs moved away from each other and turned around sideways so its feet where facing each other like it wanted to clap them together. Big steel claws like meat hooks that must have been hidden somewhere in its hollow legs came out of its feet very fast and its belly opened up and something like a long rotary file and a drill and a buzzsaw all at the same time came out and started whirling so fast it was just a blur even though it didn't make any noise like a drill or a buzzsaw usually would.

The duck had finally gotten to just at the edge of the dividing line between the shadow and the sunlight and I knew that if it came any further it would be out in the sun and just go back to being a fake duck, so I used the bamboo stick that I'd tied to the hoe to turn it around facing the other way so I could see what it would do. But it just used one wing and not the other to turn itself around in a circle so it was coming at me again and this time I let it get itself out into the sunlight so it would turn itself off.

As soon as its head was out in the sun the claws went back into its feet and the drill-thing stopped turning and started to go back into its stomach. I got a better look at it this time, and it was all covered with little barbs like fish hooks and other little knives of all sorts that looked like they turned around on their own, not always in the same direction as the whole thing, but before I could get a better look at what it was like its stomach closed up again to where they should be so it was just a fake duck lying on its back again.

It couldn't seem to turn itself back over so I used the bamboo end of the hoe to tip it back into the right position.

I sat down in one of the lawn chairs and watched it struggle back to the center of the yard.

It was too slow and clumsy in the daytime to be any use if I just left it in the backyard, especially because it wouldn't come near metal and all but one of the lawn chairs had metal frames. I was sorry we didn't have a swimming pool and tried to think of a way I could get to use Beth's pool but I couldn't think of one that would be any good. But even though I couldn't see any way to make the duck work right except maybe just by throwing it on somebody it was still good to know that the duck would chase things and try to kill them even if they were people and not other other birds.

But then I thought that that was just what the duck did in the daytime when it got cloudy and that it had a whole different way of attacking things at sunset, when it used its wings a bit and went a lot faster over the surface of the water to cut off the other ducks' heads. So maybe that would work. Only if it did work I didn't want to be there in the backyard with the duck when it attacked.

For a while I thought about getting a dog or a cat or something and putting it in the backyard with the duck to see what happened but the idea made me sick and I couldn't do it. Then I thought about going back down to El Estero Lake and catching another real duck but it would probably make a lot of noise when I was catching it unless I killed it, and if I got caught killing a duck what with the way everybody knew how I liked to go down to the lake and watch the ducks all the time everybody'd be suspicious of me and wonder how many other ducks I'd killed and maybe notice that there were a lot less ducks there on the lake than there usually were and think that I was crazy or evil, so that if someone got killed after that they'd be sure I did it.

But then I thought, it didn't have to be a real duck at all, not a live one, I had more than enough money to go down to the poultry shop in Monterey and buy myself one that was ready to cook, and I could probably even get one with the feathers and head and everything all on it. So I rode my bike down to the poultry shop, but they didn't have any ducks that weren't already plucked and the chickens were all plucked too, so I had to buy a goose, which cost a lot more than I wanted to spend. I got it anyway and they put it in a plastic bag for me and gave me a little sheet of paper with instructions for how to cook it even though I said it was for my mother.

I put it in the backyard, about five feet away from the duck so it wouldn't have to go too far to get it, then changed my mind and put it halfway across the yard, so I could see how fast the duck could go when it was after something.

It was pretty late but the sun wasn't down yet, so I went back inside and took care of father, then put some fresh clothes on him in case Mother was going to be coming home tonight even though she'd said she wouldn't, and then fixed us TV dinners. There was a movie on the cable channel, *Casablanca* with Humphrey Bogart and right after it *Shanghai Express* with Marlene Dietrich, and I would have liked to have seen both of them even though I'd seen *Casablanca* before, but it started right after dinner and I wasn't sure I'd have time to finish it before the sun went down. I tried to watch a little of it anyway with Father but I couldn't get interested in it at all so I went back into the kitchen where I could watch the backyard out the window just like I could've from the living room if I hadn't closed the curtains there so I could be sure Father wouldn't see anything.

But when the sun went down and the light went away until it was completely dark out, there wasn't even any moon, the duck didn't even try to do anything to the goose. It just turned back into a log and stuck its lily pads a little ways out of the ends of its broken-off branches. I went back into the living room in time to see the very end of *Casablanca* and all of *Shanghai Express*. *Shanghai Express* was pretty good, but not as good as *Casablanca* had been the time before.

I'd been refilling Father's drinking bottle with beer all day and he was pretty drunk by the time the movie was over but instead of getting sleepy the way he usually did he was wide awake and something in the movies had made him all angry and sad at the same time. It was really awful.

First he got angry at Mother and started yelling and telling me what a bitch she was, how she treated him like shit the way she did and even brought her mess sergeant home with her as if it didn't make any difference what Father thought and even told him that at least Don—that was the mess sergeant's name, but I didn't like to use it even though he asked me to because that would make it too much like he was my friend or an uncle or something—could help her with him when she had to get his wheelchair into the car to take him to the beach or somewhere else nice and that Don was a lot of help too with getting him in and out of the bathtub and cleaning him up, as if that wasn't worse, having to let his wife's lover clean him up when he'd dirtied himself because he couldn't get out of his wheelchair to go to the bathroom on his own and they were too busy in the bedroom to waste the time to come and help him. Like he was a baby and it was OK if they changed his diaper every day or two.

He'd been yelling for most of this, but then he got real sad again, and that was even worse, he started talking about what a good wife Mother'd been back when he could take care of her and when he'd been handsome and strong and everything Don was now only a lot better and how she would have been a perfect wife to him if only he hadn't had the accident and it wasn't her fault that he couldn't be a husband to her and even if she got angry at him a lot and had to find someone else to do all the things that it'd been his duty to do for her as a husband he couldn't blame her, because at least she hadn't divorced him or put him in a home or anything like that.

It went on and on and after a while he was crying, and then he was yelling again. His bottle was empty so I went and got him another one, only I put half a Librium in it like I'd sometimes seen Mother do when she wanted to make sure he got to sleep and after a little while he calmed down and went to sleep.

I went out in the backyard and put the log in its sack and put it in the shed. I didn't even bother to use the stick or anything this time, because I was sure it wouldn't do anything to me now that it was late enough at night so the light had been gone for a long time. I put the sack behind the TV set under the bench but I couldn't really think of what to do with the goose because it would probably rot if I just left it in the shack but if I put it in the freezer or the refrigerator Mother'd probably find it if she came home tomorrow and I couldn't think of any reason to tell her why there was a goose in the freezer.

Then I thought, what I'll tell her is I bought it with my savings because since she'd been away working all that time I wanted to cook it for her for a kind of celebration when she got home and I'd gotten all the directions for cooking it and everything, only they looked too hard. And if she asked me why I'd gotten a goose instead of something like a turkey I'd tell her it was because I'd never had a goose and I'd heard that they were something special that people had for Christmas in England and that I wanted this to be very special. She'd have to believe me even though it was a pretty silly story because she wouldn't be able to think of any other reason why I'd have a goose to put in the freezer. Unless I'd stolen it, and I had the receipt and the piece of paper with the instructions on it to show her and she could always check back with the man at the poultry store if she was really suspicious.

Then I put fresh sheets on Father's bed and got him out of his wheelchair and into it. It really *was* like he was a baby, only even though I was real strong for how big I was he was twice as heavy as I was and I almost dropped him like I'd done a few times before, but I didn't.

And anyway I was growing fast so it was getting easier all the time. I was taller than all but one or two of the other girls in my class, and I was real strong and muscular just like Mother was and like Father'd been in the pictures when he used to be on the Police Basketball Team. I was good at sports, too, especially gymnastics and swimming and soccer, but Mother said I'd have to start being careful about what I ate and about doing real exercises and not just playing around pretty soon if I didn't want to end up getting fat and flabby like Father, though she said that right now everything was OK and I was still just solid.

I still wasn't sleepy, even though it was pretty late. What with getting up early every morning and everything I'd gotten into the habit of not sleeping too much. I took a bath and washed my hair and tried to watch TV but there wasn't anything on worth watching, and I didn't feel like reading or anything like that, so I went and got another TV dinner out of the freezer and put it in the oven.

It was a fried chicken dinner and when I took the tin foil off at the end and saw it I thought, maybe that's how the duck figures out whether something's alive or not, because if it's alive it's got a temperature just like I do, 98.6, though it probably wasn't the same thing for birds. But even if it wasn't the same the duck had chased me just like it had chased the ducks and swans so that wouldn't make that much difference.

Unless the reason it hadn't tried to kill the goose was because the goose had just been lying still there on the grass and not moving at all. But some of the real ducks I'd seen the robot duck attack hadn't been moving, at least not so I could see, and part of the time my duck had been flopping across the lawn after me I'd just been standing still watching it, not moving at all. So if Mother still wasn't home tomorrow I'd put the goose in the microwave just before sunset and get it out in the yard all hot right when the sun went down to see if that would make the duck attack it.

Mother called in the next morning while I was cleaning up after breakfast to say she was going to be gone at least two more days because she had to take over liaison duty with the state police on an arson charge. I asked her if she'd had a chance to find out anything for me about James Patrick Dubic. She said, yes, he was still in prison, but even though his behavior there was very good and he was not only doing some sort of on-the-job-training program for some outside company that would look good to the parole board but had also volunteered for something called Aversion Therapy that was going to make it impossible for him to ever touch another bird again without getting sick and passing out, they *still* weren't going to let him out for at least three or four more years.

It wasn't quite eight in the morning yet but I could still hear what sounded like a party in the background, a lot of drunks and yelling and music and laughing, or maybe she was in a bar or a gambling casino in Lake Tahoe or Reno or Las Vegas or wherever she was. I could tell she wasn't anywhere close like she pretended she was because there was so much static on the line I could barely hear her.

She told me to go down and see one of her friends at the station after school, Desk Sergeant Crowder, and he'd have twenty-five dollars for what she called my "baby-sitting time." That made me really angry again, not that she was trying to bribe me to keep me on her side but that it was Sergeant Crowder who was covering up for what she was doing with the mess sergeant because even though he didn't come around to see us nearly as much anymore as he used to, he'd always been one of Father's best friends and Father thought he still was.

After Mother hung up I told Father that she wasn't going to be home for another two days but I didn't mention anything about Sergeant Crowder. He looked unhappy, more miserable and hopeless than angry for a minute, but then he grinned at me even though I could tell he was making himself do it and said that in that case maybe I'd better dial the school for him so he could tell them that even though I was starting to feel a little better he wanted to keep me home with him for two more days to be sure.

After the phone call I wheeled him into the living room and set everything up right for him and put a beer in his bottle, then I went back to the shed and got the duck. I didn't bother to be extra careful this time, I just picked up the sack and dumped the log out of it into the middle of the backyard, then made sure the backyard gate was locked. I waited until the log started to hump in on itself then went back inside and drew all the curtains and locked the back door, so that nobody who happened to come by would see the duck.

I played checkers and cards with father most of the morning—I moved all the checkers for him and we had a little rack set up so he could see the cards in his hand even when I couldn't that he used when his friends came over to play poker—and I let him win a lot, even though I was better than he was. I fixed him a hot lunch around noon and refilled his bottle with beer two or three times and cleaned him up a bit before I left him in the living room with a new Ed McBain mystery in his reader because the afternoon TV looked pretty boring.

Then I went down to the lake to watch the ducks for a while and think about my duck and what I was going to do with it, but also to keep a lookout and find out if there was anybody else there watching and trying to learn what'd happened to my duck. I didn't think there would be, not with Dubic still in prison, and there wasn't.

About four o'clock I rode my bike over to the station and got the money from Sergeant Crowder. One of the other cops, somebody I didn't know, came over just as if it was something he'd thought of doing on the spur of the moment and told me what a good job my mother was doing and how much she was sacrificing for her work and how they hoped that pretty soon she could get the kind of rest she needed and stay at home like she wanted. I said that it was OK for me, I had school and everything, but that Father got a little lonely sometimes and Sergeant Crowder said it'd been too long since he'd come by to see us and that he'd drop in on us as soon as he had a few hours free. I said that would be nice.

I got Father cleaned up before dinner, then put a whole Librium in his beer so I could cook the goose and everything without him smelling it or noticing I was doing anything strange. He fell asleep right at the table and I took him into his bedroom and put him to bed with plenty of time to get the goose cooked before sunset.

I waited until the sun was almost entirely down, then put the goose in the microwave and turned it on to get it really, really hot. All the feathers got singed and it smelled really awful when I took it out because I had to leave it in a little longer than I'd planned so that I didn't get it out in the yard too early, or it would have been too cold for the duck to attack it when the light went away. And I didn't want to risk putting it out there too late, because then the duck might attack *me*, and I didn't know how fast it could go on land when it was doing its scissors thing and not the thing where it came up from underneath the ducks like some sort of meatgrinder with claws.

I propped the goose's head up in position with toothpicks and then ran out and put it down at least ten yards away from the duck, then ran as fast as I could back into the house and slammed the door.

The duck was already getting ready to attack the goose by the time I got turned around again with the door closed so I could watch it out the window. It had its neck stuck forward with its mouth wide open and it was doing its paddling thing and even though the way it was beating its wings wasn't quite enough to make it really fly it was still close enough so that the duck was sort of half-running and half-hopping across the lawn and it was going as fast as I could have run or maybe even faster until it got to the goose and then the scissors came out of its mouth and I was close enough this time to see the scissor blades were all jagged-edged like the saws butchers use before the duck cut the goose's head off.

The scissors went back into the duck's mouth and it closed its bill and did that thing it'd done before, when it'd tried to dive down through the ground to get at me, only this time after it paddled a little it just stopped and turned back into a log.

So I knew that all I had to do was get Mother out in the backyard away from any metal or the fences or the house when the sun went away and the duck would kill her. I could do it tomorrow night when she came home if I wanted to, or whenever I wanted to after that.

It made me feel good. I wrapped the goose in tin foil and put it back in the freezer in case I found another use for it, then put the log back in its sack and hid it back in the shed. I was real excited and I rode my bike all the way to Lover's Point and the Asilomar beaches in Pacific Grove because I felt so good and I was laughing to myself all the way there and back. Then I watched a late movie on TV, *Thoroughly Modern Millie*, and it was sort of stupid but fun anyway and I even laughed two or three times.

But the next morning Father woke me up yelling because I was late with his breakfast and he had a hangover and because I'd put him to sleep so early the night before all of yesterday's beer had still been in him and he'd wet his bed in the middle of the night and when he woke up and his bed was all sticky and wet and disgusting he had to yell and yell and yell to get me to wake up and come help him. He was really angry with me just the way he was always really angry with Mother, even after I cleaned him up and got him breakfast and set him up for the day in front of the TV with his reader.

And when he yelled at me again at lunch I realized something that I should've realized a long time before. He really *was* just like a big baby, and with Mother gone there'd be no one left to take care of him but me and pretty soon he'd hate me just the same way he hated Mother and I'd hate him just the same way Mother hated him. With maybe a little love left that would come back to the surface every now and then when we remembered what it'd been like before, but less and less until all that we had left was that we hated each other.

Only it wouldn't even be that, because they'd probably put me in a foster home and put him in some sort of nursing home, the one thing Mother'd promised never to do him where she'd kept her promise, until I was old enough to go back to taking care of him. I'd have to get a job and pay for him along with me for the rest of his life, and I'd never be able to go away or get married or even have boyfriends or do anything because he'd be jealous of me the way he was of Mother even though he loved me.

He hated what he was and the only way he could stand hating himself like that was to take it out on somebody else. It wasn't his fault, he couldn't do anything about it, but that's what it was, he had to hate somebody and make them miserable and if it wasn't Mother it was going to be me.

I couldn't get away with just running off and leaving him, either, not with the new interstate runaway laws they'd been lecturing us about at school, at least not until I was fifteen or sixteen. Besides, I didn't have anywhere to run to, not yet, and no way to keep myself alive even if I got away.

Unless I killed Father first. He wouldn't mind, not really, not if he was drunk enough and I put two or three Librium in his beer so he wouldn't feel anything. He probably would've killed himself a long time ago, if he'd been able to and if his mother hadn't raised him a Catholic. I'd heard him tell Mother that a lot of times when he wanted her to really *know* how horrible she made him feel.

And then the duck would go back to being just a log again and I could hide it away until I was fifteen or sixteen before I used it to get Mother. Nobody'd ever guess what it was if I kept it hidden someplace dark.

Only what if when the other police came all they found were my footprints and they took the log in to examine it because maybe they found blood on it? If they didn't figure out what it really was they might blame me and then be sure it was me when I got Mother later, and if they did figure out what it was they wouldn't blame me but I wouldn't be able to use it again. And all they'd have to do was pick it up and they'd know it was too heavy to be a real log.

But what if they never found his body, he just disappeared, like those ducks that my duck pulled under out in the lake?

What did it do with their bodies? Why hadn't I ever found even a feather with a piece of skin attached to it?

The thing that came out of my duck's stomach looked like some sort of cross between a drill and a meatgrinder. Maybe it ground up their bodies so small there weren't any pieces left.

He wouldn't feel anything if there was enough Librium in his beer and he drank enough beer. Or if he did it wouldn't be much, not much worse than it was like for him every day just to be alive anyway.

And with him gone Mother wouldn't be angry with me all the time, wouldn't always be finding something else for me to do around the house so she could go get away from him. She might even go back to being more like she was before, the way he told me she'd been when she married him.

And if she didn't, I'd still have the duck. But I had to find out what happened to the bodies of the ducks my duck pulled under when it killed them.

Father was watching a football game turned up loud. I went into the living room, refilled his beer bottle.

The duck was still back in the shed. I went into the bathroom and checked. It was in the corner of the house, with big windows on each side and a skylight Father'd put in when he first bought the house. There'd be bright sunlight in it for the rest of the afternoon.

I opened the windows as wide as possible, so the glass wouldn't screen out any of the sunlight in case that made a difference like it did when you wanted to get a tan, then got the sack out of the shed and dumped the log out of it into the bathtub. It was a big, big bathtub, all long and deep, made out of that white stuff they use for sinks and bathtubs and toilet bowls. The only metal in it was the faucet and the drain plug.

Maybe forty-five minutes later the duck was floating at the far end of the tub. It didn't seem bothered at all by the walls around it. Maybe they were pushing the same on it from all four sides so it didn't have to try to go anywhere else.

I put the headless goose in the microwave until it got hot, then tossed it in the tub. I used the curtain hook to pull the curtain for the skylight, then quick went back out into the hall and closed the bathroom door. I ran out the back door and around and closed the shutters for both windows, not quite all the way because I didn't want the duck to think it was nighttime, but enough so there wasn't very much light coming in.

And my duck dipped its bill in the water like it was taking a drink, then dived down under the goose, grabbed it in its meathook-claws and used its meatgrinder drill to rip it into tiny, tiny pieces. It took about five minutes, and then the duck left what was left of the goose on the bottom of the tub like some sort of mud and went back to floating at the other end.

I opened the shutters wide to let the sun in, then got the hoe so I could hold the metal between me and the duck, even though I didn't think it would attack me with the sun shining on it. I went back in the bathroom and pulled back the skylight curtain with the curtain hook, then kept the duck at the far end of the tub with the hoe while I pulled the bathtub plug.

What was left of the goose drained out of the tub with the water, all except a few small fragments of bone. And when I picked them up they weren't at all hard and brittle like they should've been, they were all sort of soft and rubbery, like pieces of cauliflower. So the duck had to have something, some kind of poison or acid it used, to make sure that even the little pieces that were left dissolved.

But if it could do that I didn't know why it left the headless ducks floating on the surface of the water every night. Unless it was James Patrick Dubic's way of making sure that when he got out of jail he could come back to the park and watch his robot duck killing ducks for him even if what they'd done to him made it so he couldn't touch the ducks to kill them himself.

I ran the water down the drain for a few minutes. It didn't seem to be stopped up.

I went back into the living room. Father was still watching his football game. His bottle was empty. I emptied his urine bag, refilled the bottle with beer, added four Librium. He was still half-awake when he finished the bottle, though he was passing out fast, so I gave him three more Librium by telling them they were vitamins he was supposed to take. He was too groggy to wonder why I wanted him to take them.

I went back to the bathroom and filled the tub two-thirds full of water. With him in it it would be all the way full. Then I pushed his wheelchair into the bathroom and got him out of it into the tub the way I always did.

The duck stayed down at the other end of the tub, away from him.

I pulled the skylight curtains closed, went outside and shut the shutters. Not all the way, just enough to cut down the light like it was a cloudy day. I didn't look, just walked around the yard looking up at the sky, out at the fences, over them to the neighbor's houses, anywhere but at the bathroom windows.

Then I closed the shutters completely but I still didn't look in through them. I went back inside the house, turned off the television, turned it back on, walked around, finally opened the bathroom door and turned on the light so I could see what had happened.

The bottom of the tub was covered with red-brown mud. The log was half-buried in it.

I pulled the plug, watched the sludge drain out of the tub. I kept the water running a lot longer to make sure the drain wasn't going to get plugged up, then pushed the log under the running water so I could clean the last of the sludge off it. When it was clean I picked it up and put it in the sack again, then took the sack and hid it out under the floorboards of the shed.

I poured some Draino down the hole to make sure nothing got clogged up and washed the tub with cleanser, then put the wheelchair and the urine bottle and all of Father's clothes back in the living room and turned the TV on. There was another football game going, a replay of some sort of championship from a few years back.

I called up Beth and asked her if I could come over and go swimming with her for a while. She said yes. We swam for a while and then I said maybe it would be a good idea if we went back down to my house, I had some money back there and we could buy some ice cream or maybe go get some hamburgers at McDonalds, and anyway I still owed her for that time she'd bought me milk and given me half her sandwich.

So we rode our bikes back down to my house and when we found Father gone I called Sergeant Crowder and told him I was scared, Father was gone but his wheelchair was still there and I didn't know what had happened to him, whether they'd taken him to the hospital or somebody'd kidnapped him or what.

He said he'd send somebody right over.

Julie: 1991

That was three years ago. I'm fourteen now. A year after Father disappeared Mother married Don but even without Father to take care of she was as bad as ever, maybe even worse, and he divorced her less than a year later. The duck's still back under the shed and it still works—I took it out to check it a little over a week ago, when Mother was gone for a weekend somewhere, and it turned from a log back into a duck in the morning and then back from a duck into a log when it got dark out. So I can use it on Mother whenever I want. It would be better if I could wait two years but I don't think I can stand it that much longer. It might be better just to have them put me in a foster home for a year or two.

And anyway, I don't know if I can wait any longer at all, now. Three weeks ago Judge

Hapgood disappeared and a week ago Thom Homart, the one that wrote those articles in the *RAG* that Dubic's lawyers sued them for, also disappeared. And The Forbidden City—the Chinese restaurant that changed their name from The Ivory Pagoda after they were convicted of buying sea gulls and cats from Dubic ten years ago—burned down and its owner died in the fire just last week.

I've been going down to the lake to feed the ducks almost every day now since Father disappeared. It's not so much that I've learned to like them or anything, though I guess I like them a lot better than I used to, but just that I wanted to be there watching in case another robot duck like my mallard ever appeared.

There's another one there now. A mallard, but a female this time, brown with black speckle-marks with bright blue on its sides—what the bird books call its mirror or speculum—and an orange and brown bill. It's been there almost a month. And every day now, for just a little over a month and a half, a skinny middle-aged man comes down to sit on a bench and watch the ducks. He comes down early in the morning and he never leaves until dark and he never, never feeds the ducks or swans or pigeons, even though he spends all day watching them.

Mother tells me that James Patrick Dubic was released from prison three months ago. So that has to be him, down there watching his robot killing the ducks he can't kill for himself anymore. I don't know what he thinks happened to his other robot.

And while he's sitting there on his bench watching the ducks, or maybe at night after he drives away, he's killing all the people who helped put him in jail. I don't know how, maybe with a robot person or taxicab or something else that works just like the ducks.

Mother's one of those people, so if he gets to her before I do he'll save me a lot of trouble and I won't have to worry about getting caught. And in a way it's a good thing to know that if I don't get her he'll get her for me for sure.

But the thing is, I'm another one of the people who helped put him in jail. Maybe even the main person, except for Mother, especially if you believe what all the newspaper articles they wrote about me said. And from the way the skinny man watches me sometimes when I'm feeding the ducks I'm sure he knows who I am and that he's watching me.

But he's too smart to try to get us all at the same time, at least not unless he's figured out enough different ways to kill us all so that nobody'll see the connection between all our deaths. So he's probably going to want to wait a while before he tries to get me or Mother. And I've still got his duck, and I've spent years now thinking about the best ways to use it.

So I think what I'm going to do is put a lot of the Librium I had after Father disappeared in Mother's whisky glass tonight if she's alone, or tomorrow night or the night after if she's not, so that she'll still be knocked out the next morning when it's light enough out for me to get her into the bathtub with the duck. Only this time it won't be like Father and I want to watch it all happen.

And then that same evening when the sun's going down and before Dubic has a chance to find out about Mother I'll take the duck down to the park and watch it jump on him and cut his head off with its scissors.

I've got it all figured out and I'm not really scared at all.

This time it's going to be fun.

Thomas Ligotti (b. 1959)

Notes on the Writing of Horror: A Story

Thomas Ligotti is the most startling and talented horror writer to emerge in recent years. Exclusively a short story writer thus far in his career, he published all of his early stories in semiprofessional and small press genre magazines for several years, remaining obscure. An American writer, his first trade collection of stories, *Songs of a Dead Dreamer* (1990), was published in England, the result of a gradually growing reputation among the avid genre readers. His second collection, *Grimscribe* (1991), was published at the end of 1991. Perhaps the most startling thing about his work, aside from the extraordinary stylistic sophistication (one is reminded of the polished prose and effects of Robert Aickman's strange stories), is his devotion to horror, which is positively Lovecraftian—as is his bent for theory and knowledge of the history of the literature. This present piece selected is his masterpiece to date. "Few other writers," says Ramsey Campbell, "could conceive a horror story in the form of notes on the writing of the genre, and I can't think of any other writer who could have brought it off." It is no less than an instructional essay on the writing of horror, transformed by stylistic magic and artful construction into a powerful work of fiction. Writing students I have taught have found it a revelation. It is included for your delight and instruction.

For much too long I have been promising to formulate my views on the writing of supernatural horror tales. Until now I just haven't had the time. Why not? I was too busy churning out the leetle darlings. But many people, for whatever reasons, would like to be writers of horror tales, I know this. Fortunately, the present moment is a convenient one for me to share my knowledge and experience regarding this special literary vocation. Well, I guess I'm ready as I'll ever be. Let's get it over with.

The way I plan to proceed is quite simple. First, I'm going to sketch out the basic plot, characters, and various other features of a short horror story. Next, I will offer suggestions on how these raw elements may be treated in a few of the major styles which horror writers have exploited over the years. Each style is different and has its own little tricks. This approach will serve as an aid in deciding which style is the right one and for whom. And if all goes well, the novitiate teller of terror tales will be saved much time and agony discovering such things for himself. We'll pause at certain spots along the way to examine specific details, make highly biased evaluations, submit general commentary on the philosophy of horror fiction, and so forth.

At this point it's only fair to state that the following sample story, or rather its rough outline form, is not one that appears in the published works of Gerald K. Riggers, nor will it ever appear. Frankly, for reasons we'll explore a little later, I just couldn't find a way to tell this one that really satisfied me. Such things happen. (Perhaps farther down the line we'll analyze these extreme cases of irreparable failure, perhaps not.) Nevertheless the unfinished state of this story does not preclude using it as a perfectly fit display model to demonstrate how horror writers do what they do. Good. Here it is, then, as told in my own words. A couple-three paragraphs, at most.

The Story

A thirtyish but still quite youthful man, let's name him Nathan, has a date with a girl whom he deeply wishes to impress. Toward this end, a minor role is to be played by an impressive new pair of trousers he intends to find and purchase. A few obstacles materialize along the way, petty but frustrating bad luck, before he finally manages to secure the exact trousers he needs and at an extremely fair price. They are exceptional in their tailoring, this is quite plain. So far, so good. Profoundly good, to be sure, since Nathan intensely believes that one's personal possessions should themselves possess a certain substance, a certain quality. For example, Nathan's winter overcoat is the same one his father wore for thirty winters; Nathan's wristwatch is the same one his grandfather wore going on four decades, in all seasons. For Nathan, peculiar essences inhere in certain items of apparel, not to mention certain other articles small and large, certain happenings in time and space, certain people, and certain notions. In Nathan's view, yes, every facet of one's life should shine with these essences which alone make things really real. What are they? Nathan, over a period of time, has narrowed the essential elements down to three: something magic, something timeless, something profound. Though the world around him is for the most part lacking in these special ingredients, he perceives his own life to contain them in fluctuating but usually acceptable quantities. His new trousers certainly do; and Nathan hopes, for the first time in his life, that a future romance—to be conducted with one Lorna McFickel—will too.

So far, so good. Luckwise. Until the night of Nathan's first date. Miss McFickel resides in a respectable suburb but, in relation to where Nathan lives, she is clear across one of the most dangerous sectors of the city. No problem: Nathan's ten-year-old car is in mint condition, top form. If he just keeps the doors locked and the windows rolled up, everything will be fine. Worst luck, broken bottles on a broken street, and a flat tire. Nathan curbs the car. He takes off his grandfather's watch and locks it in the glove compartment; he takes off his father's overcoat, folds it up neatly, and snuggles it into the shadows beneath the dashboard. As far as the trousers are concerned, he would simply have to exercise great care while attempting to change his flat tire in record time, and in a part of town known as Hope's Back Door. With any luck, the trousers would retain their triple traits of magicality, timelessness, and profundity. Now, all the while Nathan is fixing the tire, his legs feel stranger and stranger. He could have attributed this to the physical labor he was performing in a pair of trousers not exactly designed for such abuse, but he would have just been fooling himself. For Nathan remembers his legs feeling strange, though less noticeably so, when he first tried on the trousers at home. Strange how? Strange as in a little stiff, and even then some. A little funny. Nonsense, he's just nervous about his date with lovely Lorna McFickel.

To make matters worse, two kids are now standing by and watching Nathan change the tire, two kids who look like they recently popped up from a bottomless ash pit. Nathan tries to ignore them, but he succeeds a little too well in this. Unseen by him, one of the kids edges toward the car and opens the front door. Worst luck, Nathan forgot to lock it. The kid lays his hands on Nathan's father's coat, and then both kids disappear into a rundown apartment house.

Very quickly now. Nathan chases the kids into what turns out to be a condemned building, and he falls down the stairs leading to a lightless basement. It's not that the stairs were rotten, no. It *is* that Nathan's legs have finally given out; they just won't work anywhere. They are very stiff and feel funnier than ever. And not only his legs, but his entire body below the waist . . . except, for some reason, his ankles and feet. They're fine. For the problem is not with Nathan himself. It's with those pants of his. The following is why. A few days before Nathan purchased the pants, they were returned to the store for a cash refund. The woman returning them claimed that her husband didn't like the way they felt. She lied. Actually, her husband couldn't have cared less how the pants felt, since he'd collapsed from a long-standing heart ailment not long after trying them on. And with no one home to offer him aid, he died. It was only after he had lain several hours dead in those beautiful trousers that his unloving wife came home and, trying to salvage what she could from the tragedy, put her husband into a pair of old dungarees before making another move. Poor Nathan, of course, was not informed of his pants' sordid past. And when the kids see that he is lying helpless in the dust of that basement, they decide to take advantage of the situation and strip this man of his valuables . . . starting with those expensive-looking slacks and whatever treasures they may contain. But after they relieve a protesting, though paralyzed Nathan of his pants, they do not pursue their pillagery any further. Not after they see Nathan's legs, which are the putrid members of a man many days dead. With the lower half of Nathan rapidly rotting away, the upper must also die among the countless shadows of that condemned building. And mingled with the pain and madness of his untimely demise, Nathan abhors and grieves over the thought that, for a while anyway, Miss McFickel will think he has stood her up on the first date of what was supposed to be a long line of dates destined to evolve into a magic and timeless and profound affair of two hearts. . . .

Incidentally, this story was originally intended for publication under my perennial pen name, G.K. Riggers, and entitled: "Romance of a Dead Man."

The Styles

There is more than one way to write a horror story, so much one expects to be told at this point. And such a statement, true or false, is easily demonstrated. In this section we will examine what may be termed three primary techniques of terror. They are: The *realistic* technique, the *traditional Gothic* technique, and the *experimental* technique. Each serves its user in different ways and realizes different ends, there's no question about that. After a little soul-searching, the prospective horror writer may awaken to exactly what his ends are and arrive at the most efficient technique for handling them. Thus . . .

The realistic technique. Since the cracking dawn of consciousness, restless tongues have asked: is the world, and are its people, real? Yes, answers realistic fiction, but only when it is, and they are, normal. The supernatural, and all it represents, is profoundly abnormal, and therefore unreal. Few would argue with these conclusions. Fine. Now the highest aim of the realistic horror writer is to prove, in realistic terms, that the unreal is real. The question is, can this be done? The answer is, of course not: one would look silly attempting such a thing. Consequently the realistic horror writer, wielding the hollow proofs and premises of his art, must settle for merely *seeming* to smooth out the ultimate paradox. In order to achieve this effect, the supernatural realist must really know the normal world, and deeply take for granted its reality. (It helps if he himself is normal and real.) Only then can the unreal, the abnormal, the supernatural be smuggled in as a plain brown package marked Hope, Love, or Fortune Cookies, and postmarked: the Edge of the Unknown. And of the dear reader's seat. Ultimately, of course, the supernatural explanation of a given story depends entirely on some irrational principle which in the real, normal world looks as awkward and stupid as a rosy-cheeked farmlad in a den of reeking degenerates. (Amend this, possibly, to rosy-cheeked degenerate . . . reeking farmlads.) Nevertheless, the hoax can be pulled off with varying degrees of success, that much is obvious. Just remember to assure the reader, at certain points in the tale and by way of certain signals, that it's now all right to believe the unbelievable. Here's how Nathan's story might be told using the *realistic* technique. Fast forward.

Nathan is a normal and real character, sure. Perhaps not as normal and real as he would like to be, but he does have his sights set on just this goal. He might even be a little too intent on it, though without passing beyond the limits of the normal and the real. His fetish for things "magic, timeless, and profound" may be somewhat unusual, but certainly not abnormal, not unreal. (And to make him a bit more real, one could supply his coat, his car, and grandfather's wristwatch with specific brand names, perhaps autobiographically borrowed from one's own closet, garage, and wrist.) The triple epithet which haunts Nathan's life—similar to the Latinical slogans on family coats-of-arms—also haunts the text of the tale like a song's refrain, possibly in italics as the submerged chanting of Nathan's undermind, possibly not. (Try not to be too artificial, one recalls this is realism.) Nathan wants his romance with Lorna McFickel, along with everything else he considers of value in existence, to be magic, timeless, and the other thing. For, to Nathan, these are attributes that are really normal and really real in an existence ever threatening to go abnormal and unreal on one, anyone, not just him.

Okay. Now Lorna McFickel represents all the virtues of normalcy and reality. She could be played up in the *realistic* version of the story as much more normal and real than Nathan. Maybe Nathan is just a little neurotic, maybe he needs normal and real things too much, I don't know. Whatever, Nathan wants to win a normal, real love, but he doesn't. He loses, even before he has a chance to play. He loses badly. Why? For the answer we can appeal to a very prominent theme in the story: Luck. Nathan is just unlucky. He had the misfortune to brush up against certain *outside* supernatural forces and they devastated him body and soul. But *how* did they devastate him, this is really what a supernatural horror story, even a realistic one, is all about.

Just how, amid all the realism of Nathan's life, does the supernatural sneak past Inspectors Normal and Real standing guard at the gate? Well, sometimes it goes in disguise. In realistic stories it is often seen impersonating two inseparable figures of impeccable reputation. I'm talking about Dr. Cause and Prof. Effect. Imitating the habits and mannerisms of these two, not to mention taking advantage of their past record of reliability, the supernatural can be accepted in the best of places, be unsuspiciously abandoned on almost any doorstep—not the bastard child of reality but its legitimized heir. Now in Nathan's story the source of the supernatural is somewhere inside those mysterious trousers. They are woven of some fabric which Nathan has never seen the like of; they have no labels to indicate their maker; there is something indefinably alluring in their make-up. When Nathan asks the salesman about them, we introduce our *first cause:* the trousers were made in a foreign land—South America, Eastern Europe, Southeast Asia—which fact clarifies many mysteries, while also making them even more mysterious. The realistic horror writer may also allude to well-worn instances of sartorial magic (enchanted slippers, invisible-making jackets), though one probably doesn't want the details of this tale to be overly explicit. Don't risk insulting your gentle reader.

At this point the alert student may ask: but even if the trousers are acknowledged as magic, why do they have the particular effect they eventually have, causing Nathan to rot away below the waist? To answer this question we need to introduce our *second cause*: the trousers were worn, for several hours, by a dead man. But these "facts" explain nothing, right? Of course they don't. However, they may seem to explain everything if they are revealed in the right manner. All one has to do is link up the first and second causes (there may even be more) within the scheme of a realistic narrative. For example, Nathan might find something in the trousers leading him to deduce that he is not their original owner. Perhaps he finds a winning lottery ticket of significant, though not too tempting, amount. (This also fits in nicely with the theme of luck.) Being a normally honest type of person, Nathan calls the clothes store, explains the situation, and they give him the name and phone number of the gentleman who originally put those pants on his charge account and, afterward, returned them. Nathan puts in the phone call and finds out that the pants were returned not by a man, but by a woman. The very same woman who explains to Nathan that since her husband has passed on, rest his soul, she could really use the modest winnings from that lottery ticket. By now Nathan's mind, and the reader's, is no longer on the lottery ticket at all, but on the revealed fact that Nathan is the owner and future wearer of a pair of pants once owned (and worn? it is interrogatively hinted) by a *dead man*. After a momentary bout with superstitious repellance, Nathan forgets all about the irregular background of his beautiful, almost new trousers. The reader, however, doesn't forget. And so when almost-real, almost-normal Nathan loses all hope of achieving full normalcy and reality, the reader knows why, and in more ways than one.

The *realistic* technique.

It's easy. Now try it yourself.

The traditional Gothic technique. Certain kinds of people, and *a fortiori* certain kinds of writers, have always experienced the world around them in the Gothic manner, I'm almost positive. Perhaps there was even some little stump of an apeman who witnessed prehistoric lightning as it parried with prehistoric blackness in a night without rain, and felt his soul rise and fall at the same time to behold this cosmic conflict. Perhaps such displays provided inspiration for those very first imaginings that were not born of the daily life of crude survival, who knows? Could this be why all our primal mythologies are Gothic? I only pose the question, you see. Perhaps the labyrinthine events of triple-volumed shockers passed, in abstract, through the brains of hairy, waddling things as they moved around in moon-trimmed shadows during their angular migrations across lunar landscapes of craggy rock or skeletal wastelands of jagged ice. These ones needed no convincing, for nothing needed to *seem* real to their little minds as long as it *felt* real to their blood. A gullible bunch of creatures, these. And to this day the fantastic, the unbelievable, remains potent and unchallenged by logic when it walks amid the gloom and grandeur of a Gothic world. So much goes without saying, really.

Therefore, the advantages of the *traditional Gothic* technique, even for the contemporary writer, are two. One, isolated supernatural incidents don't look as silly in a Gothic tale as they do in a realistic one, since the latter obeys the hard-knocking school of reality while the former recognizes only the University of Dreams. (Of course the entire Gothic tale itself may look silly to a given reader, but this is a matter of temperament, not technical execution.) Two, a Gothic tale gets under a reader's skin and stays there far more insistently than other kinds of stories. Of course it has to be done right, whatever you take the words *done right* to mean. Do they mean that Nathan has to function within the massive incarceration of a castle in the mysterious fifteenth century? No, but he may function within the massive incarceration of a castlelike skyscraper in the just-as-mysterious twentieth. Do they mean that Nathan must be a brooding Gothic hero and Miss McFickel and ethereal Gothic heroine? No, but it may mean an extra dose of obsessiveness in Nathan's psychology, and Miss McFickel may seem to him less the ideal of normalcy and reality than the pure Ideal itself. Contrary to the realistic story's allegiance to the normal and the real, the world of the Gothic tale is fundamentally unreal and abnormal, harboring essences which are magic, timeless, and profound in a way the realistic Nathan never dreamed. So, to rightly do a Gothic tale requires, let's be frank, that the author be a bit of a lunatic, at least while he's authoring, if not at all times. Hence, the well-known inflated rhetoric of the Gothic tale can be understood as more than an inflatable raft on which the imagination floats at its leisure upon the waves of bombast. It is actually the sails of the Gothic artist's soul filling up with the winds of ecstatic hysteria. And these winds just won't blow in a soul whose climate is controlled by central air-conditioning. So it's hard to tell someone how to write the Gothic tale, since one really has to be born to the task. Too bad. The most one can do is offer a pertinent example: a Gothic scene from "Romance of a Dead Man," translated from the original Italian of Geraldo Riggerini. This chapter is entitled "The Last Death of Nathan."

Through a partially shattered window, its surface streaked with a blue film of dust and age, the diluted glow of twilight seeped down onto the basement floor where Nathan lay without hope of mobility. In the dark you're not anywhere, he had thought as a child at each and every bedtime; and, in the bluish semiluminescence of that stone cellar, Nathan was truly not anywhere. He raised himself up on one elbow, squinting through tears of confusion into the filthy azure dimness. His grotesque posture resembled the half-anesthetized efforts of a patient who has been left alone for a moment while awaiting surgery, anxiously looking around to see if he's simply been forgotten on that frigid operating table. If only his legs would move, if only that paralyzing pain would suddenly become cured. Where were those wretched doctors, he asked himself dreamily. Oh, there they were, standing behind the turquoise haze of the surgery lamps. "He's out of it, man," said one of them to his colleague. "We can take everything he's got on him." But after they removed Nathan's trousers, the operation was abruptly terminated and the patient abandoned in the blue shadows of silence. "Jesus, look at his legs, look," they had screamed. Oh, if only he could now scream like that, Nathan thought among all the fatal chaos of his other thoughts. If only he could scream loud enough to be heard by that girl, by way of apologizing for his permanent absence from their magic, timeless, and profound future, which was in fact as defunct as the two legs that now seemed to be glowing glaucous with putrefaction before his eyes. Couldn't he now emit such a scream, now that the tingling agony of his liquifying legs was beginning to spread upwards throughout his whole body and being? But no. It was impossible—to scream that loudly—though he did manage, in no time at all, to scream himself straight to death.

The *traditional Gothic* technique.

It's easy. Now try it yourself.

The experimental technique. Every story, even a true one, wants to be told in only one single way by its writer, yes? So, really, there's no such thing as experimentalism in its trial-and-error sense. A story is not an experiment, an experiment is an experiment. True. The "experimental" writer, then, is simply following the story's commands to the best of his human ability. The writer is not the story, the story is the story. See? Sometimes this is very hard to accept, and sometimes too easy. On the one hand, there's the writer who can't face his fate: that the telling of a story has nothing at all to do with him; on the other hand, there's the one who faces it too well: that the telling of the story has nothing at all to do with him. Either way, literary experimentalism is simply the writer's imagination, or lack of it, and feeling, or absence of same, thrashing their chains around in the escape-proof dungeon of the words of the story. One writer is trying to get the whole breathing world into the two dimensions of his airless cell, while the other is adding layers of bricks to keep that world the hell out. But despite the most sincere efforts of each prisoner, the sentence remains the same: to stay exactly where they are, which is where the story is. It's a condition not unlike the world itself, except it doesn't hurt. It doesn't help either, but who cares?

The question we now must ask is: is Nathan's the kind of horror story that demands treatment outside the conventional realistic or Gothic techniques? Well, it may be, depending on whom this story occurred to. Since it occurred to me (and not too many days ago), and since I've pretty much given up on it, I guess there's no harm in giving this narrative screw another turn, even if it's in the wrong direction. Here's the way mad Dr. Riggers would experiment, blasphemously, with his man-made Nathanstein. The secret of life, my ugly Igors, is time . . . time . . . time.

The experimental version of this story could actually be told as two stories happening "simultaneously," each narrated in alternating sections which take place in parallel chronologies. One section begins with the death of Nathan and moves backward in time, while its counterpart story begins with the death of the original owner of the magic pants and moves forward. Needless to say, the facts in the case of Nathan must be juggled around so as to be comprehensible from the beginning, that is to say from the end. (Don't risk confusing your worthy readers.) The stories converge at the crossroads of the final section where the destinies of their characters also converge, this being the clothes store where Nathan purchases the fateful trousers. On his way into the store he bumps into a woman who is preoccupied with counting a handful of cash, this being the woman who has just returned the trousers.

"Excuse me," says Nathan.

"Look where you're going," says the woman at the same instant.

Of course at this point we have already seen where Nathan is going and, in a way too spooky to explain right now, so has he.

The *experimental* technique. It's easy, now try it yourself.

Another Style

All the styles we have just examined have been simplified for the purposes of instruction, haven't they? Each is a purified example of its kind, let's not kid ourselves. In the real world of horror fiction, however, the above three techniques often get entangled with one another in hopelessly mysterious ways, almost to the point where all previous talk about them is useless for all practical purposes. But an ulterior purpose, which I'm saving for later, may thus be better served. Before we get there, though, I'd like, briefly, to propose still another style.

The story of Nathan is one very close to my heart and I hope, in its basic trauma, to the hearts of many others. I wanted to write this horror tale in such a fashion that its readers would be distressed not by the personal, individual catastrophe of Nathan but by his very existence in a world, even a fictional one, where a catastrophe of this type and magnitude is possible. I wanted to employ a style that would conjure all the primordial powers of the universe independent of the conventional realities of the Individual, Society, or Art. I aspired toward nothing less than a pure style without style, a style having nothing whatever to do with the normal or abnormal, a style magic, timeless, and profound . . . and one of great horror, the horror of a god. The characters of the story would be Death himself in the flesh, Desire in a new pair of pants, the pretty eyes of Desiderata and the hideous orbs of Loss. And linked hand-in-hand with these terrible powers would be the more terrible ones of Luck, Fate, and all the miscellaneous minions of Doom.

I couldn't do it, my friends. It's not easy, and I don't suggest that you try it yourself.

The Final Style

Dear horror writers of the future, I ask you: what is the style of horror? What is its tone, its *voice?* Is it that of an old storyteller, keeping eyes wide around the tribal campfire; is it that of a documentarian of current or historical happenings, reporting events heard-about and conversations overheard; is it even that of a yarn-spinning god who can see the unseeable and reveal, from viewpoint omniscient, the horrific hearts of man and monster? I have to say that it's none of these, sorry if it's taken so long.

To tell you the truth, I'm not sure myself what the voice of horror really is. But throughout my career of eavesdropping on the dead and the damned, I know I've heard it; and Gerry Riggers, you remember him, has tried to put it on paper. Most often it sounds to me very simply like a voice calling out in the middle of the night, a single voice with no particular qualities. Sometimes it's muffled, like the voice of a tiny insect crying for help from inside a sealed coffin; and other times the coffin shatters, like a brittle exoskeleton, and from within rises a piercing, crystal shriek that lacerates the midnight blackness. These are approximations, of course, but highly useful in pinning down the sound of the voice of horror, if one still wants to.

In other words, the proper style of horror is really that of the *personal confession*, and nothing but: manuscripts found in lonely places. While some may consider this the height of cornball melodrama, and I grant that it is, it is also the rawhead and bloody bones of true blue grue. It's especially true when the confessing narrator has something he must urgently get off his chest and labors beneath its nightmarish weight all the while he is telling the tale. Nothing could be more obvious, except perhaps that the tale teller, ideally, should himself be a writer of horror fiction by trade. That really is more obvious. Better. But how can the *confessional* technique be applied to the story we've been working with? Its hero isn't a horror writer, at least not that I can see. Clearly some adjustments have to be made.

As the reader may have noticed, Nathan's character can be altered to suit a variety of literary styles. He can lean toward the normal in one and the abnormal in another. He can be transformed from fully fleshed person to disembodied fictional abstraction. He can play any number of basic human and nonhuman roles, representing just about anything a writer could want. Mostly, though, I wanted Nathan, when I first conceived him and his ordeal, to represent none other than my real life self. For behind my pseudonymic mask of Gerald Karloff Riggers, I am no one if not Nathan Jeremy Stein.

So it's not too farfetched that in his story Nathan should be a horror writer, at least an aspiring one. Perhaps he dreams of achieving Gothic glory by writing tales that are nothing less than magic, timeless, and you know what. Perhaps he would sell his soul in order to accomplish this fear, I mean *feat*. But Nathan was not born to be a seller of his soul or anything else, that's why he became a horror writer rather than going into Dad's (and Grandad's) business. Nathan is, however, a buyer: a haunter of spectral marketplaces, a visitant of discount houses of unreality, a bargain hunter in the deepest basement of the unknown. And in some mysterious way, he comes to procure his dream of horror without even realizing what it is he's bought or with what he has bought it. Like the other Nathan, *this* Nathan eventually finds that what he's bought is not quite what he bargained for—a pig in a poke rather that a nice pair of pants. What? I'll explain.

In the confessional version of Nathan's horror story, the main character must be provided with something horrible to confess, something fitting to his persona as a die-hard horrorist. The solution is quite obvious, which doesn't prevent its also being freakish to the core. Nathan will confess that he's gone too far into FEAR. He's always had a predilection for this particular discipline, but now it's gotten out of hand, out of control, and out of this world.

The turning point in Nathan's biography of horror-seeking is, as in previous accounts, an aborted fling with Lorna McFickel. In the other versions of the story, the character known by this name is a personage of shifting significance, representing at turns the ultra-real or the super-ideal to her would-be romancer. The confessional version of "Romance of a Dead Man," however, gives her a new identity, namely that of Lorna McFickel herself, who lives across the hall from me in a Gothic castle of high-rise apartments, twin-towered and honeycombed with newly carpeted passageways. But otherwise there's not much difference between the female lead in the fictional story and her counterpart in the factual one. While the storybook Lorna will remember Nathan as the creep who spoiled her evening, who disappointed her—Real Lorna, Normal Lorna feels exactly the same way, or rather felt, since I doubt she even thinks about the one she called, and not without good reason, *the most digusting creature on the face of the earth*. And although this patent exaggeration was spoken in the heat of a very hot moment, I believe her attitude was basically sincere. Even so, I will never reveal the motivation for this outburst of hers, not even under the throbbing treat of torture. (I meant, of course, to write *threat*. Only a tricky trickle of the pen's ink, nothing more.) Such things as motivation are not important to this horror story anyway, not nearly as important as what happens to Nathan following Lorna's revelatory rejection.

For he now knows, as he never knew before, how weird he really is, how unlike everyone else, how abnormal and unreal fate has made him. He knows that supernatural influences have been governing his life all along, that he is subject only to the rule of demonic forces, which now want this expatriate from the red void back in their bony arms. In brief, Nathan should never have been born a human being, a truth he must accept. Hard. (The most painful words are "never again," or just plain "never!") And he knows that someday the demons will come for him.

The height of the crisis comes one evening when the horror writer's ego is at low ebb, possibly to ebb all the way back to the abyss. He has attempted to express his supernatural tragedy in a short horror story, his last, but he just can't reach a climax of suitable intensity and imagination, one that would do justice to the cosmic scale of his pain. He has failed to embody in words his semi-autobiographical sorrow, and all these games with protective names have only made it more painful. It hurts to hide his heart within pseudonyms of pseudonyms. Finally, the horror writer sits down at his desk and begins whining like a brat all over the manuscript of his unfinished story. This goes on for quite some time, until Nathan's sole desire is to seek a human oblivion in a human bed. Whatever its drawbacks, grief is a great sleeping draught to drug oneself into a noiseless, lightless paradise far from an agonizing universe. This is so.

Later on there comes a knocking at the door, an impatient rapping, really. Who is it? One must open it to find out.

"Here, you forgot these," a pretty girl said to me, flinging a woolly bundle into my arms. Just as she was about to walk away, she turned and scanned the features of my face a little more scrupulously. I have sometimes pretended to be other people, the odd Norman and even a Nathan or two, but I knew I couldn't get away with it anymore. Never again! "I'm sorry," she said. "I thought you were Norman. This is his apartment, right across and one down the hall from mine." She pointed to show me. "Who're you?"

"I'm a friend of Norman's," I answered.

"Oh, I guess I'm sorry then. Well, those're his pants I threw at you."

"Were you mending them or something?" I asked innocently, checking them as if looking for the scars of repair.

"No, he just didn't have time to put them back on the other night when I threw him out, you know what I mean? I'm moving out of this creepy dump just to get away from him, and you can tell him those words."

"Please come in from that drafty hallway and you can tell him yourself."

I smiled my smile and she, not unresponsively, smiled hers. I closed the door behind her.

"So, do you have a name?" she asked.

"Penzance," I replied. "Call me Pete."

"Well, at least you're not Harold Wackers, or whatever the name is on those lousy books of Norman's."

"I believe it's *Wickers*, H.J. Wickers."

"Anyway, you don't seem at all like Norman, or even someone who'd be a friend of his."

"I'm sure that was intended as a compliment, from what I've gathered about you and Norm. Actually, though, I too write books not unlike those of H.J. Wickers. My apartment across town is being painted, and Norman was kind enough to take me in, even loan me his desk for a while." I manually indicated the cluttered, weeped-upon object of my last remark. "In fact, Norman and I sometimes collaborate under a common pen-name, and right now we're working together on a manuscript." That was an eternity ago, but somehow it seems like the seconds and minutes of those days are still nipping at our heels. What tricks human clocks can play, even on us who are no longer subject to them! But it's a sort of reverse magic, I suppose, to enshackle the timeless with grandaddy's wrist-grips of time, just as it is the most negative of miracles to smother unburdened spirits with the burdensome overcoat of matter.

"That's nice, I'm sure," she replied to what I said a few statements back. "By the way, I'm Laura—"

"O'Finney," I finished. "Norman's spoken quite highly of you." I didn't mention that he had also spoken quite lowly of her too.

"Where is the creep, anyway?" she inquired.

"He's sleeping," I answered, lifting a vague finger toward the rear section of the apartment, where a shadowy indention led to bathrooms and bedrooms. "He's had a hard night of writing."

The girl's face assumed a disgusted expression.

"Forget it," she said, heading for the door. Then she turned and very slowly walked a little ways back toward me. "Maybe we'll see each other again."

"Anything is possible," I assured her.

"Just do me a favor and keep Norman away from me, if you don't mind."

"I think I can do that very easily. But you have to do something for me."

"What?"

I leaned toward her very confidentially.

"Please die, Desiderata," I whispered in her ear, while gripping her neck with both hands, cutting short a scream along with her life. Then I really went to work.

"Wake up, Norman," I shouted a little later. I was standing at the foot of his bed, my hands positioned behind my back. "You were really dead to the world, you know that?"

A little drama took place on Norman's face in which surprise overcame sleepiness and both were vanquished by anxiety. He had been through a lot the past couple nights, struggling with our "Notes" and other things, and really needed his sleep. I hated to wake him up.

"Who? What do you want?" he said, quickly sitting up in bed.

"Never mind what I want. Right now we are concerned with what *you* want, you know what I mean? Remember what you told that girl the other night, remember what you wanted her to do that got her so upset?"

"If you don't get the hell out of here—"

"That's what *she* said too, remember? And then she said she wished she had *never met you*. And that was the line, wasn't it, that gave you the inspiration for our fictionalized adventure. Poor Nathan never had the chance you had. Oh yes, very fancy rigmarole with the enchanted trousers. Blame it all on some old bitch and her dead husband. Very realistic, I'm sure. When the real reason—"

"Get out of here!" he yelled. But he calmed down somewhat when he saw that ferocity in itself had no effect on me.

"What did you expect from that girl. You did tell her that you wanted to embrace, what was it? Oh yes, a headless woman. A headless woman, for heaven's sake, that's asking a lot. And you did want her to make herself look like one, at least for a little while. Well, I've got the answer to your prayers. How's this for headless?" I said, holding up the head from behind my back.

He didn't make a sound, though his two eyes screamed a thousand times louder than any single mouth. I tossed the long-haired and bloody noggin in his lap, but he threw the bedcovers over it and frantically pushed the whole business onto the floor with his feet.

"The rest of her is in the bathtub. Go see, if you want. I'll wait."

He didn't make a move or say a word for quite a few moments. But when he finally did speak, each syllable came out so calm and smooth, so free of the vibrations of fear, that I have to say it shook me up a bit.

"Whooo are you?" he asked as if he already knew.

"Do you really need to have a name, and would it even do any good? Should we call that disengaged head down there Laura or Lorna, or just plain Desiderata? And what, in heaven's name, should I call you—Norman or Nathan, Harold or Gerald?"

"I thought so," he said disgustedly. Then he began to speak in an eerily rational voice, but very rapidly. He did not even seem to be talking to anyone in particular. "Since the thing to which I am speaking," he said, "since this thing knows what only I could know, and since it tells me what only I could tell myself, I must therefore be completely alone in this room, or perhaps even dreaming. Yes, dreaming. Otherwise the diagnosis is insanity. Very true. Profoundly certain. Go away now, Mr. Madness. Go away, Dr. Dream. You made your point, now let me sleep. I'm through with you."

Then he lay his head down on the pillow and closed his eyes.

"Norman," I said. "Do you always go to bed with your trousers on?"

He opened his eyes and now noticed what he had been too deranged to notice before. He sat up again.

"Very good, Mr. Madness. These look like the real thing. But that's not possible since Laura still has them, sorry about that. Funny, they won't come off. The imaginary zipper must be stuck. Gee, I guess I'm in trouble now. I'm a dead man if there ever was one, hoo. Always make sure you know what you're buying, that's what I say. Heaven help me, please. You never know what you might be getting into. Come off, damn you! Oh, what grief. Well, so when do I start to rot, Mr. Madness? Are you still there? What happened to the lights?"

The lights had gone out in the room and everything glowed with a bluish luminescence. Lightning began flashing outside the bedroom window, and thunder resounded through a rainless night. The moon shone through an opening in the clouds, a blood-red moon only the damned and the dead can see.

"Rot your way back to us, you freak of creation. Rot your way out of this world. Come home to a pain so great that it is bliss itself. You were born to be bones not flesh. Rot your way free of that skin of mere skin."

"Is this really happening to me? I mean, I'm doing my best, sir. It isn't easy, not at all. Horrible electricity down there. Horrible. Am I bathed in magic acid or something? Oh, it hurts, my love. Ah, ah, ah. It hurts so much. Never let it end. If I have to be like this, then never let me wake up, Dr. Dream. Can you do that, at least?"

I could feel my bony wings rising out of my back and saw them spread gloriously in the blue mirror before me. My eyes were now jewels, hard and radiant. My jaws were a cavern of dripping silver and through my veins ran rivers of putrescent gold. He was writhing on the bed like a wounded insect, making sounds like nothing in human memory. I swept him up and wrapped my sticky arms again and again around his trembling body. He was laughing like a child, the child of another world. And a great wrong was about to be rectified.

I signaled the windows to open onto the night, and, very slowly, they did. His infant's laughter had now turned to tears, but they would soon run dry, I knew this. At last we would be free of the earth. The windows opened wide over the city below and the profound blackness above welcomed us.

I had never tried this before. But when the time came, I found it all so easy.